The Complete Morgaine

C.J. CHERRYH

THE FOREIGNER UNIVERSE

THE ALLIANCE-UNION UNIVERSE

OTHER WORKS:

THE COMPLETE MORGAINE

GATE OF IVREL
WELL OF SHIUAN
FIRES OF AZEROTH
EXILE'S GATE

C. J. CHERRYH

DAW BOOKS, INC.
DONALD A. WOLLHEIM, FOUNDER
375 Hudson Street, New York, NY 10014

ELIZABETH R. WOLLHEIM
SHEILA E. GILBERT
PUBLISHERS
www.dawbooks.com

DAW Book Collectors No. 1705

Published by DAW Books, Inc.
375 Hudson Street, New York, NY 10014

DAW TRADEMARK REGISTERED
U.S. PAT. OFF AND FOREIGN COUNTRIES
—MARCA REGISTRADA
HECHO EN U.S.A.

ISBN 978-0-7564-1123-7

148620803

Introduction

by Andre Norton

There are those among us who are compulsive readers—who will even settle a wandering eye on a scrap of newspaper on the bus floor if nothing better offers. Books flow in and out of our lives in an unending stream. Some we remember briefly, others bring us sitting upright, tense with suspense, our attention enthralled until the last word on the last page is digested. Then we step regretfully from the world that author has created, and we know that volume will be chosen to stand on already too tightly packed shelves to be read again and again. In addition one is going to call other readers, wave this trophy bannerwise in the air—see what *I* have found!—proud to be the first among friends to have the great excitement of discovery.

This excitement does not come too often in a reader's lifetime of turning hundreds of pages. I have felt it perhaps only a dozen times in more than forty years of extensive reading. For me it was sparked by such books as *The Lord of the Rings,* the work of David Mason, a couple of A. Merritt's titles (which opened at the time a whole new world of speculation), plus some other favorites which I continue to reread with as much pleasure the second, fifth, tenth time as I did the first.

But never since reading *The Lord of the Rings* have I been so caught up in any tale as I have been in *Gate of Ivrel.* I do not know the author, but her talent is one I must envy. She has drawn an entirely believable hero on an alien and enchanting world, working in bits of customs, beliefs, and history so cleverly that it now certainly exists—somewhere. For such a creation does not remain only in the mind, it begins to take on life and breath, depth, to stand complete forever.

The usual flaw in any fantasy novel is that the hero is the typical super strongman so it needs frantic action and constant movement to preserve the illusion of life. Ms. Cherryh's dour Vanye is already alive from the moment he steps onto the stage she has set for him. Certainly he is no matchless hero of the Conan type, but he possesses a strong code of honor, which holds him to a course of action he inwardly loathes and fears. The reader can *believe* fully in each of his doubts, understanding his wavering, and his constant fight against what he considers his weaknesses. One cheers when he pulls some small triumph from the shadow of defeat, even when he breaks the honor, which is his last pathetic possession, because he sees there is something here greater than all conventional oaths and codes.

In *Gate of Ivrel* there are indeed no supermen or superwomen—rather there are very human beings, torn by many doubts and fears, who are driven by a sense of duty to march ahead into a dark they are sure holds death. Ancient evils hang like noisome cobwebs, the stubbornness of unbelievers wrecks again and again their quest. Wounded, nearly at the edge of their strength, shamefully forsworn in the eyes of all they could once call kin, they continue to push on to the last test of all.

Few books have produced such characters as to draw a reader with them, completely out of this mundane world. Here the careful evocation of a highly complex alien civilization is so skillfully managed that one accepts it all without any longer remembering that this is a creation of an imagination. It might be actual history—from another plane.

Reading *Gate of Ivrel* was an exciting experience for me, and I think I dare claim a wide background for knowing such books. My personal question rises:

"Why can't I write like this?"

I very much wish that I did.

The Complete Morgaine

WELL OF SHIUAN:
For Andre Norton, a lady of lovely and gentle magics

FIRES OF AZEROTH:
To Audrey, who is Kurshin at heart . . .
and to Brad, who asked the right questions.

Andur-Kursh

Hjemur

Kath Svejur

Ra-hjemur

Ra-baien

Baien-an

Irn-Svejur

Ivrel

Baien-ei

Alis Kaje

San-morij

Ra-morij

Ra-koris

Morija

Koris

Lake Domen

Ra-leth

Erd

Cedur Maje

Morgaine's Tomb

Pyvvn

Aenor

Lun

Gate of Ivrel

ᴄ Prologue

1

The gates were the ruin of the qhal. They were everywhere, on every world, had been a fact of life for millennia, and had linked the whole net of qhal civilizations— an empire of both Space and Time, for the Gates led into elsewhen as well as elsewhere . . . except at the end.

At first the temporal aspect of the Gates had not been a matter of great concern. The technology had been discovered in the ruins of a dead world in the qhal system—a discovery that, made in the first few decades in space, suddenly opened for them the way to the stars. Thereafter ships were used only for the initial transport of technicians and equipment over distances of light-years. But after each World Gate was built, travel to that world and on its surface became instantaneous.

And more than instantaneous. Time warped in the Gate-transfer. It was possible to step from point to point across light-years, unaged, different from the real time of ships. And it was possible to select not alone where one would exit, but when—even upon the same world, projecting forward to its existence at some different point along the course of worlds and suns.

By law, there was no return in time. It had been theorized ever since the temporal aspect of the Gates was discovered, that accidents forward in time would have no worse effect than accidents in the Now; but intervention in backtime could affect whole multiples of lives and actions.

So the qhal migrated through future time, gathering in greater and greater numbers in the most distant ages. They migrated in space too, and thrust themselves insolently into the affairs of other beings, ripping loose a segment of their time also. They generally despised outworld life, even what was qhal-like and some few forms that could interbreed with qhal. If possible they hated these potential rivals most of all, and loathed the half-qhal equally, for it was not in their nature to bear with divergence. They simply used the lesser races as they were useful, and seeded the worlds they colonized with the gatherings of whatever compatible worlds they pleased. They could experiment with worlds, and jump ahead in time to see the result. They gleaned the wealth of other, non-qhal species, who plodded through the centuries at their own real-time rate, for use of the Gates was restricted to qhal. The qhal in the end had little need left, and little ambition but for luxury and novelty and the consuming lust for other, ever-farther Gates.

Until someone, somewhen, backtimed and tampered—perhaps ever so minutely.

The whole of reality warped and shredded. It began with little anomalies, accelerated massively toward time-wipe, reaching toward the ends of Gate-tampered time and Gate-spanned space.

Time rebounded, indulged in several settling ripples of distortion, and centered at some point before the over-extended Now.

At least, so the theorists from the Science Bureau surmised, when the worlds that survived were discovered, along with their flotsam of qhal relics that had been cast back up out of time. And among the relics were the Gates.

2

The Gates exist. We can therefore assume that they exist in the future and in the past, but we cannot ascertain the extent of their existence until we use them. According to present qhal belief, which is without substantiation, world upon world has been disrupted; and upon such worlds elements are greatly muddled. Among these anomalies may be survivals taken from our own area, which might prove lethal to us if taken into backtime.

It is the Bureau's opinion that the Gates, once passed, must be sealed from the far side of space and time, or we continually risk the possibility of another such time-implosion as ruined the qhal. It is theorized by the qhal themselves that this area of space has witnessed one prior time-implosion of undetermined magnitude, perhaps of a few years of span or of millennia, which was occasioned by the first Gate and receptor discovered by the qhal, to the ruin first of the unknown alien culture and subsequently of their own. There is therefore a constant risk so long as there will ever exist a single Gate, that our own existence could be similarly affected upon any instant. It is therefore the majority opinion of the Bureau that utilization of the Gates should be permitted, but only for the dispatch of a force to close them, or destroy them. A team has been prepared. Return for them will of course be impossible; and the length of the mission will be of indeterminate duration, so that, on the one hand, it may result in the immediate entrapment or destruction of the team, or, on the other, it may prove to be a task of such temporal scope that one or a dozen generations of the expeditionary force may not be sufficient to reach the ultimate Gate.

Journal, Union Science Bureau, Vol. XXX, p. 22

3

Upon the height of Ivrel standen Staines y-carven with sich qujalish Runes, the which if man touche, given forth sich fires of witcherie as taken soul and bodie withal. To all these Places of Powers, grete forces move, the which qujalish sorceries yet werken. Ye may knowe qujalish blude herewith, if childe be born of gray eyen, in stature considerable, and if he flee gude and seek after sich Places, for qujal lacken soules, and yet by sorceries liven faire and younge more yeares than Men.

—Book of Embry, Hait-an-Koris

4

In the year 1431 of the Common Reckoning, there arose War between the princes of Aenor, Koris, Baien, and Korissith, against the hold of Hjemur-beyond-Ivrel. In that year the lord of Hjemur was the witch-lord Thiye son of Thiye, lord of Rahjemur, lord of Ivrel of the Fires, which shadows Irien.

Now in this time there came to the exiled lord of Koris, Chya Tiffwy son of Han, certain five Strangers whose like was never before seen in the land. They gave that they had come from the great Southe, and made themselves hearth-welcome with Chya Tiffwy and the lord of Aenor, Ris Gyr son of Leleolm. Now it was clearly observed that One of these five strangers was surely of Qujalin blood, being a woman of pale coloring and stature as great as most ordinary Men, while Another of the partie was of golden coloring, yet withal not unlike unto such as be born by Nature in Koris of Andur, the others being dark and seeming men. Now surely the eyes of both Gyr and Tiffwy were blinded by their great Desire, they being sisters' sons, and Tiffwy's kingdom being held by the lord from Ivrel of the Fires. Then persuaded they by great Oaths and promises of rewardes the lords of Baien-an, the chiefest among whom was also Cousin to them, this being lord Seo, third brother's son of the great Andur-lord Rus. And of Horse they gathered seven thousands and of Foot three thousands, and with the promises and Oath of the five, they set forth their Standards against lord Thiye.

Now there standeth a Stone in the vale of Irien, Runecarven, which is like to the standing stones in Aenor and Sith and much like to the great Span of the Witchfire in Ivrel, by general report, and it was always avoided, howbeit no great harm had come therefrom.

To this place the lords of Andur rallied behind Tiffwy Han's-son and the Five, to make assault on Ivrel and Hjemur-keep. Then it became full clear that Tiffwy had been deceived by the Strangers, for ten thousands rode down Grioen's Height into the vale of Irien at the foot of Ivrel, and of them all perished, save one youth from Baien-an, hight Tem Reth, whose mount fell in the course and so saved his life. When he woke from his swoon there was nothing living upon the field of Irien, neither man nor beast, and yet no Enemy had possessed the field. Of the ten thousands there remained but few Corpses, and upon them there was no Wounding found. This Reth of Baien-an did quit the field alive, but much grieving on this account did enter into the Monastery of Baien-an, and spent his days at Prayers.

Having accomplished such Evil the Strangers vanished. It was widely reported however by the folk in Aenor that the Woman returned there, and fled in terror when they sought arms against her. By them it is given that she perished upon a hill of Stones, by them hight Morgaine's Tomb, for by this name she was known in Aenor-Pyvvn, though it is reported that she had many Names, and bore lord-right and titles. Here it is said she sleeps, waiting until the great Curse be broken and free her. Therefore each Yeare the folk of the village of Reomel bring Giftes and bind great Curses there also, lest perchance she wake and do them ill.

Of the Others, there was no trace found, neither at Irien nor in Aenor.

—Annals of Baien-an

✍ Chapter 1

To be born Kurshin or Andurin was a circumstance that mattered little in terms of pride. It only marked a man as a man, and not a savage, such as lay to the south of Andur-Kursh in Lun; nor tainted with witchery and *qujalin* blood, such as the folk of Hjemur and northward. Between Andur of the forests and Kursh of the mountains was little cause of rivalry; it was only to say that one was hunter or herder, but both were true men and godly men, and once—in the days of the High Kings of Koris—one nation.

To be born of a particular canton, like Morija or Baien or Aenor—this was a matter that deserved loyalty, a loyalty held in common with all Morijin or Baienen or Aenorin of whatever rank, and there was fierce love of home in the folk of Andur-Kursh.

But within each separate canton there were the clans, and the clans were the true focus of love and pride and loyalty. In most cantons several ruling clans rose and fell in continual cycles of rivalry and strivings for power; and there were the more numerous lesser clans, which were accustomed to obey. Morija was unique in that it had but one ruling clan and all five others were subject. Originally there had been the Yla and Nhi, but the Yla had perished to the last man at Irien a hundred years past, so now there remained only the Nhi.

Vanye was Nhi. This was to say that he was honorable to the point of obsession; he was a splendid and brilliant warrior, skilled with horses. He was however of a quicksilver disposition and had a recklessness that bordered on the suicidal. He was also stubborn and independent, a trait that kept the Nhi clan in a constant ferment of plottings and betrayals. Vanye did not doubt these truths about himself: this was after all the well-known character of the whole Nhi clan. It was expected of all who carried the blood, as each clan had its attributed personality. A Nhi youth spent all his energies either living up to expectations or living in defiance of his less desirable traits.

His half-brothers possessed these attributes too, as of course did lord Nhi Rijan, who was father to the lot of them. But Vanye was Chya on his Korish mother's side; and Chya were volatile and artistic, and pride often ruled their good sense. His half-brothers were Myya, which was a Morij warrior-clan, subject, but ambitious, and its folk were secretive and cold and sometimes cruel. It was in Vanye's nature to be reckless and outspoken as it was in the nature of his two half-brothers to keep their own counsel. It was in his nature to be rash, while it was in that of his brothers to be unforgiving. It was no one's fault, unless it was that of Nhi Rijan, who had been reckless enough to beget a bastard Chya and two legitimate Nhi-Myya and to house all three sons under one roof.

And upon an autumn day in the twenty-third year of Nhi Rijan in Ra-morij, a son of Rijan died.

Vanye would not go into the presence of Nhi Rijan his father: it needed several of the Myya to force him into that torchlit room, which reeked so strongly of fire and fear. Then he would not look his father in the eyes, but fell on his face on the floor, and touched his brow to the cold stone paving and rested there unmoving while Rijan attended to his surviving heir. Nhi Erij was sorely hurt: the keen longsword had nearly severed the fingers of his right hand, his swordhand, and sweating priests and old San Romen labored with the moaning prince, giving him drafts and poultices to ease his agony while they tried to save the damaged members.

Nhi Kandrys had not been so fortunate. His body, brows bound with the red cord to tie his soul within until the funeral, rested between death-lights upon another bench in the armory.

Erij stifled a scream at the touch and hiss of iron, and Vanye flinched. There was a stench of burned flesh. Eventually Erij's moans grew softer as the drugged wine had effect. Vanye lifted his head, fearing this brother dead also—some died under the cautery, of the shock, and the drugged wine together. But his half-brother yet breathed.

And Nhi Rijan struck with all the force of his arm, and cast Vanye sprawling and dazed, his head still ringing as he crawled to resume his kneeling posture, head down at his father's feet.

"Chya murderer," his father said. "My curse, my curse on you." And his father wept. This hurt Vanye more than the blow. He looked up and saw a look of utter revulsion. He had never known Nhi Rijan could weep.

"If I had put an hour's thought into your begetting, bastard son, I would have gotten no sons on a Chya. Chya and Nhi are an unlucky mixing. I wish I had exercised more prudence."

"I defended myself," Vanye protested from bruised lips. "Kandrys meant to draw blood—see—" And he showed his side, where the light practice armor was rent, and blood flowed. But his father turned his face from that.

"Kandrys was my eldest," his father said, "and you were the merest night's amusement. I have paid dearly for that night. But I took you into the house. I owed your mother that, since she had the ill luck to die bearing you. You were death to her too. I should have realized that you are cursed that way. Kandrys dead, Erij maimed—all for the likes of you, bastard son. Did you hope to be heir to Nhi if they were both dead? Was that it?"

"Father," Vanye wept, "they meant to kill me."

"No. To put that arrogance of yours in its place—that, maybe. But not to kill you. No. You are the one who killed. You murdered. You turned edge on your brothers in practice, and Erij not even armed. The fact is that you are alive and my eldest son is not, and I would it were the other way around, Chya bastard. I should never have taken you in. Never."

"Father," he cried, and the back of Nhi Rijan's hand smashed the word from his mouth and left him wiping blood from his lips. Vanye bowed down again and wept.

"What shall I do with you?" asked Rijan at last.

"I do not know," said Vanye.

"A man carries his own honor. He knows."

Vanye looked up, sick and shaking. He could not speak in answer to that. To fall upon his own blade and die—this, his father asked of him. Love and hate were so confounded in him that he felt rent in two, and tears blinded him, making him more ashamed.

"Will you use it?" asked Rijan.

It was Nhi honor. But the Chya blood was strong in him too, and the Chya loved life too well.

The silence weighed upon the air.

"Nhi cannot kill Nhi," said Rijan at last. "You will leave us, then."

"I had no wish to kill him."

"You are skilled. It is clear that your hand is more honest than your mouth. You struck to kill. Your brother is dead. You meant to kill both brothers, and Erij was not even armed. You can give me no other answer. You will become *ilin.* This I set on you."

"Yes, sir," said Vanye, touching brow to the floor, and there was the taste of ashes in his mouth. There was only short prospect for a masterless *ilin,* and such men often became mere bandits, and ended badly.

"You are skilled," said his father again. "It is most likely that you will find place in Aenor, since a Chya woman is wife to the Ris in Aenor-Pyvvn. But there is lord Gervaine's land to cross, among the Myya. If Myya Gervaine kills you, your brother will be avenged, and it will be without blood on Nhi hands or Nhi steel."

"Do you wish that?" asked Vanye.

"You have chosen to live," said his father. And from Vanye's own belt he took the Honor blade that was the peculiar distinction of the *uyin,* and he seized Vanye's long hair that was the mark of Nhi manhood, and sheared it off roughly in irregular lengths. The hair, Chya and fairer than was thought honest human blood among most clans, fell to the stone floor in its several braids; and when it was done, Nhi Rijan set his heel on the blade and broke it, casting the pieces into Vanye's lap.

"Mend that," said Nhi Rijan, "if you can."

The wind cold upon his shorn neck, Vanye found the strength to rise; and his numb fingers still held the halves of the shortsword. "Shall I have horse and arms?" he asked, by no means sure of that, but without them he would surely die.

"Take all that is yours," said the Nhi. "Clan Nhi wants to forget you. If you are caught within our borders you will die as a stranger and an enemy."

Vanye bowed, turned and left.

"Coward," his father's voice shouted after him, reminding him of the unsatisfied honor of the Nhi, which demanded his death; and now he wished earnestly to die, but it was no longer help for his personal dishonor. He was marked like a felon for hanging, like the lowest of criminals: exile had not demanded this further punishment—it was lord Nhi Rijan's own justice, for the Nhi had also a darker nature, which was implacable and excessive in revenge.

He put on his armor, hiding the shame of his head under a leather coif and a peaked helm, and bound about the helm the white scarf of the *ilin,* wandering warrior, to be claimed by whatever lord chose to grant him hearth-right.

Ilinin were often criminals, or clanless, or unclaimed bastards, and some religious men doing penance for some particular sin, bound in virtual slavery according to the soul-binding law of the *ilin* codes, to serve for a year at their Claiming.

Not a few turned mercenary, taking pay, losing *uyin* rank; or, in outright dishonor, became thieves; or, if honest and honorable, starved, or were robbed and murdered, either by outlaws or by hedge-lords that took their service and then laid claim to all that they had.

The Middle Realms were not at peace: they had not been at peace since Irien and the generation before; but neither were there great wars, such as could make an *ilin*'s life profitable. There was only grinding poverty for mid-lands villages, and in Koris, the evil of Hjemur's minions—dark sorceries and outlaw lords much worse than the outlaws of the high mountains.

And there was lord Myya Gervaine's small land of Morij Erd which barred his way to Aenor and separated him from his only hope of safety.

It was the second winter, the cold of the high passes of the mountains, and a dead horse that finally drove him to the desperate step of trying to cross the lands of Gervaine.

A black Myya arrow had felled his gelding, poor Mai, that had been his mount since he first reached manhood; and Mai's gear now was on a bay mare he had of the Myya—the owner being beyond need for her.

They had harried him from Luo to Ethrith-mri, and only once had he turned to fight. Hill by hill they had forced him against the mountains of the south. He ran willingly now, though he was faint with hunger and there was scant grain left for his horse. Aenor was just across the next ridges. The Myya were no friends of the Ris in Aenor-Pyvvn, and would not risk his land.

It was late that he realized the nature of the road he had begun to travel, that it was the old *qujalin* road and not the one he sought. Occasional paving rang under the bay mare's hooves. Occasional stones thrust up by the roadside and he began to fear indeed that it led to the dead places, the cursed grounds. Snow fell for a time, whiting everything out-stopping pursuit (he hoped that, at least). And he spent the night in the saddle, daring only to sleep a time in the early morning, after the movings in the brush were silenced and he no longer feared wolves.

Then he rode the long day down from the Aenish side of the pass, weak and sick with hunger.

He found himself entering a valley of standing stones.

There was no longer doubt that *qujalin* hands had reared such monoliths. It was Morgaine's vale: he knew it now, of the songs and of evil rumor. It was a place no man of Kursh or Andur would have traveled with a light heart at noontide, and the sun was sinking quickly toward dark, with another bank of cloud rolling in off the ridge of the mountains at his back.

He dared look up between the pillars that crowned the conical hill called Morgaine's Tomb, and the declining sun shimmered there like a butterfly caught in a web, all torn and fluttering. It was the effect of Witchfires, like the great Witch-fire on Mount Ivrel where the Hjemur-lord ruled, proving *qujalin* powers were not entirely faded there or here.

Vanye wrapped his tattered cloak about his mailed shoulders and put the exhausted horse to a quicker pace, past the tangle of unhallowed stones at the base of the hill. The fair-haired witch had shaken all Andur-Kursh in war, cast half the Middle Realms into the lap of Thiye Thiye's-son. Here the air was still uneasy, whether with the power of the Stones or with the memory of Morgaine, it was uncertain.

> *When Thiye ruled in Hjemur*
> *came strangers riding there,*
> *and three were dark and one was gold,*
> *and one like frost was fair.*

The mare's hooves upon the crusted snow echoed the old verses in his mind, an ill song for the place and the hour. For many years after the world had seen the welcome last of Morgaine Frosthair, demented men claimed to have seen her, while others said that she slept, waiting to draw a new generation of men to their ruin, as she had ruined Andur once at Irien.

> *Fair was she, and fatal as fair,*
> *and cursed who gave her ear;*
> *now men are few and wolves are more,*
> *and the Winter drawing near.*

If in fact the mound did hold Morgaine's bones, it was fitting burial for one of her old, inhuman blood. Even the trees hereabouts grew crooked: so did they wherever there were Stones of Power, as though even the nature of the patient trees was warped by the near presence of the Stones; like souls twisted and stunted by living in the continual presence of evil. The top of the hill was barren: no trees grew there at all.

He was glad when he had passed the narrow stream-channel between the hills and left the vicinity of the Stones. And suddenly he had before him a sign that he had run into better fortunes, and that heaven and the land of his cousins of Aenor-Pyvvn promised him safety.

A small band of deer wandered belly-deep in the snows by the little brook, hungrily stripping the red *howan* berries from the thicket.

It was a land blessedly unlike that of the harsh Cedur Maje, or Gervaine's Morij Erd, where even the wolves often went hungry, for Aenor-Pyvvn lay far southward from Hjemur, still untouched by the troubles that had so long lain over the Middle Realms.

He feverishly unslung his bow and strung it, his hands shaking with weakness, and he launched one of the gray-feathered Nhi shafts at the nearest buck. But the mare chose that moment to shift weight, and he cursed in frustration and aching hunger: the shaft sped amiss and hit the buck in the flank, scattered the others.

The wounded buck lunged and stumbled and began to run, crazed with pain and splashing the white snow with great gouts of blood. Vanye had no time for a second arrow. It ran back into Morgaine's valley, and there he would not follow it. He saw it climb—insane, as if the queerness in that valley had taken its fear-hazed wits and driven it against nature, killing itself in its exertions, driving it toward that shimmering web which even insects and growing things avoided.

It struck between the pillars and vanished.

So did the tracks and the blood.

The deer grazed, on the other side of the stream.

He gazed at the valley of the Stones, where there was no doubt that *qujalin* hands had reared such monoliths. It was Morgaine's vale: he knew it. The sight stirred something, a sense of *déjà-vu* so strong it dazed him for a moment, and he passed the back of his hand over his eyes, rubbing things into focus. The sun was sinking quickly toward dark, with another bank of cloud rolling in off the ridge of the mountains, shadowing most of the sky at his back.

He looked up between the pillars that crowned the conical hill called Morgaine's Tomb, and the declining sun shimmered there like a puddle of gold just disturbed by a plunging stone.

In that shimmer appeared the head of a horse, and its fore-quarters, and a rider, and the whole animal: white rider on a gray horse, and the whole was limned against the brilliant amber sun so that he blinked and rubbed his eyes.

The rider descended the snowy hill into the shadows across his path— substantial. A pelt of white *anomen* was the cloak, and the stranger's breath and that of the gray horse made puffs on the frosty air.

He knew that he should set spurs to the mare, yet he felt curiously numb, as though he had been wakened from one dream and plunged into the midst of another.

He looked into the tanned woman's face within the fur hood and met hair and brows like the winter sun at noon, and eyes as gray as the clouds in the east.

"Good day," she gave him, in a quaint and gentle accent, and he saw that beneath her knee upon the gray's saddle was a great blade with a golden hilt in the fashion of a dragon, and that it was Korish-work upon her horse's gear. He was sure then, for such details were in the songs they sang of her and in the book of Yla.

"My way lies north," she said in that low, accented voice. "Thee seems to go otherwise. But the sun is setting soon. I will ride with thee a ways."

"I know you," he said then.

The pale brows lifted. "Has thee come hunting me?"

"No," he said, and the ice crept downward from heart to belly so that he was no longer sure what words he answered, or why he answered at all.

"How is thee called?"

"Nhi Vanye, ep Morija."

"Vanye—no Morij name."

Old pride stung him. The name was Korish, mother's-clan, reminder of his illegitimacy. Then to speak or dispute with her at all seemed madness. What he had seen happen upon the hilltop refused to take shape in his memory, and he began to insist to himself that the hunger that had made him weak had begun to twist his senses as well, and that he had encountered some strange high-clan woman upon the forsaken road, and that his weakness stole his senses and made him forget how she had come.

Yet however she had come, she was at least half-*qujal,* eyes and hair bore witness to that: she was *qujal* and soulless and well at home in this blighted place of dead trees and snow.

"I know a place," she said, "where the wind does not reach. Come."

She turned the gray's head toward the south, as he had been headed, so that he did not know where else to go. He went as in a dream. Dusk was gathering, hurried on by the veil of cloud that was rolling across the sky. The wraithlike pallor of Morgaine drifted before him, but the gray's hooves cracked substantially into the crusted snow, leaving tracks.

They rounded the turning of the hill and startled a small band of deer that fed upon *howan* by the streamside. It was the first game he had seen in days. Despite his circumstance, he reached for his bow.

Before he could string it, a light blazed from Morgaine's outstretched hand and a buck fell dead. The others scattered.

Morgaine pointed to the hillside on their right. "There is a cave for shelter. I have used it before. Take what venison we need: the rest is due smaller hunters."

She rode away upon the slope. He took his skinning-knife and prepared to do her bidding, though he liked it little. He found no wound upon the body, only a little blood from its nostrils to spot the snow, and all at once the red on the snow brought back the dream, and made him shiver. He had no stomach for a thing killed in such a way, and the wide-eyed horned head seemed as spellbound as he—unwilling dreamer too.

He glanced over his shoulder. Morgaine stood upon the shoulder of the hill holding the gray's reins, watching him. The first flakes of snow drifted across the wind.

He set his knife to the carcass and did not look it in the eye.

⌒ Chapter 2

A fire blazed in the shallow cave's mouth, putting a wall of warmth between them and the driving snow. He did not want the meat, but he was many days weak with hunger, so that his joints ached and the least exertion put a tremor in his muscles. He must sit and smell it cooking, and when she had cooked and offered a bit to him, it looked no different than other meat, and smelled so achingly good that his empty belly ruled his other scruples. A man would not lose his soul for a little bit of venison, however the beast had been slain.

The night was beyond. Occasional snowflakes pelted past the barrier of the fire's heat, driven on a fierce gust. Outside, the horses, witch-horse and ordinary bay, stood together against the unfriendly wind; and when hot venison had taken the shaking from Vanye's limbs and put strength into him, he took a portion of what grain he had left and went outside, fed half to each. The gray—of that famous breed of Baien, so men sang—nuzzled his hands as eagerly and warmly as his own little mare. His heart was touched by the beauty of the gray stud. For the moment he forgot the evil and smoothed the pale mane and gazed into the great pale-lashed eyes and thought (for the Nhi were breeders of good horses) that he would much covet the get of that fine animal, in any herd: they were the breed of the lost High Kings of Andur, those great gray horses. But there were no more High Kings, only the lords of clans; and the breed had passed as the glories of Andur had passed.

Now of great kings there remained only the Hjemur-lord, far different than the brave bright kings of golden Koris-sith and Baien, that breed of men apart from clans, and greater. An older thing, a darker thing had stirred to life when the Hjemur-lord arose, and more than an army had gone down to die in Irien.

With that thought he shivered in the ice-edged wind and returned to the fire, to the center of all things unnatural in the night, where Morgaine sat wrapped in her snowy furs, beside her horse's gear and the dragon-blade glittering in its plain sheath. The silence between them had been as deep as that between old friends.

The wind whirled snow through the cave's mouth. It was a great storm. He reckoned for the first time that he would have died this night, unsheltered, weak from hunger. Had it not been for the meeting on the road, the deer, the offering of the cave, then he would have been in the open when the storm came down, and he much doubted that his failing strength could have endured an Aenish storm.

There was wood piled up by the door. How it had been cut he was loath to know, only that it gave them warmth. And when he came to put a little more upon the fire, to keep the barrier between them and the insistent wind, he saw Morgaine kneeling upon a place at the back of the cave and seeking for something beneath a pile of small stones.

I have used this place before, she had told him.

He looked in doubtful curiosity and saw that she drew forth a leather sack that was stiff and moldering, and when she poured into her hand it was only powder that came down. She snatched her hand from that as if she had touched something foul, and wiped her fingers on the earth. A bloody streak was upon her arm, parting the black leather of her sleeve where she had thrust the arm forth from the enveloping cloak, and her clean hand stole to that.

She sat there shivering, like one in the grip of some great fear. He sank down on his heels near her, puzzled, even pitying her, and wondering in the back of his mind how she had chanced to hurt herself in so short a time: no, it looked old; it was drying. She must have done it while he was busy at the deer's carcass.

"How long?" she asked him. "How long have I been away?"

"More than a hundred years," he said.

"I had thought—rather less." She moved her hand and looked down at the hurt, brushed at it, seemed to decide to ignore it, for it was not deep enough to be dangerous, only painful.

"Wait," he said, and obtained his own kit, and would gladly have tried to treat the wound for her: he thought he owed her that at least for this night's shelter. But she would have none of it, and insisted upon her own. He sat and watched uneasily while she drew out her own things, small metal containers, and other things he had no knowledge of. She treated her own injury, and did not bandage it, but a pinkish film covered it when she had done, and it did not bleed. *Qujalin* medicines, he judged; and perhaps she could not abide honest remedies, or feared they had been blessed, and might be harmful to her.

"How came you by that?" he asked, for it looked like an ax-stroke or sword-cut; but she had no tools, however the wood had been cut, and high on her arm as it was he could not judge how she could have chanced to do it.

"Aenorin," she said. "Lord Ris Heln Gry's-son, he and his men."

Heln was nearly a hundred years in his own grave. Then he felt an uneasiness at his stomach and well understood the look Morgaine had had. She had ridden out of the Aenorin's chase and across his path—a hundred years in what by that wound had been the blink of an eye.

It was insane. He bowed down upon his face and then retreated, glad to leave her to her own thoughts.

And because he was saddle-weary and harried beyond any immediate concern of magics or fear of beasts, he wrapped himself in his thin cloak and leaned against the rock wall to sleep.

The crash of a new piece of wood into the fire awakened him, still unrested, and he saw Morgaine brush snow from her cloak and settle again in her accustomed place. Her eyes went to him, fixed unwelcomely upon his, so that he could not pretend he slept.

"Is thee rested?" she asked of him, and that curious Korish accent was of long ago, and chilled him more than the wind or the stone at his back.

"Somewhat," he said, and forced stiff muscles to set him upright. He had slept in armor many a night, and occasionally he had slept colder; but there had been too many days in the saddle lately, and too little rest between, and none at all the night before.

"Vanye," she said.

"Lady?"

"Come, near the fire. I have questions for thee."

He did so, not gladly, and settled wrapped in his threadbare cloak and cherished the heat. She sat wrapped in her furs, her face half in shadow, and gazed into his eyes.

"Heln found this place," she said. "A hunter I did not kill told him. Aenor-Pyvvn rose in arms then. They sent an army after me—" She laughed, the merest breath. "An army, to take this little cave. Of course I knew their coming. How not? They filled the southern field. I fled at once—yet it was close. But they even dared the valley of Stones; so I fled where they could not—would not—follow. And there I must wait until someone freed me. I am no older; I knew nothing of the years. But things have gone to dust, else the horses and we would fare better tonight. Thee fears me—"

It was so, it was clearly so: from a man his enemy he would have resented those words; Morgaine he feared and he was not ashamed. His heart beat painfully at each direct glance of those gray, unhuman eyes. If he did not know of a certainty that he would die, he would flee this little place and her company; but there was the storm. It howled outside with the fury of winter. He knew the mountains. Sometimes there was no break in the snow for days. Men unprotected died, turned up in spring all twisted and stiff in the melting snow, along with carcasses of horses and deer that the wolves had somehow missed.

"There is no harm in words between us," she said. She offered him wine of her own flask. He took it hesitantly, but the night was chill, and he had already shared food with her. He drank a little and gave it back. She wiped the mouth fastidiously and drank also, and stopped the flask again.

"I beg thee tell me the end of my tale," she said. "I was not able to know. What became of the men I knew? What was it I did?"

He stared into her eyes, this most cursed of all enemies of Andur-Kursh, the traitor guide that had sent ten thousand men to die and sunk half the Middle Kingdoms into ruin. And those words would not come to him. He would easily say them of her to someone else: but in that fair and unguarded face there was something that unfolded to him, that strangled the curse in his throat.

He found no words for her at all.

"I do not think then," she said, "that it has a pleasant ending, since thee does not want to say. But say it, Nhi Vanye."

"There is no more to tell," he said. "After Irien, after so great a defeat for Andur-Kursh, Hjemur took Koris, took all the lands from Alis Kaje east. You were not to be found, not after the chase the Aenorin gave you. You vanished. What allies you had left surrendered. All that followed you died. They say that there were prosperous villages and holds in south Koris in your day. There are none now. It is as desolate as these mountains. And Irien itself is cursed ground, and no one enters there, even of Hjemur's men. There is rumor," he added, "that the Thiye who rules now is the same that ruled then. I do not know if that is true. The Hjemur-lord has always been called Thiye Thiye's-son. But the country people say that it is the same man, kept young a hundred years."

"It could be done," she said in a low and joyless voice.

"That is the end of it," he said. "Everyone died." And he thrust from his mind what she said of Thiye, for it occurred to him that she was living proof that it could be done, that things could be done for which he wanted no explanation. He must share this place with her: he wanted to share nothing else.

She let him be then, asking no more questions, and he retreated to the other side of the fire and curled up again to sleep.

The morning came, miserable and still spitting snow. But soon there began to be a break in the clouds, which cheered Vanye's heart. He had feared one of those storms that stayed for days, that might seal him in this place with her unwelcome company, while the poor horses froze outside.

And she cooked strips of venison over the fire for their breakfast, and offered him a little of the wine too. He cut bits from the steaming venison with his knife against his thumb, and watched even with amusement as she, more delicate, cut hers most awkwardly into bits, and dusted each piece and inspected it, and only then cooked it further and prised it off the dagger tip for eating, tiny bites and manageable.

Then she wrapped up the rest in a square of leather that he had of his gear for the purpose.

"Will you not keep some," he asked, "or are you taking it all?"

"What means the white scarf?" she asked him.

He swallowed the last bit of venison as if it had turned to dust in his mouth. All at once the rest that he had eaten and drunk turned to sickness in his belly.

"I am *ilin*," he said.

"Thee has sheltered with me, taken food," she said. "And the Chya of Koris gave me clan-welcome, and gave me lord-right, *ilin*."

He bowed his head to his hands upon the floor. She spoke the truth: alone of women, this was true of Morgaine, killer of armies. He raged at himself, even while his stomach knotted in fear; he had not even reckoned of it, for her being a woman; he had sheltered at her fire as he would have taken shelter at that of some Aenish farmwife. Such folk had no claim to make against an *ilin*.

Morgaine did.

"I beg exception," he said from that position. He was entitled to ask that, and he had no shame in asking. He dared look up at her. "I have kinsmen in Aenor-Pyvvn. I was going there. Lady, I am exiled in every province of Morija— I dare not go back there. I am little help to anyone." He took the helmet from his head—he had set it on again to go out into the cold—and, which he had not done, even for sleeping, he unlaced his coif at the throat and slipped it back from the shame of his shorn head, the fair brown hair falling free about his ears and across his brow. "I am outlawed in my clan: the Nhi and the Myya hunt me. So I became *ilin*. But I can find shelter only in Aenor-Pyvvn, and there you have said yourself you cannot go."

"For what was this done to thee?" she asked him, and he saw that he had succeeded in bringing shock even to the eyes of Morgaine.

"For murder, for brother-killing." He had told this to none, had avoided men and shelters even of country folk. The words came with difficulty to his lips. "It was a fight he forced, lady, but I killed my brother—my half-brother—and he was Myya. So there are two clans with blood-debt against me, and I am no help to you. I am grateful for the shelter—I thank you: but it is no use to you to make claim against me. Only name me some reasonable service and I will do that for you in payment. You cannot stay here, you are cursed in every hold in Andur-Kursh, and no one that hears your name or sees you will refrain from your life. Listen, for all that you are, you have been generous with me, and I am giving you good advice for it: the pass south of here leads through Aenor, and I am bound that way. I will somehow guide you through that land. I will bring you safely to the south of Aenor, where lands are warm, into Eriel, into the plains of Lun. They are savages that live there, but at least they have no bloodfeud with you and you can live there in safety. Listen to me and let me pay you with that thanks. That is the best that I can do for you, and I will do that honestly, grudging nothing."

"I refuse to grant exception," she said then, which was her right.

He swore, both foully and tearfully, and left her and went out and laid hands upon his horse's halter. He had time to think then, of the holy oath he had already made as *ilin,* and that oath-breaking was no light thing for his honor and least of all for his soul. He laid hand against the bay's rough cheek, and his head against its warm neck, and stayed there, shivering in the cold, but numb to it. Easy it would be if he could die there in the wind, robbed of warmth, to sink into the numbing snow and simply die, untouched by *qujalin* oaths.

New snow crunched beneath Morgaine's boots. She came and stood beside him, waiting for him to decide which he would, to yield up his soul by oath-breaking, or to risk it by serving the likes of her. For a man who was lost in either case, the only thing left was life: and life was sure to be longer by running now than by staying with Morgaine Frosthair.

Then he thought of the deer, and already he felt a twitching at the back of his shoulders as if she sought his life. He would not be able to outrace that: other weapons, perhaps, but not the thing that had slain the deer and left no wound.

"It is lawful," she said, "what I ask."

"With you," he objected, "that year is likely to be the last of my life. And after that, I would be a marked man in Andur-Kursh."

"I will admit that is true. My own life is likely to be no longer. I have no pity to spare for thee."

She held out her hand for his. He yielded it, and she drew the ivory-hilted Honor blade from her belt and cut deeply, but not wide: the dark blood welled up slowly in the cold. She set her mouth to the wound, and then he did the same, the salt hot taste of his own blood knotting his stomach in revulsion. Then she went inside, and brought ash to stop it with, smearing it with the clan-glyph of the Chya, writ in his blood and her hearth-ash across his hand, the ancient custom of Claiming.

Then he bowed to his forehead in the burning snow, and the ice numbed the fire in his hand and made it cease throbbing. She had certain responsibilities for him now: to see that he did not starve, neither he nor his horse, though certain of the hedge-lords were scant of that obligation, and kept the miserable *ilinin* they claimed lean and hungry and their horses in little better state when the *ilinin* were in hall.

Morgaine was of poorer estate: she had no hall to shelter either of them, and the clan she signed him—his own birth-clan—would as lief kill him as not. For his part, he must simply follow orders: no other law bound him now. He could even be ordered against homeland or blood kin, though it was no credit to the lord's honor if an *ilin* were so cruelly used. He must fight her enemies, tend her hearth—whatever things she required of him until a year had passed from the day of his oath.

Or she might simply name him a task to accomplish, and he would be bound to that task even beyond his year's time, until it was done. And that also was exceedingly cruel, but it was according to the law.

"What service?" he asked of her. "Will you let me guide you from here southward?"

"We go north," she said.

"Lady, it is suicide," he cried. "For you and for me."

"We go north," she said. "Come, I will bind up the hand."

"No," he said. He clutched snow in his fist, stopping the bleeding, and held the injured hand against him. "I want no medicines of yours. I will keep my oath. Let me tend to myself."

"I will not insist," she said.

Another thought, more terrible, occurred to him. He bowed in request another time, delaying her return to the cave.

"What else?" she asked him.

"If I die you are supposed to give me honorable burial. I do not want that."

"What—not to be buried?"

"Not by *qujalin* rites. No, I had rather the birds and the wolves than that."

She shrugged, as if that did not at all offend her. "Birds and wolves will likely care for both of us before all is done," she said. "I am glad thee sees the matter that way. I probably should have no time for amenities. Care for thyself and gather thy gear and mine. We are leaving this place."

"Where are we bound?"

"Where I will to go."

He bowed acceptance with a heavy heart, knowing of increasing certainty that he could not reason with her. She meant to die. It was cruel to have laid claim to an *ilin* under that circumstance, but that was the way of his oath. If a man survived his year, he was purged of crimes and disgrace. Heaven would have extracted due penance for his sins.

Many did not survive. It was presumed Heaven had exacted punishment. They were counted honorable suicides.

He bound up his hand with the cleanly remedies that he knew, though it hurt with dull persistence; and then he gathered up all their belongings, his and hers, and saddled both the horses. The sky was beginning to clear. The sun shone down on him as he worked, and glittered coldly off the golden hilt of the blade he hung upon the gray's saddle. The dragon leered at him, fringed mouth agape, clenching the blade in its teeth; his spread legs made the guard; his back-winding tail guarded the fingers.

He feared even to touch it. No Korish work, that, whatever hand had made the plain sheath. It was alien and otherly, and when he ventured in curiosity to ease the awful thing even a little way from its sheath, he found strange letters, the blade itself like a shard of glass—even touching it threatened injury. No blade ever existed of such substance: and yet it seemed more perilous than fragile.

He slipped it quickly back into its sheath, guilty as he heard Morgaine's tread behind him.

"Let it be," she said harshly. And when he stared at her, knowing of a surety he had done wrong, she said more gently: "It is a gift of one of my companions— a vanity. It pleased him. He had great skill. But if thee dislikes things *qujalin,* then keep hands from it."

He bowed, avoiding her eyes, and began working at his own gear, tying his few possessions into place at the back of the saddle.

The blade's name was *Changeling.* He remembered it of the songs, and wondered could a smith have given so unlucky a name to a blade, even were he *qujal.* His own sword was of humbler make, honest steel, well-tempered, name-less as befitted a common soldier or a lord's bastard son.

He hung it on his saddle, swung up to mount and waited upon Morgaine, who was hardly slower.

"Will you not listen to me?" He was willing to try reason a last time. "There is no safety for you in the north. Let us go south to Lun. There are tribes there that know nothing of you. You would be able to make your way among them. I have heard tell that there are cities far to the south. I would take you there. You could live. In the north, they will hunt you and kill you."

She did not even answer him, but guided the gray downhill.

⤳ **Chapter 3**

The wolves had been at the deer's carcass in the night, after the snow had ceased to fall so quickly. The area around the tattered bones was marked and patterned with the paws of wolves, and some of those tracks were wondrously large. Vanye looked down as their own trail crossed the trampled snow, and he saw the larger tracks he knew beyond doubt for beasts of Korish woods, more hound than wolf.

The carnage cast a further pall upon the morning, which was clearing to that ice-crystal brightness that blinded the senses, veiling all sins of ugliness into brilliance under a blue sky; but already the veil had been soiled for them. Death was with them, four-footed. Of natural wolves he had no great fear— they seldom bothered men, save in the most desperate winters. But Koris-beasts were another breed. They killed. They killed and never meant to eat—a perversion in nature.

Morgaine looked down at the tracks too, and seemed unperturbed; perhaps, he thought, she had never seen the like in her time, before Thiye learned to warp the lightness of nature into shapes he chose. Perhaps magics had grown more powerful than she remembered, and she did not know the dangers toward which they rode.

Or perhaps—it was the worse thought—he himself failed to realize with what he rode, knee to knee and peaceful on this bright morning. He feared her for her reputation: that was natural. And yet, he thought, perhaps he did not hold fear enough of her presence. She could kill without touching and without wound: he could not rid his mind of the deer's wide-eyed look, that ought by rights not to have been dead.

A gnawed bone lay athwart their path. His horse shied from it.

They rode back into the valley of the Stones, crossing the frozen stream, cracking the yet thin ice, and rode the winding trail beside the great gray rocks, under the shadow of the mound called Morgaine's Tomb. Despite the snow, the sky shimmered between the two carven pillars with the look of air above heated rocks.

Morgaine looked up at it as they rode. There was upon her face a curious loathing. He began to understand that it had been far from Morgaine's will to have ridden into such a thing with Heln's men behind her.

"Who freed you?" he asked suddenly.

She looked back at him, puzzled.

"You said that someone must free you from this place. What is it? How were you held there? And who freed you?"

"It is a Gate," she said, and into his mind there flashed the nightmare image of white rider against the sun: it was hard to remember such madness. Like dreams, it tended to fade, for the sake of sanity.

"If it is a gate," he said, "then from where did you come?"

"I was *between* until something should disturb the field. That is the way with Gates that are not set. It is like a shallow pool of time, ever so shallow. I was washed up again, on this shore."

He gazed up at it, could not understand, and yet it was as good an explanation of what he had seen as any other.

"Who freed you?" he asked.

"I do not know," she said. "I rode in with men at my heels; a shadow passed me; I rode out again. It was like closing my eyes. No—not that either. It was just *between*. Only it was thicker than any *between* I have ever ridden. I think that thee was—thee says, *you*—were—the one that did free me. But I do not know how, and I doubt that you know."

"It is impossible," he said. "I never came near the Stones."

"I would not wager anything on that memory," she said.

She turned her head; he rode behind her here, for the path was narrow at the bottom of the hill. He had view of the gray's white swaying tail and Morgaine's white-cloaked and insolent back; and the presence of this structure she called a Gate cast a pall upon all his thoughts. He had leisure to repent his oath in this ill-omened place, and knew that in a year with Morgaine he was bound to see and hear many things an honest and once religious man would not find comfortable.

He had a sudden and uncomfortable vision as he saw her riding ahead of him upon that stretch of the old paved road up between the lesser monoliths: that here was another kind of anachronism, like a man visiting the nursery of his childhood, surrounded by sad toys. Morgaine was indeed out of the long-ago; and yet it was known that the *qujal* had been evil and wise and able to work things that men had happily forgotten. Not needing transport, not needing such things as mortal weapons, *qujal* only wished and practiced sorceries, and what they wished became substance—until they grew yet more evil, and ruined themselves.

And yet Morgaine rode, live and powerful, and carried under her knee a blade of forgotten arts, in the ruins of things she might well have known as they once had been.

It was said that Thiye Thiye's-son was immortal, renewing his youth by taking life from others, and that he would never die so long as he could find unfortunates on whom to practice this. He had tended to scoff at the rumor: all men died.

But Morgaine had not, not in more than a hundred years, and still was young. She found the hundred years acceptable. Perhaps she had known longer sleeps than this.

The higher passes were choked with snow. Gray and bay fought drifts, struggling with such effort that they made little time. They must often pause to rest the animals. Yet by afternoon they seemed to have made it through the worst places, and without meeting any of the Myya or seeing tracks of beasts.

It was good fortune. It was bound not to last.

"Lady," he said during one of their rests, "if we go on as we are we will be in the valley of Morij Erd; and if we enter there, chances are you will not find welcome for either of us. This horse of mine is out of that land; and Gervaine its lord is Myya and he has sworn a great oath to have my head on a pike and other parts of me similarly distributed. There is no good prospect for you or for me in this direction."

She smiled slightly. She had been in lighter humor since the morning, when they had quitted the valley of Stones and entered the more honest shades of pine woods and unhewn crags. "We bear east before then, toward Koris."

"Lady, you know your way well enough," he protested glumly. "Why was it needful to snare me for a guide?"

"How should I know otherwise that Gervaine is lord of Morij Erd?" she asked, still smiling. The eyes did not. "Besides, I did not say that you were to be a guide in these lands, *ilin*."

"What, then?"

But she did not answer. She had that habit when he asked what displeased her. More human folk might dispute, protest, argue. Morgaine was simply silent, and against that there was no argument, only deep frustration.

He climbed back into his saddle and saw thereafter that they bore more easterly, toward Koris, toward that land that was most firmly in Thiye's hands.

Toward dusk they were in pine forest again. Gray-centered clouds sailed across the moon increasingly frequent as the night deepened, and yet they rode, fearful of more storms, fearful for the horses, for there was little grain remaining in both their saddlebags, and they wished to make what easy time they could, hopeful of coming to the lower country before the winter set a firm grip on the passes before them. The bright moon showed them the way.

But at last the clouds were thick and the trail became hardly passable, trees crowding close and obscuring the sky with their bristling shadow. A downed tree beside the road promised them at least a drier place to rest, and wood for fire. They stopped and Vanye hacked off smaller branches and heaped them into a proper form for a damp-wood fire.

How the fire came to be, Vanye did not see: he turned his back to fetch more wood, and turned again and it was started, a tiny tongue of fire within the damp branches. It smoked untidily: wet wood; but it remained, Morgaine leaning close to encourage it, and he gingerly fed it tinder.

"There is a certain danger in this," he advised Morgaine, looking at her closely over the little fire. "There may be men hereabouts to see the light or smell the smoke, and no men in these woods are friendly to any other. I do not care to meet what this may attract, and it is best we keep it small and not keep it the night long."

She opened her hand and in the dim light showed him a black and shiny thing, queer and ugly. It revolted him: he could not determine why, only that it would not be made by any hand he knew, and there was a foul unloveliness about the thing in her fair slim hand. "This is sufficient for brigands and for beasts," she said. "And I trust you are somewhat skilled with sword and with bow. *Ilinin* otherwise do not long survive."

He nodded silent acknowledgement.

"Fetch our gear," she bade him.

He did so, clearing snow from the great tree and resting all that could be harmed by damp upon that. She began to make a meal for them of the almost frozen meat, while he doled out a bit of the remaining grain to the poor horses. They nudged him in the ribs and coaxed pitiably, wanting the rest of it: but he steeled his heart against them, grieved and out of appetite for the good venison they had. Kurshin that he was, he could not eat with his animals in want. A man was to be judged by his horses and the fitness of them; and had it been grain they themselves were eating he would gladly have given them his share and gone hungry.

He went and settled glumly by the fire, working his stiffening hand, which was affected by the cold. "We must somehow get down from this height," he said, "by tomorrow, even if it takes us by some more dangerous road. We are out of grain but for one day. These horses cannot force drifts like these and go hungry too. We will kill them if we keep on."

She nodded quietly. "We are on a short road," she said.

"Lady, I do not know this way, and I have ridden the track from Morija to Koris's border to Erd several ways."

"It is a road I knew," she said, and looked up at the clouding sky, the pine-tops black against the veiled moon. "It was less overgrown then."

He made a gesture against evil, unthought and reflexive. He thought then that it would anger her. Instead she glanced down briefly, as if avoiding reply.

"Where are we going?" he asked her. "Are we looking for something?"

"No," she said. "I know where it lies."

"Lady," he asked of her, for she seemed about to sink into another of her silences. He made a bow, earnestly; he could not bear another day of that. "Lady, where? Where are we going?"

"To Ivrel." And when in dread he opened his mouth to protest that madness: "I have not told you yet," she said, "what service I claim of thee."

"No," he agreed, "you have not."

"It is this, *ilin*. To kill the Hjemur-lord Thiye and to destroy his citadel if I die."

A laugh escaped him, became a sob. This was the thing she had promised the six lords she would do. Ten thousand men had died in that attempt, so that many surmised she had never been enemy to Thiye of Hjemur, but friend and servant-witch, set out to ruin the Middle Lands.

"Ah, I will go with thee," she said. "I do not ask you to do this thing alone; but if I am lost, that is your service to me."

"Why?" he asked abruptly. "For revenge? What wrong have I done you, lady?"

"I came to seal the Gates," she said, "and if I should be lost, that is the means to do it. I do not think I can teach you otherwise. But take my weapons and strike at the heart of Hjemur's hold: that would do it as well as I ever could."

"If you wish to rain the Gates," he said bitterly, for he did not half believe her, "there was a beginning to be made at Aenor-Pyvvn's fires, and you rode past it."

"Pointless to meddle with it. They are all dangerous; but the master Gate is that you call the Witchfires: without it all the others must fade. They all once led to there: now they only exist, without depth or direction. They are the one thing that Thiye has not fully discovered how to manage. He cannot stop or use them singly. Thiye is no blood of mine, but he has had instruction. He plays with things he only half understands, although it may be," she added, "that a hundred years have increased his wisdom."

"I understand nothing at all," he protested. "Set me free of this thing. It does no honor to you to ask such a thing of me. I will go with you, I swear this: I will do you *ilin*'s service until you have seen through what you will do, no matter how mean or how miserable things you ask of me. I swear that, even beyond my year, even to Ivrel, if that is where you are going. But do not ask me to do this thing and hang my oath as *ilin* on it."

"All these things," she said softly, "I have of the oath you have already given me." And then her voice became almost kindly: "Vanye, I am desperate. Five of us came here and four are dead, because we did not know clearly what we faced. Not all the old knowledge is dead here; Thiye has found teachers for himself, and perhaps he has indeed grown in knowledge: in some part I hope he has. His ignorance is as dangerous as his malice. But if I send you, I will not send you totally ignorant."

He bowed his head. "Do not tell me these things. If you need a right arm, I am there. No more than that."

"Well enough," she said, "well enough for now. I will not force any knowledge on thee that does not have to be."

And she applied knife to a twig and sharpened it to hold the strips of venison.

He slipped his helmet off, for it hurt his brow from long wearing, but he did not slip the coif: it was cold and shame still prevented him, even in her sight. He wrapped the cloak about him and undertook to cook his own food, and shared wine with her. He went over to the log after that, and stretched himself upon the higher part of it, and she upon the lower a time later. It was a peculiar sort of bed, but better by far than the cold snow below them; and he tucked himself up like a warrior on a bier, his longsword clasped upon his breast, for he did not want to let it out of his grasp on this night, and in this place. He did not even keep it in its sheath.

And late, when the fire had become very low, he became uneasy with the impression that there was something stirring besides the wind that cracked the icy branches, something large and of weight; and he strained his eyes and hearing and held his breath to see and listen to what it might be.

Suddenly he saw Morgaine's hand seek toward her belt beneath her cloak, and he knew that she was awake.

"I will put wood upon the fire," he said, this also for any watcher. He rolled off the log into a crouch, almost expecting a rush of something.

Brush cracked. Snow crunched, rapidly receding.

He looked at Morgaine.

"It was no wolf," she said. "Go feed the fire, and keep an eye to the horses. If we ride out now we are perhaps no better target than we are sitting here, but I fear this trail has changed too much to chance it in the dark."

It was an uneasy night thereafter. The clouds grew thicker. Toward morning there came the first siftings of snow.

Vanye swore, heartbreakingly, with feeling. He hated the cold like death itself; it closed in about them until all the world was white, and they drifted through the veiling wind as they rode, like wraiths, nearly losing one another upon occasion, until the lowering sky ceased to sift down on them and they had an afternoon free of misery.

The trail ceased to be a trail at all, yet Morgaine still professed to know the way: she had, she avowed, ridden it only a few days ago, when trees were still young that now were old, where others stood that now did not, and the path was fair and well-ridden. Yet she insisted she would not mistake their way.

And toward evening they did indeed come to what seemed a proper road, or the remnant of one, and made a camp in a pleasant place that was at least sheltered from the rising wind, a hollow among rocks that looked out upon an open meadow—rare in these hills. With the wind up and no dry bed for their rest, he did what he could with pine boughs, and tried beneath the snow for grass for the horses, but it was too deep, and iced. He fed the animals the last of the grain, wondering what would become of them on the morrow, and then returned to the fire that Morgaine had made, there to sit hunched in his cloak like a winter bird, miserable and dejected. He slept early, taking what rest he could until Morgaine nudged him with her foot. Thereafter she slept in the warm place he had quitted, and he sat slumped against a rock and wrapped his arms and legs about his longsword, trying against his weariness to hold himself alert.

He nodded, unintended, jerked erect again. One of the horses snorted. He thought that he himself had startled it by his sudden movement, but the uneasiness nagged at him.

Then he rose up with unsheathed sword in hand and walked out to see the horses.

A weight hit his back, snarling and spitting and sounding human. He cried out and spun, wrist shocked as the sword bit bone; and something went loping off, hunched and shadowy in the dark. There were others joining it in its retreat. He saw a light flash, spun about to see Morgaine.

For an instant he cringed, fearing what she held no less than he feared beasts out of Koris, and still trembling in every limb from the attack.

She waited for him, and he came back to her, knelt down on the mat of boughs and zealously cleaned his sword in snow and rubbed it dry. He loathed the blood of Koris-things upon the clean steel. His hurts were numb; he hoped that there had not been any to break the skin. He did not think they had pierced the mail shirt.

"These are not natural beasts," she said.

"No," he agreed. "They are far from natural. But they can die by natural weapons."

"Is thee hurt?"

"No," he judged, surprised, even pleased that she had asked; he nodded his head in a half-bow, tribute to courtesy which *liyo* did not owe *ilin*. "No, I do not think so."

She settled again. "Will rest? I will wake a while."

"No," he said again. "I could not sleep."

She nodded, settled, and curled herself back to sleep.

The snows had passed by morning; the sun rose clear and bright upon them, beginning even to melt a little of the snow, and they took their way down the other side of the mountain ridge, among pines and rocks and increasing openness of the road.

Upon a height they suddenly had view of lower lands, of white shading into green, where lesser altitudes had gained less snow, and forest lay as far as the eye could see into lesser Koris and into the lower lands.

Far away beyond the haze lay the ominous cone of Ivrel, but it was much too far to see. There were only the hazy white caps of Alis Kaje, mother of eagles, and of Cedur Maje, which were the mountain walls of Morija, dividing Kursh from Andur, Thiye's realms from those of men.

They rode easily this day, found grass for the horses and stopped to rest a time, rode on farther and in lighter spirits. They came upon a fence, a low shepherd's fence of rough stones, the first indication that they had found of human habitation.

It was the first sight of anything human that Vanye had seen since the last brush of a Myya arrow, and he was glad to see the evidence of plain herder folk, and breathed easier. In the last few days and in such company as he now rode one could forget humanity, farms and sheep and normal folk.

Then there was a little house, a homely place with rough stone walls and a garden that had gone to weeds, snow-covered in patches. The shutters hung.

Morgaine shook her head, incredulity in her eyes.

"What was this place?" he asked her.

"A farm," said Morgaine, "a fair and pleasant one." And then: "I spent the night here—hardly a month of my life ago. They were kindly folk who lived here."

He thought to himself that they must also have been fearless to have sheltered Morgaine after Irien; and he saw by leaning round in his saddle when they had passed to the far side of the house, that the back portion of the roof had fallen in.

Fire? he wondered. It was not a surprising vengeance taken on people that had sheltered the witch. Morgaine had an uncommon history of disasters where she passed, most often to the innocent.

She did not see. She rode ahead without looking back, and he let his bay— he called the beast Mai, as all his horses would be Mai—overtake the gray. They rode knee to knee, morose and silent. Morgaine was never joyous company. This sight made her melancholy indeed.

Then, upon a sudden winding of the trail, as the pines began to crowd close upon them and upon the little fence, there sat two ragged children.

Male and female they seemed to be, raggle-taggle, shag-haired little waifs of enormous dark eyes and pinched cheeks, sitting on the fence itself despite the snow. They scrambled up, eyes pools of distress, stretching out bony hands.

"Food, food," they cried, "for charity."

The gray, Siptah, reared up, lashing with his hooves; and Morgaine reined him aside, narrowly missing the boy. She had hard shift to hold the animal, who shied, wide-nostrilled and round-eyed until his haunches brought up against the wall upon the other side, and Vanye curbed his Mai with a hard hand, cursing at the reckless children. Such waifs were not an uncommon sight in Koris. They begged, stole shamelessly.

There but for Rijan, Vanye thought occasionally: lord's bastards sometimes came to other fates than he had known before his exile. The poor were frequent in the hills of Andur, clanless and destitute, and poor girls' fatherless children generally came to ill ends. If they survived childhood they grew up as bandits in earnest.

And the girl perhaps would spawn more of her own kind, misery breeding misery.

They could not be more than twelve, the pair of them, and they seemed to be brother and sister—perhaps twins. They had the same wolf-look in their eyes, the same pointed leanness to their faces as they huddled together away from the dangerous hooves.

"Food," they still pleaded, holding out each a hand.

"We have enough to spare." Vanye directed his words to Morgaine, a request, for their saddlebags were still heavy with the frozen venison of days before. He pitied such as these children, loathsome as they were, always gave them charity when he could—for luck, remembering what he was.

And when Morgaine consented with a nod he leaned across and lifted the saddlebag from Siptah's gray back and was about to open it when the girl, venturing close to Mai, snatched his saddleroll off the rear of the saddle, slashing one of its bindings.

He cursed volubly, wiser than to drop their food and give chase to one while the boy lingered: he tossed the leather-wrapped packet at Morgaine, flung his leg over the horn. The boy fled too, vaulting the wall. Vanye went close after him.

"Have a care," Morgaine wished him.

But the fleeing urchins dropped his belongings. Content with that, he pushed to gather things up, annoyed that they returned to jeer at him like the naughty children they were, dancing about him.

He snatched as the boy darted too close to him, meaning no more than to cuff him and shake him to sober sense; the boy twisted in his grip and gave forth a stream of curses, and the girl with a shriek rushed at him and clawed at his hold upon the boy—a bodkin in her hand. It pierced deep, enough that he snatched back his hand.

They shrieked and ran, leaving him with the spoils, and vanished among the trees. He was still cursing under his breath when he returned to Morgaine, sucking at the painful wound the little minx had dealt his hand.

"Children of imps," he muttered. "Thieves. Misbegotten brigands." He had lost face before his *liyo*, his lady-lord, and swung up into Mai's saddle with sullen grace, having tied his gear behind. Until this time he had felt unworthily used, taken in treachery and unworthily on *her* part: it was the first time he had to feel that he had fallen short in his obligation, and that made him doubly debted, disgracing both himself and his *liyo*.

And then he began to feel strangely, like a man having drunk too much wine, his head humming and his whole person strangely at variance with all that was about him.

He gazed at Morgaine in alarm, reluctant to plead for help, but suddenly he felt he needed it. He could not understand what was the matter with his senses. It was like the onset of fever. He swayed in the saddle.

Morgaine's slim arm stayed him. She put Siptah close to him, holding him. He heard her voice speaking sharply to him and sternly ordering him to hold himself up.

He centered his weight and slumped, wit enough to do that, at least, distributing his failing body over Mai's neck. The saddlehorn was painful; the bending cut off his wind. He could not even summon the strength in his arms to deal with that.

Morgaine was afoot. She had his injured hand. He felt pain in it, distantly, felt her warm mouth touch it. She dealt with it like snakebite, spitting out the poison, cursing at him or at her own fell spirits in a tongue he could not understand, which frightened him.

He tried to help her. He could not think of anything for a time, and was surprised to find that she had moved again, and was upon Siptah, leading his horse by the reins, and that they were taking again to the snowy road. She had on his own plain cloak: the furs were warming him.

He clung to the saddle until his numb body finally told him that she had bound him so that he could not fall. He let himself go then, and yielded to the horse's notion. Thirst plagued him. He could not summon the will to ask for anything. He was dimly aware of interludes of travel, interspersed with darkness.

And the darkness was growing in the sky.

He was dying. He became sure of it. It began to trouble him that he might die and she forget her promise and send him into the hereafter with alien rites. He was terrified at the thought: for that terror alone he refused to die. He fought every lapse into unconsciousness. At times he almost gained will and wit enough to speak to her, but all his words came out twisted, and she generally ignored him, assuming him fevered, or not caring.

Then he knew that there were riders about them. He saw the crest upon him that led them, that of wolf with a deer within its jaws, and he knew the mark and tried desperately to warn her.

Still even they took his words for raving. Morgaine fell in with them, and they were escorted down into the vale of Koris, toward Ra-leth.

ᥫ **Chapter 4**

There was a tattered look about the hall, full of cobwebs in the corners, the mortar crumbling here and there, making hollow gaps between the big irregular stones so that spiders had abundant hiding places. The wooden frame did not quite meet the stone about the door. The bracket for the burning torch hung most precariously by a single one of its four bolts.

The bed itself sagged uncomfortably. Vanye searched about with his left hand to discover the limits of it: his right hand was sorely swollen, puffed with venom. He could not clearly remember what had been done, save that he lay here while things came clear again, and there was a person who hovered about him from time to time, fending others away.

He realized finally that the person was Morgaine, Morgaine without her cloak, black-clad and slim in men's clothing, and yet with the most incongruous *tgihio*—overrobe—of silver and black: she had a barbaric bent yet unsuspected; and the blade *Changeling* was hung over her chair, and her other gear propping her feet—most unwomanly.

He gazed at her trying to bring his mind to clarity and remember how they had come there, and still could not. She saw him and smiled tautly.

"Well," she said, "thee will not lose the arm."

He moved the sore hand and tried to flex the fingers. They were too swollen. What she had said still frightened him, for the arm was affected up to the elbow, and that hurt to bend.

"Flis!" Morgaine called.

A girl appeared, backing into the room, for she had hands full of linens and a basin of steaming water.

The girl made shift to bow obeisance to Morgaine, and Morgaine scowled at her and jerked her head in the direction of Vanye.

The hot water pained him. He set his teeth and endured the compresses of hot towels, and directed his attention instead to his attendant. Flis was dark-haired and sloe-eyed, intensely, hotly female. The low peasant bodice gaped a bit as she bent; she smiled at him and touched his face. Her bearing, her manner, was that of many a girl in hall that was low-clan or no-clan, who hoped to get of some lord a child to lift her to honorable estate. No seed of his could ennoble anyone, but she surely plied her arts with him because he was safe at the moment and he was a stranger.

She soothed his fever with her hands and gave him well-watered wine to drink, and talked to him in little sweet words which made no particular sense. When her hands touched his brow he realized that she made no objection of his shorn hair, which would have warned any sensible woman of his character and his station and sent her indignantly hence.

Then he remembered that he was surely in the hall of clan Leth, where outcasts and outlaws were welcome so long as they bore the whims of lord Kasedre and were not particular what orders they obeyed. Here such a man as he was no novelty, perhaps of no less honor than the rest.

Then he saw Morgaine on her feet, looking at him over the shoulder of the girl Flis, and Morgaine gave him a faintly disgusted look, judgment of the awkwardly predatory maid. She turned and paced to the window, out of convenient view.

He closed his eyes then, content to have the pain of his arm attended, required to do nothing. He had lost all the face a man could lose, being rescued by his *liyo*, a woman, and given over to servants such as this.

Leth tolerated Morgaine's presence, even paid her honor, to judge by the splendor of the guest-robe they offered her, and indulged her lord-right, treating her as equal.

Flis' hand strayed. He moved it, indignant at such treatment in his *liyo's* presence, and her a woman. Flis giggled.

Brocade rustled. Morgaine paced back again, scowled and nodded curtly to the girl. Flis grew quickly sober, gathered up her basin and her towels with graceless haste.

"Leave them," Morgaine ordered.

Flis abandoned them on the table beside the door and bowed her way out.

Morgaine walked over to the bed, lifted the compress on Vanye's injured hand, shook her head. Then she went over to the door and slid the chair over in such fashion that no one outside could easily open the door.

"Are we threatened?" Vanye asked, disturbed by such precautions.

Morgaine busied herself with her own gear, extracting some of her own unguents from the kit. "I imagine we are," she said. "But that is not why I barred the door. We are not provided with a lock and I grow weary of that minx spying on my business."

He watched uneasily as she set her medicines out on the table beside him. "I do not want—"

"Objections denied." She opened a jar and smeared a little medication into the wound, which was wider and more painful than before, since the compress. The medication stung and made it throb, but numbed the wound thereafter. She mixed something into water for him to drink, and insisted and ordered him to drink it.

Thereafter he was sleepy again, and began to perceive that Morgaine was the agent of it this time.

She was sitting by him when he awoke, polishing his much-battered helm, tending his armor, he supposed, from boredom. She tilted her head to one side and considered him.

"How fare you now?"

"Better," he said, for he seemed free of fever.

"Can you rise?"

He tried. It was not easy. He realized in his blindness and his concern with the effort itself, that he was not clothed, and snatched at the sheet, nearly falling in the act: Kurshin were a modest folk. But it mattered little to Morgaine. She estimated him with an analytical eye that was in itself more embarrassing than the blush she did not own.

"You will not ride with any great endurance," she said, "which is an inconvenience. I have no liking for this place. I do not trust our host at all, and I may wish to quit this hall suddenly."

He sank down again, reached for his clothing and tried to dress, one-handed as he was.

"Our host," he said, "is Kasedre, lord of Leth. And you are right. He is mad."

He omitted to mention that Kasedre was reputed to have *qujalin* blood in his veins, and that that heredity was given as reason for his madness; Morgaine, though unnerving in her oddness, was at least sane.

"Rest," she bade him when he had dressed, for the effort had taxed him greatly. "You may need your strength. They have our horses in stables downstairs near the front entry, down this hall outside to the left, three turns down the stairs and left to the first door. Mark that. Listen, I will show you what I have observed of this place, in the case we must take our leave separately."

And sitting on the bed beside him she traced among the bedclothes the pattern of the halls and the location of doors and rooms, so that he had a fair estimation of where things lay without having laid eye upon them. She had a good faculty for such things: he was pleased to learn his *liyo* was sensible and experienced in matters of defense. He began to be more optimistic of their chances in this place.

"Are we prisoners," he asked, "or are we guests?"

"I am a guest in name, at least," she said, "but this is not a happy place for guesting."

There was a scratching at the door. Someone tried it. When it did not yield, the visitor padded off down the hall.

"Do you have any wish to linger here?" he asked.

"I feel," she said, "rather like a mouse passing a cat: probably there is no harm and the beast looks well-fed and lazy; but it would be a mistake to scurry."

"If the cat is truly hungry," he said, "we delude ourselves."

She nodded.

This time there was a deliberate knock at the door.

Vanye scrambled for his longsword, hooked it to his belt, convenient to the left hand. Morgaine moved the chair and opened the door.

It was Flis again. The girl smiled uncertainly and bowed. Vanye saw her in clearer light this time, without the haze of fever. She was not as young as he had thought. It was paint that blushed her cheek and her dress was not country and innocence: it was blowsy. She simpered and smiled past Morgaine at Vanye.

"You are wanted," she said.

"Where?" asked Morgaine.

Flis did not want to look up into Morgaine's eyes: addressed, she had no choice. She did so and visibly cringed: her head only reached Morgaine's shoulders, and her halo of frizzled brown seemed dull next to Morgaine's black and silver. "To hall, lady." She cast a second wishing look back at Vanye, back again. "Only you, lady. They did not ask the man."

"He is *ilin* to me," she said. "What is the occasion?"

"To meet my lord," said Flis. "It is all right," she insisted. "I can take care for him."

"Never mind," said Morgaine. "He will do very well without, Flis. That will be all."

Flis blinked: she did not seem particularly intelligent. Then she backed off and bowed and went away, beginning to run.

Morgaine turned about and looked at Vanye. "My apologies," she said dryly. "Are you fit to go down to hall?"

He bowed assent, thoroughly embarrassed by Morgaine, and wondering whether he should be outraged. He did not want Flis. Protesting it was graceless too. He ignored her gibe and avowed that he was fit. He was not steady on his feet. He thought that it would pass.

She nodded to him and led the way out of the room.

Everything outside was much the same as she had described to him. The hall was in general disrepair, like some long abandoned fortress suddenly occupied and not yet quite liveable. There was a mustiness about the air, a queasy feeling of dirt, and effluvium of last night's feasting, of grease and age and untended cracks, and earth and damp.

"Let us simply walk for the door," Vanye suggested when they reached that lower floor and he knew that the lefthand way led to the outside, and their horses, and a wild, quick ride out of this place of madmen. "*Liyo*, let us not stay here. Let us take nothing from this place, let us go, now, quickly."

"Thee is not fit for a chase," she said. "Or I would, gladly. Be still. Do not offend our hosts."

They walked unescorted down the long corridors, where sometimes were servants that looked like beggars that sometimes appeared at hold gates, asking their three days of lawful charity. It was shame to a lord to keep folk of his hall in such a state. And the hold of Leth was huge. Its stones were older than Morgaine's ride to Irien, older by far in all its parts, and in its day it had been a grand hall, most fabled in its beauty. If she had seen it then, it was sadly otherwise now, with the tapestries in greasy rags and bare stone showing through the tattered and dirty carpets on the floors. There were corridors which they did not take, great open halls that breathed with damp and decay, closed doors that looked to have remained undisturbed for years. Rats scurried sullenly out of their path, seeking the large cracks in the masonry, staring out at them with small glittering eyes.

"How much of this place have you seen?" he asked of her.

"Enough," she said, "to know that there is much amiss here. Nhi Vanye, whatever bloodfeuds you have with Leth, you are *ilin* to me. Remember it."

"I have none with Leth," he said. "Sensible men avoid them altogether. Madness is like yeast in this whole loaf. It breeds and rises. Guard what you say, *liyo*, even if you are offended."

And of a sudden he saw the lean face of the boy leering out at them from a cross-corridor, the sister beside him, rat-eyed and smiling. Vanye blinked. They were not there. He could not be sure whether he had seen them or not.

The door to the main hall gaped ahead of them. He hastened to overtake Morgaine. There were any number of bizarre personages about, a clutch of men that looked more fit to surround some hillside campfire as bandits—they lounged at the rear of the hall; and a few high-clan *uyin* that he took for Leth, who lounged about the high tables in the hall. These latter were also lean and hungry and out-at-the-elbows, their *tgihin* gaudy, but frayed at hems: to do justice to their charity and hospitality to Morgaine, they were indeed less elegant than what they had lent to her.

And there was a man that could only have been Leth Kasedre, who sat in the chair of honor at center, youngish to look upon—he could surely have been no more than thirty, and yet his babyish face was sallow, beneath a fringe of dark hair that wanted trimming: no warrior's braid for this one, and much else that went to make up a man seemed likely wanting too. His hair hung in twining ringlets. His eyes were hunted, darting from this to that; his mouth was like that of a sick man, loose, moist at the edges. He exuded heat and chill at once, like fever.

And his clothing was splendor itself, cloth-of-gold, his narrow chest adorned with brooches and clasps and chains of gold. A jeweled Honor blade was at his belt, and a jeweled longsword, which added decoration useless and pathetic. The air about him was thick with the reek of perfumes that masked decay. As they came near him there was no doubt. It was a sickroom smell.

Kasedre arose, extended a thin hand to offer place to Morgaine, who tucked up her feet and settled on the low bench courtiers had vacated for her, a place of honor; she wore *Changeling* high at her back and released the hook that secured the shoulderstrap at her waist, letting strap and blade slide to her hip for comfort, sitting. She bowed gracefully; Kasedre returned the courtesy.

Vanye must perforce kneel at the Leth's feet and touch brow to floor, respect which the Leth hardly deigned to acknowledge, intent as he was on Morgaine. Vanye crept aside to his place behind her. It was bitter: he was a warrior—had been, at least; he had been proud, though bastard, and certainly Nhi Rijan's bastard ranked higher than this most notorious of hedge-lords. But he had seen *ilinin* at Ra-morij forced to such humiliation, refused Claiming, forgotten, ignored, no one reckoning what the man might have been before he became *ilin* and nameless. It was not worth protest now: the Leth was supremely dangerous.

"I am intrigued to have the likes of you among us," said Leth Kasedre. "Are you truly that Morgaine of Irien?"

"I never claimed to be," said Morgaine.

The Leth blinked, leaned back a little, licked the corners of his mouth in perplexity. "But you are, truly," he said. "There was never the like of you in this world."

Morgaine's lips suddenly acquired a smile as feral as Kasedre's could be. "I am Morgaine," she said. "You are right."

Kasedre let his breath go in a long sigh. He performed another obeisance that had to be answered, rare honor for a guest in hall. "How are you among us? Do you come back—to ride to other wars?"

He sounded eager, even delighted at the prospect.

"I am seeing what there is to be seen," said Morgaine. "I am interested in Leth. You seem an interesting beginning to my travels. And," a modest lowering of eyes, "you have been most charitable in the matter of my *ilin*—if it were not for the twins."

Kasedre licked his lips and looked suddenly nervous. "Twins? Ah, wicked, wicked, those children. They will be disciplined."

"Indeed they should be," said Morgaine.

"Will you share dinner with us this evening?"

Morgaine's precise and delighted smile did not vary. "Most gladly, most honored, Leth Kasedre. My *ilin* and I will attend."

"Ah, but ill as he is—"

"My *ilin* will attend," she said. Her tone was delicate ice, still smiling. Kasedre flinched from that and smiled also, chanced in the same moment to look toward Vanye, who glared back, sullen and well sure of the murder resident in Kasedre's heart: hate not directed at Morgaine—he was in awe of her—but of the sight of a man who was not his to order.

Of a sudden, wildly, he feared Morgaine's own capabilities. She slipped so easily into mad Kasedre's vein, well able to play the games he played and tread the maze of his insanities. Vanye reckoned again his worth to his *liyo*, and wondered whether she would yield him up to Kasedre if need be to escape this mad hall, a bit of human coin strewn along her way and forgotten.

But so far she defended her rights with authoritative persistence, whether for his sake or in her own simple arrogance.

"Have you been dead?" asked Kasedre.

"Hardly," she said. "I took a shortcut. I was only here a month ago. Edjnel was ruling then."

Kasedre's mad eyes glittered and blinked when she casually named a lord his ancestor, dead a hundred years. He looked angry, as if he suspected some humor at his expense.

"A shortcut," she said, unruffled, "across the years you folk have lived, from yesterday to now, straightwise. The world went wide, around the bending of the path. I went through. I am here now, all the same. You look a great deal like Edjnel."

Kasedre's face underwent a rapid series of expressions, ending in delight as he was compared to his famous ancestor. He puffed and swelled so far as his narrow chest permitted, then seemed again to return to the perplexities of the things she posed.

"How?" he asked. "How did you do it?"

"By the fires of Aenor above Pyvvn. It is not hard to use the fires to this purpose—but one must be very brave. It is a fearful journey."

It was too much for Kasedre. He drew a series of deep breaths like a man about to faint, and leaned back, resting his hands upon that great sword, staring about at his gape-mouthed *uyin,* half of whom looked puzzled and the other part too muddled to do anything.

"You will tell us more of this," said Kasedre.

"Gladly, at dinner," she said.

"Ah, sit, stay, have wine with us," begged Kasedre.

Morgaine gave forth that chill smile again, dazzling and false. "By your leave, lord Kasedre, we are still weary from our travels and we will need a time to rest or I fear we shall not last a late banquet. We will go to our room and rest a time, and then come down at whatever hour you send for us."

Kasedre pouted. In such as he the moment was dangerous, but Morgaine continued to smile, bright and deadly, and full of promises. Kasedre bowed. Morgaine rose and bowed.

Vanye inclined himself again at Kasedre's feet, had a moment to see the look that Kasedre cast at Morgaine's back.

It was, he was glad to see, still awestruck.

Vanye was shaking with exhaustion when they reached the security of their upstairs room. He himself moved the chair before the door again, and sat down on the bed. Morgaine's cold hand touched his brow, seeking fever.

"Are you well?" she asked.

"Well enough. Lady, you are mad to sample anything of his at table tonight."

"It is not a pleasant prospect, I grant you that." She took off the dragon sword and set it against the wall.

"You are playing with him," said Vanye, "and he is mad."

"He is accustomed to having his way," said Morgaine. "The novelty of this experience may intrigue him utterly."

And she set down in the other plain chair and folded her arms. "Rest," she said. "I think we may both need it."

He eased back on the bed, leaning his shoulder against the wall, and brooded over matters. "I am glad," he said out of those thoughts, "that you did not ride on and leave me here senseless with fever as I was. I am grateful, *liyo.*"

She looked at him, gray eyes catwise and comfortable. "Then thee admits," she said, "that there are some places worse to be *ilin* than in my service?"

The thought chilled him. "I do admit it," he said. "This place being chief among them."

She propped her feet upon her belongings: he lay down and shut his eyes and tried to rest. The hand throbbed. It was still slightly swollen. He would have gladly gone outside and packed snow about it, reckoning that of more value than Flis' poultices and compresses or Morgaine's *qujalin* treatments.

"The imp's knife was plague-ridden," he said. Then, remembering: "Did you see them?"

"Who?"

"The boy—the girl—"

"Here?"

"In the downstairs corridor, after you passed."

"I am not at all surprised."

"Why do you endure this?" he asked. "Why did you not resist them bringing us here? You could have dealt with my injury yourself—and probably with them too."

"You perhaps have an exaggerated idea of my capacities. I am not able to lift a sick man about, and argument did not seem profitable at the moment. When it does, I shall consider doing something. But you are charged with my safety, Nhi Vanye, and with protecting me. I do expect you to fulfill that obligation."

He lifted his swollen hand. "That—is not within my capacity at the moment, if it comes to fighting our way out of here."

"Ah. So you have answered your own first questions." That was Morgaine at her most irritating. She settled again to waiting, then began instead to pace. She was very like a wild thing caged. She needed something for her hands, and there was nothing left. She went to the barred window and looked out and returned again.

She did that by turns for a very long time, sitting a while, pacing a while, driving him to frenzy, in which if he had not been in pain, he might also have risen and paced the room in sheer frustration. Had the woman ever been still, he wondered, or did she ever cease from what drove her? It was not simple restlessness at their confinement. It was the same thing that burned in her during their time on the road, as if they were well enough while moving, but any untoward delay fretted her beyond bearing.

It was as if death and the Witchfires were an appointment she was zealous to keep, and she resented every petty human interference in her mission.

The sunlight in the room decreased. Things became dim. When the furniture itself grew unclear, there came a rap on the door. Morgaine answered it. It was Flis.

"Master says come," said Flis.

"We are coming," said Morgaine. The girl delayed in the doorway, twisting her hands.

Then she fled.

"That one is no less addled than the rest," Morgaine said. "But she is more pitiable." She gathered up her sword, her other gear too, and concealed certain of her equipment within her robes. "Lest," she said, "someone examine things while we are gone."

"There is still the chance of running for the door," he said. "*Liyo,* take it. I am stronger. There is no reason I cannot somehow ride."

"Patience," she urged him. "Besides, this man Kasedre is interesting."

"He is also," he said, "ruthless and a murderer."

"There are Witchfires in Leth," she said. "Living next to the Witchfires as the Witchfires seem to have become since I left—is not healthful. I should not care to stay here very long."

"Do you mean that the evil of the thing—of the fires—has made them what they are?"

"There are emanations," she said, "which are not healthful. I do not myself know all that can be the result of them. I only know that I do not like the waste I saw about me when I rode out at Aenor-Pyvvn, and I like even less what I see in Leth. The men are more twisted than the trees."

"You cannot warn these folk," he protested. "They would as lief cut our throats as not if we cross them. And if you mean something else with them, some—"

"Have a care," she said. "There is someone in the hall."

Steps had paused. They moved on again, increasing in speed. Vanye swore softly. "This place is full of listeners."

"We are surely the most interesting listening in the place," she said. "Come, and let us go down to the hall. Or do you feel able? If truly not, I shall plead indisposition myself—it is a woman's privilege—and delay the business."

In truth he faced the possibility of a long evening with the mad Leth with dread, not alone of the Leth, but because of the fever that still burned in his veins. He would rather try to ride now, now, while he had the strength. If trouble arose in the hall, he was not sure that he could help Morgaine or even himself.

In truth, he reckoned that among her weapons she had the means to help herself: it was her left-handed *ilin* that might not make it out.

"I could stay here," he said.

"With *his* servants to attend you?" she asked. "You could not gracefully bar the door against them yourself, but no one thinks odd the things I do. Say that you are not fit and I will stay here and bar the door myself."

"No," he said. "I am fit enough. And you are probably right about the ser-

vants." He thought of Flis, who, if she entertained everyone in this loathsome
hall with the same graces she plied with him, would probably be fevered herself, or carry some more ugly sickness. And he recalled the twins, who had
slipped into the dark like a pair of the palace rats: for some reason they and
their little knives inspired him with more terror than Myya archers had ever
done. He could not strike at them as they deserved; that they were children still
stayed his hand; and yet they had no scruples, and their daggers were razor-
sharp—like rats, he thought again, like rats, whose sharp teeth made them
fearsome despite their size. He dreaded even for Morgaine with the likes of
them skittering about the halls and conniving together in the shadows.

She left. He walked at his proper distance half a pace behind Morgaine,
equally for the sake of formality and for safety's sake. He had discovered one
saw things that way, things that happened just after Morgaine had glanced
away. He was only *ilin*. No one paid attention to a servant. And Kasedre's servants feared her. It was in their eyes. That was, in this hall, great tribute.

And even the bandits as they entered the hall watched her with caution in
their hot eyes, a touch of ice, a cold wind over them. It was curious: there was
more respect in the afterwave of her passing than the nonchalance they showed
to her face.

A greater killer than any of them, he thought unworthily; they respected
her for that.

But the Leth, the *uyin* that gathered at the high tables, watched her through
polite smiles, and there was lust there too, no less than in the bandits' eyes, but
cold and tempered with fear. Morgaine was supremely beautiful: Vanye kept
that thought at a distance within himself—he was tempted to few liberties with
the *qujal*, and that one last of all. But when he saw her in that hall, her pale head
like a blaze of sun in that darkness, her slim form elegant in *tgihio* and bearing
the dragon blade with the grace of one who could truly use it, an odd vision
came to him: he saw like a fever-dream a nest of corruption with one gliding
serpent among the scuttling lesser creatures—more evil than they, more deadly,
and infinitely beautiful, reared up among them and hypnotizing with basilisk
eyes, death dreaming death and smiling.

He shuddered at the vision and saw her bow to Kasedre, and performed his
own obeisance without looking into the mad, pale face: he retreated to his
place, and when they were served, he examined carefully and sniffed at the
wine they were offered.

Morgaine drank; he wondered could her arts make her proof against drugs
and poisons, or save him, who was not. For his part he drank sparingly, and
waited long between drafts, toying with it merely, waiting for the least dizziness
to follow: none did. If they were being poisoned, it was to be more subtle.

The dishes were various: they both ate the simple ones, and slowly. There was an endless flow of wine, of which they both drank sparingly; and at last, at long last, Morgaine and Kasedre still smiling at each other, the last dish was carried out and servants pressed yet more wine on them.

"Lady Morgaine," begged Kasedre then, "you gave us a puzzle and promised us answers tonight."

"Of Witchfires?"

Kasedre bustled about the table to sit near her, and waved an energetic hand at the harried, patch-robed scribe who had hovered constantly at his elbow this evening. "Write, write," he said to the scribe, for in every hall of note there was an archivist who kept records properly and made an account of hall business.

"How interesting your Book would be to me," murmured Morgaine, "with all the time I have missed of the affairs of men. Do give me this grace, my lord Kasedre—to borrow your Book for a moment."

Oh mercy, Vanye thought, *are we doomed to stay here a time more?* He had hoped that they could retreat, and he looked at the thickness of the book and at all the bored lordlings sitting about them flushed with wine, looking like beasts thirsting for the kill, and reckoned uneasily how long their patience would last.

"We would be honored," replied Kasedre. It was probably the first time in years that anyone had bothered with the musty tome of Leth, replete as it must be with murderings and incest. The rumors were dark enough, though little news came out of Leth.

"Here," said Morgaine, and took into her lap the moldering book of the scribe, while the poor old scholar—a most wretched old man and reeking of drink—sat at her brocaded knee and looked up at her, wrinkle browed and squinting. His eyes and nose ran. He blotted at both with his sleeve. She cracked the book, disturbing pages moldered together, handling the old pages reverently, separating them with her nail, folding them down properly as she sought the years she wanted.

Somewhere at the back of the hall some of the less erudite members of the banquet were engaged in riotous conversation. It sounded as if a gambling game were in progress. She ignored it entirely, although Kasedre seemed irritated by it; the lord Leth himself squatted down to hear her, hanging upon her long silence in awe. Her forefinger traced words. Vanye's view over her shoulder showed yellowed parchment and ink that had turned red-brown and faint. It was a wonder that one who lisped the language as uncertainly as she did could manage that ancient scrawl, but her lips moved as she thought the words.

"My dear old friend Edjnel," she said softly. "Here is his death—what, murdered?" Kasedre craned his neck to see the word. "And his daughter—ah, little Linna—drowned upon the lakeshore. This is sad news. But Tohme did rule, surely—"

"My father," interjected Kasedre, "was Tohme's son." His eyes kept darting to her face anxiously, as if he found fear of her condemnation.

"When I remember Tohme," she said, "he was playing at his mother's knee: the lady Aromwel, a most gracious, most lovely person. She was Chya. I rode to this hall upon a night . . ." She eased the fragile pages backward. "Yes, here, you see:

"*. . . came She even to Halle, bearing sad Tidings from the Road. Lorde Aralde . . .*—brother to Edjnel and to my friend Lrie, who went with me to Irien, and died there—*Lorde Aralde had met with Mischance upon his faring in her Companie that attempted the Saving of Leth against the Darke, which advanceth out of . . .* Well, well, this was another sad business, that of lord Aralde. He was a good man. Unlucky. An arrow out of the forest had him; and the wolves were on my trail by then . . . *herein she feared the Border were lost, that there would none rallye to the Saving of the Middle Realms, save only Chya and Leth, and they strippt of Men and sorely hurt. So gave she Farewell to Leth and left the Halle, much mourned . . .* Well, that is neither here nor there. It touches me to think that I am missed at least in Leth." Her fingers sought further pages. "Ah, here is news. My old friend Zri—he was counselor to Tiffwy, you know. Or do you not? Well . . . *Chye Zri has come to Leth, he being friend to the Kings of Koris.*" A feral grin was on her face, as if that mightily amused her. "Friend,"— she laughed softly—"aye, friend to Tiffwy's wife, and thereon hung a tale."

Kasedre twisted with both hands at his sleeve, his poor fevered eyes shifting nervously from here to the book and back again. "Zri was highly honored here," he said. "But he died."

"Zri was a fox," said Morgaine. "Ah, clever, that man. It was surely like him *not* to have been at Irien after all, although he rode out with us. Zri had an ear to the ground constantly: he could smell disaster, Tiffwy always said. And Edjnel never trusted him. But unfortunately Tiffwy did. And I wonder indeed that Edjnel took him in when he appeared at the gates of Leth. . . . *he has honored us by his Presence, tutor . . . to the younge Prince Leth Tohme . . . to guide in all divers manner of Statecraft and Publick Affaires, being Guardian also of the Lady Chya Aromwel and her daughter Linna, at the lamented Decease of Leth Edjnel . . .*"

"Zri taught my grandfather," said Kasedre when Morgaine remained sunk in thought. He prattled on, nervous, eager to please. "And my father for a time too. He was old, but he had many children—"

One of the *uyin* tittered behind his hand. It was injudicious. Leth Kasedre turned and glared, and that *uyo* bowed himself to his face and begged pardon quickly, claiming some action in the back of the hall as the source of his amusement.

"What sort was Tohme?" asked Morgaine.

"I do not know," said Kasedre. "He drowned. Like aunt Linna."

"Who was your father?"

"Leth Hes." Kasedre puffed a bit with pride, insisted to turn the pages of the book himself, to show her. "He was a great lord."

"Tutored by Zri."

"And he had a great deal of gold." Kasedre refused to be distracted. But then his face fell. "But I never saw him. He died. He drowned too."

"Most unfortunate. I should stay clear of water, my lord Leth. Where did it happen? The lake?"

"They think"—Kasedre lowered his voice—"that my father was a suicide. He was always morose. He brooded about the lake. Especially after Zri was gone. Zri—"

"—drowned?"

"No. He rode out and never came back. It was a bad night. He was an old man anyway." His face assumed a pout. "I have answered every one of your questions, and you promised my answer and you have not answered it. Where were you, all these years. What became of you, if you did not die?"

"If a man," she said, continuing to read while she answered him, "rode into the Witchfires of Aenor-Pyvvn, then he could know. It is possible for anyone. However, it has certain—costs."

"The Witchfires of Leth," he said, licking moisture from the corners of his mouth. "Would they suffice?"

"Most probably," she said. "However, it is chancy. The fires have certain potential for harm. I know the safety of Aenor-Pyvvn. It could do no bodily harm. But I should not chance Leth's fires unless I had seen them. They are by the lake, which seems to take so much toll of Leth. I should rather other aid than that, lord Leth. Seek Aenon-Pyvvn." She still gave him only a part of her attention, continuing to push the great moldering pages back one after another. Then her eyes darted to the aged scholar. "Thee looks almost old enough to remember me."

The poor old man, trembling, tried the major obeisance at being directly noticed by Morgaine, and could not make it gracefully. "Lady, I was not yet born."

She looked at him curiously, and then laughed softly. "Ah, then I have no friends left in Leth at all. There are none so old." She thumbed more pages, more and more rapidly. ". . . *This sad day was funeral for Leth Tohme, aged seventeen yeares, and his Consort . . . lady Leth Jeme . . .* Indeed, indeed—at one burying."

"My grandmother hanged herself for grief," said Kasedre.

"Ah, then your father must have become the Leth when he was very young. And Zri must have had much power."

"Zri. Zri. Zri. Tutors are boring."

"Had you one?"

"Liell. Chya Liell. He is my counselor now."

"I have not met Liell," she said.

Kasedre bit at his lips. "He would not come tonight. He said he was indisposed. I"—he lowered his voice—"have never known Liell indisposed before."

". . . *Liell of the Chya . . . has given splendid entertainments . . . on the occasion of the birthday of the Leth, Kasedre, most honorable of lords . . . two maidens of the . . .* Indeed." Morgaine blinked, scanned the page. "Most unique. And I have seen a great many entertainments."

"Liell is very clever," said Kasedre. "He devises ways to amuse us. He would not come tonight. That is why things are so quiet. He will think of something for tomorrow."

Morgaine continued to scan the pages. "This is interesting," she assured Kasedre. "I must apologize. I am surely wearying you and interfering with your scribe's recording of my visit, but this does intrigue me. I shall try to repay your hospitality and your patience."

Kasedre bowed very low, thoughtlessly necessitating obeisance by all at the immediate table. "We have kept in every detail the records of your dealings with us in this visit. It is a great honor to our hall."

"Leth has always been very kind to me."

Kasedre reached out his hand, altogether against propriety—it was the action of a child fascinated by glitter—and his trembling fingers touched the arm of Morgaine, and the hilt of *Changeling*.

She ceased to move, every muscle frozen for an instant; then gently she moved her arm and removed his fingers from the dragon blade's hilt.

Vanye's muscles were rock-hard, his left hand already feeling after the release of his nameless sword. They could perhaps reach the midpoint of the hall before fifty swords cut them down.

And he must guard her back.

Kasedre drew back his hand. "Draw the blade," he urged her. "Draw it. I want to see it."

"No," she said. "Not in a friendly hall."

"It was forged here in Leth," said Kasedre, his dark eyes glittering. "They say that the magic of the Witchfires themselves went into its forging. A Leth smith aided in the making of its hilt. I want to see it."

"I never part with it," said Morgaine softly. "I treasure it greatly. It was made by Chan, who was the dearest of my own companions, and by Leth Omry, as you say. Chan carried it a time, but he gave it to me before he died in Irien. It never leaves me, but I think kindly of friends in Leth when I remember its making."

"Let us see it," he said.

"It brings disaster wherever it is drawn," she said, "and I do not draw it."

"We *ask* this."

"I would not"—the painted smile resumed, adamant—"chance any misfortune to the house of Leth. Do believe me."

A pout was on Leth Kasedre's features, a flush upon his sweating cheeks. His breathing grew quick and there was a sudden hush in the hall.

"We *ask* this," he repeated.

"No," said Morgaine. "This I will not."

He snatched at it, and when she avoided his grasp, he spitefully snatched the book instead, whirled to his feet and cast it into the hearth, scattering embers.

The old scholar scuttled crabwise and sobbing after the book, spilling ink that dyed his robes. He rescued it and sat there brushing the little charring fire from its edges. His old lips moved as if he were speaking to it.

And Kasedre shrieked, railing upon his guests until the froth gathered at the corners of his mouth and he turned a most alarming purple. Ingratitude seemed the main burden of his accusations. He wept. He cursed.

"*Qujalin* witch," he began to cry then. "Witch! Witch! Witch!"

Vanye was on his feet, not yet drawing, but sure he must.

Morgaine took a final sip of wine and gathered herself up also. Kasedre was still shouting. He raised his hand to her, trembled as if he did not quite have the courage to strike. Morgaine did not flinch; and Vanye began to ease his blade from the sheath.

Tumult had risen in the hall again: it died a sudden death, beginning at the door. There had appeared there a tall, thin man of great dignity, perhaps forty, fifty years in age. The silence spread. Kasedre began instead to whimper, to utter his complaints under his breath and petulantly.

And incredibly this apparition, this new authority, walked forward to kneel and do Kasedre proper reverence.

"Liell," said Kasedre in a trembling voice.

"Clear the hall," said Liell. His voice was sane and still and terrible.

There was no noise at all, even from the bandits at the rear; the *uyin* began to slink away. Kasedre managed to put up an act of defiance for a moment. Liell stared at him. Then Kasedre turned and fled, running, into the shadows behind the curtains.

Liell bowed a formal and slight courtesy to them both.

"The well-renowned Morgaine of the Chya," he said softly. Here was sanity. Vanye breathed a soft sigh of relief and let his sword slip back. "You are not the most welcome visitor ever to come to this hall," Liell was saying, "but I will warn you all the same, Morgaine: whatever brought you back will send you hence again if you bait Kasedre. He is a child, but he commands others."

"I believe we share clan," she said, cold rebuff to his discourtesy. "I am adopted, kri Chya; but of one clan, you and I."

He bowed again, seemed then to offer true respect. "Your pardon. You are a surprise to me. When the rumor came to me, I did not believe it. I thought perhaps it was some charlatan with a game to play. But you are quite the real thing, I see that. And who is this, this fellow?"

"It is all family," Vanye said, a touch of insolence, that Liell had not been courteous with Morgaine. "I am Chya on my mother's side."

Liell bowed to him. For a moment those strangely frank eyes rested directly upon him, draining him of anger. "Your name, sir?"

"Vanye," he said, shaken by that sudden attention.

"Vanye," said Liell softly. "Vanye. Aye, that is a Chya name. But I have little to do with clan Chya here. I have other work. . . . Lady Morgaine, let me see you to your rooms. You have stirred up quite a nest of troubles. I heard the shouting. I descended—to your rescue, if you will pardon me."

Morgaine nodded him thanks and began to walk with him. Vanye, ignored now, fell in a few paces behind them and kept watch on the doors and corridors.

"I truly did not believe it at first," said Liell. "I thought Kasedre's humors were at work again, or that someone was taking advantage of him. His fantasies are elaborate. May I ask why—?"

Morgaine used that dazzling and false smile on Liell. "No," she said. "I discuss my business with no one I chance to leave behind me. I will be on my way soon. I wish no help. Therefore what I do is of no moment here."

"Are you bound for the territory of Chya?"

"I am clan-welcome there," she said, "but I doubt it would be the same warmth of welcome I knew if I were to go there now. Tell me of yourself, Chya Liell. How does Leth fare these days?"

Liell waved an elegant hand at their surroundings. He was a graceful man, handsome and silver-haired; his dress was modest, night-blue. His shoulders lifted in a sigh. "You see how things are, lady, I am well sure. I manage to keep Leth whole, against the tide of events. As long as Kasedre keeps to his entertainments, Leth thrives. But its thin blood will not breed another generation. The sons and grandsons of Chya Zri—who, I know, found no favor in your eyes—still are the bulwark of Leth in its old age. They serve me well. That in hall—that is the get of Leth, such as remains."

Morgaine refrained from comment. They began to mount the stairs. A pinched little face peered at them from the turning, withdrew quickly.

"The twins," said Vanye.

"Ah," said Liell. "Hshi and Tlim. Nasty characters, those."

"Clever with their hands," said Vanye sourly.

"They are Leth. Hshi is the harpist in hall. Tlin sings. They also steal. Do not let them in your rooms. I suspect it was Tlin who is responsible for your being here. The report was very like her misbehaviors."

"Hardly necessary that she trouble herself," said Morgaine. "My path necessarily led to Ra-leth. I had the mood to come this way. The girl could prove a noisome pest."

"Please," said Liell. "Leave the twins to me. They will not trouble you. . . . What set Kasedre off tonight?"

"He became overexcited," said Morgaine. "I take it that he does not often meet outsiders."

"Not of quality, and not under these circumstances."

They wound up the remaining stairs and came into the hall where their apartments were. The servants were busy at their tasks, lighting the lamps. They made great bows as Liell and Morgaine swept past them.

"Did you eat well?" Liell asked.

"We had sufficient," she said.

"Sleep soundly, lady. Nothing will trouble you." He made a formal bow as Morgaine went inside her own door, but as Vanye would have followed her, Liell prevented him with an outthrust arm.

Vanye stopped, hand upon hilt, but Liell's purpose seemed speech, not violence. He leaned close, set a hand upon Vanye's shoulder, a familiarity a man might use with a servant, talking to him quickly in whispers.

"She is in great danger," said Liell. "Only I fear what she may do. She must leave here, and tonight. Earnestly I tell you this." He leaned closer until Vanye's back was against the wall, and the hand gripped his shoulder with great intensity. "Do not trust Flis and do not trust the twins above all else, and beware of any of Kasedre's people."

"Which you are not?"

"I have no interest in seeing this hall ruined—which could happen if Morgaine takes offense. Please. I know what she is seeking. Come with me and I will show you."

Vanye considered it, gazed into the dark, sober eyes of the man. There was peculiar sadness in them, a magnetism that compelled trust. The strong fingers pressed into the flesh of his shoulder, at once intimate and compelling.

"No," he said. It was hard to force the words. "I am *ilin*. I take her orders. I do not arrange her business for her."

And he tore himself from Liell's fingers and sought the door, trembling so that he missed the latch, opened it and thrust it closed, securely, behind him. Morgaine looked at him questioningly, even offering concern. He said nothing to her. He felt sick inside, still fearing that he should have trusted Liell, and yet glad that he had not.

"We must get out of this place," he urged her. "Now."

"There are things yet to learn," she said. "I only found the beginnings of answers. I would have the rest. I can have, if we remain."

There was no disputing Morgaine. He curled up near their own little hearth, a small and smoky fireplace that heated the room from a common duct, warming himself on the stones. He left her the bed, did she choose to use it.

She did not. She paced. Eventually the restlessness assumed a kind of rhythm, and ceased to be maddening. Just when he had grown used to that, she settled. He saw her by the window, staring out into the dark, through a crack in the shutters, an opening that let a further draft into their chill room.

"Folk never seem to sleep in Leth-hall," she commented to him finally, when he had changed his posture to keep his joints from going stiff. "There are torches about in the snow."

He muttered an answer and sighed, glanced away uncomfortably as she turned from the window then and began to turn down the bed. She slipped off the overrobe and laid it across the foot, laid aside her other gear, hung upon the endpost, and cloth tunic and the fine, light mail, itself the worth of many kings of the present age, boots and the warmth of her leather undertunic, stretched in the luxury of freedom from the weight of armor, slim and womanly, in riding breeches and a thin lawn shirt. He averted his eyes a second time toward nothing in particular, heard her ease within the bed, make herself comfortable.

"Thee does not have to be overnice," she murmured when he looked back. "Thee is welcome to thy half."

"It is warm here," he answered, miserable on the hard stone and wishing that he had not seen her as he had seen her. She meant the letter of her offer, no more; he knew it firmly, and did not blame her. He sat by the fire, *ilin* and trying to remind himself so, his arms locked together until his muscles ached. Servant to this. Walking behind her. To lie unarmored next to her was harmless only so long as she meant to keep it so.

Qujal. He clenched that thought within his mind and cooled his blood with that remembrance. *Qujal,* and deadly. A man of honest human birth had no business to think otherwise.

He remembered Liell's urging. The sanity in the man's eyes attracted him, promised, assured him that there did exist reason somewhere. He regretted more and more that he had not listened to him. There was no longer the excuse of his well-being that kept them in Ra-leth. His fever was less. He examined his hand that her medications had treated, found it scabbed over and only a little red about the wound, the swelling abated. He was weak in the joints but he could ride. There was no further excuse for her staying, but that she wanted something of Kasedre and his mad crew, something important enough to risk both their lives.

It was intolerable. He felt sympathy for Liell, a sane man condemned to live in this nightmare. He understood that such a man might yearn for something other, would be concerned to watch another man of sense fall into the web.

"Lady." He came and knelt by the bed, disturbing her sleep. "Lady, let us be out of here."

"Go to sleep," she bade him. "There is nothing to be done tonight. The place is astir like a broken hive."

He returned to his misery by the fire, and after a time began to nod.

There was a scratching at the door. Minute as it was, it became sinister in all that silence. It would not cease. He started to wake Morgaine, but he had disturbed her once; he did not venture her patience again. He sought his sword, both frightened and self-embarrassed at his fear: it was likely only the rats.

Then he saw, slowly, the latch lift. The door began to open. It stopped against the chair. He rose to his feet, and Morgaine waked and reached for her own weapon.

"Lady," came a whisper, "it is Liell. Let me in. Quickly."

Morgaine nodded. Vanye eased the chair aside, and Liell entered as softly as possible, eased the door shut again. He was dressed in a cloak as if for traveling.

"I have provisions for you and a clear way to the stables," he said. "Come. You must come. You may not have another chance."

Vanye looked at Morgaine, shaped the beginning of a plea with his lips. She frowned and suddenly nodded. "What effect on you, Chya Liell, for this treason?"

"Loss of my head if I am caught. And loss of a hall to live in if Kasedre's clan attacks you, as I fear they will, with or without his wishing it. Come, lady, come. I will guide you from here. They are all quiet, even the guards. I put *melorne* in Kasedre's wine at bedside. He will not wake, and the others are not suspecting. Come."

There was no one stirring in the hall outside. They trod the stairs carefully, down and down the several turns that led them to main level. A sentry sat in a chair by the door, head sunk upon his breast. Something about the pose jarred the senses: the right hand hung at the man's side in a way that looked uncomfortable for anyone sober.

Drugged too, Vanye thought. They walked carefully past the man nonetheless, up to the very door.

Then Vanye saw the wet dark stain that dyed the whole front of the man's robe, less conspicuous on the dark fabric. Suspicion leapt up. It chilled him, that a man was killed so casually.

"Your work?" he whispered at Liell, in Morgaine's hearing. He did not know whom he warned: he only feared, and thought it well that whoever was innocent mark it now and be advised.

"Hurry," said Liell, easing open the great door. They were out in the front courtyard, where one great evergreen shaded them into darkness. "This way lie the stables. Everything is ready."

They kept to the shadows and ran. More dead men lay at the stable door. It suddenly occurred to Vanye that Liell had an easy defense against any charge of murder: that they themselves would be called the killers.

And if they refused to come, Liell would have been in difficulty. He had risked greatly, unless murder were only trivial in this hall, among madmen.

He stifled in such dread thoughts. He yearned to break free of Leth's walls. The quick thrust of a familiar velvet nose in the dark, the pungency of hay and leather and horse purged his lungs of the cloying decay of Leth-hall. He had his own bay mare in hand, swung up to her back; and Morgaine thrust the dragon blade into its accustomed place on her saddle and mounted Siptah.

Then he saw Liell lead another horse out of the shadows, likewise saddled.

"I will see you safely to the end of Leth's territories," he said. "No one here questions my authority to come and go. I am here and I am not, and at the moment, I think it best I am not."

But a shadow scurried from their path as they rode at a quiet walk through the yard, a shadow double-bodied and small. A patter of feet hurried to the stones of the walk.

Liell swore. It was the twins.

"Ride now," he said. "There is no hiding it longer."

They put their heels to the horses and reached the gate. Here too were dead men, three of them. Liell sharply ordered Vanye to see to the gate, and Vanye sprang down and heaved the bar up and the gate open, throwing himself out of the way as the black horse of Liell and gray Siptah hurtled past him, bearing the two into the night.

He hurled himself to the back of the bay mare—poor pony, not the equal of those two beasts—and urged her after them with the sudden terror that death itself was stirring and waking behind them.

ꙡ Chapter 5

The lake of Domen was ill-famed in more than the Book of Leth. The old road ran along its shore and by the bare-limbed trees that writhed against the night sky. It did not snow here: snow was rare in Korish lands, low as they were, although the forests nearest the mountains went wintry and dead. The lake reflected the stars, sluggish and mirrorlike—still, because, men said, parts of it were very deep.

They rode at a walk now. The horses' overheated breath blew puffs of steam in the dark, and the hooves made a lonely sound on the occasional stretch of stones over which the trail ran.

And about them was the forest. It had a familiar look. Of a sudden Vanye realized it for the semblance of the vale of Aenor-Pyvvn.

The presence of Stones of Power: that accounted for the twisting, the unusual barrenness in a place so rife with trees as Koriswood. It was the Gate of Koris-leth that they were nearing. The air had a peculiar oppression, like the air before a storm.

And soon as they passed along the winding shore of the lake they saw a great pillar thrusting up out of the black waters. In the dim moonlight there seemed some engraving on it. Soon other stumps of pillars were visible as they rode farther, marking old and *qujalin* ruins sunk beneath the waters of the lake.

And two pillars greater than the others crowned a bald hill on the opposite shore.

Morgaine reined in, gazing at the strange and somber view of sunken city and pillars silhouetted against the stars. Even at night the air shimmered about the pillars and the brightest stars that the shimmer could not dim gleamed through that Gate as through a film of troubled water.

"We are safe from pursuit," said Liell. "Kasedre's clan fears this lakeshore."

"They seem prone to drowning," Morgaine observed. She dismounted, rubbed Siptah's cheek and dried her hand on the edge of his blanket.

Vanye slid down as they did, and caught his breath, reached for Siptah's reins and those of Liell's black horse. The two beasts would not abide each other. Exhausted, out of patience, he walked Siptah and his own bay mare to cool them and spread his own cloak over Liell's ill-tempered black in the meantime. The air was chill. They had ridden such a pace that the two greater horses were spent and his own little Mai had nearly burst her heart keeping up with them. Long after the two blooded horses were cooled and fit he was still tending to Mai, rubbing her to keep her from chill, until at last he dared let her drink the icy water and have a little grain from their stores. He was well content afterward to curl up on his cloak which he had recovered from the black, and try to sleep, shivering himself in what he feared was a recurrence of fever. He heard Liell's soft voice and that of Morgaine, discussing the business of Leth, discussing old murders or old accidents that had happened on this lakeshore.

Then Morgaine disturbed his rest, for she never parted from *Changeling*, and wanted it from her gear. She slipped the dragon blade's Korish-work strap over her head and hung it from her shoulder to her hip, and walked the shore a time with Liell's black figure beside hers.

Then, in the great stillness, Vanye heard the coming of distant riders. On that impulse he sprang up, flung saddle upon Siptah first: *she* was his first duty;

and by this time Morgaine and Liell seemed to have heard, for they were coming back. Vanye pulled Siptah's girth to its proper tension and secured it, then furiously began to saddle poor Mai. The mare would die. If they were harried much farther, the little beast would go down under him. He hurt for her: the Nhi blood in him loved horses too well to use them so, though Nhi could be cruel in other ways.

Liell flung saddle to the black himself. "I still much doubt," he said, "that they will come to this shore."

"I trust distance more than luck," said Morgaine. "Do as you will, Chya Liell."

And she swung up to Siptah's back, having settled *Changeling* in its accustomed place at the saddle, and laid heels to the gray.

Vanye attempted to mount and follow after. Liell's hand caught his arm, pulled him off balance, so that he staggered and looked at the man in outrage.

"Do not follow her," hissed Liell. "Listen to me. She will have the soul from you before she is done, Chya. Listen to me."

"I am *ilin*," he protested. "I have no choice."

"What is an oath?" Liell whispered urgently, all the while Siptah's hooves grew faint upon the shingle. "She seeks the power to ruin the muddle lands. You do not know how great an evil you are aiding. She lies, Chya Vanye. She has lied before, to the ruin of Koris, of Baien, of the best of the clans and the death of Morij-Yla. Will you help her? Will you turn on your own? *Ilin*-oath says betray family, betray hearth, but not the *liyo;* but does it say betray your own kind? Come with me, come with me, Chya Vanye."

For an aging man, Liell had surprising power in his hand: it numbed the blood from Vanye's hand by its grip upon his elbow. The eyes were hard and glittering, close to him in the dark. The sound of pursuit was nearer.

"No," Vanye cried, ripping loose, and started to mount. Pain exploded across the base of his skull. The world turned in his vision and he had momentary view of Mai's belly passing over him as the mare bolted. She jumped him, managing to avoid him with her hooves; he scrambled up against the earthen bank, half-blind, seeking to draw his sword.

Liell was upon him then, wresting his hand from the hilt, close to overpowering him, dazed as he was; but the thought of being taken by Leth animated him to frenzy. He twisted, not even trying to defend himself, only to tear free, to reach Morgaine's side and keep his oath for his soul's sake. Mai was out of reach; the black was at hand. He sprang for that saddle and laid heels to him before he was even sure of the reins, gathering them up and settling low in the saddle from his precarious balance. Black legs flashed long in the dark, muscles reached and gathered, bounding obstacles, splashing over inlets of the lake, surging up rises of the shore.

The black at last had run all he chose to run, beyond the shore and far upon the trail: Vanye laid heel to him again, merciless in his fear. The animal gathered himself and plunged forward again.

Morgaine's pale form was ahead. At last she looked around, seeming to hear him; she whipped up Siptah, and he cried out to her in despair, urging the black to further effort.

And she held back, pulling up, weapon in hand until he had come closer.

"Vanye," she exclaimed softly as he drew alongside. "Is thee thief too? What came of Liell?"

He reached behind his head, felt a tenderness at the back of his head despite the leather coif. Dizziness assailed him, whether of the blow or of the fever, he did not know.

"Liell is no friend of yours," he said.

"Did you kill him?"

"No," he breathed, and was content to hang over the saddlebow a moment until his sight cleared. Then he urged the black into a gentle pace, Siptah keeping with him: no horses that had run all the distance from Ra-leth could overtake them now.

"Is thee much hurt?" she asked.

"No."

"What did he? Did he lift weapon against you?"

"Tried to hold me—tried to persuade me to break oath."

And the other thing he would not tell her, the urging and then the vile feeling he had had of the look in Liell's eyes, a feverish anxiousness that had wanted something of him, a touch that had twice sunk cruelly into his arm, an avarice matching the hunger in his eyes.

It was not a thing he could tell anyone: he did not know what to name it, or why he had provoked it, or what it aimed at, only that he would die before he fell into the hands of Leth, and most especially those of Liell.

His back had been turned: the man could easily have cut him across the backs of the knees, quickest way to disable a man elsewhere armored, slain him out of hand; instead he had fetched him a crack across the skull, had risked greatly taking him hand to hand when he could have killed him safely: he had wanted him alive.

He could not remember it without shuddering. He wanted nothing of the man. It filled him with loathing to possess the gear and the horse that he had stolen: the black beast with its ill temper was a creature more splendid and less honest than his little Mai, and leaving his little mare in those hands grieved him.

Deep forest closed about them, straight and proper trees now, and they walked the horses until there was no sky overhead, only the interlacing branches. The horses were spent and they themselves were blind with weariness.

"This is no place to stop," he protested when Morgaine reined in. "Lady, let us sleep in the saddle tonight, walk the horses while they may. This is Koriswood, and it may have been different in your day, but this is the thick of it. Please."

She sighed in misery, but for once she looked at him and listened, and consented with a nod of her head. He dismounted and took the reins of both horses, both too weary to contest each other, and led them.

She rested a time, then leaned down and bade him stop, offered to take the reins and walk and lead the horses; he looked at her, tired as he was, and had not wit to argue with her. He only turned his back and kept walking, to which she consented by silence.

And eventually she slept, Kurshin-wise, in the saddle.

He walked so far as he could, long hours, until he was stumbling with exhaustion. He stopped then and put his hand on Siptah's neck.

"Lady," he said softly, not to break the hush of the listening wood. "Lady, now you must wake because I must sleep. Things are quiet."

"Well enough," she agreed, and slid down. "I know the road, although this land was tamer then."

"I must tell you," he continued hoarsely, "I think Chya Liell will follow when he can gather the forces. I think he lied to us in much, *liyo.*"

"What was it happened back there, Vanye?"

He sought to tell her. He gathered the words, still could not. "He is a strange man," he said, "and he was anxious that I desert you. He attempted twice to persuade me—this last time in plain words."

She frowned at him. "Indeed. What form did this proposal take?"

"That I should forget my oath and go with him."

"To what?"

"I do not know." The remembering made his voice shake; he thought that she might detect the tremor, and quickly gathered up the black's reins and flung himself into the saddle. "The first time—I almost went. The second—somehow I preferred your company."

Her odd pale face stared up at him in the starlight. "Many of the house of Leth have drowned in that lake. Or have at least vanished there. I did not know that you were in difficulty. I would not gladly have left you. I did judge that there was some connivance between you and Liell: so when you did not follow—I dared not delay there between two who might be enemies."

"I was reared Nhi," he said. "We do not oath-break. We do not oath-break, *liyo.*"

"I beg pardon," she said, which *liyo* was never obliged to say to *ilin,* no matter how aggrieved. "I failed to understand."

And at that moment the horses shied, exhausted as they were, heads back and nostrils flaring, whites of the eyes showing in the dim light. Something reptilian slithered on four legs, whipping serpentwise into the thicker brush. It had been large and pale,-leprous in color. They could still hear it skittering away.

Vanye swore, his stomach still threatening him, his hands managing without his mind, to calm the panicked horse.

"Idiocy," Morgaine exclaimed softly. "Thiye does not know what he is doing. Are there many such abroad?"

"The woods are full of beasts of his making," Vanye said. "Some are shy and harm no one. Others are terrible things, beyond belief. They say the Koris-wolves were made, that they were never so fierce and never man-killers before—" He had almost said, before Irien, but did not, in respect of her. "That is why we must not sleep here, lady. They are made things, and hard to kill."

"They are not made," she said, "but brought through. But you are right that this is no good place to rest. These beasts—some will die, like infants thrust prematurely into too chill or too warm a place: some will be harmless; but some will thrive and breed. Ivrel must be sweeping a wide field. Ah, Vanye, Thiye is an ignorant man. He is loosing things—he knows not what. Either that or he enjoys the wasteland he is creating."

"Where do they come from, such things as that?"

"From places where such things are natural. From other *tonights,* and other Gates, and places where *that* was fair and proper. And there will be no native beasts to survive this onslaught if it is not checked. It is not man that such an attack wars on—it is nature. The whole of Andur-Kursh will find such things straying into its meadows. Come. Come."

But he had lost his inclination to sleep, and kept the reins in his own hand. He closed his eyes as Morgaine set them on their way again, still saw the pale lizard form, large as a man, running across the open space. That was one of the witless nonsensities in Koriswood, more ugly than dangerous.

Reports told of worse. Sometimes, legend said, carcasses were found near Irien, things impossible, abortions of Thiye's art, some almost formless and baneful to the touch, and others of forms so fantastical that none would imagine what aspect the living beast had had.

His only comfort in this place was that Morgaine herself was horrified; she had that much at least of human senses to her. Then he remembered her coming to him, out of the place she called *between,* washed up, she said, *on this shore.*

He began to have dim suspicion what she was, although he could not say it in words: that Morgaine and the pale horror had reached Andur-Kursh in the same way, only she had come by no accident, had come with purpose.

Aimed at Gates, at Thiye's power.

Aimed at dislocating all that lay on this shore, as these unnatural things had come. Standing where the Hjemur-lord stood, she would be no less perilous. She shared nothing with Andur-Kursh, not even birth, if his fears were true, and owed them nothing. *This* he served.

And Liell had said she lied. One of the twain lied: that was certain. He wondered in an agony of mind how it should be if he learned of a certainty, that it was Morgaine.

Something else fluttered in the dark—honest owl, or something sinister; it passed close overhead. He tautened his grip upon his nerves and patted the nervous black's neck.

It was long until the morning, until in a clear place upon the trail they dared stop and let sleep take them by turns. Morgaine's was the first sleep, and he paced to keep himself awake, or chose an uncomfortable place to sit, when he must sit, and at last fell to meddling with the black horse's gear, that the horse still bore, for in such place they dared not unsaddle, only loosened the girths. It shamed him, to have stolen a second time; and he felt the keeping of more than he needed of the theft was not honorable, but all the same it was not sense to cast things away. He searched the saddlebags and kit to learn what he had possessed and, it was in the back of his thoughts, to learn something of the man Liell.

He found an object which answered the question, such that set his stomach over.

It was a medal, gold, set in the hilt of a saddle knife, the sort many a man bore beneath the skirt of his saddle; and on it was a symbol of the blockish, ugly look he had seen graven on the Stones. It was *qujalin*. Whenever any strange and long-ago things were found, folk called them *qujalin* and avoided them, or burned them, or cast them into deeps and tried to lose them. Most such were likely only forgotten oddities, Kurshin and harmless. Somehow he did not think this was such as that.

He showed it to Morgaine when she wakened to take her turn at watch.

"It is an *irrhn*," she said to him. "A luck-piece. It has no other significance." But she turned it over and over in her hands, examining it.

"It is no luck," said Vanye, "to a human man."

"There is *qujalin* blood mixed in Leth," she said, "and Liell is its tutor. Tutors have ruled there nigh a hundred years. Each of the heirs of Leth has produced a son and drowned within the year. If Kasedre is capable of siring a son, he will most probably join his ancestors, and Liell will still be tutor to the son. I wonder," she added irrelevantly, looking at the blade, "who sired Hshi and Tlin."

"And on what," Vanye muttered sourly. "Keep the blade, *liyo*. I do not want to carry it, and perhaps it may bring luck to you."

"I am not *qujal*," she said.

That assertion, he reflected, might have filled him with either doubt or relief some days ago, at their meeting; now it fitted uncomfortably well with the thing he had begun to suspect of her.

"Whatever you are," he said, "spare me the knowing of it."

She nodded, accepting his attitude without apparent offense. She slipped the knife within her belt and rose.

A green-feathered arrow hit the ground between her feet.

She reached to her back, hand to weapon, quick as the arrow itself. And as quick, Vanye seized her and pushed her, heedless of hurting: Chya warning, that arrow. If she fired, they would both be green-feathered in an instant.

"Do not," he appealed to her, and turned, both arms wide, toward their unseen observers. "Hai, Chya! Chya! will you put kin-slaying on your souls? We are clan-welcome with you, cousins."

Brush rustled. He watched the fair, tall men of his own mother's kindred slip out of the shadows, where surely a few more kept arrows trained upon their hearts; and he set himself deliberately between them and Morgaine's own arrogance, which was like a Myya's for persistence, and likely to be the death of her.

They did not even ask names of them, but stood there waiting for them to speak and identify themselves. Looking at the living person of one who had been minutely described in ballads a century ago, wondering perhaps if they were not mad—he could estimate what passed in their minds. They only stared at Morgaine, and she at them, furiously, in her hand a weapon that could deal death faster than their arrows.

They would kill her of course, if she could die; but she would have done considerable damage: and her *ilin* who was her shield would be quite dead. He had heard of a certain Myya who strayed the border and was found with three Chya arrows lodged in his heart, all touching. Clan Chya lived in a hard land. They were impressed by few threats. It was typical of them that they had not yielded and begged shelter from the encroaching beasts, as had other folk; or died, as had two others. They used Hjemur's vile beasts for game, and harried the border of Hjemur and kept Thiye contained out of sheer Chya effrontery.

Vanye placed hands on thighs and made a respectful bow, which Morgaine did not: she did not move, and it was possible that the Chya did not know that they were in danger.

"I am Nhi Vanye, i Chya," he said, "*ilin* to this lady, who is clan-welcome with Chya."

The leader, a smallish man with the simple braid of a second-*uyo*, cousin-kin to the main clan, grounded his longbow and set both hands upon it, eyes upon him. "Nhi Vanye, cousin to Chya Roh. You are i Chya, that is true, but I thought it was understood that you are not clan-welcome here."

"She is," he said, which was the proper answer: an *ilin* was not held to his own law when he served his *liyo*: he could trespass, as safe or as threatened as she was. "She is Morgaine kri Chya, who has a clan-welcome that was never withdrawn."

They were frightened. They had the look of men watching a dream and trying not to become enmeshed in it. But they looked from her to the gray horse Siptah and back again, and swords stayed sheathed and bows lowered.

"We will take you to Ra-koris," said the little man. "I am Taomen, *tan-uyo*."

Then Morgaine gave him a bow of courtesy, and Vanye kept his silence hereafter, as befitted a servant whose *liyo* had finally deigned to take matters into her own hands.

The Chya were not happy at the meeting, it was clear. Clan-welcome had not been formally withdrawn because surely it had seemed a pointless vengeance on the dead. And the young lord of Chya, Chya Roh, his own cousin, whom he had never seen, still pursued bloodfeud with Nhi for the sake of his mother's dishonor at the hands of Rijan. Roh would as soon put an arrow through him as would Myya Gervaine, he was sure, and probably with greater accuracy.

There was a vast clearing in the Koriswood, that the noon sun blessed with a pleasant glow; the whole of it was full of sprawling huts of brush and logs—Chya, the only clan without a hall of stone. Once there had been the old Ra-koris, a splendid hall, home of the High Kings; its ruin lay some distance from this, and it was alleged to be haunted by angry ghosts of its proud defenders, that had held last and hardest against the advance of Hjemur. The grandsons and great-grandsons of the warriors of Morgaine's age kept only this wooden hall, their possessions few and their treasures gone, only their bows and their skill and the gain of their hunting between them and starvation. Yet none of them looked sickly, and the women and children watching them as they rode in were straight and tall, though plain: there was beauty in this people, much different from the blighted look of clan Leth.

Boys raced ahead of them, yet all was strangely silent, as though they maintained hunter's discipline even in their home.

At the great arch of the main hut the greatest number of people had gathered, and here they dismounted, escorted still by Taomen and his men. They retained their weapons, and all was courtesy, men yielding back for them in haste.

Ra-koris was a smoky, earth-floored hall of rough logs, yet it had a certain splendor: it had two levels and many halls opening off the main room. Tasseled and wrought hides were the hangings, antlers and strange horns adorned its posts. It was lit by torches even at noontime, and by a hearth larger than many halls of stone could boast, its only masonry, that great hearth and its venting.

"Here you will be lodged until Roh can be called," said Taomen.

Morgaine chose to settle at the main hearth, and by the timorous charity of the hall women, they were served a plain meal of waybread and venison and Chya mead, which they found good indeed after the suspect fare of Leth.

But folk avoided them, and watched them from the shadows of the wooden hall, whispering together.

Morgaine ignored them all and rested. Vanye nursed his sore hand and finally, troubled by the heat in the hall, at last gave up his pride and removed helm and coif, probing the soreness of the base of his skull, where Liell had struck him. A youth of the Chya laughed: a youth who did not yet even wear the braid; and Vanye looked at him angrily, then bowed his head and ignored the matter. He was not in such a position that he could complain of their treatment of him. Morgaine must be his chief concern, and she theirs.

And late in the day, when the bit of sky visible through the little windows of the high arch had gone from sun to shadow, there was a stir at the door and hunters came, men in brown leather, armed with bows and swords.

And among them was one that Vanye knew would be close kin of his, even before the youth came forward and met them as lord of the hall: for he had seen high-clan Chya before; when he was a child, and this was the image of all of them—of himself as well. The young lord looked more like a brother than his own brothers did.

"I am Chya Roh," he said, stepping to the center of the *rhowa*, the earthen platform at the head of the hall. His lean, tanned features were set with anger at their presence, boding no good for them. "Morgaine kri Chya is dead," he said, "a hundred years ago. What proof do you bear that you are she?"

Morgaine unfolded upward from her cross-legged posture with rare grace, smooth and silken, and without a bow of courtesy offered an object into Vanye's hand. He arose with less grace, paused to look at the object before he passed it into Roh's hand: it was the antlered insignia of the old High Kings of Koris, and when he saw that he knew it for a great treasure, and one that might have formed part of the lost crown treasury.

"It was Tiffwy's," she said. "His pledge of hospitality—should I need it, he said, to command of his men what I would."

Roh's face was pale. He looked at the amulet, and clenched it in his fist, and his manner was suddenly subdued. "Chya gave you what you asked a hundred years ago," he said, "and not a man of the four thousand returned. You have much blood on your hands, Morgaine kri Chya; and yet I must honor my ancestor's word—this once. What do you seek here?"

"Brief shelter. Silence. And whatever knowledge you have of Thiye and Hjemur."

"All three you may have," he said.

"Did Chya's record survive?"

"The Ra-koris you know is ruin now. Wolves and other beasts have it to themselves. If Chya's Book survives, that is where it lies. We have no means nor leisure for books here, lady."

She bowed in courtesy. "I have a warning to give you: Leth is roused. We left them in some little stir. Guard your borders."

Roh's lips were thin. "You are gifted with the raising of storms, lady. We will set men to watch your trail. It may be Leth will come this far, but only if they are desperate. We have taught Leth manners before."

"They are mightily irritated. Vanye's horse is Leth-bred, and we quit their hospitality suddenly, in a dispute with lord Kasedre and his counselor Chya Liell."

"Liell," said Roh softly. "*That* black wolf. I commend the quality of your enemies, lady. How much welcome do you ask?"

"The night only."

"Are you bound north?"

"Yes," she said.

Roh bit his lip. "That old quarrel? They say Thiye lives. It has never been in our imagination that you could survive too. But we are through giving you men, lady. That is done. We have none left to spare you."

"I ask none."

"You take *this*?" It was Roh's one acknowledgement that Vanye lived; his proud young eyes shifted aside and back again. "You could do better, lady."

But then he went and bade his women make place for Morgaine in the upper levels of the hall, and separate place for Vanye by the hearth. This Morgaine allowed, for Chya was a proper hall, and they were indeed under its peace as they had not been in Leth. And after that Morgaine and Roh talked together some little time, asking and answering, until she finally took her leave and passed upstairs.

Then Vanye gratefully put off his armor, down to his shirt and his leather breeches, and prepared the blankets they had given him by the warm hearthside.

Taomen came, spoke to him softly and bade him come to Roh; it was a thing he could not refuse. Roh sat cross-legged on the *rhowa*, with other men about him.

Of a sudden Vanye's feeling of ease left him. There was merry noise elsewhere in the hall, busy chatter of women and of children; it continued, masking softer words, and there were men ringed about so that no one outside the circle could see what was done there.

He did not kneel, not until they made it clear he must; then all the *uyin* of the Chya sank down on their haunches about him and about Roh, swords laid before them, as when clan judgment was passed.

He thought of crying aloud to Morgaine, warning her of treachery; but he did not truly fear for her, and his own pride kept him silent. These were his kin: to trouble an *ilin* for a family matter violated honor, violated the very concepts of honor under the *ilin*-codes, but Roh's offense was a powerful one. He did not know this cousin of his: his hope of Roh's honor was scant, but it kept him from utter panic.

"Now," said Roh, "and truthfully, Nhi Vanye, account for her and for your business with her."

"Nothing she told you was a lie and nothing less than the truth. She is Morgaine, and I am an *ilin* to her."

Roh looked him over, long and harshly. "So Rijan threw you out. You robbed him of one of his Myya wife's precious nestlings and he banished you. But you are due no kinship from us. My aunt did not choose your begetting. I only blame her because she did not leave Morija and come back to us. She was no captive by then, great with child as she was."

"To what should she come back—to your welcome?" Temper overcame sense, for Roh's words stung. "I honor her, Chya. And Chya's honor would not have taken her back as she had been, not after Rijan had had her, whether or not she was willing. She gave me life and died doing it, and I know the misery she had of Rijan better than you folk, that had not the stomach for coming into Morija to get her back, after Rijan rode into Chya lands to take her from you. Where is your honor, men of Chya?"

The stillness was absolute. Suddenly the hall was deserted but for them. The fire crackled. A log fell, showering embers.

"What became of her?" asked Roh at last, tilting the balance toward life and reason. "Was it death in childbirth, as they said?"

"Yes."

Roh let go his breath slowly. "Better had Rijan drowned you. Perhaps he regretted that he did not. But you are here. So live, Nhi Vanye, Rijan's bastard. Now what shall we do with you?"

"Do as she asked and let us pass from this hall tomorrow."

"Do you serve her willingly?"

"Yes," he said, "it was fair Claiming. I was in need. Now I am in her debt and I must pay it."

"Where is she going?"

"She is my lady," he said, "and it is not right for me to say anything of her business. Look to your own. You will have Leth at your borders for her sake."

"Where is she going, Nhi Vanye?"

"Ask her, I say."

Roh snapped his fingers. Men reached for the blades laid before them. They unsheathed them so that the points formed a ring about him. Somewhere in hall a dish fell. A woman ran cat-footed into the corridor beyond, drew the curtain and was gone.

"Ask Morgaine," Vanye said again; and when his breathing space grew less and an edge rested familiarly on his shoulder, he maintained his composure and did not flinch, though his heart was beating fit to burst. "If you continue, Chya Roh, I shall decide there is no honor at all in Chya. And I shall be ashamed for that."

Roh considered him in silence. Vanye went sick inside: his nerves were strung, Waiting, the least pressure from them likely to send from his lips a shout to raise the hall and Morgaine from sleep. He was not brave. He had long ago discovered in himself that he had no courage for enduring pain or threat. His brothers had discovered that in him before he had. It was the same feeling that churned in him now, the same that he had known when they, out of old San Romen's protective witness, had bullied him to his knees and brought tears to his eyes. That one fatal time he had seized arms against Kandrys' tormenting of him, one time only: his hands had killed, not his mind, which was blank and terrified, and had his hands not been filled with a weapon they would have found him as always, as he was now.

But Roh snapped his fingers a second time and they let him alone. "Get to your place," said Roh, *"ilin."*

He rose then, and bowed, and walked—it was incredible that he could walk steadily—to the place he had left at the hearth. There he lay down again, and wrapped himself in his cloak and clenched his teeth and let the fire warm the tremors from his muscles.

He wanted to kill. For every affront ever paid him, for all the terror ever set into him, he wanted to kill; and he squeezed the tears from his eyes and began to reckon that perhaps his father had been right, that his hand had been more honest than he knew. He feared a great many things: he feared death; he feared Morgaine and he feared Liell and the madness of Kasedre; but there never was fear such as there was in being alone among kinsmen, among whom he was always bastard and outcast.

Once, when he was a child, Kandrys and Erij had lured him into the storage basements of Ra-morij, and there overpowered him and hung him from a beam in the deep cellars, alone in the dark and with the rats. They had only come after him after the blood had left his hands and he could not find the strength to scream any longer. Then they had come with lights, and cut him down, hovering over him white-faced and terrified for fear that they had killed him. Afterward they had threatened worse if he showed the cruel marks the ropes had made.

He had not complained to anyone. He had learned the conditions of his welcome in Nhi even then, had learned to clutch his scraps of honor to himself in silence, had practiced, had bit his lip and kept his own counsel, until he had fairly won the honor of the warrior's braid, and until the demands of *uyin* honor must keep Kandrys and Erij from their more petty tormentings of him.

But the looks were there, the subtle, hating looks and secret contempt that became evident when he committed any error that cost him honor.

Even the Chya tried him, in the same way—scented fear and went for it, like wolves to a deer.

Yet something there was in him that yearned to like the lord of Chya, this man so like himself, that showed kindred blood in his face and in his bearing. Roh was legitimate: Roh's father had virtually abandoned the lady Ilel to her fate, captive and bearing Rijan's bastard, that must in nowise return to confound the purity of Chya—to contest with his son Roh.

And Chya both feared him, and scented fear, and would have gone for his throat if not for their debt to Morgaine.

Late, late into the long night, his not-quite-rest was disturbed by a booted foot crunching a cinder not far from his head, and he came up on his arm as Roh dropped to his haunches looking down at him. In panic he reached for the sword beside him; Roh clamped his hand down on the hilt, preventing him.

"You came from Leth," said Roh softly. "Where did you meet her?"

"At Aenor-Pyvvn." He sat up, tucked his feet under him, tossed the loose hair from his eyes. "And I still say, ask Morgaine her business, not her servant."

Roh nodded slowly. "I can guess some things. That she still purposes what she always did, whatever it was. She will be the death of you, Nhi Vanye i Chya. But you know that already. Take her hence as quickly as you can in the morning. We have Leth breathing at our borders this night. Reports of it have come in. Men have died. Liell will stop her if he can. And there is a limit to what service we will pay this time in Chya lives."

Vanye stared into the brown eyes of his cousin and found there a grudging acceptance of him: for the first time the man was talking to him, as if he still had the dignity of an *uyo* of the high clan. It was as if he had not acquitted himself so poorly after all, as if Roh acknowledged some kinship between them. He drew a deep breath and let it go again.

"What do you know of Liell?" he asked of Roh. "Is he Chya?"

"There was a Chya Liell," said Roh. "And our Liell was a good man, before he became counselor in Leth." Roh looked down at the stones and up again, his face drawn in loathing. "I do not know. There are rumors it is the same man. There are rumors he in Leth is *qujal*. That he—like Thiye of Hjemur—is *old*. What I can tell you is that he is the power in Leth, but if you have come from Leth, you know that. At times he is a quiet enemy, and when the worst beasts have come into Koris-wood, the worst sendings of Thiye, Liell's folk have been no less zealous than we to rid Koris of the plague: we observe hunter's peace on occasion, for our mutual good. But our harboring Morgaine will not better relations between Leth and Chya."

"I believe your rumors," said Vanye at last. Coldness rested in his belly, when he thought back to the lakeshore.

"I did not," said Roh, "until this night, that *she* came into hall."

"We will go in the morning," said Vanye.

Roh stared into his face yet a moment more. "There is Chya in you," he said. "Cousin, I pity you, your fate. How long have you to go of your service with her?"

"My year," he said, "has only begun."

And there passed between them the silent communication that that year would be his last, accepted with a sorrowful shake of Roh's head.

"If so happen," said Roh, "if so happen you find yourself free—return to Chya."

And before Vanye could answer anything, Roh had walked off, retiring to a distant corridor of the rambling hall that led to other huts, warrenlike.

He was shaken then by the thing that he had never dreamed to receive: Chya would take him in.

In a way it was only cruelty. He would die before his year was out. Morgaine was death-prone, and he would follow; and in it he had no choice. A moment ago he had had no particular hope.

Only now there was. He looked about at the hall, surely one of the strangest of all holds in Andur-Kursh. Here was refuge, and welcome, and a life.

A woman. Children. Honor.

These were not his, and would not be. He turned and clasped his arms about his knees, staring desolately into the fire. Even should she die, which was probably the thought in Roh's mind, he had his further bond, to ruin Hjemur.

If so happen you find yourself free.

In all the history of man, Hjemur had never fallen.

ᔧ **Chapter 6**

The whole of Chya seemed to have turned out in the morning to see them leave, as silent at their going as they had been at their arrival; and yet there seemed no ill feeling about them now that Roh attended them to their horses, and himself held the stirrup for Morgaine to mount.

Roh bowed most courteously when Morgaine was in the saddle, and spoke loudly enough in wishing her well that the whole of Chya could hear. "We will watch your backtrail at least," he said, "so that I do not think you will have anyone following you through Chya territories very quickly. Be mindful of our safety too, lady."

Morgaine bowed from the saddle. "We are grateful, Chya Roh, to you and all your people. Neither of us has slept secure until we slept under your roof. Peace on your house, Chya Roh."

And with that she turned and rode away, Vanye after her, amid a great murmuring of the people. And as at their coming, so at their going, the children of Chya were their escort, running along beside the horses, heedless of the proprieties of their elders. There was wild excitement in their eyes to see the old days come to life, that they had heard in songs and ballads. They did not at all seem to fear or hate her, and with the delightedness of childhood took this great wonder as primarily for their benefit.

It was, Vanye thought, that she was so fair it was hard for them to think ill of her. She shone in sunlight, like sun on ice.

"Morgaine!" they called at her, softly, as Chya always spoke, "Morgaine!"

And at last even her heart was touched, and she waved at them, and smiled, briefly.

Then she laid heels to Siptah, and they left the pleasant hall behind, with all the warmth of Chya in the sunlight. The forest closed in again, chilling their hearts with its shadow, and for a very long time they both were silent.

He did not even speak to her the wish of his heart, that they turn and go back to Chya, where there was at least the hope of welcome. There was none for her. Perhaps it was that, he thought, that made her face so downcast throughout the morning.

As the day went on, he knew of a certainty that it was not the darkness of the woods that bore upon her heart. Once they heard a strange wild cry through the branches, and she looked up, such an expression on her face as one might have who had been distracted from some deep and private grief, bewildered, as if she had forgotten where she was.

That night they camped in the thick of the wood. Morgaine gathered the wood for the fire herself, making it small, for these were woods where it was not well to draw visitors. And she laughed sometimes and spoke with him, a banality he was not accustomed to in her: the laughter had no true ring, and at times she would look at him in such a way that he knew he lay near the center of her thoughts.

It filled him with unease. He could not laugh in turn; and he stared at her finally, and then suddenly bowed himself to the earth, like one asking grace.

She did not speak, only stared back at him when he had risen up, and had the look of one unmasked, looking truth back, if he could know how to read it.

Questions trembled on his lips. He could not sort out one that he dared ask, that he did not think would meet some cold rebuff or what was more likely, silence.

"Go to sleep," she bade him then.

He bowed his head and retreated to his place, and did so, until his watch.

Her mood had passed by the morning. She smiled, lightly enough, talked with him over breakfast about old friends—hers: of the King. Tiffwy, how his son had been, of the lady who was his wife. It was that kind of thing one might hear from old people, talk of folk long dead, not shared with the young; the worse thing was that she seemed to know it, and her gray eyes grew wistful, and searched his, seeking understanding, some small appreciation of the only things she knew how to say with him.

"Tiffwy," he said, "must have been a great man. I would like to have known him."

"Immortality," she said, "would be unbearable except among immortals." And she smiled, but he saw through it.

She was silent thereafter, and seemed downcast, even while they rode. She thought much. He still did not know how to enter those moods. She was locked within herself.

It was as if he had snapped whatever thin cord bound them by that word: *I would like to have known him.* She had detected the pity. She would not have it of him.

By evening they could see the hills, as the forest gave way to scattered meadows. In the west rose the great mass of Alis Kaje, its peaks white with snow: Alis Kaje, the barrier behind which lay Morija. Vanye looked at it as a stranger to this side of the mountain wall, and found all the view unfamiliar to him, save great Mount Proeth, but it was a view of home.

And thereafter the land opened more to the north and they stood still upon a hillside looking out upon the great northern range.

Ivrel.

The mountain was not so tall as Proeth, but it was fair to the eye and perfect, a tapering cone equal to left and to right. Beyond it rose other mountains, the Kath Vrej and Kath Svejur, fading away into distance, the ramparts of frosty Hjemur. But Ivrel was unique among all mountains. The little snow there was atop it capped merely the summit: most of its slopes were dark, or green with forests.

And at its base, unseen in the distance that made Ivrel itself seem to drift at the edge of the sky, lay Irien.

Morgaine touched heels to Siptah, startled the horse into motion, and they rode on, downslope and up again, and she spoke never a word. She gave no sign of stopping even while stars brightened in the sky and the moon came up.

Ivrel loomed nearer. Its white cone shone in the moonlight like a vision.

"Lady." Vanye leaned from his saddle at last, caught the reins of the gray. "*Liyo*, forbear. Irien is no place to ride at night. Let us stop."

She yielded then. It surprised him. She chose a place and dismounted, and took her gear from Siptah. Then she sank down and wrapped herself in her cloak, caring for nothing else. Vanye hurried about trying to make a comfortable camp for her. These things he was anxious to do: her dejection weighed upon his own soul, and he could not be comfortable with her.

It was of no avail. She warmed herself at the fire, and stared into the embers, without appetite for the meal he cooked for her, but she picked at it dutifully, and finished it.

He looked up at the mountain that hung over them, and felt its menace himself. This was cursed ground. There was no sane man of Andur-Kursh would camp where they had camped, so near to Irien and to Ivrel.

"Vanye," she said suddenly, "do you fear this place?"

"I do not like it," he answered. "—Yes, I fear it."

"I laid on you at Claiming to ruin Hjemur if I cannot. Have you any knowledge where Hjemur's hold lies?"

He lifted a hand, vaguely toward the notch at Ivrel's base. "There, through that pass."

"There is a road there, that would lead you there. There is no other, at least there was not."

"Do you plan," he asked, "that I shall have to do this thing?"

"No," she said. "But that may well be."

Thereafter she gathered up her cloak and settled herself for the first watch, and Vanye sought his own rest.

It seemed only a moment until she leaned over him, touching his shoulder, quietly bidding him take his turn: he had been tired, and had slept soundly. The stars had turned about in their nightly course.

"There have been small prowlers," she said, "some of unpleasant aspect, but no real harm. I have let the fire die, of purpose."

He indicated his understanding, and saw with relief that she sought her furs again like one who was glad to sleep. He put himself by the dying fire, knees drawn up and arms propped on his sheathed sword, dreaming into the embers and listening to the peaceful sounds of the horses, whose sense made them better sentinels than men.

And eventually, lulled by the steady snap of the cooling embers, the whisper of wind through the trees at their side, and the slow moving of the horses, he began to struggle against his own urge to sleep.

She screamed.

He came up with sword in hand, saw Morgaine struggling up to her side, and his first thought was that she had been bitten by something. He bent by her, seized her up and held her by the arms and held her, she trembling. But she thrust him back, and walked away from him, arms folded as against a chill wind; so she stood for a time.

"*Liyo?*" he questioned her.

"Go back to sleep," she said. "It was a dream, an old one."

"*Liyo—*"

"Thee has a place, *ilin*. Go to it."

He knew better than to be wounded by the tone: it came from some deep hurt of her own; but it stung, all the same. He returned to the fireside and wrapped himself again in his cloak. It was a long time before she had gained control of herself again, and turned and sought the place she had left. He lowered his eyes to the fire, so that he need not look at her; but she would have it otherwise: she paused by him, looking down.

"Vanye," she said, "I am sorry."

"I am sorry too, *liyo*."

"Go to sleep. I will stay awake a while."

"I am full awake, *liyo*. There is no need."

"I said a thing to you I did not mean."

He made a half-bow, still not looking at her. "I am *ilin,* and it is true I have a place, with the ashes of your fire, *liyo,* but usually I enjoy more honor than that, and I am content."

"Vanye." She sank down to sit by the fire too, shivering in the wind, without her cloak. "I need you. This road would be intolerable without you."

He was sorry for her then. There were tears in her voice; of a sudden he did not want to see the result of them. He bowed, as low as convenience would let him, and stayed so until he thought she would have caught her breath. Then he ventured to look her in the eyes.

"What can I do for you?" he asked.

"I have named that," she said. It was again the Morgaine he knew, well armored, gray eyes steady.

"You will not trust me."

"Vanye, do not meddle with me. I would kill you too if it were necessary to set me at Ivrel."

"I know it," he said. "*Liyo,* I would that you had listened to me. I know you would kill yourself to reach Ivrel, and probably you will kill us both. I do not like this place. But there is no reasoning with you. I have known that from the beginning. I swear that if you would listen to me, if you would let me, I would take you safely out of Andur-Kursh, to—"

"You have already said it. There is no reasoning with me."

"Why?" he asked of her. "Lady, this is madness, this war of yours. It was lost once. I do not want to die."

"Neither did they," she said, and her lips were a thin, hard line. "I heard the things they said of me in Baien, before I passed from that time to this. And I think that is the way I will be remembered. But I will go there, all the same, and that is my business. Your oath does not say that you have to agree with what I do."

"No," he acknowledged. But he did not think she heard him: she gazed off into the dark, toward Ivrel, toward Irien. A question weighed upon him. He did not want to hurt her, asking it; but he could not go nearer Irien without it growing heavier in him.

"What became of them?" he asked. "Why were there so few found after Irien?"

"It was the wind," she said.

"*Liyo?*" Her answer chilled him, like sudden madness. But she pressed her lips together and then looked at him.

"It was the wind," she said again. "There was a gate-field there—warping down from Ivrel—and the mist there was that morning whipped into it like smoke up a chimney, a wind . . . a wind the like of which you do not imagine. That was what passed Irien. Ten thousand men—sent through. Into nothing. *We* knew, my friends and I, we five; we knew, and I do not know whether it was more terrible for us knowing what was about to happen to us than for those that did not understand at all. There was only starry dark there. Only void in the mists . . . But I lived of course. I was the only one far back enough: it was my task to circle Irien, Lrie and the men of Leth and I—and when we were on the height, it began. I could not hold my men; they thought that they could aid those below, with their king, and they rode down; they would not listen to me, you see, because I am a woman. They thought that I was afraid, and because they were men and must not be, they went. I could not make them understand, and I could not follow them." Her voice faltered; she steadied it. "I was too wise to go, you see. I am civilized; I knew better. And while I was being wise—it was too late. The wind came over us. For a moment one could not breathe. There was no air. And then it passed, and I coaxed poor Siptah to his feet, and I do not clearly remember what I did after, except that I rode toward Ivrel. There was a Hjemurn force in my way. I fell back and back then, and there was only the south left open. Koris held a time. Then I lost that shelter; and I retreated to Leth and sheltered there a time before I retreated again toward Aenor-Pyvvn. I meant to raise an army there; but they would not hear me. When they came to kill me, I cast myself into the Gate: I had no other refuge left. I did not know it would be so long a wait."

"Lady," he said, "this—this thing that was done at Irien, killing men without a blow being struck . . . when we go there, could not Thiye send this wind down on us too?"

"If he knew the moment of our coming, yes. The wind—the wind was the very air rushing into that open Gate, a field cast to the Standing Stone in Irien. It opened some gulf between the stars. To maintain it extended more than a moment as it was would have been disaster to Hjemur. Even he could not be that reckless."

"Then, at Irien—he knew."

"Yes, he knew." Morgaine's face grew hard again. "There was one man who began to go with us, who never stood with us at Irien—he that wanted Tiffwy's power, that betrayed Tiffwy with Tiffwy's wife—that later stood tutor of Edjnel's son, after killing Edjnel."

"Chya Zri."

"Aye, Zri, and to the end of my days I will believe it, though if it was so he was sadly paid by Hjemur. He aimed at a kingdom, and the one he had of it was not the one he planned."

"Liell." Vanye uttered the name almost without thinking it, and felt the sudden impact of her eyes upon his.

"What makes you think of him?"

"Roh said that there was question about the man. That Liell is . . . that he is old, *liyo,* that he is old as Thiye is old."

Morgaine's look grew intensely troubled. "Zri and Liell. Singularly without originality, to have drowned all the heirs of Leth—if drowned they were."

He remembered the Gate shimmering above the lake, and knew what she meant. Doubts assailed him. He ventured a question he fully hated to ask. "Could you—live by this means, if you wished?"

"Yes," she answered him.

"Have you?"

"No," she said. And, as if she read the thing in his mind: "It is by means of the Gates that it is done, and it is no light thing to take another body. I am not sure myself quite how it is done, although I think that I know. It is ugly: the body must come from someone, you see. And Liell, if that is true, is growing old."

He shivered, remembering the touch of Liell's fingers upon his arm, the hunger—he read it for hunger even then—within his eyes. *Come with me and I will show you,* he had said. *She will have the soul from you before she is done. Come with me, Chya Vanye. She lies. She has lied before.*

Come with me.

He breathed an oath, a prayer, something, and stumbled to his feet, to stand apart a moment, sick with horror, sensitive for the first time to his youth, his trained strength, as something that had been the object of covetousness.

He felt unclean.

"Vanye," she said, concern in her voice.

"They say," he managed then, turning to look at her, "that Thiye is aging too—that he has the look of an old man."

"If," she said levelly, "I am dead or lost and you go against Hjemur alone—do not consider being taken prisoner there. I would not by any means, Vanye."

"Oh Heaven," he murmured. Bile rose in his throat. Of a sudden he began to comprehend the stakes in these wars of *qujal* and men, and the prize there was for losing. He stared at her—he knew, like the veriest innocent, and met a lack of all proper horror.

"Would you do this?" he asked.

"I think that one day," she said, "to do what I must do, I would have to consider it."

He swore. For a very little he would have left her in that moment. She began at last to show concern of it, the smallest impulse of humanity, and it was that which held him.

"Sit down," she said. He did so.

"Vanye," she said then. "I have no leisure to be virtuous. I try, I try, with what of me there is left. But there is very little. What would you do, if you were dying, and you had only to reach out and kill—not for an extended old age, with pain, and sickness, but for another youth? For the *qujal* there is nothing after, no immortality, only to die. They have lost their gods, or lost whatever belief they ever had. That is all there is for them—to live, to enjoy pleasure—to enjoy power."

"Did you lie to me? Are you of their blood?"

"I have not. I am not *qujal*. But I know them. Zri . . . if you are right, Vanye, it explains much. Not for ambition, but of desperation: to live. To save the Gates, on which he depends. I had not looked for that in him. What did he say to you, when he spoke with you?"

"Only that I should leave you and come with him."

"Well that you had better sense. Otherwise—"

And then her eyes grew guarded, and she took the black weapon from her belt: he thought in the first heartbeat that she had perceived some intruder, and then to his shock he saw the thing directed at him. He froze, mind blank, save of the thought that she had suddenly gone mad.

"Otherwise," she continued, "I should have had such a companion on my ride to Ivrel that would assure I did not live, such a companion as would wait until the nearness of the Gate lent him the means to deal with me—alive. I left you upon a bay mare, Chya Vanye, and you chose Liell's horse thereafter. That was who I thought it was when first I saw you riding after me, and I was not anxious for Liell's company alone. I was surprised to realize that it was you, instead."

"Lady," he exclaimed, holding forth his hands to show them empty of threat. "I have sworn to you . . . lady, I have not deceived you. Surely—it could not happen, it could not happen and I not know it. I would know, would I not?"

She arose, still watching him, constantly watching him, and drew back to the place where rested her cloak and her sword.

"Saddle my horse," she bade him.

He went carefully, and did as she ordered him, knowing her at his back with that weapon. When he was done, he gave back for her, and she watched him carefully, even to the moment that she swung up into the saddle.

Then she reined about and toward the black horse. All at once he read her thoughts, to kill the beast and leave him afoot, since she would not kill him, *ilin.*

He hurled himself between, looked up with outraged horror; it was not honor to do such a thing, to abuse the *ilin*-oath, to kill a man's horse and leave him stranded. And for one moment there was such a look of wildness on her face that he feared she would use the weapon on him and the beast.

Suddenly she jerked Siptah's head about to the north and spurred off, leaving him behind.

He stared after her a moment, dazed, knowing her mad.

And himself likewise.

He cursed and heaved up his gear, flung saddle on the black, secured the girth, hauled himself into the saddle and went—the beast knowing full well he belonged with the gray by now. The horse needed no touch of the heel to extend himself, but ran, downhill and around a turning, across a stream and up again, overtaking the loping gray.

He half expected a bolt that would take him from the saddle or tumble his horse dead instead; Morgaine turned in the saddle and saw him come. But she allowed it, began to rein in.

"Thee is an idiot," she said when he had come alongside. And she looked then as if she could give way to tears, but she did not. She thrust the black weapon into the back of her belt, under the cloak, and looked at him and shook her head. "And thee is Kurshin. Nothing else could be so honorably stupid. Zri would surely have run, unless Zri is braver than he once was. We are not brave, we that play this game with Gates; there is too much we can lose, to have the luxury to be virtuous, and to be brave. I envy you, Kurshin, I do envy anyone who can afford such gestures."

He pressed his lips tightly. He felt simple, and shamed, realizing now she had tried to frighten him; none of it made sense with him—her moods, her distrust of him. His voice turned brittle. "I am easy to deceive, *liyo,* much more than you could be; any of your simplest tricks can amaze me, and no few of them frighten me."

She had no answer for him.

At times she looked at him in a way he did not like. The air between them had gone poisonous. *Go away,* the look said. *Go away, I will not stop you.*

He would not have left her hurt and needing him; there was oath-breaking and there was oath-breaking, and to break *ilin*-bond when she was able to care for herself was a heavy matter, but there was that in her manner which convinced him that she was far from reasoning.

The light grew in the sky, into a cold, dreary morning, with clouds rolling in from the north.

And early in that morning the land fell away below them and the hills opened up into the slope of Irien.

It was a broad valley, pleasant to the eye. As they stopped upon the verge of that great bowl, Vanye was not sure that this was the place. But then he saw that its other side was Ivrel, and that there was a barrenness in its center, far below. They were too far to see so fine a detail as a single Standing Stone, but he reckoned that for the center of that place.

Morgaine slid down from Siptah's back and troubled to unhook *Changeling* from its place, by which he knew she meant some long delay. He dismounted too; but when she turned and walked some distance away along the slope he did not estimate that she meant him to follow. He sat down upon a large rock and waited, gazing into the distances of the valley. In his mind he imagined the thousands that had ridden into it, upon one of those gray spring mornings that cloaked the valleys with mist, where men and horses moved like ghosts in the fog—of darkness swallowing up everything, the winds, as she had said, drawing the mist like smoke up a chimney.

But upon this morning there were the low-hanging clouds and a winter sun, and grass and trees below. A hundred years had repaired whatever scars there had been left, until one could not have reckoned what had happened there.

Morgaine did not return. He waited long past the time that he had begun to grow anxious about her; and at last he gathered up his resolve and rose and walked the way that she had gone, about the curve of the hill. He was relieved when he found her, only standing and gazing into the valley. For a moment he almost dared not go to her; and then he thought that he should, for she was not herself, and there were beasts and men in these hills that made Irien no place to be alone.

"*Liyo,*" he called to her as he came. And she turned and came to him, and walked back with him to the place where they had left the horses. There she hung the sword where it belonged, and took up the reins of Siptah, and paused again, looking over the valley. "Vanye," she said, "Vanye, I am tired."

"Lady?" he asked of her, thinking at first she meant that they would stop here a time, and he did not like the thought of that. Then she looked at him, and he knew then it was a different tiredness she spoke of.

"I am afraid," she admitted to him, "and I am alone, Vanye. And I have no more honor and no more lives to spend. Here,"—she stretched out her hand, pointing down the slope—"here I left them, and rode round this rim, and from over there—" She pointed far off across the valley, where there was a rock and many trees upon the rim. "From that point I watched the army lost. We were a hundred strong, my comrades and I; and over the years we have grown fewer and fewer, and now there is only myself. I begin to understand the *qujal*. I begin to pity them. When it is so necessary to survive, then one cannot be brave anymore."

He began then to understand the terror in her, the same intense terror there was in Liell, he thought, who also wished something of him. He wished no more truth of her: it was the kind that wrought nightmares, that held no peace, that asked him to forgive things that were unthinkable.

Spare us this, he wanted to say to her. *I have honored you. Do not make this impossible.*

He held his tongue.

"I might have killed you," she said, "in panic. I frighten easily, you see, I am not reasonable. I have ceased to take risks at all. It is unconscionable—that I should take risks with the burden I carry. I tell myself the only immorality I have committed is in trusting you after aiming at your life. Do you see, I have no luxury left, for virtues."

"I do not understand," he said.

"I hope that you do not."

"What do you want of me?"

"Hold to your oath." She swung up to Siptah's back, waited for him to mount, then headed them not across the vale of Irien, but around the rim of the valley, that trail which she had followed the day of the battle.

She was in a mood that hovered on the brink of madness, not reasoning clearly. He became certain of it. She feared him as if he were death itself making itself friendly and comfortable with her, feared any reason that told her otherwise.

And forbore to kill, forbore to violate honor.

There was that small, precious difference between what he served and what pursued them. He clung to that, though Morgaine's foreboding seeped into his thoughts, that it was that which would one day kill her.

The ride around the rim was long, and they must stop several times to rest. The sun went down the other part of the sky and the clouds began to gather thickly over Ivrel's cone, portending storm, a northern storm of the sort that sometimes whirled snow down on such valleys as this, north of Chya, but more often meant tree-cracking ice, and misery of men and beasts.

The storm hovered, sifting small amounts of sleet. The day grew dimmer. They paused for one last rest before moving onto the side of Ivrel.

And chaos burst upon them—their only warning a breath from Siptah, a shying of both their horses. Another moment and they would have been afoot. Half-lighting, Vanye sprang back to the saddle, whipped out his longsword and laid about him in the twilight at the forms that hurtled at them from the woods and from the rocks, men of Hjemur, fur-clad men afoot at first, and then men on ponies. Fire laced the dark, Morgaine's little weapon taking toll of men and horses without mercy.

They spurred through, reached the down-turning of the trail. The slope was alive with them. They clambered up on foot, dark figures in the twilight, and not all of them looked human.

Knives flashed as the horde closed with them, threatening the vulnerable legs and bellies of the horses, and they fought and spurred the horses, turning them for whatever least resistance they could find for escape. Morgaine cried out, kicked a man in the face and rode him down. Vanye drove his heels into the black's flanks and sent the horse flying in Siptah's wake.

There was no hope in fighting. His *liyo* was doing the most sensible thing, laying quirt to the laboring gray, putting the big horse to the limit, even if it drove them off their chosen way; and Vanye did the same, his heart in his throat no less for the way they rode than for the pursuit behind them—skidding down a rocky slope, threading the blind shadows along unknown trail and through a narrow defile in the rocks to reach the flat to Irien's west.

There, weary as their horses were, they had the advantage over the Hjemurn ponies that followed them, for the horses' long legs devoured the ground, and at last pursuit seemed failing.

Then out of the west, riders appeared ahead of them, coming from the narrow crease of hills, an arc of riders that swept to enclose them, thrusting them back.

Morgaine turned yet again, charging them at their outer edge, trying to slip that arc before it cut them off from the north, refusing to be thrust back into the ambush at Irien. Siptah could hardly run now. He faltered. They were not going to make it. And here she reined in, weapon in hand, and Vanye drew the winded black in beside her, sword drawn, to guard her left.

The riders ringed them about on all sides now, and began to close inward.

"The horses are done," Vanye said. "Lady, I think we shall die here."

"I have no intention of doing so," she said. "Stay clear of me, *ilin*. Do not cross in front of me or even ride even with me."

And then he knew the spotted pony of one that was at the head of the others, ordering his riders to come inward; and near him there was the blaze-faced bay that he expected to see.

They were Morij riders, that ran the border by Alis Kaje, and sometimes harried even into this land when Hjemur's forces or Chya's grew restive.

He snatched at Morgaine's arm, received at once an angry look, quick suspicion. Terror.

"They are Morij," he pleaded with her. "My clan. Nhi. *Liyo,* take none of their lives. My father—he is their lord, and he is not a forgiving man, but he is honorable. *Ilin's* law says my crimes cannot taint you: and whatever you have done, Morija has no bloodfeud with you. Please, lady. Do not take these men's lives."

She considered; but it was sense that he argued with her, and she must know it. The horses were likely to die under them if they must go on running. There would likely be more Hjemurn forces to the north even if they should break clear now. Here was refuge, if no welcome. She lowered her weapon.

"On your soul," she hissed at him. "On your soul, if you lie to me in this."

"That is the condition of my oath," he said, shaken, "and you have known that as long as I have been with you. I would not betray you. On my soul, *liyo.*"

The weapon went back into its place. "Speak to them," she said then. "And if you have not a dozen arrows hit you—I will be willing to go with them on your word."

He put up his sword and lifted his hands wide, prodding the exhausted black a little forward, until he was within hailing distance of the advancing riders, whose circle had never ceased to narrow.

"I am *ilin,*" he cried to them, for it was no honor to kill *ilin* without reckoning of his lord. "I am Nhi Vanye. Nhi Paren, Paren, Lellen's-son—you know my voice."

"Whose service, *ilin* Nhi Vanye?" came back Paren's voice, gruff and familiar and blessedly welcome.

"Nhi Paren—these hills are full of Hjemur-folk tonight, and Leth too, most likely. In Heaven's mercy, take us into your protection and we will make our appeal at Ra-morij."

"Then you serve some enemy of ours," observed Nhi Paren, "or you would give us an honest name."

"That is so," said Vanye, "but none that threatens you now. We ask shelter, Nhi Paren, and that is the Nhi's right to grant or refuse, not yours, so you must send to Ra-morij."

There was a silence. Then: "Take them both," came across the distance. The riders closed together. For a moment as they were closely surrounded, Vanye had the overwhelming fear that Morgaine might suddenly panic and bring death on both of them, the more so as Paren demanded the surrender of their weapons.

And then Paren had his first clear sight of Morgaine in the darkness, and exclaimed the beginning of an invocation to Heaven. The men about him made signs against evil.

"I do not think that it will be comfortable for you to handle my weapons, being that your religion forbids," said Morgaine then. "Lend me a cloak and I will wrap them, so that you may know that I will not use them, but I will continue to carry them. I think that we were well out of this area. Vanye spoke the truth about Hjemur."

"We will go back to Alis Kaje," Paren said. And he looked at her as if he thought long about the matter of the weapons. Then he bade Vanye give her his cloak, and watched carefully while she wrapped all her gear within the cloak and laid it across her saddlebow. "Form-up," he bade his men then, and though they were surrounded by riders, he put no restraint on them.

They rode knee to knee, he and Morgaine, with men all about them; and before they had ridden far, Morgaine made to pass the cloak-wrapped arms to him. He feared to take it, knowing how the Nhi would see it; and it was instant: weapons crowded them. A man of clan San, more reckless than the others, took them from him, and Vanye looked at Morgaine in distress, knowing how she would bear that.

But she was bowed over, looking hardly able to stay in the saddle. Her hand was pressed to her leg. Threads of blood leaked through her pale fingers.

"Bargain us a refuge," she said to him, "however you can, *ilin*. There is neither hearth-right nor bloodfeud I have with clan Nhi. And have them stop when it is safe. I have need to tend this."

He looked on her pale, tense face, and knew that she was frightened. He measured her strength against the jolting ride they would have up the road into Alis Kaje, and left her, forced his way through other riders to reach Nhi Paren.

"No," said Paren, when he had pleaded with him. It was firm. It was unshakable. He could not blame the man, in the lands where they were. "We will stop at Alis Kaje."

He rode back to her. Somehow she did keep the saddle, white-lipped and miserable. The sleet-edged wind made her flinch at times; the horse's motion in the long climb and descent wrung now and then a sound from her: but she held, waiting even as they found their place to halt, until he had dismounted and reached up to help her down.

He made a place for her, and begged her medicines of the one who had her belongings. Then he looked round at the grim band of men, and at Paren, who had the decency to bid them back a distance.

He treated the wound, which was deep, as best he could manage with her medicines: his soul abhorred even to touch them, but he reasoned that her substance, whatever it was, would respond best to her own methods. She tried to tell him things: he could make little sense of them. He made a bandage of linen from the kit, and at least had slowed the bleeding, making her as comfortable as he could.

When he arose, Nhi Paren came to him, looked down at her and walked back among his men, bidding them prepare to ride.

"Nhi Paren." Vanye cursed and went after him, stood among them in the dark with men on all sides already mounting. "Nhi Paren, can you not delay at least until the morning? Is there such need to hurry now, with the mountains between us?"

"You are trouble yourselves, Nhi Vanye," said Paren. "You and this woman. There is Hjemur under arms. No. There will be no stopping. We are going through to Ra-morij."

"Send a messenger. There is no need to kill her in your haste."

"We are going through," said Paren.

Vanye swore blackly, choked with anger. There was no cruelty in Nhi Paren, only Nhi obdurate stubbornness. He changed his own saddleroll to the front of his saddle, lashing it to pad it. Anger still seethed in him.

He turned to lead the horse back to Morgaine. "Bid a man help me up with her then," he said to Paren through his teeth. "And be sure that I will recite the whole of it to Nhi Rijan. There is justice in him, at least; his honor will make him sorry for this senseless stubbornness of yours, Nhi Paren."

"Your father is dead," said Paren.

He stopped, aware of the horse pushing at his back, the reins in his hand. His hands moved without his mind, stopping the animal. All these things he knew, before he had to take account of Paren, before he had to believe the man.

"Who is the Nhi?" he asked.

"It is your brother," said Paren. "Erij. We have standing orders, should you ever set foot within Morija, to take you at once to Ra-morij. And that is what we must do. It is not," Paren said in a softer tone, "to my taste, Nhi Vanye, but that is what we will do."

He understood then, numb as he was. He bowed slightly, acknowledged reality; which gesture Nhi Paren received like a gentleman, and looked embarrassed and distressed, and bade men help him take Morgaine up so that he could carry her.

Morij-keep, Ra-morij, was alleged to be impregnable. It sat high upon a hillside, tiered into it, with all of a mountain at its back and its walls and gates made double before it. It had never fallen in war. It had been sometimes the possession of Yla and lately of Nhi, but that had been by marriages and by family intrigue and lastly by the ill-luck of Irien, but never by siege against the fortress itself. Rich herds of horses and of cattle grazed the lands before it; in the valley its villages nestled in relative security, for there were no wolves nor riders, nor Koris-beasts troubling the land as they did in the outside. The keep frowned over the fair land like some great stern grandfather over a favored daughter, his head bearing a crown of crenelated walls and jagged towers.

He loved it still. Tears could still swell in his throat at the sight of this place that had been so much of misery to him. For an instant he thought of his boyhood, of spring, and of fat, white-maned Mai, the first Mai—and both his brothers racing with him on one of those days when there was such warmth in the air that not even they could find hate for each other, when blooms were on the orchards and the whole of the great valley lay studded with pink and white clouds of trees.

Before him now there was the light of a dying winter sun upon the walls, and the clatter of armed riders about him, and Morgaine's weight in his arms. She slept now, and his arms were numb and his back a column of fire. She knew little of the ride, exceedingly weak, though the bleeding had ceased and the wound already showed signs of healing. He thought that she might have fought against the weakness, but she did not know that things were amiss, and the men of Nhi were kindly with her. They did whatever it was possible to do for her, short of touching her or her medicines; and their fear of her seemed to have much abated.

She was very fair, and young-seeming, and capable of innocence when her gray eyes were closed. Even with women of quality men of low-clan made coarse jokes, well-meant; with women of the countryside even high-clan men were far more direct. There was none of that where Morgaine was involved— because she had lord-right, perhaps, and because there attended her an *ilin* who must defend her, and that, weaponless as he was, there was no honor in that; but most probably it was because she was reputed to be *qujal,* and men did not make light with anything *qujal.*

Only sometimes Nhi Paren would ask how she fared, and some of the others would ask the same, and wonder that she slept so.

And of one, Nhi Ryn, son of Paren, there were looks of awe. He was very young; his head was full of poets and of legends, and he had a skill with the harp that was beyond what most high-clan men learned. That which resided in his eyes was purely astonishment at first, and then worship, which boded ill for the welfare of his soul.

Nhi Paren had seemed to see it developing, and had sharply ordered the youth to the rear guard, far back along the line.

Now there was an end of such care of them: the horses' hooves rang upon paving as they approached the gates. Nhi Rej had built the channeling and the paving fifty years ago, restoring the work of Yla En—no luxury, for otherwise the whole of the hill would begin to wash down with the spring rains.

The Red Gate admitted them, and red it was, bravely fluttering with the Nhi standards with their black writing. There was no sound but the snap of the flags in the wind and the clatter of hooves on stone as they entered the courtyard.

One servant ran out and bowed to Nhi Paren. Orders and information passed back and forth.

Vanye sat the saddle, patient until some decision was reached, and at last the youth Ryn and another man came to help him lift Morgaine down from the saddle. He had expected arrest, violence—something. There was only quiet discussion as if they had been any ordinary travelers. It was decided to put Morgaine in the sunny west tower, and they carried her there, the three of them, and the guards following. There they gave her into the hands of frightened serving women, who clearly did not relish their service.

"Let me stay with her," Vanye pleaded. "They do not know how to care for her as need be. . . . At least leave her own medicines."

"The medicines we will leave," said Paren. "But we have other orders with you."

And they took him down the stairs and to a lower hall, into a hall that was home: for there upon the left was Erij's room, and there the stairs that had led up to the middle tower room that had been his. But they took him instead to that which had belonged to Kandrys: the door bolt resisted with the obstinacy of a lock long undisturbed.

Vanye glanced frightened protest at Paren. This was insane, this prison they meant for him. Paren looked intensely uncomfortable, as if he did not relish his orders in the least, but he ordered him inside. Must and mildew and age came out at them. It was cold, and the floor was covered with dust, for dust sifted constantly through Ra-morij, through barred windows and through cracks and crevices.

One servant brought in rush lights. Others brought wood, and a bucket of coals to start the fire. He scanned the room by the dim light, finding it as he had remembered. Nothing must have been disturbed since the morning of Kandrys' death. He saw his doting father's hand in that morbid tenderness.

There were the clothes across the back of the chair, the muddy boots left by the fireside for cleaning, the impression still in the dusty bedclothes where Kandrys had last lain.

He swore and rebelled at that, but firm hands kept him from the door, and men with weapons were outside. There was no resisting the insanity.

Men brought in water for washing, and a plate of food, and wine. All these things they set on the long table by the door. There was an extra armload of wood, and this they unloaded beside the fireplace, that now blazed up quite comfortably.

"Who ordered this?" Vanye asked finally. "Erij?"

"Yes," said Paren, and his tone said clearly that he did not approve of the business. There was a touch of pity in his eyes, for all that none was owed an outlaw. "We must not leave you your armor, either, nor any weapon."

That was clearly the way things would be. Vanye unlaced and slipped off both leather tunic and mail and undertunic, surrendering them to one of the men, as they had taken his helm earlier, and endured in silence their searching him for concealed weapons. He had besides his boots and leather breeches only a thin shirt, and that was no protection against the chill that still clung to the room. When they left him alone he was glad to crouch down upon the hearth and warm himself; and eventually he found appetite enough to take the food and wine they had offered, and to wash, heating the water in the little kettle that was by the hearth.

And at last the weariness that was upon him overcame the rest of his scruples. He thought that he was probably meant to spend the night guilty and miserable, crouching at the hearth rather than sleep in that ghastly bed.

But he was Nhi enough to be contrary, and determined that he would not let himself be prey to the ghost that hovered about this room, angry at its murder. He drew back the covers and settled himself in, stripped only of boots, though it was the custom of men that slept in hall to sleep naked. He did not trust the hospitality of Morija that far. It was a weary time since he had had relief of the weight of the mail even at night, and that alone was enough to make him comfortable. He slept as soon as he had warmed the cold bedclothes with his body, as soon as the tension had passed from his muscles, and if he dreamed, he did not remember it.

⤷ Chapter 7

There was the scrape of a step on stone, something hovering over him. Vanye in sudden panic turned onto his back, flinging his arm and the covers aside, seeking to rise.

Then a man in black and silver stepped back from him and Vanye stopped, one bare foot on the floor. The fire had almost died. Daylight poured wanly through the narrow slit of a window, accompanied by a cold draft.

It was Erij—older, harder of face, the black hair twisted into the different braid that was for hall-lord. The eyes were the same—insolent and mocking.

Vanye thrust himself to his feet, seeing at once that they were alone in the room and that the door was shut. There would be men outside. He had no illusions of safety. He put up a brave face against Erij and ignored him for the moment, going about the necessary business of getting his boots on. Then he went over to the leavings of last night's wine and had a sip of the wretched stuff, returning to the fireside to drink it, for the chill crept quickly into his bones. All this Erij let him do without troubling him.

And then while he knelt feeding the fire to life he heard Erij's tread behind him, and felt the gentle touch of Erij's long fingers gather back his hair, which hung loose about his shoulders. It was long enough to gather in the hand, not yet long enough to resume the braid that marked a warrior. Erij tugged at it gently, as a man might a child's.

He lifted his head perforce. He did not try to turn, but braced himself for the cruel wrench he was sure would come. It did not.

"I would have thought," said Erij, "that the honors bestowed on you at your leaving would have counseled you against coming back."

Erij let go his hair. Vanye seized the chance to turn and rise. Erij was taller than he: he could not help looking up at his elder brother, close as he stood to him. His back was to the hearth. The heat was unpleasant, Erij did not back a pace to let him away from it.

And then he saw that Erij had no right hand: the member that he kept thrust within the breast of his tunic was a stump. He stared, horrified, and Erij held it up the better for him to see.

"Your doing," said Erij. "Like much else."

He did not offer his sorrow for it; he could not say at the moment that he felt it, or anything else save shock. Erij had been the vain one, the skilled one, his hands clever with the sword, with the harp, with the bow.

The pain of the fire in his legs was intense. He pushed free of Erij. The wine cup spilled on the floor and rolled a trail of red droplets darkly across the thirsty dust.

"You come in strange company," said Erij. "Is she real?"

"Yes," said Vanye.

Erij considered that. He was Myya and coldly practical; Myya doubted much and believed little: they were not notoriously religious. It was doubtful which side in him would win, god-fearing Nhi or cynical Myya. "I have had a look at some of the things she carried," he said. "And that would seem to support it. But she bleeds like any mortal."

"There are enemies on her trail and mine," he said hoarsely, "that will be no boon to Morija. Let us be on our way as soon as she can ride, and we will be no trouble to you and neither will they. Hjemur will be far too busy with the both of us to trouble with Morija. If you try to hold her here, it may well be otherwise."

"And if she dies here?"

He stared at Erij, gauging him, and began to reckon with the two years and what they had wrought: the boy was dead, and the man would kill, cold-bloodedly. Erij had been a creature of tempers, of vanities, of sometime kindness—different than Kandrys. Erij's features now seemed those of a man who never smiled. A new scar marred one cheek. There had come to be lines about the eyes.

"Let her pass," said Vanye. "They will want her and all that ever was hers; you cannot deal with Hjemur. There is no dealing with them at all, and you know it."

"Is that where she is going?" he asked.

"The less Morija has to do with her the better. She has bloodfeud with them, and she is more danger to them than to you. I am telling you the truth."

Erij thought upon that a moment, leaned upon the fireplace and thrust the maimed limb within his tunic once more. His dark eyes rested upon Vanye, hard and calculating. "The last I heard of you was through Myya Gervaine, the matter of a killing and a horse-theft in Erd."

"It took the better part of two years to pass the land of your cousins of Myya," Vanye acknowledged. "I lived off them; and took the horse in trade for mine."

Erij's lips tightened in grim mirth at the insolence. "Before you acquired a service, I take it?"

"Before that, yes."

"And how was it that you acquired that service?"

Vanye shrugged. He was cold. He returned to the fire, folding his arms against the chill. "Carelessness," he said. "I sheltered where I ought not—too intent on the woman to remember that she had lord-right. It was fair Claiming."

"Do you sleep with her?"

He looked up at his brother in shock. "*Ilin* with *liyo*, and the like of her? No, I do not. Did not."

"She is beautiful. She is also *qujal*. I do not like having her under roof. She claims no hearth-right here, and I do not intend she should obtain it."

"She does not wish it," said Vanye. "Only send us on our way."

"What is the term of your service to her? What does she claim of you?"

"I do not think I am at liberty to say that. But it has nothing to do with Morija. We only turned here after we were harried in this direction by Hjemur."

"And if released, she will go—where?"

"Out of your lands, by the quickest means." He looked his brother in the face, dropping all arrogance: Erij was due his revenge, had had it in the hospitality he gave them. "I swear it, Erij; and I hold nothing against you for this welcome of yours. If you let us go I will take every care that it brings no trouble on the land—on my life, Erij."

"What do you ask of me, what help?"

"Only return to us the gear you took from us. Give us provisions, if you would. We are scant of everything. And we will go as soon as she can ride."

Erij stared into the fire, sidelong; his eyes flicked back again, frowning. "There is a charge on that charity."

"What charge?"

"You." And when Vanye only stared at him, blank and hardly comprehending: "I will release her," said Erij, "today, with provisions, with horses, with all your gear; and she may go where she will. But you I will not release. That is the charge on my hospitality."

Bargain us a refuge, she had ordered him before she sank into delirium, *however you can.* He knew that it dishonored her, to abandon him, but he knew the compulsion there was in Morgaine: she lived for that, and for nothing else, her face set toward Hjemur. She would gladly spend his life if it would set her safe at Hjemur's border: she had said that in her own words.

"When I have fulfilled my service with her," he offered, trying that, "I will come back to Morija."

"No," said Erij.

"Then," he said at last, "for such a bargain you owe me fair payment: swear that she will go from here with all that is ours, horses and weapons and provisions adequate to see her to any of our borders she chooses: and let her ride free away from the very gate—no double-dealing."

"And for your part?" asked Erij. "If I grant this, I will have no curse from you or from her?"

"None," said Vanye; and Erij named his oath and swore: it was one that even a half-Myya ought to respect.

And Erij left. Vanye was overcome with cold thereafter and knelt on the hearth, feeding the wood in slowly, until the blaze grew intense. The room was still. He looked into the shadows beyond the light and saw only Kandrys' things. He had never much credited the beliefs that the unhappy dead hovered close about the living, though he served one who should have been dead a century ago; but there remained a chill about the room, a biding discomfort that might be guilt, or fear, or some power of Kandrys' soul that lingered here.

Eventually there was a clatter in the courtyard. He went to the slit of a window and looked out, and saw the black and Siptah saddled, saw men about them.

And, aided by two men, Morgaine was brought down and set upon her horse. She scarcely had the strength to stay the saddle, and caught the reins with an awkward gesture that showed she had almost dropped them.

Anger churned in him, that she was being turned out in such condition. Erij meant for her to die.

He forced his shoulder through the narrow opening, shouted down at her. *"Liyo!"* he cried, his voice carried away on the biting wind. But she looked up, her eyes scanning the high walls. *"Liyo!"*

She lifted her hand. She saw him. She turned to those about her, and the attitude of her body was one of anger, and theirs that of embarrassment. They turned from her, all save those that must hold the horses.

Then he grew afraid for her, that she would take arms and be killed, not knowing the case of things.

"The matter of a bargain," he shouted down at her. "You are free on his oath, but do not trust him, *liyo!*"

It seemed then she understood. She suddenly turned Siptah's head and laid heels to him, putting him to a pace headed for the gate, such that he feared she would fall at the turning. The black that had been Liell's followed, jerked along by the rein made fast to Siptah's saddle. There was a pack on the black's saddle—his own gear.

And one other followed, before the gate swung shut again.

Ryn the singer, harp slung to his back, spurred his pony after her. Tears sprang to Vanye's eyes, though he could not say why; he thought afterward that it was anger, seeing her take another innocent as she had taken him to ruin.

He sank down by the fireside again, bowed his head upon his arms and tried not to think of what lay in store for him.

"Father died," said Erij, "six months ago." He stretched his legs out before the fire in his own clean and carpeted apartments, which had been their father's, and looked down where Vanye sat cross-legged upon the hearthstones, unwilling guest for the evening. The air reeked of wine. Erij manipulated cup, then pitcher, upon the table at his left hand, by gesture offered more to Vanye. He refused.

"And you killed him," Erij added then, as if they had been discussing some distant acquaintance, "in the sense that you killed Kandrys: Father grew morbid over Kandrys. Kept the room as you see it. Everything the same. Harness down in the stable—the same. Turned his horse out. Good animal, gone wild now. Or maybe gone to the wolves, who knows? But Father made a great mound down there by the west woods, and there he buried Kandrys. Mother could not reason with him. She fell ill, what with his moods—and she died in a fall down the stairs. Or he pushed her. He was terrible when he was in one of his moods. After she died he took to sitting long hours out in the open, out on the edge of the mound. Mother was buried out there too. And that was the way he died. It rained. We rode out to bring him in perforce. And he took ill and died."

Vanye did not look at him, only listened, finding his brother's voice unpleasantly like that of Leth Kasedre. The manner was there, the casual cruelty. It had been terrible enough when they were children: now that a man who ruled Nhi sat playing these same games of pointless cruelty, it had a yet more unwholesome flavor.

Erij nudged him with his foot. "He never did forgive you, you know."

"I did not expect that he would," Vanye said without turning around.

"He never forgave me either," said Erij after a moment, "for being the one of us two legitimate sons that lived. And for being less than perfect afterward. Father loved perfection—in women, in horses—in his sons. You disappointed him first. And scarred me. He hated leaving Nhi to a cripple."

Vanye could bear it no longer. He turned upon his knees and made the bow he had never paid his brother, that of respect due his head-of-clan, pressing his brow to the stones. Then he straightened, looked up in desperate appeal. "Let me ride out of here, brother. I have duty to her. She was not well, and I have an oath to her that I have to keep. If I survive that, then I will come back, and we will settle matters."

Erij only looked at him. He thought that perhaps this was what Erij was seeking after all, that he lose his pride. Erij smiled gently.

"Go to your room," he said.

Vanye swore, angry and miserable, and rose up and did as he was bidden, back to the wretchedness of Kandrys' room, back to dust and ghosts and filth, forced to sleep in Kandrys' bed, and wear Kandrys' clothes, and pace the floor in loneliness.

It rained that night. Water splashed in through the crack in the unpainted and rotting shutters, and thunder crashed alarmingly as it always did off the side of the mountains. He squinted against the lightning flashes and stared out into the relief of hills against the clouds, wondering how Morgaine fared, whether she lived or had succumbed to her wound, and whether she had managed to find shelter. In time, the rain turned to sleet, and the thunder continued to roll.

By morning a little crust of snow lay on everything, and Ra-morij's ancient stones were clean. But traffic back and forth in the courtyard soon began, and tracked the ground into brown. Snow never stayed long in Morija, except in Alis Kaje, or the cap of Proeth.

It would, he thought, make things easier for any that followed a trail, and that thought made him doubly uneasy.

All that day, as the day before, no one came, not even to supply him with food. And in the evening came the summons that he expected, and he must again sit with Erij at table, he at one side and Erij at the other.

This evening there was a Chya longbow in the middle of the table amid the dishes and the wine.

"Am I supposed to ask the meaning of it?" Vanye said finally.

"Chya tried our border in the night. Your prediction was true: Morgaine does have unusual followers."

"I am sure," said Vanye, "that she did not summon them."

"We killed five of them," said Erij, self-pleased.

"I met a man in Ra-leth," said Vanye, thin-lipped, the while he poured himself wine, "whose image you have grown to be, legitimate brother, heir of Rijan. Who kept rooms as you keep them, and guests as you keep them, and honor as you keep it."

Erij seemed amused by that, but the cover was thin. "Bastard brother, your humor is sharp this evening. You are growing over-confident in my hospitality."

"Brother-killing will be no better for you than it was to me," Vanye said, keeping his voice quiet and calm, far more so than he felt inside. "Even if you are able to keep your hall well filled with Myya, like those fine servants of yours the other side of the door—it is Nhi that you rule. You ought to remember that. Cut my throat and there are Nhi who will not forget it."

"Do you think so?" Erij returned, leaning back. "You have no direct kin in Nhi, bastard brother: only me. And I do not think Chya will be able to do any-thing—if they cared, which I much doubt they do. And *she* was quick enough to leave you. I would that I knew what there was in the witch that could turn the likes of you into the faithful servant, Vanye the self-serving, Vanye the coward. And no bed-sharing, either. That is a great sorcery, that you would give that loyal a service to anyone. You were always much better at ambushes."

Some that Erij said of him he owned for the truth: younger brother against the older, bastard against the heir-sons, he had not always stayed by the terms of honor. And they had laid ambushes of their own, the more so after his nurse died and he came to take up residence in the fortress of Ra-morij.

That was, he recalled, the time when they had ceased to be brothers: when he came to live in the fortress, and they perceived him not as poor relation, but as rival. He had not understood clearly how it was at the time. He had been nine.

Erij was twelve, Kandrys thirteen: it was at that age that boys could be most mindfully, mindlessly cruel.

"We were children," Vanye said. "Things were different."

"When you killed Kandrys," said Erij, "you were plain enough."

"I did not want to kill him," Vanye protested. "Father said he never struck to kill, but I did not know that. Erij, he drove at me: you saw, you saw it. And I never would have struck for you."

Erij stared at him, cold and void. "Except that my hand chanced to be shielding him after he had got his death-wound. He was down, bastard brother."

"I was too pressed to think. I was wrong. I am guilty. I do penance for it."

"Actually," said Erij, "Kandrys meant to mar you somewhat: he never liked you, not at all. He did not find it to his liking that you were given a place among the warriors: he said that he would see you own that you had no right there. Myself, it was neither here nor there with me; but that was how it was: Kandrys was my brother. If he had decided to cut your throat, he was heir to the Nhi and I would have considered that too. Pity we aimed at so little. You were better with that blade than we thought you were, else Kandrys would not have baited you in the casual way he did. I have to give you due credit, bastard brother: you were good."

Vanye reached for the cup, swallowed the last, the wine souring in his mouth. "Father had a fine choice of heirs, did he not? Three would-be murderers."

"Father was the best of all," said Erij. "He killed our mother: I am sure of it. He pushed Kandrys to his death, favoring you as much as he did once. No wonder he saw ghosts."

"Then purify this hall of them. Let me ride out of here. Our father was no better to you than he was to me. Let me go from here."

"You keep asking; I refuse. Why do you not try to escape?"

"I thought that you expected me to keep my given word," he said. "Besides, I would never reach the ground floor of Ra-morij."

"You might be sorry later that you missed the chance."

"You want to frighten me. I know the game, Erij. You were always expert at that. I always believed the things you told me, and I always trusted you more than I did Kandrys. I always wanted to think that there was some sense of honor in you—whatever it was that he was lacking."

"You hated the both of us."

"I was sorry about you; I was even sorry about Kandrys."

Erij smiled and rose from the table, walked near the fire, where it was warm. Vanye joined him there. Erij still had his cup in hand, and took his accustomed chair, while Vanye settled on the warm stones. There was silence between them for a long time, almost peace. Two more cups of wine passed from Erij's cup, and his tanned face grew flushed and his breathing heavy.

"You drink too much," said Vanye at last. "This evening and last—you drink too much."

Erij lifted the stump of his arm. "This—pains me of cold evenings. For a long time I drank to ease my sleep at night. Probably I shall have to stop it, or come to what Father did. It was the wine that helped ruin him, I well know that. When he drank, which was constantly after Kandrys died, he grew unreasonable. When he would get drunk he would go out and sit by his tomb and see ghosts. I should hate to die like that."

It was the rationality in Erij that made him seem most mad; at times Vanye almost thought him amenable to reason, to forgiveness. A man could not speak so with an enemy. At such times they were more brothers than they had ever been. At such times he almost understood Erij, through the moods and the hates and the lines that began to be graven into his face, making him look several years older than was the truth.

"Your lady," said Erij then, "has not quitted Morija as you said she would."

Vanye looked up sharply. "Where is she?"

"You might know," said Erij, "since I think you know full well what she is about."

"That is her business."

"Shall I recall her and ask her or shall I ask you again?"

Vanye stared at him, beginning suddenly to see purpose within the madness, the sickly, fragile humors. He liked it no less. "Her business is with Hjemur, and she is no friend of Thiye. Let that suffice."

"Truly?"

"It is truth, Erij."

"All the same," said Erij, "she had not quitted Morija. And all my promises were conditional on that."

"So were mine," said Vanye, "conditional."

Erij looked down at him. There was no mirth there at all. Of a sudden it was Nhi Rijan in that look, young and hard and full of malice. "You are dismissed."

"Do nothing against her," Vanye warned him.

"You are dismissed," said Erij.

Vanye gathered himself up and took his leave with a scant bow, maintaining the slender thread of courtesy between them. There were the guards outside to take him—there always were: Myya; Erij trusted no Nhi to do this duty, walking him to and from his quarters.

But they had doubled since he had come into the room. There had been two. Now four waited.

Suddenly he tried to retreat back within the room, heard the whisper of steel and saw Erij drawing his longsword from its sheath. In that instant of hesitation they hauled him back and tried to hold him.

He had nothing to lose. He knew it, and flung himself at his brother, intent on cracking his skull at least: there should no Myya whelp lord it in Ra-morij, that benefit for the unfortunate Nhi if nothing else.

But they overhauled him, stumbling over each other and overturning furniture in their haste to seize him; and Erij's fist, guarded by the pommel, came hard against the side of his head, dropping him to his knees.

He knew these nether portions of the fortress, those carved deep into the hill for the holding of supplies in the event of siege, a veritable warren of tunnels and rooms of dripping ceilings, frozen in winter. It was this which made the whole east wing unsafe, so that no one lived there: collapse had been reckoned imminent as long as anyone could remember, though the tunnels were shored up and the storerooms braced with pillars and some filled with dirt. As children they had been forbidden these places: as children they had used the upper storerooms on the safe west for their amusements in the bitter days of winter and the heat of summer.

And one time after he came to live in Ra-morij, his brothers had dared him to come with them down to the nethermost depths: they had taken a single lamp and ventured into this place of damp and cold and moldering beams and crumbling masonry.

Here they had left him, where his screams could in nowise be heard above.

And it was into this place that the Myya sealed him, without light and without water, with only his thin shirt against the numbing cold. He fought against them, dazed as he yet was, panicked by the fear that they would bind him here as Kandrys had; fled their grasp and meant to fight them.

They closed the door on him, plunged him into utter dark; the bolt outside crashed across and echoed.

He tried his strength against it until he was exhausted, his shoulder bruised and his hands torn. Then he sank down against it, the only sure point in this absolute dark, the only place that was not cold earth and stone. He caught his breath and heard for a time only the slow and distant drip of water.

Then the rats began to stir again, timid at first, stopping when he would make a sound. Gradually they grew bolder. He heard their small feet, both along the walls and overhead, in the maze of unseen beams.

He loathed them, since that nightmare in the basement of Ra-morij; he hated even seeing them in light, despising them there: the very sight of them brought back the memory, reminding him of dark places where they thrived in numbers, a realm within the walls, under foundations, where they were the terror and he small and helpless.

He no longer dared lie there. They generally avoided a man who was awake: he knew this sensibly, in spite of his fear; but he had heard too much of what they might do to a man asleep. He paced to keep himself awake, and once, when he did lie down to rest, and felt something light skitter over his leg, he came up with a shuddering cry that echoed madly through the dark, and gathered himself to his feet.

The sound made a pause in all the scurryings—only a moment. Then they proceeded fearlessly about their business.

Sometime, eventually, he would have to sleep. There had to be a time that he would fall down exhausted. Already his knees were shaking. He paced until he had to take his rest by leaning against the walls, until he had long moments of knowing nothing, and woke again in the midst of a fall to the ground, to scramble up again, dusting his hands and shuddering, holding himself on his shaking legs with difficulty.

Then, at last, came a clatter in the hall, a light under the door, and it opened, blazing torchlight into his face, dark figures of men. He went to them as to dear friends, flung himself into their arms as into a place of refuge.

They brought him back upstairs, back to the fine hall that was Erij's apartment. It was night outside the window, so that he knew it had been a night and a day since he had slept; and now his knees were shaking and his hands almost incapable of handling the utensils as he seated himself at the accustomed table opposite his brother.

He reached for the wine first, that began to take the chill from his belly, but he could not eat. He picked at a few bites, and ate some of the bread, and a bit of cheese.

The knife clattered from his hand and he had had enough. He shoved his chair back without Erij's leave, withdrew to the warm hearth and lay down there while Erij finished his dinner. His senses dimmed, exhaustion taking him, and he wakened to Erij's boot in his ribs, gently applied.

He gathered himself up, willing to stave off a return to that place by conversation, by applying himself most earnestly to Erij's humors, but the Myya guards were there. They set hands on him to take him back to that place of darkness and rats, and he fought them and cried aloud, sobbing, clawing free of them: he found the table, snatched a knife and laid a man's arm open with it before they wrested it away from him and pulled him down in a clatter of spilling dishes. A booted foot slammed into his head; when he went down his only thought was that they would take him back unconscious, and that the rats would have him. For that reason he fought them; and then a second blow to the stomach drove the wind from him and he ceased to know anything.

He still lay upon the floor. He knew light and heat and felt carpet with his fingers. Then he felt a cold edge prison one wrist against the floor, and opened his eyes upon Erij, who sat against the arm of the chair; upon the bright length of a longsword that rested over him.

"You have more staying power than you used to have, bastard brother," said Erij. "A few years ago you would have seen reason two days ago. Is it so much you owe her that you will not even say why she has come?"

"I will tell you," he said, "though I myself do not understand it. She says that she came to destroy the Witchfires. I do not know why. Perhaps it is some matter of her honor. But they never were anything but harm to Andur-Kursh; so she is no harm to Morija."

"And you do not know what gain that would be to her."

"No. She only says—somehow—she means to kill Thiye, and that is not . . ." He moved his arm. The blade sliced skin and he decided against it. "Erij, she is not the enemy."

Erij's mouth twisted into a sour smile. "There have been more than Thiye that aspired to what Thiye holds. And none of those have meant us good."

"Not to possess what he holds. To destroy it."

The blade lifted. Vanye struggled to his knees, aching in head and belly, where he had been kicked. He met Erij's cynicism with absolute earnestness.

"Little brother," said Erij, "I think you actually believe the witch. And you have gone soft in the wits if that is so. Look at me. Look at me. I swear to you—and you know that I keep my word—that if you forsake that allegiance in truth, I will not collect the price you owe me." The longsword flicked at his wrist. Vanye snatched it back, horrified. The blade instead leveled at his eyes, holding him like the eyes of a serpent.

"Bastard brother," said Erij, "it has taken me these two years to learn some skill with my left hand. All for a careless, useless gesture. Romen's efforts notwithstanding, I lost the fingers. They went before the hand. Need I tell you how I have sworn I would do if ever I had you in reach, bastard brother? Kandrys may have deserved what he had of you; but I only tried to shield him at that moment—only to keep you from striking him again, I not even in armor. There was no honor for you in what you did, little brother. And I have not forgiven you."

"That is a lie," said Vanye. "You would as gladly have killed me, and I was less skilled than either of you: I always was."

Erij laughed. "There is the Vanye I know. Kandrys would have cursed me to my face and gone for my throat if I threatened him. But you know I will do it, and you are afraid. You think too much, Chya bastard. You always had too keen an imagination. It made you coward, because you never learned to put that wit of yours to good advantage. But I will own you were outmatched then. The years have put weight on you, and half a hand to your stature. I am not sure I should like to take you on now, left-handed as I am."

"Erij." He cast everything upon an appeal to reason, put utmost heart into his tone. "Erij, will you have this hall reputed like that of Leth? Let me pass from here. I am outlawed. I admit I deserve it, and I was mad to come here asking charity of Father. I would never have dared come if I had known I would have to ask any grace of you. That was my mistake. But Nhi will lose honor for you. You know that Nhi will have no part of it, or else you would not have to use Myya guards with me."

"For what are you asking me?"

"To treat me as Nhi, as your brother."

Erij smiled faintly, drew from his belt the shortsword, the Honor blade, and cast it ringing onto the stones of the hearth. Then he walked out.

Vanye stared after him, shuddered as the door slammed and the heavy bolt went across. Fear settled into him like an old friend, close and familiar. He did not even look at the sword for a moment. He had not asked for this, but for his release; and yet it honorably answered, more than honorably answered, all that he had asked of Erij.

At last he turned upon his knees and sought the hilt of the blade, picked it up and could not find it comfortable in his hand, even less could find the courage to do with it what was required of him to do.

It was, perhaps, safe refuge from Erij, and Erij's last mercy was this offering: there were pains far worse than the honorable one of this blade.

But it required an act of will, of courage, toward which Erij challenged him—knowing, thoroughly knowing, that his Chya brother would not be able to do it.

And Vanye knew well enough that Erij, in his place, could. So might Kandrys, or their father. There was the bloodiness in them; they would do it if only to spite their enemy and rob him of revenge.

He set it against the floor, at the length of his arms, shut his eyes and stayed there. All that it took from this point was one forward impulse. His arms, his whole body, shook with the strain.

And after a time he ceased to be afraid, for he knew that he was not going to do it. He let fall the blade and crept over to the fireside and lay down, shivering in every muscle, his stomach heaving, his jaws clamped against the further shame of sickness.

The daylight found him exhausted and placid in his exhaustion, though he did not truly sleep, save one time in the thickest darkness of the night. He heard steps returning now in the hall and had only one fleeting impulse toward doing belatedly what should have been done in dignity.

He did not even meditate killing Erij with the blade. It would be in the one case futile, for he would die for it, shamefully; and in the other, the act would be void of any honor or vindication for himself.

There were several of them that came in. Erij sent the other men away to wait outside, crossed the carpets and gathered up the abandoned blade, returned it to its sheath at his belt.

"I did not think you would," he said. "But you cannot complain of me that *I* disgraced you." And he set his one hand upon Vanye's shoulder and dropped to his knee, took him by the arm and pulled at him, to have him up.

Vanye wept: he did not wish to, but like other battles with Erij, this one was futile and he recognized it. Then to his further shame he found Erij's arm about him, offering him shelter, and it was good simply to fall against that and be nothing. His brother's arms were about him after so long without sight of home or kin, and his about Erij, and after a time he realized that Erij also wept. His brother cuffed him to self-control and to sense with a rough blow and held him at arm's length: there was the moisture of tears on Erij's hard face.

"I am breaking oath," said Erij, "because I swore that I would kill you."

"I wish that you had," Vanye answered him, and Erij embraced him in his hard grip and treated him like the little brother he had always felt himself to be with Erij, roughed his hair, which was boy's length, and set him back again.

"You could never have done it," Erij said. "Because you love life too much to die. That is a gift, brother. It makes you a bad enemy."

Like Morgaine, he thought. Had that come from her? But he had had in the beginning of his wandering the broken halves of his own Honor blade, that his father had shattered; his weakness was not Morgaine's doing, but that he truly did not deserve the honor of an *uyo* of the Nhi. There were prices of such things, that sometimes had to be paid at the end of possessing them; and he would never be fit to pay such a price.

And he wept again, knowing that. Erij cuffed his ear gently, made him look at him. "You robbed me," Erij said hoarsely, "of brother, mother, father, and a piece of myself. Do you not owe me some recompense? Do you not at least owe me something for it?"

"What do you want from me?"

"We made you an enemy. Kandrys hated you and set out to be rid of you, and Father always found you inconvenient. Myself, I had a brother to be loyal to then. I owed things to him. How do you feel toward me? Hate?"

"No."

"Will you come home? Your *liyo* has left you of her own choice. You are deserted. Your service is at an end if I pardon you so that you do not have to be *ilin* and go out to risk another Claiming. I can do that: I can pardon you. I need you, Vanye. There is only myself left of the family, and I—I have trouble even cutting meat at table. Someday I should need a brother with two good hands, a brother that I could trust, Vanye."

It moved too quickly for him, this quicksilver mood of Erij: he was left amazed, and vaguely troubled, but there had been void so long where there should be family; and the solid pressure of his brother's hand upon his arm and the offer of home and honor where he had none smothered other senses for the moment.

Almost.

He shook his head suddenly. "So long as she lives," he said, "and even beyond that, I have bond to her. That is why she could leave me. I am bound to kill Thiye, to destroy the Witchfires: this she has set on me."

"She has set something else on you," his brother pronounced after a moment, his expression greatly troubled. "Heaven defend a madman. Do you hear your own words, Vanye? Do you realize what she is asking of you? You could not lift your hand against yourself last night; and do you think that what she has set on you is any easier? She has ordered you to kill yourself, that is all."

"It was fair Claiming," he said, "and she was within her right."

"She left you."

"You sent her from me. She was hurt and had no choice."

Erij gripped his arm painfully. "I would give you place with me. Instead of being outlaw, instead of being dead in this impossible thing, you would be in Ra-morij, honored, second to me. Vanye, listen to me. Look at me. This is human flesh. This is human. She is Witchfire herself, that woman—cold company, dangerous company for anything born of human blood. She has killed ten thousand men—all in the name of the same lie, and now you have believed the lie too. I will not see one of my house go to that end. Look at me. See me. Can you even be comfortable to look her in the eyes?"

You do not know how great an evil you are aiding. She lies, she has lied before, to the ruin of Koris. Ilin-oath says betray family, betray hearth, but not the liyo; but does it say betray your own kind?

Come with me, Chya Vanye.

Liell's words.

"Vanye." His brother's hand slipped from him. "Go. I shall have them set you in your own room, your own proper room, in the tower. Sleep. Tomorrow evening you will know sense when you hear it. Tomorrow evening we will talk again, and you will know that I am right."

He slept. He had not thought it possible for a man who had been deprived of conscience and reason at once, but his body had its own demands to satisfy and after such a time simply closed off other senses. He slept deeply, in his own bed that he had known from childhood, and awoke aching and bruised from the treatment he had had of the Myya.

And awoke to the more painful misery of realizing that he had not dreamed the night in the basement or that in Erij's hall; that he had indeed done the things he remembered, that he had broken and wept like a child, and that the best there was left for him was to assume a face of pride and try to wear it before other men.

Even that seemed useless. He knew that it was a lie. So would everyone else in Morij-keep, most especially Erij, with whom it mattered most. He lay abed until servants brought in water for washing, and this time there was a razor for shaving; he made use of it, gratefully, and put off the clothing he had slept in, and washed his minor hurts before he dressed again in the clean clothing the servants provided him. In a morbid turn of mind he considered doing to himself again what Nhi Rijan had done, cutting off what growth of hair had come in the two years of his exile; and suddenly he gathered it back in his hand and did so, under the shocked eyes of the servants, who did not move to stop him. This a warrior decided, and whether it would please their lord, it was a matter among warriors and the *uyin*. In four uneven handfuls he severed the locks, and cast the razor on the table, for the servants to bear away.

In that attitude he went to his nightly meeting with his brother.

Erij did not appreciate the bitter humor of it.

"What nonsense is this?" Erij snapped at him. "Vanye, you disgrace the house."

"I have already done that," Vanye said quietly. Erij stared at him then, displeased, but he had the sense to let him alone upon the matter. Vanye set himself at table and ate without looking up from his plate or saying many words, and Erij ate also, but pushed away his own plate half-eaten.

"Brother," said Erij, "you are trying to shame me."

Vanye left the table and went over to stand by the hearth, the only truly warm place in all the room. After a moment Erij followed him and set his hand on his shoulder, making him look at him.

"Am I free to go?" Vanye asked, and Erij swore.

"No, you are not free to go. You are family and you have an obligation here."

"To what? To you, after this?" Vanye looked up at him and found it impossible to be angry; there was truly misery on Erij's face at the moment, and he had never known prolonged repentance in his brother. He did not know how to judge it. He walked back to the table and cast himself down there. Erij followed him back and sat down again.

"If I gave you weapons and a horse," Erij asked him, "what would you? Follow her?"

"I am bound by an oath," he said, "still." And then, to see if he could wring it from Erij: "Where is she?"

"Camped near Baien-ei."

"Will you give me the weapons and the horse?"

"No, I will not. Brother, you are Nhi. I pardon your other offenses. I hold nothing against you."

"I thank you for that," said Vanye quietly. "So do I yours against me."

Erij bit his lip; almost the old temper flared in him, but he restrained it. He bowed his head and nodded: "They have been considerable," he acknowledged, "of which this latest has been one of the lesser. But I swear to you, you will be my brother, heir next my own children. And it would be a greater Morija than either I or our father ruled, if you came to your senses."

Vanye reached for the wine cup. Something of the words jarred within him. He set it down again. "What is it you want of me?"

"You know the witch. You are intimate with her. You know what she seeks and I would wager that you know how it is to be had: that is implicit in the commission she gave you. I will warrant you have seen her use whatever powers she holds in those weapons of hers; you have passed together through Koriswood. I would even suspect that you know *how* they are used. I am not a man that believes in magic, Vanye, and neither, I suspect, are you, for all your

Chya heritage. Things happen through the hands of men, not by wishes upon wands and out of thin air. Is that not so?"

"What has this to do with me and you?"

"Show me how these things are done. Keep your oath to kill Thiye if you will: but with my help. Remember that you are of human blood; and remember what loyalties you owe to your own kind.—Listen to me! Listen. Not since Irien has there been a power in Andur-Kursh save that of Hjemur, and this was of her making, out of her lies and her leading. Our father's kingdom once ranked high in the Middle Realms. The old High Kings are gone now and so is that power we once held, thanks to her. And it is within our hands to win it back again, yours and mine. Look at me, little brother! I swear to you—I swear to you that you will be second only to me."

"I am still *ilin*," he protested, "and I am safe from all your promises. Morgaine's power is in what she wields, and unless you are a liar, she still holds it. Do not challenge her, Erij, or she will be the death of you: she will kill. And I do not want to see that happen."

"Listen to me. Whatever she means to do with the Witch-fires, whatever she means to do with Thiye's power once she has possessed it—she is no friend of ours. We exchange one Thiye for another, she holding what he held, and she more unhuman than ever he was. Look at what Thiye has done with it, and he at least in some part man. But she . . . the use of such powers is like the breath of air to her, the element in which she moves; and she is ambitious, for revenge, for power, for what else we do not know. What were you to her against the ambition that moves her? Think on that, brother."

"You said that she is camped near Baien-ei," Vanye answered. "That does not sound to me like what she would do if she had utterly deserted me. She is waiting. She expects me to come if I can."

Erij laughed, and the grin slowly died in Vanye's cold, unhappy stare. "You are naive," said Erij then. "What she is waiting for is not you, not so small a thing as that to her."

"What, then, would that be?"

"Will you show me the manner of the power she uses?" Erij asked him. "I do not ask you to break oath. If she seeks the death of Thiye and the fall of Hjemur, I have no quarrel with that; but if she seeks power for herself, then has she not used you shamefully, Vanye? Is that the oath you swore to her, that you would help set her in power over your own people? If that were so, it was a shameful oath."

"She means to break the power of Thiye," he said, "there was nothing said of creating any other power."

"Oh, come," said Erij. "And having rained him . . . what? To live in poverty, to retreat to obscurity? Or to risk being overtaken by the bloodfeuds of so many enemies? Having taken power—she will hold it. You are nothing to her; I offered her to have you back, at the exchange of her word to go south again. She refused."

Vanye shrugged, for he had known of her that he had no importance when he ceased to serve her purposes: she had never deluded him in that.

"She simply threw you aside," said Erij. "And what might a heart like that do once in power in Hjemur, when she needs nothing? She will grow the more cold, and the more dangerous. I had rather an enemy with tempers and honest hates. I had rather a human enemy. Thiye is old and half-mad; he muddles about with his beasts and his self-indulgence, and seldom stirs. He has never made war on us, neither he nor his ancestors. But can you see the like of Morgaine being content with things as they are for long?"

"And what would you create of it, Erij?" he asked harshly. "The like of what I have seen in Ra-morij?"

"Look about you at Morija," said Erij. "Look at its people. It does not fare too badly. Did you see anything amiss, anything in the land or the villages that would be better changed? We have our law, the blessing of church, the peace of our fields and our enemies in Chya fear us. That is my work. I am not ashamed of what I have done here."

"It is true that Morija is faring well now," Vanye said. "But you, yourself, you cannot handle the things that Morgaine does; and she will not yield them. Seek her for an ally if you will. That is the best thing you can do for yourself and Morija."

"Like the ten thousand at Irien that she and her allies helped?"

"She did not kill them. That much is a lie."

"But that is what came of her help, all the same. And I would not lay Morija and Nhi open to the same kind of thing. I would not trust her. But this—*this*—I would trust, that she values powerfully." Excitedly he rose from his place and from the cabinet near the table he drew out a cloth-wrapped bundle. When he took it in his hand the cloth fell away at the top and Vanye saw to his dismay the dragon-hilt of *Changeling*. "This is what holds her encamped at Baien-ei, her desire for this. And I would wager, brother, that you know something of it."

"I know that she bids me keep my hands from it," said Vanye. "Which you had better heed, Erij. She says there is danger in it and that it is a cursed blade, and I believe it."

"I know that she values this above your life," said Erij, "and more than all else she possessed. That was plain." He jerked it back as Vanye tentatively extended his hand toward it. "No, brother. But I will hear your explanation of what value it bears to her. And if you are my brother, you will tell me this willingly."

"I will tell you honestly that I do not know," he said, "and that if you are wise you will let me return this thing to her before it does harm. Of all things she possesses, this is one she herself fears."

A second time he reached for it, beginning to be frightened for what Erij purposed with the blade: for it was a thing of power; he knew it by the way Morgaine treated it, who never let it leave her. Of a sudden Erij raised his voice in a shout. The door crashed back: the four Myya were with them.

And Erij shook the sheath from the blade one-handed, and held it naked in his hand. The blade went from translucent ice to a shimmer of opalescent fire, and all the air sang in their ears, a horrid shimmer of air at its tip that of a sudden Vanye knew.

"No!" he cried, flung himself aside. The air roared into a darkness and a wind that sucked at them, and the Myya were gone, whipped away into some vast expanse that had opened between them and the door.

Erij flung the blade away, sent it slithering sideways across the floor, ripping ruin after it, and of a sudden Vanye caught the sheath and scrambled for the abandoned blade, caught it up in his hand as other men poured through the door. The same starry dark caught them up, and his arm went numb.

He knew then the sensation that had prompted Erij to drop the blade, gut-deep loathing for such power, and suddenly he heard his brother's voice shout and felt a hand claw at his arm.

He ran, wiser than to turn and destroy . . . free down the hall and free upon the stairs downward once the *uyin* there saw the unworldly shimmer of the witchblade in his hand.

He knew his way. There was the outer door. He heaved back the bolt and ran for the stable court, feverishly cursed the weeping stableboy into saddling a good horse for him; and all the while from Ra-morij there was a silence. He kept himself clear from the arrow-slits of the windows, knowing that for his greatest peril, and bade the boy creep down in the shadows and open the gate for him.

Then he sprang to horse, keeping reins and sheath in one hand, holding the shimmering blade in the other, and rode. Arrows hissed about him. One plunged within the well of darkness at *Changeling's* tip and was lost. Another scraped his horse's rump and stung the beast to a near stumble. But he was through. Frightened warders unbarred the gates under the menace of that blade and he was free of the outer gate, clattering down the height of the paved road and onto the soft earth of the slopes.

There was no rush to follow him. He imagined Erij cursing his men to order, trying to find some who would dare it—and that Erij himself would follow he did not doubt. He knew his brother too well to think that he would cease what he had decided to do.

And Erij would well know what road he would ride. If he were not Morij-bred, he would have no chance to evade them, to ride the shorter trails and the quick ones, but he had as fine a knowledge of the web of unmarked roads in the country as did Erij.

It was a matter of reaching Baien-ei and Morgaine, if it were possible, before the Myya and their arrows.

ᕲ Chapter 8

The pursuit was behind him again. When he looked back against some patch of unmelted snow in the starlight, he could see a dark knot atop a hill or along the road; but the laboring bay kept the same distance between them.

They had not delayed long. There were most of all the arrows to fear. If they had him once within arrow range, he could not survive it; and he did not doubt that they were Myya, and keen on killing him—it was the only way to safely wrest away the thing he carried.

It was the stopping that was the most dangerous. At times he had to stop and rest the horse; and he chose such times as he did not see them behind him and reckoned that they were doing the same, well knowing that at some time he might make an error, or fail to run again in time. They had come a day across the plain of Morija, and the signal fires were still lit: he could see their glow on hilltops, warning the whole land that there was an enemy abroad, a stranger that meant no good to Morija. That net of signals was the countryside's defense. All good men would turn out to patrol the roads, to challenge any comer near the vital passes, and he had no wish to kill—or whatever it was the witchblade did to them that fell within its power; besides, some of the country-men, of clans San and Torin, were no mean archers themselves, and he feared any meeting with them.

At their first stopping he had contrived to sheathe the horrid blade, fearing to expose his own flesh to the danger of that fire, which was that about the Gates themselves. He laid the sheath on the ground and eased the point within, fearful that even that could not contain it. But the light ceased the moment the point had gone within, and then it was possible to lift and bear it like any nor-mal sword.

It was the look of the four men of Myya that he could not get from his mind, that awful lostness as they whirled away into that vast and tiny darkness, men who could not understand how they were dying.

If it were possible he would gladly have hurled *Changeling* from him, have rid himself of that dread weight and let it lie for some other unfortunate master. But it was his in charge, and it was for Morgaine, who had sense enough to keep it sheathed. He himself dreaded the thought of drawing it again, almost more than he dreaded the arrows behind him. There was sinister power about it that was far more lingering than the ugliness of Morgaine's older—lesser—weapons. His arm still hurt from wielding it.

In the hours' passing he tried at last just to keep the bay moving, stopping dead only when he must; he knew that the animal was going to fade long before he could make Baien-ei and Morgaine's camp. There were villages: the Myya could have remounts; they would run him to the bay's death. His insides hurt from the constant jolting, already bruised from the beating he had had of them. He began to have the taste of blood in his mouth and he did not know if this was from his bruised jaw or from somewhere inside.

And when he looked back of a sudden the Myya were no longer with him.

There was no hope left but to go off the main road, to try to confuse pursuit and hope that he could fight through ambush at the end, at Baien-ei. The next time that he saw the chance of another lane, one already well marred with tracks since the melting of the snow, he took that road and coaxed the poor horse to what pace he could maintain.

He knew the road. A little village lay a distance past the second winding, the hamlet of San-morij, a clan that possessed a score of smaller villages hereabouts—common and unpretentious as the earth they held, kindly folk, but fierce to enemies. There was a farmhouse that he well remembered, that of the old chief armorer of Ra-morij, San Romen; he owed a great debt to that old tutor of his, who alone of men in Ra-morij had shown some sympathy for a lord's bastard, who had soothed his hurts and treated the hidden wounds with drafts of rough affection.

It was a debt that deserved better payment than he was about to give; but desperation smothered any impulses to honor. He knew where the stable was, around at the back of the little house, a place where he and Erij had watered their mounts once upon a better time. He left the bay tied to a branch by the side of the road, and took *Changeling* upon his shoulder, and slipped down the ditch by the roadside until he was within sight of the stable.

Then he ran across the yard, skidded into the shadows and flung open the door, already hearing the livestock astir: the men of Romen's house would be waking, seeking arms at any moment, and running out to see what was among them. He chose the likeliest pony he could in the dark, already haltered in its stall: he put a length of rope in the halter ring, the only thing there was to hand, flung open the stall door and backed the pony out.

Running footsteps pelted up to the door. He expected its opening, swung up to the pony's bare back with the halter rope for a rein, and as the door was flung open, he rammed his heels into the pony's flanks and the frightened animal bolted out into the yard—an honest horse and unused to such treatment. It ran for the road, scrambled up the side of the ditch, and he wrapped his legs about its fat ribs and clung, unshakable. He wrenched its head over in the direction he wanted it to go, and when he reached the crossroads over by San-hei, he turned there, heading for Baien-ei by a slightly longer road, but a lonelier one.

There was a rider on the road ahead, sai-uyo, Vanye thought, uyo of the lesser clans, but uyo, and armored: he rode like a warrior. There was no hope that the little beast he rode could match a proper horse. There was no avoiding the meeting. Vanye rode along at leisure, legs dangling, like any herder-boy returning at evening. Only upon the heights the warning-fires still gleamed, and the roads were watched; and he for his part could not look to be a herdsman, for boots and breeches were of weathered leather such as was proper to an uyo, not a countryman, he carried a great sword, and his shirt of white lawn marked him for a man untimely rushed from some great hall, high-clan: dai-uyo, Nhi.

This man, he thought unhappily, he might have to kill. He reached to the belt, unhooked the sheath, and gripped the sheath of *Changeling* in one hand and the hilt in the other, and the *sai-uyo* on his fine dappled charger came closer.

And perhaps he already recognized what quarry he had started, for he moved his leg and lifted his blade from its place on the saddle, and rode also with his sheathed blade in hand.

It was one of Torin Athan's sons: he did not know the man, but the look of the sons of Athan was almost that of a clan apart: long-faced, almost mournful men, with a dour attitude at variance with most of the flamboyant men of Torin. Athan was also a prolific family: there were a score of sons, nearly all legitimate.

"*Uyo,*" Vanye hailed him, "I have no wish to draw on you: I am Nhi Vanye, outlawed, but I have no quarrel with you."

The man—he was surely one of the breed of Athan—relaxed somewhat. He let Vanye ride nearer, though he himself had stopped. He looked at him curiously, wondering, no doubt, what sort of madman he faced, so dressed, and upon such a homely pony. Even fleeing, a man might do better than this.

"Nhi Vanye," he said, "we had thought you were down in Erd."

"I am bound now for Baien. I borrowed this horse last night, and it is spent."

"If you look to borrow another, *uyo,* look to your head. You are not armored, and I have no wish to commit murder. You are Rijan's son, and killing you even outlawed as you are would not be a lucky thing for the likes of a *sai-uyo.*"

Vanye bowed slightly in acknowledgment of that reasoning, then lifted up the sword he carried. "And this, *uyo,* is a blade I do not want to draw. It is a named-blade, and cursed, and I carry it for someone else, in whose service I am *ilin* and immune to other law. Ask in Ra-morij and they will tell you what thing you narrowly escaped."

And he drew *Changeling* part of the way from its sheath, so that the blade remained transparent, save only the symbols on it. The man's eyes grew wide and his face pale, and his hands stayed still upon his own blade.

"To whom are you *ilin*," he asked, "that you bear a thing like that? It is *qujalin* work."

"Ask in Ra-morij," he said again. "But under *ilin*-law I have passage, since my *liyo* is in Morija, and you may not lawfully execute Rijan's decree on me. I beg you, get down. Strip your horse of gear and I will exchange with you: I am a desperate man, but no thief, and I will not ride your beast to the death if I have any choice about it. This pony is of San. If yours knows the way home, I will set him loose again as soon as I can find a chance."

The man considered the prospects of battle and then wisely capitulated, slid down and busily stripped off saddle and belongings.

"This horse is of Torin," he said, "and if loosed anywhere in this district can find his way; but I beg you, I am fond of him."

Vanye bowed, then gripped the dapple's mane in his hands and vaulted up, turned the animal and headed off at a gallop, for there was a bow among the *sai-uyo*'s gear, which he reckoned would be shortly strung, and he had no wish for a red-feathered Torin arrow in his back.

And from place to place across the face of Morija, his pursuers would have found ready replacements for their mounts, fine horses, with saddles and all their equipment.

The night was falling again, coming on apace, and the signal fires glowed brighter upon the hilltops, one blaze upon each of the greater hills, from edge to edge of Morija.

And when that *uyo* managed to reach San-morij with the little pony— Vanye intensely imagined the man's mortification, his fine gear borne by that shaggy little beast—then there would be two signals ablaze on the hill by San-morij and upon that by San-hei, and no doubt which fork of the road he had gone. There would be the whole of San and now the clan of Torin riding after him, and the Nhi and the Myya upon the other road, to meet him at Baien-ei.

To have stripped the man of weapons and armor which he so desperately needed would likely have meant killing him: but *Changeling* was not the kind of blade that left a corpse to be robbed. To have killed the man would have been well too, but he had not, would not: it was his nature not to kill unless cornered; it was the only honor he still possessed, to know there was a moral limit to what he would do, and he would not surrender it.

It would not be paid with gratitude when Torin caught him, and least of all when they brought him to Nhi and Myya.

Now he and the whole of Ra-morij—and if messengers had sped in the wake of his pursuers, the whole of the midlands villages by now—knew where he must run. There was a little pass at Baien-ei, and hard by it a ruined fort where every lad in Morija probably went at some time or another in their farings about the countryside. The best pasturage in all of Morija was in those hills, where ran the best horses; and the ruined fort was often explored by boys that herded for their fathers; and sometimes it served as rendezvous for fugitive lovers. It had had its share of tragedies, both military and private, that heap of stones.

And Morgaine's guide was a Nhi harper with the imagination of a callow boy on a lovers' tryst, who would surely know no better than to lead her there for shelter, into a place that had but one way out.

There were men guarding the hillside. He had known there must be even before he set out toward it. Any break from Baien-ei by riders had to be through this narrow pass, and with archers placed there, that ride would be a short one.

He left the dapple tethered against the chance he might have to return; the branch he used was not stout, and should mischance take him or he find what he sought, the animal would grow restless and eventually pull free, seeking his own distant home. He took the sheathed sword in hand and entered the hills afoot.

All the paths of the hills of Baien-ei could not be guarded: there were too many goat tracks, too much hillside, too many streams and folds of rock: for this reason Baien-ei had been an unreliable defense even in the purpose for which it was built. Against a massive assault, it was strong enough, but when the *fein*, the peasant bowman, had come into his own, and wars were no longer clashes between *dai-uyin* who preferred open plain and fought even wars by accepted tradition, Baien-ei had become untenable—a trap for its holders more than a refuge.

He moved silently, with great patience, and now he could see the tower again, the ruined wall that he remembered from years ago. Sometimes running, sometimes inching forward on his belly and pausing to listen, he made himself part of the shadows as he drew near the place: skills acquired in two years evading Myya, in stealing food, in hunting to keep from starvation in the snowy heights of the Alis Kaje, no less wary than the wolves, and more solitary.

He came up against the wall and his fingers sought the crevices in the stonework, affording him the means to pull himself up the old defensework at its lowest point. He slipped over the crest, dropped, landed in wet grass and slid to the bottom of the little enclosure on the slope inside. He gathered himself up slowly, shaken, feeling in every bone the misery of the long ride, the weakness of hunger. He feared as he had feared all along, that it was nothing other than a trap laid for him by Erij: Myya deviousness, not to have told him the truth. That his brother should have committed a mistake in telling him the truth and in trusting him was distressing. Erij's mistakes were few. His shoulders itched. He had the feeling that there might be an arrow centered there from some watcher's post.

He yielded to the fear, judging it sensible, and darted into shadows, rounded the corner of the building where it was tucked most securely against the hill. There was a crack in the wall there that he well remembered, wide as a door, and yet one that ought to be safest to use, sheltered as it was.

He crept along the wall to that position, caught the stable-scent of horses. Large bodies moved within.

"*Liyo!*" he hissed into the dark. Nothing responded. He eased his way inside, the pale glimmer of Siptah to his left, to his right, blackness.

"Do not move," came Morgaine's whisper. "Vanye, thee knows I mean it."

He froze, utterly still. Her voice was from before him. Someone—he judged it to be Ryn—moved from behind him, put his hands at his waist and searched him cursorily for some hidden weapon before taking hold of the sword belt. He moved his head so that the strap could pass it the more easily: he was unaccountably relieved at the passing of that weight, as if he had been in the grip of something vile and were gently disentangled from it and set free.

Ryn carried it to her: he saw the shadow pass a place of dim starlight. For his own part his knees were trembling. "Let me sit," he asked of her. "I am done, *liyo*. I have been night and day in the saddle reaching this place."

"Sit," she said, and he dropped gratefully to his knees, would gladly have collapsed on his face and slept, but it was neither the place nor the moment for it. "Ryn," she said, "keep an eye to the approaches. I have somewhat to ask of him."

"Do not trust him," Ryn said, which stung him with rage. "The Nhi would not have made him a gift of the sword and set him free for love of you, lady."

Fury rose in him, hate of the youth, so smooth, so unscarred, so sure of matters with Morgaine. He found words strangled in his throat, and simply shook his head. But Ryn left. He heard the rustle of Morgaine's cloak as she settled kneeling a little distance from him.

"Well it was thee spoke out," she said softly. "A dozen or so have tried that way these past two days, to their grief."

"Lady." He bowed and pressed his forehead briefly to earth, pushed himself wearily upright again. "There is a large force, either on its way or here already. Erij covets Thiye's power, thinking he can have it for himself."

"You cried at me not to trust him," she said, "and that I did believe. But how do I trust you now? Was the sword gift or stolen?"

What she said frightened him, so much as anything had power to frighten him, tired as he was: he knew how little mercy there was in her for what she did not trust, and he had no proof. "The sword itself is all that I can give you to show you," he said. "Erij drew it; it killed, and he feared to hold it. When it fell, I took it and ran—it is a powerful key, lady, to gates and doors."

She was silent for a moment. He heard the whisper of the blade drawn partway, the soft click as it slipped back to rest. "Did thee hold it, drawn?"

She asked that in such a tone as if she wished otherwise.

"Yes," he said in a faint voice. "I do not covet it, *liyo*, and I do not wish to carry it, not if I go weaponless." He wished to tell her of the men of Myya, what had happened: he had no name for it, and saw in his mind those lost faces. In some deeper part of him, he did not want to know what had become of them.

"It taps the Gates themselves," she said, and moved in the dark. "Ryn, do you see anything?"

"Nothing, lady."

She settled back again, this time in the dim starlight that fell through the crack, so that he could see her face, half in shadow as it was, the light falling on it sideways. "We must move. Tonight. Does thee think otherwise, Vanye?"

"There are archers on the height out there. But I will do what you decide to do."

"Do not trust him," Ryn's voice hissed from above. "Nhi Erij hated him too well to be careless with him or the blade."

"What does thee say, Vanye?" Morgaine asked him.

"I say nothing," he answered. Of a sudden the weariness settled upon him, and it was too much to argue with a boy. His eyes stayed upon Morgaine, waiting her decision.

"The Nhi gave me back all but *Changeling*," she said, "not knowing. I suspect, that some of the things they returned were weapons: they recognized the sword as what it was, but not these others. They also gave me back your belongings, your armor and your horse, your sword and your saddle. Go and make yourself ready. All the gear is in the corner together. I do not doubt but that you are right about the archers; but we have to move: all this coming and going of yours cannot have gone entirely unmarked."

He felt his way, found the corner and the things she described, the familiar roughness of the mail that had been his other skin for years. The weight as he settled it upon him was greater than he remembered: his hands shook upon the buckles.

He considered the prospect of the ride they would make, down that throat of a pass, and began to reckon with growing fear that there was not enough left in him to make such a ride. He had spent and spent, and there was little more left in him.

It was not likely, he thought, that they would escape from this unscathed: Myya arrows were a sound that had come to strike a response in his flesh. He had escaped too many of them, in Erd and in Morija. The odds were in favor of the arrows.

Morgaine came upon him, sought his hand, took it and turned his wrist upward. The thing that hit was like a weapon, unexpected, and he flinched. "Thee does not approve," she said. "But I will have it so. I have little of that to spend: unlike my other things, the sun does not renew it, and when it is gone, it is gone. But I will not lose thee, *ilin*."

He rubbed at the sore place, expecting a wound, finding none, and beginning to feel something amiss with himself, the tiredness melting, his blood moving more strongly. It was *qujalin,* or whatever race she named as her origin, and once the thing she had done would have terrified him: once she had promised him she would not do such things with him.

I will not lose thee, ilin.

She had lingered in this snare in Morija because of *Changeling.* He knew that in his heart and did not blame her. But there was in that word a small bit of concern for the *ilin* who served her, and that, from Morgaine, was much.

He set to work about his preparations with the determination that he would not be lost, that so long as he had a horse under him he would make it down the pass and into Baien's hills.

They had three horses: Siptah; the ungrateful black, who tried to bite and desisted sullenly with a rap of the quirt along his jaw; and Ryn's dun horse, hardly fine-blooded, but long in the legs and deep in the chest. Vanye estimated that the beast might hold the courses they set, at least as long as need be; and the youth could ride: he was Morij, and Nhi.

"Leave the harp," Vanye protested when he saw the thing slung on the youth's back, as they led their horses out into the starlight. "The rattle of it will kill us all."

"No," said the youth flatly, which was what one might expect of Nhi Ryn Paren's-son. And rather than snatch it from him and delay for argument, Vanye cast a stern look at Morgaine, for he knew that the boy would heed her word.

But she forbore to do anything, and, effectively set in his place, Vanye led the black after Siptah's tail, until they were at the corner. There was a gate to be opened: he led the black to that point and heaved back the rusty bolt, shouldered it wide; and Morgaine and Ryn thundered through, Vanye only an instant slower, springing to the saddle and laying heels to the animal. Siptah's white tail flipped gay insolence as the big gray took the retaining wall, warning Vanye what he had forgotten over the years: that there was a jump there. Ryn took it; his own black gathered and jolted down to a landing, skidding downslope, haunches down like a bird in landing, for the grass was wet.

And arrows flew. Vanye tucked down to the black's opposite side, making himself as inconspicuous as possible. He hoped the others had the same sense. But through the black's flying mane he saw a streak of red fire, Morgaine's handweapon; and there was silence from that quarter then, no more arrows. Whether she had hit anything firing blind, he did not know, but they were Morij, those men, and in his heart he hoped that the archers had simply lost heart and run.

Bruising force hit his side. He gasped and nearly lost his grip for the pain of it, and he knew that he had been hit: but no arrow at that range could pierce the mail. His worst fears were for the vulnerable horse. It went against Morij honor to hit a man's horse, but here was no chivalry. These men must face Erij if they let them through, and that was no pleasant prospect for them.

They were near the end of the pass. He laid heels to the black and drove him harder, and the panicked beast gathered himself, saliva spattering back against Vanye's leg as the horse took the rein he wanted. He passed even Siptah, answered to main force as Vanye hauled his head round toward the north again, toward the cleft of Baien's pass through the hills, and leaped forward under the brutal impact of Vanye's heels. In that instant he almost loved the vile beast: there was heart in him.

Morgaine, low in the saddle, was by him again: Siptah's head, nostrils wide, was alongside with the starlight in his white mane. Unaccountably Morgaine laughed, reached out a hand to him that did not touch, and clung again to the mane.

And they were through. Beyond all range of archers, safe on Baien's level plain, they were through, and Vanye reined down the snorting black and brought him to a stop, only then remembering the youth who rode in their wake. He came, a good bowshot behind them, and they both waited—silent, Vanye reckoned, in the same concern, that the boy might have been hit, for he rode low in the saddle.

But he was well enough, pale-faced in the dim light when he rode in between them, but unscathed. The dun horse was spent, his rump sinking on one side as if he favored that leg, and Vanye dismounted to see to it: an arrow had ripped the hide and perhaps hung for a time. He explored the wound with his fingers, found it not dangerously deep.

"He will last," Vanye pronounced. "There will be time later."

"Then let us be off," Morgaine said, rising in the stirrups to look behind them, even while he climbed back into the saddle. "The surprise of the matter will not last long. They had not seen me fire before; now they have, and they will accustom themselves to the idea and recover their courage about it."

"Where will you?" Vanye asked.

"To Ivrel," she answered.

"Lady, Baien's hold lies almost athwart our path. They were hearth-friends to you once. It may be we could shelter there a time if we reached them before Erij."

"I do not trust hold or hall this near Ivrel," she said. "No."

They rode, an easy pace now, for the horses were spent and might be called on again to run; and soon the fire of whatever thing had entered his veins was spent as well, and he felt his senses going. His side hurt miserably. He felt of the place and found broken links in the mesh, but little hurt beneath. Assured then that was not bleeding his life away, he hooked one leg over the high bow of the saddle, and wrapped his arms tightly about him for support, and so gave himself to sleep.

Bells woke him.

He looked up and eased cramped muscles out of their long-held position, and saw to his shame that Ryn led his horse, and that it was well into morning. They filed along a peaceful pineshaded lane by the side of a stone wall.

He leaned forward and took the reins, beginning to realize where they were, for he had visited this place in his youth. It was the Monastery of Baien-an, the largest in all Andur-Kursh that still remained safe and occupied by the Gray Fathers. He rode forward to join Morgaine, wondering whether she knew what this place was, or if she had been led to it on Ryn's advice, for here was an abundance of witnesses to her passing, and a place that could not be friendly to her.

Brothers tending their wall paused at their work in wonder. A few started forward as they might to welcome travelers, and then hesitated, and seemed to abandon the idea altogether, their faces bewildered. They were gentle men. Vanye had no fear of them.

And there was a terrible weariness upon Morgaine's face, pain, as if her wound troubled her. He saw that, and bit his lip in reckoning. "Do you think to stay here?" he asked of her.

"I do not think that the abbot would abide that," she said.

"I do not think that you are fit for much further riding," he said. And he saw also the youth Ryn, who was shadow-eyed, and miserable; and he reckoned that pursuit would not look to find them here.

He reined the black in by the gate, for he remembered a guesthouse that was kept by the abbey, probably little used in winter, but it was there for such persons as were not acceptable within the holy walls.

He brought them there, asking no permission, taking them past the wondering eyes of the Brothers in the yard, and into the privacy of the house beyond its evergreen hedge. There he dismounted, and held up his hands to help Morgaine down as he might a lady: she tried awkwardly to accept his help, better suited to dismounting on her own, but her leg gave with her when she touched the ground, and she leaned upon his arm, thanking him with a weary nod and a look of her gray eyes.

"There is sanctuary here," he said. "It is the law. There will none touch us here, and if the place is surrounded . . . well, we will reckon with that when it happens."

She nodded again, plainly at the end of her strength, and a sorry three they were, she and the youth and a warrior so stiff with bruises and wounds that he could scarcely manage to climb the steps himself.

There were no other guests. He was thankful for that, and helped Morgaine to the first of the several cots, before he went out to tend the horses and bring Morgaine's gear into the room: she was concerned with that above all else, he knew, and she gave him a grateful look before she tucked the dreadful sword into her arms and sank down upon the bare mattress.

Ryn helped him with the horses, and carried all their gear and their saddles into the guesthouse; and afterward Ryn joined him in the stables and stood by with concern in his eyes as Vanye applied some of their cooking oil to the wound in the dun's rump.

"He will not go lame," Vanye judged. "It was an arrow mostly spent, and it is not the season for pests to infest the wound. Oil will ease it, but it will scar, I think."

Ryn walked with him back to the guesthouse, a short distance hence, among the tall pines and the hedge. The bells had fallen silent now, the Brothers filing in to their prayers.

There was a difference in Ryn. He did not quickly decide what it was, but that a boy had slung harp on his back and ridden after Morgaine from Ramorij; it was a tired, older youth that walked beside him in the daylight and observed things in silence. Ryn carried himself differently. He walked with a bearing as out of place in these pine-rimmed lanes as Vanye's own. They had ridden out of Baien-ei and he had ridden hindmost; there was a new hardness to his eye that had learned to reckon more than to wonder.

Vanye took account of that new silence in him, estimated it, clapped a weary hand upon his shoulder when they had come into the guesthouse. He lowered his voice, for Morgaine seemed asleep.

"I shall watch," Vanye said. "I am not good for long; yours is next, then hers."

The youth Ryn might have found some silly protest; he had been sullen at his father's orders when they first rode together into Morija. Now he nodded assent to that justice of things, and sought a bare cot himself, while Vanye took his sword and set himself on the front steps of the guesthouse, point set between his feet, hands gripping the quillons, head leaned against its hilt. In such position he could stay awake enough. In such a manner he had watched many a night on the road.

And considering himself then, he reflected wryly that he had seen such occupations of Morija's lower guesthall only when there was some marginally honorable hill-clan passing through, bound for other pastures and asking road-right. Some bandit chief asleep in the guesthouse, his men lounging about swilling cheap wine and scarring the furniture with their feet, while, seal upon the door, some man more villainous looking than the rest sat the steps as door-warden, sword in arms and a sour expression on his face, terrifying the boys who lurked to see what visitors had come among them.

It was a warning to other would-be guests that they would be mad to seek that shelter, and must look elsewhere. Villainy had possessed the only beds, and unless the lords in the hall would take arms and dispossess them, so it would remain until the morning.

So the Brothers found him.

He came fully awake at the first tread upon the flagstone walk, and sat there with his sword between his knees while the gray-robed Brothers came cautiously up to the steps with earthen jars of food.

They bowed, hands tucked in robes. Vanye recognized innocent courtesy when it was offered and made as profound a bow as he could from his seated posture.

"May we ask?" It was the traditional question. It could be refused. Vanye bowed again, full courtesy to the honest Brothers.

"We are outlaws," he said, "and I have stolen, and we have killed no few men in the direction from which we come: but none in Baien. We will not touch flock nor herd, nor field of yours, nor do violence to any of the house. We ask sanctuary."

"Are—" There was hesitance in the question, which was always asked, if questions were asked at the granting of sanctuary. "Are all among you true and human blood?"

Morgaine had not worn the hood when she rode in; and she was, in the white furs and with her coloring, very like the legends, one survivor of which had come to die a holy man at Baien-an.

"One of us may not be," he acknowledged, "but she avows at least she is not *qujal*." Their gentle eyes were much troubled at that answer; and perhaps through the legends they knew who and what she was, if sanity would let them believe it.

"We give shelter," they said, "to all that enter here under peace, even to those of tainted blood and those that company with them, if they should need it. We thank you for telling us. We will purify the house after you have gone. This was courtesy on your part, and we will respect your privacy. Are you a human man?"

"I am human born," he said, and returned their bows of farewell. "Brothers," he added when they began to turn away. They looked back, suntanned faces and gentle eyes and patient manner all one, as if one heart animated them. "Pray for me," he said; and then because some charity on his part was usually granted for that: "I have no alms to give you."

They bowed together. "That is of no account. We will pray for you," said one. And they went away.

The sunshine felt cold when they had done so. He could not sleep, and watched far beyond the time that he should have called Ryn to take his place. As last, when he was very weary, he went down the steps and gathered up the earthen jars and took them inside, letting Ryn replace him on the step.

Morgaine wakened. There was black bread and honey and salted butter, a crock of broth and another of boiled beans, which both were cooling, but wonderful to Morgaine, whose fare had been less delicate than his the last many days, he suspected; and he took Ryn his portion out upon the step, and the youth ate as if he were famished.

The Brothers brought down great armloads of hay and buckets of grain for their horses, which Vanye saw to, storing the grain in saddlebags against future need; and in the peace of the evening, with the sun headed toward the western mountains, Ryn sat in the little doorway and took his harp and played quiet songs, his sensitive fingers tuning and meddling with the strings in such a way that even that seemed pleasant. Some of the Brothers came down from the hill to stand by the gate and listen to the harper. Ryn smiled at them in an absent way. But they grew grave and sober-eyed when Morgaine appeared in the doorway; some blessed themselves in dread of her, and this seemed greatly to sadden her. She bowed them courtesy all the same, which most returned, and retired to the inner hearth, and the warmth of the fire.

"We must be out of this place tonight," she said when Vanye knelt there beside her.

He was surprised. "*Liyo,* there is no safer place for us to be."

"I am not looking for a refuge: my aim is Ivrel, and that is all. This is my order, Vanye."

"Aye," he said, and bowed. She looked at him when he straightened again and frowned.

"What is this?" she asked of him, and gestured toward the back of her own neck, and his hand lifted, encountered the ragged edge of his hair, and his face went hot.

"Do not ask me," he said.

"Thee is *ilin,*" she said, a tone that reproved such a shameful thing. And then: "Was it done, or did thee—?"

"It was my choice."

"What chanced in Ra-morij, between you and your brother?"

"Do you bid me tell you?"

Her lips tightened, her gray eyes bore into him, perhaps reading misery. "No," she said.

It was not like her to leave things unknown, where it might touch her safety. He acknowledged her trust, grateful for it, and settled against the warm stones of the hearth, listening to the harp, watching Ryn's rapt face silhouetted against the dying light, the pine-dotted hill beyond, the monastery and church with the bell-tower. This was beauty, earthly and not, the boy with the harp. The song paused briefly: a lock of hair fell across Ryn's face and he brushed it back, anchored it behind an ear. Not yet of the warriors, this youth, but about to be, when he made his choice. His honor, his pride, were both untouched.

The hands resumed their rippling play over the strings, quiet, pleasant songs, in tribute to the place, and to the Brothers, who listened.

Then the vesper bell sounded, drawing the gray lines of monks back into their holiness on the hill, and the light began to leave them quickly.

They finished the food the Brothers gave them, and gave themselves by turns to sleep for most of the night.

Then Morgaine, whose watch it was, shook them and bade them up and make ready.

The red line of dawn was appearing on the horizon.

They were quickly armed and the horses saddled, and Morgaine warmed herself a last time by the fire and looked about the room, seeming distressed. "I do not think that they would have any parting-gift of me," she said at last. "And there is nothing I have anyway."

"They bade us be free of the matter," Vanye assured her, and it was certain that his own gear was innocent of anything valuable to the Brothers.

Ryn searched his own things, took out a few coins and left them on the bed, a few pennies—it was all.

It was upon the road with the morning light still barely bringing color to things that Vanye remembered the harp, and did not find it about the person of Ryn.

There was instead only the bow slung from his shoulders, and he was strangely sorry for that. Later he saw Morgaine realize the same thing, and open her lips to speak; but she did not. It was Ryn's choice.

It was said by men of Baien that Baien-an was a fragment left from the making of Heaven. However that was, it was true that this place surpassed even Morija for fairness. Winter though it was, the golden grass and green cedar gave it grace, and the mighty range of Kath Vrej and Kath Svejur embraced the valley with great ridges crowned with snow. There was a straight road, with hedges beside it—one did not see hedges kept so anywhere else but in Baien—and twice they saw villages off the road, golden-thatched and somnolent in the wintry sun, with white flocks of sheep grazing near like errant clouds.

And once they must pass through a village, where children huddled wide-eyed at their mothers' skirts and men paused with their work in hand, as if they were held between rushing to arms or bidding them good day. Morgaine kept her hood upon her at that time, but if there was not the strangeness of her, riding astride and with the sword-sheath under her knee, there was Siptah himself, who had been foaled in this land, before all the great herd of king Tiffwy had been taken by Hjemur's bandits. Mischance had befallen them, and they had been seen no more: Baienen said that it was because they were the horses of kings, and would not carry the likes of their Hjemurn masters.

But perhaps the villagers blinked again in the sunlight, and persuaded themselves that they had no proper business with travelers going east: it was only those who came from it, out of Hjemur, that need trouble them to take arms; and there were gray horses foaled who were not of the old blood. Siptah had grown leaner; he was muddy about legs and belly; and he spent none of his strength on high-blooded skittishness, although his ears pricked up toward any chance move and his nostrils drank in every smell.

"*Liyo,*" said Vanye when they were quit of the town, "they will hear of us in Ra-baien by evening."

"By evening," she said, "surely we will be in those hills."

"If we had turned aside there, and sought welcome at Ra-baien," he insisted, "they might have taken you in."

"As they did in Ra-morij?" she answered him. "No. And I will accept no more delays."

"What is our haste?" he protested. "Lady, we are all tired, you not least of all. After a hundred years of delay, what is a day of rest? We should have stayed at the monastery."

"Are you fit to ride?"

"I am fit," he acknowledged, which was, under less compulsion, a lie. He ached, his bones ached, but he was well sure that she was in no better case, and shame kept him from pleading his own. She had that fever in her again, that burning compulsion toward Ivrel; he knew how it was to stand in the way of that, and if she would not be reasoned into delay, it was sure that there was little else would stop her.

Then, when the sun was at their backs, reddening into evening upon the snows of Kath Svejur before them, Vanye looked back along the road they had come as he did from time to time.

This time the thing he had constantly dreaded was there.

They were pursued.

"*Liyo,*" he said quietly. Both she and Ryn looked. Ryn's face was pale.

"They will surely have changed horses in Ra-baien," Ryn said.

"That is what I have feared," she said, "that there is no war nor feud between Morija and Baien."

And she put Siptah to a slightly quicker pace, but not to a run. Vanye looked back again. The riders were coming steadily, not killing their horses either, but at a better pace than they.

"We will make the hills and choose a place for them to overtake us as far as we can toward the border," said Morgaine. "This is a fight I do not want, but we may have it all the same."

Vanye looked back yet again. He began to be sure who it was, and there was a leaden feeling in his belly. He had already committed one fratricide. To fight and to kill at a liyo's order was the duty of an *ilin,* even if he were ordered against family. That was cruel, but it was also the law.

"They will be Nhi," he said to Ryn. "This fight is not lawful for you. You are not *ilin,* and until you lift hand against Erij and your kinsmen, you are not an outlaw. Go apart from us. Go home."

Ryn's young face held doubt. But it was a man's look too, not the petulance of a boy, which was not going to yield to his reason.

"Do as he tells you," Morgaine said.

"I take oath," he said, "that I will not."

That was the end of it. He was a free man, was Ryn; he rode what way he chose, and it was with them. It pained Vanye that Ryn had no more than the Honor blade at his belt, no longsword; but then, boys had no business to attempt the longsword in a battle; he was safest with the bow.

"Do you know this road?" Morgaine asked.

"Yes," said Vanye. "So do they. Follow."

He put himself in the lead, minded of a place within the hills, past the entry into Koris, where Erij might be less rash to follow, near as it was to Irien. The horses might be able to hold the pace, though it was climbing for some part. He cast a look over his shoulder, to know how things were with those behind.

The Morijin had fresh mounts surely, to press them so, grace of the lord of Ra-baien, and how much Baien knew of them or how Baien felt toward them was yet uncertain.

There was the matter of Baien's outpost of Kath Svejur, manned by a score of archers and no small number of cavalry. There was that to pass beneath.

He chose pace for them and held it, not leaving the highroad despite Morgaine's expressed preference for the open country.

They had speed to take them through, unless there were some connivance already arranged between Baien's lord and Erij—some courier passed at breakneck speed during the night, to cut off their retreat. He hoped that had not happened, that the pass was not sealed: otherwise there would be a hail of arrows, to match what rode behind them.

Those behind were willing enough to kill their mounts, that became certain; but there was the pass ahead of them, the little stone fort of Irn-Svejur high upon its crag.

"We cannot pass under that," Ryn protested, thinking, no doubt, of arrows. But Vanye whipped up his horse and tucked low, Morgaine likewise.

They were within arrowshot both from above and from behind. Doubtless in their fortress the guards looked down and saw the mad party on the road and wondered which was friend and which was foe: yet there was in both Morija and Baien that simple instruction that what rode east was friend, and what rode west was enemy; and here rode two bands madly eastward.

Vanye cast a look back as they won through. A rider left pursuing them to mount the trail to the fort. He breathed an oath into the wind, for there would be men of Irn-Svejur after them shortly, and Ryn's dun was faltering, dropping behind them.

Here, upon the open road and with precious scant cover, the cursed dun spelled end to their flight. Vanye began to pull in, where a bend of rock gave a little shelter before the brush began. Here he leaped down, bow and sword in hand, and let the black take what way he would down the road. Morgaine alighted into cover also, bearing *Changeling* in the one hand, and the black weapon at her belt, he doubted not. And breathlessly last came Ryn; he stayed to strike the dun and make it move, and the poor beast took an arrow then, reared up and crashed down, flailing with its hooves.

"Ryn!" Vanye roared, his voice cracked and hoarse, and Ryn came, stumbled in, his arm all bloody with the black stump of an arrow broken in the flesh. He could not flex to string the bow he carried, and it was useless. The riders pressed them, came in, close quarters—men of Nhi and Myya, and Erij with them.

Vanye ripped his longsword from its sheath, too late for other defenses; and he saw Morgaine do the same, but what she drew, he would not attempt to flank to protect her. The opal blade came to life, sucked arrows amiss, bent them up and otherwhere, and sent a man after them, screaming.

The winds howled within that vortex, the sword sure, a hand that knew it upon its hilt; and nothing touched them, nothing passed the web of shimmer that it wove. Through watery rippling he saw Erij's black and furious form. Erij pulled up, but some did not, and rushed toward nothingness.

And one was Nhi Paren, and another Nhi Eln, and Nhi Bren, spurring after.

"No!" Vanye cried, snatched at Ryn, who cried the same, and flung himself from cover, between blade and riders.

And ceased to be.

One instant Morgaine flung the blade aside, a saving reaction too late: her face bore horror—a rider thundered past, struck down at her, drove her stumbling aside.

Vanye cut at horse, dishonorable and desperate, tumbled beast, tumbled rider, and killed Nhi Bren, who had never done him harm. He whirled about then to see the red beam dropping beast and man indiscriminately, corpses and dying, writhing wounded. The mass of them that came reined back into better cover, still pursued by lancing fire that started conflagrations in the brush and in the grass—full twenty beasts and men lay stretched upon the road, the visible dead, and tongues of flame leaped up in the dry trees, whipped by the wind, *Changeling* still unsheathed in her right hand.

They fled, these others. Vanye saw with relief that Erij was among those that fled: though he knew that his brother had never run from anything, Erij fled now.

Vanye fell to his knees, leaned upon his sword's hilt, and gazed about at what they had wrought. Morgaine too stood still, the glimmer of *Changeling* dim in her hand now, still opal. She sought its sheath and it became like fine glass again, slipping into its natural home.

And so she rested, one hand upon the rock, until at last with a gesture like one grown old she felt her way back from that place and turned to look at him.

"Let us find the horses before they gather courage for another attack," she said. "Come, Vanye."

She did not weep. He gathered himself up, caught her, fearing that she would fall, for she walked like one that would; and he thought then that she would have tears, but she leaned against him only a moment, shivering.

"*Liyo,*" he pleaded with her, "they will not come back. Stay, let me go find the horses."

"No." She freed herself of him, returned the black weapon to her belt, tried to lift the strap of *Changeling* to her shoulder, and her hands trembled too much. He helped her with it. She accepted its weight, eased it on her shoulder, and cast one backward look, before she began with him to seek the way the horses had gone.

And, brush rustling, there were with them brown men, gray men, men in green and mottled; men of Chya, who placed themselves across their path. With the men was Taomen, and another and another that they had seen before: they were Chya of Ra-koris, and leading them, last to appear, was Roh.

The eyes of the master of Chya swept the road behind them, gazed with horror on the thing that they had done.

Then with a quiet gesture he called Taomen, and gave orders to him, and Taomen led the others away, back into the wood.

"Come," said Roh. "One of my men is holding your horses a little distance down the road. We knew them. It was they that brought us to help you, when we saw them bolt from this direction."

Morgaine looked at him, as if doubtful whether she would trust this man, though she had slept lately in his hall. Then she nodded and set out, unneedful now of Vanye's arm. He paused to clean his sword upon the grass before he overtook her: her blade needed no such attention.

It was indeed some distance. Men other than Roh walked with them all the same: there were rustlings in the forest about them, shadows whose nature they could not determine in the gathering dusk, but it was sure that they were Chya, or Roh would have been alarmed.

And there stood the horses, being tended and rubbed with dry grasses: the Chya were not riders, but they took tender care of the beasts, and Vanye for his part thanked the men when they took their animals back in hand. Then Morgaine thanked them too. He had thought her in such a mood she would not.

"May we camp with you?" Vanye asked of Roh, for the night was gathering fast about them and he was himself so weary he felt like to die.

"No," Morgaine interrupted him with finality. She slipped the strap of *Changeling*, and hung the weapon on her saddle, then gathered the reins about Siptah's neck.

"Liyo." Vanye seldom laid hands on her. Now he caught her arm and tried to plead with her, but the coldness in her eyes froze the words in his throat.

"I will come," he said quietly.

"Vanye."

"Liyo?"

"Why did Ryn choose to die?"

Vanye's lips trembled. "I do not think he knew he would. He thought he could stop you. He was not *ilin*, not under *ilin* law. One of the men was his lord, my brother. Another was Paren, his own father. Ryn was not *ilin*. He should have gone from us."

He thought then that Morgaine would show some sign of grief, of remorse, if it was in her. She did not. Her face stayed hard, and he turned from her lest he shame himself—from anger, no less than grief. Half-blind, he sought his horse's rein and flung himself to its back. Morgaine had mounted: she laid heels to Siptah and sped him down the road.

Roh held his rein a moment, looked up at him. "Chya Vanye, where does she go?"

"That is her concern, Chya Roh."

"We of Chya have both eyes and ears in Morija, well-placed. We knew how you must come if you came from Kursh into Andur. We waited, expected a fight. Not—*that.*"

"I am falling behind, Roh. Let go my rein."

*"Ilin-*oath is more than blood," said Roh. "But, Chya Vanye, they were kin to you."

"Let go, I say."

Roh's face drew taut with some weight of thought. Then he held the rein yet tightly, a hand within the bridle. "Take me up," he said. "I will see you to the edge of my lands, and I know you will not stay for a man afoot. I want no more mischances with Morgaine. You stirred us up Leth, and they are still aprowl; you brought us Nhi and Myya, and Hjemur at once; and now all Baien is astir. This woman brings wars like winter brings storms. I will see you safely through. My presence with you will be enough for any men of Chya you meet, and I will not have their lives taken as she took those of Nhi."

"Up, then," said Vanye, moving his foot from the stirrup. Roh was a slender man; his weight was still cruelty to the hard-ridden horse, but it was all that could be done. He feared to lose Morgaine if he were delayed more.

Roh landed behind him, caught hold, and Vanye set heels to the black. The horse tried a quick gait, could not hold it, settled at once to a slower pace when Vanye reined back in mercy.

Morgaine would not kill Siptah. He knew that when her fury had passed, she would slow. And after a time of riding he saw her, where the road became a mere trail through an arch of trees, a pale glimmering of Siptah's rump and her white cloak in the dark.

Then he put the black to a quicker pace, and she paused and waited when she heard his coming. The black weapon was in her hand as they rode up, but she put it away.

"Roh," she said.

There was moisture on her cheeks. Vanye saw it and was glad. He nodded courtesy to her, which she returned, and then she bit her lip and leaned both hands upon the saddlebow.

"We will camp," she said, sensible and calm, the manner Vanye knew in her, "in whatever place you can find secure."

↫ Chapter 9

Ivrel was all the horizon now, snow-crowned and perfect amid the jagged rubble of the Kath Vrej range, anomaly among mountains. The sky was blue and still stained with sunrise in the east, as much as they could see of the sky in that direction. A single star still remained high and to the left of Ivrel's cone.

It was beautiful, this place upon the north rim of Irien. It was hard to remember the evil of it.

"Another day," said Morgaine, "perhaps yet one more camp, will set us there." And when Vanye looked at her he saw no yearning in her eyes such as he had thought to see, only weariness and misery.

"Is it then Ivrel you seek?" Roh asked.

"Yes," she said. "As it always was." And she looked at him. "Chya Roh, this is the limit of Koris. We will bid you goodbye here. There is no need that you take us farther."

Roh frowned, looking up at her. "What is there that you have to gain at Ivrel?" he said. "What is it you are looking for?"

"I do not think that is here or there with us, Roh. Good-bye."

"No," he said harshly, and when she would have urged Siptah past, ignoring him: "I ask you, Morgaine kri Chya, by the welcome we gave you, I ask you. And if you ride past me I will follow you until I know what manner of thing I have helped, whether good or evil."

"I cannot tell you," she said. "Except that I will do no harm to Koris. I will close a Gate, and you will have seen the last of me. I have told you everything in that but you still do not understand. If I wished to leave you the means to raise another Thiye, I might pause to explain, but it would take too long and I should hate to leave that knowledge behind me."

Roh gazed up at her, no better comforted than before, and then turned his face toward Vanye. "Kinsman," he said, "will you take me up behind?"

"No," said Morgaine.

"I do not have her leave," Vanye said.

"You will slow us, Roh," said Morgaine, "and that could be trouble for us."

Roh thrust his hands into the back of his belt and scowled up at her. "Then I will follow," he said.

Morgaine turned Siptah for the northeast, and Vanye with heavy heart laid heels to his own horse, Roh trudging behind. Though they would go easily, wanting to spare the horses, they were passing beyond the bounds of Koris and of Chya, and there was no longer safety for Roh or for any man afoot. He could follow, until such time that they came under attack of beasts or men of Hjemur. Morgaine would let him die before she would let him delay her.

So must he. In a fight he dared not have his horse encumbered. In flight, his oath insisted he must keep to Morgaine's side, and he could not do that carrying double, nor risk tiring the horse before the hour of her need.

"Roh," he pleaded with his cousin, "it will be the end of you."

Roh did not answer him, but hitched his gear to a more comfortable position on his shoulder, and walked. Being Chya-reared, Roh would be able to walk for considerable distances and at considerable pace, but Roh must know also that he stood almost certainly to lose his life.

Had it been his own decision, Vanye thought, he would have ridden far ahead at full gallop, so that Roh must realize that he could not keep up and abandon this madness; but it was not his to decide. Morgaine walked her horse.

That was the pace she set; and at noon rest Roh was able to overtake them and share food with them—this grace she granted without stinting; but he fell behind again when they set out.

But for knowing where they were, the land was still fair for some considerable distance; but when pines began to take the place of lowland trees, and they climbed into snowy ground, then Vanye suffered for Roh and looked back often to see how he fared.

"*Liyo,*" he said then, "let me get off and walk a time, and he will ride. That can tire the horse no more."

"His choice to come was his affair," she said. "If trouble comes on us unexpectedly, I want you, not him, beside me. No. Thee will not."

"Do you not trust him, *liyo*? We slept in Ra-koris in his keeping, and there was chance enough for him to do us harm."

"That is so," she said, "and of men in Andur-Kursh, I trust Roh next to you; but thee knows how little trust I have to extend; and I have less of charity."

And then he fell to thinking of the night and day ahead, which he had yet to serve, and that she had said that she would die. That saddened him, so that for a time he did not think of Roh, but reckoned that there was something weighing on her mind.

She spoke of the same matter, late in the afternoon, when the horses had struck easier going along a ridge. Crusted snow cracked under them, and their breath hung in frosty puffs even in sunlight, but it was an easy place after the rocks and ice that they had passed.

"Vanye," she said, "thee will find it difficult to pass from Hjemur after I am gone. It would be best if thee had a place to go to. What will thee do? Nhi Erij will not forgive thee for what I have done."

"I do not know what I will do," he said miserably. "There is Chya, there is still Chya, if only Roh and I both come through this alive."

"I wish thee well," she said softly.

"Must you die?" he asked her.

Her gray eyes went strangely gentle. "If I have the choice," she said, "I shall not. But if I do, then thee is not free. Thee knows what thee has to do: kill Thiye. And perhaps then Roh might serve thee well: so I let him follow. But if I live, all the same, I shall pass the Gate of Ivrel, and in passing, close it. Then there will be an end of Thiye all the same. When Ivrel closes, all the Gates in this world must die. And without the Gates, Thiye cannot sustain his unnatural life: he will live until this body fails him, and be unable to take another. So also with Liell, and with every evil thing that survives by means of the Gates."

"And what of you?"

She lifted her shoulders and let them fall. "I do not know where I shall be. Another place. Or scattered, as the men were at Kath Svejur. I shall not know until I pass the Gate where can make it take me. That is my task, to seal Gates. I shall go until there are no more—and I shall not know that, I fear, until I step out the last one and find nothing there."

He tried to grasp the thing she told him, could not imagine, and shivered. He did not know what to say to her, because he did not know what it meant.

"Vanye," she said, "you have drawn *Changeling*. You have a proper fear of it."

"Aye," he acknowledged. Loathing was in his voice. Her gray eyes reckoned him up and down, and she cast a quick look over her shoulder at Roh's distant figure.

"I will tell thee," she said softly, "if something befall me, it could be that thee would need to know. Thee does not need to read what is written on the blade. But it is the key. Chan wrote it upon the blade for fear that all of us would die, or that it would come to another generation of us—hoping that with that, Ivrel still might be sealed. It is to be used at Ra-hjemur, if thee must: its field directed at its own source of power would effect the ruin of all the Gates here. Or cast back within the Gate itself, the true Gate, it would be the same: unsheath it and hurl it through. Either way would be sufficient."

"What are the writings on it?"

"Enough that could give any able to read them more knowledge of Gates than I would wish to have known. That is why I carry it so close. It is indestructible save by Gates. I dare not leave it. I dare not destroy it. Chan was mad to have made such a thing. It was too great a chance. We all warned him that *qujalin* knowledge was not for us to use. But it is made, and it cannot be unmade."

"Save by the Witchfires themselves."

"Save by that."

And after they had ridden a distance: "Vanye. Thee is a brave man. I owe it to thee to tell thee plainly: if thee uses *Changeling*, as I have told thee to do, thee will die."

The cold seeped inward, self-knowledge. "I am not a brave man, *liyo*."

"I think otherwise. Can thee hold the oath?"

He gathered the threads of his thoughts, scattered and snarled for a moment with the knowledge she had given him. He was strangely calm-then, what he had known from the beginning settling into place as it ought to be.

"I will hold to it," he said.

"He is coming," said Vanye with relief. Snow crunched underfoot beyond the place where they had stopped to wait, around the bend of the trees and the hillside. It was dark. Snow lit by the stars was all about them, bright save in the shadow of the pines. They had lost sight of Roh for a time. "Let me ride back to him."

"Hold where you are," she said. "If it is Roh, he will arrive all the same."

And eventually, a mere shadow among the barred shadows of the pines on the lower slope, there trudged Roh, stumbling with weariness.

"Ride down to him," said Morgaine then, the only grace she had shown the bowman for his efforts.

Vanye did so gladly, met Roh halfway down the hill and drew his horse to a halt, offering stirrup and hand.

Roh's face was drawn, his lips parted and the frosted air coming in great raw gasps. For a moment Vanye did not think that Roh would accept any kindness of him now: there was anger there. But he dismounted and helped his cousin up, and rose into the saddle after. Roh slumped against him. He urged the horse uphill at a walk, for the air grew thin here, and hurt the lungs.

"This is a proper place for a camp," said Morgaine when they joined her. "It is defensible." She indicated a place of rocks and brush, and it was true: however acquired, Morgaine had an eye to such things.

"Surely," said Vanye, "we had better do without the fire tonight."

"I think it would be wise," she agreed. She slid down, shouldered the strap of *Changeling*, and began to undo her saddle. Siptah pawed disconsolately at the frozen earth. There was still grain left from the supply the Brothers had given them; there was food left too. It would not be a bitter camp, compared to others they had spent near Aenor-Pyvvn.

Vanye let Roh slide to the ground, and slid down after. The bowman fell, began at once to try to gather himself up, but Vanye knelt beside him and offered him drink, unfrozen, the flask carried next the horse's warmth. Then he began to chafe warmth into the man. There was danger of freezing in his extremities, particularly in his feet. Roh was not dressed for this.

Morgaine silently bent and exchanged her cloak for Roh's, and the bowman nodded gratitude, his eyes fixed on her with thanks and anger so mingled in him that it was hard to know which prevailed.

They fed the horses and ate, which warmed them. There was little spoken. Perhaps there would have been, had Roh not been there; but Morgaine was not in the mood for speech.

"Why?" Roh asked, his voice almost inaudible from cold. "Why do you insist to go to this place?"

"That is the same question you asked before," she said.

"I have not yet had it answered."

"Then I cannot answer it to your satisfaction," she said.

And she held out Roh's cloak to him, and took her own again, and went over to a rock where there was shelter from the wind. There she slept, *Changeling* in her arms as always.

"Sleep," said Vanye then to Roh.

"I am too cold," said Roh; which complaint Vanye felt with a pang of conscience, and looked at him apologetically. Roh was silent a time, his face drawn in misery and fatigue, his limbs huddled within his thin cloak. "I think—" Roh's voice was hoarse, hardly audible. "I think that I shall die on this road."

"It is only another day more," Vanye tried to encourage him. "Only one day, Roh. You can last that."

"It may be." Roh let his arms fall forward on his knees and bowed his head upon them, lifting his head after a moment, his eyes sunk in shadow. "Cousin. Vanye, for kinship's sake answer me. What is it she is after, so terrible she cannot have me know it?"

"It is nothing that threatens Chya or Koris."

"Are you sure enough to take oath on that?"

"Roh," Vanye pleaded, "do not keep pressing me. I cannot keep answering question and question and question. I know what you would do, to have me defend my way step by step into answering you as you wish, and I will not, Roh. Enough. Leave the matter."

"I think that you yourself do not know," said Roh.

"Enough. Roh, if things go amiss at Ivrel, then I will tell you all that I do know. But until that time, I am bound to remain silent. Go to sleep, Roh. Go to sleep."

Roh sat a time with his arms folded again about him and his knees drawn up, plunged in thought, and at last shook his head. "I cannot sleep. My bones are still frozen through. I will stay awake a little while. Go and sleep yourself. My oath I will see you take no harm."

"I have an oath of my own," said Vanye, though he was bone-weary and his eyes were heavy. "She did not give me leave to trade my watch to you."

"Must she give you leave in everything, kinsman?" Roh's eyes were kind, his voice gentle as a brother's ought to be. It recalled a night in Ra-koris, when they had sat together at the hearth, and Roh had bidden him return someday to Chya.

"That is the way of the thing I swore to her."

But after an hour or more, the forest still, the weight of the long ride and days of riding and sleeplessness before began to settle heavily upon him. He had a dark moment, jerked awake to find a shadow by him, Roh's hand on his shoulder. He almost cried out, stifled that outcry as he realized in the same instant that it was only Roh, waking him.

"Cousin, you are spent. I tell you that I will take your watch."

It was reasonable. It was sensible.

He heard in his mind what Morgaine would say to such a thing. "No," he said wearily. "It is her time to watch. Rest. I will move about a while. If that will not wake me, then she will wake and take the watch. I have no leave to do otherwise."

He rose, stumbled a little in the action, his legs that numb with exhaustion and cold. He thought Roh meant to help him.

Then pain crashed through his skull. He reached out hands to keep himself from falling, hit, lost most senses; then the weight hit his skull a second and third time, and he went down into dark.

Cords bound him. He was chilled and numb along his body, where he had been lying on his face. It was almost all that he could do to struggle to his knees, and he did so blindly, fearing another assault upon the instant. He turned upon one knee, saw a heap of white that was Morgaine—Roh, standing over her with *Changeling*, sheathed, in his hands.

"Roh!" Vanye called aloud, breaking the stillness. Morgaine did not stir at the sound, which sent a chill of fear through him, sent him stumbling to his feet. Roh held the sword as if he would draw it, threatening him.

"Roh," Vanye pleaded hoarsely. "Roh, what have you done?"

"She?" Roh looked down, standing as he was above Morgaine's prostrate form. "She is well enough, the same as you. An aching head when she wakes. But you will not treat me as you have, Chya Vanye—as she has. I have the right to know what I sheltered in my hall, and this time you will give me answer. If I am satisfied, I will let you both go and cast myself on your forgiveness, and if I am not, I do swear it, cousin, I will take these cursed things and cast them where they cannot be found, and leave you for Hjemur and the wolves to deal with."

"Roh, you are vain and a madman. And honorless to do this thing."

"If you are honest," said Roh, "and if she is, then you have your right to outrage. I will admit it. But this is not for pride's sake. Thiye is enough. I want no more Irien, no more wars of *qujal*, no more of the like of Hjemur. And I do think that we are safer with Thiye alone than with Thiye and an enemy let loose to our north. *We* are the ones who die in their wars. I gave her help, would have defended her at Kath Svejur had she needed it. I would have helped her, kinsman. But she has treated me as an enemy, as a cast-off servant. I think that is all we in Koris will ever be in her mind. She treats free men as she treats you, who have to be content; and maybe you are content with that, maybe you enjoy your station with her, but I do not."

"You are mad," Vanye said, came forward a step nearer than Roh wished: Roh's hands drew *Changeling* partway from the sheath.

"Put it down!" Vanye hissed urgently. "No, do not draw that thing."

Then Roh saw the nature of the thing he held, and looked apt to drop it upon the instant: but he rammed it safely into its sheath again, and cast it in abhorrence across the snow.

"*Qujalin* weapons and *qujalin* wars," Roh exclaimed in disgust. "Koris has suffered enough of them, kinsman."

Morgaine was stirring to wakefulness. She came up of a sudden, hands bound, nearly fell. Roh caught her, and had he been rough with her, Vanye would have hurled himself on Roh as he was. But Roh adjusted her cloak about her and helped her sit, albeit he looked far from glad to touch her.

Morgaine for her part looked dazed, cast a glance at Vanye that did not even accuse: she seemed bewildered, and no little frightened. That struck him to the heart, that he had served her no better than this.

"*Liyo,*" Vanye said to her, "this kinsman of mine took me from behind; and I do not think he is an evil man, but he is a great idiot."

"Get apart," said Roh to him. "I have had what words I will have with you. Now I will ask her."

"Let me go," said Morgaine, "and I will not remember this against you."

But there was a sound intruding upon them, soft at first, under the limit of hearing, then from all sides, the soft crunch of snow underfoot. It came with increasing frequency about them.

"Roh!" Vanye cried in anguish, hurled himself across the snow toward the place where *Changeling* lay.

Then dark bodies were upon them, men that snarled like beasts, and Roh went down beneath them, mauled under a black flood of them, and the tide rushed over Vanye, hands closed upon his legs. He twisted over onto his back, kicked one of them into writhing pain, and was pinned, held about his knees. Cord bit into his ankles, ending all hope of struggle.

They let him alone then, to try to wrench himself up to his knees, laughing when he failed twice and fell. On his third effort he succeeded, gasping for air, and glowered into their bearded faces.

They were not Hjemurn, or of Chya.

Men of Leth, the bandits from the back of the hall: he recognized the roughest of them.

There was quiet for a moment. He had had most of the wind knocked from him, and bent over a little to try to breathe, lifted his head again to keep a wary eye upon their captors.

They were prodding at Roh, trying to force him to consciousness. Morgaine they let alone, she with ankles bound the same as he, and now with her back to a rock, glaring at them with the warmth of a she-wolf.

One of the bandits had *Changeling* in hand, drew it partway, Morgaine watching with interest, as if in her heart she urged the man on in ignorance.

But riders were coming up the hill. The sword slammed into its sheath, in guilty hands. The bandits stood and waited, while men on horses came onto the hill into the clearing, horses blowing frost in the starlight.

"Well done," said Chya Liell.

He dismounted and looked about the clearing, and one presented to him the things that had been taken, all of Morgaine's gear; and *Changeling*, which Liell received into respectful and eager hands.

"Chan's," he said, and to Morgaine paid an ironic bow. He considered Roh, half-conscious now, laughed in pleasure, for he and the young lord of Chya were old enemies.

And then he came to Vanye, and while Vanye shuddered with disgust knelt down by him and smiled a faithless smile, lordly-wise, placed a hand upon his shoulder like some old friend, and all too possessively. "*Ilin* Nhi Vanye i Chya," he said softly. "Are you well, Nhi Vanye?"

Vanye would have spit at him: it was the only recourse he had left; but his mouth was too dry. He had a Lethen's hand in his collar behind, holding him so that he was half-choking; he could not even flinch, and Liell's gentle fingers touched and brushed at a sore place on his temple.

"Be careful with him," said Liell then to the Lethen. "Any damage or discomfort he suffers will be mine shortly, and I will repay it."

And to those about them:

"Set them on horses. We have a ride to make."

The day sank toward dark again, reddening the snows that stretched unmarred in front of them. They moved slowly, because of those on foot, and because of the thinner air. Liell rode first. He had taken back his own black horse and his gear. *Changeling* hung from his saddle, beneath his knee.

Several Lethen riders were between him and Morgaine, and two men afoot led Siptah, as two led also the horse they had borrowed for Roh, who had no strength to walk; and the black mare that Vanye rode was Liell's grace, personal, offered with cynical courtesy—exchange of the mare for the one he had stolen.

And bound as he was, hands behind, even feet bound securely by ropes under the mare's ribs, he could not even stretch his legs against the torment of the long ride, much less be aid to Morgaine. She and Roh were in no better case. Roh hung in the saddle much of the time, giving the appearance of a man who would as likely collapse and fall if the cords let him. Morgaine at least seemed unhurt, though he could guess the torment there was in her mind.

Liell was *qujal* and knew the ancient science. Perhaps he could even read the runes of *Changeling*, and then Thiye, whom Morgaine had called ignorant, a meddler in sciences, would have a rival he could not withstand.

They came among trees again, pines, rough brush, sometime outcroppings of black rock. And the trees began to be twisted and stunted things, writhing out of all true shape for their kind. Bare limbs held tufts of sickly needles, bare trunks described horrid, frozen evolutions.

And in the snow they saw a dead dragon.

At least so it seemed to be—an object leathery and twisted, and the horses shied from it. It was monstrous, frozen in its death throes so that it was yet less lovely. One membranous wing was half unfolded, stiff and stark. The other side was bare bone, taken by other beasts.

The Lethen described a wide path about that corpse. Vanye stared back at the thing as they passed and the bile rose in his throat.

Other things they saw dead too. Most were small. One resembled a man, but the wolves had had it.

The light faded in this place of evil. They moved among the twisted pines in twilight, and went carefully. Men had bows ready, eyes constantly scanning the forest.

Then the trees thinned out, quite abruptly. Upon the great shoulder of the mountain was a lesser rise, and upon that were broken pillars, fair-colored, rune-graven, out of place among the black rocks of Ivrel's cone.

And the Gate.

It was vast, unlike that of Aenor-Pyvvn or Leth at Domen: metal uncorroded by the years, casting a web of shimmer that had depth, stars winking in a black arch against the twilit white side of Ivrel. The air here worked at the nerves. The horses fought to shy off—men that rode dismounted, and prepared to wait.

Morgaine was helped down first, her ankles freed, and she was made fast against one of the few twisted pines that grew this near the Gate. Next Roh was similarly treated, though he strove to fight them. Finally Vanye was lifted down, and he thought that they would do the same with him, but instead Liell ordered him brought forward in the line.

He kicked a man, threw him to the ground writhing in pain, and a Lethen hit him, kicked him down and laid a quirt to him: Vanye tucked down against the blows, unhurt by reason of the mail, save where the quirt hit neck or hands.

And of a sudden Liell was by him, cursing the man, other Lethen hauling Vanye up, and the man that had struck him cringed away.

"No hand on him!" Liell said. "No harm to him. I will kill the man that puts a mark on him." And carefully he unlaced the cloak from Vanye, and gave it to a man, walked all about him, full circle. Then he made to lay hands on him and Vanye flinched back, constrained to bear it in patience while Liell gently probed bones, as if to see whether they were sound or no. In bitter humor he cherished the ache in his skull, the worse pain in his legs and joints where the ride bound to the saddle had bruised him—his only revenge on Liell. It was a sorry, sad thing, he thought of a sudden, that he had been taken so easily, and it was no comfort at all that Roh was about to pay dearly for his idiocy.

And by that time, there would be nothing left of Nhi Vanye, though his body would continue to move and live, housing for Liell-Zri, which would take revenge upon Roh, upon Morgaine.

That image struck him as Liell began to climb that last distance, and they began to force him up the long barren slope. It took from him what courage he had left, such that he would have fallen if not for the men on either side of him. He stumbled on the loose rocks, Liell striding surefootedly beside him, up in that clear place where air cut at the lungs like the edge of ice. There was only the Gate above them, and the stars within, and wind that gently sucked at them, aiming into that gulf.

It grew as they walked, until there was no more sky. The Lethen with them balked, and Vanye thought for one wild soaring moment that they would lose their courage and fail to hold him. But Liell cursed them and threatened them, and they drew him up and up, until they stood swaying in that awesome wind, poised upon a level place near the Gate.

There Liell bade them unbind his hands and hold him fast: "I will not enter an impaired shelter," he said. And this they did, but held his numb arms and strengthless wrists still wrenched behind him with such cruel force that he could not struggle free. He stared up into that great gulf, dizzied, faltered and lost his balance even standing still.

"How is it done?" he asked of Liell. He did not want to know, but his courage was never proof against the unknown: he feared that he would shame himself at the last, crying out, if he did not know. He knew Morgaine's things, that there were laws and realities that governed them; he insisted to believe so even in this.

"It is less pleasant for me than for you," said Liell. "I must ruin this present body of mine, enough to die; but you—you will only seem to fall for a moment. You will never reach bottom. Do not fear; you will not suffer."

Liell knew his fear and mocked him with it. Vanye set his lips and forbore to say anything, head bowed.

"Those companions of yours," Liell said. "Have you fondness for them?"

"Yes," he said.

Liell's lips made a slight smile, which his eyes did not share. "As for Chya Roh, that is an old and personal matter, which I shall enjoy settling. That which you are about to bequeath me is well capable of handling the lord of Chya, of claiming what he rules, by the blood you share; and claiming Morija too. You never appreciated your heredity as I do. And do not fear so much for Morgaine. Without her weapons she is harmless, and she has knowledge that will be of great interest to me. And in other ways, with your youth, she is of interest. Flis is tiresome."

Vanye made a sound like spitting, at which Liell was neither amused nor troubled, and they began to climb again. He balked, had his arms painfully wrenched, and gave up resistance, lost in what loomed over them.

Dark was all their vision now, stars more numerous than shone in the sky, clouds upon clouds of stars. The air was dead. It numbed. The vision seemed about to drink them into that shimmering nothing—though they climbed, it seemed a pit, a downward plunge into which one could fall and fall, and that they leaned impossibly above it. The mountain on which they walked seemed out of proper alignment with earth. The wind skirled about them, maleficent and voiced, humming with power, blurring senses.

Liell reached the Gate and touched its arch; his fingers moved upon it, and all at once there was utter dark within the Gate. The wind ceased. The humming altered its tone, higher pitched. The opalescence of *Changeling* itself burst and coruscated within the arch, flung light at them.

The Lethen faltered. Vanye spun, flung himself downslope, lost footing and slid, brought up against a level place and staggered to his feet, dazed, blinded, aware of shouting ahead and behind in the gathering dark.

Out, was the only thing his senses grasped at the moment; and hard upon that single light of reason: *Morgaine.*

He could not help her. They would have a dozen men upon him before he could free her.

Changeling.

He ran, sliding, mail-protected, but leaving skin of his hands on rocks, battering himself in one spill and another. Men tried to head him off at the bottom. He gasped air, spun left, veering off from Morgaine and Roh, scattering horses as he fled. Then there was the familiar black before him: he vaulted for the saddle, shied the beast and clung, clawed his way firmly into the saddle and caught the flying reins. The beast knew him, gathered himself and sprang forward under his guidance.

Riders were already starting after him. Tumult and shouting were in his wake, though no arrows flew. He did not even seek the hill, to brave that weight of air, that awful climb, not with pursuit and enemies and a frightened horse to confound matters. He headed back along their trail.

If the Gate were barred to him, there was still Ra-hjemur, where Thiye ruled. There was *Changeling* under his knee, its dragon-hilt familiar to his anxious fingers. With that in hand and the power of the Gate to feed it, he could force his way to the heart of Thiye's power, destroy its source, whatever it was, destroy the Gate—destroy himself and Morgaine too, he knew.

And Liell.

The world had not yet seen what Liell could do with the power of Morgaine added to his own. Thiye was small compared to that evil.

He rode the horse without mercy, whipped the poor beast down snowy slopes and across trails and down, doing all he could to clear Ivrel.

Even Liell must have care of him now. Even Morgaine's other weapons were nothing to the power of the opal blade, that drank attack and cast it elsewhere, that drank lives and cast them into nothing. And armed as he was, with that power in his hands, it was madness to kill the horse that was his best hope of reaching Hjemur: he came to his senses when he had cleared the steepest portion of the road, and come to the main trail. There he slowed his pace at last, let the horse breathe.

Around the limb of the lower slope the main road led, bending toward Rahjemur. It must be. There was no other place in Hjemur that could even boast a road.

He kept the horse to a holding pace. Lethen might be reluctant to follow, but Liell would drive them to it—timid as Morgaine avowed herself to be, able to spend others' lives before her own, she was capable of fearful risks when it became necessary; and Liell surely would prove no different: when caution would not serve, then there would be nothing reserved, nothing. When Liell knew finally that the Gates themselves were at stake, he would surely follow. The only hope was that he had yet to understand what *Changeling* was, or that a Morij *ilin* might understand what had to be done with the blade.

A shadow thundered out at him. The black screamed shrilly and shied, and an impact hit his shoulder, tumbling him inexorably over the black's rump, head over heels, and into snow and hard ice.

Joints moved, bones unbroken, but shaken; he tried to gain command of his battered limbs and move, but a shortsword pressed under his chin, forcing his head down again into the numbing snow. A body hovered over him, the arm that rested across the figure's knee ending abruptly.

"Brother," said Erij, whispering.

⌁ Chapter 10

"Erij." Vanye tried a second time to rise, and in a sudden move Erij moved back and let him. Then he snapped the Honor blade back into his belt and stalked up the road a space where his horse stood, along with Vanye's black.

Vanye stumbled up from the ditch, limping, trying vainly to overtake him and prevent him, saw to his dismay that Erij had already found what the black horse bore on its saddle.

A fierce grin spread over Erij's face as he took the sheathed blade in hand,

and with the sheath in the crook of his arm and his hand upon its hilt, he waited Vanye's coming.

Vanye stopped short of the threat he posed him, still shaking in all his limbs, trying to gather his breath and his wits and frame some reasonable argument.

"There is a *qujal* out of Leth," he began, his voice hardly audible. "Erij, Erij, there are Lethen and the devil himself behind me. We are both in danger. I will go with you clear of this road—not try at escape, at least that far. I swear, I swear it, Erij."

Erij considered, his dark eyes fluid in the dark. Then he nodded abrupt decision, hooked the sheath of *Changeling* to his own belt—one-handed as he was, he wore it at his hip, not his back—and swung up to mount.

Vanye hauled his aching body into the saddle on a second effort, sent the black galloping down the road in Erij's company, down side trails into forest, though at every turn the forest looked more ominous in itself. The horses went at a careful pace now, wending their way down into rocky ground. Here were still patches of snow in which to leave prints, but brush and woods were so thick that pursuit of them could not be easy for any group of men, and their trail was somewhat obscured. It held no feeling of safety, this place—rather, the same kind of queasiness that all of Erij's ambushes had held, from boyhood up, screaming alarm, such that he thought, like another dream by Aenor-Pyvvn, that he might have ridden this place in some bad dream, wherein he had died. The trees, the rocks etched themselves into his sight, his senses clinging to them as strongly as fingers might cling to some last handhold on solidity. *I am losing these,* he thought, and: *I am mad to go with him like this.* But he had no strength left, and Erij held *Changeling*, held his duty as *ilin* to hostage: Erij could reason, could be reasoned with—his hope insisted so.

Then, in a clear place among the trees, Erij reined in and ordered him down.

Panic struck him. Almost he did lay heels to the horse. But he found himself climbing down, careful of strained knees as he caught his balance on the ground. He moved out uncertainly as Erij motioned him to the center of the clearing.

"Where is she?" Erij asked then, and as he asked, climbed down, and unhooked the sheath of *Changeling*.

Then he knew of a certainty that Erij meant to kill him when he had answered; and *Changeling* slipped inexorably from its sheath, Erij knowing the nature of the blade now, well able to wield it.

Vanye hurled himself at Erij waist-high, grappled and came down with him, *Changeling* falling still sheathed.

Erij's elbow crashed into his face, blinding him. Vanye was suddenly underneath again, losing, as he had always lost, as it had always been with his brothers. He could not see, could not breathe, could not feel for a moment. With his last effort he heaved over and clung, fighting only for leverage. Then his hands were slamming Erij's head into the snowy ground, again and again, until Erij's limbs weakened and ceased to struggle. He scrambled up to find *Changeling*, his mind next clearing as he reached his horse, holding the sword-sheath, groping blindly for the reins.

The horse shied. Erij's rush carried into his lower back, hurling him, stunned, almost under the hooves. *Changeling* flew from his nerveless fingers, beyond reach, and when he struggled after it, Erij kicked him over by the shoulder. He came halfway up, staggered, and met Erij's fist, which laid him backward into the snow. Then Erij fell upon him with a knee upon his chest and his maimed arm still strong enough to strike his arm aside: Erij ripped the Honor blade from his belt and slipped it within the throat-laces of his armor, cutting down the thongs like so much rotten thread.

"A third of Nhi died at Irn-Svejur," Erij gasped at him, hoarse and out of breath. "Your doing—and hers. Where is she?"

Vanye swallowed against the blade's pressure, unable to answer. He fought instinctively to breathe and froze, trembling with the effort, when he felt moisture trickling down the sides of his neck. Raw pain rode on the edge of the blade as it eased slightly.

"Answer me," Erij hissed.

"Leth." He moved an arm as heavy as his whole body ought to be, ceased. "*Qujal*—men from Leth caught her—to make her give them what she knows. Erij—Erij, no, do not kill me. They will have her knowledge—theirs—Thiye's—together—against us."

The pressure eased altogether, but it was there. The faint hope there was of Erij's interest sent the sweat coursing over him, Erij's knee hampered his breathing: he felt himself losing touch with his senses again, dizzied and numb. "And you, bastard?" Erij asked him. "What are you doing loose and alone?"

"Hjemur—the source. That can stop them. I am to kill Thiye—take Ra-hjemur. Erij, let me go."

"Bastard, I have chased you from Irn-Svejur. The others had no stomach for Hjemur's territory and Morgaine's weapons, but I swore to them that I would go where I had to go to bring back your head. I would bring back the whole of you alive, but one-handed as I am, I know I cannot manage that. For Nhi and for Myya, for San and Torin—most especially for Nhi and its dead, I will do this thing, and then find how to put this gift you have given me to best use. I have no enemies I need fear so long as I wield that. If it would bring you safely to Ra-hjemur, then it could bring me there too."

"Go with me there, then."

"I offered you the chance of sharing power once, bastard, and I meant it; but you loved the witch more than you loved Morija, enough to kill Nhi for her."

"Erij, you know at least that I will not break an oath. Help me—to Ra-hjemur. Now. Before our enemy takes it. Let me have my revenge on Thiye—for Morgaine; on the *qujal* too if I can. I am speaking sense, Erij. Listen to me. There are weapons in Ra-hjemur, surely—and if our enemy lays hands on them, even holding *Changeling* might not be enough to take the citadel. Do this. Come with me. That is my oath to her—to deal with Thiye. After that, anything that is between us will be between us, and I will not cry foul at anything."

Erij's shadowed eyes took on a narrow, reckoning look. "You were condemned to be *ilin* by our father's law, for Kandrys; and you will be clean of that if I listen to you. But you have me yet to satisfy. Suppose I were to sentence you to another year."

"I would think that was too slight a thing to satisfy you."

"Swear," said Erij, "by that oath you regard with her, that you will stay for Claiming by me, no treachery, no aid from her if she should somehow live. And that will not be a year that you will thank me for, Chya bastard, and it will not stop me from turning you over to the kinsmen of Paren and Bren when it is finished. But if it is worth the price to you, I will refrain from cutting your throat here and now. I will even go with you to Ra-hjemur. Is that the way you want it, bastard? Will you pay that?"

"Yes," Vanye said without hesitating; but Erij's blade still rested under his chin.

"And I will wager," said Erij, "that you know the use of the sword and that you know the witch herself better than any now living. If taking Hjemur purges you of her—that being the service she named for you, and not merely a year—then let us agree, my brother, that when Hjemur falls, it is mine, and you are mine—from that moment. And you will not speak of this oath of ours—not to her, not to Thiye, not to anyone."

He saw the trap then, which Erij wove for Morgaine, treachery suspecting treachery in everyone, and admired the cunning of the man: Myya to the heart, thinking of all possibilities save one—that neither of them would survive the taking of Hjemur.

He did not like the oath: it was woven too tightly.

"I will agree," he said.

"And upon your soul you will not betray me," Erij said. "You will hand me Hjemur and hand me Thiye and the witch and this *qujal* himself."

"As many as live," Vanye agreed.

"That you will not desert me or raise hand against me before then."

"I agree."

"Your hand," said Erij.

It was not right to do: by *ilin*-law he ought not to yield another oath, and any crossing of the two obligations was on his soul, his own fault; but Erij insisted, and he yielded up his hand and clenched his teeth as Erij drew the black across the palm. Then Erij touched it with his mouth, and Vanye likewise, spat blood into the snow. It was not Claiming, for there was no signing with it, but it was an oath and a binding one, and when Erij released him to get to his feet, he knelt clenching numbing snow in his fist as he had knelt once in a cave in Aenor-Pyvvn, shaking this time in utter misery, such that his senses threatened to leave him.

The *liyo* he served could by rights curse his soul to perdition; he had yielded his brother the same right. And yet he knew that he would have mercy of Morgaine, and none at all of Erij. He knew his *liyo*, that though she was cruel in other ways, she would not curse him; and that knowledge of her perversely made him sure which oath he would follow.

And kill his brother, as he had killed a third of Nhi.

He had done this for his *liyo*, serving her: *ilin*-oath had bound him, and he had killed kinsmen. There had seemed no worse act that he could be drawn to commit.

Until this, that he oath-broke, and murdered his brother by his silence.

I owe it to thee to tell thee plainly; if thee uses Changeling *as I have told thee to do—thee will die.*

Changeling was not selective in its destructions.

"Come, on your feet," said Erij. He hooked the blade to his saddle-harness, displacing his own to the useless right-hand fastenings. Then he gathered reins and climbed up, waiting for him.

Vanye gathered himself up and sought the black, who stood, reins dangling, some distance away across the clearing. He set foot in the stirrup and rose into the saddle with a wince of strained muscles.

"You are guide," said Erij. "Lead. And be mindful of your oath."

He retraced the way that they had come, then cut north, aiming to come out upon the highroad at a different place than they had left it. When they had it in sight among the trees he was relieved to see that there were as yet no tracks marring the snow.

Only as they came out into the open road, something fluttered through the trees, alarmed by their passing—a rapid clap of wings in the dark. Erij stared after it with hate in his face, the honest loathing of a human man for things that frequented these woods.

Vanye had even ceased to shudder at such things. He set a good pace, reckoning that they were laying a clear trail for Liell and his men if they would follow; but it could not be helped. There was one quick way to Hjemur's heart, and they were on it.

The black was laboring. It was impossible to drive the horse further, hard-put as he had been on the road to Ivrel. And at last Vanye reined in, looked back and considered stopping. It was an uncomfortable place. Forest was on one side, high rocks upon the other.

"Let us be moving," Erij said.

"I am not going to kill this horse," Vanye protested, but he kept the animal at a walk all the same, and did not stop.

Then Erij spurred his own horse and the black dutifully matched the pace. Vanye smothered his temper and hoped that the horse would last to the gates of Ra-hjemur.

And they came upon tracked snow, where an unexpected road intersected theirs at an angle from the direction of Ivrel. Men afoot—horses—the short-footed sign of the smallish northerners, Hjemurn mixed with the larger prints of men: Andurin.

And blood upon the snow, and bodies lying in the road, abandoned.

Vanye swung down, Erij ordering him otherwise: he ignored his brother, went quickly from one body to the other, turning them to see the faces. Two were Lethen. The other three were the small, dark men of Hjemur, and one fair, like *qujal*. Relief flooded over him.

Erij hissed, drawing his attention: suddenly there was a stirring, a crunch of snow and a rattling of rocks, and he pulled himself out of his thoughts, looked up to see a dark shadow crouched upon the ledge overhanging the road.

He ran, sprang for the horse, hauled himself into the saddle as the startled animal began to run: he gathered reins awkwardly and tucked low as Erij did.

"Erij," he gasped when he could, "Hjemurn have come in behind, but Chya Liell and the Lethen are on the road ahead of us—the Hjemurn could not hold them. Ease off, ease off, or we will be riding into them."

"Then," said Erij, "we will be one enemy the less."

Morgaine too, and Roh, if they still lived: Erij, who held the sword, would as gladly kill them both as Chya Liell and Lethen: Nhi's bloodfeud with Chya was old and well-exercised, and that with Morgaine was as fresh as Irn-Svejur, and still painful.

"Give me a sword," Vanye asked of him then, for he had not so much as a dagger. "If not hers, then at least some weapon."

"Not at my back," said Erij, insulting the oath there was between them. But that was Erij's privilege: it did not lessen the oath.

Vanye pressed his lips tightly in anger and kept with him, counting Erij for a madman, to press both horses so, to ride unshielded after any company containing Morgaine after his bitter lesson at Irn-Svejur. He regretted his oath for a new reason: that Erij would kill the both of them and hand *Changeling* to the enemy, madder than Chya Roh and almost as great an idiot.

The road was winding, the turns blind, woods and rocks cutting off their view upon the right, trees almost taking the road in places upon the left.

And they met it, inevitably: the rear of Liell's column, men warned by their noise and braced to receive them with a hedge of spears, a bristling shadow in the dark.

Erij ripped *Changeling* loose and let its sheath slide, lost, nothing hesitating. He spurred his uncertain horse and drove the beast at the spears, while the blade flared into opal and a peculiar starry dark hovered at its tip. The Lethen that touched it were quickly nothing: others fled aside, closed in, in renewed determination as Vanye tried to ride through, but few, few of them. Instead came dark, fur-clad bodies off the ridge, dropping thick upon his path—Hjemurn, howling their blood-chilling cries. In his last clear sight of the column ahead he saw a glimmer of white—Siptah among those horses: and the Lethen riders began to run, abandoning those on foot, perhaps knowing what pursued them.

Dark bodies poured between, Vanye kicked his faltering horse, himself and the beast being pulled down together. A spear rammed at his ribs and rocked him badly. Weaponless, he seized the shaft with both hands and tried to wrench it free from its owner.

Then the horse collapsed, and arms encircled him, pulling him to the ground at the same moment. A blade flashed down and rebounded off his mail, surprising the would-be killer. Others hacked at him, with the same result, bruising, driving the wind from him. He was smothered in bodies and sinking into dark.

And as suddenly released.

He scrambled for his feet, still dazed, and sprawled in the stained snow. Screams were in his ears, then silence, a howl of wind, hollow and abruptly silenced too.

He struggled to one knee as steps crunched up to him, looked dazedly upon Erij, who held the sword in the sheath. There were no bodies, and there were no Hjemurn to be seen, only themselves, and the horses standing side by side.

Quickly, he twisted about to look in the direction the riders had taken. There was nothing to be seen there either.

"The riders," Vanye said. "Killed or fled?"

"Fled," said Erij. "If you had not fallen—but that must be the Chya blood in you. Get up."

He rose, steadied unexpectedly by Erij's hand, and he was surprised into a closer look at his brother, that same dark expression he had known in

Ra-morij—anger compounded by something else violent; but the hand that still held him was solidly gentle.

"Why stay for me?" Vanye taunted him, for he truly suspected some brotherly sentiment in the man. "Did you want revenge that badly?"

Erij's lips trembled in anger. "Bastard that you are, I will not leave even Nhi refuse for the Hjemurn. Get mounted."

And out of the contradictions that were Erij, he pushed him and hit him at once, no cuff, but a blow that brought him to one knee, dizzy as he was. Vanye gathered himself to rise, went after Erij, and halted as Erij's own longsword hit the snow between them. He seized it up without hesitating.

And there was Erij by his horse, glaring at him with hate and fear staring naked out of his eyes.

If he had not known Erij he would have thought him mad as Kasedre himself; but of a sudden he knew the feeling himself, an old one, and familiar. Erij did fear him. Maimed by him, his former skill cut away by him, Erij feared, and likely wakened in the night in such dreams as Vanye himself knew, dreams of Rijan, of Kandrys, and a morning in the armory court.

Father loved perfection, Erij had told him once. *He hated leaving Nhi to a cripple.*

He never forgave me either, for being the one of us two legitimate sons that lived. And for being less than perfect afterward.

But Erij had sense enough finally to arm him, in spite of all instincts otherwise. A one-handed man coming alone into Hjemur . . . he perhaps feared to die less than he feared to be proved weak.

Vanye bowed an awkward respect to his brother. "Likely we will die," he said, that sure knowledge a weight of guilt at his heart. "Erij, lend me *Changeling* instead. I do swear to you, I will go through with it—myself. Whatever can be done by a man carrying that thing, I will do. I will hand you Ra-hjemur if I live, and if I do not, then it was impossible anyway. Erij, I mean it. I owe you to do that."

Erij gave a short and uneasy laugh, tucked his handless arm behind him. "Your gratitude is unnecessary, bastard brother. The fact is, I dropped the sword-sheath and came back after it."

"You came back in time," Vanye insisted doggedly. "Erij, do not make it nothing. I know what you did; and I say I would do this."

"You are expert in treachery, and I am not about to trust you, especially where *she* is concerned. You are trying to delay me now, and there is an end of it. Get mounted."

He could not hold the course Erij set. He came near to falling as they took a slippery downslope, hung on grimly, but dropped a rein. The horse stopped at the bottom as a consequence, well-trained, stood with its own sides heaving between his knees, and Vanye slowly bent over the saddle, trying to clear his vision and making no effort to recover the lost rein.

Erij rode close to him, hit his horse and started it forward. He clung, but the horse stopped again, and he disregarded Erij and used his remaining strength to climb down and walk, leading his horse, toward a place where a flat rock promised a place to sit. He walked like a drunken man, and ached so that he more fell down than sat down when he reached it. He lay over on his side, tucked his limbs up against the cold and simply ignored Erij's attempts to rouse him: a time to let the pain leave his gut—it was all he asked.

Erij pulled at him roughly, and Vanye realized finally that Erij was attempting to lift his head upon his maimed arm; and himself took the wine flask and drank.

"You are chilled," Erij said distantly. "Sit, sit up."

He understood then that Erij was trying to put his cloak about him, and leaned against his brother, warmed against him so that finally he began to shiver and abused muscles began to knot up in reaction to cold.

"Drink," said Erij again. He drank. Then, briefly, he slept.

He meant it to be brief, only a closing of his eyes. But he awoke with the sun warming him, and Erij sitting nearby with *Changeling* tucked within his arms as Morgaine was wont to rest. Erij did not sleep: Vanye's first move brought him alert and sharp-eyed with suspicion.

"There is food," said Erij after a moment. "Get to horse and we will eat in the saddle. We have wasted enough time."

He did not contest the order, but dragged his aching limbs up and obeyed. There was an edge to the wind when they were out of the fold of the hill; he was glad of the little bit of wine Erij shared with him, and the coarse, crumbling bread and strong cheese. Food put strength into him. He looked at his brother in the daylight and saw a man equally haggard, shadow-eyed, hollow-cheeked, unshaven; but at a sane pace and with provisions to last them, he reckoned their chances of reaching Ra-hjemur better, at least, than he had reckoned them last night.

"They are surely making little better time than we," he said to Erij. "Ahead of us that they are . . . still, there is a limit to their horses, and their strength."

"It is possible that we can overtake them," said Erij. "It is at least possible."

Erij seemed soberly sane after the impulses of the night had run themselves out: for a moment there seemed even implied apology in his tone. Vanye snatched at it instantly.

"I am stronger," Vanye said. "I could go on. Listen to me. You have made a kind of Claiming; and once I am quit of my oath to her, then I serve your interests at that point, and I will hold Ra-hjemur for you."

"And of course the witch would let you."

"She has no ambitions for Ra-hjemur: only to settle with Thiye and then to go her own way. She will not come back. She is no threat to you, none. Erij, I beg you, I earnestly beg you, do not seek to kill her."

"You have to ask that, of course, being *ilin* to her; I respect that. But knowing that—of course I have to go with you into Ra-hjemur and above all I will not put this blade into your loyal hands, bastard brother. You had me willing to believe you once, and that cost me, that cost me bitterly in lives and in honor. Do not expect me to make the same mistake twice."

Then, Vanye concluded, he must obtain the blade from Erij by force or by theft, or somehow deceive Erij so that Erij himself would do what had to be done—oath-breaking and murder at once.

And ever since he had known of Morgaine what must be done, he had begun to suspect what manner of death there would be for him when he had obeyed her orders.

Its field directed at its own source of power would effect the ruin of all the Gates, she had said. And: *Cast back within the Gate itself, it would be the same: unsheathe it and hurl it through. Either way should be sufficient.*

Changeling fed upon the Witchfires of Ivrel. The black void beyond the Gate was that tiny nothingness that glimmered at *Changeling*'s tip, to seize whole men and whirl them through, winds howling into skies where men could not survive, as the dragon had perished in the snow . . . other skies where there was never day. *Changeling* aimed at the Gate would be void aimed at void, wind sucking into wind, ripping at its own substance and drawing all things in.

And perhaps even Ra-hjemur itself would follow it, and all within it. The force that had taken ten thousand men upon the winds at Irien and left no trace behind could not be so delicate as to take one man, if rent wide open, destroying itself.

He thought with a shudder of the retreating faces of those he had seen drawn into the field, the horror, the bewilderment, like men new arrived in Hell.

This would be theirs, this ending for the surviving sons of Nhi Rijan, for all their hate and striving against each other.

He kept his face turned from Erij until the wind had dried the tears upon his face, and gave himself up finally to do what he had given oath to do.

There lay before them the greatest valley in the north, and of Hjemur's hold, a grassy land ringed about by snow-capped peaks, fair to be seen save in one place, and that bare and blighted, even from such a distance.

"That," said Vanye, pointing to the ugliness, and thinking of the waste the Gates made about them, "that would be Ra-hjemur." And when he strained his eyes he could see the imagining of a rise there, a hill such as might be Ra-hjemur, hazy in distance.

They had not, after all, overtaken Liell. There lay the road. Nothing moved upon it. They seemed alone in all the land.

"It is too fair," said Erij, "too open. I should feel naked upon that road, by daylight."

"By night?"

"That seems the only good sense."

"I can tell you better," Vanye said, persistent to the last. "That you let me do this."

Erij stared at him and seemed to estimate him, so fearful in his own expression that fear of discovery wound itself through Vanye's belly. Almost he expected some harsh words, some flaring suspicion.

"What is it?" Erij asked, his tone curiously earnest. "What is it you expect down there? Has she warned you?"

"Brother," said Vanye, "the both of you have me by oath; and if my proper *liyo* is alive and with them . . . I have one responsibility to Morgaine, another to you. Between the two of you, you will be the death of me, and I could think more clearly if there were not the two of you in one place, about to go for each other's throats."

"I will give you this much," said Erij, "that if she does not seem to need killing, I will not. I have never killed a woman. I do not like the idea."

"Thank you for that," Vanye said earnestly.

And then, thinking of Liell: "Erij. If it comes to being captured—die. Those tales of Thiye's long life are true. If they took you, your body would go on ruling either in Ra-hjemur or Morija, but it would not be your soul in it."

Erij swore softly. "Truth?"

"For my sake, you have an ally if Morgaine is alive. Help me set her free and our chances of living become a thousandfold better."

Erij merely stared at him, hard-eyed.

"I am almost as ignorant as you are," Vanye protested. "I do not know the half of what is contained down there. I think she does. And for her own sake she would take our side. It is sure that no one else would. If you are going to start by killing our only possible ally in this business, or in keeping her helpless, well, then, you might as well tie me hand and foot before we go, since I am hers for a time yet . . . the hands, of which her science is the mind in this matter: and you would be wiser if you made use of both."

Erij gave him no answer, yet it seemed he thought seriously about his words, and they rode down together into a wooded place where they could no longer see the valley.

"We will rest here a time," said Erij, "and come in by night. Will Thiye resist Liell's entry?"

"I do not know," answered Vanye. "I think Morgaine thinks Thiye once was master and Liell his servant, at least at Irien; and that they had some falling-out. But if Liell brings Morgaine to Thiye, she may be the key that opens doors for him. And then, I think, if the same ambitions move *qujal* as move human men—which I do not know—then there may be treachery, and we may have either Thiye or Liell to deal with, whichever one wins the throw. I think perhaps Liell has waited a very long time to find some key that would admit him to Ra-hjemur. But this is my estimation: Morgaine said nothing of her own reckoning of their plans." He added, as Erij sat still upon his horse, listening, "I am not sure that Thiye is *qujal* or whether he is not simply some human man who employed a *qujal* for a servant and is now about to reap his reward for meddling; meddler is what Morgaine called him, and ignorant, and the Witchfires have no healthful effect on anything living. For some reason, if rumor is true, at least, he has let himself grow old. So Thiye may not be *qujal* at all, and I know that Morgaine is not, whatever you believe—but Liell is. That is the sum of it, Erij. Thiye is the matter of my oath, but I extend that oath to Liell most of all: and in good sense, you will let me do that."

"You wish to free the witch, that is what."

"Yes. But in doing that, I will kill Liell, who is a threat to both our causes, and I want your help in it, Erij. I want you to understand that I have business in Ra-hjemur beyond Thiye, and that freeing Morgaine would not be treachery against you."

Erij slid down. Vanye did not, and Erij looked up at him, face drawn against the winter sun. "There is one clear point in all of this: you will guard my life and help me take Ra-hjemur for myself. That is the sum of matters."

"You have taken my oath," Vanye said, miserable at heart. "I know that that is the sum of matters."

There was no moon, and clouds had moved in. There was that help, at least.

Ra-hjemur sat upon a low, barren hill, a citadel surely of the *qujal*, for it was simply a vast cube, unadorned, untowered, without protecting ring-walls or any defense evident to the eye. A stony path ran up to its gate; no grass grew upon it, but then, no grass grew anywhere on the hill.

They crouched a time by the bend of the knoll where they had left their horses, merely surveying the place. There was no stir of life.

Erij looked at him as if seeking his opinion.

"The sword can breach the door," Vanye said. "But beware of traps, brother, and mind that I am behind you: I do not care to die by the same chance that Ryn did."

Erij nodded understanding, then slipped from cover, seeking other shadows,

Vanye quick to follow. They came not directly up the road to the gate, but up under the walls, and in their shadow, to the gate itself.

It was graven with runes upon its metal pillars, but the gate was iron and wood, like the door of many an ordinary fortress; and when Erij drew *Changeling* and touched its black field to the joining of the doors the air sang with the groan of metals. The doors parted their joinings, and the pillars too, and stone rumbled, loosed from its supports. Dust choked them, and when it cleared a mass of rubble partly blocked the entry.

Erij gazed but a moment at the destruction he had wrought, then clambered over the rubble and sought the echoing inside of the place, which burned with light no fires supplied.

Vanye hurried through, asweat with dread, snatched up a sizable rock in the process, and as Erij started to look back at him, smashed it to Erij's helmeted skull. It was not enough. Erij fell, but still retained half-senses and heaved up with the blade.

Vanye saw it coming, twisted to evade the shimmer, kicked Erij's arm so that it wrung from him a cry of pain, and the sword fell.

He snatched it up then, gazed down on his brother, whose face was contorted with fury and fear. Erij cursed him, deliberately and with thought, such that it chilled his blood.

He took the sheath from Erij, who did not resist him; and upon an impulse to pity for Erij, he cast down Erij's own longsword.

Arrows flew.

He heard their loosing even before he whirled and knew they had come from the stairs, but *Changeling* in his warding hand made an easy path to elsewhere for the arrows, and they both remained unharmed. He knew the sword's properties, had seen Morgaine wield it, and knew its uses in ways Erij did not. Erij would as likely have taken an arrow as not.

And perhaps Erij understood that fact, or understood at the least that continuing their private dispute could be fatal to them both: Erij gathered up the longsword with but a glowering promise in his eyes, and rose, following as Vanye began to lead the way.

Killing a man from behind was an easy matter, even were he in mail; but Erij needed more hands than one: he risked everything on it.

And quickly he dismissed the threat of Erij from his mind, overwhelmed by the alien place. Breath almost failed him when he considered the size of the hall, the multitude of doors and stairs. Morgaine had sent him here ignorant, and there was nothing to do but probe every hall, every hiding place, until he either found what he was seeking or his enemies found his back.

Save that, held straight before them, *Changeling* gave forth a brighter glow, and when lifted, sent a coursing of impulses through the dragon-hilt, such that it seemed to live.

Carefully, Erij treading in his wake, he took the stairs to the level above.

They found a hall very like the one below, save that at its end there was a metal door, of that shining metal very like the pillars of the Witchfires. *Changeling* began to emit a sound, a bone-piercing hum that made his fingers ache; it grew stronger as he neared it. He ran toward that gate, figuring speed their best defense against a rally from Hjemurn: and froze, startled, as that vast door lightly parted to welcome him.

And startled more by the sight of gleaming metal and light that stretched away into distance, glowing with colors and humming with the power of the fires themselves. *Changeling* throbbed, his arm growing numb from holding it.

The field directed at its own source of power would effect the ruin of all the Gates.

The pulsing of conflicting powers reached up his arm into his brain, and he did not know whether the blade's wailing was in the air or in his own outraged senses.

He lifted it, expecting death, found instead that it did not much worsen, save when he angled it right. Then the pain increased.

"Vanye," Erij shouted at him, catching his shoulder. He saw stark fear on his brother's face.

"This is the way," Vanye said to him. "Stay here, guard my back." But Erij did not. He knew his brother's presence close behind him as he entered that hall.

He understood now: it greatly disagreed with Morgaine's careful nature, to have expected him to carry out so important a thing with so few instructions. There had been no need: the sword itself guided them, by its impulses of sound and pain. After a time of walking down that glowing corridor of *qujalin* works, the sound wiped out other senses until nothing but vision was left.

And in that vision stood an old man, hairless and wrinkled and robed in gray, who held out hands to them and mouthed silent words, pleading. Blood marred his aged face.

Vanye lifted the sword, threatening with that dreadful point, but the vision would not yield, barring their path with his very life.

Thiye, some sense told him: Thiye Thiye's-son, lord of Hjemur.

All at once the old man fell, clawing at the air, and there was an arrow in the robes at his back, and the red blood spreading.

A figure stood clear of the hall behind, gray and green, the young lord of Chya, lowering his bow. With sudden, breathless haste, Roh started toward them, slinging his strung bow to his back.

Vanye sought *Changeling*'s sheath at once, hope surging in him. The sudden silence in the air as that point found its proper haven was overwhelming: his abused ears could hardly hear Roh's voice. He felt Roh's eager hands grasp his arms, distant even from that sensation.

"Vanye, cousin," Roh cried, ignoring the threat of his blood-enemy Erij who stood beside, sword in hand. "Cousin, Thiye—Liell—they are at odds. Morgaine escaped them both, but—"

"Is she alive?" Vanye demanded.

"Alive, aye, well alive. She has the hold, Vanye. She means to destroy it. Come, come, clear this place. It will tumble down stone from stone. Hurry."

"Where is she?"

Roh's eyes gestured up, toward the stairs. "Barricaded up there, with her weapons in her possession again, and willing to kill anyone who comes within range. Vanye, do not try to reach her. She is mad. She will kill you too. You cannot reason with her."

"Liell?"

"Dead. They are all dead, and most of Thiye's servants are fled. You are free of your oath, Vanye. You are free. Escape this place. There is no need of your dying."

Roh's fingers tugged at him, his dark eyes full of agony; but of a sudden Vanye broke the hold and began to run toward the stairs upward. Then he looked back. Roh hesitated, then began to run in the other direction, vanishing quickly toward the safety of the downward stairs, a wraith in green. Erij cast a look in either direction, as if torn between, then raced toward the ascending stairs, longsword in hand, pointed it at Vanye, his eyes wild.

"Thiye is dead," Erij said. "He is dead. Your oath to the witch is done. Now stop her."

The fact of it hit him like a hammer blow: he stared helplessly at Erij, owning the justice of his claim, trying to think where his obligation truly lay. Then he shook off everything and suspended thought: his duty to either one lay in reaching Morgaine with all possible speed.

He turned and ran, taking the steps two at a time, until he came up, breathless, into yet another hall like the one below.

And confronted Morgaine, as Roh had warned him, hale and well and facing them both with the deadly black weapon secure in her hand.

"*Liyo!*" he cried, flung up his empty hand as if that alone could ward off harm, and with the other cast *Changeling* at her feet.

"No!" Erij cried in fury, but bit off further protest as Morgaine smoothly gathered the sheathed blade up, yet keeping the black weapon trained upon them. Then she lowered it.

"Vanye," said Morgaine. "Well met."

And she joined them, and began to descend the stairs from which they had come, carefully, trusting Vanye at her back; of a sudden he surmised what she sought thus cautiously.

"Thiye is dead," he said.

Her gray eyes cast back an unexpected look of agony. "Your doing?"

"No. Roh's."

"Not Roh's," she said. "Thiye freed me—that being his only hope of defeating Liell and keeping his life. He gave me this slim chance. I would have saved his life if I could. Is Roh down there?"

"He ran," said Vanye, "saying you meant to destroy this place." Horrid suspicion came over him. "It was not Roh, was it?"

"No," said Morgaine. "Roh died at Ivrel, in your place."

And she raced them down the stairs, pausing only to be careful at the turning, and came into that dread hall of *qujalin* design.

It was empty, save for Thiye's sprawled corpse in a widening pool of blood.

Morgaine ran, her footsteps echoing upon the floor, and Vanye followed, knowing that Erij was still with them, and little caring at the time. Anger seethed in him for Liell's mocking treachery with him; and dread was in him too for what Morgaine might intend with these strange powers.

She reached the very end of the hall, where there rose a vast double pillar of lights, and her hand abandoned the sword upon the counter an instant, while she wove a sure, practiced pattern among the lights. Noise thundered from the walls, voices gibbered ghostlike in unknown languages. Lights flared up and down the pillars, and began to pulse in increasing agitation.

She made it all cease, as quick as a move of her hand, and leaned against the counter, head bowed, like one who had suffered some mortal blow.

Then she turned and lifted her head, her eyes fixed earnestly on Vanye's.

"You and your brother must quit this place as quickly as you can," she said. "Liell spoke the truth in one thing: it will be destroyed. The machine is locked in such a way I cannot free it, and Ra-hjemur will be rubble in the time a rider could reach Ivrel. You are free of your oath. You have paid it all. Good-bye."

And with that she brushed past him and walked quickly down the long aisle alone, headed for the stairs.

"*Liyo!*" he cried, stopping her. "Where are you going?"

"He has locked the Gate open on a place of his choosing, and I am going after him. I have not much time: he has a good start on me, and surely he has allowed only what he thinks enough time for himself. But he is timid, this Liell: I am hoping that he has given himself too much grace, too much margin."

And with that she turned again, and began to walk and more quickly, and at last to run.

Vanye started forward a pace. "Brother," Erij reminded him. He stopped. She vanished down the stairs.

When the last sound of her footsteps was gone he turned again, of necessity, to face the anger in his brother's face. He went down upon the chill floor and pressed his forehead to it, making the obeisance his oath made due Erij.

"Your humility is a little late," said Erij. "Get up. I like to see your eyes when you answer questions."

He did so.

"Did she tell the truth?" Erij asked then.

"Yes," said Vanye. "I think it was the truth. Or if you doubt it, at least doubt it from a day's-ride distance from here. If you see it still standing after that, then it was not the truth."

"What is this of Gates?"

"I do not know," he said, "only that sometimes there is another side to the Witchfires and sometimes not, and that once she goes, she will be nowhere we can reach. I am sorry. It was not a thing she explained clearly. But she will not be back. Ivrel is a Gate that will close when this place dies, and after that there will be no more Witchfires, no more Thiyes, no more magics in the world."

He looked around him at the place, for that complexity was like the living insides of some great beast, though its veins were conduits of lights and its heart and pulse glowed and faded slowly.

"If you do not want to die, Erij," he said, "I suggest we take her advice and be as far from here as possible when it happens."

The horses were where they had left them, patiently waiting in the gray dawn, cropping the sparse grass as if there were nothing unusual in the day. Vanye checked the girths and heaved himself up, and Erij did the same. They rode the open and faster road this time, pausing for a view of the great cube of Ra-hjemur, which looked, with its breached gate, like a creature with a mortal wound.

Then they set out together for Morija.

"There is no more lord of Hjemur," said Vanye at last. "You and Baien are all the clan-lords left of any stature at all. It is within your reach to gain the High Kingship without Hjemurn magics after all, and perhaps that will be better for human folk."

"Baien's lord is old," said Erij, "and has a daughter. I do not think that he will want a war to cloud his old age and ruin his land. I will perhaps be able to make an alliance with him. And Chya Roh left no heirs. His people will be less trouble to us. Pyvvn's lady is Chya, and with Chya in Koris in our hands, Pyvvn will submit." Erij sounded almost cheerful, counting his prospects and reckoning lightly of a few wars.

But Vanye gazed to the road ahead, where it wound out of sight and into view again toward the south, hoping earnestly to see her, seeing her in his mind, at least, as she had ridden that evening out of Aenor-Pyvvn's Gate.

"You are not listening," Erij accused.

"Aye," he said, blinking and breaking the spell, and looking again toward Erij.

And ever and again after that, he saw Erij look curiously at him. There was a growing sourness on Erij's face, as if whatever alliance there had been to make them brothers this dawn in Ra-hjemur was fast shredding asunder. He held out little hope for his peace as he saw that sullen estimation grow more and more grim.

"There is none of the high-clan blood in Morija left, but us," said Erij that noon, when the sun was almost warm, and they rode still knee to knee.

Oh Heaven, Vanye thought, looking out upon the sunlight and the hills with regret, *now it comes;* for he had long since come to the conclusion he was sure would occur to Erij: that, enemies as they were, Erij was mad to flaunt a high-clan prisoner in Morija. Without Ra-hjemur from which to rule, he had not power enough to bear a taint of dishonor—or a rival. Politics and ambitions would swarm about a bastard Chya like flies to honey. Such conclusions as Erij had no doubt reached were dishonorable, better meditated in the dark of night than in such a fair day.

"Bastard that you are," said Erij, "you could make yourself a threat to me, if you were minded to do so. There is no lord in Chya. It comes to me, bastard brother, that you are heir to Chya, if you were to claim it, and that no lord can be claimed as *ilin.*"

"I have not laid any claim to Chya," said Vanye. "I do not think I could, and I do not intend to."

"They had rather own you than me, I do not doubt it at all," said Erij. "And you are still the most dangerous man to me in all of Andur-Kursh, so long as you live."

"I am not," said Vanye, "because I regard my oath. But you do not regard your own honor enough to trust mine."

"You did not regard your oath in Ra-hjemur."

"You were not in danger from Morgaine. I did not have to."

Erij gazed long at him, then reached across. "Give me your hand," he said, and Vanye, puzzling, yielded it to his left-handed handclasp. His brother pressed it in almost friendly fashion.

"Leave," said Erij. "If I hear of you after this I will hunt you down . . . or if you come to Morija. I will set Claim on you and let you work off that year you owe me. But I do not think you will come to Morija."

And he gestured with a nod to the road ahead.

"If she will have you—go."

Vanye stared at him, then gripped his brother's strong, dry hand the more tightly before he broke the clasp.

Then he set heels to the horse, dismissing from his mind every thought that he was weaponless and that Morgaine would have opened a wide lead on them during the morning.

He would gain that distance back. He would find her. He realized much later to his grief that he had not even looked back once at his brother, that he had severed that tangled tie without half the pain he thought it must have cost Erij to let him go.

In that loosing, he thought, Erij had paid for everything; he wished that he had spoken some word of thanks.

Erij would have sneered at it.

He did not find her on the road. In the second day, he cut off the track the two had used, and took the one on which Liell had come from Ivrel, the one he thought Morgaine would surely choose. Ivrel was close and there was no more time left for stopping, though he was aching from the ride and the horse's breath came in great gasps, such that he must dismount and half pull the beast up the steeper places of the trail. The delay tormented him and he began to fear that he had lost the way, that he would lose her once for all.

And yet, finally, finally, when he came out upon the height, there stood Ivrel's great side to be seen, and the barren shoulder of the mountain where the Gate would be. He urged the black to what speed the horse could bear and climbed, sometimes losing sight of his goal, sometimes finding it again, until he entered the forest of twisted pines and lost it altogether.

In the snow were footprints, the old ones of many men, and some of animals, and some of those not good to imagine what had made them; but now and again he could sort out new ones.

Roh-Liell-Zri, upon the black mare, most likely, and Morgaine upon his trail.

Breath hung frozen in the sunlight, and air cut the lungs. He had at last to walk the horse, out of mercy, and scanned the black sickly pines about him, remembering all too keenly that he had no weapons at all, and a horse too weary for headlong fight.

Then through those pines he caught a glimmer of movement, a white movement amid the blaze of sun on snow, and he whipped up his horse and made what speed he could on the trail.

"Wait!" he cried.

She waited for him. He came in beside her breathless with relief, and she leaned from the saddle and reached for his hand.

"Vanye, Vanye, you ought not to have followed me."

"Are you going through?" he asked.

She looked up at the Gate, shimmering dark again, stars and blackness above them in the daylight. "Yes," she said, and then looked down at him. "Do not delay me further. This following me is nonsense. I do not know how the Gate is behaving, whether that will bring me through to the same place that Zri has fled or whether it will fling me out elsewhere. And you do not belong. You were useful for a time. You with your *ilin*-codes and your holds and your kinships . . . this is your world, and I needed a man who could maneuver things as I needed them. You have served your purpose. Now there is an end of the matter. You are free, and be glad of it."

He did not speak. He supposed finally that he merely stared at her, until he felt her hand slip from his arm, and she moved away. He watched her begin the long slope, Siptah refusing it at first. She took firm grip on the reins and began to force the animal against his will, driving him brutally until he decided to go, gathering himself in a long climb into the dark.

And was gone.

We are not brave, we that play this game with Gates; there is too much we can lose, to have the luxury to be virtuous, and to be brave.

He sat still a moment, looked about the slope, and considered the tormented trees and the cold, and the long ride to Morija, cast off by her, begging Erij to bear his presence in Andur-Kursh.

And there was pain in every direction but one: as the sword had known the way to its own source, his senses did.

Of a sudden he laid heels to his horse and began to drive the beast upslope. There was only a token refusing. Siptah had gone: the black understood what was expected of him.

The gulf yawned before him, black and starry, without the wind that had howled there before. There was only enough breeze to let him know it was there.

And dark, utter dark, and falling. The horse heaved and twisted under him, clawing for support.

And found it.

They were running again, on a grassy shore, and the air was warm. The horse snorted in surprise, then extended himself to run.

A pale shape was on the hill before them, under a double moon.

"*Liyo!*" he shouted. "Wait for me!"

She paused, looking back, then slid off to stand upon the hillside.

He rode in alongside and slid down from his exhausted horse even before the animal had quite stopped moving. Then he hesitated, not knowing whether he would meet joy or rage from her.

But she laughed and flung her arms about him, and he about her, pressing her tightly until she flung back her head and looked at him.

It was the second time he had ever seen her cry.

Well of Shiuan

Book One

"... Last of all only the woman Morgaine survived, skilled in qujalin witchcrafts and bearing still that Sword that casts to death. Much of evil she did in Morija and Baien, rivaling all other evils she had committed ... but she fled thereafter, taking with her Nhi Vanye i Chya, once of this house, who was ilin to her and therefore bound by his oath."

—*Nhi Erij i Myya, in the Book of Ra-morij*

"Chya Roh i Chya, lord of Ra-koris ... followed the witch Morgaine, for his cousin's sake ... but Nhi Erij in his writing avows that Chya Roh perished on that journey, and that the Soul that possessed the likeness of Roh thereafter was qujal, and hostile to every Godly man. ...."

—*the Book of Baien-an*

∽ Chapter 1

Seven moons danced across the skies of the world, where there had been one in the days of the ancients. In those days the Wells of the Gods had been open, providing power and abundance to the *khal*-lords who had governed before the time of the Kings. Now the Wells were sealed, beyond the power of men or *khal* to alter. Long ago there had been vast lands on all sides of Shiuan and Hiuaj; but the world now was slowly drowning.

These were the things that Mija Jhirun Ela's-daughter believed for truth.

For all of Jhirun's young life, she had known the waters encroaching relentlessly on the margin of the world, and she had watched Hiuaj diminish by half and the gray sea grow wider. She was seventeen, and looked to see Hiuaj vanish entirely in her lifetime.

When she had been a child, the village of Chadrih had stood near the Barrow-hills of Hiuaj; and beyond that had stood a great levee and a sea wall, securing fields that gave good crops and pasturage for sheep and goats and cattle. Now there was reed-grown waste. The three parcels of land that had supported Chadrih were gone, entirely underwater save for the boundary posts of stacked stone and the useless remnant of the ancient sea wall. The gray stone buildings of the village had become a ruin, with water trickling even at low tide through what had been its streets, and standing window-high at Hnoth, when the moons combined. The roofless houses had become the nesting places of the white birds that wheeled and cried their lonely pipings over the featureless sea.

The people of Chadrih had moved on, those who survived the collapse of the sea wall and the fever and the famine of that winter. They had sought shelter, some among the marsh dwellers at Aren, a determined few vowing to go beyond into Shiuan itself, seeking the security of holds like fabled Abarais of the Wells, or Ohtij-in, among the halfling lords. The Barrows had heard tidings of those that had reached Aren; but what had befallen the few who had gone the long road to Shiuan, none had ever heard.

The breaking of the sea wall had happened in Jhirun's tenth year. Now there was little dry land in all Hiuaj, only a maze of islets separated by marsh, redeemed from the killing salt only by the effluence of the wide Aj, that flowed down from Shiuan and spread its dark, sluggish waters toward the gray sea. In storm the Aj boiled brown with silt, the precious earth washed seaward, in flood that covered all but the hills and greater isles. At high tide, when the moons moved together in Hnoth, the sea pressed inland and killed areas of the marsh, where green grass died and standing pools reeked of decay, and great sea fishes prowled the Aj. Now throughout Hiuaj, there remained only sparse pasturage for goats and for the wild marsh ponies. The sea advanced in the face of the Barrows and the widening marsh ate away at their flank, threatening to sever Hiuaj from Shiuan and utterly doom them. Land that had been sweet and green became a tangle of drowned trees, a series of small hummocks of spongy earth, reed-choked passages that were navigable only by the flat-bottomed skiffs used by marsh folk and Barrowers.

And the Barrow-hills became islands in these last years of the world.

It was Men that had reared these hills, just after the days of the Darkness. They were the burials of the kings and princes of the Kingdoms of Men, in those long-ago days just after the Moon was broken, when the *khal* had declined and Men had driven the *khalin* halflings into their distant mountains. In those days, Men had had the best of the world, had ruled a wide, rich plain, and there had been great wealth in Hiuaj for human folk.

Men had buried their great ones in such towering mounds, in cists of stone: warrior-kings proud with their gold and their gems and their iron weapons, skillful in war and stern in their rule over the farmer-peasantry. They had sought to restore the ancient magics of the Wells, which even the halfling *khal* had feared. But the sea rose and destroyed their plains, and the last Kings of Men fell under the power of the halflings of Shiuan. So the proud age of the Barrow-kings passed, leaving only their burial places clustered about the great Well called Anla's Crown, that had swallowed up their wealth and returned them only misery.

In the end there were only scattered villages of Men, farmer-folk who cursed the memory of the Barrow-kings. The old fortresses and burial places were piously avoided by later generations on the river-plain. Chadrih had been nearer the Barrows than any other village wished to be; but it had perished last of all the villages in Hiuaj, for all that—which gave Chadrih folk a certain arrogance, until their own fate took them. And the Barrow-hills themselves became the last refuge of all; the Barrow-folk had always lived beyond the pale of lowland respectability—tomb-robbers now, sometimes herders and fishermen, accused (while Chadrih stood) of stealing livestock as well as buried gold. But Chadrih died and the despised Barrow-folk lived, southernmost of all Men, in a hold that was a Barrow-king's ruined fortress atop the last and greatest rock in all Hiuaj, save Anla's Crown itself.

This was Jhirun's world. Sunbrowned and warm, she guided her flat skiff with practiced thrusts of the pole against the bottom of the channels that, at this cycle of the tides, were hardly knee deep. She was barefoot, knowing shoes only in winter, and she wore her fringe-hemmed skirt tucked above the knees because there was none to see her. A stoppered jar of bread and cheese and another of beer were nestled in the prow; and there was also a sling and a handful of smooth stones, for she was skillful with the sling to bring down the brown marsh fowl.

There had been rain last night and the Aj was up somewhat, enough to fill some of the shallower channels, making her progress through the hills quicker. There would be rain again before evening, to judge by the gathering of haze in the east, across the apricot sun; but high tide, Hnoth, was some days off. The seven moons danced in order across the watery sky and the force of the Aj was all that sighed against the reeds. The Barrows that were almost entirely awash at Hnoth were bravely evident despite the rains, and the Standing Stone at Junai was out of the water entirely.

It was a holy place, that hewn stone and its little isle. Nearby was a finger of the deep marshes, and marsh-folk came here to Junai's stone to meet on mid-cycle days with Barrowfolk to trade—her tall kinsmen with the surly small men of the deep fens. Meat and shell and metals were their trade to the marshes; wood and Ohtija grain out of Shiuan and well-made boats and baskets were what the marshlanders brought them. But more important than the trade itself was the treaty that let the trade happen regularly, this seasonal commerce that brought them together for mutual gain and removed occasion for feuds, so that any Barrower could come and go in Barrows-land in safety. There were outlaws, of course, men either human or halfling, cast out of Ohtij-in or Aren, and such were always to be feared; but none had been known this far south for four years. The marshlanders had hanged the last three on the dead tree near the old *khalin* ruin at Nia's Hill, and Barrows-men had given them gold for that good service. Marshlanders served as a barrier to the folk of Barrows-hold against every evil but the sea, and returned them no trouble. Aren was far into the marsh, and marshlanders kept to it; they would not even stand in a Barrows-man's shadow when they came to trade, but uttered loud prayers and huddled together under the open sky as if they dreaded contamination and feared ambush. They preferred their dying forests and their own observances, that made no mention of Barrow-kings.

Out here on the edge of the world lay Barrows-land, wide and empty, with only the conical hills above the flood and the wide waters beyond, and the flight of the white birds above. Jhirun knew each major isle, each stone's-throw expanse of undrowned earth, knew them by the names of kings and heroes forgotten outside the lore of Barrows-folk, who claimed the kings for ancestors and could still sing the old words of the chants in an accent no marshlander could comprehend. Some few of these hills were hollow at their crest, caps of stone, earth-covered, that had long ago yielded up their treasure to the plundering of Jhirun's ancestors. Other mounds still defied efforts to discover the cists buried there, and so protected their dead against the living. And some seemed to be true hills, that had no hollow heart of man-made chambers, with king-treasures and weapons. Such as did give up treasure sustained the life of Barrows-hold, providing gold that Barrows-folk remade into rings and sold anew to marshlanders, who in turn bought grain of Shiuan and sold it at Junai. Barrows-folk had no fear of the angry ghosts, their own ancestors, and hammered off the ancient symbols and melted down the gold, purifying it.

And besides the grain the gold bought, they kept goats and hunted, and thus secured a small source of food independent of that trade. Daily Jhirun and her cousins cut grass and loaded it on skiffs or on the back of the black marsh pony that they used in the inner hills. By such means they stored up against the days of Hnoth, and fed their livestock, and had surplus of cheeses and domestic meat that the marshlanders valued as much as the gold.

The little skiff reached a stretch of faster-moving water, that place where the current of the Aj reached into the bordering islets, and Jhirun maneuvered into the shallows, holding that margin with care. Afar off she could see the edge of the world, where the Aj met the devouring sea, and horizon and sky merged in gray haze. Hereabouts, a great rolling expanse above the flood, was the hill of Anla's Crown.

She did not mean to go near that place, with its ring of Standing Stones. None ever approached that hill save at Midyear's Day, when the priests came— her grandfather for Barrows-hold, and aged Haz for the folk of Aren. Once even Shiua priests had come to it, down the long road from Ohtij-in: it was that important, one of the two true Wells. But none had come since the sea wall broke. The rites were now only the concern of Hiua, but they were by no means neglected. And even on that day the priests remained fearful and ventured no closer than a stone's cast, Haz of Aren and her grandfather approaching separately because of their differences. In the old days, Barrow-kings had given men to the Wells there, but that custom had lapsed when the Barrow-kings fell. The sacrifices had not enlivened the Wells nor healed the Moon. The Standing Stones stood stark and empty against the sky, some crazily tilted; and that vast hill that none dared approach save on the appointed day remained a place of power and tainted beauty, no refuge for men or halflings. Each priest spoke a prayer and retreated. It was not a place to be alone; it was such that the senses prickled with unease even when one was coming with many kinsfolk, and the two priests and the chanting—a stillness that underlay the singing and made every noise of man seem a mere echo. Here was the thing the Barrow-kings had sought to master, the center of all the eeriness of the Barrows, and if anything would remain after the waters had risen and covered all Hiuaj, it would be this hill and those strange stones.

Jhirun skirted widely away from that place, working out of the current, among other isles. Marks of the Old Ones as well as the Barrow-kings were frequent here, scattered stones upstanding in the water and on the crests of hills. Here was her favorite place when she worked alone, here on the margin of Anla's Crown, far, far beyond the limit that any marshlander would dare to come save on Midyear's Day; and out of the convenient limits that her kinsmen cared to work. She enjoyed the silence, the solitude, apart from the brawling chaos of Barrows-hold. Here was nothing but herself and the whisper of reeds, the splash of water, and the lazy song of insects in the morning sun.

The hills glided past, closing in again, and she tended now toward the righthand bank of the winding channel, to the hill called Jiran, after which she was named. It had a Standing Stone at its crest, like others just downstream at water's edge, and Jiran, like the other hills that clustered here, was green with grass fed by the sweet water of the Aj. She stepped out as the skiff came to ground, her bare feet quick and sure on the damp landing. She seized the mooring rope and hauled the skiff well up on the bank so that no capricious play of current could take it. Then she set to work.

The insect-song stopped for a time when she began to swing her sickle, then began again as the place accepted her presence. Whenever she had done sufficient for a sheaf, she gathered the grasses and bound them with a twist of their own stalks, leaving neat rows behind her. She worked higher and higher on the hill in a wheel-pattern of many spokes, converging at the Standing Stone.

From time to time she stopped and straightened her back and stretched in pain from the work, although she was young and well-accustomed to it. At such times she scanned the whole horizon, with an eye more to the haze gathering in the east than to the earth. From the hilltop, as she neared the end of her work, she could see all the way to Anla's Crown and make out the ring of stones atop it, all hazy with the distance and the moisture in the air, but she did not like to look toward the south, where the world stopped. When she looked north, narrowing her eyes in the hope—as sometimes happened on the clearest of days—of imagining a mountain in the distant land of Shiuan, all she could see was gray-blue, and a dark smudge of trees against the horizon along the Aj, and that was the marsh.

She came here often. She had worked alone for four years—since her sister Cil had wed—and she cherished the freedom. For now she had her beauty, still was straight and slim and lithe of muscle; she knew that years and a life such as Cil's would change that. She tempted the gods, venturing to the edge of Anla's hill; she flaunted her choice of solitude even under the eye of heaven. She had been the youngest—Cil was second-born, and Socha had been eldest—three sisters. Cil was now Ger's wife and always heavy with child, and began to have that leaden-eyed look that her aunts had. Their mother Ewon had died of birth-fever after Jhiran, and their father had drowned himself, so the men said—and therefore the aunts had reared them, added duty, to bow these grim women down with further self-pity. The three sisters had been close, conspirators against their cousins and against the female tyranny of their aunts. Socha had been the leader, conniving at pranks and ventures constantly. But Cil had changed with marriage, and grew old at twenty-two; only Socha remained, in Jhirun's memory, unchanged and beautiful. Socha had been swept away that Hnoth when the great sea wall broke; and Jhirun's last memory of her was of Socha setting out that last morning, standing in that frail, shallow skiff, and the sunlight streaming about her. Jhirun had dreamed ill dreams the night before—Hnoth always gave her nightmares—and she had told her dreams to Socha and wept, in the dark. But Socha had laughed them away, as she laughed at all troubles, and set out the next morning, thus close to Hnoth.

Still happier Socha than Cil, Jhirun thought, when she reckoned Cil's life, and how few her own months of freedom might be. There was no husband left for her in Barrows-hold but her cousins, and the one that wanted her was Fwar, brother of Cil's man Ger and of the same stamp. Fwar was becoming anxious; and so Jhirun was the more insistent on working apart from her cousins, all of them, and never where Fwar might find her alone. Sometimes in bitter fancy she thought of running off into the deep marsh, imagining Fwar's outrage at being robbed of his bride, Ela's fey daughter, the only unwed woman in Barrows-hold. But she had seen the marshlanders' women, that came behind their men to Junai, women as grim and miserable as her aunts, as Cil; and there were Chadrih folk among them, that she feared. Most pleasant imagining of all, and most hopeless, she thought of the great north isle, of Shiuan, where the gold went, where halfling lords and their favored servants lived in wealth and splendor while the world drowned.

She thought of Fwar while she attacked the grass with the sickle, putting the strength of hate into her arm, and wished that she had the same courage against him; but she did not, knowing that there was nothing else. She was doomed to discontent. She was different, as all Ewon's fair children had been, as Ewon herself had been. The aunts said that there was some manner of taint in Ewon's blood: it came out most strongly in her, making her fey and wild. Ewon had dreamed dreams; so did she. Her grandfather Keln, priest of Barrows-hold, had given her *sicha* wood and seeds of *azael* to add to the amulets she wore about her neck, besides the stone Barrow-king's cross, which were said to be effective against witchery; but it did not stop the dreams. Halfling-taint, her aunt Jinel insisted, against which no amulets had power, being as they only availed for human-kind. It was told how Ewon's mother had met a halfling lord or worse upon the Road one Midyear's Eve, when the Road was still open and the world was wider. But Ela's line was of priests; and grandfather Keln had consoled Jhirun once by whispering that her father as a youth had dreamed wild dreams, assuring her that the curse faded with age.

She wished that this would be so. Some dreams she dreamed waking; that of Shiuan was one, in which she sat in a grand hall, among halflings, claimed by her halfling kindred, and in which Fwar had perished miserably. Those were wish-dreams, remote and far different from the sweat-drenched dreams she suffered of doomed Chadrih and of Socha, drowned faces beneath the waters— Hnoth-dreams that came when the moons moved close and sky and sea and earth heaved in convulsions. The tides seemed to move in her blood as they did in the elements, making her sullen and prone to wild tempers as Hnoth drew near. During the nights of Hnoth's height, she feared even to sleep by night, with all the moons aloft, and she put *azael* sprigs under her pillow, lying sleepless so long as she could.

Her cousins, like all the house, feared her speaking of such things, saying that they were ill-wishes as much as they were bad dreams. Only Fwar, who respected nothing, least of all things to which his own vision did not extend, and liked to make mock of what others feared, desired her for a wife. Others had proposed more immediate and less permanent things, but generally she was left alone. She was unlucky.

And this was another matter that held her to Barrows-hold, the dread that the marshlanders, who had taken in the Chadrih folk, might refuse her and leave her outlawed from every refuge, to die in the marsh. One day she might become resolved enough to risk it, but that day was not on her yet. She was free and solitary, and it was, save when she had had both Socha and Cil, the best time of her life, when she could roam the isles at will. She was not, whatever the rumors of her gossiping aunts, born of a halfling lord, nor of the little men of Aren, born neither to dine off gold nor to trade in it—but Barrows-born, to dig for it. The sea might have all Hiuaj in her lifetime, drowning the Barrow-hills and all within them; but that was distant and unthreatening on so warm a day.

Perhaps, she thought, with an inward laugh, she was only slightly and sometimes mad, just as mad as living on world's-edge ought to make one. Perhaps when she dreamed her terrible dreams, she was sane; and on such days as this when she felt at peace, then she was truly mad, like the others. The conceit pleased her.

Her hands kept to their work, swinging the sickle and binding the grasses neatly. She was aware of nothing about her but the song of the insects. At early afternoon she carried all her load down to the bank and rested, there on the slope near the water; and she ate her meal, watching the eddies of the water swirling past the opposing hill. It was a place she knew well.

And the while she gazed she realized that a new and curious shadow lay on that other bank, that indeed there was a gaping wound in that hill, opened just beneath that outcrop of rock. Suddenly she swallowed down a great mouthful of her meal and left everything lying—jars, sickle, sheaves of grass—and gathered up the rope and boat-pole.

Cist. A burial chamber, torn open by last night's rain. She found her hands sweating with excitement as she pushed the boat out and poled it across the narrow channel.

The other hill was perfectly conical, showing scars about its top as most such suspicious hills did thereabouts, wounds made by earlier Barrow-folk probing to see whether burial had been made there. Those searchers had found nothing, else they would have plundered it and left it gaping open to the sky.

But the waters, searching near the base, had done what men had failed to do and found what men never had: treasure, gold, the purchase of luxuries here at world's end.

The skiff scraped bottom among the reeds and Jhirun waded ashore up to the knees in water until she could step up on the clay bank. She heaved the skiff onto solid ground, there near the shelf that overshadowed the breach. She trembled with excitement seeing how that apparent rock outcrop was squared on the edge, proving it no work of nature; the rain had exposed it for the first time to light, for she had been here hardly a hand of days ago and had not seen it. She flung herself down by the opening and peered in.

There was a cold chill of depth about that darkness—no cist at all, but one of the great tombs, the rich ones. Jhirun swallowed hard against the tightness in her throat, wiped her hands on her skirt and worked her shoulders in, turning so that she could fit the narrow opening. For a moment she despaired, reckoning such a find too much for her alone, sure that she must go back and fetch her cousins; and those thieving cousins would leave her only the refuse—if it were still intact when she brought them back. She remembered the haze across the east, and the likelihood of rain.

But as her eyes grew accustomed to the dark, she could see that there was light breaking in from some higher aperture; the top of the tomb must have been breached too, the dome broken. She could not see the interior from this tunnel, but she knew that it must surely be a whole, unrobbed tomb; no ancient robber would have entered a dome-tomb from the top, not without winning himself a broken neck. The probing of some earlier searcher seeking only a cist atop the hill had likely fallen through, creating the wash at the lower level. And that chance had given her such a prize as generations of Barrowers dreamed in vain of finding, a tale to be told over and over in the warm security of Barrowshold so long as the world lasted.

She clutched the amulets on the cord about her neck, protection against the ghosts. With them, she did not fear the dark of such places, for she had been in and about the tombs from childhood. The dangers she did fear were a weak ceiling or an access tunnel collapsing. She knew better than to climb that slope outside, weakened as it was. She had heard a score of times how great-uncle Lar had fallen to his death among the bones in the opening of the king-hill called Ashrun. She expelled her breath and began to wriggle through where she was, dragging her body through, uncaring for the tender skin of her arms in her eagerness.

Then she lay in what had been the approach to the tomb, a stone-paved access that seemed to slant up and up to a towering door, the opening of which was faintly discernible in the dim light. She rose and felt with her hands the stones she knew would be about her. The first joining was as high as her head, and she could not reach the top of the next block. By this she became certain that it was a tomb of one of the First Kings after the Darkness, for no other men ever built with such ambition or buried in such wealth.

Such a hill this was, without even the name of a King. It was old and forgotten, among the first to be reared near Anla's hill, in that tradition that ringed the Kings' burials nearest the forces they had wished to master, from which legend said they had come and to which they always sought to return. A forgotten name: but he had been a great one, and powerful, and surely, Jhirun thought with a pounding of her heart, very, very rich.

She walked the access, feeling her way in the dark, and another fear occurred to her, that the opening might have given some wild thing a lair. She did not think such was the case, for the air held no such taint; but all the same she wished that she had brought the boat-pole, or better yet the sickle; and most of all that she had a lamp.

Then she came into the area of the dome, where sunlight shafted down, outlining the edges of things on the floor, the ray itself an outline in golden dust. It fell on stone and mouldering ruin. Her least stirring echoed fearsomely in the soaring height above her head.

Many a tomb had she seen, the little cists often hardly larger than the king buried there, and two great dome-tombs, that of Ashrun and that of Anla, and those long-robbed, Ashrun a mere shell open to the sky. She had been at the opening of one cist-tomb, watching her uncles work, but she had never been alone, the very first to breach the silence and the dark.

The stone-fall from the dome had missed the bier, and the slanting light showed what must have been the king himself, only rags and bones. Against the arching wall were other huddled masses that must once have been his court, bright ladies and brave lords of Men: in her imaginings she saw them as they must have been the day that they followed their king into this place to die, all bedight in their finest clothing, young and beautiful, and the dome ringing with their voices. In another place would be the mouldering bones of their horses, great tall beasts that had stamped and whinnied in fear of such a place, less mad than their doomed masters—beasts that had run plains that now were sea; she saw the glint of gilded harness in the dust.

She knew the tales. The fables and the songs in the old language were the life and livelihood of the Barrows, their golden substance the source of the bread she ate, the fabric of her happier dreams. She knew the names of kings who had been her ancestors, the proud Mija—knew their manners, though she could not read the runes; she knew their very faces from the vase paintings, and loved the beauty of the golden art they had prized. She was sorry when these precious things must be hammered and melted down; she had wept much over seeing it when she was a child, not understanding how such beautiful objects were reckoned unholy and unlucky by marshlanders, and that without that purifying, the gold was useless in trade. The fables were necessary for the house to teach the children, but there was no value for beauty in the existence of the Barrows, only for gold and the value that others set on having it.

She moved, and in doing so, nudged an object beside the doorway. It fell and shattered, a pottery sound, loud in that vast emptiness. The nape of her neck prickled and she was overwhelmingly aware of the silence after the echo, and of the impudence of Jhirun Ela's-daughter, who had come to steal from a king.

She thrust herself out from the security of the wall and into the main area, where the light streamed down to the bier of the king and gleamed on dusty metal.

She saw the body of the king, his clothes in spidery tatters over his age-dark bones. His skeletal hands were folded on his breast, on mail of rusted rings, and over his face was a mask of gold such as she had heard was the custom of the earliest age. She brushed at the dust that covered it, and saw a fine face, a strong face. The eyes were portrayed shut, the high cheekbones and delicate moulding of the lips more *khalin* than man. The long-dead artist had graven even the fine lines of the hair of brows and lashes, had made the lips and nostrils so delicate it was as if they might suddenly draw breath. It was a young man's face, the stern beauty of him to haunt her thereafter, she knew, when she slept beside Fwar. Cruel, cruel, that she had come to rob him, to strip away the mask and reveal the grisly ruin of him.

At that thought she drew back her hand, and shivered, touching the amulets at her throat; and retreated from him, turning to the other hapless dead that lay along the wall. She plundered them, rummaging fearlessly among their bones for golden trinkets, callously mingling their bones to be sure the ghosts were equally muddled and incapable of vengeance on Midyear's Eve.

Something skittered among them and frightened her so that she almost dropped her treasure, but it was only a rat, such as sheltered in the isles and fed on wreckage and drowned animals, and sometimes housed in opened tombs.

Cousin, she saluted him in wry humor, her heart still fluttering from panic. His nose twitched in reciprocal anxiety, and when she moved, he fled. She made haste, filling her skirts with as much as she could carry, then returning to the access and laboriously bringing bit after bit down that narrow tunnel and out into daylight. She crawled out after, and loaded the pieces in the skiff, looking all about the while to be sure that she was alone: wealth made her suspect watchers, even where such were impossible. She covered over everything with grass in the skiff's bottom and hurried again to the entrance, pausing to cast a nervous glance at the sky.

Clouds filled the east. She knew well how swiftly they could come with the wind behind them, and she hurried now doubly, feeling the threat of storm, of flood that would cover the entrance of the tomb.

She wriggled through into the dark again, and felt her way along until her eyes reaccustomed themselves to the dark. She sought this time the bones of the horses, wrenching bits of gold from leather that went to powder in her hands. Their bones she did not disturb, for they were only animals, and she was sorry for them, thinking of the Barrows-hold's pony. If they would haunt anyone, it would be harmless, and she wished them joy of their undersea plains.

What she gained there she took as far as the access and piled in a bit of broken pottery, then returned to the bones of the courtiers. She worked there, gathering up tiny objects while the thunder rumbled in the distance, filling her skirt as she worked slowly around the wall among the bones, into a shadow that grew deeper and colder.

Cold air breathed out of an unseen recess in that shadow, and she stopped with the gold in her lap, peering into that blind dark. She sensed the presence of another, deeper chamber, black and vast.

It fretted at her, luring her. She remembered how at Ashrun's tomb there had been a treasure chamber that yielded more wealth than any buried with king or court. Long moments she hesitated, fingering the amulets that promised her safety. Then she cursed her cowardice and convinced herself; the thunder walked above the hills, reminding her that there was only this one chance, forever.

With a whispered invocation to Arzad, who protected from ghosts, she edged forward, kneeling, cast a seal-gem into that dark. It struck metal; and thus encouraged, she leaned forward and reached into that darkness.

Her fingers met mouldering cloth, and she recoiled, but in doing so her hand hit metal, and things spilled in a clatter that woke the echoes and almost stopped her heart. Cascading about her knees were dusty gems and plates and cups of gold, treasure that made the objects in her lap seem mere trinkets.

She cursed in anguish for the shortness of the time. She gathered what she could carry and returned to the tunnel to push each piece out into the daylight. Drops of rain spattered the dust as she finally worked her own body out, touched her with chill as she carried the heavy objects to the boat, her steps weaving with exhaustion.

Looking up, she saw the clouds black and boiling. The air had gone cold, and wind sighed noisily through the grasses. Once that storm broke, then the water would rise swiftly; and she had a horror of being shut in that place, water rising over the entrance, to drown her in the dark.

But one piece she had left, a bowl filled with gold objects, itself heavy and solid.

With feverish anxiety she lay down and crawled back into the dark, feeling her way until her eyes cleared and she walked again into the main chamber, where the king lay on his bier.

It was useless to have spared him. She resolved suddenly to make good her theft, for the water would have all in the end, the mask as well. She went to the bier—the only place that the declining light shone, and that dimmed by clouds. A few drops of rain fell on the mask like tears, puddling the dust there, and the wind skirled violently through the double openings, tugging at her skirts, bidding her make urgent haste. But she saw again how fair he had been, and alone now, robbed, his companion ghosts all destroyed, here at the end of time. He had seen the fields wide and green, had ruled holds and villages beside which Chadrih was nothing. To have enjoyed power and never felt hunger, and to have lain down to die amidst all these good things, she thought, was a happy fate.

But at the end he was robbed by a Barrows-girl, his descendant, whose fondest wish was to have a warm cloak and enough to eat; and once to see the green mountains of Shiuan.

Her hand strayed a second time from the mask that covered him; and a curious object in his skeletal fingers caught her eye. She moved the bones aside and took it: a bird, such as she knew today over the marshes—not a lucky symbol to have been worn by a warrior, who often risked death, nor had it been part of his armor. She thought rather of some grieving woman who had laid it there, a death-gift.

And it was strange to think that so homely a creature as a gull could be common to his age and hers, that he also had seen the birds above some more distant shore, not knowing them the heirs of all he possessed. She hesitated at it, for the white sea birds were a figure of death, that came and went beyond the world's edge; but, Barrows-bred that she was, she carried even among the amulets a white gull feather, and reckoned it lucky, for a Barrows-girl, whose livelihood was from the dead. The figure was golden, delicate: it warmed in her hands as it had not done in centuries. She touched the fine detail of the wings—and thrust it into her bodice when she saw the dusty jewels beside the king. But they proved only seal-gems, worthless, for the symbols on them could not be polished away, and the marshlanders thought them unlucky.

The rain struck her face, and spotted the dusty bones and washed upon the mask. Jhirun shivered in the cold wind and knew by the sound of the water rushing outside that she had waited dangerously long. Thunder crashed above the hill.

In sudden panic she fled, gathered up what she had come to fetch, and ran to the exit, wriggled through the tunnel pushing her treasure out ahead of her, out into the dim light and the pelting rain. The water in the channel had risen, beginning to lift and pull the boat from its safety on the bank.

Jhirun looked at that swirling, silt-laden water—dared not burden the boat more. In anguish she set aside her heavy bowl of trinkets, to wait high upon the bank. Then fearfully she loosed the mooring rope and climbed aboard, seized up the pole. The water snatched at the boat, turned it; it wanted all her skill and strength to drive it where she would, across the roaring channel to Jiran's Hill—and there she fought it aground, poured rain-washed treasure into her skirts and struggled uphill, not to lose a trinket on that slope that poured with water. She spilled her skirt-full of gold at the foot of the Standing Stone, made trip after trip to heap up there what she had won, by a sure marker, where it would be safe.

Then she tried to launch the skiff again toward the Barrow, the rain driving along the battered face of the waters in blowing sheets, torn by the wind. The boat almost pulled from her hands, dragging at the rope; she could not board it—and with a desperate curse, she hauled back on the rope, dragging the boat back to land, higher and higher, legs mudstreaked and scratched and her skirts a sodden weight about them. She reached a level place, sprawled backward with the rain driving down into her face, the blaze of lightnings blinding her. The boat was saved: that, at the moment, was more than gold.

And driven at last by misery, she gathered herself and began to seek relief from the cold. There was a short paddle and an oiled-leather cover in the skiff. She wrestled the little boat completely over, heaved the bow up with her shoulder and wedged the paddle under, making a shelter, however slight. She crawled within and wrapped her shivering limbs in the leather, much regretting now the meal she had not finished, the jars the flood had already claimed.

The rain beat down on the upturned bottom of the boat with great violence, and Jhirun clenched her chattering teeth, enduring, while water crept higher up the banks of the hills, flooded the access of the tomb, covered the treasure she had been forced to abandon on that other hill.

Of a sudden, a blink of her eyes in the gray-green light of storm, and the fore part of the Barrow began to slide into the channel, washed through, the bones and dust of the king gone sluicing down the flood to a watery rest. She clutched her amulets and muttered frantic prayers to the six favorable powers, watching the ruin widen, remembering the stern, sleeping face of the mask. Tales were told how ghosts went abroad on Hnoth and Midyear's Eve, how the kings of the sunken plain hosted drowned souls of Barrow-folk and villagers in their ghostly courts, and lights could be seen above the marsh—lights that marked their passage. She reckoned that she had killed some few ghosts by breaking the spells that held them to earth. They might go where they were doomed to go hereafter, no longer bound to their king, with storm to bear them hence.

But about her neck she wore the joined brass links of Bajen and Sojan the twin kings, that were for prosperity; and Anla's silver ring, for piety; the bit of shell that was for Sith the sea lord, a charm against drowning; the Dir-stone for warding off fevers; the Barrow-king's cross, that was for safety; and the iron ring of Arzad, favorable mate to the unfavorable seventh power . . . to Morgen-Angharan of the white gull feather, a charm that Barrowers wore, though marshlanders used it only to defend their windows and doorways. By these things Jhirun knew herself protected against the evils that might be abroad on the winds; she clung to them and tried to take her mind from her situation.

She waited while the day waned from murky twilight to starless night, when it became easier to take any fears to heart. The rain beat down ceaselessly, and she was still stranded, the waters too violent for the light boat.

Somewhere across the hills, she knew, her cousins and uncles would be doing the same, sheltering on some high place, probably in greater comfort. They had gone to gather wood at the forest's edge, and likely sat by a warm fire at the ruins on Nia's Hill, not stirring until the rain should cease. No one would come searching for her; she was a Barrower, and should have sense enough to do precisely what she had done. They would reckon correctly that if she had drowned she was beyond help, and that if she had taken proper precautions she would not drown.

But it was lonely, and she was afraid, with the thunder rolling overhead from pole to pole. Finally she collapsed the shelter entirely, to keep out the prying wind, wrapped in her leather covering and with the rain beating down above her with a sound to drive one mad.

ᐦ **Chapter 2**

At last the rain ceased, and there was only the rush of water. Jhirun wakened from a brief sleep, numb in her feet, like to smother in the dark. She sneezed violently and heaved up the shelter of her boat and looked about, finding that the clouds had passed, leaving a clear sky and the moons Sith and Anli to light the night.

She turned the boat onto its bottom and staggered to her feet, brushed back her sodden hair. The waters were still running high, and there was still lightning in the north—ominous, for rains came back sometimes, hurled back from the unseen mountains of Shiuan to spread again over Hiuaj.

But there was peace for the moment, satisfaction simply in having survived. Jhirun clenched her gelid hands and warmed them under her arms, and sneezed again. Something pricked her breast, and she felt after it, remembering the gull as her fingers touched warm metal. She drew it forth. The fine traceries of it glittered in the moonlight, immaculate and lovely, reminding her of the beauty that she had not been able to save. She fingered it lovingly and tucked it again into her bodice, grieving over the lost treasure. This one piece was hers: her cousins should not take this from her, this beautiful thing, this reward of a night of misery. She felt it lucky for her. She had a collection of such things, pictures on broken pottery, useless seal-gems, things no one wanted, but a gold piece—that she had never dared. They had their right, and she was wrong, she knew, for all the hold had good of the gold that was traded.

But not the gull, never the gull.

There would be a beating instead of a reward, if her kinsmen ever suspected how much of the gold she had failed to rescue from the flood, if ever she breathed to them the tale of the king in the golden mask, that she had let the water have. She knew that she had not done as well as she might, but—

—But, she thought, if she shaped her story so that she seemed to have saved everything there was, then for a few days nothing would be too good for Jhirun Ela's-daughter. Folk might even soften their attitudes toward her, who had been cursed for ill luck and ill-wishing things. At the least she would be due the pick of the next trading at Junai; and she would have—her imagination leaped to the finest thing she had ever desired—a fine leather cloak from Aren in the marshes, a cloak bordered in embroideries and fur, a cloak to wear in hall and about the home island, and never out in the weather, a cloak in which to pretend Barrows-hold was Ohtij-in, and in which she could play the lady. It would be a grand thing, when she must marry, to sit in finery among her aunts at the hearth, with a secret bit of gold next her heart, the memory of a king.

And there would be Fwar.

Jhirun cursed bitterly and wrenched her mind from that dream. The cloak she might well gain, but Fwar spoiled it, spoiled all her dreams. Sharing her bed, he would find the gull and take it, melt it into a ring for trade—and beat her for having concealed it. She did not want to think on it. She sneezed a third time, a quiet, stifled sneeze, for the night was lonely, and she knew that her lot would be fever if she must spend the night sitting still.

She walked, and moved her limbs as much as she could, and finally decided that she might warm herself by gathering up her gold on the hilltop and bringing it down to the boat. She climbed the hill with much slipping on the wet grass, using the tufts of it to pull herself up the steepest part, and found things safe by the Standing Stone.

She flung back her head and scanned all her surroundings under the two moons, the place where the other hill had stood and hardly a third remained. She gazed at the wide-spread waters dancing under the moonlight, the lightning in the south.

And Anla's Crown.

It glowed, a blaze of light like the dead-lights that hovered sometimes over the marsh. She rubbed her eyes, and gazed on it with a cold fear settling into her stomach.

Nothing was atop Anla's hill but the stones and the grass, nothing that the lightning might have set ablaze, and there was no ruddiness of living fire about it. It was ghostly, cold, a play of witchfires about the stones of the Crown.

Almost she had no courage to delay atop the hill, not even for the precious gold. She felt naked and exposed, the Standing Stone that was the sister-stone to those of Anla's Crown looming above her like some watching presence.

But she knelt and gathered up the gold that she could carry, and slid down to the skiff, loaded it aboard, went back for more, again and again. And each time that she looked toward Anla's hill the lights still hovered there.

Jiran's Hill was no longer a refuge from whatever was happening at Anla's Crown: it was altogether too close, on the verge of what strangeness passed there. She dared not wait until morning; the sun itself would seem no comfort, but a glaring eye to mark her presence here too near to Anla.

Better the danger of the currents: against the waters she had some skill, and of them she had less fear. She eased the loaded boat downslope, the long pole and the paddle laid accessible within. Carefully she let it into the edge of the current and felt the pull, judged that she might possibly manage it.

She climbed in; the current seized the skiff, whirled it like a leaf on the flood for an instant before she could bring the pole to bear and take control. She fended herself from impact with the rocks, spun dizzyingly round again, found bottom and almost lost the pole.

It did not hold. She saved the pole and shipped a little water doing it, and suddenly the skiff whipped round the bend of a hill and out, toward the great rolling Aj, toward a current she could in no wise fight.

There was no bottom here. She used the paddle now, desperately, went with the rush and worked to its edge, broke into the shallows again and managed to fight it into the lesser channel between Anla's height and the Barrows. She averted her eyes from the unnatural glow that hovered, that danced upon the waters—used paddle and pole alternately, knowing that she must go this way, that the channels near Anla's great rise would be shallowest, where once the ancient Road had run. The current pulled, trying to take her to the Aj, and thence to the sea, where Socha had died, lost, drowned. But here, while she held to the newly flooded margins, where the skiff whispered over reeds, the waters were almost calm.

She was going home.

Jhirun rested from time to time, drawing up on the shoulder of a Barrow, driving herself further as soon as she had drawn breath. The horror that she had seen at Anla's Crown seemed impossible now, irretrievable to the memory as the interior of the tomb, a thing of the night and the edge of realities. The fear still prickled at the nape of her neck, but more present, more urgent, was the cloud in the north, the fitful flash of lightning.

She feared the hills themselves, that became refuges for small creatures with which she did not care to share the night—rats that skittered shadow-wise over the banks as she passed, serpents that disturbed the grasses as she rested.

And the flood had opened new channels, places not at all familiar, the flooding making even known hills look different. She guided herself by the currents that she fought, by the stars that began to be obscured by clouds. She felt herself carried south, riverward, and ceased to be sure where she was.

But at last before her rose jagged shapes in the water, the ruined buildings of Chadrih. Her heart leaped with joy, for she knew the way from here beyond a doubt, through shallow channels.

The murmur of the water, the frantic song of the frogs and the other creatures of the tall grasses, made counterpoint to the movement of the boat, the slap of water against the bow, the whispers of reeds under the bottom. Jhirun gathered herself to her feet in the skiff, bravely confident now, balanced evenly on her bare feet. The pole touched the sunken stones that she remembered.

Chadrih: she remembered being nine and being thrust out of a house of Chadrih, folk making gestures to avert the evil of a Barrows-child who was known to be fey, to dream dreams. She remembered a sinful satisfaction to see that house deserted, and the windows all naked and empty. The Halmo men had stayed on last, they that had most hated and despised Barrows-folk; and they had drowned when she was twelve. The water had taken them and she could not even remember now what they had looked like.

She swayed her weight and pushed with the pole and sent the skiff down that narrow channel that had once been a cobbled street. The jagged, roofless buildings like eyeless brooding beasts shape-shifted past her. The ruins rustled with wings, the nesting birds disturbed by her passage; and the frogs kept up their mad chorus in the reeds. When she reached the edge of Chadrih she could see the first of the northern Barrows against the lightning-lit sky, and beyond it would lie Barrows Rock and home.

Hills began to pass her again on one side and the other, great conical mounds, shadows that momentarily enfolded her and gave her up again to the clouding sky. And there, just where she knew to look, she first saw the light that would be Barrows-hold tower, a flickering behind wind-tossed trees, a star-like gleam in the murk.

The water was calm here and shallow. Jhirun ventured a glance back between the hills, and could see only empty darkness. She made herself forget that, and looked forward again, keeping her eyes fixed on that friendly beacon, slipping the boat in and out among the hills.

The light flickered the harder, and suddenly the wind began to rise, whipping at her skirts and ruffling the water. There were little whisperings in the reeds and in the brush that overgrew these marshward Barrows. The storm was almost on her, and lightning danced on the black waters. Jhirun drew an aching breath and worked harder as the first heavy drops hit her, unwilling to yield and shelter miserably so close to home.

And alternate with the strokes she made she heard a rippling and splash of water, like a man striding, perhaps just the other side of the hill she was passing.

She stopped for a moment, drifting free, and the sound continued.

Perhaps a stray animal out of the marsh, storm-driven; there were wild ponies there, and occasional deer left. She let the boat glide where it would and listened to the sound, trying to judge just where it was, whether it went four-footed or two, and cold sweat prickled on her ribs.

So close, so close to home: perhaps it was one of her kinsmen, seeking home. But it moved so relentlessly, unregarding of the noise her boat had made, and no voice hailed her. She felt the hair rise on her neck as she thought of outlaws and beasts that came seldom out of the deep fens—things such as might be stirred out of lairs by flood and storm.

A cry came, thin and distorted by the air and the hills.

And then she knew it for the bleating of a silly goat; she was that near home. She felt a wild urge to laugh; some of their own livestock, surely. She hoped so. The boat had begun to move with more rapidity than she liked and she feared the noise she might make using the pole to restrain it. She had let it slip into the main current, where the water curled round the hills; she must stop it. She used the pole carefully, making a rippling despite her efforts to move noiselessly. She was fearfully conscious of the gold that glittered under the lightning, scattered at her feet—treasure to tempt any outlaw, ghost-things and unhallowed as they were. Here in the dark, not alone, she was acutely aware whence the objects had come, and aware too of the gull amulet between her breasts, that made a sharp pain at every push she made, this thing that had last lain between the fingers of a dead king.

She misjudged the channel in her preoccupation; the pole missed purchase and she drifted, helpless, balancing and waiting for the current to take her where she could find bottom again. The skiff whipped round in an eddy and slowed as it rounded the curve of an isle.

And she spun face to face with a rider, a shadowy horseman whose mount went belly-deep in the water—and that rider glittered here and there with linked mail. She thrust for bottom desperately, borne toward him. Strength deserted her hands and she could not hold. The rider loomed close at hand, the face of a young man, pale, beneath the peaked helm. His black horse shied aside, eyes rolling in the lightning flash.

She could not cry out. He reached and shouted at her, a thin voice, lost on the wind as the current pulled her on.

Then she remembered the pole in her nerveless hands and leaned on it, driving the boat to another channel, seeking a way out of this maze.

Water splashed behind her, the black horse—she felt it without looking back. She moved now with more frenzy than skill, her hair blinding her when at last she had to look and know. Through its strands she saw his shape black on the lightning-lit waters behind her.

She whipped her head round again as the skiff passed between two hills, and there, there ahead was the light of Barrows-hold tower, the safety of doors and lights and her own kinsmen ahead. She exerted all her strength and skill, put out of her mind what followed her—the black king under the hill, the king in the mask, whose bones she had let lie undisturbed. She was cold, feeling not her hands nor the balance of her feet, nor anything but her own heart crashing against her ribs and the raw edge of pain on which she breathed.

Barrows-hold filled all her vision, the slope of the landing before her. She drove for it, felt the skiff go aground on mud and reeds, then glide through. She leaped out on shore, turned to look, saw the black rider still distant; and even then she thought of the gold and the precious boat that was their livelihood. She hurled the pole to the ground and gathered up the rope and pulled and heaved the skiff aground, she skidding and sliding in the mud; a last look at the advancing rider, the water curling white about the horse's breast as it came, and she heaped pieces of gold into her skirts.

Then she turned and began to run, bare feet seeking tufts of grass to aid her climbing. Above her loomed the house, the cracks of its shuttered windows agleam with light, and the old tower lit to guide the Barrows' scattered children home. She dropped a piece of treasure, gathered it again, stumbling. Rain was falling, the wind hurling the drops into her eyes with stinging force, and thunder cracked. She heard the suck of water behind her, the heave of a large body, and looking back, she saw the black horse and the rider. Lightning glittered coldly off ring-mail, illumined a pale face. The dogs began barking frantically.

She touched her luck amulets with one hand and held the knotted burden in her skirts with the other and ran, hearing the rider coming after. The grass was slick. She spilled a piece of her gold and this time did not stop. Her feet skidded again on the slick stone paving before the door. She recovered, hurled herself at the closed door.

"Grandfather!" she cried, pounding at the insensate wood. "Hurry!"

She heard the rider behind her, the wet sound of the animal struggling on the slope, the ring of metal and the panting whuffs of his breathing.

She cast a look over her shoulder and saw the rider alight to aid his horse in the climb. His leg gave with him. He caught his balance and struggled up the slope, holding out his hand to her. She saw him in the jerking flashes of the lightning.

"Grandfather!" she screamed.

The door came open. She fled into that light and warmth and turned, expecting the rider to have vanished, as all such things should. He had not; he was almost at the door. She seized the door from her grandfather's indecisive hand and slammed it, helped him drop the bar into place, the gold scattering. Plates and cups clanged against the stones and rattled to a stop.

Jhirun turned and looked at the others, awe-stricken female faces ringed about the room, women and children, boys too young to be with the men.

There were Cil and aunt Jinel and aunt Zai; but there was no man at all but grandfather Keln.

And she cast a look at him, desperate, fearing that for once her grandfather had no answer. Sprigs of *azael* and Angharan's white feathers hung above doorways of house and stable, above the windows of both floors, wherever there was an access. They jested about them, but they renewed them annually, they that robbed the dead; there were laws, and it was taken for granted that the dead obeyed them.

"The signal," her grandfather breathed; his hands shook more than usual as he waved the women toward the stairs. "Zai, go! All the house, upstairs, and hide."

Plump Zai turned and fled stableward, by the west door, toward the tower—hers to care for the signal-beacons. The others began to herd frightened children toward the stairs to the loft. Some were crying. The dogs were barking furiously; they were shut in the yard, useless.

Old Jinel stayed, her sharp chin set; Cil stayed, her belly swollen with her third child, her other children at her skirts. Cil took off her warm brown shawl and cast it about Jhirun's shoulders, hugged her. Jhirun hugged her back, almost giving way to tears.

Outside came the ring of hooves on stone, circling back and forth before the door, back and forth, to the window. The shutters rattled, ceased.

Then for a long time there was nothing but the shaking of harness and the breathing of the animal outside at the window.

"Ohtija outlaw?" Grandfather asked, looking at Jhirun. "Where did he start trailing you?"

"Out there," she managed to say, clenching her teeth against the impulse to chatter. She tried to gather an explanation.

Steps reached the door, and there was a splintering impact. The children screamed and clung to Cil.

"Go," said Grandfather. "Hurry. Take the children upstairs."

"Hurry," Jhirun echoed, pushing at Cil, who tried to make her come with her, clinging to her. But there was no leaving her grandfather, fragile as he was. Jinel stayed too. Cil fled, her children beside her, for the stairs.

The battering at the door assumed a rhythm, and white wood broke through on the edge of an axe. Jhirun felt her grandfather's arm go about her, and she held to him, trembling, watching the door riven into ruin. It was never meant to withstand attack; no outlaws had ever assaulted the hold.

An entire plank gave way: the door hung ajar, and a man's armored arm reached through, trying to move the bar inside.

"No!" Jhirun cried, tore from her grandfather and ran to seize the great butchering knife from the scullery, her mind only then thinking of tangible defenses; but there was a crash behind her, the bar hitting the floor. She whirled in midstep, saw the door crash open.

There in the rain stood the warrior-king. He had an axe in his hand and a bow slung at his back, the hilt of a sword riding at his shoulder. The rain sheeted down and made his face look like the drowned dead. He stood there with the black horse behind him and looked about the room as if he were seeking something.

"Take the gold," her grandfather offered him, his old voice stern as it was when he served as priest; but the stranger seemed disinterested in that— reached for the reins and led the tall animal forward, such a horse as had not been seen in Hiuaj since the sea wall broke. It shied at the strange doorway, then came with a rush, and its hindquarters swung round and broke the ruined door farther from its hinges. A golden cup was crushed under its hooves, spurned like a valueless stone.

None of them moved, and the warrior made no move at them. He towered in the center of their little hall and looked about him, he and the horse dripping muddy water onto the stones of the floor; and mingled with that water was blood that flowed from a wound on his leg.

Children were crying upstairs; he looked at the stairs and up toward the loft, while Jhirun's heart pounded. Then he turned his eyes instead to the fireplace. He drew on the reins of the horse and led it forward, toward warmth, himself limping and leaving a trail of blood and water.

And there, his back to that blazing fire, he turned and gazed at them, his eyes wild and anguished. They were dark, those eyes, and dark his hair, when every lord of the north she had heard of was fair. He was tall, armored in plain and ancient style; there was fineness about him that for all his misery made their little hold seem shabby.

She knew what he was; she knew. The gull lay like guilt against her breast, and she longed to thrust it into his hands and bid him go, leave, become what he was. She met his eyes without wanting to, a chill running through her. Here was no wisp of cobweb to fade in firelight: he cast tall shadows across the floor, left tracks of blood and water. Rain dripped from his hair and made him blink, long hair, in a warrior's knot, such as the ancient Kings had worn. His chest rose and fell strongly in ragged breathing; he drew a great breath, and his sigh was audible.

"A woman," he said, his voice nearly gone with hoarseness; and it was a lilting accent she had never heard—save in the songs. "A woman, a rider all— all white—"

"No," Jhirun said at once, touching at the white feather amulet. "No." She did not want him to go on speaking. In her desperation she opened her mouth to bid him gone as she might some trespassing marshlander; but he was not that, he was far from that, and she felt herself coarse and powerless in the face of him. There was no move from her grandfather, a priest, whose warding charms had failed; no word from Jinel, who had never lacked words before. Outside the hall the thunder rolled and the rain sheeted past the ruined door, a surety that the men would be held from returning, barred by risen water.

The visitor stared at them with a strange, lost expression, as if he wanted something; and then with awkwardness and evident pain he turned, and with the axe blade, hooked the kettle that hung over the fire and swung it outward. Steam rolled up from it, fragrant with one of Zai's stews. There was a stack of wooden bowls on the mantel. He filled one with the ladle and sank down where he was, braced his back against the stones. The black horse shook itself of a sudden, spattering the whole room and everyone in it with muddy water.

"Get out!" Grandfather Keln cried, his thin voice cracking with outrage.

The stranger looked at him, no answering rage, only a tired, perplexed look. He did not move, save to lift the steaming bowl to his lips to sip at the broth, still staring at them warily. His hand shook so that he spilled some of it. Even the black horse looked sorrowful, head hanging, legs scored by the passage through the flood. Jhirun hugged her dry shawl about her and forced herself to stop shivering, deciding that they were not all to be murdered forthwith.

Suddenly she moved, went to the shelves across the room and pulled down one of the coarse blankets they used for rain chill and rough usage. She took it to the invader of their home, where he sat on their hearthside; and when he, seeing her intention, leaned forward somewhat, she wrapped it about him, weapons and all. He looked up, the bowl in one hand, gathering the blanket with the other. He gestured with the bowl at the kettle, at her, at all the house, as if graciously bidding them be free of their own food.

"Thank you," she said, struggling to keep her voice from shaking. She was hungry, miserably so, and cold. And to show that she was braver than she was, she pulled the kettle over to herself and took another bowl, dipped up a generous helping. "Has everyone else eaten?" she asked in a perfectly ordinary voice.

"Yes," said Jinel.

She saw by the grease mark on the black iron that this was so; enough remained for the men. It occurred to her that the stranger might suspect others yet unfed, might take note by that how many there were in the house. She pulled the kettle as far out of his view as she could, sat down on the opposite side of the hearth and ate, forcing the food down despite the terror that still knotted her stomach.

Azael sprigs and white feathers: she suspected them nothing, her grandfather's power nothing. She had been where she should not; and came *this* where he ought not. It was on her he looked, as if no one else existed for him, as if he cared nothing for an old man and an old woman who owned the food and the fire he used.

"I wish you would leave our house," Jhirun declared suddenly, speaking to him as if he were the outlaw her grandfather called him, wishing that this would prove true.

His pale, beard-shadowed face showed no sign of offense. He looked at her with such weariness in his eyes it seemed he could hardly keep them open, and the bowl started to tumble from his hand. He caught it and set it down. "Peace," he murmured, "peace on this house." And then he leaned his head against the stone and blinked several times. "A woman," he said, taking up that mad illusion of his own, "a woman on a gray horse. Have you seen her?"

"No," said Grandfather sternly. "None such. Nothing."

The stranger's eyes strayed toward him, to the shattered door, with such a look that Jhirun followed the direction of his gaze half expecting to see such a woman there. But there was only the rain, a cold wind blowing through the open doorway, a puddle spreading across the stones.

He turned his attention then to the other door, that in the west wall. "Where does that go?"

"The stable," Grandfather said; and then, carefully: "The horse would be better there."

But the stranger said nothing, and gradually his eyes grew heavy, and he rested his head against the stones of the fireplace, nodding with the weariness that pressed upon him.

Grandfather quietly gathered up the reins of the black horse, the stranger not protesting: he led it toward that door, and aunt Jinel bestirred herself to open it. The beast hesitated, with the goats bleating alarm inside; but perhaps the warm stable smell drew it; it eased its way into that dark place, and Grandfather pulled the door shut after.

And Jinel sat down on a bench amid her abused house and clenched her thin hands and set her jaw and wept. The stranger watched her, a troubled gaze, and Jhirun for once felt pity for her aunt, who was braver than she had known.

A time passed. The stranger's head bowed upon his breast; his eyes closed. Jhirun sat by him, afraid to move. She set her bowl aside, marked suddenly that Jinel rose, walked quietly across the room. Grandfather, who had been by Jinel, went to the center of the room and watched the stranger; and there was a creaking on the stairs.

Jinel reached up to the wall for that great knife they used for butchering, tucked it up in a fold of her skirts. She came back to Grandfather.

A board creaked. Cil was on the stairs; Jhirun could see her now. Her heart beat painfully; the supper lay like a stone in her belly. They were no match for the warrior-king; they could not be. And Cil, brave Cil, a loyal sister, heavy with child: it was for her sake that Cil ventured downstairs.

Jhirun moved suddenly to her knees, touched the stranger. His eyes opened in panic and he clutched the axe that lay across his lap. Behind her in the room she sensed that things had stopped, her house with its furtive movements frozen where matters stood. "I am sorry," Jhirun said, holding his eyes with her own. "The wound—will you let me treat it?"

He looked confused for a moment, his eyes ranging beyond her. Perhaps, she thought in terror, he saw what had been proceeding.

Then he bowed his head in consent, and moved his injured leg to straighten it, moved the blanket aside so that she could see how the leather was rent and the flesh deeply cut. He drew the bone-handled dagger from his belt and cut the leather further so that she could reach the wound. The sight of it made her weak at the stomach.

She gathered herself up and crossed the room to the shelves, sought clean linen. Jinel met her there and tried to snatch the cloth from her fingers.

"Let me go," Jhirun hissed.

"Slut," Jinel said, her nails deep in her wrist.

Jhirun tore free and turned, dipped clean water from the urn in the corner and went back to the stranger. Her hands were shaking and her eyes blurred as she started to work, but they soon steadied. She washed the cut, then forced a large square of cloth through the opening and tied it tightly from the outside, careful not to pain him. She was intensely aware of her grandfather and Cil and Jinel watching her, their eyes on her back—herself touching a strange man.

He laid his hand on hers when she had done; his hands were fine, long-fingered. She had never imagined that a man could have such hands. There were scars on them, a fine tracery of lines. She thought of the sword he carried and reckoned that he had never wielded tools . . . hands that knew killing, perhaps, but their touch was like a child's for gentleness; his eyes were likewise. "Thank you," he said, and showed no inclination to let her go. His head went back against the wall. His eyes began to close, exhaustion claiming him. They opened; he fought against the impulse.

"Your name," he asked.

One should never give a name; it was power to curse. But she feared not to answer. "Mija Jhirun Ela's-daughter," she said; and daring much: "What is yours?"

But he did not answer, and unease crept the more upon her.

"Where were you going?" she asked. "Were you only following me? What were you looking for?"

"To live," he said, with such simple desperation it seized at her heart. "To stay alive." And he almost slipped from his senses, the others waiting for his sleep, the whole house poised and waiting, nearly fifty women and an old man. She edged closer to him, put her shoulder against him, drew his head against her. "The woman," she heard him murmur, "the woman that follows me—"

He was fevered. She felt of his brow, listened to his raving, that carried the same mad thread throughout. He slipped away, his head against her heart, his eyes closed.

She stared beyond him, meeting Cil's troubled gaze, none others'.

A time to sleep, a little time for him, and then a chance to escape. He had done nothing to them, nothing of real hurt; and to end slaughtered by a house of women and children, with kitchen knives—she did not want that nightmare to haunt Barrows-hold. She could not live her life and sit by the fire and sew, work at the kitchen making bread, see her children playing by such a hearth. She would always see the blood on those stones.

No wraith, the stranger: his warmth burned fever-hot against her; his weight bruised her shoulder. She had lost herself, lost all sense where her mad dreams ended, no longer tried to reason. She saw the others lose their courage, settle, waiting; she also waited, not knowing for what. She remembered Anla's Crown, and knew that she had passed that edge where human folk ought to stop, had broken ancient warding-spells with as blithe a disdain as the stranger had passed the bits of feather at the door, innocent of fear that would have been wise to feel.

If there had been opportunity she would have begged her grandfather to explain; but he was helpless, his warding spells broken, his authority disregarded. For the first time she doubted the power of her grandfather as a priest—doubted the power of all priests. She had seen a thing her grandfather had never seen— still could not see; had been where no foot had trod since the Kings.

The hold seemed suddenly a tiny and fragile place amid all the wild waste of Hiuaj, a place where the illusion of law persisted like a light set in the wind. But the reality was the dark, that lay heavy and breathing against her shoulder.

They should not destroy him, they in their mad trust in law and their own sanity. She began to wonder if they even questioned what he was, if they saw only an exhausted and wounded outlaw, and never doubted their conclusion. They were blind, that could not see the manner of him, the ancient armor and the tall black horse, that had no place in this age of the world, let alone in Hiuaj.

Perhaps they did not want to see, for then they would have to realize how fragile their safety was.

And perhaps he would not go away. Perhaps he had come to ruin that peace of theirs—to take Barrows-hold down to the same ruin as Chadrih, to ride one last course across the drowning world, one last glory of the Hiua kings, who had tried to master the Wells and failed, as the halfling Shiua had failed before them.

She had no haste to wake him. She sat frozen in dread while the storm fell away to silence, while the fire began to die in the hearth and none dared approach to tend it.

⌐ Chapter 3

Toward dawn came a stirring outside, soft scuffing on the pavement. Jhirun looked up, waking from half-sleep, her shoulder numb with the stranger's weight.

Came Zai, shivering and wet, stout Zai, who had run to set the beacon. She entered blue-lipped with chill and dripping about the hem of her skirts, and moved as silently as she could.

And behind Zai crept others, out of the mist that had followed the rain: the men came, one after the other, armed with skinning knives and their boat-poles. None spoke. They moved inside, their eyes hard and wary and their weapons ready. Jhirun watched and her heart pounded against her ribs; her lips shaped silent entreaty to them, her cousins, her uncles.

Uncle Naram was first to venture toward the hearth; and Lev after him, with Fwar and Ger beside him. Cil rose up of a sudden from the bench by the door; but Jinel was by her and seized her arm, cautioning her to silence. Jhirun cast a wild look at her grandfather, who stood helplessly at the stable door, and looked back at the men who edged toward her with drawn weapons.

Perhaps her arms tightened the least bit; perhaps there was some warning sound her numbed hearing did not receive; but the stranger wakened of a sudden, and she cried out to feel the push of his arms hurling her at them.

He was on his feet in the same instant, staggering against the mantel, and they rushed on him, rushing over her, who sprawled on the floor. And Fwar, more eager to lay hands on her than on the enemy, seized her and cruelly twisted her arm in hauling her to her feet. In the loft a baby cried, swiftly hushed.

Jhirun looked, dazed by the pain of Fwar's grip, on the stranger who had backed to the corner. She saw his move, quicker than the beat of a bird's wing, that sent his dagger into his hand.

That gave them pause; and in that pause he ripped at the harness at his side and that great sword at his back slid to his hip. He unhooked the sheath of it one-handed.

They panicked, rushed for him in a mass, and of a sudden the sheath flashed across the room loose, and the bright blade was in his two hands, a wheeling arc that scattered blood and hurled her kinsmen back with shrieks of pain and terror.

And he leaned there in his corner a moment, hard-breathing; but the fresh wounds were on his enemies and none had they set on him. The stranger moved, and Fwar gave back, wrenching Jhirun's arm so hard that she cried out, Cil's scream echoing upon her own.

The stranger edged round the room, gathered up his fallen sheath, still with an eye to them; and her kinsmen gave back still further, none of them willing to rush that glittering blade a second time. In the loft were frightened stirrings, back into shadows.

"What will you?" Jhirun heard her grandfather's voice ask from behind her. "Name it and go."

"My horse," he said. "You, old man, fetch all my gear—all of it. I shall kill you otherwise."

And not a muscle did he move, staring at them with the great sword in his hands; nor did they move. Only her grandfather sidled carefully to the stable door and opened it, going to do the stranger's bidding.

"Let her go," the stranger said then to Fwar.

Fwar thrust her free, and she turned and spat at Fwar, shaking with hate. Fwar did nothing, his baleful eyes fixed on the stranger in silent rage, and she walked from him, never so glad to walk away from anything—went from him and to the side of the stranger, who had touched her gently, who had never done her hurt.

She turned there to face them all, these brute, ugly cousins, with thick hands and crass wit and no courage when it was likely to cost them. Her grandfather had been a different man once; but now he had none to rely on but these: brigands, no different at heart than the bandits they paid the marshlanders to catch and hang—save that the bandits preyed on the living.

Jhirun drew a deep breath and tossed her tangled hair from her face and looked on Fwar, hating, seeing the promise of later vengeance for his shame—on her, whom he reckoned already his property. She hated with a depth that left her shaking and short of breath, knowing her hopelessness. She was no more than they; the stranger had taken her part because of his own pride, because it was what a king should have done, but it was not because she was more than her cousins.

He had dropped his dagger to use the sword. She bent, slowly, picked it up, he none objecting; and she walked slowly to the other corner and slashed the strings by which sausages and white cheeses were hung. Jinel squealed with outrage, provoking a child's outcry from the loft; Jinel stifled her cry behind bony hands.

And such prizes Jhirun gathered off the floor and brought back to him. "Here," she said, dropping them at his side on the hearthstones. "Take whatever you can."

This she said to spite them all.

The stableward door opened, and Grandfather Keln led the black horse back in, the beast apprehensive of the room and the men. The warrior gathered the reins into his left hand and tugged at the saddle, testing the girth, but he never stopped watching the men. "I will take the blanket, if you will," he said to Jhirun quietly. "Tie the food into that and tie it on."

She bent down and did this, under her kinsmen's outraged eyes, rolled it all into a neat kit bound with some of the cheese strings and bound it behind the saddle as he showed her. She had to reach high to do this, and she feared the tall horse, but she was glad enough to do this for him.

And then she stood aside while he tugged on the reins and led the black horse through their midst to the open door, none daring to stop him. He paused outside, still on the paving, already greyed by the mist that whitened the morning outside. She saw him rise to the saddle, turn, and the mist took him, and swiftly muffled even the sound of the hooves.

There was nothing left of him, and it was as she had known it would be. She shivered, and shut her eyes, and realized in her hand was still one relic of their meeting, one memory of ancient magics: the hilt of a bone-handled dagger, such as the old Kings had borne to their burials.

She looked on her kinsmen, who were bleeding with wounds and ragged and ill-smelling, which *he* had never been, though he came from the flood, hard-riding; and there was hate in their faces, which he had not given her, though he was set upon and almost killed. She regarded Cil, sallow-faced, with her strength wasted; and Jinel, from whose face all liveliness and love had long since departed.

"Come here," said Fwar, and reached out to jerk her by the arm, his courage regained.

She whipped the knife across his face, struck flesh and heard him scream, blood across his mouth; and she whirled and ran, slashed this way and that among them, saw Cil's face a mask of horror at her madness, her grandfather drawing Cil back for protection. She held her hand then, and ran, free, through their midst, out into the cold and the fog.

The shawl slipped from her shoulders to trail by a corner; she caught it and ran again, through the black brush that appeared out of the mist. The dogs barked madly. She found the corner of the rough stone shelter on the west corner of the hold, and there in the brush she sank down, clutching the knife in bloody fingers and bending over, near to being sick. Her stomach heaved at the memory of Cil's horrified face. Her eyes stung with tears that blurred nothing, for there was only blank mist about her. She heard shouting through the distorting fog, her cousins seeking her, cursing her.

And Cil's voice, full of love and anguish.

Then she did weep, hot tears coursing down her face. She remembered the Cil that had been, when they were three sisters and the world was wider; then Cil could have understood—but Cil had made her choice, for safety, for her children. She was a faithful wife to Ger; and Jhirun knew Ger, who was faithful to nothing, who had laid hands on Jhirun herself in the drunkenness of Midyear, careless of his wife's feelings. Jhirun still had nightmares of that escape; and Ger had a scar to remember it.

And Fwar; she knew she had scarred him badly. He would have revenge for it. She had taken the petty measure of him before them all, and he could not live without revenge for that. She sat trembling in the cold white blankness and clutched against her breast the gull-token of the dead king, and the bloody dagger with it.

"Jhirun!"

That was her grandfather's voice, frantic and angry. Even to him she could not explain what she had done, why she had turned a knife on her own cousins, or what set her shuddering when she looked on her own sister. *Fey*, he must say, which others had always believed; and he would sign holy signs over her, and cleanse the house and renew the broken warding spells.

It was without meaning, she thought suddenly, the chanting and the spells. They lived all their lives in the shadow of world's end; and her children to Fwar or any man would be born to a worse age; and their children to the end of the world. They tried to live as if it were unimportant that the sea was eating away at the marsh and the quakes shaking the stones of the hold. They lived as if gold could buy them years as it bought them grain. They sought safety and warmth and comfort as if it would last, and saw nothing that was real.

There was no peace. The Barrow-king had swept through their lives like a wind out of the dark; and peace was at an end, but they saw nothing.

To accept Fwar, until she had no spirit left; or until she killed him or he killed her, that was the choice she was given.

She drew a great mouthful of air, like one drowning, and stared into the white nothingness and knew that she was not going back. She gathered her limbs under her, and rose and moved quietly through the mist.

Her kinsmen were down by the bank, calling to each other, seeking whether she had left in the boat. Soon they found the gold that was left there, abandoned in the night. Their voices exclaimed in profane greed. Already they were fighting over the prizes she had brought.

She cared nothing for this. She had no more desire for gold or for anything that they valued. She moved quietly round by the stable's outside door, cracked it so that she could see in without being seen. The goats bleated and the birds stirred in the loft, so that her heart froze in her and she knew that the houseward door would be flung open and her presence in the outer stable discovered upon the instant. But there was no stir from the house. She could still hear the shouting down by the boat, distant and angry voices. There would be no better chance than this.

She slipped inside, went to the pony's stall and eased the gate open. Then she took the halter from its peg and slipped it on him, backed him out. He did not want to leave his stable when she reached the outside door, laid back his ears at the weather, but he came when she tugged on the rope—stolid, thick-necked little pony that bore their burdens and amused the children. She grasped the clipped mane and rolled up onto his back, her legs finding pleasant the warmth of his fat sides, and she nudged him with her bare heels and set him moving downslope, having to fight him at first: he thought he knew the trail she wanted, and was mistaken, and had to be persuaded otherwise.

The water had sunk away in the channel this morning, and kept to center. The pony's hooves made deep gouges in the mire, betrayal when the sun should clear the mist away, and the pony had careful work to find a way up the next bank: marshbred, the little beast, that knew his way among the flooded isles, far sturdier for such travelling than the slender-legged horse of the stranger-king. Jhirun patted his neck as they came up safely on the next hill, her legs wet to the knees; and the pony tossed his head and blew a puff of excitement, moving quickly, sensing by now that things were not ordinary this morning, that it was not a workday.

In and out among the Barrow-hills they travelled, in places so treacherous she must often dismount and lead the pony. Her bare feet were muddy and numb with cold, and the mist clung as it could on chill days. She felt the aches of her flight of the night before, the weariness of a night without sleep, but she had no desire to rest. Fwar would find the tracks; Fwar would pursue, if none of the others would. The thought of him coming on her alone, without his father and brother to restrain him, made her sick with fear.

Eventually in the mist she found the way she sought, the stones of the old Road, and solid footing for the pony. She climbed astride again, absorbing the warmth of the pony's sides, her damp shawl wrapped about her. She congratulated herself on having eluded pursuit, began for the first time to believe she might make it away clear. Even the pony moved gladly, his unshod hooves sounding hollowly on the stones and echoing back off unseen hills.

It was the only Road left in all Hiuaj, *khal*-made and more ancient than the Kings. Any who followed her must find her if she delayed; but they must come afoot, and she had the pony's strength under her.

Somewhere ahead, she believed, rode the stranger-king, for a northward track had brought him to Barrows-hold, and there was no way but this for a rider to take. She had no hope of overtaking him on that fine long-legged horse, not once they had both reached the Road itself; but in her deepest hopes she thought he might expect her, wait for her—that he would become her guide through the terror of the wide marsh.

But already he faded in her mind, a vision that belonged to the dark; and now things were white and gray. Only the gull-image at her heart and the bone-handled dagger in the waistband of her skirt proved that he had ever existed, and that she was most coldly sane, more than all her kinsmen.

In her common sense she knew that she was bound for grief, that she was casting herself into the hands of marshlanders or worse, who would learn, as her cousins knew, that she dreamed dreams, and hate her, as Chadrih-folk hated her, Ewon's fey daughter. But all the terror her nightmares had ever held seemed this morning at her back, hovering about Barrows-hold with a thickness that made it impossible to breathe. Death was there; she felt it, close, close and waiting. Away from Barrows-hold was relief from that pressure; it grew less and less as she rode away . . . not to Aren, to hope for that drab misery, within constant reach of Fwar. She chose to believe that she travelled to Shiuan, where holds sat rich and secure, where folk possessed Hiua gold. It was not so important to reach it as it was to go, now, now, now: the urgency beat in her blood like the heat of fever, beyond all reason.

Socha had smiled the morning she parted from them; Jhirun recalled her wrapped in sunlight, the boat gliding from the landing as it parted into that golden light: Socha had taken such a leave, at Hnoth, when madness swelled as the waters swelled in their channels. Jhirun let herself wonder the darker thoughts that she had always chased from her mind, whether Socha had lived long, swept out into the great gray sea—what night might have been for her, adrift in so much water, what horrid plunging of great monsters sporting near the shell of a boat, and in what mind Socha had come to the end—whether she had wept for Barrows-hold and a life such as Cil had accepted. Jhirun did not think so.

She drew the gull amulet from between her breasts, safe to see it now in daylight, safe where no one would take it from her; and she thought of the king under the hill, and the stranger—himself driven by a nightmare as her own drove her.

The white rider, the fair rider, the woman behind him: day and white mist, as he was of the dark. In the night she had shuddered at his ravings, thinking of white feathers and of what lay against her heart, that seventh and unfavorable power—that once had prisoned him, before a Barrows-girl had come where she ought not.

The gull glittered coldly in her hand, wings spread, a thing of ancient and sinister beauty, emblem of the blankness at the edge of the world, out of which only the white gulls came, like lost souls: Morgen-Angharan, that the marsh-landers cursed, that the Kings had followed to their ruin—the white Queen, who was Death. A nagging fear urged her to throw the amulet far into the marsh. Hnoth was coming, as it had come for Socha, when earth and sea and sky went mad and the dreams came, driving her where no sane person would go. But her hand closed firmly about it, possessing it, and in time she slipped it back into her bodice to stay.

She could not see what lay about her in the mist. The pony's hooves rang sometimes on bare stone, sometimes splashed through water or trod on slick mud. The dim shapes of the hills loomed in the thick air and passed her slowly like humps of some vast serpent, submerged in the marsh, now on this side of the Road and now on the other.

Something tall and thin stood beside the roadway. The pony clopped on toward it, and Jhirun's heart beat faster, her fingers clenched upon the rein, the while she assured herself that the pony would not so blithely approach any dangerous beast. Then it took shape clearly, one of the Standing Stones, edge-wise. She knew it now, and had not realized how far she had ridden in the mist.

More and more of such stones were about her now. She well knew where she was: the ruined *khalin* hold of Nia's Hill was nearby, stones which had stood before the Moon was broken. She rode now on the border of the marshlands.

The little pony walked stolidly on his way, small hooves ringing on stone and now muffled by earth; and all that she could see in the gray world were the nearest stones and the small patch of earth on which the pony trod, as if creation itself were unravelled before and behind, and only where she rode remained solid. So it might be if one rode beyond the edge of the world.

And riding over soft ground, she looked down and saw the prints of larger hooves.

The Road rose again from that point, so that earth no longer covered it, and the ancient stone surface lay bare. Three Standing Stones made a gathering of shadows in the mist just off the Road. Distantly came an echo off the Stones, slow and doubling the sound of the pony's hooves. Jhirun little liked the place, that was old before the Barrows were reared. Her hands clenched on the pony's short mane as well as on the rein, for he walked warily now, his head lifted and with the least uncertainty in his gait. The echoes continued; and of a sudden came the ring of metal on stone, a shod horse.

Jhirun drove her heels into the pony's fat sides, gathering her courage, forcing the unwilling animal ahead.

The black horse took shape before her, horse and rider, awaiting her. The pony balked. Jhirun gave him her heels again and made him go, and the warrior stayed for her, a dark shadow in the fog. His face came clear; he wore a peaked helm, a white scarf about it now. She stopped the pony.

"I came to find you," she said, and his lack of welcome was already sending uncertainties winding about her heart, a sense of something utterly changed.

"Who are you?" he asked, which totally confounded her; and when she stared at him: "Where do you come from? From that hold atop the hill?"

She began to reckon that she was in truth going mad, and pressed her chilled hands to her face and shivered, her shaggy pony standing dwarfed by that tall black horse.

With a gentle ripple of water, a ring of shod hooves on stone, a gray horse appeared out of the mist. Astride him was a woman in a white cloak, and her hair as pale as the day, as white as hoarfrost.

A woman, the warrior had breathed in his nightmare, *a rider all white, the woman that follows me—*

But she came to a halt beside him, white queen and dark king together, and Jhirun reined aside her pony to flee the sight of them.

The black horse overrushed her, the warrior's hand tearing the rein from her fingers. The pony shied off from such treatment, and the short mane failed her exhausted fingers. His body twisted under her and she tumbled down his slick back, seeing blind fog about her, up or down she knew not until she fell on her back and the Dark went over her.

Book Two

⤿ Chapter 4

It was not, even within the woods, like Kursh or Andur. Water flowed softly here, a hostile whisper about the hills. The moon that glowed through the fog was too great a moon, a weight upon the sky and upon the soul; and the air was rank with decay.

Vanye was glad to return to the fire, bearing his burden of gathered branches, to kneel by warmth that drove back the fog and overlay the stench of decay with fragrant smoke.

They had within the ruin a degree of shelter at least, although Vanye's Kurshin soul abhorred the builders of it: ancient stones that seemed once to have been the corner of some vast hall, the remnant of an arch. The gray horse and the black had pasturage on the low hill that lay back of the ruin, and the shaggy pony was tethered apart from the two for its safety's sake. The black animals were shadow-shapes beyond the trees, and gray Siptah seemed a wraith-horse in the fog: three shapes that moved and grazed at leisure behind a screen of moisture-beaded branches.

The girl's brown shawl was drying on a stone by the fire. Vanye turned it to dry the other side, then began to feed branches into the fire, wood so moisture-laden it snapped and hissed furiously and gave off bitter clouds of smoke. But the fire blazed up after a moment, and Vanye rested gratefully in that warmth—took off the white-scarfed helm and pushed back the leather coif, freeing his brown hair, that was cut even with his jaw: no warrior's braid—he had lost that right, along with his honor.

He sat, arms folded across his knees, staring at the girl who lay in Morgaine's white cloak, in Morgaine's care. A warm cloak, a dry bed, a saddlebag for a pillow: this was as much as they could do for the child, who responded little. He thought that the fall might have shaken her forever from her wits, for she shivered intermittently in her silence, and stared at them both with wild, mad eyes. But she seemed quieter since he had been sent out for wood—a sign, he thought, either of better or of worse.

When he was warmed through, he arose, returned quietly to Morgaine's side, from which he had been banished. He wondered that Morgaine spent so much attention on the child—little enough good that she could do; and he expected now that she would bid him go back to the fire and stay there.

"You speak with her," Morgaine said quietly, to his dismay; and as she gave place for him, rising, he knelt down, captured at once by the girl's eyes—mad, soft eyes, like a wild creature's. The girl murmured something in a plaintive tone and reached for him; he gave his hand, uneasily feeling the gentle touch of her fingers curling around his.

"She has found you," she said, a mere breath, accented, difficult to understand. "She has found you, and are you not afraid? I thought you were enemies."

He knew, then. He was chilled by such words, conscious of Morgaine's presence at his back. "You have met my cousin," he said. "His name is Chya Roh—among others."

Her lips trembled, and she gazed at him with clearing sense in her dark eyes. "Yes," she said at last. "You are different; I see that you are."

"Where is Roh?" Morgaine asked.

The threat in Morgaine's voice drew the girl's attention. She tried to move, but Vanye did not loose her hand. Her eyes turned back to him.

"Who are you?" she asked. "Who are you?"

"Nhi Vanye," he answered in Morgaine's silence, for he had struck her down, and she was due at least his name for it: "Nhi Vanye i Chya. Who are you?"

"Jhirun Ela's-daughter," she said, and added: "I am going north, to Shiuan—" as if this and herself were inseparable.

"And Roh?" Morgaine dropped to her knee and seized her by the arm. Jhirun's hand left his. For a moment the girl stared into Morgaine's face, her lips trembling.

"Let be," Vanye asked of his liege. "*Liyo*—let be."

Morgaine thrust the girl's arm free and arose, walked back to the fireside.

For some little time the girl Jhirun stared in that direction, her face set in shock. "*Dai-khal*," she murmured finally.

Dai-khal: high-clan *qujal*, Vanye understood that much. He followed Jhirun's glance back to Morgaine, who sat by the fire, slim, clad in black leather, her hair a shining pallor in the firelight. Here too the Old Ones were known, and feared.

He touched the girl's shoulder. She jerked from his fingers. "If you know where Roh is," he said, "tell us."

"I do not."

He withdrew his hand, unease growing in him. Her accents were strange; he hated the place, the ruins—all this haunted land. It was a dream, in which he had entrapped himself; yet he had struck flesh when he rode against her, and she bled, and he did not doubt that he could, that it was well possible to die here, beneath this insane and lowering sky. In the first night, lost, looking about him at the world, he had prayed; increasingly he feared that it was blasphemy to do so in this land, that these barren, drowning hills were Hell, in which all lost souls recognized each other.

"When you took me for him," he said to her, "you said you came to find me. Then he is on this road."

She shut her eyes and turned her face away, dismissing him, weak as she was and with the sweat of shock beading her brow. He was forced to respect such courage—she a peasant and himself once a warrior of clan Nhi. For fear, for very terror in this Hell, he had ridden against her and her little pony with the force he would have used against an armed warrior; and it was only good fortune that her skull was not shattered, that she had fallen on soft earth and not on stone.

"Vanye," said Morgaine from behind him.

He left the girl and went to the side of his liege—sat down, arms folded on his knees, next to the fire's warmth. She was frowning at him, displeased, whether at him or at something else, he was not sure. She held in her hand a small object, a gold ornament.

"She has dealt with him," Morgaine said, thin-lipped. "He is somewhere about—with ambush laid, it may well be."

"We cannot go on pushing the horses. *Liyo*, there is no knowing what we may meet."

"She may know. Doubtless she knows."

"She is afraid of you," he objected softly. "*Liyo*, let me try to ask her. We must rest the horses; there is time, there is time."

"What Roh has touched," she said, "is not trustworthy. Remember it. Here. A keepsake."

He held out his hand, thinking she meant the ornament. A blade flashed into her hand, and to his, sending a chill to his heart, for it was an Honor-blade, one for suicide. At first he thought it hers, for it was, like hers, Koris-work. Then he realized it was not.

It was Roh's.

"Keep it," she said, "in place of your own."

He took it unwillingly, slipped it into the long-empty sheath at his belt. "Avert," he murmured, crossing himself.

"Avert," she echoed, paying homage to beliefs he was never sure she shared, and made the pious gesture that sealed it, wishing the omen from him, the ill-luck of such a blade. "Return it to him, if you will. That pure-faced child was carrying it. Remember that when you are moved to gentility with her."

Vanye sank down from his crouch to sit crosslegged by her, oppressed by foreboding. The unaccustomed weight of the blade at his belt was cruel mock-ery, unintended, surely unintended. He was weaponless; Morgaine thought of practicalities—and of other things.

Kill him, her meaning was: *it is yours to do*. He had taken the blade, lacking the will to object. He had abandoned all right to object. Suddenly he felt every-thing tightly woven about him: Roh, a strange girl, a lost dagger—a net of ugly complexities.

Morgaine held out her hand a second time, dropped into his the small gold object, a bird on the wing, exquisitely wrought. He closed his hand on it, slipped it into his belt. *Return that to her*, he understood, and consented. *She is yours to deal with.*

Morgaine leaned forward and fed bits of wood into the fire, small pieces that charred rapidly into red-edged black. Firelight gleamed on the edge of silver mail at her shoulder, bathed her tanned face and pale eyes and pale hair in one unnatural light in the gathering dark. *Qujal*-fair she was, although she dis-claimed that unhuman blood. He himself was of the distant mountains of Andur-Kursh, of a canton called Morija; but that was not her heritage. Perhaps her birthplace was here, where she had brought him. He did not ask. He smelled the salt wind and the pervading reek of decay, and knew that he was lost, as lost as ever a man could be. His beloved mountains, those walls of his world, were gone. It was as if some power had hurled down the limits of the world and shown him the ugliness beyond. The sun was pale and distant from this land, the stars had shifted in their places, and the moons—the moons defied all reason.

The fire grew higher as Morgaine fed it. "Is that not enough?" he asked, forc-ing that silence that the alien ruins held, full of age and evil. He felt naked be-cause of that light, exposed to every enemy that might be abroad this night; but Morgaine simply shrugged and tossed a final and larger stick onto the blaze.

She had weapons enough. Perhaps it was her enemies' lives she risked by that bright fire. She was arrogant in her power, madly arrogant at times—

though there were moments when he suspected she did such things not to tempt her enemies, but it some darker contest, to tempt fate.

The heat touched him painfully as a slight breeze stirred, the first hint they had had of any wind that might disperse the mist; but the breeze died and the warmth flowed away again. Vanye shivered and stretched out his hand to the fire until the heat grew unbearable, then clasped that hand to his ribs and warmed the other.

There was a hill beyond the flood, and a Gate among Standing Stones, and this was the way that they had ridden, a dark, unnatural path. Vanye did not like to remember it, that moment of dark dreaming in which he had passed from *there* to *here,* like the fall at the edge of sleep: he steadied himself even in thinking of it.

Likewise Morgaine had come, and Chya Roh before them, into a land that lay at the side of a vast river, under a sky that never appeared over Andur-Kursh.

Morgaine unwrapped their supplies, and they shared food in silence. It was almost the last they had, after which they must somehow live off this bleak land. Vanye ate sparingly, wondering whether he should offer to Jhirun, or whether it was not kinder to let her rest. Most of all he doubted Morgaine would favor it, and at last he decided to let matters be. He washed down the last mouthful with a meager sip of the good wine of Baien, saving some back; and sat staring into the fire, turning over and over in his mind what they were to do with the girl Jhirun. He dreaded knowing. No good name had Morgaine among men; and some of it was deserved.

"Vanye. Is thee regretting?"

He looked up, saw that Morgaine had been staring at him in the ruddy light, eyes that were in daylight sea-gray, world-gray, *qujal*-gray. That gentle, ancient accent had power more than the wind to chill him, reminding him that she had known more Gates than one, that she had learned his tongue of men long dead; she forgot, sometimes, what age she lived in.

He shrugged.

"Roh," she said, "is no longer kin to you. Do not brood on it."

"When I find him," he said, "I will kill him. I have sworn that."

"Was it for that," she asked him finally, "that you came?"

He gazed into the fire, unable to speak aloud the unease that in him when she began to encircle him with such questions. She was not of his blood. He had left his own land, abandoned everything to follow her. There were some things that he did not let himself reason to their logical end.

She left the silence on him, a stifling weight; and he opened his hand, twice scarred across the palm with the Claiming by blood and ash. By that, he was *ilin* to her, bound in service, without conscience, honorless save for her honor, which he served. This parting-gift his clan had bestowed on him, like the shorn hair that marked him felon and outlaw, a man fit only for hanging. Brother-slayer, bastard-born: no other liege would have wanted such a man, only Morgaine, whose name was a curse wherever she was known. It was irony that *ilin*-service, penance for murder, had left him far more blood-guilty than ever he had come to her.

And Roh remained yet to deal with.

"I came," he said, "because I swore it to you."

She thrust at the fire with a stick, sending sparks aloft like stars on the wind. "Mad," she judged bitterly. "I set thee free, told thee plainly thee had no possible place outside Kursh, outside the law and the folk thee knows. I wish thee had believed it."

He acknowledged this truth with a shrug. He knew the workings of Morgaine's mind better than any living; and he knew the Claim she had set on him, that had nothing to do with his scarred hand; and the Claim that someone else had set on her, crueller than any oath. Her necessity lay sheathed at her side, that dragon-hilted sword that was no true sword, but a weapon all the same. It was the only bond that had ever truly claimed her, and she hated it above all other evils, *qujal* or human.

I have no honor, she had warned him once. *It is unconscionable that I should take risks with the burden I carry. I have no luxury left for virtues.*

Another thing she had told him that he had never doubted: *I would kill you too if it were necessary.*

She hunted *qujal*, she and the named-blade *Changeling*. The *qujal* she hunted now wore the shape of Chya Roh i Chya. She sought Gates, and followed therein a compulsion more than half madness, that gave her neither peace nor happiness. He could understand this in some part: he had held *Changeling* in his own hands, had wielded its alien evil, and there had come such a weight on his soul afterward that no penance of *ilin*-service could ever cleanse him of remembering.

"The law is," he said, "that you may bid me leave your service, but you cannot order it. If I stay, I remain *ilin*, but that is my choice and not yours."

"No one ever refused to leave service."

"Surely," he said, "there have been *ilinin* before me that found no choice. A man is maimed in service, for instance; he might starve elsewhere, but while he stays *ilin*, his *liyo* must at least feed him and his horse, however foul the treatment he may receive in other matters. You cannot make me leave you, and your charity was always more generous than my brother's."

"You are neither halt nor blind," Morgaine retorted; she was not accustomed to being answered with levities.

He made a gesture of dismissal, knowing for once he had touched through her guard. He caught something bewildered in her expression in that instant, something terrified. It destroyed his satisfaction. He would have said something further, but she glanced aside from him with a sudden scowl, removing his opportunity.

"There was at least a time you chose for yourself," she said at last. "I gave you that, Nhi Vanye. Remember it someday."

"Aye," he said carefully. "Only so you give me the same grace, *liyo*, and remember that I chose what I wanted."

She frowned the more deeply. "As you will," she said. "Well enough." And for a time she gazed into the fire, and then the frown grew pensive, and she was gazing toward their prisoner, a look that betrayed some inner war. Vanye began to suspect something ugly in her mind, that was somehow entangled with her questions to him; he wished that he knew what it was.

"*Liyo*," he said, "Likely the girl is harmless."

"Thee knows so?"

She mocked him in his ignorance. He shrugged, made a helpless gesture. "I do not think," he said, "that Roh would have had time to prepare any ambush."

"The time of Gates is not world-time." She hurled a bit of bark into the flames, dusted her hands. "Go, go, we have time now that one of us could be sleeping, and we are wasting it. Go to sleep."

"She?" he asked, with a nod toward Jhirun.

"I will speak with her."

"You rest," he urged her after a moment, inwardly braced against some irrational anger. Morgaine was distraught this night, exhausted—they both were. Her slim hands were tightly laced about her knee, clenched until the strain was evident. Tired as he was, he sensed something greatly amiss. "*Liyo*, let me have first watch."

She sighed, as if at that offer all the weariness came over her at once, the weight of mail that could make a strong man's bones ache, days of riding that wore even upon him, Kurshin and born to the saddle. She bowed her head upon her knee, then flung it back and straightened her shoulders. "Aye," she said hoarsely, "aye, that I will agree to gladly enough."

She gathered herself to her feet, *Changeling* in her hand; but to his amazement she offered it to him, sheathed and crosswise.

It never left her, never. By night she slept with that evil thing; she never walked from where it lay, not more than a room's width before she turned and took it up again. When she rode, it was either under her knee on the gray horse's saddle, or across her shoulders on her sword belt.

He did not want even to touch it, but he took it, and gathered it to him carefully; and she left him so, beside the fire. Perhaps, he thought, she was concerned that the warrior who guarded her sleep not do so unarmed; perhaps she had some subtler purpose, reminding him what governed her own choices. He considered this, watching her settle to sleep in that corner of the ruin where the stones still made an arch. She had their saddles for pillow and windbreak, the coarse saddleblankets, unfolded, for a covering: he had lost his own cloak the same way he had lost his sword, else it would have been his cloak that was lent their injured prisoner, not hers. The consciousness of this vexed him. He had come to her with nothing that would have made their way easier, and borrowed upon what she had.

Yet Morgaine trusted him. He knew how hard it was for her to allow another hand on *Changeling*, which was obsession with her; she need not have lent it, and did; and he did not know why. He was all too aware, in the long silence after she seemed to have fallen asleep, how clear a target the fire made him.

Roh, if his hands retained any of their former skill, was a bowman of the Korish forests; and a Chya bowman was a shadow, a flitting ghost where there was cover. Likely too the girl Jhirun had kinsmen hereabouts seeking her, if Roh himself did not. And perhaps—Vanye's shoulders prickled at the thought—Morgaine set a trap by means of that bright fire, disregarding his life and hers; she was capable of doing so, lending him her chiefest weapon to ease her conscience, knowing that this, at least, he could use.

He rested the sword between his knees, the dragon-hilt against his heart, daring not so much as to lie down to ease the torment of the mail on his shoulders, for he was unbearably tired, and his eyes were heavy. He listened to the faint sounds of the horses grazing in the dark, reassured constantly by their soft stirrings. Nightsounds had begun, sounds much like home: the creak of frogs, the occasional splash of water as some denizen of the marsh hunted.

And there was the matter of Jhirun, that Morgaine had set upon him.

He tucked a chill hand to his belt, felt the rough surface of the Honorblade's hilt, wondering how Roh fared, wondering whether he were equally lost, equally afraid. The crackling of the fire at his side brought back other memories, of another fireside, of Ra-koris on a winter's evening, of a refuge once offered him, when no other refuge existed: Roh, who had been willing to acknowledge kinship with an outlawed *ilin*.

He had been moved to love Roh once, Roh alone of all his kinsmen; an honest man and brave, Chya Roh i Chya. But the man he had known in Ra-koris was dead, and what possessed Roh's shape now was *qujal*, ancient and deadly hostile.

The Honor-blade was not for enemies, but the last resort of honor; Roh would have chosen that way, if he had had the chance. He had not. Within Gates, souls could be torn from bodies and man and man confounded, the living with the dying. Such was the evil that had taken Chya Roh; Roh was truly dead, and what survived in him wanted killing, for Roh's sake.

Vanye drew the blade partly from its sheath, touched that razor edge with gentle fingers, a tightness in his throat, wondering how, of all possessions that Roh might have lost, it had been this, that no warrior would choose to abandon.

She has found you, the girl had said, mistaking them in their kinsmen's resemblance. *Are you not afraid?*

It occurred to him that Roh himself had feared Morgaine, loathed her, who had destroyed his ancestors and the power that had been Koris.

But Roh was dead, Morgaine, who had witnessed it, had said that Roh was dead.

Vanye clenched both hands about *Changeling*'s cold sheath, averted his eyes from the fire and saw Jhirun awake and staring at him.

She had knowledge of Roh. Morgaine had left the matter to him, and he loathed what he had asked, realized it for what it truly was—that he did not want the answers.

Suddenly the girl broke contact with his eyes, hurled herself to her feet and for the shadows.

He sprang up and crossed the intervening distance before she could take more than two steps—seized her arm and set her down again on the cloak. *Changeling* safely out of her reach in the bend of his other arm. She struck him, a solid blow across the temple, and he shook her, angered. A second time she hit him, and this time he did hurt her, but she did not cry out—not a sound came from her but gasps for breath, when woman might have appealed to woman—not to Morgaine. He knew whom she feared most; and when she had stopped struggling he relaxed his grip, reckoning that she would not run now. She jerked free and stayed still, breathing hard.

"Be still," he whispered. "I shall not touch you. You will be wiser not to wake my lady."

Jhirun gathered Morgaine's white cloak up about her shoulders, up to her chin. "Give me back my pony and my belongings," she said. Her accent and her shivering together made her very difficult to understand. "Let me go. I swear I will tell no one. No one."

"I cannot," he said. "Not without her leave. But we are not thieves." He searched in his belt and found the gull-ornament, offering it. She snatched it, careful not even to touch his hand, and clenched it with the other hand under her chin. She continued to stare at him, fierce dark eyes glittering in the firelight. The bruised cheek gave the left eye a shadow. "You are his cousin?" she asked. "And his enemy?"

"In my house," he said, "that is nothing unusual."

"He was kind to me."

He gave a sour twist of the lips. "You are fair to look upon, and I would hardly be surprised at that."

She flinched. The look of outrage in her eyes was like a physical rebuff, reminding him that even a peasant girl was born with honor, a distinction that he could not claim. She looked very young, frightened of him and of her circumstances. After a moment it was he that looked aside.

"I beg pardon," he said; and when she kept a long silence, still breathing as if she had been running: "How did you meet him, and when?"

"Last night," she said, words that filled him with relief, on many accounts. "He came to us, hurt, and my folk tried to rob and kill him. He was too quick for us. And he could have killed everyone, but he did not. And he was kind to me." Her voice trembled on the word, insistent this time on being understood. "He went away without stealing anything, even though he was in need of everything. He only took what belonged to him, and what I gave him."

"He is *dai-uyo*," he answered her. "A gentleman."

"A great lord."

"He has been that."

Her eyes reckoned him up and down and seemed perplexed. *And what are you?* he imagined her thoughts in that moment, hoping that she would not ask. The shame of his shorn hair, the meaning of the white scarf of the *ilin*—perhaps she understood, reckoning the difference between him and Chya Roh, highborn, cousin. He could not explain. *Changeling* rested across his knee; he was conscious of it as if it were a living thing: Morgaine's forbidding presence, binding him to silence.

"What will you do with him when you have found him?" Jhirun asked.

"What would you have done?"

She gathered her knees up within the fur and stared at him. She looked as if she were expecting him to strike her, as if she were prepared to bear that—for Roh's sake.

"What were you doing," he asked her, "riding out here with no cloak and no food? You cannot have planned to go far."

"I am going to Shiuan," she said. Her eyes brimmed with tears, but her jaw was set. "I am from the Barrow-hills, and I can hunt and fish and I had my pony—until you took him."

"How did you get the dagger?"

"He left it behind."

"It is an Honor-blade," he said harshly. "A man would not so casually leave that behind."

"There was the fight," she said in a low voice. "I was going to give it back when I found him. I was only going to use it until then."

"To gut fish."

She flinched from the spite in his voice.

"Where is he?" he asked.

"I do not know, I do not know. He said nothing. He only left."

Vanye stared at her, weighing her answers, and she edged back from him as if she did not like his expression. "Go to sleep," he bade her suddenly, and rose and left her there, looking back nevertheless to be sure she did not make some rash bid to escape. She did not. He settled again on his stone by the fire, so that he could watch her. For a time she continued to stare at him through the flames; abruptly she flung herself down and hid herself in the cloak.

He set his hands together on *Changeling*'s pommel, resting against it, all his peace destroyed by the things that she had said.

He understood her loyalty to Roh, even as a stranger; he knew his cousin's manner, that way of reaching for the heart of any who dealt with him—as once Roh had drawn him in spite of Roh's other failings. It was painful to know that this aspect of the man was still intact, that he had his former gentleness, his honesty—all those graces that had been Chya Roh.

But it was illusion. Nothing of Roh's soul or essence could survive. Morgaine had said it, and therefore it was so.

Return it to him, Morgaine bade him, arming him.

He thought of facing Roh at weapons' edge, and another nightmare returned to him, a courtyard in Morija—a flash of blades, a brother's dying. Of that he was guilty. To destroy, to plunge home that blade when it was Roh's face and voice, for this possibly he could prepare himself. . . . *But, o Heaven*, he thought, sickness turning in him, *if it should be more than outward seeming—*

He was kind to me, the girl had said. *He went away without stealing anything, even though he was in need of everything.*

There was no kindness in the *qujal*, who had sought his life and taken Roh's in its place, nothing so simple, or so human as kindness, only sweet persuasiveness, the power to convince with seeming logic, to play on a man's worst fears and darkest impulses and promise what he had no intention of giving.

Nor was there honor—the manner of a high-clan warrior, a clan lord, who would not stoop to thievery, not even in great need: that was not the manner of the being who had lied and murdered and stolen through three generations of men, taking what he desired—even the body in which he lived. Generosity was unknown to him.

That was not the *qujal*. It was the manner of Roh himself, Chya and more prideful than practical, the blood they both shared; it was Roh.

"Vanye."

He spun toward the whisper, the tread upon leaves, heart frozen at the sight of the shadowy figure, even when he knew it was only Morgaine. He was embarrassed that he had not heard her moving, though she was herself adopted Chya, and walked silently enough when she chose; but the more he was disturbed for the thoughts in which she had come upon him—thoughts that betrayed his oath, while she trusted him.

For a moment he felt that she read him. She shrugged then, and settled beside the fire. "I am not disposed to sleep," she said.

Distress, displeasure—with what, or whom, he could not tell; her eyes met his, disturbing him, striking fear into him. She was capable of irrationality.

Knowing this, still he stayed with her; at such times he remembered that he was not the first who had done so—that she had far more of comrades' blood to her account than that of enemies—that she had slain far more who had shared bread with her than ever she had of those she had wished to harm.

Roh was one such that had crossed her path, and deserved pity for it; Vanye thought of Roh, and of himself, and in that instant there was a distance between himself and Morgaine. He thrust Roh from his mind.

"Do we move on?" he asked her. It was a risk and he knew it, that she might seize upon it in her present mood; he saw that it tempted her sorely—but since he had offered, she was obliged to use reason.

"We will move early," she said. "Go rest."

He was glad of the dismissal, knowing her present mood; and his eyes burned with fatigue. He took the sword in his hands and gave it to her, anxious to be rid of it, sensing her distress to be parted from it. Perhaps, he thought, this had disturbed her sleep. She folded it into her arms and leaned forward to the fire, as if having it comforted her.

"It has been quiet," he said.

"Good," she answered, and before he could gather himself to his feet: "Vanye?"

"Aye?" He settled back to his place, wanting, and not wanting, to share her thoughts, the things that had robbed her of sleep.

"Did thee trust what she said?"

She had heard then, listening to all that had passed. He was at once guiltily anxious, trying to remember what things he had said aloud and what he had held in his heart; and he glanced at Jhirun, who still slept, or pretended to. "I think it was the truth," he said. "She is ignorant—of us, of everything that concerns us. Best we leave her in the morning."

"She will be safer in our company a time."

"No," he protested. Things came to mind that he dared not say aloud, hurtful things, the reminder that their company had not been fortunate for others.

"And we will be the safer for it," she said, in a still voice that brooked no argument.

"Aye," he said, forcing the word. He felt a hollowness, a sense of foreboding so heavy that it made breath difficult.

"Take your rest," she said.

He departed the warmth of the fire, sought the warm nest that she had quitted. When he lay down amid their gear and drew the coarse blankets over him, every muscle was taut and trembling.

He wished that Ela's-daughter had escaped them when she had run—or better still, that they had missed each other in the fog and never met.

He shifted to his other side, and stared into the blind dark, remembering home and other forests, knowing that he had entered an exile from which there was no return.

The Gate behind them was sealed. The way lay forward from here, and it occurred to him with increasing unease that he did not know where he was going, that never again would he know where he was going.

Morgaine, his arms, and a stolen Andurin horse: that comprised the world that he knew.

And now there was Roh, and a child who had about her the foreboding of a world he did not want to know—his own burden, Jhirun Ela's-daughter, for it was his impulse that had laid ambush for her, when by all other chances she might have ridden on her way.

↪ Chapter 5

"Vanye."

He wakened to the grip of Morgaine's hand on his arm, startled out of sleep deeper than he was wont.

"Get the horses," she said. The wind was whipping fiercely at the swaying branches overhead, drawing her fair hair into a stream in the darkness. "It is close to dawn. I let you sleep as long as I could, but the weather is turning on us."

He murmured a response, arose, rubbing at his eyes. When he glanced at the sky he saw the north flashing with lightnings, beyond the restless trees. Wind sighed coldly through the leaves.

Morgaine was already snatching up their blankets and folding them. For his part he left the ring of firelight and felt his way downslope among the stones of the ruins, across the narrow channel and up again to the rise where the horses were tethered. They snorted alarm at his coming, already uneasy at the weather; but Siptah recognized him and called softly—gray Siptah, gentler-mannered than his own Andurin gelding. He took the gray and Jhirun's homely pony together and led them back the way he had come, up again into the ruins.

Jhirun was awake. He saw her standing as he came into the firelight, opened his mouth to speak some gentle word to her; but Morgaine intervened, taking the horses. "I will tend them," she said brusquely. "See to your own."

He hesitated, looking beyond her shoulder to Jhirun's frightened face, and felt a deep unease, leaving her to Morgaine's charge; but there was no time for disputes, and there was no privacy for argument. He turned and plunged back into the shadows, making what haste he could, not knowing against what he was racing, the storm or Morgaine's nature.

Dawn was coming. He found the black gelding, a shadow in a dark that was less than complete, although the boiling clouds held back the light. He freed the horse, hauled firmly on the cheekstrap as the ungentle beast nipped at him, then in his haste swung up bareback and rode back with halter alone, down across the stream and up again among the trees and the ruins.

He was relieved to find Jhirun calmly sitting by the dying fire, wrapped in her brown shawl, eating a bit of bread. Morgaine was doing as she had said, tending to Siptah's saddling; and she bore *Changeling* on her shoulder harness, as she would when she judged the situation less than secure.

"I have told her that she is coming with us," Morgaine said, as he alighted and flung the blanket up to the gelding's back. He said nothing, unhappy in Morgaine's intention. He bent and heaved the saddle up, settled it and reached under for the girth. "She seemed agreeable in the matter," Morgaine said, seeming determined to draw some word from him on the subject.

He gave attention to his work, avoiding her eyes. "At least," he said, "she might ride double with me. She has a head wound. We might give her that grace—by your leave."

"As you will," said Morgaine after a moment. She rolled her white cloak into its oiled-leather covering and tied it behind her saddle. With a jerk of the thongs she finished, and gathered up Siptah's reins, leading the horse toward the fire, where Jhirun sat.

Jhirun stopped eating, and sat there with the morsel forgotten in her two hands. Like something small and trapped she seemed, with her bruised eyes and bedraggled hair, but there was a hard glitter to those eyes nonetheless. Vanye watched in unease as Morgaine stopped before her.

"We are ready," Morgaine said to her. "Vanye will take you up behind him."

"I can ride my own pony."

"Do as you are told."

Jhirun arose, scowling, started to come toward him. Morgaine reached to the back of her belt, a furtive move. Vanye saw, and dropped the saddlebag he had in hand.

"No!" he cried.

The motion was sudden, the girl walking, the sweep of Morgaine's hand, the streak of red fire. Jhirun shrieked as it touched the tree beside her, and Vanye caught the gelding's bridle as the animal shied up.

Morgaine replaced the weapon at the back of her belt. Vanye drew a shaken breath, his hands calming the frightened horse. But Jhirun did not move at all, her feet braced in the preparation of a step never taken, her arms clenched about her bowed head.

"Tell me again," Morgaine said softly, very audibly, "that you do not know this land, Jhirun Ela's-daughter."

Jhirun sank to her knees, her hands still clenched in her hair. "I have never been further than this down the road," she said in a trembling voice. "I have heard, I have only heard that it leads to Shiuan, and that was before the flood. I do not know."

"Yet you travel it without food, without a cloak, without any preparation. You hunt and you fish. Will that keep you warm of nights? Why do you ride this road at all?"

"Hiuaj is drowning," Jhirun wept. "Since the Wells were closed and the Moon was broken, Hiuaj has been drowning, and it is coming soon. I do not want to drown."

Her mad words hung in the air, quiet amid the rush of wind, the restless stamp and blowing of the horses. Vanye blessed himself, the weight of the very sky pressing on his soul.

"How long ago," asked Morgaine, "did this drowning begin?"

But Jhirun wiped at the tears that spilled onto her cheeks and seemed beyond answering sanely.

"How long?" Morgaine repeated harshly.

"A thousand years," Jhirun said.

Morgaine only stared at her a moment. "These Wells: a ring of stones, is that not your meaning? One overlooks the great river; and there will be yet another, northward, one master Well. Do you know it by name?"

Jhirun nodded, her hands clenched upon the necklace that she wore, bits of sodden feather and metal and stone. She shivered visibly. "Abarais," she answered faintly. "Abarais, in Shiuan. *Dai-khal, dai-khal*, I have told you all the truth, all that I know. I have told everything."

Morgaine frowned, and at last came near the girl, offering her hand to help her rise, but Jhirun shrank from it, weeping. "Come," said Morgaine impatiently, "I will not harm you. Only do not trouble me; I have shown you that . . . and better that you see it now, than that you assume too far with us."

Jhirun would not take her hand. She struggled to her feet unaided, braced herself, her shawl clutched about her. Morgaine turned and gathered up Siptah's reins, rose easily into the saddle.

Vanye drew a whole breath at last, expelled it softly. He left his horse standing and went to the fireside, gathered up his helmet and covered his head, lacing the leather coif at his throat. Last of all he paused to scatter the embers of their campfire.

He heard a horse moving as he turned, recoiled as Siptah plunged across his path, Morgaine taut-reining him to an instant stop. He looked up, dismayed at the rage with which she looked at him.

"Never," she hissed softly, "never cry warning against me again."

"*Liyo*," he said, stricken to remember what he had done, the outcry he had made. "I am sorry; I did not expect—"

"Thee does not know me, *ilin*. Thee does not know me half so well as thee trusts to."

The harshness chilled. For a moment he stared up at her in shock, fixed by that cold as Jhirun had been, unable to answer her.

She spurred Siptah past him. He sought the pony's tether, half blind with shame and anger, ripped it from its branch and tied it to his own horse's saddle. "Come," he bade Jhirun, struggling to keep anger from his voice, with her who had not deserved it. He rose into the saddle, cleared a stirrup for her, suddenly alarmed to see Morgaine leaving the clearing, a pale flash of Siptah's body in the murk.

Jhirun tried for the stirrup and could not reach it; he reached down in an agony of impatience, seized her arm and pulled, dragged her up so that she could throw her leg over and settle behind him.

"Hold to me," he ordered her, jerked her shy hands about his waist and laid spurs to the gelding, that started forward with a suddenness that must have hurt the pony. He pursued Morgaine's path, only dimly aware of branches that raked his face in the passage. He fended them with his right hand and used the spurs a second time. One thing he saw, a pallor through the trees, fast opening a lead on him.

Soul-bound: that was *ilin*-oath, and he had strained the terms between them. Morgaine's loyalty lay elsewhere, to a thing he did not understand or want to know: wars of *qujal*, that had ruined kingdoms and toppled kings and made the name of Morgaine kri Chya a curse in the lands of men.

She sought Gates, the witchfires that were passage between world and world, and sealed them after her, one and another and another. His world had changed, he had been born and grown to manhood between two beats of her heart, between two Gate-spanning strides of that gray horse. The day that he had given her his oath, a part of him had died, that sense of the commonplace that let ordinary men live blind and numb to what terrible things passed about them. He belonged to Morgaine. He could not stay behind. For a stranger's sake he had riven what peace had grown between them, and she would not bear it. It was that way with Morgaine, that he be with her entirely or be numbered among her enemies.

The trees cut off all view: for a wild moment of terror he thought that in this wilderness he had lost her. She rode against time, time that divided her from Roh; from Gates, that could become a fearful weapon in skilled hands. She would not be stayed longer than flesh must rest—not for an hour, an instant. She had forced them through flood and against storm to bring them this far— all in the obsessive fear that Roh might be before them at the Master Gate, that ruled the other Gates of this sad land—when they had not even known beyond doubt that Roh had come this way.

Now she did know.

Jhirun's arms clenched about him as they slid on the downslope. The pony crashed into them with bruising force, and the gelding struggled up another ridge and gained the paved road, the pony laboring to keep the pace.

And there to his relief he saw Morgaine. She had paused, a dim, pale figure on the road beneath the arch of barren trees. He raked the gelding with the spurs and rode to close the gap, reckless in their speed over the uncertain trail.

Morgaine gazed into the shadows, and when he had reined in by her, she simply turned Siptah's head and rode, sedately, on her way down the road, giving him her shoulder. He had expected nothing else; she owed him nothing.

He rode, his face hot with anger, conscious of Jhirun's witness. Jhirun's arms were clenched about him, her head against his back. At last he realized how strained was her hold upon him, and he touched her tightly locked hands. "We are on safe ground now," he said. "You can let go."

She was shivering. He felt it. "We are going to Shiuan," she said.

"Aye," he said. "It seems that we are."

Thunder rolled overhead, making the horses skittish, and rain began to patter among the sparse leaves. The road lay in low places for a time, where the horses waded gingerly in shallow water. Eventually they passed out of the shadow of the trees and the overcast sun showed them a wide expanse where the road was the highest point and only landmark. Rainpocked pools and sickly grasses stretched to left and right. In places the water overflowed the road, a fetid sheet of stagnant green, where dead brush had stopped the cleansing current.

"Jhirun," said Morgaine out of a long silence. "What is this land named?"

"Hiuaj," said Jhirun. "All the south is Hiuaj."

"Can men still live here?"

"Some do," said Jhirun.

"Why do we not see them?"

There was long silence. "I do not know," Jhirun said in a subdued voice. "Perhaps they are afraid. Also it is near Hnoth, and they will be moving to higher ground."

"Hnoth."

"It floods here," Jhirun said, hardly audible. Vanye could not see her face. He felt the touch of her fingers on the cantle of the saddle, the shift of her grip, sensed how little she liked to be questioned by Morgaine.

"Shiuan," Vanye said. "What of that place?"

"A wide land. They grow grain there, and there are great holds."

"Well-defended, then."

"They are powerful lords, and rich."

"Then it is well," said Morgaine, "that we have you with us, is it not, Jhirun Ela's-daughter? You do know this land after all."

"No," Jhirun insisted at once. "No, lady. I can only tell you the things I have heard."

"How far does this marsh extend?"

Jhirun's fingers touched Vanye's back, as if seeking help. "It grows," she said. "The land shrinks. I remember the Shiua coming into Hiuaj. I think now it must be days across."

"The Shiua do not come now?"

"I am not sure the road is open," Jhirun said. "They do not come. But marshlanders trade with them."

Morgaine considered that, her gray eyes thoughtful and not entirely pleased. And in all their long riding she had no word save to Jhirun.

By noon they had reached a place where trees grew green at a little distance from the road. The storm had blown over, giving them only a sprinkling of rain as it went, to spend its violence elsewhere. They drew off to rest briefly, on the margin where the current had made a bank at the side of the causeway, and where the grass grew lush and green, a rare spot of beauty in the stagnant desolation about them. The watery sun struggled in vain to pierce the haze, and a small moon was almost invisible in the sky.

They let the horses graze and rest, and Morgaine parcelled out the last of their food, giving Jhirun a third share. But Jhirun took what she was given and drew away from them as far as the narrow strip of grass permitted; she sat gazing out across the marsh, preferring that dismal view, it seemed, and solitude.

And still Morgaine had spoken no word. Vanye ate, sitting cross-legged on the bank beside her, finally having decided within himself that it was not anger that kept her silent now: Morgaine was given to such periods when she was lost in her own thoughts. Something weighed upon her mind, in which he thought he was far from welcome.

"She," Morgaine said suddenly, startling him, softly though she spoke, "was surely desperate to come this road alone. For fear of drowning, says she; Vanye, does it occur to thee to wonder why out of all the years of her life, she suddenly set out, with nothing in preparation?"

"Roh can be persuasive," he said.

"The man is not Roh."

"Aye," he said, disturbed in that lapse, avoiding her eyes.

"And she speaks what we can understand, albeit the accent is thick. I would I knew whence she comes, Vanye. She surely did not have her birth from the earth and the fog yesterday noon."

"I think," he said, gazing off in the direction Jhirun stared, ahead, where the forest closed in again, great trees overshadowing the road, "I think her folk are surely in that hold we passed, and Heaven grant they stay there."

"They may be looking for her."

"And we," he said, "may come into trouble on her account, or what is more likely—she will meet it on ours. *Liyo*, I ask you earnestly, send her away—now, while she is near enough home she can find her way back."

"We are not taking her against her will."

"I suppose that we are not," he agreed, not happily. "But we are on a track they cannot mistake."

"The horses do confine us to the roadway," she said, "and this land has shown us one fellow-traveller, and not a breath of others. It occurs to me, Roh being ahead of us, it would be simple for folk hereabouts to choose some place of meeting to their advantage. I do think I saw a shadow move this morning, before you came down the trail."

Cold settled about him—and self-anger; he remembered his reckless ride, how she had turned her back to him and stayed silent when he had joined her. He had taken it for rebuff. "Your sight was clearer than mine," he said. "I was blind to it."

"A trick of the light, perhaps. I was not sure."

"No," he said. "I have never known you prone to visions, *liyo*. I would you could have given me some sign."

"It did not seem good then to discuss it," she said, "nor later, with our guest at your back. Mind, she met us either by design or by chance. If by design, then she has allies—Roh himself, it may be—and if by chance, why, then, she feels herself equal to this ugly land, and she is not delicate. Mind thy back in either case; thee is too good-hearted."

He considered this, which he knew for good sense, and he was ashamed. In all the time that they had ridden this land, he had felt himself lost, had forgotten every lesson of survival he had learned of his own land, as if any place of earth and stone could be utterly different. Blind and deaf he had ridden, like a man shaken from his senses; and little good he had been to her. She had reason for her anger.

"Back there," he said, "this morning: I was startled, or I would not have cried out."

"No more of it."

"*Liyo*, I take oath it was not a thing I would have done; I was surprised; I did not reckon—I could not believe that you would do murder."

"Does that matter?" she asked. "Thee will not appoint thyself my conscience, Nhi Vanye. Thee is not qualified. And thee is not entitled."

The horses moved, quietly grazing. Water sighed under the wind. His pulse dimmed awareness of all else; even the blood seemed dammed up in him, a beating of anger in his veins. He met her pale eyes without intending to; he did not like to look at them when she had this mood on her.

"Aye," he said after a moment.

She said nothing. It was not her custom to argue; and this was the measure of her arrogance, that she disputed with no one, not even with him, who had given her more than his oath. Still one recourse he had with her: he bowed, head upon his hands, to the earth, and sat back, and gave her cold formality, the letter of the *ilin*-oath she had invoked. She hated to be answered back; and he did it so that she was left with nothing to say, and no argument.

Her frown darkened. She cast a stone into the water, and suddenly arose and gathered up Siptah's reins, hurled herself to the saddle. She waited, anger in the set of her jaw.

He stood up and took the reins of his own gelding, the black pony still tethered to the saddle-ring; and he averted his eyes from Morgaine and rose into the saddle, reined over to Jhirun, who waited on the bank.

"Come," he said to her, "either with me or on the pony, whichever pleases you."

Jhirun looked up at him, her poor bruised face haggard with exhaustion, and without a word she held up her hand to be drawn up behind him. He had not thought she would choose so; he had wished that she would not, but he saw that she was nearly spent. He smothered the rage that was still hammering in him, knowing the look on his face must be enough to frighten the girl, and he was gentle in drawing her up to sit behind him. But when she put her arms about him, preparing for their climb to the roadway, he suddenly remembered Morgaine's advice and the Honor-blade that was at his belt. He removed it to the saddle-sheath at his knee, where her hands could not reach it.

Then he turned the horse upslope, where Morgaine awaited him on the road. He expected her to ride ahead, scorning him, but she did not. She set Siptah to walking beside the gelding, knee to knee with him, though she did not look at him.

It was tacit conciliation, he suspected. He gathered this knowledge to himself for comfort, but it was far down the road before there was a word from her, when the cold shadow of the trees began to enfold them again.

"My moods," Morgaine said suddenly. "Forget them."

He looked at her, found nothing easy to say. He nodded, a carefully noncommittal gesture, for the words were painfully forced from her, and he did not think she wanted to discuss the matter. In truth, she owed him nothing, neither apology nor even humane treatment; that was the nature of *ilin* law; but that was not the way between them. Something troubled her, something heart-deep, and he wished that he could put a name to it.

The strangeness of the land was wearing at them both, he decided; they were tired, and nerves were tautly strung. He felt in his own body the ache, the weight of mail that settled with malevolent cunning into the hollows of a man's body, that galled flesh raw where there was the least fold in garments beneath. Therein lay reason enough of tempers; and she feared—feared Roh, feared ambush, feared things, he suspected uneasily, the like of which he did not imagine.

"Aye," he murmured at last, settling more easily into the saddle. "We are both tired, *liyo.* That is all."

She seemed content with that.

And for many long hours they passed through land that was low and all the same, alternate tracts of cheerless, unhealthy forest and barren marsh, where the road was passable and in most places well above the water. *Qujal*-made, this road, Vanye reckoned to himself—wrought by ancient magics—*qujalin* works lasted, strange, immune to the ages that ate away at the works of men, some seeming ageless, while others crumbled away suddenly as if they had become infected with mortality. There was a time not so long ago when he would have sought any other road than this, that led them so well in the direction Morgaine sought: *qujalin* roads surely led to *qujalin* places—and surely such was this called Abarais, in Shiuan, which Morgaine sought.

And better, far better, could they ride that way alone, unseen, unmarked by men. He felt Jhirun's weight against his back, balancing his own, she seemed to sleep for brief periods. It was a warm and altogether unaccustomed sensation, the nearness of another being: *ilin,* outlaw, bastard motherless from birth, he could recall few moments that any had laid hands on him save in anger. He found it disturbing now, this so harmless burden against him, that weighed against him, and against his mind.

He watched Morgaine, who glanced constantly to this side and that as they rode, searching every shadow; and it came to him what kept his mind so ill at ease; that Morgaine, arrogant as she was, seemed afraid—that she, who had no sane regard for her life or his, was greatly afraid, and that somewhere in that fear rested the child that rode sleeping at his back.

The forest closed in upon the road in the late afternoon and did not yield them up again, a way that grew more and more darksome, where it seemed that evening came premature. The trees here lived, growing in interlaced confusion, thrusting roots out into the channels, reaching branches overhead, powerless against the closely fitted megaliths that were the body of the road. Brush crowded over the margins, making it impossible for two horses to go abreast.

Morgaine, her horse unencumbered, led in this narrow way, a shadow among shadows, riding a pale horse. That pale hair of hers was an enemy banner for any hereabouts who did not love *qujal*; and they rode blindly, unable to see beyond this tangle of brush that had found root, where seeds and earth piled up against the enduring stones. *Cover your hair,* Vanye wished to tell her, but he felt still that mood in her, that unreason that he did not want to meet yet another time. This forest was not a time or place for quarrels.

Clouds again began to veil the sky, and that veil grew constantly darker, plunging the forest into a halflight that destroyed all perspective, that made of the aisles of trees deep caverns hung with moss, and of the roadway a trail without beginning or end.

"I am afraid," Jhirun protested suddenly, the only word she had volunteered all day long. Her fingers clutched Vanye's shoulder-belt as if pleading for his intercession. "The sky is clouding. This is a bad place to be in a storm."

"What is your counsel?" Morgaine asked her.

"Go back. There is known road behind us. Please, lady, let us ride back to higher ground as quickly as we can."

"High ground is too far back."

"We do not know whether the road even goes on," Jhirun urged, desperation in her voice. She wrenched at Vanye's sleeve. "Please."

"And leave ourselves," said Morgaine, "on this side of a flood and Roh safely on the other."

"Roh may drown," Vanye said, set ill at ease by the suspicion that the girl was reasoning more clearly than his liege at the moment. "And if he drowns, all we need do is survive and proceed at leisure. *Liyo*, I think in this the girl is giving us good advice. Let us turn back, now."

Morgaine gave him not even the grace of an answer, only laid heels to Siptah and put the gray stud to a quicker pace, that in level places became almost a run.

"Hold on," Vanye bade Jhirun, grim anger in his heart. Her arms went about him, locked tightly as the gelding took a broken stretch of the road and picked up the clear paving again, dragging the exhausted pony after them. A misstep, a pool deeper than it looked—he feared the reckless pace that Morgaine chose, and feared equally the prospect of being caught in this lowest and darkest part of the land when the storm came down. There was no promise of higher ground as they went further and further, only of worse, and Morgaine, blindly insistent on the decision she had made, led them into it.

The clouds gathered yet more darkly and wind ruffled the water of the pools. Once something large and dark slid into the water as Siptah leaped it— vanishing beneath the murky surface. Birds started from cover with a clap of wings and raucous cries, startling the horses, but they did not slack their pace more than an instant.

The road parted in a muddy bank, a place riven as if stone had pulled from stone, a channel flowing between, and Siptah took that plunge, hooves sliding in the mud, hindquarters bunching as he drove for the other rise. Vanye sent the gelding in his wake, and the pony went down on the slide. The gelding recovered from the impact with a wrench that wrung a cry from Jhirun, and stood still on the upslope, trembling—but the pony lacked the strength or the inclination to rise. Vanye slid off and took the pony's halter, hauled against it with his full weight and brought the animal to its feet, but it simply stood there and stared at him with ears down and coat standing in points of mud, its eyes wells of misery.

He slipped the halter from it. "No," Jhirun protested, but he pushed its head around and slapped it on its muddy rump, sending it wandering, dazed, back down the bank. He had dim hope for the animal, but more than he held for their own fortunes.

He looped the empty rope and halter to the saddle, then took the reins and led his own horse up the opposing slope. Morgaine was no longer in sight when he reached the crest.

He swore, rose the awkward way into the saddle, passing his leg in front, avoiding even so much as a backward glance at Jhirun. She held to him as he spurred the exhausted animal; he felt her sobbing against his back, whether for grief over the pony or for terror for herself, he was not sure. Upon his face now he felt the first drops of rain, and panic rose in him, the bitter surety of disaster shaping about them.

A moment more brought Morgaine in view—she refused to hold back now, he thought, because she also had begun to realize that there was no safety, and she sought desperately to bring them through this place, to find an end of it as there had been an end of all other such forested entanglements.

The pattering fall of rain among the leaves began in earnest, scarring the smooth faces of the pools and chilling the air abruptly.

Soon enough there was no more running. The stone causeway began to be awash in the low places, and the horses picked their way through overgrowth. The rain slanted down, borne on strong wind, blinding, making the horses shy.

The gelding stumbled on a root, recovered with an effort that Vanye felt in his own muscles, a failing shudder. He flung his leg over the horn and slid down, beginning to lead the horse, finding its way with his own feet, lest it cripple itself. Ahead of him Siptah walked, slowly now.

"*Liyo,*" he shouted over the roar of the water, that swallowed all lesser sounds. "Let me to the fore."

She heard him and reined back, letting him lead the gelding past. He saw her face when he looked back, haggard and drawn and miserable with weariness—remembered how little she had slept. Now she surely realized that she had chosen amiss in her stubbornness, that she should have heeded Jhirun, who knew this land; but she did not offer even yet to direct them back. Jhirun offered nothing, no word, no objection; she only clung to the saddle, her hair streaming with water, her shawl a soaking rag about her shoulders. She did not even lift her head.

Vanye turned his face into the wind and the rain and led, his feet rapidly numb in the cold water, his boots soaked through. Mud held his feet and wrenched at his joints, and he fought it, moving as rapidly as he could, gasping with exhaustion.

Night was settling about them. The road was lost in twilight. Before them were only hummocks of earth that supported a tree apiece, and the channels between had become torrents. Only an occasional upthrust of rock or the absence of the largest trees in a given line betrayed the presence of the road that underlay the flood.

A vast stele heaved up beside the road, vine-covered and obscured by a tree that had forced it over at an angle and then died, a skeletal ruin. On most such stones the persistent rains had worn away the carvings, but this was harder stone. Here Morgaine paused, leaned in her saddle to seize and pull aside the dead vines, reading the ancient glyphs as if by them she hoped to find their way.

"*Arrhn*," she said. "Here stood a place called Arrhn. There is nothing else."

"Aren," said Jhirun suddenly. "Aren is the marshlanders' hold."

"Where?" Vanye asked. "Where would it lie?"

"I do not know," Jhirun insisted. "But, lady—lady, if it is near—they will shelter us. They must. They will not turn you away. They would not."

"Reasonably," said Morgaine, "if it was *qujalin*, it would have some connection with the road."

Of sound for the moment there was the singing of the wind that tossed the branches, and the mind-numbing roar of the waters that rushed and bubbled about them, elements that had their own argument, that persuaded that even strange shelter was a way to survive.

She set Siptah moving again, and Vanye struggled to keep the lead, the breath tearing in his lungs. He waded up to his knees in some places, and felt the force of the water in his shaking muscles.

"Ride," Morgaine called at him. "Change with me; I will walk a while."

"You could not," he looked back to shout at her—saw her tired face touched with anguish. "*Liyo*," he added, while he had the advantage of her, "I think that you might have used better sense if I were not with you. Only so much can I do." He shook the water from his eyes and swept off the helm that was only added weight, that made his shoulders ache. "Take it for me," he asked of her. The armor too he would have shed if he could have taken the time, but there was none to spare. She took the helm and hung it to her saddlebow by its inside thong.

"You are right," she said, giving him that consolation.

He drew a deep breath and kept moving, laced his fingers in the gelding's cheekstrap and felt his way through the swirling dark waters in a darkness that was almost complete. He walked over his knees now, in a current that almost swept him off his feet. He had feared for the horses' fragile legs. Now he feared for his own. At one moment he went into a hole up to his waist, and thought with increasing panic that he had not much more strength for guiding them: the way ahead looked no better, dark water boiling among the trees.

Something splashed amid the roar of water as he delayed, staring at that prospect before them; he looked back and saw Morgaine waist-deep in the flood, struggling with the current and leading Siptah to reach his side. He cursed tearfully, fought his way to meet her and bid her use good sense, but she caught his arm instantly as he began to object, and drew his attention away to the left, pointing through the murk of night and storm.

The lightning showed a dark mass in that direction, a hill, a heap of stones, massive and dark and crowned with trees, a height that well overtopped any further rise of the waters.

"Aye," he said hoarsely, hope leaping up in him; but he trusted nothing absolutely in this land, and he shook at Jhirun's leg to rouse her and point out the same to her. She stared over his head where he pointed, her eyes shadowed and her face white in the lightning.

"What is that place?" he shouted at her. "What would it be?"

"Aren," she answered, her voice breaking. "It looks to be Aren."

But Morgaine had not delayed. Vanye turned his head and saw her already moving in that direction, their sounds masked from each other by the rush of water—she wading and leading Siptah in that flood. He wiped his eyes and struggled to overtake her, dreading no longer alien ruins or devils or whatever folk might live in this marsh. It was the water he feared, that ripped at his body and strained his knees. It boiled up about them, making a froth on the side facing the current, waist-deep, chest-deep. He saw the course that Morgaine was seeking, indirectly, to go from high point to high point where the trees were; he drew even with her, shook the blinding drops from his eyes and tried to take the reins from Morgaine's hand.

"Go on," he shouted at her, overwhelmed with fear for her. Her lighter weight was more vulnerable to the current that tore at them, her strength perilously burdened by the armor she wore. But she refused vehemently, and he realized then that he was asking something impossible of her: she was too light to dare let go; she clung to the saddle on the other side, Siptah laboring in the strong current. Vanye himself fought the current almost shoulder-deep of a sudden, and the horses began to swim, great desperate efforts of their tired bodies.

"Lord!" Jhirun screamed.

He turned his head to look back at her, turned again in the direction of her gaze to see a great mass coming down on them in the lightning-lit waters, a tree uprooted and coming down the current end toward them.

"*Liyo!*" he cried warning.

It hit, full into the gelding's side, drove against his armor and tore him from the reins, driving him against the gray. Siptah swung under the impact, spilling him under, drove at him with threshing hooves. Roots speared at him, tangled and snagged at his armor. He fought upward against them, had purchase on the jagged mass itself. It rolled with him, spilling him under again, pulling him down with it.

There was a moment of cold, of dark, an impact.

He embraced the obstacle, the tree stabbing at his back with all the force of the current, roots snapping against his armored back. He felt stone against his face. He could breathe for a moment, inhaling air and foaming water. Then the tree tore past, ripping at him, and he slipped, pinned by the force of the current against the rock, breathing the froth boiling about his head. His fingers gripped the rock again, and he hauled himself a painful degree upward and gasped a mouthful of air, saw other stones in the near-dark, the bank close at hand, promising safety.

In desperation he loosed his hold, helpless to swim at the best of times, fighting without skill and weighted by armor and exhaustion. At once he knew it had been a mistake. He could not make it so far against the current. The rush of water dragged him down and whirled him like a leaf around the bend—belly-on to the rock, breath driven from him, skull battered by a second impact as he slipped into yet another stone, numb legs tucked, realizing dully that they were bent because he was aground. He moved, heavy with water and without strength in his limbs, drove again through shallow water and a maze of reeds to sprawl at the bank, to crawl ashore among the stones. For a moment he was numb, the force of the pelting rain painful against his back even through the armor.

There was a time of dark, and at last the rain seemed less violent. He moved, rolled over and stared up, with a sudden clutch of fear as he recognized the cursed stones in the lightning—Standing Stones, *qujalin* ruins that had intercepted his body and saved his life. The monoliths leaned over him like a gathering of giants in the dark and the rain.

"*Liyo!*" he shouted into the roar of waters and the wind. "Morgaine!"

There was no answer.

◦ͽ **Chapter 6**

The dawn was beginning, the murky clouds picking up indirect light. Vanye splashed across a shallow channel, came up against the bank and rested against a log that had fallen into the water. It might be the same from which he had started this circle of his search, or different. He no longer knew. In the light things began to take on different shapes.

There was only the persistent roar of the flood, the patter of gentle rain on the leaves, always the water, numbing the senses.

"Morgaine!" he cried. How many times he had called, what ground he had covered, he did not remember. He had searched the night long, through ruins and from one islet to another, between moments that he had to sink down and rest. His voice was all but gone. His armor pressed on his shoulders with agonizing weight, and now it would have been far, far easier for his knees to bend, letting him sink down into the cold and the mud and the waters that were likely to have him in the end.

But he would not give way without knowing what had become of his liege. Other trusts in his life he had failed, to kinsmen, to friends, and some of those were dead, but they had had others on whom to rely—Morgaine had no other, none at all.

He leaned forward, elbows tucked against his belly and the log, dragged his feet one and then the other from the mud that pulled at tendons and muscles and claimed him whenever he rested at all. The rotting trunk became his bridge to higher ground. He climbed it to the bank, used brush for a handhold and struggled to the crest of the hill. Dark gathered about him, his pulse loud in his ears, pressure in his temples. He walked. All that he knew at times was touch, the rough wetness of bark, the stinging slap of leaves and branches he could not see to avoid, the slickness of wet leaves beneath his fingers as he fought his way up yet another rise.

He thought himself in Morija once more, Myya archers on his trail; or something pursued him. He could not remember where this place was, why he was so cruelly tried, whether he pursued or was pursued; it was like a thousand other nightmares of his life.

And then he would remember, when the ghosts flitted mockingly through his memory, so that it was impossible to sort out image from reality. He knew that he was beyond Gates, and that he was lost.

That Morgaine was dead occurred to him; he rejected the possibility not with logic, but with belief. Men died, armies perished, but Morgaine survived, survived when others could not, when she herself wished otherwise; she might be lost, might be hurt, might be stranded alone and afoot in this land: these images tormented him. Anything else was impossible.

She would have guarded herself first when the mass came down upon them, would have done that while he tried to guard her, the girl Jhirun forgotten. Siptah had been between Morgaine and the impact, and so had the gelding. She would—his mind began at last to function more clearly on this track now that he had convinced himself of a means by which she might have lived—she would instinctively have let him go down, sought the bank at once, for she carried *Changeling*, and therefore she would have fought to live. Such were the reflexes by which she existed. For her there was one law: to seek the Gates at whatever cost. Panic would direct her simply to live, all else forgotten.

And perhaps when that panic passed, she might have delayed to seek him, as long as she thought it likely he might have survived. But she knew also that he did not swim, and she would not search forever. He pictured her shedding a tear or two—he flattered himself by that—and when morning came and there was no sign of him, then she would take her bearings anew and heed the *geas* that drew her.

And that would set her face northward, toward the Master Gate, and a leavetaking from this sad, drowning earth.

Suddenly he realized that she would have trusted him to understand her obligations, to trust that she would do the rational, the necessary thing—and make for the one landmark in all this quaking marsh as soon as possible: the one place where all travelers met.

The *qujalin* road. She would be there, confident that her *ilin* would be there, would follow if he could, knowing what she would do.

He cursed himself: his driving fear was suddenly that she would have found the road before him, that in the night and the storm she would have gone on— that she might have saved one of the horses, while he was afoot, incapable of overtaking a rider.

He reckoned by the flow of the current which way the road must lie, and walked, tearing his way through the brush on as straight a course as his strength could make him.

He came upon the first stones at midmorning, and everything lay smooth as an unwritten page, no marks at all on the new sheet of mud laid by the flood, only the crooked trail of a serpent and the track of a lizard.

He cast about with all his skill to find any smallest remnant of a track left during the ebb of the flood, and found nothing. Exhausted, he leaned against a low branch and wiped thickly mudded hands on his sodden breeches, trying to think clearly. There was such desperation welling up in him now, his best hope disappointed, that he could have cried his anger and grief aloud to the listening woods. But now that he thought it unlikely that she was nearby to hear, he could not even find the courage to call her name aloud, knowing that there would be silence.

She was moving ahead of him, joining the road further on; or she was yet to come. The other possibility occurred this time with frightening force. He thrust it quickly from his mind.

His one hope, that answered either eventuality, was to be at the place she sought, to reach Abarais as quickly as human strength could carry him and pray—if prayers were heard in this Hell, and for Morgaine—that she would either stay for him or overtake him. He would wait, if he reached Abarais, holding the Gate for her, against men, against Roh, against whatever threat, until she came or until he died.

He gathered himself, fought dizziness as he did at each sudden move, coughed and felt a binding pain in his chest. His throat was raw. Fever burned in him. He had been ill on the run before, and then, with his kinsmen on his trail, it had been possible to sweat the fever out, to keep moving, relying on the horse's strength to carry him.

This time it was his own shaking limbs that must bear him, and the waters and the inhabitants of them waited for his fall below that dark surface.

He walked a staggering course down the road, seeking some sign on the earth—and then he realized that he should leave one of his own, lest she take his track for Roh's, and hang back. He tore a branch from a tree, snapped it and drove its two ends into the mud, a slanting sign that any who had ranged Andur-Kursh could read like the written word: *Follow!* And by it he wrote in the mud the name-glyph of clan Nhi.

It would last until the waters rose again, which in this cursed land gave the life of the message to be short indeed; and with this in mind, he carried a stone from the paving of the buried road and cut a mark now and again upon a tree by the road.

Every caution he had learned in two years of outlawry, fleeing clan Myya, cried out that he guided none but enemies at his back. Men lived in this land, and they were furtive and fearful and would not show themselves; and therefore there were things in this land that men should rightly fear.

Nevertheless he held the center of the road, fearing more being missed than being found.

And came the time that he ran out of strength, and what had been a tightness in his chest swelled and took his breath away. He sank down in his tracks and drew breath carefully, feeling after ribs that might well be cracked; and at times the haze came over his mind again. He found a time when he had not been aware what passed about him, and some moments later he was afoot and walking with no memory of how he had risen or how far he had come.

There were many such gaps after that, periods when he did not know where he was going, but his body continued, obedient to necessity and guided by the road.

At last he was faced with a gap in the road where a channel had cut through; he stared at it, and simply sank down on the slope at water's edge, reckoning how likely he was to drown attempting it. And strength left him, the exhaustion of a night without sleep stretching him full-length on the muddy slope. He was cold. He ceased to care.

*   *   *

A shadow fell over him, a whisper of cloth. He waked violently and struck out, seeing bare feet and a flash of brown skirt; and in the next moment a staff crashed into his arm—his head, if his arm had not been quick. He hurled himself at his attacker, mailed weight and inconsiderable flesh meeting: she went down, still trying for his face, and he backhanded the raking attack hard enough that it struck the side of her face. Jhirun. He realized it as her face came clear out of the shock of the attack.

The blow had dazed her, much as he had restrained it at the last instant; and seeing her, who might know of Morgaine, he was overcome with fear that he had killed her. He gathered her up and shook at her in his desperation.

"Where is she?" he asked, his voice an unrecognizable whisper; and Jhirun sobbed for breath and fought and protested again and again that she did not know.

After a moment he came to his senses and realized the girl was beyond lying; fear was knotted in him so that he found it hard to relax his hands; he was shaking. And when he had let her go she collapsed on the muddy bank sobbing for breath.

"I do not know, I do not know," she kept saying through her tears. "I did not see her or the horses—nothing. I only swam and swam until I came out of the current, that is all."

He clutched this to him, the only hope that he could obtain, that he knew Morgaine could swim, armored though she was; and Jhirun had survived; and he had survived, who could not swim at all. He chose to hope, and stumbled to his feet, gathering up Jhirun's abandoned staff. Then he began to seek the other side of the channel, using the staff to probe the shallowest way. It became waist-deep before it grew shallow again, and he climbed out on the other side, with the staff to help him on the slope.

A splash sounded behind him. He turned, saw Jhirun wading the channel with her skirts a sodden flower about her. Almost the depth became too much for her, but she struggled across the current, panting and exhausted as she reached the bank and began to climb.

"Go back," he said harshly. "I am going on from here. Go home, wherever that is, and count yourself fortunate."

She struggled further up the bank. Her face, already bruised, had a fresh redness across the brow: his arm had done that. Her hair hung in spiritless tangles. She reached the crest and shook the hair back over her shoulders.

"I am going to Shiuan," she said, her chin trembling. "Go where you like. This is my road."

He looked into her tear-glazed eyes, hating her intrusion, half desiring it, for he was lost and desperate, and the silence and the rush of water were like to drive a man mad. "If Abarais lies in Shiuan," he said, "I am going that way. But I will not wait for you."

"Nor for her?"

"She will come," he said; and was possessed by the need for haste, and turned and began to walk. The staff made walking easier on the broken pavings, and he did not give it up, caring little whether Jhirun needed it or no. She walked barefoot, limping; but the pain of his own feet, rubbed raw by water-soaked boots that were never meant for walking, was likely worse, and somewhere in the night he had wrenched his ankle. He gave her no hand to help her; he was in pain and desperate, and during the long walk he kept thinking that she had no reason whatever to wish him well. If he left her, she could find him in his sleep eventually and succeed at what she had already tried; if he slept in her presence, she could do the same without the trouble of slipping up on him: and as for binding the child to some tree and leaving her in this flood-prone land, the thought shamed him, who had been *dai-uyo*, whose honor forbade dealing so even with a man. At times he looked down on her, wishing her unborn; and when she looked up at him he was unnerved by the distracted look in her eyes. *Mad*, he thought, *her own folk have cast her out because she is mad. What other manner of girl would be out on this road alone, following after a strange man?*

And came one of those times that he lost awareness, and wakened still walking, with no memory of what had happened. Panic rose in him, exhaustion weakening his legs so that he knew he could as well have fallen senseless in the road. Jhirun herself was weaving in her steps.

"We shall rest," he said in the ragged voice the cold had left him. He flung his arm about her, feeling at once her resistance to him, but he paid it no heed—drew her to the roadside where the roots of a tree provided a place less chill than earth or stone. She tried to thrust free, mistaking his intention; but he shook her, and sank down, holding her tightly against him. She shivered.

"I shall not harm you," he said. "Be still. Rest." And with his arm about her so that he could sense any movement, he leaned his head against a gnarled root and shut his eyes, trying to take a little sleep, still fearing he would sleep too deeply.

She remained quiet against him, the warmth of their bodies giving a welcome relief from the chill of wet garments; and in time she relaxed across him, her head on his shoulder. He slept, and wakened with a start that frightened an outcry from her.

"Quiet," he bade her. "Be still." He had tightened his arm by reflex, relaxed it again, feeling a lassitude that for the moment was healing, in which all things, even terrible ones, seemed distant. She shut her eyes; he did the same, and wakened a second time to find her staring at him, her head on his chest, a regard disturbing in its fixedness. Her body, touching his, was tense, her arm that lay across him stiff, fist clenched. He moved his hand upon her back, more of discomfort than of intent, and felt her shiver.

"Is there none," he asked her, "who knows where you are or cares what becomes of you?"

She did not answer. He realized how the question had sounded.

"We should have sent you back," he said.

"I would not have gone."

He believed her. The determination in that small, hoarse voice was absolute. "Why?" he asked. "You say Hiuaj is drowning; but that is supposition. On this road, you may drown for certain."

"My sister has already drowned," she said. "I am not going to." A tremor passed through her, her eyes focused somewhere beyond him. "Hnoth is coming, and the moons, and the tides, and I do not want to see it again. I do not want to be in Hiuaj when it comes."

Her words disturbed him: he did not understand the sense of them, but they troubled him—this terror of the moons that he likewise shuddered to see aloft. "Is Shiuan better?" he asked. "You do not know. Perhaps it is worse."

"No." Her eyes met his. "Shiuan is where the gold goes, where all the grain is grown; no one starves there, or has to work, like Barrowers do."

He doubted this, having seen Hiuaj, but he did not think it kind to reason with her delusion, when it was likely that neither of them would live to know the truth of it. "Why do not all the Hiua leave, then?" he asked. "Why do not all your folk do what you have done, and go?"

She frowned, her eyes clouded. "I do not think they believe it will come, not to them; or perhaps they do not think it matters, when it is the end. The whole world will die, and the waters will have everything. But she—" The glitter returned to her eyes, a question trembling on her lips; he stayed silent, waiting, fearing a question he could not answer. "She has power over the Wells."

"Yes," he admitted, for surely she had surmised that already.

"And you?"

He shrugged uncomfortably.

"This land," she said, "is strange to you."

"Yes," he said.

"The Barrow-kings came so. They sang that there were great mountains beyond the Wells."

"In my land," he said, remembering with pain, "there were such mountains."

"Take me to that place." Her fist unclenched upon his heart; her eyes filled with such earnestness that it hurt to see it, and she trembled against him. He moved his hand upon her shoulders, wishing that what she asked were possible.

"I am lost myself," he said, "without Morgaine."

"You believe that she will come," she said, "to Abarais, to the Well there."

He gave no reply, only a shrug, wishing that Jhirun knew less of them.

"What has she come to do?" Jhirun asked it all in a breath, and he felt the tension in her body. "Why has she come?"

She held some hope or fear he did not comprehend: he saw it in her eyes, that rested on his in such a gaze he could not break from it. She assumed that safety lay beyond the witch-fires of the Gates; and perhaps for her, for all this land, it might seem to.

"Ask Morgaine," he said, "when we meet. As for me, I guard her back, and go where she goes; and I do not ask or answer questions of her."

"We call her Morgen," said Jhirun, "and Angharan. My ancestors knew her—the Barrow-kings—they waited for her."

Cold passed through him. *Witch*, men called Morgaine in his own homeland. She was young, while three generations of men lived and passed to dust; and all that he knew of whence she came was that she had not been born of his kindred, in his land.

When was this? he wanted to ask, and dared not. *Was she alone then?* She had not come alone to Andur-Kursh, but her comrades had perished there. *Qujal*, men called her; she avowed she was not. Legends accounted her immortal; he chose not to believe them all, nor to believe all the evil that was laid to her account, and he asked her no questions.

He had followed her, as others had, now dust. She spoke of time as an element like water or air, as if she could come and go within its flow, confounding nature.

Panic coiled about his heart. He was not wont to let his mind travel in such directions. Morgaine had not known this land; he held that thought to him for comfort. She had needed to ask Jhirun the name and nature of the land, needing a guide.

A guide, the thought ran at the depth of his mind, to this age, perhaps, as once in Andur she had been confounded by a forest that had grown since last she had ridden that path.

"Come," he said brusquely to Jhirun, beginning to sit up. "Come." He used the staff to pull himself to his feet and drew her up by the hand, trying to shake off the thoughts that urged upon him.

Jhirun did not let go his hand as they set out again upon the road; in time he grew weary of that and slipped his arm about her, aiding her steps, seeking by that human contact to keep his thoughts at bay.

Jhirun seemed content in that, saying nothing, holding her own mind private; but there was a difference now in the look she cast up at him—hope, he realized with a pang of guilt, hope that he had lent her. She looked up at him often, and sometimes—unconscious habit, he thought—touched the necklace that she wore, that bore a cross, and objects that he did not know; or touched the center of her bodice, where rested that golden image that he had returned to her—a peasant girl, who possessed such a thing, a bit of gold strangely at variance with her rough dress and work-worn hands.

My ancestors, she had said, *the Barrow-kings.*

"Have you clan?" he asked her suddenly, startling her: her eyes gazed at him, wide.

"We are Mija," she said. "Ila died out. There is only Mija left."

Myya. Myya and Yla. His heart seemed to stop and to begin again, painfully. His hand fell from her shoulder, as he recalled Morija, and that clan that had been his own undoing, blood-enemy to him; and lost Yla, that had ruled Morija once, before the Nhi.

"Myya Geraine Ela's-daughter," he murmured, giving her foreign name the accents of Erd, that lay among mountains her folk had almost forgotten.

She looked at him, speechless, with her tangled hair and bruised face, barefoot, in a dress of coarsest wool. She did not understand him. Whatever anger there was between him and Myya, it had no part with Jhirun Ela's-daughter; the blood-feud the Myya had with him carried no force here, against a woman, in the drowning wastes of Hiuaj.

"Come," he said again, and gathered her the more closely against his side, beginning to walk again. The clans were known for their natures: as Chya was impulsive and Nhi was stubborn, clan Myya was secretive and cold—of cruelty that had bided close to him all his life, for his half-brothers were Myya, and she who had mothered them, and not him.

Myya hated well, and waited long for revenge; but he refused to think such things of Jhirun; she was a companion, on a road that was otherwise alien, and seemed endless, in a silence that otherwise was filled with the wind and the bubbling waters.

There were things worse than an enemy. They lay about him.

In the evening, with the light fading into streamers of gold and red, they walked a place where the marsh had widened and trees were few. Reeds grew beside the road, and great flocks of white birds flew up in alarmed clouds when they drew near. Serpents traced a crooked course through the stagnant pools and stirred the reeds.

And Vanye looked at the birds that taunted them and swore in desire, for hunger was a gnawing pain in his belly.

"Give me a strip of leather," Jhirun asked of him while they walked; and in curiosity he did so, unlacing one of the thongs the ring at his belt held for use on harness. He watched while her strong fingers knotted it this way and that, and understood as she bent to pick up a stone. He gave her a second strip to improve her handiwork, and the sling took shape.

A long time they walked afterward, until the birds began to wing toward them; and of a sudden she whirled the sling and cast, a skilled shot. A bird fell from the sky; but it fell just beyond the reeds, and almost as it hit the water something rose out of the dark waters and snapped it up. Jhirun simply stood on the bank and looked so wretched that his heart went out to her.

"Next time," she said.

But there were no more birds. Eventually, with night upon them, Jhirun pulled up a handful of reeds, and peeled them to the roots, and ate on this, offering one to him.

It eased the ache in his belly, but it had a bitter taste, and he did not think a man could live long on such fare. Ahead stretched a flat and exposed land, the road the only feature in it; and in the sky the moons began to shine, five in number.

The Broken Moon, Jhirun named them for him as they walked; and stately Anli, and demon Sith, that danced with Anli. Only the greatest moon, Li, had not yet risen, but would appear late in the night, a moon so slow and vast the fragments of the Broken Moon seemed to race to elude it.

"In the old days," Jhirun said, "there was only one.

> *"Whole Moon and whole land;*
> *and then the Wells gave weal;*
> *came the Three and rived the Moon,*
> *and then the Wells were sealed.*

That is what the children sing."

"Three what?"

"The three moons," she said. "The Demon and the Ladies. The Moon was broken and then the world began to sink; and some say when there is only the sea left, then Li will fall into it and the world will shatter like the Moon. But no man will be alive to see that."

Vanye looked at the sky, where what she named as Anli rode, with the tiny orb of Sith beside it. By night there was a cloud in which the moons moved: moondust, Morgaine had called it. He thought that apt, a sorcery of the perishing world, that it perish at least in beauty, a bow of light to form the path of the moons. He remembered Li, that hung as a vast light above the clouds two nights past, and shuddered to think of it falling, for it looked as if it truly might.

"Soon," said Jhirun, "will be Hnoth, when Li overtakes the others, and then the waters rise. It is close—and then this road will be all underwater."

He considered this, brooding upon it. Of Morgaine there had been no sign, no track, no trace; Jhirun's warning added new anxiety. But Morgaine would not delay on low ground; she might at the moment be no farther behind them than the trees that lay on the horizon.

He marked how wearily Jhirun walked, still striving to match his stride, never once complaining, though she breathed hard in her effort. He felt his own legs unsteady with exhaustion, the armor he wore a torment that set his back afire.

And Morgaine might be only a little distance behind them.

He stopped, where a grassy bank faced the shallowest tract of marsh; he took Jhirun by the arm and brought her there, and cast himself down, glad only to have the weight of mail distributed off his back and shoulders. Jhirun settled with him, her head on his chest, and spread her bedraggled shawl wide to cover as much of them both as might be.

"We will walk again before sunrise," he said.

"Yes," she agreed.

He closed his eyes, and the cessation of pain was such that sleep came quickly, a weight that bore his mind away.

Jhirun screamed.

He jerked awake, hurling her back from him; and looked about, realizing that they were alone. Jhirun wept, and the forlorn sound of it oppressed him. He touched her, finding her shaking, and gathered her to him, his own heart still laboring.

She had dreamed, he thought; the girl had seen enough in their journey that she had substance enough for nightmares. "Go back to sleep," he urged her, holding her as he might have held a frightened child. He settled back again, his arms tight about her, and his mind oppressed by a dread of his own, that he was not going to find Morgaine. She had not come; she had not overtaken them; he began to think of delaying a day in this place, giving her surely enough time to overtake him.

And thereby he might kill himself and Jhirun, being out upon this flat stretch of road when next a storm came down and the water rose. For Jhirun's sake, he thought that he should keep moving until they found safety, if safety existed anywhere in this land.

Then, without Jhirun, he could settle himself to wait, watching the road, to wait and to hope.

Morgaine was not immortal; she, like Roh, could drown. And if she were gone—the thought began to take root in him—then there was no use in his having survived at all—to become again what he had been before she claimed him.

Hunted now, it might well be, by other Myya, for Jhirun's sake.

Morgaine had seen a forest grow; against his side breathed something as terrible.

Jhirun still wept, her body racked by long shudders, whatever had terrified her still powerful in her mind. He tried to rest, and so to comfort her by his example, but she would not relax. Her whole body was stiff.

Sleep weighed him into darkness again, and discomfort brought him back, aware first that the land was bright with moonlight and then that Jhirun was still awake, her eyes fixed, staring off across the marsh. He turned his head, and saw the risen disc of Li, vast, like a plague-ridden countenance; he did not like to look upon it.

It lit all the land, bright enough to cast a shadow.

"Can you not sleep?" he asked Jhirun.

"No," she said, not looking at him. Her body was still tense, after so long a time. He felt the fear in her.

"Let us use the light," he said, "and walk some more."

She made no objection.

By noon, wisps of cloud began to roll in, that darkened and grew and spread across the sky. By afternoon there was cloud from horizon to horizon, and the tops of the occasional trees tossed in a wind that boded storm.

There were no more rests, no stopping. Jhirun's steps dragged, and she struggled, gasping in her efforts, to hold the pace. Vanye gave her what help he could, knowing that, if she ever could not go on, he could not carry her, not on a road that stretched endlessly before them.

In his mind constantly was Morgaine; hope began to desert him utterly as the clouds darkened. And beside him, on short, painful breaths, Jhirun began nervously to talk to him, chattering hoarsely of her own hopes, of that refuge to which others of her land had fled, those that dared the road. Here lay wealth, she insisted, here lay plenty and safety from the floods. She spoke as if to gather her own courage, but her voice distracted him, gave him something to occupy him but his own despair.

And of a sudden her step lagged, and she fell silent, dragging on his arm. He stopped, cast her a glance to know what had so alarmed her, saw her staring with vague and frightened eyes at nothing in particular.

There was a sound, that suddenly shuddered through the earth. He felt it, caught at Jhirun and sprawled, the both of them nothing amid such violence. He pulled at her arms, drawing her from the water's edge, and then it was past and quiet. They lay facing each other, Jhirun's face pale and set in terror. Her nails were clenched into his wrists, his fingers clenched on hers, enough to bruise. He found his limbs trembling, and felt a shudder in her arms also. Tears filled her eyes. She shook her tangled hair and caught her breath. He felt the terror under which Jhirun lived her whole life, who claimed her world was dying, whose very land was as unstable as the storm-wracked heavens.

He gathered her up, rising, held her to him, no longer ashamed by his own fright. He understood. He brushed mud from her scraped elbows, from her tear-stained cheek, realizing how desperately she was trying to be brave.

"Only little shakings, usually," she said, "except when the sea wall broke and half of Hiuaj flooded; this one was like that." She gave a desperate and bitter laugh, an attempt at humor. "We are only a hand's breadth closer to the sea now, that is what we say."

He could not laugh, but he pressed her close against his side in appreciation of her spirit, and shivered as the wind bore down on them, bringing heavy drops of rain.

They started walking, together. In places even the road was buckled, the vast paving-blocks pulled awry. Vanye found himself still shaken, in his mind unconvinced that the earth would stay still; and the crack of thunder that rolled from pole to pole as if the sky were tearing made them both start.

The rain began in earnest, the sky darkened to a sickly greenish cast, and the sound of it drowned all other sounds, the sheeting downpour separating them from all the world save the area of the causeway they walked. In places the surface of the road was ankle-deep in rapid water, and Vanye probed the stones with the staff lest they fall into a wash and drown.

It became evening, the rain coming with less violence, but steadily; and hills enfolded them as if by magic, as if they had materialized out of the gray-green murk and the curtains of rain. Of a sudden they were there, in the west, brought into dream-like relief by the sinking light; and quickly more took shape ahead of them, gray and vague as illusion.

"Shiuan," breathed Jhirun; and her hand tightened on his arm. "We have come through; we have reached Shiuan."

Vanye answered nothing, for at once he thought of Morgaine, and that destroyed any joy he had in his own survival. He thought of Morgaine, and reckoned with a last stubborn hope that the flooding had not been impassable or without warning: some little chance yet remained. But Jhirun's happiness was good to see; he answered the pressure of her hand with a touch of his own.

The hills began to enfold them closely as they walked, while the day waned. The road clung to the side of one and then the other, and never again sank below the water. Beside it, water poured, and spilled down ridges and between hills in its haste to reach the marsh.

Vanye stopped, for something strange topped the highest hill in their sight: a hulk that itself took shape out of the rain—gray towers, a little lighter than the clouds that boiled above them in the storm-drowned twilight.

"It is Ohtij-in," Jhirun shouted up at him through the roar of the rain. "It is Ohtij-in, the first of the holds of Shiuan."

Joy filled her voice at the sight of that grim place; she started forward, but he stood fast, and she stopped, holding her shawl about her, beginning to shiver in the chill that came rapidly when they stopped moving.

"They are well-fortified," he said, "and perhaps—perhaps we should pass them by in the night."

"No," she argued. "No." There were tears in her voice. He would gladly have dismissed her, bidden her do as it pleased her; and almost he did so, reckoning that for her it might be safety enough.

Then he remembered how much she knew of Morgaine, and where Morgaine might be sought; of him, too, and where he was bound.

"I would not trust it," he said to her.

"Marshlands and Ohtij-in trade," she pleaded with him, shaking as she hugged her shawl about her, drenched as it was. "We are safe here, we are safe; o lord, they must give us food and shelter or we will die of this cold. This is a safe place. They will give us food."

Her light clothing clung to her skin. She was suffering cruelly, while he had the several layers of his armor, burden though it was; their bellies were empty, racked sometimes with cramps; his own legs were weak with exhaustion, and she could scarcely walk. It was reason that she offered him, she who knew this land and its people; and in his exhaustion he began to mistrust his own instincts, the beast-panic that urged him to avoid this place, all places that might hem him in. He knew outlawry, the desperate flights and sometime luck that had let him live—supplied with weapons, with a horse, with knowledge of the land equal to that of his enemies. There had been game to hunt, and customs that he knew. Here he knew not what lay down the road, was lost apart from that track, vulnerable on it; and any enemies in this land could find him easily.

He yielded to the tug of her hand. They walked nearer, and he could see that the whole of the place called Ohtij-in was one hold, a barrel within a great wall that followed the shape of the hill on which it sat. Many towers rose about the central keep, part of the wall, each crazily buttressed, as if each support had been an affair of ingenuity and desperation never amended by later effort. Brush grew up about the walls; black trees that supported leaves only at the extremities of their branches, already inclined southward, inclined still further in the force of the storm wind, reaching fingers toward the lichen-blotched walls. The whole place seemed time-worn, a place without sharp edges, where decay was far advanced, dreaming away to death.

He rubbed at his eyes in the rain and tried to focus on it.

"Come," Jhirun was urging him, her teeth chattering with cold.

Perhaps, he thought confusedly, Morgaine would pass this way; she must; there was no other.

Jhirun drew at his arm and he went; he saw, as they left the road on the short spur that led toward the hill, that there was a solid wooden gate in the arch facing them, younger by far than the stones that framed it, the first thing in all this waste that looked new and strong.

Best, he thought, to assume confidence in his bearing, to approach as innocent folk that feared nothing and brought no threat with them.

"Hail!" he shouted up at the frowning walls, trying to outshout the wind, and he found his voice a weary and strangled sound that lacked all the confidence he attempted. "Hail! Open your gates!"

A light soon winked in the tower nearest the gate; a shuttered window opened to see them in that almost-darkness, and a bell began to ring, high-pitched and urgent. From that open shutter it was certain that they suffered the scrutiny of more than one observer, a series of black shapes that appeared there and vanished.

Then the shutter was closed again, and there was silence from the bell, no sound but the rush of water that sluiced off the walls and gathered on the stone paving before the gate. Jhirun shivered miserably.

Came the creak of a door yielding; the sally-port beside the main gate opened, veiled in the rain, and one man put his head forth to look at them. Black-robed he was, with a cloak about him so that only his face and hands were visible. Timidly he crept forward, opening the gate wider, holding his rain-spattered cloak about him and standing where a backward step would put him within reach of the gateway.

"Come," he said. "Come closer."

⤳ Chapter 7

"A priest," said Jhirun. "A Shiua priest."

Vanye let go a careful breath, relieved. The black robes were of no order that he knew, not in his homeland, where vesper and matin bells were a familiar and beloved sound; but a priest, indeed, and in all this gray and dying land there was no sight so welcome, the assurance that even here were human and godly men. He was still cautious in coming forward as they were summoned, for there were likely archers in the shadows atop the wall, bows drawn and arrows well-aimed. So would many a border hold in Kursh and Andur receive night-coming travellers, using the sally port for fear of a concealed force, keeping the archers ready if things went amiss.

But throughout all Andur-Kursh, even in the hardest years, there was hospitality, there was hearth-law, and halls were obliged to afford charity to wayfarers, a night's shelter, be it in hall, be it in a lowly guest-house without the walls. Vanye kept his hands in sight, and stopped and stood to be seen clearly by the priest, who gazed at them both in wonder, face white and astonished within the cowl, a white spot in the descending night.

"Father," said Vanye, his voice almost failing him in his hoarseness and his anxiety, "Father, there is a woman, on a gray horse or a black or, it might be, afoot. You have not seen her?"

"None such," said the priest. "None. But if any other traveler passes Ohtij-in, we will know it. Come in, come in and be welcome."

Jhirun stepped forward; Vanye felt an instant's mistrust and then ascribed it to exhaustion and the strangeness of the place. It was too late. If he would run, they could hunt him down easily; and if they would not, then here was shelter and food and he was mad to reject it. He hesitated, Jhirun tugging at his hand, and then he came, by the sally port, into a space between two walls, where torches flared and rain steamed on their copper shieldings.

A second priest closed the sally port and barred it; and Vanye scanned with renewed misgivings the strength of the gates, both inner and outer; a double wall defended this approach to Ohtij-in. The second priest pulled a cord, ringing the bell, and ponderously the inner gates swung open, upon torchlight, rain, and armed men.

There was no flourish of weapons, no rush at them, only an over-sufficient escort—pikemen standing beneath the windblown glare of torches, light gleaming wetly on bronze half-face helms that bore on the brow the likeness of grotesque faces—on armor that was long-skirted scale and plate, with intricate embellishment—on pikes with elaborate and cruel barbs.

It was a force far stronger than any hold at peace would keep under arms on a rainy night. The sense of something utterly amiss wound coldly through Vanye's belly: the terror of the strange armor, the excessive preparation for defense in an unpeopled land. Even Jhirun seemed to have lost all her trust in the place, and kept close to his side.

A priest tugged at the staff he yet held; he tightened his grip on it, trying to make sense of such a welcome, to know whether there might be more profit in resisting or in appealing to their lord. He let the staff go, thinking as he did so that it was small defense in any case.

Weapons were turned, and their escort opened ranks to receive them into their midst. The priests stayed by them, the pikemen on all sides; and beyond them, even in the rain, stood a horde of silent men and women, folk wrapped in ragged cloaks. A moment of peace lasted, then an outcry began among them, a wild shriek from one that rushed forward; others moved, and cries filled the courtyard. Hands reached through the protective screen of pikes to touch them. Jhirun cried out and Vanye held her tightly, glad now to go where the grotesquely armored guards bade them; he stared at mad eyes and open mouths that shouted words that he could not understand, and felt their hands on his back, his shoulders. A pikeshaft slammed out into hysterical faces, bringing blood: their own people they treated so. Vanye gazed at that act in horror, and cursed himself for ever having come toward this place.

It was to the keep that they were being taken, that vast central barrel that supported all the rest of the structure. Above the wild faces and reaching hands

Vanye saw those lichen-covered walls; and against them was a miserable tangle of buildings huddled under the crazy buttresses. The cobbled yard was buckled and cracked, splits filled with water, and rain-scarred puddles filled the aisle between the rough shelters that leaned against wall and towers. Next to the keep also were pent livestock, cattle and goats; and soil from those pens and the stables joined the corruption that flowed through the courtyard and through the shelters. Against the corner of the steps as they drew near the keep was a sodden mass of fur, dead rat or some other vermin lying drowned, an ugliness flushed out by the rains.

Men lived in such wretchedness. No lord of repute in Andur-Kursh would have kept his people so—would have even permitted such squalor, not even under conditions of war. Madness reigned in this place, and misery; and the guards used their weapons more than once as they cleared the steps.

A gate, barred and chained and guarded within, confronted them; a gate-keeper unlocked and ran back the chain to admit them all. Surely, Vanye thought, a lord must needs live behind chains and bars, who dwelled amid such misery of his people; and it promised no mercy for strangers, when a man had none for his own folk. Vanye wished now never to have seen this place; but the bars gaped for them, swallowed them up and clanged shut again. Jhirun looked back; so did he, seeing the keeper replacing the chain and lock at once, while the mob pressed at the gate, hands beginning to reach through the bars, voices shouting at them.

The inner doors opened to admit them, thundered shut after. They faced a spiral ramp, and with the priest and four of the escort bearing torches from the doorway, they began their ascent. The ramp led slowly about a central core with doors on this side and that, and echoes rang hollowly from the heights above. The whole of the place had a dank and musty smell, a quality of wet stone and age and standing water. The corridor floor was uneven, split in not a few places, with cracks in the walls repaired with insets of mortared rubble. The guards kept close about them the while, two torchbearers behind and three before, shadows running the walls in chaos. Behind them was the fading sound of voices from the gate; and softly, softly as they climbed, began to come the strains of music, strange and wild.

The music grew clearer, uncanny accompaniment to the iron tread of armed men about them; and the air grew warmer, closer, tainted with sweet incense. Jhirun was breathing as if she had been running, and Vanye also felt the dizziness of exhaustion and hunger and sudden heat; he lost awareness of what passed about him, and cleared his senses only slowly as the guards shifted about and encountered others, as soft voices spoke, and doors opened in sequence before them.

The music died, wailing: golden, glittering figures of men and women paused in mid-movement, tall and slim and silver-haired.

Qujal.

Jhirun's touch held him, else he would have hurled himself at guards and doors and died; her presence, frightened, at his side, kept him still as the foremost of the tall, pale men walked toward him, surveyed him casually with calm, gray eyes.

An order was given, a language he did not know; the guards laid hand on his arms and turned him to the left, where was another door; and certain of the other pale lords left their places and came, quietly, as they were withdrawn from that bright hall and into an adjoining room.

It was a smaller hall, with a fire blazing in the fireplace, a white dog lying at the hearth. The dog sprang up and began to bark frantically, sending mad echoes rolling through the halls, drowning the music that had begun again next door, until one of the guards whipped her yelping into silence. Vanye stared at the act, jarred by that mistreatment of a beast, and looked about him, at wealth, luxury, carved woods, carpets, bronze lamps—and the *qujal*-lords gathered by the door, resplendent in brocades and jewels, talking together in soft, astonished accents.

Three moved to the fore, to seat themselves at the chairs of the long table: an old man, in green and silver, he it was who had come first to look at them—and because he was first and because of his years, Vanye reckoned him for lord in the hall. At his right sat a youth in black and silver; at his left, another youth in blue and green of fantastical design, whose eyes were vague and strange, and rested in distant speculation on Vanye's when he looked him in the face. Vanye flinched from that one, and felt Jhirun step back. His impulse even now was to run, deserting her, though guards and chains and double gates lay between him and freedom: nothing that could befall Jhirun in this place seemed half so terrible as the chance that they would realize what he was, and how he had come.

Morgaine's enemies: he had come her road, and set himself against her enemies, and this was the end of it. They stood studying him, talking together in whispers, in a language he could not understand. A black-robed figure edged through that pale and glittering company, past the scale-armored guards, and deferentially whispered to the seated lords: the priest, who deferred to *qujalin* powers.

They have lost their gods, Morgaine had told him once; yet here was a priest among them. Vanye stood still, listening to that whispered debate, watching: a priest of demons, of *qujal*—this he had trusted, and delivered himself into their hands. The room grew distant from him, and the buzz of their soft voices as they discussed him was like that of bees over a Kurshin meadow, the hum of flies above corruption, the persistent rush of rain against the shuttered windows. He grew dizzy, lost in the sound, struggling only to keep his senses from sliding away.

"Who are you?" the old man asked sharply, looking directly at him; he realized then it was the second asking.

And had it been a human lord in his own hall, he would have felt obliged to bow in reverence: *ilin* that he was, he should bow upon his face, offering respect to a clan lord.

He stood still and hardened his face. "Lord," he said in the whisper that remained of his voice, "I am Nhi Vanye i Chya." He touched the hand of Jhirun, which rested on his arm. "She is Myya Jhirun i Myya Ela's-daughter, of a hold in Hiuaj. She calls this an honorable hold, and says," he added in grim insolence, "that your honor will compel you to give us a night's shelter and send us on our way in the morning with provisions."

There was a silence after that, and the lesser lords looked at each other, and the old lord smiled a wolf-smile, his eyes pale and cold as Morgaine's.

"I am Bydarra," said the old lord, "master of Ohtij-in." A gesture of his hand to left and right indicated the youth in black and him in blue, whose vague, chill eyes were those of one dreaming awake. "My sons," said Bydarra, "Hetharu and Kithan." He drew a long breath and let it go again, a smile frozen upon his face. "Out of Hiuaj," he murmured at last. "Does the quake and the flood scour out more lostlings to plague us? You are of the Barrow-hills," he said to Jhirun; and to Vanye, "and you are not."

"No," Vanye agreed, having nothing else to say; his very accent betrayed him.

"From the far south," said Bydarra.

There was a hush in the room. Vanye knew what the lord implied, for in the far south were only waters, and a great hill crowned with a ring of Standing Stones.

He said nothing.

"What is he?" Bydarra asked suddenly of Jhirun. Vanye felt her hand clench: a peasant girl, barefoot, among these glittering unhuman lords.

And then it occurred to him that she was, though human, *of* them: of their priest, their gods, their sovereignty.

"He is a great lord," she answered in a faint, breathless voice, with a touch of witlessness that for a moment seemed dangerous irony; but he knew her, and they did not. Bydarra looked on her a moment longer, distastefully, and Vanye inwardly blessed her subtlety.

"Stranger," said Hetharu suddenly, he in black brocade: Vanye looked toward him, realizing something that had troubled him—that this one's eyes were human-dark, despite the frost-white hair, but there was no gentleness in voice or look. "You mentioned a woman," Hetharu said, "on a gray horse or a black, or afoot, it might be. And who is she?"

His heart constricted; he sought an answer, cursing his rashness, and at last simply shrugged, refusing the question, hoping that Jhirun too would refuse it;

but she did not owe them the courage it would take to keep up her pretense of ignorance. There would come a time, and quickly, when they would not ask with words. And Jhirun—Jhirun knew enough to ruin them.

"Why are you here?" asked Hetharu.

For shelter from the rain, he almost answered, insolent and unwise; but that might advise them how Jhirun had subtly mocked them. He held his peace.

"You are not *khal*," said Kithan from the other side, his dreaming eyes half-lidded, his voice soft as a woman's. "You are not even halfling. You style yourself like the southern kings. This is a charade. Some find it impressive. But if you are expert with the Wells, o traveller—then why are you at our gate, begging charity? Power—ought to be better fed and better clothed."

"My lord," the priest objected.

"Out," said Kithan, in that same soft tone. "Go impress the rabble in the courtyard . . . *man*."

Bydarra stirred, rose stiffly to his feet, leaning on one arm of the chair. He looked at the priest, pursed his lips as if he would speak, and refrained. His gaze swept the other lords, and the guards, and lastly returned to Kithan and Hetharu.

Hetharu glowered; Kithan leaned back, eyes distant, moved a languid hand in a gesture of inconsequence.

The priest remained, silent and unhappy, and slowly Bydarra turned to Vanye, an old man in his movements, the seams of years and bitterness outlining his pale eyes and making hard his mouth. "Nhi Vanye," he said quietly. "Do you wish to answer any of the questions my sons have posed you?"

"No," said Vanye, conscious of the men at his back, the demon-helms that doubtless masked more of their folk. In Andur-Kursh, *qujal* had been fugitives, fearing to be known; but here *qujal* ruled. He recalled the courtyard where men lived, true men, who had cried out and reached for them, and instead they had trusted to *qujal*.

"If it is shelter you seek," said Bydarra, "you shall have it. Food, clothing— whatever your needs be. Ohtij-in will give you your night's hospitality."

"And an open gate in the morning?"

Bydarra's lined face was impassive, neither appreciating the barb nor angered by it. "We are perplexed," said Bydarra. "While we are thus perplexed, our gates remain closed. Doubtless these matters can be quickly resolved. We will watch the roads for the lady you mention, and for you—a night's hospitality."

Vanye bowed the least degree. "My lord Bydarra," he said, the words almost soundless.

They walked the winding corridor again, still ascending. Vanye kept Jhirun against his side, lest the guards think to separate them without resistance; and Jhirun hung her head dispiritedly, seeming undone, hardly caring where they were taken. About them a flurry of brown-clad servants bore trays and linens, some racing ahead, others rushing back again, shrinking against the walls motionless as they and their armored escort passed, averting their faces in terror unheard of in the worst bandit holds of Andur-Kursh.

Each bore a dark scar on the right cheek; Vanye noticed it on servant after servant they passed in the dim light, realized at last that it was a mark burned into the flesh, distinguishing the house servants from the horde outside. Outrage struck him, that the lords of Ohtij-in should mark men, to know their faces, as if this were the sole distinction of those who served them in their own hall.

And that men accepted this—to escape, perhaps, the misery outside—frightened him, as nothing human in this land had yet done.

The spiral branched, and they turned down that corridor, entered yet another spiral that wound upward yet a little distance, so that they seemed to have entered one of the outer towers. An open door welcomed them, and they were together admitted to a modest hall that was cheerful with a fire in the hearth, carpeted, with food and linens set on the long table in the midst of the room.

The servants who yet remained in the room bowed their heads and fled on slippered feet, pursued by the harsh commands of the chief of the escort. The guards who had entered withdrew; the door was closed.

A bar dropped down outside, echoing the truth of *qujalin* hospitality. Vanye stared at the strength of that wooden door, anger and fear roiling within him, and forbore the oath that rose in him; instead he hugged Jhirun's frail shoulders, and brought her to the hearth, where it was warmest in the room, that still bore a chill—settled her where she might rest against the stones. She held her shawl tightly about her, head bowed, shivering.

Gladly enough he would have cast himself down there to rest, but the urge of hunger was by a small degree greater, the sight of food and drink too much to resist.

He brought the platter of meat and cheese to the hearth and set it by Jhirun; he gathered up the bottle of drink, and cups, his hands shaking with exhaustion and reaction, and set them on the stones between them as he knelt down. He poured two foaming cups and urged one into Jhirun's passive hand.

"Drink," he said bitterly. "We have paid enough for it, and of all things else, they have no need to poison us."

She lifted it in her two hands and swallowed a great draught of it; he sipped the brew and grimaced, loathing the sour taste, but it was wet and eased his throat. Jhirun emptied hers, and he gave her more.

"O lord Vanye," she said at last, her voice almost as hoarse as his. "It is ugly, it is ugly; it is worse than Barrows-hold ever was. The ones that came here would have been better dead."

The refuge toward which the Hiua had fled . . . he recalled all her hopes of sanctuary, the bright land in which they would escape the dying of Hiuaj. It was a cruel end for her, no less than for him.

"If you find the chance," he said, "go, make yourself one of those in the yard outside."

"No," she said in horror.

"Outside, there is some hope left. Look at the ones that serve here—did you not see? Better the courtyard: listen to me—the gates may be opened during the day; they must open sometime. You came by the road; you can return by it. Go back to Hiuaj, go back to your own folk. You have no place among *qujal.*"

"Halflings," she said, and spat dryly. She tossed her tangled hair and set her jaw, that tended to quiver. "They are halfblood or less, and doubtless I can say the same, if the gossip about my grandmother is true. We were the Barrow-kings, and halflings were the beggars then; they were no better than the low-landers. Now, now we rob our ancestors for gold and sell it to halflings. But I will not crawl in the mud outside. These lords—only the high lords, like Bydarra—they are—they are of the Old Ones, Bydarra and his one son—" She shivered. "They have the blood—like *her.* But the priest—" The shiver became a sniff, a shrug of disdain. "The priest's eyes are dark. The hair is bleached. So with many of the others. They are no more than I am. I am not afraid of them. I am not going back."

All that she said he absorbed in silence, cold to the heart; that even a Myya could prize a claim to *qujalin* blood—he did not comprehend. He swore suddenly, half a prayer, and leaned against the lintel of the fireplace, forehead against his arm, staring into the fire and tried to think what he could do for himself.

Her hand touched his shoulder, gently, timidly; he turned his head and looked at her, finding only a frightened girl. The heat at his side became painful; he suffered it deliberately, not willing to think clearly in the directions that opened before him.

"I am not going back," she repeated.

"We shall leave here," he said, which he knew for a lie, but he thought that she wanted some promise, something on which to build her courage. He said it out of his own fear, knowing how easily she could tell the lords of Ohtij-in all that she knew: with this promise he meant to purchase her silence. "Only continue to say nothing, and we shall find a way to leave this foul place."

"For Abarais," she said. Her voice, hoarse as it was, came alive. The light danced in her eyes. "For the Well, for your land, and the mountains."

He lied this time by keeping silent. They were the greatest lies he had ever told, he who had once been a *dai-uyo* of Morija, who had fought to possess honor. He felt unclean, remembering her courage in the hall, and swore to himself that she would not come to hurt for it, not that he could prevent. But the true likelihood was that she would come to hurt, and that he could do nothing.

He was *ilin*, bound to a service; and this one essential truth he did not think she understood, else she would not trust her life to him. This also he did not say, and was ashamed and miserable.

She offered him food, and a second cup of drink, attacking the food herself with an appetite he lacked. He ate because he knew that he must, that if there was hope in strength, it must be his; he forced each mouthful down, hardly tasting it, and followed it with a heavy draught of the sour drink.

Then he rested his back against the fireplace, his shoulders over-warm and his legs numb from the stones, and began to take account of himself, his water-soaked armor and ruined boots. He began to work at the laces at his throat, having to break some of them, then at the buckles at his side and shoulder, working sodden leather through.

Jhirun moved to help him, tugging to free the straps, helping him as he slipped off first the leather surcoat and then the agonizing weight of the mail. Freed of it, he groaned with relief, content only to breathe for a moment. Then came the sleeveless linen haqueton, and that sodden and soiled, and bloody in patches.

"O my lord," Jhirun murmured in pity, and numbly he looked at himself and saw how the armor had galled his water-soaked skin, his linen shirt a soaked rag, rubbing raw sores where there had been folds. He rose, wincing, stripped it off and dropped it to the floor, shivering in the cold air.

Among the clothes on the table he found several shirts, soft and thin, that came of no fabric he knew; he disliked the feel of the too-soft weaving, but when he drew one on, it lay easily upon his galled shoulders, and he was grateful for the touch of something clean and dry.

Jhirun came, timidly searching among the *qujalin* gifts for her own sake. She found the proper stack, unfolded the brown garment uppermost, stood staring at it as if it were alive and hostile—a brown smock such as the servants wore.

He saw, and swore—snatched it from her hands and hurled it to the floor. She looked frightened, and small and miserable in her wet garments.

He picked up one of the shirts and a pair of breeches. "Wear these," he said. "Yours will dry."

"Lord," she said, a tremor in her voice. She hugged the offered clothing to her breast. "Please do not leave me in this place."

"Go dress," he said, and looked away from her deliberately, hating the appeal and the distress of her—who looked to him, who doubtless would concede to anything to be reassured of his lies.

Who might the more believe him if she were thus reassured.

Unwed girls of the countryside of Andur and of Kursh were a casual matter for the *uyin* of the high clans—peasant girls hoping to bear an *uyo's* bastard, to be kept in comfort thereafter: an obligation to the *uyo*, a matter of honor. But therein both parties knew the way of things. Such a thing was not founded in lies or in fear.

"Lord," she said, across the room.

He turned and looked at her, who still stood in her coarse peasant skirts, the garments held against her.

The tread of men approached the door outside, an ominous and warlike sound. Vanye heard it, and heard them pause. Jhirun started to hurry to his side.

The bar of the door crashed back. Vanye looked about as it opened, whirling a chill draft into the room and fluttering the fire; and there in the doorway stood a man in green and brown, who leaned on a sheathed longsword—fronted him with a look of sincere bewilderment.

"Cousin," said Roh.

⮑ **Chapter 8**

"Roh," Vanye answered, and heard a rustle of cloth at his left: Jhirun, who drew closer to him. He did not turn his head to see, only hoping that she would stay neutral. He himself stood in shirt and breeches; and Roh was armored. He was weaponless, and Roh carried a longsword, sheathed, in his hand.

There had been no weapons in the room, neither knife with the food nor iron by the fire. In desperation Vanye reckoned what his own skill could avail, a weaponless swordsman against a swordsman whose primary weapon had been the bow.

Roh leaned more heavily on the sword's pommel and shouted over his shoulder a casual dismissal of the guards in the corridor, then stood upright, cast wide his arm in a gesture of peace.

Vanye did not move. Roh tossed his sword and caught it midsheath in one hand; and with a mocking flourish discarded it on the table by the door. Then he came forward several paces, limping slightly, bearing that sober, slightly worried expression that was Roh's very self.

And his glance swept from Vanye to Jhirun, utterly puzzled.

"Girl," he said wonderingly, and then shook his head and walked to a chair and sat down, elbows upon the chair's arms. He gave a silent and humorless laugh. "I thought it would be Morgaine. Where is she?"

The plain question shot through other confusions, making sense—Roh's presence making sense of many matters in Ohtij-in. Vanye set his face against him, grateful to understand at least one enemy, and wished Jhirun to silence.

"She *is*," Roh said, "hereabouts."

It was bait he was desired to take: he burned to ask what Roh knew, and yet he knew better—shifted his weight and let go his breath, realizing that he had been holding it. "You seem to have found welcome enough here," he answered Roh coldly, "among your own kind."

"I have found them agreeable," said Roh. "So might you, if you are willing to listen to reason."

Vanye thrust Jhirun away, toward the far corner of the room, "Get back," he told her. "Whatever happens here, you do not want to be part of it."

But she did not go, only retreated from his roughness, and stood watching, rubbing her arm.

Vanye ignored her, walked to the table where the sword lay, wondering when Roh would move to stop him; he did not. He gathered it into his hands, watching Roh the while. He drew it part of the way from the sheath, waiting still for Roh to react; Roh did not move. There was only a flicker of apprehension in his brown eyes.

"You are a lie," Vanye said. "An illusion."

"You do not know what I am," Roh answered him.

"Zri . . . Liell . . . Roh . . . How many names have you worn before that?"

Liell, sardonic master of Leth, whose mocking humor and soft lies he well knew: he watched sharply for that, waited for the arrogant and incalculably ancient self to look out at him through Roh's human eyes—for that familiar and grandiose movement of the hands, some gesture that would betray the alien resident within his cousin's body.

There was nothing of the like, Roh sat still, watching him, his quick eyes following each move: afraid, that was evident. Reckless: that was like Roh, utterly.

He drew the sword entirely. *Now*, he thought. *Now, if ever—before conscience, before pity.* His arm tensed. But Roh simply stared at him, a little flinching when he moved.

"*No!*" Jhirun cried from across the room. It came near loosing his arm before he had consciously willed it; he stayed the blow—Jolted to remember a courtyard in Morija, and blood, and sickness that knotted in him, robbing him suddenly of strength.

With a curse he rammed the sword into sheath, knowing himself, as Roh had known him.

Coward, his shorn hair marked him. He saw the narrow satisfaction in Roh's eyes.

"It is good to see you," Roh said in a hollow, careful voice. "Nhi Vanye, it is good to see any kindred soul in this forsaken land. But I am sorry for your sake. I had thought that you would have used good sense and ridden home. I never thought that you would have come with her, even if she ordered it. Nhi honor: it is a compulsion. I am sorry for it. But the sight of you is very welcome."

"Liar," Vanye said between his teeth; but the words, like a Chya shaft, flew accurately to the mark. He felt the wound, the desperation of exile, in which Roh—anyone who could prove that the things he remembered had ever existed—was a presence infinitely precious. The accents of home even on an enemy's lips were beautiful.

"There is no point in quarreling before witnesses," said Roh.

"There is no point in talking to you."

"Nhi Vanye," said Roh softly, "come with me. Outside. I have sent the guards elsewhere. Come." He rose from the chair, moved carefully to the door, looking back at him. "Alone."

Vanye hesitated. That door was what he most earnestly desired, but he knew no reason that Roh should wish him well. He tried to think what entrapment Roh needed use, and that was none at all.

"Come," Roh urged him.

Vanye shrugged, went to the fireside, where his armor lay discarded—slung his swordbelt over his shoulder and hung the sword from it, ready to his hand: thus he challenged Roh.

"As you will," Roh said. "But it is mine; and I will ask it back eventually."

Jhirun came to the fireside, her eyes frightened, looking from one to the other of them: many, many things she had not said; Vanye felt the reminder in her glance.

"I would not leave her alone," he said to Roh.

"She is safe," Roh said. He looked directly at Jhirun, took her unresisting hand, and gone in him was every guardedness and ungentle tone. "Do not fear anything in Ohtij-in. I remember a kindness and return it doubled if I can, as I return other things. No harm will come to you. None."

She stayed still, seeming to trust nothing. Vanye delayed, fearing to leave her, fearing that might be Roh's purpose: to separate them; and in another mind, fearing what evil he might do her by holding to her, linking her with him, when he had only enemies in Ohtij-in.

"I do not think I have a choice," he said to her, and did not know whether she understood. He turned his back on her, feeling her stare as he walked to the door. Roh opened it, brought him out into the dim corridor, where a cold wind hit his light clothing and set him shivering.

There were no guards in sight, not a stir anywhere in the corridor.

Roh closed the door and dropped the bar. "Come," he said then, motioned to the left, toward the ascent of the spiral ramp.

Turn after turn they climbed, Roh slightly in the lead; and Vanye found his exhaustion such that he must put a hand on the core wall to steady his step. Roh climbed, limping only slightly, and Vanye glared at his back, his hand on the sword, waiting for Roh to show sensible fear of him and glance back only once; but Roh did not. *Arrogant*, Vanye thought, raging in his heart; but it was very like Roh.

At last they arrived at a level floor, and a doorway, up low steps. Roh opened that door, admitting a gust of wind that skirted violently into the tower, chilling the very bones. Outside was night, and the scent of recent rain.

He followed Roh outside, atop the very crest of the outermost tower of Ohtij-in, where the moons' wan light streamed through the ragged clouds: Anli and Sith were overhead, and hard behind them hurtled the fragments of the Broken Moon, while on the horizon was the vast white face of Li, pocked and scarred. The wind swept freely across the open space. Vanye hung back, in the shelter of the tower core, but Roh walked to the edge, his cloak held closely about him in the blast of the wind.

"Come," Roh urged him, and Vanye came, knowing himself mad even to have come this far, alone with this *qujal* in man's guise. He reached the edge and looked down, dizzied at the view down the tower walls to the stones below; he caught at the solidity of the battlement with one hand and at the sword's hilt with the other.

If Roh meant to destroy him, he thought, there was ample means for that. He ignored Roh for an instant, cast a look at all the country round about, the glint of moonlight on black flood-waters that wove a spider's web about the drowning hills. Through those hills lanced the road that he could not reach, subtle torment.

Roh's hand touched his shoulder, drawing his attention back. His other hand described the circuit of the land, the hold itself.

"I wanted you to see this," Roh said above the howl of wind. "I wanted you to know the compass of this place. And *she* will finish it, end all hope for them. That is what she has come to do."

He turned a hard look on Roh, leaned against the stonework, for he had begun to shiver convulsively in the wind. "It is impossible for you to persuade me," he said, and held up his scarred hand to the moonlight. "Roh or Liell, you should remember what I am, at least."

"You doubt me," said Roh.

"I doubt everything about you."

Roh's face, hair torn by the wind, assumed a pained earnestness. "I knew that she would hunt me. She was always our enemy. But from you, Nhi Vanye i Chya, I hoped for better. You took shelter from me. You slept at my hearth. Is that nothing to you?"

Vanye flexed his fingers on the corded hilt of the sword, for they were growing numb with cold. "You are supposing," he said hoarsely, "what passed between Roh and me—what was surely common knowledge throughout Chya—and I do not doubt you had your spies. If you want me to believe you, then tell me again what Roh told me last in Ra-koris, when there was none to hear."

Roh hesitated. "To come back," he said, "free of her."

It was truth. The unexpectedness of it numbed him. He leaned against the stonework, ceasing even to shiver, and abruptly turned his face from Roh. "And it might be that Roh counseled with others before saying that to me."

Roh pulled him about by the shoulder, grimacing into the wind.

"So you could say, Vanye, for any other thing you might devise to try me. You cannot be sure, and you know it."

"There is one thing you cannot answer," Vanye said. "You cannot tell me why you are here in this land. Roh would not have fled the road we took; he had no reason to—but Liell had every reason. Liell would have run for his life; and Roh had no reason to."

"He is here," Roh said, a hand upon his heart. "Here. So also am I. My memories—all are Roh's—they are both."

"No," he said. "No. Morgaine said that would not happen; and I would rather take her word than yours—in any matter."

"I am your cousin. I could have taken your life; but I am your cousin. You have the sword. There is no witness here to say it was no fair fight—if the Shiua lords cared. You are already known for a kinslayer many times over. Use it. Or listen to me."

He flung off Roh's hand, blind as a turn of his head brought his own shorn hair into his eyes. He shook it free, stalked off across the battlements, stood staring down into the squalor of that courtyard, the wind pushing at his back, fit to tear him from the edge and cast him over.

"Nhi Vanye!" Roh called him. He turned and looked, saw Roh had followed him. He stubbornly turned his head toward the view downward, toward the paving and the poor shelters huddled against the keep walls. He felt the breaking of the force of the wind as Roh stepped between it and him.

"If you are kinsman to me," Vanye said, "free me from this place. Then I will believe your kinship."

"Me? And care you nothing for that child that came with you?"

He looked back, stung, unable to argue. He affected a shrug. "Jhirun? Here is where she wanted to be, in Shiuan, in Ohtij-in. This is the land she wished for. What is she to me?"

"I had thought better of you," Roh said after a moment, "So, surely, had she."

"I am *ilin*. Nothing else. There are human folk here, men, and so she can survive. They have."

"*There* are men," said Roh, and pointed at the squalid court, where beasts and men shared neighboring quarters. "That is the lot of men in Ohtij-in. That is their life, from birth to death. Men now. Tomorrow the rest that survive in this land will live in that poverty, and the *qujal*-lords know it. Of their charity, of their *charity*, Nhi Vanye, these lords have let men shelter within their walls; of their *charity* they have fed them and clothed them. They owed them nothing; but they have let them live within their gates. You—you are not so charitable—you would let them die, that girl and all the rest. That is what you would do to me. The sword's edge is kinder, cousin, than what is waiting for all this land. Murder—is kinder."

"I have nothing to do with what is happening to these people. I cannot help them or harm them."

"Can you not? The Wells are their hope, Vanye. For all that live and will live in this world, the Wells are all the hope there is. They had no skill to use them; but by them, these folk could live. I could do it. Morgaine surely could, but she will not, and you know that she will not. Vanye, if that ancient power were used as it once was used, their lot would be different. Look on this, look, and remember it, cousin."

He looked, perforce. He did not wish to remember the sight, and the faces that had raged wildly beyond the guards' pikes, the desperate hands that had reached through the grate. "All this is a lie," he said. "As you are a lie."

"The sword's edge," Roh invited him, "if you believe that beyond doubt."

He lifted his face toward Roh, wishing to see truth, wishing something that he could hate, finding nothing to attack—only Roh, mirror-image of himself, more alike him than his own brothers.

"Send me from here," he challenged him who wore the shape of Roh, "if you believe that you can convince me. At least you know that I keep my sworn word. If you have a message for Morgaine herself, then give it to me and I will deliver it faithfully—it I can find her, of which I have doubts."

"I will not ask you where she is," Roh said. "I know where she is going; and I know that you would not tell me more than that. But others might ask you. Others might ask you."

Vanye shivered, remembering the gathering in the hall, the pale lords and ladies who owed nothing to humanity. A fall to the paving below was easier than that. He stepped forward to the very edge, inwardly trying whether he had the courage.

"Vanye," Roh cried, compelling his attention. "Vanye, she will have little difficulty destroying these folk. They will see her, they will flock to her, trusting, because she is fair to see—and she will kill them. It has happened before. Do you think that there is compassion in her?"

"There has been," he said, the words hanging half soundless in his throat.

"You know its limits," said Roh. "You have seen that, too."

Vanye cursed aloud, flung himself back from the battlements and sought the door, sought warmth, fought to open it against the force of the wind. He tore it open, and Roh held it, came in after him. The torches in the hall fluttered wildly until the door slammed. Roh dropped the latch. They remained on opposite sides of the little corridor, facing one another.

"Say to them that you could not persuade me," Vanye said. "Perhaps your hosts will forgive you."

"Listen to me," said Roh.

Vanye unhooked the sheathed sword and cast it across the corridor; Roh caught it, midsheath, and looked at him in perplexity.

"God forgive me," Vanye said.

"For not committing murder?" Roh said. "That is incongruous."

He stared at Roh, then tore his eyes from him and began to walk rapidly down the corridor, descending the ramp. There were guards below. He stopped when their weapons levelled toward him.

Roh overtook him and set his hand on his arm. "Do not be rash. Listen to me, cousin. Messengers are going out, have already sped, despite the storm, bearing warnings of her throughout the whole countryside, to every hold and village. She will find no welcome among these folk."

Vanye jerked free, but Roh caught his arm. "No," said Roh. The guards stood waiting, helmed, faceless, weapons ready. "Will you be handled like a peasant for the hanging," Roh whispered in his ear, "or will you walk peaceably with me?"

Roh's hand tightened, urged. Vanye suffered the grip upon his arm, and Roh led him through the midst of the guards, walked with him down the windings of the corridors; and they did not stop at the door of the room that confined Jhirun, but went farther, into a branching corridor, that seemed to lead back to the main tower. The guards walked at their backs, two bearing torches.

"Jhirun," Vanye reminded Roh, as they entered that other corridor.

"I thought that was a matter of no concern to you."

"She is a chance meeting," he said. "And no more than that. She set out looking for you, hoping better from you than she had where she was: the measure of that, you may know better than I. You were kind to her, she said."

"She will be safe," said Roh. "I also keep my word."

Vanye frowned, glanced away. Roh said nothing further. They entered a third corridor, that came to an end in a blind wall; and in a narrow place on the right was a deeply recessed doorway. Shadows ran the walls as the guards overtook them, while Roh opened the door.

It was a plain room, with a fire blazing in the hearth, a wooden bench by the fire, table, chairs. And Hetharu waited there, Bydarra's dark-eyed son, seated, with a handful of others likewise seated about him—pale-haired men, although only Hetharu seemed so by nature, his long locks white and silken about his shoulders. He leaned elbows upon his knees, warming his hands at the fire; and by the fire stood a priest, whose brittle, bleached hair described a nimbus about his balding head.

Vanye stopped in the doorway, confused by the situation of things, so important a man, so strangely assorted the company. Roh set his hand on his shoulder and urged him gently forward. The guards took up stations inside and out as the doors were closed and the gathering became a private one. Helms were removed, revealing faces thin and pale as those of the higher lords, eyes as dark as Hetharu's: young men, all that were gathered here, save the priest, furtive in their quiet. There was the brocaded finery of the lords, the martial plate-and-scale of the men-at-arms, the plainness of the furnishings. Guards had been posted outside as well as within the room. These things touched uneasily at Vanye's mind, warning of something other than mere games of terror with him. The gathering breathed of something ugly, that concerned the *qujal* themselves, powers and alliances within their ranks.

And he was seized into the midst of it.

"You won nothing of him?" Hetharu asked of Roh. Roh left Vanye's side and took the vacant bench beside the fire, one booted foot tucked up, disposing himself comfortably and at his ease, leaving Vanye as if he were harmless.

In peevish insolence Vanye shifted his weight suddenly, and hands reached for daggers and swords all about the room; he tautened his lips, a smile that rage made slight and mocking, and slowly, amid their indecision, moved to take his place beside Roh on the bench, near the fire's warmth. Roh straightened slightly, both feet on the floor; and the look in Hetharu's eyes was angry. Vanye met that stare with a stubborn frown, though within, he felt less than easy: here was, he thought, a man who would gladly resort to force, who would enjoy it.

"My cousin," said Roh, "is a man of his word, and reckons that word otherwise bestowed . . . although this may change. As matters stand now, he does not recognize reason, only the orders of his liege: that is the kind of man he is."

"A dangerous man," said Hetharu, and his dark, startling eyes rested full on Vanye's. "Are you dangerous, Man?"

"I thought," said Vanye slowly, with deliberation, "that Bydarra was lord in Ohtij-in. What is this?"

"You see how he is," said Roh. And on faces round about there was consternation: guilt, fear. Hetharu glowered. Vanye read the tale writ therein and liked it less and less.

"And his liege?" asked Hetharu. "What has he to say of her?"

"Nothing," said Roh. And in their long silence, Vanye's heart beat rapidly.

"It is of little profit," said Roh, "to question him on that account. I will not have him harmed, my lord."

Vanye heard, not understanding, not believing Roh's defense of him; but he saw in that moment that a hint of caution appeared in Hetharu's manner—uncertainty that held him from commanding Roh.

"You," said Hetharu suddenly, looking at Vanye, "do you claim to have come by the Wells?"

"Yes," Vanye answered, for he knew that there was no denying it.

"And can you manage them?" the priest asked, a husky, quiet voice. Vanye looked up into the priest's face, reading desire there, not knowing how to deal with the desires that gathered thickly in this room, centered upon him and upon Roh. He did not want to die; abundantly, he did not want to die, butchered by *qujal*, for causes he did not understand, that had nothing to do with him.

He did not answer.

"You are a Man," said the priest.

"Yes," he said, and noticed that the priest carried a knife at his belt, curious accoutrement for a priest; and that all the others were armed. The priest wore a chain of objects about his neck, stone and shell and bone—familiar—Vanye realized all at once where he had seen such, daily, along with a small stone cross, profaned by nearness to such things. He stared at the priest, the rage that he could maintain against armed threat ebbing coldly in the consideration of devils, and those that served them—and the state of his soul, who served Morgaine, and who companied with a human girl who wore such objects about her neck.

Only let them keep the priest from him. He tore his gaze away from that one, lest the fear show, lest he give them a weapon.

"Man," said Hetharu, looking on him with that same fixed stare, "is this truly your cousin?"

"Half of him was my cousin," Vanye said, to confound them all.

"You see how he tells the truth," Roh said softly, silk-over-metal. "It does not always profit him, but he is forward with it: an honest man, my cousin Vanye. He confuses many people with that trait, but he is Nhi; you would not understand that, but he is Nhi, and he cannot help this over-nice devotion to honor. He tells the truth. He makes himself enemies with it. But in your honesty, cousin, tell them why your liege has come to this land. What has she come to do?"

He saw the reason for his presence among them now, how he had been, in his cleverness, guided to this. He knew that he should have held his peace from the beginning. Now silence itself would accuse, persuasive as admission. His muscles tautened, mind numbed when he most needed it. He had no answer.

"To seal the Wells forever," Roh said. "Tell me, my honest, my honorable cousin—is that or is that not the truth?"

Still he held his peace, searching desperately for a lie, not practiced in the art. There was none he could shape that could not be at once unravelled.

"Deny it, then," said Roh. "Can you do that?"

"I deny it," he said, reacting as Roh thrust at him what he most wanted; and even as it slipped his lips he knew he had been maneuvered.

"Swear to it," Roh said; and as he began to say that also; "On your oath to her," Roh said.

By your soul: that was the oath; and their eyes were all on him, like wolves in a circle. His lips shaped the words, knowing the effort for useless, utterly useless; on his soul too was his duty to Morgaine, that bade him try.

But Roh set his hand on his arm, mercifully stopping him, leaving him trembling with sickness. "No," Roh said. "Spare yourself the guilt, Vanye; you do not wear it well. You see how it is, lord Hetharu. I have shown you the truth. My cousin is an honest man. And you, my lord, will swear to me that you will set no hand on him. I bear him some affection, this cousin of mine."

Heat mounted steadily to Vanye's face. There seemed no profit in protesting this baiting defense. He met Hetharu's dark and resentful eyes. "Granted," Hetharu said after a moment, and glanced at Roh. "He is yours. But I cannot answer for my father."

"No one," said Roh, "will set hand on him."

Hetharu glanced down, and aside, and frowned and rose. "No one," he echoed sullenly.

"My lords," said Roh, likewise rising. "A safe sleep to you."

There was a moment of silence, of seething anger on the part of the young lord. Surely it was not accustomed that Bydarra's son receive his dismissal from a dark-haired guest. But fear hovered thickly in the room when Roh looked at them all in their turn: eyes averted from his, to one side and the other, pretending to find interest in the stones of the floor or the guarded door.

Hetharu shrugged, a false insouciance. "My lords," he said to his companions. "Priest."

They filed out with rustling brocade and the clash of metal, those slim fair lords with their attendant guard, half-human—until there was only Roh, who quietly closed the door, making the room again private.

"Give me the sword again," Vanye said, "cousin."

Roh regarded him warily, hand on the hilt. He shook his head and showed no inclination to come near him now. "You do not seem to understand," Roh said. "I have secured your life, and your person from some considerable danger. I have a certain authority here—while they fear me. It does not serve your own cause to fight against me."

"It is your own life you have secured," Vanye said, and arose to stand with his back to the fire, "so that they will not try me too severely and find your kinsman is only human."

"That too," said Roh. He started to open the door, and hesitated, looking back. "I wish that I could persuade you to common sense."

"I will go back to the room where I was," Vanye said. "I found it more comfortable."

Roh grinned. "Doubtless."

"Do not touch her," Vanye said. Roh's grin faded; he faced him entirely, regarded him with an earnest look.

"I have said," Roh said, "that she would be safe. And she will be safer—apart from you. I think you understand this."

"Yes," Vanye said after a moment.

"I would help you if you would give me the means."

"Good night," Vanye said.

Roh delayed, a frown twisting his face. He extended his hand, dropped it in a helpless gesture. "Nhi Vanye—my life will end if your liege destroys the Wells—not suddenly, but surely, all the same. So will everything in this land . . . die. But that is nothing to her. Perhaps she cannot help what she is or what she does. I suspect that she cannot. But you at least have a choice. These folk—will die, and they need not."

"I have an oath to keep. I have no choice at all."

"If you had sworn to the devil," Roh said, "would it be a pious act to keep your word?"

Unthought, his hand moved to bless himself, and he stopped, then with deliberation completed the gesture, in this place of *qujal*, where priests worshipped devils. He was cold, inside.

"Can she do as you have done?" asked Roh. "Vanye, is there any land where she has traveled where she is not cursed, and justly? Do you even know whether you serve the side of Men in this war? You have an oath; you have made yourself blind and deaf because of it; you have left kinsmen dead because of it. But to what have you sworn it? Do you wonder what was left in Andur-Kursh? You will never know what you wrought there, and perhaps that is well for your conscience. But here you can see what you do, and you will live in it. Do you think the Wells have kept these folk in misery? Do you think the Wells are the evil? It was the loss of them that ruined this land. And this is the likeness of Morgaine's work. This is what she does, what she leaves behind her wherever she passes. There is nothing more terrible that could befall you than to stay behind where she has passed. You and I know it; we were born in the chaos she wrought in our own Andur-Kursh. Kingdoms fell and clans died under her guidance. She is disaster where she passes, Nhi Vanye. She kills. That is her function, and you cannot prevent her. To destroy is her whole purpose for being."

Vanye turned his face aside and gazed at the barren walls, at the single slit of a window, slatted with a wooden shutter.

"You are determined not to listen," said Roh. "Perhaps you are growing like her."

Vanye glanced back, face set in anger. "Liell," he named Roh, the name that had been his last self, that had destroyed Roh. "Murderer of children. You offered me haven too, in Ra-leth; and I saw what a gift *that* was, what prosperity you brought those that came under your hand."

"I am not Liell any longer."

I.

Vanye felt a tightness about his heart, himself caught and held by that level gaze. "Who is talking to me?" he asked in a still voice. "Who are you, *qujal?* Who were you?"

"Roh."

Bile rose into his throat. He turned his face away. "Get out of here. Get away from me. Do me that grace at least. Let me alone."

"Cousin," said Roh softly. "Have you never wondered who Morgaine was?"

The question left silence after it, a numbness in which he could be aware of the sounds of the fire, the wind outside the narrow window. He found it an effort to draw breath in that silence.

"You have wondered, then," said Roh. "You are not entirely blind. Ask yourself why she is *qujal* to the eye and not to the heart. Ask whether she always tells the truth . . . and believe me, that she does not, not where it is most essential, not where it threatens the thing she seeks. Ask how much of me is Roh, and I will tell you that the essence of me is Roh; ask why you are kept safe, hostile to me as you are, and I will tell you it is because we are—truly—cousins. I feel that burden; I act upon it because I must. But ask yourself what *she* became, this liege of yours. My impulses are human. Ask yourself how human she is. Less than any here—whose blood is only halfling. Ask yourself what you are sworn to, Nhi Vanye."

"Out!" he cried, so that the door burst open and armed guards were instant with lowered weapons. But Roh lifted his hand and stopped them.

"Give you good night," Roh murmured, and withdrew.

The door closed. A bolt shot into place outside.

Vanye swore under his breath, cast himself down on the bench by the fire.

A log crashed, glowing ruin, stirring a momentary flame that ran the length of the charred edge and died. He watched the shifting patterns in the embers, heart pounding, for it seemed to his blurring senses that the floor had shifted minutely, a fall like the Between of Gates.

Animals bleated outside. He heard the distant murmur of troubled voices.

The realization that it had been no illusion sent sweat coursing over his limbs, but the earth stayed still thereafter.

He let go his pent breath, stared at the fire until the light and heat wearied his eyes and made him close them.

⤳ **Chapter 9**

Guards intruded in the morning, servants bringing food and water, a sudden flurry of footsteps, crashing of bolts and doors; savory smells came with the dishes that rattled in the servants' hands.

Vanye rose to his feet by the dying fire. He ached; the pain of his swollen, chafed feet made him stagger violently, brace himself against the stonework. The pikes in the hands of the guards lowered toward him a threatening degree. The servants stared at him, soft-footed men, marked on the faces by the sign of a slashed circle—marked too in the eyes by a fear that was biding and constant.

"Roh," he asked of the servants, of the guards, his voice still hoarse. "Send for Roh. I want to see him." For this morning he recalled a lost dagger, lost with Morgaine, and a thing that he had sworn to do; and things he had said in the night, and not said.

None answered him now. The servants looked away, terrified. The demon-helms shadowed the eyes of the halfling guards, making their faces alike and expressionless toward him.

"I need a change of clothing," he said to the servants; they flinched from him as if he had a devil, and made haste to put themselves in the shadow of the guards, beginning to withdraw.

"The firewood is almost gone," he shouted at them, irrational panic taking him at the thought of dark and cold in the room thereafter. "It will not last the day."

The servants fled; the guards withdrew, closing the door. The bolt went home.

He was trembling, raging at what he knew not: Roh, the lords of this place—at himself, who had walked willingly into it. He stood now and stared at the door, knowing that no force would avail against it, and that no shouting would bring him freedom. He limped over to the table and sat down on the end of the bench, reckoning coldly, remembering every door, every turning, every detail of the hold inside and out. And somewhere within Ohtij-in—he tried to remember that room too—was Jhirun, whom he could not help.

He drank of what the servants had left—sparingly, reckoning that if his hosts were unwilling to give him firewood to keep him warm they would likely bring him nothing else for the day; he ate, likewise sparingly, and turned constantly in his mind the image he could shape of the hold, its corridors, its gates, the number of the men who guarded it, coming again and again to the same conclusion: that he could not pass so many barriers and remain a fugitive across a land that he did not know, afoot, knowing no landmark but the road—on which his enemies could swiftly find him.

Only Roh came and went where he would.

Roh might set him upon that road. There would be a cost for that freedom. The food went tasteless in his mouth the while he considered what it might cost him, to be set at Abarais, to obtain Roh's trust.

To destroy Roh: this was the thing she had set him last to do, a matter as simple as his given word, from which there was no release and no appeal, be it an act honorable or dishonorable: honor was not in question between *ilin* and *liyo*.

It was not necessary to wonder what would befall him thereafter; it did not matter thereafter to what he had sworn—it was a weight no longer on his conscience, a last discharge of obligations.

He became strangely comfortable then, knowing the limits of his existence, knowing that it was not necessary any longer to struggle against Roh's reasoning. He had, for the first time in his life, accounted for all possibilities and understood all that was necessary to understand.

None came near the room. The long day passed. Vanye went earliest to the window, that he thought a mercy of his jailers, narrow though it was, a kindness to allow him access to the sky—until he eased back the wooden slat that covered it. There was nothing beyond but a stone wall that he could almost touch with outstretched arm; and when he leaned against the sill and tried to see downward, there was a ledge below. On the left was a buttress of the tower, that cut off his view; on the right was another wall, likewise near enough to touch.

He left the window unshuttered, despite the blindness of it and despite the occasional chill draft. So long accustomed to the sky above him, he found the closeness of walls unbearable. He watched the daylight grow until the sun shone straight down the shaft, and watched it fade into shadow again as the sun declined in the sky. He listened to the wailing of children, the sounds of livestock, the squealing of wheels, as if the gates of Ohtij-in were open and some manner of normal traffic had begun. Men shouted, accented words that he did not recognize, but he was glad to hear the voices, which seemed coarsely ordinary and human.

A shadow began to fall, more swiftly than the decline of the day; thunder rumbled. Drops of rain spattered the tiny area of ledge visible beneath the window—drops that ceased, began again, pattering with increasing force as the sprinkling became a shower.

And the last of the wood burned out, despite his careful hoarding of the last small logs and pieces. The room chilled. Outside, the rain whispered steadily down the shaft.

Metal clattered up the hall, the sound of armed men. It was not the first time in the day: occasionally there had come sounds from within the tower, distant and meaning nothing. Vanye only stirred when he realized they were growing nearer—rose to his feet in the almost-darkness, hoping for such petty and precious things as firewood and food and drink, and fearing that their business might be something else.

Let it be Roh, he thought, trembling with anxiety, the anticipation of all things at an end, only so the chance presented itself.

The bolt went back. He blinked in the flare of torches that filled the opening door, that made shadows of the guards and the men until they were within the room: light glittered on brocade, gleamed on bronze helms and on pale hair.

Bydarra, he recognized the elder man; and with him, Hetharu. The combination jolted against the memory of the night—of furtive meetings within this prison of his, of young lordlings and secrecies.

Vanye stood still by the fireplace, while the guards set their torches in place of the stubs in the brackets. The room outside those interlocked circles of light was dark by comparison, the rainy daylight a faint glow in the recess, less bright than the torches. The character of the room seemed changed, a place unfamiliar, where *qujal* intervened, contrary to all his own intentions. He looked at the guards that waited in the doorway, the light limning demon-faces and outlandish scale. He looked on them with a slowly growing terror, the consciousness of things outside the compass of himself and Roh.

"Nhi Vanye," Bydarra hailed him, not ungently.

"Lord Bydarra," he answered. He bowed his head slightly, responding to the soft courtesy, though the guards about them denied that any courtesy was meant, though Hetharu's thin, wolfish face beside his father's held nothing of good will. Vanye looked up again, met the old lord's pale eyes directly. "I had thought that you would have sent for me to come to you."

Bydarra smiled tautly, and answered nothing to that insolence. Of a sudden there was about this gathering too the hint of secrecies, the lord of Ohtij-in intriguing within his own hold, not wishing a prisoner moved about the halls with what noise and notice would attend such moving. Bydarra asked no questions, proposed nothing immediate, only waited on his prisoner, with what purpose Vanye felt hovering shapeless and ominous among the lords of Ohtij-in.

And in that realization came a horrid suspicion of hope: that of ruining Roh, there was a chance here present. It was not the act of a warrior: he felt shame for it, but he did not think that he could reject whatever means offered itself. He made himself numb to what he did.

"Have you come," Vanye asked of the *qujal,* "to learn of me what things Roh would not tell you?"

"And what might those things be?" Bydarra asked softly.

"That you cannot trust him."

Again Bydarra smiled, this time with more satisfaction. His features were an aged mirror of Hetharu's, who was close beside him—a face lean and fine-boned, but Bydarra's eyes were pale: Morgaine's features, he thought with an inward shudder, horrified to see that familiar face reflected in her enemies. No pure *qujal* had been left in Andur-Kursh. He saw one for the first time, and thought, unwillingly, of Morgaine.

Ask yourself, Roh had said, taunting him, *what you are sworn to.*

"Go," Bydarra bade the guards, and they went, closing the door; but Hetharu stayed, at which Bydarra frowned.

"Dutiful," Bydarra murmured at him distastefully; and he looked at Vanye with a mocking twist of his fine lips. "My son," he said with a nod at Hetharu. "A man of indiscriminate taste and energetic ambitions. A man of sudden and sweeping ambitions."

Vanye glanced beyond Bydarra's shoulder, at Hetharu's still face, sensing the pride of this man, who stood at his father's shoulder and heard himself insulted to a prisoner. For an irrational instant Vanye felt a deep impulse of sympathy toward Hetharu—himself bastard, half-blood, spurned by his own father. Then a suspicion came to him that it was not casual, that Bydarra knew that he had reason to distrust this son, that Bydarra had reason to come to a prisoner's cell and ask questions.

And Hetharu had urgent reason to cling close to his father's side, lest the old lord learn of meetings and movements that occurred in the night within the walls of Ohtij-in. Vanye met Hetharu's eyes without intending it, and Hetharu returned his gaze, his dark and human eyes promising violence, seething with ill will.

"Roh urges us," said Bydarra, "to treat you gently. Yet he calls you his enemy."

"I am his cousin," Vanye countered quietly, falling back upon Roh's own stated reasoning.

"Roh," said Bydarra, "makes vast and impossible promises—of limitless arrogance. One would think that he could reshape the Moon and turn back the waters. So suddenly arrived, so strangely earnest in his concern for us—he styles himself like the ancient Kings of Men, and claims to have power over the Wells. He seeks our records, pores over maps and old accounts of only curious interest. And what would you, Nhi Vanye i Chya? Will you likewise bid for the good will of Ohtij-in? What shall we offer you for your good pleasure if you will save us all? Worship, as a god?"

The sting of sarcasm fell on numbness, a chill, to think of Roh, a Chya bowman, a lord of forested Koris, searching musty *qujalin* records, through runic writings that Men did not read—save only Morgaine. "Roh," Vanye said, "lies to you. He does not know everything; but you are teaching it to him. Keep him from those books."

Bydarra's silvery brow arched, as if he found the answer different from his expectation. He shot a look at Hetharu, and walked a distance to the far recess of the room, by the window slit, where wan daylight painted his hair and robes with an edge of white. He looked out that viewless window for a moment as if he pondered something that did not need sight, and then looked back, and slowly returned to the circle of torchlight.

"We," said Bydarra, "we are the heirs of the true *khal*. Mixed-blood we all are, but we are their heirs, nonetheless. And none of us has the skill. It is not in those books. The maps are no longer valid. The land is gone. There is nothing to be had there."

"Hope," said Vanye, "that that is so."

"You are human," Bydarra said contemptuously.

"Yes."

"Those books," Bydarra said, "contain nothing. The Old Ones were flesh and bone, and if men will worship them, that is their choice. Priests—" The old lord made a shrug of contempt, nodding toward the wall, by implication toward the court that lay below. "Parasites. The lowest of our halfling blood. They venerate a lie, mumbling nonsense, believing that they once ruled the Wells, that they are doing some special service by tending them. Even the oldest records do not go back into the time of the Wells. The books are worthless. The Hiua kings were a plague the Wells spilled forth, and they tampered with the forces of them, they hurled sacrifices into them, but they had no more power than the Shiua priests. They never ruled the Wells. They were only brought here. Then the sea began to take Hiuaj. And lately—there is Roh; there is yourself. You claim that you have arrived by the Wells. Is that so?"

"Yes," Vanye answered in a faint voice. The things that Bydarra said began to accord with too much. Once in Andur a man had questioned Morgaine; the words had long rested in a corner of his mind, awaiting some reasoned explanation: *The world went wide,* she had answered that man, *around the bending of the path. I went through.* And suddenly he began to perceive the *qujal*-lord's anxiety, the sense that in him, in Roh, things met that never should have met at all . . . that somewhere in Ohtij-in was a Myya girl, far, far from the mountains of Erd and Morija.

"And the woman," asked Bydarra, "she on the gray horse?"

He said nothing.

"Roh spoke of her," Bydarra said. "You spoke of her; the Hiua girl confirms it. Rumor is running the courtyard: talk, careless talk, before the servants. Roh hints darkly of her intentions; the Hiua girl confounds her with Hiua legend."

Vanye shrugged lest he seem concerned, his heart beating hard against his ribs. "The Hiua set herself on my trail; I think her folk had cast her out. Sometimes she talks wildly. She may be mad. I would put no great trust in what she says."

"Angharan," Bydarra said. "Morgen-Angharan. The seventh and unfavorable power: Hiua kings and Aren superstition are always tangled. The white queen. But of course if you are not Hiua, this would not be familiar to you."

Vanye shook his head, clenched his hand over his wrist behind his back. "It is not familiar to me," he said.

"What is her true name?"

Again he shrugged.

"Roh," said Bydarra, "calls her a threat to all life—says that she has come to destroy the Wells and ruin the land. He offers his own skill to save us—whatever that skill may prove to be. Some," Bydarra added, with a look that made Hetharu avoid his eyes sullenly, "some of us are willing to fall at his feet. Not all of us are gullible."

There was silence, in which Vanye did not want to look at Hetharu, nor at Bydarra, who deliberately baited his son.

"Perhaps," Bydarra continued softly, "there is no such woman, and you and the Hiua girl are allied with this Roh. Or perhaps you have some purposes we in Ohtij-in do not know yet. Humankind drove us from Hiuaj. The Hiua kings were never concerned with our welfare, and they never held the power that Roh claims for himself."

Vanye stared at him, calculating, weighing matters, desperately. "Her name is Morgaine," he said. "And you would be better advised to offer her hospitality rather than Roh."

"Ah," said Bydarra. "And what bid would she make us? What would she offer?"

"A warning," he said, forcing the words, knowing they would not be favored. "And I give you one: to dismiss him and me and have nothing to do with any of us. That is your safety. That is all the safety you have."

The mockery left Bydarra's seamed face. He came closer, his lean countenance utterly sober, pale eyes intense: tall, the halflings, so that Vanye found himself meeting the old lord eye to eye. Light fingers touched the side of his arm, urging confidentiality, the while from the edge of his vision Vanye saw Hetharu leaning against the table, arms folded, regarding him coldly. "Hnoth is upon us," Bydarra said, "when the floods rise and no traveling is possible. This Chya Roh is anxious to set out for Abarais now, this day, before the road is closed. He seems likewise anxious that you be sent to him when he is there, directly as it becomes possible; and what say you to this, Nhi Vanye i Chya?"

"That you are as lost as I am if ever you let him reach Abarais," Vanye said. The pulse roared in him as he stared into that aged *qujalin* face, and thought of

Roh in possession of that Master Gate, with all its power to harm, to enliven the other Gates, to reach out and destroy. "Let him ever reach it and you will find yourself a master of whom you will never free yourself, not in this generation or the next or the next. I know that for the truth."

"Then he can do the things he claims," said Hetharu suddenly.

Vanye glanced toward Hetharu, who left the table and advanced to his father's side.

"His power would be such," Vanye said, "that the whole of Shiuan and Hiuaj would become whatever pleased him—pleased *him,* my lord. You do not look like a man that would relish having a master."

Bydarra smiled grimly and looked at Hetharu. "It may be," said Bydarra, "that you have been well answered."

"By another with something to win," said Hetharu, and seized Vanye's arm with such insolent violence that anger blinded him for the moment: he thrust his arm free, one clear thread of reason still holding him from the princeling's throat. He drew a ragged breath and looked to Bydarra, to authority.

"I would not see Roh set at Abarais," Vanye said, "and once your own experience shows you that I was right, my lord, I fear it will be much too late to change your mind."

"Can you master the Wells yourself?" Bydarra asked.

"Set me at Abarais, until my own liege comes. Then—ask what you will in payment, and it will go better with this land."

"Can you," asked Hetharu, seizing him a second time by the arm, "manage the Wells yourself?"

Vanye glared into that handsome wolf-face, the white-edged nostrils, the dark eyes smoldering with violence, the lank white hair that was not, like the lesser lords', the work of artifice.

"Take your hands from me," he managed to say, and cast his appeal still to Bydarra. "My lord," he said with a desperate, deliberate calm, "my lord, in this room, there was some bargain struck—your son and Roh and other young lords together. Look to the nature of it."

Bydarra's face went rigid with some emotion; he thrust Hetharu aside, looked terribly on Vanye, then turned that same look toward his son, beginning a word that was not finished. A blade flashed, and Bydarra choked, turned again under Hetharu's second blow, the bright blood starting from mouth and throat. Bydarra fell forward, and Vanye staggered back under the dying weight of him—let him fall, in horror, with the hot blood flooding his own arms.

And he stared across weapon's edge at a son who could murder father and show nothing of remorse. There was fear in that white face: hate. Vanye met Hetharu's eyes and knew the depth of what had been prepared for him.

"Hail me lord," said Hetharu softly, "lord in Ohtij-in and in all Shiuan."

Panic burst in him. "Guard!" he cried, as Hetharu lifted the bloody dagger and slashed his own arm, a second fountain of blood. The dagger flew, struck at Vanye's feet, in the spreading dark pool from Bydarra's body. Vanye stumbled back from the dagger as the door opened, and there were armed men there in force, pikes lowered toward him. Hetharu leaned against the fireplace in unfeigned shock, leaking blood through his fingers that clasped his wounded arm to his breast.

"He—" Vanye cried, and staggered back under the blow of a pikeshaft that sent him sprawling and drove the wind from him. He scrambled for his feet and hurled himself for the door, barred from it by others—thrown aside, seized up the dagger that lay in the pool of blood, and drove for Hetharu's throat.

An armored body turned the blade, a face before him grimacing in pain and shock: more blood flooded his hands, hot, before the others dragged him back and crashed with him over a bench. The blows of pikestaves and boots overwhelmed him and he lay half-sensible in a pool of blood, his own or Bydarra's, he no longer knew. They moved his battered arms and cords bit into his wrists.

Shouts echoed. Throughout the halls there began a shriek of alarm, the sounds of women's voices and the deeper mourning of men. He listened to this, on the edge of consciousness, the shrieks part of the torment of chaos that raged about him.

He remained on the floor, untouched. Men came for Bydarra's body, and they carried it forth on a litter in grim silence; and another corpse they carried out too, that of a man-at-arms, that Vanye dimly realized was to his charge. And thereafter, when the room was clear and more torches had been brought, men gathered him up by the hair and the arms, and bowed him at Hetharu's feet.

Hetharu sat, while a priest wound his arm about with clean linen soaked in oils; and there was in Hetharu's shock-pale face a taut and wary look. Armed men were about him, and one, bare-faced, his coarse bleached hair gathered back in a knot, handed Hetharu a cup of which he drank deeply. In a moment Hetharu sighed, and returned the cup, and leaned back in the chair while the priest tied the bandage.

A number of other lords came, elegant and jewelled, in delicate fabrics. There was silence in the room, and the constant flow of whispers in the corridor outside. As each lord came forward to meet Hetharu there was a slight bow, an obeisance, some only scant. It was the passing of power, there in that bloody cell—many an older lord whose obeisance was cold and hesitant, with looks about at the armed guards that stood grimly evident; and younger men, who did not restrain their smiles, wolf-smiles and no evidence of mourning.

And lastly came Kithan, waxen-pale and languid, attended by a trio of guards. He bowed to kiss his brother's hand, and suffered his brother's kiss upon his cheek, his face cold and distant the while. He stumbled when he attempted to rise and turn, steadied by the guards, and blinked dazedly, and stared down at Vanye.

Slowly the distance vanished in those dilated pale eyes, and something came into them of recognition, a mad hatred, distraught and violent.

"I had no weapon," Vanye said to him, fearing the youth's grief as much as Hetharu's calculation. "The only weapon—"

An armored hand smashed across his mouth, dazing him; and no one was interested in listening not even Kithan, who simply stared at him, empty-eyed, unasking what he would have said. After a moment someone took Kithan by the arm and led him out, like a confused child.

Women had come, pale-haired and cold, who bowed and kissed Hetharu's hand and returned on silent feet to the corridor, a whisper of brocade and a lingering of perfume amid the oil and armor of the guards.

Then, a stir among the departing mourners, brusque and sudden, came Roh, himself attended by guards, one on either side. Roh was armored, and cloaked, and bore his bow and his longsword slung on his back for travel.

Vanye's heart leaped up in an instant's forlorn hope that died when he reminded himself of the illusion that was Roh, when Roh ignored him, and addressed himself to the patricide, Bydarra's newly powerful son.

"My lord," Roh murmured, and bowed, but he did not kiss Hetharu's hand or make any other courtesy, at which faces clouded, not least of them Hetharu's. "The horses are saddled," Roh said. "The tide is due at sunset, I am told; and we had best make some small haste."

"There will be no delay," said Hetharu.

Again Roh bowed, only as much as need be; and turned his head and for the first time looked down on Vanye, who knelt between his guards. "Cousin," Roh said sorrowfully, as a man would reproach a too-innocent youth. Heat stung Vanye's face; and something in him responded to the voice, all the same. He looked up into Roh's brown eyes and lean, tanned face, seeking Liell, struggling to summon hate. It only came to him that they two had known Andur-Kursh, and that he would not see it again; and that when Roh had left, he would be alone among *qujal*.

"I do not envy you," Vanye said, "your company on the road."

Roh's eyes slid warily to Hetharu, back again; and Roh bent then, and took Vanye's arm, drawing him to his feet in spite of the guards. His hand lingered, kindly as a brother's.

"Swear to my service," Roh said in a low voice, for him alone. "Leave hers, and I will take you with me, out of here."

Vanye jerked his head in refusal, setting his jaw lest he show how much he desired it.

"They will not harm you," Roh said, which he needed not have said.

"What you will is not law for them," Vanye said. "I did not kill Bydarra: on my oath, I did not. They have done this to spite you; I am nothing to them but a means of touching you."

Roh frowned. "I will see you at Abarais. With *her*, I will not compromise—I cannot—but with you—"

"Take me with you now if you hope for that. Do not ask an oath of me; you know I cannot give it. But will you rather trust them at your back? You will be alone with them, and when they have what they want—"

"No," Roh said after a moment that trust and doubt had seemed closely balanced. "No. That would not be wise of me."

"At least take Jhirun out of this place."

Again Roh hesitated, seeming almost to agree. "No," he said. "Nothing to please you: I do not think you hope for my long life. She stays here."

"To be murdered. As I will be."

"No," said Roh. "I have made an understanding for your welfare. And I will see it kept; we have bargained, they and I. I will see you at Abarais."

"No," said Vanye. "I do not think you will."

"Cousin," said Roh softly.

Vanye swore and turned away, bile rising in his throat. He shouldered through his guards, who lacked orders and stood like cattle, confused. None checked him. He went to the window slit and looked out at the rain-glistening stones, ignoring all of them as they made their arrangements to leave, with much clattering of arms and shouting up and down the corridors.

Group by group, to their various purposes, the gathering dispersed. Roh was among the first to leave. Vanye did not turn his head to see. He heard the room deserted, and the door heavily sealed, and distantly in the halls echoed the tramp of armed men.

Out in the yard there began a tumult among the people, and the clatter of horses on the pavings. Voices of men and women pierced the commotion, for a moment clear and then subdued again.

One lord was leaving Ohtij-in; the former could not possibly have been buried yet. Such was Hetharu's haste, to ride with Roh, seeking power; and such Roh had doubtless promised him, with promises and threats and direct warnings to bring him quickly to Abarais, before flood should come, before the way should be closed. Perhaps Bydarra had opposed such a journey, inventing delays, but Bydarra would no more oppose anything—perhaps at Roh's urging; it was Hetharu's cruel humor that had placed the blame where Roh least wanted it.

Vanye heard the number of horses in the yard and reckoned that most of the force of Ohtij-in must be going.

And if Morgaine lived, she would have to contend with *that* upon the road—if she had not already, more wary and more wise than her *ilin*, skirted round Ohtij-in and passed toward Abarais.

It was the only hope that remained to him. If Morgaine had done so, Roh was finished, powerless. This was surely the fear in Roh's mind, that drove him to create chaos of Ohtij-in, that drove him to accept allies that would turn on him when first they could. If Roh came too late, if Morgaine had passed, and the Wells were dead and sealed against him, then those same allies would surely kill him; and then would be another bitter reckoning, at Ohtij-in, for the hostage for a dead enemy.

But if Roh was not too late, if Morgaine was in truth lost, then there were other certainties: himself bidden to Abarais, to serve Roh—masterless *ilin,* to be Claimed to another service.

There was nothing else, no other choice for him—but to seek Roh's life; and the end of that, too, he knew.

A door closed elsewhere, echoing in the depths; a scuff on stone sounded outside, steps in the corridor. He thought until the last that they were bound elsewhere: but the bolt of the door crashed back.

He looked back, the blood chilling in his veins as he saw Kithan, with armed men about him.

Kithan walked to the end of the table, steady in his bearing; his delicate features were composed and cold.

"They are leaving," Kithan said softly.

"I did not," Vanye protested, "kill your father. It was Hetharu."

There was no reaction, none. Kithan stood still and stared at him, and outside there was the sound of horses clattering out the gates. Then those gates closed, booming, inner and outer.

Kithan drew a long, shuddering breath, expelled it slowly, as if savoring the air. He had shut his eyes, and opened them again with the same chill calm. "In a little time we shall have buried my father. We do not make overmuch ceremony of our interments. Then I will see to you."

"I did not kill him."

"Did you not?" Kithan's cloud-gray eyes assumed that dreaming languor that formerly possessed them, but now it seemed ironical, a pose. "Hetharu would have more than Ohtij-in to rule. Do you think that Roh of the Chya will give it to him?"

Vanye answered nothing, not knowing where this was tending, and liking it little, Kithan smiled.

"Would this cousin of yours take vengeance for you?" asked Kithan.

"It might be," Vanye answered, and Kithan still smiled.

"Hetharu was always tedious," Kithan said.

Vanye drew in a breath, finally reading him. "If you aim at your brother—free me. I am not Roh's ally."

"No," said Kithan softly. "Nor care I. It may be that you are guilty; or perhaps not. And that is nothing to me. I see no future for any of us, and I trust you no more than Hetharu should have trusted your kinsman."

"Hetharu," Vanye said, "killed your father."

Kithan smiled and shrugged, turned his shoulder to him. He made a signal to one of the men with him, toward the door. That man summoned others, who held between them a small and tattered shadow.

Jhirun.

He could not help her. She recognized him as he moved a little into the torch-light. Her shadowed face assumed a look of anguish. But she said nothing, seeing him, nor cried out. Vanye lowered his eyes, apology for all things between them, lifted them again. There was nothing that he could say to ease her plight, and much that he could say to make it worse, making clear his regard for her.

He turned from the sight of her and of them, and walked back to stare out the window.

"Make a fire in the west tower hall," Kithan bade one of the guards.

And they withdrew, and the door closed.

⌐ Chapter 10

The thunder rumbled almost constantly, and in time the torches, whipped by the wind that had free play through the small cell, went out, one by one, leaving dark. Vanye sat by the window, leaning against the stones, letting the cold wind and spattering rain numb his face as his hands long since were numb. The cold eased the pain of bruises; he reckoned that if it also made him fevered, if they delayed long enough, then that was only gain. He blinked the water from his eyes and watched the pattern of lightning on the raindrops that crawled down the stones opposite the narrow window. So far as it was possible, he concentrated entirely on that slow progress, lost in it.

Somewhere by the gate a bell began to ring, monotone and urgent. Voices shouted, lost in the thunder. The burial party had returned, he thought, and sharper fear began to gather in him; he fought it with anger, but the taste of it was only the more bitter, for he was angry most of all that he was without purpose in his misery, that he was seized into others' purposes, to die that way: child-innocent, child-ignorant—he had trusted, had expected, had assumed.

Likewise Roh was being slowly ensnared, carefully maneuvered, having taken to himself allies without law, adept in treacheries of a breed unimagined in Andur-Kursh. Best that Roh perish—and yet he did not entirely wish it: rather that Hetharu would find himself surprised, that Roh would repay them—bitterly.

There was nothing else.

The bell still rang. And now there came the tread of many men in the corridors, echoing up and down the winding halls—a scrape of stone in the hall outside, the bolt crashing back.

There were guards, rain still glistening on their demon-faced helms and the scale of their armor in the torchlight they brought with them. Vanye gathered himself to his feet on the second try, came with them of his own accord as far as the hall, where he might reckon their number.

There were eight, ten, twelve of them. *So many?* he wondered bitterly, astonished that they could so fear him, reckoning how his hands were tied and his legs, numb with cold, unsteady under him.

They seized him roughly and brought him down the corridor, and down and down the spirals, past the staring white faces of delicate *qujalin* ladies, the averted eyes of servants. Cold air struck him as the door at the bottom of the spiral opened, and there before them was the barred iron gate, the keeper running back the chain to let them out.

Outside was rain and torchlight, and a confused rabble, a mass of faces shouting, drowning the noise of the bell.

Vanye set his feet, resisted desperately being brought out into that; but the guards formed about him with pikes levelled, and others forced him down the steps. Mad faces surrounded them, rocks flew: Vanye felt an impact on his shoulder and jerked back as fingers seized on his shirt and tried to pull him away from the guards. A man went down then with a pike through his belly, writhing and screaming, and the men-at-arms hurried, broke through the mass: Vanye no longer resisted the guards, fearing the mob's violence more.

And the bell at the gate still tolled, adding its own mad voice to the chaos. A door in the barbican tower opened, more guards ready to take them into that refuge, a serried line of weapons to defend it.

A pikeman went down, stone-struck. The mob surged inward. Vanye recoiled into the hands of his guards as the rabble seized on him, almost succeeding this time in taking him. There was a skirmish, sharp and bloody, peasants against armored pikemen, and the guards moved forward over wounded and dying.

The insanity of it was beyond comprehension, the attack, the hatred, whether they aimed it at him or at their own lords . . . knowing that Bydarra was slain, that the greater force of the hold had departed. The guards seemed suddenly fearfully few; the power that Kithan held was stretched thin in Ohtij-in amid this violence that surged within the court, outside its doors. The madness cared no longer what it attacked.

There was a sound, deep and rumbling, that shook the walls, that wrung horrified screams from the surging mob—that stopped the guards in their tracks.

And the gate vanished in a second rumbling of stones: the arch that had spanned it collapsed, the stones whirling away like leaves into darkness, so that little rubble remained. It was gone. The mob shrieked and scattered, abandoned improvised weapons, a scatter of staves and stones on the cobbles; and the guards levelled futile weapons at that incredible sight.

In that darkness where the gate had been was a shimmer, and a rider, white-cloaked, on a gray horse, a shining of white hair under the remaining torches; and the glimmering was a drawn sword.

The blade stayed unsheathed. It held darkness entrapped at its tip, darkness that eclipsed the light of torches where it was lifted. The gray horse moved forward a pace; the crowd shrieked and fled back.

Morgaine.

She had come to this place, come after him. Vanye struggled to be free, feeling a wild urge to laughter, and in that moment his guards cast him sprawling and fled.

He lay still, for a moment dazed by his impact on the wet paving. He saw Siptah's muddy hooves not far from his head as she rode to cover him, and he did not fear the horse; but above him he saw Morgaine's outstretched hand, and *Changeling* unsheathed, shimmering opal fires and carrying that lethal void at its tip: oblivion uncleaner than any the *qujal* could deal.

He feared to move while that hovered over him. "Roh—" he tried to warn her; but his hoarse voice was lost in the storm and the shouting.

"*Dai-khal,*" he heard cry from the distance. "*Angharan . . . Angharan!*" He heard the cry repeated, echoed off the walls, warning carried strangely by the wind; and thereafter quiet settled in the courtyard, among humans and *qujal* alike.

Siptah swung aside; Vanye struggled to reach his knees, did so with a tearing pain in his side that for a moment took his breath away. When his sight cleared, he saw Kithan and the other lords in the unbarred doorway of the keep, abandoned by the guards. There was no sound, no movement from the *qujal*. Their faces, their white hair whipping on the wind, made a pale cluster in the torchlight.

"This is my companion," Morgaine said softly, above the rush of rain; and it was likely that there was no place in the courtyard that could not hear her. "Poor welcome have you given him."

There was for a moment only the steady beat of the rain into the puddles, the restless stamp of Siptah's feet, and came the sound of hooves behind, another rider coming through the ruined gate: the black gelding, ridden by a stranger, who swung down from the saddle and waited.

Vanye gathered his feet under him, careful of the fire of *Changeling*, that gleamed perilously near him. "*Liyo,*" he said, forcing sound into his raw throat, trying to shout. "Roh, by the north road, before the sun set. He has not that much start—"

She whipped her Honor blade from her belt left-handed, letting Siptah stand. "Turn," she said, and leaned from the saddle behind him, slashed the cords that held his hands. His arms fell, leaden and painful; he looked at her, turning, and she gestured toward his horse, and the man that held it.

Vanye drew a deep breath and made what effort he could to run, reached the waiting horse and hauled himself into the saddle, head reeling and hands too stiff to feel the reins that the man thrust into his possession. He looked down into that stranger's scarred face, stung with irrational resentment, rage that this man had been given his belongings, had ridden at her side: he saw that resentment answered in the peasant's dark eyes, the grim set of scarred lips.

Stone rattled. Dark shapes moved in the misting rain, creeping over the massive stones of the shattered gateway, the ruined double walls: men—or less than men. Vanye saw, and felt a prickling at his neck, beholding the dark shapes that moved like vermin amid the vast, tumbled stones.

With a sudden shout at him, Morgaine reined about and rode for that broken gateway, sending the invaders scrambling aside; and Vanye jerked feebly at the reins, the black gelding already turning, accustomed to run with the gray. He caught his balance in the saddle as the horses cleared the ruined gate and hit even stride again, down the rain-washed stones, passing a horde of those small, dark men. Downhill they rode, clattering along the paving, faster and faster as the horses found clear road ahead. Morgaine led, and never yet had she sheathed the sword, that was danger to all about it; Vanye had no wish to ride beside her while she bore that naked and shimmering in her hand.

Stonework yielded to mud, to brush, to stonework again, and the jolting drove pain into belly and lungs, and the rain blinded and the lightning redoubled: Vanye ceased to be aware of where he rode, only that he must follow. Pain ate at his side, a misery that clutched at muscle and spread over all his mind, blotting out everything but the sense that kept his hand on the rein and his body in the saddle.

The horses spent their first wind, and slowed: Vanye was aware when *Changeling* winked out, going into sheath—and Morgaine asked things to which he gave unclear answer, not knowing the land or the tides. She laid heels to Siptah and the gray leaned into renewed effort, the gelding following. Vanye used his heels mercilessly when the animal began to flag, fearful of being left behind, knowing that Morgaine would not stop. They rounded blind turns, downslope and up again, through shallow water and over higher ground.

And as they mounted a crest where the hills opened up, a wide valley spread before them, black waters as far as the eye could see, froth roaring and crashing about the rocks and the stonework, swallowing up the road.

Morgaine reined in with a curse, and Vanye let the gelding stop, both horses standing with sides heaving. It was over, lost. Vanye bowed upon the saddle-horn with the rain beating at his thinly clad back, until the pain of his side ebbed and he could straighten.

"Send he drowns," Morgaine said, and her voice trembled.

"Aye," he answered without passion, coughed and leaned again over the saddle until the spasm had left him.

Siptah's warmth shifted against his leg, and he felt Morgaine's touch on his shoulder. He lifted his head. The lightning showed her face to him, frozen in a look of concern, the rain like jewels on her brow.

"I thought," he said, "that you would have left, or that you were lost."

"I had my own difficulties," she said; and with anguish she slammed her fist against her leg. "Would you could have found a chance to kill him."

The accusation shot home. "When the rain stops—" he offered in his guilt.

"This is the Suvoj," she said fiercely, "by the name that I have heard, and that is not river-flood: it is the sea, the tide. After Hnoth, after the moons—"

She drew breath. Vanye became aware of the malefic force of the vast light that hung above the lightning, that lent the boiling clouds strange definition. And when next the flashes showed him Morgaine clearly, she had turned her head and was gazing at the flood with an expression like a hunting wolf. "Perhaps," she said, "perhaps there are barriers that will hold him, even past the Suvoj."

"It may be, *liyo*," he said. "I do not know."

"If not, we will learn it in a few days." Her shoulders fell, a sigh of exhaustion; she bowed her head and threw it back, scattering rain from her hair. She drew Siptah full about.

And perhaps the lightning showed him clearly for the first time, for her face took on a sudden look of concern. "Vanye?" she asked, reaching for him. Her voice reached him thinly, distantly.

"I can ride," he said, although for very little he would have denied it. The prospect of another such mad course was almost more than he could bear; the pain in his ribs rode every breath. But the gentleness fed strength into him. He began to shiver, feeling the cold, where before he had had the warmth of movement. She unclasped the cloak from about her throat and flung it about his shoulders. He put up his hand to refuse it.

"Put it on," she said. "Do not be stubborn." And gratefully he gathered it about him, taking warmth from the horse and from the cloak she had worn. It made him shiver the more for a moment, his body beginning to fight the cold. She took a flask from her saddle and handed it across to him; he drank a mouthful of that foul local brew that stung his cut lip and almost made him gag, but it eased his throat after it had burned its way down, and the taste faded.

"Keep it," she said when he offered to return it.

"Where are we going?"

"Back," she said, "to Ohtij-in."

"No," he objected, the reflex of fear; it leapt out in his voice, and made her look at him strangely for a moment. In shame he jerked the gelding's head about toward Ohtij-in, started him moving, Siptah falling in beside at a gentle walk. He said nothing, wished not even to look at her, but pressed his hand to his bruised ribs beneath the cloak and tried to ignore the panic that lay like ice in his belly—Roh safely sped toward Abarais, and themselves, themselves returning into the grasp of Ohtij-in, within the reach of treachery.

And then, a second impulse of shame for himself, he remembered the Hiua girl whom he had abandoned there without a thought toward her. It was his oath, and that was as it must be, but he was ashamed not even to have thought of her.

"Jhirun," he said, "was with me, a prisoner too."

"Forget her. What passed with Roh?"

The question stung; guilt commingled with dread in him. He looked ahead, between the gelding's ears. "Lord Hetharu of Ohtij-in," he said, "went with Roh northward, to reach Abarais before the weather turned. I walked into this place, thinking to claim shelter. It is not Andur-Kursh. I have not managed well, *liyo*. I am sorry."

"Which first—Roh's leaving or your coming?"

He had deliberately obscured that in his telling; her harsh question cut to the center of the matter. "My coming," he said. "*Liyo—*"

"He let you live."

He did look at her, tried to compose his face, though all his blood seemed gathered in his belly. "Did I seem to be comfortable there? What do you think that I could have done? I had no chance at him." The words came, and immediately he wished he had said nothing, for there was suddenly a lie between them.

And more than that: for he saw suspicion in her look, a quiet and horrid mistrust. In the long silence that followed, their horses side by side, he wished that she would rebuke him, quarrel, remind him how little caution he had used and what duty he owed her, anything against which he could argue. She said nothing.

"What would you?" he cried finally, against that silence. "That you had come later?"

"No," she said in a voice strangely subdued.

"It was not for me," he surmised suddenly. "It was Roh you wanted."

"I did not," she said very quietly, "know where you were. Only that Roh had sheltered in Ohtij-in: that I did hear. Other word did not reach me."

She fell silent again, and in the long time that they rode in the rain he clutched her warm cloak about him and reckoned that she had only given him the truth that he had insisted on knowing—more honest with him that he had been with her. Roh had named her liar, and she did not lie, even when a small untruth would have been kinder; he held that thought for comfort, scant though it was.

"*Liyo,*" he asked finally, "where were you? I tried to find you."

"At Aren," she replied, and he cursed himself bitterly. "They are rough folk," she said. "Easily impressed. They feared me, and that was convenient. I waited there for you. They said that there was no sign of you."

"Then they were blind," he said bitterly. "I held to the road; I never left it. I thought only that you would leave me and keep going, and trust me to follow."

"They knew it, then," she said, a frown settling on her face. "They did know."

"It may be," he said, "that they feared you too much."

She swore in her own tongue, at least that was the tone of it, and shook her head, and what bided in her face then, lightning-lit, was not good to see.

"Jhirun and I together," he said, "walked the road; and it brought us to Ohtij-in, out of food, out of any hope. I did not know what I would find; Roh was the last that I expected. *Liyo,* it is a *qujal*-ruled hold, and there are records there, in which Roh spent his time."

The oath hissed between her teeth. She opened her lips to say something; and then, for they were rounding the turn of a hill, from the distance came a sound carried on the wind, the sound of distress, of riot; and she stopped, gazing at a sullen glow among the hills.

"Ohtij-in," she said, and set heels to Siptah, flying down the road. The gelding dipped his head and hurled himself after; Vanye bent, ignoring the pain of his side, and rode, round the remembered bendings of the road, turn after turn as the shouting came nearer.

And suddenly the height of Ohtij-in hove into view, where the inner court blazed with light and roiling smoke through the riven gates, where black, diminutive figures struggled amid the fires.

Shadow-shapes huddled beside the road, that became women and ragged children, bundles and baggage. The gray horse thundered near them, sent the wretched folk shrieking aside, and the black plunged after.

Into the chaos of the inner court they rode, where fire had ravaged the shelters, rolling clouds of bitter smoke up into the rainy sky, where dead animals lay and many a corpse besides, among them both dark-haired and white, both men and halflings. At the keep gate, against the wall, a remnant of the guard was embattled with the peasants, and heaped up dead there thicker than anywhere else.

Men scattered from the hooves of the gray horse, shrieks and screams as the witch-sword left its sheath and flared into opal light more terrible than the fires, with that darkness howling at its tip. A weapon flew; the darkness drank it, and it vanished.

And the guard who had cast it fled, dying on the spears of the ragged attackers. It was the last resistance. The others threw down their arms and were cast to their faces by their captors, down in the mire and blood of the yard.

"*Morgen!*" the ragged army hailed her, raising their weapons. "*Angharan! Angharan!*" Vanye sat the gelding beside her as folk crowded round them with awed hysteria in their faces, he and his nervous horse touched by scores of trembling hands as they touched Siptah, rashly coming too near the unsheathed blade; shying from it, they massed the more closely about him, her companion. He endured it, realizing that he had been absorbed into the fabric of legends that surrounded Morgaine kri Chya—that he himself had become a thing to frighten children and cause honest men to shudder—that they had condemned him to all he had suffered, refusing to tell his liege what they surely had known; and that those of Ohtij-in would lately have killed him.

He did not strike, though he trembled with the urge to do so. He still feared them, who for the hour hailed him and surrounded him with their insane adoration.

"Angharan!" they shouted. "Morgaine! Morgaine! Morgaine!"

Morgaine carefully sheathed *Changeling*, extinguishing its fire, and slid to the ground amid that press, men pushing at each other to make way for her. "Take the horses," she bade a man who approached her with less fear than the others, and then she turned her attention to the keep. There was silence made in the courtyard at last, an exhausted hush. She walked through their midst to the steps of the keep, *Changeling* crosswise in her hands, that it could be drawn in an instant. There she stood, visible to them all, and ragged and bloody men came and paid her shy, awkward courtesies.

Vanye dismounted, took up her saddle kit, that she would never leave behind her, and fended off those that offered help, no difficult matter. Men fled his displeasure, terrified.

Morgaine stayed for him, her foot on the next step until he had begun to ascend them, then passed inside. Vanye slung the saddlebag over his shoulder and walked after, up the steps and into the open gateway, past the staring dead face of the gatekeeper, who lay sprawled in the shadows inside.

Men took up torches, leading their way. Vanye shuddered at what he saw in the spiral halls, the dead both male and female, both *qujal* and guiltless human servants, the ravaged treasures of Ohtij-in that littered the halls. He kept walking, up the spiraling core that would figure thereafter in his nightmares, limping after Morgaine, who walked sword in hand.

She will finish it, Roh had prophesied of her, *end all hope for them. That is what she has come to do.*

⤸ Chapter 11

In the lord's hall too there was chaos, bodies lying where they had fallen. Even the white dog was dead by the hearth, in a pool of blood that stained the carpets and the stones, and flowed to mingle with that of its master and mistress. A knot of servants huddled in the corner for protection, kneeling.

And in the other corner men were gathered, rough and ragged folk, who held prisoner three of the house guard, white-haired halflings, stripped of their masking helms, bound, and surrounded by peasant weapons.

Vanye stopped, seeing that, and the sudden warmth of the fire hit him, making breath difficult; he caught for balance against the door frame as Morgaine strode within the room and looked about.

"Get the dead out of the hold," she said to the ragged men who awaited her orders. "Dispose of them. Is their lord among them?"

The eldest man made a helpless gesture. "No knowing," he said, in an accent difficult to penetrate.

"*Liyo*," Vanye offered, from the doorway, "a man named Kithan is in charge of Ohtij-in, Hetharu's brother. I know him by sight."

"Stay by me," she ordered curtly; and to the others: "Make search for him. Save all writings, wherever found, and bring them to me."

"Aye," said one of that company at whom she looked.

"What of the rest?" asked the eldest, a stooped and fragile man. "What of the other things? Be there else, lady?"

Morgaine frowned and looked about her, a warlike and evil figure amid their poor leather and rags; she looked on prisoners, on dead men, at the small rough-clad folk who depended on her for orders in this tumult, and shrugged. "What matter to me?" she asked. "What you do here is your own affair, only so it does not cross me. A guard at our door, servants to attend us—" Her eyes swept to the corner where the house servants cowered, marked men in brown livery who had served the *qujal*. "Those three will suffice. And Haz, give me three of your sons for guards at my quarters, and no more will I ask of you tonight."

"Aye," said the old man, bowed in awkward imitation of a lord's courtesy; he gestured to certain of the young men—small folk, all of them, who approached Morgaine with lowered eyes, the tallest of them only as high as her shoulder, but broad, powerful young men, for all that.

Marshlanders, Vanye reckoned them: *men of Aren*. They spoke among themselves in a language he could not comprehend: men, but not of any kind that his land had known, small and furtive and, he suddenly suspected, without any law common to men that he knew. They were many, swarming the corridors, wreaking havoc; they had failed deliberately to find him for Morgaine— and yet she came back among them as if she utterly trusted them. He became conscious that he was not armed, that he, who guarded her back, had no weapon, and their lives were in the hands of these small, elusive men, who could speak secrets among themselves.

A body brushed past, taller than the others, black-robed; Vanye recoiled in surprise, then recognized the priest, who was making for Morgaine. In panic he moved and seized the priest, jerked at the robes, thrust him sprawling to the floor.

Morgaine looked down on the balding, white-haired priest, whose lean face was rigid with terror, who shook and trembled in Vanye's grip. In a sudden access of panic as Morgaine stepped closer, the priest sought to rise, perhaps to run, but Vanye held him firmly.

"Banish him to the court," Vanye said, remembering how this same priest had lured him into Ohtij-in, promising safety; how this priest had stood at Bydarra's elbow. "Let him try his fortunes out there, among men."

"What is your name?" Morgaine asked of the priest.

"Ginun," the slight halfling breathed. He twisted to look up at Vanye, dark-eyed, an aging man—and perhaps more man than *qujal*. Fear trembled on his lips. "Great lord, many would have helped you, many, many—*I* would have helped you. Our lords were mistaken."

"Where were you?" Vanye asked, bitterness so choking him he could hardly speak; he thrust the man free. "You knew your lord, you knew what would happen when you led me to him."

"Take us with you," Ginun wept. "Take us with you. Do not leave us behind."

"Where," asked Morgaine in a chill voice, "do you suppose that we will go from here?"

"Through the Wells—to that other land."

The hope in the priest's eyes was terrible to see as he looked from one to the other of them, chin trembling, eyes suffused with tears. He lifted his hand to touch Morgaine, lost courage and touched Vanye's hand instead, a finger-touch, no more. "Please," he asked of them.

"Who has told you this thing?" Morgaine asked. "Who?"

"We have waited," the priest whispered hoarsely. "We have tended the Wells and we have waited. Take us through. Take us with you."

Morgaine turned her face away, not willing more to talk with him. The priest's shoulders fell and he began to shake with sobs; at Vanye's touch he looked up, his face that of a man under death sentence. "We have served the *khal*," he protested, as if that should win favor of the conqueror of Ohtij-in. "We have waited, we have waited. Lord, speak to her. Lord, we would have helped you."

"Go away," said Vanye, drawing him to his feet. Unease moved in his heart when he looked on this priest who served devils, whose prayers were to the works of *qujal*. The priest drew back from his hands, still staring at him, still pleading with his eyes. "She has nothing to do with you and your kind," Vanye told the priest. "Nor do I."

"The Barrow-kings knew her," the priest whispered, his eyes darting past him and back again. He clutched convulsively at the amulets that hung among his robes. "The lord Roh came with the truth. It was the truth."

And the priest fled for the door, but Vanye seized him, hauled him about, others in the room giving back from him. The priest struggled vainly, frail, desperate man. "*Liyo*," Vanye said in a quiet voice, fearful of those listening about them; prepared to strike the priest silent upon the instant. "*Liyo*, do not let him go. This priest will do you harm if he can. I beg you listen to me."

Morgaine looked on him, and on the priest. "Brave priest," she said in a voice still and clear, in the hush that had fallen in the room. "Fwar!"

A man came from the corner where the house guards were held, a taller man than most, near Morgaine's height. Square-faced he was, with a healing slash that ran from right cheek to left chin, across both lips. Vanye knew him at once, him that had ridden the gelding into the courtyard—the face that had glared sullenly up at him. Such a look he received now; the man seemed to have no other manner.

"Aye, lady?" Fwar said. His accent was plainer than that of the others, and he bore himself boldly, standing straight.

"Have your kinsmen together," Morgaine said, "and find the *khal* that survive. I want no killing of them, Fwar. I want them set in one room, under guard. And you know by now that I mean what I say."

"Aye," Fwar answered, and frowned. The face might have been ordinary once. No more; it was a mask in which one most saw the eyes, and they were hot and violent. "For some we are too late."

"I care not who is to blame," Morgaine said. "I hold you, alone, accountable to me."

Fwar hesitated, then bowed, started to leave.

"And, Fwar—"

"Lady?"

"Ohtij-in is a human hold now. I have kept my word. Whoever steals and plunders now—steals from you."

This thought went visibly through Fwar's reckoning, and other men in the room stood attentive and sobered.

"Aye," Fwar said.

"Lady," said another, in a voice heavy with accent, "what of the stores of grain? Are we to distribute—?"

"Is not Haz your priest?" she asked. "Let your priest divide the stores. It is your grain, your people. Ask me no further on such matters. Nothing here concerns me. Leave me."

There was silence, dismay.

One of the marshlanders pushed at the *qujalin* guards, directing them to the door. In their wake went others, Fwar, Haz; there were left only Haz's three sons, claimed as guards, and the weeping priest, Ginun, and the three servants, who knelt cowering in the far corner.

"Show me," said Morgaine to the servants, "where are the best lodgings with a solid door and some secure room nearby where we can lodge this priest for his own protection."

She spoke softly with them. One moved, and the others gathered courage, kneeling facing her, eyes downcast. "There," said the oldest of them, himself no more than a youth, and pointed toward the door that led inward, away from the central corridor.

There was a small, windowless storeroom opposite a lordly hall. Here Morgaine bade the priest disposed, with a bar across that door, and that chained, and the door visible by those who would guard their own quarters. It was Vanye's to put the priest inside, and he did so, not ungently.

He hated the look of the priest's eyes as he was set within that dark place, forbidden a light lest he do himself and others harm with it. The priest's terror fingered at nightmares of his own, and he hesitated at closing the door.

Priest of devils, who would have worshipped at Morgaine's feet, an uncleanness that attached itself to them, saying things it was not good to hear, Vanye loathed the man, but that a man should fear the dark, and being shut within, alone—this he understood.

"Keep still," he warned Ginun last, the guards out of hearing. "You are safer here, and you will be safe so long as you do keep still."

The priest was still staring at him when he closed the door, his thin face white and terrified in the shadow. Vanye dropped the bar and locked the chain through it—made haste to turn his back on it, as on a private nightmare, remembering the roof of the tower of his prison—Roh's words, stored up in this priest, waiting to break forth. He thought in agony that he should see to it that the priest never spoke—that he, *ilin,* should take that foulness on his own soul and never tell Morgaine, never burden her honor with knowing it.

He was not such a man; he could not do it. And he did not know whether this in him was virtue or cowardice.

* * *

The sons of Haz had taken up their posts at the door. Morgaine awaited him in the hall beyond. He went to her, into the chambers that had been some great lord's, and dropped the saddlebags that he had carried onto the stones of the hearth, staring about him.

More bodies awaited them: tapestries rent, bodies of men-at-arms and the one-time lords lying amid shattered crystal and overturned chairs. Vanye knew them. One was the body of an old woman; another was that of one of the elder lords, he that had made most grudging obeisance to Hetharu.

"See to it," Morgaine said sharply to the servants. "Remove them."

And while this was being attended, she righted a heavy chair and put it near the fire that still blazed in the hearth for its former owners, extended her legs to it, booted ankles crossed, paying no attention to the grisly task that went on among the servants. *Changeling* she set point against the floor and leaning by her side, and gave a long sigh.

Vanye averted his eyes from what passed in the room. Too much, too many of such pathetic dead: he had been of the warriors, but of a land where men fought men who chose to fight, who went armed, in notice of such intention. He did not want to remember the things that he had seen in 'Ohtij-in, alone or in her company.

And somewhere in Ohtij-in was Myya Jhirun, lost in this chaos, hidden or dead or the possession of some rough-handed marshlander. He thought of that, sick at heart, weighed his own exhaustion, the hazard of the mob outside, who spoke a language he could not understand, but he was obliged. For other wretched folk within the hold, for other women as unfortunate, he had no power to stop what happened—only for Jhirun, who had done him kindness, who had believed him when he said he would take her from Ohtij-in.

"*Liyo*," he said, and dropped to his knees at the fireside, by Morgaine. His voice shook, reaction to things already past, but he had no shame for that; they were both tired. "*Liyo*, Jhirun is here somewhere. By your leave I am going to go and do what I can to find her. I owe her."

"No."

"*Liyo*—"

She stared into the fire, her tanned face set, her white hair still wet from the rain outside. "Thee will go out in the courtyard and some Shiua will put a knife in thy back. No. Enough."

He thrust himself to his feet, vexed by her protection of him, exhausted beyond willingness to debate his feelings with her. He started for the door, reckoning that she had expressed her objection and that was the sum of it. He was going, nonetheless. He had seen to her welfare, and she knew it.

"*Ilin*," her voice rang out after him. "I gave thee an order."

He stopped, looked at her: it was a stranger's voice, cold and foreign to him.

She was surrounded by men he did not know, by intentions he no longer understood. He stared at her, a tightness closing about his heart. It was as if she, like the land, had changed.

"I do not need to reason with you," she said.

"Someone," he said, "should reason with you."

There was long silence. She sat and stared at him while he felt the cold grow in her.

"I will have your belongings searched for," she said, "and you may take the horse, and the Hiua girl, if she is still alive, and you may go where you will after that."

She meant it. Outrage trembled through him. Almost, almost he spun on his heel and defied her—but there was not even anger in her voice, nothing against which he could argue later, no hope that it was unthought or unmeant. There was only utter weariness, a hollowness that was beyond reaching, and if he left, there would be none to reach her, none.

"I do not know," he said, "to what I have taken oath. I do not recognize you."

Her eyes remained focused somewhere past him, as if she had already dismissed him.

"You cannot send me away," he cried at her, and his hoarse voice broke, robbing him of dignity.

"No," she agreed without looking at him. "But while you stay, you do not dispute my orders."

He let go a shaking breath, and came to where she sat, knelt down on the hearthstones and ripped off the cloak she had lent him, laid it aside and stared elsewhere himself until he thought that he could speak without losing his self-control.

She needed him. He convinced himself that this was still true; and her need was desperate and unfair in its extent and therefore she would not order him to stay, not on her terms. Jhirun, he thought, would be on his conscience so long as he lived; but Morgaine—Morgaine he could not leave.

"May I," he asked finally, quietly, "send one of the servants to see if he can find her?"

"No."

He gave a desperate breath of a laugh, hoping that it was an unthought reaction in her, that she would relent in an instant, but laugh and hope died together when he looked at her directly and saw the coldness still in her face. "I do not understand," he said. "I do not understand."

"When you took oath to me," she said in a thin, hushed voice, "one grace you asked of me that I have always granted so far as I could: to remain untouched by the things I use and the things I do. Will you not grant that same grace to this girl?"

"You do not understand. *Liyo,* she was a prisoner; they took her elsewhere. She may be hurt. The women out there—they are a prey to the marshlanders and the mob in the court. Whatever else, you are a woman. Can you not find the means to help her?"

"She may be hurt. If you would heal her, leave my service and see to it. If not, have mercy on her and leave her alone." She lapsed into silence for a moment, and her gray eyes roamed the room, with its torn tapestries and shattered treasures. From the courtyard there was still shouting and screaming, and her glance wandered to the windows before she looked back to him. "I have done what I had to do," she said in an absent, deathly voice. "I have loosed the Barrows and the marshlands on Shiuan because it was a means to reach this land most expediently, with force to survive. I do not lead them. I only came among them. I take shelter here only until it is possible to move on. I do not look at what I leave behind me."

He listened, and something inside him shuddered, not at the words, which deserved it, but at the tone of them. She was lying; he hoped with all his heart that in this one thing he understood her, or he understood nothing at all. And to rise now, to walk out that door and leave her, took something he did not possess. In this, too, he did not know whether it was courage or cowardice.

"I will stay," he said.

She stared at him, saying nothing. He grew afraid, so strange and troubled her look was. There were shadows beneath her eyes. He reckoned that she had not slept well, had rested little in recent days, with no companion to guard her sleep among strangers, with no one to fill the silence with which she surrounded herself, implacable in her purpose and disinterested in others' desires.

"I will make discreet inquiry," she said at last. "It may be that I can do something to have her found without finding her . . . only so you know clearly what the conditions are."

He heard the brittleness in her voice, knew that it masked, and bowed, in shaken gratitude, touched his brow to the hearthstones, sat up again.

"There is surely a bed to be had," she said, "and an hour or more before I shall be inclined to need it."

He looked beyond her, to the open arch of the shadowed next room, where the servants had begun stirring about, the removal of the former owners completed. There was a light somewhere within, the opening and closing of cabinets, the rustle of fabrics. A warm bed: he longed toward it, exhausted—luxury that he seldom knew, and far different from the things he had expected at the end of this ugly day.

It was far different, he thought, from what many others knew this night: Jhirun, if she still lived, Kithan, bereft of power, Roh—fled into the storm and the flood this night, in his private nightmare that centered upon Morgaine—Roh, with Abarais before him and the chance of defeating them.

But Morgaine gazed down on him now with a face that at last he knew, tired, inexpressibly tired, and sane.

"You take first rest," he said. "I shall sit by the fire and keep an eye on the servants."

She regarded him from half-lidded eyes, shook her head. "Go as I told you," she said. "I have eased your conscience, so far as I can. Go on. You have given me matters to attend yet; now let me attend them."

He gathered himself up, almost fell in doing it, his feet asleep, and he steadied himself against the mantel, looked at her apologetically. Her gaze, troubled and thoughtful, gave him benediction; and he bowed his head in gratitude.

Nightmares surrounded her at times. There was one proceeding in the courtyard and elsewhere in the hold this night. *Stop it,* he wanted to plead with her. *Take command of them and stop it. You can do it, and will not.*

She had led an army once; ten thousand men had followed her before his age, and had been swept away into oblivion, lost. Clans and kingdoms had perished, dynasties ended, Andur-Kursh plunged into a hundred years of poverty and ruin.

So clan Yla had perished in her service, to the last man, lost in the void of Gates; so passed much of Chya, and many a man of Nhi and Myya and Ris. Horrid suspicion nagged at him.

He looked back at her, where she sat, a lonely figure before the fire. He opened his mouth to speak to her, to go back and tell her what things he had begun to fear of this land, to hear her say that they were not so.

There were the servants, who would overhear and repeat things elsewhere. He dared not speak, not before them. He turned away toward the other room.

There was the softness of a down mattress, the comfort of fabrics smooth and soft; of cleanliness, that most of all.

She would call him, he reckoned, in only a little while; there was not that much of the night remaining. He slept mostly dressed, in clean clothing that he had discovered in a chest, the former lord as tall as he and no whit slighter, save in the length of arm and breadth of shoulder. The fine cloth rested easily on his hurts; it was good to feel it, to have stripped away the stubble of days without a razor, and to rest with his hair damp from a thorough scrubbing . . . in a place warm and soft, fragrant with a woman's care, be she servant or murdered *qujalin* lady.

He wrestled his mind from such morbid thoughts, determined not to remember where he was, or what things he had seen outside. He was safe. Morgaine watched his sleep, as he would watch hers in turn. He cast himself into trusting oblivion, determined that nothing would rob him of this rest that he had won.

Small sounds disturbed him now and then; once the opening of the outer door alarmed him, until he heard Morgaine's soft voice speaking calmly with someone, and that door then close, and her light tread safely in the room next his. Once he heard her in the room with him, searching the closets and chests, and knew that soon enough she would call him to his watch; he headed himself back into a few treasured moments of sleep. He heard the splash of water in the bath, the room mostly dark save for a single lamp there and the fireplace in the next room; grateful for the small remaining time, pleased to know she also took the leisure for such comforts as he had enjoyed, he shut his eyes again.

And the rustle of cloth woke him, the sight of a woman, *qujal,* in a white gown, ghost-pale in the darkness. He did not know her for an instant, and his heart crashed against his ribs in panic, thinking murder, and of the dead. But Morgaine drew back the coverlet on her side of the great bed, and he, with some embarrassment, prepared to quit the other before she must bid him do so.

"Go back to sleep," she said, confounding him. "The servants are out and the door is bolted on our side. There is no need for either of us to stay awake, unless thee is overnice. I am not."

And in her hand was *Changeling,* that always slept with her; she laid it atop the coverlet, a thing fell and dangerous, in the valley that would be between them. Vanye rested very still, felt the mattress give as she settled beside him and drew the covers over her, heard the gentle sigh of her breath.

And felt the weight of *Changeling,* that rested between.

He held no more urge to sleep, his heart still beating rapidly. It was that she had startled him, he told himself at first—he found it disturbing that for that single instant he had not known her—*frost-fair, frost-fair,* an old ballad sang of her, and like frost, burning to the touch. It was kindness that she had not displaced him to the hearthside; it was like her that she was considerate in small things. Perhaps she would not have rested, having sent him to a pallet on the hard stone. Perhaps it was amends for the harsh words she had used earlier.

But it was not the same as campfires they had shared, when they had shared warmth, both armored, companions in the dark, one always waking in dread of ambush. He listened to her breathing, felt the small movements that she made, and tried to distract his mind to other thoughts, staring at the dark rafters. He cursed silently, half a pious prayer, wondering how she would understand it if he did withdraw to the hearthside.

Woman that she was, she might not have thought overmuch of the gesture; perhaps she did not understand.

Or perhaps, he thought in misery, she wished him inclined to defy that barrier, and tormented him deliberately.

She had asked him why he came with her. *Your charity,* he had told her lightly, *was always more generous than my brother's.* The remark had stung her; he wished to this day that he had asked why, that he understood why it had angered her, or why in all that bitter day it had seemed to set her at odds with him.

He was human; he was not sure that she was. He had been a godfearing man; and he was not sure what she was. Logic did not avail, thus close to her. All Roh's arguments collapsed, thus close to her; and he knew clearly what had drawn him this side of Gates, although he still shuddered to look into her gray and alien eyes, or to lie thus close to her; the shudder melded into quite another feeling, and he was horrified at himself, who could be moved by her, his liege, and thousandfold murderer, and *qujal,* at least to the eye.

He was lost, he thought, and possessed only this resolve, that he tried to remember that he was Kurshin, and Nhi, and that she was cursed in his land. Half that men told of her were lies; but much that was as terrible he had seen himself.

And that logic likewise was powerless.

He knew finally that it was neither reason nor virtue that stood in his way, but that did he once attempt that cold barrier between, she might lose all trust for him. *Ilin,* she had said once, hurtfully, *thee has a place—Ilin,* she had said this night, *I have given thee an order.*

Pride forbade. He could not be treated thus; he dreaded to think what torment he could create for them, she trying to deal with him as a man, he trying to be both man and servant. She had a companion older than he, a demanding thing, and evil, that lay as a weight against his side; no other could be closer than that.

And if she had regard for him, he thought, she surely sensed the misery that she could cause him, and kept him at a distance, until this night, that she, overpractical, over-kindly, omitted to send him to his place.

He wondered for whose sake she had placed the sword between, for her peace of mind or for his.

↶ Chapter 12

Something fell, a weight upon the floor.

Vanye wakened, flung an arm wide, to the realization that Morgaine's place beside him was vacant and cold. White daylight shone in the next room.

He sprang up, still half-blind, fighting clear of the sheets, and stumbled to the doorway. He blinked at Morgaine, who was dressed in her accustomed black armor and standing by the open outer door. A mass of gear—armor—rested on the hearthside; it had not been there the night before. Books and charts were heaped on the floor in a flood of daylight from the window, most of them open and in disorder. Servants were even then bringing in food, dishes steaming and savory, setting gold plates and cups on the long table.

And just outside the door, in conversation with Morgaine, stood a different set of guards: taller, slimmer men than the run of marshlanders. She was speaking with them quietly, giving orders or receiving reports.

Vanye ran a hand through his hair, let go his breath, deciding that there was nothing amiss. He ached; his lacerated wrists hurt to bend after a night's rest, and his feet—he looked down, grimacing at the ugly sores. He limped back into the bedroom and sought a fresh shirt from the supply in the wardrobe, and found a pair of boots that he had set aside the night before, likewise from the wardrobe. He sat in the shadow, on the bed, working the overly tight boots onto his sore feet, and listened to Morgaine's voice in the next room, and those of the men with whom she spoke. He did not make sense of it; the distance was too great and their accent was difficult for him. It seemed awkward to go into the other room, breaking in upon her business. He waited until he had heard Morgaine dismiss them, and heard the servants finish their arranging of breakfast and leave. Only then he arose and ventured out to see what matters were between them in cold daylight.

"Sit," she offered him, bidding him to the table; and with a downcast expression and a shrug: "It is noon; it is still raining occasionally, and the scouts report that there is no abating of the flood at the crossing. They give some hope that matters will improve tonight, or perhaps tomorrow. This they have from the Shiua themselves."

Vanye began to take the chair that she offered, but when he drew it back to sit down, he saw the stain on the carpet and stopped. She looked at him. He pushed the chair in again, then walked round the table and took the opposite one, not looking down, trying to forget the memory of the night. Quietly he moved his plate across the narrow table.

She was seated. He helped himself after her, spooned food onto gold plates and sipped at the hot and unfamiliar drink that eased his sore throat. He ate without a word, finding it wildly incongruous to be sharing table with Morgaine, stranger than to have shared a bed. He felt it improper to sit at table in her presence: to do so belonged to another life, when he had been a lord's son, and knew hall manners and not the ashes of the hearthside or the campfire of an outlaw.

She also maintained silence. She was not given to much conversation, but there was too much strangeness about them in Ohtij-in that he could find that silence comfortable.

"They do not seem to have fed you well," she remarked, when he had disposed of a third helping, and she had only then finished her first plate.

"No," he said, "they did not."

"You slept more soundly than ever I have seen you."

"You might have waked me," he said, "when you wakened."

"You seemed to need the rest."

He shrugged. "I am grateful," he said.

"I understand that your lodging here was not altogether comfortable."

"No," he agreed, and took up his cup, pushing the plate away. He was uneasy in this strange humor of hers, that discussed him with such persistence.

"I understand," Morgaine said, "that you killed two men—one of them lord of Ohtij-in."

He set the cup down in startlement, held it in his fingers and turned it, swirling the amber liquid inside, his heart beat as if he had been running. "No," he said. "That is not so. One man I killed, yes. But the lord Bydarra—Hetharu murdered him, his own son—murdered him, alone in that room with me; and I would have been hanged for it last night, that at the least. The other son, Kithan—he may know the truth or not; I am not sure. But it was very neatly done, *liyo*. There is none but Hetharu and myself that know for certain what happened in that room."

She pushed her chair back, turning it so that she faced him at the corner of the table; and she leaned back, regarding him with a frowning speculation that made him the more uncomfortable. "Then," she said, "Hetharu left in Roh's company, and took with him the main strength of Ohtij-in. Why? Why such a force?"

"I do not know."

"This time must have been terrible for you."

"Yes," he said at last, because she left a silence to be filled.

"I did not find Jhirun Ela's-daughter. But while I searched for her, Vanye, I heard a strange thing."

He thought that the color must long since have fled his face. He took a drink to ease the tightness in his throat. "Ask," he said.

"It is said," she continued, "that she, like yourself, was under Roh's personal protection. That his orders kept you both in fair comfort and safety until Bydarra was murdered."

He set the cup down again and looked at her, remembering that any suspicion for her was sufficient motive to kill. But she sat at breakfast with him, sharing food and drink, while she had known these things perhaps as early as last night, before she lay down to sleep beside him.

"If you thought that you could not trust me," he said, "you would be rid of me at once. You would not have waited."

"Is thee going to answer, Vanye? Or is thee going to go on evading me? Thee has omitted many things in the telling. On thy oath—on thy oath, Nhi Vanye, no more of it."

"He—Roh—found welcome here, at least with one faction of the house. He saw to it that I was safe, yes; but not so comfortable, not so comfortable as you imagine, *liyo*. And later—when Hetharu seized power—then, too—Roh intervened."

"Do you know why?"

He shook his head and said nothing. Suppositions led in many directions that he did not want to explore with her.

"Did you speak with him directly?"

"Yes." There was long silence. He felt out of place even to be sitting in a chair, staring at her eye to eye, when that was not the situation between them and never had been.

"Then thee has some idea."

"He said—it was for kinship's sake."

She said nothing.

"He said," he continued with difficulty, "that if you—if you were lost, then— I think he would have sought a Claiming . . ."

"Did you suggest it?" she asked; and perhaps the revulsion showed on his face, for her look softened at once to pity. "No," she judged. "No, thee would not." And for a moment she gazed on him with fearsome intentness, as if she prepared something from which she had long refrained. "Thee is ignorant," she said, "and in that ignorance, valuable to him."

"I would not help him against you."

"You are without defense. You are ignorant, and without defense."

Heat rose to his face, anger. "Doubtless," he said.

"I could remedy that, Vanye."

Become what I am, accept what I serve, bear what I bear . . .

The heat fled, leaving chill behind. "No," he said. "No."

"Vanye—for your own sake, listen to me."

Hope was in her eyes, utterly intense: never before had she pleaded with him for anything. He had come with her: perhaps then she had begun to hope for this thing that she had never won of him. He remembered then what he had for a time forgotten, the difference there was between Morgaine and what possessed Chya Roh: that Morgaine, having the right to order, had always refrained.

It was the thing she wanted most, that alone might give her some measure of peace; and she refrained.

"*Liyo*," he whispered, "I would do anything, anything you set me to do. Ask me things that I can do."

"Except this," she concluded, in a tone that pierced his heart.

"*Liyo*—anything else."

She lowered her eyes, like a curtain drawn finally between them, lifted them again. There was no bitterness, only a deep sorrow.

"Be honest with me," he said, stung. "You nearly died in the flood. You nearly died, with whatever you seek to do left undone; and this preys on your mind. It is not for my sake that you want this. It is for yourself."

Again the lowering of the eyes; and she looked up again. "Yes," she said, without a trace of shame. "But know too, Vanye, that my enemies will never leave you in peace. Ignorance cannot save you from that. So long as you are accessible to them, you will never be safe."

"It is what you said: that one grace you always gave me, that you never burdened me with your *qujalin* arts; and for that, for that I gave you more than ever my oath demanded of me. Do you want everything now? You can order. I am only *ilin*. Order, and I will do what you say."

There was warfare in the depths of her eyes, yea and nay equally balanced, desperately poised. "O Vanye," she said softly, "thee is asking me for virtue, which thee well knows I lack."

"Then order," he said.

She frowned darkly, and stared elsewhere.

"I tried," he said in that long silence, "to reach Abarais, to wait for you. And if I could have used Roh to set me there—I would have gone with him—to stop him."

"With what?" she asked, a derisive laugh; but she turned toward him again, and even yet her look pleaded with him. "If I were lost, what could you have done?"

He shrugged, searched up the most terrible thing that he could envision. "Casting *Changeling* within a Gate: that would suffice, would it not?"

"If you could set hands on it. And that would destroy you; and destroy only one Gate." She took *Changeling* from her side and laid it across the arms of her chair. "It was made for other use."

"Let be," he asked of her, for she eased the blade fractionally from its sheath. He edged back, for he trusted her mind, but not that witch-blade; and it was not her habit to draw it ever unless she must. She stopped; it lay half-exposed, no metal, but very like a shard of crystal, its magics restrained until it should be wholly unsheathed.

She held it so, the blade's face toward him, while opal fires swirled softly in the *qujalin* runes on its surface. "For anyone who can read this," she said, "here is the making and unmaking of Gates. And I think thee begins to know what this is worth, and what there is to fear should Roh take it. To bring this within his reach would be the most dangerous thing you could do."

"Put it away," he asked of her.

"Vanye: to read the runes—would thee learn simply that? Only that much—simply to read the *qujalin* tongue and speak it. Is that too much to ask?"

"Do you ask it for yourself?"

"Yes," she said.

He averted his eyes from it, and nodded consent.

"It is necessary," she said. "Vanye, I will show you; and take up *Changeling* if ever I am lost. Knowing what you will know, the sword will teach you after—until you have no choice, as I have none." And after a moment: "*If* I am lost. I do not mean that it should happen."

"I will do this," he answered, and thereafter sat a cold hardness in him, like a stone where his heart had been. It was the end of what he had begun when he had followed her; he realized that he had always known it.

She rammed the dragon sword back into its sheath and took it in the curve of her arm—nodded toward the fireside, where armor lay, bundled in a cloak. "Yours," she said. "Some of the servants worked through the night on it. Go dress. I do not trust this place. We will settle the other matter later. We will talk of it."

"Aye," he agreed, glad of that priority in things, for as she was, she might win yet more of him, piece by piece: perhaps she knew it.

And there was an ease in her manner that had not been there in many a day, something that had settled at peace with her. He was glad for that, at least. He took it for enough; and arose from the table and went to the fireside—heard her rise and knew her standing near him as he knelt and unfolded the cloak that wrapped his recovered belongings.

His armor, familiar helm that had been in her keeping: he was surprised and pleased that she had kept it, as if sentiment had moved her, as if she had hoped to find him again. There was his mail, cleaned and saved from rust, leather replaced: he received that back with great relief, for it was all he owned in the world save the black horse and his saddle. He gathered it up, knowing the weight of it as he knew that of his own body.

And out of it fell a bone-handled dagger: Roh's—an ill dream recurring. It lay on the stones, accusing him. For one terrible instant he wondered how much in truth she knew of what had passed.

"Next time," she said from behind him, "resolve to use it."

His hand went to his brow, to bless himself in dismay; he hesitated, then sketchily completed the gesture, and was the more disquieted afterward. He gathered up the bundle, dagger and all, and carried it into the other room where he might have privacy, where he might both dress and breathe in peace.

He would die in this forsaken land the other side of Gates, he thought, jerking with trembling fingers at the laces of his clothing; that much had been certain from the beginning—but that became less terrible than what prospect opened before him, that little by little he would lose himself, that she would have all. Murder had sent him to her, brother-killing; *ilin*-service was just condemnation. But he reckoned himself, what he had been, and what he had become; and the man that he was now was no longer capable of the crime that he had done. It was not just, what lay before him.

He set himself into his armor, leather and metal links in which he had lived the most part of his youth; and though it was newly fitted and most of the leather replaced, it settled about his body familiar as his own skin, a weight that surrounded him with safety, with habits that had kept him alive where his living had not been likely. It no longer seemed protection.

Until you have no choice, Morgaine had warned him, *as I have none.*

He slipped Roh's dagger into the sheath at his belt, a weight that settled on his heart likewise: this time it was with full intent to use it.

A shadow fell across the door. He looked up. Morgaine came with yet another gift for him, a longsword in its sheath.

He turned and took it from her offering hands—bowed and touched it to his brow as a man should when accepting such a gift from his liege. It was *qujalin,* he did not doubt it: *qujalin* more than *Changeling* itself, which at least had been made by men. But with it in his hands, for the first time in their journey through this land, he felt a stir of pride, the sense that he had skill that was of some value to her. He drew the blade half from the sheath, and saw that it was a good double-edged blade, clean of *qujalin* runes. The length was a little more than that of a Kurshin longsword, and the blade was a little thinner; but it was a weapon he knew how to use.

"I thank you," he said.

"Stay armed. I want none of these folk drawing for your naked back; and it would be the back, with them. They are wolves, allies of chance and mutual profit."

He hooked it to his belt, pulled the ring on his shoulder belt and hooked that, settling it to a more comfortable position at his shoulder. Her words touched at something in him, a sudden, unbearable foreboding, that even she would say what she had said. He looked up at her. "*Liyo,*" he said in a low voice. "Let us go. Let us two, together . . . leave this place. Forget these men; be rid of them. Let us be out of here."

She nodded back toward the other room. "It is still misting rain out. We will go, tonight, when there is a chance the flood will ebb."

"Now," he insisted, and when he saw her hesitate: "*Liyo,* what you asked, I gave; give me this. I will go, now, I will find us a packhorse and some manner of tent for our comfort. . . . Better the cold and the rain than this place over our heads tonight."

She looked tempted, urgently tempted, struggling with reason. He knew the restlessness that chafed at her, pent here, behind rock and risen water. And for once he felt that urge himself, an instinct overwhelming, a dark that pressed at their heels.

She gestured again toward the room beyond. "The books . . . I have only begun to make sense of them . . ."

"Do not trust these men." Of a sudden all things settled together in his mind, taking form; and some were in those books; and more were pent in the shape of a priest, locked in the dark down the hall. She could be harmed by these things, these men. The human tide that lapped about the walls of Ohtij-in threatened her, no less than the *qujal*-lords.

"Go," she bade him suddenly. "Go. See to it. Quietly."

He snatched up his cloak, caught up his helm, and then paused, looking back at her.

Still he was uneasy—parted from her in this place; but he forbore to warn her more of these men, of opening the door to them: it was not his place to order her. He drew up the coif and settled his helm on, and did not stay to put on the cloak. He passed the door, between the new guards, and looked at those three with sullen misgivings—looked too down the hall, where the priest Ginun was imprisoned, without drink or food yet provided.

That too wanted tending. He dared not have the guards wait on that man, a priest of their own folk, treated thus. Something had to be done with the priest; he knew not what.

In haste he slung the heavy cloak about him and fastened it as he passed the door out of the corridor, uneasy as he walked these rooms that were familiar to him under other circumstances—as he passed marshlanders, who turned and stared at him and made a sign he did not know. He entered the spiral at the core of the keep, passed others, feeling their stares at his back as he walked that downward corridor. Even armed, he did not feel safe or free here. Torches lit the place, a bracket at every doorway, profligate waste of them; and the smallish men of Aren came and went freely up and down the ramp, no few of them drunken, decked in finery incongruous among their peasant clothes. Here and there passed other men, tall and grim of manner, who did not mix with the marshlanders: Fwar's kindred, a hard-eyed lot; something wrathful abode in them, that touched at familiarity.

The Barrows and the marshlands, Morgaine had said, naming them that followed her; *Barrow-folk,* Vanye realized suddenly.

Myya.

Jhirun's kinsmen.

He hastened his pace, descending the core, the terror that breathed thickly in the air of this place now possessing a name.

The courtyard was quieter than the keep, a dazed quiet, the misting rain glistening on the paving stones, a few folk that might be Shiua or marshlanders moving about wrapped in cloaks and shawls. There was a woman with two children at her skirts: it struck him strangely that nowhere had there been children among the *qujal*, none that he had seen; and he did not know why.

The woman, the children, the others—stopped and looked at him. He was afraid for a moment, remembering the violence that had surged across these stones; but they showed no disposition to threaten him. They only watched.

He turned toward the pens and the stables, where their horses waited. Cattle lowed in the pens to his right, beasts well cared-for, better than the Shiua. The roofs of the shelters on his left were blackened, the windows eaten by fire. Folk still lived there; they watched him from doorways, furtively.

He looked behind him when he reached the stable doors, fearful that more might have gathered at his back; the same few stood in the distance, still watching him. He dismissed them from his concern and eased open the stable door, entered into that dark place, that smelled pleasantly of hay and horses.

It was a large, rambling structure, seeming to wind irregularly about the keep wall, with most of the stalls empty, save those in the first row. On the right side he counted nine, ten horses, mostly bay; and on the left, apart from the others, he saw Siptah's pale head, ears pricked, nostrils flaring at the presence of one he knew; in an empty stall farther stood a shadow that was his own Andurin gelding.

Racks at the end of the aisle held what harness remained: he saw what belonged to Siptah, and reckoned his own horse's gear would be near it. He delayed at the stalls, offered his hand to Siptah's questing nose, patted that great plate of a cheek, went further to assure himself his own horse was fit. The black lipped at his sleeve; he caught the animal by the mane and slapped it gently on the neck, finding that someone had been horseman enough to have rubbed both animals down, when he had not. He was glad of this: Kurshin that he was, he was not accustomed to leave his horse to another man's care. He checked feet and found them sound: a shoe had been reset, not of his doing; it had been well-done, and he found nothing of which to complain, though he searched for it.

And then he set himself to prepare them. There would be need of grain, that as much as the supplies they would need for themselves: their way was always too uncertain to travel without it. He searched the likely places until he had located the storage bins, and then cast about to see whether there was, amid all the gear remaining, a packsaddle. There was nothing convenient. At last he filled his own saddlebags with what he could, and took Morgaine's gear and his own, and slung it over the rails of the respective stalls, ready to saddle.

Something moved in the straw, in the shadows. At first he took it for one of the other horses, but it was close. The sudden set of the gelding's ears and the sound at once alarmed him: he whirled, reaching for the Honor-blade, wondering how many there were, and where.

"Lord," said a small voice out of the dark, a female voice, that trembled.

He stood still, set his back against the rails of the stall, though he knew the voice. In a moment she moved, and he saw a bit of white in the darkness at the racks, where the windows were closed.

"Jhirun," he hailed her softly.

She came, treading carefully, as if she were yet uncertain of him. She still wore her tattered skirt and blouse; her hair showed wisps of straw. She held to the rail nearest with one hand and kept yet some distance from him, standing as if her legs had difficulty in bearing her weight.

He slid the blade back into sheath, stepped under the uppermost rail and into the aisle. "We looked for you," he said.

"I stayed by the horses," she said in a thin voice. "I knew *she* had come. I did not know whether you were alive."

He let go a long breath, relieved to find this one nightmare an empty one. "You are safe. They are Hiua that have this place now: your own people."

She stayed silent for a long moment; her eyes went to the saddles on the rails, back again. "You are leaving."

He took her meaning, shook his head in distress. "Matters are different. There is no safety for you with us. I cannot take you."

She stared at him. Tears flooded her eyes; but suddenly there was such a look of violence there that he recalled how she had set out the marshland road, alone.

And that he must, having saddled the horses, go back to Morgaine and leave the animals in Jhirun's care, or deal with her in some fashion.

"At least," she said, "get me out of Ohtij-in."

He could not face her. He started to take up one of the saddles, to attend his business with the horses.

"Please," she said.

He looked back at her, eased the saddle back onto the rail. "I am not free," he said, "to give and take promises. You are Myya; you have forgotten a great deal in Hiuaj, or you would have understood by looking at me that I am no longer *uyo* and that I have no honor. You were mistaken to have believed me. I said what I had to say, because you left me no choice. I cannot take you with me."

She turned her back, and walked away; he thought for a moment that she was going back into the shadows to sit and weep for a while, and he would allow her that, before he decided what he must do with her.

But she did not return into the dark. She went to the harness rack and took bridle and saddle, tugging the gear into her arms and staggering with the weight of it. He swore, watching her come down the aisle toward him, dangling the girth in the foul straw and near to tripping on it, hard-breathing with the effort and with her tears.

He blocked her path and jerked it from her hands, cast it into the straw and cursed at her, and she stood empty-handed and stared up at him, her eyes blind with tears.

"At least when you go," she said, "you could give me help as far as the road. Or at least do not stop me. You have no right to do that."

He stood still. She bent, trying to pick up the saddle from the ground, and was shaking so that she had no strength in her hands.

He swore and took it from her, slung it up to the nearest rail. "Well enough," he conceded. "I will saddle a horse for you. And what you do then, that is your business. Choose one."

She stared at him, thin-lipped, and then walked to the stall halfway down, laid a hand on that rail that enclosed a bay mare. "I will take her."

He came and looked at the mare, that was deep enough of chest, but small-ish. "There might be better," he said.

"This one."

He shook his head, reckoning that she would have what she wished, and that perhaps a girl whose experience of horses extended most to a small black pony judged her limits well enough. He did as she wished.

And with Jhirun's mare saddled, he returned to his own horse, and to Siptah—took meticulous pains with their own gear, that might have to stand a hard ride and few rests: he appropriated a coil of harness leather, and a braided leather rope as well; and at last he closed the stalls and prepared to leave.

"I have to go advise my lady," he told Jhirun, who waited by her mare. "We will come as quickly as possible. Something might delay us a little time, but not for long."

Anguish crossed her face: he frowned at it, turned all the same to leave, reckoning at least that the horses were safe while Jhirun had some gain from aiding them.

"No," Jhirun whispered after him, ran suddenly and caught his arm; he looked back, chilled at the terror in her face: a sense of ambush prickled about him.

"Lord," she whispered, "there is a man hiding here. Do not leave, do not leave me here."

He seized her arm so hard that she winced. "How many more? What have you arranged for me?"

"No," she breathed. "One. He—" With her head she gestured far off across the stalls, into the dark. "He is there. Do not leave me with him, not now, with the horses—Kithan. It is Kithan."

She stifled a cry; he opened his hand, realizing he had wrenched her arm, and she rubbed the injured wrist, making no attempt to run.

"When the attack came," she said, "he came here and could not get out. He has slept—I took a hayfork, and I came on him to kill him, but I was afraid.

Now he will have heard us moving—he will come here when he thinks it safe, when you are gone."

He slipped the ring of his sword, drew it carefully from sheath. "You show me where," he said. "And if you are mistaken, Myya Jhirun i Myya—"

She shook her head. "I thought we were leaving," she whispered, through tears. "I thought it would be all right, no need, no need for killing—I do not want to—"

"Quiet," he said, and seized her wrist, pushing her forward. She began to lead him, as silently as possible, into the dark.

Small, square windows gave light within the stable, shafts of dusty light, and a maze of aisles and stalls, sheaves of straw, empty racks for harness. The building curved, irregularly, following the keep wall, and the aisles were likewise crooked, row upon row of box stalls, empty—a hay loft, a nesting-place for birds that fluttered wings and stirred restlessly.

Jhirun's hand touched his, cautioning. She pointed down a row of stalls, where the shadow was darkest. He began to go that way, drawing her with him, watching the stalls on either side of him, aware how easily it could prove ambush.

A white shape bolted at the end of the stalls, running. Vanye jerked at Jhirun's wrist, darted into a cross-aisle, into the next row.

The man raced—white hair flying—for a farther aisle. Vanye let Jhirun go, and ran, pursuing him, in time to see him scale a rail barrier and scramble for open windows. The lead was too great. The *qujal* disappeared outside, hurling himself through, as Vanye reached the stall railing.

He stood, cursing inwardly, whirled about on guard as a sound reached his ears; Jhirun came running to him. He let fall his sword arm.

And outside he heard the hue and cry, human hounds a-hunt, and Kithan loose for their quarry, the whole of Ohtij-in astir: they would not be long in taking him.

He swore, an oath that he had never used, and shook Jhirun's fingers roughly from his arm and started back toward the front of the stable, she struggling along beside him, hard-breathing.

"Stay here," he said. "Mind the horses. I am going to Morgaine. We are leaving here as quickly as may be."

ᔆ **Chapter 13**

There was chaos in the courtyard, men raced from doorways. Vanye walked through it, shouldered his way through a press that was coming out of the keep, folk giving back from him in fright when they saw him. He kept his sword, sheathed, in his left hand, and entered the halls of the keep, moving as quickly as he could without running. He would not run: there was panic enough ready to break loose, and he was known as Morgaine's servant.

He reached the lords' halls, high in the tower, crossed through to the inner chambers and startled the guards that were on watch there, who snatched at weapons and then confusedly moved out of his path, recognizing his right to pass. He flung the door open and slammed it behind him, for the first time daring draw the breath he needed.

Morgaine faced him—she standing by the window, her hand upon the sill. Distress was in her look. Distantly the cries of men could be heard from the courtyard below.

"Thee's stirred something?" she asked him.

"Kithan," he said. "*Liyo*, the horses are saddled, and we only need go—now, quickly. Someone will come into that stable and see things prepared if we wait overlong, and I do not think long farewells are fit for this place."

A cry went up, outside. She turned and leaned upon the sill, gazing down into the yard. "They have taken him," she said quietly.

"Let us go, *liyo*. Let us go from here, while there is time."

She turned toward him a second time, and there was a curious expression in her eyes: doubt. Panic rose in him. In one thing he had lied to her, and the lie gathered force, troubling all the peace that had grown between them.

"I do not think that it would be graceful of us," she said, "to try to pass them in the hall. They are bringing him into the hold. Doubtless they are bringing him here.—So short a time from my sight, Vanye, and so much difficulty. . . . Was it a chance meeting?"

He drew breath, let it go quickly. "I swear to you. Listen to me. There are things the lord Kithan can say that do not bear saying, not before these men of yours. Do not question him. Be rid of him, and quickly."

"What should I not ask him?"

He felt the edge in that question, and shook his head. "No. *Liyo*, listen to me. Unless you would have all that Roh said made common knowledge in Ohtij-in—avoid this. There can be questions raised that you do not want asked. There is a priest down the hall . . . and Shiua out in the court, and servants, and whatever *qujal* are still alive . . . that would raise questions if they lost all care of their lives. Kithan will do you no good. There is nothing he can say that you want to hear."

"And was it a chance meeting, Vanye?"

"Yes," he cried, in a tone that shocked the silence after.

"That may be," she said after a moment. "But if you are correct—then it would be well to know what he has said already."

"Are you ready," he asked her, "to leave upon the instant?"

"Yes," she said, and indicated the fireside, where her belongings were neatly placed; he had none.

Outside, in the halls, there was commotion. It was not long in reaching them—the sounds of shouting, the heavy sound of steps approaching.

A heavy hand rapped at the door. "Lady?" one asked from outside.

"Let them in," Morgaine said.

Vanye opened it, and in his other hand only his thumb held the sheath upon the longsword: a shake would free it.

Men were massed outside, a few of the marshlanders; but chief among them was the scarred Barrows-man, Fwar, with his kinsmen. Vanye met that sullen face with utter coldness, and stepped back because Morgaine had bidden it, because they were hers—violent men unlike the Aren-folk: he surmised seeing them now who had done most of the slaughter in Ohtij-in, that were murder to be ordered, they would enjoy it.

And among them, from their midst, they thrust the disheveled figure of the *qujal*-lord, thin and fragile-seeming in their rough hands. Blood dabbled the satin front of Kithan's brocade garment, and his white hair was loose and wild, matted with blood from a cut on his brow.

Fwar cast the dazed halfling to the floor. Morgaine settled herself in a chair, leaned back, *Changeling* balanced on her knee, under her hand; she watched calmly as the former lord of Ohtij-in gathered himself to rise, but they kept him on his knees. Vanye, moving to his proper place at Morgaine's shoulder, saw the force of the *qujal's* gray eyes, no longer full of dreams, no longer distant, but filled with heat and hate.

"He is Kithan," said Fwar, his scarred lips smiling.

"Let him up," Morgaine said; and such hate there was in Kithan that Vanye extended his sheathed sword between, cautioning him; but the captured halfling had some sense. He stumbled to his feet and made a slight bow of the head, homage to realities.

"I shall have you put with the others," Morgaine said softly. "Certain others of your folk do survive, in the higher part of this tower."

"For what?" Kithan asked, with a glance about him.

Morgaine shrugged. "For whatever these men allow."

The elegant young lordling stood trembling, wiped a bloody strand of hair from his cheek. His eyes strayed to Vanye's, who returned him no gentleness, and back again. "I do not understand what is happening," he said. "Why have you done these things to us?"

"You were unfortunate," said Morgaine.

The arrogance of that answer seemed to take Kithan's breath away. He laughed after a moment, aloud and bitterly. "Indeed. And what do you gain of such allies as you have? What when you have won?"

Morgaine frowned, gazing at him. "Fwar," she said, "I do not think it any profit to hold him or his people."

"We can deal with them," said Fwar.

"No," she said. "You have Ohtij-in; and you have my order, Fwar. Will you abide by it, and not kill them?"

"If that is your order," said Fwar after a moment, but there was no pleasure in it.

"So," said Morgaine. "Fwar's kindred and Haz of Aren rule in Ohtij-in, and you rule your own kind. As for me, I am leaving when the flood permits, and you have seen the last of me, my lord Kithan."

"They will kill us."

"They may not. But if I were you, my lord, I would seek shelter elsewhere—perhaps in Hiuaj."

There was laughter at that, and color flooded Kithan's white cheeks.

"Why?" Kithan asked when the coarse laughter had died. "Why have you done this to us? This is excessive revenge."

Again Morgaine shrugged. "I only opened your gates," she said. "What was waiting outside was not of my shaping. I do not lead them. I go my own way."

"Not looking to what you have destroyed. Here is the last place where civilization survives. Here—" Kithan glanced about at the fine tapestries that hung slashed and wantonly ruined. "Here is the wealth, the art of thousands of years, destroyed by these human animals."

"Out there," said Morgaine, "is the flood. Barrows-hold has gone; Aren is going; there is nothing left for them but to come north. It is your time; and you chose your way of meeting it, with such delicate works. It was your choice."

The *qujal* clenched his arms across him as at a chill. "The world is going under; but this time was ours, tedious as it was, and this land was ours, to enjoy it. The Wells ruined the world once, and spilled this Barrows-spawn into our lands—that drove other humans into ruin, that plundered and stole and ruined and left of us only halfbreeds, the survivors of their occupations. They tampered with the Wells and ruined their own lands; they ruined the land they took and now they come to us. Perhaps *he* is of that kind," he said, with a burning look at Vanye, "and came through the Wells; perhaps the one named Roh came likewise. The Barrow-kings are upon us again, no different than they ever were. But someone did this thing to us—someone of knowledge more than theirs. Someone did this, who had the power to open what was sealed."

Morgaine frowned, straightened, drawing *Changeling* into her lap; and of a sudden Vanye moved, seized the slight halfling to silence him, to take him from the room: but Morgaine's sharp command checked him. None moved, not he nor the startled peasants, and Morgaine arose, a distraught look on her face.

She withdrew a space from them, looked back at him, and to Fwar, and seemed for a moment dazed.

"The Barrow-kings," she said then: there was a haunted expression in her eyes. . . . Vanye saw it and remembered Irien, ghosts that followed her, an army, lost in that great valley: ten thousand men, of which not even corpses remained.

His ancestors, that were to her but a few months dead.

"*Liyo,*" he said quietly, his heart pounding. "We are wasting time with him. Set the halfling free or put him with the others, but there are other matters that want attention. Now."

Sanity returned sharply to Morgaine's gaze, a harsh look bestowed on Kithan. "How long ago?"

"*Liyo,*" Vanye objected. "It is pointless."

"How long ago?"

Kithan gathered himself with an intake of breath, assumed that pose of arrogance that had been his while he ruled, despite that Vanye's fingers bit into his arm. "A very long time ago.—Long enough for this land to become what it is. And surely," he shot after that, pressing his advantage, "you are about to bid equally with the man Roh: life, wealth, restoration of the ancient powers. Lie to me, ancient enemy. Offer to buy my favor. It is—considering the situation— purchasable."

"Kill him," Fwar muttered.

"Your enemy has gone," Kithan said, "to Abarais—to possess the Wells; to take all the north. Hetharu is with him, with all our forces; and eventually they will come back."

Fear was thick in the room. Morgaine stood still. The Barrows-men seemed hardly to breathe.

"The Shiua spoke the same," said one of the marshlanders.

"When the flood subsides," said Morgaine, "then there will be a settling with Roh; and he will not return to Ohtij-in. But that is my business, and it need not concern you."

"Lady," said Fwar, fear distorting his face, "when you have done that— when you have reached the Wells—what will you do then?"

Vanye heard, mind frozen, the halfling held with one hand, the other hand sweating on the grip of his sword. It was not his to answer: with his eyes he tried to warn her.

"We have followed you," a Barrows-man said. "We are yours, we Barrowers—We will follow you."

"*Take them,*" Kithan laughed, a bitter and mocking laugh; and of a sudden the foremost of the Aren-folk fled, his fellows with him, thrusting their way through the tall Barrows-men, running.

Still Kithan laughed, and Vanye cursed and hurled him aside, into the midst of the Barrows-men, who hurled him clear again; Vanye unsheathed the sword, and Kithan halted, within striking distance of him, and knowing it.

"No," Morgaine forbade him. "No." And to the Barrowers: "Fwar, stop the Aren-folk. Find me Haz."

But the Barrowers too remained as if dazed, pale of face, staring at her. One of them touched a luck-piece that he wore hanging from a cord about his neck. Fwar bit at his lip.

And Kithan smiled a wolf-smile and laughed yet again. "World's-end, world's-end, o ye blind, ye Barrows-rabble. She has followed you through the Wells to repay you for all you have done . . . your own, your personal curse. An eyeblink for her, from there till now, but there is no time in the Wells, nor distance. *We are avenged.*"

A knife whipped from sheath: a Barrows-man drew—for Morgaine, for Kithan, unknown which: Vanye looked toward it, and that man backed away, whey-faced and sweating.

There was silence in the room, heavy and oppressive; and of a sudden there was a stir outside, as the animals in the pens began bawling all at once. Furniture quivered, and the surface in the wine pitcher on the table shimmered and then men sprang one way and the other as chairs danced and the floor heaved sickeningly underfoot, masonry parting in a great crack down the wall that admitted dusty daylight. The fire crashed, a burning log rolled across the carpet, and there were echoing crashes and screams throughout the hold.

A rumbling shook the floor, deafening, sudden impact jolting the very stones of the hold.

Then it was done, and anguished screams resounded outside and throughout the keep. Vanye stood clinging to the back of a chair, Kithan to the table, the laughter shaken from him, and the Barrows-men stood white and trembling against the riven wall.

"Out," Morgaine shouted at them. "Out of here, clear the hold. Out!"

There was panic. The Hiua rushed the doorway in a mass, pushing and cursing at each other in their haste; but Vanye, sword's point levelled at Kithan, saw Morgaine delay to gather her belongings from the fireside.

"Go," he told her, reaching for her burden. She did not yield it, but left, quickly. Vanye abandoned Kithan, intent on staying with Morgaine; and the halfling darted from the door, raced the other way down the hall, a way that led upward.

"His people," said Morgaine; and Vanye felt an instant's respect for the *qujal*-lord, realizing what he was about.

And as he looked he saw another thing—broken timbers, a doorframe riven and shattered, and a door ajar.

The priest.

"Go!" he shouted at Morgaine; and turned back, running, slid to a stop and pulled that jammed door wide, splintering wood as he did so.

The storeroom was empty. The priest was a slight man, the opening he had forced sufficient for the body of so slender a man, and the priest was gone.

He turned and ran, back the way Morgaine should have gone, past a cabinet that was overturned and shattered, a wall that leaned perilously. He saw her, redoubled his effort and overtook her just as she reached the main corridor.

Terror reigned in that long spiral: few had torches, and the fall of some in the corridor had darkened areas of the passage. Servants gained courage to push and shove like free men: screaming women and children of the Aren-folk fought with hold servants for passage, and men pushed ruthlessly where strength would avail in their haste. One of the sons of Haz fought his way to Morgaine's side, pleading for comfort, babbling words almost impossible to understand. Morgaine tried to answer, caught for balance on his arm as they came to the riven place that had always been in the corridor. It was the width of a man's body now. A child fell, screaming, and Vanye seized it by its clothing and deposited it safely across, hearing a stone crumble. It hit water far below.

And Morgaine, with the marshlander to make way for her, had kept moving. Vanye saw her gone and fought his own way through, ruthless as the others, desperate.

The gate at the bottom was not barred: it had not been since the attack. He saw Morgaine step clear, onto the steps, in the drizzling rain, and caught his own breath as he overtook her, dazed, dimly conscious that they were still being jostled by those that poured out behind.

But his eyes, like hers, fixed in shock on the gate, for the barbican tower had fallen, leaving a wider gap beside the ruined gates; and pitiful folk clambered over the rubble in the falling rain, where the uppermost stones had fallen among the shelters, crushing them, crushing flesh and timbers alike under megaliths the size of two men.

Shiua saw Morgaine standing there, and there went up a cry, a wailing. They came, dazed and fearfully; and Vanye gripped his sword tightly in his fist, but he realized then that they came for pity, pleading with their gestures and their outcries. There gathered a crowd, both marshlanders and folk of the shelters, Hiua and Shiua mingled in their desolation. None reached her: she stepped off the last step and walked among them, they giving back to give her place, pressing at each other in their zeal to avoid her. Vanye went at her back, sword in hand, fearful, seeing the mob that once had threatened him now pleading desperately with them both. Hands touched him as they would not touch Morgaine, but they were pleas for help, for explanation, and he could not give it.

Morgaine slung her cloak about her and put up the hood as she walked across the yard, and there, in the clear of threatening stones, she turned and looked back at the keep.

Vanye looked, a quickly stolen glance, for fear of those about them, and saw that the tower that had fallen had taken one of the buttresses too, riving it away from the keep. There was a crack in that vast tower, opening it widely to the elements and promising further ruin.

"I would give nothing for its chance of standing the hour," Morgaine said. "There will be other shocks." And for the instant she gazed about the yard, seemed herself in a state of shock. Over the babble of prayers and panicked questions rose the steady keening of men and women over their dead.

And suddenly she flung back her head and shouted to those of the Aren-folk near her: "There is no staying here. It will all collapse. Gather what you must have to live, and go, get out of here!"

Panic spread at that dismissal; she did not regard the questions others shouted at her, but seized at Vanye's sleeve. "The horses. Get our horses out before that wall goes."

"Aye," he agreed, and then realized it meant leaving her; half a step he hesitated, and saw her face with that unreasoning fixedness, saw the folk that crowded frantically about her, that in their fear would cling to her: she could not get away. He fled, steps quickening, avoiding this man and that, racing across the puddled yard to the stable, remembering Jhirun, left to her own devices, panicked horses and the damage of the quake.

The stable door was ajar. He pushed it open. Chaos awaited him inside that warm darkness, planks down where horses had panicked and broken their barriers. There was a wild-eyed bay that had had the worst of it: it bolted when he flung the stable door wide. Other horses were still in stalls.

"Jhirun," he called aloud, seeing with relief Siptah and his own horse and Jhirun's mare still safe.

No voice responded. There was a rustling of straw—many bodies in the darkness.

Fwar stepped into the light, his kinsmen emerging likewise from the shadows, from within a stall, over the bars of another: armed men, carrying knives. Vanye spun half about, caught a quick glimpse of others behind him.

He slung the sheath from his sword and sent it at them, whirled upon the man at his left and toppled him writhing in the straw, bent under a whistling staff and took that man too: his comrade fled, wounded.

A crash attended those behind, Siptah's shrill scream. Vanye turned into a knife attack, ducked under the clumsy move and used the man's arm to guide his blade, whipped it free and came on guard again, springing back from the man that sprawled at his feet.

The others scattered, what of them survived, save Fwar, who tried to stand his ground: a shadow moved, a flash of a bare ankle—Fwar started to turn, knife in hand, and Vanye sprang for him, but the swing of harness in Jhirun's hands was quicker. Chain whipped across Fwar's head, brought him down screaming: and in blind rage he tried to scramble up again.

Vanye reversed the blade, smashed the hilt into Fwar's skull, sprawled the man face-down in the straw. Jhirun stood hard-breathing, still clenching the chain-and-leather mass in her two hands; tears streamed down her face.

"The quake," she murmured, choking, "the rains, and the quake—oh, the dreams, the dreams, my lord, I dreamed . . ."

He snatched the harness from her hands, hurting her as he did so, and seized her by the arm. "Go," he said. "Get to horse."

It was in his mind to kill Fwar: of all others that had perished, this one he would have wished to kill, but now it was murder. He cursed Jhirun's help, knowing that he could have taken this man in clean fight, that after killing kin of his, this was the wrong man to leave alive.

Jhirun came back to his side, leading the bay mare. "Kill him," she insisted, her voice trembling.

"This is kin of yours," he said angrily—minded as the words left his mouth that she had once said something of the same to him. "Go!" he shouted at her, and jerked her horse's head about, pushed her up as she set foot in the stirrup. When she landed astride he struck the mare on the rump and sent it hence.

Then he flung open the stalls of Siptah and his own horse, dragged at their reins and led the horses down the aisle, past the bodies. His sword sheath lay atop the straw; he snatched it up and kept moving, paused only in the light of the doorway to settle his sword at his side and mount up.

The gelding surged forward: he fought to control the vile-tempered animal with the Baien stud in tow; and overtook Jhirun, who was having difficulty with the little mare in the press of the yard. Vanye shouted, cursing, spurred brutally, and the crowd parted in terror as the three horses broke through. About them, folk already streamed toward the shattered gates, their backs laden with packs, some leading animals or pulling carts. Women carried children, older children carried younger; and men struggled under unwieldy burdens that would never permit them long flight.

And from the keep itself folk came streaming out, bearing gold and all such things as were useless hereafter—men who had come to possess the treasures of Ohtij-in and stubbornly clung to them in its fall.

Morgaine stood safely by the ruin of the tower, a stationary figure amid the chaos, waiting, with solid stone at her back and *Changeling,* sheathed, in her two hands.

She saw them: and suddenly her face set in anger, such that Vanye felt the force of it to the depth of him; but when he rode to her side, ready to swear that

Jhirun's presence was no planning of his, she said not a word, only caught Siptah's reins from his hand and set her foot into the stirrup, settling herself into the saddle and at once checking the gray's forward motion. A cry went up from the crowd. A loose cow darted this way and that in bovine panic through the crowd, and the horses shied and stamped.

"Give me time," Vanye shouted at Morgaine, "to go back and free the horses in the stalls."

And of a sudden the earth heaved again, a little shudder, and a portion of the keep wall slid into ruin, another tower toppling, with terrible carnage. The horses plunged, fighting restraint. The wails of frightened people rose above the sound that faded.

From the shaken keep poured other fugitives, the *qujal*-folk, and the black robes of a priest among them—pale folk and conspicuous in the crowd, dazed, ill-clothed for the cold, save for a few house guards in their armor.

"No," Morgaine answered Vanye's appeal to her. "No. There is no lingering here. Let us go."

He did not dispute it, not with the threat of further ruin about them: his Kurshin soul agonized over the trapped horses, and over another ugliness that he had left, half-finished. The collapse of the keep would end it, he thought, burying the dead and the living, ending a thing that should have ended long ago, however the Myya had come through into this land: he took it upon his own conscience, never to tell Morgaine what was pointless to know, never to regret those several lives, that had betrayed her and tried to murder him.

The horses moved, Morgaine riding in the lead, seeking their way through the slow-moving crowd more gently than the war-trained gray would have it. Vanye kept close at Morgaine's back, watching the crowd, and once, that a sound first drew his attention in that direction, looking at Jhirun, who rode knee to knee with him. He met her eyes, shadowed and fierce, minding him how she had lately urged him to murder—this the frightened child that he had taken back with them, Myya, and living, when he would gladly have known the last of her kind dead.

With all his heart he would have ridden from her now, and with Morgaine have sought some other, unknown way from Ohtij-in; but there was none other, and the Suvoj barred their way within a few leagues. There was no haste, no need of hurrying, only sufficient to clear the walls, where yet a few desperate folk still searched for bodies beneath the massive stones, beyond help and hope.

A line of march stretched out northward from Ohtij-in; and this they joined, moving more quickly than the miserable souls that walked.

And when they were well out on the road came another rumble and shudder of the earth. Vanye turned in his saddle and others turned and looked, seeing the third tower fallen: and even as he gazed, the center of Ohtij-in sank down into ruin. The sound of it reached them a moment later, growing and dying. Jhirun cried out softly, and a wail arose from the people, a sound terrible and desolate.

"It has gone," Vanye said, sickened to the heart to think of the lives that surely were extinguished there, an unconscious enemy, and the wretched, the innocent, who would not leave off their searching.

Morgaine alone had not turned to see, but rode with her face set toward the north. "Doubtless," she said after they had ridden some distance further, "the breach at the gate removed stability for the barbican tower; and the fall of the barbican prepared the fall of the next, and so it began—else it might have gone on standing."

Her doing, who had breached the gate. Vanye heard the hollowness in her voice, and understood what misery lay beneath it. *I do not look,* she had said, *at what I leave behind me.*

He wished that he had not looked either.

The rain whispered down into the grass on the hills and into the puddles on the road, and a stream ran the course between the hills, frothing and racing over brush and obstacles. Now and again they rode past a man with his family that had wearied and sat down on the slope to rest. Sometimes they passed abandoned bundles of goods, where some man had cast them down, unable to carry them farther. And once there was an old man lying by the roadside. Vanye dismounted to see to him, but he was dead.

Jhirun hugged her shawl about her and wept. Morgaine shrugged helplessly, nodded for him to get back to horse and forget the matter.

"Doubtless others will die," she said, and that was all—no tears, no remorse.

He climbed back into the saddle and they kept moving.

Overhead the clouds had begun to show ragged rents, and one of the moons shone through in daylight, wan and white, a piece of the Broken Moon, that passed more quickly than the others; the vast terror that was Li had yet to come.

The hills cut them off from view of what lay behind, gray-green hills that opened constantly before them and closed behind; and gradually their steady pace brought them to the head of the long line of weary folk. They rode slowly there, for there was nowhere to go but where the column went, and no profit in opening a wide lead.

They were first to reach the hillside that overlooked the lately flooded plain, the rift of the Suvoj, where still great pools showed pewter faces to the clouded sky, small lakes, rocks that upthrust strange shapes, stone more solid than the water had yet availed to wear away; it was a bleak and dead place, stretching far to the other hills, but the road went through it until the river, and there the stones made only a ripple under the surface of the flood.

A stench went up from the rotting land, the smell of the sea mingled with dying things. Vanye swore in disgust when the wind carried it to them, and when he looked toward the horizon he saw that the hills ended and melted into gray, that was the edge of the world.

"The tide comes in here," murmured Jhirun. "It overcomes the river, as it does the Aj."

"And goes out again," said Morgaine, "tonight."

"It may be," said Jhirun, "it may be. Already it is on the ebb."

The noise of others intruded on them, the advance of the column that came blindly in their wake. Morgaine glanced over her shoulder, reined Siptah about, yet holding him.

"This hill is ours," she said fiercely. "And company will not be comfortable for us. Vanye—come, let us stop them."

She led Siptah forward, toward the van of the column, that were strong men, Aren-folk, who had fled early and marched most strongly: and Vanye slung his sword across the saddle-bow and kept pace with her, a shadow by her side as she gave orders, directed sullen, confused men to one side and the other of the road, bidding them set up shelters and make a camp.

Two of the Barrows-men were there, grim, tall men: Vanye noticed them standing together and cast them a second, anxious look, wondering had they been two of the number with Fwar—or whether they were innocent of that ambush and did not yet know the bloodfeud that was between them. They gave no evidence of it.

But there was yet another matter astir among them, sullen looks toward the hill where Jhirun waited, standing by the bay mare, her shawl clutched about her in the cold, damp wind.

"She is ours," one of the two Barrowers said to Morgaine.

Morgaine said nothing, only looked at him from the-height-of Siptah's back, and that man fell silent.

Only Vanye, who rode at her back, heard the murmuring that followed when Morgaine turned away; and it was ugly. He turned his horse again and faced them, the two Barrows-men, and a handful of marshlanders.

"Say it louder," he challenged them.

"The girl is fey," said one of the marshlanders. "Ela's-daughter. She cursed Chadrih, and it fell. The quake and the flood took it."

"And Barrows-hold," said one of the Barrows-men. "Now Ohtij-in."

"She brought the enemy into Barrows-hold," said the other of the Barrowers. "She is fey. She cursed the hold, killed all that were in it, the old, the women and the children, her own sister. Give her to us."

Vanye hesitated, the gelding restless under him, misgivings gathering in him, remembering the dream upon the road, the mad-eyed vagaries, the tense body pressed against his.

Oh, the dreams, the dreams, my lord, I dreamed. . . .

He jerked the gelding's head about, spurred him past their reaching hands, sought Morgaine, who moved alone among the crowds, giving orders. He joined her, saying nothing; she asked nothing.

A camp began to take shape, makeshift huddles of stitched skins and brush and sodden blankets tied between trees or supported on hewn saplings. Some had brought fire, and one borrowed to the next, wet wood smoking and hissing in the mist, but sufficient to stay alight.

The column was still straggling in at dusk, finding a camp, finding their places in it, seeking relatives.

Morgaine turned back to the hill that she had chosen, where she had permitted no intrusion; and there Jhirun waited, shivering, with wood she had gathered for a fire. Vanye dismounted, already searching out with his eye this and that tree that might be cut for shelter. But Morgaine slid down from Siptah's back and stared balefully at the flood that raged between them and the other side, dark waters streaked with white in the dusk.

"It is lower," she said, pointing to the place where the road made a white-frothing ridge in the flood. "We might try it after we have rested a bit."

The thought chilled him. "The horses cannot force that. Wait. Wait. It cannot be much longer."

She stood looking at it still, as if she would disregard all his advice, staring toward that far bank, where mountains rose, where was Roh, and Abarais, and a halfling army.

The flood would not be sufficient to have delayed Roh this long; Vanye reckoned that for himself, and did not torment her with asking or saying it. She was desperate, exhausted; she had spent herself in answering questions among the frightened folk behind them, in providing advice, in settling disputes for space and wood. She had distracted herself with these things, gentle when he sensed in her a dark and furious violence, that loathed the clinging, terrified appeals to her, the faces that looked to her with desperate hope.

"Take us with you," they wept, surrounding her.

"Where is my child?" a mother kept asking her, clinging to the rein until the nervous, war-trained gray came near to breaking control.

"I do not know," she had said. But it had not stopped the questions.

"Will my daughter be there?" asked a father, and she had looked at him, distracted, and murmured *yes,* and spurred the gray roughly through the press.

Now she stood holding her cloak about her against the chill and staring at the river as at a living enemy. Vanye watched her, not moving, dreading that mood of hers that slipped nearer and nearer to irrationality.

"We camp," she said after a time.

⌁ Chapter 14

There was one mercy shown them that evening. The rain stopped. The sky tore to rags and cleared, though it remained damp everywhere, and the smoke of hundreds of fires rolled up and hung like an ugly mist over the camp. Scarred Li rose, vast and horrid, companionless now. The other moons had fled; and Anli and demon Sith lagged behind.

They rested, filled with food that Morgaine had put in her saddlebags. They sat in a shelter of saplings and brush, with a good fire before them; and Jhirun sat beside them, eating her share of the provisions with such evident hunger that Morgaine tapped her on the arm and put another bit of bread into her lap, charity that amazed Jhirun and Vanye alike.

"I have not lacked," Morgaine said with a shrug—for it must come from someone's share.

"She hid in the stable," Vanye said quietly, for Morgaine had never asked: and that lack of questions worried at him, implying anger, a mood in which Morgaine herself was unwilling to discuss the matter. "That was why your searchers could not find her."

Morgaine only looked at him, with that impenetrable stare, so that he wondered for a moment had there been searchers at all, or only inquiry.

But Morgaine had promised him; he thrust the doubt from his mind, effort though it needed.

"Jhirun," Morgaine said suddenly. Jhirun swallowed a bit of bread as if it had gone dry, and only slightly turned her head, responding to her. "Jhirun, there are kinsmen of yours here."

Jhirun nodded, and her eyes slid uneasily toward Morgaine, wary and desperate.

"They came to Aren," Morgaine said, "hunting you. And you are known there. There are some Aren-folk who know your name and say that you are halfling yourself, and in some fashion they blame you for some words you spoke against their village."

"Lord," Jhirun said in a thin voice, and edged against Vanye, as if he could prevent such questions. He sat stiffly, uncomfortable in the touch of her.

"A quake," said Morgaine, "struck Hiuaj after we three parted company.

There was heavy damage at Aren, where I was; and the Barrows-folk came then. They said there was nothing left of Barrows-hold."

Jhirun shivered.

"I know," said Morgaine, "that you cannot seek safety among your own kinsmen . . . or with the Aren-folk. Better that you had remained lost, Jhirun Ela's-daughter. They have asked me for you, and I have refused; but that is for now. Vanye knows—he will tell you—that I am not generous. I am not at all generous. And there will come a time when we cannot shelter you. I do not care what quarrel drove you out of Barrows-hold in the first place; it does not concern me. I do not think that you are dangerous; but your enemies are. And for that reason you are not welcome with us. You have a horse. You have half our food, if you wish it; Vanye and I can manage. And you would be wise to take that offer and try some other route through these hills, be it to hide and live in some cave for the rest of your days. Go. Seek some place after the Ohtija have dispersed. Go into those mountains and look for some place that has no knowledge of you. That is my advice to you."

Jhirun's hand crept to Vanye's arm. "Lord," she said faintly, plaintively.

"There was a time," Vanye said, hardly above a breath, "when Jhirun did not say what she might have said, when she did not say all that she knew of you, and stayed by me when it was not convenient. And I will admit to you that I gave her a promise . . . I know—that I had no right to give any promise, and she should not have believed me, but she did not know that. I have told her that she should not have believed me; but would it be so wrong, *liyo*, to let her go where we go? I do not know what other hope she has."

Morgaine stared at him fixedly, and for a long, interminably long moment, said nothing. "Thee says correctly," she breathed at last. "Thee had no right."

"All the same," he said, very quietly, "I ask it, because I told her that I would take her to safety."

Morgaine turned that gaze on Jhirun. "Run away," she said. "I give you a better gift than he gave. But on his word, stay, if you have not the sense to take it. Unlike Vanye, I bind myself to nothing. Come with us as long as you can, and for as long as it pleases me."

"Thank you," Jhirun said almost soundlessly, and Vanye pressed her arm, disengaging it from his. "Go aside," he said to her. "Rest. Let matters alone now."

Jhirun drew away from them, stood up, left the shelter for the brush, beyond the firelight. They were alone. Across the camp sounded the wail of an infant, the lowing of an animal, the sounds that had been constant all the evening.

"I am sorry," Vanye said, bowed himself to the ground, expected even then her anger, or worse, her silence.

"I was not there," Morgaine said quietly. "I take your word for what you did, and why. I will try. She will stay our pace or she will not; I cannot help her. *That*—" She gestured with a glance toward the camp. "That also has its desires, that are Jhirun's."

"They believe," he said, "that there is a way out for them. That it lies through the Wells. That they will find a land on the other side."

She said nothing to that.

"*Liyo*—" he said carefully, "you could do that—you could give them what they believe—could you not?"

A tumult had arisen, as others had arisen throughout the evening, on the far side of the camp, distant shouts carrying to them: disputes, dissents, among terrified people.

Morgaine set her face and shook her head abruptly. "I could, yes, but I will not."

"You know why they have followed you. You know that."

"I care nothing for their beliefs. I will not."

He thought of the falling towers of Ohtij-in: *only a hand's breadth closer to the sea.* Jhirun had laughed, attempting humor. Somewhere the child was still crying. Among the rabble there were the innocent, the harmless.

"Their land," he said, "is dying. It will come in the lifetime of some that are now alive. And to open the Gates for them—would that not—?"

"Their time is finished, that is all. It comes to all worlds."

"In Heaven's good name, *liyo*—"

"Vanye. Where should we take them?"

He shook his head helplessly. "Are we not to leave this land?"

"There are no sureties beyond any Gate."

"But if there is no other hope for them—"

Morgaine set *Changeling* across her knees. The dragon eyes of the hilt winked gold in the firelight, and she traced the scales with her fingers. "Two months ago, Vanye, where were you?"

He blinked, mind thrust back across Gates, across mountains: a road to Aenor, a winter storm. "I was an outlaw," he said, uncertain what he was bidden remember, "and the Myya were close on my trail."

"And four?"

"The same." He laughed uneasily. "My life was much of the same, just then."

"I was in Koris," she said. "Think of it."

Laughter perished in him, in a dizzying gap of a hundred years. Irien: massacre—ancestors of his had served Morgaine's cause in Koris, and they were dust. "But it *was* a hundred years, all the same," he said. "You slept; however you remember it, it was still a hundred years, and what you remember cannot change that."

"No. Gates are outside time. Nothing is fixed. And in this land—once—an unused Gate was flung wide open, uncontrolled, and poured men through into a land that was not theirs. That was not *theirs,* Vanye. And they took that land . . . men that speak a common tongue with Andur-Kursh; that remember *me.*"

He sat very still, the pulse beating in his temples until he was aware of little else. "I knew," he said at last, "that it might be; that Jhirun and her kindred are Myya."

"You did not tell me this."

"I did not know how. I did not know how to put it together; I thought how things would stray the Gate into Andur-Kursh, lost—to die there; and could not men—"

"Who remember *me,* Vanye."

He could not answer; he saw her fold her arms about her knees, hands locked, and bow her head, heard her murmur something in that tongue that was hers, shaking her head in despair.

"It was a thousand years," he objected.

"There is no time between Gates," she answered him with an angry frown; and saw his puzzlement, his shake of the head, and relented. "It makes no difference. They have had their time, both those that were born to this land and those that invaded it. It is gone. For all of them, it is gone."

Vanye frowned, found a stick in his hands, and broke it, once, twice, a third time, measured cracks. He cast the bits into the fire. "They will starve before they drown. The mountains will give them ground whereon to stand, but the stones will not feed them. Would it be wrong, *liyo,* would it be wrong—once, to help them?"

"As once before it happened here? Whose land, shall I give them, Vanye?"

He did not have an answer. He drew a breath and in it was the stench of the rotting land. Down in the camp the tumult had never ceased. Shrieks suddenly pierced the heavier sounds, seeming closer.

Morgaine looked in that direction and frowned. "Jhirun has been gone overlong."

His thoughts leaped in the same direction. "She would have had more sense," he said, gathering himself to his feet; but in his mind was the girl's distraught mood, Morgaine's words to her, his dismissal of her. The horses grazed, the bay mare with them, still saddled, although the girths were loosened.

Morgaine arose, touched his arm. "Stay. If she has gone, well sped; she survives too well to fear she would have gone that way."

The shouting drew nearer: there was the sound of horses on the road, of wild voices attending. Vanye swore, and started of a sudden for their own horses. There was no time left: riders were coming up their very hill, horses struggling on the wet slope.

And Jhirun raced into the firelight, a wild flash of limbs and ragged skirts. The riders came up after, white-haired lord and two white-haired house guards.

Jhirun raced for the shelter, as Vanye slipped the ring of his longsword and took it in hand: but Morgaine was before him. Red fire leaped from her hand, touching smoke in the drenched grass. Horses shied: Kithan—first of the three—flung up his arm against the sight and reined back, stopping his men.

And at that distance he faced Morgaine. He shouted a word in his own tongue at her, in an ugly voice, and then in a shriek of desperation: "Stop them, stop them!"

"From what," she asked, "Kithan?"

"They have murdered us," the *qujal* cried, his voice shaking. "The others— stop them; you have the power to stop them if you will."

There was ugly murmuring in the camp; they could hear it even here: it grew nearer—men, coming toward the slope.

"Get the horses," Morgaine said.

Two lights appeared behind the screen of young trees, lights that moved; and a dark mass moved behind them. The halflings turned to look, terror in their faces. Vanye spun about, encountered Jhirun, seized her and thrust her again toward the shelter. "Pick up everything!" he shouted into her dazed face.

She moved, seized up blankets, everything that lay scattered, while he ran for the horses, adjusted harness, that of their own horses and Jhirun's bay mare as well. The stubborn gelding shied as he started to mount: he seized the saddlehorn and swung up in a maneuver he had hardly used since he was a boy, armored as he was: and he saw to his horror that Morgaine had made herself a shield for the three *qujal*, they at her back, the mob advancing not rapidly, but with mindless force.

He grasped Siptah's reins, leaning from the saddle, and spurred forward, through the *qujal*, reined in with Siptah just behind Morgaine.

She stood still, with him at her back; and faced the oncoming men afoot. Vanye stared at what came, panic surging in him, memory of the courtyard—of a beast without reason in it.

And in the torchlight at the head of them he saw Barrows-folk, and Fwar . . . Fwar, his scarred face no better for a dark slash across it. They came with knives and with staves; and with them, panting in his haste, came the priest Ginun.

"*Liyo!*" Vanye said, with all the force in him. "To horse!"

She moved, questioning nothing, turned and sprang to the saddle in a single move. He kept his eye on Fwar in that instant, and saw murder there. In the next moment Morgaine had swung Siptah around to face them, curbing him hard, so that he shied up a little. She unhooked *Changeling*, held it across the saddlebow.

"Halflings!" someone shouted, like a curse; but from other quarters within the mob there were outcries of terror.

Morgaine rode Siptah a little distance across the face of the crowd, and paced him back again, a gesture of arrogance; and still they feared her, and gave back, keeping the line she drew.

"Fwar!" she cried aloud. "Fwar! What is it you want?"

"Him!" cried Fwar, a beast-shout of rage. "Him, who killed Ger and Awan and Efwy."

"You led us here," shouted one of the sons of Haz. "You have no intention of helping us. It was a lie. You will ruin the Wells and ruin us. If this is not so, tell us."

And there arose a bawling of fear from the crowd, a voice as from open throat, frightening in its intensity. They began to press forward.

A rider broke through the *qujal* from the rear: Vanye jerked his head about, saw Jhirun, a great untidy bundle on the saddle before her, saw the dark arm of the mob that had broken through the woods attempting to encircle them; Jhirun cried warning of it.

In blind instinct Vanye whirled in the other direction—saw a knife leave Fwar's hand. He flung up his arm: it hit the leather and fell in the mud, under his hooves. Jhirun's cry of warning still rang in his ears.

The mob surged forward and Morgaine retreated. Vanye ripped out his sword, and fire burned from Morgaine's hand, felling one of the Barrowers. The front rank wavered with an outcry of horror.

"Angharan!" someone cried; and some tried to flee, abandoning their weapons and their courage; but weapons were hurled from another quarter, stones. Siptah shied and screamed shrilly.

"Lord!" Jhirun cried; Vanye reined about as Shiua came at them, seeking to attack the horses. The gelding shied back, and Vanye laid about him with desperate blows, the *qujal* striking what barehanded blows they could.

Vanye did not turn to see what had befallen his liege; he had enemies of hers enough before him. He wielded the longsword with frenzied strength, spurred the gelding recklessly into the attackers and scattered their undisciplined ranks, only then daring turn, hearing screams behind him.

Bodies lay thickly on the slope; fires burned here and there in the brush; the mob broke in flight, scattering down the hillside in advance of Siptah's charge.

And Morgaine did not cease: Vanye spurred the gelding and followed her, blind to tactic and strategy save the realization that she wanted the road, wanted the hill clear of them.

Folk screamed and scattered before them, and Vanye felt the gelding avoid a body that had fallen before him, then recover and stretch out running as they gained the level ground, the *qujalin* road. Morgaine turned, heading out for the causeway across the Suvoj, scattering screaming enemies that had turned the wrong way.

On either side stretched flooded land, a vast expanse of shallow water, and the road ran as a narrow thread across it, toward the flooded crossing, where water swirled darkly over the stones. Here, well out upon that roadway, Morgaine stopped, and he with her, reining about as four riders came after them to the same desperate refuge—three terrified *qujal* and a Barrows-girl, this all their strength, and the roar of the Suvoj at their backs.

On the hillside that they had left, the Hiua regrouped, gathering their forces and their courage, and there was much of shouting and crying. Torches were waved. The glow of fire lit the center of their rallying place, and on that hillside was a tree, from which dangled objects—the aspect of which filled Vanye with apprehension.

"They have hanged them!" Kithan cried in anguish.

But neither Kithan nor his two men ventured forward against those odds. *His people,* Vanye understood, reckoning the number of dangling corpses against his memory of the band of *qujal* that had fled crumbling Ohtij-in, a pitiable group, among them women and old ones. *Qujal* they might be, but bile rose in his throat as he gazed on that sight.

And of a sudden came a shout from that gathering by the tree, and the wave of a torch, exhorting a new attack against them.

"Get back," Morgaine bade their companions; and the rush came, a dark surge of bodies pouring out onto the causeway. *Changeling* came free of its sheath, opal color flickering up and down its blade, that ominous darkness howling at its tip, and the first attacker mad enough to fling himself at Morgaine entered that dark and whirled shrieking away within it, sucked into that oblivion.

The mob did not retreat. Others swept against them, wild-eyed and howling their desperation. Vanye laid about him with his sword, reining tightly to keep the gelding from being pushed over the brink.

And suddenly those men that attacked him were alone. Morgaine spurred Siptah into that oncoming horde, swept the terrible blade in an arc that became vacant of enemies and corpses, a crescent that widened.

With a shout she rode farther, driving them in retreat before her, taking any man that delayed, the blade flickering with the cold opal fire, slow and leisurely as it took man after man into that void, dealing no wound, sparing none.

"*Liyo!*" Vanye cried, and spurred after her, shouldering a screaming marshlander over the brink. "*Liyo!*" He rode to land's edge; and there perhaps his voice first reached her. She reined about, and he saw the arc of the sword, the sudden eclipse of the light as it swung toward him. He reined over, hard, and the gelding slid on the wet stones, skidding. He recovered. The horse trembled and fretted under him, Morgaine's wild face staring at him in the balefire of *Changeling.*

"Put it up," he urged her in what of a voice remained to him. "No more. No more."

"Get back."

"No!" he cried at her. But she would not listen to him: she turned Siptah's head toward the people that gathered on the hillside, and spurred forward onto the muddy earth. Women and children cried out and ran, and men held their ground desperately, but she came no farther, circling back and forth, back and forth.

"*Liyo!*" Vanye screamed at her; and when she would not come, he rode forward, carefully, reining in a few paces behind, where he was safe from her as well as from the enemy.

She stopped, sat her horse facing the great empty space that she had made between the causeway and their attackers. There was, after that confusion and madness, a terrible silence made. And she kept the sword unsheathed, waiting, while time passed and the silence continued.

A voice broke the stillness, distant and its owner well hidden in the darkness. There were curses spoken against her, who had deceived them; there were viler things shouted. She did not move, nor seem provoked, although at some of the words Vanye trembled with rage and wished the man within reach. Almost he answered back himself; but something there was about Morgaine's silence and waiting against which such words, either attacking or defending, were empty. He had held *Changeling*: he knew the agony that grew in one's arm after long wielding of it, the drain upon one's very soul. She did not move, and the voice grew still.

And at last Vanye gathered his resolve and toed the gelding forward. "*Liyo,*" he said, so that she would know that it was he. She did not protest his approach now; nor did she turn her head from the darkness she was watching.

"It is enough," he urged her quietly. "*Liyo*—put it away."

She gave no answer, nor moved for a time. Then she lifted *Changeling* so that the darkness at its tip aimed toward the huddle of tents and shelters, and that one great tree, whereon corpses dangled and twisted above a dying fire.

And then she lowered her arm, as if the weight of the sword suddenly grew too much. "Take it," she said hoarsely.

He eased close to her, stretched out both his hands and gently disengaged her rigid fingers from the dragon grip, taking it into his own hand. The evil of it ran through his bones and into his brain, so that his eyes blurred and his senses wavered.

She did not offer him the sheath, which was all that might damp its fires and render it harmless. She did not speak.

"Go back," he said. "I will watch them now."

But she did not answer or offer to move. She sat, straight and silent, beside him—believing, he was sure, that did it come to using the sword he had less willingness than she; lives and nations were on her conscience. His crimes were on a human scale.

And they sat their horses side by side, the two of them, until he found the sword making his arm ache, until the pain of it was hard to bear. He counted only his breaths, and watched the slow passage of Li's descent; and the horses grew weary and restless under them.

From the camp there was no stirring.

"Give it back," Morgaine said at last; he did so, terrified in the passing of it, the least touch of it fatal. But her hand was strong and sure as she received it.

He looked behind him, at the rift of the Suvoj, where the others waited. "The waters are lower," he said. And after a moment: "The Hiua will not dare come. They have given up. Put it away."

"Go," she said; and harshly: "*Go back!*"

He drew his horse's head about and rode back to the others, the *qujal* at one side of the roadway, Jhirun at the other, holding the mare's reins as she sat on the stone edge.

And the girl gathered herself up as she saw him coming, staggered with exhaustion as she went forward to meet him. "Lord," she said, holding the gelding's reins to claim his attention, "lord, the halflings say we might perhaps cross. They are talking of trying it." There was a wild, desperate grief in her face, like something graven there, incapable of changing. "Lord—will she let us go?"

"Go, now," he bade her on his own, for there was no reasoning with Morgaine; and as he sat watching them mount up and begin to take their horses out onto that dangerous passage, he was dismayed at his own callousness, that he could send men and a woman ahead to probe the way for his liege—in his place, because she valued him and not them.

Such he began to be, obedient to Morgaine. He made his heart cold, though his throat was tight with shame for himself, watching those four lone figures struggling across that dangerous flooded stonework.

And when he saw that they were well past the halfway point and still able to proceed, he turned and rode back to Morgaine's side.

"Now," he said hoarsely. "Now, *liyo*. We can cross."

ꕥ Chapter 15

Vanye set himself in the lead, riding the skittish gelding toward the rift that thundered and echoed with flood. The retreating water had left the land glittering with water under the moon. A number of uprooted trees lay about the pool-studded plain, several having rammed the causeway, creating heaps of brush that loomed up on the side where the current had been, skeletal masses festooned with strings of dead grasses and leaves.

Then the causeway arched higher above the rocky shelf, pierced by spans above the water: a bridge that extended in vast arches out across the rift.

Please Heaven, Vanye thought, contemplating what lay before them, *let the earth stay still now.* The horse slowed, sidestepping; he touched it with his heels gently and kept it moving.

The current thundered and boiled through the spans that had lately been entirely submerged. Vast megaliths formed that structure, that as yet neither quake had dislodged nor flood eroded. A tree hung on the edge of the roadway, itself dwarfed by the spans, so that it seemed only some dangling bit of brush, but its roots thrust up taller than horse and rider. Vanye avoided looking directly down into the current, that dizzied the senses—save once: saw the waters sweeping down on the one side and through into endless water on the other, an expanse that seemed to embrace all creation. In the midst of it hung the thread of the bridge, and themselves small and lost amid the crash and roar that flung up spray as a mist about them.

He turned his head—suddenly, unreasoningly anxious about Morgaine, at once comforted to know her close behind him. She bore *Changeling* sheathed at her shoulders; her pale hair seemed to glow in the half-light, whipped on the wind as she also turned to look back.

Torches massed at the beginning of the causeway, like so many stars flickering there, beginning to stream out onto it.

What they had loosed on Ohtij-in was still following them, violent and desperate. Morgaine turned forward again; so did he, anxious for their safety on the bridge. The roadway was wide: it would have been possible to run, but the roar of the water and the sight of it had the animals wild-eyed with distress. It was not a place to let them go.

Yet ahead the small party with Jhirun had left the bridge, even now riding the security of the farther causeway and climbing the slope of the far-side road.

Dawn grew as they traversed that last, agonizingly slow distance; light showed them the way ahead more clearly, and the river had sunk yet more, so that it was worse to look down, where white froth rumbled and boiled about the arches of *qujalin* design and vast size, the water slipping down into a chasm as the Suvoj became a river and no longer a sea.

The brink of the far cliff came within reach. Vanye spurred his horse and it began to gather speed, sending a scatter of water from an occasional puddle. At the last he cast a look over his shoulder, obsessed with the dread that Morgaine might decide to turn and finish on that dizzying bridge what she had begun—for safety's sake.

She did not. Siptah likewise leaned into a run, following, and Vanye turned his face again, seeing the safety of the mountains ahead, a rise in the stone road that bore them upward to the hills.

To Abarais.

The dawn, breaking over the long slash of the Suvoj, showed a road well-kept that ascended steadily among the hills. For a time they rode hard, until they were within a stone's cast of the *qujal* and of Jhirun, and found leisure to walk their horses, until they had caught their breath.

Jhirun, riding somewhat apart from the halflings, looked back as if she might rein back and join them . . . but she did not; nor did the halflings.

Then of a sudden Morgaine laid heels to Siptah and rode through, startling the weary party and starting the horses to running again, along the ascending road among the hills. Vanye, staying with her, felt the fading strength of the Andurin gelding and the unsureness in his stride, the animal's shoulders slick with sweat and froth; and by now the others were dropping behind, their horses spent.

"For pity," he shouted across at Morgaine, when the gelding's bravest effort could not keep stride, burdened with a man's weight; and the Baien gray was drenched with sweat. "*Liyo,* the horses—enough."

She yielded, slowed; the horses walked again, their breath coming in great lung-tearing puffs, and Morgaine turned in the saddle to look back—not, it was likely, at the *qujal,* who struggled to stay with them, but dreading the appearance of others on the road behind them.

The light grew, flung misty peaks into outline, a central body of mountains rounded and clustered together, a last refuge. There was a desolation about them that struck to the heart. Vanye recalled the vast chains of his own mountains, reaching sharp ridges at the sky, stretching as far as the eye could see and the heart could imagine. Of these there was immediate beginning and end, and they had a blurred, aged quality, weathering that was of many ages, a yielding likewise toward the sea.

Yet on the hillsides began to be signs of habitations, fields under cultivation, protected by terraces, and stonework to carry away the flooding: recent works, the hand of farmers, small fields and orchards that were flooded in many areas, but a sign that here lay the true strength of Shiuan, a still-solid wealth that had supported the glittering lords and the humanity that had crowded within their walls.

And on the crest of a long hill, from which it was possible to see the road in all directions, Morgaine reined in, leaned on the saddlebow a moment, then dismounted. Vanye did likewise, himself aching in all his bones, and took Siptah's reins from her nerveless hand.

She stared past him, down the long road where the halflings were only beginning that hill. "A time to rest," she said.

"Aye," he agreed gladly enough, and busied himself loosening girths and slipping bits to ease the horses, tending to them while Morgaine withdrew a little to that rocky upthrust that was the cap of the hill, where flat stones afforded a place to sit other than the damp earth.

He finished his task, and brought the flask of Hiua liquor and a wrapped bit of food, and offered them to her, hoping against expectation to the contrary that she would accept them. She sat with *Changeling* unhooked and leaning against her shoulder, her right arm cradled in her lap in an attitude of evident pain; but she lifted her head and bestirred herself to take a share of what he offered, as much to avoid dispute with him, he thought, as because she had appetite for anything. He drank and ate a few mouthfuls himself; and by this time the halflings were drawing near them, with Jhirun lagging far behind.

"*Liyo,*" Vanye said carefully, "we would do well to take what chance we have to rest now. We have pushed the horses almost as far as possible. We are climbing; there looks to be more of it, and there may be a time ahead that speed will serve us better than it does now."

She nodded, mutely accepting his argument, whether or not it coincided with her own reasons. Her eyes were void of interest in what passed about her. He heard the approach of the halflings with a private anguish, not wanting strangers near her when this mood was on her. He had seen it before, that soulless energy that seized her and kept her moving, responding only to the necessity that drove her. At the moment she was lost . . . knew him, perhaps, or confused him with men long since dust; the time was short for her, who had passed Gate and Gate and Gate in her course, and confounded then and now, who but months ago had ridden into a war in which his ancestors had died.

A hundred years lay in that gap for him. For Jhirun. . . . He gazed upon her distant figure with a sudden and terrible understanding. A thousand years. He could not conceive of a thousand years. A hundred were sufficient to bring a man to dust; five hundred reached into a time when nothing had stood in Morija.

Morgaine had ridden across a century to enter his age, had gathered him to her, and together they had crossed into a place a thousand years removed from Jhirun's beginnings, whose ancestors lay entombed in the Barrows . . . men that Morgaine might have known, young, and powerful in that age of the world.

He had crossed such a gap, not alone of place, but of time.

O God, his lips shaped.

Nothing that he had known existed. Men, kinsmen, all that he had ever known was aged, decayed, gone to sifting dust. He knew then what he had done, passing the Gate. It was irrevocable. He wanted to pour out questions to Morgaine, to have them answered, to know beyond doubt what things she had never told him, for pity.

But the *qujal* were with them. Horses drew up on the margin. Lord Kithan, armorless, bareheaded, swung down from his saddle and walked toward them with one of his men, while the other attended the horses.

Vanye rose and slipped the ring that held his sword at his shoulder, setting himself between Kithan and Morgaine; and Kithan stopped—no longer the elegant lord, Kithan: his thin face was weary; his shoulders sagged. Kithan lifted a hand, gestured no wish to contend, then sank down on a flat stone some distance from Morgaine; his men likewise settled to the ground, pale heads bowed, exhausted.

Jhirun rode in among the *qujal's* horses, slid from the saddle and held to it. In a moment she made the effort to loosen the girth of her horse, then led the animal to a patch of grass, too unsure of it to let it go. She sat down, holding the reins in her lap, and stayed apart from them all, tired, seeming terrified of everything and everyone about her.

"Let go the reins," Vanye advised her. "The mare will likely stand, with other horses about; she has run too far to be interested in running."

And he held out his hand, bidding her to them; Jhirun came, and sank down on the bare ground, arms wrapped about her knees and her head bowed. Morgaine took note of her presence, a stare she might have given one of the animals, disinterested. Vanye settled his back against a rock, his own head throbbing with lack of sleep and the conviction that the earth still lurched and swayed with the motion of the horse.

He dared not sleep. He watched the halflings from slitted eyes until the rest had at least given him space to breathe, and until thirst became an overwhelming discomfort.

He rose, went back to his horse and took the waterflask that hung from the saddlebow, drank, keeping an eye to the *qujal,* who did not stir. Then he slung it over his shoulder and returned, pausing to take from Jhirun's saddle the awkward bundle she had made of their blankets.

He cast the bundle down where he had been sitting, to remake it properly; and he offered the flask to Morgaine, who took it gratefully, drank and passed it to Jhirun.

One of the *qujal* moved; Vanye turned, hand on his sword, and saw one of the house guards on his feet. The *qujal* came toward them, grim of face and careful in his movements; and he addressed himself to Jhirun, who had the waterflask. He held out his hand toward it, demanding, insolent.

Jhirun hesitated, looking for direction; and Vanye sullenly nodded consent, watching as the halfling took the flask and brought it back to Kithan. The halfling lord drank sparingly, then gave it to his men, who likewise drank in their turn.

Then the same man brought it back, offered it to Vanye's hand. Vanye stood, jaw set in a scowl, and nodded toward Jhirun, from whom the man had taken it. He gave it back to her, looked again to Vanye with a guarded expression.

And inclined his head—courtesy, from a *qujal*. Vanye stiffly returned the gesture, with no grace in it.

The man returned to his lord. Vanye grasped the ring at his shoulder, drew it down to hook it, then settled again at Morgaine's feet.

"Rest," he bade her. "I will watch."

Morgaine wrapped herself in her cloak and leaned against the rocks, closing her eyes. Quietly Jhirun curled up to sleep; and likewise Kithan and his men, the frail *qujal*-lord pillowing his head on his arms, and in all likelihood suffering somewhat from the wind, in his thin hall garments.

It grew still, in all the world only the occasional sound of the horses, and the wind that sighed through the leaves. Vanye gathered himself to his feet and stood with his back against a massive rock, so that he might not yield to sleep unknowing. Once he did catch himself with his eyes closed, and paced, his knees weak with exhaustion, so long as he could bear it: he was, Kurshin-fashion, able to sleep in the saddle, far better than Morgaine.

But there was a limit. "*Liyo,*" he said after a time, in desperation, and she wakened. "We might move on," he said; and she gazed at him, who was unsteady with weariness, and shook her head. "Rest," she said, and he cast himself down on the cold earth, the world still seeming to move with the endless motion of the horse. It was not long that he needed, only a time to let the misery leave his back and arm, and the throbbing leave his skull.

Someone moved. Vanye wakened with the sun on him, found the *qujal* awake and the day declined to afternoon. Morgaine sat as she had been, with *Changeling* cradled against her shoulder. When he looked up at her, there was a clarity to her gray eyes that had been lacking before, a clear and quiet sense that comforted him.

"We will be moving," Morgaine said, and Jhirun stirred from her sleep, holding her head in her hands. Morgaine passed him the flask; he sipped at it enough to clear his mouth, and swallowed with a grimace, gave it back to her.

"Draw breath," she bade him, when he would have risen at once to see to the horses. Such patience was unlike her. He saw the look of concentration in her gaze, that rested elsewhere, and followed it to the halflings.

He watched Kithan, who with trembling hands had taken an embroidered handkerchief from his pocket, and extracted from it a small white object that he placed in his mouth.

For a moment Kithan leaned forward, head in hands, white hair falling to hide his face; then with a movement more graceful, he flung his head back and restored his handkerchief to its place within his garment.

"*Akil*," Morgaine murmured privately.

"*Liyo?*"

"A vice evidently not confined to the marshlands. Another matter of trade, I do suppose . . . the marshlands' further revenge on Ohtij-in. He should be placid and communicative for hours."

Vanye watched the halfling lord, whose manner soon began to take on that languid abstraction he had seen in hall, that haze-eyed distance from the world. Here was Bydarra's true, his *qujalin* son, the heir that surely the old lord would have preferred above Hetharu; but Kithan had arranged otherwise, a silent abdication, not alone from the defense he might have been to his father and his house, but from all else that surrounded him. Vanye regarded the man with disgust.

But neither, he thought suddenly, had Kithan resorted to it last night, when a mob had murdered his people before his eyes; not then nor, he much suspected, despite what he had seen in that cell—had Kithan taken to it the hour that Bydarra was murdered, when he had been compelled to pay homage to his brother, stumbling when he tried to rise: his recovery after Hetharu's departure from Ohtij-in had been instant, as if it were a different man.

The *akil* was real enough; but it was also a convenient pose, a means of camouflage and survival: Vanye well understood the intrigues of a divided house. It might have begun in boredom, in the jaded tastes and narrow limits of Ohtij-in; or otherwise.

I dreamed, Jhirun had wept, who looked further than the day, and could not bear what she saw. She had fled to Shiuan in hope; for the Shiua lord, there was nowhere to flee.

Vanye stared at him, trying to penetrate that calm that insulated him, trying to reckon how much was the man and how much the *akil*—and which it was that had stood within his cell that night in Ohtij-in, coldly planning his murder only to spite Hetharu, by means doubtless lingering and painful.

And Morgaine took them, Kithan and his men, who had no reason to wish her well: she delayed for them, while the halfling lord retreated into his dreams: he chafed at this, vexed even in their company.

"This road," Morgaine said suddenly, addressing Kithan, "goes most directly to Abarais."

Kithan agreed with a languorous nod of his head.

"There is none other," said Morgaine, "unmapped in your books."

"None horses might use," said Kithan. "The mountains are twisted, full of stonefalls and the like; and of lakes; of chasms. There is only this way, save for men afoot, and no quicker than we go. You do not have to worry for the rabble behind us, but," he added with a heavy-lidded smile of amusement, "you have the true lord of Ohtij-in ahead of you, with the main part of our strength, a-horse and armed, a mark less easy than I was in Ohtij-in. And they may afford you some little inconvenience."

"To be sure," said Morgaine.

Kithan smiled, resting his elbows on the shelf of rock at his back; his pale eyes fixed upon her with that accustomed distance, unreachable. The men that were with him were alike as brothers, pale hair drawn back at the nape, the same profile, men dark-eyed, alike in armor, alike in attitude, one to his right, one to his left.

"Why are you with us?" Vanye asked. "Misplaced trust?"

Kithan's composure suffered the least disturbance; a frown passed over his face. His eyes fixed on Vanye's with obscure challenge, and a languid pale hand, cuffed in delicate lace, gestured toward his heart. "On your pleasure, Barrows-lord."

"You are mistaken," Vanye said.

"Why," asked Morgaine very softly, "*are* you with us, my lord Kithan, once of Ohtij-in?"

Kithan tossed his head back and gave a silent and mirthless laugh, moved his wrist in the direction of the Suvoj. "We have little choice, do we not?"

"And when we do meet with Roh and with Hetharu's forces, you will be at our backs."

Kithan frowned. "But I am your man, Morgaine-Angharan." He extended his long legs, crossed, before him, easy as a man in his own hall. "I am your most devoted servant."

"Indeed," said Morgaine.

"Doubtless," said Kithan, regarding her with that same distant smile, "you will serve me as you served those who followed you to Ohtij-in."

"It is more than possible," said Morgaine.

"They were your own," Kithan exclaimed with sudden, plaintive force, as if he pleaded something; and Jhirun, flinching, edged against the rocks at Vanye's side.

"They may have been once," Morgaine said. "But those that I knew are long buried. Their children are not mine."

Kithan's face recovered its placidity; laughter returned to his half-lidded eyes. "But they followed you," he said. "I find that ironic. They knew you, knew what you had done to their ancestors, and still they followed you, because they thought you would make an exception of them; and you served them exactly as you are. Even the Aren-folk, who hate you, and tie up white feathers at their doorways—" He smiled widely and laughed, a mere breath. "A reality. A fixed point in all this reasonless universe. I am *khal.* I have never found a point on which to stand or a shrine at which to worship—till now. You *are* Angharan; you come to destroy the Wells and all that exists. You are the only rational being in the world. So I also follow you, Morgaine-Angharan. I am your faithful worshipper."

Vanye thrust himself to his feet, hand to his belt, loathing the *qujal's* insolence, his mockery, his elaborate fancies: Morgaine should not have to suffer this, and did, for it was not her habit to avenge herself for words, or for other wrongs.

"At your pleasure," he said to Kithan.

Kithan, weaponless, indicated so with an outward gesture, a slight hardness to his eyes.

"Let be," Morgaine said. "Prepare the horses. Let us be moving, Vanye."

"I might cut their reins and their girths for them," said Vanye, scowling at the halfling lord and his two men, reckoning them, several, a moderately fair contest. "They could test their horsemanship with that, and we would not have to give them further patience."

Morgaine hesitated, regarding Kithan. "Let him be," she said. "His courage comes from the *akil.* It will pass."

The insouciance of Kithan seemed stung by that. He frowned, and leaned against the rock staring at her, no longer capable of distance.

"Prepare the horses," she said. "If he can hold our pace, well; and if not— the Hiua will remember that he companied with me."

There was unease in the guards' faces, a flicker of the same in Kithan's; and then, with a bow, a taut smile: "*Arrhthein,*" he said to her. "*Sharron a thrissn nthinn.*"

"*Arrhtheis,*" Morgaine echoed softly, and Kithan settled back with an estimating look in his eyes, as if something had passed between them of irony and bitter humor.

It was the language of the Stones. *I am not qujal,* Morgaine had insisted to him once, which he believed, which he still insisted on believing.

But when he had gone, at Morgaine's impatient gesture, to attend the horses, he looked back at them, his pale-haired liege and the pale-haired *qujal* together, tall and slender, in all points similar; a chill ran through him.

Jhirun, human-dark, a wraith in brown, scrambled up and quitted that company and ran to him, as he gathered up the reins of her mare and brought it to the roadside. He threw down there the bundles she had made of their supplies and began rerolling the blankets, on his knees at the side of the stone road. She knelt down with him and began with feverish earnestness to help him, in this and when he began to tie the separate rolls to their three saddles, redistributing supplies and tightening harness.

Her mare's girth too he attended, seeing that it was well done, on which her life depended: She waited, hovering at his side.

"Please," she said at last, touching at his elbow. "Let me ride with you; let me stay with you."

"I cannot promise that." He avoided her eyes, and brushed past her to attend the matter of his own horse. "If the mare cannot hold our pace, still she is steady and she will manage to keep you ahead of the Hiua. I have other obligations. I cannot think of anything else just now."

"These men—lord, I am afraid of them. They—"

She did not finish. It ended in tears. He looked at her and remembered her the night that Kithan had visited his cell, small and wretched as she had been in the hands of the guards, men half-masked and anonymous in their demon-helms. Her they had seized, and not him.

"Do you know these men?" he asked of her harshly.

She did not answer, only stared at him helplessly with the flush of shame staining her cheeks; and he looked askance at Kithan's man, who was likewise caring for his lord's horse. Privately he thought of what justice Kursh reserved for such as they: her ancestors had been, though she had forgotten it, *tan-uyin,* and honorable, and proud.

He was not free to take up her quarrel. He had a service.

He set his hand on hers; it was small, but rough, a peasant's hand, that knew hard labor. "Your ancestors," he said, "were high-born men. My father's wife was Myya, who gave him his legitimate sons. They are a hard-minded clan, the Myya; they 'my lord' only those that they respect."

Her hand, leaving his, went to her breast, where he remembered a small gold amulet that once he had returned to her. The pain her eyes had held departed, leaving something clear and far from fragile.

"The mare," he said, "will not run that far behind, Myya Jhirun."

She left him. He watched her, at the roadside, bend and gather a handful of smooth stones, and drop them, as she straightened, into her bodice. Then she gathered up the mare's reins and set herself into the saddle.

And suddenly he saw something beyond her, at the bottom of the long hill, a dark mass on the road beyond the knoll that rose like a barrow-mound at the turning.

"*Liyo*," he called out, appalled at the desperate endurance of those that followed them, afoot. Not for revenge: for revenge they surely could not follow so far or so determinedly . . . but for hope, a last hope, that rested not with Morgaine, but with Roh.

There were Shiua and the priest, who knew what Roh had promised in Ohtij-in; and there was Fwar: for Fwar, it would be revenge.

Morgaine stood at his side, looked down the road. "They cannot keep our pace," she said.

"They need not," said Kithan; and gone now was the slurring of his speech; fear glittered through the haze of his eyes. "There are forces between us and Abarais, my lady Morgaine, and one of them is my brother's. Hetharu will have ridden over whatever opposition he meets: he is not loved by the mountain lords. But so much the more will forces be on the move in this land. Your enemy has sent couriers abroad: folk here will know you; they will be waiting for you; and being mad, they are, of course, interested in living. We may find our way quite difficult."

Morgaine gave him a baleful look, took *Changeling* from her shoulder and hooked it to her saddle before she set foot in the stirrup. Vanye mounted, and drew close to her, thinking no longer of what followed them or of Myya Jhirun i Myya; it was Morgaine he protected, and if that should entail turning on three of their companions, he would be nothing loath.

The land opened before them, rich with crops and dark earth; and closed again and opened, small pockets of cultivated earth hardly wider than a field or two between opposing heights, and occasionally a small marsh and a reed-rimmed lake.

Crags rose towering on all sides of them, a limit to the sky that in other days Vanye would have found comfortable, a view much like home; but it was not his land, and nowhere was there indication what might lie ahead. He looked into the deep places of the weathered rocks, the recesses that were often overgrown with trees and man-tall weeds, and knew that in one thing at least Kithan had told the truth: that there was no passage for a horseman off this road; and if there were trails in the hills, as surely there were, even a runner must needs be born to this land to make much speed.

They did not press the horses, that like themselves had gone without sleep and rest; Kithan rode with them, his two men trailing, and last rode Jhirun, whose bay mare was content to lag by several lengths.

And at dusk, as they came through one of the many narrows, there appeared stones by the road, set by men; and against the forested cliffs beyond was a stone village, a sprawling and untidy huddle next the road.

"Whose?" Morgaine asked of Kithan. "It was not on the maps."

Kithan shrugged. "There are many such. The land hereabouts is Sotharra land; but I do not know the name of the village. There will be others. They are human places."

Vanye looked incredulously at the halfling lord, and judged that it was likely the truth, that a lord of Shiuan did not trouble to learn the names of the villages that lay within reach of his own land.

Morgaine swore, and came to a slow stop on the road, where they were last screened by the trees and the rocks. A spring flowed at the roadside, next the trees. She let Siptah drink, and herself dismounted and knelt upcurrent, drinking from her hand. The *qujal* followed her example, even Kithan drinking from the stream like any peasant; and Jhirun overtook them and cast herself down from her mare to the cool bank.

"We shall rest a moment," Morgaine said. "Vanye—"

He nodded, stepped down from the saddle, and filled their waterflasks the while Morgaine watched his back.

And constantly, while they let the horses breathe and took a little of their small supply of food, Morgaine's eye was on their companions or his was, while the dusk settled and became night.

Jhirun held close, by Morgaine's side or his. She sat quietly, for the most part, and braided her long hair in a single plait down the back, tied it with a bit of yarn from her fringed skirt. And there was something different in her bearing, a set to her jaw, a directness to her eyes that had not been there before.

She set herself with them as if she belonged: Vanye met her eye, remembered how she had intervened in Fwar's ambush in the stable, and reckoned that were he an enemy of Myya Jhirun i Myya, he would well guard his back. A warrior of clan Myya, restrained by codes and honor, was still a bad enemy. Jhirun, he remembered, knew nothing of such restraints.

It was at the men of Kithan that she stared in the darkness, and they would not look toward her.

And when they remounted, Jhirun rode insolently across the path of Kithan and his men, turned and glared at Kithan himself.

The *qujal*-lord brought up short, and seemed not offended, but perplexed at such arrogance in a Hiua peasant. Then, with elaborate irony, he reined his horse aside to give her place.

"We are going through," said Morgaine; "and from now on I do not trust we will be able to rest for more than a few moments at any stopping. We are near Sotharrn, it seems; and we are, from Sotharrn, within reach of Abarais."

"By tomorrow, *liyo?*" Vanye asked.

"By tomorrow night," she said, "or not at all."

⌒ Chapter 16

The village sprawled at the left of the road, silent in the dark, beneath a forested upthrust of rock that shadowed it from Anli's wan light: a motley gathering of stone houses, surrounded by a wall as high as a rider's head.

The horses' hooves rang unevenly off the walls as they rode by. There was no stirring within, no light, no opening of the shuttered windows that over-topped the wall, no sound even of livestock. The gate was shut, a white object affixed to its center.

It was the wing of a white bird, nailed there, the boards smeared blackly with the blood.

Jhirun touched the necklace that she wore and murmured something in a low voice. Vanye crossed himself fervently and scanned the shuttered windows and overshadowing crags for any sign of the folk that lived there.

"You are expected," Kithan said, "as I warned you."

Vanye glanced at him, and at Morgaine—met her eyes and saw the shadow there, as it had been at the bridge.

And she shivered, a quick and strange gesture, full of weariness, and set Siptah to a quicker pace, to leave the village behind them.

The pass closed about them, a place where rock had tumbled to the very edge of the road, boulders man-large. Vanye gazed up at the dark heights, and with a shiver of his own, used the spurs. They came through the throat of that place at a pace that set the echoes flying, and there was no fall of stones, no stir of life from the cliffs.

But when, halfway across the next small valley, he turned and looked back, he saw a red glow of fire atop those cliffs.

"*Liyo*," he said.

Morgaine looked, and said nothing. The Baien gray had struck that pace that, on level ground, he could hold for some space; and the gelding could match him stride for stride, but not forever.

The alarm was given: henceforth there was no stopping. What Roh had not known was spread now throughout the countryside.

Soon enough there was another, answering fire among the hills to their left.

*   *   *

The towers appeared unexpectedly in the morning light, half-hidden in forested crags: walls many-turreted and more regular than those of Ohtij-in, but surely as old. They dominated the widest of the valleys that they had seen; and cultivated fields lay round about.

Morgaine reined back briefly, scanning that hold, that guarded the pass before them.

And far behind them, horses unable to stay their pace, rode the three *qujal,* and last of all, Jhirun.

Vanye unhooked his sword and secured the sheath, marking the smoke that hung above those walls. He laid the naked blade across the saddlebow. Morgaine took *Changeling* from its place beneath her knee, and laid it, still sheathed, across her own.

"*Liyo,*" Vanye said softly. "When you will."

"Carefully," she said.

She let Siptah go; and the gelding matched pace with him, at an easy gait, toward the towers and the pass.

Smoke rose there steadily, as it had from many a point about the valleys, fire after fire passing the alarm.

But it was not, as the others had been, white brush-smoke; it spread darkly on the sky, and as they rode near enough to see the walls distinctly, they could see in that stain upon the heavens the wheeling flight of birds, that hovered above the hold.

The gates stood agape, battered from their hinges: they could see that clearly from the main road. A dead horse lay in the ravine beside the spur of road that diverged toward those gates; birds flapped up from it, disturbed in their feeding.

And curiously, across that empty gateway were cords, knotted with bits of white feather.

Morgaine reined in—suddenly turned off toward that gate; and Vanye protested, but no word did she speak, only rode warily, slowly toward that gateway, and he made haste to overtake her, falling in at her side the while she approached that strange barrier. The only sound was the ring of hooves on stone and the hollow echo off the walls—that, and the wind, that blew strongly at the cords.

Ruin lay inside. A cloud of black birds, startled, fluttered up from the stripped carcass of an ox that lay amid the court. On the steps of the keep sprawled a dead man; another lay in the shadow of the wall, prey to the birds. He had been *qujal.* His white hair proclaimed it.

And some three, hanged, twisted slowly on the fire-blackened tree that had grown in the center of the courtyard.

Morgaine reached for the lesser of her weapons, and fire parted the strands of the feathered cords. She urged Siptah slowly forward. The walls echoed to the sound of the horses and to the alarmed flutter of the carrion birds. Smoke still boiled up from the smoldering core of the central keep, from the wreckage of human shelters that had clustered about it.

Riders clattered up the stones outside. Morgaine wheeled Siptah about as Kithan's party came within the gates and reined to a dazed halt.

Kithan looked slowly about him, his thin face set in horror; there was horror too in the face of Jhirun, who arrived last within the gateway, her mare stepping skittishly past the blowing strands of cords and feathers. Jhirun held tightly to the charms about her neck and stopped just inside the gates.

"Let us leave this place," Vanye said; and Morgaine took up the reins, about to heed him.

But Kithan suddenly hailed the place, a loud cry that echoed in the emptiness; and again he called, and finally turned his horse full circle to survey all the ruined keep, the dead that hung from the tree and that lay within the yard, while the two men with him looked about them too, their faces white and drawn.

"Sotharrn," Kithan exclaimed in anguish. "There were better than seven hundred of our folk here, besides the Shiua." He gestured at the fluttering cords. "Shiua belief. Those are for fear of you."

"Would Hetharu have gathered forces here," Morgaine asked him, "or lost them? Was this riot, or was it war?"

"He follows Roh," Kithan said. "And Roh has promised him his heart's desires—as he doubtless would promise others, halfling and human." He gazed about him at the shelters that had housed men, that were empty now, as—Vanye realized suddenly—the village in the night had lain silent, as the valleys and hills between had been vacant, with only the alarm fires to break the peace.

And of a sudden one of the guards reined about, and spurred through the gates. The other hesitated, his pale face a mask of anguish and indecision.

Then he too rode, whipping his tired horse in his frenzy, and vanished from sight, deserting his lord, seeking safety elsewhere.

"No!" cried Morgaine, checking Vanye's impulse to pursue them; and when he reined back: "No. There are already the fires: they are enough to have warned our enemies. Let them go." And to Kithan, who sat his horse staring after his departed men: "Do you wish to follow them?"

"Shiuan is finished," Kithan said in a trembling voice, and looked back at her. "If Sotharrn has fallen, then no other hold will stand long against Hetharu, against Chya Roh, against the rabble that they have stirred to arms. What you will do—do. Or let me stay with you."

There was no arrogance left him. His voice broke, and he bowed his head, leaning against the saddlebow. When he lifted his face again, the look of tears was in his eyes.

Morgaine regarded him long and narrowly.

Then without a word she rode past him, for the gate where the feathered cords fluttered uselessly in the wind. Vanye delayed, letting Jhirun turn, letting Kithan go before him. Constantly he felt a prickling between his own shoulders, a consciousness that there might well be watchers somewhere within the ruins—for someone had strung the cords and tried to seal the gate from harm, someone frightened, and human.

No attack came, nothing but the panic flight of birds, a whispering of wind through the ruins. They passed the gate on the downward road, riding slowly, listening.

And Vanye watched the *qujal*-lord, who rode before him, pale head bowed, yielding to the motion of the horse. Without choices, Kithan—without skill to survive in the wilderness that Shiuan had become, helpless without his servants to attend him and his peasants to feed him . . . and now without refuge to shelter him.

Better the sword's edge, Vanye thought, echoing something that Roh had said to him, and then dismayed to remember who had said it, and that it had been true.

At the road's joining, Morgaine increased the pace. "Move!" Vanye shouted at the halfling, spurring forward, and struck Kithan's horse with the flat of his blade, startling it into a brief burst of speed. They turned northward onto the main road, slowing again as they came beyond arrowflight of the walls.

On sudden impulse Vanye looked back, saw on the walls of Sotharrn a brown, bent figure, and another and another—ragged, furtive watchers that vanished the instant they realized they had been seen.

Old ones, deserted, while the young had been carried away with the tide that swept toward Abarais: the young, who looked to live, who would kill to live, like the horde that followed still behind them.

The land beyond Sotharrn bore more signs of violence, fields and land along the roadway churned to mire, as if the road itself could no longer contain what poured toward the north. Tracks of men and horses were sharply defined beside the road and in mud yet unwashed from the paving stones.

"They passed," Vanye said to Morgaine, as they rode knee to knee behind Jhirun and Kithan, "since the rain stopped."

He tried to lend her hope; she frowned over it, shook her head.

"Hetharu delayed here, perhaps," she said in a low voice. "He would be enough to deal with Sotharrn. But were I Roh, I would not have delayed for such an untidy matter if there were a choice: I would have gone for Abarais.

And once there, then no hold will stand. I would be glad to know where Hetharu's force is; but I fear I know where Roh is."

Vanye considered that; it was not good to think on. He turned his mind instead to forces that he understood. "Hetharu's force," he said, "looks to have gathered considerable number; perhaps two, three thousand by now."

"There are also the outlying villages," she said. "—Kithan."

The halfling reined back somewhat, and Jhirun's mare, never one to take the lead, lagged too, coming alongside so that they were four abreast on the road. Kithan regarded them placidly, his eyes again vague and hazed.

"He is only half sensible," Vanye said in disgust. "Perhaps he and that store of his were best parted."

"No," said Kithan at once, straightening in his saddle. He made effort to look at them directly, and his eyes were possessed of a distant, tearless sadness. "I have listened to your reckoning; I hear you well . . . Leave me my consolation, Man. I shall answer your questions."

"Then say," said Morgaine, "what we must expect. Will Hetharu gain the support of the other holds? Will they move to join him?"

"Hetharu—" Kithan's mouth twisted in a grimace of contempt. "Sotharrn always feared him . . . that did he succeed to power in Ohtij-in, then attack would come. And they were right, of course. Some of our fields flooded this season; and more would have gone the next; and the next. It was inevitable that the more ambitious of us would reach across the Suvoj."

"Will the other holds follow him or fight him now?"

Kithan shrugged. "What difference to the Shiua; and to us—Even we bowed and kissed his hand in Ohtij-in. We who wanted nothing but to live undisturbed . . . have no power against whoever does not. Yes, most will be with him: to what purpose anything else? My guards have gone over to him: that is where they are going. There is no question of it. They saw my prospects, and they know defeat when they smell it. So they went to him. The lesser holds will flock to do the same."

"You may go too if you like," Morgaine said.

Kithan regarded her, disturbed.

"Be quite free to do so," she said.

The horses walked along together some little distance; and Kithan looked at Morgaine with less and less assurance, as if she and the drug together confused him. He looked at Jhirun, whose regard of him was hard; and at Vanye, who stared back at him expressionless, giving him nothing, neither of hatred nor of comfort. Once more he glanced the circuit of them, and last of all at Vanye, as if he expected that some terrible game were being made of him.

For a moment Vanye thought that he would go; his body was tense in the saddle, his eyes, through their haze, distracted.

"No," Kithan said then, and his shoulders fell. He rode beside them sunk in his own misery.

None spoke, Vanye rode content enough in Morgaine's presence by him, a nearness of mind in which words were needless; he knew her, that had they been alone she would have had nothing to say. Her eyes scanned the trail as they rode, but her mind was elsewhere, desperately occupied.

At last she drew from her boot top a folded and age-yellowed bit of parchment, a map cut from a book; and silently, leaning from the saddle, she indicated to him the road. It wound up from the Suvoj, that great rift clearly recognizable; but the lands of Ohtij-in were shown as wide, plotted fields, that no longer existed. There were fields mapped on this side also, along the road and within the hills; and holds besides that which seemed to be Sotharrn, scattered here and there about the central mountains.

And amid those mountains, a circular mark, lay Abarais: Vanye could not read the runes, but her finger indicated it, and she named it aloud.

He lifted his eyes from the brown ink and yellowed page to the mountains that now loomed before them. Greenish-black evergreen covered their flanks. Their rounded peaks were bald and smooth and their slopes were a tumble of great stones, aged, weather-worn—a ruin of mountains in a dying land.

Above them passed the Broken Moon, in a clear sky; the weather held for them, warm as the sun reached its zenith; but when the sun declined toward afternoon, the hills seemed overlain with a foul haze.

It was not cloud; none wreathed these low hills. It was the smoke of fires, from some far place within the mountains, where other holds had been marked on the map.

"I think that would be Domen," said Kithan, when they questioned him on it. "That is next, after Sotharrn. On the far side of the mountains lie Marom and Arisith; and Hetharu's forces will have reached for those also."

"Still increasing in number," said Morgaine.

"Yes," said Kithan. "The whole of Shiuan is within his hands—or will be, within days. He is burning the shelters, I would judge: that is the way to move the humanfolk, to draw them with him. And perhaps he burns the holds themselves. He may want no lords to rival him."

Morgaine said nothing.

"It will do him no good," Vanye said, to dispossess Kithan of any hopes he might still hold. "Hetharu may have Shiuan—but Roh has Hetharu, whether or not Hetharu has yet realized it."

Stones rose beside the road, Standing Stones, that called to mind that cluster beside the road in Hiuaj, near the marsh; but these stood straight and powerful in the evening light.

And beyond those Stones moved a white-haired figure, leaning on a staff, who struggled to walk the road.

They gained upon that man rapidly; and surely by now the traveler must have heard them coming, and might have looked around; but he did not. He moved at the same steady pace, painfully awkward.

There was an eeriness about that deaf persistence; Vanye laid his sword across the saddlebow as they came alongside the man, fearing some plan concealed in this bizarre attitude—a ruse to put a man near Morgaine. He moved his horse between, reining back to match his pace.

Still the man did not look up at them, but walked with eyes downcast, step by agonized step with the staff to support him. He was young, wearing hall-garments; he bore a knife at his belt, and the staff on which he leaned was the broken remnant of a pike. His white hair was tangled, his cheek cut and bruised, blood soaked the rough bandages on his leg. Vanye hailed him, and yet the youth kept walking; he cursed, and thrust his sheathed sword across the youth's chest.

The *qujal* stopped, downcast eyes fixed on something other and elsewhere; but when Vanye let fall the sword, he began to walk again, struggling in his lameness.

"He is mad," Jhirun said.

"No," said Kithan. "He does not wish to see you."

Their horses moved along with the youth, slowly, by halting paces; and softly Kithan began to question him, in his own tongue—received an anguished glance of him, and an answer, spoken on hard-drawn breaths, the while he walked. Names were named that touched keenly Vanye's interest, but no other word of it could he grasp. The youth exhausted his supply of breath and fell silent, walked on, as he had been before.

Morgaine touched Siptah and moved on. Vanye at her side; and Jhirun with them. Kithan followed. Vanye looked back, at the youth who still doggedly, painfully, struggled behind them.

"What did he say?" Vanye asked of Morgaine. She shrugged, not in a mood to answer.

"He is Allyvy," said Kithan in her silence. "He is of Sotharrn; and he has the same madness as took the villagers: he says that he is bound for Abarais, as all are going, believing this Chya Roh."

Vanye looked at Morgaine, found her face grim and set; and she shrugged. "So we are too late," she said, "as I feared."

"He has promised them," said Kithan, "another and better land: a hope to live; and they are going to take it. They are gathering an army, to march toward it; holds are burned: they say there is no need of them now."

He looked again at Morgaine, expecting some answer of her. There was none. She rode with her eyes fixed, no more slowly, no more quickly, passing the ruined fields. He saw in her a tautness that trembled beneath that placid surface, something thin-strung and fragile.

Violence, terror: it flowed to his own taut nerves.

Let us retreat, a thing in him wanted to say. *Let us find a place, lost in the hills, when all of them have passed, when the Wells are sealed. There is life enough for us, peace—once you have lost and can no longer hope to follow him. We could live. We might grow old before the waters rose to take these mountains. We would be alone, and sealed, safe, from all our enemies.*

She knew her choices, he reckoned to himself, and chose what she would; but he began to think, in deep guilt, what it would be did they find Roh gone: that that was earnestly to be hoped, else she would hurl herself against an army, taking all with her.

It was a traitorous thought; he realized it, and crossed himself fervently, wishing it away—met her eyes and feared suddenly that she understood his fear.

"*Liyo,*" he said in a quiet voice, "whatever wants doing, I will do."

It seemed to reassure her. She turned her attention back to the way they rode, and to the hills.

Night began to fall, streaks of twilight that shaded into dark among the smokes across the hills, a murky and ugly color. They rode among stones that gathered more and more thickly about the road, until it became clear that here had been some massive structure, foundations that lay naked and exposed in great intersecting rectangles and circles and bits of arches. Constantly the earth bore signs that vast numbers had traveled this way, and lately.

And there was a dead man by the road. The black birds rose up from his body like shadows into the dark, a heavy flapping of wings.

Violence within the army's own ranks attended them, Vanye reckoned: desperate men, frightened men; and men and halflings massed together. They were not long in coming upon other dead, and one was a woman, and one was a black-robed priest, frail and elderly.

"They are beasts," Kithan exclaimed in anguish.

None disputed him.

"What shall we do," asked Jhirun, who had remained silent most of the day, "what shall we do when we reach Abarais, if they are all gathered there?"

It was not a witless question; it was a desperate one . . . Jhirun, who knew less than they what must be done, and who endured all things patiently in her hope. Vanye looked at her and shook his head helplessly, foreseeing what he thought Jhirun herself began to foresee, what Morgaine had tried earnestly to warn her, weaponless as the Barrows-girl was, and without defenses.

"You also," said Morgaine, "are still free to leave us."

"No," Jhirun said quietly. "Like my lord Kithan, I have nothing to hope for from what follows us; and if I cannot get through where you are going, at least—" She made a helpless gesture, as if it were too difficult a thing to speak. "Let me try."

Morgaine considered her a moment as they rode, and finally nodded in confirmation.

The dark fell more and more heavily about them, until there was only the light of the lesser moons and the bow in the sky in which the moons traveled, a cloudy arc across the stars. From one wall of the wide valley to the other were the dark shapes of vast ruins, no longer Standing Stones, but spires, straight on their inner, roadward faces, with a curving slant on their outer. They were aligned with the road on either side, and began to set inward to enclose it.

Their way became an aisle, so that they no longer had clear view of the hills; the stone spires began to encroach the very edge of the paving, like ribs along the spine of the road.

The horses' hooves echoed loudly down that passage, and the shifting perspectives of that vast aisle, lit only by the moons, provided ample cover for ambush. Vanye rode with his sword across the saddlebow, wishing that they might make faster passage through this cursed place, and knowing at the same time the unwisdom of racing blindly through the dark. The road became entirely blind at some points, as it turned and the spires cut off their view on all sides.

And thereafter the road began to climb as well as wind, in long terraced steps that led ultimately to a darkness—a starless shadow that as they neared it began to take on the detail of black stonework, that lay as a wall before them: a vast cube of a building that overtopped the spires, that diverged to form an aisle before it.

"An-Abarais," murmured Kithan. "Gateway to the Well."

Vanye gazed at it with foreboding as they rode: for once before he had seen the like; and beside him Morgaine took *Changeling* into her hand. The gray horse blew nervously, side-stepping, then started forward again, taking the narrowing terraces; Vanye spurred the gelding to make him keep pace, put from his mind their two companions that trailed them.

It was no Gate, but a fortress that could master the Gates; *qujal*, and full of power. It was a place that Roh would not have neglected.

There was no other way through.

✍ Chapter 17

The road met the fortress of An-Abarais: and it vanished into a long archway, black and cheerless, with night and open sky at its other end. But the slanted spires shaped another road, fronting the fortress; and in that crossing of ways Morgaine reined in, scanning all directions.

"Kithan," she said, as their two companions overtook them. "You watch the road from here. Jhirun: come. Come with us."

Jhirun cast an apprehensive look at all of them, left and right; but Morgaine was already on her way down that right-hand aisle, a pale-haired ghost on a pale horse, almost lost in shadow.

Vanye reined aside and rode after, heard Jhirun clattering along behind him in haste. What Kithan would do, whether he would stay or whether he would flee to their enemies—Vanye refused to reckon: Morgaine surely tempted him, dismissed him for good or for ill; but her thoughts would be set desperately elsewhere at the moment, and she needed her *ilin* at her back.

He overtook her as she stopped in that dark aisle, where she had found the deep shadow of a doorway; she dismounted, pushed at that door with her left hand, bearing *Changeling* in her right.

It yielded easily, on silent hinges. Cold breathed forth from that darkness, wherein the moonlight from the doorway showed level, polished stone. She led Siptah forward, within the door, and Vanye bent his head and rode carefully after, shod hooves ringing irreverently in that deep silence. Jhirun followed, afoot, tugging at the reluctant mare, a third clatter of hooves on the stone. When she was still, there was no sound but the restless shift of leather and the animals' hard breathing.

Vanye slid his sword from its sheath and carried it naked in his hand; and suddenly light glimmered from Morgaine's hands as she began to do the same, baring *Changeling*'s rune-written blade. The opal shimmer grew, flared into brilliance enough to light the room, casting strange shadows of slanting spires, a circular chamber, a stairway that wound its way among the spires.

From *Changeling* came a pulsing sound, soft at first, then painful to the senses, that filled all the air and made the horses shy. The light brightened when Morgaine swept its tip up and leftward; and by this they both knew the way they must go, reading the seeking of the blade toward its own power.

And did they meet, unsheathed blade and living source, it would end both: whatever madness had made *Changeling* had made it indestructible save by Gates.

Morgaine sheathed it as quickly as might be; and the horses stood trembling after. Vanye patted the gelding's sweating neck and slid down.

"Come," Morgaine said, looking at him. "Jhirun—watch the horses. Cry out at once if something goes in the least amiss; put your back against solid stone and stay there. Above all else do not trust Kithan. If he comes, warn us."

"Yes," she agreed in a thin voice; and half a breath Vanye hesitated, thinking to lend her a weapon—but she could not use it.

He turned, overtook Morgaine, emptied his mind of all else—watching her back, watching the shadows on whatever side she was not watching. Right hand and left the shadows passed them, and as soon as the darkness became absolute, a light flared in Morgaine's hand, a harmless, cold magic, for it only guided them: little as he liked such things, he trusted the hand that held it. Nothing she might do could fright him here, in the presence of powers eldritch and *qujalin:* the sword of metal that he bore was a useless thing in such a place, all his arts and skills valueless—save against ambush.

A door faced them; it yielded noisily to Morgaine's skilled touch, startling him; and light blazed suddenly in their faces, a garish burst of color, of pulsing radiance. Sound gibbered at them; he heard the echo of his own shameful outcry, rolling through the halls.

It was the heart of the Gates, the Wells, the thing that ruled them: and though he had seen the like before and knew that no mere noise or light could harm him, he could not shame away the clutch of fear at his heart, his traitor limbs that reacted to the madness that assailed them.

"Come," Morgaine urged him: the suspicion of pity in her voice stung him; and he gripped his sword and stayed close at her heels, walking as briskly as she down that long aisle of light. Light redder than the sunset dyed her hair and her skin, glittered bloodily off mail and stained *Changeling's* golden hilt: the sound that roared about them drowned their footfalls so that she and he seemed to drift soundlessly in the glow. Morgaine spared not a glance for the madness on either side of them: *she belongs here,* he thought, watching her—who in Andurin armor, of a manner a hundred years older than his own, paused before the center of those blazing panels. She laid hands on them with skill, called forth flurries of lights and sound that drowned all the rest and set him trembling.

Qujal, he thought, *as they were.*

As they would wish to be.

She looked sharply back at him, beckoned him; he came, with one backward look, for in that flood of sound anyone might steal upon them from the doorway unawares. But she touched his arm and commanded his attention upon the instant.

"It is locked," she said, speaking above the roar, "wide open. There is a hold upon it that cannot be broken: Roh's work. I knew that this would be the case if he reached it first."

"You can do nothing?" he asked of her; and beyond her shoulder saw the pulsing lights that were the power and life of the Gates. He had borne as much as he wished to bear, and more than he wanted to remember; but he knew too what she was telling him—that here was all the hope they had, and that Roh's hand had sealed it from them. He tried to gather his thoughts amid the noise: sight and sound muddled together, chaos he knew he would not remember, as he could not remember the between of Gates: he did not know how to call what he saw, and his thoughts would not hold it. Once before he had walked such a hall; and he remembered now a patch of blood on the floor, a corridor, a stairway that was different—as if elsewhere in this building a door lay in ruins and at his side stood a brother he had lost.

Who was dust now, long dead, nine hundred years ago.

The confusion became too much, too painful. He watched Morgaine turn and touch the panel again, doing battle with something he did not understand nor want to know. He understood it for hopeless.

"Morgaine!"

Roh's voice, louder than the noise about them.

Vanye looked up, the sword clenched in his fist; and Roh's shape drifted amid the light and the sound, pervisible, larger than life.

It spoke: it whispered words in the *qujalin* tongue, a whisper that outshouted the sounds from the walls. Vanye heard his own name on its insubstantial lips, and crossed himself, loathing this thing that taunted him, that whispered his name to Morgaine, whispered things he could in no wise understand: his cousin Roh. He saw the face that was so nearly his own, alike as a brother's—the brown eyes, the small scar at the cheek that he remembered. It was utterly Roh.

"Are you there, cousin?" the image asked suddenly, sending cold to his heart. *"Perhaps not. Perhaps you remain safe at Ohtij-in. Perhaps only your liege has come, and has forgotten you. But if you are beside her, remember what we spoke of on the rooftop, and know that my warning was true: she is pitiless. I seal the Wells to seal her out, and hope that it may suffice; but, Nih Vanye, kinsman, you may come to me. Leave her. Her, I will not let pass; I dare not. But you I will accept. For you, there is a way out of this world, as I give it to others, if she would permit it. Come and meet me at Abarais: so long as you can hear this message, there is still a chance. Take it, and come."*

The image and the voice faded together. Vanye stood stricken for a moment; and then he dared look at Morgaine, to find question in the look that she returned him—a deadly mistrust.

"I shall not go," he insisted. "There was nothing agreed between us, *liyo*—ever. On my life, I would not go to him."

Her hand, that had slipped to the weapon at the back of her belt, returned to her side; and of a sudden she reached out and took his arm, drew him to the counter and set his hand there, atop the cold lights.

"I shall show you," she told him. "I shall show you; and on your life, *ilin*, on your *soul*, do you not forget it."

Her fingers moved, instructing his; he banished to a far refuge in him his threatened soul, that shuddered at the touch of these cold things. She bade him thus and thus and thus, a patterned touch on the colors, upon one and the other and the next; he forced it into his memory, branded it there, knowing the purpose of what he was given, little as it might avail here, with Roh's touch to seal the power against their tampering.

Again and again she bade him repeat for her the things that she had taught; mindlessly Roh's ghost overhung them, repeating things that mocked them, endlessly, blind, void of sense. Vanye's hands shook when that began again, but he did not falter in the pattern. Sweat prickled on him in his concentration; yet more times she bade him do what she had shown him.

He finished yet again, and looked at her, pleading with his look that it be enough, that they quit this place. She gazed at him, face and hair dyed with the bloody light, as if searching him for any fault; and above her yet again Roh's face began to mouth its words into the throbbing air.

And suddenly she nodded that it was enough, and turned toward that door by which they had come.

They walked the long aisle of the room. Vanye's nerves screamed at him to take flight, to run; but she did not, and he would not. His nape prickled as Roh's voice pursued them; he knew that did he turn and look there would be Roh's face hovering in the air—urging at him with reasonings that no longer had allure: better to sit helpless while the seas rose, than to surrender to that, which had lied to him from the beginning, which for a time had made him believe that a kinsman lived in this forsaken Hell, in this endless exile.

The darkness of the stairway lay before them; Morgaine shut the door and sealed it, shook him from his bewilderment to show him how it was done. He nodded blank, heartless understanding, his senses still filled with the sound and the light, and the terror of knowing what she had fed into his mind.

He held what men and *qujal* had murdered to possess; and he did not want it, with all his heart he did not. He put out his hand to the wall, still blind, save for the beam that Morgaine carried; he felt rough stone under his fingertips, felt the steps under his feet; and still his mind was dazed with what he had seen and felt. He wished it all undone; and he knew that it was too late, that he had been Claimed in a way that had no release, no freedom.

Down and down the curving stair they went, until he could hear the stamp and blowing of the horses—friendly, familiar sound, native to the man who had ascended the stairs; it was as if a different man had come down, who could not for a moment realize that the things he knew outside that terrible room could still exist, untouched, unshaken by what had shaken him.

Morgaine put out the light she bore as they stepped off the last step, and Jhirun came to them, full of whispered questions—her tearful voice and frightened manner reminding him that she also had endured the terror of this place—and knew nothing of what it held. He envied her that ignorance— touched her hand as she gave the reins of his horse to him.

"Go back," he told her. "Myya Jhirun, ride back the way we came and hide somewhere."

"No," said Morgaine suddenly.

He looked toward her, startled, dismayed; he could not read her face in the darkness.

"Come outside," she said; and she led Siptah through the doorway, waiting for them in the moonlight. Vanye did not look at Jhirun, having no answers for her; he led the gelding out, and heard Jhirun behind him.

"Jhirun," said Morgaine, "go watch the road with Kithan."

Jhirun looked from one to the other of them, but ventured no word in objection: she started away, leading her horse down the long aisle of slanting spires to the place where Kithan sat, a shadow among shadows.

"Vanye," said Morgaine softly, "would thee go to him? Would thee take what he offers?"

"No," he protested upon the instant. "No, upon my oath, I would not."

"Do not swear too quickly," she said; and when he would have disputed her: "Listen to me: this one order—go to him, surrender—go with him."

He could not answer for a moment; the words were dammed in his throat, refusing utterance.

"My order," she said.

"This is a deception of yours," he said, indignant that she did not take him into her trust, that she thus played games with him. "You are full of them. I do not think that I deserve it, *liyo*."

"Vanye—if I cannot get through, one of us must. I am well known; I am disaster to you. But you—go with him, swear to his service; learn what he can teach you that I have not. And kill him, and go on as I would do."

"*Liyo*," he protested. A shiver set into his limbs; he wound his cold fingers into the black horse's mane, for all that he had trusted dropped away beneath him, as the mountains had vanished that morning beyond the Gate, leaving all about him naked and ugly.

"You are *ilin*," she said. "And you take no guilt for it."

"To take bread and warmth and then kill a man?"

"Did I ever promise thee I had honor? It was otherwise, I think."

"Oath-breaking . . . *Liyo,* even to him—"

"One of us," she said between her teeth, "*one* of us must get through. Remain sworn to me in your mind, but let your mouth say whatever it must. Live. He will not suspect you; he will come to trust you. And this is the service I set on you: kill him, and carry out what I have shown you, without end—without end, *ilin.* Will you do this for me?"

"Aye," he said at last; and in his bitterness: "I must."

"Take Kithan and Jhirun; make some tale that Roh will believe, how Ohtij-in has fallen, of your release by Kithan—omitting my part in it. Let him believe you desperate. Bow at his feet and beg shelter of him. Do whatever you must, but stay alive, and pass the Gate, and carry out my orders—to the end of your life, Nhi Vanye, and beyond if thee can contrive it."

For a long moment he said nothing: he would have wept if he had tried to speak, and in his anger he did not want that further shame. Then he saw a trail of moisture shine on her cheek, and it shook him more than all else that she had said.

"Be rid of the Honor-blade," she said. "It will raise a question with him you cannot answer."

He drew it and gave it to her. "Avert," he murmured, the word almost catching in his throat; she echoed the wish, and slipped it through her belt.

"Beware your companions," she said.

"Aye," he answered.

"Go. Make haste."

He would have bowed himself at her feet, an *ilin* taking final, unwilling leave; but she prevented him with a hand on his arm. The touch numbed: for a moment he hesitated with a thing spilling over in him that wanted saying, and she, all unexpected, leaned forward and touched her lips to his, a light touch, quickly gone. It robbed him of speech; the moment passed, and she turned to take up the reins of her horse. What he would have said seemed suddenly a plea for himself, and she would not hear it; there would be dispute, and that was not the parting he wanted.

He hurled himself into the saddle, and she did likewise, and rode with him as far as the crossing of the road and the aisle, the arch that led through into Abarais, where Jhirun and Kithan awaited them.

"We are going on," he said to them, the words strange and ugly to him, "we three."

They looked puzzled, dismayed. They said nothing, asked nothing; perhaps the look of the two of them, *ilin* and *liyo,* made a barrier against them. He turned his horse into the passage, into the dark, and they went with him. Suddenly he looked back, in dread that Morgaine would already be gone.

She was not. She was a shadow, she and Siptah, against the light behind them, waiting.

Fwar and his kind, whatever remained of them, would be coming. Suddenly he realized the set of her mind: the Barrows-folk, that she once had led—ages hence. There was a bond between them, an ill dream that was recent in her mind, a *geas* apart from *Changeling*. He remembered her at the Suvoj, sweeping man after man away into oblivion—and the thing that he had seen in her eyes.

They were your own, Kithan had protested, even a *qujal* appalled at what she had done. They followed her; she waited for them this time, as time after time he had feared she might turn and face them, her peculiar nightmare, that would not let her go.

She waited, while the Gate prepared to seal. Here she stopped running; and laid all her burden upon him. Tears blurred his eyes; he thought wildly of riding back, refusing what she had set him to do.

And that she would not forgive.

They exited the passage into the light of rising Li, saw the valley of Abarais before them, the jagged spires of ruins, and in the far distance—campfires scattered like stars across the mountains: the host of all Shiuan.

He looked back; he could not see Morgaine any longer.

He rammed the spurs into the gelding's flanks and led his companions toward the fires.

⌒ Chapter 18

The vast disc of Li inclined toward the horizon. There was a stain of cloud at that limit of the sky, and wisps of cloud drifted across the moon-track overhead.

The sinking moon yet gave them light enough for quick traveling—light enough too for their enemies. They were exposed, in constant view from the cliffs that towered on either side of the road, above the ruins. Ambush was a constant possibility: Vanye feared it with a distant fear, not for himself, but for the orders he had been given—the only thing he had left, he thought, that was worth concern. That at some moment a shaft aimed from those cliffs should come bursting leather and mail links and bone—the pain would be the less for it, and quickly done, unlike the other, that was forever.

Until you have no choice, her words echoed back to him, a persistent misery, a fact that would not be denied. *Until you have no choice—as I have none.*

Once Jhirun spoke to him; he did not know what she had said, nor care—only stared at her, and she fell silent; and Kithan likewise stared at him, pale eyes sober and present, purged of the *akil* that had clouded them.

And the watchfires grew nearer, spreading before them like a field of stars, red and angry constellations across their way, that began to dim at last like those in the heavens, with the first edge of day showing.

"There is nothing left," Vanye told his companions, realizing that their time grew short, "only to surrender to my cousin and hope for his forbearance."

They were silent, Jhirun next to him and Kithan beyond. Their faces held that same restrained fear that had possessed them since they had been hastened, without explanation, from An-Abarais. They still did not ask, nor demand assurances of him. Perhaps they already knew he had none to give.

"At An-Abarais," he continued while they rode, walking the horses, "we learned that there was no choice. My liege has released me." He suppressed the tremor that would come to his voice, set the muscles of his jaw and continued, beginning to weave the lie that he would use for Roh. "There is more kindness in her than is apparent—for my sake, if not for yours. She knows the case of things, that Roh might accept me, but never her. You are nothing to her; she simply does not care. But Roh hates her above all other enemies; and the less he knows of what truly passed at Ohtij-in, the more readily he will take me—and you. If he knows that I have come directly from her, and you likewise from her company—he will surely kill me; and for me, he has some affection. I leave it to you how much he would hesitate in your case."

Still they said nothing, but the apprehension was no less in their eyes.

"Say that Ohtij-in fell in the quake," he asked of them, "and say that the marshlanders attacked when Aren fell—say whatever you like of the truth; but do not let him know that we entered An-Abarais. Only she could have passed its doors and learned what she learned. Forget altogether that she was with us, or I shall die; and I do not think that I will be alone in that."

Of Jhirun he was sure; there was a debt between them. But there was one of a different nature between himself and Kithan: it was the *qujal* that he feared, and the *qujal* that he most needed to confirm his lie as truth.

And Kithan knew it: those unhuman eyes took on a consciousness of power, and a smug amusement.

"And if it is not Roh who gives the orders," Kithan said, "if it is Hetharu, what shall I say, Man?"

"I do not know," Vanye said. "But a father-slayer will hardly stick at brother-killing; and he will share nothing with you . . . not unless he loves you well. Do you think that is so, Kithan Bydarra's-son?"

Kithan considered it, and the smugness faded rapidly.

"How well," Kithan asked, scowling, "does your cousin love you?"

"I will serve him," Vanye answered, finding the words strange to his lips. "I am an *ilin* now without a master; and we are of Andur-Kursh, he and I . . . you do not understand, but it means that Roh will take me with him, and I will serve him as his right hand; and that is something he cannot find elsewhere. I need you, my lord Kithan, and you know it; I need you to set myself at Roh's side, and you know that you can destroy me with an ill-placed word. But likewise you need me—else you will have to deal with Hetharu; and you know that I bear Hetharu a grudge. You do not love him. Stand by me; and I will give you Hetharu, even if it takes time."

Kithan considered, his lips a thin line. "Aye," he said, "I do follow your reasoning. But, Nhi Vanye, there are two men of mine that may undo it all."

Vanye recalled that, the house guards that had fled, that added a fresh weight of apprehension to his mind; he shrugged. "We cannot amend that. It is a large camp. If I were in the place of such men, I would not rush to authority and boast that I had deserted my lord."

"Are you not doing so now?" Kithan asked.

Heat flamed in his face. "Yes," he admitted hoarsely. "By her leave; but those are details Roh need not know . . . only that Ohtij-in has fallen, and that we are escaped from it."

Kithan considered that a moment. "I will help you," he said. "Perhaps my word can bring you to your cousin. Seeing Hetharu discomfited will be pleasure enough to reward me."

Vanye stared at him, weighing the truth behind that cynical gaze, and looked questioningly also at Jhirun, past whom they had been talking. She looked afraid in that reckoning, as if she, a peasant, knew her worth in the affairs of lords who strove for power.

"Jhirun?" he questioned her.

"I want to live," she said. He looked into the fierceness of that determination and doubted, suddenly; perhaps she saw it, for her lips tightened. "I will stay with you," she said then.

Tears shone in her eyes, of pain or fear or what other cause he did not know, nor spare further thought to wonder. He had no care for either of them, Myya nor halfling lord, only so they did not ruin him. His mind was already racing apace, to the encamped thousands that lay ahead, beginning to plot what approach they might make so that none would slay them out of hand.

Whatever their need for haste, it could be measured by the fact that none of the horde that followed Roh had yet begun to move: the watchfires still glowed in the murky beginnings of dawn. It was best, he thought, to ride in slowly, as many a party must have done, come to join the movement that flowed toward the Well: anxiously he measured the rising light against the distance to the far edge of the fires, and liked not the reckoning. They could not make it all before the light showed them for the ill-assorted companions they were.

But there was no other course that promised better.

* * *

Soon they rode out of the ruin altogether, and among the stumps of young trees, saplings that had been hewn off the beginning slope of the mountain— for shelters, or to feed the fires of the camp. And soon enough they rode within scent of cookfires, and the sound of voices.

Sentries started from their posts, seizing up spears and advancing on them. Vanye kept riding at a steady pace, the others with him; and when they had come close in the dim light, the sentries—dark-haired Men—stood confused by the sight of them and backed away, making no challenge. Perhaps it was the presence of Kithan, Vanye thought, resisting the temptation to look back; or perhaps—the thought came to him with peculiar irony—it was himself, cousin to Roh, similar in arms and even in mount, for the two horses, Roh's mare and his gelding, were of the same hold and breeding.

They entered the camp, that sprawled in disorder on either side of the paved road. At a leisurely pace they rode past the wretched Shiua, who huddled drowsing by their fires, or looked up and stared with furtive curiosity at what passed them in the dawning.

"We must find the Well," Vanye observed softly; "I trust that is where we will find Roh."

"Road's-end," answered Kithan, and nodded toward the way ahead, that began to wind up to the shoulder of the mountains. "The Old Ones built high."

Somewhere a horn sounded, thin and far, a lonely sound off the mountain-slopes. Over and over it sounded, sending the echoes tumbling off the valley walls; and about them the camp began to stir. Voices began to be heard, strained with excitement; fires began to be extinguished, sending up plumes of smoke.

Jhirun looked from one side to the other in apprehension. "They are begin-ning to move," she said. "Lord, surely the Well is open, and they are beginning to move."

It was true: everywhere men were stripping shelters and gathering their meager belongings; children were crying and animals were bawling in alarm and disturbance. In moments, those lightest burdened had begun to seek the road, pouring out onto that way that led them to the Well.

Roh's gift, Vanye thought, his heart pained for the treason he felt, his human soul torn by the sight of the overburdened folk about him, that edged from the path of their horses. Morgaine would have doomed them; but they were going to live.

He came, to bow at Roh's feet—and one day to kill him; and by that, to betray these folk: he saw himself, an evil presence gently threading his way among them, whose faces were set in a delirious and desperate hope.

He served Morgaine.

There was at least a time you chose for yourself, she had said.

Thee will not appoint thyself my conscience, Nhi Vanye. Thee is not qualified.
He began to know.

With a grimace of pain he laid spurs and reins' ends to the black gelding, startling Shiua peasants from his path, frightened folk yielding to him and his two companions, that held close behind him. Faces tore away in the dim light before him, stark with fear and dismay.

The road wound steeply upward. An archway rose athwart it, massive and strange. They passed beneath, passed through the vanguard of the human masses that toiled up the heights, and suddenly rode upon forces of *qujal,* demon-helmed and bristling with lances, whose women rode with them, pale-haired ladies in glittering cloaks, and, very few among them, a cluster of pale, grave-eyed children, who stared at the intrusion with the sober mien of their elders.

A band of *qujal* amid that mass reined themselves across the road, where its turning made passage difficult, with a dizzying plunge into depths on the right hand. Authority was among them, bare-headed, white hair streaming in the wind; and his men ranged themselves before him.

Vanye reined back and reached for his sword. "No," Kithan said at once. "They are Sotharra. They will not stop us."

Uneasily Vanye conceded the approach to Kithan, rode at his shoulder and with Jhirun at his own rein hand, as they drew to a slow halt before the half-flings, with levelled pikes all about them.

Little Kithan had to say to them: a handful of words, of which one was Ohtij-in and another was Roh and another was Kithan's own name; and the Sotharra lord straightened in his saddle, and reined aside, the pikes of his men-at-arms flourishing up and away.

But when they had ridden through, the Sotharra rode behind them at their pace; and Vanye ill-liked it, though it gave them passage through the other masses of halflings that rode the winding ascent. Hereafter was no retreat: he was committed to the hands of *qujal,* to trust Kithan, who could say what he wished to them.

And if Roh had already passed, and if it were Hetharu who must approve his passage: Vanye drove that thought from his mind.

A turning of the road brought them suddenly into sight of a round hill, ringed about by throngs of halfling folk: the horses slowed of their own accord, snorting, walking skittishly, weary as they were.

It grew upon the senses, that oppression that Vanye knew of Gates, that nerve-prickling unease that made the skin feel raw and the senses over-weighted. It was almost sound, and not. It was almost touch, and not.

He saw the place to which they went, in a day that yet had a murkiness in its pastel clouds: there were tents; there were horses; and the road came to an end in a place shadowed by slanted spires.

And the Well.

It was a circle of Standing Stones, like that of Hiuaj: not a single Gate, but a gathering of them, and they were alive. Opal colors streamed within them, like illusion in the daylight, a constant interplay of powers that filled the air with uneasiness; but one Gate held the azure blue of sky, that was terrible with depth, that made the eyes ache with beholding it.

Kithan swore.

"They are real," the *qujal* said. "They are real."

Vanye forced the reluctant gelding to a steady walk, shouldered into Jhirun's mare by a sudden rebellion of the horse, and saw Jhirun's eyes, dazed, still fixed upon the horror of the Gates; her hand was at her throat, where bits of metal and a white feather and a stone cross offered her what belief she knew. He spoke her name, sharply, and she tore her gaze from the hillside and kept by his side.

The camp at the base of the hill was already astir. Shouts attended their arrival, voices thin and lost in that heaviness of the air. Men fair-haired and armored gathered to stare at them: "*Kithan l'Ohtija,*" Vanye heard whispered: he unhooked his sword and rode with it across the saddle as they rode slowly past pale, gray-eyed faces, forcing a way until the press grew too thick to do so without violence.

Kithan asked a question of them. It received quick answer; and Kithan raised his eyes toward the edge of the hill and reined in that direction. Vanye stayed beside him, Jhirun's mare at his flank as the hedge of weapons slowly parted, letting them pass. He heard his own name spoken, and Bydarra's; he saw the sullen, wondering faces, the hateful looks, the hands that gripped weapons: Bydarra's accused murderer—he kept his face impassive and kept the horse moving steadily in Kithan's wake.

Riders came through the crowd, demon-helmed and armored, spreading out, shouldering the crowd aside, spreading out athwart their path. An order was shouted: and among them, central amid a hedge of pikemen, rode an all-too-familiar figure, silver-haired, with the beauty of the *qujal* and the eyes of a man.

Hetharu.

Vanye shouted, ripped the sword free and spurred for him, into a shielding wall of pikes that shied his horse back, wounded. One of the pikemen fell; Vanye slashed at another, reined back and back, and whirled on those threatening his flank. He broke free; Hetharu's folk scattered back, forgetful of dignity, scale-armored house guards massing in a protective arc before their lord.

Vanye drew breath, flexed his hand on the sword, measured the weakest man—and heard other riders come in on his flank. Jhirun cried out; he reined back, risked a glance in that quarter, beyond Jhirun, beyond Kithan—and saw him he hoped desperately to see.

Roh. Bow slung across his shoulders, sword across his saddlebow, Roh had reined to a halt. Ohtija and Sotharra gave back from him, and slowly he rode the black mare into what had become a vacant space.

Vanye sat the sweating gelding, tight-reining him, who turned fretfully this way and that, hurt, and trembling when he stood still.

Another rider moved in; he cast a panicked glance in that direction: Hetharu, who sat his horse sword in hand.

"Where," Roh asked him, drawing his attention back, "is Morgaine?"

Vanye shrugged, a listless gesture, though he felt the tension in every muscle.

"Come down from your horse," said Roh.

He wiped the length of the sword on the gelding's black mane, then climbed down, sword still in hand, and gave the reins of the horse to Jhirun. He sheathed the sword then, and waited.

Roh watched him from horseback; and when he had put away the weapon, Roh likewise dismounted and tossed the reins to a companion, hung his sword at his hip and walked forward until they could speak without raising voices.

"Where is she?" Roh asked again.

"I do not know," Vanye said. "I have come for shelter, like these others."

"Ohtij-in is gone," Kithan said suddenly from behind him. "The quake took it, and all inside. The marshlands are on the move; and some of us they hanged. The man Vanye and the Barrows-girl were with me on the road, else I might have died; my own men deserted me."

There was silence. There should have been shock, outcry—some emotion on the faces of the Ohtija *qujal* who surrounded them.

"*Arres,*" Hetharu's voice said suddenly; riders moved up, and Vanye turned in alarm.

Two helmless men were beside Hetharu: scale-armored, white-haired, and alike as brothers—shameless in their change of lords.

"Yours," Kithan murmured, and managed an ironical bow. The accustomed drugged distance crept into his voice.

"To protect my brother," Hetharu answered softly, "from his own nature—which is well-known and transparent. You are quite sober, Kithan."

"The news," said Roh, from the other side, "outran you, Nhi Vanye. Now tell me the truth. Where is she?"

He turned and faced Roh, for one terrible moment bereft of all subtleties: he could think of nothing.

"My lord Hetharu," Roh said. "The camp is on the move. Uncomfortable as it is, I think it time to move your forces into position; and yours as well, my lords of Sotharrn and Domen, Marom and Arisith. We will make an orderly passage."

There was a stir within the ranks; orders were passed, and a great part of the gathering began to withdraw—the Sotharra, who were prepared already to move, began to ascend the hill.

But Hetharu did not, not he nor his men.

Roh looked up at him, and at the men that delayed about them. "My lord Hetharu," Roh said, "lord Kithan will go with you, if you have use for him."

Hetharu gave an order. The two house guards rode forward and set themselves on either side of Kithan, whose pale face was set in helpless rage.

"Vanye," Roh said.

Vanye looked at him.

"Once again," Roh said, "I ask you."

"I have been dismissed," Vanye said slowly, the words difficult to speak. "I ask fire and shelter, Chya Roh i Chya."

"On your oath?"

"Yes," he said. His voice trembled. He knelt down, reminding himself that this must be, that his liege's direct order absolved him of the lie and the shame; but it was bitter to do so in the sight of both allies and enemies. He bowed himself to the earth, forehead against the trampled grass. He heard the voices, numb in the Well-cursed air, and was glad in this moment that he could not understand their words of him.

Roh did not bid him rise. Vanye sat back after a moment, staring at the ground, shame burning his face, both for the humiliation and for the lie.

"She has sent you," Roh said, "to kill me."

He looked up.

"I think she has made a mistake," said Roh. "Cousin, I will give you the sheltering you ask, taking your word that you have been dismissed from your service to her. By this evening's fire, elsewhere—a Claiming. I think you are too much Nhi to forswear yourself. But she would not understand that. There is no pity in her, Nhi Vanye."

Vanye came to his feet, a sudden move: blades rasped loose all about him, but he kept his hand from his.

"I will go with you," he said to Roh.

"Not at my back," Roh said. "Not this side of the Wells. Not unsworn." He took back the reins of the black mare, and rose into the saddle—cast a look toward the hill, where row on row of Sotharran forces had marshalled themselves, toward which the first frightened lines of human folk labored.

The lines moved with feverish speed behind: those entering that oppressive air hesitated, pushed forward by the press behind; horses shied, of those forces holding the hill, and had to be restrained.

And of a sudden a tumult arose, downtrail, beyond the curve of the mountainside. Voices shrieked, thin and distant. Animals bawled in panic.

Roh reined about toward that sound, the least suspicion of something amiss crossing his face as he gazed toward that curving of the hill: the shouting continued, and somewhere high atop the mountain a horn blew, echoing.

Vanye stood still, in his heart a wild, sudden hope—the thing that Roh likewise suspected: he knew it, he knew, and suddenly in the depth of him he cursed in anguish for what Morgaine had done to him, casting him into this, face to face with Roh.

Vanye whirled, sprang for his horse and ripped the reins from Jhirun's offering hand as the *qujal* closed on him; a rake of his spurs shied the gelding up, buying him time to draw. A pike-thrust hit his mailed side, half-throwing him; he hung on with his knees, and the sweep of his sword sent the pikeman screaming backward, that man and another and another.

"*No!*" Roh's voice shouted thinly in his roaring ears; he found himself in ground free of enemies, a breathing space. He backed the gelding, amazed to see part of the force break away: Roh, and his own guard, and all of fifty of the Ohtija, plunging toward the hill, and the Sotharra, and the screaming hordes of men that surged toward the Wells, lines confounded by panicked beasts that scattered, laboring carts, and a horde that pressed them behind. The Sotharra ranks bowed, began to break. Into that chaos Roh and his companions rode.

And the Ohtija that remained surged forward. Vanye spurred into the impact, wove under one pike-thrust, and suddenly saw a man he had not struck topple from the saddle with blood starting from his face. A second fell, and another to his blade; and a second time the Ohtija, facing more than a peasant rabble, fell back in confusion. Air rushed; Vanye blinked, dazed, saw a stone take another of the Ohtija—the house guard that had betrayed Kithan.

Jhirun.

He reined back and back, almost to the cover of the tumbled stones of the hillside; and yet another stone left Jhirun's sling, toppling another man from the saddle and sending the animal shying into others, hastening the Ohtija into retreat, leaving their dead behind them.

Jhirun and Kithan: out of the tail of his eye he saw the halfling still with him, leaking blood from fingers pressed to his sleeve. Jhirun, barefoot and herself with a scrape across the cheek, swung down from her little mare and quickly gathered a handful of stones.

But the Ohtija were not returning. They had headed up, across the slope, where the ranks of the Sotharra had collapsed into utter disorder.

Men, human-folk, poured in increasing numbers up the slope, this way and that, fleeing in terror.

And came others, small men and different, and armed, adding terror to the rout: pitiless they were in their desperation, making no distinction of halfling or human.

"Marshlanders," Jhirun cried in dismay.

The horde swept between them and the Well.

"Up!" Vanye cried at Jhirun, and delayed only the instant, spurred the exhausted gelding toward that slope, beyond thinking whether Jhirun or Kithan understood. Marshlanders recognized him, and cried out in a frenzy, a few attacking, most scattering from the black horse's hooves. Who stood in his way, he overrode, wielded his sword where he must, his arm aching with the effort; he felt the horse falter, and spurred it the harder.

And across the slope he saw her, a flash of Siptah's pale body in a gap she cut through the press: enemies scattered from her path and hapless folk fled screaming, or fell cowering to the ground. Red fire took any that chose to stand. She had lured all the force of the rabble pursuing her, to fling *them* at Roh and her *qujalin* enemies. *That* was where she had gone.

"*Liyo!*" he shouted, hewed with his sword a man that thrust for him, broke into the clear and headed across the slope on a converging line with her. She saw him; he drove the spurs in mercilessly, and they two swung into a single line, black horse and gray, side by side as they took the slope toward the Wells, enemies breaking from their path in a wide swath.

But at the first of the Ohtija lines, there riders massed, and moved to stop them. Morgaine's fire took some, but the ranks filled, and others swept across the flank of the hill. Arrows flew.

Morgaine turned, swept fire in that direction.

And the Ohtija broke and scattered, all but a handful. Together they rode into that determined mass, toppled three from their saddles. Siptah found a space to run and leaped forward; and Vanye spurred the gelding after.

Suddenly the horse twisted under him, screaming pain—a rush of earth upward and the sure, slow knowledge that he was horseless, lost—before the impact crumpled him upon shoulder and head and flung him stunned against a pile of stones.

Vanye fought to move, to bring himself to his feet, and the first thing that he saw was the black gelding, dying, a broken shaft in its chest. He staggered to his feet leaning against the rocks and bent for his fallen sword, and gazed upslope, blinking clear the sight of opal fires and Siptah's distant shape, Morgaine at the hill's crest.

Enemies were about her. Red laced the opal shimmerings, and the air was numb with the presence of the Gates above them.

And riders came sweeping in toward her, half a hundred horses crossing that slope. Vanye cursed aloud and thrust himself out from the rocks, trying to climb the slope afoot; pain stabbed up his leg, laming him.

She would not stay for him, could not. He used the sword to aid him and kept climbing.

A horseman rushed up on him from behind; he whirled, seized a pikethrust between arm and body and wrenched, pulled the halfling off, asprawl with him; the horse rushed on, shying from them. Vanye struck with the longsword's pommel, dazed the halfling and staggered free, struggling only to climb, half-deaf to the rider that thundered up behind him.

He saw Morgaine turning back, giving up ground won, casting herself back among enemies. "No!" he shouted, trying to wave her off; the exhausted gray could not carry them, double weight in flight. He saw what Morgaine, intent on reaching him, could not see: the massing of a unit of horse on her flank.

A bay horse rushed past him, a flash of bare legs as he turned, lifting the sword: Jhirun reined in hard and slid down. "Lord!" she cried, thrusting the reins into his hand, and, "Go!" she shouted at him, her voice breaking.

He flung himself for the saddle, felt the surge of the horse as life itself; but he delayed, taut-reined, offered his bloody hand to her.

She stumbled back, hand behind her, the shying horse putting paces between them as she backed away on the corpse-littered slope.

"Go!" she screamed furiously, and cursed him.

Dazed, he reined back; and then he looked upslope, where Morgaine delayed, enemies broken before her. She shouted something at him; he could not hear it, but he knew.

He spurred the mare forward, and Morgaine reined about and joined with him in the climb. Ohtija forces wavered before them, broke as horses went down under Morgaine's fire. Peasants scattered screaming, confounding the order of cavalry.

They mounted the crest of the hill, toward an enemy that fled their path in disorder, peasants and lords together, entering into that great circle that was the Well of Abarais, where opal lights surged and drifted among the Stones, where a vast blue space yawned bottomlessly before them, drinking in men and halfling riders, seeming at once to hurtle skyward and downward, out of place in the world that beheld it, a burning blue too terrible against Shiuan's graying skies.

Siptah took the leap in one long rush; the bay mare tried to shy off, but Vanye rammed his spurs into her and drove her, cruel in his desperation, as they hurtled up and into that burning, brighter sky.

There was a moment of dark, of twisting bodies, of shadow-shapes, as they fell through the nightmare of Between, the two of them together; and then the horses found ground beneath them again, the two of them still running, dreamlike in their slowness as the legs extended into reality, and then rapidly, cutting a course through frightened folk that had no will to stop them.

None pursued, not yet; the arrows that flew after them were few and ill-aimed; the cries of alarm faded into the distance, until there was only the sound of the horses under them, and the view of open plains about them.

They drew rein and began to walk the exhausted animals. Vanye looked back, where a newly arrived horde massed at the foot of Gates that still shimmered with power: Roh's to command, those who gathered there, still lost, still bewildered.

About them stretched a land as wide and flat as the eye could reach, a land of grass and plenty. Vanye drew a deep breath of the air, found the winds clean and untainted, and looked at Morgaine, who rode beside him, not looking back.

She would not speak yet. There was a time for speaking. He saw the weariness in her, her unwillingness to reckon with this land. She had run a long course, forcing those she could not lead.

"I needed an army," she said at last, a voice faint and thin. "There was only one that I could manage, that could breach his camp. And it was very good to see thee, Vanye."

"Aye," he said, and thought it enough. There was time for other things.

She drew *Changeling*, by it to take their bearings in this wide land.   ·

Book Three

↶ Chapter 19

The men passed, carts and wagons and what animals could be forced, unwilling, into that terrible void. Jhirun lay between the cooling body of the black horse and the jumble of rocks, and gazed with horror up that hill, at the swirling fires that were the Well, that drank in all that came. Straggling horsemen on frightened mounts; peasants afoot; rank on rank they came, all the host of Shiuan and Hiuaj, women of the Shiua peasants and of the glittering *khal*, men that worked the fields and men that bleached their hair and wore the black robes of priests, fingering their amulets and invoking the blind powers that drank them in. Some came with terror and some few with exaltation; and the howling winds took them, and they passed from view.

Came also the last stragglers of the Aren-folk, women and children and old ones, and a few youths to protect them. She saw one of her tall cousins of Barrows-hold, who moved into the light and vanished, bathed in its shimmering fires. The sun reached its zenith and declined, and still the passage continued, some last few running in exhausted eagerness, or limping with wounds, and some lingered, needing attempt after attempt to gather their courage.

Jhirun wrapped her shawl about her and shivered, leaning her cheek against the rock, watching them, unnoticed, a peasant girl, nothing to those who had their minds set on the Well and the hope beyond it.

At last in the late afternoon the last of them passed, a lame halfling, who spent long in struggling up the trampled slope, past the bodies of the slain. He vanished. Then there was only the unnatural heaviness of the air, and the howling of wind through the Well, the fires that shimmered there against the gray-clouded sky.

She was the last. On stiff and cramped legs she gathered herself up and walked, conscious of the smallness of herself as she ascended that slope, into air that seemed too heavy to breathe, the wind pulling at her skirts. She entered that area of light, the maelstrom of the fires, stood within the circle of the Well and shuddered, blinking in terror at the perspective that gaped before her, blindingly blue. The winds urged at her.

Her cousins had gone; they had all gone, the Aren-folk, the Barrowers, Fwar, the lords of Ohtij-in.

This she had set out to find; and Fwar had possessed it instead, he and the Aren-folk. They would shape the dream to their own desires, seeking what they would have.

She wept, and turned her back on the Well, lacking courage—hugged her shawl about her, and in doing so remembered a thing that she had carried far from its origin.

She drew it from between her breasts, the little gull-figure, and touched the fine work of its wings, her eyes blurring the details of it. She turned, and hurled it, a shining mote, through the pillars of the Wells. The winds took it, and it never fell. It was gone.

He was gone, he at least, into a land that would not so bewilder him, where there might be mountains, and plains for the mare to run.

They would not take him, Fwar and his enemies. She believed that.

She turned and walked away, out of the fires and into the gray light. Halfway down the hill the winds ceased, and there was a great silence.

She turned to look; and even as she watched, the fires seemed to shimmer like the air above the marsh; and they shredded, and vanished, leaving only the gray daylight between the pillars of the Well, and those pillars only gray and ordinary stone.

Jhirun blinked, finding difficulty now even to believe that there had been magics there, for her senses could no longer hold them. She stared until the tears dried upon her face, and then she turned and picked her way downhill, pausing now and again to plunder the dead: from this one a waterflask, from another a dagger with a golden hilt.

A movement startled her, a ring of harness, a rider that came upon her from beyond the rocks, slowly: a bay horse and a man in tattered blue, white-haired and familiar at once.

She stood still, waiting; the *khal*-lord made no haste. He drew to a halt across her path, his face pale and sober, his gray eyes clear, stained with shadow. A bloody rag was about his left arm.

"Kithan," she said. She gave him no titles. He ruled nothing. She saw that he had found a sword; strangely she did not fear him.

He moved his foot from the stirrup, held out a slender, fine-boned hand; his face was stern, but the gray eyes were anxious.

He needed her, she thought cynically. He was not prepared to survive in the land. She extended her hand to him, set her foot in the stirrup, surprised that there was such strength in his slender arm, that drew her up.

There were villages; there were fields the water would not reach in their lifetime. There were old ones left, and the timid, and those who had not believed.

The bay horse began to move; she set her arms about Kithan, and rested, yielding to the motion of the horse as they descended the hill. She shut her eyes and resolved not to look back, not until the winding of the road should come between them and the hill.

Thunder rumbled in the heavens. There were the first cold drops of rain.

Fires of Azeroth

"Records are pointless. There is a strange conceit in making them when we are the last—but a race should leave something. The world is going . . . and the end of the world comes, not for us, perhaps, but soon. And we have always loved monuments.

"Know that it was Morgaine kri Chya who wrought this ruin. Morgen-Angharan, Men named her: the White Queen, she of the white gull feather, who was the death that came on us. It was Morgaine who extinguished the last brightness in the north, who cast Ohtij-in down to ruin, and stripped the land of inhabitants.

"Even before this present age she was the curse of our land, for she led the Men of the Darkness, a thousand years before us; her they followed here, to their own ruin; and the Man who rides with her and the Man who rides before her are of the same face and likeness—for now and then are alike with her.

"We dream dreams, my queen and I, each after our own fashion. All else went with Morgaine."

—A stone, on a barren isle of Shiuan.

⌐ Chapter 1

The plain gave way to forest, and the forest closed about, but there was no stopping, not until the green shadow thickened and the setting of the sun brought a chill to the air.

Then Vanye ceased for a time to look behind him, and breathed easier for his safety . . . his and his liege's. They rode further until the light failed indeed, and then Morgaine reined gray Siptah to a halt, in a clear space beside a brook, under an arch of old trees. It was a quiet place and pleasant, were it not for the fear which pursued them.

"We shall find no better," Vanye said, and Morgaine nodded, wearily slid down.

"I shall tend Siptah," she said as he dismounted. It was his place, to tend the horses, to make the fire, to do whatever task wanted doing for Morgaine's comfort. That was the nature of an *ilin*, who was Claimed to the service of a liege. But they had ridden hard for more than this day, and his wounds troubled him, so that he was glad of her offer. He stripped his own bay mare down to halter and tether, and rubbed her down and cared for her well, for she had done much even to last such a course as they had run these last days. The mare was in no wise a match for Morgaine's gray stud, but she had heart, and she was a gift besides. Lost, the girl who had given her to him; and he did not forget that gift, nor ever would. For that cause he took special care of the little Shiua bay—but also because he was Kurshin, of a land where children learned the saddle before their feet were steady on the earth, and it sat ill with him to use a horse as he had had to use this one.

He finished, and gathered an armload of wood, no hard task in this dense forest. He brought it to Morgaine, who had already started a small fire in tinder—and *that* was no hard task for her, by means which he preferred not to handle. They were not alike, she and he: armed alike, in the fashion of Andur-Kursh—leather and mail, his brown, hers black; his mail made of wide rings and hers of links finely meshed and shining like silver, the like of which no common armorer could fashion; but he was of honest human stock, and most avowed that Morgaine was not. His eyes and hair were brown as the earth of Andur-Kursh; her eyes were pale gray and her hair was like morning frost . . . *qhal*-fair, fair as the ancient enemies of mankind, as the evil which followed them—though she denied that she was of that blood, he had his own opinions of it: it was only sure that she had no loyalty to that kind.

He carefully fed the fire she had begun, and worried about enemies the while he did so, mistrusting this land, to which they were strangers. But it was a little fire, and the forest screened them. Warmth was a comfort they had lacked in their journeyings of recent days; they were due some ease, having reached this place.

By that light, they shared the little food which remained to them . . . less concerned for their diminishing supplies than they might have been, for there was the likelihood of game hereabouts. They saved back only enough of the stale bread for the morrow, and then, for he had done most of his sleeping in the saddle—he would gladly have cast himself down to sleep, well-fed as he was, or have stood watch while Morgaine did so.

But Morgaine took that sword she bore, and eased it somewhat from sheath . . . and that purged all the sleep from him.

Changeling was its name, an evil name for a viler thing. He did not like to be near it, sheathed or drawn, but it was a part of her, and he had no choice. A sword it seemed, dragon-hilted, of the elaborate style that had been fashioned in Koris of Andur a hundred years before his birth . . . but the blade was edged crystal. Opal colors swirled softly in the lines of the runes which were finely etched upon it. It was not good to look at these colors, which blurred the senses. Whether it was safe to touch the blade when its power was thus damped by the sheath, he did not know nor ever care to learn—but Morgaine was never casual with it, and she was not now. She rose before she drew it fully.

It slipped the rest of the way from its sheath. Opal colors flared, throwing strange shadows about them, white light. Darkness shaped a well at the sword's tip, and into that it was even less wholesome to look. Winds howled into it, and what that darkness touched, it took. *Changeling* drew its power from Gates, and was itself a Gate, though none that anyone would choose to travel.

It forever sought its source, and glowed most brightly when aimed Gate-ward. Morgaine searched with it, and turned it full circle, while the trees sighed and the howling wind grew, the light bathing her hands and face and hair. An imprudent insect found oblivion there. A few leaves were torn from trees and whipped into that well of darkness and vanished. The blade flickered slightly east and west, lending hope; but it glowed most brightly southward, as it had constantly done, a pulsing light that hurt the eyes. Morgaine held it steadily toward that point and cursed.

"It does not change," she lamented. "It does not change."

"Please, *liyo,* put it away. It gives no better answer, and does us no good."

She did so. The wind died, the balefire winked out, and she folded the sheathed sword in her arms and settled again, bleakness on her face.

"Southward is our answer. It must be."

"Sleep," he urged her, for she had a frail and transparent look. "*Liyo,* my bones ache and I swear I shall not rest until you have slept. If you have no mercy on yourself, have some for me. Sleep."

She wiped a trembling hand across her eyes and nodded, and lay down where she was on her face, caring not even for preparing a pallet on which to rest. But he rose up quietly and took their blankets, laid one beside her and pushed her over onto it, then threw the other over her. She nestled into that with a murmur of thanks, and stirred a last time as he put her folded cloak under her head. Then she slept the sleep of the dead, with *Changeling* against her like a lover: she released it not even in sleep, that evil thing which she served.

They were, he reflected, effectively lost. Four days past, they had crossed a void the mind refused to remember, the *between* of Gates. That way was sealed. They were cut off from where they had been, and did not know in what land they now were, or what men held it—only that it was a place where Gates led, and that those Gates must be passed, destroyed, sealed.

Such was the war they fought, against the ancient magics, the *qhal*-born powers. Their journey was obsession with Morgaine, and necessity with him, who served her . . . not his concern, the reason she felt bound to such a course; his reason was his oath, which he had sworn to her in Andur-Kursh, and beyond which he had stayed. She sought now the Master Gate of this world, which was that which must be sealed; and had found it, for *Changeling* did not lie. It was the selfsame Gate by which they had entered this land, by which their enemies had entered, behind them. They had fled that place for their lives . . . by bitter irony, had fled that which they had come to this world to find, and now it was the possession of their enemies.

"It is only that we are still within the influence of the Gate we have just left," Morgaine had reasoned in the beginning of their flight northward, when the sword had first warned them. But as the distance widened between them and that power, still the sword gave the same disturbing answer, until there re-mained little doubt what the truth was. Morgaine had muttered things about horizons and the curving of the land, and other possibilities which he by no means comprehended; but at last she shook her head and became fixed upon the worst of her fears. It was impossible for them to have done other than flee. He tried to persuade of her that; their enemies would surely have overwhelmed them. But that knowledge was no comfort to her despair.

"I shall know for certain," she had said, "if the strength of the sending does not diminish by this evening. The sword can find lesser Gates, and it is possible still that we are on the wrong side of the world or too far removed from any other. But lesser Gates do not glow so brightly. If I see it tonight as bright as last, then we shall know beyond doubt what we have done."

And thus they knew.

Vanye eased himself of some of the buckles of his armor. There was not a bone of his body which did not separately ache, but he had a cloak and a fire this night, and cover to hide him from enemies, which was better than he had known of late. He wrapped his cloak about him and set his back against an aged tree. His sword he laid naked across his knees. Lastly he removed his helm, which was wrapped about with the white scarf of the *ilin*, and set it aside, shak-ing free his hair and enjoying the absence of that weight. The woods were quiet about them. The water rippled over stones; the leaves sighed; the horses moved quietly at tether, cropping the little grass that grew where the trees were not. The Shiua mare was stablebred, with no sense of enemies, useless on watch; but Siptah was a sentinel as reliable as any man, war-trained and wary of strangers, and he trusted to the gray horse as to a comrade in his watch, which made all the world less lonely. Food in his belly and warmth against the night, a stream when he should thirst and surely game plentiful for the hunting. A moon was up, a smallish one and unthreatening, and the trees sighed very like those of Andur's lost forests—it was a healing thing, when there was no way home, to find something so much like it. He would have been at peace, had *Changeling* pointed some other way.

Dawn came softly and subtly, with singing of birds and the sometime stirring of the horses. Vanye still sat, propping his head on his arm and forcing his blurred eyes to stay open, and scanned the forest in the soft light of day.

All at once Morgaine moved, reached for weapons, then blinked at him in dismay, leaning on her elbow. "What befell? Thee fell asleep on watch?"

He shook his head, shrugged off the prospect of her anger, which he had already reckoned on. "I decided not to wake you. You looked overtired."

"Is it a favor to me if you fall out of the saddle today?"

He smiled and shook his head yet again, inwardly braced against the sting of her temper, which could be hurtful. She hated to be cared for, and she was too often inclined to drive herself when she might have rested, to prove the point. It should of course be otherwise between them, *ilin* and *liyo,* servant and liege lady . . . but she refused to learn to rely on anyone . . . *expecting I shall die,* he thought, with a troubling touch of ill-omen, *as others have who have served her; she waits on that.*

"Shall I saddle the horses, *liyo?*"

She sat up, shrugged the blanket about her in the morning chill and stared at the ground, resting her hands at her temples. "I have need to think. We must go back somehow. I have need to think."

"Best you do that rested, then."

Her eyes flicked to his, and at once he regretted pricking at her—a perversity in him, who was fretted by her habits. He knew that temper surely followed, along with a sharp reminder of his place. He was prepared to bear that, as he had a hundred times and more, intended and unintended, and he simply wished it said and done. "It likely is," she said quietly, and that confounded him. "Aye, saddle the horses."

He rose and did so, troubled at heart. His own moving was painful; he limped, and there was a constant stitch in his side, a cracked rib, he thought. Doubtless she hurt too, and that was expected; bodies mended; sleep restored strength . . . but most of all he was concerned about the sudden quiet in her, this despair and yielding. They had been travelling altogether too long, at a pace which wore them to nerve and bone; no rest, never rest, world and world and world. They survived the hurts; but there were things of the soul too, overmuch of death and war, and horror which still dogged them, hunting them—to which now they had to return. Of a sudden he longed for her anger, for something he understood.

"*Liyo,*" he said when he had finished with the horses and she knelt burying the fire, covering all trace of it. He dropped down, put himself on both knees, being *ilin.* "*Liyo,* it comes to me that if our enemies are sitting where we must return, then sit they will, at least for a time; they fared no better in that passage than we. For us—*liyo,* I beg you know that I will go on as long as seems good to you, I will do everything that you ask—but I am tired, and I have wounds on me that have not healed, and it seems to me that a little rest, a few days to freshen the horses and to find game and renew our supplies—is it not good sense to rest a little?"

He pleaded his own cause; did he plead his concern for her, he thought, then that instinctive stubbornness would harden against all reason. Even so he rather more expected anger than agreement. But she nodded wearily, and further confounded him by laying a hand on his arm—a brief touch; there were rarely such gestures between them, no intimacy . . . never had been.

"We will ride the bow of the forest today," she said, "and see what game we may start, and I agree we should not overwork the horses. They deserve a little rest; their bones are showing. And you—I have seen you limping, and you work often one-armed, and still you try to take all the work from me. You would do everything if you had your way about it."

"Is that not the way it is supposed to be?"

"Many the time I have dealt unfairly with you; and I am sorry for that."

He tried to laugh, passing it off, and misliked more and more this sudden sinking into melancholy. Men cursed Morgaine, in Andur and in Kursh, in Shiuan and Hiuaj and the land between. More friends' lives than enemies' were to the account of that fell *geas* that drove her. Even him she had sacrificed on occasion; and would again; and being honest, did not pretend otherwise.

"*Liyo,*" he said, "I understand you better than you seem to think—not always *why,* but at least *what* moves you. I am only *ilin*-bound, and I can argue with the one I am bound to; but the thing you serve has no mercy at all. I know that. You are mad if you think it is only my oath that keeps me with you."

It was said; he wished then he had not said it, and rose and found work for himself tying their gear to saddles, anything to avoid her eyes.

When she came to take Siptah's reins and set herself in the saddle, the frown was there, but it was more perplexed than angry.

Morgaine kept silent in their riding, which was leisurely and followed the bendings of the stream; and the weariness of his sleepless night claimed him finally, so that he bowed his head and folded his arms about him, sleeping while they rode, Kurshin-style. She took the lead, and guarded him from branches.

The sun was warm and the sighing of leaves sang a song very like the forests of Andur, as if time had bent back on itself and they rode a path they had ridden in the beginning.

Something crashed in the brush. The horses started, and he came awake at once, reaching for his sword.

"Deer." She pointed off through the woods, where the animal lay on its side.

Deer it was not, but something very like unto it, oddly dappled with gold. He dismounted with his sword in hand, having respect for the spreading antlers, but it was stone-dead when he touched it. Other weapons had Morgaine besides *Changeling, qhalur*-sort also, which killed silently and at distance, without apparent wound. She swung down from the saddle, and gave him her skinning-knife, and he set to, minded strangely of another time, a creature which had been indeed a deer, and a winter storm in his homeland's mountains.

He shook off that thought. "Had it been to me," he said, "it would have been small game and fish and precious little of that. I must have myself a bow, *liyo.*"

She shrugged. In fact his pride was hurt, such of it as remained sensitive with her, that he had not done this, but she; yet it was her place to provide for him, her *ilin.* At times he detected hurt pride in her, that the hearth she gave him was a campfire, and the hall a canopy of branches, and food often enough scant or lacking entirely. Of all lords an *ilin* could have been ensnared to serve, Morgaine was beyond doubt the most powerful, and the poorest. The arms she provided him were plundered, the horse stolen before it was given, and their provisions likewise. They lived always like hedge-bandits. But tonight and for days afterward they would not have hunger to plague them, and he saw her slight hurt at the offense behind his words; with that he dismissed his vanity and vowed himself grateful for the gift.

It was not a place for long lingering: birds' alarm, the flight of other creatures—death in the forest announced itself. He took the best and stripped that, with swift strokes of the keen blade—skill gained in outlawry in Kursh, to hunt wolf-wary in the territories of hostile clans, to take and flee, covering his traces. So he had done, solitary, until a night he had sheltered with Morgaine kri Chya, and traded her his freedom for a place out of the wind.

He washed his hands from the bloody work, and tied the hide bundle on the saddle, while Morgaine made shift to haul the remnant into the brush. He scuffed the earth about and disposed of what sign he could. Scavengers would soon muddle the rest, covering their work, and he looked about carefully, making sure, for not all their enemies were hall-bred, men of blind eyes. One there was among them who could follow the dimmest trail, and that one he feared most of all.

That man was of clan Chya, of forested Koris in Andur, his own mother's people . . . and of his mother's close kin; it was at least the shape he lately wore.

*   *   *

It was an early camp, and a full-fed one. They attended to the meat which they must carry with them, drying it in the smoke of the fire and preparing it to last as long as possible. Morgaine claimed first watch, and Vanye cast himself to sleep early and wakened to his own sense of time. Morgaine had not moved to wake him, and had not intended to, he suspected, meaning to do to him what he had done to her; but she yielded her post to him without objection when he claimed it: she was not one for pointless arguments.

In his watch he sat and fed the fire by tiny pieces, making sure that the drying was proceeding as it should. The strips had hardened, and he cut a piece and chewed at it lazily. Such leisure was almost forgotten in his life—to have a day's respite, two—to contemplate.

The horses snuffed and moved in the dark. Siptah took some interest in the little Shiua mare, which would prove difficulty did she breed; but there was no present hazard of that. The sounds were ordinary and comfortable.

A sudden snort, a moving of brush . . . he stiffened in every muscle, his heart speeding. Brush cracked: that was the horses.

He moved, ignoring bruises to rise in utter silence, and with the tip of his sword reached to touch Morgaine's outflung hand.

Her eyes opened, fully aware in an instant; met his, which slid in the direction of the small sound he had sensed more than heard. The horses were still disturbed.

She gathered herself, silent as he; and stood, a black shape in the embers' glow, with her white hair making her all too much a target. Her hand was not empty. That small black weapon which had killed the deer was aimed toward the sound, but shield it was not. She gathered up *Changeling*, better protection, and he gripped his sword, slipped into the darkness; Morgaine moved, but in another direction, and vanished.

Brush stirred. The horses jerked madly at tethers of a sudden and whinnied in alarm. He slipped through a stand of saplings and something he had taken for a piece of scrub . . . moved: a dark spider-shape, that chilled him with its sudden life. He went further, trying to follow its movements, cautious not least because Morgaine was a-hunt the same as he.

Another shadow: that was Morgaine. He stood still, mindful that hers was a distance-weapon, and deadly accurate; but she was not one to fire blindly or in panic. They met, and crouched still a moment. No sound disturbed the night now but the shifting of the frightened horses.

No beast: he signed to her with his straight palm that it had gone upright, and touched her arm, indicating that they should return to the fireside. They went quickly, and he killed the fire while she gathered their provisions. Fear was coppery in his mouth, the apprehension of ambush possible, and the urgency of flight. Blankets were rolled, the horses saddled, the whole affair of their camp undone with silent and furtive movements. Quickly they were in the saddle and moving by dark, on a different track: no following a spy in the moonless dark, to find that he had friends.

Still the memory of that figure haunted him, the eerie movement which had tricked his eye and vanished. "Its gait was strange," he said, when they were far from that place and able to talk. "As if it were unjointed."

What Morgaine thought of that, he could not see. "There are more than strange beasts where Gates have led," she said.

But they saw nothing more astir in the night. Day found them far away, on a streamcourse which was perhaps different from the one of the night before, perhaps not. It bent in leisurely windings, so that branches screened this way and that in alternation, a green curtain constantly parting and closing as they rode.

Then, late, they came upon a tree with a white cord tied about its trunk, an old and dying tree, lightning-riven.

Vanye stopped at the evidence of man's hand hereabouts, but Morgaine tapped Siptah with her heels and they went a little further, to a place where a trail crossed their stream.

Wheels rutted that stretch of muddy earth.

To his dismay Morgaine turned off on that road. It was not her custom to seek out folk who could as easily be left undisturbed by their passing . . . but she seemed minded now to do so.

"Wherever we are," she said at last, "if these are gentle people we owe them warning for what we have brought behind us. And if otherwise, then we shall look them over and see what trouble we can devise for our enemies."

He said nothing to that. It seemed as reasonable a course as any, for two who were about to turn and pursue thousands, and those well-armed, and many horsed, and in possession of power enough to unhinge the world through which they rode.

Conscience: Morgaine claimed none . . . not altogether truth, but near enough the mark. The fact was that in that blade which hung on the saddle beneath her knee, Morgaine herself had some small share of that power, and therefore it was not madness which led her toward such a road, but a certain ruthlessness.

He went, because he must.

∽ Chapter 2

There were signs of habitation, of the hand of some manner of men, all down the road: the ruts of wheels, the cloven-hoofed prints of herded beasts, the occasional snag of white wool on a roadside branch. *This is the way their herds come to water,* Vanye reasoned. *There must be some open land hereabouts for their grazing.*

It was late, that softest part of afternoon, when they came upon the center of it all.

It was a village which might, save for its curving roofs, have occupied some forest edge in Andur; and a glamour of forest sunlight lay over it, shaded as its roofs were by old trees, a gold-green warmth that hazed the old timbers and the thatched roofs. It was almost one with the forest itself, save for the fanciful carving of the timbers under the eaves, which bore faded colors. It was a cozy huddle of some thirty buildings, with no walls for defense . . . cattle pens and a cart or two, a dusty commons, a large hall of thatch and timbers and carved beams, no proper lord's hold, but rustic and wide-doored and mainly windowed.

Morgaine stopped on the road and Vanye drew in beside her. A boding of ill came on him, and of regret. "Such a place," he said, "must have no enemies."

"It will have," said Morgaine, and moved Siptah forward.

Their approach brought a quiet stirring in the village, a cluster of dusty children who looked up from their play and stared, a woman who looked out a window and came out of doors drying her hands on her skirts, and two old men who came out of the hall and waited their coming. Younger men and an old woman joined that pair, with a boy of about fifteen and a workman in a leather apron. More elders gathered. Solemnly they stood, . . . human folk, dark-skinned and small of stature.

Vanye looked nervously between the houses and among the trees that stood close behind, and across the wide fields which lay beyond in the vast clearing. He scanned the open windows and doors, the pens and the carts, seeking some ambush. There was nothing. He kept his hand on the hilt of his sword, which rode at his side; but Morgaine had her hands free and in sight . . . all peaceful she seemed, and gracious. He did not scruple to look suspiciously on everything.

Morgaine reined in before the little cluster that had gathered before the hall steps. All the folk bowed together, as gracefully and solemnly as lords, and when they looked up at her, their faces held wonder, but no hint of fear.

Ah, mistrust us, Vanye wished them. *You do not know what has come among you.* But nothing but awe touched those earnest faces, and the eldest of them bowed again, and addressed them.

Then Vanye's heart froze in him, for it was the *qhalur* tongue that these Men spoke.

Arrhthein, they hailed Morgaine, which was *my lady;* little by little as they rode, Morgaine had insisted to teach him, until he knew words of courtesies and threat and necessities. Not *qhal* in any case, these small dark folk, so courteous of manner . . . but the Old Ones were clearly reverenced here, and therefore they welcomed Morgaine, taking her for *qhal,* which she was to the eye.

He reasoned away his shock: there was a time his Kurshin soul would have shuddered to hear that language on human lips, but now it passed his own. The speech was current, Morgaine had persuaded him, wherever *qhal* had been, in whatever lands Gates led to, and it had lent many words to his own language— which disturbed him to realize. That these folk spoke it nearly pure . . . that amazed him. *Khemeis,* they addressed him, which sounded like *kheman:* accompany . . . *Companion,* perhaps, for *my lord* he was not, not where *qhal* were honored.

"Peace," he bade them softly in that language, the appropriate greeting; and "How may we please you and your lady?" they asked in all courtesy, but he could not answer, only understand.

Morgaine spoke with them, and they with her; after a moment she looked across at him. "Dismount," she said in the *qhalur* tongue. "Here are friendly people." But that was surely for show and for courtesy; he dismounted as she ordered him, but he did not let down his guard or intend to leave her back unguarded. He stood with arms folded, where he could both see those to whom she spoke and keep a furtive watch on the others who began to join the crowd—too many people and too close for his liking, although none of them seemed unfriendly.

Some of what was said he followed; Morgaine's teaching with him had encompassed enough that he knew they were being welcomed and offered food. The accent was a little different than Morgaine's, but no worse than the shift from Andurin to Kurshin in his mother tongue.

"They offer us hospitality," Morgaine said, "and I am minded to take it, at least for tonight. There is no immediate threat here that I can see."

"As you will, *liyo.*"

She gestured toward a handsome lad of about ten. "He is Sin, the elder Bythein's grandnephew. He is offered to care for the horses, but I had rather you did that and simply let him help you."

She meant to go among them alone, then. He was not pleased at that prospect, but she had done worse things, and, armed, she was of the two of them the more dangerous, a fact which most misjudged. He took *Changeling* from her saddle and gave it to her, and gathered up the reins of both horses.

"This way, *khemeis,*" the boy bade him; and while Morgaine went into the hall with the elders, the boy walked with him toward the pens, trying to match his man's strides and gawking at him like any village lad unused to arms and strangers . . . perhaps amazed also at his lighter complexion and his height, which must seem considerable to these small folk. No man in the village reached more than his shoulder, and few that much. Perhaps, he thought, they reckoned him halfling *qhal,* no honor to him, but he did not mean to dispute it with them.

The boy Sin chattered at him busily when he reached the pens and began to unsaddle the horses, but it was conversation all in vain with him. Finally the realization seemed to dawn upon Sin, who asked him yet another question.

"I am sorry; I do not understand," he answered, and the boy squinted up at him, stroking the mare's neck under her mane.

"*Khemeis?*" the boy asked of him.

He could not explain. *I am a stranger here,* he could say; or *I am of Andur-Kursh;* or other words, which he did not intend to have known. It seemed wisest to leave all such accountings to Morgaine, who could listen to these people and choose what to reveal and what to conceal and argue out their misconceptions.

"Friend," he said, for he could say that too, and Sin's face lighted and a grin spread across it.

"Yes," Sin said, and fell to currying the bay mare with zeal. Whatever Vanye showed him, Sin was eager to do, and his thin features glowed with pleasure when Vanye smiled and tried to show satisfaction with his work . . . a good folk, an open-handed people, Vanye thought, and felt the safer in their lodgings. "Sin," he said, having composed his sentence carefully, "you take care for the horses. Agreed?"

"I shall sleep here," Sin declared, and adoration burned in his dark eyes. "I shall care for them, for you and for the lady."

"Come with me," Vanye told him, slinging their gear on his shoulder, saddlebags which held things they needed for the night, and food that might draw animals, and Morgaine's saddle kit, which was nothing to be left to the curiosity of others. He was pleased in the company of the boy, who had no shyness or lack of patience in speaking with him. He set his hand on Sin's shoulder and the boy swelled visibly with importance under the eyes of the other children, who watched from a distance. They walked together back to the hall, and up the wooden steps to the inside.

It was a high-raftered place, the center filled with a long row of tables and benches, a place for feasts; and there was a grand fireplace, and light from the many wide windows which—like the unwalled condition of the village— betokened a place that had never taken thought for its defense. Morgaine sat there, a bit of pallor black-clad and glittering with silver mail in the dusty light, surrounded by villagers both male and female, young and old, some on benches and some at her feet. At the edge of that circle mothers rocked children on their laps, keeping them still, themselves seeming curious to listen.

Way was made for him, folk edging this way and that to let him through at once. He found a bench offered him, when his place was sitting on the floor, but he took it; and Sin managed to work eelwise to his feet and settle there against his knee.

Morgaine looked at him. "They offer us welcome and whatever we have need of, equipage or food. They seem most amazed by you; they cannot conceive of your origins, tall and different as you are; and they are somewhat alarmed that we go so heavily armed . . . but I have explained to them that you entered my service in a far country."

"There are surely *qhal* here."

"I would surmise so. But if that is the case, they must not be hostile to these folk." She made her voice gentle then, and lapsed back into the *qhalur* tongue. "Vanye, these are the elders of the village: Sersein and her man Serseis; Bythein and Bytheis; Melzein and Melzeis. They say that we may shelter in this hall tonight."

He inclined his head, assenting and offering respect to their hosts.

"For now," Morgaine added in Andurin, "I only ask questions of them. I counsel thee the same."

"I have said nothing."

She nodded, and speaking to the elders, turned again to the *qhalur* language, with fluency he could not follow.

It was a strange meal they took that night, with the hall aglow with torches and with firelight from the hearth, and the board laden with abundance of food, the benches crowded with villagers young and old. It was the custom here, Morgaine explained, that all the village take the evening meal together as if they were one house, as indeed was the custom of Ra-koris in Andur, but here even children attended, and played recklessly among their elders, suffered to speak at table with abandon that would have fetched a Kurshin child, be he lord's son or peasant, a ringing ear and a stern march outside to a more thorough chastisement. Children here filled their bellies and then slid down from table to play noisily in the pillared wings of the hall, laughing and shouting above the roar of conversation.

It was not, at least, a hall where one feared an assassin's knife or poison. Vanye sat at Morgaine's right—an *ilin* should stand behind, and he would rather have tasted the food that she was offered to be certain, all the same; but Morgaine forbade that, and he gave up his apprehensions. In the pen outside, the horses fed on good hay, and they sat in this bright, warm hall amid folk who seemed more inclined to kill them by overfeeding than by ill will. When at last no one could eat any more, the children who did not wish to be quiet were cheerfully dismissed into the dark outside, the oldest of that company leading the youngest, and there seemed no thought in anyone that the children might be in any danger in the dark outdoors. Within the hall, a girl began to play on a tall, strangely tuned harp, and sang beautifully with it. There was a second song which everyone sang, save themselves; and then they were offered the harp as well—but playing was long-past for him. His fingers had forgotten whatever childish skill they had once had, and he refused it, embarrassed. Morgaine also declined; if there was ever a time when she had had leisure to learn music, he could not imagine it.

But Morgaine spoke with them instead, and they seemed pleased by what she said. There followed a little discussion, in which he could not share, before the girl sang one last song.

Then dinner was done, and the villagers went their own way to beds in their houses, while the oldest children were quick to make their guests a place nearest the fire . . . two pallets and a curtain for privacy, and a kettle of warm water for washing.

The last of the children went down the outside steps and Vanye drew a long breath, in this first solitude they had enjoyed since riding in. He saw Morgaine unbuckle her armor, ridding herself of that galling weight, which she did not do on the trail or in any chancy lodging. If she were so inclined, he felt himself permitted, and gratefully stripped down to shut and breeches, washed behind the curtain and dressed again, for he did not utterly trust the place. Morgaine did likewise; and they settled down with their weapons near them, to sleep alternately.

His watch was first, and he listened well for any stirring in the village, went to the windows and looked out on this side and on the other, on the forest and the moonlit fields, but there was no sign of movement, nor were the village windows all shuttered. He went back and settled at the hearth in the warmth, and began to accept finally that all this bewildering gentleness was true and honest.

It was rare in all their journeying that there awaited them no curse, no hedge of weapons, but only kindness.

Here Morgaine's name was not yet known.

The morning brought a smell of baking bread, and the stir of folk about the hall, a scatter of children who were hushed to quiet. "Perhaps," Vanye murmured, smelling that pleasant aroma of baking, "a bit of hot bread to send us on our way."

"We are not going," Morgaine said, and he looked at her in bewilderment, not knowing whether this was good news or ill. "I have thought things through, and you may be right: here is a place where we can draw breath, and if we do not rest in it, then what else can we do but kill the horses under us and drive ourselves beyond our strength? There is no surety beyond any Gate. Should we win through—to another hard ride, and lose everything for want of what we might have gathered here? Three days. We can rest that long. I think your advice is good sense."

"Then you make me doubt it. You have never listened to me, and we are alive, all odds to the contrary."

She laughed humorlessly. "Aye, but I have; and as for my own plans, some of the best of those have gone amiss at the worst of times. I have ignored your advice sometimes at our peril, and this time I take it. I reckon our chances even."

They broke fast, served by grave-faced children who brought them some of that hot bread, and fresh milk and sweet butter besides. They ate as if they had had nothing the night before, for such a breakfast was not a luxury that belonged to outlawry.

Three days went too quickly; and the courtesy and gentleness of the folk brought something that Vanye would have given much to see: for Morgaine's gray eyes grew clean of that pain which had ridden there so long, and she smiled and sometimes laughed, softly and merrily.

The horses fared as well: they rested, and the children brought them handfuls of sweet grass, and petted them, and combed their manes and curried them with such zeal that Vanye found nothing to do for them but a bit of smithing—in which the village smith was all too willing to assist, with his forge and his skill.

Whenever he was at the pens with the horses, the children, particularly Sin, hung over the rails and chattered merrily to him, trying to ask him questions of the animals and Morgaine and himself, little of which he even understood.

"Please, *khemeis* Vanye," said Sin, when he leaned to rest on the edge of the watering-keg, "please may we see the weapons?" At least so he put the words together.

He recalled his own boyhood, when he had watched in awe the *dai-uyin,* the high-clan gentlemen with their armor and their horses and weapons . . . but with the bitter knowledge of bastardy, which—for he had been a lord's bastard, gotten on a captive—made the attainment of such things desperate necessity. These were only village children, whose lives did not tend toward arms and wars, and their curiosity was that which they might hold toward the moon and stars . . . something remote from them, and untainted by understanding.

"Avert," he murmured in his own tongue, wishing harm from them, and unhooked the side ring of his sheathed sword, slipped it to his hand. He drew it, and let their grimy fingers touch the blade, and he let Sin—which filled the boy with delight—hold the hilt in his own hand and try the balance of it. But then he took it back, for he did not like the look of children with such a grim thing, that had so much blood on it.

Then, pointing, they asked to see the other blade that he carried, and he frowned and shook his head, laying his hand on that carven hilt at his belt. They cajoled, and he would not, for an Honor-blade was not for their hands. It was for suicide, this one, and it was not his, but one he carried, on his oath to deliver it.

"An *elarrh* thing," they concluded, in tones of awe; and he had not the least idea of their meaning, but they ceased asking, and showed no more desire to touch it.

"Sin," he said, thinking to draw a little knowledge from the children, "do men with weapons come here?"

At once there was puzzlement on Sin's face and in the eyes of the others, down to the least child. "You are not of *our* forest," Sin observed, and used the plural *you*—surmise which shot all too directly to the mark. Vanye shrugged, cursing his rashness, which had betrayed him even to children. They knew the conditions of their own land, and had sense enough to find out a stranger who knew not what he should.

"Where are you from?" a little girl asked. And, wide-eyed, with a touch of delicious horror: "Are you *sirren?*"

Others decried that suggestion in outrage, and Vanye, conscious of his helplessness in their small hands, bowed his head and busied himself hooking his sword to his belt. He pulled on the ring of the belt that crossed his chest, drawing the sword to his shoulder behind, hooked it to his side. Then: "I have business," he said, and walked away. Sin made to follow. "Please no," he said, and Sin fell back, looking troubled and thoughtful, which in no wise comforted him.

He walked back to the hall, and there found Morgaine, sitting with the clan elders and with some of the young men and women who had stayed from their day's work to attend her. Quietly he approached, and they made place for him as before. For a long time he sat listening to the talk that flowed back and forth between Morgaine and the others, understanding occasional small sentences, or the gist of them. Morgaine sometimes interrupted herself to give him an essential word—strange conversation for her, for they spoke much of their crops, and their livestock and their woods, of all the affairs of their village.

Like, he thought, *a village discussing with its lord their state of affairs.* Yet she accepted this, and listened more than she spoke, as was ever her habit.

At last the villagers took their leave, and Morgaine settled next the fire and relaxed a time. Then he came and rested on his knees before her, embarrassed by what he had to confess, that he had betrayed them to children.

She smiled when he had told her. "So. Well, I do not think it much harm. I have not been able to learn much of how *qhal* may be involved in this land, but, Vanye, there are things here so strange I hardly see how we could avoid revealing ourselves as strangers."

"What does *elarrh* mean?"

"It comes from *arrh,* that is *noble,* or *ar,* that is *power.* The words are akin, and it could be either, depending on the situation . . . either or both: for when one addressed a *qhal*-lord in the ancient days as *arrhtheis,* it meant both his status as a *qhal* and the power he had. To Men in those days, all *qhal* had to be *my lord,* and the power in question was that of the Gates, which were always free to them, and never to Men . . . it has that distressing meaning too. *Elarrh* meant something belonging to power, or to lords. A thing—of reverence or hazard. A thing which . . . Men do not touch."

Qhalur thoughts disturbed him, the more he comprehended the *qhalur* tongue. Such arrogance was hateful . . . and other things Morgaine had told him, which he had never guessed, of *qhalur* maneuverings with human folk, things which hinted at the foundations of his own world, and those disturbed him utterly. There was much more, he suspected, which she dared not tell him. "What will you say to these folk," he asked, "and when—about the trouble we have brought on their land? *Liyo,* what do they reckon we are, and what do they think we are doing among them?"

She frowned, leaned forward, arms on knees. "I suspect that they reckon us both *qhal,* you perhaps halfling, . . . but after what fashion or with what feeling I can find no delicate means to ask. Warn them? I wish to. But I would likewise know what manner of thing we shall awaken here when I do so. These are gentle folk; all that I have seen and heard among them confirms that. But what defends them . . . may not be."

It well agreed with his own opinion, that they trod a fragile place, safe in it, but perilously ignorant, and enmeshed in something that had its own ways.

"Be careful always what you say," she advised him. "When you speak in the Kurshin tongue, beware of using names they might know, whatever the language. But henceforth you and I should speak in their language constantly. You must gather what you can of it. It is a matter of our safety, Vanye."

"I am trying to do that," he said. She nodded approval, and they occupied themselves the rest of the day in walking about the village and the edge of the fields, talking together, impressing in his memory every word that could be forced there.

He had expected that Morgaine would choose to leave by the next morning, and she did not; and when that night came and he asked her would they leave on the morrow, she shrugged and in talking of something else, never answered the question. By the day after that, he did not ask, but took his ease in the village and settled into its routine, as Morgaine seemed to have done.

It was a healing quiet, as if the long nightmare that lay at their backs were illusion, and this sunny place were true and real. There was no word from Morgaine of leaving, as if by saying nothing she could wish away all hazard to them and their hosts.

But conscience worried at him, for the days they spent grew to many more than a handful. And he dreamed once, when they slept side by side—both slept, for sitting watch seemed unnecessary in the center of so friendly a place: he came awake sweating, and slept again, and wakened a second time with an outcry that sent Morgaine reaching for her weapons.

"Bad dreams in such a place as this?" she asked him. "There have been places with more reason for them."

But she looked concerned that night too, and lay staring into the fire long afterward. What the dream had been he could not clearly remember, only that there seemed something as sinister in his recollection as the creeping of a serpent on a nest, and he could not prevent it.

These folk will haunt me, he thought wretchedly. They two had no place here, and knew it; and yet selfishly lingered, out of time and place, seeking a little peace . . . taking it as a thief might take, stealing it from its possessors. He wondered whether Morgaine harbored the same guilt . . . or whether she had passed beyond it, being what she was, and impelled by the need to survive.

He was almost moved to argue it with her then; but a dark mood was on her, and he knew those. And when he faced her in the morning, there were folk about them; and later he put it off again, for when he faced the matter, the odds against them outside this place were something he had no haste to meet: Morgaine was gathering forces, and was not ready, and he was loath to urge her with arguments . . . when the *geas* fell on her, she passed beyond reason; and he did not want to be the one to start it.

So he bided, mending harness, working at arrows for a bow which he traded of a villager who was an excellent bowyer. It was offered free, once admired, but in his embarrassment Morgaine intervened with the offer of a return gift, a gold ring of strange workmanship, which must have lain buried in her kit a very long time. He was disturbed at that, suspecting that it might have meant something to her, but she laughed and said that it was time she left it behind.

So he had the bow, and the bowyer a ring that was the envy of his companions. He practiced his archery with the young folk and with Sin, who dogged his tracks faithfully, and strove to do everything that he did.

In the pen and agraze on the grassy margin of the fields, the horses grew sleek and lazy as the village's own cattle . . . and Morgaine, always the one who could not rest in an hour's delay, sat long hours in the sun and talked with the elders and the young herders, drawing on a bit of goatskin what became a great marvel to the villagers, who had never seen a map. Though they had the knowledge of which it grew, they had never seen their world set forth in such a perspective.

Mirrind, the village was named; and the plain beyond the forest was Azeroth; the forest was Shathan. In the center of the great circle that was Azeroth, she drew a skein of rivers, feeding a great river called the Narn; amid that circle also was written *athatin,* which was *the Fires*—or plainly said, the Gate of the World.

So peaceful Mirrind knew of the Gate, and held it in awe: *Azerothen Athatin.* Thus far their knowledge of the world did extend. But Morgaine did not question them on it closely. She made her map and lettered it in *qhalur* runes, a fine fair hand.

Vanye learned such runes . . . as he learned the spoken language. He sat on the step of the meeting hall and traced the symbols in the dust, learning them by writing all the new words that he had learned, and trying to forget the scruples in such things that came of being Kurshin. The children of Mirrind, who thronged him when he would tend the horses or who had such zeal to fetch his arrows that he feared for their safety, quickly found this exercise tedious and deserted him.

"*Elarrh*-work," they pronounced it, which meant anything that was above them. They had awe of it, but when there was no amusement to come of it, and no pictures, they drifted away—all but Sin, who squatted barefoot in the dust and tried to copy.

Vanye looked up at the lad, who worked so intently, and poignant recollection stirred in him, of himself, who had never been taught, but that he had sought it, who had insisted on having the things his legitimate brothers were born to have—and thereby gained what learning his mountain home could offer.

Now among all the children of Mirrind, here sat one who reached and wanted beyond the others, and who—when they had taken their leave—would be most hurt, having learned to desire something Mirrind could not give. The boy had no parents; they had died in some long-ago calamity. He had not asked into it. Sin was everyone's child, and no one's in particular. *The others will be only ordinary,* he thought, *but what of this one?* Remembering his sword in Sin's small hand, he felt a chill, and blessed himself.

"What do you, *khemeis?*" Sin asked.

"I wish you well." He rubbed out the runes with his palm and rose up, with a great heaviness on him.

Sin looked at him strangely, and he turned to go up the steps of the hall. There was a sudden outcry somewhere down Mirrind's single street . . . not the shrieks of playing children, which were frequent, but a woman's outcry; and in sudden apprehension he turned. Hard upon it came the shouting of men, in tones of grief and anger.

He hesitated, his pulse that had seemed to stop now quickening into familiar panic; he hung between that direction and Morgaine's, paralyzed in the moment, and then habit and duty sent him running up the steps to the shadowy hall, where Morgaine was speaking with two of the elders.

He needed not explain: *Changeling* was in her hand and she was coming, near to running.

Sin lingered at the bottom of the steps, and tagged after them as they walked the commons toward the gathering knot of villagers. The sound of weeping reached them . . . and when Morgaine arrived the gathering gave way for her, all but a few: the elders Melzein and Melzeis, who stood trying to hold back their tears; and a young woman and a couple in middle years who knelt holding their dead. To and fro they rocked, keening and shaking their heads.

"Eth," Morgaine murmured, staring down at a young man who had been one of the brightest and best of the village: hardly in his twenties, Eth of clan Melzen, but skilled in hunting and archery, a happy man, a herder by trade, who had laughed much and loved his young wife and had no enemies. His throat had been cut, and on his half-naked body were other wounds that could not have brought death in themselves, but would have caused great pain before he was killed.

They gave him his death, Vanye thought fearfully. *He must have told them what they wanted.* Then he reckoned what kind of man he had become, who could think foremost of that. He had known Eth. He found himself trembling and close to being sick as if he had never looked on the like.

Some of the children were sick, and clung to their parents crying. He found Sin against his side, and set his hand on the boy's shoulder, drew him over to his clan elders and gave him into their care. Bytheis took Sin in his arms and Sin's face was still set and stricken.

"Should the children look on this?" Morgaine asked, shocking them from their daze. "You are in danger. Set armed men out on the road and all about the village and let them watch. Where was he found? Who brought him?"

One of the youths stepped forward—Tal, whose clothes were bloody and his hands likewise. "I, lady. Across the ford." Tears ran down his face. "Who has done this? Lady—*why?*"

Council met in the hall, the while the Melzen kindred prepared the body of their son for burial; and there was unbearable heaviness in the air. Bythein and Bytheis wept quietly; but Sersen-clan was angry in its grief, and its elders were long in gathering the self-possession to speak. The silence waited on them, and at last the old man of the pair rose and walked to and fro across the fireside.

"We do not understand," he cried at last, his wrinkled hands trembling as he gestured. "Lady, will you not answer me? You are not our lady, but we have welcomed you as if you were, you and your *khemeis*. There is nothing in the village we would deny you. But now do you ask a life of us and not explain?"

"Serseis," Bytheis objected, his old voice quavering, and he put a hand on Serseis' sleeve to restrain him.

"No, I am listening," Morgaine said.

"Lady," said Serseis, "Eth went where you sent him: so say all the young folk. And you bade him not tell his elders, and he obeyed you. *Where* did you send him? He was not *khemeis;* he was his parents' only child; he never went to that calling. But did you not sense that the desire was in him? His pride made him take risks for you. To what did you send him? May we not know? And who has done so terrible a thing?"

"Strangers," she answered. Not all the words could Vanye understand, but he understood most, and filled in the rest well enough. At the feelings which gathered in the air of this hall now, he stood close to Morgaine. *Shall I get the horses?* he had asked her in his own tongue, before this council met. *No,* she had answered, with such distraction that he knew she was pulled both ways, with anxiety to be moving and guilt for Mirrind's danger. She lingered, and knew better, and he knew better, and sweat gathered on his sides and trickled under the armor. "We had hoped they would not come here."

"From where?" Sersein asked. The old woman laid her hand on the rolled map that lay atop the table, Morgaine's work. "Your questions search all the land, as if you are looking for something. You are not our lady. Your *khemeis* is not of our village nor even of our blood. From some far land you surely come, my lady. Is it a place where things like this are common? And did you expect such a thing when you sent Eth out against it? Perhaps you have reasons that are too high for us, but, o lady, if it takes the lives of our children—and you knew—could you not have told us? And will you not tell us now? Make us understand."

There was utter stillness for a time in which could be heard the fire, and from somewhere outside the bleating of a goat, and the crying of a baby. The shocked faces of the elders seemed frozen in the cold light from the many windows.

"There are," Morgaine said at last, "enemies abroad; and they are spread throughout Azeroth. We watch here and rest, and through your young men, I have kept watch over you as best I could . . . for your young folk know these woods far better than we. Yes, we are strangers here; but we are not of their kind, that would do such a thing. We hoped to have warning—not a warning such as this. Eth was the one—as you say—who ranged farthest and risked himself most. I knew this. I warned him. I warned him urgently."

Vanye bit his lip and his heart beat painfully in anger that Morgaine had said nothing of this to him . . . for he would have gone, and come back not as Eth did. She had sent innocents out instead, boys who little knew what quarry they might start from cover.

But the elders sat silent now, afraid more than angry, and hung on her words.

"Do none," asked Morgaine, "ever come from Azeroth?"

"You would best know that," Bythein whispered.

"Well, it has happened," Morgaine said. "And you are near to the plain, and there are Men massed there, strangers, armed and minded to take all the plain of Azeroth and all the land round about. They could have gone in any direction, but they have chosen this one. They are thousands. Vanye and I are not enough to stop them. What befell Eth was the handiwork of their outriders, seeking what they could find; and now they have found it. I have only bitter advice to give now. Take your people and walk away from Mirrind; go deep into the forest and hide there; and if the enemies come further, then flee again. Better to lose houses than lives; better to live that way than to serve men who would do what was done to Eth. You do not fight; and therefore you must run."

"Will you lead us?" Bythein asked.

So simple, so instant of belief: Vanye's heart turned in him, and Morgaine sadly shook her head.

"No. We go our own way, and best for you and for us if you forget that we have ever been among you."

They bowed their heads, one after the other, and looked as if their world had ended . . . indeed it had.

"We shall mourn more than Eth," said Serseis.

"This night you will rest here," said Sersein. "Please."

"We ought not."

"Please. Only tonight. If you are here, we shall be less afraid."

It was truer than Sersein might understand, that Morgaine had power to protect them; and to Vanye's surprise, Morgaine bowed her head and consented.

And within the same degree of the sun, there was renewed mourning in Mirrind, as the elders told the people what they had learned and what was advised them to do.

"They are naive people," said Vanye heavily. "*Liyo*, I fear for what will become of them."

"If they are simple enough to believe me utterly, they may live. But it will be different here." She shook her head and turned away for the inside of the hall, for there came the women and children down the midst of the commons, to begin the preparation of the evening meal.

Vanye went to the horses, and made sure that all was in readiness for the morning. He was alone when he went, but when he reached the gate, he heard someone behind him, and it was Sin.

"Let me go where you go," Sin asked of him. "Please."

"No. You have kin who will need you. Think of that and be glad that you have them. If you went where we go, you would never see them again."

"You will never come back to us?"

"No. Not likely."

It was direct and cruel, but it was needful. He did not want to think of the boy building dreams about him, who least deserved them. He had encouraged him too much already. He made his face grim, and attended to his work, in the hope that the boy would grow angry and go away.

But Sin joined him and helped him as he always had; and Vanye found it impossible to be hard with him. He set Sin finally on Mai's back, which was Sin's constant hope, whenever they would take the horses out to graze, and Sin stroked the mare's neck, and suddenly burst into tears, which he tried to hide.

He waited until the boy had stopped his crying, and helped him down again, and they walked together back to the hall.

Dinner was a mournful time. There were no songs, for they had buried Eth at sundown and they had no heart for singing. There was only hushed conversation and few even had appetite, but there were no animosities, no resentment shown them, not even by Eth's closest kin.

Morgaine spoke to the people in the midst of dinner, in a hush in which not even a child cried: babes slept in arms, exhausted by the day's madness, and there was a silence on all the children.

"Again I advise you to leave," she said. "At least tonight and every day hereafter, have your young men on guard, and do what you can to hide the road that leads here. Please believe me and go from this place. What Vanye and I can do to delay the evil, we will do, but they are thousands, and have horses and arms, and they are both *qhal* and Men."

Faces were stricken, the elders themselves undone by this, which she had never told them. Bythein rose, leaning on her staff. "What *qhal* would wish us harm?"

"Believe that these would. They are strangers in the land, and cruel, even more than the Men. Do not resist them; flee them. They are too many for you. They passed the Fires out of their own land, that was ruined and drowning, and they came here to take yours."

Bythein moaned aloud, and sank down again, and seemed ill. Bytheis comforted her, and all clan Bythen stirred in their seats, anxious for their elder.

"This is an evil we have never seen," said Bythein when she had recovered herself. "Lady, we understand then why you were reluctant to speak to us. *Qhal!* Ah, lady, what a thing is this?"

Vanye filled his cup with the ale that Mirrind brewed and drank it down, trying with that to wash the tautness from his throat . . . for he had not shaped what followed them and now threatened Mirrind, but he had had his hand on it while it formed, and he could not rid himself of the conviction that somehow he might have turned it aside.

One thing of certainty he might have done, and that regarded the Honor-blade which he carried, a kinslaying that might have averted all this grief. In pity, in indecision, he had not done it. To save his life, he had not.

And Morgaine: indeed she had launched what pursued them, more than a thousand years ago as Men reckoned time . . . men who had not trespassed in Gates. Her allies once, that army that followed them—the children's children of men that she had led.

There was much that wanted drowning this night. He would have gotten himself drunk, but he was too prudent for that, and the time was too hazardous for self-indulgence. He stopped short of it, and, likewise in prudence, ate—for the wolves were at their heels once more, and a man ought to eat, who never knew whether the next day's flight would give him leisure for it.

Morgaine too ate all that was set before her, and that, the same as his, he thought, was not appetite but common sense. She survived well . . . it was a gift of hers.

And when the hall was clear, she gathered up what supplies they could possibly carry, and made two packs of it . . . more than to distribute the weight: it was their constant fear that they could be separated, or one fall and the other have to continue. They carried no necessity solely on one horse.

"Sleep," she urged him when he would have stood watch.

"Trust them?"

"Sleep lightly."

He arranged his sword by him, and she lay down with *Changeling* in her arm . . . unarmored, as they had both slept unarmored since the first night in Mirrind.

↩ Chapter 3

Something moved outside. Vanye heard it, but it was like the wind, stirring the trees, and did not repeat itself. He laid his head down again and shut his eyes, drifted finally back to sleep.

Then came a second sound, a creak of boards; and Morgaine moved. He flung himself over and came up with his sword in hand before his eyes were even clear; Morgaine stood beside him, doubtless armed, confronting what suddenly appeared as three men.

And not Men. *Qhal.*

Tall and thin they were, with white hair flowing to their shoulders; and they bore that cast of features that was so like Morgaine's, delicate and fine. They carried no weapons and did not threaten, and they were not of that horde that had come through at Azeroth: there was nothing of that taint about them.

Morgaine stood easier. *Changeling* was in her hand, but she had not unsheathed it. Vanye straightened from his crouch and grounded his blade before him.

"We do not know you," said one of the *qhal.* "The Mirrindim say that your name is Morgaine and your *khemeis'* is Vanye. These names are strange to us. They say that you send their young men into the forest hunting strangers. And one of them is dead. How shall we understand these things?"

"You are friends of the Mirrindim?" Morgaine asked.

"Yes. Who are you?"

"Long to tell; but these folks have welcomed us and we would not harm them. Do you care to protect them?"

"Yes."

"Then guide them away from this place. It is no longer safe for them."

There was a moment's silence. "Who are these strangers? And who, again, are you?"

"I do not know to whom I am speaking, my lord *qhal.* Evidently you are peace-loving, since you come empty-handed; evidently you are a friend of the Mirrindim, since they raised no alarm; and therefore I should be willing to trust you. But call the elders of the village and let them urge me to trust you, and then I may answer some of your questions."

"I am Lir," said the *qhal,* and bowed slightly. "And we are where we belong, but you are not. You have no authority to do what you have done, or to tell the Mirrindim to leave their village. If you would travel Shathan, then make clear to us that you are friends, or we must consider that what we suspect is the truth: that you are part of the evil that has come here, and we will not permit you."

That was direct enough, and Vanye clenched his hand on the hilt of his sword and held his senses alert, not alone for the three who stood before them in the hall, but for the undefended windows about them. In the firelight, they were prey for archers.

"You are well-informed," said Morgaine. "Have you spoken with the Mirrindim? I think not, if you consider us enemies."

"We have found strangers in the woods, and dealt with them. And we came to Mirrind and asked, and so we were told of you. They speak well of you, but do they truly know you?"

"I will tell you what I told them: your land is invaded. Men and *qhal* have come through the Fires at Azeroth, and they are a hungry and a dangerous people, from a land in which all law and reason has long since perished. We fled them, Vanye and I . . . but we did not lead them here. They are prowling, hunting likely prey, and they have found Mirrind. I hope your dealing with them let none escape back to their main force. Otherwise they will be back."

The *qhal* looked disturbed at that, and exchanged looks with his companions.

"Have you weapons," Morgaine asked, "with which you can protect this village?"

"We would not tell you."

"Will you at least take charge of the village?"

"It is always in our keeping."

"And therefore they welcomed us . . . not knowing us, save as *qhal*."

"Therefore you were welcomed, yes."

Morgaine inclined her head as in homage. "Well, I understand a great many things that puzzled me. If Mirrind shows your care, then it speaks well for you. This I will tell you: Vanye and I are going back to Azeroth, to deal with the folk who have it now . . . and we go with your leave or without it."

"You are arrogant."

"And are not you, my lord *qhal*? You have your right . . . but no more right than we."

"Such arrogance comes of power."

Morgaine shrugged.

"Do you ask leave to travel Shathan? You must have it. And I cannot give it."

"I should be glad of your people's consent, but who can give it, and on what authority, if you will forgive the question?"

"Wherever you go, you will be constantly under our eye, my lady—whose speech is strange, whose manners are stranger still. I cannot promise you yea or nay. There is that in you which greatly alarms me, and you are not of this land."

"No," Morgaine admitted. "When we began our flight, it was not at Azeroth. It is your misfortune that the Shiua horde chose this direction, but that was not our doing. They are led by a halfling *qhal* named Hetharu; and by a halfling man named Chya Roh i Chya; but even those two do not fully control the horde. There is no mercy in them. If you try to deal with them face to face, then expect that you will die as Eth did. I fear they have already shown you their nature; and I wish above all else that they had come against me and not against Eth."

There were looks, and at last the foremost inclined his head. "Travel north along the stream; north, if you would live. A little delay to satisfy our lord may save your lives. It is not far. If you will not, then we shall count you enemies with the rest. Friends would come and speak with us."

And without further word the three *qhal* turned—the one in the shadow was a woman. They departed as noiselessly as they had come.

Morgaine swore softly and angrily.

"Shall we take this journey?" Vanye asked. He had no eagerness for it, but likewise he had no eagerness to gather more enemies than they had.

"If we fought, we would work enough ruin that these innocent folk would lie exposed to the Shiua; and probably we would lose our own lives into the bargain. No, we have no choice, and they know it. Besides, I do not completely believe that they came here unasked."

"The Mirrindim? That is hard to think."

"We are not theirs, Sersein said. This afternoon when Eth was killed and they doubted us—well, perhaps they sought other help. They were anxious to keep us here tonight. Perhaps they saved our lives by holding us here. Or perhaps I am too suspicious. We shall go as they asked. I do not despair of it; I have felt from the beginning that the *qhalur* hand on this place was both quiet and not greatly remote."

"They are gentler than some *qhal* I have met," he said, and swallowed heavily, for he still did not like proximity to them. "It is said, *liyo,* that in a part of Andur's forests that are called haunted, the animals are very tame and have no fear . . . having never been hunted. So I have heard."

"Not unapt." Morgaine turned back toward the fire. She stood there a moment, then laid down *Changeling* and gathered her armor.

"A leave-taking?"

"I think we should not linger here." She looked back at him. "Vanye, gentle they may be; and perhaps they and we act for similar reasons. But there are some things—well, thee knows. Thee well knows. I trust no one."

"Aye," he agreed, and armed himself, drew up the coif and set on his head the battered helm he had not worn since their coming to Mirrind.

Then they departed together to the pen where the horses were.

A small shadow stirred there as they opened the gate . . . Sin, who slept near the horses. The boy came forth and made no sound to alarm the village . . . shed tears, and yet lent his small hands to help them saddle and tie their supplies in place. When all was done, Vanye gave his hand as to a man . . . but Sin embraced him with feverish strength; and then to make the pain quick, Vanye turned and rose into the saddle. Morgaine set herself ahorse, and Sin stood back to let them ride out.

They rode the commons quietly, but doors opened along their way all the same. Sleepy villagers in their nightclothes turned out to watch, silent in the moonlight, and stood by with sad eyes. A few waved forlornly. The elders walked out to bar their way. Morgaine reined in then, and bowed from the saddle.

"There is no need for us now," she said. "If the *qhal*-lard Lir is your friend, then he and his will watch over you."

"You are not of them," said Bythein faintly.

"Did you not suspect so?"

"At the last, lady. But you are not our enemy. Come back and be welcome again."

"I thank you. But we have business elsewhere. Do you trust yourselves to them?"

"They have always taken care for us."

"Then they will now."

"We will remember your warnings. We will post the guards. But we cannot travel Shathan without their leave. We must not. Good journey to you, lady; good journey, *khemeis.*"

"Good fortune to you," Morgaine said. They rode from the midst of the people, not in haste, not as fugitives, but with sadness.

Then the darkness of the forest closed about them, and they took the road past the sentries, who hailed them sorrowfully and wished them well in their journey—then down to the stream, which would lead them.

There was no sign of any enemy. The horses moved quietly in the dark; and when they were far from Mirrind, they dismounted in the last of the night, wrapped themselves in their blankets and cloaks and slept alternately the little time they felt they could afford.

By bright morning they were underway again, travelling the streamside by trails hardly worthy of the name, through delicate foliage that scarcely bore any mark of previous passage.

From time to time there came a whispering of brush and a sense that they were being watched: woodswise, both of them, so that it was not easy to deceive their senses, but neither of them could catch sight of the watchers.

"Not our enemies," Morgaine said in an interval when it seemed to have left them. "There are few of them skilled in woodcraft, and only one of them is Chya."

"Roh would not be here; I do not think so."

"No, I do not doubt it. They must be the *qhal* who live here. We have escort."

She was uneasy in it; he caught that in her expression, and agreed with it.

A hush hung all about them as they went further. The horses moved with their necessary noise, breaking of twigs and scuff of forest mold . . . and yet something insisted there was another sound there, wind where it should not be, a whispering of leaves. He heard it, and looked behind them.

Then it was gone; he turned again, for the trail bent with the stream, and they were entering a place not meant for riders, where often branches hung low and they must lean in the saddle to pass under . . . a wood wilder and older than the area where they had entered the forest, or that which surrounded Mirrind's placid fields.

Again something touched at hearing, leftward.

"It is back," he said, becoming vexed at this game.

"Would it would show itself," she said in the *qhalur* tongue.

They had ridden hardly around the next bending when an apparition stepped into their path—a youth clad in motley green, and tall and white-haired . . . empty-handed.

The horses snorted and shied up. Morgaine, in the lead, held Siptah, and Vanye moved up as close as he could on the narrow trail.

The youth bowed, smiling as if delighted at their startlement. There was at least one more; Vanye heard movement behind, and his shoulders prickled.

"Are you one of Lir's friends?" Morgaine asked.

"I am a friend of his," said the youth, and stood with hands in his belt, head cocked and smiling. "And you wished for my company, so here I am."

"I prefer to see those who share a road with me. You are also going north, I take it."

The youth grinned. "I am your guard and guide." He swept an elaborate bow. "I am Lellin Erirrhen. And you are asked to rest tonight in the camp of my lord Merir Mlennira, you and your *khemeis*."

Morgaine sat silent a moment, and Siptah fretted under her, accustomed to blows exchanged at such sudden meetings. "And what of that one who is still watching us? Who is he?"

Another joined Lellin, a smallish dark man armed with sword and bow.

"My *khemeis*," said Lellin. "Sezar," Sezar bowed with the grace of the *qhal*-lord, and when Lellin turned to lead the way, taking for granted that they would follow, Sezar went at his heels.

Vanye watched them ghost through the brush ahead, somewhat relieved in his apprehensions, for Sezar was a Man like the villagers, and went armed while his lord did not. *Either well-loved or well-defended,* he thought, and wondered how many more there were thereabouts.

Lellin looked back and grinned at them, waiting at a branching of the way, and led them off again on a new track, away from the stream. "Quicker than the other way," he said cheerfully.

Morgaine said. "We were advised to stay by the streamside."

"Think nothing of that. Lir gave you a sure road; but you would be till to-morrow on that track. Come. I would not mislead you."

Morgaine shrugged, and they went.

They called halt of their guides at noon, and rested a time; Lellin and Sezar took food of them when it was offered, but disappeared thereafter without a word, and did not reappear until they grew tired of waiting and began to follow the dim trail on their own. Now and again came birdsong which was unnatural with so much moving; now and again either Lellin or Sezar would disappear from the trail, only to reappear at some far turning ahead . . . there seemed even shorter ways, though perhaps none that a horseman could take.

Then in late afternoon there was the faint scent of woodsmoke in the air, and Lellin returned from one of his and Sezar's absences to stand squarely in their path. Hands in belt, he bowed with flippant grace. "We are near now. Please follow me closely and do nothing rash. Sezar has gone on to advise them we are coming in. You are quite safe with me; I have the utmost concern for your safety, since I stand so close to you. This way, if you will."

And Lellin turned and led them onto a trail so overgrown that they must dismount and lead the horses. Morgaine delayed to take *Changeling* from her saddle and hook it to her shoulder-belt, the matter of an instant; and Vanye took not only his sword but his bow and quiver, and walked last, looking over his shoulder and round about him, but no threat was visible.

It was not quite a clearing, not in the sense of Mirrind's broad circle. Tents were placed here among wide-spaced trees—and one tree dwarfed all the tents: nine or ten times a man's height it rose before it even branched. Others at the far side of the camp soared almost that high, and spread wide branches, so that shadow dappled all the tents.

Their coming brought a stir in the camp, with *qhal* and Men lining the aisle down which they walked, where the light came greenly down, and the only sky showed golden-white in comparison to the shadowing branches.

None threatened them. There were tall, white-haired *qhal*, male and female; and small dark human-folk . . . a few elders of both kindreds stood among them, robed, old Men and old *qhal*, alike even to the silver hair at the last, though Men were sometimes bearded and *qhal* were not; and Men balded, and *qhal* seemed not to. The younger folk whatever their sex or kind wore breeches and tunics, and some were armed and some were not. They were a goodly-looking folk together, and walked with a free step and cheerfully, moving along with the strangers who had come to them as if all that animated them were curiosity.

But Lellin stopped and bowed before they had quite crossed the camp. "Lady, please leave your weapons with your *khemeis*, and come with me."

"As you have remarked," said Morgaine softly, "we two have outlandish ways. Now, I have no objection to handing my weapons to Vanye, but how much more are you going to ask?"

"*Liyo*," Vanye said under his breath, "no, do not allow it."

"Ask your lord," said Morgaine to Lellin, "whether he will insist on it. For my own opinion, I am minded not to agree, and to ride out of here . . . and I can do that, Lellin."

Lellin hesitated, frowning, then strode away to the largest of the tents. Sezar remained, arms folded, waiting, and they waited, holding the reins of the horses.

"They are gentle-seeming," Vanye said in his own tongue, "but first they separate us from our horses, and you from your arms, and me from you. If they go on, we shall be divided into very small pieces, *liyo*."

She laughed shortly, and Sezar's eyes flickered, puzzled. "Do not think I mean to let that start," she said. "But bide easy until we know their minds; we need no unnecessary enemies."

It was a longish wait, and all about them the folk of the camp stood staring at them. No weapon was drawn, no bow bent, no insult offered them. Children stood with parents, and old ones remained in the forefront of the gathering: it was not the aspect of a people who expected violence.

And at last Lellin returned, frowning still, and bowed. "Come as you wish. Merir will not insist, only I do ask you leave the horses; you cannot expect to take them too. Sezar will see that they are safe and cared for. Come with me, and see that you keep peace and do not threaten Merir, or we will show you quite another face of us, strangers."

Vanye turned and took from Siptah's saddle Morgaine's personal kit, and shouldered the strap of that. Sezar took the reins of both horses and led them away, while he trailed Morgaine, and she walked beside Lellin to the green tent, that largest one of all in the camp.

The flaps were back, reassuring, indicating less chance of outright ambush; and the *qhal* inside were elders, robed and unarmed, with old Men, who looked too advanced in years to use the daggers they generally wore. In their midst sat an old, old *qhal*, whose white hair fell thickly about his shoulders, confined with a gold band about his brow in the manner of a human king. His cloak was green as the spring leaves, the shoulders done in layers of gray feathers, smooth and minutely black-edged, a work of remarkable skill and beauty.

"Merir," said Lellin softly, and bowed, "lord of Shathan."

"Welcome," Merir bade them, a low and gentle voice, and a chair was unfolded and offered Morgaine. She settled, while Vanye stood at her shoulder.

"Your name is Morgaine; your companion's is Vanye," said Merir. "You stayed in Mirrind until you took it upon yourself to bid its young folk venture into Shathan, and lost one of them. You say now that you are going to Azeroth, and you warn of invasion out of the Fires. You are not Shathana, neither of you. Are all these reports true?"

"Yes. Do not expect, my lord Merir, that we understand much of what passes in your land; but we are enemies of those who have massed out on the plain. We are on our way to deal with them, such as we can; and if we must have your permission, then we ask it."

Merir gazed on her a long time, frowning, and she on him, nothing yielding. At last Merir turned and spoke briefly to one of the elders. "You have ridden far," he said then. "You are at least due hospitality while we talk, you and your *khemeis*. You seem impatient. If you know of some imminent attack, say, and I assure you we will act; or if not, then perhaps you will take the time to speak with us."

Morgaine said nothing, and sat easily, the while such hospitality was arranged, and while the old lord gave instruction for the preparation of a tent and shelter for them. For his part, Vanye stood with his hand on the back of Morgaine's chair, watching every move and listening to every whisper . . . for they two had knowledge of Gates, and of the powers of them, knowledge which some *qhal* had lost and which some would kill to learn. Whatever the gentleness of the folk, there was that to fear.

Drink was brought and offered them both; but Vanye leaned forward and took the drink from Morgaine's hand, sipped at it first and gave it back to her before he took a drink of his own. She simply held the cup in her hand, though Merir drank of his.

"Are these your customs?" Merir asked.

"No," said Vanye out of turn, "but they are, among our enemies."

The other *qhal* looked displeased at that forwardness with the old lord. "No," Merir said. "Let be. I shall speak with them. Go, all who should. We shall speak," he added then, "of things belonging to the inner councils of our people. Although you have insisted that your *khemeis* must remain with you, still it might be well if you dismissed him as far as the outside of the tent."

"No," said Morgaine. Not all the *qhal* had departed. Those remaining settled, some on the mats and the oldest ones in chairs. "Sit down," she said aside. Vanye unslung his bow and tucked his sword aside to sit crosslegged at her feet. It was a posture less than formal, and he kept the cup in one hand the while, sipped at it a second time, for he had felt no ill from the first taste. Morgaine tasted hers then, and crossed her booted ankles and extended her legs before her, easy in her attitude and bordering on too much casualness for the *qhal's* liking. She did it deliberately; Vanye knew her well enough to sense the tension in her. She sought their limits and had not yet found them.

"I am not accustomed to be summoned," she said. "But this is your land, lord Merir, and I do owe you the courtesy I have paid in coming here."

"You are here because it is expedient . . . for both of us. As you say: it is my land, and the courtesy I ask is an accounting of your purpose in it. Tell us more of what you told the Mirrindim. Who are these folk that have come here?"

"My lord, there is a land called Shiuan, the other side of the Fires . . . I think you understand me. And it was a miserable place, the people starving, Men first, and then *qhal. Qhal* had wealth and Men lived in poverty . . . but the floods that threatened their land were going to take them both all the same. Then came a Man named Chya Roh, who knew the workings of the Gates, which the *qhal* in that land had forgotten completely. He was not himself from Shiuan, this Chya Roh, but from beyond Shiuan's own Gates. From Andur-Kursh, as we two are. And that is how we came to be in Shiuan: we were following Roh."

"Who taught a Man these things?" one of the elders demanded. "How is it in the land called Andur-Kursh . . . that Men make free of such powers?"

Morgaine hesitated. "My lord, it is possible . . . that man and man may change by those powers. Is that known here?"

There was utter silence, and looks exchanged: terror; but Merir's face remained a mask.

"It is forbidden," Merir answered. "We do know; but we do not permit that knowledge outside our high councils."

"I am encouraged to see so many—*elder* folk in places of power among you. Old age evidently takes its course here; perhaps I am among people of restraint and good sense."

"It is an evil thing, this changing."

"But one known to a few ruthless folk in Andur-Kursh. Chya Roh . . . There was once a great master of the powers of the Gates . . . *qhal,* at least in the beginning, although I have no proof of it: all the guises I have known him to use were Men. Man after man he has murdered, taking bodies for his own use, extending his life over many generations of Men and *qhal.* He was Chya Zri; he was Chya Liell; and lastly he took the body of Chya Roh i Chya, a lord of his land—Vanye's own cousin. So Vanye's knowledge of Gates, my lord, is a bitter one.

"After that, Roh fled us, because he knew that his life was in danger from us . . . life: I do not know how many lives he has known from the beginning, or whether he was first male or female, or whether he was born to Andur-Kursh or arrived there from beyond. He is *old,* and very dangerous, and reckless with the powers of the Gates. So for one reason and the next, we pursued him to Shiuan, and there he found himself trapped . . . in a land that was dying—a thing fearful enough for the people who were born there, who might have had several generations more before the end; but for a being who looked to live forever . . . that death was imminent enough. He went among the *qhal* of that land, and among Men, and declared to them that he had the power to open the Gates that had been so long beyond their own knowledge, and to bring them through to a new land, which they might take for their own . . . thus he had a way out and an army about him.

"We failed to stop him, Vanye and I. He was ahead of us on the road, and we simply could not overtake him in time. It was all we could do to come through the passage ourselves. We were exhausted after that, and we ran . . . until we chanced into the forest, and then into Mirrind. We rested there, trying to find out what manner of land this is and whether there was any force in it that could stop this horde from its march. We did not want to involve the Mirrindim; they are not fighters and we saw that: our watch was meant to protect them. Now we see that there is no more time left, and we are going back to Azeroth to see to the matter as best we can. That is the sum of it, my lord."

There was dismay among them, murmurings, distressed looks cast to Merir. The old qhal sat with dry lips pressed tautly, the mask at last broken.

"This is a terrible tale, my lady."

"Worse to see than to tell. Whether Vanye and I can do anything against them, well, we shall see. There is little hope that the horde will not reach for Mirrind. They would have come there sooner or late . . . and on no account did I urge the Mirrindim to meet them. What I should have realized is that the Mirrindim would fear them no more than they feared us. I warned them; I warned them. But likely Eth walked innocently into their hands, fearing them no more than me, and that thought grieves me."

"You had no authority," said another, "to send Men into Shathan. They thought that you did, and they went, as they would go for us . . . eager to please you. You sent that Man to his death, beyond doubt."

Vanye glowered at that elder. "The Man was warned."

"Peace," said Merir. "Nhinn, could one of us have done better, alone and with a village to defend? We were at fault too, for these two moved so skillfully and settled so peacefully among the Mirrindim that we never realized their presence until this violence came. There could have been a far worse result . . . for this evil could have come on Mirrind utterly by stealth, with no one there to protect them. We were remiss; let us not pass the blame to them. These two and the others passed our defenses in small numbers, and that was my fault."

"Eth may have been questioned," Morgaine said. "If so, that means some of the qhal of the horde came into Shathan, for only they could have spoken to Eth: Men in Shiuan do not speak the same language. Your folk speak of invaders killed; you might judge how much the horde now knows by knowing if qhal were among them and if any escaped. But either a report from Eth's murderers or the mere failure of that force to return to the main body of the horde . . . will prick the interest of their leaders. Whatever else they are, they are not the sort to retreat from challenge. You might ask Lir. And I understand that you do not permit the Mirrindim to travel; if you have regard for them, I hope that you will reconsider that, my lord. I am very much afraid for their future there."

"My lord." It was Lellin, who had come in unnoticed, and all eyes turned to that young and uninvited voice. "By your leave."

"Yes," said Merir. "Go tell Nhirras to tend to that matter. Take no chances." The old *qhal* settled back in his chair. "No light thing, this uprooting of a village; but the things you tell us are no light matter either. Tell me this. How do you two alone think to reckon with these enemies of yours?"

"Roh," Morgaine said without hesitation. "Chya Roh is the principal danger, and next to him is Hetharu of Ohtij-in in Shiuan, who leads the *qhal*. First we must be rid of Roh; and Hetharu next. Leaderless, the horde will divide. Hetharu murdered his own father to seize power, and ruined other lords. His folk fear him, but they do not love him. They will split into factions without him, and turn on each other or on the Men, which is more likely. Men in the horde likewise have three factions at least: two kindreds which have always hated one another, the Hiua and the marshlands folk; and there are the Men of Shiuan, for the third. Roh is the piece that holds the whole together; Roh must be dealt with first . . . and yet not so simply done; the two of them are surrounded by thousands, and they sit securely by the Gate in Azeroth. It is the Master Gate, is it not, my lord Merir?"

Merir nodded slowly, to the consternation of his people. "Yes. And how have you means to know that?"

"I know. And there is a place which governs it . . . is there not, my lord?"

There was a stir among the elders. "Who are you," one asked, "to ask such questions?"

"Then you do know. And you may believe me, my lords, or you may go and ask Chya Roh his side of the tale . . . but I do not advise that. He has skill to use such a place; he has force to take it when he locates it . . . as he will. But for me, I come asking you: *where,* my lords?"

"Do not be in haste," said Merir. "We have seen your handiwork and theirs, and thus far prefer yours. But the knowledge you ask . . . ah, my lady, you do well understand what you ask. But we—we cherish our peace lady Morgaine. Long and long ago we were cast adrift here . . . perhaps you understand me, for your skill in the ancient arts must be considerable to make the passage you have made and to ask questions so aptly, and your knowledge of the past may match it. There were Men here, and ourselves, and our power had been overthrown. It could have been the end for us. But we live simply, as you see. We do not permit bloodshed among ourselves or quarrels in our land. Perhaps you do not understand how grievous a thing you do ask, even in seeking permission to pursue your enemies. We enforce the peace with our law; and shall we yield up our authority to keep order in our own land, and give you leave to hunt across the face of it and dispense life and death where and as you will? What of our own responsibility to our people? What then when another rises up from among us and demands similar privilege outside the law?"

"First, my lord, neither we nor our enemies are of this land; this quarrel began outside it and you are safest if it is contained in Azeroth and never allowed to affect your people at all. That is my hope, faint as it is. And second, my lord, if you mean that your own power is sufficient to deal with the threat entire, and to stop it at once, pray do so. I like not the odds, the two of us against their thousands, and if there were another way, believe me that I would gladly take it."

"What do you propose?"

"Nothing. My intent is to avoid harming the land or its people, and I do not want any allies of your people. Vanye and I are a disharmony in this land; I would not do it hurt, and therefore I would touch it as little as possible."

She bordered on admitting something they would not like to hear, and Vanye grew tense, though he tried not to betray it. Long Merir considered, and finally smoothed his robes and nodded. "Lady Morgaine, be our guest in our camp tonight and tomorrow; give us time to think on these things. Perhaps I can give you what you ask: permission to travel Shathan. Perhaps we shall have to reach some further agreement. But fear nothing from us. You are safe in this camp and you may be at ease in it."

"My lord, now you have asked me much and told me nothing. Do you know what passes at Azeroth now? Do you have information that we do not?"

"I know that there are forces massed there, as you said, and that there has been an attempt to draw upon the powers of the Gate."

"Attempt, but not success. Then you do still hold the center of power, apart from Azeroth."

Merir's gray eyes, watery with age, looked on her and frowned. "Power we do have, perhaps even to deal with you. But we will not try it. Undertake the same, lady Morgaine, I ask you."

She rose and inclined her head, and Vanye gathered himself to his feet. "On your assurance that there is yet no crisis, I shall be content to be your guest, . . . but that attempt of theirs will be followed by worse. I urge you to protect the Mirrindim."

"They are hunting you, are they not, these strangers? You fear that Eth betrayed your own presence there, and therefore you fear for the Mirrindim."

"The enemy would wish to stop me. They fear the warning I can give of them."

Merir's frown deepened. "And perhaps other things? You had a warning to give from the very beginning, and yet you did not give it until a man was dead at Mirrind."

"I do not make that mistake again. I feared to tell them, I admit it, because there were things in the Mirrindim that puzzled me . . . their carelessness, for one. I trust no one whose motives I do not know . . . even yours, my lord."

That did not please them, but Merir lifted his hand and silenced their protests.

"You bring something new and unwelcome about you, lady Morgaine. It adheres to you; it breathes from you; it is war, and blood. You are an uncomfortable guest."

"I am always an uncomfortable guest. But I shall not break the peace of your camp while your hospitality lasts."

"Lellin will see to your needs. Do not fear for your safety here, from your enemies or from us. None comes here without our permission, and we are respectful of our own law."

"I do not completely believe them," Vanye said, when they had been settled in a small and private tent. "I fear them. Perhaps it is because I cannot believe that any *qhal*'s interests—" He stopped half a breath, held in Morgaine's gray and unhuman gaze, and continued, defying the suspicion that had lived in him from the beginning of their travels, "—that any *qhal*'s interests could be common with ours . . . perhaps because I have learned to distrust all appearances with them. They seem gentle; I think that is what most alarms me . . . that I am almost moved to think they are telling the truth of their motives."

"I tell thee this, Vanye, that we are in more danger than in any lodging we have ever taken if they are lying to us. The hold we are in is all of Shathan forest, and the halls of it wind long, and known to them, but dark to us. So it is all one, whether we sleep here or in the forest."

"If we could leave the forest, there would still be only the plains for refuge, and no cover from our enemies there."

They spoke the language of Andur-Kursh, and hoped that there was none at hand to understand it. The Shathana should not, having had no ties at all to that land, at whatever time Gates had led there; but there were no certainties about it, . . . no assurance even that one of these tall, smiling *qhal* was not one of their enemies from off the plains of Azeroth. Their enemies were only half-flings, but in a few of them the blood brought forth the look of a pure *qhal*.

"I will go out and see to the horses," he offered at last, restless in the little tent, "and see how far we are truly free."

"Vanye," she said. He looked back, bent as he was in leaving the low doorway. "Vanye, walk very softly in this spider's web. If trouble arises here, it may take us."

"I shall cause none, *liyo*."

He stood clear, outside, looked about him at the camp—walked the tree-darkened aisles of tents, seeking the direction in which the horses had been led away. It was toward dark; the twilight here was early and heavy indeed, and folk moved like shadows. He walked casually, turning this way and that until he had sight of Siptah's pale shape over against the trees . . . and he walked in that direction with none offering to stop him. Some Men stared, and to his surprise, children were allowed to trail after him, though they kept their distance . . . *qhal*-children with them, as merry as the rest: they did not come near, nor were they unmannered. They simply watched, and stood shyly at a distance.

He found the horses well-bedded, with their saddle-gear hung well above the damp of the ground, suspended on ropes from the limb overhead. The animals were curried and clean, with water sitting by each, and the remnant of a measure of grain . . . *Trade from villages,* he thought—*or tribute: such does not grow in forest shade, and these are not farmer-folk by the look of them.*

He patted Siptah's dappled shoulder, and avoided the stud's playful nip at his arm . . . not all play: the horses were content and had no desire for a setting-forth at this late hour. He caressed little Mai's brown neck, and straightened her forelock, measuring with his eye the length of the tethers and what chance there was of entanglement: he could find no fault. Perhaps, he thought, they did know horses.

A step crushed the grass behind him. He turned. Lellin stood there.

"Watching us?" Vanye challenged him.

Lellin bowed, hands in belt, a mere rocking forward. "You are guests, nonetheless," he said, more sober than his wont. "*Khemeis,* word has passed through the inner councils . . . how your cousin perished. It is not something of which we may speak openly. Even that such a thing is possible is not knowledge we publish, for fear that someone might be drawn to such a crime . . . but I am in the inner councils, and I know. It is a terrible thing. We offer our deep sorrow."

Vanye stared at him, suspecting mockery at first, and then realized that Lellin was sincere. He inclined his head in respect to that. "Chya Roh was a good man," he said sadly. "But now he is not a man at all; and he is the worst of our enemies. I cannot think of him as a man."

"Yet there is a trap in what this *qhal* has done—that at each transference he loses more and more of himself. It is not without cost . . . for one evil enough to seek such a prolonged life."

Cold settled about his heart, hearing that. His hand fell from Mai's shoulder, and he searched desperately for words enough to ask what he could not have asked clearly even in his own tongue. "If he chose evil men to bear him, then part of them would live in him, ruling what he did?"

"Until he shed that body, yes. So our lore says. But you say that your cousin was a good man. Perhaps he is weak; perhaps not. You would know that."

A trembling came on him, a deep distress, and Lellin's gray eyes were troubled.

"Perhaps," said Lellin, "there is hope—that what I am trying to tell you. If anything of your cousin has influence, and it is likely that it does, if he was not utterly overwhelmed by what happened to him, then he may yet defeat the man who killed him. It is a faint hope, but perhaps worth holding."

"I thank you," Vanye whispered, and moved finally to pass under the rope and leave the horses.

"I have distressed you."

Vanye shook his head helplessly. "I speak little of your language. But I understand. I understand what you are saying. Thank you, Lellin. I wish it were so, but I—"

"You have reason to believe otherwise?"

"I do not know." He hesitated, purposing to walk back to their tent, knowing that Lellin must follow. He offered Lellin the chance to walk beside him. Lellin did, and yet he found no words to say to him, not wanting to discuss the matter further.

"If I have troubled you," Lellin said, "forgive me."

"I loved my cousin." It was the only answer he knew how to give, although it was more complicated than that simple word. Lellin answered nothing, and left him when he turned off on the last aisle to the tent he shared with Morgaine.

He found his hand on the Honor-blade he carried: Roh's . . . for the honorable death Roh had been given no chance to choose, rather than become the vessel for Zri-Liell. An oath was on him to kill this creature. Lellin's hope shattered him, that the only kinsman he had yet living . . . still might live, entangled with the enemy who had killed him.

He entered the tent and settled quietly in the corner, picked up a bit of his armor and set to adjusting a lacing, working in the near dark. Morgaine lay staring at the ceiling of the tent, at the shadows that flickered across it. She cast him a brief look as if she were relieved that he was back without incident, but she did not leave her own thoughts to speak with him just then. She was given, often, to such silences, when she had concerns of her own.

It was false activity, his meddling with the harness—he muddled the lacing over and over again, but it gave him an excuse for silence and privacy, doing nothing that she would notice, until the trembling should leave his hands.

He knew that he had spoken too freely with the *qhal,* betraying small things that perhaps it was best not to have these folk know. He was almost moved to open his thoughts utterly to Morgaine, to confess what he had done, confess other things: how once in Shiuan he had talked alone with Roh, and how even then he had seen no enemy, but only a man he had once owned for kinsman. The weapon had failed his hand in that meeting, and he had failed her . . . self-deceived, he had reasoned afterward, seeing what he had wished to see.

He wanted now desperately to seek Morgaine's opinion on what Lellin had said to him . . . but deep in his heart was suspicion, long-fostered, that Morgaine had always known more of Roh's double nature than she had told him. He dared not, for the peace which was between them, challenge her on that, or call her deceitful . . . for he feared that she had deceived him. She might not trust him at her side if she thought his loyalties might be divided, might have misled him deliberately to have Roh's death: and something would sour in him if he learned her capable of that. He did not want to find out such a thing, more than he longed to learn the other. Roh's nature could make no difference in his own choices; Morgaine wanted Roh dead for her own reasons, which had nothing to do with revenge; and if she meant to have it that way, then there was an oath to bind him: an *ilin* could not refuse an order, even against friend or kinsman: for his soul's sake he could not. Perhaps she thought to spare him knowledge . . . meant her deception for kindness. He was sure it was not the only deception she had used.

There was, he persuaded himself at last, no help for himself or Roh in bringing the matter up now. War was ahead of them. Men died, would die—and he was on one side and Roh on the other, and truth made no difference in that.

There would be no need to know, when one of them was dead.

⤳ Chapter 4

By night, fires blazed fearlessly throughout the camp, and in a clear space there burned a common-fire, where songs were sung to the music of harps. Men sang tunes that at times minded one of Kursh: the words were *qhalur,* but the burden of them was Man, and some of the tunes seemed plain and pleasant and ordinary as the earth. Vanye was drawn outside to listen, for their tent was near to that place and the gathering extended to their very door. Morgaine joined him; and he brought out their blankets, so they might sit as most did in the camp, and listen. Men came and brought them food and drink along with all the others as they sat there, for dinner was prepared in common as in Mirrind, and served in this fashion under the stars. They took it gratefully, and feared no drug or poison.

Then the harp passed to the *qhalur* singers, and the music changed. Like wind it was, and the harmony of it was strange. Lellin sang, and a young *qhalur* woman kept him harmony, that ranged the eerie scale fit to send chills coursing down a human back.

"It is beautiful," Vanye whispered at last to Morgaine, "for all it is not human."

"There was a time when thee could not have seen it."

It was true, and the realization weighed on him, the more when he considered Morgaine, who saw beauty in what she came to destroy . . . who had always been able to see it.

This will pass, he thought, looking out over all the camp of *qhal* and Men. *It will pass when she and I have done what we came to do, and killed the power of their Gates. It cannot help but change them. We will destroy all this no less than we shall destroy Roh.* It saddened him, with that sadness he had often seen in Morgaine's eyes and never understood until now.

There came a stirring at their backs. Morgaine turned, and so did he; it was a young Woman who bowed to speak with them. "Lord Merir sends," she whispered, not to disturb the listeners nearby. "Please come."

They rose up and followed the young Woman, delaying to put their blankets inside, and Morgaine took her weapons, though he did not. Their guide brought them into Merir's tent. One light burned there, and within were only Merir and a young *qhal*. Merir dismissed her and the Woman, so that they were quite alone.

Both trust and power, it was . . . that this frail elder received them thus; Morgaine bowed courtesy, and Vanye did.

"Sit down," Merir offered them. He was himself wrapped in a cloak of plain brown, and a brazier of coals smoldered at his feet. Two chairs sat vacant, but Vanye took the floor out of respect: an *ilin* did not insult a lord by sitting on a level with him.

"There is refreshment by you, if you wish," said Merir, but Morgaine declined it, and therefore Vanye refused it also. His place was comfortable, on the mat nearest the brazier, and he settled at his ease.

"Your hospitality has been kind," said Morgaine. "We have been served all that we can use; your courtesy encourages me."

"I cannot call you welcome. Your news is too grim. But for all that, your steps lie easily on the forest; you bruise no branch nor harm its people . . . and therefore we make place for you here. For the same reason I am encouraged to believe that you do oppose the invaders. You are perhaps—dangerous to have for enemies."

"And dangerous to have for friends. I still ask nothing more than leave to pass where I must."

"Secrecies? But this is our forest."

"My lord, we perplex each other. You look on my work and I on yours; you create beauty, and I honor you for that. But not all that is fair is trustworthy. Forgive me, but I have not come so far as I have by scattering all that I know to every wind. How far, for instance, does your power extend? How much could you help me? Or would you be willing? And the Men here: do they support you out of love or of fear? Could they be convinced to turn on you? I do doubt it, but my enemies are persuasive, and some of them are Men. What skill have these *khemi* of yours in arms? Things here look to be peaceful, and it might be that they would scatter in terror from the first moment of conflict; or if they are practiced in war, then where are your enemies, and what would befall me at their hands if I took your part? How is this community of yours ordered, and where are decisions made? Have you power to promise and to keep your word? And even if the answer to all these questions should please me, I am still reluctant to let this matter pass into other hands, which have not fought this battle so long or so hard as I."

"Those questions are direct and very apt. And I do read much of the nature of you and your enemies in the suspicions you hold of us. I do not think that I like that accounting. As for answers . . . my lady, that someone has passed the Fires and come here frightens me in itself. We have not found it good to make use of that passage."

"Then you are wise."

"Yet you have done so."

"Our enemy has no reluctance in the matter. And he must be stopped. You know of other worlds. You are too knowledgeable of the Gates not to know where they lead. So you will understand me if I say that the danger is to more worlds than this one. This is a man who will not scruple to use Gates recklessly in all their powers. How much more need I say to a man who understands?"

A great fear crept into Merir's eyes. "I know that much passing of that barrier may work calamity. One such disaster came on us, and we abandoned use of that passage, and made peace with Men, and gave up all that tempted us to that evil. So we have remained at peace . . . and there is none hungry but that we will feed him, none harmed—no thief or murderer nor abuser of his people. We live in the consciousness of what we can do . . . and do not. That is the foundation on which all law rests."

"I was at first amazed," said Morgaine, "that here *qhal* and Men are at peace. It is not so elsewhere."

"But it is the only sanity, lady Morgaine. Is it not very evident? Men multiply far more rapidly than we. Shorter lives, but ever more of them. And should we not have respect for that abundant vitality? Is it not a strength, as wisdom is a strength, or bravery? They can always overcome us . . . for war with them we can never win, not over the passing of much time." He leaned forward and set his hand on Vanye's shoulder, a gentle touch, and his gray eyes were kind. "Man, you are always the more powerful. We reached beyond our knowledge in bringing your kind among us, and though you were not the beginning of our sorrow, you have the power to be the end-all of it . . . save we make you our adopted sons, as we have tried to do. How is it that you travel with lady Morgaine? Is it for revenge for your kinsman?"

The heat of embarrassment rose to his face. "I swore her an oath," he said: half the truth.

"Long ago, Man, there was your like here. You are reckless in your lives, having so much life. But we took *khemi,* and that life agreed well with such Men and left others free to lead quiet lives in the villages. The hands of the *khemi* administer justice and do unpleasant things that want doing, and sometimes brave things, risking themselves in the aid of others. Such recklessness is natural to Men. But when a *qhal* dies young, he often leaves none behind him, for once and perhaps twice do we bear, and that after some years. In hostile times our number shrinks rapidly. It is always in our interest to keep peace, and to deal fairly with those who have such an advantage over us. Do you not see that it is so?"

The thought amazed him; and he realized how seldom he had seen children of the *qhal,* even among halflings.

Merir's hand left his shoulder, and the old lord looked across at Morgaine. "I shall lend you help, lady, asked or unasked. This evil has come, and we must not let it touch Shathan. Take Lellin with you, him and his *khemeis.* I send my heart with you. He is my grandson, my daughter's child, of a line that is fast fading. He will guide you where you will to go."

"Has Lellin consented in this? I would not take anyone who did not clearly reckon the danger."

"He asked to be the one, if I reached the conclusion that I should send someone."

She nodded sorrowfully. "May he come home safely to you, my lord. I will watch over him with all the force that I have."

"That is much, is it not?"

Morgaine did not answer that probing, and silence hung between them a moment. "My lord, I asked you once for help to reach the master-hold, that would control the Gate at Azeroth. And I still ask that."

"Its name is Nehmin, and it is well defended. I myself would not be allowed to pass there freely. What you ask of me is—more than difficult."

"That comforts me. But Roh's allies spend lives recklessly, and they will simply spend them until they have broken its defenses. I must have access there."

Merir sat a moment, the fires of the lamp leaping upon his downcast features. "You ask power over us."

"No."

"But you do . . . for with your hand there, you have choices, regarding more than your enemy. Perhaps you would choose what we would choose . . . but you are utterly a stranger, and I wonder if that is likely. And might you not, in that power, be as deadly to us as the enemy you fight?"

Morgaine had no answer, and Vanye sat still, fearful, for Merir surely understood . . . if not the whole truth, surely truth enough. But the old *qhal* sighed heavily. "Lellin will guide you; and there will be others along the way who will help you."

"And yourself, my lord? Surely you will not be idle . . . and should I not know where you will be? I have no wish to harm you or to expose you to the enemy by mistake."

"Trust to Lellin. We will go our own way." He rose stiffly. "The Mirrindim were amazed at your map-making. Bring the lamp, young Vanye, and let me show you a thing that may help you."

Vanye gathered up the lamp from its hook and followed the ancient *qhal* to the tent wall. There was a map hung there, age-faded, and Morgaine came and looked on it.

"Here is Azeroth," said Merir, stretching forth his hand to the great circle in the center. "Shathan is all the forest; and the great Nam and its tributaries feed the villages—see: each has accessible water. And this is a walk of many days—Mirrind is here."

"Such circles cannot be natural."

"No. In some places the trees fail, and yet there is water; and Men have cleared the rest. And where forest fails too much, they have planted hedges and thickets to change the land so that trees may grow and wild things have their place. The circles are orderly and boundaries between farm and forest are thus distinct. It gives quiet passage for our folk . . . we do not like the open lands; and Men do, who farm and herd. Also . . ." he added, and laid his hand on Vanye's shoulder, "it has prevented war and strife over boundaries. Once men rode in great hordes where they would, and there was war. They endangered us . . . but the vitality of Shathan itself is even greater than that of Men; they turned fire against us, and that was worst . . . always we are vulnerable to that kind of attack. But the woods regrew in the end; and the barricades of hedges were maintained by Men who sheltered with us. We are not the only forest or the only place where such a thing has been done; but we are the oldest. There are places outside, where Men have run to themselves, and make wars and ruin and—in some places—make better things, beautiful things. Of these folk too we have hope, but we cannot live as their neighbors; we are too fragile. We cannot admit them here above all, to the place of power; *that* must remain outside their reach. The *sirrindim*, we call them, these Men outside; they are horsemen and avoid our forests. But do you perceive why I am distressed, lady Morgaine, with the like of the *sirrindim* suddenly camped about Azeroth?"

"Nehmin is one dire concern, and I suppose that it is somewhere close about Azeroth, though I do not see it on your map. But the Narn itself . . . could become a threat, a road to lead them through your heart."

"Indeed you do see. It leads too close to the land of the *sirrindim*. It is a threat much beyond Mirrind . . . we do see that. In war, we would swiftly decline and die. The invaders must be held in Azeroth . . . above all they must not open a way to the northern plains. Of all directions they might have gone, that is the most deadly to us . . . and I think that is the direction they will choose, for you are here, and they will surely find that out."

"I understand you."

"We will hold them." There was sorrow etched deep in the old *qhal's* face. "We shall lose many of our numbers, I fear, but we shall hold them. We have no choice. Go now. Go and sleep. In the morning you will go with Lellin and Sezar, and we shall hope that you keep faith, lady Morgaine: I have shown you much that could greatly harm us."

She inclined her head, respecting the old *qhal*. "Good night, my lord," she murmured and turned and left. Vanye replaced the lamp carefully on its hanging chain near the old lord's chair, thinking of his comfort, and when the aged *qhal* sat down, he bowed too, the full obeisance he would have shown a lord of his own people, forehead to the ground.

"Man," said Merir gently, "for your sake I have believed your lady."

"How, lord?" he asked, for it bewildered him.

"Your manner—that you are devoted to her. Self-love shows itself first that *qhal* and Man cannot trust one another. But neither you nor she is afflicted by that evil. You serve, but not because you fear. You affect the manner of a servant, but you are more than that. You are a warrior like the *sirrindim,* and not like the *khemi.* But you show respect to an elder, and him not of your blood. Such small things show more truth than any words. And therefore I am moved to trust your lady."

He was stricken by this, knowing that they would fail that trust, and he was frightened. All at once he felt himself utterly transparent before the old lord, and soiled and unclean.

"Protect Lellin," the old *qhal* asked of him.

"Lord, I will," he whispered, and this faith at least he meant to keep. Tears stung his eyes and choked his voice, and a second time he inclined himself to the mat, and sat back again. "Thank you for my lady, for she was very tired and we are both very weary of fighting. Thank you for this time you have given us, and for your help to cross your lands. Have I leave to go, my lord?"

The old *qhal* dismissed him with a soft word, and he rose and left the tent, sought Morgaine's in the dark, on the rim of the gathering. The merriment there still continued, the eerie sounds of *qhalur* singing.

"We shall both sleep," Morgaine said. "And the armor is useless. Sleep soundly; it may be some time before we have another chance."

He agreed, and put up a blanket for a curtain between them, suspended from the cross-pole; gladly he stripped of the armor, and of clothing, wrapped himself in a blanket and lay down, and Morgaine did likewise, a little distance away on the soft furs provided for their beds. The makeshift curtain did not reach the floor, and the light of the fires outside cast a dim glow within. He saw her gazing at him, head pillowed on her arm.

"What kept thee with Merir?"

"It would sound strange if I said it."

"I ask."

"He—said that he trusted you because of me . . . that if there were evil in us, it would show—between you and myself; of course they take you for one of their own."

She made a sound that might have been a laugh, bitter and brief.

"*Liyo,* we shall ruin these people."

"Be still. Even in Andurin, I would not discuss that; Andurin is laced with *qhalur* borrowings, and I do not feel secure in it. Besides, who knows what tongues these *sirrindim* speak, or whether some *qhal* here may not know it? Remember that when we travel with Lellin."

"I shall."

"Yet thee knows I have no choice, Vanye."

"I know. I understand."

Her dim face seemed touched by that, and a great sorrow was on it.

"Sleep," she said, and closed her eyes.

It was the best and only counsel in the matter.

↩ Chapter 5

Their setting out was by no means furtive or quiet. The horses were brought up before Merir's tent, and there Lellin took leave of his grandfather and his father and mother and great-uncle . . . grave, kind-eyed folk like Merir. His parents seemed old to have a son as young as Lellin, and they took his leaving hard. Sezar too they bade an affectionate farewell, kissing his hands and wishing him well, for the *khemeis* seemed to have no kinfolk among the Men in the camp: it was of Lellin's family that he took his leave.

They were offered food, and they took it, for it was well-prepared for keeping on the trail. Then Merir came forward and offered to Morgaine a gold medallion on a chain, intricate, beautiful work. "I lend this," he said. "It is safe passage." And another he brought forth and gave to Vanye, a silver one. "With either of these, ask what you will of any of our people save the *arrha,* who regard no authority of mine. Even there it might avail something. These are more protection in Shathan than any weapon."

Morgaine bowed to him in public respect, and Vanye likewise . . . Vanye at his feet, and not grudgingly, for without the old lord's help, the passage which now lay so easily before them would have been a terrible one.

Then they went to their horses, Siptah and Mai glistening from a bath and content with good care. Someone had twined star-like blue flowers in long chains from Siptah's mane, and white in Mai's—the strangest accouterment that ever a Kurshin warrior's horse bore, Vanye thought . . . but the gesture was like these graceful folk, and touched him.

There were no horses for Lellin or Sezar. "We will have," Lellin explained, "farther."

"Do you know where we are going?" Morgaine asked.

"Where you will, after I have taken you clear of this camp. But the horses will be there."

And by this it was clear that they would be under more eyes than Lellin's during their journey.

They set out down the main aisle of the camp, while the people both Men and *qhal* inclined to them in a bow like the rippling of wind through tall grass—as if they honored old friends; the rippling flowed with their passage almost to the edge of the wood.

There Vanye turned and looked back, to convince himself that such a place had been real at all. There was the forest shade on them, but a golden-green light fell over the encampment, which was all tents and movable—and would, he suspected, swiftly vanish from the place.

They entered the forest then, where the air was at once cooler. They took a different path than that by which they had come: Lellin avowed they must follow it until noon. And Lellin strode along by Siptah's head, while Sezar vanished shadow-wise into the brush. The *qhal* whistled a few clear notes from time to time, which were echoed from ahead, evidence where Sezar might be . . . and sometimes, for what seemed Lellin's own joy, the notes trilled into a snatch of *qhalur* song, wild and strange.

"Do not be too reckless," Morgaine bade him after one such. "Not all our enemies are unskilled in the forest."

Lellin turned as he walked and swept a slight bow . . . he seemed too happy by nature to keep the spring from his step, and a smile came naturally to his face. "We are surrounded at the moment by our own people . . . but I shall remember your warning, my lady."

He had a fragile look, this Lellin Erirrhen, but today, against what seemed the habit of his people, he went armed . . . with a smallish bow and a quiver of brown-feathered arrows. It was probable, Vanye reckoned to himself, that this tall, delicate-looking *qhal* could use them, with the same skill that he and his *khemeis* could travel the woods unheard. Doubtless the noise they must make in riding seemed so loud to their young guide that he felt he might as well whistle songs into the bargain . . . but thereafter he heeded Morgaine's wish and signaled only. He still seemed cheerful, songs or no.

They rested at noon, and Lellin called Sezar back, to sit beside them at a stream-side, while the horses drank and they took the leisure for a bit to eat. They had become well-fed in their recent travels, accustomed to meals at regular tunes and abundant provisions, when before, their travelling and their scant rations had worn them so that they had made new notches in their armor straps. Now they were back to the old, and rested in a patch of warm sun. It would have been easy to fall under Shathan's whispering spell. Morgaine's eyes were half-lidded and lazy, but she did watch, and observed their two guides as if her thoughts much turned upon them.

"We must move," she declared sooner than they would have wished, and rose; dutifully they gathered themselves up, and Vanye took up their saddle-kits.

"My lady Morgaine says our enemies are forest-wise," Lellin said then to Sezar. "Be most careful in your walking."

The Man set his hands in his belt and gave a short nod. "It is quiet all about, no sign of trouble."

"There is bloodshed likely before we are done with this journey," Morgaine said. "And now we come to a point where we are clear of your camp and choose our own way. How far will you two be with us?"

The two looked at her with apparent dismay, but Lellin was the first to recover himself, and bowed ceremoniously. "I am your appointed guide, wherever you will go. If we are attacked, we will defend; if you attack others, we will stand aside, if it is a matter of going into the plains: we do not go there. Yet if your enemies come into Shathan—we will deal with them and they will not come to you."

"And if I bid you guide us to Nehmin?"

Now Lellin faced her with more directness than he was wont, and his look was sad. "I was warned that this was your desire, and now I warn you, my lady: the place is dangerous, and not alone because of your enemies. It has its own defenders, the *arrha*, against whom my grandfather warned you. Your safe-conduct is not valid there."

"But it will take me there."

"So will I, my lady, but if you attack that place—well, you would not be wise to do that."

"If my enemies attack it, it may not stand; and if it falls, then Shathan will fall. I have discussed it with my lord Merir, and he likewise warned me, but he set me free to do what I would in the matter. And he set you to watch me, did he not?"

"Yes," said Lellin, and now all joy and lightness in his face was replaced by dread. "If you have deceived us, doubtless Sezar and I could not stand against you, for you could always take us by stealth if nothing else. Yet I wish to believe that this is not the case."

"Believe that it is not. I have promised lord Merir that I will see you come home safely, and I will keep that promise to the best of my ability."

"Then I shall take you where you wish to go."

"Lellin," said Sezar, "I do not like this."

"But I cannot help it," said Lellin. "If Grandfather had said do not go to Neh-min, then we should not be going; but he did not, and therefore I must do this."

"At your—" Sezar began to say, and stopped; and all froze in each small movement. A horse moved, untimely, drowning the faint sound that had come to them, a bird calling. It was caught up again, nearby.

"We are not safe any longer," said Lellin.

"How do you read such signs?" Vanye asked, for it seemed a good thing to know; and Lellin bit his lip in reluctance, then shrugged.

"It is in the pulses. The more rapid the trill, the more certain and imminent the hazard. There are other songs for other purposes, and some carry words, but this was a watch-song."

"We should be moving," said Sezar, "if we wish to avoid the matter, and I hope that is your wish."

Morgaine frowned, and nodded, and they quit the place and rode further.

There were warnings sometimes about them, and all that day they tended east, bending about the arc of Azeroth . . . and it seemed, though the route they took was different, the lay of the land was familiar. "We are near Mirrind," Morgaine observed finally, which agreed with Vanye's own sense of direction, abused though it was by their crooked journeyings and the strangeness of another sky.

"You are right," Lellin said. "We are north of it; best we stay as much withdrawn from the rim of Azeroth as possible. So the signals advise."

By evening they had passed the vicinity of Mirrind and crossed one little stream and another, hardly enough to wet the horses' hooves. Then they came upon a stand of trees many of which were bound with white cords, a-flutter in the breeze.

"What are those?" Vanye asked of Lellin, for he had seen them about Mirrind; and because they had ominous meaning in Shiuan, he had avoided asking. Lellin smiled and shrugged.

"Cut-mark. We are nearing the village of Carrhend, and so we mark the trees for them that are proper to cut, for wood at need, so that the best trees live and they take the least shapely. This we do throughout Shathan, for their use and ours."

"Like tenders of gardens," Vanye observed, amazed by such a thought, for in Andur, forested as it was, and even in Kursh, men cut where they would and the trees still outpaced them.

"Aye," said Lellin, and seemed amused and pleased by such a thought. He patted the shadowy trunk of an old tree they passed in the gathering dusk. "We wander, but I have wandered more in this wood than in any other, and I daresay I know these trees as villagers know their goats. That old fellow has guided me since I was a boy and he was a little slimmer. Gardeners indeed! And if weeds spring up, why, we tend to that too."

That, Vanye thought, had a chilling undertone to it having nothing at all to do with trees.

"It is coming time for camp," Morgaine said. "And have you a place in mind, Lellin?"

"Carrhend. They will take us into their hall."

"And shall we endanger another village? I would rather the woods than that."

Lellin sketched a bow, a backward step as they walked. "I believe you would, my lady, but there is no need. Our horses will find us there in the morning, and everything there is quite secure. You will find folk there you know: some of the Mirrindim have elected to come to Carrhend for their safety, such as did not choose to stay by their own fields."

Morgaine looked to Vanye, and he ventured no opinion, but he was privately glad when she accepted. More than two years he had spent under the open sky, but Mirrind had re-taught him the luxuries he had put from his mind forever, being Morgaine's companion. In his mind was a strong memory of Mirrind's mornings, and fine hot bread and butter, so vivid he could taste it. He was, he thought, losing his keen edge. The Shathana style of travel seemed all too easy ... and yet they had covered much ground in the day's ride, and evaded some manner of trouble.

Sezar turned up again in their path, walking with them in the gathering dark. Soon enough they saw the forest's edge and a broad expanse of fields. They skirted that open space, keeping within the forest shade, and came into Carrhend at the very last of the daylight.

The village spilled out to meet them. "Sezar! Sezar!" the children cried with abandon, and they trooped round the *khemeis* and caught his hands and made much of him.

"This is Sezar's village," Lellin said as they dismounted. "His parents and sister and four brothers live here, so you see we could not pass by this hospitality; I would not be forgiven."

They had been maneuvered, but not to their hurt, and even Morgaine took it in good humor, smiling as the elders of Carrhend presented themselves. Three clans lived here: Salen, Eren, and Thesen . . . and Sezar, who was of clan Thesen, kissed his elders both, and then his parents, and his brothers and sister. There was not overmuch astonishment in this visit, as if it were a frequent thing; but Vanye felt for the young *khemeis* they took perforce into danger with them, and reckoned why he would have been anxious to make this particular stop on their way to Nehmin.

Lellin also had his welcome with them. Neither young nor old had much awe of him. He took the hands of the kin of Sezar, and was kissed on the cheek by Sezar's mother, which gesture he repaid in kind.

But suddenly there were the Mirrindim, spilling down the steps of the common-hall, as if they had waited on their hosts' courtesies. Now they came. Bythein and Bytheis, and the elders of Sersen and Melzen, and the young women . . . some of them running in their joy to greet them.

There was Sin, among the other children. Vanye caught him up out of their midst and the boy grinned with delight when he lifted him up to Mai's back. Sin set himself astride and looked quite dazed when Vanye passed him up the reins . . . but Mai was too tired to give him trouble and would not leave Siptah.

Morgaine received the elders of Mirrind—embraced old Bythein, who had been their staunchest friend, and there was a chorus of invitations to hall and meal.

"Some of the men are still in Mirrind," Bytheis explained when Morgaine asked after their welfare. "They will keep the fields. Someone must. And the *arrhendim* are watching over them. But we know that our children are safest here. Welcome, welcome among us, lady Morgaine, *khemeis* Vanye."

And perhaps the Mirrindim were no less pleased to find them now in the company of their own legitimate lords, assurance that they had not given their hospitality amiss.

"See to the horses," Morgaine said, when all the turmoil was past; and Vanye took Siptah's reins and Sin followed on Mai, the proudest lad in Carrhend.

Sezar walked with him to show him the way, while a cloud of children walked about them, Carrhendim and Mirrindim, male and female. They crowded in behind as they put the horses in the pen, and there was no lack of willing hands to bring them food or curry them. "Have care of the gray," Sin was quick to tell them, lord over all where it concerned the horses. "He kicks what surprises him," which was good advice, for they crowded too close, disrespecting the warhorse's iron-shod heels; but Siptah as well as Mai had surprising patience in this tumult, having learned that children meant treats and curryings. Vanye surveyed all that was done and clapped Sin on the shoulder.

"I will take care of them as always," Sin assured him; he had no doubt this would be so.

"I will see you in hall at dinner; sit by me," Vanye said, and Sin glowed.

He started back to the hall then, and Sezar waited for him at the gate, leaning on the rail of the pen. "Have a care. You may not know what you do."

Vanye looked at him sharply.

"Do not tempt the boy," said Sezar, "to seek outside. You may be cruel without knowing."

"And if he wishes to go outside?" Anger heated him, but it was the way of
Andur-Kursh itself, that a man was what he was born . . . save himself, who had
always fought his own fate. "No, I understand you," he admitted.

Sezar looked back, and a thoughtful look was in his eyes. "Come," he said
then, and they walked back to the hall with a few of the children at their heels,
trying to imitate the soft-footed stride of the *khemeis*. "Look behind us and
understand me fully," Sezar said, and he looked, and did. "We are a dream
they dream, all of them. But when they grow past a certain age—" Sezar
laughed softly, "they come to better sense, all but a few of us . . . and when the
call comes, we follow, and that is the way of it. If it comes to that boy, let it
come; but do not tempt him so young. He may try too early, and come to grief
for it."

"You mean that he will walk off into the forest and seek the *qhal*."

"It is never said, never suggested . . . forbidden to say. But those who will
come, grow desperate and come, and there is no forbidding them, then, if they
do not die in the woods. It is never said . . . but it is a legend among the children; and they say it. At about twelve, they may come, or a little after; and then
there is a time that it is too late . . . and they have chosen, simply by staying. We
would not refuse them . . . no child dies on his journey that we can ever help.
But neither do we lure them. The villages have their happiness. We *arrhendim*
have ours. You are bewildered by us."

"Sometimes."

"You are a different kind of *khemeis*."

He looked down. "I am *ilin*. That—is different."

They walked in silence, almost to the hall. "There is a strangeness in you,"
said Sezar then, which frightened him. He looked up into Sezar's pitying eyes.
"A sadness . . . beyond your kinsman's fate, I think. It is about both of you. And
different, for each. Your lady—"

Whatever Sezar would have said, he seemed to think better of saying, and
Vanye stared at him resentfully, no easier in his mind for Sezar's intimate ob-
servations.

"Lellin and I—" Sezar made a helpless gesture. "*Khemeis,* we suspect things
in you that have not been told us, that you—Well, something weighs on you
both. And we would offer help if we knew how."

Prying after information? Vanye wondered, and looked on the man narrowly; the words still afflicted him. He tried to smile, but it was effort, and did

not come convincingly. "I shall mend my manner," he said. "I did not know that I was such unpleasant company."

He turned and climbed the wooden stairs into the hall, where dinner was being prepared, and heard Sezar on the treads behind him.

The village had already begun the cooking before they came, but there was enough for guests and to spare . . . a prosperous place, Carrhend, and the Mirrindim in their well-ordered fashion took a share of the work as well as of food. Cooks laughed together and children made friends, and old ones smiled and talked by the fireside, sewing. There seemed no strife from the mixing: the elders could lay down stern edicts when they must, and the *qhalur* law was clearly set forth and respected.

"We have so much to exchange," said Serseis. "We long for Mirrind already, but we feel safer here." Others agreed, though clan Melzen still mourned for Eth, and they were very few here: most of the younger folk of Melzen, male and female, had elected to stay in Mirrind, a determination for Eth's sake, and showing a tough-mindedness that lay deep within the Men of Shathan.

"If any of these evil strangers pass through," Melzein said, "they will not pass back out again."

"May it not happen," Morgaine said earnestly. To that, Melzein inclined her head in agreement.

"Come to the tables," called Saleis of Carrhend then, desperate effort to restore cheer. Folk moved in eagerly, and the benches filled.

Sin scurried in and wedged himself into his promised place. The lad had no words during the meal, contenting himself with quick looks and much listening. He was there; that was enough for Sin; and Sezar caught Vanye's eye during the meal and flicked a glance at the boy, strangely complacent—as if he had seen something clear to be seen.

"It will come," Sezar said then, which Vanye understood and none else might. A weight lifted from him. He saw Morgaine puzzled by that exchange, and felt strange to have one single thought in which she had no part, a single concern that did not touch her affairs—to that extent their lives were bound together.

Then a chill came on him. He remembered what he was, and that no good had ever come of friendship with those along their way; most that they touched—died of it.

"Vanye," Morgaine said, and caught his wrist, for he laid down his spoon of a sudden and it clattered even amid the noise of voices. "Vanye?"

"It is nothing, *liyo.*"

He calmed himself, tried not to think of it, and tried not to let himself go grim with the boy, who had no thought of what fear passed in him. Food went down with difficulty for a time, and then more easily; and he put it from his mind, almost.

A harp silenced the talk after dinner, announcing the accustomed round of singing. The girl Sirn, who had sung in Mirrind, sang here; then a boy of Carrhend sang a song for Lellin, who was their own *qhal:* they teased Lellin for it, fondly.

"My turn," said Lellin afterward, took the harp and sang for them a human song.

Then, still holding the harp, he struck a chord to silence them, looked round at them all, strangely fair as all his folk, pale in that dim hall, among their faces. "Take care," he wished them. "With all my heart, Carrhendim, take care in these days. The Mirrindim can have told you only a part of your danger. You are guarded, but your guards are few and Shathan is wide." His fingers touched the strings nervously, and the strings sighed in that silence. "'The Wars of the Arrhend' . . . I could harp you that, but you have heard it many times . . . how the *sirrindim* and the *qhal* warred, until we could drive the *sirrindim* from the forest. In those days Men fought against Men, and they fought us with fire and axe and ruin. Be on your guard. There are such *sirrindim* at Azeroth, and renegade *qhal* are with them. It is the old war again."

There was frightened murmuring in the hall.

"Ill news," Lellin said. "I grieve to bear it. But be alert and be ready to walk away even from Carrhend if it comes to you. Possessions are nothing. Your children are precious. The *arrhend* will help you rebuild with stone and wood, with our own hands and of all that we have; so must you be ready to aid any village that should be in need. Trust at least that we are moving to deal with it; the *arrhendim* are not always there to be seen, and so they serve you best. Let us do what may be done in the way we know; it may suffice. If not, then it will be your arrows that defend us." The strings sighed softly into a *qhalur* song, and folk listened as if it cast some spell over them. There was neither outcry nor debate. When it was done, the hush remained. "Go to your homes, Carrhendim, and Mirrindim to your sheltering; we four guests will leave early in the morning. Do not disturb yourselves to see us go."

"Lord," said one of the young Carrhendim. "We will fight now if we can help."

"Help by defending Carrhend and Mirrind. Your help in that is much needed."

That one bowed, and joined his friends. The Carrhendim left, each bowing to their guests; but the Mirrindim stayed, for they were bedded down in the wings of the hall.

Only Sin departed. "I shall sleep by the horses," he declared, and Vanye did not deny him that.

"Lellin," said Sezar, and Lellin nodded. Sezar left, likely to his kinfolk for the night, or perhaps to some young woman.

The hall was long in settling. There were fretful children and restless young folk. Blankets hung on cords curtained the wings, making a sort of privacy, and leaving the area nearest the fire for their guests.

At last there was quiet, and they settled comfortably, without armor, sharing with Lellin a few sips of a flask that Merir had sent with him.

"Things are well done here," Morgaine said, in the whisper the hour and the sleeping children demanded. "Your folk are very well organized to have lived so long at peace."

The *qhal's* eyes flickered, and he cast off the sober mood that had lain on him like a mantle. "Indeed, we have had fifteen hundred years to meditate on the errors we made in the wars. So long ago we settled on what we would do if the time came; it has, and we will do it swiftly."

"Is it," asked Vanye, "that long since a war in the land?"

"Aye," answered Lellin, compassing with that more than the known history of Andur-Kursh, where strife was frequent. "And may it be longer still."

Vanye thought on that long after they had taken to their pallets, with the *qhal*-lord resting beside him.

Fifteen hundred years of peace. In some measure the thought distressed him, who was born to warfare. To be locked within such long and changeless tranquility, in Shathan's green shadow—the thought distressed him; and yet the pleasantness of the villages, the safety, the order—had their appeal.

He turned his head and looked on Morgaine, who slept. Theirs was a heavy doom, endlessly to travel . . . and they had seen enough of war for any lifetime. *Might we not stay here?* he wondered, brief traitor thought: and pushed it aside, trying not to think of their existence and Mirrind side by side.

Morning was not yet sprung where there came a sound of horses in Carrhend. Vanye rose, and Morgaine, sword in hand; Lellin padded after them to the windows.

Riders had come in, with two saddled horses in tow; they tied them to the rail of an empty pen and rode away.

"Well," said Lellin, "they came in time. They have ridden in from the fields of Almarrhane, not far from here, and I hope they have care riding home."

At the doorstep of one of the nearest houses Sezar appeared, lingering to kiss his parents and his sister, and then, slinging his bow and his gear to his shoulder, he walked across the commons, waved back at his family and then came toward the hall.

They went back to the fireside and armed, quietly gathering their belongings, trying not to disturb the sleeping Mirrindim. Vanye slipped out to saddle the horses and found Sin awake, already beginning that task.

"Are you going to Azeroth to fight *sirrindim?*" Sin asked, and while they both worked . . . no longer innocent, the Mirrindim: they had seen Eth's fate, and had been driven from their homes.

"Where I go next I can never say. Sin, seek the *qhal* when you are old enough; I should not tell you that, but I do."

"I would go with you. Now."

"You know better. But someday you will go into Shathan."

The fever burned in the dark young eyes. The Men of Shathan were all smallish. Even so, Sin would never be tall among them, but there was a fire in him that began already to burn away his childhood. "I will find you there, then."

"I do not think so," Vanye said; sorrow settled deep in Sin's eyes, and all at once a pain stabbed him to the heart. *Shathan will not be the same for him,* he thought. *We will go, and destroy the Gates; and it is his hope we are going to kill. It will all change, in his lifetime . . . either at our enemies' hand—or ours.* He gripped Sin's shoulder then, gave him his hand.

He did not look back.

They were not quiet enough for the village; despite their wish to depart quickly and quietly, there was no preventing the Mirrindim, who rose to bid them farewell; or Sezar's mother, who brought them bread hot from the ovens—she had risen long before dawn, baking for them; and Sezar's father, who offered them some of his finest fruit wine for their journey; and the brothers and sister who turned out to bid Sezar farewell. They laughed gently when Lellin planted a kiss on the sister's cheek, picking her up and setting her down again, for though she was a budding woman, she was tiny next to a *qhal*. She laughed at the kiss, but glanced down shyly and up again with a look that held her heart in her eyes.

Then they mounted up and rode out quietly among the trees, past sentries who were themselves little more than shadows in the trees. Leaves curtained them from Carrhend, and they soon had only the sound of the forest about them.

Sezar was downhearted after the leavetaking, and Lellin looked at him in frowning concern. His mood needed no inquiry, for surely Sezar and perhaps Lellin would have been glad to stay for Carrhend's protection, and the duty which drew them off lay heavy on them at the moment.

Finally Lellin gave a low whistle . . . and in time there came an answer, slow and placid. At that Sezar looked somewhat cheered, and they all felt better for his sake.

ᶜ Chapter 6

They kept to the streamcourse for a road after Carrhend and made good time. The horses that the two *arrhendim* had acquired . . . both bays, Lellin's with three white stockings . . . kept well from Siptah's vicinity, so that Lellin and Sezar generally kept the lead by some small space.

The two talked together in soft voices which they, who rode behind, could not quite hear, but they had no distrust for it, and sometimes conversed themselves in private, though usually in the *qhalur* tongue. Morgaine was never inclined to conversation, not in all the time he had known her, but she spoke idly and often since they had come to this land . . . teaching, at first, deliberately making him speak, correcting him often. Then she seemed to have fallen into the habit of talking more than she once would. He was glad of it, and though she never spoke of her own self beyond Andur-Kursh, he found himself speaking of home, and of the better moments of his youth in Morija.

They could speak of Andur-Kursh now, as one finally could speak of the dead, when the pain was gone. He knew his own age; she knew that of a hundred years before his birth; and grim as some of the tales they passed back and forth might be, there was pleasure in it. Time-wanderer she was; and now he was of her kind, and they could speak of it.

But once she mentioned Myya Seijaine i Myya, clan-lord of the Myya when she had led the armies of Andur-Kursh . . . and then her eyes clouded and she fell silent, overcome by memory—for that was one of the scatterings in time which had begun what sat at Azeroth, clan Myya, clan Yla, clan Chya—men who had served her once, and who had become lost in Gates and time. Myya survived. Their children's children a thousand years removed had dwelt in Shiuan, recalling her only as an evil-legend, confounding her with myth . . . until Roh came to rouse them.

"Seijaine was a fell sort," she said after a moment, "but good and generous to his friends. So are his children, but I am not among their friends."

"It looks," he said with desperate irrelevance, "as if it might rain."

She looked perplexed by his bent of thought, then looked up at the clouds that were only slightly gray-edged, and at him again. She laughed. "Aye. Thee's good for me, Vanye. Thee is—very good."

She went sober after, and found something to look at which did not necessitate meeting his eyes. Something swelled up in him that was bitter and sweet at once. He savored it briefly, but then, his eyes on Lellin's back—Lellin, whose pale, spidery grace was the very like of Morgaine's—he despaired, and put a different interpretation on what she had said to him . . . recovered the good sense which had long saved him from making a mistake with her which would sever them.

He laughed aloud at himself, which drew from her a strange look. "An odd fancy," he explained, and quickly led the talk to stopping for noon rest; she did not probe more deeply.

The rain proved an empty threat. They had feared a wet camp and a hard night, but the clouds passed over with only a slight sprinkling at evenfall, and they lay down on the stream-side haying made good progress during the day, well-fed, and under a clear sky on dry ground. It was as if all the wretchedness that had attended their other rides were a bad dream, in this land too kindly to do them harshness.

Vanye chose first watch . . . even in this matter they were more comfortable, for the four of them sharing watches meant longer sleep. He yielded his post afterward to Lellin, who rubbed his eyes and propped himself against a tree, standing, while he lay down to sleep without a qualm of apprehension of treachery.

But he was roused again by a touch on his back, and at once terror seized on him. He rolled over and saw Lellin likewise touch Morgaine. Sezar was already awake. "Look," Lellin whispered.

Vanye strained his eyes against the dark, following the fix of Lellin's stare. A shadow stood among the trees on the other side of the stream. Lellin gave a low trilling whistle, and it moved . . . manlike, but not a Man. It waded the stream with soft splashes, long-limbed and jerking in its precise movements. A chill tightened Vanye's skin, for he knew now that he had seen such a creature before, and in the same vicinity.

Lellin arose, and so did they all, but they stayed where they were, while Lellin walked to the stream and met the creature. Its height was greater than Lellin's; its limbs were arranged like those of a Man, but the articulation was different. When the creature looked up, the eyes were all dark in the starlight, and the features were thin and the mouth pursed, very small for the enormity of the eyes. The legs when it moved flexed like those of a bird, knees bent opposite the direction of a Man's. Vanye crossed himself at the sight, and yet more in awe than in fear, for there seemed less menace in it than difference.

"*Haril,*" Morgaine whispered in his ear. "Only once have I seen the like."

It came onto the bank, wary, and looked them all over with its large eyes. Whether it was male or female was impossible to tell. The body, dusky-hued, was ambiguous under its thick, fibrous robes, which were short and matched the shade of its skin, whatever the color was in daylight. Lellin spoke softly and signed to it. The *haril* answered in a lisping chitter and made a gesture of its own. Then it turned and waded the stream, heron-like in its cant of body and its movements.

"There are strangers," said Lellin. "It is distressed. Something is fearfully amiss that a *haril* has approached us. It wants us to follow."

"What are they?" Vanye asked. "How much can you understand of what it wants?"

"They are from long ago. They live in the deepest parts of Shathan, the wild parts where we seldom go, and generally they have nothing to do with *qhal* or Men. Their speech is their own; we cannot learn it and they cannot learn ours . . . nor wish to, I suppose . . . but they will sign—and if a *haril* has come asking us to do something, then we should do it, my lady Morgaine. There is something vastly amiss to urge it to that."

The *haril* waited, across the stream.

"We will go," Morgaine said. Vanye spoke no word of objection, but there was a tightness at his belly that settled in like an old friend. He gathered up their gear and started for the horses in haste and quietly. Whatever they had evaded in these last slow days was suddenly upon them, and from now on, there seemed no hope of coming peacefully to Nehmin.

They rode across the stream, moving as quietly as the horses might, and the *haril* went before them, a shadow that the horses did not like. It chose ways difficult for riders, and often they must bend beneath branches or negotiate difficult slopes. At each delay the *haril* waited, silent, until they had overcome the obstacle and began to close the gap.

"Madness," Vanye said under his breath, but Morgaine did not regard him. The *haril* stayed in sight, but now and again there was another presence: the horses detected it and threw their heads and would as gladly have fled. It flitted now on this side and now on the other, a tail-of-the-eye presence that was gone before one could turn the head, or which rustled a leaf and stopped before one could fix the place of it.

Another, Vanye reckoned . . . or maybe more than one. He slipped the ring which let his sword fall to his hip, and ducked low against Mai's neck as they took a new turn through dense branches and down a slope.

The trees thinned. Their guide brought them out into the midst of an almost-clearing, where something like a white butterfly seemed suspended above a shadowy form . . . a little nearer and they saw it for a body, *haril,* and dead. The butterfly was the fletching of the arrow in its back. Their guide chittered a string of words that seemed to reproach them.

Lellin dismounted and signed what looked like a question. The *haril* stood still and did not respond.

"It is no arrow of ours," said Sezar; and while Morgaine and Sezar stayed ahorse, Vanye slid down and went carefully to the dead *haril,* examined the arrow more closely in the starlight. The feathering it bore would not give it near the accuracy of the *arrhendim's* brown-fletched shafts at long range. This was the feather of a sea-bird, here in Shathan woods.

"Shiua," he said. "Lellin, ask them: *where?*"

"I cannot be—" Lellin began, and then looked about in alarm. Morgaine's hand went to her back, where she carried the lesser of her weapons, for all about them were tall, stalking shadows, heron-like in their movements. No brush rustled. They were simply there.

"Please," Lellin breathed, "do not do anything. Do not move." He faced the first *haril,* and repeated the question-sign, adding to it several others.

The *harilim* chittered reply all together. There was anger in that sound, which was that of mice or rats, but deeper. One came forward to stand by the dead, and Vanye backed a step, but only a step, lest they mistake it for flight. He stood very close to that one, and dark, enormous eyes flickered over him minutely. A spidery arm extended and it touched him; fingers ran lightly over his clothing, clinging slightly at each touch. He did not move. Starlight shone on the creature's smooth dark skin, showed the gauzy weave of its thick garments. He shuddered involuntarily as it moved behind him and touched his back, and he cast a glance at Morgaine, seeking counsel. Her face was pale and set, and in her hand was the weapon which had killed the deer. If she used it, he thought, then he would not be riding out with her: he much feared so.

Signs passed between the *haril* and Lellin, angry on the *haril's* part, urgent on Lellin's. "They believe you part of the strangers' force," Lellin said. "They ask why we ride with you. They have seen you two here before, alone."

"Near Mirrind," Vanye said very quietly, "there was one. I know what it was now. It ran away when we chased it." The *haril's* hand descended on his shoulder from behind, gentle as wind, and tightened, betraying enormous strength, wanting him to turn. He did so, and faced it, heart beating wildly as he stared up into that dark, strange face.

"It is you," Sezar said from horseback. "It is you that disturb them . . . a tall Man, and too fair for a Shathana. They know that you are not of our blood."

"Lellin," said Morgaine, "I advise you do something before I do."

"Please, lady, do nothing. We are all alone here. Our folk have given no warning of this, and I do not think there are any of the *arrhendim* in the vicinity . . . little they could help if they were. These woods are the *harilim's* just now, and our chances of escape are not good. They are not violent . . . but they are very dangerous."

"Bring one of my arrows," Vanye said; and when no one moved: "Bring it!"

Lellin did so, moving very carefully. Vanye held it so that the *haril* could see it and indicated the feathering, which was brown; and pointed at the arrow in the corpse, which bore white feathers. The *haril* spoke something to its fellows; they responded in tones that seemed at least less angry.

"Tell him," Vanye asked of Lellin, "that those Men out there in Azeroth are not our friends; that we come to fight them."

"I am not certain I can," Lellin said in despair. "There is no system to the signs; subtleties are almost impossible."

But he tried, and perhaps succeeded. The *haril* spoke to its fellows, and some of them gathered up the body of their dead and bore it into the woods.

Then the one behind set hand on Vanye and began to draw him away too. He resisted, planting his feet, and now he was very frightened, for the thing was strong and they were still completely surrounded.

Lellin put himself in the *haril*'s path and signed a negative. The *haril* spat back a chittering retort, and beckoned.

"They want us all to come," Lellin said.

"*Liyo*—get out of here."

She did not. Vanye turned his head, trying to reckon his chances of breaking for his horse and living to reach it. Morgaine did not move, doubtless weighing other considerations.

Sezar muttered something he did not hear clearly. "Their weapons are poisoned," Morgaine said more loudly. "Vanye, their darts are poisoned. I think Lellin has been persuaded by that from the beginning. We are in somewhat of a difficulty, and I fear that there are more of them that we do not see."

Sweat trickled down his face, cool as it was in the night. "This is a ridiculous situation. I apologize for it. What do you advise, *liyo*?"

"Vanye asks for advice," she said to Lellin.

"I think we have no choice but to go where they wish . . . and not to do anything violent. I do not think they will harm any of us unless they are threatened. They cannot speak to us; I think that they want to assure themselves of something or to demonstrate something. Their minds are very different; they are changeable and excitable. They rarely kill; but we do not enter their woods, either."

"Are these their woods, where you have led us?"

"They are ours, and we are now nearer Azeroth than I would have liked to come, following this one. Your enemies have roused something that we may all regret. *Khemeis* Vanye, I do not think they will let you go until they have what they want, but I do not think they will harm you."

"*Liyo?*"

"Let us go with this a little way and see."

Lellin translated an affirmative sign. The *haril* tugged gently at Vanye's arm, and he went, while the others were allowed to go ahorse: he heard them following. The *haril*'s hand slid to his wrist, a gentle grip, dry as old leaves and unpleasantly cold. The creature turned and chittered at him now and again as they came to rough ground, helped him up slopes, and when a time had passed in their journey, it let him go seeming to judge that he would stay with it. Then his fear diminished despite the strangeness of the face which occasionally turned to him in the dark. They were being urged to haste, but not threatened.

He looked back more than once, to be sure that they had not lost the others; but the riders stayed with them, more slowly and by a course the horses could follow. Sezar brought Mai along, which he was glad to see. But when his looking back delayed him, a touch came on his shoulder: shuddering, he faced the *haril,* which seized him a time and hurried him on.

He tried signs of his own, making what among Andurin signed for *where?*— A pass of the open palm back and forth supine. The *haril* seemed not to comprehend. It touched his face with clinging, spidery fingers, replied with a sign he did not understand, and hurried him on, through the thicket and up slopes and on and on until he was panting.

They came briefly into the open between trees. The *haril* seized his arm again to be sure of him, for suddenly there was a dead man at their feet, and another, as they crossed that area, bodies almost hidden in the dark and the leaves. He saw the leather and cloth in the starlight and knew them for the enemy. One carried arrows, white-feathered. He resisted the *haril* enough to bend and gather one up, showing the creature the nature of the feather. The *haril* seemed to understand, and took the arrow from him and threw it down. *Come, come,* it beckoned him.

He glanced over his shoulder and for a moment panicked, for he no longer saw the others. Then they came into view, and he yielded to the *haril*'s pulling at him. It began to go very quickly, so that he was rapidly exhausted by the pace, for he was in armor and the creature strode wide with its stalking gait.

Then they were at a complete break in the forest: trees ceased, and starlight fell clearly across a wide plain. Something else glowed there, the glare of fires spangled across the open. Where they stood there was wood hewn, trees felled, their wounds stark in the faint light. The *haril* pointed to those, to the camp, and signed at him, at *him,* accusingly.

No, he signed back. Whatever it wanted or suspected that had to do with himself and that camp, the answer was no. Morgaine and the others overtook them now, and *harilim* were all about them. He looked up at her, and she gazed at the campfires of the enemy.

"This is not their main strength," she whispered for Lellin's benefit; and that was true, for the camp was not nearly large enough—nor would Roh or Hetharu likely give up possession of the Gate of Azeroth's center.

"This is what the *harilim* brought us to see," Lellin said. "They are angry . . . for the trees, for the killing. They blame us that this has been allowed."

"Vanye," Morgaine said softly. "Try; mount up quickly."

He moved, without prelude or hesitation, flung himself for Mai's side and scrambled into the saddle. There was a stir among the *harilim,* but none moved to stop him. He remembered the poisoned weapons and sat the nervous horse with his heart pounding against his ribs.

Morgaine turned Siptah slowly, to regain the shelter of the woods. *Harilim* stood gathered in the way, stick-like arms uplifted, refusing them passage.

"We are not wanted here," Lellin said. "They will not harm us, but they do not want us in the area."

"Will they cast us out onto the plains?"

"That seems their intent."

"Liyo," Vanye said for a sudden he read her mind and liked not what he read. "Please. If we strike at them, then we will not ride far in the forest before there are others. These creatures are too apt to ambushes."

"Lellin," she said, "why have not your people been hereabouts? Where are the *arrhendim* who should have warned us of this intrusion of enemies?"

"The *harilim* probably forced them out . . . as they mean to do with us. We do not dispute passage with the dark folk. Lady, I fear for Mirrind and Carrhend. I fear greatly. That is surely where the other *arrhendim* have retreated, to protect and warn those places with all haste; they would not have come this far when they knew the dark folk were here. Lady, forgive me. I have failed miserably in my charge. I led you into this and I do not see a way out. None of the *arrhendim* hereabouts had reason to suspect there were those who would ride past their warning-signals. They gave them, but we rode through. I thought only of *sirrin-dim,* that we could resist. I did not reckon that the *harilim* had taken possession here. Lady, it may be that the keepers of Nehmin have stirred them up."

"The *arrha?"*

"There is rumor that the keepers of Nehmin can call them. It is possible that they are part of Nehmin's defense, summoned against *that.* If that is so, then I myself would be surprised; they are as difficult to reason with as the trees themselves; and they hate both Men and *qhal.*"

"But if it is true, then it is possible that Nehmin itself is under attack."

"It is possible, lady, that this is so."

She said nothing for a moment. Vanye felt it too, the sense that beneath the peace of Shathan, which had wrapped them securely thus far, things had been going dangerously, utterly amiss.

"Beware, all of you," she said, and slipped *Changeling* from her shoulder to her hip. Holding one palm aloft, in a gesture which somewhat stilled the *harilim's* chittering apprehension, she unhooked the sheath.

Then, two-handed, she drew it slowly, and the opal light of the blade swirled softly in the dark. The light glittered in the dark eyes of the *harilim,* and grew as she drew it forth. Suddenly it blazed full, and the well of darkness at the tip burst into being. The *harilim* drew back, their large eyes reflecting it, red mirrors of that cold light. The wind of otherwhere stirred the trees and whipped at their hair. The *harilim* covered their faces with spidery hands and backed and bowed at that howling sound.

She sheathed it then. Lellin and Sezar slid from their horses and came and bowed at Siptah's hooves. The *harilim* kept their distance, chittering softly in fear.

"Now do you understand me?" she asked.

Lellin looked up, his pale face stark with dread. "Lady, do not—do not loose that thing. I understand you. I am your servant. I was given to be, and I must be. But has my lord Merir knowledge of that thing?"

"Perhaps he suspects. He gave you for my guide, Lellin Erirrhen, and he did not forbid my seeking Nehmin. Tell the *harilim* we will go through their forest and see what their mind is now."

Lellin rose and did so, signing quickly; the *harilim* melted backward into the trees.

"They will not stay us," he said.

"Get to horse."

The *arrhendim* remounted, and slowly Morgaine urged Siptah forward. The gray horse threw his head and snorted his displeasure at the *harilim,* but they passed freely back into the forest, while the *harilim* stayed with them like shadows.

"Now I know the grief that is on you," Sezar whispered as they came near in the dark. Vanye looked at him, and at Lellin, and a weight sat at his heart, for it was true that the *arrhendim* began to understand them, who carried *Changeling . . .* recognized the evil of it, and the danger.

But they served it, as he did.

ᔐ Chapter 7

The *harilim* moved about them still, shadows in the first fading of the stars. They rode as quickly as they could in the tangled wood, and the *harilim* did not hinder, but neither did they help; while Lellin and Sezar, beyond the woods that they knew, could only guess at the quickest way.

Then at the very last of the night the forest gave way before them, and dark waters glistened between the trees.

"The Narn," Lellin said as they drew rein within that last fringe of trees. "Nehmin lies beyond it."

Morgaine stood in the stirrups and leaned on the saddlebow, stretching. "Where can we cross?"

"There is supposedly a ford," Sezar said, "halfway between the Marrhan and the plain."

"An island," said Lellin. "We have never ridden this far east, but we have heard so. It should be only a little distance north."

"Day is coming on us," Morgaine said. "The riverside is exposed. Our enemies are likely near at hand. We cannot afford errors in judgment, Lellin . . . nor can we linger overlong and risk being cut off from Nehmin."

"If they have hit Mirrind and Carrhend," Vanye reasoned, "they will have learned which way we rode, and some of them would not be long at all in understanding the meaning of that." He saw Sezar's stricken face as he said it; the *khemeis* knew well his meaning and understood the danger his people were in. "Can we find an answer of the *harilim,* whether the strangers have crossed the Narn?"

Lellin looked about; there was nothing behind them, not a breath, not a whisper of leaves . . . no sign, suddenly, of their shadowy companions.

Morgaine swore softly. "Perhaps they do not like the coming daylight; or perhaps they know something we do not. You lead, Lellin. Let us come to this crossing as quickly as we can, and if there is night enough left, we will try it."

Lellin eased his horse into the lead northward, trying to keep within the trees as they rode, but there were washes and flood-felled trees that made their progress slow. At times they must go down onto the bank, exposing themselves to view of any watchers on the far side. At others they must withdraw far into the forest, almost losing sight of the river.

And they were tired, the better part of the night without sleep, constantly tried by obstacles, the branches of the trees tearing at them, the horses stumbling often over impossible ground, or exhausting themselves in climbs up and down tributary washes. Dawn began, almost enough that they could see color on the forest's edge.

Yet in that first coloring they came to their islet, a long bar, bearing a crown of brush, with logs piled up at the upstream end.

They hesitated. Morgaine sent Siptah forward, down that slope toward the crossing. Vanye put the spurs to Mai and followed, little caring whether Lellin and Sezar stayed with them or no; but he heard them coming. Morgaine hastened: the fever was on her now . . . enemies behind, the thing which they sought ahead of them; in any doubt, he knew what she would choose, and that was to go, to make ground while they could, nothing hesitating.

The horses slowed as they hit the water, fighting current which rose about their knees. Siptah hit a hole, struggled out of it; Vanye rode around it, with the *arrhendim* in his wake. The horses waded breast-deep now, the water dark and strong. Mai slipped often, struggling after Siptah . . . shouldered into Sezar's horse. Almost Vanye dismounted then, but she found firmer footing, and the water fell briefly as they passed the halfway mark, the point of the isle. Siptah kept going, strongest of their mounts, and in anxiety Vanye used the spurs to force the mare into the second half of the crossing, cursing Morgaine's stubbornness. Soon the gray horse began to rise from the water a second time, coming out on the bank. Morgaine reined about to look back at them.

Something flew, hissing, and hit; she went over, flung nearly out of the saddle. Siptah shied wildly, and Vanye cried out and rammed spurs into the mare. Somehow, by desperate strength, Morgaine was still ahorse, clinging by the mane and by one heel across the saddle, her pale hair a wild banner against the shadow, a white-feathered arrow driven somewhere the armor was not. Siptah spun once, confused, then ran, arrows hailing faster. Vanye bent low and drove the mare in desperate flight down the bank after her . . . somehow Morgaine pulled herself back into the saddle, enough to hold on.

"Riders!" Sezar shouted behind him.

He did not turn to look. His eyes were only for Morgaine, who slumped now across Siptah's neck, and the sand over which the mare's hooves flew was spotted with dark drops.

The mare slowed, faltered, froth spattering her and him. Sezar and Lellin overtook him—passed him now as the mare broke stride. Sezar started to draw back for him. "No!" Lellin cried, and Sezar whipped the horse on to stay with Lellin. Further and further the distance widened between him and *arrhendim*.

"Get her to safety!" Vanye screamed after them. To do that, had they come within reach, he would have cast one of them from the saddle and thrown him to the enemy. Perhaps Lellin sensed it, and would not delay in his reach. "Help her!"

Mai was done, staggering badly. In desperation he turned for the trees up the incline of the bank, drove her for that, to dismount and run for cover afoot.

But she betrayed him at the last. Her strength failed in the loose sand and she went down nose-first while they were still on the flat. He sprawled, and she heaved down on him before he cleared the saddle, rolled as dead weight, neck broken, limp.

He twisted round as he heard the riders bearing down on him—grimaced, for his leg was pinned and he could not drag it free nor get leverage against Mai's heavy body.

He had no hope of anything further, even that all would give up the chase and delay for him; they did not. Most of them thundered past, spraying him with sand and gravel, but four reined back to deal with him. He had his sword still, and managed to get it into his hand, reckoning even so that it was futile, that they would put an arrow into him at safe distance and end it.

They were not halfling Shiua, but Men. He recognized them as they left their horses and came to him, and he cursed as they grinned in triumph, making a half-ring about him, out of his reach.

Myya Fihar i Myya . . . Mija Fwar, a Hiua accent made the name: there was no mistaking that face, scarred and twisted about the lips with a knife-mark. Fwar had been Morgaine's lieutenant once, before their ways parted in violence. The others were Fwar's kinfolk, all Myya, all with blood-debt against him.

They laughed at his plight, and he bided quietly, no longer anticipating the arrow, hoping that Fwar in particular would come within reach. "Bring that branch over here," Fwar ordered one of his cousins, Minur. The man brought it, a sandy length of still-sound wood, tall as a Hiua and thick as a man's wrist.

Not for levering, that; they were wiser. Vanye saw the intent in Fwar's eyes and tucked down as the blow came . . . clutched the sword against him, but blow after blow to his helmed skull stunned him, and finally they rammed the end of the branch at him and broke his grip on the sword. They were on him then; he tried for the dagger, and though he had it from sheath and put a wound on at least one of them, they pinned him and wrested it from him. Then they found cords and tried to bind his hands back; but he fought that wildly, and twice they had to daze him before that was done.

Then he was finished, and knew it . . . lay still with his face against the dry sand, gathering his forces for whatever came next. One kicked him in the belly for good measure, and he doubled reflexively, not even focusing his eyes to look at them. They were Myya, of a cold and vengeful clan, which had hated him in Kursh and sworn his death there. But these descendants of the proud Kurshin Myya, lost in Gates a thousand years and more . . . knew nothing of honor, despised it as they despised everything beyond themselves. Fwar hated him with a burning and personal hatred.

They levered Mai off of him finally. He had thought that the leg might be broken where she had fallen on him, but the sand had saved him from that. He had some hope then; but the knee gave with a stab of blinding pain when they seized him up and expected him to stand, and not all their blows and curses could amend that. Then he gave up all hope of winning free of them.

"Put him on a horse," Fwar said. "There might be friends of his hereabouts . . . and we want time to pay you your due, Nhi Vanye i Chya, for all my brothers and our kinfolk that you killed."

Vanye spat at him. It was all the recourse he had left, and that too failed of the mark. Fwar's eyes raked him over and calculated . . . not stupid, this man: Morgaine would not have had a dull-witted man in her service. "He would like us to stay near here as long as possible, I suppose. But the *khal*-lords will see to *her,* and we can deal with them later. We had better take our prize downriver a ways."

One of them brought a horse near. Vanye kneed the hapless beast in the flank and sent it screaming and plunging away from him; but the Hiua had an answer for that too, and bound his ankles and flung him over another saddle belly down, lashed him in place so that he could not further delay them. The helm fell; one of them gathered it up and set it mockingly on his own head.

Then they started off down the riverside, moving rapidly, and from that head-down jolting Vanye began to slip from consciousness . . . now wholly unaware, but there were long darknesses in which he found no refuge.

And worse than other pain was the thought of Morgaine, whether the Shiua riders had overtaken her or whether she had fallen to her wound . . . he recalled the blood on the sand, sick at heart. But he must live, then. If she were alive, she needed him. If she were dead, he still must contrive to live; he had sworn so.

He had not been reckoning of that when he had fought the Hiua, trying to win of them a quick death and honest; but when he had had time to think of what she had set on him by oath, he gave up fighting his enemies and gathered his strength for another and longer fight, in which there was no honor at all.

The Hiua stopped at midmorning. Vanye was aware of the horse slowing, but of little else until they freed him of the saddle and flung him roughly to the sand. There he lay still and ignored them, staring at the dark waters of the Narn which flowed a stone's throw away . . . a black thread that still bound this place to that where she was: the sight of it comforted him, that they were not yet lost, one from the other.

One of the Hiua seized hold of him and lifted his head, put a flask to his lips. He drank what they would give him; they poured more of it on his face and struck him, trying to restore him. He reacted little to either, although he was aware enough.

Fwar came, seized him by the hair, shook at him until his eyes fixed on him. "Ger, Awan," he named his dead brothers, "and Efwy. And Terrin and Ejan and Prafwy and Ras, Minur's kin here; and Eran, that was Hul's brother; and Sithan and Ulwy that were Trin's . . ."

"And our wives and our children and all those that died before that," said Eran. Vanye looked at him, reading there a hate which equalled Fwar's. He had killed Fwar's brothers with his own hand. Perhaps he had killed the others they named too: many had died in pursuit of them. The women and children had died with their dead hold, no doing of his . . . but that made no difference in their minds. He was a hate they could seize upon, an enemy they had in hand, and for all the grief they had ever suffered, for Morgaine who had led their ancestors to grief in Irien and tried to bind them in drowning Shiuan—for her too they had such burning hate: but he was Morgaine's, and he was in hand.

He gave them no answer; none would serve. Trin hit him a dazing blow, and

Vanye twisted over and spat blood on him, with more accuracy than before. Trin hit him a second time, but Fwar stopped him from a third.

"We have all day, and all night and after that."

They looked pleased at that thought, and the talk afterward was foul and ugly, at which Vanye simply set his jaw and stared at the river, ignoring their attempts to bait him. A great deal of their threatening was wasted on him, for they spoke a rough sort of Kurshin well-laden with *qhalur* and marshlands borrowings, much changed from his own tongue . . . and he had learned Hiua of a young woman whose speech was gentler. He could guess at enough of it.

He was angry. That fact dully amazed him, in the far distance to which his thinking mind had retreated . . . that he would feel more rage than terror. He had never been a brave man. He had come to every grief that had driven him from home and hold and honor because he imagined pain too vividly and came undone at his kinsman's slow tormenting . . . a boy's misery: he had been all too vulnerable then, loving them more than he had understood.

He had no love for these, these scourings of Hiuaj's Barrowhills, these fallen Myya. He seethed with anger that of all the enemies he had, he had fallen to them . . . to Fwar, whose worthless life he had spared, being too much Nhi to kill a downed enemy. Now he had his reward of that mercy. Morgaine too they attacked with their foul laughter, and he had to bear it, still hoping that somewhere in their confidence they would make the mistake of freeing his hands with Fwar in reach.

They did not. They had learned him too well, and devised to get him from his armor without freeing him, throwing a noose about his ankles and suspending him from the limb of one of the trees like a slaughtered deer. They amused themselves in that too, pushing him to and fro while the blood pounded in his head and his senses were near to leaving him. Then they had easier work to free his hands and take the armor from him. Even so he succeeded in getting his hands on Trin, but he could not hold him. They struck him for their amusement until the blood ran down his arms and spotted the sand beneath him. Eventually his senses faded.

Horsemen, in number.

He heard the thunder of the hooves that merged with the pulse in his ears. Bodies rushed about him, with panting and blowing of horses.

More of them, returned from upriver. He remembered Morgaine and struggled back to consciousness, trying to focus his blurred eyes to see whether they had found her or not. Upside down in his vision, all the horses were dark shadows: Siptah was not there. One rider came near, aglitter with scale, white-haired.

Khal. Shiua *qhal.* "Cut him down," the *khal*-lord ordered. Finally there came a sawing at the rope. Vanye tried to lift his stiffened arms to protect his head, knowing that he must fall. But armored riders locked arms beneath him, eased him to the ground upright. He did not struggle after he realized their support . . . fell less hard than he might. They were not Fwar's: no more his friends than Fwar's men, and likely crueler; but their immediate purpose involved his living, and he accepted it. He lay still on the sand at the horses' feet, while the blood flowed back to his lower limbs and his heart labored with the strain of it. In his ears were the *khal*-lord's curses for the Men who had almost killed him.

Morgaine, he thought, *what of Morgaine?* But nothing they said gave him any clue.

"Ride off," the lord bade Fwar and his cousins. "He is ours."

Eventually—for in Shiuan as here, *qhal* were the more powerful—Fwar and his men mounted and rode away, without a word of a threat of vengeance . . . and that, in a Barrows-man and a Myya, boded ill for an enemy's back when the time came.

Vanye struggled to his elbows to see them go; but he had view of nothing but horses' legs and a few *khal* afoot, scale-armored and wearing helms which gave them the faces of demons—all helmed, save their lord, who remained ahorse, his white hair flowing in the wind. It was not one of the Shiua lords he knew.

The men-at-arms cut the cords that bound his ankles and tried to make him stand. He shook his head at that. "The knee . . . I cannot walk," he said hoarsely and as they spoke . . . in the *qhalur* tongue.

They were startled at that. Men in Shiuan did not speak the language of their masters, although *khal* spoke that of Men; he remembered that they were Shiua when one hit him across the face for his insolence.

"He will ride," said the lord. "Alarrh, your horse will bear this Man. Gather up all that is strewn here; the humans have no sense of order. They will leave all this for enemies to read. You"—for the first time he spoke directly to Vanye, and Vanye stared up at him sullenly. "You are Nhi Vanye i Chya."

He nodded.

"That means yes, I suppose."

"Yes." The *khal* had spoken the language of Men, and he had answered again in *qhalur.* The lord's pale, sensitive face registered anger.

"I am Shien Nhinn's-son, prince of Sotharrn. The rest of my men are hunting your mistress. The arrow that took her was the only favor for which we thank the Hiua cattle, but it is a sorry fate for a high-born *khal,* all the same. We will try to better it. And you, Vanye of the Chya—you will be welcome in our camp. Lord Hetharu has a great desire to find you again . . . more desire for your lady, to be sure, but you will find him overjoyed to see you."

"I do not doubt," he murmured; but he did not resist when they bound his hands and brought a horse for him, heaving him into the saddle upright. The pain of his wounds almost took his senses from him; he swayed with dizziness as the horse shied off, and the Shiua began to dispute bitterly who should foul his hands and his person in seeing that he stayed ahorse, bloody and half-naked and human as he was. "I am Kurshin," he said then between his teeth. "While the horse stays under me, I shall not fall off. I will have no *khal's* hands on me either."

They muttered at that and spoke of teaching him his place; but Shien bade them to horse. They started off down the sandy bank with speed that jolted, likely malice rather than needful haste. They gave it up after a time, and Vanye bowed his head and gave to the horse's moving, exhausted. He roused only when they made the fording of the Narn, and the wide plain of Azeroth lay open before them.

After that it was grassland under the horses' hooves, and they went smoothly and easily.

He lived: that was for now the important thing. He smothered his anger and kept his head down as they expected of a Man awed by them. They would not anticipate trouble of him, these folk who marked their own hold-servants with brands on the face, to know them from other Men . . . reckoning no Man much more than animal.

It was not uncharacteristic of them that they found a means to splint his knee at their first rest, caring for him with the same detachment that they might have spent on a lame horse, no gentler and no rougher than that; yet no one would give him a drink because it meant his lips touching something they must use. One did throw him a morsel of food when they ate, but it lay on the grass untouched, for they would not unbind his hands and he would not eat after that fashion, as they wished. He sullenly averted his face, and was no better for that stop except that he could at least stand once he had been put on his feet. They saw to that, he reckoned, simply because it saved them having to work so much getting him on and off a horse.

"There was a *khal* with you besides your mistress," Shien said to him, riding close to him that afternoon. "Who?"

He did not look up or give indication that he had heard.

"Well, you will find time to think of it," Shien said, and spurred disdainfully ahead, giving up the question with an ease curious in his kind.

And that *who* seemed to desire a name in answer, as if they had taken Lellin to be one of their own, renegade to them. As if—he thought, hope stirring in him—as if they had not yet realized the existence of the *arrhend,* or realized a presence in this land besides that of Men. Perhaps Eth had held back more than seemed likely; or perhaps his killers had not left Shathan alive.

He lifted his head despite himself, and looked at the horizon before him, which was grassy and flat as far as the eye could see, an expanse unbroken save for a few bushes or thorn-thickets randomly scattered. The unnatural shape of Azeroth was not evident to the man who stood amid it: it was too vast to grasp at once. Perhaps there was much still secret from the Shiua . . . indicating that as yet none of Lellin's folk had fallen into their hands, and that the Mirrindim might yet be safe.

He hoped so with a fearful hope, although he held out little for himself.

They camped in the open that night, and this time they yielded to practicality and freed his hands briefly, standing over him with swords and pikes as if he could run, lame as he was. He ate a little, and one of them condescended to pour a little water into his hands that he might drink, thus saving the purity of his waterflask. But they restored the bonds for the night, hand and foot, securing him to one of their heavy saddles on the ground, so that he could not slip off into the dark. Lastly they threw a cloak over him, that he not freeze, for he had no clothing on his upper body.

Then they slept, insolently secure, posting no guard. He fretted long, trying his bonds, with an eye to stealing a horse and running for it; but the knots were out of his reach and the cords were too tight. Exhausted, he slept too, and woke in the morning with a kick in the ribs and a *khal*'s curse in his ears.

It was more of the same the next day: no food nor water until the evening, enough to keep him alive, but little more. He nursed his anger, for it kept him fed the same as the food did; but he kept his senses too, and bore their arrogance without resistance. Only once it failed him, when a guard seized him by the hair; he rounded on the halfling . . . and the guard stepped back at what he saw in him. They struck him to the ground then, for no more than that—that he had dared look one of them in the eyes. Their treatment of him worsened thereafter. They began to torment him with mindful spite when they must handle him, and began to talk among themselves, for they knew that he could understand, of what might befall him at their hands.

"You have the grace of your Barrows-ancestors," he said to them finally, and in their own tongue. One of them struck him for this. But Shien frowned, and curtly bade his own men to silence, and to let him be.

That night, when they made camp by a new tributary of the Narn, Shien stared at him long and thoughtfully after the others had begun to settle to sleep, stared with a concentration which began to disturb him . . . the more so when Shien roused his men and dismissed them out of hearing.

Then Shien came and settled at his side.

"Man." It was an inflection that only a *khal* could give that word. "Man, it is said that you are close kin to the halfling Chya Roh."

"Cousin," he answered, unnerved by this approach. No word before this had they drawn from him in questions. He resolved to say nothing more. But Shien stared at him in pensive curiosity.

"Fwar's handiwork has disturbed the resemblance, but it is there; I see it. And this Morgen-Angharan . . ." he used the name by which Morgaine was known to them, and laughed. "Can Death die?" he asked, for Angharan was a deity among the marshlanders of Shiuan, and that was her nature, the white queen.

He knew *khalur* humor, which believed in nothing and reverenced no gods, and he shut his ears to this pointless baiting. But Shien drew his dagger and laid it along his cheek, turning his face back with that, lest he soil his hands. "What a prize you are, Man . . . if you know what Roh knows. Do you realize that you could become both free and comfortable if you hold what I think you may, man who speaks our language. And I would not disdain to seat you at my table and give you—other—privileges. Gods, you have some grace of bearing, more than some who go boasting their tiny portion of *khalur* blood. You are not of the Hiua's kind. Do you know how to be reasonable?"

He stared into Shien's eyes . . . pale gray they were by daylight, as so few of the halflings' were: near full-blood, this prince. He was shaken to reckon that he could be what Shien said, a prize among *khal*, a commodity of value among the powerful: he had knowledge of Gates, the lore which they had lost, knowledge by which Roh himself had gained power among these folk.

"What of Roh?" he asked.

"Chya Roh has made mistakes, which may well prove fatal to him. You might avoid those same mistakes. You might even expect that Hetharu could be persuaded to forget his vexation with you."

"And you will present that solution to Hetharu, is that it? I work at your orders, give what I know to you, and you regain what power Hetharu has taken from you."

The blade turned, and bit slightly. "Who are you to talk of our affairs?"

"Hetharu brought all the Shiua lords to their knees because he had Roh to give him power. Do you love him for it?"

He thought for an instant that Shien would kill him outright. His expression was ugly. Then Shien flipped the knife back into sheath at his belt. "You have need of a patron, Man. I could help you. But you want to play games with me."

"If there is a way out of my situation, make it clear to me."

"It is very clear. Give me the knowledge that you have, and I will be able to help you. Otherwise not."

He stared into Shien's eyes and read it for half-truth. "And if I give you knowledge enough to contest with Hetharu and Roh, then my usefulness is ended there, is it not? Give you knowledge so that you can politic with it and trade influence with your brother-lords? Not in Hetharu's game. Be braver than that, Shiua lord, or do not think that you can use me for a weapon. Break with them both and I will serve you and give you the power that you want, but not otherwise."

"The *khal* who rode with you . . . who?"

"I will not tell you."

"You think that you are in a position to refuse?"

"Those men of yours . . . how well can you trust them? You think there is not one among them who would bear information to Hetharu for reward? How you killed me out here, trying for knowledge Hetharu would not approve you having . . . why else did you send them out of hearing? No. If you are going to break with Hetharu, you need me alive and healthy. I will *tell* you nothing; but I will help you get what you want."

Shien sat on his heels and stared at him, arms folded. He knew that he had gone very far with this *khalur* prince. He saw a veil come over Shien's eyes, and hope failed him.

"It is said," Shien murmured, "that you killed Hetharu's father. And do you hope to deal with him after that?"

"A lie. Hetharu killed his father, and blamed me for it to save his reputation."

Shien laughed wolfishly. "Aye, so do we all think. But that is the kind of lord Hetharu is, and so he dealt with you once when you trifled with him . . . so he dealt with his own lord and father; and now do you propose that if I refuse your mad scheme you will throw yourself on his mercy again? You do not learn readily, Man."

A chill came on him, remembering, but he shook his head nevertheless. "Then you also know him well enough to know that you will never profit by serving him. Take my way, lord of Sotharrn, and have what you want—or have nothing. I learn too readily to hand any *khal* the only thing that makes my life valuable."

Shien's white brows knit into a frown. For a moment thoughts passed visibly through his eyes, none of them good to behold. "You assume that you know how to deal with us, and how I must deal with the other lords. You do not know us, Man."

"I know that I am dead when you have what you want."

Shien's frown bent slowly into a smile, "Ah, Man, you are too unsubtle. One does not accuse his possible benefactor of lying. I might even have kept my word."

"No," he said, though the doubt was planted in him.

"Think of it, tomorrow, when we deliver you to Hetharu."

And Shien rose then and settled some distance away. Vanye turned his head to stare at him, but Shien poured himself a cup from his flask and sat with his face averted, drinking delicately.

Beyond him sat the others, halflings aping *khal,* with bleached hair and coarse arrogance, and a hate for Men that was the greater because of their own human blood.

Shien turned his head and smiled at him thinly, lifting the cup in mockery.

"Tomorrow," Shien promised him.

They forded two shallow rivers, one at dawn and one at noon. Vanye reckoned well now where they were, nearing the Gate that stood in Azeroth. He grew afraid, as it was impossible not to fear contemplating that power, which could drink in substance and ravel it.

But no sign of the Gate was yet visible, not in the long ride they made that afternoon. There were few rests; Shien had promised that they would come to Hetharu's camp in this day and seemed determined on it if it exhausted them. Vanye said nothing to Shien as the distance wore away under the horses' hooves. Shien had nothing more to say to him, save now and again to gaze at him brooding speculation. He reckoned again what his chances were if he yielded on the Shiua lord's terms, and averted his face from temptation.

They did not stop at dusk, even to rest, and the night turned bitterly cold. He asked them for a cloak, but they refused it, though the guard who had lent it before would not wear it himself; they took pleasure in refusing. After that he bowed his head, trying to ignore them. They taunted him with threats which this time Shien did not silence, but he said nothing, cared nothing for them.

Then there appeared a glow on the horizon . . . cold, like the moon; but the moon was aloft, and the light was far brighter.

The Gate of Azeroth, that Men called the Fires.

He lifted his face, staring at that terrible presence, seeing now where they were bound, for nearer at hand were the dimmer red lights of woodfires, and ungainly shapes: tents and shelters.

They passed sentries who sat their posts concealed in shelters of grass; and rode past picket lines, where horses stood . . . few in proportion to the vast sprawl of the Shiua camp . . . the camp of a nation spread over the vast plains under the Gate; of more than a nation: of the remnant of a world.

And it aimed at the heart of Shathan.

Morgaine and I have done this thing, he could not forbear thinking. *My doing as much as hers. Heaven forgive us.*

They passed the fringes of the camp. Suddenly Shien put the company to a gallop, passing the sprawling shelters of grass and cloth which hemmed them about on all sides.

Men stared at their passage . . . dark shapes, small: true Men, of Shiuan's marshes. Vanye saw the stares and went cold as someone sent up a thin, hysterical cry.

"*Her* man. *Hers!*"

Men rushed out to bar their way, scattered from the hooves of the horses when the *khal* kept coming. The marshlanders knew him, and would gladly tear him limb from limb if he fell among them. The *khal* whipped their horses and thundered through, reckless of human lives, and into a quieter portion of the camp, where demon-helms quickly parted and shut a barricade of brush and sharpened stakes, and backed it with a row of barbed pikes.

The mob no longer pursued; the gate sufficed. They slowed, the horses blowing and panting in exhaustion, stretching at the reins and seeking air. They rode slowly up to a sprawling shelter, the largest in the compound.

The structure was patched, cobbled together of various bits of cloth and bundles of reeds and grass, and part of it was a tent. Light blazed within, showing through the canvas; and there was music, but not such as the *arrhendim* had played. They halted there, and guards came to take the horses.

They lifted him down from the saddle. "Be careful," said Shien when one of them jerked at him. "This is a very valuable Man."

And Shien himself took him by the elbow and brought him toward the door of the tent. "You were not wise," Shien said.

He shook his head, uncertain whether he had rejected a trap that would have killed him or whether he had rejected the only hope he had. It was impossible. A *khal* would scarcely keep faith with *khal*. That one would keep faith with a Man was not to be believed.

He blinked, suddenly thrust into the light and warmth within.

⤙ Chapter 8

Hetharu.

Vanye stopped, with Shien at his back, steadied himself on his wounded leg; and of all in that gathering, he recognized that tall, black-clad lord. The music died away with a hiss of strings, and noble lords and ladies of Shiuan stopped what half-clad diversions they were practicing and came to slow, studied attention where they lounged on sacks and cushions within the tent, against walls of bound reeds.

Of sacks and brocade cloaks was the throne to which Hetharu settled. A cluster of halfling guards was about him, some far gone in stupor, others alert, armored and armed. A naked Woman shrank into the shadows of the corner. Hetharu stared at the intrusion, blank with amazement for the instant, and then pleasure grew on his countenance . . . thin and shadow-eyed that face, the more startling for the human eyes which looked darkly out from what were otherwise pure *qhalur* features. His white hair lay lank and silken on his shoulders. His black brocade was somewhat worn, the lace frayed; the ornate sword that he wore still looked serviceable. Hetharu smiled, and about him settled the miasma of all that was Shiuan, drowning and rotting at once.

"Nhi Vanye," Hetharu murmured. "And Morgaine?"

"That matter must be cared for by now," said Shien. Vanye clenched his jaw and stared through all of them, trying to use his wits; but that callous reckoning of Morgaine's life hit him suddenly with more force than he had yet felt.

Kill Hetharu? That was one of the thoughts that he had entertained over recent days; and suddenly it seemed useless, for here were thousands like him. Gain power among them? Suddenly it seemed impossible; he was a Man, and what else was here of humankind crouched naked and ashamed and weeping in the corner.

He took a step forward. Though his hands were bound, the guards were uneasy; pikes inclined marginally toward him. He stopped, sure that they would not be careless with him.

"I hear," he said to Hetharu, "that you and Roh have quarreled."

That set them back. There was an instant's silence, and Hetharu's face was whiter than usual.

"Out!" Hetharu said suddenly. "All of you who have no business here, out."

That included many: the Woman, the majority of the *khal* who had disported themselves about the fringes of the gathering. One half-conscious lordling reclined at Hetharu's side, leaning against the sacks and the brocade with unfocused gray eyes and a dreaming smile that mocked all reality. A middle-aged *khalur* woman remained; and a handful of lords; and all the guards, although some of them were far-departed in dreams, and knelt near Hetharu and about the other lords with their eyes distant and their hands loose on their weapons. Enough still remained who had all their wits about them. Hetharu leaned back in his makeshift throne and regarded him with old and familiar hate.

"Shien, what have you been telling this Man?"

Shien shrugged. "I have been pointing out his situation, and his possible value."

Hetharu's dark eyes swept over Shien narrowly. "Knowledge such as Roh has? Is that your meaning?"

"It is possible that he has it. He is reticent."

"He," said the woman suddenly, "might be more reasonable than Roh has been. After all, the human rabble hates him bitterly, and he cannot gain any followers among them. That is one sure advantage over Roh."

"There are personal issues," Hetharu said, and the lady laughed unpleasantly.

"We know the truth of those. Do not waste a valuable resource, my lord Hetharu. Who here cares about the past . . . things done and not done? Shiuan is behind us. Here is important. You have an opportunity to rid us of the so-named halfling and his followers. Use it."

Hetharu was not pleased by that, but the lady spoke as one who was accustomed to be heard, and she was of the old blood, gray-eyed and white-haired, with guards about her none of whom were hazy in their look. One of the hold-lords, Vanye reckoned her: not Sotharra like Shien, but perhaps of Domen or Marcom or Arisith. The Shiua lords were not firmly held in Hetharu's hand.

"You are too credulous, lady Halah," said Hetharu. "This Man is quite capable of turning in the hand that holds him. He surprised Roh, who should know him; and my lamented brother Kithan. And would you not attempt to surprise us in the same way, Man?"

Vanye said nothing. Debate with Hetharu could win nothing. The hope was rather in playing one and the other of his subordinates against him.

"Of course you would," Hetharu answered for him, and laughed. "And you plan to. You are not the sort who will ever thank us for the handling you have had . . . at my hands and now at Shien's.—Beware this one, Shien. He is not hand-broken, though he may try to let you think so. His cousin says that he does not know how to lie; but he does know how to keep secrets, do you not, Vanye of the Chya? Morgen-Angharan's—" and he used a word that Vanye did not know; but he suspected, and set his jaw the harder, looking through Hetharu. "Ah, glare at me. We are better acquaintances than the others, you and I. So this Morgen is missing. Where?"

He did not answer.

"Over by the great river," Shien said. "In the midst of our deepest penetration into the forest, with a Hiua arrow in her. Our riders have her trail, and if they have not found her by now, she will scarcely survive the wound. My lord, there was a *khal* with her and another human. And that is another thing this prisoner does not like to talk about."

"Kithan?"

Vanye bowed his head and concealed his surprise, for Hetharu's brother had not come through, then, and he would have reckoned otherwise . . . *my lamented brother,* Hetharu had said. He was sorry to know Kithan was not in the camp, for with him there might have been some hope; that Kithan would have joined them instead was a natural conclusion for Hetharu. He shrugged.

"Find him," Hetharu ordered. There was a frantic edge to his voice, more disturbance than Hetharu was wont to show.

Morgaine's weapons, Vanye thought suddenly; *here is a man scarcely clinging to his position.*

"My lord," said Shien, "my men are trying to do so. Perhaps they have."

Hetharu was silent then, biting at his lip, and what passed between him and Shien was plain enough.

"I brought you this one alive," Shien said very softly. "And I had to pull him out of the Hiua's keeping. Else he would be in other hands, my lord."

"We are grateful," Hetharu said, but his eyes were dead, cold. They traveled back to lock with Vanye's. "Well. You are in a sorry position, are you not, Nhi Vanye? There is not a human in that camp out there but would skin you alive if he set hands on you; they know you well, do you see? And there are the Hiua, who are Roh's dogs. And your mistress is not coming here, if ever she comes anywhere again. You can hardly look for friendship from Chya Roh. And you know what love we bear you."

"Yet you must keep Roh's favor, must you not, Shiua lords?"

Anger flared in the others; and guards fingered the hafts of their weapons. Hetharu only smiled.

"Now," said Hetharu, "there are things we could do, regarding Chya Roh. But since he has been the only storehouse of the information we want, why, we have handled him with utmost respect. He is dangerous. Of course we know that. But now you have given us some latitude, have you not? You know what Roh knows, and you are not, now, dangerous. If we should happen to lose your life in the process, why—we still have Roh. So we can dice with it, can we not?—You are dismissed, Shien, with our—thanks."

There was no stir of movement. Hetharu lifted his hand and the pikes inclined.

And Shien and his men strode out. One of the lordlings gave a low laugh. The others relaxed, easing back into comfort, and Hetharu smiled tautly.

"Did he try to persuade you to his cause?" Hetharu asked.

Vanye said nothing, his heart sinking with the knowledge that he had turned from one who might have done what he promised. Hetharu read his silence, and nodded slowly.

"You know the choice we give you," Hetharu said. "You may volunteer that information . . . and you may live . . . while Roh will someday be surprised to discover that we do not need him. Now if you will do that, you will be wise. Or we can seek it against your will, and you will be sorry for that. So make your choice, Man."

Vanye shook his head. "There is nothing I could tell you, only show you. And I need to be present at the Gate to do that."

Hetharu laughed, and so did his men, for that was transparent. "Ah, you would like to find yourself there, would you not? No, what you can demonstrate, you can tell. And tell us you shall."

Again he shook his head.

Hetharu's hand crept to the shoulder of the *khal* who dreamed, eyes open, at the side of his seat. He urged at that one gently until the dazed face lifted to his. "Hirrun, give me a double portion of what you have . . . aye, I know you have more with you. And give it to me—if you are wise."

A mean and ugly look came on Hirrun's handsome face, but he flinched under the grip of Hetharu's fingers, and dug in his belt-pouch, brought forth something which he offered with shaking hands into Hetharu's palm. Hetharu smiled and gave it to the guard next to him.

Then he looked up. "Hold him," he said.

Vanye understood then, and moved, flung himself backward, but others were behind him and he had no chance. The splinted leg lost its footing, and he sprawled along with his guards. They weighed him down and forced his jaws apart, rammed the pellets down his throat. Someone poured liquor after, to the laughter of the others, a sound that pealed like bells. He tried to spit them out, but they held him until it was swallow or choke. Then they let him go, amid much laughter, and he rolled onto his side and tried to vomit the drug up, but it was too late for that. In a moment he began to feel the haze of it—*akil*, that vice too common among the *khal* and the marshlanders who provided it to them, that stole his sense and sent a horrid languor over him. It was strange; it did not diminish the fear, but it sent it to some far place where it did not influence what he did. A warmth stole over him, and a curious lack of pain, in which the touch of anything was pleasurable.

"No!" he screamed in outrage, and they laughed, a gentle and distant rippling of sound. He screamed again, and tried to turn his face from them, but the guards gathered him up and held him on his feet.

"There is more," said Hetharu, "when that fades. Let him stand, let him stand."

They let him go. He could not move in any direction. He feared for his balance. His heart was beating painfully and there was a roaring in his ears. His vision was hazy save in the center of focus, and there was a blackness between himself and that center. But worst was the warmth which crawled over his skin, destroying all sense of alarm; he fought that with all the mind that was left to him.

"Who is the *khal* who rode with you?"

He shook his head, and one of the guards seized his arm, distracting him so that he could not recall anything. The guard hit him, but the blow was nothing but bewildering. The blackness that centered upon Hetharu abruptly slipped wider. It seemed ready to tear asunder and drop him into it.

"Who?" Hetharu repeated, and shouted at him. "*Who?*"

"Lellin," he answered in his startlement, and knew what he was doing and that he must not. He shook his head and recalled Mirrind, and Merir, and all that he could betray to them. Tears ran down his face, and he pulled away from the guard and stumbled, caught his balance.

"Who is Lellin?" Hetharu asked someone else, and the voice echoed in the emptiness. Others answered that they did not know. "Who is Lellin?" Hetharu asked of him, and he shook his head and shook it again, desperately, trying to hold to the fear that was his life, his sanity.

"Where were you going when the Hiua ambushed you?"

Again he shook his head. They had not asked him that before, and the answer of it was deadly; he knew it, and knew that they could shake that out of him as well.

"What is the knowledge you have of the old powers?" the woman Halah asked, a female voice which confused him in this gathering.

"Where were you going?" Hetharu asked, shouting at him, and he flinched from that horrid sound and stumbled against the guards.

"No," he said.

And suddenly the wall of the tent went back. Men stood there . . . Fwar, and others, with drawn bows. The pikes swung about to face that intrusion; but the bowmen parted slightly, and Roh walked out of the dark into the light of the tent.

"Cousin," Roh said.

The voice was gentle; that kinsman's face looked concerned for him, and kind. Roh held out his hand, and no *khal* dared forbid him. "Come," Roh said, and again: "Come."

He recalled why he should fear this man: but Roh's human face promised something more honest than surrounded him. He came, trying not to see the dark at the edges. Roh's hand caught him by the arm, helped him walk as Fwar's bowmen closed to guard their retreat, a human curtain between them and the *khal.*

Then the cold wind outside hit him, and he had not even the control of his limbs to shiver.

"My tent is this way," Roh said, bearing him on his feet. "Walk, curse you."

He tried, although the splinted leg was the only steady one. It was a long blank time until he found himself lying against a wall of bound reeds in Roh's shelter. A ring of Hiua at Roh's shoulder leaned on their bows and stared down at him, shadows in the dim light of a fire, the smoke of which curled up to an opening in the roof. Fwar was there, foremost of them.

"Go, get out of here," Roh bade the Hiua. "All of you. Keep an eye on the *khal.*"

They went, though Fwar lingered last . . . gave him a broad and disturbing grin before he went out the door.

Then Roh dropped down on his heels. He put forth a hand to his face, turned it to him and stared him in the eyes. *"Akil."*

"Yes." The haze of it was too thick to fight any longer. He turned his face away, shuddering, for the warmth made the touch like that on a burn . . . not painful, but too sensitive.

"Where is Morgaine? Where would she have gone?"

That alarmed him. He shook his head vehemently.

"Where?" Roh repeated.

"The river . . . Fwar knows."

"The control is there, is it not?"

The question shot through all his refusals. He looked at Roh and blinked, and realized afterward that his reaction had betrayed the truth.

"Well," Roh said, "we have suspected it. We have been searching all that area. She dares not come back here, Master Gate though this is . . . aye, I know that too; and therefore she must have that which controls the Gate. She will seek that point, reliable as a lodestar . . . if she is not dead. Do you think that she is?"

"I do not know," he admitted, and the tears surprised and overwhelmed him, flowing down his face. He could not stop them, nor tell how much or what he had said that he ought not; all his sense was undone, and, he feared, his memory with it.

"She was badly hurt, Fwar said."

"Yes."

"What worries me now is the thought of that sword of hers. Think of that in Hetharu's gentle hands. That must not happen. That must not happen, Vanye. You must prevent that. Where would she go?"

The words were reasoning, the touch gentle and pleasant. He drew back from it and shook his head, swore. Roh's hand fell and Roh rested on his heels staring at him as at a perplexing problem, his face, so like a brother's to him, furrowed between the brows with distress. He shut his eyes.

"How much did they give you? How much of the *akil?*"

He shook his head, not knowing the answer. "Let me be. Let me be. It has been days since I rested; Roh, let me sleep."

"Stay awake. I fear for you if you do not."

That had not the incongruity it might have held; it was not the first time he had seen this face of his enemy, that which had been his cousin. He blinked with dull perception, trying to think through Roh's words, flinched as Roh put his hands on his splinted knee.

"Fwar told me that a horse went down on you. And these other hurts?"

"Fwar knows."

"I thought so." Roh took the knife from his belt—hesitated as Vanye saw it and recognized it. "Ah, yes. You carried it . . . to return to me, I do not doubt. Well, it is back. Thank you." He cut the binding on the splint, and that pain stabbed even through the *akil,* touching all other nerves. But Roh felt of the joint with great gentleness. "Swollen . . . torn. Probably not broken. I will do what I can with it. I will free your hands—or not, as you will have it. You tell me."

"I will make no trouble for the meanwhile."

"Sensible man." Roh bent him forward and cut the cords, then sheathed the blade and massaged his torn hands until some life returned to his swollen and discolored fingers. "You are clear-minded enough to know where you are, are you not?"

"The Gate," he recalled, and recalled what had befallen Roh at such a place. Panic took him. Roh's fingers bit into his wrist, stopping him from a wild move, and the leg shot fire through the arch of the knee, pain and the *akil* almost taking his senses.

"You are going nowhere, crippled as you are," Roh hissed into his ear, and thrust his arm free. "What do you expect? That anyone could want the carrion they have left of you? I have no such designs. Use your wits. I would not have let you free if I had."

He blinked, trying to think clearly, trying to flex the life back into his fingers. He was shaking, sweat cold on him.

"Be still," Roh said. "Believe me. Body-changing is nothing pleasant. The one I have suffices . . . although," he added in cold mockery, "one of the Hiua might find yours an improvement. Fwar, for instance. His face gives him no joy."

He said nothing. The *akil* set even this at distance. The pain faded back into the warmth.

"Peace," Roh said softly. "I assure you, you are safe from that."

"Which are you? Liell now, is it not?"

Roh's face smiled. "More than not."

"Roh—" he pleaded, and the smile faded and the frown came back, an indefinable shift of the eyes.

"I say I will not harm you."

"Who is 'I,' Roh?"

"I—" Roh shook his head and rose. "You do not understand. There is no separation, no division. I—" He went across the shelter, there dipped up a pan of water . . . and on an apparent other thought, poured some into a handle-broken cup and brought it back to him. "Here."

He drank, thirstily. Roh knelt and took the cup back when he was finished, tossed it aside into the straw, then dipped a cloth into the pan of cold water and began, very gently, to wash the dirt from his wounds, starting with his face. "I will tell you how it is," Roh said. "At the first is utter shock . . . and then a few days that are like a dream. You *are* both. And then part of the dream begins to fade, and you know that it was once there, but you cannot recall it in daylight. I was Liell once. Now I am Chya Roh. I think that I like this shape well. But then I probably liked the other. And the others before that. I am Roh now.

Everything that he is, all that he remembers—all that he loves or hates. All, in short—that he is or ever was—I contain."

"Except his soul."

A touch of irritation came over Roh's face. "I would not know about that."

"Roh would have."

Roh's hands resumed the gentle ministering they had for an instant ceased, and he shook his head. "Cousin—sometimes—there is a perverseness in me that I cannot help. I would not harm you, but do not prick at me. Do not. I do not like it when I have done such a thing."

"O Heaven, I pity you."

The cloth found a raw spot and he winced. "Do not prick at me," Roh repeated between his teeth. The touch gentled again. "You do not know what trouble you have caused me . . . this whole camp. You know the marshlanders are across that barricade trying to figure how to get their hands on you."

He gazed at Roh, distantly.

"Wake up," Roh insisted. "They have put too much of that into you. What did you tell them?"

He shook his head, confused. For a time he truly did not remember. Roh seized his shoulder and forced his attention.

"What, confound you? Will you have them to know and not me? Think it through."

"They asked—asked me to tell what I knew of the Gates. They are tired of relying on you. They said—that because the Men in this camp want to kill me, they would have more hold on me than on you . . . that was Shien's thought . . . or someone's . . . I cannot remember. But Hetharu . . . meant to have what I know—and not to tell you until a time suited him—"

"What you know. And what do you know of Gates? Has she given you knowledge enough to be dangerous?"

He thought over the hazard of truth with Roh. Nothing would focus.

"Have you such knowledge?" Roh asked.

"Yes."

"And what did you tell them?"

"Nothing. I told them nothing. You came."

"I heard that they had brought you in. I guessed as much as you have told me."

"They will cut your throat when they can."

Roh laughed. "Aye, that they will. And yours, sooner, without my protection. What do you know that you did *not* tell them?"

Panic flashed through him, muddled with the *akil*. He shook his head desperately, not trusting to speak.

"I will tell you what I suspect," Roh said. "That Morgaine has had help staying out of sight. She has been in a certain village; I have learned that much:

Hetharu knows it too. Men live here, elusive as they are, and there are others too, are there not?"

He said nothing.

"There are. I know that. And I think that there are *qhal*—are there not, cousin? And you have friends. Perhaps that is who rode off with her, when she fled. Allies. Native allies. And she thought to go to the high place and seize control of the Gate and destroy me. Well, is that not her purpose? It is the only sane course for her. But I am less worried about what Morgaine will and will not, in the state she must be in now, than I am worried for who has his hands on that weapon of hers. A *qhal* and a Man are with her. So Fwar reports. And who are they, and what would either of them do with such a weapon as that sword in his hands?"

The thoughts tumbled chaotically about him: *Merir*, he thought. *Merir would use it well.* But then he doubted, and recalled that he and Morgaine held purposes at odds with the *arrhendim*.

"Fwar brought me something," Roh said. "Oh, he did not want to give it, but Fwar has a great respect for my anger, and he most readily gave it up for his health's sake." He drew from his belt a silver circlet on a chain . . . Merir's gift. "You wore this. I find it very strange workmanship, nothing like home, nor even like Shiuan. See, it is written over with *qhalur* runes. *Friendship* is the inscription. Whose friend are you, Nhi Vanye?"

He shook his head and his eyes hazed. He was exhausted. Of a sudden the fear that had stayed remote began to trouble him, nearer and nearer, stalking him.

"Hardly honorable . . . to worry at you when you are full of that foul stuff— is it? You are easy as a new-written page. Well, I shall not, any more. But I do tell you this that you may think on when you are sober again . . . that what I have asked of you I have not asked with purpose to harm you. And you must stay awake, Vanye. Come, keep your eyes clear. Look at me with sense."

He tried. Roh hit him, enough to sting, but not with malice. "Stay awake. I will make you angry with me if that is what it takes. Your eyes are still hazed with that drug, and until that goes, you will stay awake, whatever I have to do to keep you that way. I have seen men die of it in this camp. They sleep to death. And I want you alive."

"Why?"

"Because I have put my neck on the block for you tonight and I want reward of it."

"What do you want?"

Roh laughed. "Your company, cousin."

"I warned you—warned you that you would not find your companions grateful when you joined them. You are a Man, and they hate you for it."

"Am I?" Roh laughed again. "You admit it then, that I am your cousin."

"A *qhal*..."—*told me,* he almost said, *what it was like for you.* But he was not quite hazed enough to let it slip, and stopped himself in time. Roh looked at him strangely, and then shrugged and let it pass, beginning again to wash at his injuries. Roh's touch hurt, and he winced: Roh swore softly.

"I cannot help it," Roh said. "Thank Fwar for this. I am as careful as I can be. Be glad of the *akil* for a while."

Roh was indeed careful, and skilled; he cleaned the wounds and dressed them with hot oil, and tended those that were fevered. He put hot compresses on the knee, changing them often. In time Vanye let his head fall. Roh disturbed him to look at his eyes, and finally let him sleep, rousing him only when he changed the compresses. It was far into the night, Vanye judged at one of these wakings, and yet Roh disturbed him again, putting heat on the knee. "Roh?" he asked, perplexed by this.

"I would not have you lame."

"Someone else might see to it."

"Who? Fwar? I am scant of servants in this grand hall. Go to sleep, cousin."

He did so, a quiet sleep, for the first time since Carrhend. This last and better effect the *akil* left on him, that its passing exhausted him and he was able to rest.

⌐ Chapter 9

Roh roused him again with daylight flooding through the door and hazing through the smoke from the opening overhead. There was food; Vanye bestirred himself and took it, bread and salted fish and a little of Shiuan's sourish drink—for the first time in days, enough to eat, poor though it was and foul with the memory of Shiuan.

His jaw hurt in eating, and there was little of him elsewhere that was not bruised or wounded. But the knee had freedom of movement this morning, and the pain there, which had become so constant he had ceased even to realize it, had somewhat abated. He did not dress again, but sat with a length of cloth wrapped about him, and Roh saw to it that the hot compress stayed on the knee even at breakfast, a bit of rag constantly aboil in a pot on the fire, one and then the other.

"Thank you," Vanye said in sum of everything.

"What, honest gratitude? That is more than I had of you in our last meeting. I think you meant to cut my throat, cousin."

"I have sense enough to know what I owe you."

Roh smiled a twisted smile and poured another panful of water into the pot on the fire, then settled and poured himself a cup of the Shiua liquor. He drank of it and grimaced. "Because I did not take advantage of you as I could have done? They would have gone on and on with that drug until you had no sense left what you were doing, and if they had had long enough—well, you would have handed them everything you know, and that would have been enough to save your life . . . of sorts. You would have lived—perhaps . . . so long as humiliating you amused them. You do well to thank me. But of course I had to get you out of there; it was only practical. You would have ruined me. For the rest, well, you do owe me, do you not? At least you owe me better than to turn on me."

Vanye turned up his scarred palm, that was Morgaine's mark, sealed in blood and ash. "I cannot say that, and you know it. Whatever I have done and will do—is under *ilin*-law. No promise of mine is binding where it crosses that; I have no honor."

"But you have enough to remind me of it."

He shrugged, troubled, as Roh had always been able to seize his heart and turn it in him. "You should have looked well on what was happening in that tent last night. They dare not lay hands on you—yet. But they will find a way someday."

"I know. I know how far I can trust Hetharu, and we passed the borders of that territory long ago."

"So you surround yourself with the likes of Fwar. You know surely that he and his kindred served Morgaine once. They turned on her when they did not gain of her what they wanted. They will do the same for you the first time you cross their wishes. And that is not my hate speaking. That is the truth."

"I expect it daily. But the fact remains that Fwar and his men had rather serve me than the *khal*, reckoning how much the *khal* love them. The *khal* have alienated every human in this camp, Hiua, marshlanders—all who have any experience of independence; but the marshlanders do not love Fwar, no, not in the least. Fwar and his Hiua lads are few, hard Men as they are, and he knows that if ever he slips, the marshlanders will put his face in the dirt. Fwar loves power. He must have it, many as his enemies have become. He joined Morgaine while he thought that she would give it to him, while it looked likely that he could remain lieutenant and lord it over conquests. He joined me only when it was clear that he could not deal with the *khal* and when he realized that I am also a power in this camp. Fwar keeps the marshlanders under his heel and that is useful to me. He is essential to my survival here; he is nothing without me and he knows it . . . but so long as I have him in my employ, the *khal* do not rule Hiua or marshlanders in this camp. And arrogant as the *khal* are, they do realize that they are outnumbered, and that the Men who still serve them are cattle, of their own making. No Shiua human is a match for marshlander or Hiua, and of course not all the Men who have lived under the *khal* truly love their masters, not even those Men who wear the brand on their faces. The *khal* are really quite terrified of their own servants, and so they redouble their cruelties to keep them cowed . . . but that is not a thing to say openly. For one thing, it would not be good to have Men find it out, would it?—Another bit of bread?"

"I cannot."

"Things among them have changed since Hetharu came to power," Roh continued with a shake of his head. "There was an urge to decency in some of these folks. But in the passage, only the strongest survived; they were generally not the fittest to live."

"You chose Hetharu for your ally . . . when you had other choices."

"I did, yes." Roh refilled both their cups. "To my lasting sorrow, I chose him. I have always been unfortunate in my allies.—Cousin . . . *where* do you reckon Morgaine is?"

Vanye swallowed at a bit suddenly gone dry and reached for the cup, drank deeply and ignored the question.

"The place she attempted to reach over by the river," Roh said, "is surely the control itself . . . I believe so; Hetharu surely does. Hetharu's patrols will scour that area . . . will have been doing so in searching for her. Hetharu wants the Hiua sent back out on her trail. I am not eager to send Fwar from me, for obvious reasons; Fwar himself is not at all anxious to go, but that even he sees the danger if that weapon of hers goes to Hetharu's men. Hetharu himself is terrified, I do not doubt, of someone like Shien . . . of even his own folk getting possession of it. I do not, I confess, like to think of Fwar holding it either. Of course Fwar should have let you lie under that horse and gone after her; he realizes that now, in cold blood, but . . . he is afraid of her: he has faced her weapons before, and it was fear that obscured his good sense—fear and his obsessive hate of you. He dared an arrow against her at distance, but facing *Changeling* . . . well, that is quite another matter, at least in his thoughts of the moment. Fwar sometimes needs time to reckon clearly where his advantage truly lies; his instincts for survival on the instant sometimes overwhelm those for the long range. He regrets that choice now; but the moment has passed— saving your help, of course."

"Then it has passed," he said; the words almost choked him. "I will not help you."

"Peace, peace, I advise you against any attack on me. And put *khalur* tactics from your mind; I could have done the same as they last night, if I would. No, I am the only safety you have here."

"Liell tended to allies like Fwar: bandits, cutthroats—a hall that would have had fit place in Shiuan, for all it was human-held. I find you unchanged—and my chances equal, here and there."

Roh's eyes clouded, cleared again slowly. "I do not blame you. I loathe my companions, as you warned me I would . . . but you forced me to them. They will kill me when they can; of course they will. You are safe here just as I am . . . only because Hetharu still fears a rising in the human camp if he comes and tries to take you; I could do that to him, and he fears it. Besides, he has reason to wait."

"What reason?"

"The hope that at any hour one of his patrols may ride in bearing Morgaine's weapons . . . and in that hour, my friend, we are both dead men. And there is yet another danger: that perhaps you and I and Morgaine are not the only ones in this land who can use the power of the Gate; perhaps there is knowledge to be had elsewhere in this land. And if that is so—Is it so, Vanye?"

He said nothing, trying to keep all reaction from his face.

"I suspect that there could be," Roh said. "Whatever else we have to fear, the sword is beyond doubt. It was madness ever to have made such a thing. Morgaine knows it, I am sure. And the thought of that . . . I know what is written in the runes on that blade, at least the gist of it. And that should never have been written."

"She knows it."

"Can you walk? Come here. I will show you something."

He strove to rise, and Roh lent his hand and steadied him as he limped across the shelter to the far side where Roh wished to lead him. There Roh flung back a ragged curtain, and showed him the horizon.

And there was the Gate, afire with shimmering colder than moonlight. Vanye gazed at it, and shuddered at that nearness, at the presence of that power that he had learned to dread.

"It is not good to look at, is it?" Roh asked. "It drinks up the mind like water. It hovers over us here. I have lived in that presence until it burns through the curtains and the wall. There is no peace with that thing. And the Men who live here, and the *khal*—feel it. Because of *her* they have feared to leave it; and now they are beginning to fear to stay near it. Some may leave it and go out. Those who do stay here . . . will go mad."

Vanye turned from it, would have left Roh's help and risked falling, but Roh went with him and helped him down on the mat by the fire.

Roh sank down then on his heels, arms folded across his knees, and settled further, crosslegged. "So you see the other source of insanity in this place, deadlier than the *akil*. And far more powerful." He picked up his cup and drank it to the last, shuddered and swallowed heavily. "Vanye, I want you to guard *my* back for a time, as you have guarded hers."

"You are mad."

"No. I know you. There is no man more reliable. Save that other oath of yours, I know that any promise you give freely will be kept. And I am tired,

Vanye." Roh's voice broke suddenly, and pain was in the brown eyes. "I ask only that you do this until it crosses your oath to her."

"That might be at any time I decide it is. And I owe you no warning."

"I know. Still I ask you. Only that."

He was bewildered, and turned the thing over and over in his mind, finding no trap in it. At last he nodded. "Until then, I will do what I can. As I am—that is little. I do not understand you, Roh. I think you have something in mind, and I do not trust you."

"I have said what I want. For now—I will leave awhile. Sleep; do what you choose, so long as you stay in this shelter. There is clothing there if you must have it, but do not walk on that leg; keep the compresses on it, if you have any sense."

"If Fwar comes within my reach—"

"He would not come alone; you know him. Do not look for that kind of trouble. I will keep my eye in Fwar's direction, and you will not have to worry where he is." He gathered himself up and slung on his sword, but he left his bow and quiver.

And as he left he dropped the flap that curtained the door, taking most of the daylight.

Vanye lay down where he was and curled up to sleep, drawing a blanket over him. None did come to trouble his rest; and after a long while Roh returned, with no word of what he had been doing, though his face was weary.

"I am going to sleep," Roh said, and flung himself down on his unused pallet. "Wake me if it is necessary."

It was a strange vigil, to know the Gate on one side and *khalur* enemies on the other, and himself keeping watch over the kinsman he had sworn to kill. And he had leisure to think of Morgaine, counting the days since their parting . . . the fourth day, now, when any wound would have reached and passed its crisis one way or the other.

Through the day he kept the compresses on the knee, and in late afternoon, Roh changed the dressings on his wounds and left him again a time, returning with food. Then Roh let him sleep, but waked him midway through the night and wished him to sit awake again while he slept.

He looked at Roh, wondering what was afoot that Roh dared not have them both asleep; but Roh cast himself down on his face as if the weariness on him were unbearable, as if it were more than last night that he had not slept securely. He stayed awake until the dawn, and drowsed the next morning, while Roh pursued his own business outside.

He waked suddenly, at a footstep. It was Roh, and there was commotion in the camp. He looked in that direction, questioning, but Roh sat down and laid his sword on the mat beside him, then poured himself a drink. His hands were shaking.

"It will settle," Roh said finally. "There has been a suicide. A man, a woman, and two children. Such things happen here."

He looked at Roh in horror, for such things did not happen in Andur-Kursh.

Roh shrugged. "One of the *khal*'s latest. They pushed the man to it. And that is only the edge of evils here. The Gate—" He shrugged again, that became a shudder. "It broods over all here."

The curtain of the doorway was thrust back, and Vanye saw their visitors: Fwar and his men. He reached for the jug of liquor, not to drink; Roh's hand clenched on his wrist, reminding him of sense.

"It is settled," Fwar said, avoiding Vanye's eyes, staring at Roh. "The *khal* gave grain; the kin have begun to bury their dead. But it will not stay settled. Not while this other matter has them stirred up. Hetharu is pushing at us. We cannot have men there and here. We are not enough to be in both places."

Roh was silent a moment. "Hetharu is playing a dangerous game," he said in a still voice. "Sit down, Fwar, you and your men."

"I will not sit with this dog."

"Fwar, sit down. Do not try my patience."

Fwar considered it long, and sullenly sank down at the fireside, his cousins with him.

"You ask too much of me," Vanye muttered.

"Have peace with them," Roh said. "On your word to me: this is part of it."

He inclined his head sullenly, looked up at Fwar. "Under Roh's peace, then."

"Aye," Fwar answered gracelessly, but Vanye gave it no more belief than he would have given Hetharu's word . . . less, if possible.

"I will tell you why you will keep peace," Roh said. "Because we are all about to perish, between the *khal* and the marshlanders. Because *that*—" He hooked a gesture over his shoulder to the wall which concealed the Gate, and the glances that went that way were uncomfortable. "—*That* is a thing that will drive us mad if we stay here. And we need not. Must not."

"Where, then?" Fwar asked, and Vanye set his jaw and stared at the mat to conceal his own startlement. He was afraid, suddenly, mind leaping ahead to unavoidable conclusions; he trusted nothing that Roh did, but he had no choice but to accept it. Fwar was the alternative; or the others.

"Nhi Vanye has a certain usefulness," Roh said softly. "He knows the land. He knows Morgaine. And he knows his chances in this camp."

"And with the likes of *them*," Vanye said, and there was almost a dagger drawn, but Roh snatched up his sheathed longsword and thrust it at Trin's middle, stopping that with cold threat.

"Peace, I say, or none of us will live to get clear of this camp . . . or survive the journey afterward."

Fwar motioned at Trin, and the dagger went back solidly into its sheath.

"There is more than you think at stake," Roh said. "That will become clear later. But prepare for a journey. Be ready to ride tonight."

"The Shiua will follow."

"Follow they may. You have itched for killing them. You will have your chance. But my cousin is another matter. Keep your knives from his back. Hear me well, Fwar i Mija. I need him, and so do you. Kill him, and the Shiua will be on one side and the folk of this land on the other, and that is a position no better than we have now. Do you understand me?"

"Aye," Fwar said.

"Start seeing to things quietly. As for me, I am not involving myself in any of your preparations. The Shiua have been urging me to send you out on a certain mission; if you are challenged, say that you are going. And if you stir up trouble—well, avoid it. Go to it."

They gathered themselves up. Vanye did not look at them, but stared into the fire, and glanced up only when he had heard the last of them walk away.

"Whom do you betray, Roh? Everyone?"

Roh's dark eyes met his. "All but you, my cousin."

The mockery chilled. He looked down again, unable to meet that stare, which challenged him to doubt, and to do something about it.

"I will go with you."

"And guard my back?"

He glared at Roh.

"It is from Fwar that I need most guarding, cousin. I will guard you, and you, me—when Fwar and his folk hold watch during the night. One of us will be awake, and seem asleep."

"You have been planning this journey—from the hour you took me from Hetharu."

"Aye. I could not leave the Gate before, for fear of Morgaine. Now I cannot stay here, for fear of her . . . now I know what I needed to know; and you will aid me, Nhi Vanye i Chya. I am going to Morgaine."

"Not with my guidance."

"I have run out of allies, cousin. I shall go to her. It is possible that she is dead; and then we shall see—we two—what we shall do then. But she does not die easily, the witch of Aenor-Pyvvn. And if she lives, well, I shall take my chances with her all the same."

Vanye nodded slowly, a tautness in his stomach.

"You want your chance at Fwar," Roh said. "Be patient."

"Weapons."

"You will have them. Your own; I gathered everything back that the Hiua had of yours. And I will splint that knee of yours. You cannot bear the ride we must make, otherwise. There are clothes there . . . better than the Hiua rags you and I will have to wear to ride out of here."

He edged over to the bundle that Roh pointed out, gathered up his own boots, and what else he needed, and dressed: they were of a size, he and Roh. He avoided looking at Roh, holding what he did in his mind: Roh knew he meant to turn on him; Roh *knew,* by his own clear warning, and yet armed him. And there was no sense in it that pleased him, nothing.

Roh rested in the corner against the grass wall, staring at him from half-lidded eyes. "You do not believe me," Roh observed.

"No more than the devil."

"Believe this at least: that out of this camp you trust me and keep your pledge to me, or Mija Fwar will have both our skins. You can bring me down . . . but I promise you it will not profit you."

The commotion did not die away. It rose up again within the hour, and Trin thrust his head inside the shelter and hung there against the doorway, hard-breathing. "Fwar says get ready now. No waiting until dark. There is talk now of coming up here. The marshlanders want *him,* slow-cooked; him they could have, for my opinion . . . but if they once pass those guards, with the *khal* on this side—well—If you want those horses brought through, we have a chance of doing it now, quick, while they talk down there; when it gets to more than talk, we have no hope of doing it."

"Get to it," Roh said.

Trin spat in Vanye's direction, and left. Vanye sat still, his breathing choked with anger.

"How long will we need them?" he asked then.

"You may have to endure worse than that." Roh threw a bundle of cloth at him; he caught it, but did nothing more, blind with anger. "I mean it, cousin; armed you may be, but you will do nothing. You gave me a pledge, and I assume you will keep it. Smother that Nhi temper of yours and keep your head down. Leave your avenging to me until the time comes . . . act the part of an *ilin* to the letter. You still remember how, do you not?"

He was shaking, and expelled several short breaths. "I am not yours."

"Be so for a few days. Bitter days. But by that means you may survive them, and so may I; and your surviving them . . . does that not serve *her?*"

That argument shot home. "I will do it," he said, and started pulling on the Hiua garments over his own; Roh did likewise.

There were two more bundles. Roh gave one to him, and it was incredibly heavy. "Your armor," Roh said. "All your belongings, as I promised. Here is your

sword." And he unwrapped that and tossed it over, belt and all. Vanye set down
the other and buckled it only about his waist, for to fasten it at the shoulder
spoiled the Hiua garments and galled his wounds. Roh looked less Hiua than he,
he reckoned, for Roh's hair was twisted at the nape in the warrior's knot, in the
fashion of a hall-lord of Andur, and Roh was clean-shaven. His own face, bruised
as it was, had not known a razor in days; and his hair, shorn in his loss of honor,
had grown shoulder-length and a little beyond: usually that was held from his
face by helm or coif, but now it went where it would, and he let it, which hid
some of his bruises. He considered the bearing of the Hiua, and assumed in his
mind their gracelessness, their hangdog manner: there was a nakedness in the
prospect of going outside the shelter that chilled the blood in him.

Roh gathered up his own weapons, chiefest of which was a fine Andurin
bow; the shafts his quiver carried were mostly long, green-fletched Chya arrows. He had the bone-handled Honor-blade at his belt, and bore sword and
axe as well, the latter for the saddle. *Hall-lord,* Vanye thought in vexation; *he
cannot seem anything else.*

And when the horses came thundering to the front of the shelter, with the
shouts of Men audible in the distance, there was Roh's tall black mare, conspicuous among the smaller Shiua mounts: no hope of concealment; the alarm was
surely passed . . . Chya wildness—Vanye cursed it aloud, and flung himself for
the saddle of the bow-nosed sorrel allotted him, . . . cursed again as the leg shot
fire up the inside when he threw it over. He shook the hair from his eyes and
looked up—saw a cluster of *khalur* riders bearing down on them from the
center of the camp.

"Roh!" he shouted.

Roh saw it, wheeled the black mare about and plunged through the Hiua,
drawing them face-about, nigh forty riders, Hiua and a scattering of renegade
marshlanders.

"We will shake them from our heels," Roh cried. "There is no luck for them
in this direction."—For they were headed for the sprawl and clutter of the human camp, where a thin row of demon-helms manned the barricade, barring
the way of trouble coming out of it.

The guards saw them coming, hesitated in confusion. Roh drew rein,
shouted an order to open the barricade, and Hiua sprang down to do it—Roh
passed at the least opening, and Vanye stayed with him, raking his leg on the
barrier: it was all too quick, the guards without orders, not resisting. More Hiua
poured through, and they plunged for the midst of the human camp at a dead
gallop, aimed for the mob gathered there.

Swords whipped out; the mob lost its nerve at the first shock and scattered
from their charge, with only a few missiles flying. One man was hit and un-
horsed, and they took him . . . for what fate was not good to think. But they

broke through by sheer impetus and shock, with the open plain before them and a scatter of futile stones pelting from behind. Vanye kept low; he had not blooded his sword, not on men's backs, not on the side of Hiua.

Roh laughed. "The *khal* will ride into a broken hive."

He looked back then, and there was not a Man in sight; no more stones, no fight; the human folk had gone to cover, armed, and there was no sight of the Shiua riders behind them either. Either they would seek some exit that avoided the human camp, or they would make the mistake of trying to ride through, and either would take them time.

"When Hetharu knows we are gone," Roh said, "as he must by now—then there will be no shaking them from pursuing us."

"No," said Vanye, "I do not think there will be."

He looked again over his shoulder, past the dark mass of Hiua riders, and it dawned on him what should have before, that his flight with Roh would stir all the camp into action . . . the whole army would mass and move.

He said nothing, seeing finally the trap into which he had fallen—he had wanted to live, and therefore he had blinded himself to things other than his own survival.

Mirrind, he thought over and over, grieving. *Mirrind and all this land.*

⌒ Chapter 10

They pushed the horses to the limit, and it was dark before they stopped, a fireless camp, one that they would break before dawn. Vanye slid down from the saddle holding to the harness and found himself hardly able to walk; but he cared for his horse, and took his gear and limped over to Roh's side, head bowed as he passed through the midst of the men. He thought that if one of them should set hands on him he would turn and kill that man; but that was madness and he knew it. He endured one man shouldering his horse past deliberately, and kept his head down as Roh had said . . . assumed an *ilin's* humility like a garment.

When he reached Roh's side he flung his pack down and stayed standing, for it was painful to rise once down. "I would like to change clothes," he said.

"So shall I. Do so."

He stripped off the Hiua garments with distaste, and stood only in shirt and breeches, Shiua, of fine-spun cloth. The haqueton he put on, against the chill, and meditated putting on the mail-shirt as well, but the stiffness of his shoulders decided otherwise. He put on his cloak, no more. And Roh also rid himself of the disguise; and paused in that to give orders to Fwar.

"We will want sentries watching all horizons. There are Shiua riders behind us without doubt; but there could be some returning from the forest edge, and we cannot risk that meeting either."

Fwar made a sound that might be agreement, turned, and with his foot hooked Vanye's good leg.

Vanye sprawled, his knee awash with pain, and rolled and started up as best he could; but Roh was on his feet in the instant, his sword drawn. "Do that again," Roh said, "or lay any hand on him and I will have the head from your shoulders."

"For *this?*"

Vanye struggled to his feet, but Roh laid a hand on his arm and thrust him back, turned on him when he resisted, and struck him hard across the face. "You forget yourself. Morgaine's patience was longer than mine. Cause me trouble and I will give you to them."

Anger blinded him for the moment: and then he understood and bowed his head and sank down again—for good measure performed the full obeisance as an *ilin,* an awkwardness with a stiff leg. Then he sat down, head bowed. It amused the Hiua mightily. He did not react to the laughter, which, ugly as it was, lightened the air.

"He is *ilin,*" Roh said. "Is that in the old songs? Perhaps you have forgotten that custom; but he is not a free man. He is outlawed . . . Morgaine's servant, no more than that. By Andurin law, he is free of any blood he sheds: Morgaine is guilty. Now he is in my service, and he stays, Myya Fwar. Or would you rather kill him and lose our only hope of surviving? That is your choice. You are playing games with our own lives. Cripple or kill him and we have no guide, no safe passage. Hetharu is behind us. Why do you think? For me? No. I could ride out and Hetharu would bear that as he has everything else I have done, because he dares not kill me: I have the knowledge that provides him safety in this land . . . knowledge of the Gates and of *power,* my Myya friends, that is greater than Hetharu himself suspects. And because you serve me, Hetharu has feared us both. But listen to me now and I will tell you what has driven Hetharu and me to this parting of ways, why he has taken arms against us—and he has done so, if any of you care to ride back and find out. It is because he had a chance to question this man, and he knows enough now to fear my getting my hands on him. He knows that with this man I can overthrow the *khal* . . . and seize control of all this land."

There was dead silence. All the men had gathered, hearing this, and Vanye turned his face aside and kept his head bowed, his hand clenched on his sword.

"How?" Fwar asked.

"Because this man has knowledge of the forest, of its people, and of Morgaine. The *khal* have not found her. He can. And he is the means by which we can gain her weapons, and absolute control of the Gates. You have been trying to plunder *villages*. But with that power in hand, do you not think the *khal*-lords know what we will be then? They will risk everything to stop us. They are not anxious to be ruled by Men. But we will settle with them. No one . . . *no one* . . . is to set hands on this man. I have promised him his life for his help. The *khal* could get nothing from him . . . nor could you, my friends, where they failed. But me he will listen to; he knows I keep my word. Now if that is too great a matter for you to bear, ride off now and join Hetharu . . . take your chances you will survive that. But if you will stay with me, then keep your hands off him or go through life one-handed. He is too valuable to me."

"He will not always be," someone said.

"My oath," Roh shouted at that man. "Put it from your mind, Derth. Put it from your mind!"

There was sullen agreement. Derth spat on the ground, but nodded. Others muttered assent.

"Four days," Roh said, "and we will be within reach of all you came into my service to have. Does that not content you? Four days."

"Aye," Fwar said suddenly, and the rest of the pack fell in. "Aye, lord," the rest agreed, and the camp settled again, with mutterings of what would be done with the *khal*-lords when they had gained power over them.

Vanye swallowed heavily and looked up as Roh settled by him. Roh said nothing for a moment.

"Are you hurt?" Roh asked then. He shook his head for reply, stared at Roh with an uneasiness he could not shake. He dared not question; Fwar's cousins sat within earshot. This would be so for the duration of their journey. Roh could not be expected to reassure him, to do anything which would betray agreement between them. And he could not help wondering if he had not just heard Roh tell the truth.

Roh's hand clenched on his arm. "Get some sleep, cousin."

Vanye wrapped his cloak about him and lay down where the blanket was spread; he slept, but not quickly.

Roh nudged him in the mid of the night; he opened his eyes then and stayed awake while Roh closed his, as their agreement was. All about them were the sounds of men breathing, the sometime shifting of the horses, the strangeness of such a combination of men and purposes. It oppressed him.

At the first hint of dawn the camp stirred, the sentries passing among the blanketed shapes and kicking this man and that . . . no more grace had they among their own folk than with strangers. Vanye did not abide that manner of waking, but reached and shook at Roh, disappointing the Hiua who was coming his way—sat up and began putting his armor on. Already there were men saddling their horses and cursing the dark and the chill, for the Hiua went unarmored save where they had plundered somewhat from the *khal*-lords. Fwar had a scale-shirt under his Shiua-cloth garments: Vanye had already marked that for a time yet to come. He eased on his own ring-mail with a protest of his scabbed shoulders and laced up, put on the coif as well as his helm, to keep his hair from his eyes. And Roh had included a dagger for his belt, not a proper Honor-blade, but a Shiua knife.

"You carried mine so long and faithfully," Roh mocked him out of the dark, "I hate to deprive you of it."

"Avert," he said, crossing himself fervently.

"Avert," Roh echoed him, and made the gesture too, and, laughed afterward, which gave him no comfort at all.

He slid the hostile weapon into place at his belt and went to seek the horses, walking through the Hiua, as he must ride among them and sleep beside them and endure them for days more. They did not lose whatever chance they could find to trouble him. He bowed his head and took the abuse, choked with anger, reminding himself that he had grown too proud. It was no more than baiting, though uglier wishes lay beneath it. They hoped to provoke anger from him, which would bring Roh's wrath down on him . . . *Cause me trouble,* Roh had said in their hearing, *and I will give you to them.* They longed for that. But their baiting was only what an *ilin* in Andur-Kursh might endure under a harsh lord. Morgaine's service had been otherwise, even from the beginning, however hard it had been in other ways. He recalled her face and voice suddenly, and the gentleness she had given him, and thrust the memory away at once, for he could not afford to grieve.

She was not dead. He was not forever bound to the likes of these, in a world where she did not exist. His sanity insisted to believe it.

"Lord," someone said, and pointed south, in the direction of the Gate. There was a second dawn on that horizon, a glimmering of red brighter than the true one.

"Fire." The word hissed through the company on many lips.

Roh stared at it, and suddenly gestured for them to move. "The *khal* must have settled the trouble we started in the camp; there is no hope it could be any other way. That fire is their means of dislodging the lower camp and moving them on; we have seen that tactic before. They are behind us now, and their outriders will have moved out long before now. We have to ride hard hereafter. They are coming, all of them."

The smudge of smoke on the horizon was evident in full dawn, but it soon burned itself out and dissipated on the winds: the wind was steadily from the north . . . had it been otherwise, it would have been a fire perilous in the extreme. "It has come up against the south river," Roh surmised, on one occasion that he turned in the saddle to look back. "I am relieved. Their madness might have swept down on all of us on this plain."

"Their riders will not come much slower than the fire would have," Vanye said, and looked back also; but all that was to be seen was Fwar's troop, and their faces were a sight he cared for as little as Hetharu's own. He turned about again, and spoke little to Roh thereafter, reckoning that much friendliness apparent between them could make things no better for Roh.

He tended Roh's horse at rests, and did all such things as he would have done for Morgaine. The Hiua were uncommonly quiet in their malice by daylight, where all that was done had to be done under Roh's witness. There were only spiteful looks, and once Fwar smiled broadly at him and laughed. "Wait," Fwar said, and that was all. He glared steadily at Fwar, reckoning that his principal danger was a knifing in the back when the time came. Fwar was one that wanted facing all the time.

And once thereafter he saw Fwar looking at Roh's back, with quite another look than he gave to Roh's face.

This is a man, Vanye thought, *who never forgives; some cause he has with me; and perhaps with Roh—another.*

Guard my back, Roh had wished him, knowing well the men of his service.

They crossed the two rivers in the morning and the noon. Their bearing was to the north and slightly easterly, toward the ford of the Narn. Vanye chose their direction, for he rode at the head of the company with Roh and Fwar and Trin, and he bore as he would, while Roh adjusted his course to suit his at each small jostling of the horses, and Fwar and his men followed Roh's leading.

There was, he recalled, that camp of Hetharu's men or Fwar's due north, and he did not want to encounter that; there was the ford of the Narn itself, which he wanted less. But between the two, the expanse of a night's hard ride, there was a patch of forest that did not love Men, and that he chose, knowing it might be the end of them.

But having heard Roh's talk with the Hiua, he was determined on it, rather than to guide them all near Morgaine. He lived in the hourly anticipation that Fwar would discover where they were bound, and who was truly leading them, for Fwar had been in that region and might well know the danger . . . but it did not happen. He made himself as inconspicuous in his position as possible, bowing his head on his chest and feigning to give way to his wounds and to exhaustion. In fact, he did sleep a little while they rode, but not long; and he pretended hardly to be aware of what direction they took.

"Riders," Trin said of a sudden.

Vanye looked up and followed the pointing of Trin's arm. His heart pounded in sudden fright at the cloud that rose on the northwesterly horizon. "A Shiua camp was there," he said to Roh. "But they cannot yet know you have fallen out with Hetharu."

"They would know *him* quickly enough," Fwar said. "Get some covering round that armor, quick."

Fwar's advice or no, it was worth taking. Vanye slipped off his helm and unlaced his coif, shaking his hair free as the Barrows-men wore theirs. Fwar stripped off his tunic of coarse wool and gave it to him. "Put that on, Roh's bastard cousin, and drop back of us."

He did so, shrugged the unwashed garment down over his own leather and mail and reined back into the center of Fwar's pack of wolves where he was less conspicuous. His face was hot with rage for the taunt Fwar had flung at him . . . an old one, and one which only Roh could have told them, concerning the proper degree of their kinship. It disturbed him the more because the Roh he had known was his mother's close kin, and the taunt was not one that did honor to clan Chya or Roh's house.

Fwar's riders made close formation about him. Their hair was dark, and none were so tall. He made his stature as little obvious as possible. There was little more to be done. The riders were coming on them at speed now, having seen the dust they raised, and surely meant to meet them.

"The Sotharra camp," a man at his left muttered. "Shien's folk, those."

Roh and Fwar rode ahead to meet the riders at distance from the company, a wise maneuver if it were Shien. The oncoming riders slowed, breaking from a charge to an approach, and finally came to a halt, but for their three leaders, who kept riding. In Fwar's band, bows were strung and arrows readied, but there was no show of them.

It was indeed Shien. Vanye recognized the young *khal*-lord and thanked Heaven for the distance between them. The horses snorted and fretted wearily under them. There was a time that everything seemed peaceful. Then voices were raised, Shien's bidding them turn and follow his lead to his camp.

"I do not want your Barrows-scum riding where they please and cutting through our territory. They are hindrance as much as help. They take no orders."

"They take mine," Roh returned. "Out of my way, lord Shien. This is my path and you are in it."

"Go on, go on, then, but you are coming up against forest soon. Your men are no loss, but you are. Nothing has come alive out of that area, and I will use force to stop you, lord Roh. You are too much to risk."

Roh lifted his arm. Hiua bows lifted and bent. "Ride off," Roh said.

Shien stared incredulously, dazed by the sight of human defiance. "You are quite mad."

"Ride off. Or discover the limits of my insanity."

Shien backed his horse, and his escort with him; with a sudden jerk he wheeled about and rode back to his own troop, which glittered with scale-armor and pikes. One of the Barrows-men softly entreated protection of his several gods.

Roh started moving, Fwar and Trin beside him. The company moved forward, passing the Shiua riders, who stood still watching them. First their flank and then their backs were exposed to the Shiua, who remained motionless. Eventually the Shiua dwindled in the distance, and Roh started them to a gallop, which they kept until the horses could stay it no more. Even so it was well after dark before they stopped and flung down from their horses.

Fwar asked for his tunic back. Vanye surrendered it gladly enough, and tended his horse and Roh's . . . and Fwar's, for the Barrows-man flung him the reins as Roh had done, to the general laughter of the company; they mocked him: *bastard* was a taunt they had all taken up, seeing how it pricked at him.

He averted his face from their tormenting, and settled the horses and passed through the Hiua company back to Roh, where Fwar sat.

And he had no more than sat down than Fwar grasped his shoulder and pulled him roughly about.

"You are our guide, are you? The lord Roh says it. So what did Shien mean about hazards in the forest?"

He thrust off Fwar's hand. "There are," he said carefully, though rage nearly choked him, "there are hazards everywhere in the forest. I can guide you through them."

"What sort?"

"Others. *Qhal.*"

Fwar scowled and looked at Roh.

"Morgaine has allies," Roh said softly.

"What kind of trap have you led us into? We trusted *her* once and learned. I have no trust in this now."

"Then you are in a bad situation, are you not? Hetharu on one side and Shien on the other, and the forest that none of us yet have found a way to travel safely—"

"Your arranging."

"I will talk with you privately. Vanye, get out of here."

"See he does, Trin."

Vanye gathered himself up; Trin was quicker, and seized him by the arm and drew him away to the far side of the camp, where the horses were picketed.

They stopped there. Fwar and Roh spoke together, out of hearing, two shadows in the dark. Vanye stared at them, trying to hear all the same, trying to ignore his guard, who suddenly seized his collar from behind and wrenched. "Sit down," Trin advised him, and he did so. Trin stood over him and kicked several times gently at his splinted knee, naught but casual malice. "We will get you away from him sooner or later," Trin said.

He answered nothing, planning that meeting in his own way.

"Thirty-seven of us—all with reason enough to settle with you."

He still said nothing, and Trin swung his foot again. He seized it and wrenched, and Trin went down, startling the horses, crying out for help. Men poured toward them. Vanye hit the Hiua, staggered up from Trin's prostrate form and came up on one leg, whipped out his dagger and slashed a tether. The horse shied back; he seized its mane and swung up as the dark tide reached him.

The horse screamed and plunged—went over as the Hiua overwhelmed it, other horses shying and screaming and tearing at their tethers. Vanye cleared the falling animal and sprawled into a yielding mass of Hiua almost under other hooves. He slashed blindly and lost the dagger as that arm was held and strained back nearly to breaking.

They drew him up then, and one snatched him by the harness on his chest and wrenched him forward. He would have struck, but for the glitter of mail, that showed him who it was. Roh cursed him and shook him, and he flung the hair from his eyes, ready to fight the rest of them. One tried to come at him— Trin, alive, with dark blood on his face and a knife in his hand.

Fwar stopped the man, took the knife, thrust the rest of the mob back. "No," Fwar said. "No. Let be with him."

The Hiua gave back sullenly, began to move away, Vanye shivered convulsively from his anger and caught his breath. Roh had not let him go. He reached for Roh's hand and disengaged it.

"Trying to run?" Roh asked him.

He said nothing. It was obvious enough what he had tried.

Roh seized his wrist and turned his hand up, slammed the hilt of his dagger into it. "Put that away and thank me for it."

He went to the ground and performed the obeisance, and Roh stood staring at him for a moment, then turned and walked away. Fwar lingered; Vanye gathered himself up, expecting Fwar's malice, recalling to his confusion that it had been Fwar who pulled his men back.

"Someone go catch that horse," Fwar said then. A man went, walking out to the horse that had stopped its flight a little distance from the picket line.

Vanye started back to Roh. Fwar took him by the arm. "Come along," Fwar said, and guided him through the standing crowd.

No hand was laid on him else. Trin threatened; but Fwar took him aside and spoke to him in private, and Trin returned pacified. The whole camp settled.

Vanye looked about him at this sudden tolerance, and at Roh, who averted his face and began to prepare himself for the night's rest.

⌐ Chapter 11

They moved out yet again before dawn, and by the time day came full upon them, the dark line of Shathan bowed across their northern horizon.

During that day a strange tension lay over the company, which had riders dropping back to the rear by twos and threes and talking together a while before riding forward again.

Vanye saw it plainly enough, and reckoned that Roh did . . . dared not call it into question, for there was Fwar, as ever, at his side. *I am mad,* he kept thinking, *to have any trust left in him.* He was afraid, with a gnawing apprehension which Shathan's nearness did nothing to allay: to ride into that darkness . . .

He flexed the knee against the splints, and estimated that with the horse under him he was a whole man and without it a dead one. To ride with any speed through that dark maze of roots and uneven ground was impossible; to run it afoot, lame as he was, held no better hope—and the question was how far he could lead this band, before someone called halt and challenged him.

Yet Roh let him guide them still, even after Shien's warning, and what mutterings Fwar had made about it were silenced. All objections were stilled. There were only the whisperings in the back of the column.

In the afternoon they stopped and sat down with tether lines in hand, letting the horses rest, themselves taking a little food and drink, unpacking nothing which was not at once replaced, ready to move on in any instant. A gambling game started up, using knives and skill, and imaginary stakes of *khalur* plunder; that grew loud, and swiftly obscene. Roh sat unsmiling. His eyes shifted to Vanye's, and said nothing.

And suddenly flickered, fixed beyond his shoulder. Vanye turned and saw through his horse's legs a haze of dust on the southern horizon.

"I think we should move," Roh said.

"Aye," he murmured. There was no doubt what that was, by its direction: Hetharu—Hetharu with his riders, and the Shiua horde in his wake.

Fwar swore blackly and ordered his men to horse. They sprang up from their game and checked girths, adjusted bits, took to the saddle with feverish haste. Vanye swung up and reined about, taking another look.

It was more than one point of the horizon now: it was an arc that swept toward them from south and west, hemming them half about. "Shien," he said. "Shien has joined with them."

"That dust will be seen in the Sotharra camp," Fwar judged, and swore.

"There and among the ones out on Narn-side. They will lose no time riding this way either."

Roh made no answer, but set spurs to the black mare. The whole company rode after him in haste, driving their horses to desperate flight. Spur and quirt could not keep the weaker with the pace; already the company was beginning to string back. The Shiua animals, journey-worn, could not keep the Andurin mare's ground-eating stride, much as their riders belabored them. Vanye nursed his sorrel gelding as he had done from the beginning . . . an unlovely animal, burdened with a bigger man than the Hiua, and him armored; but the beast had had at least a horseman's care on the journey, and he held his own at the rear . . . not important now to be in the lead, only to be with the rest, to keep the animal running for that green line ahead of them. The *khalur* riders were gaining: he looked back and saw the glint of metal through the dust of their own riding; doubtless the *khal,* better mounted, would kill their horses if need be to overtake them, seeing the forest ahead as well as they did.

Roh's lead was now considerable, and only a few of the Hiua could keep with him. Vanye guided the sorrel around a bit of brush another rider had gone over, reckoning the land and the easiest path. He passed three of the Hiua, though he had not changed his pace. He bit at his lip and kept the gelding to what he had set.

Now there was a cloud of dust not only behind them, but eastward, closer there, ominously closer.

Others looked that way eventually, saw that force that sprang bright and glittering as if by magic over a swell of the land. The Hiua cried out in alarm, and spurred and whipped their horses near to exhaustion, as if that would help them—rode them over ground that was fit to lame them even at a slower pace.

A horse went down, screaming, in the path of another. Vanye looked back; one of the riders was a marshlander, and a comrade dropped back for that man: three gone, then. The man picked up the one rider and overtook them again, leaving the other; but soon the overburdened horse broke stride and fell farther and farther behind.

Vanye cursed; Kurshin that he was, he loved horses too well to enjoy what was happening. Roh's doing, Roh's Andurin callousness, he thought; but that was because he had somewhere to place the anger for such cruelty. He consented in it and rode, although by now the little gelding was drenched in sweat, and his own gut and joints felt every bruise the land dealt them.

The forest was all their view now, though the *khalur* riders were almost within bowshot. Arrows flew, fell short; that was waste. Archery slowed the force that fired, to no profit at this range.

He no longer rode among the last: three, four more horses that had been near the fore broke stride and dropped behind him, even within reach of the forest. The others might make it.

"*Hai!*" he shouted, and used the spurs suddenly; the gelding leapt forward, startled—passed others, began to close the gap with the foremost, gaining on Roh's Andurin mare. Vanye bent low, although the arrows still flew amiss, for now the forest lay ahead. Roh disappeared into that green shadow, and Fwar, and Trin; he came third and others followed, slowing at once in that thickening tangle. One rider did not, and a horse rushed past riderless.

Vanye ducked a limb and pressed the exhausted gelding past to the fore. "Come," he gasped, and none disputed.

The gelding was surefooted despite that it was so badly spent; Vanye wound his way this direction and that with an eye to the ground and the tangle overhead, as rapidly as the horse could bear—down one leaf-covered slope and up another.

More riders crashed after them, horses breaking a way where there was none, either their own companions or the most reckless of their pursuers. A man screamed somewhere behind them, and Vanye did not look back, caring nothing who it was. The horse's breathing between his legs was like a bellows working, the beast's legs communicating an occasional shudder of exhaustion which he felt through his own body. He tapped it with his heels, talked to it in his own tongue as if all horses understood a Morij accent. It kept moving. He looked back and Roh was still there, and Fwar and Trin a little farther, and a third and fourth man; brush crashed somewhere that he could not see. A horse broke through a screen of branches even as he watched, and labored downslope; Minur was that rider, and the horse could scarcely make the gentle climb up again.

There was a stream, hardly with water enough to cover the horse's hooves. His wanted to stop; he did not allow it, drove it up the slope, found the trail he had thought to find. He put the horse to no more speed, only enough to maintain the pace. The shadow thickened, not alone of the forest, but of the declining sun. He turned in the saddle and saw Roh with him, Fwar and Trin and Minur, others, about three near, more farther back. Fwar looked back too, and the look in his eyes when he turned showed that finally, finally he understood.

Vanye drove the spurs in, ducked low and rode, shouts pursuing him, the thunder of hooves with him still and close. The trail dipped again, where a tree was down. The gelding measured that slope, refused it, and Vanye reined about in the same move, whipped his sword from sheath.

Fwar rode into it, his own sword drawn: Vanye remembered the scale-armor and cut high. Fwar parried; Vanye rammed the spurs in and defended in turn, cut downward as the gelding shied up. Fwar screamed, tumbled under the hooves of his own backing mount as a second horse plunged past, riderless:

horses collided, went down on the slope, and Fwar was somewhere under them.

A third: Minur. Vanye spun the staggering gelding about and parried with a shock that numbed his fingers, whipped the blade about and across Minur's with a desperation Minur should have moved to counter: he had not. There was only his head in the longsword's path, and the Barrows-man died without a sound, dead before he left the saddle.

"Hai!" Vanye shouted, and spurred past blind at the others, cut right and cut left and emptied two saddles, he knew not whose. The gelding brought up short as one of the horses shouldered it, staggered. He drew rein and saw Roh in his path; but Roh faced the other way, still ahorse, and his bow was bent and one of his green-fletched shafts was trained down that dark aisle of trees, which was held only by dead men.

"Roh," Vanye called to him.

The shaft flew. Roh reined about and spurred toward him: a hail of arrows pursued, white-feathered, and none of them accurate. Vanye turned, and drove the gelding back toward the slope, weaving through the trees to avoid the obstacle at the bottom. The black mare stayed close behind.

An outcry rang out behind them, rage and anguish. Vanye took the gelding up the other slope, hearing brush break in the distance. The gelding reached the top and staggered, kept going a little farther and faltered badly. It was the end for it. Vanye slid down and slashed the leather that held the girth-ring, freeing it of the saddle, and he tore off its bridle and hit it a good slap to drive it further. Roh did the same for the black mare, though it could have borne him further—turned and nocked one of his good Chya shafts.

"We did not lose enough of them," Vanye said, in what breath remained to him; he clenched the bloody sword in his fist and regretted bitterly the bow that was lost with Mai.

The sound of pursuit crashed nearer down the trail—and stopped, simply stopped. There was silence, save for their own hard breathing.

Roh swore softly.

A man cried out, and another. All through the forest there were thin outcries, and of a sudden a crash of brush near them that nearly startled Roh into firing. A riderless horse broke through and kept going, mad with terror. There were screams of horses and brush crackled in every direction.

Then silence.

Brush whispered about them. Vanye let his sword drop to the dry leaves, stood still, gazing into the shadowing dark with the hair prickling at his nape.

"Put down your bow," he hissed at Roh. "Drop it, or we are dead men."

Roh did so, nothing questioning, and did not move.

Shadows moved here and there. There was a soft chittering.

"Their weapons are poisoned," Vanye whispered. "And they have had bitter experience of Men of our breed. Stand still. Stand still whatever they do."

Then very carefully, arms wide, he limped a little apart from Roh, in the midst of the trail where they had turned at bay. He stood still a moment, then carefully turned, faced every quarter of the wood until he saw the strange shadow that he sought . . . not on the ground. It sat like a nest of old moss in the crotch of a tree. Enormous eyes were centered on him, alive in the midst of that unlikely shape.

He signed to it as Lellin had done. And when that brought no reaction, he bent his good leg and awkwardly knelt, hands still far from his sides, that it might see he held no weapon.

It moved. It was incredible how it descended, as if it had no need of branches, but clung to the wood of the trunk. It stood then watching him, tall and stilt-limbed. Voices chittered now from all sides, and all about them in the dusk, shadows moved, stalking into the pathway.

They towered over him as he knelt. He stayed absolutely still, and they put their hands on his shoulders and arms . . . slender, powerful fingers that tugged strangely at his garments and his armor. They closed and drew him to his feet, and he turned and stared up into their faces, shivering.

They spoke to him, and tugged at his clothing; there was anger in their rapid voices.

"No," he whispered, and signed at them carefully: *friend, friend,* hand to his heart.

There was no response. Slowly he lifted his arm and pointed down the trail in the direction he wished to go, and saw that others considered Roh, who stood deathly still in their unhuman hands.

He tried to leave those about him and walk in that direction, but they would not let him walk free: they brought him to Roh, holding him firmly. His eyes roved the area, counting: ten, twenty of them. Their faces, their dark, fathomless eyes, seemed all immune to reason or passion.

"They are *harilim,*" he said to Roh softly. "And they are of the forest . . . *of* it, entirely."

"Morgaine's allies."

"No one's allies."

It was fully night now; the last twilight faded, and the shadows thickened. More and more of the *harilim* arrived, and all began to speak at once, in chittering rushes of sound that thundered like falling water; debate, perhaps, or chanting. But at last came other stalking shadows that simply stood and watched, and silence fell, so suddenly it numbed.

"The amulet," Vanye said. "Roh. The amulet. Do you still have it?"

Roh reached very slowly into his collar and drew it forth. It shone in the starlight, a silver circle trembling on Roh's hand. One of the *harilim* reached and touched it, and chirred softly.

Then one of the tall late-comers stalked forward with that heron-like gait, which halted several times and did not hurry. It too fingered the amulet, and touched Roh's face. It spoke, and the sound was deeper, like frog-song.

Tentatively Vanye lifted his arm yet again, pointing to the path that they wanted to go.

There was no response. He tried a step and none forbade. He took another, and another, and stooped very carefully and gathered up his sword and put it in its sheath. He edged back yet farther. Roh took his lead then, and moving very carefully, picked up his bow. There was no sound from the *harilim*, none anywhere in the forest. Step after step they were allowed.

A hail of twigs came down from overhead. They kept walking, and still none prevented them. They passed down the trail and met the stream again, where the trail ceased and they had only the streamcourse to guide them. Reeds rustled behind them. A chittering came from the trees.

"You planned this," Roh said hoarsely. "Shien understood. I would that I had."

"What did you plan for me?" he returned, half a whisper, for sound was fearsome in this place. "I promised only to go with you and guard your back—*cousin*. But what did you contrive with Fwar that so well pleased him?"

"What do you suppose I promised him?"

He answered nothing and kept walking, limping heavily over tangles of roots and washes in the mossy earth. The stream beside them promised water they dared not stop to drink, not until the breath was raw in their throats.

Then he fell to one knee and gathered a cold double handful to his mouth, and Roh did likewise, both of them taking what they could. Leaves rustled. A hail of twigs flew about them, leaves and debris hitting the water. They gathered themselves up as larger pieces began to fly. Shadows moved in the forest. They started walking and the shaking of branches stopped.

There came a time that they had to rest. Vanye sank down, hands clasped to his aching knee, and Roh flung himself down among the leaves, heaving with sobs for breath. They had left the stream for a trail that offered itself. There was only dark about them.

Of a sudden the shaking of branches began. A piece of wood cracked; a branch crashed dangerously near them, breaking young trees in its fall. Vanye reached for support and clawed his way to his feet, Roh springing up hardly slower. A scattering of twigs hit them. They began walking and it ceased.

"How far will they drive us?" Roh asked. His voice shook with exhaustion. "Is there a place they have in mind?"

"Till morning . . . and out of their woods." He caught the bad leg and stumbled, recovered with an effort that blurred his eyes. Almost he would have de-fied them and flung himself down to see whether they meant their threats, but he was too sure that they did. The *harilim* had done much, indeed, not to have killed them among the others . . . save that they might—at least one or two of them—recall him as a companion of the *qhal* . . . if they had memories at all, if anything like the thoughts of Men existed behind those huge dark eyes.

Cruel, cruel as any force of nature: they would have their way, their forest cleared of outsiders. He reckoned that their freedom to walk was the utmost of the *harilim's* mercy and went blindly. Once they met another, broader trail, started to take it, but a hail of twigs came down on them, in their faces, and the chittering began to be angry.

"Go back," he said, pushing at Roh, who was minded otherwise, and they turned and struggled the other, the harder trail, which took them deeper into the woods.

He fell. The leaves skidded slickly under his hands and for a moment he simply lay there, until the chittering nearby warned him, and Roh put a hand under his arm and cursed him. "Get up," Roh said, and when he had his feet under him again, Roh flung an arm about him and kept him moving until he had recovered his senses.

Day was beginning, a first grayness. The shadows which stalked them be-came more and more visible, sometimes moving along beside them with more rapidity than a Man could manage in the brush.

Then as the light increased a hush fell, and nothing now disturbed the trees, as if their herders had suddenly become one with bark and moss and limb.

"They are gone," Roh said first, and began to slow, leaned against a tree. Vanye looked about him, and again his senses began to leave him. Roh caught his arm, and he sank down where he was and sprawled on the dry leaves, numb and blank for a time.

He woke with a touch on his face, realized he was on his back now, and Roh's hand, cold and wet, bathed his brow. "There is another stream just beyond those trees. Wake up. Wake up. We cannot spend another night in this place."

"Aye," he murmured, and moved, groaned aloud for the misery in body and limbs. Roh steadied him to rise on his good leg, and helped him climb down to the water. There he drank and bathed his aching head, washed the dirt from him as best he could. There was blood on his hands and his armor: Fwar, he recalled, and bathed that off with loathing.

"Where are we?" Roh asked. "What do you expect to find here? Only their like?"

He shook his head. "I am lost. I have no idea where we are."

"Kurshin," Roh said, like a curse. Roh was Andurin, in all his lives, and forest-bred, as Kurshin were of the mountains and valley plains. "At least that way is the river." He pointed to the downstream of the brook. "And the ford where she was."

"Which lies across the *harilim* woods, and if you choose that route, go to it; I will not. It was your imagining to use me for a guide. I never claimed for myself what you claimed for me to Fwar."

Roh regarded him narrowly. "Aye, and yet you knew accurately enough how to cast us to those creatures, and you have travelled here. I think you are shading the truth with me, my Kurshin cousin. Lost you may be, but you know how to find yourself. And Morgaine."

"Go to blazes. You would have thrown me to the Hiua if the hour had needed it."

"A kinsman of mine? I fear I am too proud for that kind of bartering. Is that a reasoning you understand? No, I promised you to them, when we should have taken Morgaine . . . but I can shade the truth too, cousin. I would have shaken them from my track. I heard Shien's warning. I could have turned aside. I trusted to you. Are not a Kurshin and an Andurin match for Hiua in the woods? Do you think that I would ever have found them comfortable allies? Fwar hated me almost as he hated you. He meant to knife me in the back the moment Morgaine was no longer a threat and he had you in his hands, disarmed. That was the anticipation that sweetened his disposition. He thought he had everything he wanted, me to deal with Morgaine, and half-witted enough to strip myself of the only man who might give me warning if, they went for my back. Fwar saw himself as master of this land if he only tolerated us for a time; that I could give my trust to you, who had been my enemy—Fwar was not such a man, and therefore he could not imagine it in others. And it killed him. But you and I, Vanye—we are different men. You and I—know what honor is."

Vanye swallowed heavily, uneasily reckoning that it might remotely be truth. "I promised to guard your back . . . no more than that. I have done so. It was your own saying, that you would find Morgaine and try to speak with her. Well, do it without my help. Here our agreement ends. Go your own way."

"For a cripple, you are very confident to dismiss me."

Vanye scrambled awkwardly to his feet, hand jerking his sword from its hook; he almost fell, and braced his back against a tree. But Roh still knelt, unthreatening.

"Peace," Roh said, turning empty hands palm up. A mocking smile was on his lips. "In fact, you do think you can manage without me in this wood, and I would know why. Crippled as you are, cousin, I should hate to abandon you."

"Leave me."

Roh shook his head. "A new agreement: that I go with you. I want only to speak to Morgaine . . . if she is alive; and if she is not, cousin . . . if she is not, then you and I together should reconsider matters. You evidently have allies in this forest. You think that you do not need me. Well, that is the truth, more than likely. But I shall follow you; I promise you that. So I may as well go with you. You know that no Kurshin can shake me from his trail. Would you not rather know where I am?"

Vanye swore, clenched his hand on the sword he did not draw. "Do you not know," he asked Roh hoarsely, "that Morgaine set me under orders to kill you? And do you not know that I have no choice where it regards that oath?"

That took the smile from Roh's face. Roh considered it, and shrugged after a moment, hands loose across his knees. "Well, but you could hardly out-fence me at the moment, could you?—save I gave you a standing target, which would hardly be to your liking. I shall go with you and abide Morgaine's decision in the matter."

"No," he pleaded with him, and Roh's expression grew the more troubled.

"What, is that keeping faith with your liege—to warn her enemies that she is pitiless, that she is unbending, that she understands no reason at all where it regards a threat to her? My oldest memories are dreams, cousin, and they are long and full of her. The Hiua call her Death, and the Shiua *khal* once laughed at that. No longer. I know her. I know my chances. But the *khal* will not forgive what I have done. I cannot go back; I would have no freedom from them. I saw what they did to you—and I am quick to learn, cousin. I had to leave that place. She is all that is left. I am tired, Vanye, I am *tired*—and I have bad dreams."

Vanye stared at him. Gone was all semblance of pride, of mockery; Roh's voice trembled, and his eyes were shadowed.

"Is it in your dreams . . . what Liell would have done with me and with her?"

Roh looked up. Horror was in his eyes, deep and distant. "Do not call those things up. They come back at night. And I doubt you want the answer."

"When you—dream those things: how do you feel about it?"

"Roh hates it."

Vanye shuddered, gazing into the wildness in Roh's face, the war exposed. He sank down again on the bank of the stream, and for a time Roh wrapped his arms about himself and shivered like a man fevered. The shivering stopped finally, and the dark eyes that met his were whole again, quizzical, mocking.

"Roh?"

"Aye, cousin."

"Let us start walking."

They walked the streamside, which in Shathan was no less than a road . . . more reliable than the paths, for all the habitations of Men in Shathan were set near water. They must struggle at times, for the way was overgrown and at times the trees arched over the little stream or grew down to the very margin, or some fallen log dammed it, making deep places. They had no lack of water, hungry as they were . . . and there were fish in the stream that they might devise to take when they dared stop: not favored fare for a Kurshin, but he was not fastidious, and Roh had fared on much worse.

He limped along with Roh at his back, saying nothing of how he guided himself, though perhaps Roh could guess; he had found himself a staff and leaned on it as he walked, though it was less the knee that troubled him than other wounds, which covered the most of his body and at times hurt so that the tears came to his eyes . . . an abiding, never-ceasing misery that now had the heat of fever.

He sank down toward noon and slept, not aware even that he chose to do so. He simply came to himself lying on the ground, with Roh asleep not far from him. He rose up and shook at Roh, and they both stood up and started walking.

"We have slept too long," Roh said, anxiously looking skyward. "It is halfway through the afternoon."

"I know," he said, with the same dread. "We cannot stop again."

He made what haste he could, and several times dared whistle aloud, as close to Lellin's tones as he could manage, but nothing answered him. There was no sight of game, hardly a flicker of a bird's wings through the trees, as if they were all that lived in this section of Shathan. No qhal were near . . . or if they were, they chose to remain silent and unseen. Roh noted it; whenever he looked back he saw Roh's anxious shift of eyes over their surroundings and agreed with Roh's uneasiness. They walked through something utterly unnatural.

They came upon an old tree, corded with white. It was rotten at the heart, lightning-riven.

"Mirrind," Vanye said aloud, his pulse racing, for now he knew completely where he was, to what place the little stream had guided them.

"What is that?" Roh asked.

"A village. You should know it. The Shiua murdered one of its people." Then he repented his words, for they were both at the end of their strength and their wits, and he needed no quarrel with Roh. "Come. Carefully."

He sought the rutted road and found it, concealed as it was now by brush. He walked as quickly as he could with his limping stride, for the night was coming fast on them. From this place, he thought, he might try to find Merir's camp . . . but he was not sure of the way, and the chance was that Merir would have broken camp and left the place even if he could find it. He was only anxious now to put the harilim behind them before the dark came on them again.

Through the trees suddenly appeared a haze of open space, and when they had reached that edge there were only shells of stone and burned skeletons of timber where Mirrind had stood. He swore when he saw it, and leaned against one of the trees by the roadside. Roh wisely said nothing at that moment, and he swallowed the tightness from his throat and started forward, keeping to the shadow of trees and ruins.

The crops still grew, although weeds had set in; and the ruins of the hall were mostly intact. But the desolation, where beauty had been, was complete.

"We cannot stay here," Roh said. "This is within reach of the Sotharra camp. Shien's men. We have come too far. Use some sense, cousin. Let us get out of the open."

He lingered yet a moment, staring about him, then turned painfully and began to do as Roh had advised.

An arrow hit the dirt at their feet, quivered there, brown-feathered.

↫ Chapter 12

Roh started back from the arrow as from a serpent, reaching for his own bow. "No," Vanye said, holding him from flight.

"Friends of yours."

"Once. Maybe still.—*Arrhendim, Iher nthim ahallya Meriran!*"

There was no response. "You are full of surprises," Roh said.

"Be still," he answered. His voice shook, for he was very tired, and the silence dismayed him. If the *arrhendim* themselves had turned against him, then there was no hope.

"*Khemeis.*" The voice came from behind him.

He turned. A Man stood there, a *khemeis*. It was not any that he knew. "Come."

He began to do so, bringing Roh with him. The *khemeis* melted back into the forest, and when they had reached that place there was no sign that he had stood there. They walked further into the shadow.

Suddenly a white-haired *qhal* shifted into their view, from the shadow of the trees. His bow was bent, and a brown-feathered arrow was aimed at them.

"I am Lellin Erirrhen's friend," Vanye said. "And *khemeis* to Morgaine. This man is my cousin."

The arrow did not waver. "Where is Lellin?"

Then his heart sank, and he leaned on his staff, little caring whether the arrow was fired.

"Where is Lellin?"

"With my lady. And I do not know. I hoped that the *arrhendim* would."

"Your cousin bears lord Merir's safe-passage. But that is good only for him who bears it."

"Take us to Merir. I have an accounting to give him for his grandson."

Slowly the arrow was lowered and eased from the bowstring. "We will take you where we please. One of you does not have leave to be here. Which?"

"I," Roh confessed, lifting the amulet from his neck. He gave it into Vanye's hand.

"You will both come with me."

Vanye nodded when Roh looked questioningly at him; and he hung the amulet again about his neck and, heavily, limped in the *qhal's* wake.

There was no stopping until long after dark; and then the *arrhen* halted and settled among the roots of a large tree. Vanye sank down, Roh beside him, tucked his good leg up and rested against it, exhausted. But Roh shook at him after a moment. "They offer us food and drink," Roh said.

Vanye bestirred himself and took it, small appetite as he had now; afterward he leaned against the base of a tree and gazed at the *arrhendim* . . . two now, for the *khemeis* had joined them.

"Do you know nothing of where Lellin or my lady is?" Vanye asked them.

"We will not answer," said the *qhal.*

"Do you count us enemies?"

"We will not answer."

Vanye shook his head and abandoned hope with them, rested his head against the bark.

"Sleep," said the *qhal,* and spread his cloak and wrapped in it, becoming one with the tree against which he leaned; but the *khemeis* vanished quietly into the brush.

There was a different *qhal* and a different *khemeis* in the morning. Vanye looked at them, blinked, disturbed that they had shifted about so silently. Roh cast him a sidelong glance no less disturbed.

"I am Tirrhen," said the *qhal.* "My *khemeis* is Haim. We will take you farther."

"Nhi Vanye and Chya Roh," Vanye replied. "Where?"

The *qhal* shrugged. "Come."

"You are more courteous than the last," Roh said, and took Vanye's arm, helping him rise.

"They are Mirrind's guardians," Tirrhen replied. "Would you expect joy of them?"

And Tirrhen turned his back and vanished, so that it was Haim who walked with them a time. "Be silent," the *khemeis* said when Roh ventured to speak; it was all he said. They walked all the day save brief rests, and Vanye flung himself down at the midafternoon stop and lay still a good moment before he had caught his breath, eyes blurred and half-closed.

Roh's hand touched his. "Take the armor off. I shall carry it. You are done, otherwise."

He rolled over and began to do so, while Roh helped him. The *khemeis* watched, and finally offered them food and drink, although they had had a little at noon.

"We have sent for horses," Haim said. Vanye nodded, relieved at that.

"There is no word," Vanye said again, trying another approach, "what became of my party."

"No. Not that we know. And we know what there is to be known in this part of Shathan."

"But others might have contact elsewhere." Hope sprang up in him, swiftly killed by Haim's grim look.

"What there is of news is not good, *khemeis*. I understand your grief. I have said too much. Get up and let us be going."

He did so, with Roh's help. The lack of the armor was relief. He made it until nightfall before he was utterly winded and halted in his tracks.

It was Tirrhen with them now, and not Haim; and Tirrhen showed no intention of stopping. "Come," he said. "Come on."

Roh flung an arm about him and steadied him. They followed Tirrhen until Roh himself was staggering badly.

Then a clearing lay ahead of them in the starlight, and four *arrhendim* waited with six horses. "They mean we should keep going," Roh said, and his voice nigh broke.

Vanye looked, and knew none of them. He was helped to one of the saddleless horses, which was haltered only, and led by one of the *arrhendim*. Roh mounted the other without their help, and silently the party started to move.

Vanye leaned forward and rested against the horse's neck, instinct and habit keeping him astride over rough ground and through winding trails. The pain subsided to something bearable. The horse's patient strength comforted him. He slept at times, though once it cost him a bruise on a low branch: he bent back under it and slumped forward again, little the worse for it among so many other hurts. They moved through the night like shadows, and by morning they had reached another clearing, where more horses waited for them, with another escort.

He did not even dismount, but leaned, grasped a mane, and drew himself to the other horse. The party started forward, with no offering to them of food or water. Vanye ceased even to care, although such was finally offered at noon, without stopping. He rode numbly, silent as their escort was silent. Roh was still there, some distance behind . . . he saw that when he would look back. *Arrhendim* rode between them so that they could not speak to each other. They had not been disarmed, he realized at last, which heartened him; he trusted that Roh still had his armor and his weapons, for Roh had his own. He himself was beyond using any, and wished only for a cloak, for he was cold, even in daylight.

He asked finally, recalling that these were *qhal*, not Hetharu's halfling breed, and not by nature cruel. He was given a blanket to wrap himself in as they rode, and they offered him food and drink besides, all with little delay in their riding. Only twice in the day did they dismount even for a moment.

At nightfall there was another change of horses, and new guides took over. Vanye returned the blanket, but the *qhal* gently put it back about him and sent him on into the night with the new escort.

The *arrhendim* who had them in charge now were more than gentle with them, as if their condition aroused pity in them; but again at dawn, mercilessly, they were passed to others, and both of them now had to be helped to mount.

Vanye had no memory of how many changes there had been; it all merged into nightmare. There were always whistles and sounds about them now, as if they rode some well-marked highroad in the wood, one well-watched . . . but none of those watchers came into their view.

The trees here loomed up monstrous in size, of different sort than they had seen. The trunks were like walls beside them, and the place existed in shade that made it always twilight.

Night settled on them in that place, a starless dark beneath that canopy of branches; but there was the scent of smoke in the air, and one of their horses whinnied a greeting to another.

Light gleamed. Vanye braced his hands on the horse's moving shoulders, and stared at that soft glow, at the assemblage of tents gathered amid those great trunks, color showing in the firelight. He blinked through tears of exhaustion, fragmenting the image.

"Merir's camp?" he asked of the Man who led his horse.

"He has sent for you," that Man said, but no more would he say.

Music drifted to them, *qhalur* and beautiful. It died at their coming. Folk left the common-fire and stood as a dark line of shadows along the course that they rode into camp.

The *arrhendim* stopped and bade them dismount. Vanye slid down holding the mane, and needed the bracing of two *arrhendim* to keep his feet as they guided him, for his legs were weak and the ceaseless motion of the horses still ruled his senses, so that the very earth seemed to heave under him.

"*Khemeis!*"

A cry went up. A small body impacted his and embraced him. He stopped, freed a shaking hand and touched the dark head that rested against his heart. It was Sin.

"How did you come here?" he asked the boy, out of a thousand questions that he wondered, the only one that made clear sense.

The wiry arms did not let him go; small hands clenched in the sides of his shirt as the *arrhendim* urged him to start walking, and drew him on. "Carrhend moved," Sin said. "Riders came. It burned."

"Go away, lad," said the *khemeis* at the right—gently. "Go away."

"I came," Sin said; his hands did not unclench. "I went into the forest to find the *qhal*. They brought me here."

"Did Sezar come back? Or Lellin?"

"No. Ought they? Where is the lady?"

"Leave him," said the *khemeis*. "Lad—do as you are told."

"Go away from me," Vanye said heavily. "Sin, I am not in good favor with your people. Go away as he tells you."

The hands relaxed, withdrew. Sin lagged behind. But then as he walked Vanye caught sight of him, staying to one side, trailing them forlornly. He walked, for they would not let him do otherwise, to Merir's tent. They brought him at once inside, but Roh was left behind: he did not realize that until he was faced about in front of Merir's chair.

The old *qhal* sat wrapped in a plain gray cloak, and his eyes were sad, glittering in the light of the lamps. "Let him go," Merir said; they did, gently, and Vanye sank down to one knee and bowed himself to the mat in respect.

"You are sorely hurt," Merir said.

It was not the opening he had expected of the old lord, whose grandson was lost, whose line was threatened, whose land was invaded. Vanye bowed again, shaking with exhaustion, and sat back. "I do not know where Lellin is," he said hoarsely. "I want leave to go, my lord, to find him and my lady."

Merir's brows contracted. The old lord was not alone in the tent; grim armed Men and *qhal* were about him, force at need; and there were the elders, whose eyes were darkened with anger. But Merir's frown held more of pain than of wrath. "You do not know the state of things here. We know that you crossed the Narn. And after that, the *harilim*, the dark ones . . . have severed us from the region. Is it not so, that you went to find Nehmin?"

"Yes, lord."

"Because your lady would have it so, against my wishes. Because she was set on this thing; and warnings would not deter her. Now Lellin is gone, and Sezar; and she is lost; and war is upon us." The anger did come, and stilled, and the gray eyes brooded in the lamplight, lifted slowly once more. "I saw all these things in her. I saw in you only what I see now. Tell me, *Khemeis,* all that happened. I shall hear you. Tell me everything and spare no detail. It may be that some tiny scrap of knowledge will help us understand the rest."

He did so. His voice failed him in the midst of it, and they gave him drink; he continued, in their stark silence.

There was silence even after he had finished.

"Please," he asked of Merir, "give me a horse and one for my cousin too. Our weapons. Nothing more. We will go and find them."

The silence continued. In the weight of it, he reached to his neck and lifted off the chain that bore the amulet, tendered it to Merir. When Merir made no move to take it, he laid it on the mat before him, for his hand could not hold it longer without shaking.

"Then let us go out as we are," Vanye said. "My lady is lost. I want only to go and find her and those with her."

"Man," said Merir at last, "why did she seek Nehmin?"

He was dismayed by the question, for it shot to the heart of things that Morgaine had withheld from their knowledge. "Does it not control Azeroth?" he countered. "Does it not control the place where our enemies are?"

"Were," said another.

He swallowed, clenched his hands in his lap to keep them from trembling. "Whatever is amiss out there is my doing. I take responsibility for it. I told you why they came; they pursued me, and Nehmin has nothing to do with that. My lady is hurt. I do not know if she is still alive. I swear to you that she is not at fault in bringing attack on you."

"No," said Merir. "Perhaps she is not. But never yet have you told us all the truth. She asked truth of me. She asked trust. And trust have I given, to the very edge of war and the loss of our people's lives and homes. Yes, I see your enemies for what they are; and they are evil. But never yet have you told us all the truth. You and she crossed through the *harilim*. That is no small thing. You dared use the *harilim* in escaping your enemies; and you survive . . . and that amazes me. The dark ones hold you in uncommon regard—Man that you are. And now you ask us to trust you once more. You wish to use us to set you on your way, and never once have you told us truth. We shall not harm you, do not fear that; but loose you again to work more chaos in our land . . . no. Not with my question still unanswered."

"What will you ask, lord?" He bowed again to the mat, trembling, and sat back. "Ask me tomorrow. I think that I should answer you. But I am tired and I cannot think."

"No," said another *qhal,* and leaned on Merir's chair to speak to the old lord. "Will a night's rest improve the truth? Lord, think of Lellin."

Merir considered a moment. "I ask," he said at last, though his old eyes seemed troubled at the unkindness. "I do ask, *khemeis.* In all cases your life is safe, but your freedom is not."

"Would a *khemeis* be asked to betray his lord's confidence?"

That told upon all of them; there were doubtful looks among these honorable folk. But Merir bit his lip and looked sadly at him.

"Is there something then to betray, *khemeis?*"

Vanye blinked slowly, forcing the haze away, and shook his head. "We never wished you harm."

"Why Nehmin, *khemeis*?"

He tried to think what to answer, and could not; and shook his head yet again.

"Do we then guess that she means some harm to Nehmin? That is what we must conclude. And we must be alarmed that she has had the power to pass the *harilim*. And we must never let you go."

There was nothing else to say, and even silence was no safety. The friendship that they had enjoyed was gone.

"She wished to seize Nehmin," Merir said. "Why?"

"Lord, I will not answer you."

"Then it is an act which aims at us . . . or the answer would do no harm."

He looked at the old *qhal* in terror, knowing that he should devise something to say, something of reason. He pointed vaguely and helplessly toward Azeroth, from which he had come. "We oppose that. That is the truth, lord."

"I do not think we have truth at all until it involves Nehmin. She means to seize power there. No. Then what else might she intend? *'The danger is to more worlds than this one . . .'* Her words. They sweep much wider than Azeroth, *khemeis*. Do I dare guess she means to destroy Nehmin?"

He thought that he must have flinched. The shock was evident too in the faces that watched. There was heaviness in the air such that it was hard to draw breath.

"Khemeis?"

"We . . . came to stop the Shiua. To prevent the kind of thing that has come on you."

"Aye," said Merir after a moment, and breath was held in that place; none stirred. "By destroying the passage. By taking and destroying Nehmin."

"We are trying to save this land."

"But you fear to speak the truth to those who live in it."

"That out there . . . *that* . . . is the result of the opening of your Gate. Do you want more of it?"

Merir gazed down on him. His senses blurred; he was shaking convulsively. He had lost the blanket somewhere; he could riot remember. Someone put a cloak about him, and he held it close, shivering still.

"This Man, Roh," Merir said then. "Bring him in."

It was a moment before Roh came, and that not willingly; but he seemed too weary to fight, and when he was brought to face Merir, Vanye looked up and whispered to him: "Lord Merir, cousin; a king in Shathan, and worth respect. Please. For my sake."

Roh bowed: hall-lord and clan-lord himself, although they had taken his weapons and insulted him, he maintained his dignity, and when he had bowed, he sat down crosslegged on the floor . . . the latter a courtesy to kinsman rather than to Merir, for he should have demanded a seat on Merir's level or remained standing.

"Lord Merir," Roh said, "are we free or no?"

"That is the question, is it not?" Merir's eyes shifted to Vanye's. "Your cousin. And yet you have warned us before now what he is."

"I beg you, my lord—"

"Chya Roh." Merir's eyes flashed. "Abomination among us, this thing that you have done. Murder. And how many times have you so done?"

Roh said nothing.

"Lord," Vanye said. "He has another half. Will you not remember that?"

"That is to be reckoned . . . for he is both the evil and its victim. I do not know which I see."

"Do him no harm."

"No," said Merir. "His harm is within him." And Merir wrapped his cloak the more tightly about him and brooded in silence. "Take them," he said at last. "I must think on these things. Take them and lodge them well."

Hands settled on them, gentle enough. Vanye struggled to rise and found it beyond his strength, for his one leg was stiff and the other would scarcely hold him. *Arrhendim* helped him, one on a side, and they were led away to a neighboring tent, where there were soft skins still warm from someone's body. Here they were left, unrestrained, able to have fled, but that they had no strength left. They sprawled where they were let down, and slept.

Day came. A shadow stood against the light in the doorway of the tent. Vanye blinked. The shadow dropped down, and became Sin, squatted with his arms folded across his bare knees, patiently waiting.

A second presence breathed nearby. Vanye turned his head, saw a *qhalur* lad, his long white hair and clear gray eyes strange in a child's face; delicate, long hands propped his chin.

"I do not think you should be here," Vanye whispered to Sin.

"We may," said the *qhalur* child, with the absolute assurance of his elders.

Roh stirred, sat up reaching for weapons that were not there. "Be still," Vanye said. "It is all right, Roh. We are safe with such guards."

Roh dropped his head against his hands and drew a slow breath.

"There is food," said Sin brightly.

Vanye rolled over and saw that all manner of things had been provided them, water for washing, cloths; a tray of bread, and a pitcher and cups. Sin crawled over and sat down there, gravely poured frothing milk into a cup for him and offered it . . . offered a cup to Roh when Roh held out his hand for it. They breakfasted on butter and bread and a surfeit of goat's milk, the best fare they had had in many days.

"He is Ellur," said Sin, indicating his *qhalur* friend, who settled crosslegged near him. "I thank that I may be *khemeis* to him."

Ellur soberly inclined his head.

"Are you all right?" Sin asked, touching his splinted knee with great care.

"Yes. It is mending. I shall take that off soon."

"This is your brother?"

"Cousin," said Roh. "Chya Roh i Chya, young sir."

They inclined their heads in respect as men might.

"*Khemeis* Vanye," said Ellur, "is it true what we have heard, that many Men have come behind you against Shathan?"

"Yes," he said, for there was no lying to such children.

"Ellur has heard," said Sin, "that—Lellin and Sezar are lost; and that the lady is hurt."

"Yes."

The boys were silent a moment, both looking distressed. "And," said Ellur, "that if you go free, then there will be no *arrhendim* by the time we are grown."

He could not look away. He met their eyes, dark human and gray *qhal,* and his belly felt as if he had received a mortal wound. "That could be the truth. But I do not want that. I do not want that at all."

There was long silence. Sin gnawed at his lip until it seemed he would draw blood. He nodded finally. "Yes, sir."

"He is very tired," Roh said after a moment. "Young sirs, perhaps you should speak to him later."

"Yes, sir," said Sin, and rose up, gently reached out and touched Vanye's arm, bowed his head and exited the tent, Ellur shadowing him like a small pale ghost.

It was a mercy equal to any Roh had ever shown him. He felt Roh push at him, and lay down, shivering suddenly. Roh flung a cover over him, and sat there wisely saying nothing.

He drowsed at last, found respite in sleep. It did not last. "Cousin," Roh whispered, and shook at him. "Vanye."

A shadow fell across the doorway. One of the *khemi* crouched in the opening. "You are awake," he said. "Good. Come."

Vanye nodded to Roh's questioning look, and they gathered themselves out of the cramped confines of the tent, stood and blinked in the full daylight outside. There were four *arrhendim* waiting there.

"Will Merir see us now?" Vanye asked.

"Perhaps today; we do not know. But come and we shall see to your comfort."

Roh hung back, doubting them. "They can do what they will," Vanye said in his own tongue, and Roh yielded then and came. He limped heavily, loath to be moved anywhere, for he was dizzy and sore; but what he had told Roh was the very truth: they had no choice in the matter.

They came to an ample tent, and entered into it, where sat an old *qhalur* woman, robed in gray, who regarded them with bright stern eyes and looked them up and down, sorry as they were and filthy. "I am Arrhel," she said in a voice that cracked with authority. "Wounds I treat, not dirt." She gestured to the young *qhal* who stood in the rear corner. "Nthien, take them into the back and deal with what you may; *arrhendim,* assist Nthien where needful."

The young *qhal* parted the curtain for them, expecting no argument. Vanye went, pausing to bow to the old woman; Roh followed, and their guard trailed them.

Hot water was already prepared, carried steaming through an opening at the rear of the tent. At Nthien's urging they stripped and washed, even to the hair . . . Roh must unbind his, which was shame to any man; but so was it to be unwashed, so he only frowned displeasure and did so. Vanye had no such pride left.

The water stung in the wounds, and Vanye felt fever in his which must be dealt with; Nthien saw that at a glance and a touch, and began to make preparations in that direction. Vanye watched him with dread, for there was likely the cautery for the worst of them. Roh's injuries were scant, and a little salve sufficed for him, and a linen bandage to keep them clean; afterward Roh settled, wrapped in a clean sheet, on a mat in the corner, braiding his hair back into the warrior's knot and watching Nthien's preparations with mistrust equal to his own.

"Sit down," Nthien said then to Vanye, indicating the bench where he had set his vessels and instruments. There was no cautery at all. Nthien's gentle hands prepared each wound with numbing salve; some he must open, and he kept the *arrhendim* coming and going with instruments to be washed, but there was little pain. Vanye simply shut his eyes and relaxed after a number of the worst were done, trusting the *qhal's* skill and kindness. The numbness proceeded from the most painful to the least of his hurts, and afterward there was no bleeding; clean bandages protected them.

Then Nthien examined the knee . . . called in Arrhel, to Vanye's consternation, who laid her wrinkled hands on the joint and felt it flexing. "Leave the splint off," she said, then touched her hand to his brow, pressed his face between her hands, making him look at her. Regal she was in her aged grace, and her gray eyes were surpassing kind. "You are fevered, child."

He almost laughed in surprise, that she could call him child; but *qhal* lived long, and when he looked into those aged eyes, so full of peace, he thought that perhaps most Men to her years were children. She left them, and Roh gathered himself up off the mat, staring after her with a strangely disturbed expression.

His kind, Vanye thought, and his skin prickled at the thought. *Liell's kind . . . the Old Ones.* He was suddenly frightened for Roh, and wanted him quickly out of this place.

"We are done," said Nthien. "Here. We have found you both clean clothing."

The *khemi* offered it to them . . . soft, sturdy clothing such as the *arrhendim* wore, green and brown and gray, with boots and belts of good workmanship. They dressed, and the clean cloth next the skin was itself a healing thing, restoring pride.

Then the *arrhendim* held back the curtain and showed them again into Arrhel's presence.

Arrhel was standing at the tripod table which had not been there before. She stirred a cup, which she brought then and offered Vanye. "For the fever. It is bitter, but it will help." She gave him a small leather pouch. "Here is more of it. Once daily as long as the fever lasts, drink this steeped in water, as much as covers the center of your palm. And you must sleep much and ride not at all, nor wear armor on those wounds; and you must have wholesome food and a great deal of it. But it seems that this is not in anyone's plans. The supply is for your journey."

"Journey, lady?"

"Drink the cup."

He did so; it was bitter as promised, and he grimaced as he gave it back to her, uneasy at heart. "A journey to or from where I asked lord Merir to go?"

"He will tell you. I fear I do not know. Perhaps it depends on what you say to him." She took his hand in hers, and her flesh was soft and warm, an old woman's. Her gray eyes looked into him, so that he could not look away.

Then she let him go and turned, sat down in her chair. She set the cup on the tripod table beside her, and looked at Roh. "Come," she said; and he came, knelt when with her open hand she indicated a place before her—hall-lord though he was, he did so—and she leaned forward and took his face between her hands, gazing into his eyes. Long and long she stared, and Roh shut his eyes finally rather than bear that longer.

Then she touched her lips to his brow, and yet did not let him go. "For you," she whispered, "I have no cup to drink. There is no healing that my hands can work. I would that I could."

Her hands fell. Roh thrust himself away and to his feet and came against the warning hand of the *khemeis* who kept the door, stopped cold.

Vanye cast a look back at Arrhel, remembered courtesy and bowed; but when the lady then dismissed them, he made haste to take Roh from that place. Roh did not look back or speak, not then nor for a long time after, when they were settled again in their own tent.

Merir sent for them in the afternoon, and they went, escorted by the same several *arrhendim*. The old lord was wrapped in his feather-cloak, and bore the circlet of gold about his brow; armed Men and *qhal* were about him.

Roh bowed to Merir and sat down on the mat; Vanye knelt and performed the full obeisance, and settled as much as he could off his injured leg. Merir's face was grave and stern, and for a long time he was content only to stare at them.

"*Khemeis* Vanye," Merir said at last, "your cousin much troubles what little peace I have found in my mind. What will you that I do with him?"

"Let him go where I go."

"So Arrhel has told you that you are leaving."

"But not where, lord."

Merir frowned and leaned back, folding his hands before him. "Much evil has your lady loosed on this land. Much harm. And more is to come. I cannot wish this away. The wishes of all the folk of Shathan cannot turn this away. Even yet I fear you have not told me all that you know . . . yet I must heed you." His eyes flicked to Roh and back again. "The ally that you insist to take: would your lady approve him?"

"I have told you how we came to be allies."

"Yes. And yet I think she would warn you. So do I. Arrhel vows she will not sleep soundly for days for his sake, and she warns you. But you will not listen."

"Roh will keep his word to me."

"Will he? Perhaps. Perhaps you know best of all. See that it is so, *khemeis* Vanye. We will go to find your lady Morgaine, and you will go with us . . . So will he, since you insist; I will reserve my judgment. I have misgivings—for many things in this—but go we shall. Your weapons, your belongings, all are yours again. Your freedom, your cousin's. Only you must return me assurance that you will ride under my authority and obey my word as law."

"I cannot," Vanye said hoarsely, and turned his scarred palm toward Merir. "This means that I am my lady's servant, no one else's. But I will obey you while obeying you serves her; I beg you take that for enough."

"That is enough."

He pressed his brow to the mat in gratitude, only then daring believe they were free.

"Make ready," Merir said. "We leave very shortly, late in the day as it is. Your belongings will be returned to you."

Such haste was what he himself desired; it was more in all respects than he had dared hope of the old lord . . . and for an instant suspicion plucked at him; but he bowed again and rose, and Roh stood with him to pay his respect.

They were let out, unguarded, the *arrhendim* withdrawn.

And in their tent they found all that they owned given back to them, as Merir had said, weapons and armor, well-cleaned and oiled. Roh gathered his bow into his hand like a man welcoming an old friend.

"Roh," Vanye said, suddenly apprehensive at the dark look.

Roh glanced up. For an instant the stranger was there, cold and menacing, for all the affront the lord Merir had offered him.

Then Roh slowly shed that anger, as if he willed it so, and laid the bow down on the furs. "Let us leave off wearing the armor, at least until the next day on the trail. There is no need to bear that weight on our aching shoulders, and doubtless we are not immediately in range of our enemies."

"Roh, deal well with me and I will deal so with you."

Roh gave him a hard look. "Worried, are you? Abomination. Abomination I am to them. How kind of you to speak for me."

"Roh—"

"Did you not tell them about *her,* about your half-*qhal* liege? What else is she? Not pure *qhal.* Nor human. Doubtless she has done what I have done, no higher nor nobler. And I think you have always known it."

Almost he struck . . . held his hand, trembling with the effort; there were the *arrhendim* outside, their freedom at hazard. "Quiet," he hissed. "Be quiet."

"I have said nothing. There is much that I could say, and I have not, and you know it. I have not betrayed her."

It was truth. He stared at Roh's distraught face and reckoned that it was no more and no less than Roh believed. And Roh had not betrayed them.

"I know it," he said. "I will repay that, Roh."

"But you are not free to say so, are you? You forget what you are."

"My word is worth something . . . among them, and with her."

Roh's face tautened as if he had been struck. "Ah, you do grow proud, *ilin,* to think that. And you trade words with *qhal*-lords in their own language, and dispose of me how you will."

"You are lord of my mother's clan. I do not forget that. I do not forget that you offered me shelter, in a time when others of my kin would not."

"Ah, is it 'cousin,' now?"

There was no appeal to that hardness. It had been there since Arrhel gazed at him. Vanye turned his face from it. "I will do what I said, Roh. See you do the same. If you ask apology as my clan-lord, that I will give; if as my kinsman, that I will give; if it galls you that *qhal* speak civilly to me and not to you . . .

that involves another side of you that I have no reason to love; with *him* there is no dealing, and I will not."

Roh said nothing. Quietly they packed their belongings into what would be easy to carry on the saddles. They put on only their weapons.

"I will do what I said," Roh offered finally.

It was Roh again. Vanye inclined his head in the respect he had withheld.

In not a long time, *khemi* came to summon them.

⌒ Chapter 13

The company was forming up outside Merir's tent . . . six *arrhendim*, all told: two younger; two older, the *khemeis'* hair almost as white as his *arrhen's*, with faces well-weathered by time; and an older pair of *arrhendim*, women of the *arrhend* . . . not quite as old, for the *khemein* of that pair had hair equally streaked with silver and dark, while her *arrhen*, like all *qhal*, aged yet more slowly and had the look of thirty human years.

Horses had been readied for the two of them, and Vanye was well-pleased with them; a bay gelding for him and a sorrel for Roh, both deep-chested and strong, for all their gracefulness. Even the herds of Morija would have been proud of such as these.

They did not mount up; one horse remained riderless, a white mare of surpassing beauty, and the party waited. Vanye heaved his gear up to his saddle and bound it there, found also a waterflask and saddlebags and a good gray blanket, such things as he would have asked had he dared press at their charity. A *khemeis* from the crowd came offering them cloaks, one for him and one for Roh. They put them on gratefully, for the day was cool for their light clothing.

And when all that was done, they still waited. Vanye stood scratching the bay's chin and calming his restiveness. He felt himself almost whole again, whether by Arrhel's draught or by the touch of a horse under his hands and his weapons by him . . . fretting to be underway, to be beyond intervention or re-call, lest some circumstance change Merir's mind.

One of the *khemi* brought a chain of flowers, and bound it in the mane of the white horse; and came others, bringing such flower chains for each of the departing *arrhendim*.

But it was Ellur who brought a white one for Roh's horse, and Sin came bearing a chain of bright blue. The boy reached high to bind it into the black mane, so that they swung there like a chain of tiny bells. And then Sin looked up at him.

Premonition came on him that he was looking on the boy for the last time, that there would be—one way or another—no return for him from this ride. Sin seemed to believe it too this time. Tears brimmed in his eyes, but he held them; he had been through Shathan: he was no longer the boy in Mirrind.

"I have no parting-gift," Vanye said, searching his memory for something left that he owned but his weapons: and never had he felt his poverty as much as in that moment, that he had nothing left to spare. "Among our people we give something when we know the parting will be long."

"I made this for you," said Sin, and drew forth from his shirt a carving of a horse's head. It was made of wood, small, of surpassing skill, as there were so many talents in Sin's hands. Vanye took it, and thrust it within his collar. Then in desperation he cut a ring from his belt, plain steel and blue-black; it had once held spare leather, but he had none of that left either. He pressed it into Sin's hand and closed his brown fingers over it. "It is a plain thing, the only thing I have to give that I brought from home, from Morija of Andur-Kursh. Do not curse my memory when you are grown, Sin. My name was Nhi Vanye i Chya; and if ever I do you harm, it is not from wanting it. May there always be *arrhendim* in Shathan, and Mirrindim too. And when you are *arrhendim* yourselves, you and Ellur, see that it is so."

Sin hugged him, and Ellur came and took his hand. He chanced to look up at Roh, then, and Roh's face was sad. "Ra-koris was such a place," Roh said, naming his own hall in forested Andur. "If I had no reason to oppose the Shiua for my own sake, I would have now, having seen this place. But for my part I would save it, not take from it the only thing that might defend it."

The boys' hands were clenched in either of his; he stared at Roh and felt defenseless, without any argument but his oath.

"If she is dead," Roh said, "respecting your grief, cousin, I shall not even say evil of her—but you would be free then, and would you still carry out what she purposed? Would you take that from them? I think there is some conscience in you. They surely think so."

"Keep silent. Save your shafts for me, not them."

"Aye," Roh murmured. "No more of it." He laid his hand on his horse's neck, and looked about him, at the great trees that towered so incredibly above the tents. "But think on it, cousin."

There was a sudden murmuring in the crowd; it parted, and Merir passed through—a different Merir from the one they had seen, for the old lord wore robes made for riding; a horn bound in silver was at his side, and he bore a kit which he hung from the saddle of the white horse. The beautiful animal turned its head, lipped familiarly at his shoulder, and he caressed the offered nose and took up the reins. He needed no help to climb into the saddle.

"Be careful, Father," said one of the *qhal*. "Aye," others echoed. "Be careful."

Arrhel came. Merir took the lady's hand from horseback. "Lead in my absence," he bade her, and pressed her hand before he let it go. The others were beginning to mount up.

A last time Vanye bade the boys farewell, and let them go, and climbed into the saddle. The bay started to move of his own accord as the other horses started away; and before he had ridden far he was drawn to look back. Sin and Ellur were running after him, to stay with him while they could. He waved at them, and they reached the edge of the camp. Trees began to come between. His last sight of them was of the two stopped forlornly at the forest margin, fair-haired *qhalur* lad and small, dark boy, alike in stance. Then the green leaves curtained them, and he turned in the saddle.

The company rode mostly in silence, with the two young *arrhendim* in the lead and the eldest riding close by Merir. Vanye and Roh rode after them, and the two *arrheindim* rode last . . . no swords did they bear, unlike the *arrhendim*, but bows longer than the men's, and their slim hands were leathered with half-glove and bracer, old and well-worn. The *khemein* of that pair often lagged behind and out of sight, serving apparently as rearguard and scout as the *khemeis* of the pair in front tended to disappear ahead of them to probe the way.

Sharrn and Dev were the names of the old *arrhendim;* Vanye asked of the *arrhen* Perrin, the *qhalur* woman, who rode nearest them. Her *khemein* was Vis; and the young pair were Larrel and Kessun, cheerful fellows, who reminded him with a pang of Lellin and Sezar whenever he looked on them together.

They rested briefly halfway to dark. Kessun had vanished some time before that stop, and did not reappear when he ought; and Larrel paced and fretted. But the *khemeis* came in just as they were setting themselves ahorse again, and bowed apology, whispering something to lord Merir in private.

Then from somewhere in the far distance came the whistled signal of an *arrhen,* thin and clear as birdsong, advising them that all was well.

That was comforting to hear, for it was the first signal they had heard in all that ride, as if those who ranged the woods hereabouts were few or frightened. Lightness came on the *arrhendim* then, and a smile to Merir's eyes for a moment, though they had been sad before.

Thereafter Larrel and Kessun both parted company with them, and rode somewhere ahead.

Nor did they appear at night, when they could no longer see their way and stopped to set up camp.

They were settled near a stream, and brazenly dared a fire . . . Merir decided that it was safe enough. They sat down together in that warmth and shared food. Vanye ate, although he had small appetite: he felt the fever on him after the day's riding, and drank some of Arrhel's medicine.

He would gladly have sought his blanket then and gone to sleep, for his wounds pained him and he was exhausted from even so short a journey; but he refused to leave the fireside with Roh able to say what he would, to use his cleverness alone with the *arrhendim.* Chances were that Roh would keep his word; but he did not think it well to put overmuch temptation in Roh's way, so he rested where he was, bowed his head against his arms and sat savoring at least the fire's warmth.

Merir gave some whispered instruction to the *arrhendim,* which was not unusual in the day; quietly the *arrhendim* moved, and Vanye lifted his head to see what was happening.

It was Perrin and Vis who had withdrawn, and they gathered up their bows where they stood, deftly strung them.

"Trouble, lord?" Roh asked, frowning and tense. But the *arrheindim* made no move to depart on any business.

Merir sat unmoved, wrapped in his cloak, his old face gaunt and seamed in the firelight. All pure *qhal* had a delicate look, almost fragile; but Merir was like something carved in bone, hard and keen. "No," Merir said softly. "I have simply told them to watch."

The old *arrhendim* still sat at the fire, beside Merir; and something in the manner of all of them betokened no outside enemies. The *arrheindim* quietly put arrows to their strings and faced inward, not outward, though no bow was drawn.

"It is ourselves," Vanye said in a still voice, and a tremor of anger went through him. "I believed you, my lord."

"So have I believed you," Merir said. "Put off your weapons for the moment. I would have no misunderstanding—Do so, or forfeit our good will."

Vanye unbuckled the belts and shed the sword and the dagger, laid them to one side; and Roh did likewise, frowning. Dev came and gathered them all up, returned to Merir's side and laid them down on that side of the fire.

"Forgive us," said Merir. "A very few questions." He arose, Sharrn and Dev with him. He gestured to Roh. "Come, stranger. Come with me."

Roh gathered himself to his feet, and Vanye started to do the same. "No," said Merir. "Be wise and do not. I would not have you harmed."

The bows had drawn.

"Their manners are marginally better than Hetharu's," Roh said quietly. "I do not mind their questions, cousin."

And Roh went with them willingly enough, possessed of knowledge enough to betray them thoroughly. They withdrew along the bank of the stream, where trees screened them from view. Vanye stayed as he was, on one knee.

"Please," said Perrin, her bow still bent. "Please do not do anything, *sirren.* Vis and I, we seldom miss even small targets separately. Together, we could not miss you at all. They will not harm your kinsman. Please sit down so that we may all relax."

He did so. The bows relaxed; the *arrheindim's* vigilance did not. He bowed his head against his hands and waited, with fever throbbing in his brain and desperation seething in him.

The *arrhendim* led Roh back finally, and settled him under the watchful eye of the archers. Vanye looked at Roh; Roh met his eyes but once, and his look said nothing at all.

"Come," Sharrn said, and Vanye rose up and went with them, into the dark, down where the trees overhung and the brook splashed among the stones.

Merir waited, sitting on a fallen log, a pale figure in the moonlight, wrapped in his cloak. The *arrhendim* stopped him at a few paces' distance, and he stood, offering no respect: respect had been betrayed. Merir offered him to sit on the ground, but he would not.

"Ah," said Merir. "So you feel misused. And yet have you been misused, *khemeis,* reckoning all things into the account? Are we not here, pursuing a course you asked of us—and in spite of the fact that you have not yet been honest with us?"

"You are not my sworn lord," Vanye said, his heart sinking in him, for he was sure now that Roh had done his worst. "I never lied to you. But some things I would not say, no. The Shiua," he added bitterly, "used *akil,* and force. Doubtless you would too. I thought you different."

"Then why did you not deal with us differently?"

"What did Roh say to you?"

"Ah, you fear that."

"Roh does not lie . . . at least not in most things. But half of him is not Roh; and half of him would cut my throat and I know it. I have told you how that is. I have told you. I do not think anything he would have told you would have been friendly to me or to my lady."

"Is it so, *khemeis,* that your lady bears a thing of power?"

Had it been daylight, Merir must have seen the color wash from his face; he felt it go, and fear gathered cold and small in his belly. He said nothing.

"But it *is* so," said Merir. "She could have told me. She would not. She left me and sought her own way. She was anxious to reach Nehmin. But she has not done so . . . I know that much."

Vanye's heart beat rapidly. Some men claimed Sight; it was so in Shiuan . . . but something there was in Merir's hardness which minded him less of those dreamers than of Morgaine herself.

"Where is she?" he demanded of Merir.

"And do you threaten? Would you?"

He sprang to seize the old *qhal* to hostage before the *arrhendim* could intervene; and all at once he felt that thickness of sense that a Gate could cause. He caught at the *qhal*-lord, and as he did so his senses swam; he yet held to the robes, determined with all that was in him. Merir cried out; the dizziness increased; for a moment there was darkness, utter and cold.

Then earth. He lay on dew-slick leaves, and Merir with him. The *arrhendim* seized him—he hardly felt the grip—and drew him back. Weakly Merir stirred.

"No," Merir said. "No. Do not harm him." Steel slid back into sheath then, and Sharrn moved to help Merir, lifted him gently, set him on the log; but Vanye rested still on his knees, lacking any feeling in hands or feet. The void still gaped within his mind, dazing him, as it surely must Merir.

Gate-force. An area about the *qhal*-lord—charged with the terror of the Gates. *I know,* Merir had claimed; and know he must, for the Gates were still alive, and Morgaine had not stilled their power.

"So," Merir breathed at last, "you are brave . . . to have fought that; braver surely than to sink to violence against one as old as I."

Vanye bowed his head, tossed the hair from his eyes and met the old lord's angry stare. "Honor I left long and far from here, my lord. I only wish I could have held you."

"You know such forces. You have passed the Fires at least twice, and I could not frighten you." Merir drew from his robes a tiny case and carefully opened it. Again that shimmering grew about his hand and his person, although what rested inside was a very tiny jewel, swirling with opal colors. Vanye flinched from it, for he knew the danger.

"Yes," said Merir, "your lady is not the only one who holds power in this land. I am one. And I knew that such a thing was loose in Shathan . . . and I sought to know what it was. It was a long search. The power remained hidden. You fit well into Mirrind, invisibly well, to your credit. I was dismayed to know that you were among us. I sent for you, and heard you out . . . and knew even then that there was such a thing unaccounted for in Shathan. I loosed you, hoping that you would go against your enemies; I did believe you, you see. Yet she would seek Nehmin . . . against all my advice. And Nehmin had defenders more powerful than I. Some of them she passed, and that amazes me; but she never passed the others. Perhaps she is dead. I might not know that. Lellin should have returned to me, and he has not. I think Lellin trusted you somewhat, else he would have returned quickly . . . but I do not even know for certain that he lived much past Carrhend, I have only your word. Nehmin stands. Perhaps the Shiua you speak of have prevented her . . . or others might. You cast yourself back into our hands as if we were your own kindred—in some trust, I do think; and yet you admit with your silence what it was she wished in coming here . . . to destroy what defends this land. And she is the bearer of the power I have sensed; I know that now, beyond doubt. I asked Chya Roh why she would destroy Nehmin. He said that such destruction was her function and that he himself did not understand; I asked him why then he sought to go to her, and he said that after all he has done, there is no one else who will have him. You say he rarely lies. Are these lies?"

A tremor went through him. He shook his head and swallowed the bile in his throat. "Lord, *he* believes it."

"I put to you the same questions, then. What do you believe?"

"I—do not know. All these things Roh claims to know for truth . . . I do not; and I have served her. I told her once that I did not want to know; she gave me that—and now I cannot answer you, and I would that I could. I only know *her,* better than Roh knows—and she does not wish to harm you. She does not want that."

"That is truth," Merir judged. "At least—*you* believe that it is so."

"I have never lied to you. Nor has she." He strove to gain his feet; the *ar-rhendim* put their hands on him to prevent him, but Merir gestured to them to let him be. He stood, yet sick and dizzied, looking down on the frail lord. "It was Morgaine who tried to keep the Shiua out of your land. Blame me, blame Roh that they came here; *she* foresaw this and tried to prevent it. And this I know, lord, that there is evil in the power that you use, and that it will take you sooner or later, as it took the Shiua . . . this thing you hold in your hand. To touch that—hurts; I know that; and she knows best of all . . . she hates that thing she carries; hates above everything the evil that it does."

Merir's eyes searched over him, his face eerily lit in the opal fires. Then he closed the tiny case, and the light faded, reddening his flesh for a moment before it went. "One who bears what Roh describes would feel it most. It would eat into the very bones. The Fires we wield are gentler; hers consumes. It does not belong here. I would she had never come."

"What she brought *is* here, lord. If it must be in other hands than hers—if she is lost—then I had rather your hand on it than the Shiua's."

"And yours rather than mine?"

He did not answer.

"It is the sword—is it not? The weapon that she would not yield up. It is the only thing she bore of such size."

He nodded reluctantly.

"I will tell you this, Nhi Vanye, servant of Morgaine . . . that last night that power was unmasked, and I felt it as I have not felt it since first you came into Shathan. What would it have been, do you think?"

"The sword was drawn," he said, and hope and dread surged up in him—hope that she lived, and agony to think that she might have been in extremity enough to draw it.

"Aye, so do I judge. I shall take you to that place. You stand little chance of reaching it alone, so bear in mind, *khemeis,* that you still ride under my law. Ride free if you will; attempt Shathan against my will. Or stay and accept it."

"I shall stay," he said.

"Let him walk free," Merir said to the *arrhendim,* and they did so, although they trailed him back to the fire.

Roh was there, still under the archers' guard; the *arrhendim* signalled them, and the arrows were replaced in their quivers.

Vanye went to Roh, anger hazing his vision so that Roh was all the center of it. "Get up," he said, and when Roh would not, he seized him and swung. Roh broke the force with his arm and struck back, but he took the blow and drove one through. Roh staggered sidewise to the ground.

The *arrhendim* intervened with drawn swords; one drew blood, and he reeled back from that warning, sense returning to him. Roh tried to rise to the attack, but the *arrhendim* stopped that too.

Roh straightened and rose more slowly, wiped the blood from his mouth with a dark look. He spat blood, and wiped his mouth a second time.

"Henceforth," Vanye said in Andurin, "I shall guard my own back. Take care of yours, clan-lord, cousin. I am *ilin,* and not your man, whatever name you wear. All agreements are ended. I want my enemies in front of me."

Again Roh spat, and rage burned in his eyes. "I told them *nothing,* cousin. But have it as you will. Our agreement is ended. You would have killed me without asking. Nhi threw you out. Clan-lord I still am, and for my will, *Chya* casts you out. Be *ilin* to the end of your days, kinslayer, and thank your own nature for it. I told them nothing they did not already know. Tell him, lord Merir, for his asking: What did I betray? What did I tell you that you did not first tell me?"

"Nothing," said Merir. "He told us nothing. That is truth."

The anger drained out of him, leaving only the wound. He stood there with no argument against Roh's affront, and at last he shook his head and unclenched his bloody hand. "I bore with everything," he said hoarsely. "*Now* I strike back . . . when I am in the wrong. That is always my curse. I take your word, Roh."

"You take nothing of me, Nhi bastard."

His mouth worked. He swallowed down another burst of anger, seeing how this one had served him, and went away to his pallet. He lay down there, too distraught for sleep.

The others sought their rest; the fire burned to ash; the watch passed from Perrin to Vis.

Roh lay near him, staring at the heavens, his face set and still angry, and when Roh slept, if ever that night, he did not know it.

The camp came to slow life in the daylight, the *arrhendim* beginning to pack up and saddle the horses. Vanye rose among the first, began to put on his armor, and Roh saw him and did likewise, both silent, neither looking openly toward the other. Merir was last to rise, and insisted on breaking their fast. They did so; and quietly, at the end of the meal, Merir ordered their weapons returned to them both.

"So you do not break the peace again," Merir cautioned them.

"I do not seek my cousin's life," Vanye said in a faint voice, only for Merir and Roh.

Roh said nothing, but slipped into his sword harness, and rammed the Honor-blade into place at his belt, stalking off to attend to his horse.

Vanye stared after him, bowed courtesy to Merir; empty reflex . . . and went after him.

There were no words. Roh would not look at him but with anger, making speech impossible, and he turned instead to saddling his horse.

Roh finished; he did, and started to lead his horse into line with the others that were mounting up. And on a last and bitter impulse he stopped by Roh's side and waited for him.

Roh swung to the saddle; he did the same. They rode together into line, and the column started moving.

"Roh," he said finally, "are we beyond reasoning?"

Roh turned a cold eye on him. "You are worried, are you?" he asked in the language of Andur. "How much did they learn of *you,* cousin?"

"Probably what they did of you," he said. "Roh, Merir is armed. As she is."

Roh had not known. The comprehension dawned on him slowly. "So that is what unnerved you." He spat painfully to the other side. "And there is something here, then, that could oppose her. *That* is why you are so desperate. It was a bad mistake to set me at your throat; that is what you least need. You should not have told me. That is your second mistake."

"He would have told you when he wished; now I know that you know."

Roh was silent a time. "I do not know why I do not pay you what you have deserved of me. I suppose it is the novelty of hearing a Nhi say he was wrong." His voice broke; his shoulders sagged. "I told you that I was tired. Peace, cousin, peace. Someday we shall have to kill one another. But not . . . not without knowing why."

"Stay with me. I will speak for you. I said that I would, and I still mean it."

"Doubtless." Roh spat again to the side, wiped his mouth and swore with a shake of his head. "You loosened two of my teeth. Let it wipe out other debts. Aye, we will see how things stand . . . see whether *she* knows the meaning of reason, or whether these folk do. I have a fancy for an Andurin burial; or if things turn out otherwise, I know the Kurshin rite."

"Avert," he murmured, and crossed himself fervently.

Roh laughed bitterly, and bowed his head. The trail narrowed thereafter, and they rode no more together.

*   *   *

Larrel and Kessun returned; they were simply standing in the way as they rode around a bending of the trail, and met and talked with Merir.

"We have ridden as far as the Laur," Larrel said, and both the *arrhendim* and their horses looked weary. "Word is relayed up from Mirrind: no trouble; nothing stirs."

"This is a strange silence," Merir said, leaning on his saddle and casting a look back. "So many thousands—and nothing stirs."

"I do not know," said Vanye, for that look shot directly at him. "I would have expected immediate attack." Then another thought came to him. "Fwar's men. If any who fell behind were not killed—"

"Aye," Roh said. "They might have given warning what that forest is, if any came out again; or Shien might. And perhaps others of Fwar's folk could do us harm enough by talking."

"Knowledge where *she* is to be sought?"

"All the Shiua know where she was lost. And having lost us . . ."

"Her," Merir concluded, taut-lipped. "An attack near Nehmin."

The sword was drawn, Vanye recalled, two nights ago. There was time enough for the horde to have veered to Narnside. A fine sweat broke out on him, cold in the forest shadow. "I pray you haste."

"We are near the *harilim*'s woods," Merir said, "and there is no reckless haste, not for our lives' sake."

But they kept moving, the weary *arrhendim* falling in with them, and they rested as seldom as the horses could bear, save that they stopped at midafternoon and rested until twilight; then they saddled up again, and set out into a deeper, older part of the woods.

Dark fell on them more quickly under these monstrous old trees; and now and again came small chitterings in the brush that frightened the horses.

Then from the fore of their party flared an opal shimmer that made Merir's horse shy the more, horse and rider for a moment like an image under water. The flare died.

For a moment the forest was utterly quiet. Then the *harilim* came, stalking, rapid shapes. The first gave a chirring sound, and the horses threw their heads and fought the bits, dancing this way and that in a frenzy to run.

Then Merir led them forward, and their strange guides went about them, melting away into shadow after a time until there were only three left, which walked with Merir, chittering softly the while. It was clear that the master of Shathan had safe-passage where he would, even of these: they reverenced the power of the Fires which Merir held in his naked hand, and yielded to that, although the *arrhendim* themselves seemed afraid. Of a sudden Vanye realized what his chances had truly been, trifling with these creatures, and he shuddered recalling his passage among them: they served the Fires in some strange fashion, perhaps worshipped them. In his ignorance he had sought a passage in which even the lord of Shathan moved carefully and with dread . . . and one of them at least must have recalled him as companion to another who carried the Fires. Surely that was why he and Roh lived: the *harilim* had recalled Morgaine.

His heart beat faster as he scanned the dark, heron-like shapes ahead of him on the trail. *They may know,* he thought. *If any living know where she is, they may know.* He entertained a wild hope that they might lead them to her this night, and wished that there were some way that a human tongue could shape their speech or human ears understand them. Even Merir was unable to do that; when he did consult with them, it was entirely with signs.

The hope faded. It was not to any secret place that the *harilim* led them, but only through; they broke upon the Narn at the last of the night . . . black and wide it showed through the trees, but there was a place which might be a crossing, sandbars humped against the current. The *haril* nearest pointed, made a sign of passing, and as suddenly began to leave them.

Vanye leaped down from his horse, caught his balance against a tree and tried to stop one of them. *Three persons,* he signed to the creature. *Where?* Perhaps it understood something. The vast dark eyes flickered in the starlight. It lingered, made a sign with spidery fingers spread, hand rising. And it pointed riverward. The third gesture fluttered the fingers. And then it turned and stalked away, leaving him helpless in his frustration.

"The Fires," said Sharrn. "The river. Many."

He looked at the *qhal.*

"You took a chance," said Sharrn. "It might have killed you. Do not touch them."

"We could learn no more of them," said Merir, and started the white mare down the bank toward the water.

The *harilim* were gone. The oppression of their presence lifted suddenly and the *arrhendim* moved quickly to follow Merir. Vanye swung up to the saddle and came last but for Roh and Vis. The anxiety that gnawed at him was the keener for the scant information the creature had passed. And when they went down to water's edge he looked this way and that, for although it was not the place they had been ambushed, it was the same situation and as likely a trap. The only difference was that the *harilim* had guided them right up to the brink, and perhaps still stood guard over them in the coming of the light.

There was need of care for another reason in crossing at such a place, for quicksands were well possible. Larrel gave his horse into Kessun's keeping and waded it first; at one place he did meet with trouble, and fell sidelong, working out of it, but the rest of the crossing went more easily. Then Kessun rode the way that he had walked, and Dev followed, and Sharrn and Merir and the rest of them, the women last as usual. On the other side the young *arrhen* Larrel was soaked to the skin, shivering with the cold and the exhaustion of his far-riding and his battle with the sands. *Qhal* that he was, he looked worn to the bone, thinner and paler than was natural. Kessun wrapped him in his dry cloak and fretted about fevers, but Larrel climbed back into the saddle and clung there.

"We must get away from this place," Larrel said amid his shivering. "Crossings are too easily guarded."

There was no argument from any of them in that; Merir turned them south now, and they rode until the horses could do no more.

They rested at last at noon, and took a meal which they had neglected in their haste of the morning. No one spoke; even the prideful *qhal* sat slumped in exhaustion. Roh flung himself down on the sun-warmed earth, the only patch of sun in the cover they had found in the forest's edge, and lay like the dead; Vanye did likewise, and although the fever he had carried for days seemed gone, he felt that the marrow had melted from his bones and the strength that moved them was dried up from the heat. His hand lying before his face looked strange to him, the bones more evident than they had been, the wrist scabbed with wounds. His armor was loose on his body—sun-heated misery at the moment where it touched him; he was too weary even to turn over and spare himself the discomfort.

Something startled the horses.

He moved; the *arrhendim* sprang up; and Roh. A whistle sounded, brief and questioning. Merir stood forth to be seen, and Sharrn answered the signal in such complexity of trills and runs that Vanye's acquaintance with the system could make no sense of it. An answer came back, no less complex.

"We are advised," Merir said after it fell silent, "of threat to Nehmin. *Sirrindim* . . . the Shiua you fled . . . have come up the Narn in great numbers."

"And Morgaine?" Vanye asked.

"Of Morgaine, of Lellin, of Sezar . . . nothing. It is as if a veil has been drawn over their very existence. Alive or dead, their presence is not felt in Shathan, or the *arrhendim* this side could tell us. They cannot. Something is greatly amiss."

His heart fell then. He was almost out of hopes.

"Come," said Merir. "We have no time to waste."

⌒ Chapter 14

The trouble was not long in showing itself. Movement startled birds from cover in the thickets of the Narn's other bank, and soon there were riders in sight, but the broad Narn divided them from the enemy and there was no ford to give either side access to the other.

The enemy saw them too, and halted in consternation. It was a *khalur* company, demon-helmed, scale armored, on the smallish Shiua horses. Their weapons were pikes; but they carried more than those . . . ugly opponents. And the leader, whose white mane flowed evident in the wind of his riding when he led them forward to the water's edge: the *arrhendim* were appalled at the sight of him, one like themselves, and different . . . fantastical in his armor, the *akil*-dream elaborations of *khalur* workmanship.

"Shien!" Vanye hissed, for there was no one in the Shiua host with that arrogant bearing save Hetharu himself. The *khal* challenged them, rode his horse to the knees in water before he was willing to heed his men-at-arms and draw back.

Their own company kept moving, opposite to the direction of the Sotharra band; but Shien and his riders wheeled about and paced them, with the broad black waters of the Narn between. Arrows flew from the Sotharra side, most falling into the water, a few rattling on the stones of the shore.

The *qhal* Perrin reined out to the river's very brink and shot one swiftly aimed shaft from her bow. A demon-helmed *khal* screamed and pitched in the saddle, and his comrades caught him. A cry of rage went up from that side, audible across the water. And Vis raced her horse to the brink and shot another that sped true.

"Lend me your bow," Vanye asked then of Roh. "If you will not use it, I will."

"Shien? No. For all the grudge you bear him—he is Hetharu's enemy, and the best of that breed."

It was already too late. The Shiua lagged back of them, out of bowshot of the *arrhendim*, having learned the limits of their own shafts and the deadly accuracy of the Shathana. They followed at a distance on that other side, and there was no way to reach them and no time to stop. Perrin and Vis unstrung their bows as they rode, and the *arrhendim* kept tight formation about Merir, scanning apprehensively the woods on their own side of the river. It was speed they sought now, which ran them hard over the river shore, with nothing but an occasional wash of brushheap to deter them.

Then Vanye chanced to look back. Smoke rose as a white plume on the Shiua side.

Perrin and Vis saw the fix of his eyes and looked, and their faces came about rigid with anger.

"Fire!" Perrin exclaimed as it were a curse, and others looked back.

"Shiua signal," said Roh. "They are telling their comrades downriver we are here."

"We have no love for large fires," Sharrn said darkly. "If they are wise, they will clear the reach of that woods before night comes on them."

Vanye looked back again, at the course of the Narn which slashed through Shathan, a gap in the armor, a highroad for Men and fire and axes . . . and the *harilim* slept, helpless by day. He saw the dark shadow of distant riders, the wink of metal in the sun. Shien had done his mischief and was following again.

Again they rested, and the horses were slicked with sweat. Vanye spent his time attending this one and the other, for kindly as the *arrhendim* were with their mounts, and anxious as they were to care for them, they were foresters and the horses had come from elsewhere into their hands: they had not a Kurshin's knowledge of them.

"Lord," he said at last, casting himself down before Merir, "forest is one thing; open ground is another. We must not press the last out of the horses, not when we may need it suddenly. If the Shiua have gotten into the forest on our side and press us toward the river, the horses will not have it left in them to carry us."

"I do not fear that."

"You will kill the horses," Vanye said in despair, and left off trying to advise the old lord. He departed with an absent caress of the white mare's shoulder, a touch on the offered nose, and cast himself down by Roh, head bowed against his knees.

In a few moments more they were bidden back to the saddle, but for all Merir's seeming indifference to advice, they went more slowly.

Like Morgaine, he thought bitterly, *proud and stubborn.* And then he thought of her, and it was like a knife moving in a wound. He rode slumped in the saddle, cast a look back once, where Shien and his men still paced them, out of range. He shook his head in despair and knew what that was for: that they were apt to meet a force on their side of the Narn up by the next crossing, and Shien meant to be there to seal them up.

Roh rode close to him, so that the horses jostled one another and he looked up. Roh urged one of the *arrhendim*'s journeycakes on him. "You did not eat at the stop."

He had had no appetite, nor did now, but he knew the sense of Roh's concern, and took it and washed it down with water, though it lay like lead in his stomach. Small dark Vis rode up on his other side and offered another flask to him.

"Take," she said.

He drank, expecting fire by the smell of it, and it was, enough to make his eyes sting. He took several more swallows, and gave it back to Vis, whose dark eyes were young in her aging face, and kindly. "You grieve," she said. "We all understand, we that are *khemeis,* we that are *arrhen.* So we would grieve too." She pressed the flask back into his hand. "Take it. It is from my village. Perrin and I can get more."

He could not answer her; she nodded, understanding that too, and dropped behind. He hung the flask to his saddle, and then thought to offer some to Roh, which Roh accepted, and passed it back to him.

Night-shadow began to touch the sky. The sun burned over the dark rim of Shathan across the river, and from the east there was silence, no comforting whistles out of the dark woods, nothing.

They kept moving while there was still twilight to guide them, and bent into the forest itself, for a river barred their way, flowing into the Narn.

It was not a great river; quickly it dwindled until the trees that grew on its margin almost sufficed to span it.

And suddenly about them stealthy shadows moved, and a chittering warned them of *harilim.*

One waited on the riverside, like some large, ungainly bird standing at the water's shallow edge. It chirred at them as that kind would in perplexity, and backed when Merir would have approached it on horseback. Then it beckoned.

"We cannot go another such journey," Sharrn protested. "Lord, *you* cannot."

"Slowly," said Merir, and turned the white mare in the direction that the creature would have them go: breast-high she waded, but the current was very weak, and all of them followed, up the other bank, into wilder places.

The *haril* wanted haste: they could not. The horses stumbled on stones, faltered going up the slopes of ravines. The trees were old here, and the place beneath them much overgrown with brush. *Harilim* moved all about them, finding passage that the horses could not.

And suddenly there was a white shape before them in the dark, an *arrhen,* or like unto one, afoot and clothed in white, not forest green. His hair was loose, his whole aspect like and unlike one of the *arrhendim,* seeming more wraith than flesh in the starlight.

Lellin.

The youth lifted his hand. "Grandfather," he saluted Merir, softly. He came and took Merir's offered hand, reaching up to the saddle. Solid he was, yet there was a change on him, a sad quiet utterly unlike the youth they knew. "Ah, Grandfather, *you* should not have come."

"Why should I not?" Merir answered him. The old lord looked frightened. "What madness has taken you? Why this look on you? Why did you not send the message you promised?"

"I had no means."

"Morgaine," Vanye said, forcing his horse past Sharrn's to Lellin. "Lellin—what of Morgaine?"

"Not far." Lellin turned and lifted his arm. "A stony hill, the other side—"

He used the spurs, broke free of them and bent low, caring nothing for their protest, for *harilim* warnings. He would not bring Merir on her without warning. His horse stumbled under him, recovered; brush opposed, branches caught at him and snapped on his armor. He clung low to the saddle and the horse stayed on its feet, upslope and down, shying from this side and that as it sensed *harilim*. Pursuit was on his heels: the *arrhendim* . . . he heard them coming.

Suddenly there was a broad meadow in the starlight, and the low hill that Lellin had named hove up. He broke through a thin screen of young trees and rode for that place.

White figures appeared before him in the starlight, white robes, white hair flying in the wind, aglow like foxfire. He saw the shimmer, tried to rein over at the last instant and could not avoid it.

There was dark.

"*Khemeis.*"

A touch fell on his shoulder. He heard a horse near . . . sensed still the numbing oppression of Gate-force in the air.

"*Khemeis.*"

Lellin. Coarse grass was under his hands. He strove to push himself up. Another hand reached to help him rise. He looked into Sezar's face . . . Sezar likewise in white such as Lellin's, neither of them armed. He cast a dazed look about him, at white-robed *qhal*, at the two who had once been *arrhendim* . . . one of the *qhal* held the reins of his horse, which stood with legs braced as if it were still dazed.

And others . . . Merir, who dismounted and took his place among the *qhal* in white robes, a taint of gray among them. Roh was there at a distance, among the *arrhendim,* who grouped together as if in great fear.

"You are permitted," Lellin said, pointing toward the hill, "She sends for you. Go, now, quickly."

A moment he looked a second circuit of him, looking on the white figures, feeling the silence. His senses still swam. Gate-force worked at his nerves. He turned suddenly and went, overwhelmed with anxiety. One of them shadowed him, pointed the way that he should take up the hill, where a trail began among the trees which marched up its side. He did not run, but he wished to.

It was not a high hill, hardly more than a rocky upthrust amid the forest. At either side of him were trees aged and warped, twisted by wind or Gate-force, strange shapes in the starlight. He climbed that path carefully, his heart frozen in dread of the thing that he might find in this smothering silence.

The path bent, and she was there, a white figure like the others, as Lellin had been, standing among the rocks. Wind tugged at her white hair and her thin garments . . . unarmored and unarmed she was, when never willingly would she part from *Changeling*.

"*Liyo*," he said in half a voice, and stopped . . . human, and feeling it mortally. He did not want to come closer and find her changed; he did not want to lose her like that.

But she came to him, and there was no difference but the clothing: the strength was there, and the recklessness. Wraith she seemed, but this wraith scrambled down from the rocks with Morgaine's energy, a hand to this side and the other to catch herself, and a hand to him at the bottom. He seized her as if she might prove illusion after all, and they flung arms about each other with the desperation of sanity returned.

She said nothing. It was long before he thought of saying anything. But then he thought of her wound, and realized how thin she was, and that he might be hurting her. He drew her aside to the rocks and gave her a place to sit, cast himself to a lower stone beside her. "You are well," he breathed.

"We saw the smoke . . . from here. I hoped . . . hoped that you were somehow the cause of that alarm. I sent word, such as the *harilim* can bear. And I saw you coming . . . from this hill. I could not prevent them. I shouted, but in the wind, they did not hear, or heed. Lellin . . . Lellin found you, did he not?"

"Down near the river." His voice failed him and he rested his head against the stones at his side. "Oh Heaven, I did not know how I would find you."

"Sezar found Mai dead on the riverbank. And traces of horses about her. They searched further . . . but there were Shiua aswarm in that area and they had to come back. What happened?"

"Trouble enough." He reached for her hand, held it tightly, to assure himself she was solid and with him. "What of you? What are these folk? What are we amid here?"

"*Arrha*. Keepers of Nehmin, among other things. They are dangerous. But without them I would not have survived, whatever else we have to do one with the other."

"Are you free?"

"That is a question yet to be tried. There is nowhere to go from here. Three nights ago the marshlanders tried our defenses. They are still out there. We held them then. Lellin . . . Sezar . . . the *arrha*. I have tried to stay back from it, to avoid having them know me . . . but then I could not. Even so it was close."

A host of questions pressed on him. He felt her hand, how thin and fragile it had become. "Are you all right? Your wound—"

She moved her hand to her hip, where the leg joined. "Mending. The *arrha* are skilled healers. It was a bad one. I came close enough to dying. I do not remember the last of that ride, but that Lellin and Sezar knew where they were going . . . or thought they did. And the *arrha* . . . let us pass."

"If you had not stayed ahorse . . ." He did not finish the thought, sickened by it.

"Aye. I had the same thought for you. But you reached Merir after all. And yet you sent me no message."

He was confused for a moment, realizing then how she had misconstrued things. "Would my course had been that direct," he said, and a sudden fear possessed him, reluctance to admit what had happened . . . most of all to have her know he had been in the enemy's hands. Gate-force could change men: Roh was proof enough of that; and he recalled a time when she would have killed out of hand for any such doubt of a companion. "Forgive me," he said. "I have used allies in getting here that you will curse me for taking. And Merir knows both what you hold and what you have come to do . . . what *we* came to do. Forgive me. I trust too easily."

She was silent a moment. Fear touched her eyes. "The *arrha* know both by now, then."

"There is more, *liyo*. One of the men out there is Roh."

She drew back.

"I have been to the Gate and back again," he said hoarsely, refusing to let her go. "*Liyo*, on my soul, I had no choice; and I would not be here but for Roh."

"What of an oath you swore? What of that? You were not to let him live. And you have brought him to me?"

"He has helped us both. He asked only to see you; that was his condition. I warned him . . . I confess that I warned him and tried to persuade him to run. But—he would come. He has ran out of friends. And without him—Will you not hear him?"

She looked down. "Come with me," she said, and rose, still with her hand in his. He rose and walked with her among the rocks, down the other slope of the hill, by yet another trail. "Our camp is here," she said as they walked. "Extraordinary dispensation: no axe touches Nehmin . . . but the *arrha* brought wood from the outside, and built this for us. In some regards they have been more than kind."

A wooden shelter was almost hidden among the tall trees; a ghostly horse grazed beside it . . . Siptah. He recognized the gray Baien stud with a pang of relief, for Morgaine loved that horse, and had she lost him, she would have grieved . . . as much, he thought, as she might for him, for the gray horse had come with her farther and longer. Two other horses grazed slightly apart: Lcl lin's and Sezar's, one conspicuous for its white stockings. All of them looked sleek and well-cared for.

"Roh," she murmured as they descended toward the shelter. "The *arrha* meant to hold all of you from me at least overnight, to ask their own questions, I do not doubt. But they understand the bond of *khemeis* and *arrhen,* and when I accused them of harming you, they let you come, out of shame, I suppose. Roh's presence . . . that concerns me. I would not have him giving witness of me."

"We might try to break out of here."

She shook her head. "I fear our choice is in the Shiua's hands. They are on two sides of us at least." She drew back the curtain of the shelter, gray gauze like the *harilim*'s veils, like old moss, many layered. It swung against his face as he entered, and he did not like the feel of it.

Morgaine bent and touched a reed to a brazier of coals and transferred that tiny flame to a single-wicked lamp, so that a dim light surrounded them. "The *harilim* do not like fire," she said. "But we are very careful. Drop the curtain. Shed the armor. No enemies can come at us here without a great deal of trouble, and as for the *arrha* . . . they are of a different sort. I will find out what we have about here to eat—"

He stood motionless in the center of the small shelter as she searched through the collection of jars in the corner. There was Siptah's harness, and that of Lellin's and Sezar's horses; there were three pallets, with gray gauze veils dividing one off for privacy; Morgaine's armor, laid neatly in the corner; and *Changeling* . . . as if it were only another sword, leaned by it. Even to have walked up to the hilltop without that fell thing was something incredible in her . . . a dulling of cautions by which she had survived. There was after all a change about her, something alien and distant. In this place of familiar things . . . she was the difference. He watched her in the dim light, slender and delicate as the *qhal* in the white garments . . . and her features when she looked up at him: the tautness of pain had been there recently. *So close,* he thought with sudden anguish, *so very close to losing her; perhaps that is the mark on her.*

"Vanye?"

He reached for the straps of his armor, worked at them clumsily, managed them. She helped him pull it off, received the two-stone weight of mail into her hands and laid it aside. He unlaced the haqueton and shed it, sank down into the mat with a sigh. Then she gave him water to drink, and bread and cheese of which he could eat only a few bites. He was more content simply to lean against the support of the shelter and rest. It was warm; she was there. It was for the moment, enough.

"Do not worry about the others," she said. "Lellin and Sezar will give warning if anything threatens us, and the *arrha* refuse to lay hand on them or me.—Oh, it is good to see thee, Vanye."

"Aye," he murmured, for his voice was too taut to say more.

She sat on the mat beside the brazier, locked her hands about one knee. A moment, she gazed at him, as if taking in small details. "You have been hurt."

"It passes."

"Your fall out there—"

"I rode into that blind." He grimaced. "I thought to warn you . . . of my company."

"You succeeded." Her face grew the more concerned, deeply distressed. "Vanye. Will thee—tell me what happened?"

"Roh, you mean."

"Roh. And whatever else thee thinks good for me to know."

He glanced down, up again. "I have gone against your orders. I know that. I could not kill him. I confess to you . . . it has not been the first time. I agreed with him that I would speak to you . . . he asked nothing more, not even that much, but I told him that I would; I owed him. He is out of allies, out of hope, except to come here."

"And you believe him."

"Yes. In that—I do believe him."

Her hands clenched on her knee until the knuckles were white. "And what do you expect me to do?"

"I do not know. I do not know, *liyo*." He made the profound obeisance, which gesture she ordinarily hated, but the time demanded it. "I told him that I would speak with you. Will you let me do so, and hear me? I set my word on that."

"Do not hope that it will make any difference. My choices are not governed by what I would or you would."

"All I ask is a hearing. It is not easy to explain. In any sense, it is not easy. And I have asked few things of you, ever."

"Aye," she said softly, drew a long breath and let it go. "I will listen. I will at least listen."

"For long?"

"As long as you wish. Till the sun rises, if that is what you want of me."

He bowed his head against his hands a moment, gathering his thoughts. Nothing would make sense except from the beginning . . . and there he began, far off the matter of Roh. She looked perplexed at that . . . but she listened as she had said she would do; her gray eyes lost their anger and bore only on what he haltingly told her: things of himself, and his home, small things that she had not known of him, some of which were agony to tell . . . what it was for a half-Chya lad in Morija, what constant war Nhi and Chya had known, and how he came to be a Nhi lord's bastard. And there were things even of times that they had travelled together, things which he had seen and she had not . . . of Liell; and Roh; of the night they had spent in Roh's hall at Ra-koris; and another with him in the woods near Ivrel, when she had slept; or in Ohtij-in of Shiuan, unknown to her. He watched understanding flicker into sometime anger, and puzzlement return; she said nothing.

And he told her the rest: Fwar, and Hetharu's camp; and Merir's; and their way here. He spared nothing, least of all his pride; at the last he did not look at her, but elsewhere, close to choking on the words . . . for half of him was Nhi, and Nhi were proud, and not given to such admissions as he made.

Her hands were clenched when he had done. She loosed them after a moment, as if she had only then realized it. It was a moment before she looked up.

"Some things I would that I had known at the time."

"Aye, and some things I would that you did not know now."

"Nothing that you have told me troubles me, not on your account. Only—Roh . . . Roh. I did not reckon on that. I swear that I did not."

"You saw him. But—but perhaps—I do not know, liyo."

"It cannot make any difference. It changes nothing."

"Liyo."

"I warned you it could not make any difference . . . Roh or Liell; no difference."

"But Roh—"

"Let me alone a time. Please."

His control came close to breaking. He had said too much, too painful things, and she shrugged them off with that. "Aye," he said thickly, and thrust his way to his feet, seeking the cold, sane air outside. But she rose and prevented him with a grip on his wrist. He would hurt her if he struck out in his anger; he stood still, and the tears broke his control. He averted his face from her.

"Think of something," she hissed fiercely. "*Think* of something that I can do with this gift you have brought me."

He could not. "His word you would never take. And that is all there is . . . his word, and my faith that it is worth something. And that is nothing to you."

"You are unfair."

"I make no complaint of you."

"Keep him prisoner? He knows too much . . . more than you, more perhaps than Merir . . . in some things more than I, perhaps. I cannot trust that much knowledge . . . not with Liell's instincts."

"At times . . . at times, I think there is only Roh. He said the other was only in dreams; and perhaps the dreams are stronger than he is when there is nothing near him that Roh remembers. He says that he needs me.—But I have no knowledge of such things. I only guess. Perhaps I am the one who forced him to come here to you, because when he is with me . . . he is my cousin. I only guess."

"Perhaps," she said after a moment, "your instinct in that guess is not so far amiss."

There was a clutching pain in him. He turned and looked at her, looked into her gray eyes, the face that was utterly *qhalur*. "Roh has said . . . again and again . . . that you know all these things very well—and by your own experience."

She said nothing, but stepped back from him. He did not mean to let it go this time.

"I do not know," she whispered at last. "I do *not* know."

"He says that you are what he is. I am asking you, *liyo*. I am only *ilin*; you can tell me never to ask; and the oath I took to you does not question what you are. But *I* want to know. *I* want to know."

"I do not think you do."

"You said that you were not *qhal*. But how do I go on believing that? You said that you had never done what Liell has done. But," he added in a still voice difficult to force against the distrust in her eyes, "if you are not *qhal*—*liyo*, are you not then the other?"

"You are saying that I have lied to you."

"How can you have told me the truth? *Liyo*, a little lie, even a kindly lie at the time . . . I could understand why. If you had told me you were the devil, I could not free myself of the oath I had given you. Perhaps you meant it for kindness in that hour. It was. But after so long, so many things—for my peace—"

"Would it give you peace?"

"To understand you—yes. It would. In many ways."

The gray eyes shimmered, pained. She offered her hand to his, palm up; he closed his over it, tightly, a manner of pledge, and he marked even in doing so that her fingers were long and the hand narrow. "Truth," she said faintly. "I am what Hetharu is: halfling. A place long ago and far from Andur-Kursh . . . closed now, lost, no matter. The catastrophe did not come only on the *qhal*; they were not the only ones swept up. There were their ancestors, who made the Gates." She laughed, a lost and bitter laugh. "You do not understand. But as the Shiua are out of my past, I am out of theirs. It is paradox. The Gateworlds are full of that. Can what I have told you give you peace?"

Fear was in her look . . . anxiety, he realized numbly, for *his* opinion, as if she needed regard it. He half understood the other things, the madness that was time within gates. That anything could be older than the *qhal* . . . he could not grasp such age. But he had hurt her, and he could not bear to have done that. He let go her fingers, caught her face between his hands and set a kiss beside her lips, the only affirmation of trust he knew how to give. He had believed her a liar, had accused her, assuming so, so surely that he could dismiss such a lie and forgive, understanding her.

And he did not. A pit opened at his feet, to take in all his understanding.

"Well," she said, "at least thee is still here."

He nodded, knowing nothing to say.

"Thee surprises me sometimes, Vanye."

And when he still found no answer, she shook her head and turned away across the little shelter, her arms folded tightly, her head bowed. "Of course you came to that conclusion; there was nothing else you could think. Doubtless Roh himself believes it. And for whatever small damage it could do—Vanye, I beg you keep it to your knowledge, no one else's. I am not *qhal*. But what I am no longer has any meaning, not in this age. Not in Shathan. It no longer matters."

"*Liyo—*"

"I would not have you believing that I knew Roh's nature. I would not have you thinking I sent you against him, knowing that. I did not. I did *not*, Vanye."

"Now you have me between two oaths. Oh Heaven, *liyo*. I was thinking of Roh's life, and now I am afraid of winning it. I do not . . . I swear I do not try to pull against your good sense. I do not want that. *Liyo,* protect yourself. I should never have questioned you; this is not how I would have persuaded you. Do not listen to me."

"I know my own mind. Do not shoulder everything." She tossed her head back, thin-lipped, and looked at him. "This is Nehmin. You will see it as I have seen it; I am not anxious to spill blood in this place. We are far from Andur-Kursh . . . far from every grudge it had . . . and I pity him. I pity him, even as Liell—though that is harder: I knew his victims. Give me time to think. Go to sleep a while. Please. There is at least something of the night left, and you look so tired."

"Aye," he agreed, though it was less for weariness than that he would not dispute her, not now.

She gave him the mat by the east wall, her own. He lay down there with no real desire of sleep; but the ease it gave sent a sudden heaviness on him, so that he cared not even to move. She drew the blanket further over him, and sat down on the mat beside him, leaned there against the post, her hand over his. He shivered for no reason—if he had taken a chill he was too numb to feel it. He let his breath go, flexed his fingers against hers, enclosed them.

Then he slept, a hard, swift darkness.

⌒ **Chapter 15**

She was gone in the morning. There was food there, milk and bread and butter, and slices of cold meat. Written in a dab of butter on the side of the pitcher was a Kurshin symbol, the glyph that began *Morgaine.*

Safe, she meant. He ate, more than he had thought he could; and there was water heated for him over the coals. He bathed, and shaved . . . with his own razor, for his personal kit was there: they had recovered it from Mai, surely; and his bow was laid there with his armor, and other things that he had thought forever lost. He was glad—and dismayed, to think that they might have risked themselves, she and Lellin and Sezar, to recover them.

But her own weapons were still standing in the corner, and it began to trouble him that she stayed so long, unarmed. He went outside, unarmored, to see whether she was in sight: Siptah was gone too, though the harness was not.

Then a movement caught his eye, and he saw her coming back, riding down the slope, bareback on the gray horse, a strange figure in her white garments. She slid down and wrapped the tether-line over a branch, for she had been riding with only the halter. Her face had held a worried look for an instant; but she put on a different face when she looked up at him . . . he saw it and answered it with a faint smile, quickly shed.

"We have a little trouble from the outside this morning," she said. "They are trying us."

"Is that the way to go looking for it?" He had not meant his voice to be so sharp, but she shrugged and took no affront. The frown came back to her eyes, and they fixed beyond, back the way she had come.

He looked. Three *arrha* had followed her, and a Man walked with them, a tall man in green and brown, coming from the shadow of the trees.

It was Roh.

They brought him to the front of the shelter and stopped: they laid no hand on Roh in their bringing him, but he had no weapons either. "Thank you," Morgaine told the *arrha,* dismissing them; but they withdrew only as far as the rocks near the shelter.

And Roh bowed, as lord visiting hall-lord, with weary irony.

"Come inside," Morgaine bade him.

Roh came, passed the curtain which Vanye held aside for him. His face was pale, unshaven—and afraid, although he tried not to show it. He did not look as if he had slept.

"Sit down," Morgaine invited him, herself settling to the mat by the brazier, and Roh did so on the opposite side, cross-legged. Vanye sank down on his heels at Morgaine's shoulder. An *ilin*'s place, which said what it might to Roh. *Changeling*, he thought uneasily, for the sword was unattended in the corner, and Morgaine unarmed: he had at least placed himself as a barrier between Roh and that.

"Chya Roh," Morgaine said softly. "Are you well?"

A muscle jerked in Roh's jaw. "Well enough."

"It took me some argument to bring you here. The *arrha* were minded otherwise."

"You usually obtain what you want."

"Vanye did speak for you—and well. None could be more persuasive with me. But counting all that—and my gratitude for your help to him, Chya Roh i Chya—are we other than enemies? Roh or Liell, you have no love for me. You hate me bitterly. That was so in Ra-koris. Are you the kind of man who can change his mind that thoroughly?"

"I hoped you would be dead."

"Ah. Truth from you. That does surprise me. And then what would you?"

"The same that I did. I would have stayed . . ." His eyes shifted to Vanye's and locked, and his voice changed. "I would have stayed with you and tried to reason with you. But . . . that is not how it came out, is it, cousin?"

"And now?" Morgaine asked.

Roh gave a haggard grin, made a loose gesture of the hands.

"My situation is rather grim, is it not? Of course I offer you my service. I should be mad not to. I do not think that you have any intention of accepting; you are hearing me now to satisfy my cousin's sensibilities; and I am talking to you because I have nothing left to do."

"Because Merir and the *arrha* turned a deaf ear to you last night?"

Roh blinked dazedly. "Well, you did not expect me not to try that, did you?"

"Of course not. Now what else will you try? Harm Vanye, who trusts you? Perhaps you would not; I almost believe that. But me you never loved, not in any shape you have worn. When you were Zri you betrayed your king, your clan, all those men . . . when you were Liell, you drowned children, and made of Leth such a plague-spot, such a sink of depravity—"

Terror shot into Roh's eyes, horror. Morgaine stopped speaking, and Roh sat visibly shivering . . . gone, all pretense of cynicism. Vanye looked on him and hurt, and set his hand on Morgaine's shoulder, wishing her to let him be; but she did not regard it.

"You do not like it," she murmured. "That is what Vanye said—that you had bad dreams."

"Cousin," Roh pleaded.

"I shall not call it back for you," she said. "Peace. Roh . . . *Roh* . . . I shall say nothing more of it. Be at peace."

Roh's hands, shaking, covered his face; he rested so a moment, white and sick, and she let him be. "Give him drink," she said. Vanye took the flask she indicated with a glance, and knelt and offered it to him. Roh took it with trembling hands, drank a little. When he was done, Vanye did not leave him, but held to his shoulder.

"Are you all right now?" Morgaine asked him. "Roh?" But he would not look at her. "I have done you more harm than I wished," she said. "Forgive me, Chya Roh."

He said nothing. She rose then, and took *Changeling* from the corner . . . withdrew from the shelter entirely.

Roh did not look at that, nor at anything. "I can kill him," he breathed between his teeth, and shuddered. "I can kill him. I can kill him."

For a moment it made no sense, the rambling of a madman; and then Vanye understood, and kept hold of him. "Cousin," he said in Roh's ear. "Roh. Stay with me. Stay with me."

Sanity returned after a moment. Roh breathed hard and bowed his head against his knees.

"Roh, she will not do that again. She saw. She will not."

"I would be myself when I die. Can she not allow me that?"

"You will not die. I know her. I *know* her. She would not."

"She will manage it. Do you think that she will ever let me at her back where you stand, or rest when I am near her? She will manage it."

The veil shadowed, went back. Morgaine stood in the doorway. "I am afraid I hear you," she said quietly. "The veils do not stop much."

"I will say it to your face," Roh said, "syllable by syllable if you did not get it clear.—Will you not return the courtesy, to me—and to him?"

Morgaine frowned, rested *Changeling* point down on the floor before her. "I will say this: that there is some good chance it will make no difference what I will and will not." She nodded vaguely westward, at the other wall. "If you want to walk through that woods and take a look at the riverside, you will find enough Shiua to make any quarrel we have among ourselves quite pointless. What I say I would say if Vanye were not involved. The kindnesses I attempt generally come to worse than my worst acts. But murder sits ill with me, and . . ." She lifted *Changeling* slightly from the floor and rested it again. "I have not the options of fair fight that a man has; nor would I put that burden on Vanye, to deal with you in that fashion. You are right; I cannot trust you as I do him. I do not think I could ever be persuaded to that. I do not want you at my back. But we have mutual enemies out there. There is a land about us that does not deserve that plague on it . . . and you and I made it, did we not? You and I created that horde. Will you share in stopping it? The fortunes of war—may make it unnecessary to concern ourselves about our . . . differences."

Roh seemed dazed a moment . . . and then he set his hands on his knees and laughed bitterly. "Yes. Yes, I would do that."

"I will not ask an oath of you or take one, no great one: it would bind me to an honor I cannot afford. But if you will give your simple word, Roh—I trust *you* can bind your other impulses."

"I give it," Roh said. He rose, and Vanye with him. "You will have what you want of me. *All* . . . that you want of me."

Morgaine's lips tightened. She turned and walked to the far wall and laid down *Changeling,* gathering up her armor. "Do not be too forward in it. There is food left, probably. Vanye, see he has what he needs."

"My weapons," Roh said.

She looked at him, scowling. "Aye, I will see to that." And she turned again and began working into her armor.

"Morgaine kri Chya."

She looked up.

"You . . . did not bring me from Ra-koris; I brought myself, I. You did not aim that horde at this land. I did, no other. And I will not take food or drink or shelter of you, not—as matters stand. If you insist, I must; but if not—then I will take it elsewhere, and not inflict any obligation on myself or on you."

She hesitated, seeming stunned. Then she walked over and flung back the veil to the outside, waved a signal at the *arrha* who waited there. Roh left, pausing to offer a bow of courtesy; Morgaine let fall the veil after him, and lingered there, leaning her head against her arm. After a moment she swore, in her own tongue, and turned away, avoiding his eyes.

"You," Vanye said into that silence, "you did as much as he would have asked of you."

She looked up at him. "But you expect more."

Vanye shook his head. "I regard you too much, *liyo.* You are risking your life in giving what you have. He could kill you. I do not think so, or I would not have him near you. But he is a risk; and I know how you feel. Maybe more so. He is my cousin. He brought me here alive. But . . . if . . . he is overmuch tempted, *liyo,* then he will lose. I know that. What is more, he does. You have done the best thing you could do."

She bit her lips until the blood left them. "He is a man, your cousin. I will give him that."

And she turned and gathered up the rest of her armor, put it on with a grimace of discomfort. "He will have his chance," she said then. "Armor and bow: little use for anything else if this is like the last time . . . until they reach the rock itself. We are in no small danger."

"They are prepared?"

"Some of them are well up the Silet, the tributary river to our south; the force at Narnside began moving across to our bank at dawn."

"You permit this?"

She gave a bitter laugh. "I? Permit? I fear I am not in charge here. The *arrha* have permitted it, step by step, until we are nigh surrounded. Powerful they are, but their whole mind, their whole conception of the problem, is toward defense, and they will not hear me. I would have done differently, yes, but I have not been able to do anything until recently. Now it comes to the point that the only thing I can do is help them hold this place. It has never been a matter of what I would choose here."

He bent and gathered his armor from where he had left it.

They saddled the horses, not alone Siptah, but Lellin's and Sezar's, and gathered up all that they might need if it came to flight. What was in Morgaine's mind remained her own; but he reckoned in his own thoughts what she had told him, the isolation by wood and water of the area that was Nehmin, and the Shiua possessing the rivers that framed their refuge.

All the area about them was tangled and wooded, and that was a situation no Kurshin could find comfortable; there was no place to maneuver, no place to run. The horses were all but useless to them, and the hill was too low to hold.

They rode up the slope of the hill and among the twisted trees, down again by the winding trail among the rocks, so that they came out again on the meadow.

"No sight of them," Vanye muttered, looking uneasily river-ward.

"Ah, they have learned a slight caution of this place. But it will not last, I fear."

She turned Siptah to the right hand, and warily they rode away from that vicinity into the woods, through brush, into an area where the trees grew very large. A path guided them . . . *and our enemies next,* Vanye thought dismally. Horses had been down it recently.

"*Liyo,*" he said after a space. "Where do we go? What manner of thing have you in mind?"

She shrugged, and seemed worried. "The *arrha* have withdrawn. And they are not above abandoning us to the enemy. I am concerned for Lellin and Sezar. They have not reported back to me. I do not like to take their horses from where they expect to find them, but likewise I do not want to lose them."

"They are out there—toward the enemy?"

"That is where they should be. At the moment, I am concerned that the *arrha* are not where they should be."

"And Roh."

"And Roh," she echoed, "though in some part I doubt he is the center of this matter. He may himself be in danger. Merir . . . Merir is the one who deserves watching. Honorable he may be—but thee learns, Vanye, thee learns . . . that the good and virtuous fight us as bitterly as those who are neither good nor virtuous . . . more so, perhaps—for they do so unselfishly, and bravely . . . and we must most of all beware of them. Do you not see that I am what the Shiua name me? And would a man not be entitled to resist that . . . for himself—most of all for what the *arrhend* protects?—Forgive me. Thee knows my darker moods; I should not shed them on thee."

"I am your man, *liyo.*"

She looked at him, surprised out of the bitterness that had been her expression.

And around the bending of the trail there stood one of the *arrha,* a young *qhalur* woman. Silent, she stood among the branches and ferns, light in green shadow.

"Where are your fellows?" Morgaine asked of her.

The *arrha* lifted her arm, pointed the way that they were going.

Morgaine started Siptah forward again, slowly, for the trail wound much. Vanye looked back; the *arrha* still stood there, a too-conspicuous sentinel.

Then they passed into another space where few trees grew, and in that open space there were horses; the *arrhendim* were there, seated . . . the six who had gone out with Merir, and Roh. Roh gathered himself to his feet as they came.

"Where is Merir?" Morgaine asked.

"Off that way," Roh said, and pointed farther on. He spoke in Andurin, and looked up . . . shaven, washed, he looked more the *dai-uyo* he was, and he bore his weapons again. "No one is doing anything. Word is the Shiua are closing on us from two sides, and the old men are still back there talking. If no one moves, we will have Hetharu in our midst before evenfall."

"Come," said Morgaine, and slid down from the saddle.

"We leave the horses here." She wrapped Siptah's reins about the branch, and Vanye did the same for the horse he rode and the ones he led.

None of the *arrhendim* had done more than look up.

"Come," she bade them; and in a stronger voice: "Come with me."

They looked uncertain; Larrel and Kessun stood up, but the elder *arrhendim* were reluctant. Finally Sharrn did so, and the six came, gathering up their weapons.

Wherever they were bound, Morgaine seemed to have been this way before: Vanye stayed at her shoulder, that Roh should not walk too near her, watching either side and sometimes looking back at the *arrhendim* who trailed them on this suddenly narrower path. He was far from easy in his mind, for they were all too vulnerable to treachery, for all the power of the weapons Morgaine bore.

Gray stone confronted them through the tangle of vines and branches . . . lichen-spotted, much weathered, standing stones thrust up among the roots of trees, closer and closer, until the stones formed an aisle shadowed by the vast trees.

Then they had sight of a small stone dome at the end of that aisle. *Arrha* guarded the entry of it, one on either side of the doorway that stood open, but there was no offer to oppose their coming.

Voices echoed within, echoes that died away at their tread within the doorway. Torches lit that small dome within; *arrha* sat as a mass of white on stone seats that encompassed more than half the circuit of the walls: the center of the floor was clear, and there Merir stood. Merir was the one who had been speaking and he faced them there.

One of the *arrha* arose, an incredibly old *qhal,* withered and bent and leaning on a staff. He stepped down onto the floor where Merir stood.

"You do not belong here," that one said. "Arms have never come into this council. We ask that you go away."

Morgaine did nothing. A look of fear was on all the *arrha* . . . old ones, very old, all those gathered here.

"If we contest for power," said another, "we will all die. But there are others who hold the power we have. Leave."

"My lord Merir." Morgaine walked from the doorway to the center of the room; Vanye followed her: so did the others, taking their place before that council. His distress was acute, that she thus separated herself from the door. There were guards, *arrha,* bearing Gate-force, he suspected. He could not prevail against that. If it came to using her weapons she needed him close to her, where he was able to guard her back . . . where he was not in the way of what had taken at least one comrade of theirs. "My lords," she said, looking about her. "There are enemies advancing. What do you plan to do?"

"We do not," said the elder, "admit you to our counsel."

"Do you refuse my help?"

There was deep silence. The elder's staff rang on the floor and echoed, the slightest tap.

"My lords," she said. "If you do refuse my help, I *will* leave you. And if I leave you, you *will* fall."

Merir stepped forward half a pace. Vanye held his breath, for the old lord knew, knew utterly what she meant, the destruction of the Gate which gave them power, in her passing from this world. And surely he had told the others.

"That which you bear," said Merir, "is greater than the power of all the *arrha* combined. But it was fashioned as a weapon; and that . . . *that* is madness. It is an evil thing. It cannot be otherwise. For fifteen hundred years . . . we have used our power gently. To protect. To heal. You stand here, alive because of it . . . and tell us that if we do not bow to your demands, then you will turn that thing against us, and destroy Nehmin, and leave us naked to our enemies. But if we do as you wish—what, then? What are your terms? Let us hear them."

There was no sound or movement after.

But suddenly other footfalls whispered on the stones at the doorway.

Lellin, and Sezar.

"Grandfather," Lellin said in a hushed voice, and bowed. "Lady . . . you bade me come when the enemy had completed their crossing. They have done so. They are moving this way."

A murmur ran the circuit of the room, swiftly dying, so that the tiniest movement could be heard.

"You have been out doing her bidding," Merir said.

"I told you, Grandfather, that I went to do that."

Merir shook his head slowly, lifted his face to look on Morgaine, on all of them, on the *arrhendim* who had come with Morgaine, and all but Perrin lowered their eyes, unable to meet his.

"You have already begun to destroy us," Merir said. His voice was full of tears. "You offer your way . . . or nothing. We might have been able to defeat the Shiua, as we did the *sirrindim* who came on us long ago. But now we have come to this, that armed force has entered this place, where arms never have come before, and some have faith in them."

"Lellin Erirrhen has said," the elder *arrha* declared, "that he is *hers*, lord Merir. And therefore he insists on coming and going at her bidding, refusing ours."

"Else," Morgaine said in a loud voice, "the council would keep me blind and deaf. And Lellin and Sezar in their service to me have kept me from taking other action, my lords. They know what you do not. By serving me . . . they have served you."

Merir's lips made a taut line, and Lellin looked at the old lord, bowed to him very slowly, and to Morgaine . . . faced his grandfather again. "Of our own choice," Lellin said. "Grandfather—the *arrhendim* are needed. Please. Come and look. They cover the riverside like a new forest. Come and look on this thing." He cast an anguished glance about at all the *arrha*. "Come out of your grove and see this horde. You talk of taking it into Shathan. Of peace with it . . . as we found with the remnant of the *sirrindim*. Come and look on this thing."

"One more dangerous to us," said the elder, "is already here." And Gate-force flared, making the air taut as a drawn string. It shimmered about the elder.

And it grew. One and another of the *arrha* began to bring forth that power, until the *arrhendim* flinched back against the wall, and the whole dome sang with it.

"*Liyo,*" Vanye murmured, and whipped his sword from its sheath, for two of the *arrha* barred the doorway, and the air between shimmered with the barrier they formed.

"Cease!" Morgaine shouted.

The elder stamped the heel of his staff on the floor, a sound almost drowned in the taut air; his half-blind eyes were set rigidly. "Six of us have invoked the power. There are thirty-two. Surrender that which you bear."

"*Liyo.*"

Morgaine slipped *Changeling*'s ring and dropped the sword to her hip. Vanye looked about him, at the elders, at the frightened *arrhendim* . . . and Roh, whose face was pale, but whose hands stayed from his weapons.

"Two more," said the elder. The singing in the air grew louder, numbing hearing, and Morgaine lifted her hand.

"You know what the result will be," she cried.

"We are willing to die, all of us. The passage we open here may be wide enough to work ruin on the enemies of Shathan as well. But you who do not love this land . . . may not be willing to become part of that. One by one we shall add to the force. We do not know how many of us will be needed before the passage is complete, but we shall discover it. You cannot leave. You can try your other weapons. If you do, we will answer you with all we have. Or you can draw that sword and complete the passage beyond any doubt: its force with ours is sufficient beyond any argument. It will drink us all up, and more besides. But surrender that weapon and we shall deal well with you. Our word is good. You have nothing to fear from us."

Gate-force keened in the air. Another joined it.

"*Liyo,*" Vanye said. Very small his voice sounded in that power. "Your other weapon—"

She said nothing. He dared not look at what was happening before her, but kept his eyes to the *arrhendim,* who were at her back and armed; and Roh, Lellin and Sezar were apart from the others, fear in their faces, but they stood with arms folded and had never moved.

"My lords!" Morgaine exclaimed suddenly. "My lord *arrha!* We are gaining nothing by this. Only your enemies gain."

"We have made our choice," said Merir.

"You sat here—sat here until I should become desperate enough to try to come stir you out of it. A trap of your working, lord Merir? It is a well-devised one."

"We are utterly willing," said Merir, "to perish. We are old. There are others. But there is no need of it, unless you value power more than your own life. If we add many more jewels to the web, lady Morgaine, it will be accomplished. You sense that. So do I." He held up his hand, with the jewel-case upon it.

"Here is another mote of that power you hold. Perhaps this will complete it. It is that near. Shall I add it to the others?"

"Enough! Enough. I see that you are capable of doing it. No more."

"Surrender the sword."

She unhooked it and grounded it point-down before her. "My lords of the *arrha!* Lord Merir is right . . . that is an evil thing. And there is only one of it, and that itself is a great evil, and subtle. You hold your power divided into many hands; whoever takes this, that one will be more powerful than all the others. Which? Who of you seeks it?"

None answered.

"You have never seen a Gate opened," Morgaine said. "You have never summoned that power entire, counting that passage dangerous. You are right. Shall I show you? Damp that which you hold: I shall show you my meaning. Let me show you *why* Nehmin must cease to exist. You value reason, my lords; then listen to me. I have no terms. I come not to possess Nehmin by the threat of destroying it. I come to destroy it, whether or not the enemy is stopped. I do not want any power over you."

"You are mad," said the elder.

"Let me show you. Damp the jewels. If I do not convince you, the unveiling of only a few of them while *Changeling* is unsheathed will be sufficient for your purposes . . . and mine. You do not well reckon . . . that I also am willing to die for what I do."

The elder stepped back, bewilderment in his look. Merir made a helpless gesture. "She says well," Merir said, "We can always die."

The force ebbed, more suddenly than it had grown, jewel after jewel winking into cover. And when it was utterly gone, Morgaine eased *Changeling* forth, crystal as the jewels, which were only motes that human flesh itself could obscure unharmed. Opal fire flowed along *Changeling*'s runes, and suffused the blade, and darkness flared at the tip of it, where the wind began. Someone cried out. Its light bathed all their faces. She moved it, and the wind grew stronger, whipping at the torches, tugging at hair and robes and howling within the dome. Vanye stepped back from her side, not even aware that he moved until he found himself near Lellin.

"Here is the passage you would form!" Morgaine shouted over the roar of the wind. "Here it is open before you. Look into it. Have you courage now to add your jewels to that? A few of them would suffice, and this whole dome will be elsewhere, with us in it. The shock of air will level all the trees hereabouts, and perhaps, as you say, take a good part of the enemy with us. Or more than that, if the force leaks through to this side of here and now. This is the power that your fathers' fathers' fathers trifled with. You do well to avoid it. But what will your children do? What, when someday someone less wise than yourselves takes it up again? What, if I surrender the sword to you, and someday one of your folk draws it? On it is written the knowledge of the Gates . . . and it cannot be destroyed, save by one who will carry it unsheathed within a Gate, into the Fires. Who of you wants to go in my place? For any man who loves this world, for any man who holds this weapon and has anything of virtue left in him—there is only one choice in the end—and that is to take it out of this world, forever. Is not a calamity written in your legends? The same calamity fell everywhere that such power has been . . . and it will come again, and again. That power must have an end. Does one of you want the sword? Does one of you want to carry it under those conditions?"

She held it aloft, and the void gaped and howled. Roh was at her back; Vanye saw him, never took his eyes entirely from him. Roh's face was rigid, his eyes reflecting that opal light.

And suddenly Roh moved, fled, thrusting aside Sezar and Lellin, rushed past the *arrha* guards . . . the two of them too dazed to react. Vanye realized his sword was still in his hand. He looked on the others, on faces pale and drawn . . . turned and saw Morgaine. Her arm trembled from that force which numbed body and soul. Sweat stood on her face.

"You must seal it off," she said. "Let me take this out of your world and seal the passage forever after me. Your other choice is not one that Shathan can survive. *This—this—*does not love living things."

"Put it away," Merir said hoarsely. "Put it away, now."

"Have you seen enough? I always questioned the wisdom that made this thing. I know the evil of it. Its maker knew. And perhaps that is its only virtue: that it is shaped as what it is . . . it is something that you can see and know exactly as it is. There is no ambiguity here, no yes and no. This thing ought not to exist. Those delicate jewels of yours . . . are nothing other than this. Their beauty deludes you. Their usefulness deludes you. Someday someone will gather them together and you will know that they were all aspects of *this*. Look. Look at it!"

She swung it in a great arc, faster and faster, and the wind grew until it pulled at them, until the light blazed white, until the void widened and there seemed little air in the room. Cold numbed the skin, and the *arrha* held to their chairs, those standing staggered to the walls as if their own weight could not anchor them.

"Stop it!" the elder cried.

She did so, and returned it to sheath. The winds stopped; the howling died; the dark void and the blazing light went together, leaving the dome darkened, the light of the torches sucked out, only a shaft of daylight reaching them from the door. She grounded the sword, sheathed, before her.

"That is the power you hold, *arrha*. You have but to combine your tiny jewels into one. Did you not know that? We are armed . . . alike. And I make you free gift of that knowledge now—for someday one will discover it, and you will have to use them that way."

"No."

"Can you forget what I have told you?" she asked in a low voice. "Can you forget what you have seen? Can you take the sword and keep it forever sheathed, when the *sirrindim* rise up with cities and threaten you, when Men increase and you are few? Some evil, *qhal* or Man, someday . . . will draw it. And unlike your jewels, which will fade when the Gate is sealed, the sword is knowledge to build more such Gates."

There was deathly silence. Some of the *arrha* wept, their heads bowed into their hands.

"Give it up," Morgaine urged them. "Or leave Nehmin, and come my road, the passage that I must take. I have told you truth. I have shown you. And while Nehmin remains open, that truth will always gape at your feet to swallow you up. Seal up the passage; seal Nehmin and the stones lose their fire and Shathan stands . . . unbarriered, but living. Keep Nehmin open, and you will fall to it one day. But whatever you choose, I have no choice. I must take this sword out of the world. More than Shathan is at hazard. More than your lives. More than this world alone. The evil is as wide as all the passages that ever existed. And it is most dangerous when you think it tamed and secure. Those little stones are more evil than *Changeling* . . . because you do not see them for what they are: fragments of a Gate. Joined, they will drink you in and ruin more than your own world: they will reach to others."

The elder trembled, and looked on the others, and on Merir. Lellin wept, and Sezar, the both of them bowed to the floor; and two by two their brother *arrhendim* joined them.

"We have heard truth," Merir said. "I think we have heard the truth my grandson was quicker to hear."

The elder nodded, his hands trembling so that the staff rattled against the floor. He looked at all the *arrha* about him. There was none to say otherwise.

"Do as you will," he said then to Morgaine. "Pass. We will seal Nehmin behind you."

Morgaine let go a long slow breath, and bowed her head. After a moment she gathered *Changeling* to her side and hooked it there, drew it to her shoulder. "We have a number of Shiua to clear from our path to Azeroth. The enemy, my lords of the *arrha*, is still advancing from the river. What will you do about it?"

There was long silence. "We—must hold, this place and Nehmin. Nehmin is surrounded. The enemy has already taken all the area. We can speak to the *arrha* who hold Nehmin itself; and within the hold of Nehmin, they can work what you ask. You may ride from here. We can give you seven days . . . to reach Azeroth and pass; and then we may kill the power."

"You would fall. Shathan would be utterly open to the Shiua horde."

"We fought the *sirrindim*," said Merir. "The *arrhend* will drive these invaders back too."

Morgaine stared at them, one after another, scanning all the company. And at last she folded her arms and looked at the floor, glanced up at Vanye. He tried to say nothing with his expression. She turned last to Merir. "Will you take my help? I would not leave you with such a gift as waits out there. Aye, Vanye and I could slip past, go another route . . . reach Azeroth in seven days. But what sits out there is—mine. I do not want to leave you to that."

The elder approached her slowly, leaning on his staff. He bowed, deeply, and gazed at her when he straightened, like a man looking into the Gates themselves. "There have been—many passages for you."

"Yes, elder. I am older than you."

"Much so, I suspect." The frail hand reached, touched Vanye's arm, and the dim gray eyes turned to his. "*Khemeis* to such an *arrhen* . . . We sorrow for both of you. For both of you." He looked at Lellin, and bowed, and to Sezar and the other *arrhendim;* and lastly at Merir and Morgaine once more. "You are experienced in wars. We are not. We need you. If you are willing, we need you."

"This, at least, must be on my terms. We consult together."

"We accept that," said Merir.

"You say that you can signal those who now hold Nehmin. Bid them expect me, and soon. You shall hold here, as you can; and they must hold Nehmin until we can reach them. My lord Merir—" she nodded to him to join her, and started to the door, unsteady suddenly; at her side, Vanye felt her lean against him, and took her arm, lending his strength. The sword took, of body and soul; he had held it, and knew the pain of it. "Roh," she said suddenly, distractedly. "Where is Roh?"

He had that worry on him too; there were too many things random, too much slipping their grasp.

But Roh waited outside, a huddled figure at the base of the third standing stone, arms tucked about him. He saw them coming, and rose, torment in his eyes.

"They let you go," he said. "They let you go."

"They agreed," Morgaine said, "to seal Nehmin themselves. That was their choice."

The look went stricken, dazed; they walked past, and Roh followed after.

⌐ Chapter 16

They found the horses still safely in the clearing, with some of the *arrha* watching over them—four *qhal,* male and female, dressed in white, with faces which still were innocent of what had passed in the dome. The *arrha* offered neither courtesy nor resistance, but backed from them in seeming distress as they came close—perhaps there was a mark on all of them, Vanye thought, for there was a grimness about the *arrhendim,* the same fey desperation which had troubled him in Lellin and Sezar: he understood now that bleak, lost manner . . . that of men who had seen the limits of their world.

And of all the *arrhend,* it rested most heavily on Merir.

"My lord," said Morgaine to him. "The *arrhendim*—must be brought here. If we are to save this place—they must be brought. Can you do it?"

The old lord nodded, turned, the reins of the white horse in his hand, and stared in the direction of the river. Even through the trees the roar of many voices could be heard, shouts raised; the horde was on the march.

"I would see this thing," Merir said.

It was madness. But not even Morgaine opposed it. "Aye," she said. "Lellin, Sezar?"

"The hill is still ours," Lellin said. "Or was, lately."

Arrha stood sentinel in the woods, and farther on, in the meadow. "Do not stay here when they come," Morgaine said to the last. "You will only lose your lives. Take shelter with your elders."

They bowed, after their silent fashion. Perhaps they would heed and perhaps not. There was no dispute with men who did not speak.

There rose their own goal, the stony hill at the side of the meadow, and the trail which wound among the trees. The shouts of the horde sounded very near to this place, hardly beyond the screen of trees at the far side of the hill.

They climbed the height on horseback, and rode farther, Morgaine guiding them among the trees which crowned that slope and far to the other side. Rocks were frequent here, a tumbled basalt mass which became a naked promontory, highest of all points hereabouts.

Here Morgaine drew rein and slid down, leaving Siptah to stand. The rest dismounted and tied their horses among the aged trees, and followed her.

Vanye looked back; the last of them rode in, Roh, who left his horse too, and came. Roh might have fled. *Do so,* Vanye wished him with part of his heart;

but that which loved the man knew why he had stayed, and what he sought, that was his soul.

But he did not wait for Roh; what battle Roh fought was his own, and he feared to intervene in it. He turned instead and followed after Sharrn and Dev, up among the rocks.

The hill gave them view across the open meadow, higher than it had seemed, for it overtopped most of the trees at this one point, which upthrust broken fingers of stone. Slabs stood like standing stones on this crest, no work of *qhal*, but of nature. Morgaine and Merir stood between two of them, sheltered there, with the others of their company.

Vanye moved up carefully past Dev to the very brink next to Morgaine, and gained a view which spanned the river and showed far across into the *harilim's* woods, so subtly did the ground hereabouts slope. Trees extended into gray-green haze on all sides of this place, on this side of the river and the other, and even part of the curve of a clearing was visible.

And nearer . . . ugliness moved. It was as Lellin had said, like a new forest grown upon the shores of the Narn, a surging mass bristling with metal-tipped pikes and lances of wood, dark and foul. Occasionally there showed a small *khalur* band, conspicuous in the sunlight glancing off their armor . . . most of those were horsemen. The horde filled all the shore and surged up the throat of the low place that led to the meadow, moving steadily and in no haste. Their voices roared as if from a common throat.

"They are so many," breathed Vis. "Surely there are not so many *arrhendim* in all Shathan. We cannot find that many arrows."

"Or time to fire them," said Larrel.

Morgaine stepped closer to the edge. Vanye seized her arm, anxious, although the distance was far and the chance was small of being seen in this sheltered point against the rocks. She regarded his warning and stopped. "This place," she said, "is impossible to hold, even if we would. The slope on the other side is too wide. This height would become a trap for us. But the enemy's circle is not yet closed. If the *arrhendim* could be brought . . . before they start to work at us with fire and axe, and if we could keep the horde from breaching Nehmin's gates . . ."

"It can be done," said Lellin. "Grandfather, it must."

"We cannot fight," said Merir, "not after their fashion, armored and with horses. We are not like them, of one mind and one voice."

"Yet we must have help," Morgaine said, "of whatever fashion."

"Do not trust—" Roh said, edging forward; Vanye whipped out his dagger and Roh stopped still a distance from Morgaine, leaning against the slanting rock. "Listen to me. Do not trust appearances with the Shiua. I taught them.

Hetharu took the whole north of Shiua in a matter of days. He is a student more apt than his teacher."

"What do you reckon of them?"

Roh looked toward the river, grimacing into the wind and the light. "Eight, ten thousand there, if they extend much beyond that point of the trees. What they have coming in on the other side of Nehmin . . . three times that many. Probably more coming up that little river north of here, until they have us framed. Any riders of ours who try to escape this wedge of land now—will be cut down. They are screened in brush and on every side of us. This—*show*—is to distract us."

"And the higher crossings of the Narn? How many are we dealing with?"

"Believe that Shiua will have reckoned first of those crossings. Every possible escape will be held. And the whole number of the horde . . . that is uncounted; even the *khal* do not know. But they reckon a hundred thousands—all fighters, killers. Even the young ones. They plundered their own land and killed their own kind to come here into this one. A man who falls even to the children will be cut to pieces. Murder is common among them; murder, and theft, and every crime. They will fight; they do that well when they think their enemy helpless."

"Shall we," asked Merir, "believe that advice this one gives?"

Morgaine nodded. "Believe," she said softly, "that this man wishes you well, my lord Merir. His own land was such as Shathan, even more so in the age before him, which he may remember—in his better dreams. Is it not so?"

Roh looked at her, shaken, and reached forth a hand to the rocks, leaning there.

"My lord," said Morgaine, "I do not think even the *arrhendim* could fight with more love of the land than this man."

A moment Merir looked on him. Roh bowed his head, looked up with eyes glittering with tears.

"Aye," Merir said, "aye, I do think so."

The voices from the lower meadow chanted the louder. The sound began to strike them with immediacy, reminder of their danger.

"We cannot stay here," Vanye said. *"Liyo—"*

She stepped back; but Merir lingered, and unslung the horn which he carried . . . silver-bound and old and much cracked.

"Best you get to horse," said the old lord. "We are bound to attract notice.— It is a strange law we have, stranger-friends, . . . that no horn shall ever be blown in Shathan. And yet we do keep them, silent though they have been these fifteen hundred years. You asked the *arrhendim* be summoned. Get you to horse."

She looked beyond him, to the horde which swarmed toward the hill. Then she nodded, started back quickly with the others. Only Lellin and Sezar stayed.

"We shall not leave them," said Sharrn.

"No," Morgaine agreed. "We shall not. Ready their horses for them; I think we shall have a hard ride leaving this place."

They reached the horses and mounted up in haste.

And of a sudden came a low wailing that grew to the bright, clear peal of a horn. Vanye looked back. On the height they had quitted Merir stood, and sent forth a blast which rang out over the meadow . . . exhausted, he ceased, and gave the horn to Lellin, who lifted it to his lips. Uncertain the sound was at first, in the raging shout of the horde who took it for challenge. Then it rang out louder than all the voices of the enemy, woke echoes from the rocks, and sounded again and again and again.

There was silence for a moment; even the voices of the horde were stilled by that.

Then from far away came another horn-call, faint as the wind in leaves. A howl from the enemy drowned it, but the faces of the *arrhendim* were wild with joy.

"Come!" Morgaine shouted at the three, and now they left the high rocks, Lellin and Sezar helping the old lord.

Vanye led the white mare across their path, gave Merir the reins as the two youths helped him into the saddle; then Lellin and Sezar ran for their own horses as Morgaine turned them all for the trail off the hill.

They ran, weaving in and out the trees of the grove, around the rocks; and sudden and chilling came a howl on their right, on the gentle slope of the hill. Shiua were pouring up it toward them.

"*Angharan!*" the cry went up, "*Angharan! Angharan!*"—That to them was Death.

A bolt of red fire came from Morgaine's hand, a single arrow from Perrin's bow. Several of the horde fell, but Morgaine did not stay for more, and Vanye spurred his horse between her and them, bent low for the hazard of branches and answering fire. The down-trail was before them. They hurtled down that winding chute, the horses twisting and turning at all the speed they could manage.

The enemy had not yet reached the point of the hill; at the bottom of the trail Morgaine bent low and headed Siptah for the forest and the path concealed there, and in that moment Vanye cast a look over his left shoulder. There were Shiua aplenty running up the slope of the meadow, foot and riders, demon-helms with barbed pikes and lances.

Sharrn and Dev, Perrin and Vis and Roh: they rode rearguard, and sent a few arrows back. Larrel and Kessun were with Merir, guard to him, for Lellin and Sezar bore no weapons . . . all too vulnerable they were, with three of their number unarmed. But into that arrow-fire which shielded them the Shiua were less than willing to ride.

Vanye had his sword in hand: vanguard, he and Morgaine, and there was no use for his bow in head-to-head meeting. Morgaine would pull ahead of him . . . insisted so, for fear of taking him as she had taken one of their comrades: the black weapon and the sword needed freedom for their effective use; and in *ilin's* place at his lord's left hand, shield-side. Vanye kept there now, as best he could, while they rode a mad course through land that demanded more caution. Branches raked them; horses jostled one another avoiding obstacles or making the turns. But the *khalur* riders, less skilled, hampered with their barbed lances and half-blinding helms, could not follow so swiftly here, and in time the sounds of pursuit faded into distance behind them.

There was a flash of white in the woods; they rounded a curve in the trail and Morgaine drew up suddenly, for there stood two of the *arrha,* young women.

The *arrha* waved them past.

"No," Morgaine said. "You waste yourselves. Even the force of the jewels cannot hold back what is behind us."

"Obey her," Merir said. "Climb up with us. We have need of you."

It was Lellin and Sezar who took them up, being unarmed and least likely to involve them in fighting. The *arrha* took their hands and scrambled lightly to the rear of the saddles. Morgaine started off again, at reckless pace as they crossed the small clearing, quickly slowed by undergrowth as they veered aside from the aisle of stones and the dome.

"This way!" It was the only time that Vanye had ever heard an *arrha* speak; but the young *qhalur* woman behind Sezar pointed them another direction, and Morgaine reined instantly off upon that track.

Swiftly it became a broad way among the trees of an aged grove, cleared ground where their horses could find easy passage, without brush to hinder.

They ran them, weaving when they must, until the horses were blowing with the effort and the trees, darkening their way, grew wider spaced. The Shiua seemed now to have lost their trail. They walked for a time to rest the horses, ran again, slowed again, making what time they could without completely winding the horses.

And suddenly they burst through upon cleared ground, a vast open space, and Vanye forgot all their haste in that instant.

Two hills upthrust, the farther of incredible steepness, although all the clearing else was naked and flat, hazy with distance and the westering sun. A vast hold sat atop that high place, dominating all the land round about, looking down on clearing and on forest, square, a cube such as the great holds of power tended to be.

Nehmin.

And before them on the flat of the vast clearing was mustered the host of

Shiuan, the glitter of arms ascending the side of the rock of the fortress, shining motes, rare in the dark tide of Men, all misty with afternoon haze.

Morgaine had drawn rein yet within the cover of the woods. Dismay seldom touched her face, but it did now. The number of those about Nehmin seemed that of the stones at Narnside. They stretched as a gray surging mass across the floor of the clearing in the far distance, stretched up the farther hill like the waves of Shiuan's eroding seas beating at the rock, tendrils of humanity which straggled among the rough spires and wound constantly higher toward the stronghold.

"*Liyo,*" Vanye said, "let us work round the side of this place. To be caught between that and what already pursues us . . . little appeals to me."

She reined Siptah about so that her back was to the clearing and her face toward the woods from which they had come. There was audible again the distant sound of pursuit. "They *have* us between," she said. "There is ambush everywhere; they have come in by all three rivers. Days—*days*—before the *arrhend* can match this kind of force."

Merir's face was grim. "We will never match it. We cannot fight but singly. In time, each will come, each fight."

"And singly die," Vanye said in despair. "That is madness, to go by twos against that force."

"Never *all* die," said Sharrn. "Not while Shathan stands. But it will take time to deal with that out there. The first to oppose them will surely die, ourselves surely among them . . . and thousands may die, in days after. But this is our land. We will not let it fall to the likes of these."

"But Nehmin may fall," said Morgaine. "Enough force, enough weight of bodies and doors will yield and even the jewel-force cannot long stop them. Their ignorance—let loose in Nehmin—amid the powers *it* holds—no. No, we do not wait here for that to happen. Where, lord, is the access to Nehmin?"

"There are three hills, not apparent from this view; there is the Lesser Horn, there to the side of the greatest hill, a fortress over the road itself: gates within it face this way and the far side . . . that is the way up. Then the road winds high to the Dark Horn, which you cannot see from here, and then to the very doors of Nehmin. We cannot hope to reach more than this nearest and least, the White Hill, before they come on us."

"Come," she said. "At least we shall not be waiting here for them. We shall try. Better that than sitting still."

"They will know that horse of yours, even at distance," Roh said. "There is none such in their company, yours or Lord Merir's."

Morgaine shrugged. "Then they will know me," she said. There was distrust in her look suddenly, as if she had of sudden reckoned that Roh, armed, was at her back in a situation where none could prevent him.

But the sound of pursuit was almost upon them, and she touched the spurs to Siptah and led them forward, circling within the fringe of trees, riding the bow of the clearing.

She meant a run with the White Hill between her and Nehmin, Vanye realized; it was what he would have done, running at the horde on the flat from an angle such that they had cover for at least a portion of their ride.

"They are on us!" Kessun cried; they looked back and the foremost of their pursuers had broken through, riders stringing out in wild disorder, cutting across the open to head them off while they still rode the arc.

But at the same moment Morgaine veered out into the open, and meant to lead them from under the face of that charge, riding for the White Hill.

"Go!" she shouted. "Lellin, Sezar, Merir, ride while you can. We will shake these from our heels and overtake you. The rest of you, stay by me."

Well-done, Vanye thought; the unarmed five of their party had cover enough in which to gain ground; the nine armed had cover in which to deal with these rash pursuers. He disdained the bow: he had no skill at firing from horseback. He was Nhi when he fought, and whipped out the Shiua longsword, at Morgaine's left. Perrin and Vis, Roh, Sharrn, Dev, Larrel and Kessun: their arrows flew and riders went down; and Morgaine's lesser weapon laced red fire across the front of the charge which met them. Horses and riders went down, screaming, and even so a handful broke through. Demon-helms, their barbed lances lowered, with a straggling horde of marshlands foot panting behind.

The charge reached them: Vanye fell to the side Nhi-style, simply not there when the lance passed, and the good horse held steady as he came thrusting up again, blade aimed for that rider. The *khal* saw it coming, horrified, for the lance point was beyond and his sword inside the defense. Then his point drove into the undefended throat and the *khal* pitched over his horse's rump, carried on the force of it.

"Hai!" he heard at his side, and there was Roh, longsword flashing through *khalur* defense—no plains-fighter, the Chya lord, but there was an empty saddle where there had been a *khal* about to skewer him.

Others came on them; one rider pitched from the saddle short of them, a red streak of fire for his undoing. Vanye trusted to Morgaine's aim and took the gift, aiming for the rider hard behind, whose half-helmed face registered horror to find an enemy on him before he expected and his own guard breached. Vanye cut him down and found himself and Roh enmeshed in marshlands rabble. That dissolved in terror at what fire Morgaine sent across their mass, cutting down men indiscriminately, so that dying fell on dead. Grass was burning. The trampling of feet put it out as the horde turned in panic. *Arrhendur* arrows and Morgaine's bolts pursued them without mercy, cutting down the hindmost in windrows of dead and dying.

Vanye wheeled to turn back, chanced to look on Roh's face, which was pale and grim and satisfied. And he turned further and saw Larrel on the ground with Kessun bending over him. From the amount of blood that covered him and Kessun there was no hope he could live; a *khalur* lance had taken the young *qhal* in the belly.

Even as he watched, Kessun sprang up with bow in hand and sent three shafts in succession after the retreating Shiua. Whether they hit he did not see; the *khemeis'* face ran with tears.

"Horses!" Morgaine shouted. "*Khemeis*—get to horse! Your lord needs you!"

Kessun hesitated, his young face twisted with grief and indecision. Then Sharrn ordered him the same, and he sprang to the saddle, leaving his *arrhen* among the Shiua dead. The shock had not yet hit Kessun. Vanye hurt for him, and remembered at the same time that they had two horseless members of their company . . . one, now: Perrin had caught Larrel's.

And Roh came up leading one of the Shiua mounts, even as they started to move. They struck a gallop and held it, and Kessun rode ever and again looking back.

The White Hill lay before them, and their party neared it. Morgaine gave Siptah his head and the gray stretched out and ran with a speed which none of the *arrhendur* horses could match. Vanye dropped back in despair, but he looked on that craggy hill which rose so strangely out of the flat and of a sudden chill hit him as he considered how it seemed to stand sentinel to this approach.

Morgaine wanted the others stopped short of arrowflight of that hill; Merir's group was nearly there, moving at the best speed they could make with two horses carrying double, but she and the gray horse closed on them rapidly, the while they behind labored to stay with her. And she had their attention; the five waited at the last, seeing her desperate to overtake them, and in moments they all closed ranks, out of breath.

"Larrel," Merir mourned, seeing who it was who had fallen. Vanye recalled what Merir had said of a *qhal* dying young, and grieved for that; but he grieved more for the stricken *khemeis* who sat his horse with his hands braced on the saddle and his head bowed in tears.

"Mount up," Morgaine bade the *arrha* shortly; the young women scrambled uncertainly to the ground and Sezar helped them to the horses they were offered. Their handling of the reins was that of folk utterly unused to horses.

"The horses will stay with the group," Roh told them. "Keep the reins in your hands and do not pull back on them. Hold to the saddle if you think you will fall."

The *arrha* were frankly terrified. They nodded understanding, and held on at once when they started to move, the horses hardly more than loping. Vanye looked on the women and cursed, showed them how to turn and how to stop, thinking with horror of what must befall the helpless creatures when they rode full tilt into the Shiua horde. It was all there was time to give them. He shook his head at Roh, and received back a grim look.

"Larrel was only the first," Roh said; and that took no prophecy, for the *arrhendim* were not armed or armored for hand-to-hand. Only he, Roh, and Morgaine could fight that sort of battle. Vanye rode closer to Morgaine, taking his place by habit as much as clear thought; and it was impossible now to avoid the sight that faced them. Gray indistinct lines stretched across their whole horizon, the great rock of Nehmin behind. Their coming was not yet remarked or not yet known for attack: they might as well have been Shiua riders for all the main forces knew. The skirmish had not been seen because of the hill . . . and the approach of thirteen riders to that countless host could hardly seem threatening.

"Look!" cried one of the *arrha*, gazing back, for there was a signal fire lit on the White Hill, a plume of smoke trailing out on the wind.

And that was enough.

The sound that went up from the Shiua horde was like that of the waves of the sea, and their number—the number was unimaginable even to a man who had seen forces in the field and knew how to estimate them: all that the camp on Azeroth had spilled forth, the refuse and scourings of a drowning world. *Khalur* riders poured out toward them, a troop of demon-helms, a cold sheen of metal and a forest of lances in the fading daylight.

Then Vanye doubted their faintest hope of survival, for even if the marsh-landers would flee and confound themselves by their own numbers, the Shiua riders would not: the *khal* knew what they attacked, had made up their minds, and came at Morgaine for hate. A hundred riders, two hundred, three hundred deep and twice that wide; a shout went up, drowned in the thunder of hooves.

And of a sudden Merir drew even with them in the lead, the white mare easily matching strides with Siptah and the bay. "Fall behind," the old lord urged them. "Fall back. Here the *arrha* and I are worth something, if anywhere."

Morgaine began to do so, falling back more and more, though Vanye shuddered at the sight of the old lord, out to the fore of them, and the frail white-robed *arrha* joining him in the face of those lances. Merir and his companions spread wide, and the horses shied with the *arrha* as Gate-force suddenly shimmered about them; one lost her seat and fell, a stunning blow; but the one on the horse which had been Larrel's rode still with Merir.

The downed *arrha* scrambled for her feet, scraped and shaken, childlike in her size and her helplessness. Vanye rode down on her and in a desperate maneuver leaned from the saddle and seized the back of the clothing as they seized the prize in riders' games in Kursh . . . dragged the bemused girl belly-down across his saddle and kept going. Morgaine cursed him bitterly for his madness, and he flung her back a look of anguish.

"Stay with me," Morgaine shouted at him. "Throw her off if you must; stay with me."

"Hold on," Vanye begged of the *arrha;* he could not do more for her. His horse was already laboring with that added burden. But the frail child struggled to rise, pounding her taut fist on his leg, until at last he realized that she yet held the jewel and wished him to know it. She was sore hurt; he thrust his sword into sheath and hauled her up with one hand by her robes, knowing what pain the saddle must be giving her. Thin arms went about his neck, held desperately: she dragged at one side and he leaned to the other. She flung a leg across his, relying on his balance with more courage than he had expected. The Shathana horse held steady with this shifting, staggered only a little, and when she had gained a hold he suddenly felt the queasiness of Gate-force about them: the *arrha* had unleashed the power of her jewel.

He knew then what she wanted of him, and used the spurs, aimed himself forward with all the speed the horse had left . . . defying Morgaine's direct order for one of a few times in their partnership. He pulled out to the side at the interval of Merir and the other *arrha,* hearing someone coming hard yet farther over; and it was, as he had thought . . . Morgaine.

He gasped and the horse staggered as they joined that bridge of force, but the little *arrha* held tightly and he blinked his eyes clear as the serried line of lances came at them, near and distinct, like a forest horizontal.

It was madness. They could not hit that mass and live.

Senses denied it, even while the terror of Gate-force ripped the air along the line they held. He thought of *Changeling* added to that, and that frightened him the more; but Morgaine did not draw it. The red fire of her lesser weapon laced across the charge, merciless to horse and rider. Animals went down in a line; those behind tumbled after in a screaming tangle; and others went round them, some falling, but not enough. The lances came into their very faces.

Vanye leaned aside as the Gate-force hit the rank like a scythe, tumbling horses and riders in the area of crossing forces; but the few riders nearest stayed ahorse, unaffected, flashing past most too dazed to strike well. Vanye could but lean and evade. A blade rang on his helm and shoulder as he bowed over the saddle and shielded the *arrha* as best he could. The horse stumbled badly, recovered by a valiant effort, and they rode over corpses and the unconscious; he was hit more than once, and then they broke into the clear, the horses running. Morgaine drew ahead of him, Siptah taking free rein for a space, with the marshlanders ahead of her. The rabble tried to hold their ground; a hedge of braced spears barred her way. Then *Changeling* flashed into the open, a force that hit his nerves and sent the horse staggering even at this distance. It stopped; the *arrha* had shielded her own. For an instant he thought himself clear.

Then a hoarse shout warned him. He hurled the *arrha* off as he wheeled and leaned, holding to the mane only. Roh was there, and Lellin, and the rider that thundered past spun off over his horse's tail. More Shiua came on. Vanye gained his seat and whipped out his sword, feeling his backing horse stumble over a body, recover under the brutal drive of the spurs.

Hetharu. He saw the *khal*-lord coming down on him ahead of a trio of riders, and tried to gather himself to meet that charge. But Roh was already flashing past him, sword to sword with the *khal* with a shock of horse and metal, and Vanye veered instead for the rider at Hetharu's right—swordsman likewise. The halfling shouted hate and cut at him; Vanye whipped the sword aside and cut for the neck, knowing the man at the last instant: Hetharu's *akil*-drugged minion. He grimaced in disgust and reined about for the two that had sped behind him, expecting attack on his flank, but *arrhendur* arrows had robbed him of those. Roh needed no help; in his jolted vision he saw Hetharu of Ohtij-in flung nigh headless from the saddle, and themselves suddenly in a wide area where only corpses remained, corpses, a scattering of dazed men and horses only beginning to recover, and a handful of *arrhendim,* and the main body of the horde yet hazy with distance.

He reined full about in desperation, seeking Morgaine—but he saw her then beyond them, she, and Merir, and a wide area where no dead lay and their enemies were in confused retreat. *Changeling's* shimmer glowed moon-pale in the twilight, and his arm ached in sympathy, for he knew well what it was to wield it.

Then he recalled another companion, and looked right, turning his horse . . . saw with a pang of shame the little *arrha*, her white garments torn and bloody, who had gained her feet and caught one of the dazed horses. She could not reach the stirrup; the horse shied from her. Sezar reached her before any other, reached across the saddle from the other side and pulled her up. Then Vanye called to the rest of them and they started moving forward anxious to close the interval between themselves and Morgaine and Merir, for the Shiua were recovering themselves and their clear space was about to be invaded.

But Morgaine did not delay for them. Once she saw them coming she reined about and spurred Siptah into a charge, knifing toward the regrouping Shiua foot, driving them before her as they had scattered the first time. Arrows flashed about them, brief and short of the mark; the fleeing Shiua did not delay to fire again.

The Lesser Horn loomed now distinct and near, rising out of the twilight; a road led up to it, and marshlanders and Shiua humans scattered off it as they came. Some lingered to die, whirled away into that darkness at *Changeling's* tip;

more fled, even casting down weapons in their terror, scrambling down the rocks at the side of the road.

A vast gateway was open before them, and a dark interior with yet another open gate beyond, showing road and rocks in the fading light. Morgaine rode for that narrow shelter, and Merir beside her, the rest of them following in desperate haste, for arrows began to rattle on the stones about them. Then they gained the refuge, finding it empty—a fortress, of which the doors were splintered and riven, the near ones and the far. The horses skidded on the stone floor, hooves bringing echoes off the high arch above them, and stopped, hard breathing. Roh came in; and Lellin and Sezar; and Sharrn and Kessun and Perrin, the *arrha* with them. Vis came last and late. Perrin leaned from the saddle to embrace her, overwhelmed with relief, though the *khemein* was bloody and hurt.

"Dev is not coming," said Sharrn; tears glistening on the old *arrhen's* face. "Kessun, we must make a pair now, we two."

"Aye, *arrhen*," said Kessun steadily enough. "I am with you."

Morgaine rode slowly to the gate by which they had entered, but the Shiua seemed to have hesitance to charge the fortress, and had fallen back again. She found *Changeling's* sheath and despite the tremor of her arm, managed to slide the blade in and still the fire. Then she leaned forward on the saddle, almost fell. Vanye dismounted and came to her side, reached up and took her down into his arms, overwhelmed with fear for her.

"I am not hurt," she said faintly, though sweat beaded her face. "I am not hurt." He sank down on his knees with her and held her tightly until the trembling should leave her. It was reaction, the pain of the sword. They all settled, content for the moment simply to draw breath. The old lord was almost undone, and the little *arrha* lay down quietly sobbing, for she, like Sharrn and Kessun, was alone.

"Doors." Morgaine murmured suddenly, trying to gather herself. "Better see if there is any stir outside."

"Rest," Vanye said, and rose and left her, picking his way back to the riven farther door of the fortress. There was little means to close those gates now, little left of them but splintered wreckage. He looked at what lay farther, a road up the height, winding turns indistinct in the gathering dusk. Sight of enemies there was none.

"Lellin," Morgaine said elsewhere, and timbers crashed. She was on her feet by the other doorway, that by which they had entered, trying to move it alone. Lellin rose to help her; Vanye came to assist; others gathered themselves up, exhausted as they were. Down on the flat, in the gray distance across the clearing, there was a force massing, riders gathering, sweeping up the horde of foot and forcing them on, driving them rather than leading.

"Well," Roh said hoarsely, "they have learned. That is what they should have done before now, put the weight of bodies against us. Too late for Hetharu. But some other leader has taken them now, and they care not how many human folk they lose."

"We must get these doors closed," Morgaine said.

The hinges were broken; the doors, thick at the edges as a man's arm, grated over the stone and bowed alarmingly close to coming apart as they threw their strength against them. They moved the other half as well, and that was too free at one point, for one hinge still held, but it too grated into place, with daylight between.

"That big timber," Roh said, indicating a rough, bark-covered log which had been an obstacle in the hall, amid the other fallen beams. "Their ram, doubtless. It can brace the center."

It was the best they had. They heaved it up with difficulty, braced it hard; but the broken gates could hardly stand long at any point if the Shiua brought another ram against it. The doors were a lattice of splinters, and though they braced them up with beams and debris from the rear doors, they could not stop them from bowing at their weak points, even to one man's strength.

"It is not going to hold," Vanye declared in despair, leaning head and arms against it. He looked at Morgaine and saw the same written on her face, exhausted as she was, her face barred with the half-light that sifted through their barricade.

"If," she said in a faint voice, "if those higher up this hill have not attacked us down here it can only be for one cause: that they see the others coming. They are waiting for that, to hit us from both sides at once and pin us here. And if we do not stop them from attacking Nehmin itself, then ultimately they can batter down its gates. Vanye, we have no choice. We cannot hold this place."

"Those down below will be on our heels before we can engage those above."

"Should we sit and die here, to no account at all? I am going on."

"Did I say I was not? I am with you."

"Get to horse, then. It is getting dark, and we dare not waste the little time we have."

"You cannot go on wielding that sword. It will kill you. Give it to me."

"I shall carry it while I can." Her voice went hoarse. "I do not trust it near Nehmin. There is danger that you might not feel, a thing one senses in the sound and feel of it . . . a limit of approach. A mistake would kill us all. If it comes to you—avoid the jewels . . . avoid them. And if someone stirs up the forces channeled through the fortress—I hope you feel it in time. It would tear this rock apart, unsheathed." She thrust herself from the gateway and sought Siptah's side, took up the reins. "Stay with me."

Others began to go to their horses, weary as they were, determined to come with them. Morgaine looked about at them and said nothing. Only at Roh she looked long and hard. In her mind surely was Nehmin itself—and Roh for their companion.

Roh averted his eyes and looked instead toward their fragile barricade. The sounds of the horde were louder, the enemy almost at the foot of the road, by the sound of it. "I can keep a ram away from that barrier a little time. At least they will not be on your backs. That will give you a chance."

Vanye looked at Morgaine, wishing otherwise, but Morgaine slowly nodded. "Aye," she said, "you could do that."

"Cousin," Vanye said, "do not. You can buy too little time for your life."

Roh shook his head, desperation in his eyes. "You mean well; but I will not go up there while there is any use for me here. If I went up there, near *that* . . . I think I would break my word. There is some use for me here . . . and you underestimate my marksmanship, Nhi Vanye i Chya."

Vanye understood him then, and embraced him with a great pain in his heart, then turned and hurtled himself into the saddle.

Sezar cried out sudden warning, for there was the sound of a force advancing not only up out of the valley, but down off the height, coming down upon them.

Only Perrin and Vis stayed afoot, leaning on their bows. "Here is work for more than one bowman," Perrin said. "Three of us just might be able to change their minds; besides, if some pass you, we can keep them from Roh's back."

"Your blessing, lord," Vis asked, and Merir leaned down and took the *khemein's* half-gloved hand. "Aye," he said, "on you all three."

Then he broke away, for Morgaine turned Siptah's head and rode into the gathering dusk. Vanye followed closely, too wrapped now in their own fate to mourn others. Even for them it was a matter of time: Lellin and Sezar were with them, weaponless; the little *arrha* rode with them, bloodied and scarcely clinging to her saddle, but she stayed with Merir; and Sharrn and Kessun with their bows . . . the only two armed now but themselves.

"How far?" Morgaine asked of the *arrha*. "How many turns before the Horn? How many from there to the fortress of Nehmin itself?"

"Three before the Dark Horn; more after . . . four, five; I do not clearly remember, lady." The *arrha's* voice was hardly audible in the sounds about them, a painful breach of habitual silence. "I have only been here once."

Rocks hove up on either side of them in the near-darkness, making a wall on their left, sometimes falling away sharply to the right, so that they looked down a darkening fall to the flat. There was no more sound from above them, while shouts came distantly from the gray masses which surged toward the Lesser Horn.

Then the rocks began to rise on their right as well as on their left, and they must venture a steep, dark winding.

"Ambush," Vanye muttered as they approached that. Morgaine was already reaching for *Changeling*.

Suddenly rock hurtled down, bounding and thundering from above, and the horses shied in terror. *Changeling* whipped the air and wind howled, cold, sucking at them in that narrow chute. The moaning drank the thunder: the only rock to come near them plummeted down on their very heads and went elsewhere. Sweat ran down Vanye's sides beneath the armor.

Siptah leaned into a run; they pressed forward with arrows hailing down like invisible wasps, but the overhang of the cliff and *Changeling's* wind sheltered them from harm.

It was when they made the turning and faced the height that the arrows came truly; Morgaine held the fore, and the sword shielded them all, hurling the arrowflight into nothingness, the winds sucking such few as passed into forceless impacts. Men with wooden spears opposed them and Morgaine hit those ranks with a sweep that cleared Men and weapons elsewhere, flung them screaming into dark, and what remained Vanye caught, closer to *Changeling's* howling dark than ever he liked to come: he felt the cold himself, and Morgaine struggled to press Siptah as close to the outer margin of the road as she could, rather than risk him.

Panic seized the Shiua remaining; they turned their backs and began to flee up the road, and on them Morgaine had no mercy: she pursued them, and in her wake no bodies remained.

Blackness waited beyond the turn, the shadow of the Dark Horn itself, upthrust against the sky, a wide flat a bowshot across where the road turned and enemies massed.

Suddenly Kessun cried warning at a rattle of rock behind, for enemies poured off the rocks at their left flank, cutting them off from retreat.

Witch-sword and plain steel: they held an instant; then Morgaine began to back against the rock of the Horn. These Shiua did not break and run: *"Angharan!"* they cried, knowing Morgaine, voices hoarse with hate. With pike and staff they pressed forward, demon-helms on the one side and marshlands rabble on the other.

There was no more retreat. Lellin and Sezar, Sharrn and Kessun, had snatched themselves weapons such as they could off the dead, wooden spears and barbed lances. They set their backs against the jumbled rock of the Horn, the horses backed almost against it, and held, the while *Changeling* did its dread work.

Then there was respite, a falling back, the enemy seeming exhausted, dazed by the lessening of their ranks, and raw abrasion of Gate-force loose in the area: hearing dimmed, skin seemed raw, breath seemed close. A man could bear that only so long.

So could its wielder. Vanye spurred forward as the retreat spread, thinking

Morgaine would attempt it, but she did not; he checked his impulse at once, appalled when he saw her face in the opal light. Sweat beaded her skin. She could not sheath the sword. He pried it from her fingers and felt the numbing force in his own bones, worse than it was wont to be. With that gone, she simply slumped against Siptah's neck, undone, and he stayed beside her, the sword yet naked, for he wished to give their enemies no encouragement by sheathing it.

"Let us try," said Merir, moving up beside. "Our force added to yours. We might have distance enough here."

Morgaine sat up and shook her white hair back. "No," she exclaimed. "No. The combination is too dangerous. It might still bridge, take us all, perhaps. No. And stay back. Your kind of barrier cannot turn weapons. We have seen that. You and the *arrha*—" She looked about, for the *arrha* was not with Merir. Vanye cast a quick look back too, and saw the small white figure poised halfway up the black rock, perched there forlornly . . . horse lost in the melee. "See she stays there," Morgaine said. "Lord, go back, go back against the rock."

Then came a booming from far below, echoing up the height. Even the murmur of the enemy fell silent, and the faces of the *arrhendim* were for an instant bewildered.

"Ram," Vanye said hoarsely, shifting his grip on *Changeling*'s dragon-hilt. "The Lesser Horn will fall quickly now."

A shout arose from the enemy; they had also understood the sound and the meaning of it.

"They will wait now," Lellin judged, "till they can come at us with the help of those from the flat."

"We ought to carry the attack to these uphill of us," Morgaine said. "Sweep them from our path and try to reach Nehmin's doors."

"We cannot," Vanye said. "Our backs are at least to rock and we can hold that turning. Higher up—we have no guarantee there is a place to stand."

Morgaine nodded slowly. "If they grow cautious of us, we may last a little time—maybe long enough to make a difference for the *arrhend*. At least we carry food and water. Matters could be worse."

"We have not eaten today," Sezar exclaimed.

Morgaine laughed weakly at that, and others smiled. "Aye," she said. "We have not. Perhaps we should take the chance."

"A drink at least," said Sharrn, and Vanye realized the parchment dryness of his own throat, his lips cracked. He sipped at water of the flask Morgaine offered him, for he did not sheath the sword. And another flask went the rounds, fiery stuff that lent a little false warmth to shock-chilled bodies. In their lasting freedom from attack, Sezar broke a journeycake or two which they passed about; and Kessun went over to the *arrha* on her lonely perch, but she accepted only the drink, refusing the food.

Anything of substance lay cold in the belly, indigestible; only the *arrhendur* liquor lent any comfort. Vanye wiped his eyes with the back of a bloody hand and suddenly became aware of silence.

The ram had ceased.

"Soon now," Morgaine said. "Vanye, give me back the sword."

"*Liyo—*"

"Give it to me."

He did so, hearing that tone; and his arm and shoulder ached, not alone from the shocks they had endured, but from the little time he had held it. It was worse than ever it had been. *Jewel-force,* he thought suddenly, *in the fortress above us. Someone has one unmasked.*

And then with comforting clarity: *They know that we are here.*

Not yet did the enemy come on them. There was a growing murmur from below, from the part of the trail which wound below the Dark Horn. The sound came nearer and louder, and now their enemies above rallied, waiting eagerly.

"We simply hold," Morgaine said. "Stay alive. That is all we can do."

"They come," Kessun said.

It was so. The dark mass of riders thundered up the road in the dark. *They have erred,* Vanye thought with grim joy; *they choose speed over numbers.* And then he saw the number of them and his heart sank, for they packed the road, filled it, coming on them leftward as the marshlanders surged forward on the right, slower than the riders who plunged between.

Demon-helms, white-haired riders, and pikes and lances beyond counting in the moonlight . . . and there was one bareheaded.

"Shien!" Vanye shouted in rage, knowing now who it was who had broken Roh's defense, though Roh had spared him once. He checked his impulse on the instant: he had other concern, Shiua arrows on their flank. Morgaine fended those away, though one hit his mailed ribs and nigh drove the breath from him. Sharrn and Kessun spent their last several shafts in the other direction, into the riders . . . spent them well; and Lellin and Sezar gave good account of themselves with Shiua pikes. But constantly they were forced back against the rocks.

A charge surged at them. Shien was the heart of it, and he came hard, seeing them without retreat. Horsemen plunged about them and Morgaine drove Siptah for the midst of them, aimed at Shien himself. She could not; man and rider *Changeling* took, but there were ever more of them, more pouring up the road, deafening clamor of steel and hooves.

They were done. Vanye kept at her side, doing what he could; and only for an instant in the shying of a demon-helm from attack was there an opening. He rammed the spurs in with a manic yell and took it, broke through, swung an arm which itself was lead-weighted with sword and armor, but he was suddenly without hindrance.

Shien knew him: the *khal*-lord's face twisted in grim pleasure. The blade swung; rang off his, his off Shien's in two passes. His exhausted horse staggered as Shien spurred forward and he lurched aside and felt the blade hit his back, numbing muscles. His left arm fell useless. He drove up straight-armed with his blade with force enough to unseat his elbow, and it grated off armor and hit flesh. Shien cried a shriek of rage and died, impaled on it.

Gate-force swept near, Morgaine by him. The wind out of the dark took the man who came at him; the face went whirling away into dark, a tiny figure and lost. He reeled in the saddle, and while the reins were still tangled in the fingers of his left hand, the arm was lifeless, the horse unguided. Siptah shouldered it back; it staggered and turned with that shepherding as Morgaine tried to set herself twixt him and them.

Then her eyes fixed aloft, toward the Horn.

"No!" she cried, reining back. Vanye saw the white-robed *arrha* who stood with one arm thrust up, the shapes of men crawling up the height to reach her; but the *arrha* looked not at them, but to Morgaine, fist extended, white wraith against the rock.

Then light flared, and dark bridged from *Changeling's* tip to the Horn, cold and terrible. Rocks whirled away vast and then eye-wrenchingly small; and riders and horses, debris sucked screaming into a starry void. The white form of the *arrha* glowed and streamed into that wind, vanished. Abruptly light went, all save *Changeling* itself, while the earth shook and rumbled.

Horses shied back and forward, and part of the road went. Rock tumbled over the side, taking riders with it; rock tumbled from the height, and poured over the edge. Those riders nearest cried out in terror, and Morgaine shrieked a curse and whipped a blow that took the man nearest.

Few Shiua remained; they fled back, confounding themselves with the marshlanders. And Vanye cast his sword from his bloody fingers; with his right hand he dragged the reins from his useless left and kept with her.

Some of the enemy attempted the slide itself, scrambling down the unstable rocks to escape; some huddled together in desperate defense, and a few of their own arrows returned from *arrhendur* bows shattered that.

There was silence then. The balefire of *Changeling* lit a place of twisted bodies, riven rock, and seven of them who survived. Kessun lay dead, held in Sharrn's arms: the old *arrhen* mourned in silence; the *arrha* was gone; Sezar had taken hurt, Lellin trying with shaking hands to tear a bandage for the wound.

"Help me," Morgaine asked in a broken voice.

Vanye tried, letting go the reins, but she could not control her arm to give him the sword; it was Merir who rode to her right, Merir alone of them unscathed; and Merir who took the sword from her fingers, before Vanye could prevent it.

Power . . . the shock of it reached Merir's eyes, and thoughts were born there that were not good to see. For a moment Vanye reached for his dagger, thinking that he might hurl himself across Siptah—strike before *Changeling* took him and Morgaine.

But then the old lord held it well aside, and asked the sheath; Morgaine gave it to him. The deadly force slipped within, and the light winked out, leaving them blind in the dark.

"Take it back," Merir said hoarsely. "That much wisdom I have gained in my many years. Take it back."

She did so, and tucked it against her like a recovered child, bowed over it. For a moment she remained so, exhausted. Then she flung her head back and looked about her, drawing breath.

It was utter wreckage, the place where they had stood. No one moved. The horses hung their heads and shifted weight, spent, even Siptah. Vanye found feeling returning to his back and his fingers, and suddenly wished that it were not. He felt of his side and found riven leather and parted mail at the limit of his reach; whether he was bleeding he did not know, but he moved the shoulder and the bone seemed whole. He dismounted and limped over to pick up his discarded sword.

Then he heard shouting from the distance below, and the heart froze in him. He returned to his horse and mounted with difficulty, and the others gathered themselves up, Sharrn delaying to take a quiver of arrows from a marshlander's corpse. Lellin gathered up a bow and quiver, armed now as he preferred. But Sezar was hardly able to get to the saddle.

The sound was coming up from the foot of the road. It roared like the sea on rocks, as wild and confused.

"Let us ride higher," Morgaine said. "Beware ambush; but that rockfall may or may not have blocked off the road below us."

They rode slowly, the only strength they and the horses had left, up the winding turns, blind in the dark. Morgaine would not draw the sword, and none wished her to. Up and up they wound, and amid the slow ring of the horses' shod hooves there were sounds still drifting up at them out of the night.

A great square arch loomed suddenly before them, and a vast hold built of the very stone of the hill. Nehmin: here if anywhere there should be resistance, and there was none. The great doors were scarred and dented with blows, a discarded ram before them, but they had held.

Merir's stone flashed once, twice, reddening his hand.

Then slowly the great doors yielded inward, and they rode into a blaze of light, over polished floors, where a thin line of white-robed *arrha* awaited them.

"You are she," said the eldest, "about whom we were warned."

"Aye," Morgaine said.

The elder bowed, to her and to Merir, and all the others inclined themselves dutifully.

"We have one wounded," Morgaine said wearily. "The rest of us will go outside and watch. We have advantage here, if we do not let ourselves be attacked by stealth. By your leave, sir."

"I will go," said Sezar, though his face was drawn and seemed older than his years. "You shall not," Lellin said. "But I will watch with them for you."

Sezar nodded surrender then, and slipped down from his horse. If there had not been an *arrha* close at hand, he would have fallen.

ᴄ᷒ **Chapter 17**

Cold wind whipped among the rocks where they sheltered, and they wrapped in their cloaks and sat still, warmed by hot drink which the *arrha* brought out to them—fed, although they were so bloody and wretched that food was dry in the mouth. *Arrha* tended their horses, for they were hardly fit to care for them themselves; Vanye interfered in that only to assure himself that at least one of them had some skill in the matter, and then he returned to Morgaine.

Sezar joined them finally, supported by two of the young *arrha* and wrapped in a heavy cloak; Lellin arose to rebuke him, but said nothing after all, for joy that he was able to have come. The *khemeis* sank down at his feet and Sharrn's and rested against their knees, perhaps as warm as he would have been inside and fretting less for being where they were.

Morgaine sat outermost of their group, and looked on them little; generally she gazed outward with a bleak concentration which made her face stark in the glare from Nehmin's open doors. Her arm was hurting her, perhaps other wounds as well. She carried it tucked against her, her knees drawn up. Vanye had moved into such a position that he blocked most of the wind, the only charity she would accept, possibly because she did not notice it. He hurt; in every muscle he hurt, and not alone with that, but with the anguish in Morgaine.

Changeling had killed, had taken lives none of them could count; and more than that—it had taken yet another friend; that was the weight on her soul now, he thought: that and worry for the morrow.

There was still the tumult on the field below . . . sometimes diminishing, sometimes increasing as bands surged toward the rock of Nehmin and away again.

"The road must surely be blocked with the stonefall," Vanye observed, and then realized that would remind her of the *arrha* and the ruin, and he did not want to do that.

"Aye," she said in Andurin. "I hope." And then with a shake of her head, still staring into the dark: "It was a fortunate accident. I do not think we should have survived otherwise. Fortunate too . . . Fortunate too . . . there were none of us in the gap twixt *Changeling* and the *arrha*."

"You are wrong."

She looked at him.

"Not fortunate," he said. "Not chance. The little *arrha* knew. I bore her across the field down there. She had great courage. And I believe she thought it through and waited until it had to be tried."

Morgaine said nothing. Perhaps she took peace of it. She turned back to the view into the dark, where cries drifted up fainter and fainter. Vanye looked in that direction and then back at her, with a sudden chill, for he saw her draw her Honor-blade. But she cut one of the thongs that hung at her belt-ring and gave it to him, sheathing the blade again.

"What am I to do with this?" he asked, thoroughly puzzled.

She shrugged, looking for once unsure of herself. "Thee never told me thoroughly," she said, lapsing into that older, familiar accent, "for what thee was dishonored . . . why they made thee *ilin*, that I know; but why did they take thy honor from thee too? I would never," she added, "*order* thee to answer."

He looked down, clenching the thong taut between his fists, conscious of the hair that whipped about his face and neck. He knew then what she was trying to give him, and he looked up with a sudden sense of release. "It was for cowardice," he said, "because I would not die at my father's wish."

"Cowardice." She gave a breath of a laugh, dismissing such a thought. "Thee?—Braid thy hair, Nhi Vanye. Thee's been too long on this road for that."

She spoke very carefully, watching his face: in this grave matter even *liyo* ought not to intervene. But he looked from her to the dark about them and knew that this was so. With a sudden resolve he set the thong between his teeth and swept back his hair to braid it, but the injured arm would not bear that angle. He could not complete it, and took the thong from his mouth with a sigh of frustration. "*Liyo*—"

"I might," she said, "if thy arm is too sore."

He looked on her, his heart stopped for a moment and then beginning again. No one touched an *uyo*'s hair, save his closest kin . . . no woman except one in intimate relation with him. "We are not kin," he said.

"No. We are far from kin."

She knew, then, what she did. For a moment he tried to make some answer, then as it were of no consequence, he turned his back to her and let her strip out his own clumsy braiding. Her fingers were deft and firm, making a new beginning.

"I do not think I can make a proper Nhi braid," she said. "I have done only my own once and long ago, Chya."

"Make it Chya, then; I am not ashamed of that."

She worked, gently, and he bowed his head in silence, feeling what defied speaking. Long-time comrades, she and he; at least in distance and time as men measured it; *ilin* and *liyo*—he thought that there might be great wrong in what had grown between them; he feared that there was—but conscience in this area grew very faint.

And that Morgaine kri Chya set affection on anything vulnerable to loss— he knew what that asked of her.

She finished, took the thong from him and tied it. The warrior's knot was familiar and yet unaccustomed to him, setting his mind back to Morija in Kursh, where he had last been entitled to it. It was a strange feeling. He turned then, met her gaze without lowering his eyes as once he might. That was also strange.

"There are many things," he said, "we have never reckoned with each other. Nothing is simple."

"No," she said. "Nothing is." She turned her face to the dark again, and suddenly he realized there was silence below . . . no clash of arms, no distant shouting, no sound of horses.

The others realized it too. Merir stood and looked out over the field, of which only the vaguest details could be seen. Lellin and Sharrn leaned on the rocks to try to see, and Sezar struggled up with Lellin's help to look out over the edge.

Then from far away came thin cries, no warlike shouts, but terror. Such continued for a long time, at this point of the horizon and that.

Afterward was indeed silence.

And a beginning of dawn glimmered in the overcast east.

The light came slowly as always over Shathan. It sprang from the east to touch the gray clouds, and lent vague form to the tumbled rocks, the ruin of the great cliffs of Nehmin, and the distant breached gate of the Lesser Horn. The White Hill took shape in the morning haze, and the circular rim of the grove which ringed them about. Bodies of men lay thick on the field, blackening areas of it. Birds came with the dawn. A few frightened horses milled this way and that, riderless, unnatural restlessness.

But of the horde . . . none living.

It was long before any of them moved. Silently the *arrha* had come forth into the daylight, and stood staring at the desolation.

"*Harilim,*" said Merir. "The dark ones must have done this thing."

But then the distant call of a horn sounded, and drew their eyes northward, to the very rim of the clearing. There was a small band gathered there, which began their ride to Nehmin even as they watched.

"They came," said Lellin. "The *arrhend* has come."

"Blow the answer to them," Merir said, and Lellin lifted the horn to his lips and sounded it loud and long.

The horses began in their far distance, to run.

And Morgaine gathered herself up, leaning on *Changeling.* "We have a road to open," she said.

It was a grisly ruin, that tumbled mass on the lower road which had been the Dark Horn. They approached it carefully, and perhaps the *arrhendim* had vision of setting hands to that jumble of vast blocks, for they murmured dismay; but Morgaine rode forward and dismounted, drew *Changeling* from its sheath.

The blade shimmered into life, enveloped stone after stone with that gulf at its tip, and whirled them away otherwise . . . no random choice, but carefully, this one and the next and the next, so that some rocks fell and some slid over the brink and other were taken. Even yet Vanye blinked when it was done, for the mind refused such vision, the visible diminution of that debris whirled away into the void, carried on the wind. When even a small way was cleared, it seemed yet impossible what had stood there before.

They went past it fearfully, with an eye to the slide above them, for Morgaine had taken some care that it be secure, but the whole mass was too great and too new to be certain. There was enough space for them to pass; and below, cautiously, they must venture it again on the lower windings of the road.

The carnage was terrible in this place: the road had been packed with Shiua when the Horn came down, here and in other levels. In some places Morgaine must clear their way through the dead, and they were wary of stragglers, of ambush, by arrow or stonefall, at any moment; but they met none. The lonely sounds of their own horses' hooves rolled back off the cliff and up out of the rocks of the Lesser Horn as they wound their way down to that breached fortress.

This Vanye most dreaded; so, surely, did they all. But it had to be passed. Daylight showed through the broken doors as they rode near; they rode within and found death, dead horses and dead Men and *khal,* arrow-struck and worse. Beams and timbers from the shattered doors were scattered so that they must dismount, dangerous as it was, and lead the horses among Shiua dead.

There lay Vis, her small body almost like a marshlander's for size, fallen among her enemies, hacked with many wounds; and by the far gates was Perrin, her pale hair spilled about her and her bow yet in her dead fingers. An arrow had found her heart.

But of Roh, there was no sign.

Vanye dropped the reins of his horse and searched among the dead, finding nothing; Morgaine waited, saying nothing.

"I would find him," he pleaded, seeing the anger she had not spoken, knowing he was delaying them all.

"So would I," she answered.

He thrust this way and that among the bodies and the broken planks, the crashes of disturbed timbers echoing off the walls. Lellin helped him . . . and it was Lellin who found Roh, heaving aside the leaf of the front gate which had fallen back against the wall, the only one of the four still half on its hinges.

"He is alive," Lellin said.

Vanye worked past the obstacle, and put his shoulder beneath it, heaved it back with a crash that woke the echoes. Roh lay half-covered in debris, and they pulled the beams from him with care, the more so for the broken shaft which was in his shoulder. Roh's eyes were half open when they had him clear; Sharrn had brought his water flask, and Vanye bathed Roh's face in it, gave him a sip to drink, lifting his head.

Then with a heaviness of heart he looked at Morgaine, wondering whether having found him was kindness at all.

She let Siptah stand and walked slowly over in the debris. Roh's bow lay beside him, and his quiver that held one last arrow. She gathered up both out of the dust and knelt there, frowning, the bow clasped in her arms.

Horses were coming up the road outside. She rose then and set the weapons in Lellin's keeping, walking out into the gateway; but there was no alarm in her manner and Vanye stayed where he was, holding Roh on his knees.

They were *arrhendim,* half a score of them. They brought the breath of Shathan with them, these green-clad riders, fair-haired and dark, scatheless and wrapped in dusty daylight from the riven doors. They reined in and dismounted, hurrying to give homage to Merir, and to exclaim in dismay that their lord was in such a place and so weary, and that *arrhendim* had died here.

"We were fourteen when we came into this place," said Merir. "Two of the nameless; Perrin Selehnnin, Vis of Amelend, Dev of Tirrhend, Larrel Shaillon, Kessun of Obisend: they are our bitter loss."

"We have taken little hurt, lord, of which we are glad."

"And the horde?" Morgaine asked.

The *arrhen* looked at her and at Merir, seeming bewildered. "Lord—they turned on each other. The *qhal* and the Men—fought until most were dead. The madness continued, and some perished by our arrows, and more fled into

Shathan among the *harilim,* and there died. But very, very many—died in fighting each other."

"Hetharu," Roh whispered suddenly, his voice dry and strange. "With Hetharu gone—Shien; and then it all fell apart."

Vanye pressed Roh's hand and Roh regarded him hazily. "I hear," Roh breathed. "They are gone, the Shiua. That is good."

He spoke the language of Andur, thickly, but the brown eyes slowly gained focus, and more so when Morgaine left the others to stand above him. "Thee sounds as if thee will survive, Chya Roh."

"I could not do even this much well," Roh said, self-mocking, which was Chya Roh and none of the other. "My apologies. We are back where we were."

Morgaine frowned and turned her back, walked away. "*Arrhendim* can tend him, and we shall. I do not want him near the *arrha,* or Nehmin. Better he should be taken into Shathan."

She looked about her then, at all the ruin. "I will come back to this place when I must, but for the moment I would rather the forest, the forest . . . and a time to rest."

They made an easier ride this time across Azeroth, attended by old friends and new. They camped last beyond the two rivers, and there were *arrhendur* tents spread and a bright fire to warm the night.

Merir had come . . . great honor to them; and Lellin and Sezar and Sharrn, no holding them from this journey; and Roh: Roh, sunk much of the time in lonely silence or staring bleakly elsewhere. Roh sat apart from the company, among the strange *arrhendim* of east Shathan, well guarded by them, although he did little and said less, and had never made attempt to run.

"This Chya Roh," Merir whispered that night, while the remnant of the company shared food together, all but Roh. "He is halfling, aye, and more than that—but Shathan would take him. We have taken some even of the Shiua folk who have come begging peace with the forest, who have some love of the green land. And could any man's love for it be greater than his, who has offered his life for it?"

He spoke to Morgaine, and Vanye looked on her with sudden, painful hope, for Roh's fate had blighted all the peace of these last days. But Morgaine said nothing, and finally shook her head.

"He fought for us," said Lellin. "Sezar and I will speak for him."

"So do I," said Sharrn. "Lady Morgaine, I am alone. I would take this Man, and Dev would not reproach me for it, nor would Larrel and Kessun."

Morgaine shook her head, although with great sadness. "Let us not speak of it again tonight. Please."

*   *   *

But Vanye did, when that night they were alone, in the tent which they shared. A tiny oil lamp lent a faint glow among the shadows. He could see Morgaine's face. A sad mood was on her, and one of her silences, but he ventured it all the same, for there was no more time.

"What Sharrn offered . . . are you thinking of that?"

Her gray eyes met his, guarded at once.

"I ask it of you," he said, "if it can be given."

"Do not." Her voice had a hard edge, quiet as it was. "Did I not say: *I will never go right or left to please you?* I know only one direction, Vanye. If you do not understand that, then you have never understood me at all."

"If you do not understand my asking, hopeless as it is, then you have never understood me either."

"Forgive me," she said then faintly. "Yes, I do. Thee must, being Nhi. But consider him, not your honor. What did you tell me . . . regarding what struggle he has? How long can he bear that?"

He let go his breath and clenched his hands about his knees, for it was true; he considered Roh's moodiness, the terrible darkness that seemed above him much of the time. The Fires were near dying. The power at Nehmin had been set to fade at a given day and hour, and that hour was evening tomorrow.

"I have ordered," Morgaine said, "that his guards watch him with special closeness this night."

"You saved his life. Why?"

"I have watched him. I have been watching him."

He had never spoken with her of Roh's fate, not in all the days that they had spent in the forest about Nehmin, while Roh and Sezar healed, while they rested and nursed their own wounds, and took the gentle hospitality of Shathan's east. He had almost hoped then for her mercy, had even been confident of it.

But when they had prepared to leave, she had ordered Roh brought with them under guard. "I want to know where you are," she had told Roh; and Roh had bowed in great irony. "Doubtless you have stronger wishes than that," Roh had answered, and the look of the stranger had been in his eyes. The stranger was much with them on this ride, even to this last night. Roh was quiet, morose; and sometimes it was Roh and as often it was not. Perhaps the *arrhendim* did not fully see this; if any suspected this shifting, it was likely Merir, and perhaps Sharrn, who knew fully what he was.

"Do you doubt I consider what pain he suffers?" Vanye asked bitterly. "But I have faith in the outcome of this mood of his; and you always have faith in the worst. That is our difference."

"And we would not know until the Fires were dead, whether we should believe one thing or the other," Morgaine said. "And thee and I cannot linger this side to find it out."

"And you do not take chances."

"I do not take chances."

There was long silence.

"Never," she said, "have I power to listen to heart more than head. Thee's my better nature, Vanye. All that I am not, thee is. And when I come against that . . . Thee's the only—well, I would miss thee. But I have thought it over . . . how perhaps if I should harm this man, thee would hate me; that thee would, finally, leave me. And thee will do what thee thinks right; and so must I, thee by heart, I by head; and which of us is right, I do not know. But I cannot let myself be led by wanting this and wanting that. I must be right. It is not what Roh can do that frets me; once the Fires are dead—I hope . . . I *hope* that he is powerless."

I know what is written in the runes on that blade, Roh had said; *at least the gist of it.* The words shot back into his mind out of all the confusion of pain and *akil*, turning him cold to the heart. Little of that time he did remember clearly; but this came back.

"He knows more," he said hoarsely. "He has at least part of *Changeling*'s knowledge."

A moment she stared at him, stark-stricken, and then bowed against her hands, murmured a word in her own lost language, over and over.

"I have killed him," Vanye said. "By telling you that, I have killed him, have I not?"

It was long before she looked up at him. "Nhi honor," she said.

"I do not think I will sleep well hereafter."

"Thee also serves something stronger than thyself."

"It is as cold a bedfellow as that you serve. Perhaps that is why I have always understood you. Only keep *Changeling* from him. What wants doing—I will do, if you cannot be moved."

"I cannot have that."

"In this, *liyo*, I do not care what you will and will not."

She folded her arms and rested her head against them.

The light eventually burned out; neither of them slept but by snatches, nor spoke, while it burned. It was only afterward that Vanye fell into deeper sleep, and that still sitting, his head upon his arms.

They slept late in the morning; the *arrhend* made no haste to wake them, but had breakfast prepared when they came out, Morgaine dressed in her white garments, Vanye in the clothing which the *arrhendim* had provided. And still Roh did not choose to sit with them, nor even to eat, though his guards brought him food and tried to persuade him. He only drank a little, and sat with his head bowed on his arms after.

"We will take Roh," Morgaine said to Merir and the others when they had done with breakfast. "Our ways must part now, yours and ours; but Roh must go with us."

"If you will it so," said Merir, "but we would go all the way to the Fires with you."

"Best we ride this last day alone. Go back, lord. Give our love to the Mirrindim and the Carrhendim. Tell them why we could not come back."

"There is also," said Vanye, "a boy named Sin, of Mirrind, who wants to be *khemeis*."

"We know him," said Sharrn.

"Teach him," Vanye asked of the old *arrhen*. He saw then a touch of longing come to the *qhal*'s gray eyes.

"Aye," said Sharrn. "I shall. The Fires may go, but the *arrhend* must remain."

Vanye nodded slowly, comforted.

"We would come with you," said Lellin, "Sezar and I. Not to the Fires, but through them. It would be hard to leave our forests, harder yet to leave the *arrhend* . . . but—"

Morgaine regarded him, and Merir's pain, and shook her head. "You belong here. Shathan is in your keeping; it would be wrong to desert it. Where we go—well, you have given us all that we need and more than we could ask. We will fare well enough, Vanye and I."

And Roh? The question flickered briefly into the eyes of the *arrhendim,* and there remained dread after. They seemed then to realize, and there was silence.

"We had better go," Morgaine said. From her neck she lifted the chain, and the gold medallion, and gave it back into Merir's hands. "It was a great gift, lord Merir."

"It was borne by one we shall not forget."

"We do not ask your forgiveness, lord Merir, but some things we much regret."

"You do not need it, lady. It will be sung *why* these things were done; you and your *khemeis* will be honored in our songs as long as there are *arrhendim* to sing them."

"And that is itself a great gift, my lord."

Merir inclined his head, and set his hand then on Vanye's shoulder. "*Khemeis,* when you prepare, take the white horse for your own. None of ours can keep up with the gray, but only she."

"Lord," he said, dismayed and touched at once. "She is yours."

"She is great-granddaughter to one who was mine, *khemeis;* I treasure her, and therefore I give her to you, to one who will love her well. The saddle and bridle are hers; Arrhan is her name. May she bear you safely and long. And this more." Merir pressed into his hand the small case of an *arrha*'s jewel. "All these will die in this land as the Fires die. If your lady permits, I give you this . . . no weapon, but a protection, and a means to find your way, should you ever be parted."

He looked at Morgaine, and she nodded, well-pleased. "Lord," he said, and would have knelt to thank him, but the old lord prevented him.

"No. We honor *you. Khemeis,* I shall not live so much longer. But even when our children are dust, you and your lady and my small gift to you . . . will be yet upon your journey, perhaps not even across the simple step you will take this evening. Far, far travelling. I shall think of that when I die. And it will please me to be remembered."

"We shall do that, lord."

Merir nodded, and turned away, bidding the *arrhendim* break camp.

They armed with care for this ride, in armor partly familiar and partly *arrhendur* and each of them had a good *arrhendur* bow and a full quiver of brown-fletched arrows besides. Only Roh went unarmed; Morgaine bound his bow, unstrung, upon her saddle, and his sword was on Vanye's.

Roh seemed not at all surprised when told that they required him to ride with them.

He bowed then, and mounted the bay horse which the *arrhend* had provided him. He yet moved painfully, and used his right hand more than his left, even in rising to the saddle.

Vanye mounted up on white Arrhan, and turned her gently to Morgaine's side.

"Goodbye," said Merir.

"Goodbye," they said together.

"Farewell," Lellin offered them, and he and Sezar were first to turn away, Merir after, but Sharrn lingered.

"Farewell," Sharrn said to them, and looked last on Roh. "Chya Roh—"

"For your kindness," Roh said, almost the first words he had spoken in days, "I thank you, Sharrn Thiallin."

Then Sharrn left, and the rest of the *arrhendim,* riding quickly across the plain toward the north.

Morgaine started Siptah moving south, in no great haste, for the Fires would not die until the night, and they had the day before them with no far distance to ride.

Roh looked back from time to time, and Vanye did, until the distance and the sunlight swallowed up the *arrhendim,* until even the dust had vanished.

And no word had any of them spoken.

"You are not taking me with you," said Roh, "through the Gate."

"No," said Morgaine.

Roh nodded slowly.

"I am waiting for you," said Morgaine, "to say something in the matter."

Roh shrugged, and for a time he made no answer, but the sweat beaded on his face, calm as it remained.

"We are old enemies, Morgaine kri Chya. Why this is, I have never understood . . . until late, until Nehmin. At least—I know your purpose. I find some peace with that. I only wonder why you have insisted on my survival this far. Can you not make up your mind? I do not believe at all that you have changed your intentions."

"I told you. I have a distaste for murder."

Roh laughed outright, then flung his head back, eyes shut against the sun. He smiled, smiled still when he looked at them. "I thank you," he said hoarsely. "It is up to me, is it not? You are waiting for me to decide; of course. You bade Vanye carry that Honor-blade of mine, long since hoping. If you will give it back to me, I think that—outside the sight of the Gate—I shall have the strength to use that gift. Only—*there*—I could not say what I would do, if you bring me close to that place. There are things I do not want to remember."

Morgaine reined to a halt. There was nothing but grass about them, no sight yet of the Gate, nor of the forest, nor anything living. Roh's face was very pale. She handed across to him the bone-hilted Honor-blade, his own. He took it, kissed the hilt, sheathed it. She gave him then his bow, and the one arrow that was his; and nodded to Vanye. "Give him his sword back."

Vanye did so, and was relieved to see that at the moment the stranger was gone and only Roh was with them; there was on Roh's face only a sober look, a strangely mild regret.

"I will not speak to him directly," Morgaine said at Roh's back. "My face stirs up other memories, I think, and perhaps it is best he look on it as little as possible under these circumstances. He has avoided me zealously. But do you know him, Vanye?"

"Yes, *liyo*. He is in command of himself . . . has been, I think, more than you have believed."

"Only with you . . . in Shathan. And with difficulty . . . now. I am the worst possible company for him; I am the only enemy Roh and Liell share. He cannot go with us. Chya Roh, you have knowledge enough it is deadly to leave you here; all that I do would rest on your will to rule that other nature of yours. You might bring the Gate to life again in this land, undo all that we have done, work ruin on us, and on this land."

He shook his head. "No. I much doubt that I could."

"Truth, Chya Roh?"

"The truth is that I do not know. There is a remote chance."

"Then I give you choice, Chya Roh. That you have the means with you and the strength to leave this life: choose that, if you think that safest for you and for Shathan; but if you choose . . . if you can for the rest of your years be strong enough . . . choose Shathan."

He backed his horse and looked at her, shaken for the first time, terror on his face. "I do not believe you could offer that."

"Vanye and I can make the Gate from here; we will wait here until we see you over the horizon, and then we will ride like the wind itself and reach it before you could. There we will wait until we know that you cannot follow. That eliminates the one chance. But the other, that you might do harm here—that rests on Chya Roh. I know now which man is making the choice: Roh would not risk harm to this land."

For a long time Roh said nothing, his head bowed, his hands clenched upon the sword and the Chya longbow which lay across his saddle.

"Suppose that I am strong enough?" he asked.

"Then Sharrn will be glad to find you coming after him," said Morgaine. "And Vanye and I would envy you this exile."

A light came to Roh's face, and with a sudden move he reined about and rode—but he stopped then, and came back to them as they watched, bowed in the saddle to Morgaine, and then rode close to Vanye, leaned across and embraced him.

There were tears in his eyes. It was Roh, utterly. Vanye himself wept; a man might, at such a time.

Roh's hand pressed the back of his neck, bared now by the warrior's knot. "Chya braid," Roh said. "You have gotten back your honor, Nhi Vanye i Chya; I am glad of that. And you have given me mine. Your road I do not truly envy. I thank you, cousin, for many things."

"It will not be easy for you."

"I swear to you," said Roh, "and I will keep that oath."

Then he rode away, and the distance and the sunlight came between.

Siptah eased up next Arrhan, quiet moving of horse and harness.

"I thank you," Vanye said.

"I am frightened," Morgaine said in a still voice. "It is the most conscienceless thing I have ever done."

"He will not harm Shathan."

"And I have set an oath on the *arrha,* that should he stay in this land, they would guard Nehmin still."

He looked at her, dismayed that she had borne this intention secret from him.

"Even my mercies," she said, "are not without calculation. You know this of me."

"I know," he said.

Roh passed out of sight over the horizon.

"Come," she said then, turning Siptah about. He reined Arrhan around and touched heel to her as Siptah sprang forward into a run. The golden grass flew under their hooves.

Soon the Gate itself was in sight, opal fire in the daylight.

⤚ **Epilogue**

It was a late spring . . . green grass covered all of Azeroth's plain, with wildflowers spangling areas gold and white.

And it was an unaccustomed place for arrhendim.

Four days the two had ridden from Shathan's edge, to this place where the land lay flat and empty on all sides and the forest could not even be seen. It gave them a curious feeling of nakedness, under the eye of the spring sun.

Loneliness came on them more when they came within sight of what they had come to find.

The Gate towered above the plain, stark and unnatural. As they rode near, the horses' hooves disturbed stones in the tall grass, bits of old wood, mostly rotted, which remained of a great camp that had once sat at the base of it.

They drew rein almost beneath the Gate, in a patch of sun which fell through the empty arch. Age-pitted it was, and one of the great stones stood aslant, after only so few years. The swiftness of that ruin sent a chill upon them.

The khemeis *of the pair dismounted . . . a smallish man, his dark hair much streaked with silver. An iron ring was on his finger. He looked into the Gate, which only looked through into more of the grassland and the flowers, and stood staring at that until his* arrhen *came walking up behind him and set his hand on his shoulder.*

"What must it have been?" Sin wondered aloud. "Ellur, what was it to look on when it led somewhere?"

The qhal had no answer, only stared, his gray eyes full of thoughts. And at last he pressed Sin's shoulder and turned away. There was a longbow bound to the saddle of Sin's horse. Ellur loosed it and brought it to him.

Sin took the aged bow into his hands, reverently handled the dark, strange wood, of design unlike any made in Shathan, and strung it with great care. It was uncertain whether it had the strength to be fired any longer; it had been long since its master had set hand to it. But one arrow they had brought, green-fletched, and Sin set that to the string, drew back full, aimed it high into the sun.

It flew, lost from sight when it fell.

He unstrung the bow and laid it within the arch of the Gate. Then he stepped back and gazed there a last time.

"Come," Ellur urged him. "Sin, do not grieve. The old bowman would not wish it."

"I do not," he said, but his eyes stung, and he wiped at them.

He turned then, and rose into the saddle to put the place behind him. Ellur joined him. Four days would see them safe in forest shadow.

Ellur looked back once, but Sin did not. He clenched his hand upon the ring and stared straight ahead.

Exile's Gate

∽ Prologue

The qhal found the first Gate on a dead world of their own sun.

Who made it, or what befell those makers, the qhal of that age never learned. Their interest was in the dazzling prospect it offered them, a means to limitless power and freedom, a means to shortcut space and leap from world to world and star to star—instantaneous travel, once qhalur ships had crossed space at real-time, to carry to each new site the technology of the Gates and establish the link. Gates were built on every qhalur world, a web of eyeblink transport, binding together a vast empire in space.

That was their undoing . . . for Gates led not alone where but when, both forward and backward along the course of worlds and suns.

The qhal gained power beyond their wildest imaginings; they were freed of time. They seeded worlds with gatherings from the far reaches of Gate-spanned space . . . beasts, and plants, even qhal-like species. They created beauty, and whimsy, and leaped ahead in time to see the flowerings of civilizations they had planned—while their subjects lived real years and died in normal span, barred from the freedom of the Gates.

Real-time for qhal became too tedious. The familiar present, the mundane and ordinary, assumed the shape of a confinement no qhal had to bear . . . the future promised infinite escape. Yet once a qhal made that first forward journey, there could be no return. It was too dangerous, too fraught with dire possibilities, to open up backtime. There was the deadly risk of changing what Was. Only the future was accessible; and qhal went.

Some went further than certainty, pursuing the hope of Gates which might or might not exist where they were predicted to be built. More lost their courage completely and ceased to believe in further futures, lingering until horror overwhelmed them, in a present crowded with living ancestors in greater and greater numbers. Reality began to ripple with unstable possibilities.

Perhaps some desperate soul fled to backtime, seeking origins or a lost life or a memory; or perhaps at last the very weight of extended time and energies grew too much. Might-have-been and Was were confounded. Qhal went mad, perceiving things no longer true, remembering what had never been true in the worlds which now existed.

Time was ripping loose about them—from ripplings to vast disturbances, the overstrained fabric of space and time undone, convulsed, imploded, hurling all their reality asunder.

Then all the qhalur worlds lay ruined. There remained only fragments of their past glory . . . stones strangely immune to time in some places, and in others suddenly and unnaturally victim to it . . . lands where civilization rebuilt itself, and others where all life failed, and only ruins remained.

The Gates themselves, which were outside all time and space . . . they endured.

A few qhal survived, remembering a past which had been/might have been true.

Last came humans, exploring that dark desert of worlds the qhal had touched . . . and found the Gates.

Men had been there before . . . having been victims of the qhal and therefore involved in the ruin; Men looked into the Gates, and feared what they saw, the power and the desolation. A hundred went out those Gates, both male and female, a mission with no return. There could only be forward for them; they must seal the Gates from the far side of time, one and the next and the next, destroying them, unweaving the deadly web the qhal had woven . . . to the very Ultimate Gate or the end of time.

World after world they sealed . . . but their numbers declined, and their lives grew strange, stretched over millennia of real-time. Few of them survived of the second and third generations, and some of those went mad.

Then they began to despair, for all their struggle seemed hopeless: one Gate omitted anywhere across the web would begin it all again; one Gate, anywhen misused, could bring down on them the ruin of all they had ever done and make meaningless all their sacrifice.

In their fear they created a weapon, indestructible save by the Gates which powered it: a thing for their own protection, and containing all the knowledge they had ever gained of the Gates—a doomsday force against that paradoxical Ultimate Gate, beyond which was no passage at all—or a truth worse than all their nightmares.

They were five when that dreadful Weapon was made.

There was one who survived to carry it.

⌒ Chapter 1

Vision of horses, one gray and shadow, one star-white, both shod for war . . .
one dark rider, one pale, across void and night—

In gray lines, horses and riders appear along the river-ridge, concealed in mist
and the uncertainties of dawn. Weapons bristle up, lower, all in one nightmare
movement of the charge. It is ambush, and below them, humans ride along the
sedge-rimmed river, Ichandren's men, their weapons laid across saddlebows.
Ichandren looks up aghast at the first thin shout, the thunder that comes down
on them in morning mist, the hedge of weapons that materializes out of the
fog. The promised truce is broken, the valley has become a trap into which
shadowy riders pour off either slope.

"Back!" Ichandren yells, wheeling his horse about.

The hindmost of his men shriek and die, pierced by lances, and the riderless
horses splash along the reed-edged banks. The mist is full of shadows, shadows
of enemies, of human riders fleeing in confusion, small bands battling in isolation. Even sound is distorted, echo mingling with present orders, screams
and the clash of weapons ringing off the hills.

Some attempt retreat; but other shadows come pouring out of the mist
behind, and horns sound in wild confusion. Ichandren shouts orders, but there
is no relief, the enemy is too numerous, and his voice is lost in the confusion.

In despair he rallies such of his guard as he can, and turns and drives back
the way he has come, in a world of shades and ghosts.

Vision of horses, the gray and the white, hooves descending, slowly, all of time
and existence suspended upon that single motion—

In the opal dawn, in the mist, arrows fall like black sleet on flesh and steel, and
thunder on wooden shields, finding chinks in the failing defense. Hammer and
hammer again, blow after blow. Horses are down, threshing and screaming,
crushing the wounded and the dead. Men flee afoot, cut down by the sweep of
riders on the perimeters.

There is no more hope. Ichandren has met ambush. The fox has been out-
foxed, and the enemy riders circle, cutting down those few who evade that last
sweep.

But most rally around Ichandren, as horses go down, as men fall.

No arrows now. At the last it is swords and a battle afoot, humans against humans, Ichandren's men against those who have sold their souls to Morund.

"Bron!" Chei ep Kantory cries, seeing his brother fall, his place suddenly vacant in the defensive circle and Morund crests surging against it. He tries to gain those few feet, in that desperate knot about Ichandren, to die shielding his brother, for it is only a question of place now: weight of numbers bows their slight defense and breaks their shield-ring.

But thunder breaks behind him. Chei turns and lifts his sword, but there are two of them, helmed and masked, who come thundering toward him across the brook, throwing a fine spray in the first breaking of the sunlight.

Third stride, the gray horse and the white, stately slow, inexorable as fate—

The solemn procession reaches the killing-ground, the place of execution. They have walked this far, these last survivors of Gyllin-brook. Ichandren is not among them. The fox's head stands on a pike outside Morund-gate, his countenance strangely tranquil after so much he has suffered; and by now the crows will have claimed the eyes, as the crows and the kites have claimed so many, many others.

Carrion crows rise up here, at this end of all roads, black shapes against a pale, sickly sun, dull clap of startled wings that recalls the thunder of hooves on sand—

But that day is done, Ichandren is dead, his men have seen him die, and seen the things done to him, which made his death a mercy.

Now is their own turn. And disturbed birds settle back to the field, one solitary raven pacing on the roadside in the important way of his kind.

"Halt," lord Gault calls out, Gault ep Mesyrun, but this is not the Gault Ichandren knew, the brother in arms he once trusted. This is a different creature, who now holds lordship over Morund Keep. *Qhal* serve him, though his hair is human-dark and his body heavy and of no remarkable stature; the humans in his command fear him greatly. That is the kind of man he has become. And Gault has brought the prisoners here, to this place where crows gather, where the woods grow strange and twisted. He has cause to know this vicinity. In a place not far hence the woods grow strange indeed: no beast will go there, and no bird will fly above the heart of it. By that place Gault holds power over the south.

But they will go no further than this, for this purpose, for the disposal of enemies, here on the boundaries of law and reason. Horses shy and snort at the carrion smell of the place. White bits of bone, scattered by animals, litter the dust of the roadway, beside a bald hill—and on that hill stakes and frames stand against the sky, some vacant, some holding scraps of flesh and bone.

Blows and curses drive the prisoners staggering toward their fate, blows more cruel than the others they have suffered on this march, for even the guards fear this place and are anxious to be away. The prisoners go, bewildered; they climb most of the way up that hill before something, be it courage, be it only the breaking of a fragment of skull under a man's foot, or the regard of one black, beadlike raven eye lifting from its fixation on carrion—breaks the spell, breaks the line, and a man attempts escape. Then horses cut him off, two riders gather him up by the arms and haul him screaming to the hilltop. Other riders, humans with staffs and pikes, rain blows on the rebellion that follows, and drive the remainder to the stakes.

"I shall not leave you destitute," lord Gault follows them to say, riding his red roan horse to the crest, bones breaking under its hooves. "I leave you food. And an abundance of water. Can I do more?"

Chei ep Kantory is one who hears him, but dimly, as a voice among other voices, for the executioners have laid hands on him, as already they have taken Eranel, ep Cnary, Desynd, and red-haired Falwyn who is Ichandren's youngest cousin. He resists, does Chei, as he has been trouble on the march; but repeated blows of a pikestaff bring him down, at the last without a struggle, stunned and waiting only for whatever the enemy will do. The carrion stench is everywhere, his groping hand feels the brittle shards of bone among the silky dust on which he lies, the sky is a white, burning fire and the shadows of devils move across it, press at his body, drag at his booted ankle and clamp a grip about it which does not relax when they let him go.

A man curses. Chei recognizes it for Desynd's voice, distant and strained. Gault's laughter follows it. And because breath has come back to him and the shadows have gone he rolls over onto his hands, flinching from the bones, and tries the chain. Finally, because it is a solidity in so much that is flux, and a protection should the riders have some sport in mind, he huddles against the stake to which he is chained.

By each of them is set a water-skin. By each a parcel of food. And the lord Gault wishes them well, before he and his servants ride away.

Each of the condemned is secured alike, by the ankle to separate weathered posts; and at the fullest stretch of each chain a man is within reach of the man next at the fullest stretch of his. Their hands are not bound and they have their armor, but that is only to prolong matters.

In the evening the wolves come, dilatory, to a prey they have learned to expect when the riders are about. There is no haste. They are a bastard breed, and much of the dog is in them. It is in their eyes, in that way they creep forward, like hounds at hearth seeking some tidbit, with a kind of cunning and bravado neither breed alone would have. They retreat from such missiles as bone-chips and even handfuls of dust, they slink from shouts and threats, but in the long hours of the night they come closer, and rest, tongues lolling, one of them rising now and again to pace the line and to try the temper of this offering, whether any of them has yet weakened or determined to surrender.

By the second evening patience is rewarded. And at full stretch of the chain, in the night, the wolves and the survivors can reach truce, of sorts, while the terrible sounds proceed, of quarrels and the tearing of flesh and the crack of bone.

For the remaining nights, the wolves have leisure.

The horses stride into the world, the dapple gray and the white, in an opal shimmering, stride for stride. Their hooves touch the leafy mold of a forested hillside and their legs stretch, take their weight—like the riders, they are bemazed by the gulf, and chilled by the bitter winds.

The riders let them run. They have no knowledge where they are . . . but they have taken such strides before.

The sun came mottled through a grove of twisted shapes, saplings, trees, blighted as by some perpetual wind . . . such places as this, they had seen before, and they had passed gates before the one which hove up on the hill above them, still powerful, still baneful and flinging power into the heavy air.

The horses ran out their terror, slowed as the trees grew thicker, and walked a gentler course in a forest where, among the trees, stood stones half again taller than horse and rider together. They snorted their acquaintance with a foreign wind and the smell of this world, while the riders went in silence.

But in time they stopped of their own accord, and the riders only listened to the world, the whispering of wind and branch, and looked about them at this strangely twisted place.

"I do not like this," Vanye said, and gave a twitch of his shoulders as he leaned forward against his saddle.

Horses dapple-gray and white, male and female, like the riders: Morgaine in black and silver, Vanye in forester's gray and green, her hair *qhal*-silver and his hair human-hued, pale brown beneath a peaked steel helm, wrapped round the rim with a white scarf . . . that was the look of them. They were lost, except for the road which led them—which they trusted they would find again: for *qhal* whenever they had built, had built much of the same pattern; and to leave the Gate and its confusion was the only thing that mattered, across such a gulf as that void at their backs, that cold nightmare which lay between them and a yesterday—Heaven knew how long lost.

They went armored and armed. Morgaine was liege and Vanye was liege-man; she was—what she was, and he was Man; that was the way of things between them.

"Nor do I care for it," said Morgaine, and started the gray stud moving, a gentle, careful pace.

There was no retreat for them. That, they neither one mentioned. Vanye cast a quick look back, where the thin, spiral-twisted trees hid all view of that great span which was a *qhalur* Gate—little different than other gates they had seen, very like one he had known, in a land like this one—but this was not that land: he knew that well enough, knew it in the patterns of the rare leaves which grew in dispirited clumps at the end of limbs, lit by a wan and (he thought, and time proved) westering sun.

Although the gate behind them stood still powerful, and disturbed the air and worked at the nerves, it could not carry them back, and it could not carry them where they had now to go, or tell them their direction. For now, it was only downslope, from standing stone to standing stone, in a woods as unwholesome as the feeling in the air.

Life here—struggled. What had feet to flee, fled; what rooted, grew twisted and strange, from the trees to the brush, the shoots of which were tormented and knotted, the leaves of which were deformed and often curled upon themselves. And the horses laid back their ears and shook themselves from time to time, likeliest with that same feeling that made the fine hair stand up on the body and made the ears think that there was sound where no sound existed, until they had put more and more of the hill between them and the gate.

They rode in amid a jumble of stones and trees, finally, a leaning conspiracy of broken stone walls and twisted saplings none of which attained great age, but many of which lay rotten or broken by winds.

Vanye looked about him as his white mare danced and fretted beneath him, hooves ringing on half-buried paving in quick, nervous steps, echoing out of time to the pace of the iron-shod dapple gray. "This was a keep of some sort," he murmured, and crossed himself anxiously, forgetting as he forgot in such moments, that his soul was damned.

"A great one," Morgaine answered him, whether that was surmise or sure knowledge; and Vanye blinked and stared round him a second time as the horses moved and the ruin of walls unfolded. "We have found our road again."

Hooves on stone. Buried pavings. Vanye conceived of the Road as a thing of all places, all gates, all skies: it was one Road, and the gates inevitably led to it.

"No sign of men," he murmured.

"Perhaps there are none," Morgaine answered him. "Or perhaps there are."

He took nothing for granted. He gazed about him with a warrior's practiced eye, looking for recognizable points, things by which he could make order out of this jumbled buff and white stone. These flat stretches, these narrower places were the foundations of houses, craftshops, warehouses. People—uncountable numbers of people would have dwelt in such a place, and plied their crafts; but how much land must they till, how feed so great a number in so rough a land, except they take their provender from war and tribute? It did not suggest peace.

He tried to imagine these ruins near him as they might have stood, bare foundations rising into forms which (he could not help it) very greatly resembled the keep and the barracks and the guesting-house of Ra-morij of his birth, in distant Andur-Kursh, a courtyard cobbled and usually having a standing puddle down the middle of it, where the scullery dumped its dirty water. It was gray cobbles in his vision, not the buff stone under the mare's hooves—was an aching touch of home, however cruel it had been in his living there.

He remembered other crossings of that gulf they had just passed, the night he had looked up to see two moons, and constellations strangely warped; that night he had first looked on a sea of black water, among drowning hills; a dawn that had risen and showed him a land unwalled by mountains for the first time in his life, horizons that went on forever and a sky which crushed him beneath its weight. He blinked this ruin about him clear again, in its desolation; and the cries of birds brought back keen memory, a presentiment of danger in the sea and the omen of the gray gulls, and the threat of moons unnaturally large.

A third blink, and it was forest, and they were black ravens that cried, and the stones held no present threat.

Behind them was dust, friends were long dead, and all they had known was changed and beyond recall, although the pain of parting was for them as recent as this morning and keen as a knife. He tried to be wise as his liege and not to think on it.

But when they rode over the shoulder of that hill, the ruin and the forest gave way to barren plains on their right hand, and sunset on their left. A wolf cried, somewhere beyond the hills.

Morgaine let slip the ring of her sword-belt, letting the dragon-hilted weapon which rode between her shoulders slide down to her side.

It had a name, that sword: *Changeling*. His own nameless blade was plain arrhendur steel. Besides his sword he had a bow of arrhendur make, and a quiver of good arrows, and a stone next his heart, in a small gray pyx, as a great lord had given it to him—as memory went, it had been very recent. But the worlds shifted, the dead went to dust; and they were in a place which made that small box no comfort to him, no more than that ill-omened blade his liege handled, on the hilt of which her hand rested.

Birds rose up from that horizon, black specks against the setting sun at that hour when birds would flock and quit the field; but not birds of the field, nothing so wholesome, gathered in hills so barren.

"Death," Morgaine murmured at his side. "Carrion birds."

A wolf howled, and another answered it.

*   *   *

They were there again in the twilight, yellow-eyed and slope-shouldered, and Chei ep Kantory gathered himself on his knees and gathered up the weapons he had, which were a human bone in one hand and a length of rusty chain in the other; he gathered himself to his feet and braced his back against the pole which his efforts and the abrasion of the chain had cut deeply but not enough. The iron held. The food was gone, the water-skin wrung out to its last drops of moisture.

It would end tonight, he thought, for he could not face another day, could not lie there racked with thirst and fever, listening to the dry rustle of wings, the flutter and flap and the wafts of carrion-stench as a questing beak would delve into some cranny where flesh remained. Tonight he would not be quick enough, the jaws that scored his armor, the quick, darting advances that had circled him last night, would find his throat and end it. Falwyn was gone, last but himself. The pack had dragged Falwyn's body to the length of the chain and fed and quarreled and battled while Chei sank against the post that was the pivot and the center of all his existence. They had worried the armor to rags among the bones; the ravens helped by day, till now there was nothing but the bones and shreds of flesh, too little, perhaps, to content them.

"Bastards," he taunted them, but his voice was a croak like the birds', no more distinct. His legs shot pain through the tendons, his sight came and went. He did not know why he went on fighting. But he would not let them have his life unscathed, not do what ep Cnary had done, passing his food and water to Falwyn, to sit waiting for his death. Ep Cnary had lost a son at Gyllin-brook. It had been grief that killed him as much as the wolves. Chei grieved for a brother. But he was not disposed to quit. He worried at the chain hour by hour of his days, rubbing it back and forth on the post; he had strained himself against that limit to lay hands on the rusty links which wolfish quarrels over Desynd's body had pushed a hand's-breadth nearer: with his belt he had snagged it, some relic of a previous victim which was now his defense and his hope of freedom. He battered at the post now with all the force his legs and his failing strength could muster, and hoped that his weight could avail to snap it where he had worn it part way through; but it stood firm as the rock in which it was set: it was weathered oak, and it would not break.

The black-maned wolf moved closer, jaws agape, a distraction. It was always the notch-eared one that darted to the flank. He had seen this before, and knew her tricks. He spun and swung the chain, and notch-ear dodged: Black-mane then, and the gray one—he gave them names. He taunted them with a voice that rasped like the ravens'. "Here, bitch, try again. Try closer—"

They came in twos and threes this time. He turned with his back against the pole, his right foot failing him, swollen in the boot and the chain, a lifeless thing at the end of his leg. It was that which the wolf caught, driving in with serpent-quickness, and he swung the chain at it, jabbed down onto its shoulders with the jagged bone and felt it snap on tough hide and bone. Jaws closed on his armor at knee and elbow, teeth snapping in front of his face and a wolf dodging with a yelp as he swung the chain in the limited range he had. The pack closed about him in a snarling maelstrom, out of which the flap of wings, the thunder of riders—he saw them in a whirling confusion, the pale horses, the gleam of metal, the pale banner of hair a-flutter in the wind—

—back, then, to that moment. The wolves shied away, their grip leaving him, all but the gray bitch, and a sword flashed, the rider of the white horse leaning from the saddle to strike—

He cried out then, falling against the post, which did not belong on that river-bank. It began again. He fell, and the riders, afoot, walking their horses across the debris of bones, came to take him to torment. That was the worst cruelty, that he was lost in a dream wherein the end began it all again.

The man fought him. Well he might, though there was little strength left in him. "Have care!" Morgaine cried as the chain swung, but Vanye jerked his head out of the way, guarded himself against a knee-thrust, and with the press of his weight and a twist at the arm, disarmed the wild-haired, armored man of the chain he wielded. It did not end the fight, but he had the man, then, beyond any dispute, gripped in both arms and carried struggling to the ground.

"Be still," he said in his own language, for the man was human. "Be still. We are not your enemies."

That did no good. "We are not here to harm you," Morgaine said in the qhalur tongue. And in the human: "Hold him still."

Vanye saw what she was about and edged further from the post, dragging the struggling man with him and drawing the ankle chain taut between the man and the post, as Morgaine took that small black weapon of hers and burned it. A smell of heated metal went up. One link reddened and bent under the pull, and the man writhed and fought his hold, but Vanye freed a hand and laid it on his cheek, shielding his vision from what a man of simple beliefs might not want to see, while iron sparked and sputtered and parted.

"There, man, there. You are free of that."

"Tie him," Morgaine said, being the crueler and the more practical of them both.

"I must," Vanye said, and patted the man's face and shared a look with him, one glance into blue and desperate eyes that sought—perhaps—some hope of him, before he took the man in both his arms, wrestled him over face down and sat on him till he could work loose one of the leather thongs from his belt and tie his hands behind him.

After that, the man seemed sane, for he stopped fighting and lay inert, only turning his face out of the unwholesome dirt, his cheek against the ground, his eyes open and staring elsewhere as if nothing that proceeded could interest him further.

He was thin, beneath the armor. There was filth all about, a stench of death and human waste and wolf. Vanye got up and brushed himself off, and bent to drag the man up to his feet with him.

The man kicked, a futile effort, easily turned. Vanye shrugged it off and hauled him up to his feet with a shake at the scruff, grabbed him up in a tight embrace from behind and held him there against his struggles. "Enough," he said, and when he had gotten his breath: "*Liyo*, a drink of water might improve his opinion of us."

Morgaine fetched the water flask from her saddle, unstopped it, filled the little cup that was its cap. "Careful," Vanye said, anxious, but careful she was, standing to the side, offering it for a moment until the man turned his head and committed himself to their charity.

Rapid sips, then, a trembling throughout the man's body then and after Morgaine drew the cup away. "We will not harm you," she said. "Do you understand?"

The man nodded then, a single movement of his head. And shivered in Vanye's grip—a young man, his beard and hair sunbleached blond and matted with every manner of filth. He stank, like all the air about this hill; dirt and gall-marks were about his neck where the edge of his armor had rubbed him raw, and the chained ankle would not bear his full weight.

"Who put you here?" Vanye asked him in the *qhalur* language, as Morgaine had spoken.

"Lord Gault," he thought the answer was. Or some name like that, which told him nothing.

"We will put you on my horse," Vanye said. "We will take you somewhere safe. We will not harm you. Do you understand me?"

Again a nod. The trembling did not cease.

"Easy," Vanye said, and supported him gently; the grip became an embrace of his left arm. He slowly led him to the slope where their horses stood— well-trained and waiting, but skittish near so much wolf-smell and decay. He sought after Arrhan's reins, but Morgaine took them up and held the mare steady for him. He did not offer the man the stirrup, considering his hands were bound. He only steadied the prisoner against Arrhan's side and offered his hands for a stirrup: "Left foot. Come."

The man did as he was told. Vanye heaved him upward, pressing close with his body while Arrhan shifted and fretted, and the man landed belly down on the saddle, struggling then to right himself. Vanye set his own foot in the stirrup, stepped up and rested his leg across the low cantle and blanket roll till he could get hold of the man and haul him upright enough. Then he slid down behind him, occupying most of the saddle, all the while Morgaine held Arrhan to an uneasy standstill; and the prisoner rested against him, his leg hooked round the horn, for he had no strength to bring it over.

"I have him," Vanye said, and took the reins Morgaine handed up to him.

She had a worried look. So, he reckoned, had he; and he wanted clear of this place, wanted them on lower ground and less conspicuous, wanted the stink of death out of his nostrils—but he held it against him in human shape, inhaled it through his mouth much as he could, and thought that even his armor and his gear would hold the smell for days.

In front of him, leaning against him, the man gave a racking cough. *Disease and plague*, Vanye thought. It went with such places. He reined about carefully, following Morgaine as she mounted up on the gray. The stud was fractious too, snorting and working at the reins, but she did not let Siptah have his head. They rode carefully over the bone-littered ground.

"Are they near," Vanye asked the prisoner, "the men who did this to you?"

Perhaps the man understood. Perhaps he did not. He did not answer. Intermittently he underwent spasms of coughing, racking and harsh, then, exhausted, slumped against him, his body rolling more and more to the motion of the horse.

"He is fainting," Vanye said to Morgaine. "I think all his strength is going."

In a little time more, the man's head fell forward, and it was loose weight leaning against him. But when Vanye pressed his hand over the man's heart he felt it beating steadily. It was a strong heart, he thought, of a man stubborn beyond all reason, and such a man might touch his sympathy—might, except such a man might be fair or foul, and he had known more than one enemy and more than one madman on this Road.

Morgaine led them back to the road again, and across it, to a place where a small river ran at woods-edge. In the last light, they rode a pathless track among the trees, in a land where they already knew that there were wolves, and men who had done the like of this. It was enough to know.

They gave him water, they brought him a long dazed ride deep within the twisted forest, laid him on a streamside and there freed his hands, the man of the pair giving him a little waybread soaked in cordial so strong it stung Chei's throat.

After which they let him lie, busy at the making of their camp, and through his slitted, aching eyes, Chei saw them moving here and there in the light of a tiny fire, illusory and ominous. Chei's heart beat in panic when they would come near; it eased whenever they would seem occupied about their own business. Then he knew that he was safe for a while, as hc had known that he was safe when the wolves were feeding: and in such intervals, as then, he drifted only scantly waking.

A shadow fell between him and the fire. He came awake, saw the reach toward him, and feigned unconsciousness as a hand rested on his brow. "There is tea," a man's voice said, in the *qhalur* tongue, "here, drink."

He did not intend to break his pretense. He was still even when a hand slipped beneath his neck, though his heart was hammering in fright; he stayed quite limp as the man lifted his head and slid support under his shoulders.

But the cup which touched his lips smelled of herbs and honey. A little of it trickled between his lips, warm and wholesome, and he swallowed, risking the harm in it—a sip which touched off a spate of coughing and destroyed his pretense of unconsciousness. The cup retreated, came back to his lips. He drank again, eyes shut, tears leaking from between his lids as he fought the rawness in his throat; and drank a third sip, after which his head rested on the man's knee and a gentle hand soothed his brow.

He ventured to open his eyes, and met a face human as his own—but he had learned to doubt appearances.

All about them were twisted trees, the night, the fire. He knew that he had come to Hell, and that this *qhalur* woman from beyond the gate had laid claim to what the *qhal*-lord this side of the gate had flung away. These strangers had no use for revenge: there was nothing he personally had done to them save be born. There was nothing he knew that would be valuable to them. There was no cause at all for their mercy to him save that they had use for him, and what use the tall, lordly *qhal* had for a young and fair-haired human man he knew all too well.

They would take him through the gate with them. He would come back again, but with such a guest in him as Gault had, an old thing, a living hell which spoke with Gault's mouth and looked out through Gault's eyes, and which was a sojourner there. *Qhal* did not use *qhal* in that way, or it was rare. A healthy human body would serve, when a *qhal* outlived the one he was born with.

So they touched him gently, this *qhalur* woman and this maybe-*qhal* who did her bidding. So they gave him drink, delicate drink, perhaps because the great *qhal*-lords gave him what they themselves drank, because it did not occur to them that it was too precious to waste. So the man let his head down to the soft grass and spoke to him reassuringly, looking to the iron that banded his swollen ankle: "This is a simple lock; I can strike it off, have no fear of me, I will take good care." And he fetched a hand-axe and one flat stone and another, to Chei's misgiving—but the axe-blade was for a wedge, the one rock for a brace, the other for striking, and the woman came and with her own hands gave him more of the cordial against the shocks that ran through his nerves, gave him enough that his raw throat was soothed and his head spun while the man worked in soft, steady blows.

Surely they took good care for the body they claimed. There was something terrible in such careless use of their rich things, in the gentle touch of the woman's hand as it rested on his shoulder, and in her soft reassurances: "He will not hurt you."

It was one with the other madness, and Chei's senses spun, so that he was not sure whether the ground was level or not. The soft ringing of the metal resounded in his skull, the pain ran up from the bones of his leg and into his hip, till the iron fell away, and the man very delicately, with his knife, slit the stitching of his boot and said something to the *qhal* in words which made no sense—but Chei was far gone in the pain that began about his ankle from the moment it was free of its confinement, an ache that made him wish the chain back again, the boot intact, anything but that misery which made him vulnerable. He tried not to show it, he tried not to react when the man probed the joint; but his back stiffened, and he could not help the intake of breath.

The world was dim for a time after that shock. They went away from him. He was glad to lie still and not heave up the moisture they had given him; and he thought that he would, for a time, if he lifted his head at all. But the man brought a wet cloth warm from the fire, and washed his face and his neck and his hands with it.

"Do you want more water?" the man asked.

He did. He did not ask. It was a trick, he thought, to make him believe them, and he did not want to talk to them. Somewhere in the distance, wolves howled, and he shivered at the chill of water rolling down under his collar; that small twitch he could not suppress. For the rest he did nothing, lay still and cared as little as possible what they did.

Until he felt the man's hands at his armor buckles, unfastening them.

"No," he said then, and flinched from under that touch.

"Man, I will not hurt you. Let me rid you of this and wash the dirt off—only the worst of it. Then you can sleep till morning."

"No," he said again, and blinked the man clear in his vision—a human face, faintly lit by fire. The place was real, like the woods overhead, branches the fire lit in ghostly ways. He flinched as the touch came at his shoulder again, and struck feebly at it, being desperate.

"Man—"

"No. Let me be."

"As you will. It is your choice." Another touch, this time on his wrist, from which again he moved his hand. "Peace, peace, rest, then. Rest. Whoever did this to you is no friend of ours. You can sleep."

The words made no sense at all to him. He thought of the wolves, the ones he had named—he had known their faces, he had known their ways. They were terrible, but he knew them, what they would do, when they would do it: he had learned his enemy and he had known the limits of his misery.

But the *qhal* he could not understand. They would guard his sleep, fend away the wolves, do him whatever kindnesses pleased them: they would do no terrible thing until they had brought him to the gate, or to their own lands. There was no limit, then, no mercy such as the wolves would have shown.

"He might be a murderer," Vanye said, at the fire with Morgaine, sitting on his heels in that way that years out of hall made comfortable enough for him. "But so am I," he added with a shrug. "Whoever put him there—God requite."

"He will run," Morgaine said.

"Not with that foot. At least tonight. God in Heaven, *liyo*—"

Vanye hugged his arms about him, in the scant warmth of the fire they risked, and shook his head, and cast a glance toward the dark lump that was their guest, lying just beyond the firelight. It was a fair, green land they had left the other side of the gate. Their friends were aged and gone, a kinsman of his—was dust, he thought, for he once had thought the gates led only between lands; but now he knew that their span was years and centuries; and knew that if he looked up away from the fire he would see the too-abundant stars in no familiar pattern, the which sight he could not, this moment, bear. The breath seemed choked in him.

"We do not let him free," Morgaine said harshly. The fire shone on the planes of her face, winked redly from the eyes of the dragon sword. It had not left her side. It would not, this night.

"No," he said. "That I do know."

He felt cold, and bereft, and victim of a cruel choice which was Morgaine's doing—that she asked everything of him, every possession, every kinship, every scruple, the sum of which choices brought him here, where men fed each other to wolves. *I had everything I thought that I had dreamed of. Everything was in my hands—honor, kinship, a home that was mine—within the arrhend. There was peace—*

But Morgaine would have gone on without him. And with her, the warmth in the sun would have gone. And no one could ever have warmed him again, man or woman, kinsman or friend. The essential thing would have left his life, and beyond that, beyond that—

He had ridden into that dark gulf of the gates—it had been this morning, a bright meadow, a parting with his cousin, last save Morgaine herself who could speak the language of his homeland, last save Morgaine who knew his customs, knew the things he believed, remembered the sights of home. And it was already too late. Was dust, between two strides of the horses that bore them.

He shivered, a convulsive twitch as if a cold wind had blown over his back; and he bowed his head and rubbed the back of his neck, which the warrior's braid made bare. Honor demanded. Honor, he had back again. But he did not put off the white scarf, which made him *ilin*, a Claimed warrior, soul-bound to the liege he served; and when he asked himself why this was, his thoughts slid away from that question as it did from the things Morgaine tried to explain to him, how worlds circled suns and what made the constellations change their shapes.

So he thought, listening to the wolves, thinking that they were not alone, that this world had touched them already. They had in their care a man who depended on them for life, and who in someone's estimation had deserved to die by a terrible means.

He wished that he knew less than he did, or had seen less in their journeying.

"We cannot leave him; Heaven knows we cannot make speed carrying double. And Heaven knows—fever may take him by morning."

Morgaine stared at him, a flash of her eyes across the fire, out of a brooding silence. So he knew he had gotten to the heart of her thoughts, that she dismissed his worry for their guest as short-sighted, the matter of one life. She weighed it against other things.

"We will do what we have to," she said, and beneath that was: *I will do, and you will, or our ways part.*

There was always that choice. It was knowing that, perhaps, that made him choose to stay within *ilin*-oath and keep himself from other, more damning choices. He could not take another direction, in a strange land and outside the law he knew. And where was honor—when a man chose a woman, and refused to leave her even for his honor's sake; and a liege, and must not desert her, else he had no honor at all; and that woman and that liege lord, being one and the same, would never turn left or right for his sake, being bound by an oath still more dreadful than his.

He had no wish to serve what she served. Serving her, he served that terrible thing, as much as a man could and hold out any vestige of hope for his soul. Being Kurshin, and Nhi, and honorable, he sought after absolutes of law, and right; and that truth of hers, which killed the innocent and shattered law and right, shimmered beyond all his horizons, stark as the sword she bore—*here is absolute truth, man, here is truth beyond truths, which makes all justice void.*

Morgaine understood it. Morgaine did all that she did for that thing she served, did all that flesh and blood could do, woman or man; and took so little care for herself that she would not eat or drink, at times, would forget these things if he were not there to put food into her hand and to protest that he, he, being a natural man, needed rest even if she did not. He distracted her from her pursuit from time to time. And so few things could.

He gave her such comfort as he could, and they were not even lovers, Heaven knew and few guessed. They had shared a blanket in the beginning with her sword between, lately without so much as that caution to stay them; which was intolerable and gave him the more reason to chafe at this unwanted guest, and the demands of his own stubborn honor.

"I think," Vanye said quietly, "that he has no love of *qhal*."

"He is human," Morgaine said with a shrug. "And we do not know who left him to die."

I am not qhal, she was wont to insist, as long as he had known her—for in his own lost land the *qhal* were dreaded and damned; *halfling* had been Morgaine's ultimate admission to him, when at last he won a little of truth from her, none so many days ago as their time ran.

Now she let the implication of *qhalur* blood pass without a protestation. Perhaps she was preoccupied; perhaps she finally believed him enough to give up the lie—that pretense which had begun perhaps in kindness on her part and lasted in doubt of him.

Was that the last test, that I should ride this gate with you? But did you doubt me, liyo, *that I would keep my word?*

"Go, rest," she told him, brushing the last crumbs of their dinner into the fire. "I will watch a while."

He shifted his eyes to their guest, in the shadows. "If he has need of anything, wake me; do not go near him."

"I have no such notion," she said, and slid the pan into her saddlebag, there by her side, as if they could leave in the morning with their guest as weak as he was. But it was only prudence. They had not survived this long by leaving gear behind, if attack came on them. "If he has need of anything in your watch," she said, "you will wake me, the same."

"He is one man," Vanye said with a little indignation, and she frowned at him.

"Wake me," she said, being unreasonable on the matter.

So this land had frightened her too. And she grew irrational in little things.

"Aye," he said, and shrugged. It was little enough concession.

He loosened his armor, and wrapped himself in his cloak, wrinkling his nose from the stink the cloth had taken on from its little contact with the man, and thinking that he might never have it clean again.

In the morning, in the daylight, after sleep, he thought, the man might be reasonable—Heaven help them, they had no means to deal with a madman.

He must see what could be done to salvage the man's gear—as long as they were not traveling.

But for his part he was very weary, and his bones ached. So with his liege, he thought; but she had thinking to do, and he had none—it was Morgaine chose their way, Morgaine who decided matters, it was Morgaine who told him what he should do, and therefore he did not worry about that—only about the little matters—the horses, the gear, and how they should do what Morgaine had set them to do. And he was content enough with that arrangement.

Morgaine threw her own blanket over him as he lay there, a little settling of added warmth, in the which, his head pillowed on Arrhan's saddle, he relaxed. She patted his ankle as she let down the blanket, a gentle good night, a comfort at which he sighed, and thought after that, staring into the dark—for she had a way of doing that to him—that perhaps that gesture of hers had been intended for more than that, that if not for the damnable matter of their uninvited guest, if not for this world that threatened them and set them to sleeping turn and turn about, in their armor, that cursed, familiar burden which seemed to settle on heart and soul, with all its habits of fear—

So close they had been to being lovers. So very close.

He sighed again, but not for the same reason, and tried with all his mind to go quickly to sleep, with that good sense he had learned on this trail—that unbroken sleep was precious as food and water, and very often harder come by.

A hard lump pressed beneath his armor, against his heart. He felt after the chain which held it and pulled it loose for his comfort . . . careful of the case, for it was a perilous thing within, more perilous still as near the Gate as they were camped. The stone in it might tell him the way to another Gate. It might find another stone of its kind which was near enough. That was the virtue in it, which held so much else of danger.

It had been a parting-gift, from a man he had begun to love, one he had wished had been his father. But in Morgaine's service there were only partings—and deaths. Only the small stone and the white horse, these he owned, besides his gear, both of which he knew for foolishness and dangerous vanity—a mare, and white at that; and a stone which marked him equal to a *qhal*-lord—and reminded him of the arrhend.

That land they had traded irrevocably for this one, where the gates themselves threw out power enough to misshape the trees and make all their vicinity unwholesome.

It was that lost, beautiful forest and another, less wholesome, which haunted his sleep. He dreamed that Morgaine had left him and he could not overtake her.

He dreamed of a ride wherein he had seen a dragon frozen in the snow, beyond which time nothing had been ordinary in his life. For the most part, he thought, folk chose to be where they were born, with familiar dangers. It might be a terrible place or a good one, might be love or hate that came to them, they might have their freedom merely by turning their faces from what they knew and walking straight ahead—yet they would not go, not though the place where

they were would kill them. He might have been such a man as that. He had
hovered for two years close about the region of his exile, when he was eighteen
and an outlaw, despite his danger: he had imagined nothing beyond that.

Till Morgaine had found him.

She had shown him things which made no sense in the world he knew. And
like the dragon which perished, bewildered, in the snow—he had known he
was out of his element from the moment he had begun to follow her.

Therefore he dreamed of endless following. Therefore he waked with his fist
clenched on the stone; and lay bewildered, wondering where he was; and where
Morgaine was; and was terrified until he had found her, a familiar shadow,
beneath the ancient and twisted tree, in more starlight than any world he had
yet seen.

He drifted off again. The horses remained quiet. The wind blew and rattled
the branches, and there was no sound that did not belong.

But—a brief darkness then; and a snap like a burning log, that brought him
out of his sleep reaching for his sword, aware first that Morgaine was at his left
and that their guest was to his right and moving, staggering to his feet and
reeling away among the trees at no slight speed. Fire burned in the leaf mold.
That was the result of Morgaine's weapon: he knew it well enough—knew that
was the sound that had waked him; and he scrambled up sleep-dazed as he was
and overtook the man before he had gotten as far as the horses he strove to
reach—overtook him and seized him at the shoulders, bearing him down in a
crash to the leaves at the very hooves of the gray warhorse.

The gray reared up with a challenge and Morgaine's whistle cut the dark.
"Siptah!" she shouted, as Vanye shielded his head with his arms, the prisoner
with his body, and the iron-shod hooves came down, flinging dirt and leaves
into his face and clipping his shoulder, thunder of hooves all about them as the
warhorse scrambled over them, missing them with every stride but one. The
prisoner beneath him did not move.

"Is thee hurt?" Morgaine was asking. "Vanye, is thee hurt?"

Vanye gathered himself up off the man and caught his own breath in great
frightened gasps, looking up at his liege, who had caught firm hold of Siptah's
halter rope. He flexed the shoulder as he rose and thanked Heaven the hoof had
clipped only leather and a mail shirt.

"He could have had a knife," Morgaine raged at him. "He might have had
any sort of weapon! Thee did not know!"

He thought the same, now it was done; more, he thought of the hoof-strike
that had missed his head, and his knees went to water. The big gray had shifted
balance in mid-attack and all but fallen trying to miss him; that was what had
saved them.

At his feet the prisoner moaned and moved, a half-conscious stir of his limbs. Vanye set his foot in the man's back when he tried to get an arm under him and pressed him flat, not gently.

"He is not altogether lame," Morgaine observed dryly, then, having recovered her humor.

"No," Vanye said, still hard-breathing. The deserved reproof of his mercy stung more than the bruise did. "Nor in any wise grateful."

ᔡ Chapter 2

Dawn light grew in the clearing, and Vanye probed the ashes of their fire with a bit of kindling, as he had fed it from time to time in the hours of his watch. Yellow threads of fire climbed and sparked in the threads of inner bark of something very like willow. He added a few other twigs, then arranged more substantial pieces, deliberate in his leisure. It was a rare moment in which nothing pressed them, in which he knew that they were not riding on, and all he needed think on was the fire, the mystery that was always homelike, no matter what the sky over him, or the number of moons in it. The horses grazed in the clearing on the riverside, where the twisted trees let in enough light for grass—faithful sentries both, dapple gray Siptah wise to war and ambushes, Arrhan forest-wise and sensible. Something might escape human ears, but the horses would give alarm—and they found nothing amiss in this morning. Catastrophe had attempted them in the night—and failed.

On the other side of the fire, the glow falling on slender hand and silver hair, Morgaine slept on, which small vision he cherished in that same quiet way as he did the fire and the dimly rising sun.

"Sleep," he whispered when she stirred. Sometimes, in such rare leisure, she would yield him the body-warmed blankets, so he might sleep a little while she made breakfast—or he yielded them to her, whichever of them had sat the watch into dawn.

She half-opened her eyes and lifted her head, nose above the blankets. "Thee can sleep," she said, in the Kurshin tongue, as he had spoken—but it was an older accent, forgotten by the time he was born. It was a habit she had when she spoke to him alone, or when she was muddled with sleep.

"I am full awake," he said, which was a lie: he felt the long hours of his watch in a slight prickling in his eyes, his bruised shoulder ached, and the blankets were tempting shelter from the morning chill. But he saved her from hardship when he could—so often that it became a contest between them, of frowns and maneuverings, each favoring the other in a perpetual rivalry which tilted one way or the other according to the day and the need.

"Sleep," he said now. Morgaine sank back and covered her head; and he smiled with a certain satisfaction as he delved into their saddlebags and brought out a pan for mixing and cooking.

The prisoner too, lying prone in his cloak, showed signs of life, rolling onto his side. Vanye reckoned what his most pressing need likely was, and reckoned that it could wait a time: shepherding an escape-prone madman out to the woods meant waking Morgaine to put her on guard; or letting their breakfast go cold—neither of which he felt inclined to do, considering the prisoner was healthy enough to have sprinted for the horses last night, and considering he had won a stiff arm for his last attempted kindness.

Morgaine bestirred herself as the smell of cakes and bacon wafted into the air—enough to draw the hungry for leagues about, Vanye reckoned—the most of them bent on banditry, if what they had seen was any guide.

And another glance toward the prisoner showed him lying on his side, staring in their direction with such misery and desolation that Vanye felt his eyes on him even when he looked back at their breakfast.

"I should see to him," Vanye muttered unhappily when Morgaine came back from the riverside. He poured tea into their smallest mixing bowl, wrapped a cloth about it to keep it warm, and set out a cake and a bit of bacon on the cloth that wrapped his cooking-gear, while Morgaine sat down to eat. "Have your own," he said, "before it cools."

It did not look like a madman who stared up at him as he came over to his place among the tree-roots. It looked like a very miserable, very hungry man who hoped that food truly was coming to him. "I will free your hands," Vanye said, dropping down on his heels beside him. He set the food down carefully on the dead leaves of the forest floor. "But not your feet. Meddle with that and I will stop you, do you understand? For other necessities I trust you can wait like any civilized man." It was the *qhalur* language he spoke, and it did not go so lightly over his tongue as it ought. He was not sure, at times, what hearers did understand of him. "Do you agree? Or do I take the food back?"

"The food," the man said, a faint, hoarse voice. "Yes."

"You agree."

A nod of the head, a worried gnawing of the lip.

He turned the prisoner over and gently worked the knots free on his hands. The man only gave a great sigh and lay still on his face a moment, his arms at rest beside him, as a man would who had spent the night with his hands and shoulders going numb.

"He is quieter," he reported then to Morgaine, in his own tongue, when he settled down to breakfast beside her. He took a cup of tea and considered his hands, where he had touched the man. It was death-stink, lingering: the man was that filthy; and he could not eat until he had walked down to the river and washed his hands.

It was overdone bacon then; Morgaine kept the breakfast warm for him on the coals, along with the tea which by now was bitter-edged. He drank and made a face.

"I should have gotten up," Morgaine said.

"No," he said. "No, you ought not. I will take care of him. I will have him down to the river before the sun is much higher, and I swear to you he will be cleaner before you have to deal with him."

"I want you to talk to him."

"*Me?*"

"You can manage that."

"Aye—but—"

"Not?"

"I will do it." Rarely nowadays she put any hard task on him: and he took it, distasteful as it was, likely as he was to make a muddle of things. "But—"

"But?"

"He can lie to me. How should I know? How should I know anything he told me? I have no subtlety with lies."

"Is thee saying I do?"

"I did not say—"

She smiled, a quirk of her mouth, gray eyes flickering. "Man and man; Man and Man. That is the fact. Between one thing and the other I am not the one of us two he will trust. No. Learn what brought him here. Promise him what thee sees fit to promise. Only—" She reached out and laid a hand on his arm. "He will not go free. We cannot allow that. Thee knows what I will give—and what I will not."

"I know," he said, and thought as he said it that he had chosen the road that brought him to this pass—thought suddenly how more than one land cursed Morgaine kri Chya for the deaths she brought. He had tried in his life to be an honorable man, and not to lie.

But he had chosen to go with her.

It was far more warily the man regarded him on his return, tucked up with his back against a tree, eyes following every move he made—a filthy, desperate figure their guest was by daylight, his nose having bled into his white-blond mustache and down his unkempt and patchy beard, dirt-sores and crusted lines on his face, a trickle of dried blood having run from under the matted hair at his temple—a reminder of the night previous, Vanye thought. Likely more than the man's arms ached this morning.

But he had not touched the binding on his ankles. He had eaten every bit of the cake and the bacon off the cloth, down to the crumbs. And there was still a look on his face, as if having eaten off their charity, he felt there was a chance something else of hope might happen, but much doubted it.

"I will tell you," Vanye said, sinking down on his heels, arms on knees, in front of him, "how I am. I hold no grudge. A man in the dark and fevered—he may do strange things. I reckon that this was the case last night. On the other hand, if you take some other mad notion that endangers my liege, I shall not hesitate to break your neck, do you understand?"

The man said nothing at all. There was only a stare of wary blue eyes, beneath the tangled hair, and the stink of filth was overwhelming.

"Now I think you have been a warrior," Vanye said. "And you do not choose to be filthy or to be a madman. So I should like to take you down to the water and give you oil and salve and help you present a better face to my lady, do you understand me at all, man?"

"I understand," the man said then, the faintest of voices.

"So you should know," Vanye said, taking out his Honor-blade from his belt and beginning to undo the knots which bound the man's feet, "my lady is herself a very excellent shot, with weapons you may not like to see—in case you should think of dealing with me." He freed the knot and unwrapped the leather, tucking it in his belt to save. "There." With a touch on the man's bare and swollen right foot. "Ah. That did the swelling no good at all. Can you walk?—Have you a name, man?"

"Chei."

"Chei." Vanye rose and took his arm, and pulled the man up to take his weight on his left foot, steadying him as he tried the right. "Mine is Vanye. Nhi Vanye i Chya, but Vanye is enough outside hold and hall. There. Walk down to the water. I warn you it is cold. I would have heaved you in last night, with that gear of yours, except for that. Go on. I will find you down by the water. I *will* find you down by the water—or I will *find* you. Do you hear me?"

Thoughts of escape passed through the man's head, it was clear by the wariness in his eyes; then different thoughts entirely, and fear, the man being evidently no fool. But Vanye walked away from him, going back after his kit by the fire.

"Be careful with him!" Morgaine said sharply, as he bent down near her. *Her* eyes were on the prisoner. But he had been sure of that when he had turned his back.

Vanye shrugged and sank down a moment to meet her eyes. "Do as I see fit, you said."

"Do not make gestures."

He drew a long breath. So she set him free and then wanted to pull the jesses. It was not her wont, and it vexed him. But clearly she was worried by something. "*Liyo*, I am not in danger of a man lame in one foot, smaller than I am and starved into the bargain. Not in plain daylight. And I trust your eye is still on him—"

"And we do not know this land," she hissed. "We do not know what resources he may have."

"None of them came to him on that hilltop."

"Thee is leaving things to chance! There are possibilities neither of us can foresee in a foreign place. We do not know what he is."

Her vehemence put doubt into him. He bit his lip and got up again. He had never quite let his own eye leave the man in his walk downhill, save the moment it took to reach her; but it seemed quibbling to protest that point, the more so that she had already questioned his judgment, and justly so, last night. Beyond this it came to opinion; and there were times to argue with Morgaine. The time that they had a prisoner loose was not that moment.

"Aye," he said quietly. "But I will attend him. I will stay in your sight. As long as you see me, everything is well enough."

He gathered up one of their blankets for drying in, along with his personal kit. He walked down the hill, pausing on the way to lay a hand on Siptah's shoulder, where the big gray and white Arrhan grazed at picket on the grassy slope. He reckoned that Morgaine would have that small black weapon in hand and one eye on him constantly.

It was not honorable, perhaps, to deal with hidden weapons in the pretense of being magnanimous; but Morgaine—she had said it—did not take pointless chances. It was not honorable either, to tempt a frightened man to escape, to test his intentions, where keeping him under close guard would save his life. And other lives, it might well be.

But the man had not strayed—had attended his call of nature and limped his way down to water's edge by the time Vanye had walked the distance downslope, and he had never dared bolt from sight of them or wander behind branches. That much was encouraging. Chei had bent down to drink, with movements small and painful, there on the margin.

"Wash," Vanye said, and dropped the folded blanket beside him on the grass. "I will sit here, patient as you like."

Chei said nothing. He only sat down, bowed his head and began with clumsy efforts to unbuckle straps and work his way out of the filth- and weather-stiffened leather and mail, piece after piece of the oddly fashioned gear laid aside on the bank.

"Lord in Heaven," Vanye murmured then, sickened at what he saw—not least was he affected by the quiet of the man sitting there on the grass and taking full account, with trembling hands and tight-clamped jaw and a kind of panic about his eyes, what toll his ordeal had taken of his body—great, deep sores long festered and worn deep in his flesh. Wherever the armor had been ill-fitted, there infection and poison had set in and corruption had followed, deepening the sores, to be galled again by the armor. Wherever small wounds had been, even what might have been insect bites, they had festered; and as Chei pulled the padding beneath the mail free, small bits of skin and corruption came with it.

It was not the condition of a man confined a day or even a few days. It bespoke something much more terrible than he had understood had happened on that hill, and the man sat there, trembling in deep shock, trying stolidly to deal with what a chirurgeon or a priest should attend.

"Man—" Vanye said, rising and coming over to him. "I will help."

But the man turned his shoulder and wanted, by that gesture, no enemy's hands on him, Vanye reckoned—perhaps for fear of roughness; perhaps his customs forbade some stranger touching him; Heaven knew. Vanye sank down on his heels, arms on his knees, and bit his lip for self-restraint, the while Chei continued, with the movements of some aged man, to peel the leather breeches off, now and again pausing, seeming overwhelmed by pain as if he could not bear the next. Then he would begin again.

And there was nothing more than that, that a man could do, while Vanye watched, flinching in sympathy—Lord, in Ra-morij of his birth, a gentleman would not countenance this sort of thing—chirurgeon's business, one would murmur, and cover his nose and go absolve himself with a cup of wine and the noisy talk of other men in hall. He had never had a strong stomach with wounds gone bad.

But the man doggedly, patiently, worked out of the last of it, put his right leg down into the water, and the left, and slipped off the bank, to lose his balance and fall so suddenly that Vanye moved for the edge thinking he had gone into some hole.

Chei righted himself and clawed for the bank—held on in water only chest deep as Vanye gripped his forearm against the grass. Chei was spitting water and gasping after air, his blond hair and beard streaming water, his teeth chattering in what seemed more shock than cold.

"I will pull you out," Vanye said.

"No," Chei said, pulling away. "No." He slipped again, and all but went under, fighting his way to balance again, shivering and trying to pull free.

Vanye let him go, and watched anxiously as the prisoner ducked his head deliberately and rubbed at ingrained dirt, scrubbing at galled shoulders and arms and body.

Vanye delved into his kit and found the cloth-wrapped soap. "Here," he said, offering it out over the water. "Soap."

The man made a few careful steps back to take it and the cloth; and wet it and scrubbed. The lines about the eyes had vanished, washed away with the dirt. It was a younger face now; tanned face and neck and hands, white flesh elsewhere, in which ribs and shoulder-blades stood out plainly.

More of scrubbing, while small chains of bubbles made serpentines down the rapid current. There was danger of that being seen downstream. But there was danger of everything—in this place, in all this unknown world.

"Come on," Vanye said at last, seeing how Chei's lips had gone blue. "Come on, man—Chei. Let me help you out. Come *on*, man."

For a moment he did not think the man could make it. Chei moved slowly, arms against his body, movements slowed as if each one had to be planned. The hand that grasped Vanye's was cold as death. The other carefully, deliberately, laid the soap and the cloth in the grass.

Vanye pulled on him, wet skin slipping in his fingers, got the second hand and drew him up onto the grass, where Chei might have been content to lie. But he hauled Chei up again and drew him stumbling as far as the blanket, where he let him down on his side and quickly wrapped him against the chill of the wind, head to foot.

"There," Vanye said. "There—stay still." He hastened up again, seeing Morgaine standing halfway down the slope, there by the horses: and recalled a broken promise. He *had* left her sight. He was shamefaced a second time as he walked up to speak to her.

"What is wrong?" she asked, fending off Arrhan's search for tidbits. There was a frown on her face, not for the horse.

He had turned his back on their prisoner again. But: "He is too ill to run," Vanye said. "Heaven knows—" It was not news that would please her. "He is in no condition to ride—No, do not go down there, this is something a man should see to. But I will need the other blanket. And my saddlebags."

She gave him a distressed look, but she stopped with only a glance toward the man on the bank, a little tightening of her jaw. "I will bring them down halfway," she said. "*When* will he ride?"

"Two days," he said, trying to hasten the estimate; and thought again of the sores. "Maybe."

It was a dark thought went through Morgaine's eyes—was a thought the surface of which he knew how to read and the depth of which he did not want to know.

"It is not his planning," he said, finding himself the prisoner's defender.

"Aye," Morgaine said quietly, angrily and turned and walked uphill after the things he had asked.

She brought the things he asked back down to him, no happier. "Mind, we have no abundance of anything."

"We are far from the road," Vanye said. It was the only extenuation of their situation he could think of.

"Aye," she said again. There was still anger. It was not at him. She had nothing to say—was in one of her silences, and it galled him in the one sense and frightened him in the other, that they were in danger, that he knew her moods, and her angers, which he had hoped she had laid aside forever. But it was a fool who hoped that of Morgaine.

He took what she gave him and walked back to the bank, and there sat down, a little distance from their prisoner—sat down, trying to smother his own frustration which, Heaven knew, he dared not let fly, dared not provoke his liege to some rashness—some outright and damnably perverse foolishness, he told himself, of which she was capable. She scowled; she was angry; she *did* nothing foolish and needed no advice from him who ought well to know she was holding her temper very well indeed, Heaven save them from her moods and her unreasonable furies.

The focus of her anger knew nothing of it—was enclosed in his own misery, shivering and trying, between great tremors of cold and shock, to dry his hair.

"Give over," he said, and tried to help. Chei would none of it, shivering and recoiling from him.

"I am sorry," Vanye muttered. "If I had known this, Lord in Heaven, man—"

Chei shook his head, clenching his jaw against the spasms a moment, then lay still, huddled in the blanket.

"How long," Vanye asked, "how long had you been there?"

Chei's breath hissed between his teeth, a slow shuddering.

"Why," Vanye pursued quietly, "did they leave you there?"

"What are you? From where? Mante?"

"Not from hereabouts," he said. The sun shone warm in a moment when the wind fell. A bird sang, off across the little patch of meadow. It meant safety, like the horses grazing above them on the slope.

"Is it Mante?" Chei demanded of him, rolling onto his back and lifting his head, straining with the effort.

"No," Vanye said. "It is not." And reckoned that Mante was some enemy, for Chei seemed to take some comfort in that, for all that his jaw was still clamped tight. "Nor anywhere where they treat men as they treated you. I swear you that."

"She—" The man lay back and shifted desperate eyes toward their camp.

"—is not your enemy," Vanye said. "As I am not."

"Are you *qhal*?"

That question took the warmth from the daylight.

"No," Vanye said. "That I am not." In Andur-Kursh the fairness of his own brown hair was enough to raise questions of halfling blood. But the one who asked was palest blond; and that puzzled him. "Do I look to be?"

"One does not need to *look* to be."

It was, then, what he had feared. He thought before he spoke. "I have seen the like. My cousin—was such a man."

"How does he fare?"

"Dead," Vanye said. "A long time ago." And frowned to warn the man away from that matter. He looked up at a motion in the edge of his vision and saw Morgaine coming down the hill toward them, carefully—a warlike figure, in her black and silver armor, the sword swinging at her side, either hand holding a cloth-wrapped cup she was trying not to spill.

Chei followed his stare, tilting his head back, watching her as she came, as she reached the place where they sat and offered the steaming cups.

"Thank you," Vanye said, as he took his cup from her hand, and took Chei's as well.

"Against the chill," Morgaine said. She was still frowning, but she did not show it to Chei, who lay beneath his blanket. "Do you need anything?" she asked, deliberately, doggedly gracious. "Hot water?"

"On the inside of him will serve," Vanye said. "For the rest—the sun is warm enough when the wind falls."

She walked off then, in leisurely fashion, up the hill, plucked a twig and stripped it like some village girl walking a country lane, the dragon sword swinging at her side.

She was, he reckoned, on the edge of a black rage.

He gave Chei his cup and sipped his own, wrinkling his nose as he discovered the taste. "'Tis safe," he said, for Chei hesitated at the smell of his. "Tea and herbs." He tasted his again. "Febrifuge. Against the fever. She gives us both the same, lest you think it poison. A little cordial to sweeten it. The herb is sour and bitter."

"*Qhalur* witch," the man said, "into the bargain."

"Oh, aye," Vanye said, glancing at him with some mild surprise, for that belief might have come out of Andur-Kursh. He regarded such a human, homelike belief almost with wistfulness, wondering where he had lost it. "Some say. But you will not lose your soul for a cup of tea."

He had, he thought when he had said it, lost his for a similar matter, a bit of venison. But that was long ago, and he was damned most for the bargain, not what sustenance he had taken of a stranger in a winter storm.

Chei managed to lean over on his elbow and drink, between coughing, and spilled a good amount of it in the shaking of his hands. But sip after sip he drank, and Vanye drank his own cup, to prove it harmless.

Meanwhile too, having considered charity, and the costs of it on both sides, he delved one-handed into the saddlebags and set out a horn container, intricately carved.

And perhaps, he thought, a scrupulous Kurshin man would regard the contents of that little container as witchcraft too.

"What is that?" Chei asked warily, as he finished his cup.

"For the sores. It is the best thing I have. It will not let the wounds scab, and it takes the fire out."

Chei took the box and opened it, taking a little on his fingers and smelling of it. He tried it on the sore on the inside of his knee, his lip caught between his teeth in the patient habit of pain; but soon enough he drew several deep breaths and his face relaxed.

"It does not hurt," Vanye said.

Chei daubed away at himself, one wound and the other, the blanket mostly fallen about him, his drying hair uncombed and trailing water from its ends. Vanye took a bit on his own fingers and covered the patches that Chei could in no wise reach, those on his shoulders, then let Chei do the rest.

"Why?" Chei asked finally, in a phlegmy voice, after a cough. "Why did you save me?"

"Charity," Vanye said dourly.

"Am I free? I do not seem to be."

Vanye lifted a shoulder. "No. But what we have we will share with you. We are in a position—" He drew a breath, thinking what he should say, what loyalties he might cross, what ambush he might find, all on a word or two. "—we do not want to make any disturbance hereabouts. But then, perhaps you have no wish to be found hereabouts—"

The man said nothing for a moment. Then he reached inside the blankets to apply more of the salve. "I do not."

"Then we do have something to talk about, do we not?"

A pale blue stare flicked toward him, mad as a hawk's eye. "Have you some feud with Gault?"

"Who is Gault?"

Perhaps it was the right bent to take. Perhaps the man in his turn thought him mad—or a liar. Carefully Chei took a fresh film of salve on his fingers and applied it, and winced, a weary flinching, premature lines of sunburn and pain around the eyes. "Who is Gault?" he echoed flatly. "Who is Gault. Ask, *what* is Gault?—How should you not know that?"

Vanye gave another shrug. "How should we? I know great lords aplenty. Not that one."

"This is his land."

"Is it? And are you his man?"

"No," Chei said shortly. "Nor would I be." He lowered his voice, spoke with a quickening of breath. "Nor, unlike you, would I serve the *qhal.*"

It was challenge, if subdued and muttered. Vanye let it fly, it being so far off the mark. "She is my liege," he said in all mildness, "and she is halfling, by her own word. And in my own land folk called her a witch, which she is not. I should take offense, but I would have said the same, once."

Chei occupied himself in his injuries.

"It was this Gault left you to die," Vanye said. "You said that much. Why? What had you done to him?"

It was that hawk's stare an instant. There was outrage in it. "To Gault ep Mesyrun? He lives very well in Morund. He drains the country dry. He respects neither God nor devil, and he keeps a large guard of your kind as well as *qhal*."

"Tell me. Do you think he would thank us for freeing you?"

That told. There was a long silence, a slow and evident consideration of that idea.

"So you may reason we are not his friends," Vanye said, "and my lady has done you a kindness, which has so far gained us nothing but an alarm in the night and myself a few bruises. Had you rather fight us to no gain at all? Or will you ride with us a space—till we are off this lord Gault's land?"

Chei rested his head in his hands and remained so, sinking lower with his elbow against his knee.

"Or do you mislike that idea?" Vanye asked him.

"He will kill us," Chei said, and lifted his face to look at him sidelong, head still propped against his hand. "How did you find me?"

"By chance. We heard the wolves. We saw the birds."

"And by chance," Chei said harshly, "you were riding Gault's land."

The man wanted a key—best, it seemed, give him a very small one. "Not chance," Vanye said. "The road. And if our way runs through his land, so be it."

There was no answer.

"What did you do," Vanye asked again, "that deserved what this Gault did? Was it murder?"

"The murder was on their side. They murdered—"

"So?" Vanye asked when the man went suddenly silent.

Chei shook his head angrily. Then his look went to one of entreaty, brow furrowed beneath the drying and tangled hair as he looked up. "You have come here from the gate," Chei said, "if that is the way you have come. I am not a fool. Do not tell me that your lady is ignorant what land this is."

"Beyond the gate—" Vanye considered a second time. It was a man's life in the balance. And it was too easy to kill a man with a word. Or raise war and kill a thousand men or ten thousand. There was a second silence, this one his. Then: "I think you have come to questions my lady could answer for you."

"What do you want from me?" Chei asked.

"Simple things. Easy things. Some of which might suit you well."

Chei's look grew wary indeed.

"Ask my lady," Vanye said.

It was a quieter, saner-seeming man Vanye led, wrapped in one of their two blankets, to the fireside where Morgaine waited, Chei with his hair and beard clean and having some order about it once he had wet and combed it again. He was barefoot, limping, wincing a little on the twigs that littered the dusty ground. He had left all his gear down on the riverside—Heaven knew how they would salvage it or what scouring could clean the leather: none could save the cloth.

Chei set himself down and Vanye sat down at the fireside nearer him than Morgaine—in mistrust.

But Morgaine poured them ordinary tea from a pan, using one of their smaller few bowls for a third cup, and passed it round the bed of coals that the fire had become, to Vanye and so to Chei. The wind made a soft whisper in the leaves that moved and dappled the ground with a shifting light, the fire had become a comfortable warmth which did not smoke, but relieved what chill there was in the shade, and the horses, the dapple gray and the white, grazed a little distance away, in their little patch of grass and sunlight. There was no haste, no urgency in Morgaine.

Not to the eye, Vanye thought. She had been quiet and easy even when he had come alone up the hill bringing the cups, and told her everything he could recall, and everything he had admitted to Chei—"He knows the gates," Vanye had said, quickly, atop it all. "He believes that is how we got here, but he insists we lie if we do not know this lord Gault and that we must know where we are."

Morgaine sipped her tea now, and did not hasten matters. "Vanye tells me you do not know where we come from," she said after a moment. "But you think we should know this place, and that we have somewhat to do with this lord of Morund. We do not. The road out there brought us. That is all. It branches beyond every gate. Do you not know that?"

Chei stared at her, not in defiance now, but in something like dismay.

"Like any road," said Morgaine in that same hush of moving leaves and wind, "it leads everywhere. That is the general way of roads. Name the farthest place in the world. That road beyond this woods leads to it, one way or the other. And this Gate leads through other gates. Which lead—to many places. Vanye says you know this. Then you should know that too. And knowing that—" Morgaine took up a peeled twig to stir her tea, and carefully lifted something out of it, to flick it away. "You should know that what a lord decrees is valid only so far as his hand reaches. No further. And I have never heard of your lord Gault, nor care that I have not heard. He seems to me to be no one worth my trouble."

"Then why am I?" Chei asked harshly, with no little desperation.

"You are not," Morgaine said. "You are a considerable inconvenience."

It was not what Chei had, perhaps, expected. And Morgaine took a slow sip of tea, set the cup down and poured more for herself, the while Chei said nothing at all.

"We cannot let you free," Morgaine said. "We do not care for this Gault; and having you fall straightway into his hands would be no kindness to you and no good thing for us either. Quiet is our preference. So you will go with us, and somewhere we shall have to find you a horse—by one thing and the other I suppose you are familiar with horses. Am I wrong?"

Chei stared at her, somewhere between incredulity and panic. "No," Chei said faintly. "No, lady. I know horses."

"And our business is not truly needful for you to know, is it? Only that it has become yours, as your safety has become conditional on ours—as I assure you it is. We will find you a horse—somewhere hereabouts, I trust. Meanwhile you will ride with Vanye—as soon as you are fit to ride. In the meanwhile you eat our food, sleep in our blankets, use our medicines, and repay us with insults." All of this so, so softly spoken. "This last will change. You have naught to do today but lie in the sun, in what modesty or lack of it will not affect me, I do assure you. You do not move me.—How wide are Gault's lands? How far shall we ride before we cease to worry about his attacking us?"

Chei sat there a moment with a worried look. Then he bit his lip, shifted forward and pulled a half-burned stick out of the coals to draw in the dirt with it. "Here you found me. Here the road. Back here—" He swept a wide, vague area with the stick. "The gate from which you came." The stick moved on to inscribe the line of the road running past the hill of the wolves, and up and up northward. "On either side here is woods. Beyond that—" He gestured out beyond the trees, where the river was, and where meadow shone gold. "The forest is scattered—a woods here, another there, at some distance from the road."

"You are well familiar with this lord's land," Morgaine said.

The stick wavered, a shiver that had no wind to cause it. "The north and the west I know. But this last I do not forget. I watched where they took us." The stick moved again, tracing the way, and slashed a line across the road. "This is the Sethoy, this river. It comes from the mountains. A bridge crosses it, an old bridge. The other side of it, northward across the plain, lord Gault's own woods begin; and his pastures; and his fields; and there is his hold, well back from the old Road. In the hills, a village. A road between. He has that too. There are roads besides the Old Road, there is a track goes across it from Morund and up again by the hills; there is another runs by Gyllin-brook—that runs along these hills and through them, up toward the village. None of these are safe for you."

"Further over on either side," Morgaine said, and moved around the fire to indicate with her finger the left and the right of the road. "Are there other roads?"

"Beyond the western hills." Chei retreated somewhat from her presence, and used his stick to trace small lines.

"Habitations?"

"High in the hills. No friends of any strangers. They keep their borders against every outsider: now and again the lords from the north come down and kill a number of them—to prove whatever that proves. Who knows?"

There was perhaps a barb in that. Morgaine did not deign to notice it. She pointed to the other side. "And here to the east?"

"*Qhalur* holdings. Lord Herot and lord Sethys, with their armies."

"What would you counsel?"

Chei did not move for a moment. Then he pointed with the stick to the roads on the west. "There. Through the woods, beyond Gault's fields. Between Gault and the hillmen."

"But one reaches the trail by the old Road."

"There, lady, just short of Gault's woods. I can guide you—from there. I *will* guide you, if you want to avoid Gault's hold. I want the same."

"Where are *you* from?" Vanye asked, the thing he had not said, and moved close on the other side. "Where is your home?"

Chei drew in a breath and pointed close above Morund land. "There."

"Of what hold?" Morgaine asked.

"I was a free man," Chei said. "There are some of us—who come down from the hills."

"Well-armed free men," said Vanye.

Chei's eyes came at once back to him, alarmed.

"Are there many of your sort?" Morgaine asked.

Fear, then. True fear. "Fewer than there were," Chei said at last. "My lord is dead. *That* is my crime. That I was both armed, and a free Man. So once was Gault. But they took him. Now he is *qhal*—inside."

"Is that," Vanye asked, "the general fate of prisoners?"

"It happens," Chei said, looking anxiously from one to the other side of him.

"Tell us," Morgaine said, shifting position to point at the road where it continued. "What lies ahead?"

"Other *qhal*. Tejhos. Mante."

"What sort of place?" Vanye asked.

"I have no knowledge. A *qhalur* place. *You* would know, better than I."

"But Gault knows them."

"I am sure," Chei said in a hoarse small voice. "Perhaps you do."

"Perhaps we do not," Morgaine said softly, very softly. "Describe the way north. On the old Road."

Chei hesitated, then moved the stick and drew the line northward with a large westward jog halfway before an eastward trend. "Woods and hills," he said. "A thousand small trails. Above this—is *qhalur* land. The High Lord. Skarrin."

"Skarrin. Of Mante." Morgaine rested her chin on her hand, her brow knit, her fist clenched, and for a long moment were no more questions. Then: "And what place had Men in this land?"

Unhesitatingly, the stick indicated the west. "There." And the east, about Morund. "And there. Those in the west and those who live in *qhalur* lands. But in the west are the only free Men."

"Of which you were one."

"Of which I was one, lady." There was no flinching in that voice, which had become as quiet as Morgaine's own. "You are kinder than Gault, that is all I know. If a man has to swear to some *qhal* to live—better you than the lord that Skarrin sent us. I will get you through Gault's lands. And if I serve you well— believe me and trust my leading when you come near humans, and I will guide you through."

"Against your own," Vanye said.

"I was Gault's prisoner. Do you think human folk would trust me again? There have been too many spies. No one is alive who went through Gyllinbrook, except me. My lord Ichandren is dead. My brother is dead—Thank God's mercy for both." For a moment his voice did break, but he sat still, his hands on his knees. "No one is alive to vouch for me. I will not raise a hand against human folk. But I do not want to die for nothing. One of my comrades on that hill—he let the wolves have him. The second night. And I knew then I did not want to die."

Tears spilled, wet trails down his face. Chei looked at neither of them. His face was still impassive. There were only the tears.

"So," Morgaine said after a moment, "is it an oath you will give us?"

"I swear to you—" The eyes stayed fixed beyond her. "I swear to you—every word is true. I will guide you. I will guide you away from all harm. On my soul I will not lie to you, lady. Whatever you want of me."

Vanye drew in a breath and wrapped his arms about him, staring down at the man. Such terms he had sworn, himself, *ilin*-oath, by the scar on his palm and the white scarf about the helm—outcast warrior, taken up by a lord, an oath without recourse or exception. And hearing that oath, he felt something swell up in his throat—memory of that degree of desperation; and a certain remote jealousy, that of a sudden this man was speaking to Morgaine as his liege, when he knew nothing of her; or of him; or what he was undertaking.

God in Heaven, liyo, *do you trust this man, and do you take him on* my

*terms—have I trespassed too far, come too close to you, that now you take in
another stray dog?*

"I will take your oath," Morgaine said. "I will put you in Vanye's charge."

"Do you believe him?" Morgaine asked him later, in the Kurshin tongue, while
Chei lay naked in the sun on a blanket, sleeping, perhaps—far enough for decency on the grassy downslope of the riverside, but still visible from the
campfire—sun is the best thing for such wounds, Morgaine had said. Sun and
clean wind.

Not mentioning the salve and the oil and the matter of the man's fouled
armor, which there was some salvaging, perhaps, with oil and work.

"A man swears," Vanye said. "The oath is as good as the man. But," he said
after a moment, kneeling there beside the dying fire, "a man might sell his soul,
for something of value to him. Such as his life."

She looked at him for a long time. "The question then, is for what coin,
would it not be?"

"He believes," Vanye said, "in witchcraft."

"Does thee not, now?"

Vanye lifted his shoulders, a small, uncomfortable movement, and shifted
his eyes momentarily toward the dragon sword, which had never left her side,
not in all this perilous day. Its ruby eyes gleamed wickedly in the gold hilt; it
reminded him of that stone which he carried against his own heart, a foreign,
a dangerous thing. "I have never seen any witch-working. Only things *qhal*
have made, most of which I can manage—" A sense of dislocation came on
him, a sense of panic, fear of what he had become, remorse for the things that
he had lost. "Or I have become a witch myself," he murmured. "Perhaps that is
what witchcraft is. Chei ep Kantory would think so."

There was a great deal, he thought, on Morgaine's mind. But for a moment
he had distracted her, and she looked at him in that way that once had made
him vastly uncomfortable. Her eyes were gray and clear to the depths of that
gray like the devouring sea; her lashes were, like no human and no *qhal* he had
ever seen at such range, dark gray next the lid and shading to pale at the tips,
and that shading was on her brows but nowhere about her hair, which was altogether silver. Halfling, she had said. Sometimes he thought it true. Sometimes he did not know at all.

"Thee regrets?"

He shook his head finally. It was the most that he could say. He drew a great
breath. "I have learned your lesson, *liyo*. I look around me. That is all. Never
back."

Morgaine hissed between her teeth and flung a bit of burned stick, that with
which Chei had drawn the map. It was more than her accustomed restlessness.

She rested with her arms about her knees, and shifted to hunch forward, her arms tucked against her chest, gazing into nothing at all.

He was silent. It seemed wisest.

It was their lives she was thinking on. He was sure of that. She was wiser than he—he was accustomed to think so. He missed things, not knowing what he should see, things which Morgaine did not miss. She had taught him—skills which might well horrify their prisoner: the working of gates, the writing of *qhal*, the ideas which *qhal* held for truth—who swore by no god and looked (some of them) back toward a time that they had ruled and (some of them) forward to a time that they should recover their power, at whatever cost to the immortal souls they disavowed.

Qhal in most ancient times had taken Men, so Morgaine had told him, and changed them, and scattered them through the gates, along with plants and creatures of every sort, until Time itself abhorred their works and their confusing what Was, and mixed all elements in one cataclysmic Now—the which thought chilled his much-threatened soul, and unhinged the things Holy Church had taught him and which he thought he knew beyond any doubt.

Qhal had taken Men to serve them because they were most *qhal*-like . . . and thereby the ancient *qhal*-lords had made a dire mistake: for Men in their shorter lives, multiplied far more rapidly, which simple fact meant that Men threatened them.

In his own land, in Kursh and Andur, divided by the mountain ridge, the snowy Mother of Eagles—there *qhal* had been reduced virtually to rumor, hunted for the most part, tolerated in a few rare cases—so frost-haired Morgaine had been tolerated by the High Kings a hundred years before his birth, while in his own ruined age even his own hair had been too light a brown for Nhi clan's liking. And in this place—

In this place, *qhal* had adjusted that balance. *The lords from the north come down and kill a number of them*—Chei had said of *qhalur* raids on the hillfolk. To prove whatever that proves. Who knows?

Vanye knew. He knew it along with the other things that a man like Chei would not, he hoped, comprehend. That understanding of callous murder, that perspective which allowed him to fathom *qhalur* motives—seemed to Vanye a gulf like the gulf of life and death, the knowledge that everything behind them was dust.

What became of your cousin? Chei had asked. But he could not answer that either: he could explain to no one, except the likes of lord Gault, behind whose human eyes, Chei had said, resided a *qhal*—

—an old one, Vanye thought. Or one wounded or sick to death. A *qhal* who had learned a single way to overcome humankind, by the gates and the power they had to conserve a dying mind in a body not its own.

Qhal who use the gates, he thought suddenly, and felt a touch of ice about his heart.

"*Liyo,*" he said. "If *qhal* are using the gates here—what will prevent them going where they will?"

"Nothing prevents them," Morgaine said, and looked toward him, a sharp, quick look. "Thee understands—nothing—prevents them. It is possible they know we are here, it is possible they are tracking us already, since we disturbed the gate. These are not gentle folk. We have seen the proof of that. I will tell you what I notice: that our friend yonder is not much amazed at our horses or our gear or our companying together. Nor astonished that we should come from the gates, the precise location of which he does not know. Now, that he is not astonished may be that he knows nothing of the gates, but if the *qhal* in this world do come and go by that one gate, then they have considerable mastery of the other one." She gestured about them. "There are the trees, do you see? That twisting does not happen in one use of the gates. It is frequent that this one gate throws out power. It is not working well. But that they cannot mend it does not mean that they do not use it."

It was not a comforting thought. "Then they might come behind us."

"If what our friend believes is true, yes. They can. And if by chance someone in Mante or Tejhos was warding that gate when we came through, then they do know that it was used."

He cast a sharp look toward the man sleeping in the sun, and experienced a feeling of panic.

It was a guide *he* did not trust, a burden to slow the horses. Easiest to abandon the man, trust to speed, remembering that the man was lame in one foot and incapable of running.

—There were, to be sure, the wolves.

There was no pain finally—nothing but the wind and the sun on his bare skin, and Chei lay with his eyes shut, the light glowing red through his lids, the delirious play of sun-warmth alternate with the cool wind—in abandonment and safety unimaginable in all his life. He ought to feel shame at his nakedness, but there was little left in a man who had suffered Gault's dungeons. He ought not to be so well content, but he had learned to put all his mind into a moment, even into the trough between two waves of pain, and to find his comfort there, trusting that another such respite would come—if he ignored the pain between.

So with this day. Hell was on either side. But the day was the best he had known since the other side of Gyllin-brook, and if there was hell to come, perhaps—only perhaps—it would be like the waves of pain, the first signal of a rhythm he only now discovered in his life.

That was how he reasoned with himself. Perhaps he had grown mad on his hilltop, conversing with the wolves and calling them by name. But he was very sure that his life was better now; and that tomorrow might well be the same. He had grown comfortable indeed if he could plan for two whole days at once.

Beyond that he refused to think at all. There was danger in such thoughts— danger the moment he began to believe the earnestness in the man's eyes or the easy way this man and this *qhalur* woman spoke together, argued, shrugged and gestured—everything about them being the way of two comrades in the field, except the little frowns, or the small gestures that said male and female—

As if that could be. As if a human man could willingly go to a *qhal*—

That a *qhal* could laugh and trade barbs with her servant, and that a *qhalur* woman sat here in the woods, secret from Gault and all his doings—a *qhalur* witch with one human servant and a power which could burn iron—this was a matter that ranged far beyond the things that Chei wanted to think about.

It was only certain that they meant him to go with them; and for the moment that meant he had hope of evading Gault's patrols and a return to that hilltop. That was worth the *lady* and the bowing of his head, and even—more dangerously—the least small wondering if there was not another kind of *qhal*, and if the bargain this *qhalur* lady offered might be real—or if her human servant might wish to be his friend.

The most perilous thing, the most dangerous thing, was to give way to that manner of thinking and even once, even a moment—think that the *qhal* might take him on the same terms as her servant, or that in her—in the slender person of this *qhalur* woman—might be safety without compromise, safety such as he experienced now—even power such as a Man could have. If a man could find a *qhal*-lord so free with her servants—was a man not a fool to refuse to shelter in that shadow, when he had come to the point he would not have lived, otherwise? Was there shame in that?

He did not want to think of that overmuch either. The comfort he was in was sufficient for the day, sufficient for many days. He should turn onto his face and avoid burning his skin. That was the most onerous decision he needed make.

In a little while he moved to the shade and was content to lie still, wrapped in his blanket, his head pillowed on his arm. He slept, and waked to find the smell of cooking on the breeze, at which he wept, a foolish leaking of tears from his eyes and a desire to gather his courage and walk up the hill to them and sit down at their fire and be welcomed there—but he lay there weeping instead, and shaking with fear of trying that, fear that there would be no welcome for him, and that they would only tie him again and his aching shoulders could not bear the pain of another night like the last.

And he did not know why he should weep and shiver like a fool over the smell of cakes on the fire, except he was still alive; and others were not, his brother was not, which thoughts ranged back to the hill and the noise of wolves feeding in the dark—a safe sound, a sound with nothing at all of grief in it, because life shrank to the night, the moment, the instant . . . in which the wolves were fed and he was still alive.

That was the safe thing to remember. That was a cold time, a numb, down-to-the-rock time, when a man learned that only life was valuable, and only his own life was truly valuable. His comrades kept the wolves from him. That was all. They were there to talk to and fill the silence while they were alive, but a man only wanted to be alive a little longer at the last; and if a friend was the price of that, then a man learned he would pay that, would pay the wolf-price with his dearest friend or with his own brother. That was the safe thing to remember . . . when the smell of bread and the sound of voices waked something so painful, so terribly painful it might shatter him and make him a man again.

So quickly then, the aching knot untied itself, and the tears dried in the wind, and he lay smelling that cooking and thinking that he would sell his soul for a morsel of fresh bread and a little of human laughter. There was so little of it left to sell, so very little of what he had been. He was damned as the *qhal* and as this man who served her, and if they would take another soul for a little ease and a little food and a betrayal of his own kind, then he was apt enough for that trade.

He might have tamed the wolves, finally, and if they would let him be a wolf, then he need not fear Gault, or anything in the world—for a while. They might well be Gault's enemies: rumor was that the thing which was Gault had no love lost with his Overlord. They might be from Mante, or from somewhere— the woman had said it—that he did not understand; but if they let him be a wolf, if they took him among themselves and there was a kind of man who could walk among the *qhal* free as that one walked, and still in his own right mind—then there was hope. . . .

He shivered again, seeing Ichandren's head outside Gault's gates, seeing that dungeon again, and hearing the screams wrung from a man who was the bravest and strongest he had ever known, before they reduced him to a red and terrible lump of meat and struck off his head. . . .

. . . There was revenge. Gault would never know him by sight. It was a random choice had selected the few for the wolves. He was no one, that Gault should single him out for any personal revenge.

But if he was a wolf, there was a time Gault would learn to fear him and to curse the day he met him.

That was an aim even worth a man's soul.

For the first time the chance of a future opened up before him, like a mist clearing.

But he had met the woman's eyes by accident across the fire, and after that avoided—after that, avoided remembering, too closely, that he had felt himself in bodily danger from her. It was *that* kind of feeling, that a man did not expect to feel with a woman, that was unmanly to feel with a woman, and that one would never admit to; but if ever he remembered it, afterward, when he was with a woman, then he would have no power with her . . . no more with any woman, ever. . . .

She was indeed a witch, he thought. He knew folk who called themselves witches, and made a great deal of muttering over their herbs and potions, and mid-wived babes and horses into the world. A man did not cross them, or did so only if he had bought the token of a greater one for stronger luck—and too great a one might, the priests said, taint a man's soul.

Such great power he had felt in this one. He knew that it was. And it was better mercy by far had he gotten from her than Gault had gotten from Mante— the Gault they had honored before the *qhal* had taken him up with talk of peace; the Gault who had been Ichandren's friend, and worked the same ploy on Ichandren—God help them all.

Truce. Truce—Gault had said.

That was the faith *qhal* kept.

The man Vanye came down the hill finally: Chei watched him come—and trembled, as if in a dream; and walked with him at his invitation to share their fire.

Thereafter Chei sat wrapped in his blanket and took a meal he could not eat his share of, so weak his stomach was. But they were easy with him, the man and the woman both, and asked him few questions, and afterward let him lie over near the fire, while the witch took the pans down to the water to wash them like any woman of the bands; and Vanye after she had returned, led the horses down to water them, from their picket higher on the hill.

After that, while daylight faded, they worked on what Chei recognized for his own gear, picking bits of rust from the links of his chain-mail, scouring the metal with water and river sand, finishing it with oil.

His boots were already done, the one split as it was, but with a length of harness-leather lying looped about it, sufficient to wrap several times about the ankle and hold it.

He saw all these things, lying on his side, with only the blanket to clothe him . . . watched them work, even the witch, on these menial tasks which seemed to be for his benefit—for him, since they had no conceivable need of a pair of ruined boots or armor much poorer than the wonderful close-linked mail and supple leather that they wore.

In the deep night, when they said to each other that it was time to sleep, the man dragged his saddle and his bedding over by the horses and lay down there, while the witch wrapped herself in a dark cloak and settled against an old, thick-boled tree, to keep night-watch. They left him the warmth of the coals. They said no word to threaten him. They did not tie him.

Chei lay in the dark thinking and thinking, watching and drowsing by turns, observing every smallest move they made. Hope trembled through him, that they had already accepted him, for whatever reasons. He wept, in the dark, long and unreasonably.

He did not know why, except their kindness had broken something in him which all Gault's threats had never touched, and he was terrified it was all a lie.

⤳ Chapter 3

It was fish, the next supper they shared. There was not a rabbit to be had—the wolves, Vanye reckoned, who sang to them nightly, had seen to what hunting there was about the gate; although why the wolves themselves stayed in such an unwholesome place, he wondered.

It was the mountains to the south, Chei said; and humans; humans to the west and north; *qhal* to the north and east; and in all, Vanye reckoned, the wolves were as shy of habitations as they were in other worlds.

Excepting only, Chei said, the half-wolves. Gault's pets.

Or once, when war had made chaos of the middle lands—then Chei remembered the wild wolves coming down to human camps and villages to take the sheep. He remembered his folk moving a great deal—where, he did not know, except it had been in the hills.

"Then," Chei said, looking mostly at the fire, as if his thoughts ranged distant, "then we settled in Perot's freehold, in Aglund. We felt safe there. But that only lasted—at most, a year. Then Gault was fighting along with the other lords. I was a boy then. I remember—I remember wars, I remember having to move and move again. I remember the winters, with the snow chest-deep on the horses—and people died, many died. We came to Gault's freehold, in Morund. We were borderers, for him. Those were the good years. I rode with Ichandren. My brother, my father and I. They are dead. All."

He was silent for a time, then.

"Mother?" Morgaine asked.

Chei did not look at her. His throat worked. But the eyes never shifted from their wide gaze on the fire. "I do not know. I saw her last—" A lift of one shoulder. "I was thirteen winters. That was before Morund fell and Gault went north. He came back . . . Changed. After that—after that, he and the *qhal* from the north killed most of the human men at Morund-keep. Killed most everyone, and brought in men from the east. They would fight for Gault. Some of those from Morund might have wanted to, but if they took them at all, they marched them west, to serve the other *qhal*-lords. Gault would never trust men who had served him before he was *qhal*. Aye, nor women either. They put them all on wagons. We lost—twenty men trying to take the women from the guards. My father died then. There were just too many."

There was more of silence. The fire snapped and spat.

"But I doubt very much my mother was alive," Chei said. "Even then. My father believed it. But no one else did. She was not a strong woman. And it was a bad year."

Twenty men lost, Vanye thought, amid a man's grief, and thought by the way he had said it that twenty had been a devastating loss. *There were just too many. . . .*

He met Morgaine's eyes across the fire and knew that she had added that as quickly and set things somewhat in proportions—she, who had taught a young outlaw something beyond woodcraft and ambush; his lady-liege, who had ridden to war and sat in the affairs of kings a hundred years before he was born.

But she had led him into both war and kings' councils since then.

He rested his arms on his knees and probed the coals with a stick, watching it take fire.

"The trees," Morgaine said. "Do you mark them, Chei, how they twist here? Yet there is no present feeling of unease in this woods. Birds come here. They tolerate the gate-force very little. Why do you suppose this is?"

"I do not know," Chei said faintly.

Morgaine did not answer.

"Why would it be?" Chei asked her then.

Morgaine shifted the dragon sword to her lap, tucking one knee up, and hugged that knee against her. "If I cast leaves in the fire, it would flare. Would it not?"

"Yes, lady."

"And you would move back. Would you not?"

"Yes," Chei said, more faintly still, as if he regretted ever asking into *qhal*ish lore.

"Quickly?"

"Yes, lady."

"So the birds would fly for their comfort if that gate yonder opened this moment. And you would feel it in your bones."

Chei flinched, visibly.

"So this is a very good place for a camp," Morgaine said, "for us who have no desire for unannounced visitors. How frequently do you suppose this gate is used?"

"I would not know."

"Perhaps not. So of that use we would have warning. If we ride from here we have Gault to concern us. How long—might we ride, slowly, on the road itself, before we came to his notice?"

"If we left after sundown—" Chei's breath came rapidly. "We could make the western road and be deep in the woods before daybreak. Lady, I do not know where his riders may be, no one could say that, but I know where they are likeliest not. We could make a safe camp in that woods near his lands, stay there the day, and pick up the west road. No one would be traveling that at night; and by one more morning we can reach the hills. We rest during the day, we travel at night. That is the best thing to do."

"So," Morgaine said, and glanced Vanye's way, a quick shift of her eyes. "We can reach the woods before the dawn," she said, looking back at Chei. "You are sure of that."

"A-horse, I know that we could."

"Then we will go," she said quietly. "If our guest swears he can bear the saddle, we had best leave this place. We do not know how long our welcome will last."

Vanye nodded, agreeing, with misgivings he knew she shared, and with a quiet as carefully maintained.

The place, true, had a ward as great as any fabled witchery could provide— that they would feel any disturbance in the gate.

But it held danger too: it was remotely possible—that that flaring of power could simply take them, at this range, if there were some unshielded gate-stone to which the force might reach—and if their enemies had found them.

Vanye had one change of clothes, cloth breeches and a fine shirt—the one for those times they could lay aside the armor, which did not look likely here: light and fine, delicately sewn—a waste to wear such a gift on the trail; but the giver had insisted.

Now he laid all this at Chei's side, along with the mended boots, as Morgaine was meticulously packing and weight-measuring with their bags.

"You could not bear the armor on your shoulders," Vanye said. "My liege will carry it; I will carry you on my horse. We are taking your word we can make cover before sunrise."

Chei took up the fine cloth and frowned in surprise. Well he might, Vanye thought; and went to prepare his own gear, and to saddle the horses in the dark. *They* knew that there was a journey to come, and stamped and shifted in impatience at this meddling about.

He saddled them both, and hung his sword at Arrhan's right side, where he would not carry it on a ride like this, except he had Chei at his back. He tied a folded blanket flat under thongs bound to the rings that ordinarily held it rolled, scratched Arrhan in the soft underside of her throat, and Siptah under his chin, snatching his fingers from the stud's half-hearted nip—trouble, he thought. Siptah had been trouble of one kind before, well-trained as he was; now that he had acquired the mare, Siptah had other thoughts in his head, and Arrhan had like ones.

"Fool," he muttered to himself, that ever he had taken her, that ever he had brought her to a land like this. He was Kurshin, was a horseman from his birth. And he had been, a handful of days ago, under a fair sun, too willing to hope— Heaven save them—for something other than this.

Fool, he thought again. For disaster went about the gates. Where power was, there the worst men gathered—too rarely, the best. He had ridden out among the twisted trees, among ruins, into murder and wars—

And all his subtle plans—for Morgaine was mad, at times, and drove them too hard and wore herself to bone and will—all his plans, ill-thought that they were, involved a means to travel at a saner pace. For that, he had accepted the mare, knowing there was a risk—but hoping for a more peaceful passage, for leisure and time, even to drop a foal of the Baien stud: such thoughts the ar-rhend had made reasonable, and now they seemed mad.

Now it was his own instincts urged they run.

He hugged the mare about the neck, pressed his head against her cheek, patted her hard, all with a pang of bitter guilt. "So we go," he whispered to her. She ducked her head free and nosed him in the side with a horse's thoughtless strength.

No stopping the stallion or the mare. No stopping any horse from what it truly willed to do, even if it was a fatal thing. It was always their own vitality that killed them, a horseman knew that.

He heard a step behind him, and turned his head. It was Morgaine, bring-ing the saddlebags. She let them down at his feet, then, standing close, rested her hand on his shoulder, and walked away, so startling him by that gesture he simply stood and stared at her retreating back.

What was that? he wondered.

Apology, of a kind? Sympathy?

She did these things to him, and walked away in her silences, and left him to saddle the horses and wonder, in a kind of biding panic, what had moved her to that.

He did not even know, Heaven witness, why he should be disturbed, or why his heart was beating in panic, except it was the old familiar business of snatched sleep and arming by dark and riding through hostile lands, sleeping by turns in the daylight, tucked close in some concealment.

Except it was Morgaine who, like Heaven, decided where they should go and when; and there had been all too much of comradely understanding in that small gesture—as if she had confessed that she was weary, too, and there were no miracles.

From his liege, he did not want such admissions.

He finished his work. He overtook her at the buried fire, leading the horses; and having the horses between him and Chei, he took his Honor-blade sheathed from his belt and gave it to her without a word—for safety's sake. She knew. She slipped it into her belt next her own ivory-hilted Korish blade, and pulled and hooked the belt ring which slid the dragon sword up to ride between her shoulders, before she took Siptah's reins from his hand and climbed into the saddle. The gray stud snorted his impatience and worked at the bit.

Vanye set his foot in Arrhan's stirrup and settled himself in the saddle, reining her about, where Chei waited, dressed in his borrowed clothing and his own mended boots, and holding his sleeping blanket rolled in his arms.

"You will want that on the ride," Vanye said, taking the blanket roll into his lap, and cleared his left stirrup for the man. Chei set his foot, took his offered hand as Arrhan shifted weight, and came astride and well-balanced so quickly that Vanye gave the mare the loose rein she expected. It made the mare happier about the double load; she pricked her ears up and switched her tail and took a brisk stride behind Siptah.

Through the trees and down along the river which had guided them—by the light of an incredible starry heaven and a slivered moon, so brilliant a night as the sunlight left the sky utterly, that the pale grass shone and the water had sheen on its darkness.

Behind him, Chei wrapped the blanket about himself, for the breeze was chill here in the open; and Vanye drew an easier breath, bringing Arrhan up on Siptah's left—the left, with Morgaine, shield-side and never the perilous right. She had her hair braided for this ride: not the clan-lord's knot to which she was entitled, but the simple warrior's knot of clan Chya of Koris, like his own. *Changeling's* hilt winked moonlit gold beside the silver of her braid; bright silver sparked and flashed along the edge of her sleeves, where mail-work shone the like of which later ages had forgotten. Moonlight touched Siptah's illusory dapples, the pale ends of his mane and tail.

They were enspelled—not with magics, but with the sense of change, of passage, the night sky's softening influence that made them part of a land to which they did not belong.

And Chei had sworn, on his life, that they might expect peace for a time on this ride.

They took the same slow pace when they had come to the Road, with its ancient stone bridge across the stream. Woods gave way briefly to meadow and to woods again, a tangled, unkept forest. A nightbird called. There was the sound of their horses' hooves—on earth and occasionally on stone, and eventually on the stone and damp sand of a ford which crossed a stream, perhaps tributary to the river they had left.

"I do not know its name," Chei said when Vanye asked. "I do not know. I only know we crossed it."

They let the horses drink, and rode further, in wilderness cut well back from the road, but unthinned beyond that. No woodsmen, Vanye thought, no caretaker. It was still wild woods, overgrown and rank with vines and thorns. But the trees grew straight and clean. Gate-force did not reach to this place. They were beyond the region in which they would know if the gate were used; and they were beyond the region in which some weapon of that nature could reach to them.

He felt Chei lean against him, briefly, and recover himself; felt it again; and again the same recovery; a third time: "No matter," he said. "Rest," and: "No," Chei murmured.

But in time Chei slumped a while against him, till they faced a stream-cut to go down and up again. "Chei," Vanye said, slapping him on the knee.

Chei came awake with a start and took his balance. Arrhan took the descent and the climb with dispatch then, and quickened her pace till she had overtaken Siptah.

They were still on the Road. It began to stretch away across a vast plain, country open under fewer and fewer stars, exposed to view as far as the eye could see, and Morgaine drew rein, pointing to the red seam along the horizon.

"Chei. That is the sun over there."

Chei said nothing.

"Where are we?" she asked.

"It is still the Road," Chei protested; and: "Lady, this is not the land I know. Northward—yes. But here—I have never been but the once. We are still on the Road—we will make it—"

"How far does this go?" Her voice had an edge to it, a dangerous one. "Wake up, man. You know what I would know. You swore that you did. Do you want your enemies' attention? Or do you tell me full and free that you do not know where you are?"

"I know where I am! There is a kind of ruin, I do not know how far—I swear to you, we will reach it by morning." Chei's teeth chattered, and his breath hissed, not altogether, Vanye thought, of exhaustion and the night chill. "It was our starting-place misled me. The river must have bent. I know it is there. I swear it is. We can still come to it. But we can go wide, now." He pointed over westward, where the plain rolled away to the horizon. "We can pick up the trail yonder in the hills. Off Gault's lands."

"But equally off our way," Morgaine said, and held Siptah back, the dapple gray backing and circling. "How is Arrhan faring?"

"She will manage," Vanye said, and looked uneasily toward the lightening of the sky in the east, over low and rolling hills. "*Liyo*, I do not say yea or nay, but I had as lief be off this road. West is likely the best advice at this point."

"North," she said, and held Siptah still a moment, when he would have moved. "By morning, he swears. It is very little time."

She swung about and went on, not quickly, saving the horses.

"*Are* you mistaken?" Vanye asked of Chei.

"No," Chei said; and shivered, whether with cold he could not tell.

Morgaine had said it; there was only one way, ultimately, that they could go; and less and less he liked delay along this road, less and less he liked the prospect of a long journey aside, and more and more he disliked their situation.

"Best you be right, man."

Morgaine dropped back to ride beside. They went perforce at Arrhan's double-burdened pace, under an open sky and fading stars.

Chei hugged his blanket about him. It was terror kept him awake now. It was nightmare as dread as the wolves, this slow riding, this pain of half-healed sores and the slow, steady rhythm of horses which could go no faster, not though Gault and all his minions come riding off the horizon.

The sky brightened, the few wispy clouds in the east took faint and then pinker color, until at last all the world seemed one naked bowl of grass and one road going through it, unnaturally straight track through a land all dew-grayed green. At times Vanye and the lady spoke in a language he did not understand, a harsh speech which fell on the ear with strange rhythms, but softly spoken, little exchanges of a word and a few words. There was a grim tone to it. There was discontent. He imagined it involved him, though he dared not ask.

"Where are these ruins of yours?" Vanye asked then, and slapped him on the knee when he failed to realize that it was to him he had spoken.

"I know that they are there," he said, "I swear to you."

"Neither does the sun lie," Vanye said.

There was the beginning of daylight. There was the hint of color in things. And the white mare was weary now. Did their enemies find them, Chei thought, there was no way that the mare might run.

Did their enemies find them. . . .

But on that terrible hilltop, like a dream, he recalled light coming from Morgaine's fingers, and recalled chain melting and bending, and how Vanye had shielded him from that sight.

Weapons you may not like to see, Vanye had warned him.

He looked at the open land around him, and the treacherous roll of hills which might mask an army.

They would kill him first, he thought, if they suspected ambush. There was no doubt but what they would; he had failed them. They had cause to be angry.

The sun came up full. The land went gold and green.

And as they crested a rise of the plain and looked on a darkness that topped the rise ahead he felt a moment's dread that it was some band of riders—till his eye adjusted for the scope of the land and he knew it was woods that he saw.

They camped among ancient stones, beside a stream which crossed the low point among them, under the branches of trees which arched over and trailed their branches waterward. Among the ruins, a sparse and stubborn grass grew, on a ridge well-shielded by the trees; and there the horses grazed.

They ventured a fire only large enough to heat a little water, and ate bread Morgaine had made at the last camp, and fish they had smoked; and drank tea—Chei's prepared with herbs against the fever.

Chei had borne the ride, Vanye reckoned, very well—was weary, and only too glad to lie down to sleep, there in the sun-warmth, on the leafy bank. So, then, was he, leaving the watch to Morgaine, and listening to the water and the wind and the horses.

"It has been quiet," she whispered when she waked him, while Chei still slept. "Nothing has stirred. A bird or two. A creature I do not know came down to drink: it looked like a mink with a banded tail. There is a black snake sunning himself down on that log."

These were good signs, of a healthier vicinity. He drew a deep breath and yielded her up the blankets, and tucked himself down again in a nook out of the wind. He had a bite to eat, a quarter of the bread he had saved back from their breakfast; and a drink of clear water from the stream which ran here, more wholesome than the river had been.

And when toward dusk, Chei stirred from his sleep, he rose and stretched himself, and put together the makings of a little fire—again, hardly enough to warm water, quick to light and quick to bury, and a risk even as it was.

Morgaine roused them for tea and day-old cakes and smoked fish, and sat against the rock, sipping her portion of the tea and letting her eyes shut from time to time. Then her eyes opened with nothing of somnolence about them at all. "We might stay here a day," she said. "We have put distance between ourselves and the gate—which is very well. But this is the last place we may have leisure. Another night's riding—and we will be beyond Gault's holdings. Is that not the case?"

"That is the case," Chei said. "I swear to you."

"Bearing in mind that hereafter I will not permit Vanye's horse to carry double, and tire itself."

"I will walk. I can fend for myself, lady."

"Are you fit to walk? I tell you the truth: if you are not fit—we will give you that day's grace. But there may be other answers. Perhaps you know something of Morund's inner defenses."

Chei's eyes widened in dread. "Guarded," he said. "Well guarded."

"I," Vanye said, and rested his chin on his forearm, his knee tucked beneath his elbow. "I have stolen a horse or two in my life. I suppose Morund has pastures hereabouts. And for that matter, *liyo*, I can quite well walk."

Morgaine glanced his way. So he knew that he had guessed her intention all along, by that calm exchange. And he had had a queasy feeling in all this ride, good as the reasons were for quitting the last camp: Arrhan might carry double at a very slow pace, but not in haste—his liege not being a fool, to press one of their horses to the limit.

But that she risked them this far on this man's word had bewildered him, all the same—until she asked of Morund.

"Or," he said in the Kurshin tongue, "we might let our guide walk these trails he claims to know—alone. And we go the quicker way, the two of us, by night and by stealth, *liyo*, and get clear of this place. That is my opinion in the matter."

She gave him a sudden sidelong glance.

He gave a little lift of his shoulder. No frown was on her face, but that, he thought, was because there was a witness.

"I will have a word with thee," she said, and motioned off toward the streamside.

But: "I do not think there is overmuch to say," he said, and did not rise. "I am *ilin*. Ask. I will do it. Steal a horse? That is nothing. Perhaps I should take Morund. You hardly need trouble yourself."

"Thee is unreasonable!"

"I do not think I am unreasonable. Everything you wish, I will do. Can a man be more reasonable? Take Morund. Better that than walk in there. *Far* better than drag this poor man in there, since you are set on stirring up a trouble we could ride around. We have come this far on this man's advice. Take the rest of it, I say, and go where he bids us go, and let us go around this place."

For a moment she did not speak. There was sullen anger in the look she gave him. Then: "Oh, aye, and trust to luck and half a score human bands, shall we?"

"Better luck than this Gault, *liyo*. And what will we, do general murder? Is *that* what you want? It is what you lead us to. Someone will die, likest myself, since I have to shield you. I have a bruise the size of my fist on my right shoulder—"

"Whose fault, that?"

"—and a man by me I do not trust; or we do trust him, enough to let him free where he could cry alarm; or we do murder outright on this man—Which is it, do we kill him, do we tie him to a tree for the wolves and his enemies to find, or do we trust him to go free? Or if we trust him for that, why in Heaven's sweet reason do we not trust him down the back trail ourselves, and take ourselves clear of this damnable place before we raise hue and cry from here to the north?"

She rose abruptly to her feet and walked off. It left him Chei's frightened stare.

"We are having a dispute," Vanye said, "regarding the ease of finding horses."

Chei said nothing at all. He looked from one to the other of them, and for a long while Morgaine stood by the streamside, arms folded, staring off into the gathering dark.

Vanye buried their fire, and went down to wash the single pan they had used.

"Thee confuses me," Morgaine said, standing behind him as he rinsed the pan. "Thee considerably confuses me."

It was not, precisely, what he had expected her to say.

"Then," he said, "we confuse each other."

"What will you?"

That was not the question he was prepared for either—or it was the earnestness of it which confounded him.

"What will *you*?" He turned from the stream, for he sensed her precisely where she was, her back turned to their prisoner and the horses; and all manner of mischief possible. "I have no idea—"

"Thee does not kneel."

"I am washing the cursed dish," he retorted, "and you have your back to the man. Do you trust him that much?"

"Now thee is watching. I *trust* that thee is watching. What will thee? To let him free? Ride in among his folk, on his guidance? *Or* do we kill him or leave him for the wolves?"

"Ah. I thought it was his oath we trusted."

She drew in a sharp breath, and said nothing at all as he got to his feet. They were of a height. He stood lower on the bank. And for a long moment he did not move.

"Or," he said, "do you think we should *not* trust his guidance? Lord in Heaven, you took his oath. Did you count me so lightly? I do not recall my pledge was much different."

"Thee is *Kurshin*," she said, and recalled to him what he had forgotten: that it was more than the language she spoke, that she was, perhaps to a greater extent than he had thought—Andurin, out of the woodland cantons of his own land.

"You will not let me remember it," he said, and jutted a clenched jaw toward the man who waited by the dead fire. "He is human. But it is not considering my scruples you took his oath. You deceived him and you refused to confide in me. Why?"

"I do not deceive you."

"You do not tell the truth."

"*Thee* pleaded for his life."

"*I* had as soon have left him at the last camp, where he had some choice where to go. *I* had as soon gone further west from the beginning and come up through the hills."

She pressed her lips together in that way she had when she had said all she would. So their arguments tended to end—himself with the last word, and Morgaine lapsed into one of her silences that could last for hours and evaporate at the last as if there had never been a word of anger.

But always Morgaine did as she would—would simply ride her own way, if he would not go with her; there was no reasoning with her.

"I will get your cursed horse," he said.

She drew a sharp breath. "We will go *his* way, by the trails."

He felt his face go hot. "So we walk turn and turn."

"I did not ask that."

"That is a wounded man. How much do you think he can do?"

"I am willing to wait here. Did I not say as much?"

"Wait here! With the enemy over the next hill!"

"What would you?"

Now it was he who found no words. He only stood there a moment, half-choked with anger; then bowed his head and walked on past her, back to put the pan with their gear.

Chei looked at him with the same bewilderment, his eyes jerking from one to the other—lastly toward Morgaine, who came and sat down on her heels beside them.

Vanye sat as he was a moment, jabbing at the ground with a stick between his knees. "I reckon," he said mildly, "that we could make the back trails. If Chei and I rode and walked by turns."

Morgaine rested her arms on her knees, her brow on the heels of her hands. Then she dropped her arms and sat down cross-legged. "Myself," she said, "I am not of a mind to be inconvenienced by this Gault of Morund."

A touch of renewed panic hit him. "*Liyo—*"

"On the other hand," she said, "your suggestion is reasonable. Unless our guide knows where we might find horses, otherwise."

"Not except we raise the countryside," Chei said in a faint voice.

"How far a journey—clear of his lands?"

"By morning we are clear."

Vanye rested the stick in both his hands. "In the name of Heaven," he said in the Kurshin tongue, "he will tell you whatever he thinks will save his life: he was wrong this morning, and we rode under sun and in the open."

"Trusting him is thy advice, and first it is aye and then nay—which do I believe?"

"I am a Man. I can trust him without believing him. Or trust him in some things and not in others. He is desperate, do you understand. Wait here. I will go and steal you a horse."

"Enough on the horse!"

"I swear to you—"

"Vanye—"

"Or lord Gault's own cursed horse, if you like! But I should not like to leave you with this man. *That* would be my worry, *liyo.* Leaving you here, I *would* tie him to a tree, and I would not take his word how far it is across this cursed lord's land. I will tell you what I had rather do: I had rather do without the horse, strike out due west, far from here, and come north well within the hills."

"Except it needs much too long."

"Too long, too long—God in Heaven, *liyo,* it *needs* nothing but that we ride quietly, carefully, that we arrive in our own good time and disturb no one. I thought we had agreed."

"He named a name," Morgaine said.

"What, he? Chei? What name?"

"Skarrin, in Mante. This lord in the north."

His heart clenched up. "Someone you know?"

"Only an old name. We may be in great danger, Vanye. We may be in very great danger."

For a moment there was only the sound of the wind in the leaves.

"Of what sort?" he asked. "*Who?*"

"In the north," she said. "I am not certain, mind. It is only a very old name—and this north-lord may be an old man, *very* old, does thee mark me. And once he knows his danger, there are measures he might take which could trap us here. Does thee understand me?"

"Who is he?"

"I do not know who he is. I know *what* he is. Or I guess. And if I bind this man by oaths and any promise I can take from him—I do not loose him near that gate behind us, does thee understand? From Morund I might gain something. From Morund I might draw this north-lord south, out of reach of his own gate. But thee may be right—there is the chance too that this Gault is mad, and that there is no dealing with him."

"With a man who feeds his enemies to wolves?"

"With a *devil*, there is dealing—sometimes far easier than with an honest man. And by everything Chei has told us, there are Men enough among the *qhal* and not the other way about, so we need not worry for thy sake. But thee says trust this Man, and trust ourselves to his folk—"

"I did not say that!"

"What does thee say? Leave him? Kill him? Is that what thee is asking? Or ride on with him? We are too far into this to camp, and if this lord Gault finds us skulking about without his leave, that brings us to a fight or to Morund-gate, under worse terms."

Vanye raked his hair out of his eyes, where it fell forward of the braid, and raked it back again, resting his elbows on his knees.

In Andur-Kursh, Men would shoot a *qhal* on sight.

"Has Chei ever heard my other name? Did you by any chance tell it to him?"

"I do not know," he said, dismayed. "The one the Shiua used?" And when she nodded: "I do not know. I think not. I am not sure. I did not know—"

"Do not speak it. Ever. And do not ask me now."

He glanced at Chei, who stared at him and at her as his only hope of safety—his life, Chei surely sensed hung in the balance in this dispute he could not follow. It was a sensible man, Vanye thought, whose eyes followed all their moves, but who had the sense to hold his peace. "He is surely wondering what we say—Heaven knows what he understands of us—but in God's good mercy, *liyo*—"

She rose and walked back to Chei; and he rose and followed.

"Can you walk?" Morgaine asked in the *qhalur* tongue, looking to Chei. "Do you think you can walk through the night?"

"Yes," Chei said.

"He is telling you anything he thinks he must," Vanye said in the other. "He fears you. He fears to refuse any *qhal*, that is the trouble with him. Let him ride and I will walk, and let us go the trails he says he knows, quietly as we may. That is my advice. That is all the advice I have. Quickly and quietly, and without bruising a leaf. It is *Men* here I had rather trust. And you know that it is not my human blood makes me say it: I had no such feeling in the arrhend, and you well know it."

"My conscience," she named him. "And has thee forgotten—it is a world's honest men who will always fight us. I dread them, Vanye, I do dread them, more than the Gaults and all the rest."

"Not here," he said with conviction. "Not here, *liyo*. Nor, let me remind you, in my land, where you found me."

"Ah, no. Thee saw only the end of it. In Andur-Kursh I did my very worst. And most I killed were my friends." It was rare she would speak of that. There was a sudden bleakness in her face, as if it were carved of bone, and as if there were only the *qhal*-blood in her and nothing else. "But thee says it: this is not Andur-Kursh. Thee trusts this man, and I had rather be where I know what a man stands to gain—have I not said I have no virtue? But so be it. I do not say I have always been right, either. We will go his way."

He was frightened then, with a fear not unlike the moments before battle.

The north, she had said—an *old* enemy. And he argued against her instincts which had saved them a hundred times over, however unlikely her choices.

Heaven save them, *who* in this land could know her name, when they had never passed this way in their lives, nor had aught to do with the people of it?

"We are going on," he said to Chei, who looked at them with bewilderment. "I will walk. You ride. My liege thinks it too much risk to venture Morund for a horse."

There was still the bewilderment in Chei's eyes. And gratitude. "She is right," he said, in innocence.

He did not want to take it for omen.

He went up to the ridge and fetched the horses down. He saddled them, and arranged their gear.

"Get up," he said then to Chei, who waited, no more enlightened than before. "I am leading the horse. From time to time we will trade places."

"And hereafter," Morgaine said, touching Chei on the shoulder before he could get to the saddle, "should we meet anyone, if you have heard any other name than Morgaine and Vanye—consider your own safety and forget that ever you heard it: there are those who would do worse to you than ever Gault did, to have their hands on anyone who knew different—and you could not tell them what they would want. Do not ask me questions. For your own sake."

"Lady," Chei said to her, half-whispering. He looked straight into her eyes close at hand, and his face was pale. "Aye, lady."

Vanye walked, the *qhal*-witch rode, when they had come down the streamside and found that trail Chei knew—that narrow track the fey-minded deer and determined borderers took which ended, often with like result, on Gault's land.

Chei watched them from his vantage—the *qhalur* witch, the man who deferred to her at most times and argued with her with a reckless violence that made his gut tighten instinctively, a man knew, a Man knew lifelong, that the *qhal*-lords were not patient of such familiarity—or Vanye himself had deceived him, and was not human. But he could not believe that when he looked in Vanye's brown and often-worried eyes, or when Vanye would do him some small and unnecessary kindness or take his side—he knew that Vanye had done that—in argument.

What these two were to each other he still could not decide. He had watched all their movements, the gestures, the little instants that an expression would soften, or she would touch his arm at times when she gave an order—but never did he touch her in that same way or truly bid her anything, for all he might raise his voice and dispute her.

They are lovers, he thought sometimes. Then he was equally sure that they were not—not, in the way the man deferred to her: *my lady*, Vanye would say; or *my liege*, or a third word he did not understand, but which likely signified the same.

Now they raged at each other, argued in voices half-whisper, half-shout, in which debate he—Vanye had said it—was undoubtedly the center of matters.

It was not the threat to his life that bewildered him. It was that there was argument possible at all. And between arguments he saw a thing he had never, in all his life, beheld. He watched them in a fascination which, increasing, absorbed his fear.

Unholy, he thought. But there seemed profound affection between them. There was more than that—but not in the way of any man and any woman he had known. It was that loyalty which bound the bands together.

It was that devotion for which men had followed Ichandren till he died.

It was that motion of the heart which he thought had died in him; and it ached of a sudden, it ached so that he rode along with the branches and the leaves raking him, and the tears running down his face—not fear such as he had felt in the night, but a quiet ache, for no reason at all that he could think of except he was alone.

He reckoned even that it was a spell the witch had cast over him, that from the time she surprised him with that look into his eyes, from that moment his soul had been snared. Now he found himself weeping again—for Falwyn and the rest, and for Bron and Ichandren his lord, and even for his father, which was foolish, because his father was many years dead.

He was weak, that was all. When the lady reined back and the man stopped the horse under them, saying they would rest, he was ashamed, and pretended exhaustion, keeping his face toward the horse as he climbed down.

So he sat with them, at the side of what had become a dirt track, and tucked his knees up and bowed his head against his arms so he should not have to show his eyes damp.

He should find some means to get a weapon and break from them—in this night, in this tangle he knew and they did not. The man he had once been would have done something to resist them, be it only slide off the horse and hope that he could put brush between them and him, and lie hidden.

But he let go his hopes in all other directions. He began truly to mean the oath that he had sworn. He wiped his face, disguising tears as sweat, despite the night air, and took the cup of water they passed him, and took their concern—for all that he had thought Vanye's earlier anger was half for him, Vanye's hand was gentle on his shoulder, his voice was gentle as he inquired was he faint.

"No," he said. "No. I will walk a while."

"Horses will fly," Vanye muttered to that. "We have half the night gone. What do we look to find ahead?"

"I will know the border," he said. "We have come halfway."

"As you knew the plains yonder?"

"This, I know," he insisted, anxious, and found the stirrup as the lady mounted up. He heaved himself into the saddle and took his seat as the horse started to move, Vanye walking ahead on the road, defined in a ray of moonlight and gone again, ghostly warrior in forest-color and mail and leather, the white scarf about his helm, the sheen of the sword hilt at his shoulders the most visible aspect of him. And the lady was no more than gray horse and shadow: she had put on her cloak and the dark hood made her part of the night.

Only he himself was visible, truly visible, to any ambush—helmless, in a pale linen shirt and astride the white mare that shone like a star in the dark. He thought of arrows, thought of the gates of Morund which lay beyond the woods, across the ancient Road.

He thought of Ichandren's skull bleaching there, and the bodies of the others cast on Morund's midden heap, and shivered in the wind, taking up his gray blanket again and wrapping it about himself partly for the cold and partly that he felt all too visible and vulnerable. He trembled; his teeth chattered if he did not clench them, and every measured tread of the horse beneath him, the whisper of the wind, the small sounds of the night—seemed all part of a terrible dream begun at Gyllin-brook.

He had ridden this way, part of Ichandren's band. In those days they had been Gault's allies; in those days they had won victories. For a few years there had seemed to be a turning in their fortunes against the northlord.

It was the same road. But the boy who had traveled it, keen on revenge for both mother and father, on winning a sure victory against the thing Gault had become . . . had become a thin and beaten man, much the wiser, in the company of strangers and on a journey which at one moment seemed swift and full of turns, and in this forever-lasting night—such a peak of terror that it could not last; as the things they did to his comrades could not last; as the nights atop the hill could not last: there was always a morning, and done was done, and a man survived somehow, that was all—but O God, the hours between, that a man had to live. . . .

They rested yet again. Quietly the woman spoke—some suggestion which

Vanye refused: perhaps, Chei thought, it was to put him off the horse and make him walk a time. And Vanye would not, whatever it was, which imagined kindness reassured him and made him warmer in the long night.

But he was afraid with a growing fear—that he had not accurately reckoned their pace: the rides he recalled had been swift and none of them had been afoot. Once he had misjudged the plains: that was the mistake of a shock-dazed memory. But now he misjudged again—he knew that he had, and that safety was further than daylight at the pace they were setting; and more difficult than he had thought, for the shock was done and the mind began reckoning clearly again, that since Ichandren was lost—any situation might prevail and the borders might have moved as they did after battles: things might not be what they had been and it was not to a known land that he was returning.

Nor was it any longer a known land in which he was both guide and hostage.

And to confess to them the fact that he had twice mistaken the distance—or given them false assurance—

He moistened his lips. He shifted his weight in the saddle. "Man," he whispered. "Vanye."

Then something else came to his ears beyond wind and leaf-whisper and the sound of their own horses. Vanye stopped the horse. The lady reined back and circled back toward them, then stopped again in mid-turn.

The woods felt wrong. Hairs lifted at his nape, and he shivered again, looking about him as Vanye did, at thicket and nightbound silence. The mare stood steady, hard-muscled under Vanye's touch. The gray stud yonder had his ears up, and they angled back and twitched as he shifted round, restless and with nostrils flared.

Of a sudden, in that silence—was another definite sound, faint and far ahead.

"Get down," Vanye whispered faintly. "Get down, man. Take cover. Quietly."

Chei looked at him in panic. "Gault's men," he whispered, with one wild thought of driving in his heels and seizing control of the horse—weaponless as he was, with Gault's hunters abroad.

"My lady has a weapon aimed at you," Vanye said, "and you will get down."

Chei looked in startlement. He saw no weapon at all, only the cloaked form and the lady's face. And in that instant, quick as a snake striking, Vanye had one hand entangled in his breeches-leg, and the mare was shying the other direction—the night suddenly, irrevocably upended and his shoulders and the back of his head meeting the ground before his hips and his legs did.

Colors exploded in his skull. He was helpless for the instant, the breath driven out of him; he saw Vanye leap to the saddle, saw the white mare shy over in quiet, mincing paces and move back again as Vanye carefully, quietly, drew his sword and lifted the fallen blanket from the dust.

Vanye flung it at him off the sword-tip, and he caught it, dazed as he was; flung himself over and scrambled for the brush and safety, hugging the blanket to him as he sprawled belly down.

The white and the gray horse had moved too, like ghosts over amongst the trees, a wisp of illusion, a pallor which did not belong and which a searching eye must see.

Chei wrapped the blanket about his own white shirt and made himself part of the ground, next a deadfall, next the smell of decaying leaves and rotting wood and the pungent, herbal stink of centurel that he had bruised in lying there.

Such a small accident could kill a man. A waft of wind. A breeze. A silence when no silence should be—as there was now; or the smell of crushed leaves reaching an enemy. He held himself from shivering, pressed as tight to the cold earth as if he could by willing himself, sink into it.

⤳ Chapter 4

The sound grew in the night—riders on the road, a goodly number of them, Vanye reckoned, knee to knee with Morgaine there in the dark; and a tremor went through his muscles, the chill that was no chill but a desire to move. He felt the heavy press of Siptah's shoulder against his right leg, heard the small sounds as the warhorse pulled at the reins and worked at the bit.

Arrhan stood—arrhend-foaled and trained to stand silent at a pass of a hand over her neck and a careful hand on the reins. So the Baien gray was trained to stand and hold silent; but that was not all his training, and Morgaine's little distractions with the bit only availed so far with him. It was oil and metal, was the presence of a mare and the smell of strangers and strange horses the warhorse would have in his sensitive nostrils, and it was only a skilled and familiar hand could hold him as still as he was, frothing the bit and sweating.

It would happen, Vanye thought; horseman that he was, he felt it in the air—sensed it in the number of the horses coming, the agitation at his right, which infected the mare under him and made her shiver and work the bit—it was in the way the road lay and the startlement likely when the riders turned that bend and the shifting and fickle breeze carried sound and scent to the horses, was in the growing sound of hooves and metal, not the sound of peaceful folk, but of riders in armor, in the night and moving together.

A horse whinnied, on the road before the turning. Siptah snorted and gave half an answer before he answered to the rein, rising on his hind legs and breaking brush on his descent: Arrhan shied over and fidgeted, complaining.

There was quiet again, both their horses and the ones down the road, deathly quiet in the woods.

"That has it," Morgaine hissed, hardly above a breath. "They have stopped. They will sit there till daylight if we are lucky—and send a messenger back to their lord if we are not."

Vanye slid his sword into sheath. "My bow," he said, and made a sign in that direction.

She leaned and loosed it from her gear, along with the capped quiver, and quietly passed it over to him. The horses bided quiet, the damage done. Siptah ducked his head and worked to free more rein, but Arrhan stood steady as Vanye stepped carefully down from the saddle and felt for footing among the undergrowth. He cleared Arrhan's reins and lapped them round a sapling that might hold when Siptah moved. Heaven knew.

He took off his helm with its betraying sheen and passed it to Morgaine before he slipped past Siptah's head with a reassuring touch on a sweaty neck and insinuated his way into the brush.

It was not alone Myya deer he had hunted when he had been an outlaw. The instincts came back, with the memory of Myya arrows and hunger: a desperate Nhi-Chya boy had learned of the only tutors he had, his enemies, and was still alive, when some of his Myya kinsmen were not.

He heard them, as quiet as half a score of riders could be, all drawn aside into brushy cover—no one of them so quiet as a single Kurshin hunter could stalk them. He saw them, himself motionless and themselves as still as they could hold their horses, vague shadows in the starlight. He moved carefully beyond them. The horses knew he was there. They jerked at the reins and fretted. The men cast about them anxiously, beginning to look back the way they had come, at the woods about them.

In moves soft and still he set his bow against his instep and strung it; he uncapped his quiver and took out three arrows, brushing the protected fletchings to be sure of them in the dark. There was not an arrow he had he did not know as sound. There was not a crooked shaft or a marred feather in the lot.

He nocked the first and chose the clearest and the nearest target, rising from the thicket: there was no mail forged might stand against an arrhendur longbow full-bent at that range. His bruised shoulder held sound. The arrow flew, thumped in a solid hit and the man fell.

The others turned to look. He had another arrow nocked while they were amazed, and a second man went down with an outcry as a horse broke free and went shying off into the road.

Third arrow: the men scrambled to mount and ride, and one of them cried out and fell even as he made the saddle.

Vanye snatched another arrow from the quiver braced against his leg. He took a fourth man in the back as the troop bolted away from his fire, toward Morgaine.

Then he snatched up his quiver and ran past the fallen, caring nothing for concealment as he raced down the road after them, his heart hammering against his ribs.

He heard the outcries and the crash of brush before he reached the turning; and beyond it as he rounded the bend was Siptah and his rider in the moonlight and horses still shying off from the calamity that had spilled their masters lifeless in the dust. He saw Chei scramble from cover, bent on seizing one of the loose horses, saw Morgaine with deadly aim wheel instead toward himself and knew a moment of stark terror.

"*Liyo,*" he called out, holding the bow wide.

Then she knew him, and spun the stallion about to ride after Chei as he swung up onto the captured horse with more strength than a sick man ought to show.

He thought then that she would kill Chei outright or shoot the horse under him, and he ran with a dread like ice in his gut—he could not cry out, not stay her from what had to be: he was afoot, and Chei escaping on horseback, and she had no strength to grapple with him hand to hand—there was no way that Morgaine could stop him, else. He ran, breathless and armor-weighted, down the middle of the roadway.

But Chei was reining hard about, the panicked horse going wide on the turn and fighting the bit; and Morgaine reined back, bringing Siptah to a stop facing him.

Chei rode back to join them, of his own will. Vanye reached Morgaine's side with a stitch in his side and a roaring in his ears, sweat running beneath his armor. He saw the terror on Chei's face, the terror of a man who had just seen the deaths he had seen—and knew what might have overtaken him an instant ago and what might befall him now. But Chei had made his decision. By riding back—he had declared something, at least.

And there were eight dead back there, four dark lumps in the roadway, others where he had left them beyond the turning. There were seven horses headed wherever those horses thought to go—home and stable, eventually, with empty saddles and trodden reins.

"Did any escape?" Morgaine asked, not taking her eyes from Chei.

"No," Vanye said, "if none passed you."

"None," she said in that hard, clipped tone, "but we have horses loose and dead men lying here with marks on them that will raise questions in Morund—Chei! Whose are they? Are they Gault's?"

"Gault's," Chei said in a low voice.

Vanye drew a ragged breath. "The marks I can care for." The blood was still up in him. In an hour he would be shaking. Now the grisliest tasks seemed possible. "If it is the sword Chei's people favor."

"It will not hide the burning well enough," Morgaine said; and coldly: "*Fire* will. *Fire* in these woods will occupy them no little time. Move the bodies deep into the brush."

"God," Chei murmured in a tone of horror. "Burn the woods? Burn the land?"

"Vanye," Morgaine said flatly.

Vanye set the bow against his foot and unstrung it; and handed that and the quiver to Morgaine's left hand, the while she hardly took her eyes from Chei.

"Help him," she bade Chei in a voice still colder. "You seem fit enough."

"If any are alive—" Vanye said. The numbness was still about him. It frayed suddenly; and he tried to hold onto it, tried not to think at all except in terms of what he must do.

"Find that out," she said.

Beyond that she did not give him orders. Beyond that, surely, was her own numbness, as essential as his own. It was cowardice to ask what he should do in that case, cowardice to cast the necessity onto his liege by asking for instruction, when he knew as well as she that they could afford no delays and no second and hostile encumbrance. He walked back toward the men on the ground, slipping his sword to his side, unhooking and drawing it. He heard the two horses walking at his back, heard one rider dismount and delay a moment; he had no attention for anything but the supposed dead—men armored much as Chei had been, in leather and chain.

There was no doubt of the four Morgaine had taken. He went into the woods where Arrhan stood fretting—the white mare, the cause of so many deaths. He recovered his helm from where he had left it, freed the mare and rode back beyond the curve of the road where he had left the rest of the company, those his arrows had accounted for.

One of them was *qhal*. All of them were dead.

Thank Heaven, he thought; and was horrified at his own blasphemy.

He tied Arrhan by the road and dragged the dead men as far into the brush as he could manage; and rode back to Morgaine and Chei, where Chei tried to do the same, staggering and panting with the effort of hauling yet another armored corpse off into the brush of the roadside.

Vanye lent his help, himself staggering by the time that they had laid out the last of the bodies well within the woods.

Chei said not a word in all of it—worked with his face averted and grim, his gasps after breath the only sound except the breaking of brush as they trod back to the open road.

"Wind to the east," Morgaine said as they mounted up. Under her, Siptah sidled toward Chei or his horse and she curbed that. "I trust this road tends north, Chei—rapidly."

"Yes," Chei answered.

"On your life," Morgaine said then, and lifting her arm toward the roadside fired the black weapon she carried, taking no trouble now to conceal it, from a man who had seen it and seen the wounds it made, burning through flesh and bone.

Now it was the dry leaves it burned, and a thin line of fire traced itself along the ground where it aimed. The fire increased with a dry crackling. The horses fretted and complained at the smell of smoke, and they let them move.

All along that curve of the road as they went, Morgaine raised fire. That behind them blazed bright when Vanye looked over his shoulder.

The dawn itself was not so bright. It was well beyond the fire that they could see the sun coming, a lightening of the east that had nothing to do with that ominous glare in the woods behind them.

"It is Gault's woods," Chei muttered when they let the horses breathe, looking back from a height and a turning of the wooded road. "It is his woods we are burning, and the wind will bring the fire to his fields."

Vanye stared at the line of fire below them that now rolled smoke into a dim but increasingly sunlit sky. For himself he wanted clean water, in which he could wash his hands and wash his face and take the stink of death and burning out of his nostrils.

Lord in Heaven, there were horses loose down there, in that, no knowing whether the road would take them to safety. And the land itself—

Burn the woods? Burn the land?

He was not sure where it weighed, against ambush and murder of unsuspecting men who might, Heaven knew, have run from the sight of them; or a lord who fed his enemies to wolves; or the obscure terrors which Morgaine feared, which involved the gates and things which she tried in vain to make him comprehend.

The gates opened too far, into too much, and it was possible, Morgaine had said, that they could unravel all that was and take it into themselves. Perhaps that was so. He did not conceive of things in the way Morgaine did—he did not want to conceive of them, in the same way he did not want to know why the stars shifted, or where they were when they were between the gates and there were neither stars nor substance.

But he had felt the gate-force in his bones. He had stared into the void often enough to know it was hell itself that beckoned there.

He knew what made a man like Gault. He knew that there was, for himself and his liege, no honor such as the world counted it, and that the most irresponsible thing in the world was to have let a man of that company back there escape alive, to bring pursuit on them, for if they should fall—Morgaine had told him—the deaths would be . . . everything: all that had ever been and might be. In this she was telling the truth as she believed it, though she had lied to him in lesser things. On this one item of faith he committed himself body and soul. He even hoped—in the secrecy of his heart—that God might forgive him. For all the murder, God might forgive him and forgive her, if it was somehow right, what they did, and they were not deceived.

But he wished with all his soul, that he could feel as keen a remorse as once he might have felt for the men he had killed back there. He could not find it again. There was only horror. There was keenest anguish—but that mostly for the horses; and very little for the men, even of his own kind. He was afraid when he knew that, as if something were slipping irrevocably away from him, or he from it, and he did not know his way back from this point.

"Where have we gotten to?" Morgaine asked their guide when they had come still a little higher up the road, up where the road bent again away from the dawn and toward the still-shadowed sky; and the fire below them was a rolling of white smoke across the tops of trees. "Can we get off this road and onto the old one?"

"It is not safe," Chei said. His face by the dawning light was haggard and his hair wild, with bits of dead leaves stuck in it. His eyes held a feverish look, as well a man's might, which had seen what they had. "If you want ambush, lady, that is where to find it."

"Where were they going before dawn?" Vanye asked harshly, for that was the thing that made no sense to him; it outraged him, that men had been so foolish, and he had had to pay them for it. He felt *that*, when he wished to Heaven he could feel something like conscience.

One of them, Mother of God, had been hardly more than sixteen; and tears stung his eyes, at the same time he could have struck anything in his path.

"I do not know," Chei said. "I do not know."

"We assume they had reason," Morgaine said shortly. "We assume it was on this road and we may yet meet it, to someone's sorrow—do you understand me, Chei?"

"I do not know," Chei protested, shaking his head.

"You took a great chance," Morgaine said, "running for that horse back there in the woods. If not for that white shirt, you would be dead. Eight men are—lest they betray us. Do you still understand me, Chei?"

"Yes, lady," Chei said in a faint voice.

"Are we yet off Gault's land? Where is his border?"

"I do not know.—It is truth! We fought north of here. My lord Ichandren— is dead. Gault's forces are on the road at night—God knows, God only knows, lady, what they were doing, or where more of them are—That fire will draw them, but it will draw other attention too—God knows who, or whether they will think it an accident or set. It is Gault's land down there. His men would not burn his own land. Neither—" He hesitated a breath. "Neither have we ever fired the land we move in. That road will be Gault's when it has burned out. It will be black sticks and open to the eye, and it will be so much more land he can march through."

It was indignation, that last. Vanye leaned on the saddlebow and frowned—it was a change in Chei's voice and bearing, was even daring of a Man toward a *qhal* who threatened him, and with corpses a-smolder in the forest to prove it. "What," Vanye said, "'we'? Friends of yours? And how will *we* fare with them?"

Chei's mouth stayed open an instant. There was a wild flicker in his eyes, only the briefest of moments. Then his glance settled from him onto Morgaine and back again. "The same as I," he said. "They will kill us all, you on sight, me when they recognize me for one of Ichandren's men. Prisoners do not come back. But if we go back to the Old Road, they will take us for Gault's and kill us just the same."

It was wretched enough to be the truth.

"And where are they?" Morgaine asked. "Close enough to cause that band of Gault's to ride at night? What are we going into?"

"War," Chei said, "war, lady, beginning with that fire down there and eight men dead. If things had settled to any truce before—Gault will lay that fire to the account of human folk, and human folk will know that when they see the fire. Up there in the hills they will know it, and they will move down to strike while they can, while Gault's men are occupied putting it out—Gault knows *that* too; and he will throw every man he can spare out toward the hills to prevent it. That is the way things are. We must go up, by the remote trails, we must keep moving by night, and hope we do not have to give account of ourselves—there will be ambushes laid on every road Gault's men will take."

It seemed like the truth. It seemed very much like the truth, after so much of deception and mistake.

"Should we believe you?" Morgaine asked. "You are twice *wrong*, Chei."

"I do not want to die." Chei's voice trembled. He leaned forward in the saddle, shirt-clad shoulders taut in the chill wind. "Before God, lady—if we go the way you want we will run head-on into ambush. I know that I have been wrong. I have no excuse, except I hoped we could go faster, except—I lied—how well I knew the land down there. Here, truly, here is the place I know. I have lived to get here. And I will not, on my life, be wrong again. I swear it to you."

"We dare not tire the horses," Vanye muttered. "*Liyo*—whatever we meet, we cannot push them now."

Morgaine looked at him. For a moment there was that look in her eyes he knew and dreaded—that impatience that would kill them. Then reason returned.

"I know a place," Chei said very quietly, "not far from here, to camp."

It was a place well-hidden among the trees, where a spring broke from the rocks of the hill—not a great deal of water, Vanye saw as they rode in, but sufficient. He climbed down from the saddle, finding suddenly that his very bones ached, and that the mail weighed far more on his shoulders than it had when he had put it on two days ago. "Let me," he said, catching up Siptah's reins while Morgaine dismounted: the gray stud had decided on war with the stolen bay gelding, and his ears were back and his movements full of equine cunning—not outright challenge, but going toward it, in little increments of aggression that meant all three of their horses unsettled.

"He hates that horse," Morgaine said, and reached and jerked at the gray's chin-strap, turned his attention and rubbed the nose the stallion offered her like a maid's fat pony. "I will take him in hand, no mind. It is Arrhan has him disturbed."

A heat came to his face. It was as close to reproach on that score as she had come, and it flew straight to a sore spot.

While Chei, wisely, drew his horse well off out of reach in the little clearing among the pines—for pines they were, at last a tree like trees of Andur-Kursh; and a little scraggle of grass among the rocks.

But the while he unsaddled the mare, Vanye shot glances Chei's way, past Arrhan's shoulder—"Heaven knows," he said to Morgaine, "what is in that gear he has gotten along with the horse."

"We will find out," Morgaine said quietly, the while she took down Chei's armor, which Siptah had carried this far. "He will have his own gear to carry when we ride on, that much I know.—Hush, hush." She reached and smothered a nicker from the gray stud, and gave several sharp tugs at the halter-strap. "Do not thee make us trouble, thou."

The Baien gray muttered and shook his head and Arrhan fretted beside him. "It is the fighting," Vanye said. "Among other things."

"It is the other things," Morgaine said, and looked at him in a way that, vexed as she was, said that nature was what it was—the which stung twice over.

"I will be rid of her."

"I did not ask."

More than Chei's horse was inconvenient. He clenched his jaw and took off the mare's saddle and rubbed her down from head to foot, the while Morgaine did the same for the gray and put him in better humor.

Then Chei came walking over, bringing the saddlebags which belonged to the bay.

And with a harness-knife in his hand.

Chei lifted that hand and held it out hilt-foremost, letting the saddlebags to the ground. "I do not think you want me to have this," he said; and as Vanye reached out and took it: "Search the bags if you like. Or myself."

Vanye stood staring at him. It was a point of honor Chei put in question.

"Do that," Morgaine said, having no compunction in such things.

Or because her liegeman hesitated.

"Come with me," Vanye said to Chei. That much courtesy he returned, not to shame the man. He took him aside, against the rocks, and ascertained, to their mutual discomfort, that there was no second knife.

"I would like," Chei said, staring past him while he searched, "to borrow a razor. I would like to shave. I would like to have a knife to defend myself. I would like to have the blanket that came with this gear. I lost yours in the woods. I am freezing."

"Take the blanket," he said; and, finding nothing: "As for the razor—" He thought more of the man's suicide with it, and discarded the idea. It was not the choice of a man so determined to live. Nor was the choice which had brought him back to them—mere cowardice, in a man who had survived what this one had. "I will lend you mine.—I will search the rest of the gear, understand."

"I did not doubt it," Chei said.

Smoke drifted up in a general haze about the hills; Vanye perched low on the rocks to see what he could of the direction of the fire, and climbed down again to Morgaine's side, where she worked. "Our cookfire will draw no notice," he said.

"Is it burning east?"

"East and quickly east. There is a great deal of undergrowth. I do not think they will be able to stop it till it comes to open fields." It still troubled him, about the burning; and most, the thought of the horses haunted him. "They may not get *through* those roads if the wind shifts. Nothing may."

Morgaine said nothing for the moment, as she stirred a little salt into the meal. Then: "Would we could assure that."

Vanye dropped down to his heels and rested his arms on his knees, thinking of that map Chei had drawn for them, how far they had come and how far there was yet to go, northward to a place called Tejhos, where a gate stood, and into a land utterly *qhal*.

And never quite did Chei leave his attention, as he was under Morgaine's observation from where she sat working.

It was a stranger that emerged from under that blond thatch of hair and

straggling beard. With one of their cooking-pans full of water from the trickle
of a stream that served them, with the borrowed razor, the lump of soap, and
Morgaine's tortoise-shell comb, Chei had washed his hair and braided the sides
of it and the crown of it, which the sun was drying to its straw color; and sat
thereafter leaning forward and doggedly scraping the lathered beard off.

It was a lean face, sun-darkened above and a little paler where the beard
had covered it. It was a well-favored face, and unexpectedly young—hardly
more than two score years, if that: nothing of madness about it, nothing but a
young man of whom no one would expect an older man's experience, and who
showed a meticulous if oddly timed determination to present a better appearance to them. Chei was shivering the while, wrapped in his blanket as far as
his waist, in the thin shirt above, and scraping his skin raw with a keen razor
and cold water, his wet braids dripping water onto his shoulders and adding
to his chill.

Perhaps it was his new freedom, given a horse, given the wind of his own
hills blowing on his face.

A man of Andur-Kursh could understand such a feeling . . . who knew he
would never come to his own highlands again; who found something familiar
in the chill of the wind and the smell of pines and the manner of a young man
who for some reason had recovered his pride again—and perhaps his truthful-
ness.

Chei came back to them, to return the razor and the pan and the comb,
bringing his blanket with him and settling with a shiver at the tiny fire.

"Here," Vanye said, and offered him his own cup of tea—receiving a look
of earnest gratitude in return, so natural an expression, of a face so changed
and eyes so strangely shy of them now Chei had restored what must be his
proper self—

—A golden meadow . . . a parting. His cousin riding away, last friend, save
his liege.

And there was something so like himself in this young man who attached
himself to them, whose glances toward him were earnest and worried and
wanting—perhaps nothing more than friendliness. A man could grow that
desperate.

He remembered—remembered his house, and his brothers, and being the
bastard son, gotten on a Chya prisoner in a Nhi house and lodged under the
same roof as his father's heirs. Generally both his brothers had tormented him.
More rarely his middle brother had mitigated that. And to him, in those days,
that had seemed some sign that brother secretly loved him.

Strangely—in their last meeting, there had been something of that left,
small as it had always been.

Now it was that desperate gesture Chei had made, that glance directed at him, which touched that recollection: see, this is myself, this is Chei, am I not better than what you thought of me?

It ached, deep as an old wound. On so small a thing, his heart turned around and found the man no threat at all—which was foolish, perhaps; he told himself so. He was always too forgiving; he knew that of himself, that his brothers had set that habit in him—a foolish conviction that there was always the hope of a hope of something changing, a misguided faith which had kept him in misery all those years.

And helped him survive all they had done to him.

He ventured a dark and one-sided smile Chei's direction, a gesture, a reassurance on the side Morgaine might not see; and saw that little shift of hope in Chei's eyes—ah, it was the same pool and the same poor desperate fish come to the bait: poor boy, he thought, Heaven help you, Heaven help us both, it was Morgaine who pulled me out. Who will save *you*? God, is it *me* you look to?

He passed Chei the cake Morgaine passed him, cut a bit of cheese and passed that too, then a bit for Morgaine and for himself.

It was a small thing, the precedence of a guest, but it was not lost on Chei. His eyes lightened. He settled easier and adjusted the blanket about himself so he could lay his meal in his lap; it was a healthy appetite he had gained, too.

There had been food in the saddlebags Chei had appropriated: that went into common stores. It was rough-ground grain and a flask of oil and a bit of salt, all welcome. A sort of jerky along with it. A change of linen. And a pan and a cup, a whetstone, a rasp and blunt scraping blade, oddments of rope and leather, with a harness ring—valuable, all; a packet of doubtful herbs, the which Morgaine spread out beside her now, and asked Chei the name and properties of each.

"That is yellowroot," he said of one twisted, dry sliver. "A purgative." And of others: "Lady's-cap, for the fever. Bleeding-root, for wounds."

It had value, then. So had the blanket, since Chei had lost one of their two in the fire.

"The riders did not come from very far, or intend to stay long," Vanye said, "reckoning what they carried with them."

"No," said Chei, "they were a patrol, that was all. A few days and back to Morund land." He swallowed a mouthful of cake, and waved the back of his hand toward the hills. "There is always trouble."

"But now more of it," Morgaine said. "Very much more."

The hand fell. Chei's ebullience vanished as he looked at Morgaine. For a moment the fear was back, and what thoughts went through his head there was no knowing.

"I mean no harm to your folk," Morgaine said. "I will tell you something, Chei: *what* I am I will not argue with you; but by what you have told me, there is no harm I will do you . . . unless you have some reason to love the lord in Mante."

"No," Chei said softly.

"Nothing I intend will harm your folk in these hills," Morgaine said. "Perhaps it will do you a great deal of good. *Qhal* have reason to fear me. You do not."

"Why—" Chei's face had gone still and pale. "Why should they?"

"Because I will be sure there are no more Gaults—no more comings and goings through the gates. No more of what gives them their power over you. Humankind has only to draw back and wait. In time, you will outnumber them. And of that—they know the end. *That* is why they war against you."

Chei surely knew that he had heard a perilous thing. For a long moment he hardly seemed to breathe; then his glance flicked desperately Vanye's way.

"It is true," Vanye said. But it was not, O Heaven, so simple as that, it could never be. And surely a man grown to his manhood in war—knew that much. Morgaine was lying—by halves and portions.

"What will you do?" Chei asked of Morgaine, bewildered. "What will you do, alone?"

"I shall shut the gate. I shall tell you the absolute truth: when I do that, Vanye and I shall pass it, and we will destroy it behind us, with all its power and all its harm. Serve me as you swore you would and I will give you that same choice: pass the gate or remain behind, in this land, forever. To no one else will I give it. I shall counsel you against accepting it. But at some time you may desire it, desperate as your situation is; and if you do choose it, I will not deny you that right, if you have kept your word to us."

For a moment Chei rested still, lips parted, eyes fixed on her. Then he broke the spell with a desperate, humorless laugh. "Against Mante?"

"Against Mante and against Skarrin who rules there, if that is what opposes us. Against anything that opposes us, *qhal* or human. Our motives are very simple. Our solutions are very direct. We do not argue them. We pass where we will and best if we meet no one and share no hospitality of your folk, however well-meant."

Chei caught up the blanket that had fallen from his shoulders, as if the wind were suddenly colder. His face was starkly sober.

"Now, Chei, I have given you my truth. I will listen to yours, if there is anything that presses you to tell me, and not hold it against you, but beyond this I will hold any omission worth your life. Does anything occur to you, Chei, that you ought to tell me?"

"No." He shook his head vehemently. "No. Everything is the truth. I told you—I told you I had lied; but I did not mean to lie—"

"A second time I ask you."

"I have not lied!"

"Nor omitted any truth."

"I guide you the best that I know. I tell you that we cannot go back to that road, we have no choice but go through the hills."

"Nor claimed to know more than you do."

"I know these hills. I know the trails—*here*, here I do know where I am. This is where I fought. You asked me guide you through the other and I had only been that way the once, but here I know my way—I am trying, lady, I am trying to bring us through to the road beyond the passes; but if we go that road, through those passes, they will catch one glimpse of your hair, my lady, and we are all three dead."

"Human folk, you mean."

"Human folk. They watch the road. They pick off such as they can. They ambush *qhal* who come into the woods—"

"In this place where you lead us."

"But they expect *qhal* to come in numbers. They expect humans serving the *qhal*, in bands of ten and twenty. They do not expect three."

"It must happen," Vanye said, "that your folk fall to the *qhal*; and that such as Gault—know these selfsame trails; and that Gault's folk have guides who bring them very well through these woods."

"So my people will assume I am," Chei said. "That is exactly what they will think. That is why we do not go on that road. That is why moving quietly and quickly is the best that we can do. I am no safety to you. And you are a death sentence for me."

"I believe him," Morgaine said quietly, which was perhaps not the quarter from which Chei expected affirmation. He had that look, of a man taken thoroughly off his balance.

"So you will show us how to come on these folk," Morgaine said, "by surprise."

"I will show you how to avoid them."

"No. You will bring us at their backs."

Vanye opened his mouth in shock, to protest; and then disbelief warned him.

"To prove your good faith," Morgaine said.

Surely Chei was thinking quickly. But every hesitation passed through his eyes, every fear for himself, every hope sorted and discarded. "Aye," he said in two more heartbeats. "Ah. Now you have lied to me," Morgaine said.

"No." Chei shook his head vehemently. "No. I will bring you there."

"You are quick, I give you that; but a mortally unskilled liar, and you have scruples. Good. I wondered. Now I know the limit of what I can ask you. Rest assured I intend no such attack. Do you understand me?"

"Aye," Chei said, his face gone from white to flushed, and his breath unsteady.

"I shall not overburden your conscience," Morgaine said. "I have one man with me who reminds me I have one." She began to smother the fire with earth as if she had never noticed his discomfiture. "Have no fear I shall harm your people. You will carry your own armor when we ride out tonight—on your horse or on your person, as you choose. I have some care of your life, and, plainly put, I want the weight off my horse."

The flush was decided. Chei made a little formal bow where he sat—a quick-witted man, Vanye thought, and shamed by that deception of him, shamed again by a woman's kindly, arrogant manner with him. That she was *qhal* made it expected, perhaps—to a man attempting a new and unpalatable allegiance.

It was not a thing he could reason with, knowing Morgaine's short patience, and knowing well enough that she had that habit especially with strangers who put demands on her patience—blunt speech and a clear warning what her desires were and what she would have and not have.

She gave him the pots to scour; she re-packed the saddlebags. "Go to sleep," she bade Chei, who still sat opposite her. He was slow to move, but move he did, and went over where his saddle lay, and tucked down in his blanket.

"You are too harsh with him," Vanye said to her, returning the pans wet from the spring.

"He is not a fool," Morgaine said.

"Nor likes to be played for one."

She gave him a moment's flat stare, nothing of the sort she gave Chei. It was a different kind of honesty. "Nor do I. Lest he think of trying it."

"You are *qhal* in his eyes. Be kinder."

"And test his unbelief twice over?"

"You are a woman," he said, because he had run out of lesser reasons. "It is not the same. He is young. You shamed him just then."

She gave him a second, flatter stare. "He is a grown man. Let him manage."

"You do not need to provoke him."

"Nor he to provoke me. He is the one who needs worry where the limits are. Should I give him false confidence? I do not want to have to kill him, Vanye. *That* is where mistakes lead. Thee knows. Thee knows very well. Who of the two of us has ever laid hands on him?"

"I am a—"

"—man. Aye. Well, then explain to him that I did not shoot him when he ran and that was a great favor I did him. Explain that *I* will not lay hands on him if he makes a mistake. I will kill him without warning and from behind, and I will not lose sleep over it." She tied the strings of the saddlebags and shifted *Changeling's* hilt toward her, where it lay, never far from her. "In the meanwhile I shall be most mildly courteous, whatever you please. Go, rest. If we *trusted* this man, you and I both might get more sleep."

"*Plague take it*, if you heard any—"

Across their little shoulder of rock and soil, the horses lifted their heads. Vanye caught it from the tail of his eye and his pulse quickened, all dispute stopped in mid breath. Morgaine stopped. Her gray eyes shifted from horses to the woods which shielded them from the road, as Chei lay rolled in his blanket, perhaps unaware.

Vanye got up carefully and Morgaine gathered herself at the same moment. He signed toward Chei's horse, tethered apart: that was the one that he worried might call out, and to that one he went while Morgaine went to their own pair, to keep them quiet.

The bay gelding had its ears up, its nostrils wide. He held it, jostled the tether as he would do with their own horses, held his hand ready should it take a notion to sound an alarm. It might be some predator had attracted their notice, even some straying deer, granted no worse things prowled these pine woods.

But in moments he heard the high clear ring of harness, of riders moving at a deliberate speed—down the road, he thought, and not ascending, though the hills played tricks. He ventured a glance back at Morgaine as he held his hand on the bay's nose and whispered to it in the Kurshin tongue. Between them Chei had lifted his head: Chei lay still and tense with his blanket up to his shoulder—facing him, his back to Morgaine, who was the one of them close enough to stop some outcry, but not in a position to see him about to make it.

Chei made no move, no sound. It was the horse that jerked its head and stamped, and Vanye clamped his hand down a moment, fighting it, sliding a worried glance Chei's way.

It was a long, long while that the sounds lasted in the wind and the distance, the dim, light jingle of harness, the sound of horses moving, in full daylight and with, perhaps, Heaven grant, more attention on the part of the riders to what was happening in the valley and what they might meet on the road, than to the chance someone might have occupied this withdrawn, rocky fold of the hills.

Thank Heaven, he thought, the fire was out, and the pots were washed, and the wind was coming off the road to them and not the other way.

There was quiet finally. A bird began to sing again. He gingerly let go the horse he held, looking at Chei all the while.

He nodded at Chei after a moment.

And Morgaine left the horses to walk back to the streamside.

⤶ Chapter 5

The roan horse shied back from the fire and the rider applied the quirt, driving it through the smoke, where human servants labored with axe and wet sacking and mattocks to keep it from passing the Road. Others rode behind him, both *qhal* and the levies from the villages.

Gault ep Mesyrun was not his name: it was Qhiverin; but at times he forgot that fact, as he did now, that the rebels assailed the land itself. In this unprecedented attack on the forest, Gault's will and the self that had been Qhiverin's were of one accord.

The land burned. They had seen the plume from Morund, long before the first of the riderless horses came wandering into the pastures. There was no reasonable cause of fire on a clear night, but one; and Gault had roused the levies, rung the bell to turn out the villagers, and sent out his couriers breakneck for the east, where his fellow lords held an older and firmer control over the land. Southward to the gate, to take a shorter route to the north, he sent his lieutenant Kereys—for the change in tactics that set human folk to war against the land itself was a considerable one, and the high lord in Mante preferred too fervent a zeal for reports rather than too much complacency.

It was a humiliation of a kind Gault did not intend to let pass, more, it was an embarrassment before Skarrin, with whom he had little favor; and nothing but justice on the rebels would redeem him. He had broken the back of the rebellion at Gyllin-brook, eliminated his former ally Ichandren as a troublemaker and made examples; and since that time the man who rode beside him, on the piebald gelding, was not the human he looked to be.

His name had been Jestryn ep Desiny, but that was not the mind which lived behind that handsome, sword-marred face. It was Gault-Qhiverin's old friend Pyverrn, who had taken too grievous a wound at Gyllin-brook; and who had chosen a human shape, gate-given—one of Ichandren's own, his cousin.

There was a certain irony in it, Gault-Qhiverin thought—that two old friends rode side by side bent on vengeance, Jestryn being Gault's ally and guide in this foray to the highlands as they had once, when they were human, ridden against *qhalur* enemies at Ichandren's side.

Their friendship thus had, as Gault counted it, a certain double poesy.

It was onto the road at dusk, and the road which began in the lowlands as a track carts used, became a narrow trail cut through the pines, a pale line eroded and slotted by horse or foot, grown up in wispy grass along the margin so that it was easy to mistake some thinning of the trees for a spur off it.

There was no room, where it crossed difficult places, to have two riders abreast; and it was all too easy a place for ambush.

Ambush crossed Vanye's mind—constantly. He little liked these close spaces, little as he had liked the prospect of the open road, knowing what Chei had warned them. It was Chei in the lead now, Morgaine bringing up the rear, in this dark, pine-spiked shadow, and Chei did not have the look of a man contemplating a run for freedom: Chei had declined to wear the armor Morgaine had returned to him—the scabbed sores were still too painful, Chei had said: it was hard enough to bear the riding.

But Chei was armed again, after a fashion: he had the harness-knife, small as it was, a gesture Morgaine had made to him at their setting-out; for peace, Vanye reckoned. Or it was another test of him.

Certainly Chei had looked confused, and then: "My lady," he had said, in a respectful, astonished tone, the while Vanye's gut had knotted up and his hand clenched tight on his own blade-hilt, considering how close Morgaine stood to Chei, with the knife in his hand.

But Chei had put it away in its sheath on his saddle-skirt, and tied his armor up behind his horse with his blanket and his saddle-bags; and rode now to the fore of them, conscious, surely of his sword and of Morgaine's weapon at his back, if treachery ever crossed his mind.

It was a wooded track, Chei had assured them. It was a way they would stand less chance of being seen.

It was also a track in which they could not see the turns ahead in the night-bound forest, in which they did not know the way and were utterly dependent on their guide, the same one who had twice mistaken his way—he swore.

Vanye himself had argued for this. Morgaine would have walked brazenly into Morund and demanded hospitality, and thrust Chei into Gault's very hold and hall and forced Gault to take him for a guest . . . backed by power enough to deal with any *qhalur* hedge-lord.

He had persuaded her otherwise, into this, with the land afire and men dead, half a score of them, and a twice-mistaken guide holding their lives in his hand—

Lady, Chei called her now, not witch. If Chei thought of sorcery it was surely tempered, living near *qhal* as he did, by the knowledge that what *qhal* did came not entirely from empty air and ill intent; it was not a thoroughly superstitious belief, and Chei surely knew by now that there was a *qhalur* weapon involved. When it came to fine distinctions beyond that—

—When it came to that, Vanye himself was not well sure whether it was witchcraft, or what it was he carried against his heart, or what that blade was that Morgaine carried, and both guarded and hated with all that was in her.

If they had met some innocent folk family on the valley road, if some children—

God help them, he thought; God help us.

And tried to forget the face which lingered behind his eyes, the sixteen year old boy, open-eyed and startled and dead in the starlight of the road.

It stood for everything that had gone amiss.

He rubbed his eyes that stung with weariness—short sleep, trading watches, with the smell of smoke still hanging about the hills and the surety that by now there was commotion behind them, deadly as a river in spate—Heaven send it was not in front of them as well.

At a point where the road reached the turning and the climbing was steep to the shoulder of the hill, Chei drew rein and hesitated, drawing his horse back about in the starlight, coming even with them.

Then he gave his horse his heels and took the ascent with the impetus it needed.

I am not eluding you, that gesture was to say. Follow me.

Morgaine sent Siptah after; Vanye allowed the big gray the room he needed on the narrow track, then gave Arrhan the touch of his heel.

For a moment they were in starlight, climbing that slot among the rocks; then they came among the pines again, and into thicker brush, where boughs whispered in a ghostly voice above the creak of harness and the sound of the horses, a climb for a long, long distance until the way began to wind down again, through deep shadow, such as it was in this land where the stars shone in such numbers and so bright, and white Arrhan and even the Baien gray and his gray-cloaked rider seemed to glow by night.

Then they broke out upon a broader track, and Chei's gelding struck a faster pace, along a streamside and across shallow water that kicked up white in the night-glow.

Morgaine suddenly put Siptah to a run, so that Vanye's heart skipped a beat and he kicked Arrhan in the same moment that Arrhan leapt forward on her own: the mare cleared the water in a few reckless strides to bring him up on Morgaine's flank as she overtook Chei and cut him off with Siptah's shoulder. The gelding shied off, scrambling up against a steep bank and recovering its balance at disadvantage. Chei drew in, his eyes and hair shining pale in the starlight.

"Slower," Morgaine said. "Where do you think to go, so surely and so fast? A trail you know? To what?"

"It is a way I know," Chei said, and restrained his horse as it backed against the bank and shied and threw its head. "Where should I lead you? I swear I know this place."

"That also I wonder. We are making far too much noise for my liking."

"Vanye," Chei appealed to him, "for God's sake—"

"*Liyo,*" Vanye said, and eased Arrhan forward, his heart beating so the pulse seemed to make his hands shake. No man called his name. Few in his own land had cared to know it; excepting Nhi and Chya and Myya, and his Chya cousin, who was not wont to use a Kurshin name when he could help it, and called him only *cousin* when he was kindest. But in Chei's mouth it was not a curse, it was like a spell cast on him, was the way Morgaine used it.

Fool, he told himself. And his heart moved in him all the same.

"Where are we going?" he asked Chei.

"Where I told you from the beginning—across the hills to the road. Before God I have not lied. Vanye, tell her so. Tell—"

What sound it had been Vanye could not identify, even in hearing it. But it had been there; and none of them moved or breathed for the instant.

The black weapon was in Morgaine's hand, beneath the cloak. Vanye knew it, as well as he knew where sky and earth was. *Changeling* rode at her side tonight, since she went hooded; and there was power enough in her hand to deal with any single enemy.

Chei shook his head, faint movement. His eyes rolled toward the woods, a gleam of white in a shadowed face. "I do not know," he whispered, ever so faintly. "I swear to God I do not know who that is, I did not plan this—Please. Let me go, let me ride to them. It may be they are human—I expect that they are. If they are not, you can deal with them. If they are, then likely I can ride in on them."

"And tell them what?" Morgaine asked in a flat voice.

"After that—God knows. They may kill me. But likeliest they will want to know what they can find out." His voice trembled. His teeth were chattering, and he drew in a rough breath. "Lady, if we go on we will ride into ambush and they will raise all the hills against us. We have no choice! Let me go to them!"

"You are supposing we would ride in after you," Morgaine said.

"I am supposing," Chei whispered back, "nothing. Except we are too few to threaten them. That is all the safety we have. I can talk to them, I can tell them you are no friend of Gault's—Let me *try*, lady. It is the only way. They are bowmen. We will not have a chance if they begin to hunt us."

"He is brave enough," Vanye said in his own language.

"Brave indeed," Morgaine said. "He has courted this, curse him."

It might well be true. Honest men, Morgaine had warned him.

"What can we do now," Vanye asked with a sinking heart, "that costs less?"

"Try," Morgaine said to Chei.

"Hold." Vanye edged Arrhan up next the gelding to pull the ties free which held the heavy bundle of mail and leather atop Chei's other gear. He pulled it free and handed it to him. "Put it on."

In the case, he thought, that Chei was on their side.

Chei did not argue. He took the offered help, and took the mail on his arms, ducked his head and slid it on, leaving it unbelted.

Then he took up the reins and urged the gelding quietly ahead, up the bank and into the woods.

In a moment more there was a whistle from that direction, low and strange. Siptah threw his head and Morgaine held him steady.

It was not a safe vantage they had. Vanye interposed himself and his horse between her and the woods, on the side the bank did not shelter; but their backs he could not defend.

There was nothing then but the dark and the bubbling of the stream behind them, the sighing of the leaves.

Another sound, from their side: Morgaine unfastened the hook which held *Changeling* at her side, and brought it sheath and all, to rest crosswise on her saddle.

Doomsday. His hand went on reflex to that pyx he had beneath his armor, and he felt it like a coal against his heart.

Destruction.

Once that sword was drawn there was no peace in the world. Once that was drawn there would be deaths heaped up and uncountable.

He sat his horse still, thinking of archers beyond the trees; and that by now Chei had either fallen to some silent killer, or found the allies he had led them to, for whatever purpose.

The movements were virtually silent, the rustle of a branch, the brush of a body against leaves. The gelding shifted and snorted and stamped, breaking twigs and working at the bit; and Chei held him in place.

"Who are you?" came a voice hardly above the wind.

"A human man," Chei answered in a normal voice, and did not turn in his saddle. "Ep Kantory. Chei ep Kantory, asking passage. There are three of us, no more, two at the streamside. One of us is *qhal*."

There was long silence, very long. He heard a whisper, and another, but he could not hear the words. He did not turn his head.

"Get off your horse," the whisper came.

He did that, and drew a whole breath, though his legs wanted to shake under him. One *qhal*, he had told them. It was enigma enough to confuse them and make them ask further. He had made himself defenseless. He had ridden without true stealth. Therefore he was still alive. He stepped down in the little clear space and held his horse close to the bit, forestalling its nervous shifting as branches stirred and a shadow afoot came out of the brush into filtered starlight only slightly better than the forest dark.

That shadow came to him and took his horse's reins and led it away from him. He did not resist.

He did not resist when others came up behind him and took his arms in a painful grip.

"It is passage I ask," he said to them in a hushed voice. "The *qhal* with me is a woman, alone with one human man. They are enemies of Gault's. Gault is hunting us."

A slight weight rested on his shoulder, and moved till the cold, flat metal of a sword-blade rested against his neck. "Where do you come from?"

It was death to move. It was death to give the wrong answer, and for the moment he could think of nothing at all, the forest air seeming too thin, his senses wanting to leave him as if the world had shifted again, and he should be back on that hilltop, all that he had to tell them become a dream, a delirium. He could not even believe, for one dizzy moment, in the companions he had left on that streamside, or in the things that had happened to him, at the same time that he knew he was back among human men.

The sword turned edge-on against his neck.

"I am still human," he said. "So is the man with her. She is here on business of her own. It would be well—to find out what that is. They have told me something of it—enough I knew I ought to bring them here. I swear you have never seen anything like her. Or like the man with her—he *is* a Man, and from somewhere I do not know. Let me go back to them and I will lead them to the falls. There is no way out of that place but back. You know that there is not. We will camp there and wait, and you can ask what questions you want."

There was another long pause. Then: "Ep Kantory," the whisper in front of him said, "your brother is with us."

His heart lurched. As a trick, it was cruel. "My brother died at Gyllin-brook. Ichandren at Morund. I am the last alive."

"Bron ep Kantory is alive," the whisper said. "He is with Arunden. In our camp."

He did not know whether, then, he could stand on his feet. He was numb. He felt his breath short and anger blinded him and hope came by turns, between the conviction they were lying and hope—remotest and terrible hope, that it might be true.

"Who is this," the same voice continued to ask, "that you travel with?"

He could not speak. He could not find his voice. He had been better than this when Gault's men led him to the hilltop. He had been better than this in the depths of Morund-hall when Ichandren died. His senses came and went, as if he would faint, and here and there wavered.

"Did you think that you could do this?" the whisper asked him. "Did you think that you could deceive us?"

"I am Chei ep Kantory. My brother's name is Bron. He fell at Gyllin-brook—"

The blade pressed against his neck. A strong grip drove the blood from his hands.

"And who else are you? What other name?"

"Tell Bron I am here. Bring him. Tell him he will know if I am still his brother. Tell him that!"

A long time passed. He told himself that it had been a test. He had failed it. At any moment the one in front of him would give the order and the blade would slit the vein—or worse, they would take him with them, and ask him questions alone—

There was a chance, O God, a chance: if Bron had lain alive on Gyllin's bank, if Arunden's men had heard the rumor and had been able to reach that place before the night and the scavengers—

If only once, if he died for it, he could see his brother again—

"Let him go," the voice said.

Vanye had both hands on his own sword, across the saddlebow, as he heard the stir of a rider in the forest. Arrhan shifted nervously, and Siptah stamped once and worked at the bit.

Then one rider in unbelted mail came out into the starlight and down the slope at an easy pace. Two others followed, shadowlike, at either side and behind him.

Chei reached the flat and stopped face to face with them, then carefully got down from his horse and left it to stand while the others waited at his back.

It was to Vanye's side he walked, leftward, away from Morgaine, and it occurred to Vanye it might be attack, some means to take him down and leave Morgaine's back undefended: there was the harness-knife, for one; and Heaven knew with what Chei was armed now.

But he saw nothing in Chei's hands—Chei held them both outward from him in the starlight, and when Chei came up at Arrhan's shoulder and laid a hand on his stirrup:

"They have agreed to talk," Chei said in a low voice. "They want you to come. There are others in the woods. There are arrows aimed at us. Likely they will aim for the horses if we try to run." Strong emotion trembled in his voice. "They say my brother is alive. I do not know. It might be true. If it is—if it is, then he might convince them—whether to listen to me."

That they were surrounded was credible. The rest of it . . . Heaven knew. He was sure that Morgaine heard what Chei was saying: her ears were sharper than anyone's he knew, and likeliest she heard whatever was in the brush as well. She said nothing, and a sense of panic came over him—man and man, she had said, Man and Man, trusting his instincts to deal with this many-turning youth.

"I beg you," Chei said, and caught at his hand where it rested on his leg, gripping it hard. "I beg you. I am not sure of these trails, enough to run the horses here. It is a tangle ahead, rock and root. The stream leads to a falls and there is no way out. But if we go with them, there is the chance they will listen, and it will likely be closer to the road anyway. These men belong to Arunden ep Corys, and if they are not lying, my brother will know whether or not to believe me. Come with them. If things go wrong I will fight *with* you, I swear it under Heaven."

"And your brother? What of him?"

"I want his life. His. That is all I ask. And you have me. Heart and mind—I swear it, only so you save him and take no life you can spare. Listen to me: this is the last place free Men hold. It is the land I am fighting for, it is the land, and your lady says she has hope for us—but if becomes a war of fire, Gault and the lady—for God's own sake, Vanye—listen to me and come with me and take them for allies. They will not ask you give up your weapons. They are not unreasonable men. And when we reach their camp my brother will stand with us. I know that he will."

"As you knew the way across the plains? And the woods? As you led us here?"

Chei's hand was cold on his, cold and strong. "In the name of God, Vanye. I am your friend. You have been mine. I never betrayed you. I only wanted to live to get here; and we are here—and I am begging you—take what I give you. I have lied, I admit it. But not of malice—only of too much hope. And now I swear to you I am not lying. I have brought you where there was hope of getting through, and now that has failed us—there is this, and it is the best one, the best I could have hoped for—"

"All your hopes diminish, friend. And this one if it goes amiss, has your people's blood on it."

"There is nothing else," Morgaine said beside him, and in the Kurshin tongue, "that we can do, but see where this leads."

His advice, he thought, had brought them to this—as much as Chei's. "Aye," he said heavily. And to Chei: "My lady agrees; we will go."

Chei's hand clenched on his, desperately hard. Gratitude shone in his eyes, starlight aglimmer on tears unshed. "I swear," Chei said. "I swear to you—I am with you in this. I will not betray you. Not for my life. I know what you can do. Take me first if I betray you."

Vanye felt an unaccustomed, half embarrassed impulse, let his fingers twitch, then clench in human comfort as he looked into Chei's shadowed face.

"My brother will help us," Chei said. "I swear that too. And you will not harm him."

"We will harm no one who does not threaten us."

"And your lady—"

"Take Vanye's word," Morgaine said. "He does not know how to lie. And in this I take his advice."

The way lay up the bank, into the forest by trails only Chei and the shadowy horsemen knew; and it was well enough certain that there were other watchers about, on foot and ahorse on trails following and crossing theirs.

It was like the arrhend, Vanye thought; or the men of Koris, of his own land. One did not hope to take such a land cheaply, in lives or in time—except an enemy did the unthinkable; except it was not the land or the wealth of the woods a conqueror valued, and he was willing to use fire.

We ought not, he kept thinking with every stride of the horses, every whisper of the leaves, we ought not, we ought not to have brought the fire.

There was that in him which ached, thinking of it, as greenwood and the forest damp took the stench of smoke away—as more and more the land was like coming to his own home again, even to the smell of the trees.

O my liege, I might have stopped you from setting the fire. Why did not I speak? I am a Man. And this is a human place. Did it not occur to me?

Or am I become something else?

The trails made a maze, a narrow track down one hill and up another through one and another little dell completely unremarkable in the dark.

Chei went foremost behind their first guide. Morgaine rode at Chei's back and Vanye at hers, with the second of their mounted guides going hindmost; and at times in the shadow of the thicket there was only the sound of the horses and the creak of harness and jingle of chain; and at most the pale flash of Siptah's pale rump and white-tipped tail to keep him aware which way they were turning, each horse following the other.

To such a land Arrhan had been foaled, and there was a lightness in her step and an alertness to her busy ears as if she were reading signals no human ear heard. She was not alarmed, not yet; but by the prick of her ears and the set of her head she advised where her apprehensions were and where some sound went which he did not hear.

There is no way out of this, he kept thinking, the further and the deeper they went. Whether Chei is witting of it or no, it is a trap, this narrow passage.

Heaven help us. The last hold of free Men. Chei has lied to us; and fair enough for that: Morgaine has lied to him in turn—and we are all in the web, they and we alike.

No more deaths. No more children, Mother of God, no more mistakes, and no more blood. I dream of them.

At last Morgaine stopped; for ahead of her Chei and their guide had paused.

Arrhan came up with her head against Siptah's flank and crowded closer still as the big gray threw his head and snorted warning.

"It is soon," their forester guide said. "Be patient."

It was, Vanye reckoned, a boundary of a sort, and they were about to cross it: someone ran ahead to tell others what came visiting.

There was silence after. There were only forest sounds and the slow, fretful shifting of the horses. Morgaine did not question. Chei did not say anything, nor had he spoken since they began this ride. Their guides volunteered no word beyond that simple directive.

Somewhere a nightbird cried.

"Come," their guide said then, and turned his horse sedately and went ahead at the same deliberate walk he had used for some little time. So Chei went and so Morgaine; and himself and the last man, as the trail followed the shoulder of a wooded hill and climbed again, up among tall trees and down once again, onto the other side of the hill.

For the first time, on that breath of wind, Vanye picked up the scents of smoke and habitation. No lights showed as they came down, first into thinner trees and then among brushy lumps—huts which seemed more like thickets than dwellings—but nature never grew them, Vanye thought, as they rode sedately down the steep slope and past one such that was high as horse and rider together, a rounded shape against the straight trunks of the trees.

Not a stirring hereabouts. Not a breath of a voice, no gleam of fire. From a pen, withdrawn among the trees, came stable-smell and a restless shifting of horses, as they rode out into the clear midst of this low place.

Then their guide dismounted. "Get down," he said.

"Best we do that," Chei said, and slid down.

Well indeed, if there were archers in question. Morgaine got down from the saddle, with *Changeling* hung at her side, and Vanye did, at the same time as Chei did; and dropped the reins to let the horses stand.

Then came a little movement, and more than one shadow gliding out from among the trees and the huts.

One came and crouched on the ground in the starlight in the midst of the large clearing at the center of the huts, and poked round in a familiar way with a stick, after which coals came to a sullen glow, and a slight gleam showed: the man then piled on tinder and wood. So the village folk had taken precautions and now felt encouraged enough that the one man squatted there with the firelight leaping up brighter and brighter on his heavy-jowled face.

"My lord Arunden—" Chei said in a plaintive way, and walked forward a pace or two; and stopped as the man at the fire looked up at them with an underlit scowl.

The man called Arunden stood up, and drew the short sword that hung at his belt. The fire limned them both, Chei all dark, fire glancing on the edges of his mail; the older man all light, shadow about his features and his leather and furs and braids.

"Strange guests," Arunden said, and the voice matched the face, heavy and rough. "Stranger still that you bring them here. What does Gault want?"

"Is my brother truly alive, my lord?"

"Answer."

"Gault wants our lives, theirs and mine, my lord. I am human. So is the man. The lady is *qhal*, but she is no friend of Gault's."

"The land is burning, below. What do we do for this? How did this happen?"

Chei had no quick reply for that.

"It happened," Morgaine said, drawing a startled look from the man, and walked forward to stand, gray-cloaked and hooded figure with arms folded, the dragon-sword out of sight, riding at her hip, and Heaven knew where her other weapon was, but Vanye well guessed as he moved to take his place at her left shoulder. "The *qhal* of your land have no courtesy," Morgaine said to the lord, "and I have found more with this young human. So I have come to you. As for the burning—a matter of war, my lord, else worse would be at your borders."

There was stark silence from lord Arunden . . . stark silence too from the shadowy figures which appeared among the trees behind him. Vanye's heart began to pound in dread, his mind to sort rapidly what he could see of those about them, mapping which way they should go—what their path of escape should be, where cover was.

There would be, Chei had assured them, archers.

"Who are you," Arunden asked sharply, "riding here with your minions? What are you, Gault's jilted doxy?"

That was the limit. Vanye slipped the ring. The weight of the sword hit his hip as Morgaine lifted one empty, white hand, forestalling him without even looking to see what his move had been, and let back her hood, spilling her pale hair free to the light.

"No," she said softly, "I am not. Would you guess again, my lord Arunden?"

"My lady," Chei said, stepping between. "My lord—"

"Is she here to make threats?" Arunden asked. "Or to spy out the hills, with you for her guide?"

Morgaine glanced Chei's way with chill disdain. "You vowed this was a reasonable man."

"I am no fool!" Arunden shouted, and stamped his stick into the coals, so that coals scattered and sparks flew up.

"I am out of patience," Morgaine said to Chei, and turned aside.

"Stay," Chei said. "Wait—my lord Arunden. Do not make a mistake."

"I make no mistake. It is *your* mistake—"

"Chei!" a voice called out of the dark, and a man was coming down the slope of a sudden, limping and making his way with difficulty on the uneven ground among the trees and huts.

Vanye let his sword surreptitiously back to its sheath, as Morgaine had stopped near him, her hands shrouded in her cloak and her jaw set.

"Bron, it is not your brother," Arunden shouted uphill as that man came on, and waved him to stand off.

But: "Bron," Chei said, quietly. "O Bron—"

The man came resolutely forward, limping somewhat—unarmored, wearing only breeches and shirt and boots, weaponless; he came and he stopped in doubt a little the other side of the fire; as Chei for his part stood still—wisely, Vanye thought, with that prickling between his own shoulder-blades that weapons at his back set there.

"I am not Changed," Chei said in a voice that scarcely carried, a voice which trembled. "Bron, Ichandren is dead. Everyone is dead. Gault gave the last of us to the wolves. Myself, Falwyn, ep Cnary—" His voice did break, quiet as it was. "They died. That was what happened to them. I thought you had died on the field."

"What do you want here?" Bron asked, in a voice colder than Arunden's. "What is it you want?"

Chei turned his face away as if it he had been dealt a blow, and shook his head vehemently.

"What do you want, Chei?"

"Passage," Chei said after a moment, looking back toward his brother. "Safety. I am sworn, Bron, my lord was dead, you were dead, the lady and this man found me, they took me away from the wolves, healed my hurts—He is not *qhal*, Bron, he is a man like I am and *she* set me free and gave me a horse and tells me things that Arunden ought to know, that all of us ought to know, Bron—I swear to you, I know there is no way to prove anything I say. But you know me, you know everything I could know—try me, whether I have forgotten anything. Bron—for the love of Heaven—"

Bron's face worked, somewhere between desperation and grief.

And suddenly he held out his open arms.

"No," Arunden cried. "Fool!"

But Chei came to him, slowly, carefully. They embraced each other, and wept, for very long, till Bron set Chei back by the shoulders and looked at him as if he could discover the truth by firelight.

Vanye watched with a pang of his own—the which he could not comprehend, only something in him hurt, perhaps that a man could come home again; or that brothers could prove true.

Or that Chei had just deserted them for a deeper loyalty, whatever the issue of this place.

Fool, he thought. Well that there *be* some help for us here.

There was Morgaine beside him, who was all his own concern; and Chei at the moment was hers, he reckoned, their guide and the source of everything they knew in this world. She would wreak havoc to keep him safe, Chei was very right; had Arunden attempted to stop him or to strike him or his brother, Morgaine would have acted, fatally for Arunden and half the village before she was done.

But she and Arunden and all of them stood baffled by this, that Bron ep Kantory took his brother into his arms without being sure what he was embracing: he made himself a hostage to stop those who cared for either of them, and by one move held them all powerless.

⮜ **Chapter 6**

"Come," Bron said, his hands on Chei's shoulders, while Chei's thoughts reeled between one side and the other of the forces gathered there at odds. There was the lady and Vanye and there was Arunden ep Corys, a sudden and hard-handed lord. Calamity was possible at any instant.

But Bron held to him as if there were no chance in all the world that he was a piece of Gault's handiwork. "Come," Bron said gently, as if there were no lunacy at all in his arriving in camp in company with a *qhalur* witch and a man in strange armor. "Tell me; tell me what I can do; O my God, Chei—" Of a sudden Bron hugged him tight again and pressed his head against his shoulder; and Chei embraced him a second time, appalled at now thin his strong brother had become, how there was so little between his hands and Bron's ribs, and how there was a fragile, insubstantial feel about him.

"I am not theirs," Chei insisted, over and over again. "Not theirs. I am not lying, Bron, I swear to you I am not Changed."

"I believe you," Bron said. "I know, I know, what shall I do, what do you want me to do?"

"Just swear for me. *Talk* to Arunden."

"Tell him what? Who are they? What are they?"

"Friends. Friends to us."

Bron set him back and stared at him, bewildered, desperate—at his little brother who was a fool and could not think of anything but seeing him, until now, now that he knew what he had known from birth, that Bron would do the same as he—would believe him because he wanted to believe, and become another fool for his sake, risking his life and his soul for the remotest hope Chei was alive and still his brother. That was what was in Bron's eyes, that was the struggle to believe, while his hands trembled on Chei's arms and strayed once and twice to his face and his shoulders as if he could not believe he was flesh and blood.

"You *look* tolerably well," Bron said.

"They have been good to me, Bron, truly—they have. You—?"

"Well enough, I am well enough."

"You limp."

"Ah, well, that will mend, it will mend. So do you.—My God, my God—"

"There was a brooch Mama had—it was a marsh rose. There was a place in the wall we used to hide our special things—"

"O *God*, Chei—"

"—I gave you that scar on your chin; I hit you with a harness buckle—you teased me about a girl; her name was Meltien. She died in the winter march—"

"Brother—" Bron hugged him to silence. They wept together; and when he could speak again:

"Bron, I have sworn to take them north on the Road; and I have to do that—"

"There are arrows aimed at us." Bron took his face between his hands and looked again at him, intensely. "Who are they? You will have to tell me. I do not understand. God knows Arunden does not. What shall we do?"

"I will talk to them. *They* will talk with Arunden if he will listen—"

"He will listen," Bron said; and hugged him close against his side, so that they shielded each other as they went to Arunden, Bron armorless as he was, himself in a mail shirt that was in no wise proof against the lady's weapons.

But a man barred their way, a man with a drawn sword and the emblem on him of Holy Church; and Bron stopped still, his hand clenched on Chei's shirt.

"If you will not kill it," the priest said, "*I* will. Your soul is in danger, Bron ep Kantory."

"Your *life* is," Chei answered, and would have pushed Bron behind him, but Bron stood fast. "My lady!"

"Hold!" Arunden said.

"My lord," the priest protested.

But Arunden walked into the matter, and waved the priest off. And Chei stood with a weakness still in his knees, uncertain which of them was supporting the other. Words froze in his throat. They always did, at the worst of times.

"There is a curse in him," the priest said. "It is a curse has come to us in a friend's shape. It is Gault's gift. Kill them. Have no words with them."

"Then we would know nothing Gault wants," Arunden said. "Would we, priest?—Talk, boy. What have we here? What do you bring us, eh? More of Gault's handiwork?"

*　　*　　*

"The lord is talking, at least," Vanye said in a low voice, seeing what transpired, with the brothers and Arunden and two armed men. His hand was still on his sword, from the first Chei had called out.

And he thanked Heaven that Arunden had moved to stop the man.

"Hope that this brother's word has some weight," Morgaine said in the Kurshin tongue. "I should not have let us leave the road. That was the first mistake. Stay to my left."

"Aye," he murmured, feeling the sting of that, and his heart was pounding, the old, familiar fear, the nightmare of too many such choices. But Chei came toward them and fear shifted to a frail, desperate hope, seeing that Bron continued to talk to Arunden.

"He will speak to you," Chei said, casting an anxious glance between him and Morgaine. "I swear to you—Arunden is not a treacherous man: God witness, he is not a careful one, either—he is afraid of you, lady, and he cannot admit it. Be patient with him. That is a priest of God—that one, with the sword. Be careful of him."

Vanye looked a second time. It did not look like a priest. He drew in a quick, anxious breath. It had been long since he had found anything of the Church; and there had been so much doubtful he had had to choose on his own: so far he had come, and changed so much—and a priest—

He was starkly afraid to face anything of the Church nowadays: that was the proof that he was damned, and he did not need a priest to threaten him with Hell.

Or to threaten Morgaine, or curse her with curses she would not regard, but which would all the same bring no luck to them.

"We do not need the priest," he muttered. "Send him away."

"I do not know," Chei said in evident consternation. "I do not think—I do not see how . . . my lady—"

"No matter," Morgaine said. Gold flashed in the seam of her cloak. She rested *Changeling*'s cap on the ground, her hands on the quillons of the dragon grip. "If it saves us time, let us be done with this."

Vanye opened his mouth to protest. But it was not that Morgaine did not know the Church. There was nothing he could tell her. There was nothing he knew how to tell her.

He longed—God in Heaven, he longed for someone to tell him he had done right, and that his soul was not so stained as he thought it was, or a gentle priest like those in Baien-an or even old San Romen, who would lay hands on him and pray over him and tell him if he did thus and thus he was not damned.

But this priest did not have any gentle look. This one was damnation and hellfire, and met them with the uplifted cross of a sword.

"No further," the priest said, and drew a line in the dirt, between them and his lord. "Talk behind that."

Morgaine grounded *Changeling* just behind that line, the dragon hilt in her hands, and a hell between them that the priest could not in his wildest dreams, imagine.

"Do we talk to this?" she asked scornfully, looking past the priest to Arunden. "Is he lord in this camp? Or are you?"

"My lady," Chei cautioned her, and Bron, who had come halfway between Arunden and his brother, stopped still and looked appalled.

"I will talk with whoever is lord here," Morgaine said. "If it is this man, so be it. His word will bind you. And I will take it for yours."

"If I say talk with the camp scullions, you talk with them!" Arunden snarled.

Vanye went stiff, but Morgaine's hand was up, preventing him, before the lord Arunden had even finished speaking.

"Well and good," she said. "To *them* I will offer my help, and turn this camp upside down, lord Arunden, when they profit from what I have to say. *Or* you can listen, and profit yourself and yours, and not come to Ichandren's fate or have to ask advice of your servants."

"You are in a poor place to threaten us, woman! Have you looked around you?"

"Have *you*, my lord, and have you not noticed that *qhal* are taking your land and killing your people? I might make some difference in that. Let us talk, my lord Arunden! Let us sit down like sensible folk and I will tell you why I want to pass through your land."

"No passage!" the priest cried, and people murmured in the shadows. But:

"Sit down," Arunden said. "*Sit*, and *lie* to us before we deal with you."

More and more people appeared out of the dark and the woods, coming down into the light: a man or two at first, who stood with Arunden within the priest's line; and young women in breeches and braids, who scurried about seeing to the fire and bringing out blankets to spread by it—an appearance of decent courtesy, Vanye thought, standing by with his hand on his sword-hilt and a dart of his eye toward every move around the shadows on their own side of the line.

On his, the dour, broad-bellied hedge-lord stood by with a clutch of his own men and with Bron and Chei both across that line and talking urgently to him—he had his arms folded, and scowled continually; but made no overt gesture of hostility, only repeated ones of impatience.

The priest, for his part, drew another line when the rapidly-forming circle took shape about the fire, a mark in the dust with his sword and a holy sign over it, the which sent a cold feeling to Vanye's gut.

"Poor manners, these folk," he said to Morgaine, looking constantly to their flanks and refusing to be distracted by the priest's doings.

"No saying where the archers may be posted," Morgaine said. "I will warrant there is one or two with clear vantage—that ridge yonder, perhaps. Mark you, we do not give up the weapons—hai, there—"

One man was moving to take the horses. Vanye moved to prevent it, one hand out, one hand on his sword; and that man stopped.

Chei's horse had strayed loose, uncertain and confused, and apt, Heaven knew, to bolt; but their own had stood where the reins had dropped, where Siptah now stood and jerked his head and snorted challenge, a wary eye on the man approaching.

"I would not," he advised the man, who measured the warhorse's disposition and the owners' resolution with one nervous glance and kept his distance. "I would not touch him at all, man."

That stopped the matter. The man looked left and right as if searching for help or new orders, and edged away, leaving the warhorse and the mare and all their belongings to stand unmolested. Vanye whistled a low and calming signal, and the Baien gray grunted and shook himself, lifting his head again with a wary and defiant whuff.

"My lady," Chei came saying then. "Come. Please. Keep within the line."

Morgaine walked toward the fire. Vanye walked after her, and stood behind her—*ilin's* place, hand on sword, within the wedge-shaped scratch in the dirt that made a corridor to the fire.

So Arunden stood, with his priest, and his men—all men: the only women were the servants, who came and went in the shadows.

"Sit," Arunden muttered with no good grace, and sank down to sit cross-legged.

So Morgaine sat down in like fashion, and laid *Changeling* by her, largely shrouded in the folds of her cloak—which movement Arunden's eyes followed: Vanye saw it as he stood there.

But: "Vanye," Morgaine said, and he took her meaning without dispute, and sank down beside her, as others were settling and gathering close, Chei and Bron among them, on Arunden's side of the line, but beside them on Vanye's side.

"So you found this boy with the wolves," Arunden said. "How and why?"

"We were passing there," Morgaine said. "And Vanye did not like the odds."

"Not like the odds." Arunden chuckled darkly, and with his sheathed sword poked at the fire so that sparks flew up. "Not like the odds. Where are you from? Mante?"

"Outside."

There was long and sober silence. The fire crackled, the burning of new branches, the flare of pine needles.

"What—outside?"

"Beyond Mante. Things are very different there. I do not give my enemies to beasts. I deal with them myself."

There was another long silence.

Then: "Cup!" Arunden said.

"My lord," the priest objected vehemently, scrambling up.

"Sit *down*, priest!" And as the so-named priest sank down with ill grace: "Close up, close up, close up! Does a *qhalur woman* frighten you? Close up!"

No one stirred for a moment. Then Chei edged closer on Vanye's side. After that there was a general movement, men moving from the back of the circle forward on Arunden's side, edging closer on either side of them, blurring and obliterating the line the priest had drawn, two rough-looking men crowding close on Morgaine's side, so that Vanye felt anxiously after his sword-hilt.

"You!" Arunden jabbed his sheathed sword toward him across the fire. "Sit *down!*"

"Sit as they do," Morgaine said quietly, and Vanye drew a second nervous breath and came down off his heels to fold his legs under him, sitting cross-legged and a cursed deal further from a quick move. Morgaine reached and touched his hand, reminding him it was on the sword-hilt, forbidding him, and he let it go, glaring at Arunden with his vision wide on everything around him.

But a young woman brought a massive wooden bowl and gave it to Arunden: he held it out to the priest. "Here," he said. *"Here!"*

The priest drank. Arunden did, and passed the massive bowl to his right.

So from hand to hand it passed, all about the gathering on that side before it came to Bron and to Chei.

There was utter silence then, a profound hush in every movement in the circle.

And from Chei, as he gave it to Vanye's hands, a frightened look, a pleading look—What, Vanye wondered. That they not refuse? That there was some harm in it?

"Take it," Chei said. "You must take it."

It was honey drink, strong-smelling. Vanye looked doubtfully toward Morgaine, but he saw no likelihood of poison, seeing others had drunk, seeing that the moisture of it shone on Chei's mouth. *"Liyo?"*

She gave a slight nod, and he drank one fiery and tiny sip, hardly touching the tip of his tongue to it.

"Drink," Chei whispered from his left. "For God's sake, truly drink. They will know."

He hesitated, feeling the sting of it, tasting herbs. Panic touched him. But they would insist for Morgaine too, he thought; if there was harm in it, she had to know. He took a mouthful and swallowed it down, tracing fire all down his throat.

He passed it slowly, amid the soft murmur of those about the fire. He held onto the bowl a moment, feeling that fire hit his stomach, tasting it all the way down with the sense that he knew to use on bitter berries, unfamiliar fare at strange table. Slowly he let her take it, while the murmur grew; and there was a troubled frown on her face—full knowledge what he had done, and why.

So she looked at him and drank a very little, he thought that she truly did, her own judgment: but she was a woman, she might be delicate in her habits; it was his place to convince them, and he thought that he had, sufficient good faith for the two of them.

She passed the bowl on to the man at her right, and so it went on.

The murmur grew.

"Is there something remarkable in it?" Morgaine asked then, civilly.

"There is fen-wort in it," Arunden said. "And neverfade."

"To loosen tongues," Chei said in a small voice, at Vanye's left, "and to bring out truth."

"*Liyo—*" Vanye said, for there was of a sudden too much warmth on his tongue for one sip of honey-mead. She glanced his direction.

"It is harmless—" Chei said. The cup was finishing its course. A young woman brought a skin and filled it, and it began a second passing.

The crowd-murmur grew. "Another bowl!" the priest objected. "It is un-clean, unclean—"

But the bowl went to him. "Drink," Arunden bade him, and clenched his hand in the priest's hair and compelled him, at which there was rough laughter, at which Vanye took in his breath and stared in horror, not knowing what to do, not knowing what the priest might do, or some man who respected him.

But no one did anything.

"*Liyo,*" he said, wishing them out of this.

"Is thee all right?" she whispered back, past the laughter and the noise.

"I am all right," he said, and it was true, as the moments passed and the cup went round and the priest wiped his mouth and frowned. He felt Chei take his arm and press it. "—no harm," Chei was assuring him. "No harm in it—"

He reached that conclusion in his own reckoning, that it was very strong, that his stomach had been empty, but it was well enough: he thought that he would not fall if he rose, nor sleep if he sat, but that if he sat still a little while his head might not spin and his judgment might come back.

Chei's hand rested on his shoulder then, heavily, a friendly gesture, offering him the cup in the next round. Every detail seemed to stand out with unnatu-ral clarity—like the effects of *akil*, very like that, but milder. There were more and more cups offered about, bowls passed hand to hand, drink poured from skins, blurred voices murmuring words indistinct to him. More than one bowl came his way. He drank only a little and passed them on.

It was mad. There seemed no hostility in it, but it was all balanced on the knife's edge, a peculiar sort of intimacy in this passing of drink round and round. Yet another bowl came his way, and he only pretended to drink now, and gave it on to Morgaine, who likewise feigned drinking, and passed it on again.

"Say on now," Arunden said, whose mustache glistened with beads of liquid in the firelight. "*Now* we talk. My lady *qhal*, fine lady, who shares my drink and shares my fire—what is it you want in my land?"

"Passage through."

"Through, through, *where* through? To what—to *Mante?*"

"It is the gates," Chei said unbidden. "My lady—*tell* him."

"Chei means to say," Morgaine said quietly, in a silence that had grown so sudden and so hushed there was only the wind in the leaves about them, among a hundred, perhaps a hundred fifty men, and words rang in the air like a hammer on iron: "that Vanye and I came through the southern gate and we are going out the northern one, against the interests of the *qhal* in this world. We will pass it, we will seal it, and there will be no more taking of men and changing them, there will be no more coming and going out the southern gate, with Gault bringing whatever he likes at your backs while the north brings war against you. There will be no more gate-force. Once I am done with them, they cannot bring them back to life."

A great murmuring grew in the silence she left. "Ha," Arunden cried, and gestured to one of the women, who filled a bowl. He drank deeply, and wiped his mouth. "Who will do this?"

"No great band of men will do it," Morgaine said. "No force of arms. A Gate is far too dangerous to assault head-on."

"Aye, there you say!" He took another deep draft. "So who will do it?"

"I am enough."

"Ha!" He waved his hand. "*Drink* for our guests! *You* are enough! Woman, m'lady *qhal*, how do you propose to do that? Seduce Skarrin?"

"*Liyo,*" Vanye said, but her hand rested on his arm, and she slid her hand to his and pressed it hard.

"Gate-force," she said. "I am *qhal*—am I not? The most they have to fear—is one of their own with hostile intent."

"Who says there has never been? *Qhal* feud and fight. And what has it ever done? You are lying or you are mad, woman."

"Feud and fight they may. But they will not go that far. I will. They have no chance against you then. Do you see? I will give you the only chance you will ever have."

"And the fires—the fires—in the valley!"

"The only chance," Morgaine repeated, "you will ever have. Else Gault will widen his territory and yours will grow less and less. I set that fire—else Gault would be warned and warn his lord, and after *that*, my lord, you would see a hunt through these hills you would not wish to see. I will advise you: shelter me and mine tonight, and pass us through these woods in the morning as quietly and quickly as you can. Beyond that I can assure you the *qhal* will have other concerns; and beyond that you can do what you have never, I would surmise, been able to do: to come at Gault from the wooded south. That gate south of Morund will cease to be active. There will be no power there. Begin to think in those terms. Places you have not dared to go. Enemies you will not have when these present shapes age and fade—it is *that* which can make a *qhalur* enemy a most deadly threat, do you understand? It is the experience of a half a score lifespans fighting in the same land, against human folk who know only what they can learn in twenty years. That will cease. You will see them die. You will find their successors fewer and fewer. They do not bear half so frequently. That is what I offer you."

Arunden wiped a hand across his mouth. The bowl tilted perilously in his hand. From time to time as Morgaine spoke the gathering murmured almost enough to drown her voice, but it was quiet now.

Arunden was entirely drunk, Vanye thought. He was drunk and half numb and the visitor he had tried to ply with drink and drug had spun a spell enough to muddle a man's mind—that was the witchery Morgaine practiced. He had seen her work it on more than one man with his wits about him; and he watched now a desperate and inebriate man trying to break the strands of that web, with sweating face and glittering eyes and quickened breath.

"Lies," Arunden said.

"Wherein?"

"Because you will never do it! Because no one can get through."

"That is my worry. I have said: shelter for the night. Safe passage through to the Road. That is all."

"That is easy done," Arunden said, wiping his mouth again. He held out the bowl which had come to him. "It is empty!"

A woman hastened to fill it. There were a great number of bowls filled, and a general and rising commotion among the onlookers. Chei's hand a second time rested on Vanye's shoulder.

"Quiet!" Arunden shouted, and took another deep draft of the bowl. "Quiet!"

There was a slow ebb of noise. Wind sighed in the leaves, and bodies shifted anxiously.

"Gault will move against us," Arunden said, and motioned violently toward her with the bowl, spilling the liquor. "*That* is what you have done!"

"He may," Morgaine said.

"What does a woman know about strategy?" Arunden cried then, and seized by the shoulder one of the women who rested near with the skin of drink, and shook at her. "Eleis here—a fair shot and a fair cook, till she comes to bearing, eh, pretty?—a good many of our girls come down to the marches for a few years, but lead? Carry a sword? This arm here and mine—d' you want to go a pass with me, Eleis?"

There was rude laughter.

"What do *you* say?" Arunden asked then, and jutted his chin and waved the bowl toward Vanye.

Morgaine laid her hand on his arm again. "Patience," she said, and the laughter sank away a little.

"Go a pass with you?" Vanye asked in measured tones. "Aye, my lord. Gladly. When you are sober."

There was a moment quieter still. Then Arunden broke out in laughter, and others laughed. He pushed the young woman roughly aside, and the woman caught her balance and got up and left the circle.

"Are you human?" Arunden asked him.

"Aye, my lord."

"Your speech is strange as hers."

"That may be, my lord. I learned it of her. My own I much doubt you would understand."

"What clan are you from?"

"Nhi. I am Kurshin. You would not know that land either, my lord. It had gates—which my liege sealed. There have been others. There have been those who attacked my liege. Many of them. *She* is here with you."

That, perhaps, took some thinking for some of them. It evidently did, for Arunden, who sat frowning in a sudden quiet and perhaps wondering whether there was an affront somewhere mixed in it.

"Ha," Arunden said then. "Ha." He lifted the bowl and drained it. "So. Hospitality."

"That is what we ask," Morgaine repeated patiently.

"Weapons."

"That we have, my lord."

"Men. You need—three thousand men to storm Mante. Four thousand!"

"I need one. I have him. That is *all*, my lord. *You* will reap the benefit of it—here. You will need those three thousand men, *here*, in the hills, to wait till the *qhal* grow desperate. That is what you have to do."

"You tell *me* strategy?"

"I could not possibly, my lord. No one could."

"Ha!" Arunden said. And: "Ha! Wise woman. Witch! Is that a witch?" He elbowed the priest with his bowl. "That is a witch, is she not?"

"That is a *qhal*," the priest muttered, "my lord."

"That is the way out of these hills. That is the way of *winning* against the whole cursed breed! *Qhal* against *qhal*! *Qhalur* witch—that, they send, slip into Skarrin's own bed, hey—is that how you will do it?"

"My liege is very tired," Vanye said. "We have been days on the road. She thanks you for your hospitality; and I thank you. I would like to find her a place to rest, by your leave, my lord."

"Too much to drink, eh?"

"Travel and drink, my lord." Vanye gathered himself to his feet in one smooth motion: such as the drug had done, rage had dispelled. He reached down his hand and assisted Morgaine to stand, taking matters beyond Arunden's muddled ability to manage. "Good night to you—gracious lord."

"See to it," Arunden said, waving his bowl, and women leapt up and hurried as seated men edged aside, opening a path in their circle for the course they were about to take. Shouts went up. More drink splashed into bowls.

But Chei was on his feet too, and Bron. Vanye escorted Morgaine through the press, toward the horses, with Chei at his heels; and young women intercepted them, managing to come not at either of them, but at Chei: "This way," one said, "come, tell them come—"

"Our horses," Vanye said, and ignored the summons, he and Morgaine, walking back to where Siptah and Arrhan stood, while the crowd behind them muttered with drunken dismay. "*Liyo*, let me tend them," Vanye said. "They should not see you do such a thing."

"One of them can tend them," Morgaine said shortly. "But not with our belongings."

"Aye," he said, understanding the order to stay close by her; and caught his breath and went hurrying ahead of her, between the horses, snatched thongs loose and retrieved their saddlebags and their blankets, finding female hands all too ready to take anything he would not hold back from them, and Siptah bothered enough to be dangerous. "Take them," he said, and threw the reins at Chei's brother, who limped within range. "Get someone to rub them down—*both*, else you call me." This last because Siptah was on the edge of his temper, and he was not sure whether any man in camp was sober enough to trust with a twenty year old packhorse, let alone the Baien gray.

"They have vacated a shelter for the lady," Chei said, at his elbow.

O Heaven, he thought, get us clear of this. And aloud: "See the horses picketed near us, Chei, Bron, I trust you for that. And have our gear near us."

"Aye," Chei agreed.

He turned away, after Morgaine and the women, as they tended out of the firelight and toward the shadow of the woods, as the uproar around the fire grew wilder and more frivolous.

There was more to-do as they came to the ill-smelling little shelter of woven mats and bent saplings. Women offered blankets, offered water, offered bread and a skin of liquor. "Go," he said shortly, and pushed the ragged wool flap aside to enter the shelter where Morgaine waited. Firelight entered through the gaps in the reed walls. After a breath or two his eyes found it enough light to make out more than shadow, the glow of her pale hair, the glimmer of silver at her shoulders as she dropped the cloak, the shape of her face and her eyes as she looked at him.

"I would kill him," he said. He had done very well up till now. He found himself shaking.

She came then and embraced him, her cheek against his for a moment, her arms about his ribs; then she took his face solemnly between her hands. "You were marvelous," she said, laughing somewhat; and touched her lips to his, the whole of which confounded him in that way she could do. Perhaps it was the drug which still muddled him. It seemed only courteous not merely to stand there, but to hold to her and to return that gesture, and perhaps it was she who pressed further, he was not sure—only that he did not want to let her go now she had gotten this close and she did not let him go, but held to him and re-turned him measure for measure till the world spun.

"Vanye," Chei's voice came from outside the shelter, and he caught his breath and his balance and broke apart from her with a whispered curse; at which a second touch of Morgaine's hands, lightly this time, on his arm, sliding to trail over his fingers—

"What?" he asked, far too harshly, flinging back the door-flap.

Perhaps there was murder in his look; perhaps his rapid breaths said some-thing; or perhaps the firelight struck his face amiss, for Chei's expression went from startlement to thorough dismay.

"I was about to say," Chei said, above the uproar from about the fire, "I have told them where to picket the horses, yonder. I am going to go back to the fire, if you—I think I should—Bron and I. . . . Your pardon," Chei said suddenly, and backed and made a hasty retreat, not without a backward look; and a second, and a third, before he suddenly had to dodge a tree and vanished around it.

Vanye caught his breath and, muddled somewhere between outrage and embarrassment, let the door-flap fall again.

Morgaine's hands rested on his shoulders, and her head against the back of his neck. "We had best take the sleep," she whispered, her breath disturbing the fine hairs there.

"Aye," he said with difficulty, thinking that sleep was not going to come easily despite the liquor and the drug and the exhaustion. "They are fools out there. At least ninety and nine of them. I cannot credit that Chei is a fool with the lot of them—"

"I do not think he is," she said. "I think he has found his brother, that is all. Let him be."

Fire and clangor of arms, one brother lying dead at his hand, the other lying under the knife in hall—and after that, after that was exile, *ilin*-ban, and every kinsman's hand against him. The old nightmare came tumbling back again, of bastardy and years of torment before he reacted, once, frightened—no, *angry*—cornered in a practice match.

Kandrys had not intended his death. He had reasoned his way to that understanding: it would have been only another baiting—except it was the wrong day, the wrong moment, Kandrys' bastard brother grown better and more desperate than Kandrys knew.

And he had always wanted most that Kandrys would forgive him his existence and his parentage.

He drew a sudden, gasping breath, as if a cold wind had blown out of that dream, and brought the grave-chill with it.

"Vanye?"

"It is that cursed drink," he murmured. "Likely Chei has his ear to matters out there—my mind is wandering. I am hungry, but I think I am too tired to get into the packs. Did you drink anything of it?"

"No more than I must."

"They have left us more of the stuff. What kind of fools raise such a noise, living as they do? That is a *priest* out there—"

She leaned her head against him. "This is not Andur-Kursh. And they are fools who have fought their war too long," she said. "Fools who are losing it, year by year, and see a hope. If they are not thinking how to betray us *and* do Gault harm. How far can we trust Chei, do you think? For a few leagues still?"

"I do not know," he said. He slipped her grasp, turning to look at her, as laughter and shrieks rose from the gathering at the fire. "He may. There is no honor for a man here. He is too good for this. This is a sink, *liyo*, a man who could not hold his folk, except he binds them with that—out there. That is the game this hedge-lord plays. Only he is gone in it himself. Heaven knows about Chei's brother."

"Heaven knows when Chei knew about his brother," Morgaine said. "Curse him, he forced this, *he* has gotten us into this tangle; I do not say he was not taken by surprise, I do not know whether he wanted this from the beginning, but there is disaster everywhere about this place. They have left us bread yonder; and meat; likely it is safe enough; and we will take what food we can and prevail on Chei and his brother at least to see us to the Road. That is all we need of him, and there is an end of it."

"Aye," he said forlornly, and with a sense of anger: "It is a waste, *liyo,* this whole place is a waste. Heaven knows we could do better for him."

"Or far worse," she said.

"Aye."

She caught him by the arm and held him so. Perhaps her eyes could see him in the dark. She was faceless to him. "If he ties himself too closely to us—will they ever forget? If he stays then, is he or his brother safe, when once the gates die, and powers start to topple? Or if we take them with us—*where* are they then? Can you promise them better? Best, I say, we let him go. The eight down in the valley are only an earnest of what we shall do here. When power falls here, it will fall hard."

"Lord in Heaven, *liyo—*"

"Truth, Nhi Vanye, bitter truth. That is the ciphering I do: thee knows, thee knows I have no happier choices—except we leave him, here, near a great fool, who will vaunt his way to calamity with the power he imagines he has; and Chei, being Chei, will know when to quit this hedge-lord—or supplant him. *That* is the best gift we can give him. To leave him among his own kind and kin."

He drew several large and quietening breaths. "Aye," he said again, reasoning his way through that. "In my heart I know that."

"Then be his friend. And let him go."

"Is it that clear?"

"Vanye, Vanye—" But what else she would have said, she did not say, not for some little moment. Then: "Did I not tell thee, thee could leave me? I warned thee. Why did thee not listen?"

He said nothing for a moment, in confusion, a sudden hurt, and deep. He traced it several times, trying to understand how she had gotten to that, or what he had said or done to bring her to that offer again.

Then he realized it for her wound, not his—a doubt she could not lose.

"There will never be a time," he said. "There will never be. *Liyo,* when will you believe it? I cannot leave you. I could never leave you. When will you trust me?"

There was long silence. He wished that he could see her. The very air ached.

"I do not know," she said finally, in a voice hushed and faint. "I do not know why thee should love me."

"God in Heaven—"

But it was not a simple thing that she meant. It was all that she was. It was the whole that she was.

Chei, then, was not the one she had meant—*be his friend. Let him go.*

He took her face between his hands. He kissed her on the brow, and on either cheek, as a man might his kin. He kissed her a third time on the lips, not after the same fashion. It was desperate; it became passionate, and her arms came around him, while the tumult went on outside.

Then he remembered she had not wanted this, and he heard the arrival of the horses out beside the shelter; and reckoned that there was too much of ill in this place and too much chance of disturbance and too much that they risked. Perhaps she had the same sense of things. He separated himself from her in consternation, and she touched his face.

"I think they have brought the horses," she said, foolish for the moment as he was, one heartbeat, one way of thinking, one intention between them, and all of it sliding in that way a dream might—coming apart and passing into the ordinary.

"Aye," he said, feeling himself still breathing in time with her, and all the world having shifted in its balances, and still reeling. He drew another breath. "Best I see where the rest of our gear is."

And outside, with the horses, dealing with the several men who tried with little success to deal with the gray—"Let him be," he said, and took the reins himself. "Put the tack over there—" He gave orders while the figures at the fire moved darkly against the glare, and shouts rang out, and his mind was dangerously busier with his liege than it was with Arunden's men and with Chei and Bron, who had deserted them.

"Whoa, whoa," he whispered to the gray stud, and to the mare, the both of which were unsettled by the place, the fire, the strangers about them. He spoke to them in his own tongue, he stroked them with his hands.

It was strange that he could suddenly be so content to stay a night in this wretched place, or that he could suddenly put the matter of Chei and Chei's betrayals out of his mind. He went back in, he shared a supper of yesterday's bread and a little honey and a sip of their own arrhendur liquor, and somehow they sat closer together than they were wont, and leaned together, armored that they were—and not, after all, fools enough to shed it, whatever the temptation.

"There is time," she said against his cheek, when they were also fools enough to lie down together, because it was easier than to move elsewhere.

And what she had said somehow frightened him, like an ill omen.

There was a third presence by them, an unliving thing. She had laid *Changeling* on her other side, that fell thing without which she never slept, and with and without which she could not rest.

Against that, against the things which had begun to move in the world, he knew he had no power.

⤳ Chapter 7

There had been quiet in the camp for some time, in Vanye's restless sleep. The tumult around the fire had sunk away. Now a milky daylight was streaming through the reed walls, and he lay with his eyes open a moment content only to breathe and to feel Morgaine's warmth against his side, and to know that it was no dream that had happened. Sleep, she had bade him finally: if there was harm here they would have done it—only sleep lightly. It had thundered in the last of the night, a little flashing of lightning, a little sifting of rain against the reed roof, no more than that.

He drifted again, in that half-sleep in which he had spent the little of the night they had had left, alternate with Morgaine, when she would shake at him and tell him it was her turn for an hour of deep rest.

It was more rest, at least, than sitting awake and battling exhaustion during a first watch: as the course of things had gone, it was rare luxury, considering the weather and the night chill.

But he came wide awake again at the simultaneous realization that there was a quiet stirring in the camp, and that Morgaine had shifted onto her elbow.

"They are awake out there," he said reluctantly; and she:

"We had best take our leave of this place, gather Chei, and go."

"I will find him."

She rested her hand on his chest. "Do not stray from here." Fingers tightened on his harness. "The horses first. Then we both find Chei, if he does not come to us. We can break our fast on the way."

She was always cautious. This had other cause. He sensed that suddenly, wider awake than a moment ago, though he did not know which cause of many he could think of.

"Aye," he said. He understood it for something of instinct; he did not take his own such impulses lightly, when they came; and Morgaine's, which were reliable, set a chill into him and cleared his head faster than cold water.

He gathered himself up and moved.

All the world outside was gray and wet, in a hanging fog—except he had kept the blankets dry, and seeing the likelihood of dew, even if he had not foreseen the rain, had thrown a reed mat over the good leather of their tack—being of mountainous Morija, where heavy dew and sudden rains were ordinary. The horses blew and stamped and threw their heads when he came to saddle them, and shifted skittishly as he worked, liking the drying-off, all the same.

Around the dead fire below, the women labored, wrapped in blankets, strange moving shapes like their own huts gone animate in the mist, among the less energetic forms of men who had begun to rise and wander about the peripheries of the camp similarly shrouded.

Morgaine came out with their packs and slung them over Siptah's saddle, pausing to cast a glance downhill toward the fire-site and the moving figures.

"There will be aching heads this morning," Vanye muttered, pulling Arrhan's girth tight; and heard someone walking near them, through the brush, the which sound set his heart beating a little faster in apprehension. "Who will that be?"

Morgaine made no answer. She had her cloak slung on one-sided against the cold; and because of the weapons she had. She carried *Changeling* at her back; and she stood by Siptah's side looking in the direction of that quiet tread—more than one man was there, that much was certain.

It was Chei that came out of the mist and the trees, with Bron limping behind him.

"We are leaving," Morgaine said quietly. "Chei, one last journey and I release you from your word—guide us as far as the Road. Beyond that—you are quit of us and you can go where you like, with our thanks."

"Lady," Chei said, "you mistake me. Where I want to be, is with you and with Vanye. Myself and Bron, together. We have both decided. He understands everything. He agrees."

"There is no need," Morgaine said with a shake of her head. "Believe me: that one service is all you need do us, and then go back, find some other place, do as you choose."

"I am not helpless," Bron declared fervently—a man much like his brother in all points, but taller. It was the identical anxious look. "Lady, I limp, but I am a whole man on horseback—I shall not slow you; it is my leg that is wounded, that is all, and it is healing. I will not be lame, I have my gear, and I will not slow you."

The silence went on then, painfully. "No," she said then.

The man drew in his breath, slowly. "Then at least—do not cast Chei off for my sake."

"You do not understand," she said.

"*You* do not understand," Chei said, and held out his hand toward Vanye with that same expression. "Vanye—we were worth something to our lord, Bron and I; Bron—Bron was the one he used to say—had no fear of the devil himself. You see he is wounded; but he will heal—*I* will heal; you have never seen what I can do, and the two of us—you will never regret taking us, we will fight for you, Bron and I, against *any* of your enemies, human or *qhal*; we will never find a better lord, I believe that, and Bron believes it—He knows what you might have done here, and did not, and how you dealt with Arunden—and how you dealt with me—Tell her, Vanye. Tell my lady we will repay everything she spends on us. We will earn our keep. We are worth having, Nhi Vanye!"

"It is not your worth she disputes, Chei."

"Then what? Do you doubt us? I brought you through this. I have gotten you safe passage. I swore to you. What do you think—that I have not kept my word? Bron and I—will go with you on our own. We will prove to you what we are worth. Take us on those terms. You owe us nothing. Only for God's sake do not leave us in Arunden's debt."

Entanglement showed itself, unguessed and dark, an obscurity of honor and obligation. "You mean that Arunden has some claim on you."

"For Bron's life," Chei said. "For mine, if you leave me here; I will have to trade him everything I own; and most of everything that comes to me or Bron; and then we will never be free of him. One or the other of us he will always find a way to keep in his debt—that is the way he is. Lady, I swear we will manage, we will take nothing of your supplies—have I not brought you my own horse and gear already? Bron has his gear, he has a good horse—he traded his small-sword for it last night. He has his other. We will not slow you. We will earn our way, every step of it."

"Foolishness," Morgaine said harshly. "Two wounded Men and *qhalur* territory ahead of us. And you *would* use our supplies. We have no time for hunting."

"We have them! We have provisions—we—"

"Chei. Chei, no. This much I will do, if you have some debt here. Ride with us, both as far as the Road. I will at least get you free of here. You will see us as far as the Road and then we are quit of each other. You will have no debt to me or to Arunden, and that is as much as I can give you. I claim nothing of you."

"Did you not promise—*promise* to me—that you would take me through the gate if I chose?"

Morgaine stopped for once with her mouth open, caught. Then she shut it abruptly and frowned. "That had condition, condition you cannot meet. You know nothing about the land further on."

"I thought it was for my life's sake—for my protection. Not a few nights gone. *I will not deny you that right,* you said."

"I said I would advise you against it."

"But I will go, lady, and my brother will."

"*You,* I said. No other!"

Chei's face went paler still. "Both of us. You will not hold me to that. You will not deny me for Bron's sake, you would not do that, lady."

"You do not know *what* I would do, fool!"

"I know I will follow you. And Bron will. Both of us. And you will not turn us back. Please."

A long moment she stood still. And Chei was next to weeping, Bron's face pale and set. "You are not afraid for *that*?" She swept her hand toward the camp, the dead fire, Arunden's place and others'. "You have no fear of your priest and his curses?"

"We will follow you."

"We will talk about it again before Tejhos. By then, you may have another opinion."

"Lady," Chei said fervently, and knelt down and seized her hand, his brother after him kneeling and taking her hand and pressing it to his brow, the which she endured with a look of dread on her face.

"We are leaving," Morgaine told the brothers. "Arm and saddle and take everything you can. I would dispense with any long leave-takings with Arunden, if we can avoid that, Chei. Or if you have to deal with him, say we will remember him kindly—say whatever will keep him content and keep him off our trail."

"Aye, lady," Chei said, and Bron murmured the same, rising with a great effort not to falter in the act. Chei delayed for him and then the both of them went off directly across the camp in all the haste Bron could use.

Morgaine swore beneath her breath and shook her head.

"It is freedom you offer them," Vanye said. "Evidently they are beholden for whatever they take at Arunden's hand."

"If that is all they want," she muttered, and turned to Siptah to tie the thongs that held her blanket roll. "What would they want?"

She cast him a frown over her shoulder. "Glory. Whatever else you name it. Power. I have seen it before." She finished the tie with a vengeance. "No matter. I could be wrong."

"You do not understand them. I think that is a good man, Chei's brother. I think that Chei is trying to be. He is young, *liyo*, that is all, and too proud, and he knows too little, and acts on it too soon, that is the trouble with him. I have done that, now and again."

"Then thee generally did it younger. No, likely I do not understand: men and Men, did I not say it from the beginning? When did I say I kept my promises? I lie; thee knows I lie; *tell* this boy."

"Why am *I* always the messenger?"

"Because thee is the honest man in this company. Did I not tell thee how trouble looks for an honest face?"

"I cannot tell him—"

"Peace, peace, forbear. We will settle it later. I only want us away from here. We are already delayed. Now we have these two making noise in the camp—"

"And it is trouble if we slip out without it. You will shame this Arunden if you leave with no courtesy to him."

"A wonder, something that would shame Arunden. No, I will pay him courtesy; and well enough it were short courtesy, and ourselves well away from here." She took Siptah's reins and flung herself to the saddle, reining back as the horse started forward. "Before noon, I hope."

Vanye mounted up more carefully, and leaned to pat the white mare's shoulder as she stood quietly at Siptah's side. In the camp in general there were more folk up shambling about their private business. A little tongue of fire gleamed through the mist, where blanket-shrouded figures crouched.

And in a very little time there was the sound and the ghostly shapes of two riders coming back again through the mist, but they were not alone. A handful of bearish figures went after them afoot.

"*There* is trouble," Morgaine said between her teeth, about the time the riders broke free and came cantering their way.

They did not shake the followers. A loud shout rang through the misty air and dark shapes jogged at the riders' heels, others rousing from fireside and shelters and every occupation in the camp.

The brothers did not bring the trouble that far. They turned their horses about and stopped there, in the face of the oncoming crowd.

Morgaine sent Siptah forward and Vanye touched his heels to Arrhan, overtaking her as she reined in alongside Chei and Bron, in the face of Arunden himself and his priest, and by the size of the crowd that was rallying there, of every man in camp.

"You do not take them only," Arunden shouted at her, waving an arm at the brothers. "Here is a man in debt to me—I release him! I make no claim against him or his brother for his keep! But if it is my safe-conduct you want, by Heaven, lady, you do not have it through my land with these guides, and you do not have it without my riders. That is no lie, lady, God knows what they have told you to send you riding out like this, with no farewell cup and no advisement to me, but you are ill-advised to listen to them."

"My lord Arunden, I counsel *you*, I am traveling with all speed, and the more speed and the fewer and the more silence the safer."

"Arrows are quicker than any horse," Arunden said, and set his fists on his hips, walking forward. Siptah snaked his head for more rein and Vanye sent Arrhan sidestepping closer on his side, forming a solid wall, whereupon Arunden stopped in his tracks. "My lady Morgaine—Yonder is no trail for any *qhal*, much less a woman and a handful of men, two of them such as I would never send out on a ride like this, and who do not have leave to come and go in my land. My warders will stop you, and at best hail you back here, and at worst shoot without asking questions! Whatever these two scoundrels have told you, *I* will tell you, you do not pass through these woods or any other without a good number of reliable men around you, and you before

God do not ride that road without there be good human men around you, and men my warders know, or before Heaven, someone will take that hair of yours for a target! First cover that head of yours before someone takes you for some of Gault's own, and stand down and wait while we break camp. We will rouse you more than one clan, my lady, and I will personally see you to the Road!"

"We need no help," Morgaine said. "The four of us are enough. Do not press me, my lord Arunden. Pay your attentions to Gault, southward."

"Do not be a fool," Arunden said, and stalked off a few paces to give a wave of his hand at his gathered men. "Break camp."

The men started to obey; and froze and scrambled back as red fire cut through the mist and smoke and then flame curled up at Arunden's feet. Arunden stood confused a moment, looked down and retreated in alarm as the tiny fire grew to larger points. Then he looked back at Morgaine, wide-eyed, and Vanye settled back in the saddle with his hand still on his sword-hilt.

"Witch!" Arunden cried; and his priest held up the sword.

"You have been my host," Morgaine said coldly. "Therefore I owe you some courtesy, my lord. Therefore your land is untouched. But do not mistake me. Here I am lady, and these are men of mine, and whoever rides with me takes my orders or Vanye's orders. There are no other terms with me, and I am sure they are not to your liking. If you would have my gratitude—my lord—then be sure of that southern border, where Gault is very likely to be no little disturbed by what we have done in his lands."

A series of expressions fleeted through Arunden's eyes, from fear to other things less easy to read.

And the priest thrust himself forward with his sword for a cross, chanting prayers and imprecations at them, at the crowd, at Heaven above. *Witch*, was the general murmur in the crowd that was melting backward; and there was fear in Bron's eyes too, as he controlled his horse and glanced her way. At the priest's feet the fire had spread to a small circle, faltering in the wet grass, and he kicked at it suddenly with a vengeance, stamping it underfoot as Arunden and his men murmured behind him. "Fire," the priest cried, "such as took the woods down in the valley. Fire of your making. Who burns the woods is cursed of God! Cursed be all of you, cursed who ride with you—"

Vanye crossed himself. So Bron and Chei made some sign, and backed their horses, when the priest pressed forward with his sword uplifted hilt to Heaven; but: "Hai!" Vanye cried, seeing he was going at Morgaine, and rode forward and shouldered the priest back and back.

"Cursed and damned!" The mailed priest's sword wheeled and came down at Arrhan's neck. Vanye swung his sheathed sword up and struck the blade up, then kicked the priest sprawling in the smoking grass, the priest howling and

writhing instantly with the heat of it. "Damned!" he shouted, "Damned!"—
scrambling up and after his sword.

Arunden brought his foot down on the blade as his hand reached the hilt,
pinning it to the blackened ground.

"Is this your help?" Morgaine asked dryly. "I shall do without, my lord
Arunden."

"You will take what I give!"

"I said that I was Gault's enemy. I have told you what I will do, and where I
am going, and I will have done it before Gault spreads the alarm to his masters
if you do me the grace to do what I have said. I should take that advice, my lord,
if it were my lands bordering Gault. But far be it from me to say what a free
Man should do. That is your choice—to help or hinder."

"Do not listen to her," the priest cried, and snatched up the sword Arund-
en's stride released.

Arunden turned and interposed his arm at the same time Vanye bared steel;
and grasped the priest's sword-hilt in his hand and wrenched it away, disarming
the man and flinging the sword far across the grass. "My lady," Arunden said,
"Take my advice. I will not argue strategy with you. I will go with you myself,
with ten of my men. My lieutenant will go south and close the road, others east
and west and advise the other clansmen. Ichandren's skull is bleaching on a pole
at Morund, and it is only my word and yours that tells my warders these lads are
still human or that *he* is. I can vouch for you, and get you to Tejhos-gate never
touching the Road. My word carries weight in these hills with bands beyond
this one—there is no one says *I* am one of Gault's minions—ha? Ha, priest who
eats my food and warms at my fire? Take the curse off. *Off*, hear?"

"God remembers," the priest muttered, and made a sign, half with an eye
to Arunden.

"Well enough," Arunden said. "See? We are friends."

"*Liyo,*" Vanye said in his own language. "There is no mending this man. You
will regret any good you do him. And much more any help he gives. Do not
have any part of his offer."

Morgaine was silent a moment, in which Arunden stood looking up as
solemn and sober as he had yet been.

"You will not regret it," Arunden said. "Time will come, you will need us, my
lady—you will need someone the other clans know, a man they will listen to."

"Then prove it, now" Morgaine said. "Send messengers to the clans and
prevent Gault from your land and from the southern gate. Three of your men
can manage our safe-conduct. But all this land will regret it if Gault learns what
I am about, he or his neighbors; and if one of Gault's men reaches that gate in
the south and brings help from Mante—do me that grace, lord Arunden, and
I will freely own myself in your debt."

Arunden's face darkened, suffused with a flush. He gnawed on his lip and raked a hand back through his disordered hair, where it had come loose from its braids.

"Whoever commands that position," Morgaine said, "will command the south. When that gate dies—you will feel it in the air. When it dies you will know that I have kept my promise; and you will sit as lord at Morund. That I offer you—that and anything you can take and hold. The south will need a strong lord. I will have those three men you offer. I will send them back to you when I have cleared your lands. My own, I keep!"

She wheeled Siptah then and rode, as Arunden stood open-mouthed and with a thousand hostile and avaricious thoughts flickering through his eyes. Vanye did not turn away from him. "Go with her," he said to Chei and Bron, who had moved up beside him; and the brothers turned and rode after Morgaine, leaving only himself facing Arunden and his folk.

"My lord," Vanye said then sternly. "Your three men."

Arunden came free of his astonishment and called out three names, at which Vanye inclined his head in respect to Arunden. "I trust," Vanye said, without a trace of insolence in his tone, "that your men can track us."

Then he whirled about and rode after Morgaine and the ep Kantorei.

"Damned, who defies the priest of God!" the priest shouted after him. "Cursed are ye—!"

He cast a look back. No weapons flew. Only words. Ahead of him Morgaine waited on the slope, Bron and Chei on either side of her, dim figures among the ghosts of tall trees.

"Was there trouble?" Morgaine asked him as he reined in.

"My back is unfeathered," he said, and refrained from crossing himself. He felt more anger than distress.

"He is not much of a priest," Bron said. "No one regards him. It is only words."

"Well we were out of here," Morgaine said, "all the same." And motioned Bron and Chei to lead. "Vanye?"

Vanye drew Arrhan to a walk beside Siptah as Chei and Bron led them out of the misty clearing and in among the trees.

"Do we have the escort?" Morgaine asked.

"He did not refuse it," he said. "I said they should find us on the trail."

"Good," Morgaine said. Then, in the Kurshin tongue: "Did I not tell thee? Power. Arunden does not know what I am. He thinks he knows, and fills in the gaps himself. At least it is honest greed. And it is rarely the first rebel in any realm who ends by being king. There will far worse follow."

He looked at her, troubled by her cynicism. "Never better?"

"Rarely. I do not put treachery past him—or the priest."

"The three he is sending?"

"Maybe. Or messengers he may send ahead of us and behind."

He had reckoned that much for himself. He did not like the reckoning. He thought that he should have forced a challenge and taken off Arunden's shoulders all capacity for treachery.

He was not, he knew all too well, as wise as Morgaine, who had improvised a use for this man: but Arunden, last night, had touched on an old nightmare of hers: he had felt it in the way she had clenched his hand at the fireside.

They would not listen, she had said of that moment human lords had broken from her control; because I am a woman they would not listen.

And ten thousand strong, an army and a kingdom had perished before her eyes.

That was the beginning of that solitude of hers, which he alone had breached since that day. And what they had almost done in the night was very much for her—Heaven knew any distraction was a risk with that burden she carried, dragon-hilted and glittering wickedly against her shoulder as she rode, and trust was foreign to everything she did—trust, by her reckoning, was great wickedness.

So he was resolved, for his part, not to bring the previous night into the day, or to be anything but her liegeman under others' witness, meticulous in his proprieties.

Wet leaves shook dew down onto them as they maintained their leisurely pace and refused to give any grace to Arunden's laggard men. A fat, strange creature waddled away from the trail and into the brush in some haste, evading the horses' hooves: that was all the life they saw in the mist. Trails crossed and re-crossed in the hollows, along ravines and up their sides, in this place where Men seemed to have made frequent comings and goings.

Eventually the sound came to them of riders behind them on the trail. Morgaine drew rein. The rest of them did, waiting in a wide place on the shoulder of a low hill.

"They took long enough," Morgaine said with displeasure. She slipped *Changeling* to her side and adjusted and put up the hood of the two-sided cloak the arrhendim had given her; wrapping herself in gray—gray figure on gray horse in the misty morning; and in the next moment one and the next and the third rider appeared through the thicket across the ravine. They seemed unaware until the next heartbeat that they were observed; then the leader hesitated to the confusion of his men and their horses.

"Well we are no enemy," Vanye said under his breath as the men came on ahead, down the slope and up again toward them.

"Lady," the older of the three said as he reined in, and ducked his head in respect, a stout man with grizzled braids and scarred armor.

"My thanks," Morgaine said grimly, leaning on the saddlehorn. "I will have one thing: to go quickly and quietly. I want to find the road where it enters *qhalur* lands, and that with no harm to anyone, including yourselves. I do not need to say the other choice. Ride well ahead of us. When we come to the road, your duty is done and you will return to your lord. Do you question?"

"No, lady."

She nodded toward the trail, and the three rode on into the lead at a brisk pace. Her glance slid Bron's way, and to Chei, as she reined the gray about; and last she looked to Vanye.

"If they do not cut our throats," he muttered in the Kurshin tongue, and stayed close by her as they rode. The riders ahead had already hazed in the mist, and Bron and Chei were hindmost on the narrow trail. "Bron," he said, reining back half a length. "Do you know those three?"

"The one is Eoghar," Bron said, "and the others are his cousins—Tars, they call the dark one; and Patryn is the one with the scarred face. That is all I know, m'lord—no better and no worse than the rest of them."

"Well when we are quit of them," Chei said for his part, "but just as well we have them now. In that much Arunden told the truth."

The rain began to fall again, a light, chill mist that alternately blew and clung. The noon sun had no success with the clouds, nor was the afternoon better. Streams trickled in the low places they crossed; the rounding of a hill gusted moisture into faces and down necks, and showed the wooded flanks of further hills all hazed and vague.

It was steady progress they made, but not swift, and Morgaine chafed in silence—Vanye knew that look, read the set of her mouth and the sometime impatient glances at the sky, with frowns as if she faced some living enemy.

Time, he thought. It was time and more time lost.

"How far is it?" she had asked Chei early on; and: "Two days," Chei had said, "down to the road again." Then: "Maybe more."

Now their guides halted, waiting for them on the trail, all wrapped in their cloaks and with their horses back-eared and unhappy in the blowing mist.

"We should make camp," their leader said—Eoghar, Bron had named him. He had a wretched look, a pained look, squinting against the rain that dripped off his hair, and Vanye recalled the last night, and the campfire, and the amount of drink that had passed even before they quit the gathering.

"No," Morgaine said, and, "No," again when Eoghar argued the weather and the horses and the slickness of the rocks and the slopes. "How much worse does it get?" she asked then, looking at Chei and Bron, who had ridden up close behind them.

"More of the same," Chei said, himself in worse case, having only his blanket for a cloak, and its gray fibers beginning now to soak through. "No worse, my lady. Certainly no better."

Only looking at him and at Bron did Morgaine's frown go from annoyance to a more complex thing—worry, Vanye thought. But: "Move on," she said to Eoghar and his cousins.

"Lady," Eoghar protested, and his mustached lips shut themselves and the voice faded into something very like fear at whatever look Morgaine then sent him. "Aye, lady." And Vanye took his hand from the sword-hilt as three wet and unhappy men turned their horses about and kept going down the exposed and down-sloping trail.

To Morgaine he ventured no word, knowing her moods well enough, that a black anger was roiling in her, and he knew well enough what kind of look had likely set the men moving.

Yet she delayed a moment, looking back at Chei, and there was worry again. "Are you bearing up?" she asked.

"Well enough," Chei said, and drew a little breath, straightening in the saddle. "My lady."

It was not gratitude shone in Chei's fair eyes, with rain-chill whitening his face and the water running from his hair. It was something like adoration.

Vanye lowered his head and kept his eyes on the trail as they rode after their guides, gazing down on the tops of trees and the depths of a ravine that fell away beside Arrhan's sure, careful steps.

He did not know why that expression of Chei's should trouble him so. It was not the look of a man with a woman he wanted. He had seen it—he recollected—in chapel, candlelight off painted wood, face after identical face—

He did not know why that image out of childhood and Church came back to him again and again, stronger than the world around him, of gray mist and mist-grayed pines and slick granite, or why he thought then of Chei when he had first come to them, that fevered, mad glare that had nothing to do with the clean-faced, earnest youth who spoke so fair to Morgaine and looked at her since this morning as if she were some saint.

But he understood with a little chill of fear—knowing that behind Morgaine's careful question, that kindly, out of the ordinary question to Chei when she was otherwise distracted—Morgaine was indeed disturbed.

I am not virtuous, she was wont to say, again and again to him, warning him. I cannot afford to be.

And again, in the night: How can you love me?

And this morning: I lie; thee knows I lie; *tell* him—

It was fear he felt in her, that was what moiled in his stomach at the moment; it was a rising sense of panic, between her acceptance of Chei for his sake and Bron for Chei's sake; and the changes between himself and her; and this priest and this cursed gift from a hedge-lord. It was no time to think of such things, riding on a high trail in the company of men they could not trust, in a land which might offer ambush: he was derelict to think of anything but where they rode and what things the forest might tell him and the attitudes of the men in front of them. But it was not in the forest that he felt the danger. It was beside him, in Morgaine's silence, in the way she looked at Chei and at him.

Perhaps she mused on things the two of them had done and promised and said to each other, in the thunderous dark.

Nothing seemed now so simple or so clean now as then. He did not know what he should have done differently this morning or how he could have protected her or what he ought now to do.

Persuade Chei and his brother to leave them, that was the first thing, before worse happened.

But to cast them out in these hills, when Chei was known to have been in *qhalur* hands, and when both of them were known to have ridden with Morgaine kri Chya—that would be a death sentence for these two, for these honest, too-young men who had neither lord nor family to protect them, and not, he sensed, the ability to wrest power unto themselves.

Honest men, Morgaine had said.

⌒ Chapter 8

The rain came down in wind-borne mist by sundown, under skies flickering and glowing with lightnings, as they rode within the shelter of a rocky retreat which had not, perhaps, been a streambed until the rain fell, but which now had a waterfall spilling off the heights above the cut and boiling white along the rocks to yet another falls.

There was a sheltered camp here, Chei and Bron supported the guides in that assertion, and Vanye was only glad to hope for the overhanging cliff face Bron described or anywhere out of the wind. "There is no way out of the place but one," Bron had admitted, "but with your weapons no one could force it from the front or from above."

Vanye had had second thoughts at that description, and looked at Morgaine: warfare in world and world and world had taught him half a score of ways to attack such a place; Morgaine surely knew as many more. But Morgaine had made no objection except a misgiving glance, wet and miserable as the rest of them in this storm that mixed cold mist with the breaths they took.

Now they rode in the last of the light, into this narrow place where a waterfall thundered above the rain, and where some previous user had left standing a woven brush-work against the rock. He did not like the look of it; but the horses were spent after rough going on the slick trails, they were chilled to the bone, and the whipping of the wind up the heights and the scattering of water off pine boughs in soaking drops, threw water at them so many directions there was no fending it off: it ran down necks and got under cloaks clenched in numb hands; and that brush shelter beckoned with the promise of dry ground and rest and respite.

But: "No," Morgaine said then, ready to refuse it after all, "no more of guesting—"—at which Vanye's heart both sank in weariness and resolved itself she was altogether right. But: "It is a hunter-shelter," Chei said. "I do not expect anyone is there."

"Find out," Morgaine said to Eoghar, and with more zeal than he had done anything in the last hour, Eoghar spurred his horse up the bank to hail the place and then to dismount, draw his sword, and look into it.

Eoghar turned then and waved to them to come ahead, murky flash of his sword-blade in the dark. Vanye gave a sigh of relief and guided Arrhan carefully after Eoghar's cousins, to have an eye on them and keep his sword between them and Morgaine, should they have any notions of treachery in this dark hole.

But when they had come up and dismounted beside the shelter:

"One cannot hear in this place," Morgaine objected, the last of them still ahorse, her voice thinned by the roar of the water pouring down and running over rock. "I do not like this."

Vanye looked up at her from across Arrhan's rain-wet saddle. "Aye," he said hoarsely, knowing a second time she was right, but he felt the weight of the mail on his back and the cold of water down his neck and soaking his boots and breeches. It was her second quibble with this place. He respected her instincts; but there was in him a heart-deep vexation—Heaven save us, *liyo*, you have three men you can trust, he thought to shout at her.

But there were Arunden's three, and those men large and strong, and if they would not mutiny in the night, they were bound to if she bade them go on now.

And he, God help them, had to enforce her orders, or she had to do murder on them; and he was not sure he had a fight left in him—

"Do we ride on, *liyo*?" he asked with a deep and weary breath.

She glanced back, a shifting of her eyes toward Chei and Bron, who were already taking gear off their horses in the lightning-flashes and the mist, Chei trying in vain to keep the sodden blanket from flying in the wind, his cloth breeches wet through in places where it had blown as he rode. They were spent, man and youth both thin and worn, both recent from wounds, both vulnerable to chill and staggering with exhaustion.

"No," she said, then, in a voice weary as his own. She slid down from Siptah's back, and led him toward the shelter. "We will have a fire if we can find wood enough. At least the rain will drown the smoke. If anyone disturbs us tonight it will be his own misfortune."

It was dead branches broken off the trees back along the rocks, that they had for their fire; and the black weapon's power to set it burning, for which Vanye was earnestly grateful, for nothing but sweat and all a woodsman's skill could have gotten such a fire alight tonight, even considering the heart of the wood was dry. A quick touch of that red light into a little fibrous tinder pulled from the underbark of the nether side of the branches, a little encouragement with dead leaves pulled from the inside of the woven shelter, and there was instantly a cheerful if smoky little flame that grew with twigs and grew with kindling and branches and quickly underlit her face and the fearful countenances of their companions.

A man grew to rely on such comforts.

"It has other uses," Morgaine said to the men who watched in horror. One—Patryn, it was, signed himself. None of the three looked reassured.

To the good, Vanye thought. Chei was not troubled; he tucked his wet blanket about him and huddled close to the *qhal*-made fire, whereat Bron relaxed and even gave a shy grin between his own shivers as he pulled his boots off to dry them.

With Eoghar and his kin it was another matter—but so was their situation, men passed off by their lord into a witch's keeping, despite their priest's objections. They huddled together a little separate, and hugged themselves against the cold. The cousin named Tars sneezed mightily, and buried his head a moment in his arm, and sneezed again.

If they had begun the day with aching heads, Vanye reflected, their misery was surely complete by now. He was even moved to pity for them—not enough that he turned his back on them, but he brought them some of the wood, and brought them burning tinder in a wedge between two sticks, and left them to nurse it along and to go out in the rain if they wanted more firewood in the night: "My charity," he said dourly, "stops at the shelter's edge."

Thereafter Eoghar and Patryn took their turn out in the driving mist, wood-gathering, and he went back to Morgaine and the brothers, loosed his armor buckles and his belts, tucked himself up in his wet cloak next the fire, and rested with Chei and Bron, close by Morgaine as she boiled up tea, his back against the rock and his left shoulder next the dry leaves of the woven branches which made one wall of their shelter.

Outside, the horses complained of the rain, and Siptah snorted his displeasure either at two wet strangers wandering about outside or at the geldings picketed apart from him and the mare.

The wood-gatherers returned with their arms full, before their fire died. Inside, under the shelter of the stone overhang and the woven walls, the warmth increased. By the time there were a few coals and the first pannikin of tea had boiled, there was a closer, less peevish feeling in the air and Chei had unfolded himself somewhat and ceased to shiver.

There was smoked meat, fowl, venison, and the bread they had taken from the camp: they did not use their carefully prepared trail rations while there was that choice, and with food that would not last there was no stinting. There was tea to warm them; and by their own fire at the opposite and shallower end of the shelter, Eoghar and his cousins saw to their own supper with the supplies they had brought.

"Ah," Chei said with a little wince when he had drunk his cup, and he sighed as he leaned back against the rock wall by his brother. Bron pushed at him with an elbow, grinned, and Chei pushed back, then clapped Bron on the shoulder in a brief embrace, a glance, a quick and tender look passed between them such as brothers might exchange, who found each other alive against all expectation.

Then Chei burst into tears, and turned his face into Bron's shoulder, and the two of them held each other fast, at which Vanye found himself the fire to look at, and then Morgaine's face—as she looked distressedly toward him, and then found occupation for her hands with repacking.

There was no cursed place for privacy, except the rain. And Chei fought hard for his dignity, who was, Heaven knew and events had witnessed, not prone to tears.

After, Chei bent and rested his forehead on his knee, his braids covering his face, for a long time in which he met no one's eyes. Only Bron's hand rested on his back, until he wiped fiercely at his eyes.

It was safety did that to a man. That was all. The lifting of some terrible burden. The knowledge of trial passed. As if this place, with the rain beating down and the wind whipping outside, offered what the secure camp had not.

Freedom, perhaps. Or a brother's life.

"I am all right," Chei declared, and wiped his eyes and drew a breath and clasped his hands on the back of his neck, taking his wind.

Bron held him by the shoulder and rocked at him. There was a sheen on Bron's eyes too, as he rubbed Chei's back and wound his fingers in Chei's hair and tugged at it with a familiarity from which Vanye averted his eyes in embarrassment.

But perhaps they felt they had found kin.

"You did not know," Morgaine said, "that your brother was there. Truly."

"No," Chei said, a small, quick breath. And looked up, as if he then understood that question. "I swear I did not."

"But took us to land you knew—to friends' territory."

A frightened shift of Chei's eyes mistrusted the listeners. But there was the waterfall to cover their voices. "Ichandren's. My own lord's."

"Ah," Morgaine said, and did not glance at Eoghar herself; and Vanye dared not, putting it together, how Arunden who held a sick man in debt, had moved right gladly into a dead ally's lands.

"This Arunden seems quick to gain," he muttered.

"From everything," Chei said fiercely. "He is known for it."

"I had wondered," Morgaine said in a low voice, "how we happened to find Bron. Coincidence is the most remote chance in all the world—good coincidence even rarer. I do not trust men who seem to have it all about them. And strokes of luck are worst of all."

It was honesty. When Morgaine became obscure it was an offered confidence. Honesty with her was one thing and the other. It was Chei she meant, and Chei she looked at, and Chei looked confused as a man might. "I—do not think I have had luck, lady, except you brought it."

"Any man might have been there, at the gate. Luckier for your friends if we had been a fortnight earlier. It is finding Bron I mean."

"I had no hope of it," Chei said earnestly. "I only went home. I wanted no more mistakes. I thought—I thought—there was no way to get through without meeting ambush. When you told me—what you told me—I knew there was hope in talking. So I did not try to slip around the long way. I brought you up the short way, and took no pains to be quiet, you were right, lady. But we were dead, the other way. It was all I could do."

"And did not tell me."

There was long silence. Chei looked at her, only at her, and his face was pale in the firelight.

"But you did not know," Morgaine said, "that Bron was there."

"No, lady. On my soul, I did not know."

"He could not have known," Bron said. The fire snapped, wet wood; and scattered sparks.

"Arunden took you up," Morgaine said.

"I fell in the fighting," Bron said. "Arunden's folk came down to collect the gear. To *steal* anything they could. That is what they are."

"Gault's men leave their enemies' gear?" Vanye asked. "For others to take up?"

"This time they did," Bron said, and drew a long and shaken breath. "I do not know why. Probably they had wind of Arunden's folk close by. They took up prisoners—I saw them. I fainted then. I thought they would gather up weapons and they would find me alive and finish me. When I woke up it was one of Arunden's men had found me, that is all I know. And Gault's men had taken none of my gear."

"You were fortunate," Morgaine said. "Did I not just say how I abhor good fortune?"

Bron looked anxiously at Chei, last at Vanye, a worried look, a pleading look.

"It is truth," Bron said. "That is all I know."

Vanye shifted position, having found his arm cold from the wind gusting through the woven-work. He found his heart beating uncomfortably hard. "Arunden was an ally of your lord's?"

"We were ambushed on our way to join with him. The *qhal* may have known he was there—" The thought seemed to come to Bron then. His mouth stayed open a moment. His eyes darted and locked.

"And withdrew," Morgaine said.

Bron had nothing to say. He darted a look of his own Eoghar's way and back again. Chei's breath was rapid.

"No one would—" Bron said.

"You say yourself, changelings are not uncommon. A man too close to *qhalur* lands, a scout, a hunter—"

"We are not that careless!"

Heaven save us, Vanye thought. And aloud: "Is your enemy without guile? Or luck?"

Both the brothers were silent. At their own fire, Eoghar and his cousins talked among themselves, voices that did not carry over the water sound.

"It would be easy, then," Morgaine said, "for messengers of all sorts to come and go. From the camp, for instance."

"We do not know it is so!" Chei said.

"No," Morgaine said. "It might be coincidence. Everything might be coincidence."

Bron exhaled a long slow breath. "A treaty with Gault?"

"Possibly," Morgaine said, "you were only fortunate. There *is* chance in the world. It is only very rare—where profit is concerned."

Bron ran his fingers back through his hair and rested, his hands clenching his braids. Then he looked at Vanye and at Morgaine. "Are you, after all, from Mante? Is this something you *know*? Are you having games with us?"

"We are strangers," Morgaine said. "We are not from Gault and not from Skarrin. We do not know this land. But of treachery and of greed we have seen altogether too much. Perhaps it has occurred to you—that there is profit to be had. We do not withhold it. Anything you can gain from us, take. We will have no need of power in this world. Do you want Gault's place? Or any other—take it."

Bron caught a breath. "Everything," he said in a faint voice, "that Chei has told me about you I believe. I never—in all my life—In all my life, I never—never knew I would—come to—to owe—"

"A *qhal*?" Morgaine asked.

Bron swallowed the rest of that speech. His face was bone-white, his pain-bruised eyes set on her as if he could not find a way to move. "But," he said after, "it is you I will follow. I do not think we will live long. I do not think we will live to see Mante. But for what you did for my brother I will go with you; for what you did for both of us, I will do everything I can for you. I do not deny I am afraid of you. There is a cost—to serving *qhal*—and I do not know what you would choose, between us and others. But what you say you will do—if you seal the Gates—is a chance for every man alive; and we never had one till this. It is *worth* a life. And mine is spun out longer than I expected, since Gyllinbrook. Chei's, too. Where else shall we find a place for us?"

Morgaine looked at him long; and turned then and began to pack away their belongings. "I do not know. But I would you could find one." She looked up at them. "When we reach the road, turn back. Go somewhere far, and safe. Two more humans will be a hazard to me—only that much more likelihood that someone will know me for a stranger."

Chei had opened his mouth to protest. He shut it as she spoke and he caught a breath. "But," he said then, "they would take us for the Changed, that is all. There is no reason not."

"It is that common."

"Half the *qhal* in Morund—have human shape."

"So," she said softly, and her frown deepened and darkened. She put a last packet into the saddlebags and wrapped the ties tight. "They are using the gates that often."

"I do not know," Bron said, looking as bewildered as his brother. "I do not know how often they come and go."

"No one knows," Chei said. "None of us go south. When they want to come and go—they use Morund-gate. They do not need to ride through our land."

"Frequently?"

"Maybe—several times a year. I do not know. No one—"

"So a message has already gone to Mante."

"I think that it would have," Chei said. "When the woods burned. I think they would send for that. Gault is not friendly with Mante. With his lord. So they say."

"Rumor says," Bron amended. "Men who come and go off Gault's land. Some do, still."

"Too much here is tangled," Morgaine said; and Vanye shifted his mailed and weary shoulders back against the rock and picked up the thongs that depended from his belt, beginning to braid three of them.

"As to changelings," Vanye said, "we do not do that, with friend or enemy. You are safe with us, as safe, at least, as we are. And we intend to reach Mante, and go beyond it. But that—that, has no return. You should understand that. My lady advises you turn back. There is reason. You should listen to her."

There was silence after, except a discordant muttering from Eoghar and his cousins, about their separate fire. A little laughter drifted from them, about their own business. Doubtless Chei and Bron were distressed. He did not look up.

"Lady," Chei said.

"For your sake and ours," Morgaine said firmly.

Again there was silence, long silence, with only the noise from the other fire where, Vanye saw with a shift of his eye, the three clansmen had unstopped what he reckoned was not a water-skin, and began to pass it about. He did not like it. He did not want the quarrel now, either, with unhappiness enough in their camp. *"Liyo,"* he said in a low voice and when he had her attention, shifted his eyes to indicate the matter.

She frowned, but she said nothing. They were not boisterous at the other fire, only men taking their ease of the dark and the rain in a way as old as men on any earth.

And finally: "I do not understand you," Chei said.

Vanye jerked the braiding loose and looked up at him, frowning. "There is Hell between the gates, Chei, and we will ride through it. There is a new earth the other side, but fairer or fouler than this one, neither of us knows. Heaven knows how the worlds are ordered, but the gates bind them together in ways dangerous for all life. When we are gone it will not be the same sun that rises over us. That is all I understand of it. But that is where we will be—as if we were dead, Chei, and the other side of Hell, and you cannot go back or change your minds then, and nothing you knew will be true. That is what will become of you. This land is your home. And fair or foul, it is what you understand. Think on that. And you still will not know the extent of what will happen to you. Nothing you know will be true."

"But you go. And you are a Man. Are you not?"

Vanye shrugged. The question went deep, troubling him. "It will not matter," he said. "I cannot even reckon how old I am. The stars are not the same. I do not know where I am. I do not know how long ago my cousin died. And it was only a handful of days ago I left him. Now only my liege speaks my language. All the rest are gone." He looked up at two bewildered, sobered faces. "That is the plainest I know to tell you. There is nowhere we come from. There is nowhere we are going. We only go. Come with us if you will. Leave us, the other side of the gate. It may be you will find peace there. It may be we will fall straight into Hell, and die there. We have no way to know. If it is to glory you hope to follow us—or wealth—there is none to offer you. And whether we are right or wrong in anything we do, I do not know. I cannot offer you that either. My liege cannot. So you would be wisest to stay here. Truly you would."

"I do *not* understand you," Chei said.

"I know. But I am telling you the truth. Go with us as far as Tejhos, that is all. Then ride west. Lose yourselves in the hills, hide and wait. There will be wars. In that time—you will find a lord worth following. That is my advice to you."

"Are you a witch?" Chei asked.

"I suppose that I am."

"But not *qhal*."

"No. Not *qhal*."

"You are my friend," Chei said, and reached and pressed his arm.

He could not look at Chei. It hurt too much. He gave a sigh, and ripped out his braiding.

From the men beyond there was a burst of laughter, muted; Bron turned himself about to see what they did and looked back again, frowning, as if he were thoroughly remiss not to forbid that.

But he was not, at present, in any mind to fight with men who, whatever their lord was, brigands or no, were cheerful again, after sullenness all day.

"They will sleep the better for it," Vanye said. "And if their heads ache in the morning, that is their misfortune."

They neither one said more than that. How their thoughts ran now he could not say. They sat together, leaned together. Bron touched his brother's hair as no man would touch another, casually, even were they kinsmen, but he reckoned this was only affection, and foreign ways. They understood hospitality; their fire seemed sacred enough, and the passing of food and drink; and there were priests to confess them; and yet a lord could claim a wounded man who came to him for protection, and not let him go again. He had met men far more strange to him, whose customs troubled him less, because they were utterly strange.

Yet he reckoned they might trust two watches tonight to these brothers, and know their throats would stay uncut, and their backs defended, if it came to that. If these two were not arrhendim and did not have Kurshin ways, still they were decent men, and he felt his supper uneasy at his stomach, somewhere between regret for having them along and the fear that they would go, and the sorrow that he had finally found a friend staunch enough to stay by them—

—and it was not a man he could trust.

That Chei could lie and never know he was lying—that was a flaw he did not know how to mend. Chei simply did not know what truth was.

And he himself was Nhi as well as Kurshin, wherefore a man who deceived and twisted and turned with the agility that seemed native to this land, set his teeth on edge, in an anger at once familiar and terrifying—and he remembered suddenly why.

It was only his brothers had evoked that peculiar ambivalence in him.

And he had killed one and all but killed the other: clan Myya was his legitimate half-brothers' clan—hill bandits turned noblemen, who did not know a straight way through any door, that was Nhi's proverb for them; and again: thicker than feuds in Myya.

He opened his eyes again. It was only pale-haired Chei, and Bron, whose faces showed hurt and whose eyes sought some answer of Morgaine, since he had shut them out.

"I will take first watch," Morgaine said, rescuing him from the chance that they would go on with him. "Go to sleep. We will be on our way before light; best you all take what you can."

"Aye." He reached at his side and loosed his armor buckles, and found a place the rock fit his shoulders. He unhooked his sword from his side and laid it across his lap, considering Eoghar's company yonder. "Quiet," he shouted at those three, making a small shocked silence, astonishing himself profoundly that they looked so daunted. "Men are going to sleep here."

The trouble was in himself, he thought in the quiet that continued, who invented worries and conjured up calamities—you think too much, his brother Erij had told him once upon a time, chiding him for cowardice.

It was truth. He fell into old habits. It was fear which did that to him, fear not of enemies, but of friends. His brothers had taught him that lesson—beaten it into him, flesh and bone and nerve.

He clasped his sword to him, nevertheless, in both arms, so that Eoghar and his cousins would go on understanding their situation, if there remained any doubt.

The rain subsided to a light patter on the ground outside, an occasional gust carrying it into the shelter, but there was enough heat from the two fires and the presence of seven bodies to keep the chill away. It would have been a good night under other circumstances, Chei thought glumly, lying curled toward the fire warmth, back to back with Bron, but a different kind of cold had crept in among them, and Chei could not reason why, except somehow the lady, always cold and obscure, turned kind to them; while Vanye suddenly refused to look him in the eyes, for reasons which Chei did not, after thinking and thinking on the matter, understand. . . .

What do you want of me? A prisoner, a slave, someone to be grateful for whatever crusts you will give me?

Why could he not say once that he was glad for me, that Bron is alive?

Could not he manage anything but that scowl for it?

The thoughts turned over and over in him like pebbles in a current, one abrading the next; and one atop and then the other. He ached inside. It angered

him that the man he admired turned away from him, and it mattered in a personal way—when he ought to worry only for the consequences of being cast
out masterless, as a sane man ought.

He might, he thought, appeal to the lady who sat there in the glow of the
coals, beautiful and terrible in her fire-stained pallor, herself embodying every
fear he had had from childhood; and every mercy he had found in extremity.
She leaned on the sword that she bore, which had a fantastical beast for hilt and
quillons. Her eyes gazed toward the glow of the coals, and her face was pensive,
even gentle—it tempted a man to think she might listen to him.

He was mad, perhaps: a man who began to hope against the general ebb of
human fortunes in the world, and who began to believe in miracles—was he
not mad?

But he would not have believed at all, till he looked up from the wolf-pack
snarling about him and saw first the swordsman bearing down on him and then
the silver-haired woman—demons out of Hell he had thought them first, that
the ordinary world had rent in twain and death had come for him. He thought
of that in bleak moments of terror which intervened in his other thoughts: but
he was not dead, his delirium had left him, and it was a familiar woods he rode,
with Bron back from the dead and in company with these two who moved out
of pattern with the world and promised him humankind need not, after all,
perish.

He had ridden a knife's-edge of hope and terror thus far; and that it all
should unravel on the spite of a man he had begun to rely on in ways he had
only relied on Bron—he could not accept that. He could not believe that Morgaine would in truth send them off to die. He could not believe, now he thought
about it, that Vanye, who had dealt kindly with him when it had not been
necessary—could turn so vindictive. He must, he thought, have done something or said something—or it was Arunden's offense against the lady; or things
had not gone well between Vanye and the lady when he had walked in upon
them—

He built a score of desperate structures in the blink of an eye, each more
and more fantastical, until he found his hands clenched and his heart thumping
against his ribs, and at last rose up on his elbow.

"My lady," he whispered, very softly, not to disturb the others. His hands
were sweating as she gazed at him, a figure of shadows in the light of the coals;
his arm shook under him, which might have been the chill and the hour. He
had everything prepared to say.

Then there came a sound from outside, the low mutter of a stallion that
might be bickering with the other horses, but it was the gray: he knew the tim-
bre of it, and where that horse was, just outside the woven wall.

So Morgaine's eyes shifted, and she became still as stone. So he was, till the horse complained a second time and one of the others, further toward the falls, made a complaint of its own that was echoed farther away.

Of a sudden, with her the only one waking, cipher that she was, he was afraid. "Something is out there," he said; and by now Vanye was rising and putting the blanket aside, and Bron had waked, all the while Morgaine sat very still, with the ornate sword against her, her long fingers curving about the hilt as her eyes shifted from him to Vanye.

Vanye gathered himself to his knees and tightened the buckles of his armor. There was no sound now but the roar of the falls and the rain-swollen waters, no light but the afterglow of the coals. Chei trembled and cursed his own cowardice in the uncertainty of the hour; but he was lost, he did not know what was on them, whether it was Arunden's treachery or some hapless hunter of the clan they would have to deal with as the lady had said, more murder they had to commit, this time on innocent men; and his tongue seemed paralyzed.

"I will go out there," Bron said, and moved. "If it is human they are late on the trail—or if they are Arunden's—"

But Eoghar and the others still slept, none of them stirring.

"I will go with you," Chei said. No one prevented him. Eoghar and his cousins snored on, lost to every sense. He walked out into the drizzling rain and stood there blind to the dark and with himself and then Bron silhouetted against the fire-glow, however faint.

A rock turned, click of stone on stone, and the horses close at hand snorted in alarm.

"Arunden!" a voice called out, hoarse above the roar of water. "Eoghar!"

It was sure then that Eoghar had led them along the route where Eoghar had been told, and Chei dived back inside. "My lady—" He found himself facing the black weapon and froze in mid-motion. "It is Arunden's men," he said then, against the risk of her fire and Vanye's half-drawn sword.

But outside someone was coming, and Bron was left to meet that advance. He risked a move to escape and joined Bron out in the drifting mist, out in the dark in which some rider came down the streamside and toward them in haste.

"Who are you?" Bron called out sharply.

"Sagyn," the voice called back. "Ep Ardris."

"I know him," Bron said to Chei as the rider stopped just short of the ledge that was their shelter and slid down off his horse to lead it. "Stop there," Bron said, but the man did not.

"Riders," the man gasped out, staggering to them over the gravel. "Gault's."

"Where?" Bron asked, and drew his sword about the time Chei reached after his own knife, misliking this approach. "No closer, man, take my warning!"

"Truth," ep Ardris said, a thin and shaken voice, and stood there holding the reins of a rain-drenched and head-drooping horse. "It was Gault came on us—Gault, in the woods—"

Chei felt a sense of things slipping away. He heard the movement behind him, he heard the curses of Eoghar and his men, awakened to news like this and by now standing outside; he knew the lady's anger, and the uncertainties in everything, all their estimations thrown in disorder.

Except the lady had fired the lowland woods and begun a war as surely as Gault had come to answer it.

In Chei's hearing ep Ardris was babbling other things, how their sentries had alerted them too late, and Arunden had attempted to attack from the cover of the woods, but Gault's men had been too many and too well armed. The clan had scattered. Arunden himself was taken. Ep Ardris did not know where the others were or how many had survived.

"What of my father?" Eoghar came from the shelter with his two cousins, and laid hands on the man—and if there was a man of the lot not dissembling, it was Eoghar, whose grip bid fair to break the man's shoulders. "Did you see him? Do you know?"—to which ep Ardris swore in a trembling voice that he did not know, no more than for his own kin.

And at Chei's side, all sound of her coming drowned in the roar of the falls, the lady walked up and doubtless Vanye was behind her. "So Eoghar told his lord the places we might camp."

"He would know," Chei protested, "lady, any man of his would know—"

"So, now, might our enemies," Morgaine said darkly. "We have no way of knowing *what* they know. Saddle up. Now."

Chei stood frozen a moment, lost in the water-sound and the nightmare. Others moved. A hand closed hard on his arm.

"Come on," Vanye said harshly, as he had spoken when they had been enemies; and in his muddled sense he heard ep Ardris protesting that Gault's riders might be anywhere—Arunden was innocent, he thought, of the worst things; but if any of Arunden's folk was in Gault's hands, there was very much that they knew.

"They do not know the forest," Chei protested, the least frail hope he could think of, but no one listened, in the haste to break camp. Gault and his men had gotten *into* the forest, plainly enough.

He could not account for all of Ichandren's men. He had not thought of that for very long, since he had sat waiting for the wolves—that there were worse fates than Gault had meted out to him, and that it was Gault's spite of his own Overlord that chained healthy and fair-haired prisoners to die within reach of Morund-gate—when there might be someone in Mante with use for them. It was defiance Gault made of his master.

But he had no idea who had died on the field, who in the prison, and who might not have been taken to Morund's cellars at all.

Or who—as the lady had said—of their hunters and scouts of whatever clan might not have strayed into Gault's hands. For that reason a man never went alone to the border; for that reason they left no wounded, and carried poison among their simples and their medicines.

Someone had betrayed them, either living or dead. Someone who knew the ways in.

The roan horse picked a narrow path among the rocks, a course that others followed in the dark. They made no night camp, only took such rests as they had to have, and few of those.

There was fear in Gault ep Mesyrun, and therefore he drove them. At times thoughts surfaced in him which Gault himself would have had, and not Qhiverin—to that extent he was disturbed; and he knew that Jestryn-Pyverrn who rode near him was much more than that, to the extent that he feared for Pyverrn's self. A profound shock could affect a mind newly settled in a body, and old memories might surface, like bubbles out of dark water, from no knowing which self of the many bodies a man might have occupied, no knowing whether it might not be the latest and strongest self reorganizing itself, disastrous in a mind distracted by doubts.

Therefore Jestryn-Pyverrn himself had laughed, when first the priest had told them what they had to deal with—had looked into Gault's face with a laugh and a desperation in his eyes that quickly died, more quickly than Arunden's priest, who been all too willing to talk, for hate, it seemed, a genuine hatred of a *qhalur* woman and a man for whose sake he had suffered some slight; and thought that he had something to trade to them for his life. "That might be," Jestryn had said, "except we have no need of a priest—"

At which the priest had called out Arunden's name, pleading with him as a Man—wherefore Gault asked Arunden, the quisling they had set over the borderlands: "Dealings with Mante, now, is it?"

"They are from outside," Arunden protested, as the Man had protested everything, disavowed the fire-setting, wept and sobbed and swore he had never betrayed them, only the woman was a witch and might read everything he did.

Therefore Arunden had been compelled to entertain them, therefore he had dealt with them and had sent men with them—this woman who proposed to attack Mante.

"From outside," Gault had said then, beginning to believe this lunacy, though they had long thought there was no outside, and the very thought that there might be, implied a tottering of the world—challenging the power in

Mante, of Skarrin himself, over whose death neither he nor the men of his company would shed tears.

But an incursion from outside—

But a threat, babbled in a human witness's confused terms, against the very gates—and a *qhal* counseling humans about things which humans did not well guess—

The priest went on babbling, pleading his usefulness and his sacrosanctity. "Silence that," Gault said, and had meant that one of the others should do it.

Quick as the drawing of a sword, Jestryn cut the priest's throat and stepped back, his face all flecked with blood: Gault had seen that moment's horror, and well knew the reason the Pyverrn-self had desired that particular execution.

Exorcism, the humans would say.

They had come in the space of an hour from anger at human attack to suspect a far greater danger. "We cannot get a message south," Jestryn had said, meaning one that should pass the southern gate and speed north with the speed of thought. "There is Tejhos-gate."

"They will know that," Gault had said, and had dispatched one small part of his forces back toward the road to sweep north, under a man he trusted— which would have been Jestryn, had he thought Jestryn reliable at the moment.

Perhaps, he thought now, Jestryn had mustered anger enough to overcome his confusion. Perhaps luck would be with them and Jestryn could guide them on these trails, now they knew where their enemy had gone.

But he did not trust to Jestryn's sanity.

"Take him with us," he had said of Arunden. "Kill the rest." And headed for his horse at a run.

There was a Weapon loose. What the priest and Arunden had described could only be that. It was that which had lent absolute credence to a tale otherwise incredible.

Skarrin himself was challenged. The trouble had passed Morund with only a trifling attack. It was possible that the high lord had stirred up some trouble which bade fair to destroy him and to take the world down to chaos— it answered to things which in *qhalur* lore were only dimmest legend, that there had been such visitations once, and time itself might shift, and all reality alter.

He did not count himself a virtuous man. He did not know one—Skarrin being Skarrin and only the favored few of his lords profiting from Skarrin's rule; but Gault found himself with no choice and no one but himself to look to.

He rode without heed of the night or the rain that should keep them prudently camped. He trusted himself and his men to the guidance of a traitor and a bloodstained man struggling for sanity, because there was no time for anything else.

The war he had started out to fight was for a woods, a handful of deer and rabbits and revenge on a quisling human he thought had betrayed him.

But in a few words from a human's lips he found himself in a war for survival.

⤸ Chapter 9

"It might be a trick," Vanye said to Morgaine, beside her as they saddled in desperate haste, there by the woven wall of the shelter. He worked by feel on gear rapidly becoming rain-soaked, with their horses unsettled by the visitor out of the dark and ill-tempered at taking the trail again. It had the feel of old nightmares.

And there were Arunden's men with them; Eoghar and his lot, and ep Ardris, Bron and Chei over with them, flinging saddles onto wet, angry horses, ep Ardris' beast standing with hanging head, unfit for the trail.

"They might be waiting for us out there."

Morgaine said nothing, only flung her saddlebags over Siptah's saddle and jerked the ties tight.

"Let me go up on that ridge and have a look," Vanye said. "*I* can climb it—"

"Aye, and it would take considerable time and mesh us in a battle and separate us if the least thing went amiss."

"Nothing would go amiss. There is the water to cover the sound—"

"No," she said sharply. She finished the last tie on the other side and took up Siptah's reins, stopping face to face with him as he took up Arrhan's. "If they would be on us out in the open, they could save themselves the trouble and fire down from the ridge. Thee is too careful, thee is always too cursed careful. Let us be out of here!"

His face went hot. But there was no leisure for argument and less profit in it at the moment. "Aye," he said sharply, and threw Arrhan's reins over, on his way to the saddle.

She caught his arm with a hard grip. "Vanye." And as he stopped and looked full into her face there in the misting dark: "Take care for *thyself*, not for me, does thee hear me? I need no more fools tonight!"

"I am none," he retorted; "you mistake me,"—their voices being muffled in the sound of the falls; and she turned quickly to mount.

It was Chei she meant, Chei and Bron and every other encumbrance which had seized on her and weighed on her: that panic in her came of delays and entanglements and mortal frailties—he knew well enough that pitch of rage that he had begun to sense growing in himself, the understanding of dangers winding them about like threads, more and more of entanglements.

He flung himself to horse and reined in beside her. "If so happen," Morgaine said more sanely, "if so happen the *qhal have* Arunden for whatever cause—then it is speed will save us now, and we cannot reckon otherwise. There is the gate at Tejhos; and if Gault does come behind us, then we can reckon that from the hour he reaches either gate, north or south, the lord at Mante will know everything Gault knows."

Then, he thought, there was little now that conscience would stay her from. An old and familiar chill lapped him about, more penetrating than the rain and the wind. Morgaine turned Siptah's head and rode forward, the paler tip of Siptah's dark tail moving like a will o' the wisp above the ground and the horse himself like illusion: it was white Arrhan would draw the most attention of all their company—fool, he thought again, that he had ever taken such a gift; and he drew his sword as they rode, quietly passing the rest, sweeping up Chei and his brother with him, devil take the rest who were rising to their saddles. "Stay close," he said as they passed, half lost in nightmare. "Whatever happens, keep close."

Chei said something which he did not hear in the rush of the stream near them and in the sighing of the trees on the ridge. He blinked the water from his eyes and took his own pace from Morgaine, staying to her left, always to the left, shieldside, as the way out turned onto a narrow trail and the water-laden wind came blasting up the mountainside, under his cloak and into his eyes.

There the stream took a precipitate course and plunged down the mountain in a second falls as the land opened out. Morgaine took the right-hand bend around the rocks, close against them as possible, toward the wooded track that led higher up, and Vanye glanced behind them as they turned, to see the tail of their column leave the narrows and bolt the other way.

"*Liyo,*" he exclaimed, and reined Arrhan about as Chei and Bron also turned, drawing the weapons they had.

"My lady," Bron called out. "Arunden's men—"

"Let them go," Morgaine hissed, as she drew back even with them.

"We did not know—"

"Do you know the way from here to the road, that is what I care for!"

"We know it," Chei said with no doubt at all in his voice. "Let us to the fore, my lady. At least in this rain we will have less chance of meeting any watchers."

"Go to it," she said, and with no delay at all Chei and his brother urged their horses past and on. "Do not thee stray far back," she said then to Vanye. "Stay with me."

That suited him well enough, thinking of *qhalur* riders at their backs—of whom Eoghar and ep Ardris and the rest could have joy, he thought in dark rage: they had made no decent request to go back to their kin, if that was where they were bound, and it was as likely they were deserting outright to hide in the hills.

For his part he recollected that great westward jog in the road Chei had drawn. He tried to think where the sun had been and where they might come to it and where Gault might; and he did not like the reckoning.

He dropped back as the trail narrowed, and wended up again among the rain-dripping trees, cold, large drops falling more unpleasantly than did the fine mist, branches raking them with wet bristles where limbs pressed close on the trail.

It was climbing for a while and descent for a while, and eventually rest for the horses, who suffered with the rain and the uncertain footing, the lee of a hill being the only respite they could find on this side of the ridge.

"How much further?" Morgaine asked of Chei and Bron. Their horses, even Siptah and Chei's gelding, huddled together as they took their breath, breaking the force of the wind off each other as it skirled about them. "Do we get there tonight? Tomorrow?"

"Far yet," Chei said, at which Vanye's heart sank in greater and greater despair.

"How far for Gault's folk?" Morgaine asked. "If he sent a messenger up to Tejhos or back to Morund-gate—can we reach Tejhos first?"

"I *think* we can," Chei said. "Lady, God knows! We do not know how long ep Ardris hunted for us—we do not know how long Gault will delay—"

"The Road bends our way up ahead," Bron said. "He cannot send one of his own back to Morund except with a guide, and he has hit his own ally, if Arunden has betrayed us. He may not have men he can spare who know their way up here: they say it is not every Changed can remember—that is what has saved us before this: they get few of us and most of those remember nothing who they were—"

"Do not count on that," Morgaine said darkly. "It is *not* the case. Believe that he will have every help he needs, *curse* your optimism!"

"We are on the high trails," Chei said. "A large force cannot make good time where we are going: if there are any of Arunden's warders left, they may have to fight their way through—"

"And Arunden himself may be their safe-conduct *and* their guide and the warders may find us instead! Man, quit making excuses for our troubles and quit making allowances for our enemies! *Do* what I tell you and get us to the Road!"

"It is at least another day to get there!" Chei shouted. "For them and us—

and there is no shorter way than this—I swear there is not! We can turn and fight them—"

"*If* we could trust that they have not gone straight east to the Road, *if* we could trust ep Ardris told half the truth—It is *time* we do not have: do not question me, Chei! Do not make me delays or excuses! Lead! We will find a secure camp, rest and move on when we can make more time. That is all we *can* do now."

It was in a weary haze Chei rode at last—fending branches in the dark, feeling an uncertainty in his horse's legs as they negotiated a descent. Of a sudden the animal skidded and went down on its haunches and clawed its way sideways on the muddy hill so that he had to let the reins down and let it fight its own battle.

The horse recovered itself facing uphill and with its hindquarters braced, unmoving as the other riders came down the straightforward way, but not so steeply. Chei found himself trembling the same as the horse, weak in the legs as he dismounted there on the slope and slipped and slid to lead it around and safely down. The mail had rubbed his shoulders raw; he knew that it had, working wet cloth against wet skin; and that pain brought back the hill, and the wolves, so vividly at times he did not know this woods from the other, or remember the intervening time.

But Bron was with him. Bron urged him on, promising him rest, saying that there was shelter, and he bit his lip and concentrated on the pain there and not in his arms.

"Soon," he agreed, teeth chattering, "soon."

"We need not lose a horse," Vanye said, to which Morgaine said something Chei could not understand; but they got down where they were, on the leaf-slick floor of the ravine, and led their horses an increasingly difficult track in this dark and rain, off the main trails, all of them walking now, descending the next muddy slope and ducking low under the branches.

"Straight on," Chei said, his heart suddenly lifting as lightning-flicker showed him an ancient pine he knew. He recognized his way again. He pulled at the weary horse, taking it sideways on the slope and down again, around the boggy place between the slopes and up another rise, up and up a pine-grown slope to the crest of the hill.

It was a hunter's shelter below them, looming up like nothing more than a massive brush-heap in the constant flicker from the clouds; but Chei knew it, and when Bron said that he would go down to it: "I will go," Chei murmured, and led his horse along with Bron, down the incline as Bron hailed the place.

There was no answer. There was only the dark mass of the shelter; and neither horse seemed shy of it, which was the best indication nothing had sheltered there. Only some small creature skittered away in the brush, at which his weary horse hardly reacted, a little jerk at the reins.

"Hai-ay," Bron called out again, and with no answer and no answering hail, led his horse into the lee of the hut.

It was enough. Chei reached the place, leaned against his horse and managed the girth; and had him half unsaddled before Vanye and Morgaine had ridden in.

He dried off his horse vigorously with the blanket and rubbed down its legs, such care as he could give to ease it and protect it from soreness; and looked and saw Bron's horse unattended, which carelessness his brother would not countenance on a night like this and after such a ride.

Then he spied Bron sitting on the ground, and went to him quietly. "Bron?" he whispered, dropping down to face him, and laid a hand on Bron's shoulder.

"It is hurting," Bron said. Chei could not see his face in the dark, could hardly make out the pallor of skin and hair in the dark, but he gripped Bron's shoulder in a brotherly way and felt a cold about his heart.

"How bad is it?"

A whisper of leather and metal, a shrug beneath his hand. "Hurting," Bron said, and drew a breath. "I will make it tomorrow. They will not leave me. They will not. I will not slow you down."

He embraced Bron, hugged him tight a moment as he reckoned Vanye and the lady were paying no attention to them. "Give me your cloak," he said; and unfastened it from Bron's neck, slung it on and rose to tend Bron's horse, trying not to think of the fear, only of necessity—not turning his head, only doing his work and praying neither Vanye nor the lady would notice in the deep shadow beside the hut and the confusion of two bay geldings and two blond men and a borrowed cloak, that it was the same man on his feet.

But Vanye walked near him, leading the two pale horses into that shadow, and behind him; and stopped.

Chei dropped down and rubbed at the gelding's legs, head tucked. But he heard the step in the wet mold, heard the light ring of metal as Vanye went past him and knelt down by Bron.

He got up then and went over to him. "I am all right," Bron was saying, where he sat against the wall in the wet and the decaying leaves. And Chei, desperately: "He is all right. I will tend the horses, the gray too if he will stand—"

"We cannot go much more of this," Vanye said, and touched Bron's shoulder and rose and laid a hand on his, gently shaking at him. "My lady has her reasons. How much farther?"

"Tomorrow," Chei said. His heart was beating hard. He found himself short of breath, not knowing what was in Vanye's mind. "We will get there tomorrow."

"My lady is grateful. Truly."

"What does she want of us?" he asked desperately; and did not believe that the lady had said it at all: the lady was angry with them, had been angry since they had broken camp, and everything seemed the wrong thing with her. Now Vanye came to them, on his own, for Vanye's reasons, catching them in another deception, and fear swept over him—irrational, for they could go no faster and no further, and the lady on that iron-winded gray could not so much as find the road without them.

But honor meant very much, when there was neither clan nor kin; and the lady cursed them and shamed them, even Bron: he had brought his brother to this, and the lady cursed them for mistakes he himself had made, and shamed Bron for things not Bron's doing—

"We will make it," Vanye said. "Chei—"

"Aye," he said, and jerked his shoulder free, turning his face to his work again.

"Chei. Listen to me." Vanye put his hand on the other side of the horse's neck, stood close against its shoulder, close beside him. "She has one manner with everyone. With me as well. She is thinking, that is what she is doing, she is thinking, and what talks to us is not herself when this mood is on her. That is all I can tell you."

Chei listened in anger, down to the last, that a tendril of cold slipped into his heart. Then he recalled that they were pacted not only with a *qhal*, but with a witch. He gave a twitch of his shoulders, less angry, and more afraid, and no more certain where honor was in anything.

"She never remembers her tempers," Vanye said. "Do the best you can do. When she knows what you have done she will be grateful. *I* thank you. She would want me to. She would want me to tell you—get us as far as the Road, and if you have changed your minds, go aside: we will see to Gault."

"Mante," Chei said. "We are going to Mante."

"Do you know what is there? Do you know what we face?"

He shook his head. He had no wish to know. "The gate," he said. "Somewhere else."

"Maybe a worse place."

"It could not be. For us it could not be." He seized Vanye by the arm and drew him well aside, over by the trees, into the dark and the wind. "Vanye, my brother—he is a great man, he *is*, Vanye: he *will* be; Ichandren himself used to say that in his life he had never seen any man promise so much—"

"For whose sake are you doing this? For his? Then leave us at the road."

"That is not what I am saying!"

"There is nothing to be had from us. There is nothing we can give you. You mistake us. We have no place to go to. You are chasing after what does not exist."

"We will not go back to live like bandits! We will not find another clan! We will make a name for ourselves—we—Bron and I. Do not shame us like this."

Vanye was silent a moment. "I only try to warn you. You cannot ask too much of her. I will not let you."

"You are her lover."

An intake of breath. "What I am is my concern."

"I only mean that I know. We know you are her right hand. We do not dispute you. Only do not let her speak like that to my brother."

"My lady will speak how she chooses, to me, to Bron, or to you!—But I will talk to him."

"Do that," Chei said. The wind touched him. He shivered, having gotten less than he wanted. But he had pushed too far; he saw that.

Vanye walked away from him. Chei stood with his arms and Bron's cloak about him, waiting, while Vanye found Bron looking after the horses himself, cloakless and stubborn.

They had words together. It did not last long, but they parted with a mutual touch at shoulders, and Vanye took their own two horses in charge, while the lady stayed in shelter.

"Here," Chei said to Bron, when he had walked back to the arbor. He slung the cloak about Bron's shoulders. "Get out of the wind." And: "Did he say anything?"

Bron shrugged. "Only courtesy," Bron said. "He offered *qhalur* medicines. I said I was well enough. Do not trouble him, Chei."

The morning brought fog again, a general murk that made it uncertain exactly when it ceased to be night and began being daylight; but Vanye levered his aching bones up when there was light enough to see by, in a watch he judged by his own time-sense. "Stay and rest," he said to Morgaine: it was his watch last—they were the better by Chei and Bron having their turn at waking, in the small part of the night they had had left—and he left her and the brothers to drowse away the last few moments while he sought after their gear and carried it up to saddle up.

But Chei was up as quickly, moving about in the gray and the damp, seeing to his horse and his brother's.

"I meant to let you sleep," Vanye said, attempting to mend matters.

"We will manage," Chei said shortly.

So a company grew irritable, weary as they were, friends more quickly at odds than utter strangers. His face still burned when he recollected Chei's remark of last evening, and how Chei thought he knew more of their affairs than he knew.

Ilin and liege—and he was not sure whose doing it was, after all this time. He tried to protect their honor; but Chei—

Chei, being Chei, trod straight in on a matter that would have gotten challenge outright and unexplained, if Chei were of his own people.

But Chei, being Chei, had not understood, no more than he himself understood more than the surface of Chei's thinking. Bron had seemed dismayed when he went to ask his pardon, had seemed embarrassed, if nothing else. "Chei ought not to have done that," Bron had said. "Forgive him."

Now Bron came out into the daylight, limping pronouncedly in the first few steps; and concealed that with a grasp after one of the support poles of the shelter.

Vanye paid it no attention and offered no help. He wanted no more misunderstandings. He flung Siptah's saddle up and tightened the girth.

"We will break our fast on the trail," he said as Chei passed him; Chei nodded and said no word to him. Perhaps it was only the reaction of a man with his jaw clamped against the chill.

Or it was the reaction of a man who felt betrayed.

Morgaine came out, wrapped in her cloak, gray side out, her pale coloring one tone with the fog.

"Tonight for the open road," she said in a quiet voice, taking Siptah's reins. "So we dare not push the horses today."

"Aye," Vanye agreed, thanking Heaven one of them at least had come back to reason.

They rode out, with breakfast in hand, a little waybread and water from their flasks, ducking water-laden branches, but with the sun bringing a little warmth through the mist, and the wind having stopped. There was that for comfort.

"Here," Jestryn said, and urged his horse down a trail hardly worthy of the name, a narrow slot of stone and dirt among pines that clung desperately to a crumbling slope. Some of the men murmured dismay, but Gault followed, nothing loath, for the Road passed near a village hereabouts, a straight bare track below the truncate hill: the ancients had carved mountains, disdaining to divert their Road for any cause; and yet bent it sharply west in open ground, for reasons that no *qhal* living knew.

Now the descendants of the builders rode quietly as they could, making better time than they had been able to make in the fog, reliant on Jestryn-Pyverrn's human memory and on Arunden's thoroughly human one, under the threat of Jestryn's knife.

"I swear to you," Arunden had cried, "I swear to you—I will guide you! I am your friend—"

"Impudent Man," Jestryn had said, and laughed, as Pyverrn would, with his human, guttural laughter. "You are not *my* friend before or *after* I was human; and God knows you were never Gault's—"

Jestryn kept such human affectations, and swore and used human oaths *qhal* did not. But the sparkle in his eye was Pyverrn—past the sword-cut that raked one handsome cheek. It did not distract from his looks. Next to him, Arunden was a clumsy, shambling brute; and Arunden's wit matched his outward look.

"You will lose a finger," Jestryn had said, "for every annoyance on this trail; I counsel you, *tell* me where the warders are, and what the signals are, or you will find out what pain is—my lord Arunden."

They had taken three of the watchposts. Arunden snuffled and wept about it and protested they were disgracing him and ruining his usefulness.

But a flash of Jestryn's knife stopped the snuffling.

"You either serve us," Gault had said then, "or not. Decide now. We *can* do without you."

"My lord," Arunden had said.

Now they rode quietly as they could, with bows strung and arrows ready.

Jestryn gave a quiet call, a kind of lilting whistle, and a like signal answered it from down the slope.

The horses picked their way down with steady, small paces, to a place where the trail widened. A Man waited there, whose eyes betrayed shock the moment before Gault's arrow took him. Perhaps it had been the sight of Jestryn, back from the dead. Perhaps it had been the sight of Arunden himself, who was their own lord, beside Gault, who had been lord over the human south, not six years gone: Men to the outward sight, and armored like Men, he and Jestryn, Qhiverin and Pyverrn—both archers of Mante's warrior Societies and both deadly.

Jestryn grinned at him, an expression light and pleasant as ever Jestryn-the-Man could have used, past Arunden, who sat his horse in apparent shock.

"Let us go," Gault said, and motioned to the men who followed.

They rode forward, closer to the human camp, with the stench of its midden all too evident. It was that garrison which guarded the road; and there was dangerous work at hand—We must take them, Jestryn had said, and reach the Road there: that is the quickest way.

If only, Gault thought, they did not bog down in some day-long siege; but Jestryn promised not: Arunden would hail them out once their archers were positioned.

Gault chose three arrows as he rode quietly at Jestryn's back: he did not ride the roan, which was too well known—but on a borrowed sorrel. The rest of the column overtook them on this flat ground as the shapes of huts appeared among the pines. Gray smoke drifted up as haze in that clearing, from fires about which humans pursued domestic business, the weaving of cloth, the grinding of grain doubtless bartered or plundered from Gault's own storehouses.

There was hardly reason at first that these humans should take alarm at human riders arriving in their camp, since those riders had had to pass their sentries, even if the riders carried bows at their sides.

They could only be mildly alarmed when their own lord Arunden rode forward of the three, and in a ringing voice ordered everyone to the center of the village.

Only when those bows lifted and bent and the shafts went winging to drop those who obeyed, then the cries went up and humans rushed to the attack of two solitary archers.

Then the rest of Gault's troop appeared from the brush around the camp, and arrows came from every direction.

It was unfortunate that Arunden was not quick enough, and that a stray shaft tumbled him from his horse.

Beyond this there was little resistance. Certain humans escaped into the brush and saved their lives: do not pursue, Gault had told his men. We have no time.

When there was quiet in the clearing Gault changed horses again and rode where Jestryn beckoned him, where the height on which the village sat, dropped away sheer, and the Road showed as patches of white stone in an otherwise grassy expanse of rolling hills.

Jestryn led them down the slope of the hill to a track which human feet had worn, going and coming, laying bare the roots of pines and stripping those roots of bark, a natural series of steps in the muddy slope which gave the horses somewhat surer footing on their way down to the plains.

There was no dread of arrows now. Only of what they followed.

He could not understand why they had burned his woods and sheltered with humans; why, if they were hostile they had not attacked Morund; why, if they were not, they had not approached it. The woman whom Arunden had abundantly described was surely no halfling and the tall Man with her doubtless hosted some *qhalur* mind: they would have been welcome in Morund, if they were Mante's enemies, some shadow out of Skarrin's traffic in the gates.

But they had one and now two of Ichandren's lot to advise them: that too. Arunden had told them, among other things. That one of them was Chei ep Kantory surprised him: the pale-haired wolf-whelp had cozened Morund-gate's wolves then, longer than he would have thought: Kantory's get was hardy as its sire, whatever might presently house in that human frame—for it was well possible the strangers had taken his offering at Morund-gate.

But that the other Man was Bron ep Kantory distressed him: Bron who had carried off Gault's serfs and raided his storehouses three times in the last two years. He had thought he had taken care of that matter at Gyllin-brook, along with the rest of Ichandren's rebels.

Bron could not be *qhal*, having been near neither gate; and therefore Chei was not likely to be. Bron would have suspected a changeling—they never would have deceived him. No, it was a question of humans.

And *qhal* who dealt with them in preference to legitimate authority, for whatever purpose.

It was a ride on which Gault-Qhiverin had had ample time to think; and the thoughts which chased one another through his mind held only greater and greater uncertainty, whether he could hope to find common ground with these strangers, Mante's likely enemies, or whether he should only strike and kill and hope for reward as Skarrin's savior.

Which would last, he thought, about as long as it took for Skarrin to arrange his assassination. Gault-Qhiverin the exile was something Skarrin could ignore. Gault the hero of the south—was not.

He reached the road just behind Jestryn and with room to run, the red roan overtook Jestryn's bay with a vengeance, weary as they all were.

"We will catch them," Jestryn said. "There is still time."

It was Tejhos Jestryn was thinking of; so were they all. That was the place the enemy was going, and that was the place they would find them.

The trail led down by the last of the twilight, and deeper still the twilight under the great trees which overshadowed the trail in the descent. "Not far, not far," Bron assured them, when once Morgaine asked. Bron's face was pale in the half-light and sweat glistened on it. Constantly Chei had a worried look, but Bron did not ask to stop; neither did Chei, though Bron's riding now was generally with his shoulders hunched in pain, his hands braced against the saddle-horn against the jolts of the descent: his leg by now must be agony and Vanye hurt with a sympathetic pain, who had endured similar miserable rides.

But suddenly their trail reached a level place, and in a little more of riding the trees began to thin: the forest edge gave way to open land and hills the like of the hills in the south, open grassland.

Between the last trees, under a clearing and fading sky, a rain-puddled bit of white stone, the trace of the Road; and looking up from it, toward the hills in the dusk, it was easy to see it, a line where ancient builders had sundered hill from hill, letting nothing divert it from here to the horizon.

Exhausted as they were, the horses picked up their pace somewhat on this level ground, and they grouped two and two, Bron and Chei to the fore and himself and Morgaine behind, with all the open hills before them and the sunset at their left.

"We will make it," Bron said, dropping back a moment to ride with them. "My lady, we will make it there very soon."

"Tejhos is on the road itself," Morgaine asked him, "is it not?"

"Yes," Bron said.

"We can find our way, then, from here. Go back. Take my advice."

"No," Bron said, "my lady."

"I have warned you." She shifted in the saddle. "That is all I will do."

"I know the reports of the road," Bron said. "I have never ridden it, but I know something of where it goes. I know something of the lord in Mante. I have these things to trade. Lady—"

"As far as you will," Morgaine said after a moment, and heavily. "As far as you can. I will keep my word to you."

Chei had dropped back with them. There was heavy silence as they rode.

Chei's eyes sought toward Vanye as if even then he questioned; and Vanye shrugged and looked away, denying him any help or any encouragement.

Morgaine laid her heels to Siptah and rode from between them.

"It is kindness she meant," Vanye said, and lingered a moment more to reason with them, holding Arrhan as she made to follow Siptah, reining her about again. "That is all."

Chei answered something. Vanye held steady, sweeping his eye back to a thing in the dusk beyond Chei's shoulder, a darkness that had not been on the horizon the instant before. It might have been a rock or a tree in the first blink of the eye.

But it moved. It vanished from the horizon.

Chei and Bron turned their horses about, fallen silent. "God in Heaven," Vanye murmured, and turned and rode after Morgaine. *"Liyo,"* he said as she turned half about. "They are behind us. Someone at least—is on the Road."

She looked, and reined back somewhat. "Ground of our choosing," she said in a low voice, and brought Siptah to a halt as Chei and Bron overtook them.

She slipped the hook on *Changeling's* sheath and laid it across the saddle-bow.

ꙍ Chapter 10

"I cannot see them now," Vanye said, straining his eyes against the gathering dark, holding Arrhan steady as she would stand with Morgaine's big gray chafing at the bit and stamping the ground beside her. "We have lost them out there."

"They will come to us," Morgaine said, while Bron drew his sword and Chei waited weaponless except for his knife.

"Their horses may be no more rested than ours," Bron said.

"Then again," Morgaine said, "they may be."

"This is mad," Chei cried. "There is the woods over there. We might make it."

"Again," Morgaine said, "we might not. Put away the sword."

"My lady—"

"Do as I say, Bron. Put it away."

"My lady, for our lives—listen to me. Vanye—"

"Never ride on my lady's right," Vanye said quietly. He was excruciatingly conscious of the stone at his heart, inert and harmless as it was at the moment. He had his own sword unhooked and resting across the saddlebow, as Men would parley who met under uncertain circumstances; but he did not reckon it likely that this world knew that sign of conditional peace.

"Vanye," Chei protested, riding close, "for God's sake—"

"Have done!" He whipped the sheathed sword across Chei's chest and stopped it a finger's width from his shoulder. He glared at Chei with temper flaring in him; but this time the sword was sheathed; this time he had the control to hold it, trembling, short of touching. "There will none of them live if we come to blows. Do you understand me? Not the innocent and not the purest. We cannot let them to the gate. We cannot let one escape. It is clear targets we want, range where their archers are useless and none of them can escape. Will that satisfy you?"

Chei's face was stark and wide-eyed in the twilight. Bron had frozen in place. Vanye withdrew the sword and laid it back across his saddlebow, with a second and challenging glance toward one and the other brother.

"The dark will help us," Morgaine said quietly. Vanye did not see her face. He did not want to see it. There was in his vision a boy, staring up at him from a dusty road as if death had greatly astonished him. He saw candles and a nightmare room in Ra-morij, his brother's face all white and still.

He concentrated instead on the rolling land in front of them and on the hills about them, a constant pass of the eyes, lest the riders arrive at their flank or bring archery to bear from the hill nearest.

"I hear them," Morgaine said, and a moment later he heard them too, horses coming at considerable speed for horses long on the trail. Their own blew and shifted, and Arrhan's ribs worked less strenuously between his legs. That was the simple strategy of their position: the enemy chose to exhaust their horses overtaking on the uphill; they rested theirs by waiting.

It was a small band, ten to twenty, that crested the hill. Where are the rest of them? Vanye thought in a moment's cold panic. Then the rest poured over the hilltop, forty, eighty, a hundred and more riders sweeping out on either side of the road.

Steel rang as Bron began to draw.

"No," Morgaine said calmly. "Wait. Both of you keep constantly to Vanye's left. Do *nothing* until I tell you. I have scant patience and less charity today. Vanye—" She changed suddenly to Kurshin accents. "Do not attempt the stone. Here!"

He had reached after his bow. She flung him *Changeling*. He caught it one-handed across its sheath, in a rush of cold fear, first because she had thrown it; then that it was in his keeping—the one of her weapons that he knew how to use. He had only to look at the odds and know why.

"Chei!" he said, and flung his own arrhendur sword to Chei in the same fashion, as accurately caught, while a familiar panic loosened his joints.

He drew several breaths more, hoping neither man saw; hoping more that Morgaine did not. It was his besetting weakness, that set his palms sweating on *Changeling's* hilt and gray sheath, and his heart pounding to the hoofbeats of the oncoming riders.

Heaven save us, he thought as the line began to spread wide.

Beside him, Morgaine signaled. He reined over, and Bron and Chei took a place at equal separation in their meager line.

The centermost riders drew to a halt. The rest kept moving, a half-ring about them, still closing. *Move us,* he thought, *for the love of Heaven, backward, forward,* liyo, *one or the other!*

Morgaine leveled her hand toward their center, where the most of the *qhalur* riders were. "Halt!" a man called out, and that envelopment ceased on the instant, everything stopped, except the breathing and stamping of the horses and the leathery creak and jingle of armored riders.

Morgaine's hand did not lower. It stayed aimed at the center of the *qhalur* ranks.

"My lady," the man said to her, human face, human voice.

"Gault," Chei's voice rasped. "That is Gault, on the roan. The man by him is Jestryn ep Desiny—he was one of our company—"

"My lord Gault," Morgaine shouted back. "What have we to say to each other that you follow me so far from home?"

"We might have discovered that had you come to me." Gault rode forward a few paces and drew the roan to a halt again. "You take strange allies, my lady. Brigands. Rebels. You set them free from my justice. You burn my lands and kill my game. Am I to take this for a friendly gesture?"

"I rarely practice justice. Outright slaughter, yes. I do not call it pretty names, my lord Gault."

"What is that you hold?" Gault's big roan surged forward and he curbed it, reining aside.

"That which seems to make you prudent, my lord. Justifiably so. I see you have talked to my enemies."

"And is your report of me so foul?" Again Gault paced the horse the other direction, weaving a slow, distracting course in the deepening dusk, which Morgaine's hand followed constantly.

"It is your death, my lord. My patience is lessening with every step you take. Do you want to discover which is the fatal one?"

Another three paces. "He is delaying," Vanye muttered, scanning the hills with constant attention. "There is something else out there, and he is waiting for the dark."

"My lady," Gault called out. "You and I might have more to speak of than you think likely. And perhaps more in common than you think." Gault's voice grew gentler, and he curbed his horse's straying. "I take it that it is you I deal with and not this gentleman by you."

"It is myself," she said. "Have no doubt of that."

"What is he?"

"This is delay," Vanye said. "*Liyo,* seek no more of him. Let us be out of here."

"My companion," Morgaine answered Gault. "So—you do not know everything about me."

"Should I?" Again the horse surged forward and Gault reined it back. "You are no visitor out of Mante. Your name is Morgaine. So the humans say. Mine is Qhiverin—among others."

"*Liyo.* Break away—now! Do not listen to this serpent."

"You are a stranger here," Gault said. "A wayfarer of the gates. You see I am not deceived. You have threatened Mante. Now you will kill me and all my men, lest I reach Tejhos. You think that you have no choice. But here am I, come to parley with you when I might have stayed safe in Morund—or turned prudently south to Morund-gate, once I learned what you are. I did not. I have risked my life and my lord's favor to find you. Is this the action of an implacable enemy?"

"Do not believe him," Bron said. "My lady, do not listen!"

Gault held up one hand, took his sword from its hangings and dropped it ringing to the ground. "There. Does that relieve your suspicions?"

"Withdraw your men," Morgaine said.

Gault hesitated, seeming uncertain, then lifted his hand to the darkened sky. A black and moving hedge crested the hill eastward.

"*Riders on our left!*" Vanye cried, and ripped *Changeling* from its sheath.

The air went numb and Arrhan shied under him as that the blade came free, an opal blaze till its tip cleared the sheath and whirled free.

Then a darkness greater than the night formed at *Changeling*'s point, and drew in the air all about them. Wind shrieked and keened; men cried out in panic, and the dark lines went to chaos, some breaking forward to meet him, some turning to flee.

"*Gate,*" he heard cry throughout the enemy ranks, "*Gate!*"—for gate it was, leading to Hell itself. He swung it and a horse and rider together went whirling away into dark, screaming with one terror. Others collided with each other in their attempt to escape his attack, and them he took in one stroke and the next, merciless, for there was no stopping it, there was no delicacy in it—it ate substance and spun it out again, streaming forms of living men away into Hell and cold—

—one and the next and the next as Arrhan cut a curving swath through attackers who trampled each other trying to flee it.

"Archers!" he heard cry. It was for his liege and his comrades he had concern. He reined aside to bring the hell-thing to the defense of his own—taking missiles askew with the wind, trying to shield his liege if he could find her in the unnatural light and the blinding wind.

"*Liyo!*" he shouted, desperate, fighting when he must, when some rider rushed him. The gate-force quivered through his arm and his shoulder and deafened him with its screaming; his eyes grew full of the hell-light and the sights and the faces till he was numb and blinded.

"*Liyo!*"

"*Vanye!*" he heard, and went to that thin sound, turning Arrhan, forcing her with his heels as the mare faltered in blind confusion.

Riders swept toward him. He swung the sword up at the nearest and saw the horrified face in the light of the blade, saw the mouth open in a cry of disbelief.

"*Bron!*" he cried, wrenching the blade aside, veering so that Arrhan skidded and fought wildly for balance.

Bron was gone. The bartered horse thundered past riderless.

He guided Arrhan about in a stumbling turn, and saw Morgaine beyond, silver and black, and Siptah's eyes wild in the opal fire.

"Follow!" she ordered him, and reined about and rode for the dark and the road.

He did not even think then; he followed. He drove his heels into Arrhan's flanks and swept to her right and behind, to keep Morgaine safe from what he did not know and could not see for the shock to his soul and the blinding of his eyes. If there were enemies still behind he did not know. He held *Changeling* naked to his right, protecting them both, for in that howling wind no arrow could reach them.

Up, up and up the steep slope, until horses faltered on the wet grass, and Siptah came about and Arrhan slowed, blowing froth back from her bit.

"Sheathe it," Morgaine cried. "Sheathe it!"

He discovered the sheath safe in its place at his side: he had done that much before he lost himself, reflexive and unremembered act. He took the sheath in

a trembling hand and turned the other numbed and aching wrist to wobble the
point toward safety, the only thing that would contain *Changeling*'s fire.

That small aperture was a goal he suddenly feared he could not make without calamity. His hand began to shake.

"Give over!" Morgaine said in alarm.

He made it. He slid the point home and the fire dimmed and died, so that
he was truly blind. His right arm ached from fingers to spine. He had no
strength in it nor feeling in his fingers. "I killed Bron," he said with what voice
he could manage, quite calmly. "Where is Chei?"

"I do not know," Morgaine said, reining Siptah close to him. There was
hardness in her voice, was very steel. He could not have borne any softer thing.
"We did not take them all. Some escaped. I do not know which ones."

"Forgive—" His breath seemed dammed up in him.

"We are near Tejhos. There is a chance that Mante will mistake one gate-fire
for the other. At least for the hour." She turned Siptah on the slope and rode,
Arrhan followed by her own will, dazed and blind as he.

"Too near the gate," he heard her say. "Too cursed near. We must be nearly
on Tejhos-gate. I should *never* have given it to you."

"Bron is dead," he said again, in the vague thought that she might not have
understood him. He had to say it again to believe it. The fabric of the world
seemed thinned and perilously strained about him and what he had done
seemed done half within some other place, unlinked and without effect here.
Things that Were could not be mended piece to piece if he did not say it till it
took hold of him. "Chei may have gone with him—O God. O *God!*"

He began to weep, a leakage from his eyes that became a spasm bowing him
over his saddle.

"Is thee hurt?" Morgaine asked him sharply, grasping Arrhan's rein. They
had stopped somehow. He did not recall. "Is thee hurt?"

"No," he managed to say. "No." He felt Siptah brush hard against his leg and
felt Morgaine touch him, a grip on his shoulder which he could hardly feel
through the armor. He was alone inside, half deaf with the winds, blinded by
the light which still swung as a red bar passing continually in his vision. He was
drowning in it, could not breathe, and he was obliged to say: "No. Not hurt,"
when next he could draw a breath, because she had no time for a fool and a
weakling who killed a comrade and then could not find his wits again. He
pushed himself up by the saddlebow and groped after the reins.

"Give me the sword," she said. "Give it!"

He managed to wind the reins about his numbed right hand and to pass
Changeling back to her with his left.

"Brighter," he remembered, competent in this at least, that his mind recollected something so difficult amid the chaos. He indicated with a lifting of his

left hand toward the northeast, as the road ran. "There. There will be Tejhos-gate."

She stared in that direction; she hooked *Changeling* to her belt and they rode again at all the pace the horses could bear. His right arm ached in pulses that confused themselves with the rhythm of the horses or with his heartbeats, he could not tell which. He worked the fingers desperately, knowing the likelihood of enemies. He scanned darkened hills the crests of which swam with the blurring of his eyes.

"Gate-force," Morgaine said in time. "We are very near. Vanye, is thee feeling it?"

"Aye," he murmured. "Aye, *liyo*." It was inside the armor with him, was coiled about his nerves and his sinew, it crept within his skull and corrupted sight and reason. They must go near that thing. Perhaps ambush waited for them.

We will lose everything we have done, he thought, everything she has suffered this far—lost, for a fool who mishandled the sword. I should have sheathed it when it went amiss. I should have ridden back. I should have—

—should have—known what I struck—

O God, it could as well have been her.

"Vanye!"

He caught himself before he pitched. He braced himself against the saddle-horn and felt Siptah's body hit his right leg, Morgaine holding him by the straps of his armor, though he was upright now without that.

"Can thee stay the saddle? Shall I take the reins?"

"I am well enough," he murmured, and took the reins in his left hand and let his numbed right rest braced between him and the saddlebow. If he could do one thing right this cursed night it was to dispose himself where he could not fall off and compound his liege's troubles.

Siptah took to the lead then; and the mare lengthened her stride to match him, struggling now, on heart alone.

Where are we going? he wondered. Is it enemies she fears? Or do we go toward the gate, to hold it?

His very teeth ached now with the emanations, and he felt a pain like knives driven into every joint of his right arm, an ache that crept across his chest and into his vitals. He wished he had respite to faint away or to rest; and dutifully fought not to, for what use he was. The pain reached his spine and his skull, one with the pounding of the mare's gait, the jolts which threatened to take him from the saddle.

Hold on, he told himself, slumped over the saddle when other thought had ceased, hold on, hold on.

*   *   *

The roan horse came to a slow halt where the battle had been, and Gault clutched after its ties and its stirrup, letting himself down by painful degrees to stand amid the field. He did not know the weapon that had struck him, which had pierced through his left arm and burned across his back. But here he had fallen in the battle, here his ranks had broken in terror of the gate-weapon, and there were appallingly few corpses remaining.

Here he had flung himself at the roan horse as the slaughter started and managed to get back astride—when the gate-force broke loose and sane men quit the field as quickly as they could.

Such of them as survived had rallied again—*qhal*, and a scattering of terrified humans—most of all, that the squad he had sent wide before they came to Arunden's camp, had overtaken them now, having swept up the deserters; and had found him on the road.

Now they walked as he did, probing among the dead that were thickest here, where only the red fire had come, where the woman had wielded what they had mistakenly thought the chiefest of weapons they faced.

That was the fire that had touched him. He understood that much. He stumbled among cooling bodies and found one living, who hoarsely called his name—"Rythys!" Gault called out. "Your cousin!"—and Rythys left his desperate searching and came in haste, one of the few fortunate.

But Gault sought Jestryn on the field, and found him finally—Pyverrn the wit, Pyverrn the prankster, Pyverrn who had done an unhumorous thing at the last, and flung himself and his horse between Gault and the killing fire.

"Pyverrn," Gault-Qhiverin said, feeling after a heartbeat, and finding none, finding Jestryn's face already cold in the night wind. "Pyverrn!" he cried, for that was the oldest name, the name by which they had been friends in Mante, and fought the Overlord's battles and intrigued in the Overlord's court through their last life. *"Pyverrn!"*

He hugged the body to him, but it was only cooling human clay against his own borrowed flesh, a body Pyverrn had worn, but never truly mastered.

This was the last death, the irrecoverable one: not Tejhos-gate nor any other could save a life, once the life was gone; and Gault would have murdered one of his own men to have hosted Pyverrn's self again—he would have taken one of his own kind; his other and dearest friends.

He would have—such was the bond between them—accepted what only a few had dared to save a fading life: he would have gone into the gate with his friend and taken him into his own self, risking madness, or obliteration.

That was his love for Pyverrn.

But there was nothing left to love. There was only the cold flesh that Pyverrn had wrested from its previous owner, and no way to restore it.

His men came round him where he knelt and wept. None ventured a word to him, until he himself let the body go and stood up.

"Tejhos-gate," he said. *"We are going after them!"*

Doubtless there were some few who would have fled, had they had a choice. He knew the cowardice of some of them, that had had to be herded back. But in the southern lands there was nothing to hide them should they fail him—and now they knew he was alive.

"Two of you will go to Mante," he said when they were mounted again. "The rest of us will ride after these invaders. We will have them. *I* will have them, him and her, and they will wish they had been stillborn."

"Better?" Morgaine asked; and Vanye, sitting with his back against a standing stone, leaned his head against that unforgiving surface and nodded with his eyes shut. He did not remember much of the ride that had brought them this far. He knew that he had been upright in the saddle, but so much of it had been that kind of pain which the mind would not believe could last so keenly, so long. All that time seemed compressed; yet he knew it was leagues beyond that place where he had almost fallen. Tejhos-gate was far behind them.

And the cessation of that force left him drained, void, as if he had been gutted.

Beside them the horses caught their breath and began to show a little interest in the grass under their feet, now they had drunk of the little creek and had their legs rubbed down. He had done that much for his horse, while Morgaine saw to the Baien gray. He was a horseman from his birth: he would have done that for the brave mare with his heart's blood, after the course she had run; and Morgaine—whatever she was—had no less care for the gray.

Now she leaned against another such stone facing him—not stones of power, mere markers along the roadside. One knee propped the sword on which she leaned, the sight of which he could hardly bear and the weight of which he remembered in his bones: not balanced like an ordinary blade, the crystal length within that sheath rune-written with the secrets of the gates—for the sake of a successor, she had told him once. She had taught him writing and ciphering more than a lord's bastard needed—for what purpose he knew, and loathed, and thought about no more than he had to.

But he could read those runes. They were burned into his soul like the light into his eyes.

"Water?" she asked him.

He drank from the flask she gave him, struggled with his left hand and his right to hold it without shaking. The pain was still there, but only a dull ache, against the memory of the living blade in his hand. He gave the flask back, drew a breath and looked about him at the rolling hills, the stones, the road pale in the starlight.

"We should have gone over to Tejhos," he murmured.

"Thee could not," she said.

It was bitter truth. He would have left her to hold the place alone, would have fallen—Heaven knew where he would have fallen, or how long the fire would run in his bones if he lay within that influence.

The drawing of the sword was a dice-throw, a power either felt in Mante, if they were wary; or was mistaken for ordinary—O Heaven—*ordinary* use of the gate, in which case Mante would do nothing, until their enemies reached it and passed it and told Mante otherwise—which they would, assuredly.

Therefore they ran. Therefore they paced themselves to last now, with all the speed they could make, while they might make it.

He had a cold lump of fear at his gut. Coward, he had heard from his brothers, and from his father, and most of Morija—You think too much, his brother had told him. He had never been like them. In all too many respects.

If a man thought—if a man let himself think—backward or forward—

"It is not the first friend the sword has taken," she said finally. "Vanye, it was not your fault."

"I know," he said, and saw in his mind the harper-lad of Ra-morij, who had thrown himself between that blade in her hand and his threatened kin—had flung himself there to be a hero, and discovered Hell in the unstoppable swing of Morgaine's hand.

"They rode to your right," she said, "against all our warnings."

The excuses she made for him were doubtless those which armored her, the only and best wisdom she had to give him. He sensed the pain it cost her to expose that. And there was nothing to say against those excuses that she did not, beneath those reasonings, know—

—except the harper had known the report of the sword: who in Morija had not?

But Bron had not known, had not guessed how far its danger extended. They had never told him.

He shut his eyes, clenched them shut, as if it could banish the terrified face that was burned across his vision; or bring back the sun, and end this terrible night where visions were all too easy. The priest, he thought, had cursed him, cursed Bron, cursed Chei. He did not say that to Morgaine. But he feared it. Heaven had answered that creature, and he did not know why, except Heaven judged them worse—

Harness jingled, the sudden lifting of Siptah's head, the clink of slipped bit and snaffle ring that his ears knew before his eyes lifted. The stallion stood with ears pricked, gazing toward the road.

Morgaine rose instantly and moved to take the horses in hand and lead them inward of the stones for cover from the road.

He rose shakily to his feet and held the reins, soothing them, stroking one nose and the other—"Quiet, quiet," he said to them in the Kurshin tongue, and Siptah strained at his grip and shivered, one long twitch up his foreleg.

"One rider," Morgaine said, venturing a quick look from the edge of the stone.

"One man makes no sense."

"A good many have cause to follow us."

"Past the gate at Tejhos? Alone?"

She drew the black weapon. It was a dead man rode that track, and did not know it. He leaned his shoulders against the stone and looked out past it, as the stone was canted at an angle to the road.

The rider came on a dark horse. Mail glinted about him in the starlight.

Vanye's heart leapt and jolted against his ribs. For a moment he could not breathe. "Chei," he said, and reached for Morgaine's arm. "It is Chei."

"*Stay here.*"

He turned his head in dismay to look at her, at the weapon still in her hand. "*Liyo*, for the love of Heaven—"

"We do not know that it *is* Chei. Stay here. Wait."

He waited, leaning against the rock and breathing in shorter and shorter breaths as the faltering hoofbeats came closer.

"*Liyo,*" he whispered in horror, seeing her arm lift.

She fired as the rider came past them, a red fire breaking out in the meadow-grass; and the exhausted horse shied and fought for balance as the rider reined up and about, facing them.

Chei slid down, holding to the saddlehorn and clinging to the reins.

"Chei," Vanye said, and left the horses, walking out from between the stones.

"Stop," Morgaine said; and he stopped.

Chei only stood there, as if he were numb.

"Bring your horse in," Morgaine said. "Sit down."

Chei staggered toward them and led the horse as far as the first stone. "Where is my brother?" he asked. "Where did Bron go?"

It was not the question Vanye had expected. It took the breath out of him.

"Bron is dead," Morgaine said.

"Where did he *go*?"

"*Changeling*'s gate has no other side."

Chei slid down the face of the stone and leaned against it, his head resting against the rock. Vanye sank down facing him.

"Chei—I could not stop it. I did not know him—Chei?"

Chei neither moved nor lifted his head. There was only silence, long and deep, in which Morgaine at last moved and retrieved her flask from Siptah's saddle.

"Here," she said, offering it.

Chei looked up and took it as if his hands and his mind were far separate. He fumbled after the stopper and drank, and slowly, as if it were a thoroughly unfamiliar task, stopped it again and gave it back.

"I feared," Vanye said desperately, "that it was the both of you. I could not see, Chei."

"Rest," Morgaine said, and came close and stood with *Changeling* folded in her arms. "So long as we rest. After that, go back to your own land."

"No," Chei said with a shake of his head.

"Then take my order. You will go no further with us."

Vanye looked around at her in dismay, at a face implacable in the starlight, a figure that had as well be some warlike statue.

"*Liyo*—"

"He is a danger," she said in the Kurshin tongue. "There is a gate yonder. Has thee forgotten?"

"There is not enough time!"

"Tell me how long it takes. There were wounded aplenty back there."

"It is Chei! Would a *qhal* come asking where his brother was? Is that the kind of question a *qhal* would ask first, who *knows* what the gates are?"

"Barring other chances, there is the matter of bloodfeud. Of revenge."

"Revenge? God in Heaven, has the man come seeking revenge on me? I wish he would—I wish he *would* say something—"

"In time to come, at some point of crisis—yes. Being what he is, he may well think of revenge, when he wakes from the shock of it. I will not have him with us, at your back—or mine."

"For the love of God, *liyo!* No! I refuse this. I will not have it."

"We gave him what chance we could. Here is an end of it. He goes, Vanye."

"And where is my voice in this?"

"Thee is always free to choose."

He stared at her in shock, numb. It was the old answer. It was forever true. It was real now, an ultimatum, from which there was, on this plain, near the gates—no return within her trust.

"You will go," she said to Chei.

"Lady—"

"Life I have given you. Use it."

"You have taken my brother's!"

"Aye, and spared yours just now. Do not stay to rest. Take your horse and go. *Now.*"

"Vanye—" Chei said.

"I cannot," he said, forcing the words. "I cannot, Chei."

Chei said nothing for a moment. Then he struggled toward his feet. Vanye put out a hand to help him and he struck it away, fumbling after his horse's reins.

"At least," Vanye said to Morgaine, "let him rest here!"

"No."

Chei did not look at him until he was in the saddle, and then he was all shadow, there between the menhirs.

He rode away without a word, whipping the exhausted horse with blows Vanye felt in his own flesh.

"*Liyo,*" he said then to Morgaine, without looking at her, "I know your reasons. I know everything you would say. But, Mother of God, could we not have let him rest, could we not have tried him—?"

"Pity," she said, "will be your undoing. *I* did this. I have spared you the necessity. For your sake—and mine. And I have given him cause to hate me. That is my best gift. Best he lose his zeal for us altogether—before it kills him. *That* is the pity I have for him. And best it come from me rather than you. That is all the mercy I have."

He stared at her in the darkness, somewhere between numbness and outrage. Now it was temper from her. Now she was righteous. "Aye," he said, and sat down abruptly, deciding that numbness was better, for the night, perhaps for a good many days to come.

There was a pain behind his eyes. He rested his head on his arm and tried to make it go away, or the pain in his heart to stop, or the fear in his gut; and none of them had remedy, except that Morgaine knew that pain, Morgaine was still with him, Morgaine was sunk in her own silence and Morgaine was bearing unto herself—she had told the truth—all the cruelty of which he was not capable.

The road stretched on and on in the starlight, unremitting nightmare, and Gault-Qhiverin clung to the course with what followers he had left to him. There was a wetness all down his side, the wound broken open again, though he had bound it, and the roan horse's gait did nothing to lessen the pain of his wounds.

"Go back," his captain said to him. "My lord, let us continue. You go back. We dare not lose you—" Which was true: there were many in Gault's household who were there for reasons which had much to do with court and intrigue and the saving of their lives—lose him they dared not, for fear of who might replace him in Morund.

But they were not mortal wounds, that bled down his side and across his back. He would live to deal with consequences, and he had said things and compromised himself in front of witnesses, in ways that required personal action to redeem him: no, my lord, treason was never my purpose. I only queried them to learn their business: my offers to them were a lie.

Form meant a great deal in Mante, whatever the Overlord knew of true purposes.

There was most of all, most of all—revenge. And the saving of his reputation: Gault was never without double purposes, even in something so precious to him as his best friend's life. There were ways and ways to accomplish anything; and revenge was always best if it accomplished more than its immediate aims.

This was the common sense that had settled into Gault now the blood was cool and the purpose formed: alliance was not possible and therefore he would be virtuous, serve his own interests in the other way—and survive to deal with his and Pyverrn's enemies.

The pair of them first for himself; and, failing that, for Mante and Skarrin's gentle inquiries. That was the object of his ride.

But there was something before him on the road, a single moving darkness that advanced and gained detail at the combined speed of their horses.

"What is that?" one of his company asked. "*Who* is that?"—for Tejhos was behind them on the road, where the two members of their own company had gone message-bearing and asking after troops. This could be no answer Mante had sent—from upland, from that direction.

Closer and closer the rider came, on a horse weary and faltering in the night.

"Lord Gault!" the rider cried. "Lord Gault!"

Gault spurred the roan forward of the rest. "Who are you?" he yelled back at the oncoming rider.

And had his answer as the pale-haired rider came straight for him with a howl neither human nor *qhal.*

"Gault—!"

A sword glittered in the starlight. He whipped his own out and up, and metal rang on metal as the fool tried to leave his saddle and bear him off the horse.

But a knife was in the other hand. It scored his armor and found a chink in his belly, and he yelled in shock as he brought his own sword-hilt round, the only weapon he could bring to bear at too close a range, battering at his enemy who was ripping the knife upward in his belly before his men could close in and pull the man off.

"My lord," his men cried, holding him in their arms, lifting him from the saddle, as he clamped a hand to his gut and stared down at the wild man the rest of them had caught and pinned.

"Do not kill him!" he managed to say, while his gut leaked blood through his fingers and the chill came on him. "Do not kill this one."

The Man screamed and lunged at him, trying before the others could stop him to tear him down by the feet, by the knees; but they held him.

"Do not hurt him," Gault said again, and the man struggled and screamed at him, calling him butcher and coward and what other things Gault's dimming hearing lost track of.

"I am Chei ep Kantory," the man yelled at him. "Try again, Gault. Do you want a shape to wear? Do you need one? I will give you one—I will give you mine."

"He is mad," someone said.

"What do you want?" Gault asked, fascinated despite the pain that racked him and the cold that came on him. "What price—for this partnership?"

"For my brother," ep Kantory said. His sobs stilled. He became quite calm. "We have a common enemy. What is it worth to you—to have me willing?"

ᔐ Chapter 11

It was a procession as fraught with fear as the last trek Chei had made with Gault and his company—the same, in that many of these were the same men that had taken him to Morund-gate; but here was no one stumbling along afoot: they let him ride, and though he was bound, none of them struck him, none of them offered him any threat or harm, and their handling had put not so much as a bruise on him.

They went now with what speed they could, such that it must cost Gault agony: Chei knew and cherished that thought for the little comfort he could get from it.

Mostly, in this dreadful place of barren hills and night sky and stars, he thought of his own fate, and from time to time of Bron, but not Bron in their youth, not Bron in better times, but Bron's face when the sword had taken him. That horror was burned into his sight, every nuance of it, every interpretation of what word Bron had tried to call out and for whom he had meant it, and whether he had known what was happening to him as he fell away into nowhere at all.

And it was all to no purpose, serving allies who despised them both, who killed Bron and then cast off the faith he had tried to keep for his brother as if it was some soiled rag, himself *qhal*-tainted, henceforth not to be trusted—so much the clans might have done, for their own safety—but *something*, something, they could have said, something—anything, to make Bron's death noble, or something less horrible than it was. They might have offered regret—Forgive, they could have said: we dare not trust you. Forgive me, Vanye could have said: could have prevailed with the lady—the man who had taken him from the wolves, been his ally—

—killed Bron.

—then cast him out with a shrug of his shoulders, seeing the lady threaten him with death by fire—with the sword itself.

But that was not the fate that he had chosen.

He felt power in the air as they passed the shoulder of a hill—felt it stronger and stronger, so that the hair stood up on his head and his body, and the horses shied and fought the bit.

Men dismounted; some led Gault's horse and some led his after this, though the gelding fought and resisted and Gault's roan horse threw its head and tried to turn away.

"Not far now," one said; and Chei felt cold inside. "Not far—" As they passed that hill and the black menhirs rose up like teeth against the stars.

Beyond, atop the hill, the gate of Tejhos itself hove up against the sky, monstrous and dark, a simple square arch that framed a single bright star.

Then Chei's courage faltered. Then, his exhausted horse led perforce toward the base of that hill, he doubted everything that he had purposed, whether any revenge was worth this. He pulled furtively at the cords that held him and found them secure. He looked about and measured how far he could ride if he should kick the horse and startle it free—but the horse was doing all it could to free itself already, as men held it close by the bit and crowded it close.

Suddenly other figures came into their path, from among the rocks, accosting Gault; words passed; swords were drawn. What is this? Chei wondered numbly. It occurred to him that something threatened Gault himself, and that some other presence had arrived that had the guards all about him reaching for weapons. It was too complex. He had come into a *qhal* matter, and their deviousness and their scheming threatened to swallow him up all by accident.

But the difficulty seemed resolved. The *qhal* who had met them broke their line and allowed Gault to pass. Then they began to move again, toward the hill. They passed between the masked warders themselves, strange helmed figures with visors in the shape of demons and beasts, with naked swords that gleamed silver in the starlight.

This was Hell, and he had come to it of his own accord. They left the warders behind, he and the men who led his horse and surrounded him with force. The gate loomed above them. There was no way back and no way of escape, and he had done everything knowing that such would be the case, knowing himself now, that he was not a man who could die simply or easily, or lay down his life of his own accord.

At every step of this he had planned that they would take care of the matter for him: they would shoot him down on the road—Gault would be dead or refuse to fight him, and the whole band would ride against him—he would find them scattered on the road and kill a few of them before the odds ran out—or he would ride all the way to Morund-keep itself, and hail out *qhal* one after the other till they killed him.

Or his first purpose would succeed, Gault would answer his challenge and Gault would skewer him outright or he would kill Gault before Gault's men killed him—

And last of all they might take him prisoner and use him as they planned to now, if there was desperate need—

That was the bargain he ventured. He had heard while he was in Gault's prisons, that when they took a body, sometimes the *qhal* who tried it lost, and utter madness was the end; or now and again (so they whispered, devising vague hopes and schemes in that stinking dark) the war inside that body went on for years, mind and mind in the same flesh.

There was not a clan in the hills would have him now. There was nothing going home could offer him.

But this . . . this offered something.

He had planned this when he drove himself straight at Gault and gotten his way past Gault's guard by sheer berserk desperation, and driven a harness-knife for Gault's vitals, even while half a hundred men moved to stop him.

He kept believing it possible, as the horse fought and jolted under him, and men whipped it and forced it.

War on different grounds, he thought, you and I, inside, with no escape for either of us—I shall embrace you, Gault-my-enemy. That leaves us your hate and mine, and my anger and yours; and what I want and what you want, and which is stronger, *qhalur* lord?

Was Gault-the-Man afraid when you took him? But I am not. I welcome you. I shall welcome this fight with all my damned soul, Gault-my-enemy. I came back from Hell once, where you sent me. Do you think I will not come back again?

"A little farther," someone said.

Or seemed to say. But it was harder and harder to think at all, in the jolting steps the horse made under him in its struggles, in the sensation crawling like insects over his skin. The gate loomed nearer and nearer, and the horse shied and faltered under him, so that the men finally stopped it, as it stumbled nearly to its knees. "Get down," that voice said, and they pulled him from the saddle, their hands no longer gentle, everything passing further and further from the familiar and the known.

He looked up at the span of the gate and saw that the roan horse had gone further; but now the men lifted Gault from his saddle and carried him, while others seized his own arms and started him toward that height, toward the night sky shimmering like air over fire, within the towering frame of the gate.

Closer and closer, until he could see nothing but the sky past those pillars, and a single star within that arch, a point of light that quivered and danced in the air. There was a singing in the wind, the thrum of bowstrings, of voices, spectral and quivering in his bones.

Closer yet. The sky seemed to shift *downward* within the gate, and the thrumming was in his brain. His bowels turned to water in him, and his knees quaked, and the men holding him were all that enabled him to walk. O God, he thought, God, what can a Man hope to do here, with them?

And again: Fear is Gault's weapon. I must not be open to it. I dare not let fear in. Hate is all I have. Hate greater than his—

They reached the crest almost together, Gault holding his hand pressed to his belly, but walking at the last, leaning on the men who attended him. The black pillars seemed to throw off a kind of light, none for themselves, but a white hell-glow that played about the ground and that ran up the legs and the bodies and the faces of men who passed within its compass. Small sounds were swallowed up. The sky twisted and writhed like a gaping pit.

As far as the pillars that dwarfed them, Gault went, and leaned against the left-hand stone holding to it for his support, laying his hand on one place and another as if it were a living thing, and himself in communion with it—*qhalur* wizardry, Chei thought, breathing with difficulty, watching with small jerks of his eyes and knowing that his face betrayed terror; but so was there terror in the grip of hands which numbed his arms and held him upright despite his failing knees. They were all afraid, he, the *qhal* themselves—it was a strange reliance he began to have on them, who would defend his safety now with their own lives, who were there to hold him and keep him from failing his resolution or from tumbling untimely into that place—A little longer, a little longer, he told himself; and concentrated on the little pain they caused his arms as the only saving of his sanity: *Help me, do not let me go; we are all flesh, and flesh does not belong next this thing—*

They gathered him up; they brought him closer, and Gault staggered forth to meet him in front of that dark archway, on the edge of the sky.

"Free him," Gault bade them, and a rough sawing cut the cords on his hands. They let go their grip on him, and Chei lurched out of balance, staring at the sky which now had lost all stars, which did not show the hills beyond, or anything but night—stared helplessly at Gault's face, suddenly, as Gault caught his arms. Hell-light shimmered over them, turning flesh dead white; Gault caught him closer, as suddenly the air began to move about them, stirring Gault's hair, howling with the force of summer storm.

The gate was opening, greater than the gate the sword had made, louder than the howling of the winds which had taken Bron.

"Have you changed your mind?" Gault asked, and embraced him closer still. "Is it still willingly?"

Chei fought down his gorge and nodded, and his heart pounded in shock when he felt Gault seek his hand and press the hilt of a knife into his cold fingers. "Then you may do what you so much wish so much to do," Gault said, and slid his hand to the back of his neck, winding fingers into his hair, holding him tight. "Friend."

Chei rammed upward with the knife in a spasm of outrage, under Gault's jaw, toward the brain.

Someone pushed him. He felt the hands strike him, and the hill fell away under him and the man who was locked with him in a sickening fall of cold and wind and void.

Something began to go wrong then, his senses going out one by one: he saw things he could not name, and was blinded by light that was pain. He screamed and screamed as he fell, alone now, falling slower—a drifting dark, in which something else walked, and that thing was a thought that waked in him and called itself Chei, but it was not himself. It remembered dying, remembered the shock of a blade in its bowels, and one beneath its jaw, stopping breath and speech; the pain was all for a moment.

Then it ebbed, retreating to the past, safe and bearable.

He knew then what had happened to him, and that realization itself was fleeting, shredding away from him in the dark as something he dared not reconcile, except that he had died—he knew that recent memory had his death in it, and he did not want to delve into that, here, in the dark, naked to the winds and the cold.

He had use for his life. He discovered it and clung to it. He called it Bron and he called it Jestryn and Pyverrn, and he could not remember whether it had been brother or friend, or whether the man or the woman had killed him, but it was one and the same. He had a revenge to take, and that it was the one thing that had brought him north or south on that nightbound road, whichever direction he had been traveling, whichever horse he had been riding.

Then, having discovered his heart was whole, he was less afraid. He felt other things slipping away, pieces that might matter, but he was no longer in doubt where his course was and that the men waiting for him would follow him.

He knew all of Morund. He knew the hills. He knew Mante. He saw a hold set in the mountains, and the great Gate which ruled all gates, and knew the intricacies of politics which had sent the warders who waited below the hill: the Overlord Skarrin had received his first message and sent this handful of his

underlings to guard the approach and to discover what they could, while Skarrin questioned at length the messengers he had sent. Skarrin's men had tried to
bar him from use of the gate, until he could have permission of the high lord.

They had hoped, perhaps, that he would die.

But now, in his recollections, he had something indeed to tell them, which
would stir Skarrin out of his lethargy and bring forces south.

Tell them the urgency of it he would, but he would not tell all he knew—nor
stay for them or wait on Skarrin's pleasure. He had been Qhiverin Asfelles. He
and Pyverrn had fought in these lands between Tejhos and Mante, against various of the high lord's enemies; he knew the secret ways into the hills, off the
Road and back to it. He had utter freedom of the land, the high lord himself
had cause to fear him and his connections within the warrior Societies, and he
was as likely as any to profit by the present chaos—by whatever means turned
up under his hand. He drew a breath.

He felt the winds again, when a moment before had been only cold that
numbed all feeling.

He heard the sounds, when a moment before had been only stillness. It was
as if a ripple were sweeping through the dark, bearing him closer and closer to
the shores of the world.

He moved his limbs, finding himself weaker than he remembered, lighter
of limb. It was a young body. It was skilled and agile and had a long-muscled,
runner's strength different than the slower, mature power of the body he recalled as Gault's—was far more like Qhiverin's; was nearly as fair as a *qhal*; and
that pleased him.

He had a mature mind, too, that took the skittish thoughts of a younger and
impulsive man and calmed them and spread wider and further into connections from which he shied back, of a sudden: there was too much memory, and
it needed long meditation to reconcile it.

Witch-mind, a part of him said.

Nature, said the other, nature and knowledge.

God! part of him cried.

The other part said: Nature.

Vision cleared in a shimmer like the surface of a pond. The hill grew firm
under his feet and the men who gathered anxiously to meet him were all
friendly and familiar to him.

"Hesiyyn," he said, and laid his hand on a tall *qhal*'s shoulder with easy
humor, knowing how Hesiyyn loathed humankind.

"Lord Chei," Hesiyyn hailed him with deep irony. It was custom. It was the
penalty of the twice-and-three-times-born.

The Men among them would be confused. They would murmur things
about souls, which Chei dismissed and refused to think about. But tall, elegant

qhal had no hesitation in bowing the head and offering homage to him, to Chei ep Kantory, lord of Morund—the intimates of his household, his servants, the remnant of the human levies, even the troublesome and arrogant warders from Mante, who waited below, with their captain.

He felt wounds on him. He felt bruises. His knees ached with exhaustion. That was the penalty this body brought with it. None were unbearable.

He sought weapons—the sword which the Man had given him: that was one weapon he did not intend to lose. It was *qhalur*-work, and foreign—from further, he was sure, than merely overseas, and he delighted in it when he tried its balance.

He took his own bow; and the red roan; the lame gelding he turned out to fend for itself: perhaps it would recover.

But he declined more weapons than that, and declined to go in more than the breeches and mended boots and light mail that came with the man.

"This is the shape they will expect," he said to Hesiyyn.

"Wake," Morgaine's voice whispered out of nowhere, and muscles jumped and body tensed all in one spasm as on the edge of a fall—But it was stone at Vanye's back, and he pressed himself against it, controlling his breaths and blinking at the shadow that stood between him and the horses. "I might have hit you," he said. "Oh, Heaven—" He caught his breath and brushed loose hair out of his eyes with a trembling hand. "I dreamed—" But he did not tell those dreams, that took him back to old places, old terrors. "I did not mean to sleep."

"Best we move."

"Is there—"

"No. Only shortness of time. A little of the night left. We travel while we can."

He glanced around to see were Chei and Bron awake then, one instant's impulse, and remembered everything like a blow to the stomach; he drew a breath then and rubbed an unshaven face, and quickly gathered himself to his feet, trying not to think on anything but the road.

Fool, he thought. Do not look back. Look around you. *Look around you.* That is what caused this sorry business, nothing more and nothing less than losing track of things.

He wanted to weep. He adjusted Arrhan's gear and reached out to hold Siptah's bridle for Morgaine as she prepared to mount. "Do not be seeing to *me*," she said sharply, taking back the reins, by which she meant do not be twice a fool.

It stung. He was not in a mood to bear her temper, and she was not in a mood for debating what she wanted. He turned and flung himself to horse, and waited on her, since she was in such haste.

She mounted up and rode without a backward look. She was fey and doom-ridden, and the loss of a comrade and the driving away of another—the excessive cruelty of it, like her ultimatum to him with Chei, was all one thing.

It was because of that blade she bore. It was because of the lives it took. It was because of the things she knew that he did not, and the madness—the madness which distracted her, and which, this morning, beckoned both of them.

Her moods had been tolerable while he had been no more than *ilin* and now were enough to drive him to black, blind rage, anger to match her own.

She spoke finally. It was to remark on the land, as if there had never been a quarrel.

"Aye," he said, and: "Aye, my liege," choking down his temper—for hers was gone, vanished. That was the way of her. He was Nhi on one side of the blanket and Chya on the other and temper once it rose was next to madness, it blinded and it drove him—even to fratricide; after which he had learned to smother it under *ilin*-law. O Heaven, he thought, *ilin* to a temper-prone woman was one thing. Both lover and shieldman to a woman half-mad and geas-driven was another.

He had the warrior's braid back. The cool air on his neck, the high-clan honor that forever reminded him he could take another path, the *ilin's* oath that bound him to a liege he could in no wise leave—unwise, unwise, ever to tangle matters further, unwise to have drifted closer and closer until she could wound him, and drive him mad, and then absently forget she had struck at him at all.

But it had happened. He was snared. He had been enspelled from the beginning.

And she left him with his ghosts—thinking at one time he heard more horses than their two, thinking at another moment that Chei and Bron were behind him. They haunted the tail of his eye so that a bit of brush, a stone, a trick of the rising sun, persuaded his sight that they were there.

Both.

Chei is dead, he thought with a chill, and crossed himself. *Chei is dead.*

And he could not say why he suddenly believed this, or why it was two riders that haunted him, except it was guilt, or foreknowledge what they had sent Chei to, in a land where he had *qhal*-taint on him.

He wept, the tears running down his face, without expression. Beside him, Morgaine said some word.

"Vanye," she said then.

There was no place for a man to go, except to turn his face away.

She was silent after. The wind dried his face. There seemed nothing to say, that would not lead to things he did not want to discuss. He only gave a sigh and shifted in his saddle and looked at her, so that she would know that he was all right.

The sun came up by degrees in the sky and showed them other ghosts, the heights of hills which had not been there, showed them a land of crags and rough land ahead of them, all painted in shadows of gold and cloud.

"Rest," she said again, when they had come to water, a little pond between two hills, and this time again he took Siptah's bridle as she dismounted.

She laid her hand on his back as she walked past him, as he slipped the horses' bits to let them graze and rest a little. He felt it faintly through the armor, and it set the thoughts moiling in him, a little of relief, a great deal of reluctance to do or say anything with her. It was not a quarrel of woman and man. It was, he decided finally, that their blood was up, both, that they had killed, that she had fighting in her mind and so did he, and to expect any gentleness or to offer any was unwise.

He went and washed his hands and his face and his neck in the pond, wetting his boots in the boggy grass.

"Do not drink," she said from behind him, reminding him of cautions that he knew as well as she, and he turned half about with a sudden, trapped fury in him.

He said nothing, and rose and walked back to sit down on his heels and press his wet hands to the back of his neck and to his brow.

"Sleep," he said without looking at her. "You are due that."

"I should not have chided thee."

"No, you should have let a fool drink from standing water. It is not Kursh, or Andur, *liyo*. I know that. I was not that much fool."

"Thee can take the rest. Thee has more need."

"Why, because I am short-tempered? I have killed a man. I have killed one man I held for a friend. And we have lost the other. No matter." He wiped the hair back from his stubbled face, the wisps that had come loose from his braid and trailed about brow and ears, and he had not the will left to do more than wipe them out of his way. "I am learning."

Then the reach of what he had said shot through him. He glanced up at her face. *My God, why did I say that?*

The mask had come back over her countenance, pale as it was. She shrugged and looked aside at the ground. "Well that we save our shafts for our enemies."

"Forgive me." He went to his knees and she moved so suddenly he thought she would strike him in the face, but it was his shoulder she caught, hard, with the heel of her hand, before he could even think to bow to the ground as reflex made natural. He met her angry stare and there was nothing woman-gentle in the blow that had stopped him from the obeisance. He had meant to make peace. Now he only stared at her.

She looked dismayed too, finally, the anger fading. Her hand went gentle on his shoulder and trailed down his arm. "There is no way back," she said. "If you learn anything of me, learn that."

He felt his throat tighten. He drew breaths to find an adequate one and finally shook his head, and turned aside and got up clumsily, since she gave him no room.

"I am sorry," he said with his back to her. The arm that had wielded the sword ached again, and he rubbed at the shoulder she had struck. "I have my wits about me, better than you see. God knows, we are going to need our rest. And I do you no service to rob you of yours. I am not the first man mistook a friend in a fight, God knows I am not—" He remembered the harper, with a wince. He could not but wound her, no matter what he did or said; no more than she with him. He could not think where they would find rest, or where he would shake the phantoms in the tail of his eye, and of a sudden panic came over him, thinking what odds mounted against their passing those mountains ahead.

It was speed they needed. And human bodies and exhausted horses could only do so much before hearts broke and flesh failed.

"They are my mistakes," she said. He heard her move, and her shadow fell past him and merged with his on the thin grass, "to have taken them with us, to have given thee the sword. It was thy own strength betrayed thee, that thee kept using it. Never—*never* bear it till it wields thee. That is what happened. That, I did not make thee understand. It has happened to me. Thee learns. And sometimes even then—"

She did not finish. He looked half around at her and nodded, and refused to regard the phantom that beckoned him from the tail of his eye, a shadow on the horizon of the road. Her hand rested on his arm and his pressed hers.

Until that phantom insisted, and this time he must look, seeing a horseman atop the ridge.

"*Liyo!*" he hissed. "On the road—"

He leapt up and she did; and hurried for the horses, to tighten cinches and refit bridles: he caught Siptah first, his duty to his liege, and she left him to that for economy of motion and did the same for Arrhan, still working as he led Siptah to her.

A last buckle and she was done. He cast a glance over his shoulder and saw the oncoming riders, twenty, thirty or more.

"They are Gault's or they are out of the gate," Morgaine said, and set her foot in Siptah's stirrup. "If the latter, we have no knowledge *what* weapons they have, and I do not like this ground—Ride!"

He sprang to the saddle and reined to her left as they made the road. There was no question but that they were seen by now, but the narrowing of the road left them little choice—and that in itself put a fear into him. Many things about the gates bewildered him, but crossing from *here* to *there* did not, and if Gault's men had gone from Tejhos to Mante and back, Mante itself was warned and might have riders coming south to head them off.

It was more and more of narrow passage ahead of them: the rising sun had limned rougher land stretching eastward and north, and that meant fewer and fewer choices of any sort.

They had won so many battles. The odds grew and the land shaped itself against them. "Get off the road," he shouted at Morgaine as he rode alongside. "For Heaven's own sake, *liyo*, we cannot win straight through—we cannot out-ride them behind and before! Let us get into the hills, let them hunt us there, let them hunt us the winter long, if that is what it takes to let them grow careless—"

It was an outlaw's counsel. He had that to give. He looked at Morgaine and saw her face set and pale in that unreason that drove her. He despaired then.

"We make as much ground as we can," she called across to him, "as long as we can."

He looked back over his shoulder, where their pursuers made a darkness on either margin of the road, running beside the sporadic white stone.

"Then stop and fight them," he said. "*Liyo*, in Heaven's name, one or the other!"

"There might be others," she shouted back, meaning overland, through the hills; and he caught the gist of her fears and reckoned as she reckoned, on Mante, and stones, and gates.

The riders so easily seen might be a lure to delay or herd them.

Still, still, she was the elder and warier of them.

They crested a hill and for a time they were running alone, at an easier gait, for a long enough time that he looked back once and twice looking for their pursuers; and Morgaine looked, her silver hair whipping in the wind.

They were gone.

"I do not like this," she said as they rode.

The road which had held straight so far, through so much of the land, took a bend toward the east which Chei had never mapped.

And his own instincts cried trap.

"*Liyo*, I beg you, let us get off this!"

Morgaine said nothing, but of a sudden turned Siptah aside into a fold of the hills, keeping a quick pace on grassy and uneven ground, down the course the hills gave them.

Deeper and deeper into land in which they no longer had a guide.

They rode more quietly at last, finding their way by the sun in a wandering course through grassy hills, brush and scrub forest.

They watched the hilltops and the edges of the thickets, and from time to time looked behind them or stopped and listened and watched the flight of birds for omens of pursuers.

Morgaine did not speak now. He rode silent as she, senses wide and listening, for any hint of other presence.

Only as the sun sank: "The dark is their friend tonight," Morgaine said, "more than ours, in a land we do not know. We had best find ourselves a place and lie quiet a while."

"Thank Heaven," he muttered; and when they had found that place, a deep fold of the hills well-grown with brush, and when they had gotten the horses sheltered up against an overhang of the hills and rubbed them down and fed them, then he felt that he could breathe again and he had a little appetite for the fireless supper they made.

"Tomorrow," he said anxiously, "we will camp here, and I will go a little down the way and bring back forage for the horses—I do not think we ought to stir out of here for a few days. Listen to me!" he said, as she began to answer him. "Whatever you ask, I will do, you know that. But hear me out. Time will serve us. If it takes us months—we will live to get to Mante."

"No," she said. "No. We have no months. We have no days. Does thee understand me? This Skarrin—this lord in Mante—" She fell silent again, leaning her chin on her arm, resting on her knee, and there was a line between her brows, in the fading of the light. "There are *qhal* and there are *qhal*, and Skarrin's is an old name, Vanye, a very old name."

"Do you know him?"

"If he is what I think he is—I know *what* he is; and I tell thee there is no risk we have ever run—" Her fist clenched. "Only believe what I tell thee: we have no time with this man."

"*What* is he?"

"Something I hoped did not exist. Perhaps I am wrong." She sighed and worked the fingers of that hand. "Talk of something else."

"Of what?"

"Of anything."

He drew a breath. He cast back. It was Morija came to mind. It always did. But darker things overshadowed it—a keep surrounded with flood. A forest, haunted with things which did not love human or *qhal*. Of his cousin. But that was a memory too fraught with dark things too.

"At least we are warmer," he said, desperate recourse to the weather.

"And dry," she said.

"Good grazing here. A few days," he said. "*Liyo*—we can rest a few days. The horses will not take more of this."

"Vanye—"

"Forgive me."

"No, thee is right, but we have no choice. Vanye—I *had* no choice."

It was not their moving on that she meant. Her voice trembled.

"I know that," he said, no steadier.

She looked at him and reached out to his arm, a light touch which jolted him like hot iron, drew him out of despair and absorbed his attention so thoroughly a score of enemies could have ridden down on them and come second in his mind.

No, he had wit to think, but not much beyond that. Her arms clenched about him. Her mouth met his. There was precious little more to do, surrounded by enemies, under arms, with no rest to be had and no leisure to spend unwary.

There will never be a time, he thought, in a chill of panic, and held her the tighter, as she held him, in an armored grip become harsh and desperate, with nothing of gentleness about it. *Everyone else has failed her. Too much she has lost, too many dead—For that reason she armed me more than herself, gave me her chiefest weapon; and what did it win us but calamity to our friends, and rage at each other?*

They slept finally, turn and turn about, on the sloping, stony ground where the brush afforded them cover. He watched her as she slept. He wished—but there was no hope.

Only they managed to heal what was torn, there was that much.

Morgaine waked him toward dawn, a shadow between him and the day. He heard her voice telling him there was breakfast and he murmured an answer, rolled over and favored an aching arm, holding it across him.

"We should move," she said, "a little ways this morning."

"Oh, Heaven," he moaned, and bowed his head between his knees, arms over his neck.

She did not stay to argue. She went back to sit on her saddle, where she had laid out a cold breakfast on the leather wrappings they used for foodstuffs, knowing matters would go her way.

He followed, and sat down on the grass, and ate in silence no different than other silences.

And did not give way to temper, or venture in headlong.

"*Liyo*," he said when he was toward finishing: "Listen to me. This enemy of yours—whoever he is. You think he will run. But a man will not run, who thinks himself winning. No one can be that cautious."

She said nothing. It was not a frown on her face, only thought.

"Let them lose us," he said. "Let this Skarrin marshal some defense against us. Let him think he has turned us. A man in power—he will not want to give up what he has. He will go nowhere at all. In the meanwhile we will learn this land, we will go slowly—we will gather strength, rest, find a way to him—am I not right?"

Her lips made a taut line. There was warfare in her eyes, unbelief and consideration. "Possibly. Possibly. But being wrong, Vanye—"

"What will a man do who is cornered? He is far more apt to use the gate at Mante and escape us."

He argued for their lives, for sanity and safety.

And she gathered that *thing* into her lap in silence, the sword, that weapon which was constantly beside her, day and night, and which gave them no peace.

"*Liyo*, you drive this man and you force this man, and what will he do? You will unseat him; his own vassals will question his power, or you will make him desperate—you always strike too hard, *liyo*—listen to me: you know no moderation with your enemies. You give them no choices and while they have no warning, that serves you well—but you have no subtlety in the field. You are the kind of lord who loses lives—forgive me." His heart beat hard and he gazed up into her eyes in a dread of the things he had to say with brutal force, that the numbness of recent sleep let him say without stumbling, and the quiet of the dawn let her hear without preventing him. "If it were an army with us I should never question you: if you told me to go against any odds, then, I would do that, and trust there was good cause. But you have no army. You have one man. And he is bound, *liyo*, to cover your back and your side, as long as he can; and he will do that. But he is one man, all the same, and someday, if you keep on as you are, you will lose him, because he will die before he lets you go down first."

The frown had deepened on her face. There was storm in her eyes. "I can guard my own back. I need no fools to kill themselves, plague take you, I have had enough of fools to fling themselves in my way—"

"It is your back I am talking about."

Her breath came hard. His own did. "And I am talking about fools," she said. "Bron's sort. Chei's sort. Arunden, for another." Her enemies saw that look. It had been a long time since she had turned it on him. "Ten thousand men at Irien, who would not hold where I told them to hold, no, they must get to the fore of me, because I am there and their damnable pride makes them do what no lord could order them to do in cold blood, if it means charging a wide open gate—"

"That is what you are doing now. That is what I am objecting to, *liyo*. Do you not see it?"

There was shock in her eyes, and outrage, a shake of her head. "Thee is—"

"I am telling you that you are *wrong*. I do not do that often. And you do not want to hear me because you suppose I do not want the same thing that you want. But that is how much I love you: I do not know enough to understand all the why of the things you do, but I stake my soul that you are right; I have sworn to go on with or without you, *liyo*, and if that is true, then listen to me, will you listen, if you do not think me an utter fool?"

"I am listening," she said in a different and milder voice.

"Be the wind. Do not make our enemy afraid. If he hears reports what happened south of here, he will use his power. He has men to send. He has ten thousand things to try before he is out of resources. He will not run at the first whisper of war. He will attack. And we will be the wind again and go find him in his lair."

"So easily. Did thee ever take Myya?"

Heaven! she has a sharp edge when the swords are out.

"No," he said reasonably, quietly. It is tactic. Lord in Heaven, she knows only the attack, never defense, even with me. "But then, I was one man. They did not take me. And if I had aimed at the Myya-lord's life, I would have taken him, do you doubt it?"

She thought on that point, long and long, with that worried line between her brow.

"*Liyo*, they are all about us. They are watching the road. All we need do is stay quiet, and I do not think, I cannot believe that the rumor of a rumor will send this *qhal*-lord running with his tail tucked. No. Being a man used to power, he will likeliest strike first at his own folk, to subdue any disloyalty, and only then think of us; and when he hears we are only two—"

"With a gate-weapon. *That* is what we may well face if he has time to marshal his strength. Whatever he has, he will use."

"He might use it by the time we could get there. We *cannot* go there with enough speed. And we would be spent. So let him lay his plans. We can turn them."

She let go her breath, and slid *Changeling* between her knees, hands on the quillons that were the dragon's arms, resting her head against the hilt.

Very, very long she rested there—thinking, he knew, thinking and thinking.

He rested too, arm on knee and chin on arm, wondering where her thoughts were going, into what nooks that she would report to him, unraveling all his arguments, going far beyond him, telling him new and terrible things.

Then she lifted her head. "Aye," she said. "But it is a fearful risk, Vanye."

All along, he had used argument like weapons in drill—one tactic, the next, the next in despair that any would suffice: only now he heard what she was saying and realized it was agreement.

Then, as always when he had won some lesser point, the doubts came to him. What he truly, at the depth of his heart, yearned for, was for his liege to bring up some miracle, some assurance that she knew precisely how to get into Mante and overcome their enemy.

Knowing that she had no such resource, and that she surrendered her instincts for berserker attack, to his for stealth and stalking, against an enemy of her own kind—

It was as if a weight had come down on him, of the sort that he was not accustomed to bear. And perhaps some of it had left her shoulders. She gazed at him with an expression he could not read, but a less anguished one—perhaps thinking, perhaps planning again, at a range still beyond him.

He earnestly hoped so. For when it came to *qhal*, he had no idea at all of their limits.

ꙮ Chapter 12

The riders gathered again in a place near the road, and Chei leaned on the saddle of the big roan, weary, and feeling the weight of the mail on his shoulders, in a dizziness in which his very body seemed diminished, the light dimmed, the voices about him become strange, calling him 'my lord' and speaking to him with courtesies. The *qhal* who served him were not confused. Certainly a few of the humans with him measured the difference in his stature and saw his apparent youth and thought treasonous thoughts, but had they lifted daggers against him, there were enough of his own folk about him to protect him, and there was the captain of Skarrin's warders, who was bound, under present and ironical circumstance, to protect him.

They were a few more than twoscore—of all that company that had left Morund-keep, of the levies; and ten—those men of Skarrin's who had joined them at Tejhos-gate. The rest were dead or scattered or wounded too severely to continue; and it had needed at least half a score men to leave in charge of the wounded, but he had left six and bidden them stay camped where they were for fear the hillmen might hit them on the way back to Morund. That was how desperate things had become.

This open sky is madness, Chei thought. The open blue above them, the land laid open to any witness, shivered through his nerves as if he lay naked to his enemies, though he remembered fighting in such land before, in times that humans had come deep within the plains. Something deep as instinct pulled him in two directions, and feared nameless things.

Most of all, the one he would have turned to for advice was not there, and whenever he turned and looked about him he missed that face, which shifted and changed from silver-haired to red to palest gold like some reflection in troubled water: Pyverrn. Jestryn. Bron. The void ached in him, in a place where the voices could not reach, a point at which all memory found anchor.

Qhiverin-Gault-Chei, all alone among the men who followed him, longed for a familiar haven, even if the nature of it confounded itself between stone walls and the closeness of forest—

But his enemy, the enemy which lay hidden somewhere in this place, did not shift like sun on water: of him, of her, of the man he was and the man who pursued, he could not think clearly at all: it was like trying to look at the sun itself, a glare in which no shape was distinguishable.

"The troops from Mante are coming south to meet us," he told his followers, as he paced the red horse along the roadside, where they formed up. "The captain affirms that. We will have reinforcements. And we will not close with our enemy, now we know what we face." The red horse shifted under him and he curbed it, riding it back and forth past his listeners, silver-haired and dark, *qhal* and human. "But there are other ways. Those of you who have been loyal to me—I will reward after this. Count on it. Those of you who are human I will gift with land. Do you hear me? For those of you who follow me, I will give you the holdings of every man who fled. I will have it known how I pay loyalty— and deserters. We will settle this business, we will settle it on our terms, and give Mante's troops the leavings. Our enemies have gone into the land, that is what they have done; but they do not know their way—and we do. I want this pair. *I want them.* Need I say how much?"

"I have found a place," Vanye said, when they found each other after scouting afoot up and down the area, the gray horse and the white left in hiding the other side of the hill.

"Good," Morgaine said, wiping her brow, "because there is nothing in the other direction."

It was a place they rode to then, where the rains had washed beneath a sandstone cap, and where still a little water ran in a sandy bed, folded on either side by hills and closed round by thorn and a scattered few trees.

And no better place to hide indeed had they found.

It was cold rations and not so much as fire to boil water, but it was rest; it was respite from the pace they had set, and it was a chance for the horses to recover their strength, if it meant walking afield and bringing grass to them to keep them hidden.

So he did, and curried them both till their coats shone, did a bit of work with Siptah's left hind shoe, and afterward lay in the sun and slept, while Morgaine worked at the horses' trail-worn gear. Then it was turn about while she slept, and after that a leisurely supper of cold sausage and cheese and waybread.

It was the last of the cordial they shared, the last sweet taste of arrhendur honey.

They watched the sun go down over the hill in a film of cloud and silken colors, and they sat a while under a golden twilight, leaned shoulder against shoulder and watched the horses drink from the rill and eat the forage he had gotten for them in places he did not think cutting would be evident.

He was content. Morgaine leaned back against the hill and smiled at him in her turn, one of her rare, kindly smiles. The quiet, and the brief, fond glance of her eyes set his heart to racing as if they were both be-spelled. Twilight touched her slanted cheekbones, touched her gray eyes and silver hair and the edges of the mail of her over-sleeves, the black leather, the buckles of her armor, and—like a watchful familiar, the dragon-sword lying beside her against a stone. Its ruby eyes winked red and wicked.

I am here, it said. *I never sleep.*

But it was familiar to him too. Like Morgaine—her silences, the little shifts of her expression which he could read or thought he read—as now he read something in her level, continual stare which had the silence of the night about it, and the dying light dancing in gray, *qhalur* eyes and a face every line of which he knew in his sweetest and most terrible dreams.

"How long," she said at last, "does thee think to camp here?"

He frowned as he found himself suddenly back in an argument he had thought he had just won. "*Liyo,* do not think of it. Do not think of when. *Stay camped,* do nothing. Do not move or stir: let the enemy do that, that is my counsel in the matter."

"Until winter sets in?" A frown leapt to her eyes. "It—"

"A few days, for Heaven's own sake. A few days. Five. I do not know."

He had not wanted debate with her. He found his muscles gone tense, his breathing quickened; and she dejectedly flung a pebble into the little rill that ran at their feet.

Fret and fret, she would; she could not stay still, could not delay, could not rest, as if no other thought would stay in her head.

"We cannot wait here for the snows."

"God in Heaven, *listen* to me. Let them move. Let us find out what they will do. That is the purpose of this."

"In the meanwhile—"

"God help us. Tomorrow—tomorrow I will scout out and around."

"*We* will," she said.

"You can stay in—"

"We can gain a few leagues north. That is all. If the next camp is not so comfortable, then the one after—"

He rested his brow against his joined hands. "Aye."

"Vanye, I take your advice—we go slowly. We let the horses build back their strength. But we dare not be further from that gate than we can reach—whatever the lord in Mante decides to do."

"Let him! Whatever he will do, let him! He will come after us. He will try us. He will not bolt."

"We are risking everything on that. Thee knows."

"Why?" he asked. "Tell me why this lord should leave his people?"

"It is possible that they are *not* his people."

He had thought that he had the shape of things, in this strange war that stretched from land to land, with curving horizons and stars too few or too many and moons that came and went. He tried to make a wise answer to that, so she should not think all her teaching wasted.

"You mean that he might be a human man, in *qhalur* shape."

"It is the name," she said.

"Skarrin?" It had no *qhalur* sound. But there were *qhal* who had uncommon names.

"It is a name in a very old language. I do not know where he should have heard it. Perhaps it is all chance. Languages have coincidence. But this, on a *qhal*—this name: there are among the gate worlds, a kind older than the *qhal*. And such of them as survive—are very dangerous."

"What are you saying—older than the *qhal*? Who is older?"

"Older than the calamity the *qhal* know. Did I ever say it had only happened but the once?"

He said nothing. He scarcely understood the first calamity, how the *qhal* had made the gates and made time flow amiss, till Heaven set matters straight again, or as straight as matters could be, where gates remained live and potent, pouring their magics *(their power,* Morgaine insisted, *do not be superstitious)* into worlds where *qhal* survived.

"Thee does not understand."

He shook his head ruefully. "No."

"I do not know," she said. "Only the name troubles me. A name and not a name. In that language Skarrin means an outsider. A foreigner."

The dark was gathering. The first stars were out. He crossed himself against the omen, whatever it should mean.

"My father," Morgaine said, "was one such."

He looked at her as if some chasm had opened at his feet, and all of it dark. She had named comrades from before his time—from before he or his father before him was ever born.

Of kin she had never spoken. She might have risen out of the elements, out of moonbeams, out of the tales of his people.

I am not qhal, she had said time and again. And at one time: *I am halfling.*

"Are you saying this Skarrin—then—is kin of yours?"

"None, that I know."

"Who *was* your father?"

"An enemy." She cast another pebble into the darkening water, and did not look at him. "In a land before yours. He is dead. Let it rest."

He would not have trod on that ground for any urging.

"He was *qhal*, to your way of thinking," Morgaine said. "Give it peace. It has no significance here. Anjhurin was his name. You have heard it. Now forget ever you heard it. This Skarrin is no one I know, but my name might warn him, changed as it is."

He took in his breath and let it go again, stripping a bit of grass in his fingers, looking only at that. And for a long time neither of them spoke.

He shrugged. "I will scout out tomorrow," he said, to have the peace back, to ease her mind, however he could. "When I go for forage. There might be something over the hills."

"Aye," she said, and shifted round to lean her shoulder against his back. He sighed at the relief that gave the center of his back, against the armor-weight. "But two of us would—"

"I. Do we need start every bird and rabbit 'twixt us and Mante?" He felt a sense of impending calamity, such that his breath came in with a shiver, and he let it go again. "I will go."

"Afoot?"

"No. I can ride the stream-course. There will be no difficulty." He sighed against her weight on his shoulders, and looked at the sky in which the stars had begun to appear. "We should rest," he said sullenly.

"Is thee angry?"

He drew in his breath, and shifted about to face her. *Aye*, he was about to say. But the sober, gentle look she gave him was rare enough he hesitated to offend it.

She was always and always the same, always devil-driven, always restless, incapable even of reason.

And she had brought them through, always, somehow—was always beforehand, always quicker than her enemies expected, and not *where* they expected.

She might drive a sane man mad.

"Vanye?" she asked.

"*What more?*" he said shortly.

She was silent then, and sat back with a wounded look that shot through him and muddled all the anger he could muster.

It was not, not, Heaven knew, the face she turned to the world. Only to him. Only to him, in all the world.

He got to his feet and snatched up a wildflower at his other side, knelt and solemnly offered the poor thing to her, all closed up for the night as it was. Bruised, it had a strong grass smell, the smell of spring lilies, that reminded him suddenly of rides on a brown pony, of—Heaven knew—his boyhood.

Her eyes sought up to his. Her mouth curved at the edges, and solemnly she took it, her fingers brushing his hand. "Is this all thee offers?"

"Aye," he said, off his balance in his foolishness: she always had the better of him with words—was not, he suddenly thought, taking it for a jest; or was; he did not know, suddenly; it was like everything between them. He gestured desperately beyond his shoulder. "Or," he said briskly, deliberately perverse, "I might find others, if I walked along the stream there. I might bring you a handful."

Her eyes lightened, went solemn then, and slowly she rose up to her knees and put her arms about his neck, whereat the world went giddy as the smell of flowers.

"Do it tomorrow," she said, a long moment later; and gently she began the buckles of his armor, that she had helped him with a hundred times to different purpose.

Changeling slipped from its place and fell with a rattle as they made themselves a nest there of their cloaks and blankets. She reached out and laid the dragon sword down beside them, the hilt toward her hand, and loosed his hair from the ivory pin.

So he laid his own sword, close by the other side. They never quite forgot. There had been too many ambushes, that they could ever quite forget.

It was up and prepare to move at sunrise, in the dewy chill and the damp; and Vanye shut his eyes, wrapped in his blanket, leaning his back against Morgaine's knee and letting her comb and braid his hair this morning, carefully and at leisure, which a lady might do for her man. He sighed in that quiet, and that contentment.

There was no blight could touch the hour, nothing at all wrong with the world or with anyone in it, and the quick deft touch of Morgaine's fingers near lulled him to sleep again. He shut his eyes till she pushed his head forward to plait the braid, and rested so, head bowed, till she tied it off and brought it through and pinned it in its simple knot at the back of his neck.

So she was done with him. So it was time to think about the day. He leaned his head back against her knees and sighed to a touch of her fingers pulling at a lock by his temple. "Does thee intend to tie this someday? Or go blind by degrees?"

"Do what you like." No blade came on an *uyo's* hair, except for judicious barbering, at his own hand. But his hair was twice hacked and hewn and grown out again, and truth, some of it was often in his eyes. "Cut it," he said, nerving himself. His Kurshin half was aghast. But it was Chya clan which had taken him from his outlawry, it was a Chya he served, it had been a Chya who had proved his true kinsman; and a Chya was what he became, less and less careful of proprieties. He faced about and leaned on one hand, while she took her Honor-blade and cut the straying lock; and cut it again, and cut another.

At that he opened his mouth to protest, then shut his eyes to keep the hair out and bit his lip.

"It was another one."

"Aye," he said. He was determined not to be superstitious; he prepared himself to see her cast the locks away, he would not play the fool with her, not make her think him simple.

But she played him that kind of turn she did so often, and put the locks of hair into his hand as if she had known Kurshin ways.

He scattered them on the moving water, since they had no fire; so any omen was gone, and no one could harm his soul.

And he turned on his knee and settled again on both knees, like a man who would make a request.

"*Liyo*—"

"I have a name."

She had had some lover before him. He knew that now. But into that he did not ever want to ask. Folly to look back, profoundest folly, and against all her counsel—

She had so little she could part with. Least of all her purposes.

"Morgaine," he said, whispered. Her name was ill-omen. It burned with the legends of kings and sorceries, and too much of death. Morgaine Angharan was the other face, not the one he loved. For the woman he knew, he did not have a name at all. But he tried to fit that one around her, and took both her hands in his as he knelt and she sat on a stone as it were some high queen's throne, under the last few stars. "Listen, my liege—"

"Do not you kneel," she said harshly, and clenched her hands on his. "How often have I told thee?"

"Well, it is my habit." He began to get up; then sank back again, jaw set. "It still is."

"You are a free man."

"Well, then, I do what I please, do I not? And since you are a lord, my lady-liege, and since I am only *dai-uyo* at best, I still call you my liege and I still go on my knees when I see fit, for decency, my liege. And I ask you—" She started to speak and he pressed her hands, hard. "While I am gone, stay close, take no chances, and for the love of Heaven—trust me, however long. If I meet trouble I can wait it out until they leave. If I have to wonder about your riding into it, then I have to do something else. So do me the grace and wait here, and be patient. Then neither of us will have to worry, is that not reasonable?"

"Aye," she said quietly. "But turn and turn about. The next one is mine."

"*Liyo*—"

But he had already lost that argument for the time. He gathered himself up and dusted off his knees, and went to saddle Arrhan.

The land was difficult beyond the camp they had made—little wooded, flatter for a space: he had known that much when he had chosen the camp they had, a retreat from the furthermost point he had reached in his last searching.

Now it was careful riding, by every low spot he could find that could shelter them as they went, and a good deal of it east rather than north. It was the watercourses he had most hope in, and most fear of: it was water that bound a man to his course in land like this, water by which their enemies could find them, nearly as surely as they might have by the Road itself.

But he spent some time afoot, and finally flat on his belly on a hill from which he had vantage, scanning every rabbit-track in the grassland below, every flight of birds, and listening—listening finally alone, until the sounds of the land began to speak to him, the ordinary chirp of insects in the sun, the birds that ought to sing in the thicket and out on the meadows.

He was alone. There was no one out there: he was as sure of that as he dared be sure of anything with an unknown enemy.

Still—he found no sane way to cross that plain, except to go far to the east and as the stream bore: to cross it even by night, would leave a track plain enough for a child to follow the next day.

That was no good. If they did that, there was no good choice but to pick up speed again, and then they would be no better off than before.

A plague on her haste and her insistence. He lay with his chin on his hand and with the sun on his back overheating the layers of armor, and considered again what his chances were of reporting to her and gaining her agreement, after a day's delay, that the proper course was not northward, but considerably eastward and out of the direct course she wanted to take.

Her anger when it came to her safety was a matter of indifference to him—except that his liege, having gotten a purpose in her mind, was likely to strike out on her own in what direction she chose, leaving him to follow; and that prospect left him contemplating arguments, and reason, and unreason, and the fact that he had no means but force truly to restrain her—and restrain her by that means, he could not, by *ilin*-oath, by *uyin*-oath, by the deeper things between them, not to save either of their lives, so long as she was in her right mind.

And Heaven help them both, she was oftener right even when she was not sane, or at least retrieved her mistakes with more deftness than anyone he knew; and he was still uneasy that he had persuaded her against her instincts. Doubt ate at his gut, a continual moil of anxiety in all this ride out here separate of her, and the only solace in it was the knowledge that she was well-situated, in no likelihood of attracting attention, and in a way to defend herself if trouble happened on her.

It was that things had shifted between them, he told himself; it was the muddle things had gotten to that made him unreasonably anxious. They sinned before Heaven with his oath and hers, and with no priest, and with ten thousand trifling laws he had no regard of—laws it was mad to regard, when there were so many greater and bloody sins on them.

He was half-witted with thinking about her, he had done what he had sworn he would never do and let that thinking come between them in daylight, using that bond to gain his way—he had done one thing after another he had sworn he would not do with her. Decisions that she would make, he had argued to take onto his shoulders when he well knew he was not, of the two of them, the wiser—

If he were back in Myya lands, he thought, with his cousins hunting him, he would lie low for the whole day exactly where he had left Arrhan down under the hill. He would watch everything that moved by day, every hawk that flew, every start of game; and move again only at night. But Morgaine was left worrying back there; and he could never have persuaded her to wait day upon day on him—he could not bear the worry of it himself, to be truthful, if matters were reversed; or keep her still beyond half a day as matters were, unless he could demonstrate some danger to her.

It was a long effort for their enemies to search all the watercourses in the plains.

But long efforts bore fruit, if they had long enough.

And having thought that three times through, he could not rest where he was and he could not risk anything further. He edged down off the height and gathered up Arrhan where he had left her in a brushy hollow; and led her by the dry streambed which had been his route up to this hill.

It merged with yet another narrow water-cut, and took him back into sparsely wooded hills.

Then he mounted up and rode, quietly, back the way he had come, far and far through the hills to the place where the dry bed joined the water.

Beyond that he rode the stream itself for a space, the water only scarcely over Arrhan's hooves, but it served.

It served, certainly, better than the streamside had served another rider. He saw the mark among bent reeds, the water-filled impression of a horse's hoof, and searched his mind whether Arrhan had misstepped when he had passed this bank in the morning.

No, he thought, with the blood going colder and colder in him. No. She had not. Not here. They had gone straight along as they went now, making no track at all. He remembered the reeds. He remembered the little shelf of rock where it came down from the hill.

He saw the track merge with the stream further on, a single rider.

Morgaine would not have broken her word to him without reason. He believed that implicitly. She would not have followed, except something had gone very wrong.

There were further marks, down the stream where the water became momentarily and treacherously deeper and a rider had to take to the waterside. He had done so. So had this rider; and one mark showed a shod horse, a shoe of a pattern different than Siptah's and headed the wrong direction.

There was cold dread in him now. He scanned the hills about him.

If he had been in Myya lands again, his Myya cousins looking to have his head on a pike, he would do what he had told Morgaine he would do: he would go to earth and lie close until the hunters had passed and failed to find him for a fortnight or more.

But then he had not had a woman waiting for him, in the direction the rider was going, camped right on the stream-course as if it were some roadside, now the hunters were out. She would not be sitting blind: she would have vantage from higher on the hill—he took that for granted. But there was the horse to worry for—more visible, and tracking the ground despite all they could do to keep cover. If someone rode through, looking with a skilled eye—never grant that every man in Gault's party was a fool, even granted one of them had been careless enough to let his horse misstep in this thread of a stream.

He put Arrhan to more speed. He scanned the hills about him, dreading the sight of riders, finding only, in one place between the hills, a fan of tracks in the grass, as riders had come together and joined forces.

Thereafter tracks met the stream and the bank was well-trampled, the mud churned by the hooves of more than a score of horses.

He followed, trying desperately to recollect every stone and every vantage of the camp they had. It was well enough, he thought: their numbers were only an advantage—they could not go silently, Heaven knew that they were no woodsmen, the way they bunched together; and Morgaine with the least of her weapons could take them, once she had taken some position of defense: the greatest worry she must have was whether her companion was going to come riding in to put himself in danger.

Only—he thought of the pyx he wore against his heart and thought of gate-weapons with a lingering chill—it might not be Gault's folk. It might be something else, out of Mante.

Even if it were not, she would hesitate to use the sword that was her chiefest weapon, for fear of alerting other forces Mante might have sent out southward to find them—

Or through the gate at Tejhos, coming at them from both sides.

Heaven knew what their limit was.

And if one of them had so much as what he carried, it could reshape *Changeling*'s gate-force, warp it and draw it in such fashion that *Changeling* became wildly unpredictable, a danger to flesh and substance anywhere between: he had seen one of the *arrhim*, a gate-warder, brave that danger in the arrhend war—and lose—which sight haunted him every time he thought of what he carried.

The gift was for way-finding, was for light in dark places, for startling an ignorant enemy but not as a weapon—never as that, for someone who rode as shieldman to Morgaine Angharan.

He dared not use it now, in any hope of warning her. He had given his sword to Chei and not reclaimed it—not, in all else they had done, turned him out utterly defenseless.

He had no weapon now but his bow.

And Heaven knew how far he was behind.

He listened as he rode the center of the stream, close to their camp. He stopped Arrhan where there was brush enough to hide her, and slid down, and stood for a moment steadying her so that he could hear the least stirring of the wind.

A bird sang, natural, long-running song, but it was not a sound that reassured him. There were the tracks, evident now at this muddy bank, and hours old.

Now it was a hard choice what to do. There was no safe place further than this. He took one risk, and made a faint, careful bird-call: I am here, that said, no more than that.

No answer came to him.

He bit his lip furiously, and put a secure tie on Arrhan, took his bow and quiver and slipped away into the brush, onto the hillside. He was not afraid, not yet. There were too many answers. There was every chance she had heard him and dared not risk an answer.

He went hunter-fashion, stopping often to listen. He found the tracks again where he picked up the stream course; and when he had come within sight of the place where they had camped, beneath the hill, Siptah was gone, and with one glance he was reassured.

Good, he thought, she has taken him, the tack is gone.

But there were marks of the enemy's horses, abundant there, trampling on Siptah's and Arrhan's marks, and no matter the skill of the rider, there was no way not to leave some manner of a trail for a good tracker well sure where that trail began.

She would lead them, that was what she would do. She would lead them around this hill and that until they came straight into one of her ambushes.

But so many riders had gone away from this point, left and right, obliterating any tracks the gray stud might have made, the tracks they could have followed; and left him the necessity to cast about beyond the trampled area—and cast about widely he could not, without risking ambush.

Best, he thought, find out what was still here.

He moved, crouched behind what cover there was, along the flank of the hill, among the rocks, stopping now and again to listen. There was nothing astir but the wind.

Then a bird flew up, taking wing east of his backtrail.

He froze where he was, a long time, shifting only the minuscule degree that kept his legs from cramping.

A bird-call sounded, directly on his track.

He calmly, carefully scanned the hillsides and the points of concealment so far as he could from his own cover, not willing to give way to any feeling, not fear, not self-reproach for anything he might have done and not done: there was only the immediate necessity to get off this hillside and take the enemy, whatever had happened behind him, else he might never find her.

He waited what he judged long enough to make them impatient, then moved, quietly, behind what cover the brush and the rocks afforded, without retracing his steps into what might now be tracking him.

They meant him to go to his horse. They had found Arrhan, that was what had happened, and they were effectively advising him where the ambush was, and where he had to go, if he did not want to flee them afoot.

Where is she? was his constant thought. The whole area had become hostile ground, enemy marks everywhere, his horse discovered, and no sign of Morgaine.

If she had heard the bird-calls, she was at least warned.

He sank down behind a rock to wait a moment, to see what they would do, and there was not a sound, not a stir below.

Not even the wind breathed.

Then a pebble rolled, somewhere on the bare rock around the shoulder of the hill above him. A step whispered across stone and left it again.

Carefully he took three arrows from his quiver and fitted one to the string, braced himself comfortably and waited with the bow unbent, not to cramp his arm, for one quick shot if need be.

The step came closer and the sweat ran on his brow and down his sides, one prickling trail and another.

The sound stopped a moment, then advanced again, a man walking on the rock a moment, then disturbing the brush.

He drew a breath and bent the bow all in one motion.

And held his shot in a further intake of breath as a man in a bright mail shirt saw him and slid down the crumbling hill face. His bow tracked the target.

"Vanye," Chei breathed, landing on two feet in front of him. "For God's sake—I followed you. I *have* been following you. What did you expect when you told me go back? Put that down!"

"*Where is she?*"

"Gone. Put down the bow. Vanye—for God's sake—I saw them pass; I followed them. There was nothing I could do—"

"Where is she?"

"Northward. That is where they will have taken her."

His heart went to ice. He kept the bow aimed, desperate, and motioned with it. "Clear my path."

"Will you kill me too?" Chei's eyes were wide and outraged. "Is that what you do with your friends?"

"Out of my way."

"Your *friends*, Vanye," Chei repeated, and flattened himself against the rock as he edged past. "Do you know the word? *Vanye!*"

He turned from Chei to the way ahead, to run, remembering even then the whistle he had heard downslope; and saw an archer standing in his path as a weight smashed down between his shoulders and staggered him.

He rolled, straight down the hillside, tucked his shoulder in a painful tangle of armor straps and bow and quiver. His helm came off; he lost the bow; and went up-ended and down again on the grass of the slope.

He came up blind, and ripped his Honor-blade from its sheath, hearing the running steps and the rattle of armor, seeing a haze of figures gathering about him on the hillside, above and below him.

"Take him alive!" someone shouted. "Move!"

He yelled out at them and chose a target and a way out, cut at a *qhal* who missed his defense, met him with a shock of steel against leather and flesh; but in that stroke his foot skidded on the bloody grass and there was another enemy on him, with more coming. He recovered his balance on both feet and laid about him with a clear-minded choice of threats, finding the rhythm of their attacks and their hesitations for a moment; and then losing it as other attackers swarmed in at another angle.

A man, falling, seized him by the leg. He staggered and others hit him and wrapped a hold about him, inside his guard; and overbalanced him and bore him down in a skidding mass of bodies.

They brought up against a rock together. It jolted the men who held him and he smashed an elbow into one body and a fist into another's head as he struggled free and levered himself toward his feet, staggering against the tilted surface as he tried to clear his knife hand of the dazed man who clung to it.

Steps rushed on him, a shadow loomed out of the sun at his right, and others hit him, carrying him backward against the rock. The point of a sword pressed beneath his chin and forced his head back.

Chei's face cleared out of the haze and the glare, Chei's face with a grin like the wolves themselves, and a half a score of *qhalur* and human faces behind him.

"Ah," Chei said, "very close, friend. But not good enough."

⌒ Chapter 13

They flung him down on the trampled ground of the streamside, and he did not know for a moment where he was, except it was Chei sitting cross-legged on the grass, and Chei's face was a mask behind which lived something altogether foreign.

Chei was dead, as Bron was dead. He knew it now. As many of these men's comrades were dead, several wounded, and he was left alone with them to pay for it. That was the logic he understood. It was not an unreasonable attitude in men or *qhal*, not unreasonable what they had done in the heat of their anger, with a man who had cost them three dead on the selfsame hillside.

Not unreasonable that Chei should look on him now as he did, coldly—if it were Chei and Chei's reasons. But it was not. He was among men who fed their enemies to beasts.

Morgaine, he thanked Heaven, had ridden clear. She had escaped them, he was sure of it. She had ridden out, she was free out there, and armed with all her weapons.

She might well be anywhere in the country round about. Heaven knew, the same stream that had covered his tracks could cover hers—in the opposite direction, he thought; toward the Road; which their enemies must have thought of, and searched, and failed.

She might have fled toward the north and east as the Road led, thinking to find him by cutting into the country along the way; but that was so remote a chance. Gone on to the Gate itself . . . that was possible; but he did not think so: she would not ride off and leave him to fall into ambush.

Unless . . . O God, unless she were wounded, and had no choice.

And he did not reckon he would have the truth from these men by asking for it.

"Why are you here?" Chei asked him, as if he had a list of questions in mind and any of them would do. "Where do you come from? Where are you going?"

They had not so much as bound him. It was hard enough to lift his cheek from the mire and regard Chei through whatever was running into his eyes and blurring his vision.

"She has authority to be here," he said, which he reckoned for the truth, and perhaps enough to daunt a *qhal.*

"Are you full human?"

He nodded and shifted his position, and whatever was dripping, started down his cheek. He dragged his arms under him, and felt, beneath the mail and leather, the pressure of the little box against his heart. They had not discovered it. He prayed Heaven they would not, though they had taken his other weapons, from Honor-blade to boot knife. And the arrhendur sword in Chei's lap he well remembered.

"Is she *qhal?*"

He had answered that so often he had lied before he realized it, a nod of his head. "Aye."

"Are you her lover?"

He did not believe he had heard that question. He was outraged. Then he knew it was one most dangerous to him. And that Chei in Chei's own mind— had his own opinion. "No," he said. "I am her servant."

"Who gave her that weapon?"

"Its maker. Dead now. In my homeland." His arms trembled under him. It was the cold of the ground and the shock of injury. Perhaps also it was fear. There was enough cause for that. "Long ago—" he began, taking breath against the pain in his gut. "Something happened with the gates. It is still happening— somewhere, she says. Against that, the sword was made. Against that—"

"Bring that thing near a gate, Man, and there will *be* death enough."

He started to agree. Then it came to him that they seemed to know—at what range from a gate the sword was too perilous to use. And that put Morgaine in danger.

"What does she seek in Mante?"

The tremors reached his shoulders, tensed his gut so that the pain went inward, and he wished, for his pride's sake, he could only prevent the shaking from his voice.

"What does she seek in Mante?"

"What she would have sought in Morund," he said, "if we had not had other advice."

Chei? he wondered, gazing into that face. Chei? Is there anything left?

Can you remember, man? Is there anything human?

"What advice would that be?"

"That you were unreasonable. Chei knows." He heaved himself upward another hand's-breadth to ease the pain in his hip, where they had kicked him, and the tendon there was bruised. He determined to sit up and risk a cracked skull from the ones behind him; and discovered that there was no part of him that their kicks or the butts of their lances had not gotten to. It was blood running down his face. It splashed dark onto his leg when he sat up, and he wiped at the cut on his brow with a muddy hand. "My lady's mission here—you very well know."

"Death," Chei said, "ultimate death—for every *qhal*."

"She intends no harm to you—"

"Death."

It seemed the sum of things. There was no peace, then, once the *qhal*-lords knew what Morgaine purposed with the gates. He gazed bleakly at Chei, and said nothing.

"Where will your lady have gone?"

"To Mante."

"No," Chei said quietly. "I doubt that she has. I *remember*, friend. I remember a night in Arunden's camp—you and she together—do you recollect that?"

He did. There was altogether too much Chei knew; and he despaired now of all the rest.

"I rather imagine," Chei said, "that your lady is somewhere in these hills. I rather imagine that she would have tried to warn you—if she could reach you in time. Failing that—she will follow if we move. If we were foolish enough to kill you, then she might even come looking for revenge—would she not?"

"I do not know," he said. "She might well have ridden for Mante."

"I do not think so," Chei said. "I think she is waiting for dark."

He said nothing. He tensed muscles, testing whether he could rely on his legs if he made a lunge for Chei's throat. To kill this man might at least keep some knowledge out of the hands of the *qhal*.

It might put some enemy less dangerous in command of this band, at least.

"I think," Chei said, "she will come close to see whether you are alive. Afoot, by stealth. And perhaps for your sake she might come and talk to us a little closer."

"Set me free," Vanye said. "I will find her and give her whatever message you wish. And come back to you."

There was startled laughter.

"I am Kurshin," Vanye said. "I do not break an oath."

Chei regarded him in silence a long time, eyes flickering slowly, curiously, as if he might be reaching deep into something not *qhal* and not familiar to him. The laughter died away.

"Chei?" Vanye said, ever so quietly, seeking after whatever balance might have shifted.

"Possibly that is so," Chei said then, blinking. "I would not say that it is not. But who knows what you would bring back? No. She will come in for you. All you have to do is cry out—and you can do that with no persuasion, or with whatever persuasion it—"

He sprang, sliding in the mud, for Chei's throat; and everyone moved, Chei scrambling backward, the men around them moving to stop him. Chei fended his first hold off and he grabbed Chei's shirt and drove a hand toward Chei's throat to break it, but hands dragged at him, and the blow lost force as they bore him under a tide of bodies and against the edge of the rock.

There were more blows. He protected himself as he could and the armor saved him some of it. He hoped that he had broken Chei's neck and saved them all from the damage Chei might do—but it was a small hope, dashed when they hauled him up by the hair and Chei looked down at him from the vantage of the rock, smiling a twisted, bloodied smile.

"—with whatever persuasion it takes," Chei said.

"She is not a fool."

"—so she will know you are with us. If she comes in—she will have some care of that fact. Will she not?"

"She is not a fool."

"A fool would kill his hostage. Keep thinking of that."

He made another lunge, while he had the chance. They stopped him. They battered him to the ground and held him there while they worked at his buckles and belts, and when he fought them they put a strap around his neck and cut off his wind.

It was a man of considerable temper, Chei observed, probing with his tongue at the split in his lip: a lunatic temper, a rage that did damage as long as he could free a hand or a knee. But this was the man had wielded the gate-sword. This was the man had taken half his house guard and the most part of the levies.

Another image came to him—a chain was on his leg, and this wild man came riding down on the wolves, leaning from the white horse's saddle to wield his sword like some avenging angel, bloody in the twilight.

This same man, bowing the head to his liege's tempers—defending him with quiet words, glances from under the brow, measured deference like some high councillor with a queen—

They had him down, now, having finally discovered there was no way to deal with him without choking him senseless. "Do not kill him!" Chei shouted out, and rose from his seat on the rock and walked the muddy ground to better vantage over the situation.

They stripped him—he was very pale except his face and hands, a man who lived his life in armor. Armor lying beside the little stream—armor lying beside a river—the same man offering medicines and comfort to him—

"My lord," someone said, and asked a question. Chei blinked again, feeling dizzied and strangely absent from what they did, as if he were only spectator, not participant.

"Do what you like," he murmured to a question regarding the prisoner; he did not care to focus on it. He remembered his anger. And the dead—Jestryn, Bron. And the sight of his men vanishing into gate-spawned chaos.

It was the woman he wanted within his reach. It was the sword, against which there was no power in Mante could withstand him—the woman with her skills, and himself with a valued hostage. There was—a thought so fantastical it dizzied him—power over Mante itself, a true chance at what they had never dared aim for.

He retired to the rock, sat down, felt its weathered texture beneath his right hand. He heard commotion from his men, glanced that way with half attention. "Let him alone," he said to the man who hovered near him. "The man will not last till Mante if you go on, and then what hostage have we against the gate-weapons? Twilight. Twilight is soon enough."

It was as if the strength the gate had lent him had begun to dissipate. He heard voices at a distance. He saw them drag their captive up against one of two fair-sized trees at the edge of the brush, along the stream, saw him kick at one of them, and take a blow in return.

"Stubborn man," he murmured with a pain about him that might be Jestryn and might be Bron and might be outrage that this man he had trusted had not prevented all the ill that had befallen him.

Or it was pointless melancholy. Sometimes a man newly Changed wept for no cause. Sometimes one grew irrationally angry, at others felt resentments against oneself. It was the scattered memories of the previous tenant, attempting to find place with the new, which had destroyed it.

He had fought this battle before. He knew coldly and calmly what was happening to him, and how to deal with it—how he must to deal with the memories that tried to reorganize themselves, for his heart sped and his body broke out in sweat, and he saw the wolves, the wolves that ep Kantory mustered like demons out of the dark; he heard the breaking of bones and the mutter of wolfish voices as he walked across the trampled ground, to where his men had managed finally to bind the prisoner's hands about the tree.

"Chei—" Vanye said, looking up at him through the blood and the mud. And stirred a memory of a river-bank, and kindness done. It ached. It summoned other memories of the man, other kindnesses, gifts given, defense of him; and murder—Bron's face. "Chei. Sit. Talk with me. I will tell you anything you ask."

Fear touched him. He knew the trap in that. "Ah," he said, and sank down all the same, resting his arms across his knees. "What will you tell me? What have you to trade?"

"What do you want?"

"So you will offer me—what? The lady's fickle favor? I went hunting Gault, *friend*. That is what you left me. And I am so much the wiser for it. I should thank you."

"Chei—"

"I went of my own accord. We discovered things in common. What should I, follow after you till you served me as you served Bron? *I was welcome enough with your enemies.*"

Vanye flinched. But: "Chei," he said reasonably, "Chei—" As if he were talking to a child.

"I will send you to Hell, Vanye. Where you sent Bron."

Vanye's eyes set on his in dismay.

"I say that I was willing. Better to *be* a wolf, than to be the deer. That is what you taught me, *friend*. The boy is older, the *boy* cannot be cozened, the *boy* knows how you lied to him, and how you despised him. Never mind the face, *friend*: I am much, much wiser than the boy you lied to."

"There was no lie. I swear, Chei. On my soul.—*For God's sake, fight him, Chei—Did you never mean to fight him?*"

Chei snatched his knife from its sheath and jerked the man's head back by the braid he wore, held him so, till breath came hard and the muscles that kept the neck from breaking began to weaken. The man's eyes were shut; he made no struggle except the instinctive one, quiet now.

"No more words? No more advice? Are you finished, Man? *Eh?*"

There was no answer.

Chei jerked again and cut across the braid, flung it on the ground.

The man recovered his breath then in a kind of shock, threw his head back with a crack against the tree and looked at him as if he had taken some mortal wound.

It was a man's vanity, in the hills. It was more than that, to this Man. It was a chance stroke, and a satisfaction, that put distress on that sullen face and a crack in that stubborn pride.

Chei sheathed the knife and smiled at human outrage and human frailty and walked away from it.

Afterward, he saw the man with his head bowed, his shorn hair fallen about his face. Perhaps it was the pain of his bruises reached him finally, in the long wait till dark, and his joints stiffened.

But something seemed to have gone from him, all the same.

By sundown he might well be disposed to trade a great deal—to betray his lover, among other things: the first smell of the iron would come very different to a man already shaken; and that was the beginning of payments . . . his pride, his honor, his lover, his life; and the acquisition of all the weapons the lady held.

Always, Qhiverin insisted, more than one purpose, in any undertaking: it was that sober sense restrained him, where Chei's darkness prevailed: revenge might be better than profit; but profitable revenge was best of all.

And there were those in Mante who would join him, even yet. . . .

Unease suddenly flared in the air, like the opening of a gate. A man of his cried out, and dropped something amid the man's scattered belongings down along the streamside, a mote that shone like a star.

"Do not touch it!" Chei sprang up and strode to the site at the same time as the captain from Mante, and was before him, gathering up that jewel which had fallen before his own man could be a fool and reach for it again—a stone not large enough to harm the bare hand, not here, this far from Mante and Tejhos: but it prickled the hairs at his nape and lit the edges of his fingers in red.

And there was raw fear in the look of the man who had found it.

"My lord," the captain objected. There was fear there, too. Alarm. *That is not for the likes of you*, was what the captain would say if he dared.

But to a lord of Mante, even an exiled one, the captain dared not say that.

Chei stooped and picked up the tiny box which his startled man had dropped amid Vanye's other belongings, and shut the jewel in it. Storm-sense left the air like the lifting of a weight. "I will deliver this," Chei said, staring at the captain. His own voice seemed far away in his ears. He dropped the chain over his head. "Who else should handle it? I still outrank you—Captain."

The captain said nothing, only stood there with a troubled look.

This, a Man had carried. The answering muddle of thoughts rang like discord, for part of him was human, and part of him despised the breed. That inner noise was the price of immortality. The very old became more and more dilute in humankind: many went mad.

Except the high lord condemned some *qhal* to bear some favorite of his—damning some rebel against his power, to host a very old and very complex mind, well able to subdue even a *qhalur* host and sift away all his memories.

From that damnation, at least, his friends at court had saved him, when he had given up Qhiverin's pure blood and Qhiverin's wholly *qhalur* mind for Gault's, which memories were there too—mostly those which had loved Jestryn when Jestryn was human. And knowledge of the land, and of Gault's allies—and Gault's victims—when Gault was human: but those were fading, as unused memory would.

There were a few things worth saving from that mind, things like the knowledge of Morund's halls and the chance remembrance of sun and a window, a knowledge that, for instance, Ithond's fields produced annually five baskets of grain—some memories so crossed with his own experience at Morund that he was not sure whether they were Gault's recollections or his own.

Gault's war was over. He no longer asserted himself. It was the Chei-self, ironically, which had done it—human and forceful and flowing like water along well-cut channels: young, and uncertain of himself, and willing to take an older memory for the sake of the assurance it offered, whose superstition and doubts scattered and faded in the short shrift the Qhiverin-essence made of it: wrong, wrong, and wrong, the Qhiverin-thoughts said when Chei tried to be afraid of the stone he held. *Let us not be a fool, boy.*

This is power—and the captain has to respect it; and very much wishes he had Mante to consult. And what I can do with it and with what the lady carries, you do not imagine.

"Place your men," he ordered the captain.

"My lord," the man said. Typthyn was his name.

The serpent's man. Skarrin's personal spy.

Chei drew a long breath through his nostrils and looked at the sky, in which the sun had only then passed zenith.

The sun went down over the hill, the shadow came, and they built a fire, careless of the smoke. Vanye watched all this, these slow events within the long misery of frozen joints and swollen fingers. He had not achieved unconsciousness in the afternoon. He had wished to. He wished to now, or soon after they began with him, and he was not sure which would hurt the worse, the burning or the strain any flinching would put on his joints.

He flexed his shoulders such as he could, and moved his legs and arched his spine, slowly, once and twice, to have as much strength in his muscles as he could muster.

In the chance she might come, in the chance his liege, being both wise and clever, might accomplish a miracle, and take this camp, and somehow avoid killing him, remembering—he prayed Heaven—that there was a gate-stone loose and in the hands of an enemy.

But if that miracle happened, and if he survived, then he would have to be able to get on his feet. Then he had to go with her and not slow her down, because there was no doubt there were forces coming south out of Mante, and he must not, somehow must not, hinder her and force her to seek shelter in these too-naked hills, caring for a crippled partner.

A partner fool enough to have brought himself to this.

That was the thing that gnawed at him more than any other—which course he should take, whether he should do everything the enemy wished of him and trust his liege to stay clear-headed; or whether he should refuse for fear she would not, and then be maimed and a burden to her if she did somehow get to him.

Then there was that other thought, coldly reasonable, that love was not enough for her, against what she served. There had been some man before him.

And she traveled light, and did always the sensible thing—no need ever fear that she would do something foolish.

He told himself that: he could do what he liked, cry out or remain silent, and have the *qhal* dice him up piecemeal, and it would do neither harm nor good. He had been on his own since she rode out of here, and would be, till the *qhal* dragged him as far as Mante and either killed him or, more likely, treated his wounds and kept him very gently till some *qhal* claimed him for his own use.

Or—it was an occasional thought, one he banished with furious insistence— she might have run straight into forces sent from Mante, and be pinned down and unable to come back—or worse; or very much worse. A harried mind conjured all sorts of nightmares, in the real and present one of the smell of smoke and the unpleasant, nervous laughter of men contemplating another man's slow destruction.

The darkness grew to dusk. The *qhal* finished their supper, and talked among themselves.

When Chei came to him, to stand over him in the shadows and ask him whether he had any inclination to do what they wanted.

"I will call out to her," Vanye said, not saying what he would call out, once he should see her. "Only I doubt she is here to listen. She is well on her way down the road, that is where she is."

"I doubt that." Chei dropped down to his heels, and took off the pyx that swung from its chain about his neck. "Your property."

He said nothing to that baiting.

"So you will call out to her," Chei said. "Do it now. Ask her to come to the edge of camp—only to talk with us."

He looked at Chei. Of a sudden his breath seemed too little to do what Chei asked, the silence of the hills too great.

"Do it," Chei urged him.

He shaped a cut lip as best he could and whistled, once and piercingly. *"Liyo!"*

And with a thought not sudden, but one that had come to him in the long afternoon: "Morgaine, *Morgaine!* For God's sake hear me! They want to talk with you!"

"That is not enough," Chei said, and opened the box, so that a light shone up on his face from the gate-jewel there. The light glared; flesh crawled. Everything about it was excessive and twisted.

"You have only to feel that thing," Vanye said, "to know there is something wrong in the gate at Mante. Truth, man. I have felt others. I know when one is wrong."

"You—*know.*"

"You have no right one to compare it against. It is wrong. It is pouring force out—" He lost his thought as Chei took the jewel in his fingers and laid it down again in the box, and set the open box on the ground beside him.

"So she will know where you are. Call to her again."

"If she is there, she heard me." He had hope of that small box and its stone. The light that made him visible in the twilight, made Chei a target, if Morgaine were there, if she could be sure enough whether the man kneeling by him was the one she wanted. She might be very accurate—unlike a bowman. Several men might be on their way to the ground before they knew they were under attack.

Or she might, instead, be far on her way to Mante.

"That is not enough," Chei said, and called to the men at the fire in rising. "You can," he said then, looking down, "give her far more reason."

He was not going to put them off, then. He might shout, make a useless appeal: he spared himself that indignity and drew several quick, deep breaths before they got to him.

When the iron touched him he did not even try to hold it back.

It went on, and on. There was laughter. A human spat in his face, and some thought that amusing. Others, elegant *qhal*, simply watched.

She has gotten clear, he kept thinking, he insisted to think, like a litany, imagining gray horse, silver-haired rider, far and far across the hills. *She is far too wise for them to catch.*

And that is well. That is very well.

"*O God—!*"

Then: "M'lord!" someone said sharply, and a hand gripped his hair and a knife pricked his throat. *It is over*, he thought.

But something pale appeared and drifted like a cloud in the dark across the stream. He blinked and haze cleared momentarily on a glimmer of silver hair in the dark, black figure in the starlight, the dragon sword, sheathed, set point down in front of her.

"*Liyo,*" he cried from a raw throat. "*Archers!*"

The knife pierced his skin; Chei struck it aside.

"We have a man of yours!" Chei shouted out.

"*Liyo*, they know—"

A blow smashed into his skull, jolting everything into dark, his sense of place, of whether he had warned her or only meant to—

"Do you want me or do you want to talk?" Morgaine's clear voice rang out of the dark.

Vanye slid his eyes to the open box, the gate-jewel. She could not draw, with that unshielded, without taking him as Bron had gone. He struggled against those who held him, only to bring his legs around, tears of pain running through the sweat on his face.

"Do you want your lover back?" Chei taunted her. "Come in and bargain for him."

Vanye gave a sudden heave, swung his left leg over and brought it down on the lid. The light went out. He was blind.

Then *Changeling*'s light flared out, a bar of opal which grew to a white blaze, a shimmering into colors the eye did not want to see. *Qhal* who had faced that thing before scrambled to escape.

But Chei snatched the box and rolled to cover at Vanye's back, beside the tree.

"I have the stone in my hand," Chei yelled. "Come near my men and I uncover it!"

"Vanye?" her voice rang out. He saw her and all the brush and hill about her lit in *Changeling*'s fire. He saw her hesitate, stopped still. But the winds still blew, howling and blowing the grass. No arrow could fly true in that.

"*Liyo*, he is telling the truth. Do what you have to. They will not keep me in any comfort."

"In perfect comfort," Chei called out, "if you are reasonable."

"What do you want?"

"*Liyo*, it is Chei!"

There was silence then, and he lay back against the tree, satisfied, then, he had gotten out what would tell her everything. It was all she needed know.

Perhaps there would be a miracle. He thought not. The only thing he hoped now was that she would not try further, understanding now there was no bargain to be made—not with Chei, who knew far too much about her intentions.

"Curse you for that," Chei said at his shoulder, and surprised him into a painful laugh. It was altogether Chei's expression, plaintive and indignant.

"Let me free," he said to Chei. "It is the only bargain you can make. At the least you will have to keep me in better state than this."

"We have him," Chei shouted out into the dark. "Come near us and he will suffer for it, all the way to Mante—he will wear that stone about his neck, lest you have notions otherwise!"

"Let me tell *you*, I will take your men one by one, and you will not kill him—you will not *dare* harm him, else your men die faster, my lord, you will see how fast. And you will not kill him, for your own life's sake, because he is the only thing keeping you alive. Lest you doubt me—"

A man cried out and fell, and Chei whirled half about and clenched his hand on Vanye's shoulder.

"Now what will you do?" Vanye taunted him.

"*Damn* you—"

Vanye grinned, for all the pain it cost him.

On the slope, *Changeling*'s fire went out, leaving them blind to the dark. And Chei's men murmured in indignation and fear.

They gave him food at the dawn—not much, but a piece of waybread and a kind of porridge that was tolerable to his stomach; they let him eat with his hands free, and drink from the stream and wash, with two score men watching him and most of them close enough to fall on him and weigh him down if nothing else. The humor of it was salve for the pain which rode every breath and slightest movement. He would, he hoped, grow more limber the longer he did move, and he refused to show them the pain that he was in or to ask any consideration they dared refuse. The burns on his chest and stomach bid fair to be the worst, the more so that they intended to set him in armor again—lest, Chei argued loudly with a captain who objected, some accident take him on the road.

Chei prevailed, by shouting, and the forty-odd men watched him sullenly as he pulled on his breeches and his shirt and padding, and the mail, which weight felt ten times what it was wont; but it made his bruised and burned ribs and stomach feel the safer from chance blows. He fumbled about with the straps of the leather, and Chei cursed him, whereat he hurried no more than before, having judged Chei had no wish to try his fortunes and discommode his men before the day was even begun.

Then Chei ordered him tied. He had known that they were going nowhere until they had done it; he had known they would take what revenge they dared in the doing of it, and he resolutely disappointed them by standing quietly and yielding his hands behind him, using his strength only when they put pressure on his arms, intentionally to cause him pain.

And the stone, which had been unshielded the night long, pouring its evil into the air, Chei brought him and hung about his neck as he had said, eye to eye with him for that moment.

"There will be ways," Chei said to him.

"You can save your men, Chei. Give me my horse and let me go. That is all you have to do. You have fifty good years as you are, whether we win or lose. Otherwise you have only a handful of days—if you have that. Do you think you will be the last my lady leaves alive with me?"

There was fear in Chei's eyes. And hate. Chei drew his hand away, and smashed it across his face before he could entirely evade the blow.

There was fear, when he shook the hair back and looked past Chei at his men. There was outright resentment.

"Threats," Chei scoffed, and went to his horse. He waved his hand at the others. "Move! Mount up! We have ground to cover."

There was a small, dull sound. The man holding the red roan for him fell without an outcry, only a puff of foul smoke hanging in the air. The camp broke into chaos, the horse shied. A second man fell, further away.

Chei whirled and flung himself at Vanye, arms about his waist, and came down on top of him with an impact that drove the breath out of him and half stunned him with the blow to the back of his head. He came to himself in pain, being dragged to a sitting position with Chei's arm about him and Chei shouting orders at his men to find Morgaine.

Not likely, he thought. He did not resist being used as a shield. He sat there with his eyes shut and drew small breaths that did not hurt. "If she wants you," he murmured to Chei, "she will surely take you."

There had been forty men and two in their company last night. He had taken account. Losing one last night, two this morning, there were thirty-nine, counting himself.

"Shut up," Chei hissed at him.

He rested, that was all.

When the men, by ones and twos, trailed back from their search of the hillsides, there were thirty-seven, and Chei, standing, shouted furious orders to mount up.

"There are reinforcements coming," the second in command protested, in full hearing of the others. "We should raise a fortification and stay here. You are losing men, Qhiverin, all for your damnable insistence on going ahead with this—"

"Do as I tell you!" Chei shouted at the man. "Get to horse! We are riding out of here!"

The *qhalur* captain, tall and elegant, bowed his head with ill grace and went for his horse.

To all this Vanye said nothing at all, considering the state of his ribs and his gut. Chei grabbed him by the hair getting him on his feet and even this he bore, that and the hard grip of the men who pushed him at Arrhan. But one of them hit her when she shied from them and at that he resisted, an instant's bracing of muscles before he thought quickly that men of their ilk might as like kill her to spite him. So he struggled to get his foot into the stirrup and let them shove him up onto her back. They tied Arrhan's reins to a sorrel gelding's saddle and she did not like that either, sidestepping and jerking till he tapped her with his heels and spoke to her in the Kurshin tongue, softly, one friend in this situation, where he had as soon not have had her.

The company rode out of the camp and across country, toward the road.

He was not surprised by that. They hoped to deprive Morgaine of cover from which to strike at them. All day they would be thinking of means to save themselves and to have revenge on them both.

Himself, he gave himself up to Arrhan's gait and slept, in what stretches he could, between the pain of burns and stiff muscles and the ache of his shoulders and back, and the peculiar unpleasantness of the unshielded stone which rode close against his throat, as Chei had tied it, a sense of gate-force which reached a mind-numbing pitch and stayed there, never abating.

When Morgaine needed him to do something she would signal him. He had no doubt she would do it in some fashion—perhaps through the stone itself, if it would not likewise advise their enemy.

Beyond that he did not try to think, except where the *qhal* themselves afforded him something to wonder on. To think what the end of this might be, or to think how he had wandered into this, was too deadly a sink, a place in which he could lose himself. This much he had learned of Morgaine, to deal with the moment and keep his mind flowing with it—like swordplay, like that intricate art in which there was no time to spare for forever.

He waited, that was all.

And by afternoon another man pitched from the saddle.

There were outcries, there was shouting—some men broke and ran and the whole company did, stringing out in disorder.

Two riders veered far off toward the northwest, and kept going.

"They are cowards!" Chei yelled at the rest. "Likeliest they are dead men. Stay with the column."

"Let him go!" one of the *qhal* shouted back. "Let him *go*, let us ride back to Morund!"

"Silence!" Chei bade him. "Do you think any of us would live out the hour?"

"No one would prevent you," Vanye said. "Go home. It is your high lords who use the gates—this one is spending your lives to no—"

He ducked his head and put his shoulder in the way of Chei's sheathed sword as it came whistling round for him, ducked again from the second blow, and as Arrhan shied, drove his heels in.

The mare jerked and bolted, hitting the reins with all her weight and throwing the other horse into a wild stagger after balance. For a moment he kept her circling and shying up under the impacts of his heels.

Then other riders closed in about him and seized reins and bridles to stop her.

Chei was one. Chei shoved the sheathed sword under his chin when all was done and jerked his head up.

"Tonight," Chei told him. "Tonight."

No one spoke, except Chei bade them put a rope to Arrhan's halter and use that as well as the reins.

They gave him neither food nor water, nor any other consideration for his comfort, so that the ride became one long misery of heat and ache—no rest for him at the times they would stop to rest the horses. They drank at a stream and afforded Arrhan water, but none for him.

It was petty vengeance.

Only once, there was an outcry from the rear of their column, and Chei gave furious orders that sent men thundering back along the road toward a rider that appeared like a ghost and vanished again in the tricks of the rolling land.

He held his breath then. He could not but worry.

But the rider left the road before they came that far.

And within the hour a man pitched dead from the saddle.

"Damn you!" Chei shouted to the hills. *"Damn you!"*

The hills echoed him. That was all.

Vanye did not meet his eyes then. He kept his head bowed amid the murmuring of the others.

They were thirty-three.

Close to him, for some little time, Chei and the captain argued in muted fury, concerning a place for a camp, concerning the hazard of leaving the road for the hills.

"It is him she wants," the captain asserted finally, in hushed violence. "Put a sword in him, take the jewel, and leave him in the road. She will stop for him. No horse for him and a wounded man on her hands—*then* the balance shifts. *Then* we become the hunters. More of this is madness."

It was only too reasonable a course. Vanye listened with a sinking heart, and braced himself to cause them what trouble he could.

But: "No!" Chei said.

"It is your ambition," the captain said. "Your damnable ambition, Qhiverin! No waiting on Mante—no chance of anyone but yourself dealing with it—You will listen to me, or the high lord will when I bear the report to him—"

"You will obey orders, captain, or I will bear reports of my own of your insubordination, of your obstructing me, damn you! I am *my lord*, and Qhiverin is gone, *captain*, with all his disfavor, Gault is dead, what is more, and you do not know me, *captain*, you do not know me in the least and you do not know the enemy you are dealing with and you do not know the weapon you are dealing with. That stone around his neck keeps us alive, captain. Around yours, much as I would like to see it, it would be no more than an encouragement—it cannot take that weapon of hers, need I shout the matter aloud? Whoever holds the stone will go like a leaf in the wind, and that accursed sword will stand fast in this world—*that* is what prevents her, nothing more."

"Her lover bleeding in the dirt will prevent her." The captain ripped his sword from its sheath. "And I will carry the stone, *my lord*, and deliver the stone to Mante, *my lord*!"

Vanye drove his left heel into Arrhan's side and she wheeled, jerking hard at the reins, clear of his reach as Chei's sword came out and rang loud in the turning of that blade, a mirror-bright flash of sun, a wheeling cut and the hiss of other steel drawn, on all sides.

A thunder of hooves and a second man came at him; he drove with his heels and ducked, flat in the saddle, as the stroke grated off his armor, as the man leading his horse swung round and an arc of steel flashed over his head in the other direction, ringing off the rebel's blade close by his ear. Horses shoved and shied and Arrhan struggled in the press: there was nothing he could do but lie flat as he could against Arrhan and the heaving rump of his defender's horse for an instant as the blades rang above him, as blood spattered over him and one or the other fell—

He drove his heels in and fought for balance with an effort that tore muscles in his stomach, with steel still ringing over his head, then let go entirely and landed in a space between the horses, to scramble up again, hands bound, and run.

A shout, a rumbling behind him—riders on either side of him, and a horse shouldered him and sent him rolling; up to his feet again and a second dash for the rocks that he could see—

If Morgaine were near enough, if she could give him cover—

A horse thundered down at him. There was nothing he could do but run, and veer, spinning aside at the last moment as the horse rushed past.

But the second horse he could not evade, and fell, his helm saving his head and rolling free as he hit on his bound arms and struggled after wind and purchase to rise.

A horseman overshadowed him. An extended lance slammed against his armor and pushed him back, the point hovering an unstable distance from the pit of his throat.

He did not know which side had won until Chei's voice bade the rider back away, and men got down to gather up him and his helmet and take him back to his horse.

There were bodies on the road. The captain was one, with his skull split. There were two other *qhal* who might have been all the captain's and might have been, some of them, Chei's. They left them for the scavengers as they had left the others, and they put him on Arrhan's back again.

He slumped over such as he could to rest then, and to avoid Chei's attention.

There was no more dissent. It was a while more of riding, and very little of speaking at all, until they came into a stony place between two hills, where the Road had cut deep, and where a stream had cut deeper still into the hills beside it.

It was a sheltered place. It was a slit between the rocks where an overhang provided cover against attack, a natural fortification, and when they rode into it, and passed within that shadow, Vanye's heart sank in him as hope had trembled on the edge this last and terrible hour.

They were twenty-six as he counted them again—three dead on the road and four vanished, deserted, he thought, when the fight began to go against them. But the *qhal* had done this to themselves, and the noise of the fight ought to have reached Morgaine through the hills. There had been a real chance she might have been there when he fled, or after—at the most, that commotion should have drawn her close again, and she might have dealt them damage— might have taken some good position among the rocks and taken out man after man, giving him the chance he needed to run, on foot, if he must— beneath her covering fire.

But she had not been there. There had been nothing at all from her since early afternoon; and Chei had sent men out to hunt her.

She is hurt, he thought. *Something has happened to her or she would have come in—she would have come, she would have come—*

Now they drew into this place shadowed with premature twilight, close among rocks, where he knew that she could not reach; and that shadow closed over him, his enemies laid hands on him and pulled him off his horse and struck him once in earnest of what else they might do, and for the first time since last night he felt a cold despair.

They bound his feet and let him lie while they had their supper: for him there was not so much as a cup of water, and when in desperation he rolled over to the streamside close by him, they ignored that. It was all they would do for him, until after, that a few of the human servants came and unbound him, and then his hands were so swollen and his arms so lifeless there was little he could do for himself. They gave him leave to relieve himself, that was the sole mercy; and when he turned about again they laid hands on him and bound him and hauled him over to where the *qhal*-lords sat, the pale and the human-seeming both by the little fire they had made under the overhang; and Chei centermost among them, their faces and their eyes reflecting the white shining of the jewel he wore.

He sank down there on his knees, his head reeling from hunger and exhaustion, and the gate-force humming in his bones. He waited to hear what they would do, and heard the small shifts of the men at his back, the men who gathered close about him, yet more than a score of them.

"Did I make you a promise?" Chei asked him.

"Aye," he murmured, to stay Chei's madness. Aye to anything.

Something has happened to her, he reasoned to himself. *She is not dead, they would have reported that. But hurt, somehow held, pinned down in ambush—O God, or out there, late, perhaps ahead of us, perhaps that is where she is—*

They will want to draw her in, they will want me to draw her—

I must not do that, whatever they do, no outcry this time—

No sound, he told himself over and over, when Chei gave the order that they should take the armor off him.

But: "My lord," one of the *qhal* said. "No. He is our safety. He is all the safety we have. My lord, we stayed by you—"

Chei said nothing for a long moment. Then: "Do you intend to ride off too?"

There was silence.

"Then go, curse you, go, ride out into the dark and take your chances! Or do what I tell you. Take him!"

The servants hesitated. Of a sudden one of them bolted and ran, and another fled, and the rest after them, afoot, toward the road. One of the *qhal* gave pursuit.

And fell.

Chei sprang and Vanye rolled and resisted him as best he could, tried to get his legs to bear for a kick, but Chei caught him in his arms and held him fast against him, one arm nigh choking him while shouts and alarm rang about him.

Alive, Vanye thought; and: *"Be careful,"* he shouted out before Chei's fingers pressed at either side of his throat and began to take his consciousness. *"Liyo—"*

As one and another of the *qhal* fell and such as were left huddled close within that shelter.

They were six, Vanye saw when the night grew quiet again and consciousness came back to him, as he lay still in Chei's tight grip. Mostly there were bodies strewn out across the open; and one of the *qhal* by them called a name and crept out to reach a friend, against his lord's advice.

"Get out of here," Vanye said to that man, for a man who would take that risk seemed better to him than the rest of them. "Get on your horse and ride out of here. She will not stop you."

But it was that man who came back and seized him out of Chei's hands and battered and half-choked him before the others pulled him off.

He lay silent after that, dazed and relieved of some of the pain, so close he was to unconsciousness. But the *qhal* stirred forth, and saddled their horses in the dark, and led them close by the rock where they sheltered, horses enough for them and a relief mount for each, but Arrhan was not among them.

Then they hauled him up and put him ahorse, and they rode breakneck up the narrow way they had gotten into this place.

When day came, there were only the six of them, and himself, and they pushed the horses, changing from one to the other.

But another of them died, at one such change. It was the man, Vanye thought, who had beaten him. He regarded the man in a kind of numbness when he sprawled almost under his horse's hooves, with a black spot on his forehead and a dazed expression on his face. He was not glad of it, except he lifted his eyes toward the low hills and felt as if his liege, unseen, were looking at him this moment.

"It is that cursed stone," one of the *qhal* said, as others had muttered. "She can *see* it."

"Wrap that cursed thing," Chei said then, and one of them drew him close and dragged him down off the horse while others got down and lengthened the cord on the stone, and tucked it under his armor at his neck, against his bare skin.

The gate-sense was worse then.

It was worse yet when they had crested a long rise and suddenly found the land dropping away below them across a wide rolling plain; and the crags which had long hung rootless in morning light, faced them across this gulf.

Then the world reeled about him in a mad confusion of blue sky and golden distances and the crags of yellow rock about them. The horse moved again, and his vision cleared, but there still seemed a distance between him and the world—less of pain, but greater unease, gate-sense that crawled up and down his nerves and prickled the hair on his body.

There, he thought, lifting his face toward the high crags. Mante-gate is up there—

Without question, as he knew the whereabouts of other powers, close by it, like small pools beside an ocean, and that ocean raging with storms and like to swallow up the lives that came near it.

It wanted this stone that he wore, wanted the bearer, wanted all creation, and that was not enough to fill it.

O my God, he thought, my God, if they bring me nearer this thing, if they bring me too close—

He rode, he did not know how. He heard their voices sharp in argument. "You can feel that thing," one said, and he knew what thing they meant: it was all about them, it was in their nerves; it made the horses skittish and fractious.

But it was nothing to them who did not hold it against their bare skin.

No more died—for whatever reason, there were no more ambushes, as they shifted horses and kept a pace that even gray Siptah could not match unaided, in this place where the *qhalur* road broke down into eroded stone traces, and the riders found a course not straight, but recklessly direct, down toward the valley.

She is left behind, he thought. These crags and this rough land has forced her back to the road and she has fallen behind. They have won, in my case. Somewhere I could have done better than this. Somehow I could have done something better.

It was the first thought he had allowed himself, of might-have and could-have, and of how he had fallen to them and the things they had done, and might do. Well enough, he thought, fool, twice fool—and reviewed every move he had made on that hillside, every sign he might have missed, every chance he had had, until the pain was all that took his mind from his inward misery.

Then: fool, he thought. She has taken the odds down.

It would cost, he thought. Time would cost very dear. And chances were hard come by.

The *qhal* shared rations at midday. "We had best feed him," one said, "or he will faint." And when Chei consented, one came and fed him a strip of jerky and gave him a drink as they rode, the water splashing down his chin and front and onto the saddle, to dry again in the sun. After that his stomach was queasy, and cramped, and the pounding gait put the taste of blood in his mouth. He wished that he might fall off and simply break his neck and be done, except he was Kurshin, and his body kept the rhythm it had known from childhood, no matter how much he swayed; and the same fool who had fallen into their trap, still thought that there was a hope of delaying them, if he could find the means.

Then he put the matter together and at their next stop, when they were changing horses, as he was about to mount, brought his knee up in his horse's flank and flung himself out of the way as it went hopping and pitching and throwing the horse it was tied to into a wildly swinging panic.

The men grabbed after those and he went for the three a single man was holding, startling those with a wild yell and a shove of his shoulder before someone overhauled him from behind.

He fell, with a man atop him and one of their horses having slipped its bridle and racing off wildly across the road, one of the riders having to free his horse of his relief mount to run it down.

It was a little victory, a little one. The man who had overhauled him dragged him over onto his back and stared at him as though murder was too mild a vengeance.

Vanye brought his knee up with all the strength in him.

Two more of them pinned him to the ground and one of them paid him in kind. After that he lost sense of where he was for the moment, until he felt the weight go off him and heard a shout, and came to with Chei's blade at his throat and a dead man at his side.

And the sound of a rider coming, at full gallop.

Chapter 14

The gray horse became clear, and its rider, and Vanye took in his breath, held as he was against Chei's knee, Chei's sword across his throat. And one of the two *qhal* with him had taken up his bow, and nocked an arrow.

Vanye swung his leg around in an attempt to strike the bowman. He could not. The blade stung along his neck, taking up what room he had for breathing. "Look out!" he yelled. But Morgaine was drawing to a halt well down the road. She slid down, and started walking, through the tall grass.

The bowman drew back, aiming a high arc for a distance shot.

"You are in her range," Vanye said quietly, and the bowman eased off the draw.

"Fire!" Chei said.

The bowman drew again, with careful aim. And a second time eased off.

"Fire, curse you!"

"The wind is gusting." A third time the bowman lifted the bow and drew. His arm trembled with the strain as he sought an arc and a lull in the wind.

"Wind does not trouble her," Vanye said.

"Wait your target," Chei said then, and the bowman eased off a third time, trembling. Chei relaxed his grip on Vanye's hair, then shifted his hand to his shoulder and pressed gently. "Stay still, man, stay still."

It was worse than the other. His leg began to shake, at its unnatural angle. He moved it. And Morgaine walked closer still, the bowman's necessary arc continually diminishing.

She reached half-range. The bowman lifted his bow, made a swift draw.

"Haaaaiiii!" Vanye yelled, and Chei jerked his head back. The shaft flew.

Morgaine dropped, and sprang up again, covering ground at a run.

The blade stung, and a slow trickle ran down Vanye's neck. *"I will kill him,"* Chei yelled.

Morgaine stopped. The bowman stopped, a second arrow nocked and drawn.

"Ride off!" Chei shouted at her. "You leave me nothing to lose, woman!"

"I will bargain with you!" Morgaine's voice came faintly on the wind at full shout.

"I will, bargain with *you*, woman. Throw down the sword and I will give you both your lives. Or I will cut his throat here and now."

She walked closer, and a second shaft flew, amiss on a gust of wind.

"Curse you," Chei said to the bowman. "Fire!"

The bowman brought up another arrow. But Morgaine had stopped. She lifted her hand, aimed dead at them. "An easy shot for me. Let him free and you are free to ride south. My word on it! Any one of you that wants to live, walk clear."

The bowman lowered his bow; and: "My lord," the *qhal* on Chei's other side said, and reached, and pressed the blade back from Vanye's throat with his bare hand. "My lord. We are the last. She will kill us. Let him go. We have lost."

There was long silence. Chei's grip faltered on his shoulder and tightened again.

"Let him free!" Morgaine said.

"For a price," Chei said.

"Name it!"

"I will name it later," Chei said. "Do you want him on those terms?"

"Let him go!" Morgaine said. "And I will give you your lives and your gear— or flay the skin off you if you harm him! Let him go!"

Chei's hand loosed. The sword withdrew and Chei shoved him carefully aside and stood up, a clear target. "Free him," Chei said. "Let him go."

The second man took a knife and cut Vanye's hands free, and with a hand under his arm, helped him to his feet. He was not one of those who had been forward to do him harm—a tall, silver-haired *qhal*, expressionless even now in this shift of fortunes. His hand was firm and steady, and gently tested his balance before he let him free.

Vanye walked, the whole of the sky seeming for a moment gone to metal and his hands, lifeless and swinging beside him, seeming to belong, like his feet, to some other man. He staggered on a hole in the ground, recovered himself short of a fall, and kept walking, the gusts of wind touching the sweat on his face and stinging in the cuts on his throat.

But the sky went stranger still, peculiarly translucent, and he was on one knee without knowing how he had gotten there, Morgaine rushing up to kneel and seize him by the shoulder.

"I am all right," he said. There was a look of dismay on her face; and rage; and she whirled on one knee and aimed her weapon at their enemies.

"No," he said on a breath, and caught her arm.

She did not fire. He did not know why he had said it, only that it was one more mistake like the rest he had made. He felt the shorn hair blowing about his face and into his eyes, the most visible of the dishonors they had put on him, and her; and that expression of horror was still in her eyes. "I am sorry," he said to her, when he could say anything.

"*Curse* them for this!"

"It was their doing, not mine." He knelt there shifting glances between her and their unmoving enemy, for she had stopped paying them attention. He did not offer the head-to-ground obeisance that might have made some amends for his shame with a Kurshin liege, did not ask for duel with the man who had done this, did not do any of the things that would have driven her to fury with him. "*Liyo*, I am tired, is all."

"I have Arrhan with me. Yonder, beyond the hill." She made a motion of her head. "And all your gear. With her and Siptah to trade about, there was no way they could outrun me." She found the cord that bound the stone about his neck and pulled it from beneath his armor, which itself was great relief. She laid down the black weapon a moment to take her Honor-blade and cut it free. "Where is the case for this thing?"

"Chei has it."

"That is one thing I will get from him.—Is it Gault?"

"Yes." In the tail of his eye, he saw Chei walk toward them. "In Heaven's name, *liyo*, watch them—"

Her gray eyes flicked past his with a killing fury—for them, not for him. He knew then the measure of it, in her red-rimmed and shadowed gaze—the pace she had to have kept, to set ambush after ambush, the strain, constantly to be sure of her targets.

She gathered up her weapon. She rose to her feet, and Vanye levered himself up to stand by her.

"The matter of a price," Chei called out.

"There is no price," Morgaine shouted back, "but your *lives*, my lord, and that is for old grudges, not new ones! You have the casing for the stone. Let it fall. And get out of my sight!"

"The price, my lady!"

Her hand lifted, the weapon aimed. "You go too far with me."

"My enemies—and passage through the gate, for me and mine." Chei strode forward and stopped, hands held wide and empty. "There is no way back for us."

"No way back from *hell*, my lord, and you are treading on the brink. *Vanye* wants your life, I have no least notion why—you can thank him on your knees, before you ride out of here. Now! Drop the case, man!"

Chei's hand moved to his neck. A silver chain glittered in the sun as he lifted it over his head and dropped it.

"*On your knees, my lord, and thank him, else I will shoot the legs out from under you.*"

Chei went down.

"Thank him."

"*Liyo,*" Vanye protested.

"*Thank him!*"

"I give you my thanks, Nhi Vanye."

Morgaine dropped her hand, and stood staring as Chei got up and went to the roan horse and his remount; and the others, the *qhal* and the bowman who wore human shape, claimed their own.

"There was one more man—" Vanye recalled with a sudden chill.

"The one who chased the horses?" Morgaine asked. "That one I accounted for." She half-turned and whistled for Siptah. The gray horse threw his head and shook himself and tended in their direction, reins trailing, as they walked toward the place Chei had dropped the casing.

Chei and his men rode off, southward, with no delaying. Vanye knelt, fighting dizziness, and picked up the gray box that Chei had dropped in the trampled grass. Morgaine gave him the stone and its cord and he made a ball of it and put it inside. Its raw power left the air like the feeling after storm, and his hands were shaking as he hung it again about his neck on its proper chain, safe and still.

"What did they do?" she asked fiercely. "What did they do?"

He did not meet her eyes. He gathered up his helm, from where it had fallen. The gray horse came up to them, snorting and throwing his head, and he went and caught the trailing reins and laid his hand on Siptah's neck, for the comfort of a creature who asked no questions. "Nothing, past the time you put a fear in them. Mostly want of food and rest."

"Get up," she said. "I will ride behind. We will find Arrhan and quit this place."

He was glad enough of that. He wiped the hair back from his face, put the helm on, slung the reins over and put his foot in the stirrup with a little effort, with a greater one hauled himself onto Siptah's back and cleared the right stirrup for Morgaine. She climbed up by the cantle and her hand on his leg, and held only to the cantle when they started out, so she knew well enough he was in pain, and did not touch him as they rode. She only gave him directions, and they went over the road and beyond the further hill, where Arrhan placidly cropped the grass with a pair of Chei's strayed horses.

She slid down. He climbed down and went and gave his hands to Arrhan's offered muzzle, endured her head-butting in his sore ribs and leaned himself against her shoulder.

His bow, his quiver, hung on Arrhan's saddle, though different men had stolen them. There was a fine *qhalur* sword, that one of the lords had worn.

He looked around at Morgaine, at a face as *qhal*-pale as theirs, and a vengefulness far colder. For a moment she seemed changed far more than Chei.

Then she walked past him to take the rest that she had won, the horses that grazed oblivious to their change of politics. "Remounts," she said, leading them back. "Can thee ride, Nhi Vanye?"

"Aye," he murmured. She was brusque and distant with him, giving him room to recover himself; he inhaled the air of freedom and set his foot in his own stirrup and flung himself up to Arrhan's back, gathering up the sword as the mare began to move. He wanted that in its place at his belt first; even before water, and a little food, and a cool spring to wash in.

Even that impossible gift Morgaine gave him, finding among the hills and the rocks, a place where cold water spilled down between two hills and trees shaded the beginnings of a brook. She reined in there and got down, letting Siptah and the remounts drink; and he slid down, holding to the saddle-ties and the stirrup-leather: he was that undone, now that the fighting was done, and his legs were unsteady when he let go and sank down to drink and wash.

He looked and she was unsaddling the gray stud. "We have pushed the horses further than we ought," she said, which was all she said on the matter.

He lay down on the bank then, sprawled back and let his helmet roll from his head, letting his senses go on the reeling journey they had been trying to take. He felt his arm fall, and heard the horses moving, and thought once in terror that it had been a dream, that in the next moment he would find his brothers' hands on him, or his enemies' faces over him.

But when he slitted his eyes it was Morgaine who sat against the tree, her arms tucked about her knees, the dragon sword close by her side. So he was safe. And he slept.

He waked with the sun fading. For a moment panic jolted him and he could not remember where he was. But he turned his head and saw Morgaine still sitting where she had been, still watching over him. He let go a shaking breath.

She would not have slept while he slept. He saw the exhaustion in her posture, the bruised look about her eyes. "*Liyo,*" he said, and levered himself up on his arm, and up to his knees.

"We have a little time till dark," she said. "If thee can travel at all. Thee should tend those hurts before they go stiff. And if need be, we will spend another day here."

There was fever in her eyes, restraint in her bearing. It was one thing and the other with her, a balance the present direction of which he did not guess at, rage and anxiety in delicate equilibrium.

He felt after the straps of his armor and unbuckled it. "No," he said when she moved to help him. He managed it all himself, glad of the twilight that put a haze between her and the filth and the sores, but while time was that he would have gone out of her witness to bathe, now it seemed a rebuff to her. He only turned his body to hide the worst of it as he slid into the chill water.

Then he ducked his head and shoulders under, holding fast to the rocks on the bank, for he did not swim. Cold numbed the pain. Clean water washed away other memory, and he held there a moment and drifted with his eyes shut till Morgaine came to the bank with salves and a blanket and his personal kit, and sternly bade him get out.

"Thee will put a chill in the wounds," she said, and was right, he knew. He heaved himself up onto the dry rock and wrapped himself quickly in the blanket she flung around him. He made a tent of it to keep the wind off while he shaved and brushed his teeth, careful around the cuts and the swollen spots, and afterward sat rubbing his hair dry.

She came up behind him and laid her hands on his shoulders, and took the fold of the blanket and began to dry his hair herself.

So he knew she forgave him his disgrace. He bowed his head on his arms and did not flinch when she combed it with her fingers—only when she put her arms about his shoulders and rested her head against him. Then it was hard to get his breath.

"I did not deserve it of them," he said, in his own defense. "I swear that, *liyo*. Except my falling into their trap in the first place. For that—I have no excuse at all."

Her arms tightened. "I tried to come round north and warn thee. But I came too far. By the time I came back again it was too late. And thee had come riding in. Looking for me. True?—True. Is it not?"

"Aye," he murmured, his face afire with shame, recollecting the well-trampled stream, recollecting every mistaken reasoning. "It might have been you in their hands. I thought you were, else you would have been there—"

"To warn thee off. Aye. But I was being a fool, thinking thee was like to rush into it for fear I had been a fool; and thee knew *something* was wrong, well enough, that I was not somewhere about. It was as much my fault as thine." She moved around where she could see his face. "We cannot do a thing like this again. We cannot be lovers and fools. *Trust* me, does thee hear, and I will trust thee, and we will not give our enemies the advantage after this."

He pressed his hand over hers, drew it to his lips and then let go, his eyes shut for a moment. "Will you hear hard truth, *liyo*?"

"Yes."

"You take half my opinion and do half of yours, and whether mine is good or ill I do not know, but half apiece of two good opinions makes one very bad one, to my way of thinking. Hear me out! I beg you." His voice cracked. He steadied it. "If your way is straight down the road, straight we go and I will say no word. My way, to tell the truth, has not fared very well in recent days."

She sat hill-fashion, on her heels, her arms between her knees. "Why, I thought I had done tolerably well by your way in the last few days—I did think I had learned well enough."

"You learned nothing of me—"

"Constantly. Does thee think me that dull, that I learn nothing?"

His heart lifted a little, a very little, not that he counted himself so gullible. "Does not believe me?" she asked.

"No, *liyo*." He even managed a smile. "But it is kind."

Her mouth tightened and trembled, not for hurt, it seemed, only of weariness. She put out her hand and touched his face with her fingertips, gently, very gently. "It is true. I did not know what to do. I only thought what thee would do, if it were the other way about."

"I would have gone in straightway like a fool."

She shook her head. "Separately, we are rarely fools. That is what we have to mend." She brushed a lock of hair from his eyes. "Trust *me*, that I will not be. And trust that I trust thee."

He glanced at the dragon sword behind her shoulder, that thing she did not part with even now, that one thing for which she would leave him.

Perhaps she understood the direction of that glance. She settled back on her heels with a bruised and weary gaze into his eyes.

"With my life," he said.

It was not enough to say. He wished he had not had that thought, or given way to it.

I believed you might come, only because we were still far enough from the gate.

Beyond such a point, she had no such loyalties, nor could help herself. He believed that. With the sword, at such a time, she fought for nothing but the geas—and for her sanity.

At such a time, liyo, *you would have taken me with your enemies.*

And always that is true.

"Truth, *liyo*, I had no doubt."

She looked so weary, so desperately weary. He rose up on his knees and put his arms about her, her head against his bare shoulder, her slim, armored body making one brief shiver, hard as it was. Her arms went about him.

"We have no choice but move on," she said, her voice gone hoarse. "Chei has gone back toward Tejhos. I do not think he will go all the way south."

"Chei has done murder," he said. "He killed a captain Mante sent by way of Tejhos. The captain's men deserted."

"Was *that* the division." Her shoulders heaved to a sigh, and for a moment her weight rested against him. "None of them escaped. Plague take it—I should have killed him—long since. . . ."

"Chei," he murmured, "went to them . . . willingly, he said. And Mante knows everything he knows by now. I have no doubt they do. There may be more than a few riders out from there."

She nodded against his shoulder. "Aye. I know that."

"And neither of us is fit to ride. What could you do? What could I? Sleep."

She was limp in his arms, and moved her hand then to push away from him, and abandoned the effort, slumping bonelessly into his arms. "Not wise, not wise, of me. I know. We have to move. This place is not safe—'t is not safe at all—"

It was, perhaps, the first time in recent days she had done more than close her eyes.

Chei splashed water over his face and wiped it back over his hair, crouching at the stream. Across from him in the dusk, the remnant the witch had left to him—witch, he insisted to himself, against all the knowledge *qhalur* rationality could muster. He grew superstitious. He knew that his soul was lost, whatever that was, simply because he did not know how to believe in it any longer; or in witchcraft, except that in the workings of the world there might conceivably be prescience, and outsiders might know things he did not understand.

Ichandren had believed in unnatural forces. Bron had never doubted them. The man across the rill of water from him had known them, Rhanin ep Eorund, before he housed a *qhalur* bowman, and perhaps even yet. They were foreign only to Hesiyyn, the *qhal*, whose face was a long-eyed, high-boned mask, immune to the worry that creased Rhanin's brow—human expression, woven into the composite like so many subtle things.

Like fear. Like the moil of hate and fear and anger that boiled inside Chei's own self, seductive of both halves: revenge on the strangers; revenge on Mante, which had always been his enemy no less than Chei's; and life, life that might stretch on forever like the life that trailed behind, life that remembered jeweled Mante, and the face of the Overlord which young Chei had never seen, and of kin and friends Gault-Qhiverin had both loved and killed and betrayed for greater good—

Friends and kin the strangers had taken, as they bade fair to take all the world down to dark.

"Go back if you will," he, Chei, Gault, Qhiverin, had said to his last followers, when they had put distance between themselves and their enemies.

Rhanin had only shaken his head. There was nothing for him in Morund, only in Mante, where his kin were, and his wife, and all else Skarrin had reft away from him. The wife he had had, the human one, in the hills—she would run in terror from what Rhanin had become; and break Rhanin's heart, and with it the heart of the *qhal* inside him. And Chei knew both things.

Hesiyyn had said, with eyes like gray glass: "To live among pigs, my lord? And tend sheep? Or wait Skarrin's justice?"

He did not understand Hesiyyn. Qhiverin when he was fully *qhal* had never understood him, only that he was the son of two great families both of which disowned him for his gambling, and that he had been under death sentence in

Mante, for verses he had written. He had attached himself to Gault and gambled himself into debt even in Morund: that was Hesiyyn.

So they had ridden north again, from the place they had stopped, not having ridden far south at all.

"They cannot outrace us," Chei said, wiping a second palmful of water over his neck. "They will rest. They will seek some place to lie up for a while—but not long. They know they are hunted."

Wounds had stiffened; and Vanye bestirred himself carefully in the dark, while Morgaine slept. He made several flinching tries at getting to his feet then, cursing silently and miserably and discovering each time some new pain that made this and that angle unwise. Finally he clenched his jaw, took in his breath, and made it all in one sudden effort.

"Ah—" she murmured.

"Hush," he said, "sleep. I am only working the stiffness out."

He dressed by starlight, struggled with breeches and bandages and shirt and padding, and last of all the mail, which settled painfully onto strained muscles and shortened his breath. He fastened up the buckles of the leather that covered it, making them as loose as he dared; he fastened on his belts.

Then he walked by starlight to the place she had tethered the horses, and soothed them and made the acquaintance of the two they had from Chei's men, animals by no means to be disparaged, he thought: the Morund folk bred good horses.

Then he gathered up their blankets and bridles and saddles, the latter with an effort that brought him a cold sweat, but painful as it was, it was good to stretch and move and pleasant to feel some of the stiffness work out of him.

It was even more pleasant to sink down on his heels near Morgaine and whisper: "*Liyo*, we are ready. I have the horses saddled."

"Out on you," she said muzzily, lifting herself on her elbow; and with vexation: "Thee ought not."

"I am well enough." In the tally of the old game, he had scored highly by that; and it was like the stretch of muscles, a homecoming of sorts.

Home, he thought, better than Morij-keep or any hall he had known—home, wherever she was.

She gathered herself up and paused by him, to lay her hand on his shoulder, and when he pressed his atop it, to bend and hug him to her, with desperate strength, while he was too stiff to stand as easily. "A little further before daybreak," she said. "We will gain what we can. Then we will rest as we need to. With the—"

There was a disturbance among the horses, the two geldings and the mare and the stud in proximity ample reason for it, but Morgaine had stopped; and he listened, still and shivering in the strain of night-chill and stiff muscles.

He pressed her hand, hard, and hers closed on his and pushed at him: *I agree. Move. I do not like this.*

He got up then, silently and in one move, for all the pain it cost. He reached Arrhan and quieted her and the remounts as Morgaine took Siptah in charge.

In the starlight, downhill where the stream cut through, a solitary rider appeared, and watered his horse at the lower pool. In a little more, two more riders joined him, and watered theirs, and drank, and rode on across.

Vanye shivered. He could not help it. He bade Arrhan stand quiet with a tug at her head; the others, the remounts, he held close and kept as still as he could, while Morgaine kept Siptah quiet.

They were not Chei's folk, whatever they were. He reckoned them for riders out of Mante, hunting reported invaders—else they would ride the road and go by daylight like honest and innocent travelers.

He moved finally, carefully, and looked at Morgaine. "There will be others," he whispered. "They may search back again along the watercourses."

"Only let us hope they confuse our tracks and their own." She threw Siptah's reins over his neck and rose into the saddle. "Or better yet—Chei's."

He set his own foot into Arrhan's stirrup and heaved upward with an effort that cost pain everywhere.

If they had dared a fire, if they could have sweated the aches out with boiled cloths and herbs, if he could have lain in the sun and baked himself to warmth inside and out, instead of lying cold and rising cold and riding again—but they were too close now, to the gate, and the enemy too aware of their danger.

Turn back, he thought of pleading. Go back into the plains and the hills and let us recover our strength.

But they had come so far. And they had no friends in this land and no refuge, and he did not know whether his instincts were right any longer. He yearned, he yearned with a desperate hope for the gate and a way into some other place than this, another beginning, when this one had gone desperately amiss.

They did not try to make speed by dark, with the ground stony and uneven as it was. They rode down one long sweep of hill, passed between others, and over a brushy shoulder. They kept a pace safe for the horses and quiet as they could manage, under a sky too open for safety.

And once, that Siptah pricked up his ears and Arrhan looked the same direction, off to their left flank, his heart went cold in him. He imagined a whole hostile army somewhere about them—or some single archer, who might be as deadly. "Likely some animal," Morgaine said finally.

And further on, where they stopped to breathe within a stand of scrub: "Time, I think, we gave the horses relief," he said. "But I do not want to stop here."

"Aye," Morgaine said, and slid down, to tie Siptah's tether to his halter; and to calm the stallion, who took exception to the geldings, flattening his ears and pricking them up again, and swinging between them and Arrhan as Vanye dismounted.

"Hold," Morgaine hissed at the gray, and caught his tether-rope, which usually would stop him; but his head came up and his nostrils flared toward the wind, ears erect.

"Stay," Vanye said quietly, calmly as he could. "There is something there."

The horses were vulnerable. There was no guarantee of cover for them beyond this point. There was no guarantee they were not riding into worse. Siptah threw his head and protested softly, dancing sideways.

"Dawn could see us pinned here," she said. "That is no help."

"Then they have to come to us. *Liyo*, this once—"

"I thought thee had no more advice."

He drew in a sharp breath. Pain stabbed through bruised ribs. *"Liyo—"*

Brush cracked, somewhere up on the slope.

"I agree with you," he said. "Let us be out of this."

"Go!" she hissed, and it was Siptah she chose to carry her, war-trained and sure, for all the gray was through his first wind.

He took Arrhan on the same reasoning, the horse he knew, the one that answered to heel and knee. He had both the relief mounts in his charge, that jolted the lead against the saddle as they took the next climb over ground studded with rocks, Siptah's tail a-flash before them in the starlight, eclipsed now and again by black brush and trees, the necessary sound of hoof-falls and harness and the raking of brush sounding frighteningly loud in the night.

Down the throat of the folded hills, along the track of a minuscule stream, they kept a steady pace, until Morgaine drew in and he stopped, and panting horses bunched together, their breathing and the shift of their feet and creak of harness obscuring what small like sounds might be behind them.

"I do not hear them," he said finally.

"Nor I," Morgaine whispered, and turned Siptah uphill again, a hard climb and a long one with the two led horses tugging at Arrhan's harness.

But when they had come high up on that hill, dawn was seaming the east with a faint glow, and the stars were fading to that black before daylight.

And when they had changed off mounts and ridden the downslope on the two bays, Arrhan and Siptah led behind and too weary to object, the red edge of the sun was rising, offering a dim light, showing the distant crags of Mante's highland upthrust like a snaggled jaw against the sky beyond the hills.

The gelding missed a step and caught himself, and Vanye shifted weight; for a moment the whole of the east seemed to blur and reel, and he caught the saddlehorn, taking in breath in a reflex that hurt. He had bitten through a wound inside his cheek. He did it again, and it was one more misery atop the others.

But Morgaine had drawn up short, and she reached across to him as he caught himself, her horse crowding his amid the scrub and the rocks. "Vanye?"

"I am all right." His pulse raced with a sullen, difficult beat. The sky still spun and he felt a cold fear that he might fail her in the worst way, weighing on her, forcing her to decisions she would not make and tactics she would not use.

But not yet, he thought. Not yet. If threats and blows of his enemies could keep him in the saddle, his own determination could do as much, until the give and flex had worked the stiffness out of him and food and water had taken the dizziness from his skull.

"Beyond this," she said, "no knowing how long the ride. Vanye—we can find a place—That is what we *must* do."

He shook his head, turned the gelding's head for the downslope, and set it moving, too much in misery for courtesy.

An object hissed out of thin air and hit his shoulder like a sling-stone, spun him half-about in the saddle by force and shock: in the next heartbeat the arrow-hiss reached his mind and he knew that he had been hit and that arrows were still flying. His horse plunged in panic and shied back, and he fought it, finding life in the numbed arm, his only thought to get back to cover before Morgaine left it for his sake and tried to cover him. The horse stumbled on the brush, recovered itself, crowding Siptah and Arrhan and snagging the lead-rope as it came up against the others, but it was in cover, behind the rocks. He slid down, stumbled as the horse had on the encumbering brush, and brought up on the downhill slant against a boulder, trying to take his breath as Morgaine slid down and fetched up against the same, firing as she went, as the hillside erupted with ambush, a din of shouts.

"Is thee hurt?" Morgaine asked him. "Vanye, *is thee hurt?*"

The force of the blow had made any feeling uncertain, but the arm worked, and he pushed himself off the rock and struggled back after Arrhan and Siptah, who had wound the tether-ropes into a confusion of frightened geldings and war-trained stallion, in the midst of which was his bow. Arrows landed about him. One, spent, hit Arrhan and shied her off from him, and behind him was Morgaine's voice cursing him and bidding him take cover.

He seized the bow and ripped it loose from its ties on Arrhan's saddle, the same with his quiver; and scrambled for higher vantage, up atop a tumbled several boulders that hemmed the horses in.

The climb took his breath. He gained his knees, blind to anything but the necessity and deaf to anything but the cries of the enemy. He set the bow against the rock and his knee as he knelt, and strung it with an effort that brought sweat to his face.

Then he nocked an arrow and chose his target among those who swarmed up the hill, as if the very rocks and brush had come alive in the murky light.

He counted his shots, knowing the value of his position. He fired, calmly, carefully, with the advantage of height and the surety he was a target if he could not take their bowmen before they came to vantage on him or Morgaine, and they were trying: he picked one off, and selected another shaft, shaking the hair from his eyes and feeling the sweat running on cold skin. He wondered had the arrow pierced his armor after all before it fell away. It had hit enough to cause deep pain, the sort that caused a sweat and the weakness in his limbs and the giddiness that sent the landscape reeling.

But he could still draw. He bent the bow and drew breath and sighted all in one deliberate and enveloping focus, time after time taking targets Morgaine's straight-line fire and lower vantage could not reach, taking the archers foremost, who strove to position themselves and reach him.

But his supply of arrows dwindled.

∽ Chapter 15

The enemy found cover on the rock-studded, scrub-thicketed hill, and targets were fewer. Vanye wiped sweat with the back of his arm, and laid out his last four arrows, with care for their fletchings.

Morgaine left her vantage and climbed to another, a black-clad, white-haired figure in the gathering dawn, whose safety he watched over with an arrow nocked and ready for any move on the slope.

One tried. He quickly lifted the bow and fired, dissuading the archer, but the wind carried the shaft amiss.

Three arrows remaining.

Morgaine reached her perch and sent a few shots to places that provoked shifts in the enemy's positions, and afforded him a target he did not miss.

"We are too close here," Morgaine shouted across at him—meaning what he already understood, that *Changeling* was hazardous in the extreme in this confinement of loose boulders and brush, with the horses herded together in that narrow slot among the rocks and close to panic. "I am going for the horses! Stay where you are and give me cover!"

He drew in his breath and picked up his next to last shaft, his heart trying to come up his throat. He did not like what she proposed, riding out alone, with *Changeling* under Mante's warped touch.

He did not like, either, their chances if the enemy came up on them, and if they waited too late to gain room for the sword; and of the two of them, Morgaine *knew* the weapon. There was nothing to do but hold fast and spend his two remaining arrows to afford her the room she needed.

She edged outward on the rock and onto the slope that would lead her down to the horses.

And an arrow whisked past his position and shattered on the rock a hair's-breadth from her.

He whirled and sought a target among the crags over their heads, desperate. Morgaine's fire glowed red on stone as she fired past him and up at the cliffs.

"Get down!" she cried at him. "Get down!"

"Get to the horses!" he yelled. *"Go!"*

As an arrow hit the rock by his foot.

An arrow flew from another quarter, crosswise streak of black on pale rock, high up the ledges.

Not at them. At the hidden archer. An outcry said that it had hit. Other arrows followed, arcing downslope this time, into enemy positions, starting enemies from cover, as Morgaine turned on her slab of rock and fired again and again at targets suddenly visible.

A dark spot moved in the edge of Vanye's vision: he whirled and fired at a man coming up the throat of their little shelter, near the horses.

That man sprawled backward, his armor of no avail against an arrhendur bow at that range; and screamed as he slid down the slope, while Vanye nocked his last arrow with a deliberate effort at steadiness, as shafts sped unexplained over their heads, as the enemy broke and fled, offering their backs to the arrows and the red glow that flashed on a man and doomed him.

There were, perhaps, two or three who made it off that field. When quiet came the very air seemed numb. He still had the one arrow left. He refused to spend it on a retreating enemy. He slid off his rock and lost his footing in the landing, gathered himself up with his bow in one hand and the last arrow still nocked, and struggled through the brush to the tumbled mass Morgaine was descending.

"My lady Morgaine!" a shout came down from the heights.

He crossed the last distance with a desperate effort, to steady Morgaine as she jumped the last distance and to thrust her back where there was at least scant cover.

"No gratitude?" The mocking voice drifted down from that place of vantage. "No word of thanks?"

"Chei," Vanye muttered between his teeth, and pressed his body against Morgaine as some large object hurtled off the heights to land close by them, with a sickening impact of bone and flesh.

A helmet rolled and clanged down the rocks. Arrows scattered and rattled; and a *qhalur* body lay broken on the stone.

He bent the bow, aimed upward, hoping for a target.

"There is my gift," Chei called down to them, never showing himself. "One of Skarrin's pets, none of mine. An appeasement. Do I hear yet thanks?"

"He is mad," Vanye breathed.

"I could kill you both from here," Chei said. "I could have let Skarrin's men kill you. But I do not. I had rather come down to talk. Which shall I?"

"Mad," Vanye said. His arm was shaking as he had it braced. His breath was short. He looked at Morgaine. "There were three of them. I have the one arrow left. I can gather more out there. Cover me."

"Stay!" Morgaine said. "Do not try it."

He lowered the bow and eased the string.

"My lady," Chei's voice drifted down to them. And an arrow struck and shattered in front of them. "Is that earnest enough of good faith? Talk is what I want. On your terms."

"I cannot see the wretch," Morgaine hissed softly, looking upward with the black weapon in hand. "Curse him, he can loft his shots, and I cannot—"

"Let me—"

"We still have another choice."

"Loose rock," Vanye muttered, looking at the set of the boulders *Changeling* might dislodge. "The horses—"

"My lady—" Chei's voice came down. "They have sent a gate-jewel into the field, more than one—Do you want to talk about this?"

"I am listening," Morgaine answered him.

"The while we were on the road the jewel he wore was constantly sending. It could not but draw them. I do not deny—I fought you. But there is no more fighting. If you win, you will destroy the gate at Mante, you will destroy everything, and we die. If Skarrin wins, we die—as rebels. We have few choices left. You want Mante. I want something else. It is alliance I am proposing."

"Alliance," Vanye muttered under his breath.

"Narrow quarters," Morgaine said quietly. "And an unstable gate. And no knowing where our enemies out there have gotten to."

"It is a lie—"

She rested her hand on his shoulder, and looked up at the cliffs. "Come down!" she called to Chei.

"Under truce?" Chei asked.

"As good as your own," Morgaine shouted back. "Do you trust it?"

A pebble dropped and bounded from somewhere above.

"For God's sake, do not trust him."

"I do not. I want him in sight. Remember I have no scruples."

He drew a larger breath. His hands were shaking. From off the rock where the *qhal* had fallen, blood ran, and dripped.

And from up among the rocks, on the trail they had ridden, the sound of movement.

"There were three," Vanye said again as a rider came down, out of their view behind the hill, hoof-falls echoing among the rocks.

"We do not know how many there are now," Morgaine said. "We have a dead man for proof. Perhaps they would kill their own. Who knows?"

He drew a long, slow breath, resting back against the rock that was no shelter.

"On the other hand," Morgaine said, "Chei has already killed men of Skarrin's. Did you not say? How did that go?"

"Aye." Breath was short. He sent his thoughts back, to gather everything, putting it in one place. "Typthyn was the name. For the stone. It was the stone the captain wanted. To take it to Mante, he said. And to get clear. But do not believe him for the sake of that. Chei wanted it for himself."

A single rider came into view, on the red roan that had been Gault's, the man a slight, young figure in silver mail.

"The fool," Vanye breathed.

"Foolish or desperate."

"No!" Vanye said. "I believed him a moment too long. He lies—very well."

Her hand clenched on his shoulder, on bruises. "Be patient. We will hear him out. That at least we can afford."

She stood clear to face the rider, who, finding himself in a pocket in the maze of stone, dismounted and leapt up to the flat rock which had been Vanye's post. Vanye took his place at her left shoulder, the bow easy in his hands, aimed at the ground.

But he kept the arrow nocked.

Chei spread wide his hands. "That I have men above me, you can guess. And you have the sword." He walked forward on the slanting surface and dropped lightly off the rock to the ground facing them—spread his hands again, keeping the palms in plain view. "I think the advantage is yours."

"Come no closer," Morgaine said. "For this I have no need of the sword."

Chei stopped instantly. The mockery was gone from his face as she lifted her hand toward him. "My lady—"

"I am not your lady and whatever there is of Chei ep Kantory I should best requite by killing his enemy, *Gault*. I saved you for last, only so *you* might keep the others under your hand. I spared you once on Vanye's word—and because I should have enjoyed it too much—*Do you hear me, Gault?*"

"My men, my lady. Above us."

"We two, lord Gault, are in front of you, and this is the cleanest of my weapons, for which you may thank me. Is there something you want that is worth this?"

"What I always wanted. What I would have freely given, if you had come to Morund. What the boy gave when you befriended him—"

"Lies," Morgaine said sharply.

"Vanye!" Chei said, holding out his hands.

"I had as lief kill you," Vanye said; and bent the bow as Chei took a step closer. *"No farther!"*

Chei fell to his knees, hands outheld. "God help me, I do not know what I am, I cannot sort it out—What else do you leave me?"

"No more lies!"

"Listen to me. I know the way in. Do you want Skarrin? I will give him to you."

"Our guide," Vanye breathed, "to whom we owe so much already."

There was fear on Chei's face now. The eyes flickered desperately, distractedly for a moment, and he moistened his lips before they steadied. "The boy—misled you. I am not that boy. My men have you in sight. Will you throw away your lives—merely to have mine? It seems a poor exchange."

"We can take him with us," Vanye said in the Kurshin tongue. "I will take care of him."

"Skarrin will kill me for what I have done—he will kill all of us. *Listen* to what I am saying. I know how to mislead them. I know the way in. I will give you Skarrin . . . for your promise to take us with you." He rested back on his heels, hands on his knees, and the rising sun shone fair on Chei's curling hair, on Chei's earnest face. "And I will not betray you."

"Why not?" Morgaine asked. "You are betraying Skarrin."

"Because," Chei said with a foreign twist of the mouth, a sullen look up, as he set his hands on hips and sat back. "Skarrin is not a lord I chose, not a lord who chooses *me*, what is more. You are no fool, lady. And I am not. You have knowledge of the gates that I do not have. I made one try. You won. I have spent my life bowing down to a lord who has trod my face into the dust more than once, and the *boy*—when I will listen to him—" The young features contracted, a kind of grimace. "—the boy remembers you dealt well with him."

Vanye's breath shortened. "Let us get out of here," he said, *"liyo."*

"The boy meant to kill me," Chei said. "He *wanted* to die. He still *wants* revenge. He came to me—to pit himself against me—inside—to drive me mad, if he could." Chei's mouth jerked, neither grimace nor smile, both humorless. "But he has changed his mind about death. It never agreed with him. Or with me. And he has changed his mind about killing you. He thought you would kill him—and me. He was disturbed that you declined. Now he understands more and more what a fool he was, having acquired a man's understanding, and a warrior's good sense. And what he remembers tells me I am safer right now than I would ever be in Morund."

"He was mistaken now and again. I need no assassin at my back."

"You need *me*, my lady. And Skarrin will prove it to you, too late, if you kill me. I know the way into Mante. And you will not find it!"

"I have done harder things."

"I am not a rebel by nature, my lady! Give me a lord I can serve, give me a lord who can win against Skarrin, deal with me as you deal with your own, put me beside you, and you will find I have skill, my lady—in a command twice Morund's size, in any field, I am a man worth having, only so I have a lord more set on winning than on his fears of having me win! I do not rival you. I do not wish to. Only take me and my men and I will tell you how I will prove it: I will swear my allegiance through Vanye, I will put myself under his orders—he is a fair man. I *know* that he is a fair man—"

"But no fool," Vanye said bitterly, down the shaft of the arrow, "besides which, man, I have my own allegiance, which is to my liege, and her safety, and if I have to shoot you where you kneel I will do that before I will let you at her back." The arrow trembled and almost he lost his grip on it, so much the soreness of his joints and the lightness of his head affected him. He tightened his fingers, feeling the sweat stinging in the cut on his brow; and for all his stomach knotted up in loathing of the choices, it was not for her to do, after so many other burdens she had. *"Liyo,"* he said, and lapsed into the Kurshin tongue, looking nowhere but at the center of Chei's chest. "Let him call the others down. Let us—as you say—have them in sight. Let us get down off this hill. And I will deal with them."

She delayed her answer. The sweat stung his eyes and ran down his sides, into raw burns; the muscles of his arm began to tremble dangerously.

She touched his shoulder then. "No," she said; and the breath went out of him and the world spun so that he braced his feet as he lowered the bow. "You are Vanye's," she said to Chei. "What he does short of killing you I will not prevent." Her hand pressed hard on Vanye's shoulder. "No," she said in the Kurshin tongue, "thee cares too much."

He drew a breath and lifted the bow on the draw, half-blind and choking on the desperation in him. He fired. But her hand struck his arm up and the arrow sped past Chei's head to strike a chip from the stone wall behind him.

Everything froze in its place—Chei in front of him, white-faced; Morgaine at his side. He trembled in the aftershock of attempted murder; he felt the weakness on him with a giddiness that dimmed the light and made sounds ring in his ears.

"Aye," he said, because something seemed incumbent on him to say then, who had disregarded her orders. If there was a part of his soul undamned, he had done it by that act, excepting her forgiveness. He drew in a breath, straining bruised ribs, vision hazing—the blows to his head, he thought; the lack of food; the exertion of the fight. He wanted only to have them moving again, himself in the saddle with the horse to carry him. Rest would mend him, a night's sleep—

But, O Heaven, it was not in reach, and Morgaine listening to this man—

He could not think beyond her, not, in any case, with his head swimming and his thinking and his fears shrunk to the little space between these rocks, and the chance of an enemy which had been all too fortunate in its ambush—

And he must not kill this man. Morgaine forbade it. He had defied her order once. Twice was without excuse.

"Do you swear?" he asked Chei, knowing after he had asked, that oaths meant nothing with this creature.

"I have said," Chei said, and got to his feet. There was darkness in that stare. There was profound apprehension. Then another, more agitated way of speaking: "I swear before God. Is that enough?"

That human expression, that shift of voice, sent a chill through him.

Perhaps it was meant to.

But he let the silence go on a moment, and looked Chei in the eyes, long and steadily, until the air was a good deal colder and Chei surely knew it was not fear held his hand.

Then: "Do not cross me," he said to Chei, "and I will return you nothing of what I owe you. Where is my sword?"

Chei's eyes shifted toward the roan horse.

"I will have it back."

Chei nodded. "Aye."

"Aye—*my lord*."

"Aye, my lord."

"Call your men down here. They can ride away or they can ride with us, but if one of them missteps, I will lay his head at your feet and lay yours at my lady's. I am nothing you know, whatever you think you gained at Tejhos. I am Nhi, and my clan is not reputed to give second chances."

Perhaps Chei believed him. Chei looked once back at him as he turned to face the cliffs, and once at Morgaine.

Then he shouted up at the height. "They have agreed," he called up the cliffs. "Come down."

Three of them, Vanye kept thinking, and went and gathered up the arrows that had spilled off the cliff with the dead man—twelve he found with the fletchings and points whole, and put them in his quiver, the while Morgaine kept her eye on matters. His ribs ached.

Three of them, he kept thinking in the throbbing of his hurts and the panicked beating of his heart. She has gone mad.

It is this Skarrin—this man she fears. That is what drives her. That is what she wants to know—always, always when she does not know as much as she wishes—she doubts herself—

The Devil rather than honest men, he remembered her saying. *O my liege, you have found him.*

The two from the cliff came riding around the shoulder of the hill as Chei had come, stopped their horses by the red roan; and came to pay their respects to their recent enemy—the bowman and the *qhal*, the bowman's human face betraying intense worry, the *qhal*'s having no expression at all.

"Rhanin ep Eorund," Chei named them. "And Hesiyyn Aeisyryn, both late of Mante."

"I will give you a simple choice," Vanye said, leaning on his bow, and this time with a quiver half full of arrows. "Ride off now, and go free. Or go with us, do my liege honest service, and I will forget what I owe you. I count that more than fair."

Rhanin nodded, clear of eye and countenance; and had the likeness of truth about him. "Aye," Rhanin said, and let go a long breath, as if he had taken him at his word and had worried, until then.

Hesiyyn lowered his eyes and inclined his head, and looked up with a bland, half-lidded insolence. "Anything you will, lord human."

Vanye stared at him and thought of striking him to the ground. But then it would come to killing—not one but all of them.

The archer had fired on his liege: but in defense of his own lord. While this Hesiyyn, he judged, might do anything and everything for his own sake.

And this, this was the *qhal* who had intervened to save his life.

"If they ride with us," he said to Chei, disdaining the *qhal* with a passing glance, "remember I hold you accountable."

And he turned his back on Chei as well, feeling their stares like knives; his heart beat like a hammer in his temples, and his face was hot, the sky like brass. Morgaine said something to him of riding out, that they were well off this hillside. "Aye," he said, and shouldered his bow and his quiver, and went to untangle the horses, which had wound themselves into a predicament, their two with the nervous geldings. Siptah had braced himself, flat-eared, too trail-wise to move, despite Arrhan's lead-rope wound across his rump, and that the blaze-faced gelding had a hind leg in among the rocks, its rump against the wall, one foreleg crossing its partner's lead.

He cut both free and straightened out the leads, darting an anxious eye to Chei and the rest, but Morgaine was watching them: he saw her. He shoved Siptah with his shoulder to gain room, held Arrhan steady to re-tie the leads, and recalled his sword on Chei's saddle, uphill with the other horses.

He thought of climbing the rocks and making the exchange, but it was a warhorse in question, easier that Chei should deal with it, and he was out of breath and not wanting either the climb or any dealings with weapons at close quarters: bruised ribs and stiff muscles, he thought, leaning on Siptah's side to work past him and lead him out of the confusion.

But when he unstrung his bow to tie it with his gear on Arrhan's saddle, the weakness of his arm and his lack of wind surprised him. He had to make a second pull to slip the string. When he had gotten it tied and set his foot in the stirrup, it more than hurt to pull himself up, it sapped the strength from him and made him sweat and his head reel despite the morning chill.

It is the sun-heat on the metal, he told himself; there is no wind here. Using the bow and pushing the horses about had strained the ribs. *It will pass.*

He sat still, with the sweat running, leaning on the saddlebow, while Morgaine mounted up. *Get us moving,* he thought, feeling the sting of salt in his cuts. There was no wind in this place. He longed to be off this hill, not knowing what they might meet on that slope down there or out in the land: *best hurry before they collect a defense,* he thought; and everything conspired with delays.

"They will go first," Morgaine said, starting out. "I have told them."

"Aye," he murmured. "Let Skarrin's men have *them* for ranging-shots."

"They might have killed us," Morgaine said. "They could have taken the weapons. That much is true."

He thought about that.

"But I do not forget what they did," she said.

"Aye," he said. The hill seemed steeper than he recalled as they struck the open slope—a place littered with dead, thirty, forty or more.

And Chei and his men rode past them, dutifully taking the lead.

"Is thee all right?" Morgaine asked.

"A little faint. I am well enough. It is the heat." He urged Arrhan to a faster pace, and overtook Chei's men.

"Arrows," he said. "All we can gather. We may need them."

"Aye," Rhanin said, and veered off on that chancy slope, at hazard of further attack, from men on the ground, from Heaven knew where on the rocky heights around them.

Rhanin would not, he thought at the back of his mind, come back. The man would take his chance and ride for his own life.

"The sword," he said to Chei.

Chei took it from his saddle and reversed it, passing it over as they rode.

"A good blade," Chei said.

He said nothing. He unhooked his own from Arrhan's saddle and passed it by the hilt.

"Alayyis' sword," Chei murmured.

"My liege did not ask his name," he said harshly, and reined back and hooked the arrhendur blade to his sword-belt, waiting for Morgaine to overtake him.

O God, he thought then, *why did I say that? Why am I always a fool?*

Morgaine overtook him. He murmured an explanation for the bowman's departure, and started up again, riding after the others, a crowded trail avoiding the lumps of bodies which lay like so much refuse on the hillside. He watched carefully such dead as they did pass close at hand, wary of traps. He watched the hills about them, for any flash of armor, any flight of birds or bit of color out of place.

Far across the field, Rhanin searched, dismounted, searched again. Eventually he came riding back, carrying three quivers of arrows. "I would keep one," Rhanin said, offering two as he rode alongside—no grudging look, only an earnest and an anxious one.

"Do that," Vanye said; and the man gave him them, and turned off downslope, to overtake Chei and Hesiyyn.

He hung the two quivers from his saddlebow, and he stared at Rhanin's retreating back with misgivings. They had reached the bottom of the hill, and the last body, which lay face upward. Carrion birds had gathered. He did not look down at it as they rode their slow course past. That man was incontrovertibly dead. The hour was fraught enough with nightmares, and he had had enough of such sights in his life.

But, he thanked Heaven, there were no ambushes.

The hill beyond the next rise gave out onto the flat again, a broad valley; he blinked at the sweat in his eyes and rubbed at them to make the haze go away.

"Vanye?" Morgaine asked, as Siptah's heavy weight brushed his leg.

"Aye?" His head ached where the helm crossed his brow; the sun heated the metal, heated his shoulders beneath the armor and the pain in his ribs made his breath hard to draw.

"Is thee bearing up?"

"Well enough. Would there was more wind."

Chei had drawn rein in front of them, and scanned the ground; and waited for them with the others.

"We should bear south a little," Chei said. "Around the shoulder—" Chei pointed. "Off into the hills. One of them may well have us in sight. But the weapon you used up there—" He gave a small, humorless laugh. "—will have improved my reputation with Mante. At least for veracity. They will be very hesitant to come at us."

"Why south?"

"Because—" Chei said sharply, and pointed out over the plain, below, and to their right, toward the hills. "To reach that, necessitates crossing this, else, and if you have no liking for—"

"Courtesy, man," Vanye muttered, and Chei drew another breath.

"My lady," Chei said quietly, "it is safer. If you will take my advice—lend me the stone a moment and I can send a message that may draw their forces off us."

"Tell me the pattern," Morgaine said.

Chei took up the reins on the roan, that flattened its ears toward Siptah. "Two flashes. A simple report. I can send better than that. I can tell them the enemy has gone up into the hills. In numbers. And if you provoke them to answer you, my lady, and you cannot reply rapidly, they will *know* what you are. I can answer them."

"Do not give it to him," Vanye said, and made no move to hand over the stone.

"No," Morgaine said. "Not here and not now."

"My lady—"

"Can it be—you *have* sent?"

"Aye. From Tejhos."

"And the stone, man!"

"With that," Chei said with a reluctant shrug. "Yes. The first night."

"And *told* them it would stay unshielded. Do not evade me. I am out of patience for guesswork. *What* have you done, what do you suspect, what is out there?"

"They will have known something went amiss from the time you sealed off the stone," Chei said in a low voice. "There is rumor Skarrin's gate can tell one stone from the other, given sure position. I do not know. I only know there are two more such stones out there. I saw them, clear as I could see Tejhos."

"In the stone."

"In the stone, my lady. There may be more than that by now. When yours stopped sending—It is myself they will be hunting, along with you. I am well known for treason."

"Did you think they would forgive," Vanye asked, "the small matter of killing your lord's deputy?"

Chei's eyes lifted to his, hard and level. "No. But, then, if I had won, I would have done what we are doing now. With your weapons. It is not Mante I want. It is the gate. . . . With your weapons. I told you my bargain. And, lady, you have convinced me: I will not follow a lord in the field who cannot beat me. I should be a fool, else. You won. So I take your orders."

There was a moment's silence, only the stamp and blowing of the horses.

"Let us," Morgaine said to Chei then, "see where your ability leads us."

And in the Kurshin tongue, when they struck a freer pace, tending toward the south, into rougher land:

"Do not be concerned for it. I will choose any camp we make, and he will not lay hands on the stone, to be telling them anything.—Thee is white, Vanye."

"I am well enough," he said again.

If he confessed otherwise, he thought, she might take alarm, might seek some place to rest, where they must not—*must* not go to hiding now, when Mante knew the vicinity to search, and might throw company after company into the field. Even *Changeling* had its limits—

—had them, more and more as they drew near the aching wound that was Mante.

My fault, he kept thinking. All of this. *O Heaven,* what are we going to do?

And others, out of the muddle of heat and exhaustion: she has taken them *because* she knows I am near to falling; she needs help; she takes it where she can, against this stranger-lord in Mante—against this Skarrin—needs them in place of me—to guard her back—O God, that I leave her to these bandits—It is her own perverse way of managing them, putting them under my hand, forcing the bitter draught down their throats—lest they think they can leave me behind: it is her own stratagem, give them a captain like to spill from his horse, and let them vie for her favor, whereby she keeps Chei at bay, and in hope of succession, and he never dares strike at me, lest he lose what gratitude he might win of her later—If he has not betrayed us outright—if the ambush was not a trick, their own arrangement—

A man learned to think in circles, who companied with Morgaine kri Chya. A man learned craft, who had before thought a sword-edge the straightest way to a target.

She might manage Chei. Surely Rhanin. I should tell her to keep that man.

And: This weakness of mine may pass. It may well pass. She is winning time for me. Gaining ground.

And lastly: Why did she prevent me from Chei? Why strike my hand?

You care too much?

What did she mean by that?

Hills closed about them, brushy ravines and rock and scrub, steep heights on either side. He looked up and behind them, and never was there trace of any watcher.

Except in a fold between two hills, near a stand of scrub, where they came to a stream: there Hesiyyn drew up by the grassy margin and signaled Chei.

They were old tracks. It had surely been yesterday that some rider had paused to water his horse, and ridden along the hillside, in this place of tough, clumped grass which showed very little trace otherwise. The track there went out onto that ground on their own side, not, Vanye reckoned, hard to follow, if one had to wonder where that rider had gone, or if one were interested in finding him.

As it was: "What is this place?" he asked angrily. "A highway their riders use? A known trail?"

"Doubtless," Hesiyyn said, "my lord human. We are all anxious to die."

He sent Hesiyyn a dark look.

"We are no more anxious for a meeting than you are," Chei said. "They are out here, that is all. I told you. Skarrin is no longer taking the matter lightly.— I ask you again, lady, in all earnestness: lend me the stone."

Morgaine leaned her hands against the saddlebow and quickly restrained Siptah from edging toward the roan. It was warfare, now. The red roan's ears were flat, his eyes—red-rimmed, his least lovely feature—constantly one or the other toward the gray stud.

"No," she said shortly, and reining Siptah sharply aside to gain room, dismounted and threw her hand up to shy the roan. "Move him off! We will rest here a little. At least they *have* passed here. And it is at least some cover."

"My lady," Chei said with heavy resentment, and drew the wild-eyed roan aside, along the stream.

So the rest of them. Vanye glared a warning in their direction, threw his leg over the horn and slid down. He dropped Arrhan's reins to let her drink, and let the two horses he led move up to the water, then sank down on his knees and bathed his face and the back of his shorn neck, discovering that insult again, where it had passed in shock when Chei had done it. For this one unjustified thing he was more and more angry, an unreasoning, killing anger, of the sort he had not felt—

—since the day his brother died.

"We will rest here an hour," Morgaine said, sinking down to wash beside him, letting Siptah drink.

"Aye." He dipped up another double handful. It was spring-fed, this stream, and like ice, taking the breath. He stood up with a sudden effort.

The daylight went to gray and to dark.

"Vanye—" Morgaine said.

"Watch them!" he said to her in the Kurshin tongue, and sat down hard where he stood, his balance simply gone, his foot off the edge into the chill water, his wounds jolted so he thought he would not get the next breath at all.

"Vanye!"

"Watch them," he said again, calmly, fighting panic. He drew his foot out of the water. "*Liyo*, I will rest here a little. I am tired. That is all."

He heard her bend near him, felt her shadow take the heat of the sun from his face. He heard footsteps in the grass nearby and that frightened him.

"*Liyo*, do not turn your back on them."

She laid her hand on his brow. "Thee is fevered," she said.

"*Liyo*, in the name of Heaven—"

"We will rest here," she said. The daylight began to come back, but it was still brass and full of illusion, with her as a darkness in the center of it.

"We have no time—"

"Vanye, lie down."

He did as she asked, reckoning if they must stop an hour for his sake, he had as well not waste the time it cost them in argument. He let himself back on the grass and rested his head on his arm, and shut his eyes against the giddiness of the sky. The ground seemed to pitch and spin under him. He had not felt that dizzy when he was riding, and now that he let go it was hard not to lose all his senses. His stomach tried to heave and he refused to let it, refused the panic that lay at the bottom of his thoughts.

A little time, he told himself. They had been pushing too long to keep moving; and a battle and a ride with enemies-turned-comrades did not count for rest. An hour on his back, and he would be good for another ten.

Only, O God, he was weak. And his head spun.

And Morgaine was alone with these men.

She came back to him, knelt down by him, dampened a cloth in the cold stream and laid it on his brow.

"You are watching them," he murmured in his own tongue.

"I am watching them."

"*Liyo*, kill them."

"Hush, rest."

"Kill them!" He sat up on his elbow and caught the cloth in his hand, the pulse at once hammering in his ears and his gut hurting and his ribs a blinding pain. " 'Man and man,' you said. Then trust me to know. I am telling you these men are after the weapons; they are only waiting to see what more they can find out, whether we have anything else they want—Kill them. And do not give them any warning."

Her hand rested on his chest, pressing him to lie back. He would not yield.

"Listen to me," he said.

"Hush," she said. "Hush. I have an eye to them."

"This is a man who gave Chei to the wolves. This is the guide who lied to us, whose brother I killed. If it is sane inside it is a wonder."

"Lie back. Lie down. Do not make me trouble. Please. *Please*, Vanye."

He let go his breath and let himself back. She wet the cloth again and wrung it out and laid it on his brow. It set him shivering.

"I will ride," he said, "in an hour."

"Only lie here. I will make some tea."

"We cannot be risking a fire—"

She touched his lips with her fingers. "Still, I say. Hush. A little one. Do not fret about it. Be still."

"Willow tea," he murmured, "if you are going to do it anyway. My head aches."

He rested then with his eyes half-open, slitted on Chei and his two men, who sat apart on the stream-bank. He watched Morgaine gather up twigs and grass, and his gut tensed as he saw Chei rise and walk toward her and have words with her.

What they said he could not hear. But Morgaine settled down thereafter and made a fire with that means she could, and Chei and the others began to unsaddle the horses.

He sat up then, and began to get to his feet in dismay, but Morgaine looked at him and lifted her hand in that signal that meant no.

He fell back again, and lay in misery while the pulse beat like a hammer in his temples and the sun glared red behind closed lids.

She brought him tea to drink, infused very strongly with something bitter; and little pellets wrapped in leaves, that were from Shathan, and very precious. He took them and drank the sour-bitter tea, as large mouthfuls as he could bear, simply to get it down, and rested back again.

"I will be all right," he murmured then.

"Thee is not riding in an hour. Or two."

"Dark," he said. "Give me till dark. We can cut closer to the plain at night. Gain back the time."

But he was no better. If anything, he hurt the worse. It is because of lying still, he thought.

Then, clearly and honestly: I am getting worse.

And we are too near the gate.

He rested. It was not sleep that passed the hours into twilight, only a dimness in which Morgaine came and went, and gave him cold water to drink. "I will try," he said, then, "try to ride. Have them put me on my horse. I will stay there."

There was fear in her eyes. It verged on panic. She smoothed the hair back from his face. "We will hold this place," she said.

"With *what*? With *them*? With—" Anger brought a pain to his skull. His eyes watered, blurring the sight of her. "It is foolishness. Foolishness, *liyo*. No more time. Too many of them. When will you sleep? You cannot—cannot depend on me to stay awake. Cannot depend on me."

"I will manage."

"Do not lose for *me*! Do not think of it! Ride out of here!"

"Hush." She touched his face, bent and kissed him, weary, so very weary, her voice. Her hand shook against his cheek. "Forgive me. Trust me. Will you trust me?"

"Aye," he said, or thought he said. She unlaced his collar and took the stone from under his armor; and took it from him.

"Not to him—" he protested.

"No. I will keep it. I will keep it safe."

It was too difficult to hold on. The dark grew too deep, a place unto itself, tangled and mazed. He wanted to come back. He wanted to stay awake to listen to her.

He dreamed of dark, like that between the Gates.

He dreamed of dark, in which she walked away, and he could not so much as tell where she had gone.

Chei rested his head in his hands, weary with his own aches, with the foolishness that would not let the woman see reason.

Will not leave him, the inner voice said, and it echoed a night in Arunden's camp, a doorway—embarrassed youth, rebuffed and dismayed and made lonely all at once, in a child's way; Pyverrn, seeking exile—riding into Morund on a wretched, shaggy horse—*Ho, hello, old friend—Court grew deadly dull without you. . . .*

Thoughts upon thoughts upon thoughts. He rubbed the heels of his hands into his eyes, grimaced with the confusion of images.

"My lord," Rhanin said.

He looked up to see the lady walking toward them—with further delay, he reckoned. She looked distraught, her eyes shadowed and her face showing exhaustion.

She had to sleep. There would come a time she had to sleep. Then there was a reckoning, with the weapons in his hands, and the lady brought to see reason once for all.

He was not prepared to see her hand lift, and the black weapon in it, aimed straight at him. His heart froze in him: *death*, he thought. *Our death, only so a crazed woman dares sleep—*

"My lord Gault," she said quietly, "Qhiverin. Chei. I have a proposition for you."

"My lady?" he asked, carefully.

"I am going to rest. You will tend him, you will do everything you can for him, you will make him fit to ride, my lord; and if he is not better by morning, I will kill you all. If he cries out—*once*—I will shoot one of you at random. Do you have any doubt of that, my lord?"

"He will not *be* fit to ride—the man is fevered—he is out of his head—"

"Do you doubt my word, *my lord*? Do you want an earnest of my intentions?"

"She is mad," Hesiyyn exclaimed.

Chei gathered himself hastily to his feet. "Up," he said, dragging at Hesiyyn, at Rhanin. And cast an anxious glance at Morgaine, whose weapon stayed centered on him, whose eyes were, as Hesiyyn said—mad and beyond all reason.

∽ Chapter 16

"Vanye. *Vanye*," Morgaine's voice called him gently.

"Aye, *liyo*." He opened his eyes, trying to bring her face out of the dusk. He could not, quite.

"Vanye, will you trust me?"

"Aye, *liyo*."

"I am going to go over there and rest, the night. Listen to me. I have not the strength to take care of thee—" Her fingers brushed his cheek. Her voice shook. "Chei will help thee, he will do everything he can for thee—he has agreed, at peril of his life. Does thee understand, Vanye? I do not want thee waking and not knowing where I am. And if he hurts thee I will shoot him. And if thee does not mend I will shoot him. And he knows it."

He blinked at her. When she took that tone it was her intention beyond a doubt, even if it made no sense at all.

"Thee understands?"

"Aye," he said.

The dark swallowed him up a time, and there was movement about him—firelit faces between him and the night sky.

One was Chei's.

He forgot, then, where he was.

"Ah," he cried, and tried desperately to fight them.

"Be still," Chei said, and put his hand over his mouth. "Be still, man. Vanye. Vanye—listen to me."

He recalled then, some insanity that Morgaine was with him. Or would come. He could not remember which.

"Look." Chei lifted his head, carefully, gently, and showed him a strange sight: showed him Siptah, and at Siptah's feet a stump, or some object, and Morgaine sitting with her hands between her knees. He was afraid, until he saw *Changeling* across her lap.

"You are safe," Chei said. "You are quite safe with us."

"She has promised to shoot one of us." Hesiyyn gently unfastened a buckle at his side as Chei let his head back. "I have no doubt which one of us. My lord Chei is necessary, Rhanin wins everyone, and I am told I make enemies. I pray you know I shall be careful."

He blinked dazedly. He recalled some such thing, mad as it was, and lay still, until they needed to work the mail shirt off. But that they did gently, easing his arms as they worked it free.

It was all one with the dark, the fever, the nightmare that began to become ease of pain. They put warm compresses on his hurts, renewing them constantly; they put hot cloths over him, soaked in herbals; they made him drink something complex and musky, and breathe something that gave his throat ease. He became comfortable, finally.

And slept till Chei roused him and made him drink something else.

"No more," he said.

"Drink this," Chei said fiercely. "Damn you, drink; we will not die for your convenience."

He heard the harshness of panic in that voice. He recalled a nightmare, wherein Morgaine had asked him bear with everything.

He struggled onto his arm, dislodging compresses, to see was she safe and his memory true.

She was there. *Changeling* was still with her. Siptah stood close by her. Her head had fallen forward, her pale hair touched with fire-glow and starlight.

"Drink," Rhanin said.

He trusted them then, and drank, with a clearer head than he had had. He shivered, and the bruises hurt less. They renewed the compresses out of a pan of hot water, and smothered him in blankets.

Only his chest hurt sharply, where ribs might be cracked. But that, he thought, was bearable, if he were not so drained and weak. The burns hurt far less; the other injuries that had near taken his mind with pain, were so much relieved he seemed to drift in enervated numbness.

The *qhal* whispered among themselves, urgently, debating something they might give him. Or how much they might give him, to put him on his feet. One said no, there was risk. Another objected he had to ride, and could not else: he would never last in the saddle. And that was Chei and Hesiyyn.

He lay and thought about that. He tested his breathing, how much it hurt; he moved his right leg, to test whether it hurt as it had, and looked at the two who argued.

"Is there something," he asked faintly, in a lull, "will let me ride today?"

He shocked them, perhaps. There was a moment's utter hush.

"Yes," Chei said. "There is something that will. But the end of it is worse than the first. Best you do without it. You will ride. That is what she asked. That is what she will have. We have kept our end of the bargain."

"Do you drink it," he asked, the faintest of whispers, "or swallow it?"

"Not, I say."

"Chei—tell me what it will do."

"It will kill you, that is what it will do. And no."

"It would keep a dead man on his feet," Hesiyyn said. "It would not improve his judgment. And my lord says the truth: it would take a heavy toll."

"Give it to me. To carry. Chei, give it to me and we are quit of a great deal."

Chei gnawed at his lip—young Chei's face, a mature *qhal*'s calculation as he rested with his arm on his knee and his eyes, by firelight, flickering with changes.

"You would take only a taste of it on your tongue," he said. "I will tell you the truth, man, if you use it in extremity—you will not survive it."

He thought about that. He drew breaths against the ache in his ribs, and knew what his sword-arm or his archery was worth at the moment. He thought how far they had yet to go.

"You are not the man I would choose," he said. "But there is a great deal you could learn from my liege. There are more worlds than you know. If you knew more than you did, I think you might understand her more. You would know why she is right. More than I do. Give me this thing and do not tell her. The important thing is that we get there."

Chei looked at him in profound disturbance. His fist clenched and unclenched, of the arm which supported his chin, and his brow was ridged and glistening with sweat. "And you do what—lay this in her lap? Tell her then we tried to kill you?"

"We will have no quarrel, Chei. What do you want? That she stop somewhere further on—for my sake? That is what she *is* doing. Give it to me."

Chei delved into his belongings, and gathered out a packet. "One pellet. One. No more than that. Three and your heart would burst. I am putting it with your belongings. That is all I will do." He busied himself and mixed something with water, and boiled it.

"What is this?" he asked, when Hesiyyn intended he drink it.

"I thought we were allies," Hesiyyn said. "Drink. This is for the fever."

"Also," Hesiyyn said when he had drunk it, "it will make you sleep."

The sun came up, and Morgaine still drowsed, he saw as he lifted his head, with Siptah's tether passed across her shoulder, with the sword in her lap, her back against a rock, and the small black weapon between her knees, in both her hands.

It was Chei whose eyes had shadows. It was Chei who offered him an over-cooked porridge, with a hand that shook with exhaustion.

He took it. He forced it down. It came at too much cost to refuse.

Across the little distance, Siptah jerked his head up and snorted challenge to Rhanin's approach. Morgaine lifted her head abruptly, the weapon in her hand.

But it was a bowl Rhanin brought, offering it to her. Rhanin came no closer, and Morgaine got quickly to her feet, *Changeling* in one hand, the black weapon in the other, and stopped, staring not at Rhanin, but toward him.

He stared back at her, weak as he was, and got up on his arm, feeling the shock of cold air as the blanket fell.

For a long moment she said nothing. Then: "How does thee fare this morning?"

"Much better," he said. "Much better, *liyo*."

"I had not meant to fall so far asleep—"

He drew a breath, such as yesterday would have cost him pain. It amazed him it did not, overmuch. Only it would be very easy, just now, to weep, and he moved, suddenly, and shoved himself up with a sudden straightening of his arm so that a twinge took his mind off it. He was dizzy then. The whole world swung round.

She came to him and swept *Changeling*, sheathed and crosswise, in curt dismissal of the others, who drew back a few paces. Then she knelt and spared a glance for him.

"I think the porridge is safe," he murmured, "but I would not eat it."

"Has thee?"

"Aye," he said. "It is truly wretched."

She slid the black weapon into place at her belt, touched him with that hand, brushed the hair off his unshaven cheek. She looked tired, tired and mortally worried. "We will ride at night," she said.

"*Liyo*, we cannot wait!"

"Now how are we arguing? I take your advice and you will none of it. We are safe here for the moment. The horses are resting. We can make up the time."

"We cannot make up two days. I can ride." He sat upright and tucked his leg up; and she put her hand onto his knee.

"Thee will lie down, thee will rest, that is what. Thee will not undo everything." She touched his ribs, where Hesiyyn had wound a tight bandage. "Broken, does thee think?"

"No. Sore." He drew a breath, testing it as he had tested it again and again: if he kept his back straight it was much better. "I will manage."

"Vanye." Her hand sought his wrist and closed on it, hard. "Do not give up. Hear me? I will tell thee a thing may comfort thee—"

She hesitated, then. That reticence did not seem to herald anything that should comfort him; and ice settled into his stomach. "What?" he asked. "What would you tell me, *liyo*?"

"Thee knows—how substance goes into a gate—It . . . disarranges itself . . . and some similar arrangement comes together at the other side—"

"You have told me." He did not like to talk of such things. He did not like to think of them oftener than he must—especially now, facing a gate which was not behaving as it should. He wished she would go straight to the point.

"Thee will find—thy hurts—will not trouble thee the other side. Thee will not carry the scars of this beyond it. Thee will mend."

She could lie with such simplicity. Or with webs of truth. Except that it was something kept from him, that he would not like. In such things she would not meet his eyes. It was that simple.

"What are you saying?" he asked.

"I chose a time," she said. "I made a pattern, for thee as for me . . . a rested pattern, a whole pattern, a pattern without flaw. Within its limits—and it has them—it will always restore it. Every gate, on every world—will recognize thee, and always restore it—restore *thee*, as thee was, so far as it has substance to work with. There will be no scars. Nothing to remind thee."

It made no sense for a moment. He put his hand to his ribs, wondering could it mend more than the surface.

Or what other things they had done to him.

"There will always be the weakness in the knee," she said. "That happened before the pattern was made. Would I had done it before that. But there was never the leisure it needed."

"Shathan," he said. "Azeroth-gate."

"Aye. There. The gates will abhor any deviation from that moment. They will restore that moment, so far as they can, always. The thoughts go on. The memories. But the body—will not change."

"Will not *change*? Ever?" A sense of panic took him. He thought that he should be grateful. He thought that it was a kind of gift.

But it was Gate-given. And every Gate-magic was flawed—

"I shall grow older—"

"Never. Not in body."

"O my God," he murmured. For a moment the dizziness was back. Mortality was, reminding him with a sharp pain in his side and a twinge in the hip.

He had always had an image of himself, older, grown to his mature strength—had begun to see it, in breadth of shoulder, strength of arm. A man looked forward to such a thing.

It would never happen. His life was stopped. He thought of the dragon, frozen in snow, in mid-reach.

"My God, my God." He crossed himself, gone cold, inside and out.

"Injuries will never take their toll of thee. Age—will have no power over thee. Thee will grow wiser. But thee will always mend in a gate-passage, always shed the days and years."

"Why such as Chei, then? Why Gault? *Why Thiye, in Heaven's name?*" He wanted to weep. He found himself lost again, lost at this end of his journey as at the beginning. "If it can be done like this, why did they choose to kill—?"

"Because," she said, "they are *qhal*. And I know things they do not. Call it my father's legacy. And if they should know, Vanye, *that* secret, they would find others, that I will give no one, that are not written on the sword—that I will not *permit* anyone to know and live—" Again her hand brushed his cheek. "Forgive me. I had meant to tell thee—some better time. But best thee know, now—Forgive me. I need thee too much. And the road would grow too lonely."

He took her hand, numb in shock. He pressed it. It was all he could think to do for answer.

"Rest," she said. And rose and walked away from him, stopping for a moment to look at Chei and the rest—at Rhanin, who still had the bowl in his hands, beside the others. "I will make my own breakfast," she said; but to Chei she said nothing. She only looked at him, and then walked on, *Changeling* still in her left hand.

Vanye sat numb and incapable, for the moment, of moving. He trembled, and did not know whether it was outrage or grief, or why, except he had always thought she would betray him in one way, and she had found one he had never anticipated.

You might have ordered me, he raged at her in his mind. *If you were going to do such a thing,* liyo, *God in Heaven, could you not have bidden me, could you not have laid it on my honor, given me at least the chance to go into it of my own will?*

But he could not say these things. He could not quarrel with her, in front of strangers. Or now, that he was fighting for his composure.

It was his protection she had intended. It was for every good reason. It promised—O Heaven!—

He could not imagine what it promised.

It was, in any case, only the thought of a thought of himself she had stolen. And if she had thought him too foolish to choose for himself, that was so, sometimes. She was often right.

He reached beside him, in the folds of his mail shirt, and felt after a small, paper packet. He found it, and unfolded it, and saw the very tiny beads that lay on the red paper—eight of them.

He folded it up again, dragged his belt over and tucked the packet into the slit-pocket where he kept small flat things, where, lately, had been a small razor-edged blade. But Chei's men had taken that. He did not, given the circumstances of his losing it, look to have it back again.

He lay back to rest, then, since he had no more likelihood of persuading Morgaine than Chei did. There was justification for the delay: beyond this point, he thought, rested horses and rested men might make the difference, and Chei and his men had gotten little enough sleep last night. If the horses were rested—they might dare the fringe of the plain, and know that they had enough strength to run or to fight.

It was a risk that made his flesh crawl.

"She is staying here," Chei came to him to say, standing over him, a fair-haired shadow against the dawn. Chei was indignant. And came to him for alliance.

He found some small irony in that. "Man," he said quietly, reasonably, "she will be thinking. Go to her. Be patient with her. As thoroughly, as exactly as you can, tell her everything you know about the way ahead: make her maps. Answer her questions. Then go away and let her think. Whatever you have held back—to bargain for your lives—this is the time to throw everything you have into her hands. She will not betray you. You say you will follow her. Prove it."

It was not precisely the truth. But it was as good, he thought, as might save all their lives. Chei clearly doubted it.

But Chei went away then, and presented himself where Morgaine was busy with her gear; and knelt down with his hands on his knees and talked to her and drew on the ground, answering her questions for some little time.

Himself, he scanned the rough hills, the rocks and the scrub which rose like walls about them, watched the flight of a hawk, or something hawklike.

Morgaine was not utterly without calculation, he thought, in choosing this camp. The valley was wide and either end of it was in view. Nowhere were they in easy bowshot of the sides or cover a man could reach without crossing open ground.

Until now Chei and his company, riding ahead of them through the hills, had run the risk of a gate-force ambush, two stones bridging their power from side to side of a narrow pass. Chei had surely known that. And doubtless Morgaine would put him and his company to the fore again when they rode out of this place. Chei would not like that.

But there was small comfort having them *all* riding point, and surely neither of them would do it.

There was better food at noon: Morgaine cooked it. Vanye stirred himself to sit up in the shade, and to put his breeches on and walk about, and to take a little exercise, a little sword-drill to work the legs, and the abused shoulder, which had a great dark bruise working its way out from the arrow-strike.

It would go through several color-changes, he thought, and then thought that it might not, for one reason or the other; and put all of that to the back of his mind with a swing and flourish and extension that worked the ribs as far as he thought safe for the moment. Vanity, he chided himself, taking pleasure in Hesiyyn's respectful look, and was careful to stand very still for a moment after, before he called it enough and walked back to the shade and sat down.

He went through the arrows Rhanin had collected then, and took his harness-knife—the loss of the little razor vexed him—and sighted down the shafts and saw to the fletchings, in both quivers finding only three shafts to fault and mark with a cautioning stain on their gray feathers, and one fletching that wanted repair.

Then he gathered himself up again and went and saw to the horses, running his hands over their legs, looking for strain, looking over their feet, seeing whether there was any shoe needing re-setting. The bending and lifting was hard. And Morgaine was watching him: he felt her stare on his back, and gentled the gray stud with particular care, lulling him with all his skill to keep him from his rougher tricks—"So, so, lad, you have no wish to make me a liar, do you?"

The fine head turned, dark-eyed and thinking; the white-tipped tail lashed and switched with considerable force and he stamped once, thunderously. But: "Hai, hai, hai," Vanye chided him, and he surrendered the ticklish hind foot, with which, he thanked Heaven, there was no problem, nor with the others.

He did all these things. He wanted, looking to certain eventualities, to do them particularly well, and the way he always did.

"Sleep," he bade Morgaine, pausing to wash on his way back to the shade. "Sleep a while."

She looked at him with a worry she did not trouble to hide. He could bear very little of that.

"We have not that far to go," she said, "—Chei swears."

"Perhaps he has even learned to reckon distances."

Her eyes flickered, a grim amusement that went even to a grin and a fond look. "Aye. Perhaps. I do not think I will sleep. Go take what rest you can." She drew the chain of the pyx from over her head. "Here. Best you keep it now."

He closed his fist about it. It was not something he wanted to wear openly.

She sketched rapidly in the dirt at her feet. "This is where we are. Chei says. This is Mante. This is where we will ride. This hill, then skirting the plain and up again. There is a pass. A gatehouse, but not a Gate."

"We are that close."

"Under Skarrin's very eye, if there were a mistake with stone or sword. We will start at sundown. A single night to the pass, if we go direct." She let go her breath. "We will *ask* at his gate."

"Ask!"

"We will not come like enemies. It will be Chei's affair. He says he can pass us through. We will have the greatest difficulty beyond that. So Chei says." She sketched a pocket behind the line that represented the cliffs. *"Neisyrrn Neith.* Death's Gate. A well of stone, very wide. There are gate-stones within it—here, and here, and here."

He sank down on his heels and onto his knees. His breath grew short.

"Chei swears," Morgaine said, "there is—no other way in. In all their wars, in all their internal wars—no enemy can come at them, except by the highlands. And that, they rule utterly. *Those* lords are loyal."

"God save us." He drew breath after breath. *"Liyo*—turn back. Turn back, give this more time. We can find a way—"

"Those lords are loyal, Vanye. And the south cannot stand against them. I have thought of it. I have thought of pulling back to Morund and trying to take the south—but it could not hold. This whole southern region is a sink, Mante's midden-heap—it is where they send their exiles. It is where they breed their human replacements." She went on drawing. "Herot, Sethys, Stiyesse, Itheithe, Nenais—I forget the other names. Here, here, here—this is a vast land. And I do not doubt this Skarrin set the World-gate purposely on Morund. Perpetually on Morund, in the case any intruder, any rebel, any rival—should attempt him. Here, below these cliffs, this rift in the world—lie Men; and his exiles. Here above, across all this continent—lie the *qhalur* lands. There is irony in this. We knew our young guide was abysmally incapable of reckoning a day's ride—"

"Or lied to us."

"—had never traveled much in all his life, except the hills, except forest trails and winding roads. Straight distances bewildered him. He lived his life in so small a place. Arid he did not know anything beyond it. The distance between Morund and Herot, is less than he thought. Sethys and Stiyesse abut against marsh he did not know existed. These are little places. These are holds humans once had. *Qhal* have moved in, those exiled, those out of favor—like Qhiverin, who became Gault. The south has no resource against the north, not if the north realized its danger. And by now, since Tejhos—Skarrin does, though Chei does swear—for what it is worth—that he did not tell Skarrin our purpose here. That is the only grace we may have, if we can believe it."

He leaned his hands on his knees and bowed his head a moment. "We *should* have gone to Morund, the way you wanted to. We would have learned this. We could have dealt with whatever we found there—whatever we found there. This is my fault, *liyo*, it is *all* my—"

"It was my decision. It was *my* judgment. Do not be so cursed free with blame. It is still my decision, and all of this may be wrong. Chei has the notion we can come close before they will take alarm."

"With *our* horses—"

"Or his. That roan of his is no unremarkable beast, in itself. No, they will surely know us: they will have gotten the description from their watchers afield. It is a question of keeping them uncertain what we intend." She looked at the ground in front of her and seemed lost for a moment. "Chei says if they have thrown no great number of men into the field since yesterday, they are taking a cautious path. He talked at some length of his own difficulties with his Over-lord—he was high-born, was a member of a martial order that lost its influence at court: disastrously for him, though more so for others. Connections saved his life and sent him to Morund, to redeem himself, if ever he could—The ar-rangement by which human lords were permitted to rule in the south was collapsing, on evidence of human Gault's complicity with the rebels in Mante—*that* was how they lured the original Gault into their trap: and sentenced him and Qhiverin to one conjoined existence—on that point Qhiverin's friends in-tervened virtually to kidnap Gault from his jailers and coerce the gate-wardens to join them, to forestall enemies who would have preferred not to have Qhiv-erin at Morund."

"Where he served their interests well enough—"

"So he has done. So he fully intended to come home, someday. Except—as thee says, possibly we could have persuaded him to go against his lord from the beginning. He says so. Certainly he is quick enough to commit treason. I do not know. At least—he has had some little credit with Skarrin for setting affairs in the south in order, if, as he says, they do not take that for too *much* success, and if his connections in Mante have not lost all influence. That we have arrived in the south without a force about us—that they have lost contact with him, whom they do not trust, under uncertain circumstances, after he has faithfully sent them a report from Tejhos and seemed, there, under the witness of the wardens there, to be fighting us—all of this, he thinks, might create some de-bate among Skarrin's advisers. The question is whether we should attempt stealth—or bewilder them further. Recall that there is one way in, that we must pass within *that*, that thing they call *Seiyyin Neith*, the Gate of Exiles, and within this league-wide pit of stone, that they call Death's-gate—they can kill us with a thought. As you did say: a man who thinks he is winning—will not flee."

"No, he will send us straightway to Hell, *liyo*, and we will hardly see it coming!"

"Chei will get us to Exile's Gate. There is where they will be vulnerable."

"God in Heaven, are we leaning on this man's word?"

She lifted her eyes to him. "This man—wants to live. So do the men with him. Did I not say I trusted him more than honest men? They *have* no cause, no cause for which they would give up their lives. Skarrin cannot promise them anything they would believe. Not as deeply as they have tangled themselves. They know that."

For a moment he truly could not breathe. His eyes went involuntarily to see where Chei and the others were, but they were not in earshot, even for Hesiyyn's *qhalur* hearing, and it was the Kurshin tongue they spoke.

"The sword—" he said. "If we use it at this Gate of Exiles—will be very near those standing stones."

"The sword is unstable. Like the gate. We cannot predict. There is no way to predict—what will happen."

"Aye," he said, and wiped at the sweat which gathered on his lip, and wiped his hands on his knees.

She scratched through the map once, twice. "Go, rest, take whatever sleep thee can. Thee will need it."

He went back and lay down again, staring at the sky through the branches, counting leaves, that being better than other thoughts that pressed on him. He put the stone about his neck, and lay with his hand closed about the pyx to shield it, to be certain of its safety.

And when the sun started below the hill he rose up and dressed methodically, laced up the padding tight and worked the mail shirt on: that was worst. Morgaine came to help him with it; and with the buckles beneath the arm.

"I will saddle up," she said. "No arguments from thee. Hear?"

"Aye," he said, though it fretted him. "Pull it tight, *liyo*. It can take another notch there."

"Thee has to get on the horse."

"I have to stay there," he said.

To that she said nothing. She only tightened the strap.

They mounted up while there was still a little light beyond the hills. It was Hesiyyn who rode farthest point, Hesiyyn with his brown cloak about him, his pale hair loose about his shoulders, his weapons all covered. His horse was a fine blood bay with no white markings.

It was Hesiyyn's own reasoning that he should ride foremost, to forestall any ambushes: "It is likely the only company in which I shall ever find myself the most respectable."

With which the *qhal*-lordling put his horse well out to the fore, passing out of sight around the bending of the stream, while Chei and Rhanin went a distance behind. "Come," Morgaine said, and chose her own distance from that pair—herself cloaked in black; and Vanye swept his own cloak about him when he had gotten up, and threw up the hood over the white-scarfed helm.

Ambush was possible. Hesiyyn might betray them, signaling to some band out from Mante. Everything, henceforward, was possible—

Even that they should come to the verge of the starlit plain unmolested—a last hillside, a trail down a steep, rocky slope, on which Hesiyyn sat waiting for them, resting his horse, spinning and spinning a curious object on the surface of the slab of rock on which he sat.

"The lots come up three, three, and three: are you superstitious?"

"Curse your humor," Chei said, reining back his horse from the descent.

They changed about with the remounts, one to the three *qhal*, the blaze-faced bay going turn and turn with Siptah and Arrhan: and again Hesiyyn went to the lead, but not so far separated from them now.

Down and down to the plain, a difficult slope, a long and miserable jolting. *Hang on*, Vanye told himself, cursing every step the bay made under him. Sweat broke out, wind-chilled on his face. He clenched the saddlehorn and thought of the red packet in his belt-pocket.

Not yet, he thought. Not for this. To every jolt and every uneven spot: not for this, not for this—

Across the plain, the mountains—not the peaks of a range like the Cedur Maje of his homeland, but a wall of rock which giants might have built, as if the world had broken, and that were the breaking-point, under a sky so brilliant with stars and moon it all but cast a shadow.

"They are not preventing us this far," he said to Morgaine.

He wished in one part of his reeling mind that the enemy would turn up, now, quickly, before they were committed to this—that somehow something would happen to send them on some other and better course.

But there was no sign of it.

They came down onto the plain at last, a gradual flattening of the course they rode. Vanye turned as best he could and looked back at the track they had made as they entered the grassy flat, a trail too cursed clear under the heavens. "As well blaze a trail," he muttered. If there had been the choice of skirting the hills instead of taking Chei's proposed course across the plain, it was rapidly diminishing.

They drew their company together now, Hesiyyn riding with them as they struck out straight across.

And the cliffs which had been clear from the hillside showed only as a rim against the horizon.

Then was easier riding. Then he finally seized hold of his right leg by the boot-top and hauled it with difficulty over the saddlehorn, wrapped his arms about his suffering ribs and with a look at Morgaine that assured him she knew he was going to rest for a while, bowed his head, leaned back against the cantle and gave himself over to the bay's steady pace in a sickly exhaustion.

He roused himself only when they paused to trade mounts about. "No need," Morgaine said, sliding down from Arrhan's back. "That horse is fit enough to go on carrying you, and I will take Siptah: I weigh less."

He was grateful. He took the medicines she carried for him, washed them down with a drink from her flask, and sat there ahorse while others stretched their legs. It was not sleep, that state of numbness he achieved. It was not precisely awareness either. He knew that they mounted up again; he knew that they moved, he trusted that Morgaine watched the land around them.

No other did he trust . . . except he reasoned if betrayal was what Chei and his men intended, it did not encompass losing their own lives, not lives so long and so dearly held; and that meant some warning to them.

Some warning was all his liege needed. And half-asleep and miserable as he was, he continually rode between her and them: it was a well-trained horse, if rough-gaited, and Siptah, he thanked Heaven, tolerated it going close by him.

He did truly sleep for a while. He jerked his head up with the thought that he was falling, caught his balance, and saw the cliffs no nearer.

Or they were vaster than the eye wanted to see. His leg had gone numb. He hauled it back over, and his eyes watered as the muscles extended. Everything hurt.

And the riding went on and on, while a few clouds drifted across the stars and passed, and a wind rose and rippled through the endless grass.

Another change of horses. This time he did dismount, and walked a little, as far as privacy to relieve himself, discovering that he could, which did for one long misery; and saw to Arrhan's girth and the bay's.

But facing the necessity to haul himself up again, he stood there holding the saddlehorn and trying, with several deep breaths, to gather the wind and the courage to make that pull.

"Vanye!" Morgaine said, just as he had found it. He stopped, unnerved, with a jolt that brought tears to his eyes; and: "Chei," she said, "one of you give him a hand up."

"My lady," Chei said. And came and offered his hands for a stirrup.

Shame stung him. But he set his foot in Chei's linked hands and let Chei heave him up like some pregnant woman.

"For a like favor," Chei said to him.

He recalled it. And flinching from Chei's hand on his knee, he backed Arrhan out of his reach.

*　*　*

The cliffs cut off the sky before them, against the dimming stars, and they had left a trail a child could follow, the swath of passage in tall grass. The horses caught mouthfuls now and again: there was no time to give them more than that.

Morgaine rode the bay now; it was Siptah due the rest. And the sky above the eastern hills was showing no stars: the sun was coming.

We are beyond recall now. That was the thought that kept gnawing at him. *Wise or not, we are beyond any change of mind.*

God save us.

By sunlight, at the lagging pace of weary horses, the rock face in front of them rose and filled all their view—a plain of dry grass, a wall of living stone, so abrupt and so tall it defied the eye's logic.

It had one gap, shadow-blued within the yellow stone, in noon sunlight, and closing it—the gatehouse that Chei had named to them. *Seiyyin Neith.*

Doors—the size of which a Kurshin eye refused to understand, until a hawk flew near them, a mote against their height.

Exile's Gate.

Chei turned the roan back a half-circle as they rode, reined in alongside and lifted a hand toward it. "There," he said, "there, you see what we propose to assault. That is merely the nethermost skirt of Mante." He leaned on his saddlebow and gave a twitch of his shoulders, a shiver. "A man forgets it, whose eyes are used to Morund's size. And the boy, my friends, . . . is terrified."

He gave a flick of the reins and sent his horse thundering on ahead to join his men.

↶ Chapter 17

Another space of riding. This time it had measure, that vision of the towering cliffs which rose steadily before them. Vanye looked up at the doors, whose valves were iron, whose surface held twelve bronze panels each, of figures far more than life-size, the actions of which he could not at first understand, until he saw the detail. They were scenes of execution, and torment.

"Can such things open?" he wondered aloud, and his voice was less steady than he wished. He expected some sally-port: he looked, for it among the panels, and saw no joint.

"Oh, indeed," Chei said, "when Mante wishes to diminish its vassals—and its exiles. They do open."

"Mante has a taste for excess," Morgaine said.

"They want a man to remember," Hesiyyn said, "the difficulty of return."

Vanye looked at Rhanin, who rode alone ahead of them, weary man riding one exhausted horse, leading another, dwarfed by the scenes of brutal cruelty looming over them.

He felt something move in him then, toward all of these his enemies, a pang that went to the heart.

He saw not Seiyyin Neith, of a sudden, but a steep road down from gray stone walls, and on it, beneath those walls which had seemed so high and dreadful, a grief-stricken boy in a white-scarfed helm, with exile in front of him.

This at least they had in common. And they were brave men who did not flinch now, in the face of this thing.

This barrier, Mante reared in the name of justice. This was the face it turned to its damned and its servants. This was what the power of the world held as honorable dealings with its own subjects—men hanged, and gutted and burned alive, and what other things, higher up the doors, he had no wish to see.

He drew a copper-edged breath and leaned on the saddle, a shift of weight that sent a wearying, monotonous pain through his sides and his gut, a cursed, always-present misery. He was not certain there was life left in his legs. He had found a few positions that hurt less, and kept shifting between them. But the approach to this place meant different necessities, meant—Heaven knew what. If they must fight here, he could do that, he thought, as long as they stayed mounted.

"How is thee faring?" Morgaine asked him. "I will manage," he said.

She looked at him, long, as they rode. "On thy oath, Nhi Vanye."

That shook him. He was much too close to judgment to trifle with damnation. It was unfairly she dealt with him—but she had no conscience in such matters, he had long known it.

"Vanye, does thee leave me to guess?"

"I will stay ahorse," he said, half the truth. "I can defend myself." But he could imagine her relying on him in some rush to cover, or doing something foolish to rescue him if he should fall. He sweated, feeling a coldness in the pit of his stomach. He had not used the *qhalur* medicines. He abhorred such things. More, he did not think they could deal with a numbness that had his right leg all but useless, prickling like needles all up the inside. "It is walking I am not sure of. But my head is clear."

She said nothing then. She was thinking, he decided—thinking through things he did not know, thinking what to do, how far to believe him, and what of her plans she must now change—all these things, because he had been a fool and brought them to this pass, and now began to be a burden on her.

I shall not be, he would have protested. But he already was. And knew it.

He let Arrhan fall a little back then—the horses fretted and snorted, having the scent of strangeness in the wind, the prospect of a fight—always, always, the prospect of war wherever they came to habitations of any kind. The *qhal* cared little what he did. And Morgaine had her eyes set on the thing in front of them.

He slipped the red paper from its place and carefully, with fingers which trembled, managed to get one of the tiny pellets beneath a fingernail, and then, losing his resolve and his trust of the gift, dislodged it and let it roll back into the paper. He folded it up again, and put it back.

Fool, he thought again. Coward.

But he knew that *he* would take care for her. He was not sure what the stuff in the red paper cared for. And there was too much and too delicate hazard to deal with, which needed clear wits and good judgment.

He gained leverage as he could, took his weight mostly on his arms, hands on the saddlebow, and let the pain run as it would, while he made the right leg move, and bend, and the feeling come back in tingling misery. Sweat fell from his face and spattered his hands, white-knuckled on the horn.

He watched Chei ride up to the very doors, draw the red roan alongside that door-rim and pound with a frail human fist against that towering mass of metal, which hardly resounded to his blows.

"I am Chei ep Kantory," he shouted, in a voice that seemed far too small. "I am Chei lord of Morund, Warden of the South! I have brought visitors to the Overlord! Open the doors!"

They will not, Vanye thought then. It seemed too improbable that anyone inside could even hear them. He looked up dizzily toward the masonry that supported the great doors, expecting there, if they had any answer, the small black figures of archers, and arrows to come down on them like sleet. Fore-warning was all the grace he sought of this place—*time*, for Morgaine to draw the sword, with all the risk *that* was, this close to the gate.

But metal boomed and clanked and hinges groaned with a sound that hurt the ears and shied the horses: Arrhan came up on her hind legs and down again, braced in an instant's confusion. He caught his balance, steadied her, colliding with the panicked bay at lead, at Siptah's left.

The iron doors groaned and squealed outward, opening on a shadowed hall of scale to match them, pillars greater in girth than all but the greatest trees of Shathan.

He slipped the ring that held his sword at his back, and let it fall ready to his side.

"Not yet," Morgaine said, as Chei and his companions started forward and rode into that hall. She began to ride after, calmly, slowly as the men in front of them.

He touched Arrhan with his heels and curbed the mare's nervousness with a pat on her sweating neck. His hand was shaking.

Reason enough, he thought, as he passed between the doors that towered either side of him, greater than Ra-morij's very walls. He could not see what images were on the inside: he dared not take his eyes from where they were going, into an aisle of vast pillars wanly lit with shafts of sunlight from above.

There was a second set of doors before them, far down that forest of stone. They were closed.

Did we expect more? he asked himself, and breathed the air of the shadow that fell on them, a dank chill the worse after the noon warmth outside. He heard the clank that heralded the sealing of the doors behind them, and steadied Arrhan, who shied and danced under him. The blaze-faced bay jerked and jolted at lead, fighting it. Shod hooves clattered and echoed on pavings, under the machine-noise of iron and chain and ratchets.

And the ribbon of daylight which lay wide about them, narrowed and vanished with the meeting and sealing of the doors at their backs.

The horses settled, slowly, in a profound silence.

Footsteps sounded within the forest of pillars. A *qhal* in black armor, his silver hair loose around his shoulders, walked out into their path, into a shaft of light.

It was not the only footfall in the place. But the pillars hid what else moved about them.

"My lord Warden," Chei said, as the roan fought the rein.

"South-warden?" Seiyyin's Warden asked. He was not young nor old. The face might have been carved of bone, the eyes of cold glass.

"Yes, my lord," Chei answered him—youth's form and youth's face; but that was not what sat his horse facing this grim lord. "I was Qhiverin Asfelles."

"With?"

"Rhanin ep Eorund, once Taullyn Daras, and Hesiyyn Aeisyryn, under my orders, in the performance of my office, with persons traveling under my seal. We are escorting this lady and her companion to Mante."

The lord Warden's eyes traveled past the others to Vanye and to Morgaine, and lingered, unreadable and cold. "These are the Outsiders."

"They are, my lord. I urge you speak civilly to them. It was a mistake they ever came through Morund-gate, and due to their falling in with humans, and due to lies humans have told them, there have been costly misunderstandings. This lady is a warden herself, and she is not well-pleased with the things she has met on her way."

Wise man, Vanye thought, light-headed with the pounding of his heart. *Chei, get my lady through this and I will be your debtor, I swear it.*

And, O Heaven, the Warden's cold eyes shifted toward them with the least small fracture in his command of the affair.

Not a stupid man either. Nor one incapable of shifting footing. "Where are you warden, lady?"

Morgaine rode a little forward; Vanye moved instantly to stay beside her.

"Where I am warden," Morgaine said, "and more than warden—is something between your Overlord and myself. But I thank you, my lord, if I am about to meet more courtesy than has been my experience on this journey. It will do a great deal to mend matters."

For a long moment the Warden was silent. Then: "We will advise the authorities in Mante," the Warden said.

"I would suggest—my lord—you advise Skarrin himself, and do not waste my time with 'authorities' and deputies. He is the one who *can* say yes or no, he is the one to whom your 'authorities' have to appeal if they are not utter fools, and I assure you, lord Warden, he will be better pleased if you do *not* bring my affairs to him through a succession of subordinates, not all of whom *need* to know my name or my business, for your *safety*, my lord Warden."

It was very still in the vast hall.

Then: "I pray you," the Warden said, "leave your horses to my deputies and accept my hospitality. Advise me of whatever complaints you have, with names where you may know them. Our lord will see justice done."

A cold crept through the sudden warmth, a sense of meshes closing. "It is a trap," Vanye murmured in his own tongue. "*Liyo*, I beg you, no."

"My lord Warden," Morgaine said gravely, gently, "I should fear then—for your own well-being. I am not a comfortable guest. The Warden of Morund and his men are in my custody, as I think your lord will sanction when he hears what I have to say. The South-warden has come into more knowledge of my business than your lord may like, as it is. *And* he has created difficulties for me. I have promised him if he makes amends and if his lord will release him, I will take him and his men with me, and save their lives. But I am *not* disposed to leave this world with an entourage of half your lord's councillors and his wardens. I advise you in all earnestness, my lord of Seiyyin Neith: my affairs are secret, and I have told you enough already to put you at some risk. Do as I tell you. Send this message directly to your lord: Morgaine Anjhuran is here to see him, under circumstances you may explain to him."

"Anj—"

Morgaine spelled it. "Be precise. Be very precise, my lord. Do you understand? Your safety and his are in question."

"I—have no direct contact with the high lord. I can gain it. It will take time. I beg you—step down, rest your horses, let us offer you food and drink—"

"We will wait here."

"A drink, at least—"

"We have our own supplies, my lord. We trust your hospitality includes haste."

"My lady." The Warden looked profoundly offended, and worried. "It will be some little time. I beg you understand. Stand down and rest. Take it or no, my people will offer you what hospitality we have. Your leave, my lady."

He inclined his head and walked away into the shadows.

They were alone then, and not alone, in this chill place where the smallest move echoed, and the stamp of an iron-shod hoof rang like doom.

"We have disquieted him," Morgaine said quietly, in her most obscure Kurshin accents. "That may be good or ill. Vanye—give me the stone."

He gave it. His heart hammered against his ribs.

"Come," she said, and sent Siptah suddenly forward, down the vacant aisle, toward the sealed doors.

There were running footsteps beyond the columns behind him, a quick spurt that died away in the direction the Warden had gone.

Someone had sped to advise him.

And Morgaine veered off into shadow, the other side of a vast column three quarters of the way down the long aisle, drew in and wheeled Siptah about as Vanye arrived, as Chei and Hesiyyn and Rhanin clattered in close behind him.

"What are you doing?" Chei asked, a young voice, which rose incongruously in pitch.

Light flared, white and terrible as she opened the case of the gate-jewel. It touched columns, faces, the wild eyes of the shying horses—and damped as suddenly as she closed her hand about it, veiling it in flesh, awful as it was.

"Give it to me!" Vanye exclaimed, knowing the feel of it, imagining the pain of handling it this close to Mante. But she held it fast, letting a little of its flickering light escape to strike the stone pillar beside them.

"Watch the surrounds!" she ordered. "Chei—what is our host saying?"

There was no word for a moment, in which Vanye loosed his bow from his shoulder, set its heel in his stirrup and strung it in the strength fear lent.

"He is reporting our presence—our breach of his orders—" Chei said.

"To whom?"

"To whoever is watching—I do not know—I do not know who that would be.—He reports himself in danger. He is going to open the doors. He hopes we will leave—"

"—into their reach," Morgaine said. There was pain in her voice. "Has he sent what I bade him?"

"No—or we have not seen it—"

"Take it. *Do* it."

"Send *what*? Who *are* you, that he should know you—curse you, woman, have you lied to me?"

"Believe everything you heard me tell the Warden—*Send* the cursed message, man, send it exactly as I gave it and keep sending till we have answer, or take your chances with the lord Warden's archers! Or with that thing outside! Make your choice!"

Chei reached. For a second the stone flared bright between them, blinding, light glistening on Morgaine's pale face, on his, which grimaced as he took it, and the red roan and the gray horse shied apart, both fighting the rein.

Engines began to clank and chain to rattle at the other entrance. A seam of daylight lanced through the hall, blinding bright. The horses sidestepped and fretted, more and more panicked, doubtful between the gate-force in the air, and the racket and that view of escape.

"It is more powerful than his," Chei said between his teeth. He used the shuttering of the lid to send, less sure in his use of it than the dimmer, rapid flickers of the Warden's sending, which came through as weak pulses in his intervals. "We are drowning his sending—Rhanin! are the warders moving?"

"No, my lord," the bowman said.

"If the gate at Mante should open," Hesiyyn said, "my lord, and you are holding that thing—"

"Send and wait for an answer," Morgaine bade Chei harshly. "Again and again—the same message. Watch around us! They have only to get one gate-jewel positioned—"

"My lady!" a voice called down the aisles. "My lady, cease! You are free to go!"

"Ignore it," Morgaine said under her breath. "I take it that the lord Warden is lying."

"He is lying," Chei said, reading the silence of the stone in the intervals. "He has never reached—*Ah!*"

Opal shimmer flared, rapid pulses. Chei cupped his hand about it, and the muscles of his face tensed with pain. "Skarrin," he said hoarsely. "Skarrin himself—has just discovered treachery—has bidden silence. He—knows your presence. And your name. He—tells the Warden—let us pass—not to—oppose us.—He asks who wields this st-stone, my lady."

"Answer him. Tell him it is ours. And we have come to talk with him."

It needed a moment. Chei's face stood out in taut-jawed relief in the flashes, that came brighter from the stone, brighter than the glare from the open door.

Then: "He will hear us," Chei said, hoarsely. And shut the case, letting his arm fall. "He forbids—more use of the stone."

Morgaine was silent a moment. It was an affront she was paid, by Skarrin's order. She reined close and recovered the pyx.

"He bids us," Chei said, "come to Mante."

"On his mercy," Vanye murmured. "Among the stones out there."

"It is Shein's enemies," Chei said in a ragged voice. "*My* enemies—in court—who killed all my Society. They have made a fatal mistake, thinking this was my doing—that you were my prisoners. They thought to kill us three—that is what they are about; and gain credit for it—like the lord Warden. Only he had to ask his masters what to do. And now his own head will be on the block. They will disavow him, or try to. They will not attack us. Not now."

"They could only lose by it," Hesiyyn said. "Either the Overlord will destroy us out there—or you have favor with him. In either case, lady, we are in *Skar-rin's* hand, for good or ill."

"We came," Morgaine said, "knowing there was no other way in."

She turned Siptah's head toward the light, and rode in the shadow toward the doors.

Vanye put his heels to Arrhan, and sent her forward, jolting hard at the horse at lead. Cut it free, he thought, laying a hand on his Honor-blade, and then thought again—seeing the expanse before them, and the ride there was yet to make as they passed the second set of doors: distant cliffs in a glare of sun—distant and with the threat of the standing stones to dominate all this plain of patchy grass and sere dust, this well of stone open to the sky; and heat that hit like a hammer-blow after the coolth of the building.

For a moment Vanye felt the giddiness—for a moment Arrhan ran uncertainly, waiting direction, until he took the reins in and swung alongside Morgaine. Chei and the others overtook them on the left. He bore over again, to have it clear to them how close they dared come to Morgaine's side.

"Let be," Morgaine said, "let be—If Skarrin will kill us he will do so." She looked behind her, turning in the saddle. "No one is following us, that is sure. If he is in control of the gate—"

"He is always in control of the gate," Chei said in a faint voice. "There are men in Mante counting the hours of their lives now, and others hastening to desert them. That is the way one lives in Mante. That is the *law* in Mante."

Chei's face was pale. In Hesiyyn was no vestige of humor.

Rhanin said: "We have kin who have managed to survive in Mante. And whether they will survive this day, we do not know."

Morgaine made them no answer. Possibly she did not even hear them. She set Siptah to an even, ground-devouring run, which the most of their horses were taxed to maintain. She gazed ahead of them, where their course lay—no road to follow, except the aisle of standing stones that paced widely separated toward the cliffs—marker-stones only, carriers of the gate-force, not the deadly ones, not the ones which, at his whim, the lord of Mante might use against them.

Those stones stood—Vanye could see one in the distance—far taller, and over against the cliffs that formed this well of stone.

The way of exiles. Death-gate. Mante's enemies who breached Seiyyin Neith found themselves here, in a plain utterly dominated by those three stones.

So Mante's exiles rode to their dismissal from Seiyyin Neith, during all the crossing of the plain knowing that that ride was on sufferance, that they lived or died as Mante and Skarrin pleased.

Like crossing the very palm of God, he thought; and went cold at the blasphemy, while the sun heated the armor and the sweat ran on him and the pounding of the horse's gait drove knives into his gut.

The stones measured the course: a hundred fifty and two. Chei knew their number. They all knew. It was the number of lords admitted to council. They stood for silent accusers to the damned; eyeless, watched them; mouthless, cursed them—stood waiting, finally, to welcome the exile home, who wished once to see Mante, and surrender body or life, as the high lords pleased.

A man had to think of such things, somberly, as surely Hesiyyn and Rhanin thought of them; and thought of kindred and friends, who by now might know that their kinsman had made the choice to return.

And their enemies would know—as they would know the lady had gained Skarrin's ear, and quickly after, as the lord Warden sent all he dared send—that the South-warden had been taken for a playing piece in this game.

There would be those rushing to exert influence where they could, to save what they could.

Blood—would flow; might be flowing even now, of remotest and humblest connections Shein Society might have had, from the moment certain powers in Mante knew that Qhiverin Asfelles was returning. But all his dead company was avenged, as he had said—a revenge as perfect as he could have contrived, his enemies done to death by their own power to rule the doings at court.

There were the few lords who had supported Shein, whose mark Qhiverin's natural body had worn tattooed above the heart, whose sole survivor he was. But the high lords had their bodyguards and their own sources of rumors, and if they were taken by surprise, they were fools—the more so if his messengers had gotten to them from Morund-gate and Tejhos.

He had done well, he thought. Live or die—he had done well, and he aimed for the unthinkable.

But there was still within him a small bewildered voice, of a boy further and further from home and missing one who should have ridden with him—

Well, lad, he told it sorrowfully, *so do I. Pyverrn should have seen this day, damn us all. He would have laughed to think of the lord Warden back there, scrambling to save his neck.*

The boy did not understand what he saw, except that they rode through the region of a gate which could drink them down at any moment, at the Overlord's pleasure, and that the lady had a name that she trusted Skarrin knew.

The boy feared now, that the lady he had once followed and the man who had betrayed him—had lied to him from the beginning.

So do I fear it, he told the boy. *But we have no choice, do we?*

Never speak to it—the wisdom ran, advising against such accommodation.

But it did not go away. It was there. It watched everything, it wanted to learn of him—

Most of all it wanted not to die.

You gave me to the wolves, the boy wept. *You killed my lord.*

So I did. You were trying to kill me, at the time. As for Ichandren—I tried to spare him. It was Arunden stirred that pot—for Arunden's gain. Now Arunden is raven-bait. Stop sniveling, boy. It is death we both face. The world is like that. And better the company around us than some I have known. Gault was a liar and Ichandren a conniver and Arunden a bloody-handed traitor. Wake up and see, boy. Wake up and know *the world you were born to, Mante's refuse-heap. . . .*

More of sun and heat, of glare on dusty ground, and a cloud which rose behind and around them, a long effort for weary horses, jolting which brought the taste of blood.

The longer they delayed in this place, Vanye thought, the longer the lord in Mante had to hear other advice, change his mind, come to other conclusions— or some other power snatch its opportunity and bring the power of the World- gate at Mante to bear on the standing stones of Neisyrrn Neith.

Then the last thing they might know would be a sudden rending of the sky and ground, and the howl of winds fleeing into that rift, taking them with it— aware of their deaths, Heaven knew how long or how keenly.

That thought kept him in the saddle, though it was hard to breathe. He coughed, and wiped his mouth, and saw blood smearing the dust on his hand.

A cold feeling came on him then, a chill dizziness as if truth had been wait- ing for him to find it, before it sprang on him and shook him and all but took his wits away.

O Heaven, not here, not now, not yet, not in this place.

He spat blood, wiped his stubbled mouth, and wiped the hand on his dusty breeches. Morgaine was ahead of him. She had not seen. He measured the distance yet to go—they had come halfway, now, halfway along the aisle of stones that led to Mante, and that far again was all he might be able to do—

—at least not slow her in this place. At least cross this plain and know that she had gotten safely to its far side, where she had a chance: to draw *Changeling* here was impossible, for loosed within a gate, it would take the very world asunder.

It was too cursed late for Chei's medicines, not by the tightness in his chest, by the lack of breath; but he found the folded paper, a red haze in the dust and the darkness that threatened his vision. He pinched up what he hoped for one pellet in his fingers, but he thought was more than that—he was not sure. He almost dropped it entirely, and put the medicine into his mouth and held it through a cough that brought up more blood. He swallowed, wiped his mouth with a bright smear of scarlet across the back of his hand; and hung on and waited for the strength he hoped would come to him.

It did come. He was aware of his heart pounding, of his vision dark-edged, of a cessation of the pain, at least—but he could not get his breath. He felt his balance going, and was aware of Morgaine looking back and reining around. The strength left in a rush of heat and cold, and he knew in one terrible moment he was leaving the saddle, the ground coming up at him—

He hit, and twisted sideways, stunned, in a second impact, lost in dust and pain that lanced through the drug-haze, skull shaken, spine rattled, limbs twisted, pain like a dull knife driven through his side.

Through the dust, Morgaine's dark figure, running toward him, sliding down to her knees.

"Vanye!"

The others had stopped. Chei—behind her, on the red roan, Rhanin and Hesiyyn like ghosts in the dust.

He tried to get up, knowing it was necessary, and the pain was in abeyance for the moment. He tried to get his arm under him.

And heard the wind howl, saw Morgaine whirl and rise and reach for *Changeling's* hilt as the sky tore in two above them, showing the dark beyond, her hair and cloak streaming, dust pouring skyward like water pouring over a brink.

The world ripped. And there was only the cold and the dark between.

—He saw her hand on the hilt, that would bring the Gate in upon itself.

"No," he cried to her, because they were still alive, and the time was not yet—

The rift came full circle, and blue swallowed up the black, leaving only a rush of wind and chill.

Then he lay on his back on stone, and rolled onto his arm, to see Morgaine with the sword half-drawn, the blade shimmering crystal, its runes running with opal fires.

She slammed it home again, seeing him, and he got to his knees, dazed, disentangled himself of his bow that had come awry of his shoulder and shed it. He saw Siptah and Arrhan riderless and confused, Chei and the others fighting for control of their frightened mounts—standing stones all about them, stones like a forest of such slabs, all about the walled court of blond stone in which they had suddenly found themselves.

There was no pain. There was no ache anywhere about the bandages bound too tightly about his ribs, no hindrance in his limbs. He might have come from a morning's easy ride.

Gate-passage. The gate had flung them here, unscathed and whole except the dust and the dirt that turned Morgaine's dark armor pale and made her face a porcelain mask.

God in Heaven, he thought, remembering the fall, then, and the blood in his mouth; and then thought it might be blasphemous to thank Heaven for *qhalur* gifts. He had no idea. He only knew he could stand, and Morgaine was throwing an arm about him and embracing him, the dragon-sword in her other hand, the scarred and battered longbow in his. "We are alive," she said, and said something else urgently in a tongue he could not understand, telling him, he reckoned in his dazed state, that they were none of them dead, that they were somewhere of Skarrin's choosing—

She held him tight. He held to her as if he were drowning, and then remembered there were enemies. He scanned round about the stones which rose in a five-fold stagger between them and the walls; and looked up, at the rim of the masonry walls against the cloudless sky.

There was no one, no one but Chei and Rhanin and Hesiyyn, on horses exhausted and head-hanging, themselves hardly fit to climb from their saddles and stand.

But they, themselves—and the white horse and the gray—

"There *is* sorcery," Vanye murmured, misgiving of everything, most of all his memory, which insisted there should be pain, and broken bones, and not this unnatural strength, recovered flesh, that made the buckles and bandaging all too tight. He trembled, and wished he could shake everything from his head and begin again. "Mother of God, there is—you cannot tell me else—"

She wiped the corner of his mouth, with fingers that came away, shaking, with blood and dirt. Tears marred the dusty mask of her face. She pressed her lips tight, held him by the arm and looked up and about the slow circuit of the walls, seeking who had done this to them.

Then to Chei, in anger: "Is *this*—ordinary, Skarrin dropping his guests into this place? Is *this* the way to Mante you simply neglected to tell us?"

"I do not know." It was bewilderment. It was utter consternation. "No. Not—for what I know."

There was fear—in Chei's look, in Rhanin's—even in cold Hesiyyn's eyes. It was fear directed toward them both, for the healing the gates had done for them, and the horses they rode, and not for themselves.

"None of us know," Rhanin said, a faint voice. "Never—never that I have known of—"

"*Skarrin!*" Morgaine shouted to the walls and the sky.

"He has spared us," Vanye said. "*Liyo*, he has *spared* us—"

She turned a look on him—not the face he loved, but a *qhalur* mask in white dust, tear-streaked and implacable in purpose. "Do not believe it."

On the one side, Chei and his companions, who knew something had been done with gates such as ought not to have happened, within the laws they knew—

On the other, Morgaine—

I know things they do not. Call it my father's legacy. And if they should know, Vanye, that *secret, they would find others, that I will give no one, that are not written on the sword—that I will not* permit *anyone to know and live—*

She hooked *Changeling* to her belt. She walked a few steps and recovered his helm from the ground and threw it to him. He caught it. The wind blew at his hair, still shorn. His armor was filthy with dust and blood. Why this should be, and other things mended, he did not understand.

He did not hope to. Nor wish to. He put the helm on, slung the bow to his shoulder, and followed her across the courtyard to the horses.

She stopped there. From that angle, among the standing stones, an open gateway was visible in the masonry wall.

⤳ Chapter 18

There was no sound in the high-walled courtyard, save their own movements and those of the horses. There was nothing above them but the sky.

And the open gateway, among the standing stones.

Morgaine took Siptah in hand to look him over and Vanye looked over the exhausted bay and gathered up Arrhan's reins, as Chei and his two comrades led their exhausted horses toward them, slow clatter of iron on stone.

"There is the way out," Morgaine said. "Such as our host gives us. Do you have any reckoning where we are?"

"Neneinn," Hesiyyn said quietly. "That is where we would be, I am relatively certain of it. The citadel itself. But no one sees the inside of that, except the Overlord's own guards. And they rarely come and go in the city."

"The Gate itself?"

Hesiyyn looked about him, at the sky, the walls; and pointed off to the right of the open gateway. "There, by my guess. The gate is close—very close to Neneinn, at the crest of the same hill. That weapon of yours—I should hesitate to use anywhere about these premises."

Morgaine was silent a moment, looking at Hesiyyn. The tall *qhal*-lord wore an unwontedly anxious expression.

"Where is your loyalty?" she asked him.

"Assuredly not in Neneinn," Hesiyyn answered in a faint voice. "I am under banishment. Skarrin dislikes my poetry."

"None of us has any loyalty here," Chei said. "I assure you. Nor prospects."

There was nothing of arrogance in them. Their courage seemed frayed, their strength flagging in the face of their own unnatural vitality—men hollow-cheeked, eyes red-rimmed with exhaustion, their horses dull-coated and ill-fed beneath the dust that coated all of them. They did not ask what had happened, or why, or, indeed, venture any question at all.

"Then tell Skarrin nothing," Morgaine said shortly, and turned and hooked Siptah's left stirrup to the horn. She let out the girth no small bit, at which the warhorse grunted and sighed.

Arrhan needed the same. Vanye saw to it, hung his bow from Arrhan's saddlehorn and let out first Arrhan's girth and then the straps of his own body-armor, that were tight to the point of misery; but the bandages and the padding he could not reach, and he drew a breath and strained at them, trying to stretch against what would bind his draw and his sword arm.

Even in blackest sorcery, he thought, gathering his gear about him, there were cursedly maddening shortcomings.

Morgaine flung the stirrup down and gathered up Siptah's reins, looking back toward Chei and the rest. "I will warn you," she said, "You may be safer here. Death—may be safer than where we go. Choose for yourselves."

Chei looked astonished. It was young Chei's expression. The frown which followed was Gault's. Or Qhiverin's. "You jest, lady."

"No," she said. "I do not." And led Siptah among the tall stones, toward the open gateway.

Vanye led Arrhan after her, the blaze-faced bay following perforce, with lagging, wearied steps.

The others came behind him, then, a clatter of iron-shod hooves on stone.

He had as lief not have them at his back. He recollected the medicine Chei had given him, and what it had done to him when at last he had had to rely on it—

—Chei had warned him, he recollected. To do justice to the man, Chei had warned him clearly.

Chei had given it to him after that warning, of course—in hope, perhaps, of *not* having him between them and Morgaine—in any sense. And if he had used it before that, Heaven knew what would have been the outcome.

He kept constantly between Morgaine and the *qhal*, now, on the winding track among the stones, pale gold of standing stones and of pavings and masonry—and of more sunlit paving visible through the gateway.

Another trap, he thought.

But the gateway opened out into yet another such courtyard, this one with a single standing stone in its center . . . a flat, paved courtyard, the end of which a building closed, jumbled planes of wall and tower, and at the sides—

A sheer drop: and buildings upon buildings, upon buildings and buildings, pale gold stone, red roofs, as far as the eye could see.

He stopped in his tracks and stared—only stared, senses confounded, when he was mountain-born and used to heights and perspectives.

But not to men and the works of men so vast they spread like a blanket about the hill and across the plain—to the verge of the cliffs that dropped away into the circular abyss of Neisyrrn Neith, and along and away till the roofs lost themselves in haze and distance.

Morgaine had stopped. So had the others.

"Mante," Chei said softly. So a man might speak of Heaven and Hell in one. The others said nothing at all.

And Vanye could not forbear looking at it, though he tangled his fingers in Arrhan's coarse mane and feared irrationally that the sight might drive the horses mad, and bring them too near the edge, however far away they stood.

Morgaine led Siptah further. It was the sound of the gray's steps that woke him from trance, and brought him after her, resolutely, as she walked toward the open doorway at the end of the courtyard.

The others followed, at distance.

This door—had little sunlight about it. This one let into the very heart of the fortress, by a long narrow aisle, shadowed by columns.

They had seen such before, of many kinds. Such buildings were always near the World-gates. They held the machines to command and direct the forces.

It was what they had come to find; and Morgaine would go in. He had no doubt of it. He saw her lay her hand on the sword-hilt.

"*Liyo.*" He searched after the chain of the stone he wore about his neck, drew it from his collar and over his head as he led Arrhan quickly to overtake her. It was a weak thing—stronger by far than the Warden's mote or many another sending-stone in this land, he suspected, but not *Changeling*'s match. It was useless to him, a means to sudden death, if he matched it against anything of *Changeling*'s power.

Or against the gate Hesiyyn swore must lie close hereabouts.

"He knows you have a gate-weapon," he said. "*Take* it. It is larger than the ones they use. It may be he will mistake this for it."

She understood him then. And refused it with a shake of her head. "The sword," she said in his language. "I cannot wield both. And no—he will not."

"The sword is too dangerous," he whispered hoarsely, and started at a movement in the corner of his vision, in the deep shadow within the narrow aisle ahead—a *qhalur* man, alone, nor very old.

Some high servant, he thought, the while his heart skipped a beat and his hand went for his sword-hilt; and then he thought otherwise, seeing the eldritch figure drifted, mirage-like, and was only an image.

It spoke. It spoke words he could not understand, but he knew, whatever they were, that they were not meant for him, or for Chei, or any of them other than Morgaine. He heard Morgaine answer in that tongue, and saw the man's figure grow dimmer as it retreated down that aisle.

She walked forward.

Vanye caught at her arm, the barest touch, before she reached that threshold. She looked at him. That was all; and she turned and hit Siptah a resounding blow on the rump.

The Baien gray sprang through the door, hooves echoing on stone, off high walls, and stopped inside, unscathed.

She went, then, through the doorway, in a single step and a second one which cleared a path for him to follow. He did so, in a motion so quick he did not think of it: he was there, Arrhan was behind him, and he whipped the arrhendur blade from its sheath, for what it was worth against this illusion and the more substantial things it might call down on them.

A question then, from the man of light and shadow. The voice echoed about them, rang off the walls of this long, narrow passage.

"He does not understand you," Morgaine said.

"He is human," the image said then. "I have read everything—in the gate-field. I know what you carry. Yes. How could I fail to remark—a thing like that forming in the patterns? I read his suffering. I intervened, against my habit, to save him. I trusted there *was* a pattern—if you valued him. And I was not mistaken."

"I thank you for that," Morgaine said.

"I wished to please you—who come wandering the worlds. Anjhurin's daughter. It is likely that we are kin—remote as that kinship may be. How does Anjhurin fare?"

"He is dead," Morgaine said shortly.

"Ah." The regret seemed genuine. The image murmured something in the other language.

"Perhaps," Morgaine said, "he was weary of living. He said as much."

Again it spoke.

"No," Morgaine said. And to another query: "No." And: "I travel, my lord."
A harder voice then.

"For my companion's sake," she said. "Speak so he can understand." And
after another such: "Because he understands it and because I wish it." And
again: "That may be. I would be glad of it." She lapsed for a moment into the
other tongue. Then, gently: "It has been a long time, my lord, since I have spoken the language. It has been a long time—since I have had the occasion."

"You bring me felons and rebels." The mouth of the image quirked upward
slightly at the corners. "As well as this human warrior. You have turned my
court upside down, lifted every rotten log and sent the vermin scurrying
forth—from Morund-gate to the highest houses in Mante. What shall I do for
you in return?"

"Why, give me the three rebels in question," Morgaine said, "and the pleasure of your company, and in due time, the freedom of your gate. I am a wan-
derer. I seek no domain of my own."

"Nor to share one?"

She laughed. "We do not *share* a world. My father taught me that much. I
will find a place. Or do you give this one up, my lord of shadows, and come
wander the worlds with us."

"With a rebel, a killer, a doggerel poet and a human lordling?" Skarrin
laughed in his own turn. "Come ahead into my courtyards, my lady of light.
Wash off the dust. Take my hospitality." The drifting face became melancholy,
even wistful. "Go with you. That is a thought. That is indeed a thought. You will
sit with me, my lady, and tell me where you have traveled and the things you
have seen—convince me there is something different than one finds . . .
everywhere. . . ."

The image faded.

The voice drifted into silence, leaving the stillness of the tomb behind it.

Old, Vanye thought with a chill, *old—more than a Man can reckon*.

And he found himself staring into Morgaine's eyes, lost, beyond understanding what she did or what she meant to do any longer, and with the least
and dreadful fear—that she had found something in common with this lord
who contemned everything he ruled, who despised the *qhal*, who themselves
used human folk for cattle—

She had had to defend her companying with a human man. He had sensed
that. He imagined the questions which had gone by him, and fitted her answers
to them, his liege, his lover . . . defiant, in the beginning—toward a man of her
own kind, who could speak with her, trade words with her in a language she
had never taught him, quickly and unexpectedly draw the sort of laugh and
light answer from her such as had taken him—oh, so long to win.

"We will do as he asks," Morgaine said.

"Aye," he said. He was too far into strange territory to say anything more. He did not even agree for loyalty or love or out of common sense. He was only lost, on ground which continually shifted and threatened to shift again. They stood in a foreign lord's elegant forecourt with three confused horses in their charge, and three men awaiting their fate outside who were, surely, no less bewildered.

Then: *a clear target*, he thought, like a shock of cold water.

How else do we come at him—except she draw him out?

And how can she persuade him?

"Call Chei and the rest," she bade him in the Kurshin tongue. "Quickly."

He left Arrhan to stand and went back to the sunlight. "My lord," he said to Chei at the doorway, and lowered his voice. He was determined to observe courtesy with the man and forestall argument. "We are going ahead. We do not know into what. Be aware: the Overlord brought up the matter of your exile. My lady claimed you for her own and Skarrin gave you to her. So if you have any scruples, I think you are honorably quit of debts to him, but I do not know what favor this wins of him if things go amiss."

Chei looked at him and gnawed at his lip. It was young Chei's expression for the instant. It was doubt; and then amusement. "I was quit of debts to him when he failed to kill me," Chei-Qhiverin said. "That was *his* mistake."

Chei led his horse forward. Hesiyyn and Rhanin followed, Rhanin with his bow strung and slung over his shoulder. Vanye cleared the doorway, gathered up Arrhan's reins, and led the white mare up alongside Siptah as Morgaine began that course Skarrin chose for them.

Ambush was in his thoughts, constantly. But Morgaine went, with *Changeling* slung at her hip, and walked the long court in which the horses' pacing made a forlorn and lonely sound.

"Games," she said to the air. "I do not like games, my lord Skarrin."

At the end a door whisked open, in that way which doors could move, in such places of gate-force—on a sunlit court.

Vanye cut the lead next the bay's bridle and sent it ambling past them with one slap and another on its dusty rump. It came to no grief in the doorway. And they came through into afternoon sunlight, into a stable court clean and well-supplied with straw and haystack, rows of stables, with well and stone trough. The bay went straightway to the water, and Siptah and Arrhan flared their nostrils and pricked up their ears and approached the trough with keen interest.

"Hospitality," Vanye muttered, for the first time beginning to wonder was there good will in this beckoning of doors and corridors and ghosts. "Dare we trust it?"

"He needs no ambush," Morgaine said, and bent and washed her hands and her face, and let the water wash black, clean trails over her dusty armor. She drank from the demon-mouth that poured fresh water continually into the trough.

He took the chance for himself, doused face and hands in cool water, wiped his hair back from his eyes, washed and drank as Chei and the others arrived.

There was no one to threaten them. There was not a horse other than theirs in all the stable-court. There was no servant and no groom to serve them. Vanye stood, with the wind chilling the water on his face, scanning the walls around them, looking for some sign of life and seeing nothing but bare stone.

"Ghosts," he said aloud. "And of them this Skarrin seems chief."

"More than ghosts," Morgaine whispered in the Kurshin tongue, and caught his shoulder and leaned close to him. "We may be overheard. I do not know how many languages he may have known or where he may have traveled."

His heart leapt in him and fell again. "Even Kursh?"

"There are tracks among the Gates: thee knows. No knowing which path he has come to arrive here. There are a handful of the old blood, in all the worlds gates reach. They have no congress with one another. They are too proud. Each settles to a world—for a while—using a knowledge of the gates the *qhal* do not have—They *rule*. There is no likelihood that they will fail to rule. They direct affairs, they make changes at their pleasure. And inevitably they grow bored— and they move on, through time or space or both. Some are older than the calamity, older than the one before it. My father claimed to be."

"*What* 'one before it', what—"

"—And some are born into *this* age—of one whose life has stretched across ages. Some are born of events which cannot be duplicated, events on which vast changes depend—Some lives, in that way, anchor time itself. So the lords assure themselves of continuance—in more than one way. Such am I—but not what my father planned. *I* exist. Therefore other things do not. Therefore *he* does not."

"I do not understand. You have left me." He felt a shiver despite the sun. "What shall we do?"

"I shall court this man," she hissed softly. "By any means, Vanye, *any* means, and thee must not object, does thee understand that?"

"Let us take the sword, let us go through this place until we find him—" He felt cold to the heart now. "That is the only sense."

"He will not be there. He can retreat *within* the gate. He can leave us here. Has thee forgotten?"

"You cannot fight him hand to hand, *liyo*, in the name of Heaven, you can-not think of—"

"I will do what I have to do. I tell thee now: do not attempt *anything* with this man. I beg thee. I do not want help in this. Or hindrance. Thee says thee is still *ilin*. Nothing have I asked of thee by that oath—in very long. *This* I ask. For my sake. For thine."

"*Tell* me what we shall do!"

"On thy oath. Nothing. *I* will do it."

"And I tell you—if you hang my soul and my salvation on it—I will throw them away, if it comes to harm—"

"Thee will take the sword if it comes to that. Thee will bear it. Thee will trust Chei and the rest if it comes to that. All these things—I ask thee, as thee loves me—do. Does thee love me? Does thee understand what I ask?"

It reached him, then, the thing that she *was* asking of him, and the sense of it. It shook the breath from him for a moment. It was not the sort of thing a man wanted to agree to, who loved a woman. It was harder than dying for her, to agree to leave her to die.

"That much," he said, because anything less was betrayal, "yes, I understand. On my oath, I will." He looked up uncomfortably at their comrades, who did not understand what passed—their comrades, who expected, perhaps, betrayal prepared for themselves, in this exchange in another language.

"We will go on," Morgaine said to them, and drew Siptah away from the water.

"*Where* do we go?" Chei asked.

"Did I promise I knew?" Morgaine answered, and led the gray horse on, through the stable-court, down the empty rows.

"It makes no sense," Hesiyyn said. "There should be servants—there should be attendants. *Where* are the people?"

"Heaven knows," Chei answered him, and found no incongruity in saying so. There was an angry young man in the center of his being, as lost as he was, in this place which had dominated both their lives and ruined their separate families—and which proved, after all, only hollow and full of echoes. "People come here," he said, half to the lady, who seemed some old acquaintance of Skarrin's. "People serve the Overlord. What has become of them?"

She offered them no answer.

"Perhaps he is holding them elsewhere," Hesiyyn said under his breath, and with an anxious look toward Chei.

Death, the lady had said; and in this court which should, at least, have horses, have some evidence of occupancy and life—Chei found a scattering of memory which was human and adult and frightened—

Gault had been imprisoned here, had been hailed up from the outskirts of this fortress by his kidnappers, to the gate above these walls. *Gault* remembered. And there had been others in that dark hour, there had been servants, there had been abundant life in this court, torchlit and echoing with confused shouts as Qhiverin's friends dragged him struggling and resisting toward the hell above these walls.

"Even the horses," Chei-Gault-Qhiverin said aloud, finding a shiver down his spine and a terrible feeling of things gone amiss in this daylit, sterile vacancy, "even the horses—No." He quickened his pace, tugging at the weary roan he led, and caught Vanye's arm. "There were people here. Now even the horses are gone. *Something* is direly wrong here. It is a trap. Make the lady listen."

Vanye had rescued his arm at once. There was on his sullen face, a quick suspicion and a dark threat. The shorn hair blew across his eyes and reminded them both of things past, of miscalculations and mistakes disastrously multiplied. A muscle clenched in his jaw.

But if there was at the moment a voice of caution and reason in their company it was this Man, Chei believed it: the boy's experience told him so and Qhiverin's instincts went to him, puzzling even himself—except it was everywhere consonant with what the boy knew: a man absolute in duty, absolute enough and sane enough to lay aside everything that did not pertain to the immediate problem.

Trust him to listen, was the boy's advice. *Nothing further.*

And Qhiverin, within himself: *Boy, if the one thing, with what lies between us, then anything; and you have been a mortal fool.*

"It is for all our sakes," he said. "I swear to you, Nhi Vanye. We are walking into a trap. Every step of this is a trap. He has vacated the place. Even the horses. Even the horses. I do not know where."

"The gate," Vanye said, looking down the little distance Chei's slighter form needed.

"To Tejhos?" Chei asked. "—Or elsewhere?"

Vanye cast a look toward Morgaine, whose face was stern and pale and set on the way before them, which led toward yet another gate in this maze.

"Anything is possible," he said.

A man who is winning, he had said to Morgaine again and again, will not flee.

But the man of that face and that voice which had spoken to them—

—Go *with* you, it had said.

Convince me there is something different than one finds . . . everywhere. . . .

Older than the calamity, Morgaine had said of Skarrin.

And: *Not of human measure, not predictable by human intentions*, his own experience told him.

Deeper and deeper into this snare Morgaine went, leading the rest of them in what haste they dared—

Lest Skarrin strand them here, lest he go before them and seal the gate and leave them imprisoned here forevermore.

He did not question now. He understood the things that she had attempted to tell him throughout their journey—and he had overwhelmed her arguments, delayed her with his foolishness, his well-meant advice and his hopes and, Heaven forgive, his desire of her, which had stolen her good judgment and thrown his to the winds.

But for me, he kept thinking, the while he walked beside her: *but for me she would have ridden straight to him and stayed him from this; but for me she would have gone straightway to Morund and enlisted* qhalur *aid and learned more at the start than ever young Chei could have taught us.*

And perhaps Chei would be alive, himself, and Gault would be Gault, and their ally.

"Tell her," Chei hissed at him.

"She has always understood," he said to Chei and his murderer, "better than I. Better than any of us. She gave you the chance to turn back. It is not too late to take it."

The gate before them was open. He was not in the least surprised at that. And this one let into the building itself, into a shadowed hall which might hold more than ghosts—but he began to doubt that there need be guards or soldiery, nor any hand but Skarrin's own, which held the gate-force. He kept beside Morgaine as far as that doorway, and suddenly sent Arrhan through ahead of them, expecting no harm.

The arrhendur mare came to none, only stopped, confused, her feet striking echoes from polished pavement, in a hall supported by columns much lest vast than those of Neisyrrn Neith, but vast for all that, shaped of green stone and black.

A table was set there, set with pitchers and platters bearing fruit and bread and what else his eye did not trouble to see.

Skarrin's ghost hung before them, welcomed them, smiled at them with all beneficence and no little amusement.

"My guests," he said; then, and with less mockery: "My lady Morgaine An-jhuran, my youngest cousin—sit, take your ease. You can trust my table. Surely you know that. And you might indeed leave the horses outside my hall."

"My lord Skarrin," Morgaine said, "forgive me. I have known so many and so bizarre things in my travels—I have found folk do things for remarkable reasons, some only because they can, some only for sport—I do not know you, my lord. So I keep my horse and my arms—and my servants. My father's friends may, for all I know, be no less mad than some others I have met on the way."

The drifting image laughed, a soft sound, like the hissing of wind in grass. "And thus you decline my hospitality?"

"I do not sit at table with shadows, my lord. Our mistrust is mutual—else you would not hesitate to come and meet me face to face—if you can."

"My lady of outlaws and rebels—should I trust myself to your companions, when they think so ill of me?"

Morgaine laughed, let fall Siptah's reins, and walked over to the table, to pull out a chair and sit down. She picked up a pitcher and poured a cup of red wine.

Vanye let Arrhan stand alone too, and went and stood at the side of her chair as she lifted it and sipped it in courtesy to their shadowy host.

Whereupon Skarrin laughed softly, and drifted amid their table, severed at the waist. "You are trusting."

"No, my lord of Mante. Only interested. I knew when I heard your name from young Chei—who is host to my lord of Morund—what you *might* be. I took your gatewardens' behavior for yours—to our mutual discomfiture. No one saw fit to apprise me of the truth—in which I do fault you, my lord of Mante. So much could have been saved, of affairs in the south, if I had known. Now I leave you a humankind in war and disorder—an inconvenience, at the least, for which I do apologize."

"There are other lands. The world is wide. I weary of Mante."

"I took this for the greatest of your cities. Are there others? Truly, this one is a wonder to see."

"Ah, there are hundreds. Everywhere—there are cities, as unvarying as the worlds. Everywhere is boredom, my lady of light, until you came—traveling, as you say. With a human servant, no less—what is his name?"

"Nhi Vanye i Chya. Nhi Vanye, if you please."

"My lord," Vanye said. To say something seemed incumbent on him, when the image turned its cold eyes in his direction and the face seemed to gaze straight at him. He was in danger. He knew beyond a doubt that he was in peril of his life, only for being human, and for standing where he stood, and for more than that: it was the look a man gave a man where a woman was in question— and blood was.

The glass-gray stare passed from him and turned slowly to the others, and back again to Morgaine.

"Why have you come?"

"Why should I not?" Morgaine said. "I take my father's lesson, who found one world and a succession of worlds—far too small for him. *That* was An-jhurin." She leaned back, posing the chair on its rearmost legs, and stared up at the image. "From all you say, you have arrived at the same place as he—you have wielded power over world and world and world—am I right? And you have found this world much the same as the last."

"And the one before," Skarrin said. "And before that. You are young."

"As you see me."

"Very young," Skarrin said softly, this young man with gray, gentle eyes.

"You knew Anjhurin," Morgaine said.

"A very, very long time ago." The image became merely a face, drifting in the shadow, a handsome face, with Morgaine's own look, so like her among *qhal* it might have been a brother. "Anjhurin dead! Worlds should shake."

"They have," Morgaine said softly. "And things *change*, my lord of dust and stability. You do not love your life. Come risk it with me. Come join me."

"To what purpose?"

"The changing of worlds, my lord, change that sweeps through space and time."

"Even this, I have seen. I have ties in many ages, many worlds. I will survive even the next calamity. What new can you offer me?"

"Have you *risked* that hope, elder cousin? It is risk makes immortality bearable—to know that personal calamity is possible, oh, very possible, and tranquility, what time it exists, is precious. Anjhurin is dead. Does that not tell you that fatality is possible? Come with me. There are worlds full of chances."

"Full of cattle. Full of same choices and same tragedies and same small hearts and smaller minds which lead to them. Full of stale poets who think their ideas are a towering novelty in the cosmos. Full of rebels who think they can change worlds for the better and murderers who see no further than the selfish moment. Mostly, full of cattle, content with their mouthful of grass and their little herd and endless procreation of other cattle. And we are finite, calamity endlessly regenerate, disaster in a bubble. One day it will burst of sheer tedium. And the universe will never notice."

"No," Morgaine said, and reached and took Vanye by the arm, drawing him to the table edge. "I have news to give you, my lord. *Qhal* reached outside. They stole *his* ancestors in real-space, and his cousins voyage there, *not* with the gates, *not* within them so far as they know—"

"It will not save them."

"No. But they are widening the bubble, my lord who sees no change. They are involving all who meet them—and all who meet their allies. Do you see, my lord of shadows? There *is* chance and change. *His* kind—humankind—have realized the trap. They have refused it. More, they have set out to prick the bubble themselves."

There was long silence.

"It would doom them," Skarrin said.

"Perhaps. *Their* threads reach far beyond their own world, but they were not that deeply entangled."

"If they have taken it on themselves to do this, by that very act they are entangled."

"And they know *other* races who know others still."

Vanye listened through that silence, his heart beating harder and harder. Morgaine's light hand upon his elbow held him fast, by oath and by the surety that somewhere in this exchange he had become all humanity, and that existence was the prize of this struggle—*What must I do, what must I say, what is she telling him—of threads and bubbles?*

This man can kill us all. He has stripped this house of its servants, its goods, its cattle. He has destroyed them or he has sent them through the gate before him—and means to follow.

—Humankind—has refused the trap.

What is she telling him?

"Change," Morgaine said, "is very possible. That is the work I do."

"And *this*—for heir," Skarrin said. "This for companion. His get—for inheritors."

"Come with me," Morgaine said, "down the thread that leads to infinity. Or bind yourself more and more irrevocably to the one you have followed thus far. Eventually change *may* become impossible. But you will not find it inside the patterns; you find it linked to these—to *qhal*, and to humankind. And to *me*, lord Skarrin, and to those with me."

"So I should serve your purposes."

"Follow your own. Did I ever say I wished to share more than a road and the pleasure of your company? We will bid one another farewell—in time, in time I cannot predict, my lord Skarrin, nor can you. That is *chance*, my lord Skarrin. Have you grown too attached to this age and to what is? Have you found your own end of time, and are you content with solitude among your subjects—or do I tempt you?"

"You tempt me."

"We have a horse to spare." She held Vanye's arm the tighter, and laughed softly. "What want you, an entourage, a clutter of servants, lord Skarrin? I have my few, who will serve you the same as me. A horse, a bedroll, and the sky overhead—your bones are still young, and your heart is not that cold. Come and learn what a younger generation has learned."

The image smiled, slowly and fondly. "Was Anjhurin—fate's way of creating you—who see no wider than that?"

"Perhaps that is all there is worthwhile, my lord kinsman. *Freedom.*"

"Freedom! Oh, young cousin, lady, you mistake the roof for the sky. We are prisoners, all. *Inside* the bubble we work what we will and we shift and change. The gates end and the gates begin. And all the hope you bring me is that the contagion is spreading and the bubble widens. Is *that* cause to hope? I think not. In the wide universe we are still without significance."

"You are melancholy, my lord of shadows."

"I am a god. The cattle have made me so." There came laughter, soft and terrible. "Tell me, is that not cause for melancholy?"

"They name me Death. Is it not reasonable that I am the youngest of us, and the most cheerful?" Again she laughed, and stood and leaned against Vanye's shoulder, clasping his arm. "Few of humankind love me. But, lord of shadows, I shall live longest, and so will those who ride with me. It is helpers I seek. Come ride the wave with me, down to the last shore. Or do you want eternity in Mante, with shapes of your own devising, in a world of your own making? Another stone palace and more worshippers? Come, let us see if we can shake the worlds."

The image faded abruptly to dark. The hall was very still, except the random shift of a horse's foot, which rang like doom on the pavings.

"What are you saying?" Chei asked, suddenly breaking that peace. "What *are* you, what are you talking about—waves and shores? Who *are* you?"

"I have said," Morgaine said quietly, and her hand never left Vanye's shoulder, a calming touch. If it had not been there he would have reached for a weapon for comfort. It was; and he felt himself numb like a bird in the eye of the serpent—not afraid, not capable, he thought, of fear at all any longer. He knew her lies, even when they were told with the truth. Even when they were entirely the truth. He trusted. That was all there was left to do.

"Perhaps you can flee," Morgaine said to the others. "It seems likely. I do not think he will trouble himself with you."

Rhanin edged away. And stopped, as if he did not know what to do, or as if he had expected the others would, or as if he had had second thoughts. He only stood there.

Then distantly, softly echoing, came footsteps in the corridors.

This time, Vanye thought, it was substance which came to them; it was substance which appeared in the shadows of the corridor which let into this hall.

It was Skarrin himself who walked out into the light which was always available in such places, that power drawn of gate-force, come full in the room.

"My lady of mysteries," Skarrin said, halted there in that entry. "Am I in truth welcome?"

"Oh, indeed," Morgaine said in a still, hushed voice. "Good day to you, shadow-lord." She walked a few paces closer, and stopped, and Vanye stood with a shiver running through his limbs, a twitch that was the impulse to follow her, stay with her instantly; but that was a fool's move, to show hostility to this lord, and useless. He watched Morgaine stop and stand, hands on hips, head tilted cheerfully. "You are smaller than I thought."

For the least instant he frowned, then laughed in offended surprise. "We are well-matched." His gaze swept the room. "And this, the company you ask me to keep. You—Man. Come here."

Vanye's heart turned over. He measured the separation between him and Morgaine and between him and Skarrin with a nervous sweep of his eye, and used that small chance to bring himself even with Morgaine.

"I take my lady's orders," he said as mildly as he could, while his heart beat in panic.

"Defiance from a human?"

"From *me*," Morgaine said, and walked a little forward, to stop again with hand on hip. "Not that I am discourteous, my lord, but I do not lend my servants; I will reckon you have your own, and I will trust there are loyal folk among them. Or has this kingship of yours gotten too old and the intrigues too many? Or have you ceased to care? My folk will serve you. Bring your own servants—I care not, only so they are strong enough to last the course and honest enough to guard our backs. Let us set the gate and quit this tedious place. Keep to my path a while. I shall at very least value your company—and your advice. I am, after all, youngest. You can teach me—very much. And I can teach *you*, lord of dusty Mante—that there are new things under new suns. *I* am sufficient guarantee of that."

"You are arrogant."

"So I am told." She walked two paces forward and stood wide-legged. "I am terminus. And perhaps I am inception. Time will prove that. My origin is very recent as you measure time. I have never existed until now."

"As you dream—you have not existed."

"I am *Anjhurin's* daughter, Anjhurin who claimed to have seen the calamity. Think of *that*, my lord. And my mother came down a thread he had never known, that one which leads to stars outside, my lord. By seizing *that* he hoped to widen his power. But causality doomed him. He used force. She despised him. So, my lord, did I. And I destroyed him."

"You."

"With a will, my lord. All of Anjhurin's causality rests in *me*. That is my weight in the web of time—the youngest and the oldest of us, in one, and *I* reach outside. In me, every causality meets."

Skarrin backed a pace.

She lifted her hand so naturally and so quickly the red fire had touched the lord before Vanye could both realize the weapon was in her hand and draw in his breath.

"I cannot *die—!*" Skarrin cried; as a second time the red light touched him, from Morgaine's hand, amid the forehead: he fell with a horrified expression.

Die . . . die . . . die . . . the walls and the vaulted ceiling gave back. They echoed the heavy fall of Skarrin's body, and the nervous shifting of the horses.

Vanye caught his breath, shaken in every bone, not believing it had been so sudden or so without warning.

And knowing then by the dread in Morgaine's face as she turned that it was not over. It was far from over. It was wizardry they fought, whatever Morgaine named it; wizardry that could knit bone and heal flesh and put blood back in veins—and his liege's face was pale and desperate. "Follow me!" she cried, and ran toward the dark of the corridor.

ᥰ Chapter 19

Vanye ran, sword in hand, abandoning everything to Chei and his comrades—ran with a desperate burst of speed to close the gap between himself and Morgaine as she headed alone toward the corridor inward.

He heard someone behind him then, and spun to a halt and saw Chei and the other two coming. "Watch the horses!" he shouted at them, not wanting them at his liege's back, not wanting the horses unguarded either.

Then he raced after Morgaine, reaching the corner an instant after her—the corridor ahead filled at short range with a double rank of drawn bows and loosed arrows.

He hit her from behind in utter panic—that quickly the arrows flew and he fell to the floor atop her, did not think, except they were both like to die here, did not know what he did, except that the enemy had to nock their next arrows and he was already rolling toward them, onto his feet and toward them with a Kurshin yell—"Haaaaaiiiiiiii——Haiii!"—hurtling for the flank of their double line with sword swinging even while they were thinking some of them to shoot him and some nearest him to parry him with bowstaves and daggers.

The curved blade swept along the parry of a bowstaff and, skidding off it, came around into an unprotected arm and neck, and he laid about him left and right and round about without time to see where attack was coming from until it came within his circle, and then he killed it, with sword in his right hand and then Honor-blade in the left, for what came at him too close.

A blade scored his armor at his back; he gained room with the Honor-blade, and followed with a sword-stroke. A bow whistled round toward his head; he ducked under it, stabbed under a rash fool's chin, as some fallen enemy groped after a hold about his knees, raking the heavy leather and braces of his breeches and boots with a dagger stroke. He sprang aside from that, used his bow-arm bracer to counter a descending blade on one hand, clove a man's face horribly in a slash to the right and brought the blade back to deal with the return stroke on the left.

That enemy fell arrowshot through the neck, and he did not know where it had come from, except he saw the flash of red on a man's armor that meant Morgaine's weapon, and there were fewer and fewer enemies. He gasped for air and struck out, turning, sliding off a blade with his curved one to deal a man a blow that staggered him—hard effort then on the desperate one after, and on the parry he swept around to save his own skull. Steel rang on steel, bound and slipped as he made his sweep the faster, out of breath now, sight hazed and sweat streaming, on a carnage widening by the instant, red fire taking man after man. One man fled him; red flashed on his armor and he fell, screaming, on a heap of his comrades.

Others tried to surrender. Fire cut them down as they were halfway to their knees, and fire swept the wounded on the ground. *"Liyo!"* Vanye cried in consternation—but it was done, there were none alive as he staggered clear of the bodies and hit the wall with his back, gasping after air and gazing in horror on the slaughter.

Chei pulled his sword from a body and Hesiyyn and Rhanin stood back as Morgaine recovered herself, there at the edge of the carnage, the black weapon in her hand. *She will kill them too,* Vanye thought on the instant. There was no reason and no mercy on Morgaine's face.

Then she caught her breath and ran for the undefended door, opened it with quick passes of her hand on the studs which marked its center.

It gave back on hall and hall and hall brightly lighted, leading toward other doors.

"Hold here!" she cried. "All of you, hold the doors! Vanye—stay with them! Do not count Skarrin dead!"

She ran, before he could muster protest; and he thought then and knew he was guard of those who guarded them—to ward their retreat when it would surely be in haste.

"One of you," he shouted at Chei, "get down to the end of the hall and guard the horses!"

"Curse you, we are not your servants!"

"Dead men *have* no precedence! We are all in this, and likely to be stranded if we have no horses!"

"Rhanin!" Chei shouted, and Rhanin tucked his bow in hand and ran, vaulting dead men as he went.

That was the only one of them presently with other than a sword and dagger. Vanye longed for his own good bow, which he had left with Arrhan, and took a dead man's in its place, gathered up a quiver of arrows and slung it to his shoulder.

One arrow to the string, two others in his bow-hand. He tested the draw, and moved down to the intersection of the halls to set his shoulders against the wall where he had vantage of the right-hand corridor, while Chei took up a bow as well, and a quiver; and by the way he handled it, at least one part of him was no stranger to the weapon.

Morgaine's footfalls had died away in distance, within the farthest doorway, and he pressed his shoulders against the wall and watched, arms both at ease and ready on the instant, if there were any movement down the lighted corridor.

Such places he knew. There would be machines. There would be traps and such things as Morgaine dealt with better than ever he could in that room where she had gone, to deal with whatever Skarrin had done to the machines that controlled the gates. But he trembled as in winter cold, the reaction of muscles into which the bandages cut, and the fight which still had him drenched with sweat, and cooling now in the chill of Skarrin's keep. He blinked at the film on his eyes, shook his hair aside as it straggled into his face, his heart pounding in his chest with a kind of terror he had seldom felt in his life.

Qhalur enemies, he knew. Chei and Hesiyyn across the corridor from him made him anxious, no more than that. But this—

This man who knew the gates well enough to frighten Morgaine herself, whose mastery of them excelled hers—

What manner of enemy could die that death and not die, struck through the skull and through the heart?

Except there be witchcraft and sorcery which Morgaine denied existed.

But I am skilled in both. What matter it invokes no devils? I have met *devils left and right in her service, and slain no few, except this last, that says he cannot die—*

O Heaven, could we come so far and across so many years and fall to this, this creature, at the height of the sky, while so many men are surely going about their business in the town below, in all ignorance what passes here—if they are there— if the whole of that great city has not gone like the servants.

God deliver us. I do not know what more to do than stand here and guard her back.

Chei shivered, against the wall, looking toward that portion of hallway which was his to guard. Exhaustion ached in his knees and his gut and trembled in his hands. And the lady—

The lady had not killed them. That much they knew of her. Nothing more, that the boy had believed of her. *Nothing* more, except she was perilous as ever

Skarrin was—more than perilous: murderous and hellbent and—which she had said—more than a match for any gate-warden.

Skarrin's match—that was very clear. Of Skarrin's disposition: that remained to be seen.

Across the hall, Hesiyyn, warding the other direction; and at the opposite corner, Vanye; and the slow minutes passed, while something happened in that room down the hall—the master boards for the gates of all the world: *that* was what Morgaine Anjhuran had her hand to, who had *defeated* Skarrin—that was the fact which could hardly take hold in a shaken mind: Skarrin, who had ruled in Mante from time out of mind, Skarrin, ever-young and ruling through prox-ies, but cruel beyond measure when some rebellion came nigh him—

Skarrin, around whom conspiracies and plots continually moved, like a play acted for his amusement—

Gone—in a lightning-stroke, the simple act of a woman who had not come to parley at all.

And at whose actions with the gate, in that room—sent the lights brighten-ing and dimming as if all Neneinn were wounded.

"What is she doing?" Chei asked furiously. "What does she think to do?"

"What needs no hearers," Vanye returned shortly across span of the hall which divided them. "Trust her. If she wished you dead you would be dead with the rest."

"I have no doubt," Hesiyyn said, and tightened a buckle of his armor—wan and exhausted, Hesiyyn, as all of them, shadow-eyed and dusty. He took up his sword again from between his knees. "But whatever she is, she has done fairly by us, and that hound Skarrin is dead or dead as fire can make him." He made a kind of salute with the blade. "There is all I need know."

It was a desperate man, Hesiyyn who had no choices; and himself—himself with so much good and ill mixed in him of his varied lives that he could not see the world, either, in dark or light. And Nhi Vanye, who knew, with more confidence than either of them, where his loyalty belonged.

It was irony, Chei thought, with pain in his heart, that he, Qhiverin, found more and more reason to like this man, while the boy—the youth forgave him, *him*, Gault-Qhiverin, because of old betrayals and loss of kin and things in which they fit together like blade and sheath—never mind that some of those griefs had been at Qhiverin's hand, Qhiverin's fault, in the bloody deeds incum-bent on a warden of the warlike South—Qhiverin could find sympathy, Qhiv-erin could embrace and comfort Chei in his desolation. There *was* no more war between them, except the boy would not forgive, would not listen, would not reason—

—for too much self-blame lay within it.

Here is insanity, Chei thought in a heart-weary panic. *Peace, boy, or we both go under.*

And the boy, who did not want to die: *He will kill us if he can—finally, when we have done all they want, one or the other of them will kill us. Knowledge was all they ever wanted.*

Then they made a poor bargain, did they not? He wiped tears from his eyes. *Boy, we will guard his back. You are a fool, is all—a great fool. And would you had never made him my enemy. Your brother would have had more sense. It was yourself coming up on the man's sword-side, it was Bron drove his horse between to shy you off. That is the truth I remember.*

Liar!

And your Gault, boy—your Gault the hero was a traitor the same as Arunden. He would have sold you all for his peace. Have you never known that? He betrayed Ichandren before I did. I took him, yonder, on that hill, because I had no choice. But ah, boy, he was a scoundrel. Scoundrel and fool. What a legacy you give me.

What a cursed great—

Light and sound came from the room at the end of the hall, where the lady had gone, a high thin moan which no living throat could make, and a deep roaring like thunder sustained.

"What is she *doing*?" Hesiyyn asked hoarsely, leaning against his wall. "Lord human—"

"I do not know," Vanye said, biting his lip, and looked toward the door which lay open at the end, where red light flashed, and the wailing grew. "Hold our retreat open!"

He ran. He trusted the men for what they might be worth and raced down the slick stone hall at all the speed he could manage, down the hall and through the gaping doors and into such a place as he had seen more than once in his travels—where light dyed everything the color of blood, and inhuman voices wailed and thundered and shrieked from overhead and all about.

"Liyo!" he shouted into that overpowering racket.

"Liyo!—"

She turned, red-dyed with the light from silver hair to metal of her black armor, with the light flaring about her and behind her as the boards blinked alarm.

"He is not dead," she cried. "Vanye, he has stored his essence inside the gate—he is still alive, for the next poor soul that ventures that gate."

He tried to understand that. He stood there staring at her and thought it through twice and three times.

"*For us,*" she shouted. "He has trapped us and I cannot dislodge him!—That is the wrongness we have felt in the gates—he has kept his pattern there continually, kept it bound to him, day and night—He will *take* the next living man that enters the World-gate! He will go through, he will be free, there is no way we can stop him!" She came to him and caught at his arm, turning him for the door, not running, but walking quickly, by which and by the flashing of the lights at their back and the uncomfortable prickling in the air, he knew that the gate of Mante was set on its own destruction, on some near time which—he hoped to Heaven—she had chosen. "He had a snare set that would have sealed the gate once he was free. I broke that lock easily enough. I set it to a new time, a few hours hence. I dare not leave it longer. There is too much knowledge in this place, and the chance of someone re-opening it, except I build destruction into its pathways—that, I dare not risk."

It was old Kurshin she spoke, awkward in the things for which the *qhalur* language had ready words, which conjured the inner workings of the gates and the things she had showed him, how to redirect the power like damming one stream and opening another, to flood throughout the channels and destroy the means to reactivate it.

"I have set it to destroy the core-tap," she said in the *qhalur* tongue, meaning the line of power which ran from the earth's deep heart.

And everything round about it. Such a thing, she had told him—might cause havoc with a world, involving gate-force and the power in the earth itself. *I do not know what happens thereafter,* she had said. *No one comes through such a gate again—or any of the gates linked with it. It is no good thing for the world. And I would not willingly do it. Time itself closes in on a gate once it is shut. Ordinarily, time itself will destroy one as thoroughly in a few years without touching the core, and there is no need for such a catastrophe. And I do as little as I dare.*

He thought on the city spread about the hill of Neneinn, the countless lives, the city on the brink of a well only gate-force or cataclysm could have shaped; and his gut and his knees went to water.

It was a death-sentence. That was the wailing, that he had never heard, the threat to life all about this world's gates—Morund and Tejhos and Mante and wherever else gates had their veins of power sunk into this world's heart.

"How much time do we have?" he asked.

"Three hours," she said, *qhalur*-reckoning. He measured it against the daylight and the sun, Kurshin-fashion, and there was ice about his heart. "I dared not give it more time," she said. "This is a *qhalur* city. And there is the warden down at Seiyyin Neith, *if* he is still there and not fled with the rest—"

"One of his guards might solve matters for us," he said, reckoning—O Heaven, what was he become—to think cold-bloodedly where they should get a victim?

"We cannot know it if they do. Do not speak of it to our comrades. Does thee hear?"

He saw Chei and Hesiyyn waiting for them at the intersection of the corridors, saw their anxious faces. *"Does thee hear?"*

"Aye," he said, clutching the remnants of his soul to him; and no likelihood that fate would offer better.

Like the men who had surrendered; like the forty on the road; like the city spread below them, doomed with the gate, men and women and babes in cradle—

For the sake of all the worlds, she told him. *All* the worlds was too large a thing for a man's heart to understand, when it was the one under his feet and the lives around him and the murder and the choices were his.

Not tell them—not offer even the chance to choose or to fight—

"Come," she said to Chei and Hesiyyn, gathering them up as they strode along toward the hall where they had left the horses and where Rhanin stood guard. "We are bound for the gate. Hurry. There is not that much time. I have set it to seal behind us and there will be no following after us."

They did not question. They kept pace with weapons still in their hands, and Chei whistled to Rhanin and called to him as they came into the hall.

"We are bound for the gate," Chei told Rhanin as the archer lowered his bow and met them there, where he had herded the horses into a corner of the hall.

"Quickly. Come, man. The lady is keeping her promises."

But from Rhanin there was no such eagerness. "My lord Chei," he said. "My lady—I have a wife—"

O Heaven, Vanye thought.

"—I beg your leave," Rhanin said. "Let me go bring her."

Chei looked to Morgaine.

"No," Morgaine said. "There is no time. That gate will *seal*, and there will be no more passages; and if we do not get there in time, there will be none for us."

"How long?" Chei asked.

"An hour," Morgaine said. "Perhaps. Skarrin has done damage I cannot correct. We have no *time*, man, and your lord has need of you and I do—where we go is no place for a hallbred woman. A hard trail and a long one in sun and storm and lightning; and war, man, that I can promise you. Come with your lord, and hurry about it."

"I cannot." There was torment in Rhanin's brown eyes. "Lord Chei—I cannot leave her."

He turned and went to the horses. Morgaine lifted the black weapon in threat. "Stop!" she cried; and: "My lady!" Chei exclaimed.

Rhanin stopped, but he did not turn. After a few heartbeats he started walking again.

Morgaine let fall her hand. She stood in silence as Rhanin mounted up. "Fare well," she said quietly then. "Fare well, Rhanin."

Rhanin cut the tether of the remount he led, gave it to Hesiyyn, and saluted his lord and the rest of them, before he swung up to the saddle and rode, black shadow against the light, for the stable-court and the city below.

"Mount up!" Morgaine bade them.

Vanye swallowed against the knot in his throat and went first for Siptah's reins, to bring the gray horse to his liege while the others sought their own. He held her stirrup for her. He did not look in her eyes. She did not, for all he knew, try to meet his.

She said no word at all, nor quarreled with him that he did her these courtesies.

He must, he thought. He had no words to tell her he was with her.

He felt the shorn hair about face and neck, and it seemed apt, of a sudden, the felon's mark, the mark of an honorless man, penance for Mante, for Rhanin and his wife, for lies and for murder yet to do.

Honest men, Morgaine had said, must fight us. Brave men must.

"We have to *find* the way out in this warren," Morgaine said shortly. "And hope the stable court leads to some road up the hill—"

"No need to search for it," Chei said, drawing his horse alongside in the hall. "There is a way from the stable court. *Gault's* memory is clear enough on that. I came up from the city—but Gault was here. Follow me."

It was leftward Chei led, beyond the fountain. The blaze-faced bay lipped up some meager spillage of grain on the dirt by the stables nearby: "I will get him," Vanye said, distractedly—to leave the poor brave beast to Mante's fate seemed impossible to him, was, at least, one death he could prevent. He rode wide of the group, leaned from his saddle and snagged the reins that had fallen as the animal lowered his head. It did not want to come. It jolted his arm, then surrendered, of habit, perhaps, and followed.

He overtook the others before they had gotten to the stable-gate, never having taken his eyes off them, and Morgaine acknowledged the rescue with a worried frown, a flicker of the eyes which understood him entirely, as Chei got down from his horse and pushed at the latch. "Let it free outside," she said. "It will balk at the gate. We cannot afford difficulties."

It was true. He knew that it was. He held onto the reins as the stable-gate swung wide on a long colonnade, and Chei mounted up again. He drew the horse along with them as they rode that long course to a second gate, the latch of which was high enough for Chei to trip from horseback; and that gate opened out on a road and a barren hill, where standing stones made an aisle leading upward.

"At least the saddle," he said, then, outside; and slid down while the whole company waited, and hastily loosed the bay's girth and tumbled the saddle off; unbuckled the bridle and threw it away, and sent the confused horse off with a hard slap on the rump. He did the same for the horse Hesiyyn led, then, and sent it off after its fellow.

He came close to tears, then. He turned and flung himself to the saddle, and swallowed down that impulse.

Fool, he told himself, to weep for a pair of horses, when there is so much else we do. It belongs to this world, that is all.

And there may indeed be trouble—at the Gate.

O *God*, are we right? If only I knew that we were right.

He kept close at Morgaine's side as they struck out up the road which wound about the rocky hill, Chei and Hesiyyn close on his left.

"A great many horses," Hesiyyn said, of the trampled ground ahead of them, of the sparse brush about them, that was broken and trodden down.

"Everyone in Neneinn," Chei said.

But not, Vanye thought, heart-heavy, *not enough for all of Mante. There is no escape for them.*

He thought that if he turned, high as they climbed now, he could truly see a wondrous sight, a vantage over all Mante, over Neisyrrn Neith and Seiyyin Neith and perhaps the plains and the hills beyond, to all the distance a clear day would afford them.

But the sight of it would haunt him. *I do not look back*, Morgaine was wont to say; and he clung to that wisdom now: once through the world on a single track, a single purpose, without touching more lives than they must.

Too much knowledge here: he understood that. It had been unconscionable hazard to have left his own cousin near a faded gate, except there were warders to prevent him coming near it until it was dead beyond recall.

Here—there were no warders they could trust: a corrupt gate-warden and a twisted gate, and all too many who would rush to enliven the gate and seize power for themselves—not Skarrin's measure, it was sure, but equally deadly, in the affairs of worlds and stars and suns which Morgaine understood, and which he did not.

Now he wept over two doomed horses, and longed with all his heart for enemies.

But none presented themselves, and the storm-sense grew in the air, making the hair prickle. Arrhan sidestepped and worked at the bit, so ready to run she hardly seemed to walk on the earth; and the rest of the horses rolled their eyes and threw their heads, snorting their dislike of the place.

Skarrin's presence—a man warded from assassination and accidents because he had stored—whatever of him mattered, in such fashion that the ordinary traffic of the gates would deliver him a host virtually instantly, were it ever needed: different than *qhalur* knowledge, Morgaine had said.

Different—root and branch.

My father's legacy, Morgaine had said.

And called Skarrin kinsman—whatever Skarrin's true name was.

Or hers.

The great Gate came slowly from the unfolding of the hill, the screening of the standing stones—a towering arch of stone, within which the blue sky shimmered like fever-vision. Hesiyyn's horse fought the bit wild-eyed, and the red roan Chei rode threw his head and fretted in distress; but Siptah went with his ears laid flat and pricked up by turns, trying to get rein to go, knowing where he was bound, what he must do, and all too anxious to make that jump, till Morgaine reined him down and patted his shoulder.

Closer and closer then, at a careful pace. There were no enemies at hand. They were alone at the height, on this Road which led to a place where the very air had sound and substance; and smaller sounds, those of hoof and harness, lost themselves.

"You can see the city," Hesiyyn said, looking over his shoulder.

"Goodbye to it," Chei said and seemed lost already in the Gate's spell.

They had reached the last of the road. After this it was the barren, rocky slope leading to the Gate itself, tracked and scarred with hundreds of feet, with the hooves of horses, the wheels of wagons; and here Morgaine drew rein.

"Go through," she bade Chei and Hesiyyn with a wave of her arm. "I have yet something to see to from this side. I will overtake you, have no fear of it."

Chei drew up on his reins and used his heels, for the red roan fought to turn away, and Hesiyyn circled his horse to distract it from full flight.

"Rhanin," Chei said.

"The gate will give no warning when it seals. There is no time! If he comes, he comes. We cannot wait for him. Go through!"

Chei reined hard over and about again, holding the roan as it fought to get the bit. There was a frown on his face. He looked at Vanye then, full at him, and Vanye held his breath as Chei turned the horse yet again.

And back again, hard-reining it. This time as he came about, it was a wary look, a more and more misgiving look.

"Like the horses, is it? Send us through—*first*?"

"That you go at all is my lady's gift!" Vanye shouted at him. Gate-force oppressed the air, like impending storm. Hair crackled and metal stung when the hand brushed it, as he felt after his sword-hilt. "Go through!"

Chei's hand went to his own hilt; and in the same instant he cast a sudden and wide-eyed look toward Morgaine, toward a threat far more substantial than steel.

"My lord," Hesiyyn said anxiously, fighting his horse steady. "My lord, likely it is safe. The lady has—"

"—set the gate herself," Chei said; and looked her direction; and Vanye's, slowly, with a hard hand on the reins. "Is that it? Is it a trap, eh?"

"She set no trap," Vanye said.

"No?" There was long silence. "Then it is his you suspect. Is it not? *Is it not?*"

Vanye said nothing at all. He could think of nothing to say.

"Oh, my friend," Chei said quietly. "What are you prepared to do? Threaten us with death—to make us risk that?"

"Death is not a risk here," Morgaine said. "It is a certainty. *There*, in the gate, is the only doubt. Take it."

"Or you will kill us. What good are we then?" Again Chei turned the horse about, and drew it in with a hard hand. "How will you know? How will you ever know that it is safe?"

"The risk is to one," Morgaine said. "That is the truth. And it will not be myself; and it will not be Vanye. I promise you that." She lifted her hand. "*This* need not kill."

Chei stared at her, very long. Then he looked, slowly, toward Vanye.

"Forgive her," Vanye said. "She has no choice."

"Not forgive *you*?"

"She has no choice. I have. And for her sake—I cannot take it. I cannot even offer you fair fight."

"It is not any grudge. Is it?"

"No, my lord. Not in this. Skarrin is waiting;—within the gate. We could not dislodge him. That is the truth. That is the trap. One of us—will host our enemy."

Chei laughed—laughed, shortly and silently; and laughed a second time, reining the red horse about yet again. "He would. He would, the bastard. *That* was what he meant."

"That was what he meant."

A third laugh, shortest of all. "The boy urges me there is a logic in this. He has had his revenge. He confuses me. He urges me—we are best suited to this fight. It is his revenge on me. Or mine on him. *Damn you to hell, boy!* Damn you and all your choices!—Hesiyyn." He took up on the reins, turning aside. "Hesiyyn!"

"No, my lord!" Hesiyyn cried, and rode his horse across Chei's path.

"I will race you for it," Chei said, and cracked the rein ends down on the roan and drove with his heels. The red horse went, as Hesiyyn fought the bay about and into a run. "Let *him* choose!"

The gate took them. One—and the other. Hesiyyn did not slow at all.

Vanye shut his eyes, and rested so, a long, long moment, till he heard

Morgaine ride up beside him, until living warmth brushed against him. He looked then, at the vacant gate that loomed above them, with blue sky shimmering again where dark had showed for an instant.

"It is safe now," she said, and reached and rested her hand on his arm.

"It was Chei and Qhiverin," he said then. He was trembling, as if the gatecold had gotten to his bones. "Skarrin—is their enemy. And Hesiyyn's. But Chei is overmatched. Both of them—are overmatched."

"Skarrin has had only one body," Morgaine said.

He looked toward her then.

"Chei was right," Morgaine said, "altogether right. They are peculiarly apt for that fight. And Skarrin is their enemy." Her fingers tightened. "We have given them such as we could. It is all the charity we have. Nhi Vanye—"

There were tears in her voice finally. He was glad of that. Her burden was absolute, and older; and that she still could weep—gave him hope for himself, in such a time, after so many journeys.

He took her hand in his and held it till the horses moved apart, fingertip parting from fingertip. Siptah was bound for the gate. Arrhan followed, of her own accord.

Gray horse and white. Dark rider and light. There was no knowing where they were bound, except they went together.

Printed in the United States
by Baker & Taylor Publisher Services